Letters of Insurgents

Originally published by Black & Red Books in Detroit, Michigan, 1976
http://blackandred.org

This edition published by Left Bank Books, 2014

Left Bank Books is a not-for-profit project collectively owned & operated
by its workers, founded in 1973.

LEFT BANK BOOKS
92 Pike street
seattle, WA 98101
206//622//0195
http://www.leftbankbooks.com
publishing@leftbankbooks.com

Left Bank Books ISBN: 978-0-939306-05-3

Printed in Canada
10 9 8 7 6 5 4 3 2 1

Letters of Insurgents

by
Sophia Nachalo
and
Yarostan Vochek

as told by
Fredy Perlman

Left Bank Books
Seattle, Washington
2014

Contents

Foreword

Letters of Insurgents is an epistolary novel written, printed, and published by Fredy Perlman and Black and Red Press in 1976. It is a critical examination of the absurd, human, and contradictory nature of radical politics in the sixties and early seventies in America and Europe. It is also a touching and cruel dissection of the illusory community-at-war-with-itself-and-the-world that I have associated myself with for the past 25 years (much to my chagrin). The rummaging around in my own contradictions, illusions, and wishful thinking that *Letters* has forced me to do is the reason I have thrived in the last decade or so as I continue to find people and ideas who keep me in this terrible-but-lovely community.

Letters encourages this kind of self-reflection partly because it is not a book about winners. The victories that occur are quiet victories that make a different kind of sense to those of us who have made the cognitive break from straight society. Other kinds of people can get a lot out of the book as well, but it is targeted straight at the heart of an underachiever like me. I will never be able to put my ideas about how to live into practice other than in the most fleeting of moments and spaces. I will never turn back the tanks, hang the bureaucrats, destroy the interstates, erase the bombs and guns of states, or live in a real community that is free from property and violence. *Letters* made a convincing argument that I would never be able to make these things happen and made just as convincing of an argument that I needed to pull my head out of my books and try anyway.

I read *Letters* as a great work on how to do criticism: a humane story about two sharp people cutting each other to size in ways that are appropriate--if harsh and sometimes mean. This criticism ranges far beyond the dynamics between two writers on either side of the Berlin Wall. Each of us is confronted with a great isolation in modern society that we are unable to speak to or from due to a lack of tools, models, or closeness to each other. The critical model provided by *Letters* has been personally influential in its demonstration of each of these elements: in the first few letters the focus is on criticism (by which I also mean intimacy) and later are discussions of the tools and models by which we could imagine breaking down the colossus of the existing order.

It seems evident to me that both correspondents are correct (in their analysis and attacks on the other) but are making different points. Sophia's argument is that the power of autonomy and independent creative action (aka the class struggle) is the important part of their story, perhaps of life itself. If the choice is between politicians and their backers or the protesters and their friends, Sophia's choice is clear. In her analysis Yarostan is making group identification entirely negative. If one member of the working class is willing to act the role of the politician then are the working class dupes of the politician?

Yarostan's argument is that the specifics, or the intentions of the actors, aren't particularly important to the reality of the 20 years he spent in prison, or the not-positive impact the two of them (as individuals) had on the situation that they were in control of, not to speak of the world outside of their factory or their relationships. This distinction, between the fatalist and the optimist point of view, is the political heart of the story and echoes throughout the rest of the book.

The harshest criticism of this book is of me and those people who are around me. We have devoted ourselves to a mythology. To revolution. To destroying all the things that destroy us. To a life-long pursuit of knowledge and context and meaning. In this struggle we have not become free human beings. Or perhaps we have seen the possibility of freedom and been destroyed by it. In our shattered state we have to feel our way along. We understand complexity and it hasn't saved us. It has made us observers of life and inept at free action. The falsehood of the theory vs action divide isn't that either are better but that neither are sufficient.

The necessity of our project, of the project of *Letters of Insurgents*, and the Beautiful Idea that is anarchy, is incontrovertible AND impossible, yet we still participate in it. We are not crusaders, the revolution is not just around the corner--the means by which the world will be changed, and more importantly how we will live a meaningful life, is not simply defined or stated.

Aragorn!
LBC Books
Berkeley, CA

Dear Sophia,

Forgive me for addressing you familiarly, as a friend; I have no way of knowing if you're still the person I once knew. I can't remember the sound of your voice, the shape of your face or the feel of your hand. I vaguely remember admiring the energy and intelligence in someone so young, but I regret that you didn't leave a lasting mark, you didn't become my guide in my journey through hell.

I wouldn't even remember your name if you hadn't written me twelve years ago. My wife Mirna memorized the name and address on the envelope because she attributed a strange power to your letter. Unfortunately I never saw that letter and never learned its contents.

Part of my reason for writing you now is that the activities of our omnipotent and omniscient police have been blocked. Letters aren't being read by the eagle-eyed censors and letter-writers aren't being escorted out of their homes by middle-of-the-night visitors. So I'm told. I want to believe it. Rebellious words and even gestures are becoming frequent and I haven't seen or heard of the arrest of the rebels. Something is changing in this city, in the entire land; I don't know if the change is permanent.

This change is reviving my interest in my surroundings, in my fellow beings, in myself, in you. If there is no change, if this is another illusion, if I'm not writing to Sophia but to a benevolent protector of the people's real interests, a censor, then I'd rather be back in prison than "free." There's no joy in such freedom. Such a life is filled with dread and the only ones free of that dread are those already in prison. If the change taking place around me is an illusion or a trap, then I no longer care if I'm arrested again. Even in solitary confinement a prisoner tortured by dampness and rats is comforted by the thought that others survived it, that they weren't crushed by moving walls or descending ceilings. But the policed "free citizen" can't ever get rid of the fear that he may be dragged off at any time, wherever he is, whoever he's with; that all his friendships and all his projects can suddenly end; that the front door of his house can crash open at midnight; that the ceiling of his bedroom might start descending on him while he's asleep. In a context where any word or gesture can lead to the dreaded arrest there's no freedom. In such a context, beings vibrant with the will to live are transformed into beings for whom death is no worse than a life marked by the dread of death. The prisons and camps don't contain only those inside them but also those outside them. All human beings are transformed into prisoners and prison guards.

I don't put the blame on prison guards. They're only workers. They're not inanimate things, cement walls that can neither see nor hear nor think. Most of them didn't choose their jobs; they ended up there because they thought they had no other choice. I've spent a total of twelve years inside walls, behind bars and fences, and I've never met a prison guard in whom I saw no trace of myself. I never met a guard who had dreamed that patrolling a convict yard would be the daily content of his life. Very few of those I've met admitted to never having dreamed, never having imagined themselves proud of projects undertaken with one or several genuine friends. Was our point of departure the same, and were we at some point interchangeable? How much has each of us contributed to what each has undergone? If a guard ever dreamed, was it of prisons and camps that he dreamed, and was he my jailer-to-be already then?

I can't say I failed to write you sooner because there were censors. I could have found ways to reach you without sending a letter through their hands. I could also have devised simple ways to camouflage the letter's origin, destination and content and sent it gliding unseen past the censor's omniscient gaze.

It's now three years since my release. During the first two years I wasn't able to remain in one place long enough to write a letter. This is apparently an illness that affects many individuals released after a long imprisonment. When the day of my release was so distant that I thought I wouldn't live to experience it, I was able to formulate clear and distinct ideas ordered with an impeccable logic. In conversations with inmates and in my imagination I composed one after another book unveiling the inverted practice that seized a field intended for a garden and built a concentration camp. I thought all I needed was a table in a small room, a pen and paper and an occasional meal; I thought the ideas would flow by themselves.

When I'd been home for only half an hour after my release I rushed out of the house and spent the remainder of the day walking aimlessly. It wasn't because I wanted to see what had changed during my eight-year absence. I avoided studying the changes and gazed at the pavement. I was too familiar with the spirit in which those changes were created. Nor did I want to see or communicate with people who weren't convicts. They were altogether unfamiliar to me, almost a different type of creature, and I avoided them. I longed for the comrades I had left inside. We had shared insights and hardships, we had shared a common world, a common enemy and common hopes. I could no longer imagine myself becoming a self-policed imbecile who voluntarily put an end to his sleep so as to voluntarily reach a workshop at eight in the morning only to spend the day voluntarily turning out the number of parts which planners and managers had assigned to "his" machine. In prison such idiocy had only characterized newcomers; if they weren't quickly cured by fellow convicts, they became tools of the prison administration or else their stupidity was so abused by sadistic guards that they went insane or died of overwork.

For two years after my release I was unable to express myself in any form. I was "disoriented" and needed time to "adjust to freedom." I had grown used to the routine, the meals, the jobs, the guards; I had become attached to my comrades, to our conversations and arguments, to our imaginary common projects and breathtaking escapes. I missed all that. I was an exile, an alien among people whose activity I found incomprehensible, whose language I could neither speak nor understand, whose sympathy and communication I rejected because they seemed condescending and hypocritical. Of course I understood then as I do now that factories are prisons, foremen are not unlike prison guards, and the threat of firing or eviction causes as much terror as the threat of solitary confinement or deportation. But during those two years I concentrated on the differences between the two situations. The prisoners I had known had repressed words and gestures in the face of a rifle, but had regained their humanity when the repressive force withdrew. Among the outsiders I became aware of an altogether different type of repression: self-repression. My next-door neighbor, a Mr. Ninovo, is a cleaning man in a bar. The first time I ran into him I smiled and said "good evening." When he failed to respond to my greeting I apologized and said, "The evening obviously can't be good for someone who is about to spend it cleaning up after drunken bureaucrats." He responded by shouting, "You people are trouble-makers! They should never have let you out!" I had an urge to slap him, the same urge I'd felt in prison toward an informer. But I turned my back to him and walked away. According to Mirna, Mr. Ninovo likes his job, admires the president and is proud of "his" country. He enjoys listening to official propaganda on the radio. He has spent his life cleaning up the dirt of the bar's customers and he's satisfied with himself. I never met anyone like him in prison.

I was driven to despair by the thought that Mr. Ninovo was not the exception but the rule. It seemed to me that the last human beings were dying in prisons and camps and would leave no heirs, while a horrible mutation of the species was taking place outside. I thought of committing suicide, or of finding a way to return to my prison cell so as to live out my days among comrades and die among human beings.

But visions of horror are inverse Utopias. Recently my ten-year old daughter Yara put an end to my stupor, my "disorientation." My condition began to improve the moment she entered the house. Her manner exuded the pride of a discoverer at the moment of completing a quest. The unqualified and unashamed happiness radiated by her face was an expression I hadn't seen in years. On Yara's chest was pinned a sheet of paper with the words, "Give us back our teacher!"

"What happened to your teacher?" I asked.

"They told us he had disappeared. But my girlfriend Julia wrote a sign that said, 'People can't disappear; something happens to them!'"

"What happens to them?" I asked.

"The same thing that happened to you. He was arrested."

"How many took part in this protest?"

"All the kids in school," Yara answered enthusiastically. "Everyone whispered about it all morning and after lunch everyone went to the school yard. Not a single student went back to class."

"How did all this get started?" I asked. "Were the other teachers upset when he was fired?"

"The other teachers all seemed glad he'd disappeared," Yara told me. "Yesterday I and three others in my class made some signs and this morning we told other kids we were going to wear them in the school yard. We told them not to let any of the teachers know. I loved him. I cried when he was replaced by another teacher who wouldn't tell us when he'd come back' and told us he'd disappeared. Lots of kids loved him, and if we hadn't started making signs, other kids would have, because the schoolyard was full of signs."

"But where did you and your friends learn how to do this sort of thing?"

"You mean demonstrations? We're always being told about thousands of workers marching down the street carrying big signs. If they can do it, why can't we?"

"So you all gathered in the schoolyard —"

"It was full of kids with signs. We stood quietly for a long time. Many kids were scared. Someone started to whisper that we would all be arrested. One of the teachers came out and stood with us. A boy standing next to her hugged her and burst out crying. We knew we had won. Other teachers joined us. Finally the principal came out. He said our teacher had been called away by mistake and that he'd be back next week. Everyone knew he was lying about it being a mistake. But no one cared. Kids started screeching, wrestling, hugging each other and hugging their teachers. Some kids even ran up to the principal and threw their arms around him."

"Do you know why your teacher had been arrested?"

"Sure. He wants us to think on our own and they don't, that's why. He always told us the explanations in our books weren't the only explanations, that many things have lots of different explanations and we have to choose the one we like best."

Words are too poor to convey what I felt when Yara described her "protest." I was "cured." In one sudden leap I had rejoined the living. My species had not, after all, undergone a mutation — at least not a permanent one. Such an event would require a far greater catastrophe than the rule of an organization of prison officials. "People can't disappear." How right she is! Wherever there are people there's negation, rebellion, insurrection. When twenty-year olds repress and mutilate their humanity, the repressed humanity reappears intact among ten-year olds. I threw my arms around Yara and she danced me around the room. "Father, would you teach me different explanations of things so I can choose the ones I like best?" she asked.

Mirna burst out crying. She had stood speechless in the corner of the room during the entire scene. I had wrongly interpreted her silence as hostility toward the girl's rebellious act. Mirna ran to embrace Yara, rested her head on the girl's shoulder and sobbed.

"Don't be sad, mommy."

Mirna whispered, "I'm not sad. I'm happy for both of you."

I can't convey to you what this meant to me. Mirna too emerged unscathed. All those long years of repressed humanity were overturned with a simple gesture and a few words.

That day I regained my desire to express myself. I have an urge to write everything down. Yet I can't imagine who you are now, what you're thinking, what you've done, if you're married and have children, or even if you're alive and well. I have no right to bore you with an interminable letter which you might regard as an unwanted intervention by a complete stranger. You did send me a letter once, but not having seen it I can't assume it contained anything more than a delayed Christmas greeting. But you did write something, you did initiate some sort of correspondence, and I'm trying to write you an answer and to explain why I couldn't write sooner. I want to tell you about myself and I long to learn about you. My daughter's brave act renewed my interest in living and intensified my curiosity. Since that day I've learned that Yara's demonstration was neither exceptional nor original. Protests against dismissals and arrests of teachers have recently become frequent events in the schools. And the protests aren't limited to students. Full-fledged strikes complete with strike committees, bulletins and support groups are taking place in some large factories. Until recently everyone knew about these events yet everyone denied them. Officially they weren't taking place. Everyday language — a language impoverished by official lies — had for twenty years ceased to be an instrument for communicating about real events. When I first returned from prison Mirna was afraid I would exert a demonic influence on Yara. She warned the child daily: "Don't start anything; don't get into trouble." Trouble could only lead to imprisonment. But Yara began to experience "trouble" as something positive: trouble meant protests, demonstrations and strikes, it meant individual and collective acts of defiance. Trouble referred to the heroic deeds of individuals and groups praised in her schoolbooks. I was unaware of Yara's growing defiance until the day of her demonstration, just as I failed to notice the grumbling in the shops and on the streets, the facial expressions in the trams and busses, the defiant gestures in bars, the slogans in toilets, the shouts in the night.

Yara helped me begin to see and hear the return of the repressed, and now I yearn to see yet further and hear yet more. I started this letter several weeks ago but convinced myself it would never reach you and abandoned it twice. My curiosity defeated my doubts. I long to know why you wrote me and what you said to me twelve years ago. I long to know who you are, what you've done, with whom, why. For months after my release I wanted to escape from this city and return to the finite world enclosed by prison walls. Now I find the city itself an enclosure and I'm reaching out to you to help me see and feel a larger world, if only through a letter.

If your only connection with the Sophia I once knew is your name, then please let me ask you to do a small favor for a fellow human being who has not fared well in this bizarre world: please let me know that you received this letter. I can't hide the impatience with which I wait for your answer.

Yarostan.

Sophia's first letter

Dear Yarostan,
What a marvelous surprise! Surely you remember Luisa. She was all excited when she came with your letter last night. Sabina and Tina, my housemates, were both home. Luisa hadn't ever been in our house before. We spent the evening and most of the night reading and rereading your letter, reliving our past for Tina's sake, discussing events we've never discussed before. We were all amazed to learn how many years you'd spent in prison and we were deeply moved by the contrast between your beautiful letter and the miserable life you've led.

Luisa and I traveled twenty years backward in time, reconstructing the world of experience we shared with you. I still regard that experience as the key to my whole life. Luisa had lived through such significant events before, but for me the days I spent with you have always been unique.

As soon as she read your letter Tina asked who you were and if all three of us had known you. I started to tell her about that vast uprising we had all taken part in. "Yes, we were together — not just the four of us, but thousands of us," I told Tina. "Those events released a surge of contentment, enthusiasm and initiative throughout the whole working population. At last we were going to run our own affairs, at last the people were masters, nobody would be able to exploit our efforts for their own ends, nobody would be able to deceive us, sell us to our enemies, betray us."

"If that's what happened, then why in the world did you leave, and why did Yarostan spend half his life in jail?" Tina asked.

"That wasn't what happened," Sabina said curtly.

"What do you mean 'that wasn't what happened'? You were there too! Don't you remember?" I immediately wished I hadn't said that to Sabina, because she has a phenomenal memory: she remembers events from her childhood as vividly as events that took place yesterday.

"What did happen, then?" Tina asked Sabina.

"An old boss was thrown out and a new one replaced him, that's all. The contentment, enthusiasm and initiative were just a vast put-on," Sabina told her.

Luisa turned indignantly to Sabina and shouted, "You don't know what you're talking about! You were only twelve at the time!"

Disregarding Luisa, Sabina turned to Tina and told her, "Yarostan and two other workers, Claude and Jan, stormed into the office of the owner of a carton factory, a Mr. Zagad. I went with them. Claude threw the door open and shouted, 'We're the representatives of the plant council.' We weren't anything of the sort, but Zagad looked like a cornered rabbit. He ran straight to the coat rack, threw his coat over his arm and vanished, leaving all his important papers lying on his desk. Then another official installed himself in Zagad's office. That's what happened and that's all that happened."

"Was that all?" Luisa asked sarcastically. "Workers went into the office of a factory owner, threw him out, and that's all?"

Sabina shrugged her shoulders and turned her back to Luisa. Those two have never gotten along and they still don't.

I agreed with Luisa and was going to ask Sabina how many times in history workers have ousted their bosses.

But Luisa turned to Tina and pushed her argument in another direction. "Of course that wasn't all that happened. Sabina is only talking about the events she took part in. She didn't see past the end of her own nose. Masses of workers filled the streets for the second time in three years. The first time, when the liberation armies marched toward the city surrounded by enemy military forces, thousands of workers joined the resistance and fought to free their city. The second time, when they learned that reactionary elements were again powerful enough to resume the counter-offensive, they called a general strike."

Sabina snapped, "The workers didn't call that strike; the trade union called it."

"Whoever called it," Luisa snapped back, "it was a general strike." Mimicking Sabina, she added, "'A general strike? Is that all?'"

Tina, completely baffled, asked, "Why are you shouting at each other about something that happened twenty years ago?"

I tried to explain, "It was our most significant experience during the past twenty years and Sabina is ridiculing it."

"What were you doing at the time?" Tina asked me.

I didn't remember Mr. Zagad or the general strike or who had called it, but I did remember what I had done and the people I had done it with. "All I remember," I told Tina, "is that I was home when Luisa rushed in and told Sabina and me, 'Come on, this is no time to be sitting in the house; the workers are taking over the plant!' I got all excited. I was three years younger than you are now. I had never been inside any kind of factory. Mountains of cardboard were piled along the sides. Huge machines stood idle; I had no idea what they all did. Workers sat on top of tables smoking and laughing. I remember Claude, Yarostan, Jan and four or five others. I couldn't understand much of the discussion. But there was one thing I did understand, and I've understood it for the rest of my life. They were talking about social problems, about historical events. And they weren't just talking about them but taking part in them, defining their own actions. They were making history and I was part of that."

"What kinds of decisions did you make?" Tina asked.

Luisa turned to Tina as if to answer her question, but she addressed herself to Sabina's comments instead: "Of course in the end one boss replaced another in government offices and factories. It was the same problem I had experienced before. We confronted enemies on two different fronts: capitalists ahead of us and statists behind us. Some of us thought the danger of one was as great as that of the other. Others thought the capitalists should be defeated first."

"What did that have to do with the decisions you made?" Tina asked.

"The way we understood the situation affected the statements and slogans we put on our posters and placards," Luisa explained.

"I remember those arguments!" I shouted excitedly "Luisa wanted to attack both sides simultaneously. Everyone paid attention to whatever was said and I thought the others were particularly attentive every time you spoke, Luisa. I thought at least half the people there supported you."

"All those who seemed to support me thought something different," Luisa said, "whereas all those on the other side had one single position. Two of them were convinced the only real threat came from the owners —"

"That was Adrian and Claude," Sabina reminded us.

"And although the other two agreed that we faced enemies in front as well as behind —"

"Marc and Titus," Sabina interrupted again.

"Marc and Titus agreed about the two dangers," Luisa continued, "but they argued that unity was the first requirement, since by dividing we would be used by both sides to fight against each other."

"What was your position?" Tina asked.

"I argued that it was impossible for workers to unite with statist politicians, since after the victory over the present rulers the workers would find themselves under the rule of their former allies. This is what happened in every revolution where workers' unions allied themselves with politicians struggling for power. The workers always learned too late that their revolutionary allies got power over them."

"Didn't Yarostan agree with you, and two others as well?" I asked.

Luisa said, "Either they didn't agree or they didn't understand. That hothead Jan argued that the real battle would start when workers wrecked the machines by stuffing wrenches and bolts into the gears and rollers, when workers started tearing down the factories with saws and axes, when workers started rioting, dismantling, burning. Jasna applauded, and Yarostan laughed! That soft-spoken Adrian Povrshan, the one who never took sides until the argument was over, suggested a compromise and everyone agreed with it except Jan. Adrian suggested that the slogans need not describe what we were against, but only what we were for. For example: 'The factories should be administered by the workers themselves.' 'The people should run their own affairs.' And that was what we decided to do."

"At that moment," I told Tina, "ten separate individuals who a minute earlier had seemed unable to agree about anything became a coordinated group with a single project. Suddenly, without electing a chairman, without an assignment of tasks, everyone knew what had to be done next."

"Jan still wasn't satisfied," Luisa remembered. "He went on grumbling about the need to fight with axes and not with words."

"I remember that!" I exclaimed. "That was when Yarostan announced that while we were trying to decide whether to take over or take apart the plant, the boss was sitting in his office figuring out how much output he'd have to get out of the workers after the strike so as to make up for his losses." How well I remember that! I really admired you at that moment; I think I fell in love with you then.

"That ape Claude suggested we arm ourselves and rush to the boss's office," Luisa exclaimed.

I went on, "Yarostan asked if we couldn't simply ask the boss to leave. That's when Sabina accompanied Yarostan, Claude and Jan to the office. Before they went Adrian suggested they tell Mr. Zagad to return after the revolution since he had experience in the work and the workers would remember him. Everyone laughed. The tension was over. We became a group of friends. I had the feeling I had known everyone there for years."

Sabina put a blanket on my enthusiasm by saying, "And then we were all arrested."

Luisa retorted angrily, "It wasn't 'and then'!"

I asked, "Sabina, how can you remember some things so well and others not at all? You took part in it all and you weren't the least active among us!"

Sabina yawned. Her yawn had the same significance as her earlier statement, "And that's all that happened." Luisa must have thought Sabina's yawn an insult aimed specifically at her and didn't say another word until Sabina and Tina went to bed. But my enthusiasm was still rising and I wanted to communicate it to Tina. I told her those days were the only time in my life when I knew why I was in the world. It was the only time I knew what part I was playing in the creation of our common world, the only time I was part of a social project which wasn't imposed on me from above. I told her about the wonderful days during which you patiently taught me how to run a press, the days I spent printing and silk-screening posters on my own. During every single one of those days I learned more than I've learned during all my years in school. I described our daily meetings, our discussions of the day's tasks, I told Tina each of us could do whatever we wanted; no one was bound to a task, even for a day; no one was forced to complete anything. Yet in spite of this absolute freedom every task got carried out, decisions got made, the posters got printed. I tried to describe the bicycle trips you and I took to other plants to distribute posters and collect suggestions for new ones, about Sabina's excursions with Jan, about the joy of seeing our posters on the walls of public buildings and on busses and trams. Wherever any of us went we were among friends. It was a rehearsal for what the new world would be like.

When I finally paused, Tina asked, "Why were you arrested?"

The question made my head spin. I looked helplessly toward Luisa, but she was staring at the wall, probably still seeing Sabina's yawn and hearing "that's all that happened." I must have looked startled or even angry because Tina felt compelled to say, "I'm sorry." She didn't have to apologize. I hadn't heard any hostility in her voice when she asked the question. Yet for some reason I felt that the question itself was hostile. I groped for an explanation but didn't know where to begin. My vivid memories receded until they were again covered up by the impenetrable curtains of time. I forgot all the newly remembered names and experiences. I had never asked myself that question, and it was pointless to look in my memory for an explanation. I had experienced so much during those few days twenty years ago, so many of the events that affected my whole life had flown by so quickly, that I hadn't had the time to absorb any of them fully, to re-experience them in my memory, to analyze or explain them. And when the storm was over I found myself in a completely different world, disoriented and frightened, surrounded by beings who were incomprehensible to me.

I groped, "What happened was exactly what Luisa had feared would happen. The workers were betrayed; they were stabbed in the back by their own allies. I do remember my first clue that something was wrong. One afternoon when Luisa and I returned home, George Alberts was already there. He usually worked until late at night. But that day, he was home before dark and we could see he was upset. Luisa asked him if anything had happened. He said he'd been fired. He was told never to come back. They had even called him a saboteur and some other things,"

Tina asked, "Who fired him? I thought the workers were on strike!"

"The trade union council," Sabina answered.

I couldn't say anything more; my throat was stopped up. Sabina got up and yawned again, as if to announce that she'd been right: "That's all that happened." She reminded Tina that it was three in the morning and if Tina was going to get up and go to work she might feel better if she got some sleep. I agreed. But dozens of "explanations" started to crowd into my mind as soon as Sabina left the room. I didn't want Tina to go to bed without understanding why the events had turned out the way they had. But I didn't stop her when she got up and said goodnight. She looked sad, perhaps because she saw the tears of frustration on my face, perhaps because she wanted in some way to apologize for having asked why we had been arrested.

As soon as Sabina and Tina left, Luisa became talkative again. She too intended to go to work the following day, but she insisted on staying up the rest of the night; she said her job was so repetitive she could do it in her sleep. She has a horribly boring job in an automobile factory.

Luisa read your letter over again. Certain passages bothered her. She read them to me and we discussed them. I'd like to summarize that discussion; I hope you aren't hurt or offended.

Both of us laughed and cried when we re-read your description of the censorship. Your letter doesn't seem to have been opened. What bothered Luisa was the next section, where you identify yourself with censors and prison guards and even say that your point of departure could have been the same as theirs. This also bothered me when Luisa read the passage to me. Both of us applied the passage to ourselves, and as soon as we did, we felt there was something profoundly untrue about it. Would we have become jailers if we hadn't been arrested? For example, if George Alberts hadn't been Luisa's "husband" (which in fact he never was) we wouldn't have been directly affected by his dismissal. Would we have stayed on in the carton plant carrying on the urgent tasks of the day? Would we have sat in judgment while one worker was labeled a "counterrevolutionary" and another a "saboteur"? Would we have stayed and watched while one after another of our comrades were called "dangerous elements" and "foreign agents"? Did we misread what you wrote? Isn't this what you meant when you said we all had the same starting point? You even wonder to what extent you contributed to your own imprisonment. Should Luisa and I wonder to what extent we were implicated in your arrest, and how much we contributed to the suffering you've undergone, for the past twenty years?

I think your premise is all wrong. I'm not altogether sure what you mean by "starting point," but I am sure that my starting point as well as yours and Luisa's was not the same as the starting point of those who fired Alberts, imprisoned you, arrested Luisa and me. It's simply ridiculous to identify yourself with them. The people who arrested me weren't workers but police agents. They had never been committed to the self-liberation of workers; on the contrary, their life-long commitment was to establish a dictatorship over the workers, to transform society into a beehive and themselves into queen bees, to become the wardens of a vast prison camp. They won and we lost. That sums up the entire history of the working class. But how can you say those who fought against them contributed to their victory?

Take the people in our group. Luisa and I spent a long time reminding ourselves of them. At most you can say that some of them didn't know what they were doing. Jasna, for instance, became something like Luisa's "disciple." Luisa remembered that poor Jasna constantly repeated things Luisa had told her, but only the words and incidents, not the meanings. This doesn't mean Jasna had the same starting point as an inquisitioner or a prison guard. Or take Jan. Luisa called him a hothead. Maybe he was, but his "hotheadedness" was a healthy and human response to abuse and exploitation. There isn't even a question about any of the others. Vera and

Adrian couldn't let a stranger walk by without trying to convert him to the "self-government of the producers." I remember how I admired the speed with which Vera answered people's questions. Once, when someone asked her, "Who's going to pick up the garbage if there's no government?" she immediately retorted, "Who do you think picks it up now — the government?" Or take Marc. Luisa remembered him as being slower than Vera but more profound. He could spend hours talking about the types of social relations people would be able to create and develop as soon as they were free of authority. And he was so resourceful; whenever materials or tools were lacking, he knew either where to find them or what could be used instead. As for Claude: all I remember about him is that he seemed devoted to every project he undertook. I don't remember Titus very well either. I do remember I didn't like him; he struck me as too much of a "realist", he was always calculating the "balance of forces." But he was an old friend of Luisa's and she was always convinced of his total devotion to the workers' struggle. I also remember that you looked up to him for his knowledge and experience.

Whatever you mean by "starting point," the starting point of my life was the experience I shared with you. That was the only time in my life when I was engaged in a group project. No outside force, no institution, boss or leader defined our project, made our decisions, determined our schedules or tasks. We defined and determined ourselves. No one pushed, drove or coerced us. Each of us was free in the fullest sense. We briefly succeeded in creating a real community, a condition which doesn't exist in repressive societies and therefore isn't even understood. Our community was a ground on which individuals could grow and flower; it was totally unlike the quicksand which pulls down the seed, the root and even the whole plant. If this was our starting point, then we differed from order-givers and order-takers as much as a healthy living cell differs from a cancer cell, as much as an oak tree differs from a hydrogen bomb.

Luisa and I discussed other things in your letter, but not as thoroughly; we were both very tired. You might think this all-night discussion of your letter bizarre. I should tell you that Luisa and I hadn't seen each other since last year and we haven't had anything to say to each other in ages, partly because I chose to live with Sabina and Tina, but mainly because we've stopped having anything in common. Your letter brought to life the one subject we do still share: our past. Thanks to your letter we learned we could be "old friends"; you helped revive a relationship which had degenerated to the level of polite indifference.

The question of marriage was another thing that bothered Luisa. This hadn't bothered me at all until she started talking about it. You're "married," you have a "wife" and a "daughter." Obviously! Why wouldn't you? I accepted these things as matter-of-factly as you narrated them. But as soon as Luisa questioned all this I remembered who you were and kicked myself for having thought it all so obvious. I'm really not very observant: whenever I leave familiar surroundings I seem to lose my powers of observation and take everything for granted. Luisa said your statements about your "wife" and "daughter" seemed as strange as if you'd written us about the second coming of the savior.

My own memory has shut out everything except those wonderful days I spent with you on the streets and in the factory. Luisa reminded me that we had known you for years before that. It was Titus who first brought you to our house. You came at least once a week, and as Luisa put it, you were unquestionably one of "us." You must know what she means.

Someone whose life goal was to have a nice house, a nice family and a nice job in the bureaucracy simply didn't come into our house. Opposition to the state, religion and the family was taken for granted in anyone we considered a friend. And that's an attitude we've continued to share, whatever differences have grown up between us over the years.

Luisa had innumerable relationships (I haven't yet heard about all of them), but she never married. She always insisted she was genuinely in love only once, with Nachalo, her first companion, my father. But she was never his "wife." She adopted his name as her own the day after he was killed: that was the only "memorial" she was able to build for him. The adoption of his name may have been a caprice, or an expression of romantic sentimentality, but it was not a concession to the institution; union with a corpse doesn't count as marriage. Luisa's next "husband" was George Alberts, and as soon as Luisa figured out he was transforming her into a "wife" she chased him out of the house. Sabina had a child and never married. As for me, I never wanted children, for any number of reasons; I can summarize them by saying I was always "too much of a revolutionary."

None of us ever became institutionalized "mothers," and none of us were ever institutionalized "daughters." Surely you were aware of this. From the moment we could walk and talk, Sabina and I took part in the work, the discussions as well as the decisions. Even earlier, when Sabina was still a baby, it was I who "brought her up," not her "parents." Of course this is common among working people, but in our case it didn't happen only because our "parents" both had to work. We had genuinely eliminated every trace of the hated institution, obviously only to the extent possible in a society which had not eliminated it. I can't remember ever having thought of Luisa as "my mother": at most we were friends, once very close friends, in recent years no longer even friends.

Sabina is Tina's "mother," but I'm certain that neither of them thinks of herself or of the other as mother and daughter. And the mere thought that Tina and I are "relatives," that I'm something like Tina's "aunt," drives me up a wall. To each other and to our friends we're simply three women who live together. It's cheaper that way, we help each other, and we usually enjoy each other's company. If one of us decided she'd had enough of the other two, nothing could keep her from leaving — certainly not the thought that we're relatives. Not that it's all so easy and obvious. On legal forms we're "sisters" because of our name. And to inquisitive and hostile strangers who suspect we're not "sisters," we're bizarre: we're living proof that the world is indeed coming to an end.

You speak of "mother and father, wife and daughter" as if these were the most natural relations in the world, as if people had never lived outside these categories. Of course these things are "natural" to most people, but at one time they weren't "natural" at all to you. They were as alien to you as religion, the state and capital. Was I mistaken? Was this only the way I imagined you? Or have you changed? Luisa remembered long talks she'd had with you, not just about "politics" in the narrow sense, but also about the senselessness of promising a stuffy judge that you'd spend the rest of your life with the individual you happen to like at the time, and discussions about the horror of locking children up in the family prison. Did you adopt those attitudes only because you knew how Luisa felt, or how I felt? I can't make myself believe you were only pretending. I wouldn't have been more disturbed if you'd told us you had invested millions in a uranium mine. How could you possibly have changed so much? I can obviously understand that you might introduce Mirna to a complete stranger as "your wife." But I'm not a stranger to you. Neither are Luisa or Sabina. What do they do to people in those prisons?

Luisa and I made ourselves coffee, watched the sun rise above the buildings behind our snowy yard, and continued discussing your letter. By now you might think we spent the night dissecting it. We did in fact find another strange element in it, although by no means as bizarre as your becoming a husband to a wife and a father to a daughter.

We were moved by your tirades against the prison system, by your exposure of the petty informers and executioners our neighbors so often turn out to be, by your beautiful description of Yara's protest. Yet you treated the whole subject of rebellion in a way we thought strange. In your words rebellion became something metaphysical, something that transcends individuals of flesh and blood and refers to the core of being. "Wherever there are people there's negation." That's beautiful. I found the whole passage powerful and poetic. But we also found something wrong with it. (By "we" I mean that I noticed it after Luisa pointed it out.) Surely you didn't discover "negation, rebellion, insurrection" only a year ago, and only because schoolchildren demonstrated for a teacher! There's a war on! It's been going on for centuries — ever since human beings found themselves in class societies. And the defeat, even the repeated defeat, of one of the protagonists doesn't mean that the war is over. So long as the vanquished giant is not exterminated he'll rise again and yet again, returning to battle with ever greater fury. You of all people ought to know that — you who took part in two massive uprisings, two unforgettable acts of rebellion by the working people.

But I realize I'm being unfair and extremely insensitive. Luisa and I are obviously aware that the world of jailers and convicts is not the world in which the workers' commonwealth can be built. As I challenge conclusions you've drawn out of so much pain, I realize I've no right to challenge them and I'm ashamed. Not ashamed of what I said, but ashamed of my fairly comfortable surroundings and my generous friends. I'm ashamed that I was released two days after our arrest while you spent all those years in prison, ashamed I was arrested only once after that and was again released after only two days in jail. And I'm not even sure I agree with Luisa. I think what bothered her wasn't so much your treatment of rebellion as your description of the self-repressed "imbecile." Earlier in the evening, when Tina was reading your letter after the rest of us had already read it, she burst out laughing. We all knew she had come to the passage where you describe the imbecile who voluntarily exploits himself. Sabina and I laughed too: none of us can stand workers who "love" their jobs. But it wasn't long before my laughter nearly turned to tears: I realized that Luisa, unsmiling and shocked, saw herself as the "imbecile." Luisa has "voluntarily" gotten up every morning and gone to the same idiotic job for the past seventeen years. The schedule, the product, the task are imbecilic. Does that make Luisa an imbecile? My first impulse was to agree with you: I laughed too. But I'm not sure. When Luisa referred to your "metaphysical" attitude toward rebellion and your "simplistic" attitude toward work, I understood what she meant. I couldn't help but understand: in a few minutes she was going to rush away to her job. As soon as she left, Tina rushed into the kitchen, gulped down some juice, rushed out without saying goodbye, and slammed the door as she always does. I know she won't keep her job for as long as seventeen weeks. Yet it's Luisa, not Tina, who attends every meeting she hears about, who is the first one out in every strike, who joins every picket line and carries the biggest sign in every demonstration. Tina stays home and reads during a strike. She's as hostile to demonstrations as she is to girlie shows, and the one time in her life when she attended a "radical" meeting, her only comment was, "Every one of them thinks he's Napoleon."

The more I think about it the more disturbing I find your description of the "imbecile." Several years ago I had a bad scene with Luisa. I was staying at her house. She came home from work and started sobbing. She kept saying that her life wasn't any good to anyone, that she saw no reason for dragging it on any longer. I couldn't think of anything to say. I could only ask her what had happened that day. And of course nothing had happened either that day or the day before or the year before. She described herself as an old rag that was being squeezed drier every day. What you said in your letter passed through my mind at that time. I knew I couldn't spend every day of my life repeating the same motions, helping build the very machines that oppressed me, contributing to my own suffering, as you put it. I haven't done that, by the way: my "work record" is worse than Tina's. In practice I've agreed with you. Luisa somehow pulled out of it, although I was no help. She threw herself into new activities. And she continued to go back to work every day.

I wanted to summarize our reactions to your letter, and instead I'm summarizing my confusion. I'm no longer even sure my last few paragraphs have anything to do with your letter. They certainly don't amount to a "reasoned critique" of anything you said.

When I started to tell you about our "night with Yarostan's letter," I thought this would be a way to begin to answer your questions: who I am, what I'm thinking, what I've done, if I'm "married" and have children, if I'm still alive. I've told you some of these things, and surely you weren't expecting one-word answers. I assume you want to know as much about my life as I'd like to know about yours. Maybe it was a mistake to try to combine the story of my life with the story of our discussion. This happens to be one of the "devices" I was using on the two occasions when I started to write a novel.

Yet even if this combination of the present with the past is "only" a literary device, the novels in which I was going to use it were never anything more than answers anticipating your questions. This letter is the first chapter. Whenever I tried to imagine who my readers would be, I always focused on one and the same person: you. It was to be a novel about you and me, about the days we spent together. That was to be the "past." The "present" was to consist of my frustrated attempts to recreate those days in impossible circumstances. It was all true, exactly as it happened; I was only going to change people's names, and in my drafts I didn't even do that: I only changed the names of the people I was still with; I was too attached to the other names to change them. A lot of it would have had to be "fiction" even if the names weren't because I don't have Sabina's memory.

I was sorry you didn't mention the experience we shared. I was sad that you had almost forgotten me. The experience I shared with you has marked everything I've thought and done. My life begins with it. That experience gave me a standard, a measure which I applied to all my later experiences and to all the people I met. Complete persons once picked up a corner of the world and began to reshape it. From them I learned what people and activity could be. From them I learned that every theoretical ideal was a mere combination of words, that every intellectual Utopia was a reshuffling of present repressions. I understood the shortcomings of the people I was with because I had known people without them; I had learned that people could be more than lifeless checkers waiting to be moved or removed by superhuman hands.

Luisa had lived through an experience far richer than mine, yet her demands on the present were far more modest. After we came here she threw herself into union activity and peace demonstrations with unqualified enthusiasm; no one could have guessed that three times in her life she had experienced eruptions that undermined the world's foundations. Perhaps she nursed the illusion that every strike was the beginning of the general strike, every demonstration the signal for an insurrection, every movement the outbreak of the revolution. I threw myself into similar activities, but without the same enthusiasm. If I had shared Luisa's exhilaration whenever the same burned-out mummy was publicly exhibited as the newest spark, Sabina and Tina wouldn't have tolerated me. It's not that either of them is "conservative." When I compare Luisa's personal life to Tina's I can't help feeling that Tina is the subversive. As for Sabina: she rejects convention so uncompromisingly that everyone considers her a "crackpot." To Sabina, Luisa's "revolutionary enthusiasm" is merely another convention. In Sabina's words, all of Luisa's attitudes can be summarized in two short sentences: whenever a worker farts, the ruling class trembles; whenever a worker pisses, the tidal waves of revolution begin to flood the world. I've never heard of two individuals who had less in common.

I ought to admit that most of my seeming "wisdom" is hindsight; in the heat of events I'm every bit as hysterical as Luisa. Only last year there was a large-scale riot here. People burned stores, broke shop windows and carried home as many loads as they could carry. I came home with a television; someone handed it to me and I couldn't pass it on because everyone else's hands were full. Tina came home with a new pair of shoes which fit her perfectly. The festival turned into a massacre; police and soldiers murdered a lot of people. Sabina commented, "At least Tina had good sense." What she meant was, "That's all that happened." In purely selfish terms Tina's shoes were all we got out of the riot, since I gave my television away the following day because none of us can stand to watch it. But I refused to reduce the event to Tina's shoes. For me the glass walls of private property had at last been battered by the underlying population. The riot was the healthiest move I had seen the people of this city make in all the twenty years I've been here. I was teaching a university course at the time, and the day after the rioting ended I arrived in class full of the looting spirit. I asked which students had taken part in the riot. Then I turned to one of the students who had not taken part and asked if he had always been a good boy. It turned out he had, so I asked if as a boy he hadn't secretly wished he had joined the more intelligent kids swimming in the pond instead of sweating in Sunday school like an obedient poodle in a suit and bow tie. Predictably, the good boy reported me to the dean and I was fired next time I went to teach my class. Unlike Yara, none of my students thought of demonstrating for me. It apparently didn't occur to them. It didn't occur to me either since I hated my job, and my "riot" was the pretext I'd been looking for to quit.

The riot was a carnival before the professional killers got into it. But ultimately Sabina was right. A few people got things they actually needed, and that was all that happened. Most people got home with armloads of elephants, like mine, which they ended up storing in their attics or giving away. The walls of private property didn't crumble. Tensions that had built up for years, for ages, were let out like farts into the already polluted air. Broken shop windows were replaced by brick walls and people went back to work to produce more commodities. Then they again waited in lines to pay for them. Some people made a fuss about those who had been killed by the army and the police — rightly so. But suing the government for killing looters instead of jailing them isn't equivalent to expropriating the exploiters.

I became wise only after the fact. But Luisa! I saw her soon after the riot. She told me that when the riot broke out she locked herself up in her house and turned on the radio. When I expressed amazement, she said the workers she had fought with had attacked the system of property, not the property itself. "What good would it do them to inherit a world in ruins?" she asked. She stayed away. But the cooler it got outside the warmer she got. She started to get excited when the army was called in. And she became her enthusiastic and militant self when everything was over. That's when she joined a demonstration against police repression. When I saw her, she was working away in the dingy office of an anti-repression committee. Everything was over. The "committee" was nothing but a mop-up operation, the house-cleaning on the day after the big event. Yet Luisa was in a state of euphoria: she was positively sick with enthusiasm. For her the revolution was just beginning. I didn't even try to argue with her. I was polite and indifferent. I smiled condescendingly. I hadn't seen her for several years; I didn't see her again until your letter came.

I still haven't answered all your questions. Why did I write you twelve years ago? I had been looking for someone like you from the day I arrived here and the people I found weren't enough like you to put an end to my search. So I decided to try to reach you, and in case you couldn't be found, I tried to reach the other people in our group. I had just "finished" college (I should say it finished me: I was expelled). I had taken part in one of the earliest actions of what was later called the "student movement," and it had all come to nothing. In later years that experience wasn't even counted as part of the history of the student movement. But I won't tell about that now. What bothered me at the time wasn't the fact that no one knew what we had done, but the nightmarish quality of the experience itself: I ran with all my might and got nowhere. I couldn't orient myself. I was desperate. It seemed that ever since I'd come here I'd been seeing only walls: concrete walls, brick walls, metal walls, all of them too high to see over. I had no idea what happened on the other side of the walls nor who was behind them. I've since learned that there are workshops behind the walls, workshops where most people spend most of their lives, workshops which are probably very similar to the prisons where you've spent most of your life. But at that time I only knew that the walls kept me out, that I was excluded, and I remembered that once in my life I hadn't been excluded, that I had known live individuals and had taken part in meaningful activity; I remembered that once in my life the walls had stopped being impenetrable and had started to crumble. I thought that if I could only reach you or the others I'd find a frame of reference.

I waited and waited for an answer, but not a word came. I'm surprised to learn that Mirna had seen my letter; I had thought none of my letters had reached their destinations. I suppose you didn't see my letter because, you were in prison. Why didn't you see it afterwards? Was it lost? And why did she have to memorize the address; did she know the letter would be lost? What mystified me most was your statement that Mirna thought the letter peculiar and "attributed a strange power" to it. What in the world happened to my letter?

I want to know everything, and in detail. I want to know about the things you did and the things that were done to you, about the people you met and the people you liked. I want to know what you thought about the experiences and the people, and what you think of them now. I want to know about Yara and Mirna and about the people I knew twenty years ago.

Your letter made all of us aware of the chasm that separates your world from ours. None of us believes the official literature of either side (they're both in fact the same side: the outside), but as a result no one knows what to believe. The impenetrable walls I mentioned seem to be the world's main architecture. When you're behind one wall, you can't know that there's yet another wail on the other side of it. As for the people behind that wall: they simply don't exist. If one of them nevertheless appears among us, we're suspicious: he must be a state agent; who else could scale both walls? I've heard about such state agents: they knew as little about the people who had been my comrades as I know about the manikins at a debutante's ball, and they were every bit as contemptuous. We do learn something from them: when you hear a horror story often enough you start to assume it's true, although that's a poor way to determine what's true, especially if you know that the repetition of lies is the propagandist's stock in trade.

I was dumbfounded when you said that at one point you felt homesick for prison. I have to admit I'm one of the many who fear arrest and dread imprisonment. In spite of my brief experience with jails I still imagine prison life as consisting of long lines of silent men and women pulling iron balls and chains. Luisa reminded me that the conditions of workers are often similar to those of convicts serving long prison terms, and that these conditions stimulate feelings of mutual aid, solidarity as well as shared goals and lifelong friendships. A person who is dumbfounded by their solidarity, their camaraderie, is not one of them but an alien, an outsider, possibly an enemy. I genuinely hope you won't regard me an outsider, or what you called an "imbecile."

All my encouragement and admiration go out to you, to Yara, to Mirna, to all your still-imprisoned comrades. And if you couldn't hide your impatience for an answer, I won't even try to hide mine.

Love, *Sophia*.

Yarostan's second letter

D ear Sophia,
My picture of you was hazy when I wrote you last time but now I remember you as if I had been with you only yesterday. No one who had known you twenty years ago could fail to recognize you. You wrote me a warm, comradely letter. I'd like to answer in the same spirit. I'd like at least to be polite. But twenty years have passed. Everyone around me has changed. Your picture of yourself as

you are today is disturbingly similar to the person you thought you were twenty years ago. What I recognize in your letter is not the event we experienced together but an event we never experienced. I wrote to a living person and was answered by an imaginary person celebrating an event that never took place.

I admit that I once shared the illusion your letter celebrates. Twenty years ago you and I were like children who saw a group of people digging in a field and ran to join them. They were chanting. We misunderstood the chant; we failed to hear the suffering and resignation. We thought they were singing out of joy. We found spades and dug with them. We sang more loudly than the rest until one of them turned to us and asked, "Don't you know what you're doing?" Sophia, don't you remember that terrified face wrinkled with pain? "Look over there," he said, pointing toward rifles aimed at the group. We had joined a group of prisoners sentenced to die; we were helping them dig the mass grave into which they were to be thrown after they were shot. How can you have retained only the memory of the moment when we joyfully sang alongside them? Is it possible that after twenty years you still don't know what we helped them do?

I was disappointed by your letter and infinitely more disappointed by Luisa. Maybe you were too young and full of life to grasp the nature of what you call your key experience. But I can't make myself believe that Luisa — the Luisa I thought I knew — could nurse an illusion of this magnitude for two decades. That's why I'm sending this letter to your address instead of hers.

When I started reading your letter I was overjoyed at having reached both of you. By the second or third page my joy turned to disbelief. I started again. My impression was confirmed. You locate your birth, your starting point, in the event that tore me apart; your growth coincides with my destruction.

And Luisa encourages you. Only Sabina seems to be aware of what happened even though she was only twelve at the time. Maybe my inability to recognize the Luisa in your letter is similar to your inability to remember what we did together. I too nursed an illusion for many years, an illusion of a person called Luisa whose only common trait with the real Luisa was her name. I preserved my portrait of Luisa during my first prison term; no investigators could take it from me, no torturers could mar it, I admired and respected this Luisa. I loved her. She was the guide who led me unharmed through all the suffering, the hopelessness, the horror. She was my first real teacher. Every one of Luisa's comments, from the words about the approach of liberation armies to the description of Jan Sedlak as a hothead, disfigured the picture I had guarded so carefully. My "Luisa" is now in shreds. You rid me of an illusion. My imaginary "Luisa" is shattered and fragments of a different person are returning to my memory. These fragments had been suppressed during the years when the mythical Luisa was the only Luisa I remembered. The return of the fragments suggests that I once knew a different Luisa from the one whose portrait I preserved; I once knew a person disturbingly similar to the one in your letter. I knew such a person and rejected her because she wasn't someone I could admire, respect or love. The years of separation annihilated the traces left by the real person; the imaginary Luisa evicted the living Luisa from my memory.

I'm making this tedious effort to understand the workings of my memory so as to gain some insight into yours. Could it be that what you describe as our common experience was only partly a real event and mainly your own invention? Could it be that your illusory past experience was so gratifying, so complete, that in time you suppressed every trace of the real event? If so, and if you're attached to your illusion, then you don't have to read any further; the rest of this letter may have the same effect on you as yours had on me: my shattered illusion is being replaced by painful, long-suppressed memories; I'm seeing people and events I had warded off for two decades.

I was only fifteen when Titus Zabran first introduced me to your house. He and Luisa both worked at the carton plant. I had met Titus a year earlier, just before the end of the war; we were both in a resistance group that fought against the occupying army. I remember, even without your reminder, that Titus did not introduce me to a mother and her daughters. He introduced me to three women: Luisa, a woman in her late twenties; Sophia — you must have been twelve or thirteen — and little Sabina, nine or ten. You addressed each other by your first names, as equals. You and Sabina had prepared supper for all of us. Luisa asked Sabina if there was anything she could do to help, and the little girl answered with self-assurance: "Just sit clown and talk; everything is ready." I was fascinated. I had never before experienced such a total absence of authority in relations between children and adults.

In retrospect it might be more accurate to say that I was entranced. I fell under a. spell. I started to create my mythical picture of the three of you from the moment I met you. From then on I saw, heard and felt only those expressions and gestures that fitted with the imaginary creatures you had already become. I suppressed everything that conflicted with my picture. The suppressed elements remained somewhere in my memory, buried under the myth. These elements are returning now, perfectly preserved but fragmentary. They had never been more than fragments.

I was drawn to your house like a bee to flowers, first once a week, then two and even three times. I plied Luisa with questions about the revolution in which she had taken part ten years earlier. I couldn't hear enough about it. Titus had also taken part in it, but I didn't ask him any questions. Whenever he made a comment, it consisted of vast historical generalizations. He referred to people and events that were unfamiliar to me and I was bored, confused and embarrassed to be so ignorant. I didn't only want to learn about that revolution; I wanted to learn it from Luisa. I understood every word she spoke. Her descriptions were so clear, so vivid that as she spoke I imagined I was taking part in the events she described. She helped me live those events by comparing them to experiences I had myself lived.

Luisa compared the day of the outbreak of the revolution with the first day of the resistance, when my neighbors and friends ran out of their houses armed and filled with enthusiasm, the day when I helped build a barricade and then helped defend it. Nine years separated the two events, and in Luisa's descriptions that was all that separated them. I knew then as clearly as I know now that the two events had nothing in common except the barricades. To Luisa they had everything in common; the two events were one and the same. Yet this didn't bother me. Her comparison helped me understand. Groups of people who had never engaged in any activity together — some of them former acquaintances from the neighborhood or factory, most of them complete strangers — became the best of friends in an instant. They suddenly had everything in common: apprehensions as well as hopes, immediate tasks as well as distant projects. And I was one of them. I transferred the resistance experiences I had lived a year earlier to the revolutionary experience Luisa had lived. I became a member of a fighting community, an equal among people who were freeing themselves, a comrade among workers determined to destroy the repressive world. I was no longer the lousy kid, the vagrant, the lumpen I had been during the war.

I wasn't proud of what I'd been earlier; my recent past was out of place in the world the three of you inhabited, that mythical world where I myself lodged you. You wanted to know about my "heroic" experiences during the resistance but I never told you about them. Luisa helped me forget them; she helped me transform the real events of my life into imaginary events which I "experienced" only while listening to Luisa's stories.

My parents were taken away shortly before the war ended. I was supposed to hide in the coal bin of the house across the street. But I stood by the basement window and watched as they were escorted out of our house and helped to the back of a truck. They had both worked in factories. They'd just come home from work; it was dusk. Earlier that day, when my neighbors had forced me into the bin, I insisted on knowing why. They "explained" that my mother's father had been Jewish. This explanation told me nothing. My parents had never discussed politics or religion or anything at all except the amount of money left to meet the week's expenses. The explanation I understood was written on my neighbors' faces: my parents were stained. I was stained. All the neighbors watched as my parents were taken away. Those who couldn't see from the windows came out of their houses to look. No one did anything or said anything. It was like a funeral. All the faces were sad, yet they all expressed something other than sadness: they were relieved they didn't have Jewish grandfathers.

My neighbors, as poor as my parents and nervous as squirrels, had already gotten false papers proving I was their son. But I couldn't stay on with them. They weren't used to having a permanent guest and I knew they couldn't afford to feed me. Secondly, and I now think unjustly, I felt that just below their kindness and generosity they feared I would sooner or later stain them.

I left my "home town" and I've never felt the slightest desire to return there, even for a visit. I walked all the way to the city, sleeping in fields and barns, eating fruits and raw vegetables on the way. When I got here I roamed the streets like a stray dog, sleeping in doorways and alleys. In winter I pried open basement windows. My last "stolen home" was the storeroom of a factory, a vast gallery full of sheets and rolls of cardboard. I survived by stealing — not from the occupiers nor from the rich. One day I saw a boy my age running along the sidewalk; he snatched an old woman's grocery bag without slowing down or even losing a step and disappeared. I practiced for several hours with a garbage bag, I acquired a "skill" and I went out to the world to earn my living.

One morning I overslept. I didn't wake up until a man pulled me by the ear and shouted hysterically: "How did you get in here, you lousy vagabond? I'll take you straight to the police." Others ran in from the workshop. One of them ran up to my torturer and shouted, "Let the boy go!" "I will not! He's going straight to the police!" the man shouted back, pulling my ear so hard I thought it would break; I later learned he was the foreman. The group surrounded the foreman; my defender planted himself right in front of him. The foreman left my burning ear alone and grabbed me by the arm. My defender then said, "He's a friend of mine; he's looking for work; I asked him to meet me here. It's freezing outside and you can see he's not dressed for it. Would you stand and wait in the cold if you were able to come inside?" The foreman visibly didn't believe a word of it, but he let my arm go; he couldn't prove anything except that I had found my way out of the cold, and besides, he was surrounded. That evening I learned my defender's name: Titus Zabran. One of the people in the group that surrounded the foreman was Jasna Zbrkova. When I finally did get a job there after the war she called me "the vagabond who was caught oversleeping." I returned to the plant that evening; I wanted to thank Titus. Instead, he thanked me for waiting for him. He asked if I would have been willing to work there if there had been an opening. I had never thought of working. I told him my parents had done nothing else with their lives and in the end were taken away in the back of a truck.

Titus introduced me to his friends. One of them housed me; others took turns feeding me. They were all workers. They all begged me to stop stealing; they said it would endanger their organization; the police would come looking for me and would arrest all of them. I stopped. But then I had nothing to do. I attended all the organization meetings but was bored to tears. When they argued I stared into space; nothing they ever said had anything to do with me. They used words like "revolution" and "liberation," but in such strange ways; they seemed like exotic merchants screeching and tearing each others' hair because one had cheated the other in a transaction that had taken place years ago in a different part of the world. (Later on I took part in such discussions; in retrospect I consider my first reaction to have been the healthier one.) I wasn't idle very long. The war was nearing its end. The word "liberation" began to be used in increasingly comprehensible ways. It started to mean rifles, grenades, bullets. When it was learned that I was familiar with hiding places in every part of the city I no longer had time to steal or to stare into space during meetings.

The three days and three nights of the rising were the high point of my life. All the elements I later heard Luisa describe were present; they are probably elements of every popular uprising. But there were other elements, sinister ones; Luisa later helped me suppress them; she helped me remember those three days as if they had been the first three days of the revolution she had experienced. Yes, the cooperation, the sociability and the comradeship were all there. But I took all this for granted. After all, for several months I had used all my time and energy hiding weapons, preparing for this event; I didn't expect less from others. The only emotion I felt during those three days — an emotion whose memory traces were later driven underground by Luisa 's edifying story — was a "bloodthirsty desire for revenge. Building the barricades was a profound experience, a social project as you call it, even a type of popular architecture. And I genuinely enjoyed the work in ways that the routinized, institutionalized daily work can't be enjoyed. But the project was marred by its purpose. I worked enthusiastically, but my mind was on the enemy: I looked forward, not to the completion of the common project, but to the attack. And when they attacked, my sociability and my architectural interest vanished. I had only one goal: to lodge every single bullet in a uniformed body. At first I shot to avenge my parents. Later I just shot; my only concern was to hit.

I can already hear, "But that's not just you; that's war." Yes it is. It's just war. If we take it so much for granted, why do we suppress every memory of it? A few months earlier I had stolen the groceries of poor old women and I had been a vicious thief, a bully. Now I murdered dozens of human beings, most of them workers, many of them hardly older than I, and I was a hero. I haven't been proud of my thefts, but I never felt the need to suppress them from my memory. As for the deeds that made me a hero: I couldn't flee from them fast enough. I had to suppress them, replace them with other deeds — and even then I wasn't self-assured in my hero's pride.

Luisa helped me suppress my memory of the real uprising. She helped me drive out of my consciousness the shots, the falling bodies and the expressions on their faces. I met Luisa only a few days after the rising, when I was hired at the carton plant. Claude Tamnich. Vera Neis and Adrian Povrshan were also hired at that time. The rising had created lots of vacancies. Several workers had been killed by a single grenade as they were leaving the plant. It was probably thrown by a young worker avenging the death of his comrades, perhaps comrades I had shot some minutes or hours earlier. Even the foreman was gone; he had been killed by "our side," the day after the rising; someone had shouted "Kill the dirty collaborator!" and several people had aimed and shot him as if he had been a diseased dog; if I had been there I would have been among the first to shoot. Perhaps the man who shouted "Kill the collaborator" was a truck driver; perhaps some two years earlier he had driven a truck in the back of which two old workers were transported to a camp.

Luisa's inspiring narrative left no room for such speculations. I forgot about my resistance experiences when I listened to her describe the day when, nine years earlier, the army started to attack the population it supposedly defended. In response to the attack, the people rose; men, women, boys and girls, employed and unemployed workers began arming themselves and building barricades. The isolated cogs of the social machine became a community of human beings held together by a common project, a common goal: to defend their city and to build a new world, their own world. In my experience such a project had been neither the intention nor the outcome. But I wished it had been both, and I believed Luisa. Furthermore the three of you were living proof of the new world; at least all the proof I needed.

The climax of the story was the victory. The army was defeated. The old order crumbled. The revolution had triumphed at last. And the population was transformed. On the barricades and in the battles the passive, submissive and repressed underclass turned into a community of independent individuals. At that point a steady, unbroken process began. Churches were turned into nurseries and schools and meeting houses. Prisons were destroyed. Workers occupied the factories where they had worked and began to operate them on their own, without owners or managers. Busses and trams were operating normally only a few days after the victory. In the armaments factories workers began to produce weapons that had never before been made in those plants. The revolution spread. Peasants ousted landlords and took over the land.

How did such a sequence of victories end in such overwhelming defeat? The workers were attacked on two fronts: Luisa repeats this explanation in your letter. The power of the forces that oppressed the workers was overwhelming. The generals built powerful armies abroad; they got aid from every quarter and the workers got none. Besides which a fifth column developed internally. The revolution could have been victorious against one or the other front: it had already proved itself in its confrontation with the generals. But in the face of both it was defeated. Luisa's picture is beautiful, edifying and sad. Everything our side did spread the revolution, strengthened it, deepened it. Those who worked against it were outsiders to it, foreign to its spirit, hostile to its project.

Years later, in prison, I met Manuel, a man who had taken part in that revolution. He had been in prisons and camps for fourteen years when I met him. He was arrested by the "people's" police a few months after the revolutionary victory against the army, and he spent his life since then being transferred from one prison or camp to another. His account of the experience was similar to Luisa's only to the extent that it reminded me of the events with which Luisa had familiarized me. The language was different, but the event was the same: I recognized it, down to details. What I failed to recognize was that the fragments Manuel narrated did not fit into Luisa's picture at all. I failed to see that the language was different because it described a different picture. Luisa's descriptions of the revolution, the resistance, the uprising in which you took part, have one thing in common: they are descriptions of imaginary events. The very language she used falsified the real events and replaced them with stories that were profound, complete and edifying only because they were myths. I can see this now because your letter applied the same magic to an experience I actually lived, an experience I still remember. You sent me a distorted mirror-image of myself, similar enough to be recognizable, engaged in activity that never took place. When I see what you and Luisa did to my experience I begin to understand what she has done to her own. She experienced one of the great moments of history and she suppressed every trace of it from her memory. She saw the repressed, the maimed and the stunted transform themselves into human beings who glistened with potentialities, and she looked away so as not to be blinded. On the barricades she took part in a project that was completely her own, a project born with the group engaged in it, a project that would make all projects possible. For a moment the imaginations of free individuals roamed through a universe of infinite possibilities, for a moment the possibility of genuinely human activity was in everyone's reach. This was the peak of the revolution; everything that followed was a steep descent. Yet it is this moment that's missing from Luisa's account. Either she was looking away or she suppressed it. Instead, she glorifies the sequence of events that destroyed the possibilities, stunted the imaginations and maimed the lives of the individuals who had so briefly been free. Luisa's "revolution" is still moving upward when, on the day after the victory, "our militants" met with ousted and powerless politicians of the ruined state apparatus and constituted themselves into a "people's committee"; it is still moving upward when, instead of launching our own projects, we return to "our own" factories, busses and trams, when "our own" militants replace the foremen, managers and directors; it is still moving upward when we produce "our own" weapons in "our own" armaments plants. It begins to move downward only when outside elements using foreign force betray "our militants" on the "people's committee" and transform the committee into a police; when these elements force "our militants" to convince peasants to give their lands back to former landlords and to convince workers to accept a state-appointed manager or even the former owner as their boss; it begins to move downward only when the new "people's army" and the revitalized "people's police" begin to arrest workers who resist the reimposed boss and peasants who resist the reimposed landlord, when workers begin to be killed by "their own" bullets fired from rifles produced in "their own" plants, when the army and police parade through the streets with trucks and tanks of a type never before produced in "the workers' own" armaments plants. We were overwhelmed by external forces, by "statists" and by the "fifth column." At no point was there a trace of rot at our own core. Maybe' a few, very few, of our militants made some mistakes, but they were minor and insignificant, and everyone makes mistakes.

I believed what Luisa told me. I had to. She had been there and I hadn't. But when she uses the same language and imagery to describe the resistance which I did take part in, as well as the coup which cut away half my life, I realize she has done something drastic to reality: she has cut it out of her memory.

But what happened to you, Sophia? What have you done to your memory? How can you refer to the resistance by mentioning, in one and the same sentence, the "thousands of working people fighting and dying to free their city" and the "approach of the liberation armies"? If we fought to free the city, then we lost; the "liberation army" destroyed the city's freedom. But if we fought to free the city, why did we — thousands of us in the streets, as you say — cheer and dance when the tanks and soldiers of the "liberation army" marched into the already liberated city? If we fought to liberate the city, why didn't we turn our guns on the new occupiers? Why didn't we shoot the commanders, fraternize with the soldiers and begin building our free city? It's the same, familiar and distorted picture. We were pure; we fought for freedom. They were despotic; they fought to enslave us. This picture is false. I was one of those thousands. I shot to avenge and to kill. So did the people alongside me on the barricades. I learned that I had helped to "free the city" only after I met Luisa. And then I "remembered" having done that. But it's not true. I didn't for a moment believe that I and the people with whom I built barricades were going to create a new social activity, invent new modes of transportation, dream up new ways to relate to each other, to our activity, to our environment. I knew that gangsters, cops and soldiers had always governed in the past and I didn't think anything I did would keep them from governing in the future. I didn't relate any of that to my activity on the barricades. While I shot and while hundreds like me were killed, we cleared the streets for the "victorious liberation army." I didn't help clear their path intentionally; I wouldn't ever have risked my life to do that. Yet among the thousands you say were "freeing their city," there were some who did actually risk their lives in order to clear the path for the new occupiers. Perhaps they thought they'd be praised and rewarded by the new masters. Perhaps they were in fact rewarded. I had met some of them in the resistance organization. I suspect they couldn't have fought hard and couldn't have taken great risks since the dead can't enjoy their rewards. But maybe I'm wrong. Maybe like the noblest of slaves they risked everything, hoping that if they died the new masters would at least decorate their graves.

You refer to what happened three years later as the most significant experience in your life. "No outside force defined our project or made our decisions." You've retained this picture for as long as I retained my picture of a Luisa who rejected wage labor, the family, the state, a Luisa who rejected all illusions. Yet surely somewhere in your consciousness fragments of another experience must survive. An "outside force" did in fact define your project and make your decisions. It was none other than the politicians who three years earlier had helped clear away one army in order to make room for another. You and I merely recited the lines of a script, moved under the control of a puppeteer. Even the emotions we expressed were predesigned. You apparently liked your costume and make-up so well that you've continued to wear them after the play ended. The play was a show of the politicians' power "among the workers": the plot dealt with the "workers' struggle" against the politicians' enemies; the climax came when the workers ousted Zagad from the factory. At that point, behind the scenes, politicians ousted Zagad's friends from government offices; anyone unfriendly to the politicians was automatically Zagad's friend. The union apparatus acted as puppeteer. Union politicians initiated the strikes, prepared the spontaneous demonstrations and lectured about the solidarity, power and determination of the working class. It was our role to confirm our solidarity by reciting our scripts, to demonstrate our power by gesturing and to show our determination by making faces. The play was educational: its main purpose was to instruct the audience about their lines, gestures and feelings. The feeling you still express today: the illusion of autonomy, the illusion that we were defining our own projects and making our own decisions, was precisely the illusion the play was designed to communicate. Animated by the illusion of autonomy we didn't only perform our roles with contagious enthusiasm; we also convinced audience after audience that we genuinely considered the enemies of the politicians to be our own enemies.

Of course I was taken in as much as you were. The carnival spirit took hold of everyone. We were all on stage, most of us for the first time in our lives. Sometimes as many as five puppet shows played for each other. It was impossible to tell who wasn't on stage. Like everyone else, I took my role seriously; I wanted to perform well. When I carried a placard that said, "The factories to the workers!" I acted as if I meant what it said. I knew that politicians had arranged the demonstration, that the union had prepared it. Didn't I know, then, that my slogan could only mean, "I support the new boss"? Maybe I knew. But I didn't wish it. Maybe I thought the placards themselves would give rise to the situation they described. I did feel like an agent, an instrument, when we marched to Zagad's office like a militia of four. But I thought I was an instrument of "the working class," not an instrument of the union and the state. Yet the detail Sabina remembered should have put me on my guard. To Claude we weren't mere workers, four among many; we were "representatives of the plant council," agents of an apparatus.

I wasn't only taken in; I was taken over. The carnival atmosphere was so contagious that it infected my deepest emotions. An experience I remember vividly had to do with George Alberts. I hardly knew him; the most we ever said to each other was "good evening." Shortly before we were arrested, when slogans about "Factories to workers" had been replaced by slogans about "the enemy in our midst," Claude and Adrian approached me, to "talk about Alberts." They asked where Alberts had gone before the end of the war and why he hadn't fought in the resistance. They asked which side he had fought on. I was angry. I told them to ask Luisa, who lived with Alberts, or Titus Zabran, who had fought with him several years earlier. I told them I didn't know anything about Alberts. I had never considered it any of my business to ask where he had been or what he had done; I only knew that when he returned he was employed as a highly qualified specialist. Adrian said they didn't want to confront Titus Zabran "prematurely," before they had determined "all the facts." As for Luisa: they were going to speak to her when the "case" was complete; they were going to confront her with an ultimatum: either denounce Alberts or leave the plant. I yelled at them furiously. I said they had gone crazy. I asked if they were in the pay of the police. But their performance, like all the other performances, succeeded. It communicated its message. On that day my dislike for Alberts turned to suspicion. Yes, he became suspicious to me. He was stained exactly the same way my parents had been stained. You tell me your projects and decisions were your own. Even my feelings weren't my own. My suspicion of Alberts was no more my own than any of the rest of that "significant experience." I reproduced inside myself the "feelings" of the state.

The significance of my suspicion of Alberts became clear to me during my first year in prison. I met countless prisoners whose sole crime had been the "act" of becoming suspicious to others. Sometimes, a politician started a rumor about someone he disliked: sometimes the rumor was started by a worker who thought he'd get another's job. The victim was always helpless; everything he said and did only made the stain more visible. Soon everyone saw it, everyone was ready to turn him in. His fellow workers, his comrades, his neighbors all became police agents, pathetically pointing their fingers like my neighbor Ninovo, shouting, "You're all troublemakers; they should never have let you out."

Your letter goes on to describe the individuals who took part in this "significant experience"; you refer to them as "our group." The only traits your portraits share with the individuals I remember are their names. Since you've disabused me of my illusory portrait of Luisa, I should in fairness try to do as much for you. I had known most of those individuals for at least three years. You were with them for two weeks, during a crisis. I realize that people are often transformed by crises: they acquire traits they had never displayed in normal times, they undergo profound changes. I realize that you might have been seeing these individuals during the moment when they had ceased to be what they had been. But I vividly remember that this is not the case. Either because the crisis wasn't real, or because these individuals weren't able to shed their former personalities, they did not undergo profound changes; each of them remained what she or he had been before.

You remember the speed of Vera Neis's wit. So do I. I was grateful to her quick wit every day I spent at the plant. Everyone was. She made the routine bearable. She was like a radio that was turned on when we started to work and couldn't be turned off until we were through. In any other circumstances her quick wit would have been unbearable. In this particular circumstance it represented a great deal. She entertained us with gossip about the ruling class. Occasionally she taught us something about the machinery behind the facades. She was a missionary; apparently she really believed that as soon as all of us grasped the message of her stones, the world would change. This wasn't what we liked about her. What made her a genuine heroine in the plant was that with her continual tirades she sabotaged production from the moment work began. She considered her crusades more important than the work she had been hired to do, and she never allowed the work to interfere with her lectures. The constant arguments in which she engaged one or another of us must have cut our output at least by half. Everyone expected her to be fired. The leniency of the foreman was one of the things we had won from the resistance. When the general strike began she remained what she had been; in your words: "she couldn't let a stranger walk by without trying to convert him." But at that point her quick wit no longer represented an escape from the boring routine; it was no longer unintended sabotage; At that point she was only a missionary preaching salvation through belief in half a dozen abstractions and a mound of gossip, converting present-day Romans to a new Christianity.

You say "there's not even a question about any of the rest." Yet all you say about Adrian is "Vera and Adrian." That much is quite accurate. Before you met him, it had been "Titus and Adrian," when the strike began it was "Vera and Adrian," and before the strike ended, "Claude and Adrian." That's all that can be said about him. He was like a pin drawn to the most powerful magnet, like dough shaped by the nearest baker, a cog who could fit into any apparatus. When the unions launched the "campaign for a workers' society," Adrian became Vera's only convert. He memorized two or three abstractions and set up a mission of his own: a slow, humorless version of the same theme. When the time came to "ferret out the enemy in our midst," he became Claude's disciple, pathetically trying to simulate what you call Claude's "devotion," his contempt for his fellow workers.

Your portrait of Jasna Zbrkova was less favorable. She was the exact opposite of Claude. She was by far the warmest, the most generous person in the group. She was one of those rare human beings who are able to feel another person's pains and enjoy another's hopes. It's true that her empathy with others went to the point of feeling sorry for the "poor owner" who had so many problems running such a complex plant. It's true that her generosity was blind to political and economic realities. But in a context where Claude was ready to shoot his fellow workers, where Adrian shifted overnight from universal solidarity to universal suspicion, it was precisely this "blind" generosity that was missing.

I don't have a clear memory of Marc Glavni. He had been hired a few weeks, at most a couple of months, before the strike began. I remember staying away from him. He was a student, and was clearly on his way through the plant to something "higher." He may have been resourceful, as you say. I only remember that he thought himself resourceful.

We know about Luisa. So this leaves only Jan and Titus. You didn't like Titus. And Jan was "hotheaded." This characterization of Jan appears early in your letter. I had a hard time reading past it. That was how his executioners described him.

Titus Zabran was a "realist." At the time I thought his "realism" enabled him to see through the masquerade. He seemed to be as aware as Jan that the removal of Zagad was at most a beginning, that our victorious appropriation of the existing project was no victory at all. Unlike Jan, who was impatient, Titus seemed to have a long-range strategy; he seemed "realistic" because, he considered the present, move to be a necessary step or "stage" toward the next. Yet was Titus any more of a "realist" than Jan was a "hothead" Did Titus know that this step, this "stage," was going to eliminate the possibility of taking another step?

By the way, you're also wrong about the reasons for our arrest. Your and Luisa's connection to Alberts had nothing to do with it, no matter how suspicious Alberts became to Claude. Thanks to imaginations like yours, and mine, Luisa's and Vera's, we all took our roles seriously. And we infected everyone else, with our enthusiasm. When the strikes and demonstrations ended, when most workers realized the carnival was over and returned to work, our group continued to perform its show. We were still printing posters, gluing "Factories to Workers" on recently cleaned walls, shouting about the workers' commonwealth. At that point we became dangerous, because at that point people like us elsewhere saw that at least some had meant what they said and that the performance of a play had not been the only possibility. If others didn't realize this, at least the authorities thought they did. Only at that point did we begin to "act on our own," but we weren't aware of this. We were so carried away by our performance that we failed to see that the curtain had fallen and the carnival had ended. Instead of acting on our own we continued reciting the lines of the script and performing the rehearsed motions even though the prompter and play director had left the theater. We were arrested because we unintentionally transported our performance out of the theater into the street, because we continued to play when it was time to return to work. Because of my failure to turn off my act I spent four years moving from one dungeon to another. My overenthusiastic performance in a puppet show was interpreted by the all-knowing proletarian inquisitors as dangerous, anti-social activity, as sabotage of social means of production and therefore as a threat to the present and future well-being of the working class.

Four years later I was given an opportunity to enjoy the new society to which our significant experience had led. Much of the old society had survived in the new. Among other things, marriage. Why do you single out marriage? I remember the discussions at your house. I also remember that not only marriage but also wage labor, police, prisons, governments and schools were going to be absent from the new society. They all survived, intact, even reinforced. Or did you think our significant experience had changed all this, that marriage, wage labor and prisons had been abolished?

What I saw when I was released resembled the prison I had left more than it resembled a free city. There were inmates and guards. Officials were in automobiles, workers in busses and trams. And everyone was "in uniform." I saw functionaries, policemen, soldiers, workers, shoppers and students. I didn't see plain, uncategorized, ununiformed human-beings, I sensed that none of the people I saw met at houses like yours to discuss the abolition of marriage and wage labor. All such people had been arrested; all such discussions took place in jail.

I had no place to go since I had no family and my friends had all been jailed. Yet I was enthusiastic: the first term hadn't broken me the way the second was going to. I wanted to find work and then continue to fight, to express what I had seen and learned. I wanted to learn what was possible in the new situation. I visited the carton plant. Every face was new. Every member of the group you and I had known was gone, including the lenient foreman. That's all that was new. The machines were the same. The walls were the same; they hadn't even been painted. People worked in complete silence. I walked around and watched. People glanced at me and turned away. No one asked me who I was or what I wanted. The silence and indifference were new. Something else was new; maybe it was only a product of the indifference. Every carton I saw was poorly printed; we would have put them all in the stack of seconds. But now every stack in the plant was a stack of seconds. There were no longer any firsts. The workers were silent and seemed indifferent, but under those frightening masks they were still alive.

An old man was operating "my" press, at a snail's pace. He had turned the speed down to the lowest notch. The press creaked and squealed. It obviously hadn't been greased for four years. I didn't see a can of grease in the entire plant; apparently the planners didn't see why grease should be allocated to a carton plant. The absence of grease had caused the main cylinder bearing to turn to an ellipse. As a result there was no way to avoid printing a double image at every impression. The old man obviously couldn't be held responsible for sabotage. He was visibly being as slow and careful as he could be. He was doing his very best. And who needs perfectly printed boxes anyway? I wanted to shake his hand, to congratulate him, to laugh and share the joke with him. Instead I asked him if it was possible to apply for a job in the plant. He told me to speak to an official on the trade union council. This was another novelty, a sign of the workers' victory. Pointing in the direction of Zagad's former office, I asked where I could find these officials. I had guessed right. I must have been there before.

The trade union official at Zagad's desk was slightly chubbier than Zagad. And he called me "comrade." In all other ways he was very similar. He asked my name. He telephoned. Then he said, very politely, "Sorry, comrade. The economic situation is extremely critical. We cannot afford to hire an individual who was found guilty of sabotage."

Before leaving the plant, I stopped by the old man to ask him some questions. I wanted to find out to what extent the sabotage I saw was organized, what forms of communication the workers had succeeded in creating. But the old man was nervous; he kept looking around with a fear I had never seen on a worker's face. As far as I could see, the foreman was out for the day, the manager must have had his office elsewhere, the union official was smoking in his office, and everyone else was working. Was the old man actually afraid of being watched and heard by the other workers? Vera couldn't have lasted for a day in this plant.

I waited for him outside as I'd waited for Titus Zabran almost eight years earlier. He was more talkative. He asked if I'd been hired. "No jailbirds," I said. He looked around as he had inside; I was afraid I'd put an end to our conversation. The look on his face was a look I had seen before. No one had ever looked at me that way in prison. So this was what I had been released into! I felt intense relief when the old man said many of his friends, the "more political" ones, had also been jailed, and my growing anger left me when he said, "One day these wiseacres are going to reap what they're sowing." He was aware that his earlier look had stung me, and he became more talkative, though by no means comradely. The union, he told me, duplicated the supervisory work of the management, and both were supervised by the police. The foreman was directly responsible to the police, and one or more workers were police agents. He laughed when I asked about informal organization in these conditions. There had never been more distrust among workers. "In addition to actual police agents," he told me, "there are workers who seriously believe the factories are theirs and that therefore the workers are their own boss. They're fanatics. Such people don't remain workers very long, since their convictions lead to quick promotions. But while they're workers, they're far worse than the union officials or even the police agents. They work harder than anyone else, criticize other workers, have workers fired for sabotage and wrecking. The managers and union officials would of course like to hire only workers of this type. But this is impossible. The enthusiasm doesn't last long if the promotions don't follow. And they can't promote the entire production crew. Consequently such workers are always in a minority. But this minority effectively prevents any kind of unified action. Even grumbling can lead to arrest. But don't think they've turned us into oxen," the old man concluded. "With all their threats, arrests and harassments, with all their talk about record productivity and record output, production still hasn't reached the pre-war level."

In parting, the old man gave me strange advice. He told me not to be disappointed at not having been hired. Factory life wasn't for "political people." "The good life is in politics: that's the place for you activists," he said. He had grasped the essence of what you call your significant experience. I was going to receive the same advice again.

I looked for jobs elsewhere. Sometimes I spoke to managers, sometimes to union officials. The outcome was always the same: the same phone call, the same "Sorry comrade, four years for sabotage..." Production had not reached the pre-war level, but the centralization and communication of police files had broken all previous records and was continually climbing to new heights. The enthusiasm with which Zagad left prison vanished. I became desperate. I was running out of money. I slept in alleys, but this wasn't as easy as it had been eight years earlier. I was older and people were far more suspicious of strangers. I was afraid someone who saw

me in the street or in an alley would turn me in as a vagabond. I began to understand why the police had grown so enormous. I was trapped. I had the choice of
starving to death or killing myself. I had yet another "choice." It was then I grasped
that the police were not a different species. At least not all of them. Sooner or later
I would be arrested. I would be under a roof, I would sleep on some kind of mattress. I might even tell them, "I give up. What do I have to do to survive?" They
would smile, have me sit down, offer me a cigarette. "Yes, we've been expecting you,
comrade. We thought you would return much sooner. Times are hard. If you want
to work, we can find a job for you."

This was my mood when I decided to try to find Jan Sedlak. I stopped worrying about adding to his problems in case he'd just been released. I needed to communicate with another human being. I had little hope of finding him. I didn't know
how long his sentence had been or if he'd been released. I had been to his house
only once, shortly before our arrest. He had taken Sabina and me there one or two
days after Zagad was ousted from the carton plant. They lived in a poor working
class quarter on the outskirts of the city. They had been driven from their farm
during the war, and had moved to the section that most closely resembled a village.
Like their neighbors, mainly former peasants, they raised chickens and geese and
kept a large garden. Jan's father had found a job driving a bus during the war, and
had continued to drive the same bus through the war, the resistance, the coup and
the arrests. As I rode the tram I convinced myself the Sedlaks would no longer be
living there. Surely the old peasant had found another job and moved to the city.
Surely the one-time peasants of that quarter had finally become just workers and
had left their houses and yards to new arrivals from villages. I found the quarter.
The houses had deteriorated and many had been abandoned. Former occupants
had not been replaced by new arrivals.

But there were curtains in the windows of Jan's house. It was obviously inhabited. I knocked. The old woman who opened the door wore the same black dress
and the same black shawl she had worn before. Her face was wrinkled with age. She
was startled, as if she were looking at a ghost. Her shock gave way to an expression
which has remained engraved on my memory. I'm still convinced it was an expression of regret. With unmistakable sadness, she said. "Jan's friend," and motioned
for me to come in. She seemed to know already then the nature of the gifts I was
bringing into the Sedlak household. She fed me sweets and coffee and left me alone
in a large room.

There were several chairs and a table, but otherwise the room was barren
except for three books stacked in a corner: mathematics, zoology, and a "history
of the working class movement." I leafed through the history. I learned that the
working class had begun to move during the very moment when I thought it had
stopped moving, and that the movements of the class consisted of moves of politicians. I was relieved when I leafed through the zoology book and saw that the
names of animals had not been changed.

A young woman burst into the room carrying potatoes in her apron. She dropped them as soon as she saw me. I surmised they still kept a garden. Nothing had changed here. People were a little older, some of the neighbors had moved out, and that was all. The old man probably still drove the same bus. I assumed the young woman was Jan's wife. She was clearly a peasant in spite of her city dress. She looked at me with an expression I can only call wild: like a lone shepherdess on a desolate mountain who had unexpectedly bumped into a stranger.

Suddenly she shouted, "You're Yarostan!" She said this with such joy I thought she was going to throw her arms around me.

It was my turn to see a ghost. "How in the world do you know who I am?"

"You're Jan's friend!"

Beginning to doubt my first assumption, I nevertheless formulated the question, "And you're — Jan's wife?"

"No, silly! Don't you remember me? I'm Mirna!"

Jan's sister. How could I have remembered her, or even guessed? The last time I'd seen her she'd been at most ten or eleven years old, attending elementary school. That meant she was at most fifteen. I helped her pick up the potatoes. She said nothing more, just stared at me. I couldn't help looking at her. She became embarrassed. She carried the potatoes into the kitchen and stayed there. I was again alone in the large room. My thoughts and feelings were in chaos. Isn't it amazing how flexible we are, how quickly we can travel from one emotional extreme to another? Only two hours earlier I had been weighing and comparing my alternatives: imprisonment, suicide or capitulation. Now I was filled with enthusiasm again, filled with thoughts of living, of building a world together with these people, near this girl. I looked at the three books. I had an urge to hurl them out of the house. They were as out of place in this room as she was out of place in this city. What forces had driven this country girl away, from open fields and into authoritarian classrooms? Why? What is gained when this free being is confined to a desk and forced to recite a toady's account of the words and gestures of his patrons?

Jan's father returned from work wearing his driver's cap. He embraced me as soon as he came in. He was neither startled nor apprehensive. He acted as if I were an old friend, as if he had expected me to be there. "Living anywhere?" he asked.

I lied and told him I was renting a room in the city.

"Are your things there?"

"I have no things," I admitted.

"Mirna!" he shouted, "fix up the guest room. Jan's friend is going to stay with us."

He seemed to know that I had nothing else to do and nowhere else to go, that I had reached the end of my journey. "Relax," he told me, as if he knew what I'd been thinking earlier. "Together we'll straighten everything out."

It was only when Jan came home that I started to relax. Jan was overjoyed. He had tears in his eyes when he embraced me. He said he had known I'd turn up. Released a few months before I was, he had somehow learned the date of my release. He knew I wouldn't find a job and would have nowhere else to go. He had begun to worry when I failed to turn up; he wondered if they'd failed to release me or if I had already been arrested again.

Jan had a job in the transport depot repair shop. He got the job through an odd coincidence. A few months before his release, his father's bus had broken down and the driver had accompanied it to the repair shop. While a clerk was asking Sedlak the usual questions: name, number, route, and so on, a union official who was standing nearby asked if the driver was related to Jan Sedlak. Suspicious of all officials, Sedlak warily asked the man why he wanted to know. The official apologized very politely, admitting that under the circumstances he had been insolent to ask him such a question. He then proceeded to explain he had been Jan's friend since the war, they had worked together for several years, and he — the official — had only recently been released from prison. The day after Jan was released, he and his father went to see this official. It was Titus Zabran. The following day Jan was employed in the repair shop. He changed his first name and soon received a work booklet. Titus had discreetly recommended him as Sedlak's country nephew, a hard-working peasant who had just arrived in the city.

That night I ate supper with friends who were not prisoners for the first time in four years.

Jan and I left his house an hour before sunrise the following morning. We traveled by tram and bus to the other end of the city. The headquarters of the trade union were located next door to the repair shop. Jan knocked on the door of Titus' office. When Titus opened it, I was sure that for an instant I saw the same expression of alarm and disappointment I had seen on the face of Jan's mother: he saw a ghost. Jan convinced me later that Titus couldn't have been alarmed, since it was from him that Jan had learned the date of my release. In any case, Titus quickly recovered. He embraced me and asked if I needed money or a place to stay. Jan explained that I had "already solved" all my living problems; all I needed was a job.

Titus picked up the phone. He talked about another Sedlak newly arrived from the country. Suddenly he turned to me and asked, "Your first name?"

I fumbled. Then I almost shouted, "Miran!" And I glanced at Jan with a sheepish grin.

"Miran Sedlak," Titus told the phone. He told me I was to start driving a bus in a week. I said I had never driven anything other than a bicycle. Titus laughed. He said I'd learn in a week, and by the second week I would already be bored; there were no fine adjustments to be made (as there had been on a press). Titus embraced both of us when we left. This was the second time he had pulled me out of a trap. The first time seemed to have taken place so long ago I wasn't sure it had taken place at all; perhaps I had dreamed it.

Dinner that night was a celebration. I had rejoined humanity. I had found a home, a family, a job.

"We're almost back on our feet," Jan said. "Soon we'll be running again."

"And you'll run right back to jail," his mother grumbled.

But Jan's father didn't let his spirits be dampened. "Another relative!" he shouted. "Soon there'll be Sedlaks driving half the busses, Sedlaks in half the factories. Welcome Yarostan Sedlak!"

"Miran Sedlak," Jan corrected.

"Miran?" asked Mirna. "Then we're twins!"

"Twins!" roared the old man. "Everyone for miles around can see you're anything but twins!"

Mirna blushed, dropped her food, and ran to her room. Jan laughed. It was already understood that Mirna and I were to be married. No more was going to be said about it; the matter had been settled. I was overjoyed.

It wasn't your letter that gave rise to my first doubts. These began to rise the very next morning, when I left the house with Jan's father for my first driving lesson. What had I celebrated? What did my joy mean? Which humanity had I rejoined: a humanity of unshackled beings transforming their dreams into projects, or the humanity of home, family and job? Had I celebrated my self-betrayal? Had I become a traitor to my own commitment, to you and Luisa, to all the comrades with whom I had fought for a different world? Had the imprisonment broken me, tamed me, domesticated me? Would my betrayal of my past and my comrades have been any greater if I had joined the police or if, as you suggested, I had taken up religion or invested capital? Hadn't I spent four years in prison for rejecting everything I was now embracing, enjoying and celebrating?

At the very beginning of my prison term I had grumbled about the food. I complained that the bread was stale and the soup was lukewarm sewage. A prisoner sitting across the table from me told me he had read about people who had so little food they ate the bark of trees; when a fire destroyed their forest, they dreamed about the bark as if it were a delicacy. Sometime later I spent a week in a damp, airless dungeon. My diet then was stale bread and cold water. When I rejoined the living, the warm sewage became a delicacy. I ate it slowly, sipping it so as to enjoy the flavor of every spoonful.

I was undoubtedly broken, tamed, but not by the four years in prison. I had left prison with a certain amount of enthusiasm. I had at least been eating bark. The fire that destroyed my forest burned during the nine or ten days after my release. It was only then that I was left with nothing at all. It was only then that I was deprived of all friendship, all communication, all hopes. I was excluded from every community and from all social activity. I longed for no more than bark, but it had all burned. The worst deprivation of all was my exclusion from work. I had fought against self-selling, I had engaged in the struggle to abolish wage labor, yet now I was tortured because I couldn't sell myself for a wage. I was in pain because this exclusion was a far greater torture than solitary confinement. Though death and insanity were not infrequent results of solitary confinement, they were not inevitable. I had seen many emerge with their selves intact. It was this possibility of emerging intact that had been removed. A new arrest or starvation meant not emerging at all. Emerging by selling myself to the police meant I would murder my own self, my whole past life, and I would also suppress others like me, I would murder my other selves.

I had been excluded from humanity. This exclusion was the dungeon I emerged from when I rejoined humanity. And I sipped, with genuine enjoyment, the very soup I had rejected as sewage. I embraced a traditional, archaic, patriarchal family, and I was filled with joy. I would have been satisfied with bark and I sat in front of a complete meal, a virtual feast. I was with warm, sociable human beings who welcomed me as one of their own, with peasants who had never quite been urbanized; I was with people who were more human than my contemporaries precisely because they had been left behind, because they had not replaced kinship with civic responsibility or friendship with duty to the state. I was with people who did not experience our great society as their boon or their victory, but as their fate, their destiny, as an incomprehensible catastrophe, a punishment for unknown transgressions. And for an instant I felt I had rejoined my own. I was filled with joy. I embraced the world I had once rejected. I accepted what we had once called nepotism and was proud of myself as a nephew, a country cousin, a relative. I felt only gratitude when I was allowed to rejoin the community of wage laborers. And my happiness was crowned by the prospect of marrying the wonderful peasant girl who had remained unstained by urban corruption, unstained by the factories and prisons.

My stupor lasted for a day. I couldn't permanently turn myself inside out, become someone else, turn my back on what I had wanted until then. And I couldn't forget all those like me who were still in prison, all those who had died, all those who had emerged so maimed they could only hope for the next release.

The old peasant took me along in his bus for a week. There were hardly any passengers during two afternoon hours, when he had me drive the bus. On the fifth day he let me drive it all day. By the end of the week I was an experienced driver; all I had left to learn was the route. And by the end of the following week I was a seasoned driver. I began to recognize many of the passengers. I began to understand the nature of my useful social activity, the function of the job I had been so overjoyed to find. The morning passengers were almost all workers on their way to factories, warehouses and sometimes offices. They were in the process of selling their energy and time in exchange for a wage. The bus was the vehicle which delivered the sold item to its purchaser. The transaction was unusual because the sellers had to accompany the items they sold: they couldn't stay home while the buyer walked away with their time. As a result the bus looked like it was transporting people, but the people were merely accompanying their merchandise. It wasn't the people who were delivered every morning but only the merchandise. The afternoon passengers, generally relatives of the same workers, took the bus to shops; they bought back, not the living energy sold by the workers, but some of the objects which had consumed the energy. They spent the wage. When it was spent, the bus again delivered merchandise, this time tangible merchandise, material objects, things — the things into which the workers had poured their lives. In the evening the outer husks of the workers returned home. The specific content of each had dissolved into that homogeneous substance they had sold for a wage, it had dripped out of them during the day like liquid excrement. This excrement was the merchandise the bus had delivered in the morning. It was carried in the hands, arms, legs and eyes of the passengers. Potential energy had been transformed into a substance that could be discharged from the body and sold. Since the workers couldn't separate themselves from the item they had sold, the transaction was not completed until the item was consumed. In the evening they returned home to refill their empty shells, to regenerate the energy, only to let it flow out again during eight hours of diarrhea the following day. It was my useful function to be a middleman in this transaction, to circulate the excrement among its consumers. And as I circulated it I studied the objects into which this liquid energy had flowed, the monuments into which it had been molded. I drove past these products of human labor every day: the cramped living quarters in which the consumed energy was nightly regenerated, the forbidding structures inside which the allocation of the excrement and the speed of its discharge were daily determined. I also studied the most sophisticated products of human labor, the most important monuments shaped out of the excrement: officials, politicians and police, as they drove by me in their glossy cars. This was the victory into which our significant experience was shaped. And you tell me: "I knew exactly what part I was playing in the creation of our common world." Did you really? And are you proud, twenty years later, that you helped create this world?

My enthusiasm diminished the day after I experienced such joy at having rejoined this world, and it was all gone by the time I had driven the bus for a week. My interest in life returned. I had left prison with an intense desire to express myself, to communicate with others, to explore the possible and project the impossible. This desire returned as soon as I was "almost back on my feet" and had started "running again," as Jan had put it. I regained the posture you remember: my "militant" posture. My hosts became my audience, my potential insurgents, my revolutionary community. I began arguing with the old driver about the significance of driving a bus in a society consisting of enterprises and wageworkers. I argued about the significance of kinship relations in a society of buyers and sellers. And when he didn't respond, I argued about the dangers of housing two saboteurs, two elements who threatened the present and future well-being of the working class.

The old peasant heard nothing, but he learned that his future "son-in-law" was an agitator. And his response to this discovery was identical to that of the old worker in the carton plant. "You won't be driving a bus for long," Sedlak said. "They've got other jobs for you up there." He was proud of his future relative. Sedlak was a shrewd and calculating man. I knew that for once he was miscalculating but I couldn't have known at the time how badly he was miscalculating me, my prospects, and the situation he would find himself in because of me. His wife's expectations were far more modest, her guesses were based on more solid realities. She merely shook her head whenever I spoke and she said absolutely nothing.

I also argued with Mirna about marriage. I had not learned to consider marriage "the most natural relation in the world"; I had not convinced myself that "people never lived outside this category." I agree with everything you say in this part of your letter, and I admire the way all of you have refused to compromise with this institution. But you provoke me to ask a question. Since you are also opposed to wage labor, have you refused to compromise with this institution? If so, how have you supported yourselves?

Mirna and I took long walks in that village-like neighborhood. Only then did everyone for miles around know that Mirna and Miran were not twins. I tried to explain to her that the proposed marriage was an absurdity, a mistake, possibly even a crime. Sooner or later I would be arrested again. My term would probably be much longer since I would be a repeated offender. We would both be old when I returned, if I returned at all. I doubted that I could live through a longer term. If I died she would as likely as not think I was still alive somewhere in that under-world of the living dead. Informing relatives about such details was not one of the priorities of our record-breaking control industry. Her archaic, monogamous and patriarchal peasant neighbors would not allow her to divorce me if it was thought I was still alive. She would be chained to a buried corpse. The marriage would rob her of her young life. She wouldn't merely be bound for life to a person she might cease to love on the day after the ceremony. That possibility was at the core of every marriage. There was the additional possibility that I would be arrested the day after the marriage. The fifteen-year old girl would be bound for life to a person she might never see again.

Mirna listened to me the same way her father did. She heard nothing. Her energy, her passion and her joyful anticipation did not diminish for an instant. The marriage was simply a date on the calendar, a coming holiday that was one day closer with every sunrise. It was as unavoidable as the passage of time. There was no longer anything she or I could do about it — if we were decent. Her brother's friend, the intelligent and sensitive young man who had experienced torture and imprisonment, was obviously decent. Such a person couldn't possibly humiliate her, stain her for life, make her the laughing stock of the village by running out before the marriage. My talk didn't even suggest such a possibility. Such things did happen. Brides who were coerced to marry a person they hated, bridegrooms who were afraid to face the world, sometimes ran away just before the ceremony. But clearly neither of us had reason to run away. We loved each other and I wasn't able to communicate my misgivings. Should I have run away? Where was I to go? Back to prison? Should I have sacrificed my own life so as to avoid ruining hers? And if I did could I be sure the humiliation would be less severe to her than the marriage? Could I be sure she wouldn't torture or maim herself because I had "run out" on her, leaving her the "laughing stock of the village"?

I spoke to her parents as well. But that was like talking to stones. Her father "knew" that I'd "go far." And her mother heard nothing at all. At first I thought I could reach the old woman: she had disliked me since the day I had arrived and she seemed to foresee a catastrophic fall where her husband foresaw a steep and unlimited ascent. But the coming catastrophe might as well have taken place already. In her view we couldn't avoid our future any more than our past; all we could do was to resign ourselves to what was to come. My jabbering was mere noise, since to her I could no more undo what was to come than I could undo my arrival at their house.

Jan was the only one who heard me, but he didn't help. My arguments and my doubts angered him. He accused me of destroying the basis of all friendship and all solidarity. He argued that anyone might die of an illness the day after forming a relationship with another person and that was no reason to avoid forming such relations. As for the institutionalization of the relationship, Jan argued that if our lives were to acquire any meaning at all, we would soon be rid of the institution and Mirna and I could choose or reject each other freely.

In spite of my doubts those were the happiest moments of my life. As the day drew nearer, Mirna beamed constantly. On our evening walks she threw her arms around children and old people, she danced with perfect strangers in the street. I talked less about the possibility of my arrest and more about the possibilities of our lives together. I talked about the day when all the working people of the city would embrace each other and dance in the street.

The ceremony was archaic, patriarchal and authoritarian. I experienced it as beautiful. Mirna seemed like a feather floating through air. She didn't make the slightest effort to hide a happiness that was as clear as a cloudless sky. She literally flitted from one person to the next, infecting them all with her unrestrained joy. I had been walking on clouds from the moment I had gotten up; for me the event was a dream. I was in a stupor, as unconscious as if I hadn't woken up at all. I don't think I spoke a single coherent word all day long. All I did was laugh.

We didn't stop loving each other the day after the ceremony or later. There were times when I cursed the marriage because of the torture and misery it had carried in its train, but I never regretted it. Mirna embraced the happy moments — and there were many but they all flew past us during the first few months — with undisguised joy, and she accepted the tragedies with silent resignation, though never with her mother's absolute, unquestioning resignation.

I drove a bus for a year, during which time Mirna and I lived with her parents. Jan moved out soon after we were married. He explained that he didn't enjoy traveling across the entire city twice a day. That was undoubtedly part of his reason for moving out. He had probably also come to feel like a stranger to our happiness. He had lost his sister as well as his best friend, and the house must have started to seem crowded to him: crowded with strangers.

Toward the end of the first year Vesna was born. This unlucky, unhappy child was born into something like a pit surrounded by the unscalable walls you described so vividly in your letter. It wasn't Mirna I should have worried about, but Vesna. The baby girl born late that fall hadn't asked to be brought to this world, she hadn't asked to be born into the cage from which she was never to emerge. We had neglected this topic in our discussions at Luisa's: birth. By what right do we drag a helpless infant into a world we've left unchanged, by what right do we force another human being to breathe an air, that's suffocating us, by what right do we leave a little girl scratching her fingernails until her hands bleed in a pathetic attempt to scale a wall we could neither climb nor destroy?

I can't read Luisa's or your description of our significant experience without remembering the significance of that experience. I can't forget the significance it had for the old peasant, for his wife, for Jan and Vesna, for Mirna, for me and others like me. How can you remind me of the dreams we shared and the possibilities we anticipated while you glorify the event which deformed the dreams and destroyed the possibilities? How can you point to everything that died in that event, tell me it was born then and ask me to celebrate the birth?

I'm able to write you now only because, after twenty years, the significance of our experience is at last being exposed. I can reach you now only because those impenetrable walls have started to crack. It's not so much because of the efforts of my contemporaries, my likes, that the walls are crumbling, and certainly not because of my efforts. They're coming down more or less on their own. The city is waking up from a twenty-year long death-like sleep. Corpse-like husks with shriveled capacities, dried up imaginations and used up lives are beginning to exhibit new gleams in their eyes and new energies in their limbs.

The people of this city are suddenly realizing they've been building those walls: high and low walls, outer and inner walls, yet more walls within the inner walls; they've been building the walls that imprison them. Perhaps they're not realizing this only now; perhaps they were aware of it all along. But their awareness didn't affect their activity. They acted as if they were unaware of the walls. It was as if huge signs, massive colorful tapestries, had been hung in front of the walls. The signs depicted free human beings engaged in common projects, working people engaged in creating their own history. You and I helped to paint those signs. If people realized there were walls behind the signs they couldn't refer to the walls without being arrested; if they knew their activity wasn't the activity depicted on the signs but the activity of constructing and reinforcing the walls behind the signs, they had to keep this knowledge to themselves. The only activity they could refer to and communicate about was the activity on the signs. People saw open, vast, unlimited fields while they accommodated themselves to cramped prison cells. All of a sudden those tapestries are being torn down and the walls behind them are being attacked. It's all happening because of a quirk in the prison machinery, a mistake on the part of a prison warden. A few weeks before I wrote you my first letter, one of the normal changes of the prison guard took place. This particular change was slightly less routine than the daily changes because it was accompanied by a less frequent, though still periodic, replacement of the head warden by his understudy. Due to the fact that the prison administrators had been careless and had neglected to replace the warden many years earlier, this warden had gotten used to his job and had grown senile in his office. When the time came for him to leave his office, he refused. Instead, he and the head prison guards, who had remained faithful to him, hatched a plot: they were going to lock up all the other members of the prison administration in order to keep him in his office. But one of the guards who was to take part in the conspiracy lost faith in the senile warden and told the remaining administrators they were about to be arrested. The administrators promptly replaced the warden and blocked the conspiracy. The plotters were routed. One of them, the second or third highest official in the prison, ran off to sell himself to the prison administrators of what he had until then called the enemy camp. The administrative shuffle ended; it had been fairly routine.

Such changes had taken place before, and even the conspiracy was nothing out of the ordin49ary. Such events didn't normally create ripples among the inmates, if for no other reason than because the prison population was told nothing about them. But this time something else happened. The nearly arrested administrators discovered that all the prison guards had been involved in the conspiracy. To protect themselves, they suspended the activity of the guards. They couldn't possibly have known what they were doing. Maybe they had no choice. By suspending the guards they removed the glue that held the whole system together and it all started to fall apart. People started to pull at the tapestries, to tear them, to point to the walls behind them. "This is what we've been building, and this is all we've been building," someone shouted. And when that person wasn't shot or even locked up others started shouting and tearing down the signs. And nothing happened to any of them. People who had been silent for twenty years suddenly started to speak. Many were unable to find words. For two decades they had only spoken about the people and activities depicted on the tapestries. Suddenly people started talking about themselves and their own real activities, about jailers and prison walls, about their sacrificed lives and about the tortures. Many failed to understand. Yet still nothing happened to those who tore at the signs and spoke about the walls. Gradually those who had forgotten how to refer to themselves or their own activity began to remember or learn the words, and those who had thought their lives were described by the tapestries learned to experience their own lives. Even children who had never known any language other than the language on the signs and students who had experienced life only as it was depicted on the tapestries began tearing down signs and communicating about the prison walls. They had to invent words with which to talk about themselves and their real surroundings.

It's only because the significance of the event you glorify is finally being exposed that I'm able to write you now. If these events weren't taking place my letter probably wouldn't even reach you and I might not even be here. In my first letter I told you about a demonstration in which Yara participated at her school. In slightly different circumstances that demonstration could have led to my third and surely last imprisonment. My neighbor Mr. Ninovo, the self-repressed bar cleaner who expresses himself only in the language of the signs, learned about the demonstration and about Yara's role in it. He promptly reported me to the police. In other circumstances I would have been re-arrested, accused of instigating dangerous anti-social activity and jailed. I could hardly believe what happened instead. An official came to the house. He was extremely polite and he apologized for his visit. He told us Mr. Ninovo had reported me and then he proceeded to warn us to beware of our neighbor, telling us Mr. Ninovo was a spiteful, envious and dangerous man. (Of course in other circumstances there would have been no demonstration at Yara's school and Mr. Ninovo wouldn't have reported me for instigating it.) We've been looking for Mr. Ninovo but he apparently hasn't been coming home to sleep. There have been two more demonstrations at Yara's school since them.

An unbelievable metamorphosis has been taking place. With the exception of the Ninovos (who unfortunately aren't rare), predictable machines are turning into human beings, specialized instruments are turning into living creatures with unlimited possibilities. The emergence of so many human beings out of the shells, the husks and the cages is stupefying. The first thing it indicates is that so long as the repressive apparatus had functioned, human beings had disappeared. The human community had ceased to exist. There had only been deaf and dumb aggregates of specialized instruments, collections of Ninovos who related to each other by way of the police.

The repressed are returning in a very literal sense as well. I've heard rumors that released prisoners are starting to form clubs, to communicate their experiences and expose their significance. I want to take part in this activity but so far Mirna has kept me from contacting these groups. She doesn't believe that what we're experiencing today will last and she's convinced my contact with other former prisoners will only shorten the duration of my release.

I'd like to believe that Mirna's apprehension is exaggerated, that her fears have no basis in present reality, but I can't keep myself from hearing what she hears. The situation is still unclear, the newborn communication still contains some old and sinister sounds. The politicians still use the language and the imagery of the torn tapestries. The fawning priests who run the press still preach about the omniscience of their gods and justify the wisdom and goodness of their past, present or future patrons. But an altogether different type of communication is gradually drowning out these sounds from the past. It is a communication among likes, a communication about themselves, their lives and possibilities. It is a communication I first experienced on the barricades of the resistance twenty-three years ago, a communication whose significance I learned only when Luisa told me about the barricades of the revolution she had experienced. Such communication has so far existed only in situations of crisis, on barricades, in the face of almost certain death. Yet even if it has so far existed nowhere else, it revealed itself there as a permanent human possibility, and it's this possibility that is being grasped by those around me today.

This rebirth of communication is what stimulates me to seek out my likes, not only among other former prisoners and other workers, but everywhere in the world. I wrote you because I wanted to explore the present, to probe its possibilities, to move beyond the past. I didn't write you in order to revive the past and certainly not to celebrate the events which had put an end to all communication, at least for me. It's because we were in the throes of the victory you now celebrate that the letter you sent me twelve years ago couldn't reach me. I would have welcomed it then. That was another period of ferment, a ferment that was immediately suppressed, a ferment that created cracks in the walls but not for long enough to allow human messages to get through. That was also the moment of my second arrest. Mirna tells me the police came looking for" that letter only a few hours after it came. By sheer coincidence I didn't come home from work on the day your letter came, nor the following day, nor any day after that for the next eight years.

A few days ago I asked Mirna if she still remembered the walks we took just before we were married. She remembered the walks but not the talks. When I reminded her I had once tried to warn her not to chain herself to a convicted saboteur, a socially dangerous element, she asked furiously, "Were you God? Did you know that cursed letter was going to come years before it was even written?" Mirna holds that letter responsible for my second imprisonment. She still thinks it caused my arrest. I've tried to explain to her that the arrival of the letter on the day of my arrest was a pure coincidence, but she merely tells me, "There are no coincidences." That's why she thought the letter peculiar and attributed a strange power to it, and still does today: she thinks your letter had the power to imprison me for eight years.

Yarostan.

Sophia's second letter

Dear Yarostan,
Your letter was cruel. You were obviously aware of that. It doesn't call for an answer. It's the last word. Victims don't share their experiences with their executioners. That's clear. Why should they? Since you've defined me that way, I'm surprised your letter was so long! Why didn't you communicate exactly the same message by not answering me at all? Why did you feel you owed an explanation to that type of person?

You can't possibly imagine what a sad experience your second letter was for me. If you can then you're even crueler than your letter. For countless years I dreamed of finding you, of sharing a project with you once again, of telling you what I'd experienced since I was with you, of comparing it with what you experienced; if I failed to see you again I hoped I'd at least reach you with one after another letter, each crossing at least one of yours, each as long and full of detail as your last letter. That dream was starting to come true; at least one of the longings of my life was being fulfilled. But I never dreamed I'd get a letter from you with that content, a letter which so cruelly ended the correspondence when it had barely begun.

I can't say I never dreamed of such a content. I did in fact dream of it — in a nightmare. It was my greatest fear. It did pass through my mind that the long separation and the different experiences would create a wall between us, that we would no longer have anything to say to each other, that we would be merely polite, cold and strange to each other. But not even in a nightmare did I dream that you'd ever see me as your enemy!

The same letter wouldn't have been so cruel if you'd sent it from jail. I would have understood your anger, your desire to destroy my frame of reference. I would have understood it as resentment against someone who is not in jail. But you didn't write from jail. You wrote from a situation that's far happier than mine. You described a world which is again in ferment, a social context which is alive with hopes and possibilities. You described exactly the experience I longed to learn about and share, the experience that would heal the open wound I've carried in my being since I was torn from you. And you excluded me from that experience. Yours wasn't a letter from one in jail but from one becoming free and it was sent to one who is still in jail. Instead of sharing the joy, the promise of new life, you spat on me, pushed me aside, discarded me. Why?

I recognize the pain and suffering you've undergone. I say "recognize" because in your description I saw my own pain and suffering. The forms were different, though sometimes not so different; the pain was communicated by your letter because I had felt it too. I also recognized the bitterness, a bitterness I had felt toward those who inflicted the pain, never toward others who suffered from it. The cold, calculated cruelty is what I can't understand, a cruelty aimed at "a fellow human being" asking for help in "this bizarre world," as you said with such a different spirit in your first letter.

Do you actually think the suffering excuses and justifies that cruelty, that inhumanity toward me? Inhumanity. I can't find a better word. A complete lack of human warmth, understanding, sympathy, comradeship. A cold, dispassionate dissection of an animal. Under the guise of unmasking what you call my illusions, you tear apart my past experiences, my commitments, my few accomplishments and all my dreams.

Wouldn't silence be the most appropriate response to your letter? That might be what you expect. You would have severed me from your life for good, and my silence would confirm the truth of your analysis. But I won't keep silent! I won't let our correspondence end where you ended it. Because you're wrong. You're wrong about me, about the friendships and experiences I shared with you, about yourself. Your cruelty is blind and unjust. I won't be silent until I show you how wrong you are. And if you throw my letter into the garbage unread, you won't have confirmed the truth of your analysis but its complete falsity and its cruelty.

Unfortunately I can't refute you point by point, I can't expose every false detail and erroneous judgment in your letter because I can't get myself to read your letter yet another time. I've already drenched it with tears twice. Tears of shame and humiliation. This wasn't the only time I was excluded from my world by my comrades. It's probably not the last. But this exclusion pushes me out of the one world I thought was mine; you're the single friend who, I thought, would never push me away.

You can't simply turn my own experience upside down and tell me I remembered it wrong. You're the one who is wrong. If I carried a sign that said, "The factories to the workers!" I didn't mean "I support my new boss!" If this was what you meant then you were a hypocrite and your letter is a confession of your own hypocrisy. But you know perfectly well that neither you nor any of our friends anticipated the establishment of new bosses, the reinforcement of prisons or the enlargement of the political police. How can you be so absurd? How can your imagination even formulate the bizarre vision of thousands of people joyfully and enthusiastically anticipating their own incarceration?

I think it's not Luisa or I who have lost touch with reality, but you. I think your mind is fogged by a terrible confusion. Your first letter already contained hints of it, when you treated inmates and guards as interchangeable. You seem to have lost your ability to distinguish victory from defeat, executioner from victim. Our activity was followed by our imprisonment. Your confusion begins when you modify this sentence ever so slightly and say: our activity led to our imprisonment. Having put it this way you conclude that our activity was the cause of our imprisonment and that we were our own judges and guards, and the builders of our own prisons.

If our struggle was followed by the reinstatement of factory bosses and prison guards, then this means our struggle came to nothing. We were defeated. Our intentions were thwarted. In no way does it mean that the bosses and guards are the fruit of our victory and the realization of our intentions. The bosses and guards are what we fought against. And they won. Not because of us but in spite of us. To cement their victory they had to jail us. This is so obvious!

The world you walked into when you were released from prison wasn't the world I fought for, no matter how often you say I helped build it. Does it show a single trace of my commitment, yours, Luisa's? Where are the destroyed prisons? Where's the rubble of former government buildings? Where are the human beings engaged in projects chosen by themselves, without supervisors or guards? The world you describe hasn't a trace of the world I fought for. What you describe is the very world I fought to destroy. Don't you recognize it? You should. Your descriptions of it were vivid enough. It's the world of wage labor and capital, the world of inmates and jailers. It's the world you and I were born into. We couldn't possibly have helped build this world: it was built before we were born.

If you claim this world was the outcome of our struggle, you have to admit it's been the outcome of every struggle. So far there's been no other outcome in history. It's the outcome of struggles in which those who fought against it lost. They were defeated, as we were. You build your whole argument by omitting this small detail: the defeat. It's this omission that enables you to say that the world of bosses and jailers was rebuilt, not by those who fought to reinstate it and won, but by those who fought to destroy it and lost.

If this is what you learned in prison, then prison is not the great school Tolstoy said it was. Or else you learned your lessons very badly. Can you really be saying that insurgents only rise against the ruling order so as to reimpose it? Can you really be saying that the only dreams of rebels are dreams of authority and submission? You even accuse me of having helped deform dreams and destroy possibilities. What dreams were deformed, suppressed, destroyed? Clearly not the dreams of reimposing authority but the dreams of destroying it. You admit that insurgents fought to destroy the world of jailers. Yet you say they reimposed that very world. How? By fighting against it, by fighting to realize their dream of a world without jailers? Is this paradox the ultimate wisdom of a prison education?

I don't really understand your letter. Parts of it are so full of resentment, all of it aimed against Luisa and me. Other parts are so full of compassion, especially your descriptions of Mirna. You said Jan moved out of the house when you and Mirna were married. He felt like an outsider to your happiness. If you began to treat him the way your letter treats me, I can understand perfectly why he left. You drove him out, just as you're driving me out of your life. I'm sure he didn't feel jealous or resentful, just confused and stunned. Until the day before yesterday he'd been your best friend; suddenly he was a stranger. You wrote the first letter to one who had once been a friend, a comrade, and more: someone you had loved. Why shouldn't I remind you? You've obviously forgotten; in your first letter you even said you hardly remembered me! Well, I haven't forgotten. I can understand how I might become a stranger to you over so many years; I can even understand that we might have become enemies. What I can't understand is how you can treat me as if I'd been your enemy then, precisely during the moment when we loved each other. And we did love each other. Passionately. You can't discard that. It's already inscribed in time. You can't take that love from me no matter how often you accuse me, exclude me or insult me. Because the person I loved is not the person who wrote those accusations. The person I loved was present in your letter, not in your statements about me but in your descriptions of Mirna. I recognized your love for me in your love for Mirna. I recognized the evening walks, the conversations, even the expectation that working people would soon join us, embrace us and dance with us in the street. If you tried to present yourself to me as a completely different person from the one I once knew, you failed. You made me want to be Mirna. Not in spite of your bitterness toward me but because of it. The Sophia in your letter is a treacherous wretch who caused you only pain and suffering, whereas Mirna is a wonderful, unspoiled creature who brings you happiness. Could any conceivable reader of your letter want to be Sophia? I don't. I want to be the one who shares the embrace as well as the happiness; I want to be on the street with you when the dancing begins. Even to the point of consenting to marriage? Oh, but you've disposed of that question altogether. Yes, under the circumstances: if I'm a shepherdess, a village girl, yes. To share the happiness. I don't want to be an outsider to that happiness. I don't want to be excluded. Why can't you share it with me? I don't begrudge your moments of happiness with Mirna. On the contrary, I found joy in your descriptions of them because I found myself. How could I help it? I was exactly the same age when I knew you as Mirna was when you met her. You were younger for me, but for me you haven't aged. And the joy you described was recognizable to me because I, too, had experienced it once, though only once in my life — with you.

Pain and suffering predominated in your life. Does that justify the pain your letter inflicts on me? Pain predominated in my life too; it was undoubtedly less intense than yours, but my moments of happiness were also less intense and fewer than the ones you've described. My relationship to you, my participation in the project we shared with others, account for the happiest moments of my life. Why do you want to take that away from me now? Don't you see that your argument puts the guilt on Luisa and me because you spent twelve years of your life in prison and we didn't? Can't you see the absurdity of accusing slaves of enslaving themselves through the very act of trying to free themselves? Can't you remember that my project was to destroy the world that caused your suffering, not to reimpose it?

Can't you recognize my project in the agitation taking place around you while you wrote me? The people tearing down the signs, the tapestries — where did they come from? Did they drop from the sky? You admit they didn't. You admit they're the same individuals who were nothing but moving corpses only yesterday. Today empty shells are suddenly becoming full of life, imagination and potentiality. Dreams are once again becoming realizable. Where did that life and those dreams come from? You don't say. But I know those dreams didn't suddenly drop from the sky any more than the people did. They're dreams that have been suppressed, dreams that were held inside until the day when they could again be expressed. They're my dreams and Luisa's and yours. What you're describing is the rebirth of our struggle, our project, our hopes. Why are you so intent on excluding us — all of us: Vera, Marc, Jasna, Titus, Adrian and Claude? Were we so criminal for having tried and failed where no one else has yet succeeded?

The walls that are crumbling around you today were the prisons that suppressed our struggle. Why are you trying to prove that we ourselves imprisoned our own hopes, that we were the tombs of our dreams? I don't understand! Without that struggle, without that project we're nothing. Your letter abounds in imagery that shows how well you understand this: without those dreams we're corpses, shells, husks, instruments, machines. If you raze the rest of us to the ground you may find yourself standing very high, Yarostan, but not in a human community.

You shatter my dreams, revise my past, and then tell me I've deformed both. You're the one who deforms. I shouldn't have told you I had a poor memory. Maybe you thought I'd let your revision stand unchallenged, or even that I'd believe you. But you're telling me about my own past! And Luisa's fantasy, as you choose to call it, happens to coincide with a large part of my own life, so that I have some familiarity with that as well.

You made a cryptic reference to a certain Manuel you met in prison. He helped you see everything clearly. He provided the missing facts. He completed a picture that until then was incomplete. And the complete picture shows Luisa and her comrades stabbing each other in the back. I don't know where Manuel's facts come from but I know that mine come from several individuals who actually lived them. The reason I remember them is because they happen to be part of my own life. Nachalo, Luisa's first companion (and my father) is the first fact that doesn't fit your picture, and his whole life undermines what you learned from Manuel. I was only two years old when he was killed, but I learned about him ever since then, not only from Luisa, whose veracity you discount, but also from Alberts, who never had any illusions (or dreams). Nachalo was a peasant, like the Sedlaks, but when he met Luisa he had already divorced himself from all the village traditions, taboos and ceremonies. He was considerably older than Luisa. When they met he had already experienced a revolutionary peasant uprising which had been defeated by statists parading as revolutionaries. He had seen his village destroyed, his friends and his wife killed by a gang of murderers who called themselves a workers' army. He fled with a newborn baby, together with a handful of his comrades. He later learned that none of the insurgent peasants who stayed behind became jailers or executioners because every single one of them was killed. In exile he worked at odd jobs and drank. His daughter, whom he named Margarita, grew up as a street urchin: ragged, hungry and illiterate! On one of his jobs he met Luisa, a girl who was only three or four years older than Margarita. Luisa, in her own words, seduced him. She was fascinated, even hypnotized by Nachalo, not only by the man but also by his experiences. Her mother had died when she was a girl; her father had been shot by the police in a strike. Before she met Nachalo she had been actively involved in union activities. Nachalo brought her a totally new perspective, new hopes and possibilities. Here was a man who hadn't only fought losing defensive battles against the oppressors but who had actually gone on the offensive, routed the exploiters, and held the ground for a period of years. She couldn't hear enough from him. She followed him after work, to the bars, and then to his miserable room. She took Nachalo and Margarita to union meetings and introduced them to militant comrades. It was at one of these meetings that the three of them met George Alberts.

After I was born. Nachalo, Luisa and Margarita moved to a larger and cleaner apartment. It was so large that their comrades used it to hold meetings. Alberts was the most regular visitor; he and Margarita became inseparable.

When the army attacked the city, Nachalo was among the first workers in the neighborhood to run out armed and begin building barricades. Luisa ran after him. Margarita joined them although she was pregnant, and she refused to return home until a bullet grazed her arm. She died while giving birth to Sabina. Nachalo died two or three months later, while fighting against the combined forces of the army, the landowners and the church.

I'm not asking you for tears or even sympathy. All this happened very long ago, and I've already shed all the tears I'll ever shed over it. All I'm asking is why you sent me such a letter. How can you tell me that a certain Manuel said Nachalo, Luisa, Margarita and all their dead and wounded comrades fought only to reimpose the landlords, the state and the church? What have I become to you? Why?

You proceed to revise my equally illusory picture of the resistance. It so happens that I was there as well, and I was considerably older; I even remember some events on my own, not just from the stories told to me by others. What you tell me is that the workers of the city, some of whom I knew personally, fought to liberate themselves from a military dictatorship only to make room for another. I found your account of your own activity during the war fascinating; you had never spoken about that. But your new insight, your exposure of the true nature of the event, is neither insightful nor true. Do you really expect me to purge my memory of what you call Luisa's fantasy in order to replace it with yours? It seems to me that I'd then be even worse off than the workers in your fabricated resistance fighting in an already liberated city to make room for a military dictatorship.

You describe my activity with you as a puppet show. Your description corresponds neither to the events I experienced at the time nor to events I experienced later. I'm not misreading your letter. I think I understand perfectly well what you're saying. We thought we were acting freely while in fact we were being manipulated. Therefore we were puppets. Since we're not in fact puppets but people, we must have turned ourselves into puppets. Therefore we manipulated ourselves.

Your conclusions don't follow from your premises. I'll show you. I won't refer to my experience with you to illustrate my argument, since that experience has become so foul to you. I'll refer to a similar experience which had nothing to do with your imprisonment. Two years ago I got a job teaching a university class. The first thing I noticed was that students, especially the men, were not the same people I had gone to school with. My contemporaries had been short-haired automatons who applauded in movie houses whenever a bomb destroyed a village. The new students were almost a different species. Instead of considering the university a training ground which would magnify their power to kill, many thought of school as a way of avoiding or postponing going to war. They no longer applauded mass killings. Most of them didn't want to become professional murderers, and none of them wanted to die for the flag. Ways to avoid killing and dying constituted the main topic of their conversations. Some months after the beginning of the school year I was visited by two young people who weren't students. They called themselves revolutionary organizers. They introduced themselves to students who published the radical newspaper, to outspoken students and to what they called radical faculty members like me. They announced a meeting in the school's largest auditorium; they had made previous arrangements with students who were to be the local hosts of the event, and I agreed to be the faculty sponsor. These two organizers were no longer, subject to the military draft. They saw the draft as a lever, an "issue" around which to organize a following. They saw the protesting students as a potential "base" for their organization. In other words they were professional politicians. Over two hundred students came to the meeting. It was the largest political gathering that had taken place at this university for several decades. Students came with the hope of communicating with their likes, as you put it; they came to learn what others had learned, to help and be helped. All their hopes were thwarted. They were subjected to several hours of political harangues that were far less inspired than most of their daily lectures. The organizers had picked the speakers, among whom they had included themselves; they had defined the topics of the harangues; they had even planted people in the audience to ask questions at the end. Most of the two hundred people who had originally come to the meeting left before it was over. At the end there were only eight left besides the organizers. I stayed in the back of the auditorium until the end. Those eight students elected themselves to be the local chapter of the organization. I later learned that seven of them had already elected themselves to this office earlier. For the remainder of the year these eight students became representatives and spokesmen, not only of the two hundred students who had come to the meeting, but of all the students in the university.

In terms of your analysis, the students who originally came to the meeting shackled themselves, as well as all other students, with these political bureaucrats. They were manipulated into legitimating the power of these politicians. But that's absurd. They all left as soon as they realized the speeches came from tin cans. Only one out of two hundred was taken in by the political marmalade dished out by those political bosses who differed from professors and factory managers only in age. Of course you'll say that by the time they realized the program was canned it was too late. Their mere presence at the meeting had already validated the politicians' claim to be the spokesmen of the mass of students. After that single act they could no longer meet publicly with each other without having the politicians preside over them (which was in fact what happened). Therefore merely by attending the meeting they had muzzled themselves, bound themselves to new bosses who were more insidious than the old bosses because they came from among themselves. Therefore the students had been puppets, inert things, objects moved by forces outside themselves, dolls manipulated by puppeteers.

Your analysis reduces a two-dimensional picture to a single dimension, it reduces two sides to one. The protesting students were on one side, the politicians and all other officials were on the other. The fact that the university officials accepted the student politicians as the spokesmen of protesting students doesn't mean that any of the protesting students accepted them as their spokesmen. It merely means that officials recognized and embraced other officials and momentarily disregarded their club's age requirements. By omitting the second side you lose sight of the relation between the two sides. You leave out what we used to call the struggle between the ruling class and the repressed class, the class struggle. The fact that the rulers recruit their agents from among the repressed doesn't mean that the repressed are the agents of their own repression.

You don't only omit the fact of struggle. In one part of your letter you even make fun of Luisa's description of the external forces that suppressed revolutionary workers and peasants who had not become puppets. According to you there were no external forces. The rot is always within. Whatever happens to me is my own fault. Your profound new insight is no more than the ancient doctrine of original sin. You misunderstand Cassius' observation, "The fault, dear Brutus, is not in our stars, but in ourselves, that we are underlings." In your version, the bullets, dear Sophia, are not in their guns, but in our brains, that make us underlings.

Those who arrested you and me were not imaginary beings, nor was I arrested by myself. My memory did in fact freeze certain facts, and they've been perfectly preserved. One of these facts is that I was arrested by police agents. Another fact is that I was taken to a police station and a jail which I had not helped build: both were much older than I was. A third fact is that the statements on my posters and the words on my lips were not secret instructions to the police for your arrest. The police received their instructions from their superiors, ultimately from the politicians in the state apparatus, and not from the likes of you or me. If you think I was a puppet displaying the warrant for my own arrest, you're hallucinating, not Luisa or I.

It was absurd of me to tell Tina we were arrested because we were Alberts' relatives, since eight or nine of us were arrested and only two of us were related to Alberts. Furthermore Alberts wasn't arrested. I suppose it's this ridiculous slip of my memory that confirms your statements about my inability to remember my own real past. This slip embarrasses me, it makes me wish I had a more trustworthy memory, but it doesn't convince me that I've systematically falsified my past, it doesn't convince me that my modest exterior houses an ogre who, after exterminating her victims, makes them vanish to oblivion.

I do remember that Alberts had nothing to do with our arrest, but I don't remember that I helped paint signs and tapestries which were hung in front of prison walls; I don't remember that I helped bury a human community and drown the sound of human voices. My own life has been surrounded by those very signs and tapestries, by those very walls, by that very silence and lack of community. All my life I've longed for nothing more than to communicate with my likes on a field without signs or walls. How can I prove this to you? You reached out to me and I responded. I would have tried to reach you the day after my release from jail and every day after that if I had thought my letters would be delivered. But you know perfectly well that letters were being returned without any explanations.

I had my first real chance to reach you only twelve years ago. A friend of mine, Lem Icel, was going to be near you on his way to some international conference. I frantically wrote letters to all of you. I was terribly sad when nothing came in response to those letters. I didn't see Lem again until several years later. He told me he had been arrested because he'd been carrying my letters. He proceeded to list the horrors he had undergone in prisons and camps and concluded by telling me about his recent conversion to an ancient Egyptian religion. I hardly listened to what he told me and I didn't believe any of it. I concluded he had lost my letters and had made up the stories about the imprisonment and the tortures. I thought he was covering up his guilt by pretending I was guilty of his imprisonment. Now you tell me that one of my letters did reach its destination, though you never saw it. Lem didn't lose the letters after all. This means that the rest of his story may also have been true. I might have caused Lem's arrest. And according to Mirna I also caused yours. This makes me a dangerous schizophrenic: mild and well-intentioned during the day while at night I plot the arrest, imprisonment and torture of my friends.

I can't stand seeing myself where your letter leaves me. Can't you see there's something ridiculous about these insinuations and accusations? When I wrote you twelve years ago, and when I wrote you last time in answer to your warm and comradely first letter, I was desperately reaching for understanding, sympathy, human communication. Your last letter reduces both my gestures to terrible crimes. You, Lem and Mirna suggest I've done nothing in my life except send instructions to the police. Though I don't feel like laughing, I'm convinced something funny is going on. I'm no more schizophrenic than the rest of my contemporaries and my paranoia is generally lower than the average. I can't make myself believe that my letter had anything to do with Lem's arrest or with yours. I have no idea what Lem was doing there besides delivering my letters, but I do know that my letters didn't contain instructions to the police. They were private, personal letters. They referred solely to my own insignificant experiences and didn't contain a single reference to politics or politicians. I didn't know what the president's name was or even if there was a president. Do the police arrest, imprison and torture people for carrying such letters? Does that police really have nothing else to do? Are they madmen? Doesn't this sound awfully silly and terribly paranoid?

I had known Lem for many years and I knew that paranoia wasn't out of the question as far as he was concerned. Paranoia was the root of his conceit; it confirmed his importance and his political effectiveness. He always saw himself as persecuted. When he called himself a revolutionary he convinced himself his phone was tapped; he was forever being followed and watched. All the attention he got proved how revolutionary he was. When he later became a mystic he convinced himself that objects persecuted him. Could I believe such a person when he told me my letters caused his arrest?

I don't know what to say about Mirna's suspicions. Does she, too, have traces of paranoia? You certainly suggest as much when you tell me you don't consider my letter the cause of your arrest. I obviously can't prove anything since I don't have access to the police files. All I can say is that the accusation sounds silly.

I'm going to admit something else, because suddenly I no longer care what you make of this admission. I haven't told you all my reasons for thinking that Lem was lying to me when he told me about his arrest and imprisonment. It wasn't only because I was familiar with Lem's persecution mania that I didn't believe him. The story itself sounded phony to me. I didn't pay any attention to him. The sequence of horrors didn't only seem terribly exaggerated but was also similar, down to details, to the pictures drawn by official propagandists. I was sure he had read the whole story in a newspaper. And at that time I was convinced that those stories were pure fabrications, fictional from the first word to the last. No, I wasn't taken in by the opposite propaganda. I knew about the prisons and camps, the political purges, the state-run unions, the speed-ups and productivity campaigns. What I didn't believe were the stock stories about the priests, nuns and itty-bitty children tor-tured in medieval dungeons, since these stones were obviously journalistic fictions pulled out of dusty war-hysteria files, with names and dates changed for every occa-sion. I recognized these newspaper articles in Lem's account; I didn't recognize a single element of a world which should have been familiar to me because, as you so crudely put it, I'd helped build it. He was, after all, talking about a place where I had once known several workers who were not unlike thousands of other workers. He was telling me that all the people I had lived with and worked with, and all others like them, had simply vanished into thin air and had been replaced by chains, gates and horrifying instruments of torture. He was telling me that all those workers had either allowed those horrors to take place or else that they'd all been imprisoned and executed and that the only people left were apes or sheep. I couldn't believe any of that. I couldn't believe all those people had vanished, all the dreams I had fought for had disappeared without leaving a trace. I couldn't accept a vision similar to the one you expressed in your letter; I couldn't believe the last human beings were dying in prisons while self-repressed beings had replaced them outside.

I nursed my illusion. I deluded myself. Put it any way you want. If I had believed Lem I would either have gone straight to a mental hospital or I would have killed myself. I believed there were people like me over there, that they had retained their dreams and hopes, that they were still struggling. I tried to reach them. Does that make me a criminal? Is it criminal to have hopes and dreams which reality might invalidate? Are a prisoner's dreams about his projects after release illusions because he might die in prison? Since we all know we'll eventually die, since any of us might die tomorrow, are all our hopes and dreams illusions? Are we criminals when we fail to realize them?

You contradict your main argument. You tell me that, in spite of the uncertainty of your release, you made plans in prison. In every other paragraph you speak of projects, dreams and hopes. You write poetry about the unshackled imagination, about the possibility of creating our world in the light of our dreams. You're insincere. I think you were equally insincere when you told Mirna and her parents that you were opposed to marrying her. Your arguments against marriage seemed as hollow as your arguments about my illusions. At no point in your narrative did I feel you had the slightest doubt that you'd marry Mirna. When you told me how certain they all were that the event would take place I felt you were every bit as certain from beginning to end. And when you tell me about my illusions I'm convinced you share every last one of them. If you didn't share those illusions you wouldn't be able to describe the ferment surrounding you today; you wouldn't even be able to see it. If those in ferment today didn't share what you call my illusions there would be no ferment around you today. People without such hopes and dreams are not human beings, and only human beings can give rise to a ferment of the type you describe. You're insincere, and you're applying a double standard. When I express the hope that we'll tear down the walls that imprison us, that hope is an illusion; when you express the same hope, it becomes an intention, a project, a motive for communication, comradeship and struggle. I remember my past only in order to hallucinate whereas you remember your past in order to understand your present.

Believe it or not, I use my past exactly the same way you use yours. I don't use it as a subject for admiration, distortion or hallucination, but as a perspective from which to view my present. Exactly as you do! If I hadn't once in my life been with people who had momentarily stopped being wage workers, I would have been perfectly satisfied to remain a wage worker the first time I got a job. Just as you would still be driving that infernal bus delivering human excrement to the city's sewers. I quit my first job, as well as my second, because I had known human beings who had been more, much more, than wage workers. If I hadn't once had a genuine learning experience I would have accepted my years in high school and college as a learning experience; I couldn't have imagined education in any other form. My past experience helped me see through, expose and rebel against my present experience; it helped me see through the systematic stunting and incapacitation which passes as education. If I hadn't once experienced friendship, solidarity and communication I would never have been able to guess what was wrong with all the Mr. Ninovos who populate the world, and nothing in my life would have kept me from becoming one of them.

The people you and I once knew, the hopes we shared with them, the projects we undertook together, have served me as a standard of comparison. Perhaps imaginary people and projects would have served as well. Isn't that the sensible meaning of utopia: a standard against which to measure the present? My utopia was slightly more vivid than most people's because I had actually experienced moments of it. This is why all your accusations miss their mark. I'm not, after all, competing in a memory contest, nor writing a history, nor am I engaged in scholarly research into my past. If I were, you would have devastated my project as inept, inaccurate and totally untrustworthy. Since I'm only trying to determine who I am and what I'm doing you fail to make a point and you punch holes in an imaginary balloon. Far from trying to reconstruct the actual sequence of past events, I'm only using my own and to some extent Luisa's and Nachalo's past as a standard of comparison and guide for present decisions and actions. You've been my lifelong guide just as Luisa was yours. And you're wrong to uproot her from your memory, to discard her. You're only impoverishing yourself. By eliminating this standard you're left with nothing but the world as it is. If you deprive yourself of the ability to see what people can be and what life can be you'll only be able to see what they are and you'll conclude that's all they can be.

Yet even while you uproot Luisa from your memory, you reject the world into which you've been released. Even while you're discarding your standard of comparison you're comparing and measuring. By what standard can you define a person as a stunted human being if all conceptions of fully developed human beings are illusions? How on earth can you even know you're in prison if you can't imagine there are human beings out of prison?

If I froze the memory of my experience with you, I didn't do this to glorify the outcome of that experience, since it had no outcome, but to transport that experience to a new terrain. If I preserved the hopes and dreams I shared with you, it wasn't because I thought you and I had realized them but because I wanted to go on struggling to realize them. I brought those hopes and dreams to a world that lacked them, a world that uprooted and killed such hopes and dreams. If those dreams now seem stunted to you it's because this world to which I was brought didn't contain the soil in which they could grow. Accuse me of having dragged those dreams into an environment unfavorable to them, accuse me of having failed to realize them, but don't in the same breath accuse me of having suppressed them.

I'm sorry you didn't read my last letter in the spirit in which I wrote it. I'm sorry because our lives were not so different after we were arrested and separated. I understood perfectly the desperation you felt right after your release from prison. I understood why you considered those few days bleaker than all your years in prison. I understood because, when I wrote you twelve years ago, I considered the eight years after my release bleaker than imprisonment. I apologize for the way this sounds. When I sent that letter I had no idea you had spent four years in prison. Luisa and I were released after two days in jail and for some reason I'd thought you had been released shortly after us. Yet even if I'd known you had spent half those years in jail I would have preferred to spend those eight years as you spent them. I would at least have been in prison for acts I had known I'd committed. And on release I would once again have been in a world that was familiar to me with people who were friends. Please don't misunderstand me again. I'm not glorifying the bureaucracy and the police who installed themselves as rulers. I don't know much about them but everything I do know sends shivers down my back. That's not at all what I'm writing about. I'm trying to tell you that all my life here I've wished I had never left you, that my emigration was nothing but a big mistake, that here I wasn't able to become more than I already was when you knew me. I hope this time I'm making myself clear. You told me the world you found after your release wasn't paradise. I never thought it was. I'm trying to tell you something similar about myself. The world I came to wasn't paradise either; it wasn't even as close to paradise as my experience with you.

The world to which I was brought was publicly considered humanity's first earthly paradise, the most perfect community of happy human beings. It took me only a few minutes to learn that the happy human beings were images on signs and tapestries identical to those you described, that the milk and honey were spilled willy-nilly on a desert that contained neither community nor comradeship nor human warmth. I had been brought to this Utopia of objects for no reason at all. I was imprisoned here, not because of acts I had committed, but because someone thought he was doing me a favor by bringing me here. And in this desert paradise there's no hope of release. This is the apex of everything that can be desired, though not by human beings. All roads leading from the apex are steep descents. From here I can only go down; from here I can only be released into the prisons in which you've spent half your life.

I wish I knew what you heard me saying. How frustrating it is to communicate across such a great distance. Surely you don't again hear me saying that your imprisonment was the realization of my dreams! If I refer to my experiences with you while describing the world I was brought to, it's because those were the only experiences I'd had before coming here; they were the vantage point from which I saw where I was. You described Vesna as being born into a cage from which she never emerged. I suppose you mean she had never known life outside the cage since her earliest memories were memories of the cage. She had no other memories, not even frozen ones, to compare and contrast with her experiences in the cage. Consequently she couldn't know that she was in a cage. I do have memories and it's thanks to them that I'm able to describe this paradise as a cage. And so do you! If you didn't how would you know Vesna was born in a cage? If you didn't remember a moment of life outside the cage, no matter how brief, you, like Vesna, would think of the cage as the world, the only possible world, perhaps even the best of all possible worlds.

I remember my release from jail and my journey here as a terrible trip through a very long tunnel. My life was at the opening I was moving away from and I expected to find nothing at the other end. Released after two days in jail, I thought Luisa and I would return to our friends, I thought we would continue the work we hadn't finished; I thought the struggle had only begun. I expected to find you and all our other friends engaged in the activities from which I had suddenly been cut off. "We're leaving!" Luisa said. Leaving what? Our friends? Our project? But our project wasn't yet off the ground; the new world wasn't yet built. Was everyone leaving? Were we going to continue our struggle elsewhere? Was our world already built somewhere else? If not, why were we leaving and where were we going?

I didn't understand. I was frustrated and shocked. I froze every detail of that project and those friends as well as every hope I had shared with them. I fixed my experience in my memory as if I knew already then that I was being taken to a cage from which I would never emerge. If I hadn't frozen those memories, if I had forgotten my experiences and my friends, then like Vesna I would only have known the cage. I would have grown up like those around me who don't know any life outside. I would have accepted my cage companions as the only possible human beings and my cage experiences as the only possible human experiences. I couldn't have compared my life in the cage to the life I'd had before I was caged. If I'd forgotten you I couldn't have written you twelve years ago and I'd have no reason in the world to write you now. I wouldn't have responded to your first letter because I would have thought you alien and bizarre. I would have been a bird of paradise who couldn't possibly have understood a letter from a foreigner and even if I'd read it I wouldn't have sent a word of mine to an insurgent who was a jailbird to boot.

Luisa later told me I was sick during the entire journey, that I broke down. I was extremely hostile to Alberts, and ungrateful. I didn't show the slightest appreciation for the favor he was doing us. I was as rude to him as I had been to my jailer. Luisa acted grateful. I remember that. This was partly what made me sick. As things turned out later she had been wrong. Her gratitude only lasted a few months. I clung to Luisa but for the first time in my life I didn't trust her. I suspected she didn't know where we were going, why we were going or what we would do when we got there. And I was right. Sabina was the only one of us who knew exactly where she was going and what she would do there. Alberts had told her she was going to the land of gigantic objects and monstrous toys. (He was right.) She bubbled over with enthusiasm and couldn't wait to get there. She jumped around like a monkey released from its cage. I hated her for that enthusiasm; I did everything I could to block out the noise she made. I saw her as a chicken running around a yard cackling during the few minutes before her head is chopped off.

Sabina's wishes were fulfilled. This Eldorado was everything Alberts had promised. The original Eldorado, where streets had been paved with nuggets of gold and where people had walked on the gold and respected each other, had disappeared long ago; its inhabitants had all been exterminated. In its place had grown up another Eldorado, where gold is stored in underground vaults and the streets are paved with flesh, where objects walk on people and respect each other. It is indeed the land of gigantic toys. The toys have defeated the people. Objects rule city streets, country highways, bridges and underpasses; objects are housed, fed and nursed;

objects are displayed, praised, honored and worshipped. The people are small and fearful; they're mere attendants to the needs of the objects. When they're not nursing objects, the people are nothing more than obstacles on the paths of rushing objects. Every collision between a person and an object destroys the person while leaving the object intact. Only the objects have purposes and directions. When people aren't tending objects they drift. They don't rest; on the contrary, they're always on the alert; they keep their eyes on the objects so as to avoid colliding with them. They don't even dream about communicating with each other. They don't have the time. They know that in the time it took to establish contact with one of their likes they'd be crushed. They eavesdrop on conversations among objects. Without communication they can't launch common projects and they no longer even imagine them.

Where did I find the language and imagery with which to understand and describe this world? You know exactly where: in the carton plant twenty years ago, when I was among fearless, unintimidated human beings communicating with each other, engaged in a common project, among individuals who walked on objects and respected each other. That was my utopia, my Eldorado. Haven't you been carrying a similar picture for at least as many years? What are those barricades which existed so briefly and then only in situations of crisis but which nevertheless revealed a permanent human possibility? That's what my picture shows me: a permanent human possibility. By showing me what people can be it helps me understand what those around me have become. By showing me people engaged in common projects it informs me that drift is not the only possible content of human life.

No, I haven't been a hermit for the past twenty years. I haven't remained totally isolated from the people around me. I haven't sat in my room contemplating the picture of my one-time friends. My breakdown didn't last from then until now. I met innumerable people. I worked with many of them. I'm trying to describe how I experienced them. I'm trying to tell you who they were and what they were by contrasting them with what they weren't. I'm trying to describe a cage as the cage I experienced it to be and not as the paradise its other inmates imagine it to be. I can only do this from a vantage point outside the cage, from the vantage point of the experience I shared with you, from the vantage point of that picture I kept for all those years.

By tearing my picture to shreds as you tore your picture of Luisa, you tear my life as well. The possibilities I reached for in every encounter and every event were the only live elements of my experiences. Please don't rob me of the people who informed me of those possibilities. They're among the few people I knew who weren't puppets. They're the only human community I ever experienced. They weren't perfect. They weren't gods. They were flawed and human, identical to millions of others. That's why they revealed a human possibility. Yet you make their very humanity appear inhuman. It's you who are looking for gods. I'm only looking for more Veras, more Adrians, Marcs, Claudes.

I remember a Vera who talked, but not like a radio. The radio is an instrument which kills communication; it robs people of their tongues; it broadcasts the voice of a single individual to millions of listeners, reducing them to passive receptacles. If communication has the same root as common and community, the radio is an instrument for uprooting all three. The Vera I remember had the unmagnified voice of a single individual among thousands of other individuals; she was one of the thousands who were turning off the radios and regaining their own voices. To me she's the very opposite of the countless politicians I've met since who dreamed only of the day when their voices would be the only sound in a sea of silent listeners.

I remember an Adrian who moved with the tide. When the people around him began to throw off the muck of ages, he was infected by their spirit and did his best to liberate himself. If the spirit of liberation could spread to Adrian it could spread to all. He was living proof of what was possible. I've met many conformists since but none of them were ever infected by a spirit of liberation or by any spirit at all: they all moved within the rigid confines of official routine.

I remember a Claude who was an oaf, but I also remember that at least for an instant he was using his bulk to defend himself and his comrades. You expressed intense dislike for him. To me he was a symbol of the working class, waking up from the stupor of wage labor, at last turning its bulk against capital. The bullies I've known since have used their weight to defend their masters and oppress their peers.

You describe Marc as a self-styled expert. I thought he was a worker like the others. I remember him as a dreamer. He let his imagination wander freely over the field of possibilities (the expression is yours). He gave me a glimpse of what the world might be like if everyone's imagination wandered so freely. I've met many people who thought themselves experts, but I never wished for a world which contained more of them.

According to you these people whose emotions and projects were their own existed only in my private imagination. You have good words only for Jasna, Jan and Titus, precisely the three whom I didn't consider models or guides. I was never able to consider Titus a comrade because after Nachalo's death both he and Alberts acted as fathers toward me. But have it your way. Say the workers I remember are imaginary. Say the experience I shared with them never took place. It doesn't really matter. Even if I never lived such an experience, I can still say that my imagination once glimpsed the possibility of genuine social activity which was neither trivial nor marginal. Even if I never knew those people, I imagined insurgents who struggled to shake off their chains and not to shackle others with them. Imaginary or not, that experience and those people informed all my senses from the first moment after my release. It's because of them and because of you that I experienced my release from jail and my emigration as a descent to hell. Instead of being overjoyed I was morose. Instead of being grateful to Alberts I thought he had cut me off from the living. I didn't accept events the way Mirna's mother accepted them, as the unwinding of fate. My real or imagined experience had made me a critic.

Alberts already had a job when we came here. This had been arranged by people he had worked with during the war; I never knew them nor what he had done with them. He taught natural science in high school, although your imagery describes his activity much more accurately: he paced in front of thirty or forty teen-agers from nine to three while excrement dripped from him. I know because a year after we came I watched him drip for a whole semester. Thanks to you I know what a teacher is.

When we arrived we were greeted — I should say fawned over — by a self-appointed reception committee. They told us that freedom was the nickname of their flag, that the mortal danger of crossing the street was proof of a high standard of living, and that we would be happy when we learned to live like them. They were jingoes, war hawks. They found us a place; they called it a home, the local euphemism for the walls that separate people from their neighbors. They told us they would gladly help us solve any problems we might have, but they left us neither names nor phone numbers and we never saw any of them again.

I had my own room in our home. I had never had one before. It wasn't damp or cold and it had no roaches, mice or rats. There was a bed and there were walls. It wasn't like a prison cell because I could leave whenever I pleased. For several days I sat on the bed and stared at the walls and then it was just like a prison cell. It separated me from my friends and from my activities. My life was elsewhere, outside, far away. I was a prisoner. Luisa brought me my meals. At times she was the old Luisa: she understood, she sympathized, she regretted the journey and hated the home, the reception committee and Alberts. But at other times she was a new Luisa, the Luisa who had been grateful to Alberts and polite to the reception committee, who called me a stubborn goose and insisted I'd find new friends and forget my old ones.

Neighbors came to visit. I wanted to go out and stare at them but I stayed in my room and listened. They said they wanted to introduce themselves, but in fact they had come to snoop. They asked Luisa how old her two daughters were. They must have counted us when we moved in. I hadn't once left my room since that day. They asked Luisa why we weren't in school. Luisa told them we were learning the language. That wasn't true. Sabina was already fluent, thanks to Alberts, and I could understand most of what was said. Luisa also told them the trip had been a shock to both of us and we were recovering. That wasn't true of Sabina and the neighbors must have known Luisa was lying. Sabina had already run all around the neighborhood and no one could have thought her sick. Sabina simply refused to go to school. She argued that neither she nor Luisa nor I had come here to go to school; only Alberts had.

A few days after our neighbors' thoughtful visit, two officials came. They too asked Luisa why her daughters weren't in school. You're not the only one who has

Mr. Ninovo for a neighbor. Luisa was intimidated. She promised to pack both of us off to school the following morning. (You aim your critique at the Luisa who fought bravely in a revolution. You don't even seem aware of this second Luisa, the one who ran away from her friends and projects twice, the one who was afraid and intimidated. You're disillusioned with the wrong Luisa.)

Luisa begged me to go to school, and I was disillusioned. But I felt sorry for her and gave in, since I had never intended to spend the rest of my life in that room. Sabina was more principled than I, and Alberts was less slavish than Luisa. He telephoned someone he knew and had Sabina enrolled in a private school which she never attended. Sabina was simply told to stay out of the neighbors' sight during school hours, which she managed to do quite successfully until she and Alberts moved out several months later. She didn't spend a single day in school.

How sickeningly adaptable people are! During my first few days in school I was revolted, shocked and indignant. Lively young people sat like trained poodles and let ignorant functionaries stuff their heads with garbage, I tried to think of ways to expose and undermine the poodle-training sessions. But all I ever thought of doing was to refuse to answer questions on the ground that they were biased or trivial. Instead of taking notes about the lectures I took notes about the teachers and the students. I intended to use those notes when I wrote letters to my former comrades. I was going to describe to you what happened to human beings if they lost the struggle we had fought. I still have those notes. I reread some of them before I started this letter; I wanted to see to what extent my memory contained only experiences I had invented. I found myself innocent of your charge. I never wrote the letters those notes were intended for. Yet I continued to take notes. Later I rearranged them; I was going to write a novel comparing my past with my present. Gradually my shock, my indignation, my desire to expose the farce called education were confined to my notes. My life was confined to my notebook. I dragged myself to school mechanically, absently, as if I were taking a garbage bag to a dump. I adapted. I became like the others. Only my notebook continued to rebel, and I never showed those notes to anyone. They were intended for you. Yet now that I'm finally showing them to you I'm embarrassed; your letter makes me defensive about them. I had always been sure you'd understand. Your letter makes me suspect I did have one illusion after all: the illusion that you'd understand. In any case your letter wasn't a letter from a complete stranger. I recognized you every time you stopped talking about me; the passages where you described yourself and the people around you were the passages in which I recognized my own experience and it's because of them that I think you'll understand mine.

I understood your anger and frustration when you leafed through Mirna's history book. My history book was similar to Mirna's; it contained the same accounts of the rise of bureaucrats to government offices. Though I lived in an environment where every single human attribute and every facet of nature had been transformed into wage labor and capital, the textbook history of that environment didn't mention wage labor or capital. Though I lived in a city where the systematic despoliation and oppression of human beings had reached a level unknown to any previous human beings, the textbook history spoke only of equality and freedom. The students didn't seem to pay a whole lot of attention, but the lies nevertheless got through to them, by osmosis. One of the first students who talked to me was another foreigner. He told me his father had worked in a steel plant for two years; he had lifted a load that was too heavy for him and had injured his back; when he failed to recover and return to work, he was fired. The boy's mother had gone to work to support him and his sick father. The boy asked me: "The place where you come from — is it part of the free world too?"

The language teacher spent six months reading a single novel to the class. Can you imagine that? Since I had already read the book I spent my time elaborating my notes. There was even a class in cooking which I simply refused to attend. As soon as I refused, I was told I was free to take a class in wood-turning and carpentry. I was the only girl there; apparently no other girl refused to take the cooking class and consequently no other girl had learned she was free not to take it.

You described how out of place Mirna's schoolbooks seemed to be in her house. Books seemed at least as misplaced in the hands of some of my teachers, particularly my mathematics teacher. In addition to being the math teacher this man was the school's sports expert. He was one of the few teachers in the school who possessed the highest academic degree. He was called a doctor and it was said he had framed his diploma and hung it in his living room. It was also said the thesis for which he had been granted this degree dealt with basketball dribbling. I think both stories were true. He may in fact have been very good at writing about dribbling a basketball, but he couldn't divide fractions and I suspected he had never learned to solve simple algebraic equations. He would solve on the blackboard precisely those problems that were solved in the book. One day he made a mistake copying. In order to go to the next step he had to divide the same quantity out of both sides of the equation. He divided each side by a different quantity and nonchalantly continued copying. I was furious. "Hey, you can't do that!" I shouted. "You wouldn't have to do it if you had copied the right numbers out of the book!"

He turned red as a beet. "You Bolshies are too smart for your own good!" he shouted. The athlete then walked right up to me and slapped me. I screamed and he became as rigid as a board. Some students cheered him and shouted, "You show 'er, coach!"

Those students cheered him because they considered him the rebel. I was in a world where everything familiar to me stood on its head. The roles were inverted. The bullying teacher was seen as a rebel and the rebellious student as a representative of authority. The police were experienced as agents of freedom and insurgents as agents of repression. Authoritarian conformists considered themselves individualists and revolutionaries were called Bolshies and Commissars. The greatest inversion of all was that the most authoritarian of the authoritarians, those who glorified the state and dreamed of becoming omnipotent police chiefs, thought of themselves as revolutionaries. My friend Lem Icel, the one who later carried my letter to you, was one of these.

I met Lem the day the dribbling expert slapped me. Lem ran after me when school was over, in his suit and tie, wearing glasses, carrying his leather bag.

"I think you were right," he told me.

"What do you mean you think I was right? I know I was!" I shouted. "Look into your book!"

"Yes I know," he said. "I had the book open too. What I wanted to ask you was about that name he called you."

"You mean Bolshie? That's not my name!"

"I know it's not your name. What I mean is, is it true? Are you? Do you believe in tendencies and things?" He asked this last question in the same tone in which someone might have asked, "Do you believe the sun is going to fall into the lake the day after tomorrow and the world is going to end?" or "Do you believe every statue of Jesus bleeds every night?" And I knew he was dying to relieve himself by telling me, "So do I."

"Tendencies and things! What on earth do you mean?" I asked.

"Oh, you can tell me. I'm a Comrade. I'm no stool pigeon!" He whispered all this.

I shouted, "What are you talking about? What do you want?"

"Shh. You know what I mean. Tendencies. Forces. The Dialectic!" Yes, unfortunately I knew what he meant. It was nothing very exciting; it wasn't even altogether alive. But it was something. It was the form rebellion took in this environment, and I was extremely lonely. I'm reminded of the people you described who ate bark. Lem was a disgusting clown, a tidy bureaucrat who might someday transmit the order to exterminate thousands of workers, a stuffy state agent who was old long before his time. But I hadn't had a conversation with anyone except Luisa since we'd come here, and after I'd started going to school I had avoided Luisa. I couldn't keep myself from reaching out to Lem.

"Tendencies," I said, hesitating, as if I were remembering something. "Why yes, of course! Tendencies!" I forgot to add, "And things."

"I knew you were one of us as soon as the coach called you a Bolshie!" And I knew what Lem was going to say long before he said it.

"And did I confirm, what you already knew?"

"You sure did! We can keep it a secret from them, but not from each other!" He was obviously a novice in the conspiratorial profession, and had as yet learned nothing about security.

"Does no one else know you're one of them — I mean of us?" I asked.

"I've kept it a secret from everyone. Even from my parents," he proudly boasted.

"My! Imagine that!" I didn't even try to hide my admiration for his ability to keep secrets. "Not even your parents! You must be very courageous!"

"I thought it would be hard, but it isn't really," he explained. "My study group meets every Friday night and I tell my parents I go to movies. I used to go to movies a lot on Friday nights. I always make sure I know what's on at one of the theaters, though they haven't yet asked what I'd seen."

"And the study group," I ventured, "it must be even better than our classes in school."

"Oh yes, it's much more disciplined," he said predictably. "Anyone who did what you did today would be expelled right away."

"How marvelous!"

"Are you making fun of me?"

"Oh no!"

"Of course none of the lecturers in the study group would ever be caught making such a dumb mistake!"

"Can you tell me your name?" I asked to change the subject; I had heard enough about the study group. "Or is that a secret?" I felt silly for adding this question, and I hoped he wouldn't spoil my fun by remembering that I'd learn his name the next time the teacher revealed this secret in class.

"Oh no, I can tell you my name!" he said eagerly and obligingly. "It's Lem. Lem Icel. It comes from the Greek god Icelus. My grandfather shortened it."

"I'm Sophia."

"Yes I know. Sophia Nachalo. I saw it written on your notebook."

"You pronounced it right!" My name was the only thing he had said that pleased me.

"Does it bother you when that jock pronounces it Natural?"

"His pronunciation is his problem, not mine."

"It's obviously no better than his math," Lem said.

"Do you want me to get slapped for correcting his pronunciation as well? Why don't you correct him?"

Lem blushed. He could at least have corrected the athlete's math, since he'd had the book open too. "Objective conditions," he answered hesitantly. "You know what I mean?"

"Oh yes, of course! They weren't ripe."

"Wow! You know a lot!" He was genuinely impressed. "I only learned about that a couple of weeks ago!"

"Aren't you tired of learning by the end of the week, and wouldn't you rather go to movies on Friday nights?"

"Haven't you ever been to study groups?" he asked.

I didn't answer. I was already tired of my game, and of Lem.

"The study group is completely different," he explained as I walked away from him. "Here everything they tell you is a lie. There I learn about tendencies and forces. You know, the truth about things. You and I ought to talk more. You know. We ought to become friends, since we're already comrades."

My first friend was an admirer of those who had betrayed Luisa, arrested me, imprisoned you. The more I learned about him the less likeable he became. Lem was one of the wealthier students in the school. His father was the manager of a department store. Other people of his social class were sent to private schools, but Lem's father wanted to give his son what he considered a taste of reality. Lem's newly acquired political religion provided him with a new way of expressing his social status, and nothing more. He considered himself superior to the working class students because of his social class. He thought himself more intelligent as well, since he had been trained to memorize and obey from childhood on. And when one of the teachers introduced him to the world of tendencies and forces, he became a giant who towered above the others, being the only student in school who had been initiated into the dialectical truth about things. He was as much a member of the ruling class after his political conversion as he had been before.

I let him walk me home several days a week. We frequently went to movies together, and once I invited him to a dance. Although he insisted I accompany him to his study group, I didn't once go. I don't think we talked a great deal after our first encounter; at least I didn't record any other conversations. And because he had been friendly to me when I had been completely alone, this travesty of a rebel, this pompous leech was to cling to me for much of the rest of my life.

I don't know if I need to mention this or if I'm being clear this time: if I hadn't known you I wouldn't have seen through Lem. I might have seen him as he saw himself and as the official mythology defined him: as a rebel, an insurgent. Lem obviously didn't fill the gap I'd felt since my release.

Unlike you I didn't have any friends here; there was no Jan Sedlak I could run to. When I finally did find a genuine friend, it was someone who had something in common with the Sedlaks. Like them he moved on the fringes. He wasn't a peasant but he was just as much of an outsider. His name was Ron Matthews. I had seen him walk through the halls of the school with his three companions, all in leather jackets, long before I met Lem. I had seen him during lunch hours, heading toward a wall behind the parking lot to smoke with his companions. Other students as well as most of the teachers were afraid of them, though I had never seen any of them raise a hand against anyone. Lem called them "the lumpen." They modeled themselves after gangsters in movies and comic books. Ron, the tallest and strongest of the four, was the leader. Behind his back students called him "The Commissar," a nickname he was known to dislike. His mother taught at the school and it was said she was a subversive. She was in fact fired sometime later for her political beliefs. It was she who converted Lem; I didn't meet her until years later. Ron was repeating the first year of high school for the third time. He had left elementary school only because the school's principal had been afraid of him. His three companions were supposed to be his bodyguard, but in terms of size and strength he was obviously theirs; on their own they wouldn't have made much of an impression.

I began to look forward to the lunch hour. Boredom, loneliness and curiosity drove me further and further into the parking lot, closer to the wall. One day I walked to the other side of the wall. One of the lieutenants nudged Ron, who turned to look at me.

"Well, well, what have we got over here? Come a little closer, baby, so we can have a better look at you. You want a smoke?" While Ron spoke the other three grinned stupidly.

"I'm not a baby and I have a name!"

"Let's see. Soap-fee Natural. Is that a name, boys?"

All three nodded.

"Okay, Natural. Would you like to join us in the pleasure of smoking a cigarette?" He handed me his pack.

"Thank you, Tarzan. Pleasure is exactly what I came for." I wasn't sure exactly what role I wanted to play, nor how far I wanted to play it.

"Hey, we've been wondering about you. If you're smart enough to ace out that wise-assed coach, why d'ya let him sock you?"

"Because you weren't there to protect me, Superman!"

So far so good, but then I tripped. I burst out coughing when he lit my cigarette, and it became obvious to all four that I had never smoked before.

Roil took up the offensive again. "Now look what we're doing boys, dragging this nice girl across the state line. We're committing the Mann Act."

"Don't flatter yourself, muscles; I walked here by myself."

"What'll your boyfriend say about that? He'll say we committed the Mann Act. While we're on the boyfriend, tell us what a nice girl like you wants with that shit-on-a-stick professor."

"If I'd known there were commissars like you around, I wouldn't ever have noticed that one."

"You've got a sharp tongue. Miss Not-so-low. If you don't watch out they'll clip it right out of your mouth."

"They wouldn't dare if you four strong men protected me."

Ron laughed; his three cronies just continued to grin. He turned to them and said, "You meatheads hear that? She's just contracted us as private dicks."

That angered me and I started to walk away. "Goodbye. Tarzan. Thanks for the cigarette."

"Don't leave yet, baby. We didn't mean that the way it sounded, did we boys? We ain't even got half acquainted yet."

"I didn't hear what you meant, Tarzan, and it sounded like goodbye." I continued backing away from them.

"Not so low, baby. You get sore too easy."

"I'm not sore!"

"Prove it, Natural! How's about meeting me here around midnight tonight?"

"You're too much, Tarzan! Do you think I'd trust my body to someone who butchers my name?"

The three bodyguards responded for the first time: they laughed at Ron. I rounded the wall and started back across the parking lot. Ron followed me to the parking lot and shouted, "I get it! A nice girl like you wouldn't want to be stuck in an empty lot with a crazy ape that'll rape her and then knife her! You wouldn't want to get stuck at night, but you want to see what the ape looks like in broad daylight. Right?"

"That's right," I shouted back. "I've never seen an ape before."

For an instant before he turned his back to me, Ron looked like an injured child who was going to cry. "You bitch!" he whispered, kicking the dirt as he disappeared behind the wall. I regretted my last comment. I liked him. Under the mask of the dunce who failed all his courses I saw a lively intelligence which refused to submit to the school routine. Under the leather jacket and the gang leader's pose I thought I recognized a genuine rebel, the first one I'd met here.

I was hungry for activity that was not part of the official routine. I was hungry for the companion who had not been cast in one of the standard molds. I longed for you, for the comrades and projects I had left behind. I thought there was a strong resemblance; the form was altogether different; the content seemed the same.

I crossed the schoolyard again the following day. With his back toward me, Ron said quietly, as if he were pleading with me: "Look, lady! Do us the favor of letting us enjoy our privacy on our own grounds, by which we mean we would like for you to remove yourself from this territory."

"I apologize, Ron."

"We would like for you to get out of here," he said, still quietly.

"I didn't mean what I said yesterday," I told him.

He turned toward me; his face was flushed. The anger mounted in his voice as he said, "We don't accept apologies from the likes of you, lady! Now kindly do us the favor of getting the hell out of here!"

"It was you who put those words in my mouth, Ron," I pleaded.

All four were staring at me now. Ron turned to the other three and shouted, "Looks like the lady is deaf, boys!"

"I'll meet you here any time —"

He stepped backward and almost fell. "You'll what?"

" — of day or night," I continued, almost whispering.

"Lady, would you please repeat that?" All his anger was gone.

"What's my name?" I asked, still whispering. I was afraid.

"Sophie Nachalo," he shouted. Had he known it all along or had he learned it since the previous day?

"Set the time." My knees were trembling. I thought I'd start crying.

"Do you mean that you, Sophie Nachalo, are going to trust me —"

I didn't let him finish; I could no longer hide my nervousness. "Right here?" I asked, starting to run off. "At midnight? Tonight?" I ran as fast as I could.

I shook for hours. I thought I'd get sick. My fear didn't leave me until midnight that night. Ron was already there, sitting up against the part of the wall closest to the street lamp, smoking. He didn't look up. I sat down an arm's length away from him. He didn't move. I suddenly realized that he was as nervous as I had been. It was I who asked, "You're not afraid of me, are you?"

He looked at me. He seemed so sad. "I was going to wait here all night. But I never thought you'd come." He turned to look at the ground again and puffed on his cigarette. I saw that he had shaved and combed his hair. By himself he was only a boy: shy, nervous and lonely.

"I thought you met girls here every night," I said, although I didn't really think that.

"Are you kidding?" he asked, somewhat bitterly.

"Haven't you ever been with a girl at night?"

"Yea, sure," he said, with growing bitterness. "I've spent lots of nights with two-bit whores. The others talk a lot, but that's all they ever do. And that's right, too. You shouldn't have come out here, Sophie. No decent girl goes out at night looking for an ape."

"I'm sorry," I said, reaching for his hand.

He took my hand and squeezed it. "Yea, I know. I put the words in your mouth."

We sat like that for at least half an hour, I was relieved to learn he was harmless, but half an hour of sitting on concrete is awfully long; I got bored and extremely uncomfortable. "Is this all that's going to happen?" I asked.

He jumped up as if I'd woken him. "Would the lady like to have a guided tour of the city at night?"

"Why yes! That's exactly what the lady would like!" I said eagerly, squeezing his hand with both of mine when he helped me get up. My eagerness was genuine; I hadn't yet seen the city even in daytime.

The city Ron showed me must have been very similar to the city you knew during the war. It consisted of hideouts, danger zones, places to investigate and places to avoid. It was Ron's personal, private world; he had never shown it to anyone else; he let me share it.

"Someday I'll show you where the other half lives," he said as we walked along one after another street lined with almost identical two-storied houses. "This is where the ants live. Sometimes I come here before school starts, about six or seven in the morning. I watch them all file out of their houses with their lunch boxes, like kids coming out of johns; they all pile into their cars at the same time and then they all sit on the highway blowing their brains out because the traffic can't move. The ones who live here drive to a plant on the other side of town, and those who live there drive all the way over here. If they're not deaf when they get there, the noise in the plant finishes them off. But they honk their brains out all the way back home because they're all on the road again."

"It's not their fault, is it?" I ventured.

"You don't know what you're talking about. Some of those guys drive bulldozers. They could push the factories straight into the river if they wanted to."

We walked on. He led me through quarters that looked like forests that had burned. Pointing to an immense lot that looked like the city's garbage dump, he said, "That's what they spend all their time making in this town." As we got closer I noticed that it was a dump for wrecked cars. Beyond the lot there were two-storied houses that were more run down than the ones we tad passed earlier. Pointing to one of them he said, "The guy who lives there makes it without going to the plants. He takes batteries out of cars and resells them in a store he runs. Once I watched him and another guy clean out all the batteries in a parking lot. It's hard fucking work though."

We sat down on the sidewalk. "I know the kid next door too," Ron continued. "His old man's a cop. You'd think he'd be on to the batteries by now, but that's not his job. He spends his time patrolling this whorehouse on the other side of town: downstairs there's a bar where lots of dope is sold. He makes twice as much from the bar as he gets from his job and they go on a big trip every year. But shit, who wants to be a cop?"

We sat down and smoked. I asked Ron how he knew these people. He said he had lived here before moving near the school. "I know this other guy down the street," he said. "His old man builds motors. He works in a machine shop and every day he takes home a small part in the false bottom of his lunch box. Every six or seven months he's got a whole motor put together. Then he sells it to this place that deals in motors. I used to think that was neat. But now I think he must have his brains up his ass: he could have started his own machine shop twenty years ago and he'd have it made by now."

We got up and walked on. The structure on the corner looked like an abandoned railway car. That's what it was. On top was a sign that said, "Diner."

"That's where my old man hangs out," Ron told me.

"You mean he eats there?"

"No, he runs it. He flips the eggs and butters the toast, from eight in the morning 'til eight at night, six days a week. He saved for years to buy this dump. He thought it would make him a businessman. Me and my buddies skip afternoon classes lots of times just so as to get here around noon. That's when it's busy as hell here; everyone's hollering at him, lots of 'em are eating standing. As soon as we go through the door the hollering stops and everyone looks at us like we're dignitaries or something. My old man gets mad as hell but he doesn't let on he's ever seen me before. He skips everyone else and asks what we want, and no one objects; it's like they'd all agreed that we get served first, and he sure as hell doesn't want us standing around waiting. We really get on his ass. Eight eggs, I tell him, sunny side up, on the double, we ain't got all day. You should see him run! He moves so fast you'd think the eggs fell from the ceiling. Just like a flunkey getting an order in the army. The only thing he doesn't do is say Yessir! Some businessman! He holds it all in 'til he gets home, and then he goes off like a time bomb. I ask him why the hell he's so mad; I was just bringing him some business; that's what he's in there for, isn't it? Didn't we pay for our eggs like everyone else? Is he going to put up a sign that says No hoods, dogs or relatives allowed?"

We walked by the house where Ron used to live. "Don't know who lives here now. Must be a gardener." There were flowers on the front lawn. I asked Ron about his mother.

"She's a commie," he said, as matter-of-factly as if he were saying, "She's tall." He had considered and rejected this possibility as well. "She started being one during the depression. She likes to talk about it, but I never understood any of that shit about workers wanting commies to run the unions and factories. I never met any who wanted that. But she thought that's what they wanted and the union paid her to organize workers to want that. After the war the union threw her out on her ass and not one worker stood up for her. She still thinks that's what everyone wants. She's like this religious nut I know who thinks everyone wants to die so as to see Jesus in the sky. Now the school's getting ready to throw her out on her ass again, and those crazy bastards'll do it too. I don't understand any of that shit either. When the commies had a chance, before the war, they left them alone. Now that there are hardly any of them left and they don't have a chance, everyone's jumping on them like a gang of perverts raping a kid. Shit!" he concluded, flinging his cigarette into the gutter; "those are the bastards who say I'm the one that's dangerous!"

It was starting to get light out when Ron walked me to my house. He squeezed my hand and asked me to take a bike trip with him the following weekend. I accepted. I was happy. I had found a friend. The next day I dozed during all my classes. I looked forward to the weekend. I was in love for the second time in my life, yet I imagined I was continuing my first love. In my daydreams I imagined myself riding with leaflets under my arm and you were on the bicycle next to me.

I was out of practice and we didn't get far, though we did get out of the city. We left our bikes in a cornfield and walked until we reached a pond. We were completely alone. The road and the nearest farmhouse were at least a mile away. Ron told me the owner sometimes fished in the pond but only early in the morning; he'd been there before. Although the sun had gone down and it hadn't been a warm day, we were both sweating from the ride and the walk. Ron removed his clothes and slipped into the pond. I followed him. When we came out we made love on the grassy bank. That night a full moon made the mist on the pond look like steam; the pond seemed to be evaporating. I felt as if I were spending the night in a Dutch landscape painting. But I couldn't sleep. I had never before experienced such silence; I missed the city noises I'd grown so used to blocking out, and I concentrated on the few sounds there were, sounds that were completely unfamiliar to me;

rustling leaves, crickets, and Ron's breathing. I watched the moon fall into a field on the other side of the pond, and when it got completely dark I started worrying that the farmer would choose the next morning to come fishing. I heard the farmer coming — I imagined him coming with a rifle and not a fishing pole — whenever a squirrel or a bird stirred on a branch of a nearby tree. When the sky started to get light I woke Ron and told him I'd heard someone coming. He jumped up and we put our clothes on; we'd used them as blankets. As soon as he was dressed he stood still and listened.

"Oh shit, Sophie," he said, annoyed and somewhat angry; "that's the crickets you heard! Those people don't fish on Sunday morning! They go to church!" But when I yawned and he saw how tired I must have looked he put his arms around me and whispered, "I should have turned those crickets off before going to sleep so they wouldn't keep you awake. I heard them all night once too. You sorry you came?"

"No, I'm happy," I whispered, and to prove it I started crying, probably because I was exhausted. "I'd like to come every weekend."

We did go there two more times, but I never again saw the steam rise from the pond, nor did I listen to the crickets and leaves all night, and we didn't once meet the fisherman farmer.

The following weekend we set out on two completely different bikes. I learned that Ron had sold the previous two bicycles and stolen the new ones. "How do you think I get my spending money — from my old man?" he asked. "I've been stealing them since elementary school. It's easy. You take a pocket-sized saw to the back of any movie house and you can select whichever one you want. I only take the chained ones. I figure if a kid is so poor he can't buy a chain he wouldn't want to lose his bike. I puncture a tire and take it down to the basement and I tell my mom that kids pay me to fix and paint their bikes. She actually thinks that's what I do. The old man thinks I steal them but then he thinks I robbed a bank every time I stayed out all night so he doesn't bother making a fuss about little things like bikes. He couldn't prove much anyway unless he caught me doing it, which he'd love to do, but he loves to flip his eggs even more. A little spray paint takes care of the body, sandpaper and a little solder takes care of the number and a little sticker takes care of the registration. No sweat, and it's like new; I learned it all from my half-brother. All you have to watch is that you don't dangle the sawed-off chain in front of a cop, like one kid I know who got sent to reform school."

It sounded easy enough but I didn't volunteer to join Ron in this activity, as Sabina did sometime later. I only enjoyed the fruit of Ron's labors. For the sake of our weekend trips he started specializing in bicycles that were lighter and better suited for long journeys, and by our third or fourth excursion I could ride as far and as long as he. Two or three times we ran into storms and once we spent an afternoon and night in a barn with horses.

In addition to our sandwiches I frequently took my notebook with me on the excursions, especially when we decided ahead of time not to spend the whole weekend riding. I loved to sit under a tree in a field, or on a rock by a lake, jotting down my observations about myself and about Ron. Much of this letter is taken directly out of that very notebook. I told Ron that someday I'd write a novel about him. He assured me he'd never read it, so I could write about him if I saw a point in that, but I shouldn't bother writing it for him. I told him his name would be Yarostan. He said the name alone would keep him from recognizing himself. I did in fact intend to write a novel about Yarostan; he was going to be a composite of you and Ron. But I never got further than to jot down some of my experiences and conversations with Ron. The better I got to know him the less suitable he became for the story I had in mind. The character in my story, composed of the two of you, was going to express my own feelings, my own observations, my own choices. I gradually, and sadly, realized that Ron was not the same as I at all.

Ron became aware of this difference much sooner than I. The very first time I opened my notebook, when we had just sat down by a tree on top of a hill, he got up and said he was going for a walk. He wasn't jealous of the notebook; he didn't consider it an intruder or an obstacle that came between us; he didn't even mind when I wanted to write instead of accompanying him for a walk. The notebook instantaneously defined me as a person who would one day be very far away from him, a person he would not recognize and probably wouldn't even remember as a onetime friend. The first time I opened my notebook he knew our relationship would be short. He probably thought he would be the one to end it. If so, he was wrong only about that; I was the one who ended it, and for the very reason he thought it would end. But before it ended I did have a chance to undergo two adventures which compare with nothing I experienced before or since.

One Sunday we returned from our weekend very late at night. We had spent most of the day sleeping on a lakeside beach and both of us were wide awake. We rode to Ron's house and he asked me to accompany him to his room. I agreed, partly because I wanted to play, but mainly because I wanted to see what his room was like. As we were tiptoeing in the dark up the stairs from the basement, the light suddenly came on and a voice thundered: "Where the hell do you think you're going?"

A tall, thin, vicious-looking man wearing pajamas and an overcoat glared down at us from the top of the stairs. It was Ron's father. I was out of my wits with fright.

"Oh shit!" Ron said. "Why don't you go to bed and mind your own fucking business!"

"You punk!" the man shouted. "You're not bringing any broads into my house!"

A woman's voice, Ron's mother, shouted, "Come back to bed, Tom, and leave the kid alone for chrissake!"

"He's bringing a woman into the house!" Tom Matthews shouted.

"So what, you jackass! Haven't you ever heard of that?" she shouted back.

"You heard her, pop," Ron said, still calm. "Now go back to bed and leave us alone."

"I'm not going anywhere until you get that whore out of here!" the man said. I started trembling.

"Don't you call her that, pop," said Ron, raising his voice.

"I'm calling her a whore and I'm telling you to take her back to the whorehouse!"

I could feel Ron starting to shake; he waved his fist, took a step toward the man and shouted, "Call her that one more time and I'll —"

"You'll what, sonny boy? Kill me? You'd love to do that, wouldn't you? Don't you think I've been waiting for that every day for years? You don't think I went out and bought this thing so as to keep someone from taking twelve dollars out of my cash register, do you? I bought it just to keep you and your whore from breaking into my house!"

I heard Ron's stunned voice saying slowly: "You crazy bastard!" But I heard it as in a dream. I must have fainted. All I remembered was the gun pointing at us and that voice, which I can only describe as evil.

I didn't know how we'd gotten there, but suddenly Ron and I were in the street. He held me; I was trembling like a leaf. I couldn't walk. I asked him to take me to my house; he almost carried me. When I opened the door, I begged him to stay with me, not to go back to his house.

"Won't your father blow my head off?" He didn't know who Alberts was; he hadn't once asked me anything about myself.

"No one's going to shoot you here. I'll introduce you in the morning."

The following morning we all had breakfast together. As we told the story of our previous night's escapade, Sabina laughed and Luisa gasped. Alberts paid no attention to the story or to Ron, although when he saw Ron reach into the pocket of his leather jacket and pull out an empty cigarette pack he offered Ron a cigarette and lit it for him. Luisa visibly didn't like Ron; she made no effort to hide her fear of him. Sabina was drawn to him like a needle to a magnet.

Ron stayed with us, in my room, for a week. He didn't go to school, and he left the house only once, during school hours, when neither his father nor his mother were at home; he brought back three bicycles. That weekend, although both of them acted as if Ron and I were married, Sabina and Ron became good friends, lifetime friends; their relationship lasted until Ron was killed. We rode to a forest. At night I slept with Sabina; Ron slept by himself. The previous night had been our last night alone together.

When we got back Ron telephoned his mother (her name is Debbie). She cried all the time she talked to him, telling him she'd thought he had left for good. She had come out of her room before we had left the house and had seen Matthews pointing the gun at us. She had grabbed the gun, hysterically slapped his face with it, and told him to get out of the house and never come back. Matthews had returned two days later with a gift, begged her forgiveness and even promised to apologize to Ron. Debbie begged Ron to return, and told him the gun had been taken away with the garbage. Ron decided to go home.

I experienced my last escapade with Ron shortly after that. He came over on a weeknight and asked us to go riding. We went out expecting to find bikes. He had a car.

"It's the old man's," he explained. "He's all soft on me now. He hands me the keys and says, Here, punk, you want to take your broad for a ride?" His imitation was perfect; I believed him.

"Where are you going to take us?" I asked.

"Where would you like to go?" he asked.

"To the beach!" Sabina answered.

Ron drove us to the lake. The three of us were alone on the enormous sandy beach. It was a moonless night. Ron removed his clothes and ran to the water. Sabina ran after him. "Hey Sophie," he called. "You coming?"

"I'm cold," I yelled back. "Have fun in there."

I heard them splashing, shouting, laughing. I looked up at the stars. After a while I no longer heard them. The only sound came from the water hitting the shore.

I don't know how long we were there. When I woke up Ron was carrying me in his arms. They were both dressed. He let me down when I objected to being carried.

Sabina gently pushed me into the front seat of the car before going in, so that I sat between them. I was sure they had made love. Neither of them said anything. Making a sudden turn off the main road Ron asked, as if he'd just thought of it, "Hey Sophie, you remember that first night when I told you I'd show you how the other half lives? Well feast your eyes 'cause this is where they live."

I stared blankly at enormous mansions surrounded by fountains and gardens. The only places like it I'd seen before had been museums or public monuments; here we drove past one after another mansion, each with its own beach and dock. But the last day of my tour came to an abrupt and unpleasant end. Three boys in a sports car drove up to us and cruised next to us. They were obviously residents of the mansions. Ron said, "Oh shit, let's get out of here. Those creeps'll get the cops on me and I don't have a license."

One of the boys shouted, imitating inner-city slang, "Hey hood! What cha doin witha spare broad?"

"I'm not eating shit from a silver spoon like you, Bozo!" Ron answered. He pulled into a driveway, turned the car around and headed back toward the highway. They caught up to us at the light.

"Where did you steal that limousine, boy?" shouted another one.

Sabina stretched herself to the window and shouted, "Why aren't you in your baby carriage, mamma's boy?" to which Ron added, "Get that can off the road before I tear it up with my can opener!"

Ron pulled away at the light, but when the oncoming traffic had passed they pulled up alongside us, driving on the wrong side of the road. One of them shouted, "Thieves and whores aren't permitted on this highway," and another added, "Yea, we saw your picture in the post office and there's a posse out looking for you."

Sabina, who knew as much about cars as I did, urged Ron to drive faster. He pressed the gas pedal to the floor but they stayed alongside us shouting, "Give 'er all she's got, boy!" and "They'll sign you up in the kiddie car races." Then they flew ahead of us, swerving to avoid an oncoming car and just barely missing Ron's car.

"Those rich bastards don't give a shit if they pile up those souped up cars; they go through them like toys," Ron muttered. I, characteristically, started to tremble.

"Ron, slow down!" I pleaded. "Let's just close the windows and ignore them. They'll get bored."

Sabina objected, "Catch up to them! Run into them!" She was obviously as unconcerned about the Matthews' car as the rich boys were about theirs.

When they were alongside again, one of them shouted. "You'll never get anywhere that way, boy. Let the girls get out and push!"

Ron yelled back, "This ain't no car, kiddo; it's a bulldozer."

Sabina shouted, "We'll flatten you out and use you as rugs!"

I shouted to Sabina, "You're crazy! Tell him to slow down!"

Sabina shouted to me, "Coward! You're just like your mother!"

Suddenly we were blinded by the bright lights of an oncoming car. The sports car bumped us and apparently moved us to the extreme right side of the road, because we were heading straight into a parked car. Ron slammed on the brakes, but we piled into the car's trunk. We heard the sports car speed around a corner; they disappeared.

Ron got out. He kicked the fender and said, "Shit! It's wrecked! And the cops'll be here any minute." Suddenly he rushed into the car, grabbed the key, and said with urgency, "Come on! Let's get out of here!"

I got out. Ron and Sabina rushed around a corner but I walked along the highway. Ron came up behind me and grabbed my arm. "Come on, Sophie! You're making it easy for the police."

I shook myself loose and continued walking. I let the tears run freely down my face and could barely see where I was going. Too many things had happened that night. I was alone again. I was hurt and humiliated. I kept repeating Sabina's last comment before the crash. That caused me greater pain than everything else that had happened. She might say it today, not in anger but coldly and analytically. It's obviously true.

I must have been walking for at least an hour when Ron and Sabina rode up to me on bicycles. "Get on the bar, Sophie!" Ron said, half pleading, half ordering.

I ignored them and walked on.

"Come on, smart ass! You've still got almost ten miles to go!"

I didn't care if I had a hundred. The last thing I heard him say was, "Oh shit!" He was probably waiting to see if I'd hesitate. I didn't. I walked and sobbed. I knew I wasn't going to spend any more weekends bicycling with Ron. I also knew I wasn't ever going to write my novel about him.

I did see Ron again, twice: I saw him more than a year after the car wreck, in a courtroom, when he was on trial for a robbery. And I saw him again, for the last time, after he was released from reform school. But on both of those occasions I saw a completely different person. As I walked away from his father's wrecked car I knew that the Ron I had known, the Ron I had loved, had been an illusion. Ron may in fact have been a rebel but his rebellion wasn't one I understood; his life's project wasn't mine. I had never known Ron. As I walked home sobbing I knew I'd never use those notes I had scribbled about him. He was as out of place in my life's project as I was in his.

I learned long after the event that Tom Matthews had not in fact lent Ron the keys to the car; Ron had taken them from his father's pants pocket. After the collision, when he had rushed into the car and grabbed the keys, Ron had already planned a strategy, which succeeded up to a point. He and Sabina rode two bicycles straight out of a luxurious garage and rushed to Ron's house after they'd convinced themselves I wouldn't go along. Ron slipped the keys back into Tom's pants pocket. In the morning Ron and Sabina joined Tom and Debbie Matthews at breakfast. Ron introduced Sabina and Tom was extremely friendly toward her since he took her to be the "broad" he had almost shot. Then Ron established his alibi. "Hope we didn't wake you when we came in at one. Sure was a quiet night; no fire engines or anything." He hoped they hadn't been awake at one and that there had in fact been no nearby fires. He had guessed correctly, and had almost carried out his strategy. Matthews predictably returned to the house right after he'd left. "The car's gone!" That's when Ron almost ruined his whole plan. "Jesus Christ that's terrible, pop! We ought to call the police right away!" His concern was so excessive and so uncharacteristic that Tom became suspicious immediately and gradually convinced himself it was Ron who had wrecked the car. Characteristically Ron would have said, "What the hell did you expect?" or "It was bound to happen sooner or later." To express concern he would at most have said, "Oh shit!" Matthews' suspicions were confirmed by the police investigators, who insisted the thief must have had a key since there was no sign the car had been broken into. None of this proved Ron had stolen it since many car thieves have universal keys and the police don't always figure out just how a car is stolen. Debbie was unshakably convinced that Ron was innocent; she firmly believed Ron had come home at one and had spent a quiet night with Sabina. But Tom was firmly convinced Ron had stolen and wrecked his car. He knew he couldn't prove anything; his anger simmered for over a year, when he finally found a bizarre way to get even with his hated son.

This episode coincided with an uproar that took place at my house, about which I know nothing at all, strange as this may seem. A few nights after the car wreck, when I returned to my house from a lonely walk, I found Sabina and Alberts packing suitcases. I asked what was going on but neither of them would say a word to me. I concluded that my behavior after the car wreck was at the root of it and I became hysterical. I grabbed Sabina, shook her and screeched at her: "It's because we're cowards that you're leaving us! You're not a coward! You wanted to get us all killed!" Sabina shook herself loose and turned to me with a look of fierce hatred, saying only, "Mind your own business. Sophia!" I ran to my room and bawled. They slammed the door when they left. When Luisa came in several hours later I was still bawling. She must have heard me but she went straight to her room and closed the door I ran to her room and threw the door open. I could see she had been crying too. "What's the matter with you?" I screeched. "Go to bed, Sophia; this has nothing to do with you," was all she said, and that's all I ever learned about what had happened. I never saw Alberts again. He and Sabina moved into another house, not far from ours. I later learned that Ron moved in with them. His father's suspicions had made Ron feel unsafe in his own house. This permanent departure obviously turned his father's suspicion into certainty. Ron no longer came to visit our house. For a short time I had glimpses of him in school, but I avoided him. When his mother was fired he quit school and I no longer saw him there either.

Luisa and I were alone and I hated it. I hated being where I was. I had become nothing and had done nothing. All I could see ahead of me was an endless desert and an inner void. I shuffled to school and back as indifferently, as mechanically as I had during my first days here. But I no longer took notes and I no longer looked for people who resembled those I had once known. I don't know how fair it is to put it this way; I became what your letter seems to advocate. I lost my illusions. I stopped trying to interpret my experience, to compare it, to grasp its meaning. I simply underwent a meaningless routine passively and indifferently. I became an object. My present friends tell me I still frequently lapse into the pose I acquired during those days: I stop paying attention, stare blankly and move like a robot; they flatteringly assume I'm lost in thought but I'm not; my mind is a complete blank. I don't understand your letter because for me those moments without illusions are not moments when I experience reality. They're moments when I don't experience anything at all, moments which I imagine are very similar to death.

My only crutch during those last months in high school was Luisa. She never abandoned her dreams, she never let herself be reduced to an inert thing. If she sometimes became desperate it wasn't because she lost her grip on her past but because the present failed to live up to it.

I leaned on Luisa again after I read your letter. Yes, I showed her your letter, in spite of all the pain it caused me and in spite of your warning. It was in fact Luisa who formulated my arguments against your philosophy of universal guilt. If I hadn't shared your letter with her I wouldn't have been able to answer it. I would only have cried until it receded in my memory as yet another bad experience, until I suppressed it.

I called Luisa a few days after your letter came. I tried to warn her before she read it. I told her you had changed very much as a result of your imprisonment. She could also read on my face that I hadn't received a joyful letter. But she didn't read it as I had. She didn't cry; she wasn't torn by it. She became increasingly enraged. You were wrong about the effect your letter might have on her; your revised portrait of her can't be more accurate than the one you've suppressed.

Luisa didn't read your letter as an attack aimed at her, but as a confession about yourself. "He certainly has changed," she said. "These aren't the arguments of a comrade who is still committed to the struggle. They're the arguments of a former comrade who has become a reactionary. He's confessing that he now thinks the struggle was nothing but a trick of his memory and a youthful illusion."

Even if Luisa didn't see your letter as an attack, she must have felt attacked by it since all her reactions to it were defensive. I latched on to every one of her defensive reactions because she was defending me as well. She dismissed your treatment of our revolutionary experience as illusory: "That's nothing but a thinly disguised justification for the status quo: the present is real; opposition to it is illusory." She reminded me that she had spotted one of your characteristic arguments already in your first letter: "That Christian proposition that we're all responsible for our own condition, that serfs are responsible for feudalism and workers for capitalism. He talks as if historical systems imposed on people by force were the outcome of their struggles against them." She didn't even comment on your descriptions of her past experiences and simply dismissed all of them as reactionary arguments bolstered by fabricated facts. "He obviously didn't meet any Manuel while he was in prison. Manuel is nothing but a name he gave to his reactionary arguments. In his next letter he'll tell us he met Jesus in prison. Yarostan had a hard life. Haven't we all? But not all of us have used that as an excuse for denying our experiences and turning our backs on our comrades."

I didn't read your letter as the confessions of an insurgent who had turned reactionary. I knew you hadn't renounced our struggle for a human community; I knew you hadn't turned against the dreams we had shared. That's why I was so hurt by your letter. But Luisa nevertheless communicated her anger to me and in fact stimulated me to formulate arguments against the parts of your letter I found offensive. The most offensive are precisely the sections which deal with Luisa, the sections which contrast her supposed illusions with some supposed reality. I'm convinced that in those passages you simply don't know what you're talking about.

Luisa's experiences after her release were no more edifying than mine. The reality to which she came was not more real, meaningful or human than what you call her illusory past experiences. The shedding of illusions which you seem to advocate would not have set Luisa on her feet. Without those dreams based on past experiences she would simply have been a caged bird without hope of release, as you described Vesna. The only mystery to me is why she ever consented to coming here, why she let Alberts take her away from her struggle and her comrades. Did she actually hope to find a more meaningful struggle here? Or was Sabina's explanation complete? Did Luisa consent to that flight only because of cowardice, because she feared long imprisonment? If so, she made a tragic mistake; she escaped from a cell only to land in a tomb. She landed in an environment where she permanently remained a foreigner, an environment that did not contain more meaningful struggles nor more human comrades. What's surprising is not that she froze her memories of earlier experiences, but that she retained them at all; her new world didn't contain anything that reminded her of those experiences. After a lifetime of agitation with fellow workers, after the experience of several social dramas in which the foundation of the ruling order was shaken, she found herself in a world where the ruling order had never even been challenged.

Luisa got a job shortly after Alberts and Sabina left our house. She started working on an assembly line in an auto plant. She still has the same job today. From the very first day she tried to communicate with the people at work. She met people who were experts in watching baseball games, people who had memorized unbelievable lists of trivia from the sports pages of newspapers, people who knew nothing at all about the events she had experienced. They were not only ignorant of all the struggles in which workers had fought for themselves, but proud of their ignorance. They were workers who had become what they are for capital: labor time, the exchangeable and expendable entity you compared to excrement. They were dead as human beings. Luisa's hopes rose when she was accepted into the union. She couldn't wait to attend her first union meeting. She thought she'd find a comrade, perhaps even more than one. Instead of comrades she found comic book he-men whose model was the uniformed killer in the war-hero movies. A friend of mine — Daman (I'll tell you more about him later) — claims that the post-war generation of workers Luisa met when she started working was every bit as militant as every other generation. If he's right, then workers here are a different breed from those I used to know or else what he means by militancy is very strange. In any case, Daman derives his facts from his political ideology. The workers Luisa met aspired precisely to those things capital offered them: the house filled with commodities, the grotesque hunk of metal on wheels that has to be replaced every year, the standardized universal household appliance known as a wife, and two and a half little ones to replenish the labor market. The political commitment of these workers consisted of admiration for the army and the police: their main political observation was: "We'll smash them," and by "we" they meant "our army and our police." Never before have workers been so completely despoiled of their human characteristics. The union meetings Luisa attended couldn't have been very different from those of the state-run union you've become familiar with. Only a handful of workers attended, all of them men. These men had never dreamed of meeting with each other to discuss strategies for taking over the plants. They didn't even discuss strategies for eliminating health and safety hazards or for slowing down the pace of the work. The fact is that they didn't even have strategies for fighting for wage raises. This was the role of the gangs of racketeers who capitalized on the price of wage labor. At one meeting the union members discussed a picnic, a Sunday outing which was also to be attended by the wives and the children. What they discussed was who would bring the punch and the silverware. For these men the union meeting served the same function church meetings served for others. Luisa was as out of place at the union meeting as she would have been in a men's toilet. Several men made crude jokes about women; the biggest joke of all was her presence at the meeting. These union meetings were part of what Luisa called the workers' movement. The men could see no reason for Luisa's presence at the meeting and thought she had gone there in quest of a he-man like each of them. The workers' movement was dead. If there had once been one here then this was its corpse and the air would have stunk less if the corpse had been buried instead of being left exposed; it had become putrid.

What did Luisa have in this world except what you call her illusions? If she had shed those illusions would she have been more like the Luisa you remembered and discarded, or would she have been no more than the defeated workers on that bus you drove? Should she have accepted herself as a wage-earning machine, decorated her house, bought a car, used up her life exchanging it for objects, and forgotten that she had once experienced human life as something altogether different? She did in fact use up most of her life exchanging it for a wage, but she didn't erase her past experiences from her memory, and she didn't stop trying to realize the dreams she had failed to realize in the past. In time Luisa did find comrades with whom she was able to communicate; in time she even took part in events which had some semblance of social significance, which in some small way resembled the large events she had experienced in the past. Without her dreams, without those illusions you now find so objectionable, she wouldn't have looked for comrades who differed from the professional admirers of baseball pitchers and she wouldn't have recognized them if she had met them. It seems to me that if Luisa had followed your advice and shed her illusions she would have confronted the same hopeless situation you faced during the days after your release. If she'd had to choose between giving up the dreams for which she had fought or committing suicide I suspect she would ultimately have chosen suicide, in spite of the cowardice Sabina takes to be Luisa's main quality. Turning her back on everything she had fought for and yet remaining alive as a mere quantity of labor-time exchangeable for money would have meant remaining alive as a corpse, an entity that no longer has any life in it.

The only one of us who lived up to the standards your letter sets up is George Alberts. He shed all his illusions. But I don't really think you would hold him up as any sort of model in spite of the fact that you might feel apologetic because you were once suspicious of him. I can't say when it was that Alberts suppressed his dreams or if he ever had any. I was never close to him. I don't know how deep his commitment was when he fought alongside Nachalo, Luisa and Titus Zabran; I only know that he and Titus helped Luisa escape from that struggle when I was only two. Twelve years later he helped Luisa escape again, pulling me away from you. And I know that he had neither dreams nor illusions when we settled here; he had neither principles nor scruples.

Alberts can't always have been the unscrupulous person I knew, since Luisa respected him once and considered him a comrade. And Sabina, who is anything but uncritical, used to adore him; she considered him a god, not only when she was a child, but until her late teens, long after she had ceased to depend on him financially. Years after she and Alberts left our house Sabina mysteriously left him; she hasn't seen him since. I don't know if he suddenly changed or if Sabina suddenly saw him as I had always seen him. Most of what I know about Alberts I learned during the brief period when he lived with us after we got here. He transported Luisa and me like country relatives, like baggage he had left behind. He disposed of us as if he were the one who was responsible for our lives. He lodged us in the house as if we were furniture or exotic animals. He was our keeper; his role was to house, clothe and feed us. Our role was to cease to be exotic, to learn to behave like the furniture in all the other little houses. Luisa became aware of the nature of her relationship to him almost as soon as we got here. They never touched each other; I don't remember that they ever talked to each other. I really can't imagine how they had related to each other earlier.

Although Luisa is as unwilling to talk about him as Sabina, I think the reason she asked him to leave our house is that she knew what a despicable role he had played in an event I only learned about years later and only by chance. Alberts had begun his teaching career here during a period of reaction. Individuals who were nonconformists, or who had in the past diverged from the official model, were being fired from their jobs. Our century seems to have outrun all previous epochs in hysterical witchhunts. Subversive teachers were a choice target for inquisitions. In my school one rumor followed on the tail of another; every teacher in the school was at one or another time accused of being a subversive. I had known only the outcome: Debbie Matthews and two others-were fired; George Alberts continued to teach. Years later I learned that Alberts had been on friendly terms with the three fired teachers; he had introduced himself to them, continually engaged them in discussions and acted as if he had been their friend for years. Yet when the official inquisition began he characterized each of them in colorful detail and with dossiers of documentation as a person who had daily intercourse with the devil, as a pied piper who was pulling schoolchildren straight down to hell. He became a Mr. Ninovo, a state agent. He shed all those qualities you call illusions: solidarity, comradeship, even sheer decency. He actually did to several people what you say Claude had once wanted to do to him, only Claude failed where Alberts succeeded.

You tell me Claude and Adrian were suspicious of Alberts and then you became suspicious too. You pretend that something was wrong with the three of you while nothing about Alberts was strange. You exaggerate. I was suspicious of Titus Zabran and of Alberts as well. They were not among the people I considered my comrades. But this doesn't mean I wanted to jail them! I never in my life dreamed of a situation where I'd have the power to do that!

While Luisa was reading your letter she made a crude comment about you. I didn't consider it relevant at the time but now I think it reveals something else about Alberts. She said, "George considered him a hooligan. He was right. Yarostan moves from absolute destruction to absolute acceptance. The two extremes meet because he's moving along the circumference of a circle without ever stepping inside; he's always rejected real struggles."

I don't accept Luisa's analysis because I don't think your letter indicates absolute acceptance. What interests me is that Alberts considered you a destructive hooligan. That's revealing because that's exactly what our jailers called us. You think Claude had no reason at all to be suspicious of Alberts? I doubt that. I suspect that Claude knew something about Alberts involvement with those who arrested us. I suspect that Alberts was already then saving his skin by ranting and raving about subversives and hooligans. I suspect that Alberts had already then shed his illusions and accommodated himself to the realities. Would you like Luisa better if she had done that? I suspect not, since your portraits of Mr. Ninovo are not drawn with any great sympathy for that type of person.

Even if you're right, if Claude's suspicion was groundless, if Alberts was at that time selflessly devoted to his comrades, what would this prove? That Claude's and your suspicion of Alberts indicate a mentality similar to that of the police? That's ridiculous! My lack of trust in someone simply meant I preferred not to work with him. It couldn't possibly mean that I wanted him jailed since my entire life's project aimed at the abolition of jails and jailers. Our project was to communicate, not excommunicate.

By this point I've convinced myself that you didn't mean half of what you said in your letter. There are too many contradictions. You must have let yourself be carried away by your own rhetoric. The only person I know who seems to have lived up to your demand that we shed our illusions is George Alberts, and he's obviously not your model of a fully developed human being. Even if he were, neither Luisa nor I could have followed Alberts' path; neither she nor I could have saved our skins by selling or repressing our insides. Why would you have written me in the first place if you had thought I had suppressed my wants and had become a commodity that walks and speaks?

Isn't it enough that the world I live in mobilizes all its forces to suppress my wants and dreams? Why should I let my own will be recruited alongside those forces? Why should I let myself become a mere function of my environment? And why would you want to exchange letters with such a function? The functions are as predictable as they are dull. Shedding our illusions, repressing our wants, forgetting our possibilities: these are the slogans of the ruling order; coming from you they sound bizarre.

I became a function again a few weeks ago. After all, self-repression, even if only temporary, is still the condition for survival in this society. Yet I don't completely repress my desires even when my survival depends on it. In my first letter I told you how I lost my last job, during last year's riots. I enjoyed being unemployed since then but I don't want Tina to support me so I sold myself again. Daman Hesper, a college friend who is now a university professor, told me about an opening for something called a sociology instructor in something called a community college. My job there is to lecture to workers three evenings a week. The whole thing is designed to give some people the illusion they're moving while in fact they're standing still; it's like a simulated railway car where the moving scenery is actually a projection on a screen. First of all I've no idea what sociology is and I'm convinced it's nothing more than a job classification: someone is a sociologist the same way someone is a director or a secretary. Secondly the community college deserves every attribute except "community," which is not merely lacking, but is negated by this very institution. Thirdly the workers who attend my course are precisely those workers whose aim in life is to oppress other workers. In fact, the sole purpose of this activity euphemistically called adult education is to provide credentials to aspiring foremen, union bosses and even managers. The role of the credentials is to give these people an appearance of legitimacy as order-givers. The students experience these evening courses as one of Hercules' labors: this is one of the many arbitrary rites which are performed as part of the initiation to a higher rung on an endless ladder. Fourthly I don't give any lectures. That's my own innovation. The first day I simply sat down and waited, like everyone else. When one of the students got up to leave I asked him if he'd stay if someone in the room turned out to be the instructor. He didn't answer but he stayed. I was of course suspect number one. Someone else then got up to leave. He was quite determined and quite angry. He said he was going home since the teacher, even if present, obviously wasn't doing her job. I suggested that instead of going home he should report such a teacher to the school authorities, since he had paid his fee and wasn't getting anything in return. Everyone seemed to agree so I added: "Whenever you see someone who isn't doing his job you should report him to the authorities." At this point he lost his determination and returned to his seat. Of course at this point I had given myself away. I was asked if I intended to continue not doing my job and I said I did. An argument began. Some didn't like to be cheated; when they drop a coin into a cigarette machine they want either the cigarettes or the coin returned. Others didn't think it was right to be informers. The argument continued for half an hour after the class was scheduled to end. It was I who got up and put on my coat. I was asked if I'd be there again next time and I said I would. I should probably have said I didn't know. Every single student returned for the next session. They talked almost exclusively to each other during the entire session. Yet if they had known I wasn't going to be there none of them would have come back. Isn't that funny? If dogs were officially certified as sociology instructors a roomful of people supplied with the right dog would qualify as a sociology class. Yet some of my so-called colleagues think the students come to be ennobled by the precious words which drop like diamonds from their mouths. During an argument about sabotage — mostly about how to stop it, unfortunately — one of the students triumphantly shouted, "But this is sociology, for chrissake! I never knew it was so interesting." Everyone seemed to agree with that comment except me, although I characteristically said nothing. I disagreed because it wasn't socio-anything; it was pure time-serving for the sake of future rewards. My remuneration is immediate, theirs is deferred; the slogan that describes the activity in its entirety is "education pays." If everyone agreed that these sessions were interesting you can imagine what the other courses are like, the ones where lecturers impart wisdom to ignorant and attentive listeners. The fact is that the sessions are not interesting. The language, the concepts and even the experiences that are discussed are hardly ever an individual's own; they're almost always the stock terms, the trivial ideas and the stereotyped experiences repeated daily by the propaganda apparatus; these people speak the language and think the images on the signs you described. These sessions are nothing more than forms of adapting to boredom. They reinforce closed minds and negate the very possibility of learning. The anticipation, exploration and adventure involved in every experience of learning are lacking; there's no feeling of discovery; everything that's discussed is predictable; every insight is already known. If this is interesting what must the rest of their lives be like?

I'll obviously be fired sooner or later but by then I'll have saved up some money again and won't have to depend on Tina. If I'm not fired soon enough I'll quit. Why? Because I experienced learning, comradeship and community in that event you tried so hard to smear and distort and therefore I refuse to accept this activity as anything but a degrading sham. I decided during my first teaching job that I wasn't going to let myself be reduced to a means of production for the production of means of production. It's true that merely by accepting this job I play a role similar to the one you played when you drove your bus, but I don't do any of the driving. The only discussion in which I took any part at all was the discussion about sabotage. Only one of the students had anything good to say about sabotage: "It might be necessary in some circumstances." I eagerly asked him what types of sabotage he was personally familiar with. Although his accounts were tame and he lumped simple gestures of solidarity together with sabotage, that was the only time I felt I was communicating with someone, the only time we talked about our activity in the light of a different, unrealized yet possible activity. He was mildly interested when I told him I had known workers who had locked up the owners and had run the plant on their own. But as far as all the other students were concerned, I had started to talk in a foreign language.

I've tried to show you that my whole life has revolved around the experience I shared with you and that all my life I've sought to communicate with you. I hope

I've clarified what I mean. Without that experience my life is reduced to the life of a lifeless object: it becomes the period of time during which the object is consumed, a trivial episode in the life of capital. On my way to my job I take a bus through the part of the city where the city's "life" takes place, and I pass through there during the hours when the city's inhabitants do their "living." The city's life consists of a display of commodities: behind glass, behind concrete walls, on screens. "Life" is a proliferation of items for sale: everything from toilet bowls to human beings has a price tag. All art, philosophy, science and history, the entire past and present of humanity are enjoyed, not-by individuals, but by money. "Life" doesn't consist of projection, communication or creation, but of a wallet with bills inside. The act of "living" consists of spending the money for which living time is exchanged during the working day. The only shred of human life in this dance of objects with corpses is the struggle to destroy the dehumanizing game; the only shred of humanity in me is the memory of that struggle.

I think you're wrong when you say my memory of our struggle is frozen. I think the fact that it informs every moment of my present life means that it's very much alive. I do know someone in whom similar past experiences and hopes are frozen. That's my friend Daman, the one who helped me find my job. His one-time commitment has become his profession. His past experience is the subject of his lecture notes. He's been teaching for three or four years now. He has enacted the same revolution in his classroom year after year; he's broken it down into assignments and test questions. He froze and packaged his life's dreams and sold them to his employers; he has been thawing and serving them in sauces to customers who simply swallow them along with the other ingredients in the sauce. I haven't done that to my past.

Whether or not you intended it, you've validated the very dreams your arguments dismissed as illusions. You told me that people who had seemed to be no more than inert objects were turning into human beings. You told me that human voices could again be heard in a space where human voices had seemed forever drowned by the sounds of electrical contrivances. You told me that my hopes and Luisa's hopes were coming back to life. Yet you insist that neither Luisa nor I ever shared those hopes. Luisa was obviously wrong when she said you had become a reactionary; if you had you wouldn't be able to describe what's happening around you. But why do you insist Luisa and I were reactionaries all along? If that were true, we wouldn't understand your descriptions, we couldn't begin to grasp what you meant by a new birth of dreams, of projects, of communication.

What's alive in my memory, what you claim I froze, is precisely what causes your enthusiasm about the events you describe. Communication about such events is what I've missed ever since I've been here. Your letter brings me so close to realizing this communication — and then slams the door in my face.

I'm begging. I know it. I really don't think I deserved your letter. I wasn't your jailer. You weren't arrested either because of my relation to George Alberts or because of the letter I sent you by way of Lem. Neither Luisa nor I shackled you with a distorted view of the past. Luisa wasn't your nurse when you were too young to formulate your own thoughts and she wasn't a hypnotist who insinuated herself into your consciousness while you were in a trance. The most significant moments of my life were not moments during which I deformed your dreams and destroyed your possibilities. My previous letter was not a glorification of your imprisonment but a call for warmth, comradeship and understanding.

Please don't leave our relationship where your last letter left it. You would be killing something I've kept alive in an environment which tried repeatedly to kill it and failed. Please don't drive me out of the single context in which I haven't felt like an outsider. Please don't put an end to the only real friendship I've succeeded in forming.

Apprehensively, with love, your, *Sophia.*

Yarostan's third letter

Dear Sophia,

Your letter was comradely and I'll try to answer in the same spirit. But I don't agree with you. You make the statement: "Our project was not to excommunicate but to communicate." This is a bad joke. I'll try to show you that our project was to excommunicate, not to communicate.

I read your letter several times. Mirna read it. She's still convinced you're the ogre who caused my arrest but she now considers you a rather pleasant ogre. She even expressed a desire to get together with you and Sabina if circumstances should ever allow such a meeting. But she thought the passages where you glorify your past experience must have been taken from the speeches of our politicians.

Mirna and I were stunned to learn certain facts from your letter. I was amazed to learn that George Alberts had not been arrested at the time when you, Luisa, I and the rest of us were arrested. I also think it curious that you and Luisa were released after spending only two days in jail; I spent four years there and as far as I know very few of us were sentenced to terms shorter than that.

The reason I was amazed Alberts hadn't been arrested is because I had always thought he'd been arrested before any of the rest of us. I had thought Claude's suspicion of him a part of an official campaign designed to prepare Alberts' friends and acquaintances for his arrest. Such campaigns to stigmatize an individual as a suspicious character normally originated high up in the political hierarchy and were passed down to susceptible people like Claude. An instruction was thus transformed into a widely circulated rumor, the rumor gradually became a widely held certainty, and in time all the victim's friends acquiesced in his temporary or permanent liquidation, frequently feeling relieved to be rid of such a dangerous acquaintance. The fact that Alberts wasn't arrested suggests that the suspicion was not an instruction from the top but originated with Claude. Since Claude had never had personal contact with Alberts he must have been pointing his finger at Luisa or else at Titus Zabran or me, since we were Luisa's closest friends and therefore by extension Alberts' friends. Claude's act must have been a classical political move: he was incriminating one or all three of us in order to establish his power over the rest. His success against us would be a permanent threat he could hold over the others and his position as gang leader would be assured by his power to eliminate real or potential opponents. This wouldn't mean that Claude Tamnich was any less of a gorilla than I had remembered him to be but it would mean that he was considerably more intelligent.

Another reason I'm amazed to learn that Alberts wasn't arrested is because this conflicts with an event you mentioned in your first letter, namely with the fact that he was fired from his job. I had known about his expulsion at the time and had assumed this had been the first step toward his arrest and imprisonment. I had assumed he had been arrested for exactly the same reason we were. I had thought his firing had been something like a forecast of our arrest; he was accused of sabotage, of being a foreign agent and of representing a danger to society's productive forces. I know he wasn't the cause of our arrest but I was sure he had been arrested. Are you sure about this? I'm not asking to catch you in another slip of memory but to clarify my understanding. Since Titus Zabran as well as Luisa had long been his comrades I had assumed his activity had been similar to Luisa's, at least before he emigrated, and that consequently he had been arrested for the same reason.

The detail that upset Mirna concerned the letter you sent me twelve years ago. You make me feel I should apologize for bringing this up again. Before mentioning what bothered Mirna I should make it clear that I don't consider either you or Luisa personally responsible for my arrest or imprisonment. You apparently read my critique of our shared past activity as a critique of you and Luisa and you understood Mirna's suspicions about your letter to be part of that critique. My critique is primarily a re-evaluation of my own past and has nothing to do with Mirna's suspicions. I told you I didn't consider that letter responsible for my arrest and I didn't make the absurd suggestion that you sent instructions to the police. At the time of my second arrest thousands of people were imprisoned; they were accused of engaging in acts hostile to the state. I was arrested because of the activities in which Jan Sedlak and I and several other comrades were engaged at the time. The arrival of your letter happened to coincide with a vast uprising that broke out in Magarna, an uprising which had numerous echoes here. Jan and I were among those echoes; all the echoes were suppressed. Mirna saw a causal connection where there was nothing more than a pure coincidence. Yet my mention of Mirna's erroneous conclusion led you to think I was accusing you indirectly, backhandedly.

Such an understanding of my letter makes it difficult for me to deal with Mirna's response to your most recent letter.

Mirna was upset when she learned that the messenger who delivered your letter was arrested. This information confirms her belief that your letter was the cause of my arrest. Her belief remains groundless, but your friend's arrest does pose another question. What was he doing here besides delivering your letter? Why was he so important to the police? Did they think your letter was an important document, or was he delivering something else besides?

You didn't believe your friend's account of the experiences to which he was subjected in prison. You very honestly admitted you couldn't believe a world we had helped build could have degenerated into such a primitive torture chamber. I don't know what he told you but I know that some of the experiences I have undergone are difficult to put into words. I suspect that your greatest injustice to him was to think he was lying.

The fate of your letter illustrates a point I'm trying to make. What is the relation between the intentions of our acts and the significance our acts have to others? How do others understand and respond to our words and gestures? Mirna's response to your letter illustrates that this relationship is not as clear and obvious as you make it seem. Living in a world where arrests are frequent, where news is rarely good, where the outcome of unusual events is not anticipated with joy but with fear, Mirna saw your letter as an omen. For Mirna that letter could only have been a threat or a summons; those were the only types of messages she had ever received. My point isn't to suggest that Mirna is right in thinking your earlier letter the cause of my arrest. My point is to understand what her attitude to your letter means. What you exclude from your analysis is the social context in which our acts take place. When you wrote that letter twelve years ago your intention was to communicate about experiences we had shared. This was the content of your letter. Yet to Mirna that letter was an omen; it was an object which had nothing in common with your intentions. Mirna was wrong. But let's imagine that she was right, that your letter did have something to do with my arrest. In that case your letter would have been precisely the object Mirna saw and not the communication you had intended. In that case there would have been a great discrepancy between your intention, to communicate, and the significance of your gesture, to cause my arrest.

After my first release from prison my outlook was very similar to your present outlook. Much of what I experienced during that four-year term should have changed that outlook but failed to do so until many years later. Like you, I treated my past, my experience with you and my understanding of Luisa's experience as a standard of comparison, as a stark contrast to the world into which I was released. The four years in prison only strengthened my desire to communicate this experience to others. Like you, I wanted to bring my earlier experience back to life; I looked for comrades with whom to resume the same struggle. Like you, I didn't want to become a blind tool of the world that surrounded me. I saw through that world, I saw it as a cage, because I had experienced an outside, a Utopia, because I had struggled together with others to realize a different world.

This was my outlook when I embraced Mirna and her parents. I saw them as the common people, as typical examples of the broadest sector of the working population. I was convinced that if I could communicate my project to these few people they would themselves communicate it to all those like them and the revolutionary project would spread like a tidal wave. I was convinced that in time Mirna's father would translate into his own language his understanding that the constraints and the deadening routine were not imposed by nature like the cycle of planting and harvesting but were socially imposed, largely because he and his likes consented daily to reproduce the constraint and the routine. I was sure he'd find his own words for expressing his understanding that he and his likes had the ability to end the infernal routine and the ability to project and build an altogether different world. I was also convinced that Mirna would easily grasp that marriage, childbirth and housekeeping were not her lot, that those activities couldn't continue if she and her likes didn't submit to them. I was convinced that as soon as she translated this understanding into her own words she would communicate it to others like her, and a new field of possibilities would open up.

When Jan still lived at the Sedlak house I sensed a certain hostility toward my arguments. Though I knew he agreed with me, he never supported me. Once, after a long argument the subject of which I've forgotten, he told me he had never realized how much of a missionary I was. He treated my arguments as attempts to convert his family to a religion. I didn't try to understand his attitude. Later, when he and I worked together, I didn't draw any conclusions from the blatant difference between his behavior and mine. Like your friend Ron he flouted authority, didn't submit to discipline, avoided work whenever possible and stole as much as he could. Also like Ron and unlike you and me he didn't argue, he didn't try to convert anyone to his Utopia, he made no attempt to communicate his past experiences to others. I didn't learn the significance of Jan's hostility until several years later, when it had long been too late to let him know I finally understood what he had tried to tell me. My activity during those heated after-dinner arguments was not communication; it was missionary activity. It was exactly the type of activity that takes place in that school you described; it couldn't generate a community but only destroy it. I acted toward my hosts and future relatives as a priest, a professor, a pedagogue. My mind had transformed my past experiences into revelations of truth and I professed this truth in order to convert Mirna, her father and if possible even her mother. I had convinced myself that as soon as I communicated this truth from my head to theirs they would spread it further.

Every evening after dinner I launched into a tirade against one or another type of sold activity, usually bus driving. What Mirna's father heard was a tirade, a lecture, which referred only marginally to his own activity as bus driver and which had nothing at all to do with rebellion or insurrection. He knew people who rebelled in various ways: some came to work drunk, others damaged or wrecked busses, yet others used their busses on weekends for family outings. He may have sympathized with all of them and he understood they were all rebels in some sense. I clearly wasn't like them. My discourses on the need to abolish vehicles were not rebellion but pedagogy.

Professors of insurrection are not insurgents. Later in this letter I'll try to describe what I think they are. Most people know this. For example when Mirna read your letter she remarked that your friend Ron reminded her of her brother. Ron rejected wage labor, private property, education and his family through concrete acts; he fought against these institutions in his daily practice. Ron was an insurgent whereas you and Luisa are pedagogues, missionaries. You recognize the contradictory nature of such pedagogy in your description of your academic friend Daman but you don't seem to recognize it in Luisa or in yourself.

To Mirna's father I was neither a drunkard nor a thief nor much of a rebel. I went to work on time, drove the scheduled route, didn't get drunk and never tried to borrow the bus. Sedlak had no trouble at all understanding what I was in his world: a political pedagogue. And in his world such people were not bus drivers but politicians. He recognized me, not because of my birth or my social function but because of my behavior. He knew that in his world political philosophers didn't long remain peasants or bus drivers; they were eventually transferred to rungs on the ladders of union bureaucracies or government bureaucracies. When I tried to communicate my intentions he only heard me express the aspirations of a politician. All he saw in my gestures was the ability to satisfy such aspirations. And he related to me in terms of the way he saw me, not in terms of the projects and possibilities I thought I was communicating to him. I've already told you that he was very enthusiastic about my marriage to Mirna. His enthusiasm can't be explained by the fact that he liked me nor by the fact that he had fallen in love with my dreams and hopes, my projects, my past experiences. He was a generous and warm person but he was also a shrewd, calculating and observant peasant. The years of bus driving hadn't deprived him of the peasant's ability to orient himself to the village market. He could still sense the precise moment when the price of his commodity rose; he still knew which buyers were willing to pay the highest price. He hadn't lost the commercial instincts of peasants whose productive activity is oriented to the market. He was also aware that politicians had become the diamonds and caviar on the market of human commodities. My attempts to communicate with him had merely informed him that I was a commodity of this type. His enthusiasm for the marriage was motivated by a combination of traditional and commercial considerations. Traditionally the husband or wife of a villager had to be strong and healthy; the same standard was applied to cows and horses. A sick cow or a weak horse would constitute a burden; what was desired was an animal that would contribute to the maintenance of the peasant household and would assure the survival of the parents in old age. Sedlak applied this standard in the conditions of the society in which he found himself. The husband still had to be healthy and strong but these requirements lost their physical meaning and referred to commercial qualities. Thus healthy became equivalent to marketable, namely the quality of being useful to specific potential buyers. He had to be strong, not physically but commercially, in the quantitative sense of commanding a high price, as opposed to a weak ordinary commodity the low quality of which is proved by its low price. Consequently for Sedlak the marriage was a shrewd commercial transaction; he sold his daughter in exchange for an anticipated future which would more than recompense his original investment. He made only one mistake in his calculations, and considering the limits of his knowledge of the market his error was really very minor. His main estimates were all precise. The conditions of the market were exactly those he surmised: today's buyers do in fact pay more for politicians than for any other human commodity; our century is after all the golden age of the political racketeer. And thanks to Luisa I was in fact a commodity of that genus. His only miscalculation was caused by his lack of familiarity with the specific commodity in question. If apples had been in question he would have known that only certain types of apples were selling for an exaggeratedly high price and he wouldn't have erred by bringing the wrong apples to the market. But he wasn't as familiar with politicians as with apples. He didn't grasp the subtle differences between politicians; he didn't even know there were such differences. To him all politicians were the same. He lacked the system of classification of this commodity. This is what caused him to err. He mistakenly placed his expectations on a commodity of the right class, even the right genus, but the wrong species. He never understood his error.

My words didn't inform Sedlak about my past experiences or my hopes or my determination to struggle for a different world. They informed him about the characterics and the potential selling price of a commodity. I thought that by communicating those experiences and formulating those arguments I was ceasing to be a tool of my environment, a mere object in a world of objects. Yet the end result of my activity was a complete inversion of my intentions: I succeeded only in defining myself as a specific type of object.

My point isn't to expose a peasant's motives or idiosyncrasies but to understand what happened to the hopes and projects I once shared with you when I tried to communicate them to other human beings. How did others perceive me, my project and my past experience? Was Sedlak's perception of me distorted? Or was it my self-perception that was distorted? He recognized the pedagogue behind the speechmaker, the politician behind the pedagogue, and the repressive machinery of the state behind the politician. He recognized the political rhetoric as the main attribute of today's rulers. It was I who didn't understand the nature of my activity. I only understood it in terms of my intentions, as you still do today. At that time I shared your present commitment. That's why you're right when you compare my release after my first prison term with your experience after you emigrated. Both of us lacked and tried to reconstitute the project we had shared. I saw the Sedlaks as people with whom I could share that project; you saw Ron as such a person. But you failed to learn from Ron what I eventually learned from the Sedlaks: that I wasn't one of them but one of the pedagogues; that my teaching wasn't distinguishable from the one that had created their repressive world; that this pedagogy was nothing more than a series of rationalizations which justified the rule of pedagogues over the rest of society. When Mirna's father saw a politician behind the pedagogue he wasn't exhibiting his ignorance but rather his acute powers of observation. He saw my dreams as illusions and linked my gestures to the repressive acts of the ruling order. It was he who exposed the nature of your and my past experience, not because he was a social philosopher or critic but because he had a fairly lucid awareness of the world he inhabited and because, like a prisoner in a crowded cell, he tried to accommodate himself as well as possible without causing discomfort to others and without dehumanizing himself.

The commitment I once shared with you rebounded from the world and hit me in the face. At some point I had to reexamine that commitment. When I found that my past experience as well as my attempts to communicate it were flawed I began to reject them. I consider it highly significant that teaching happens to be the branch of activity in which you've engaged yourself. I'm sorry if I seem intentionally cruel. I know from your description of your life's activities and from your attachment to experiences I've been rejecting that you're offended by my present attitudes. When I first wrote you I wondered if you had changed and if I'd recognize you; when I read your first letter I recognized you far too well; I realized it was I who had changed. I had reexamined and rejected the qualities you had maintained. That's why I responded to your letter with a certain amount of anger. I wasn't responding to you but to myself and my own recent past, to attitudes I had only recently wrestled with and rejected in myself. If you thought my attacks were aimed specifically at you then you misunderstood me. They were aimed at a past which I share with most of my contemporaries. Today I'm one among hundreds, maybe thousands, who are rejecting and uprooting and exposing that past. Contrary to what you say repeatedly in your last letter, the ferment surrounding me today is not a continuation of any project you and I took part in. All around me in factories and schools and on the streets my contemporaries are turning their backs to the experience you celebrate in your letters and also to the dreams you and I once shared.

A few days ago I visited the plant where I had found my first job, where I had met Titus and Luisa and you. The last time I had been there was fifteen years ago after my first release. Your letters and my attempts to remember and describe the plant stimulated me to see it again. I also had a vague desire to find out what happened to the people who have played such a significant part in your life.

I was stunned by what I saw there although I should have expected it. Zagad's name has now been removed from the front of the building, from all the windows and from the cartons; it has been replaced by the word "popular." And hardly anything else in the plant has changed — in more than twenty years! In fact it is now more similar to the place I once worked in than to the plant I visited after my first release. The machinery seemed greased and oiled; everything seemed to be in working order. On the other hand the building is deteriorating, the walls haven't been painted for at least a quarter of a century, the work space is even dirtier than it had been fifteen years ago and the printing on the cartons is of even lower quality. The red posters on the walls with their messages celebrating the glorious victory of the working class are covered with grime.

The first major change that took place there during the past twenty years was taking place before my own eyes; the workers were on strike. It's the first strike there in twenty years. It started a week ago.

Everything about this strike glaringly demonstrates that it has nothing in common with the last strike that broke out in that plant, the one you and I took part in. And everyone in the plant was aware of this. I didn't even have to ask questions. As soon as I introduced myself as someone who had worked there once and had been imprisoned for sabotage, everyone started talking at once. What everyone expressed most clearly and unmistakably was relief: "It's over! The terror is over!" It's as if a war or a plague had suddenly come to an end. Various workers told me that for several weeks they'd been skeptical and cautious. They had read about the attempted coup by the president and the army and about the suspension of the police but they didn't discuss these events. They listened to the speeches of politicians, at first only on their radios at home; later a worker brought a radio to work and they listened all day. They started to talk about the speeches. But they didn't act. They were suspicious. They thought the whole sequence might be nothing more than a performance conducted by those on top, an intermission between two acts, a change of guard, a mere replacement of one repressive group by another group with different names and slogans but equally repressive. Then they began to hear of outbreaks of strikes in other plants, oustings of police agents, managers and union representatives. They learned that the workers who took part in those acts weren't arrested, imprisoned or even fired. At that point they stopped discussing the speeches on the radio and started talking about their plant. The decision to strike grew out of those discussions. It was the collective decision of the workers in the plant. It wasn't a decision taken by politicians and transmitted to the workers by union representatives or any other agents of those in power. In fact the purpose of the strike was to oust the union representative. They won this demand immediately: the official left his post as soon as the strike broke out. But the workers remained on strike. They worked out a scheme for replacing the union representative. They wanted the post to rotate among all the workers in the plant, in alphabetical order. Each worker was to occupy the post for a month. The manager insisted on a permanent and appointed union representative. The workers abandoned their initial scheme and insisted only on the right to elect a permanent representative, a demand the manager is ready to grant. I asked them why they gave up their demand and why they didn't oust the manager along with the union representative. Various workers explained that the present manager is a pliant and mediocre bureaucrat who performs his functions reluctantly and obeys instructions like everyone else whereas the previous union representative had been the real power behind the management and the most feared and hated individual in the plant. The union representative was a member of the political police and his actual function was that of prison warden. As soon as he was ousted all the minor police agents among the workers quietly disappeared. Thus the removal of this single functionary clears the air and creates an atmosphere of freedom never before experienced by most of the workers in the plant. I was told that all the other steps they might take were minor by comparison; now that they've recovered their ability to act and removed their main fetter they'll wait and see what other steps the situation makes possible. Behind this realism I sensed a certain amount of fear.

Despite their apprehension and their caution these workers are not the puppets we were. This time the project is genuinely their own. I don't want to exaggerate the importance of what they've done so far. Strikes initiated by workers have been nearly impossible here for twenty years but such strikes are not a new discovery. Nor is the ousting of a union representative a novelty. All I want to emphasize is the difference between this event and the one you and I experienced. The forces in play are almost identical. A group of politicians is jockeying for positions of power. The politicians' journalistic admirers are designing haloes and crowns for their patrons, hysterically trying to stimulate displays of reverence for one or another clique of racketeers. Professors and union bureaucrats are flying from one plant to another frantically and pathetically seeking applause for one or another bureaucratic panacea. Each political group is trying to plant its agents among workers, each group is trying to stimulate workers to demonstrate support for one or another part of its program. But unlike twenty years ago the politicians aren't succeeding. The speeches are cheered and ignored. Workers invite speakers, praise them, applaud them and then discuss the next steps to be taken with each other; the steps they take are almost always diametrically opposed to those advocated by the speech-maker they applauded. The workers I saw in the plant weren't carrying out the directives of officials but exploring and carrying out their own desires. I sensed a feeling of solidarity I hadn't felt twenty years ago; it was a solidarity cemented by mutual aid instead of mutual suspicion.

And this group of people welcomed me. Unlike my experience fifteen years ago, when the union bureaucrat told me he couldn't afford to hire a convicted saboteur, these workers invited me to join them before I even asked. Several people asked me if I had another job and since I didn't they urged me to "come back." Several openings have been created by the sudden resignation of the police agents who fled when their chief was ousted, fearing the other workers' revenge. I told them I'd think about it and they said they'd reserve a place for me. The very possibility of such an invitation is probably the greatest change in the plant's history. I wasn't being hired but invited: the difference in words alone indicates that a profound change is under way. One is hired to a job; I was being invited to take part in an experience whose content is as yet unknown. And the people inviting me were neither owners nor managers nor union bureaucrats but workers. They were inviting me to join them in an activity which was about to be transformed from a deadening routine to a project, although no one as yet knew just how it was to be transformed.

What I saw, heard and felt amounted to a complete rejection of your and my past experience. I'm sorry if this sounds cruel or callous. You sound even more callous to me when you describe our past activity as a project in which the whole population raised itself out of submission. Such a description is a travesty of the real event. Your description refers to the moment when the whole population immersed itself in unprecedented submission. The population is raising itself out of that submission only now, scarred and weakened after twenty years of bending but not defeated. What these workers are finally questioning is everything that was imposed on them twenty years ago — everything except the function of the plant itself, which Jan Sedlak and your friend Ron would have questioned but not you or I or Luisa. They've discussed everything except the nature of their activity, an activity in which people sell their lives so as to package other people's sold lives, an activity that epitomizes the cannibalism of the commercial monstrosity that nourishes itself on human lives. I have no idea whether or not these workers are going to storm that fortress. If they do, you and I will not have contributed to that struggle with our slogans about workers administering and managing their own factories.

Before I left the plant I asked the workers if any of them might know what happened to our former comrades. Several people had heard of three of our friends but they were all surprised to learn our comrades had once worked at the plant. You will surely be more surprised by what I learned than I was. The dreamer, according to you a worker like all the rest, Marc Glavni, is one of the more important bureaucrats in the state apparatus; he has been on the central committee of the state planning commission for several years. They found my ignorance more surprising than I found the news; I had to admit I never looked into newspapers. They were even more surprised when I asked about Adrian Povrshan. "Don't you listen to the radio either?" one person asked. I do listen to the radio occasionally but apparently I'm not very attentive. Our friend Adrian, to whom you say the spirit of liberation once spread, gives frequent speeches over the radio and is a well-known politician "of the new type," I was told. Like old Sedlak I can no longer distinguish between politicians.

One woman also knew Jasna Zbrkova and this surprised me a great deal more, not because Jasna has become rich and famous too, but because she teaches in Yara's school and lives in my neighborhood. I could have asked Yara about her; Jasna could just as well have asked Yara about me. I rushed to the school as soon as I left the plant.

When Yara came out of school she thought I'd come to walk her home and was pleased, since I had never done that before. I told her I had just learned an old friend of mine taught in her school.

"Do I know her?" Yara asked.

"I suppose so," I answered. "It's Jasna Zbrkova."

"Oh, not her!" Yara said, intensely disappointed. "She was the last one to join us; she stayed out of every demonstration except the last and she came out a week ago only because it's become fashionable."

I saw Jasna come out of the school while Yara was still speaking and I didn't have time to respond to Yara's perfect description; I would have told her, "Yes, that's the one, that's exactly the person I knew."

Jasna looked twenty years older. I don't think I would have recognized her if I hadn't been looking for her. She seemed embarrassed to see both of us. She greeted Yara politely. Then she ran to embrace me and burst out crying. With a voice muffled by sobs she said, "Thank god it's finally over!" Letting me go, she embraced Yara and told her, "And thank you for being the most mature and the most courageous of all of us!" Jasna began to apologize profusely to Yara and to me although neither of us had said anything. She admitted having known for years that Yara was my daughter; she apologized for never having told Yara that she knew me. She had known when I was released and that I was home. "I wanted very badly to come to see you," she told me. Turning to Yara she continued, "Just as I wanted very badly to take part in the first two demonstrations. But I stayed away. I was afraid. I was imprisoned too, not as long as Yarostan, but long enough to have filled the rest of my life with fear of being arrested."

I told Jasna about my correspondence with you and asked if she remembered you and Luisa and Sabina.

"I could no more forget them than I could forget you!" she said. "It's because I remember all of you that I began to hate myself for my fear and cowardice, for staying away from the students and the demonstrations; I felt I was betraying not only the students but everything and everyone I loved."

I asked if she was still afraid to visit our house.

"If you hadn't come today I would have come to see you," she answered. "The spell broke a week ago. I'm no longer afraid. What kept me from coming yesterday or the day before was no longer fear of arrest but embarrassment; I couldn't face your brave Yara; I was ashamed of being such a coward."

Yara reached for the teacher's hand and held it in her own; she had apparently become convinced she had misjudged our comrade.

"That fear is so irrational, so senseless and yet it holds you as if you were locked into a box," Jasna explained. "But as soon as I took part in that demonstration a week ago the fear vanished as if I had suddenly left the box. It was wonderful! Just like old times!"

To find out if she was really saying what you've been saying in your letters I asked her, "Just exactly like old times?"

The same Jasna whom you and I remember answered, "No, it wasn't really like old times at all. This was completely different. These kids have far more courage than I ever had. I never did anything unless I thought everyone else was doing the same thing. The kids began completely on their own when no one was on their side, when they didn't know what would happen to them, when all the officials and teachers were against them. And Yara was among the first."

I asked Jasna if she ever saw any of the people you and I had known. She said she had seen Titus Zabran regularly over the years. She also knew something about all the others and promised to tell me about them when she visits us; all she said about them was, "They're all doing better than I am."

That evening I told Mirna about my visit to the plant and about Jasna. I decided to accept the workers' generous invitation and go back to work in the carton plant. I asked Mirna if she would quit her job when I started working. She said she wouldn't dream of it.

When I spoke to Mirna about my intense desire to visit the recently formed political prisoners' club she again said such a visit would only cause more trouble than it could possibly be worth. However when I mentioned Jasna's reluctance to visit us and the reason for her reluctance, Mirna said, "It's one thing to be afraid to take part in a demonstration. If Yara had asked for my permission I'd never have given it to her. But it's terrible to be afraid to visit old friends. She was my brother's friend! She should have come to see me long before you were released."

"Don't you see I have as much reason to visit the prisoners club?" I asked. My concern wasn't to have her permission but to calm her fears. Mirna was once as reckless and adventurous as Yara; two decades of "paradise" have made her fearful, cautious and resigned.

I went to the prisoners' club the following day. I had the impression I was visiting the underworld of the ancient Greeks, the place where people went after they died. Everyone in the room turned to look at every newcomer; on every face there was the same question: is this another ghost of a former friend? Newcomers continually shouted with glee as they recognized their former friends. It was very moving. Men and women mostly older than I continually called out the names of people they suddenly recognized. People who had met in prison wept, people who hadn't seen each other for twenty years embraced. Each thought the other had long been dead. But it wasn't Hades. The people I saw were very much alive. They all expressed the same sense of relief I had felt everywhere else: "It's finally over!" These people were not spirits meeting in the underworld but living beings dancing on a tomb; the tomb contains what you call our project. These people are at last emerging from that project's spell, ridding themselves of its power; you are among the last who are still in a trance.

I didn't long remain an outsider observing a ceremony but quickly became one of the celebrants.

"Yarostan!" someone shouted, someone I didn't recognize. He was a grey-haired man who looked over sixty. When he embraced me and shook me to make sure I was alive, I was overwhelmed. I recognized him. "Zdenek Tobarkin!" I shouted.

I first met this one-time union organizer during my first prison term. I had thought he wasn't much older than I. He's aged terribly. He briefly told me about his experiences after his release; they were quite different from mine. He was released a few months after my first release. He too was turned down by a union bureaucrat when he tried to get his former job back. But many workers at his plant remembered him. They threatened to strike if he wasn't reinstated. What happened then was almost unheard of in those days. The workers won. Zdenek was rehired. He told me he then spent several weeks trying to locate me; he even asked a friend to do research in union files. He laughed when I told him I had become Miran Sedlak, a newly-arrived peasant.

"I've been shuffling from home to work and back home again. The only extraordinary thing I've done over these years was to come to this prisoners' club," he told me. "It's not the prisons that have to be exposed. Wherever there are prisons they're going to be the same. What has to be exposed is the activity that led workers to put up with the imprisonment of their comrades, to accept without struggle the complete destruction of their rights and the constant police surveillance."

I asked him what forms these exposures might take and he said, "I don't know but I do know it will be the most useful work I've done in my life."

My views had been similar to Zdenek's when we'd first met. I was intensely happy to learn he had undergone a similar change as I and that we again had a similar outlook. He's as convinced as I am that the type of activity to which we were committed when we first met lies at the root of the relations which have shackled us. This activity is precisely the experience which for you has become a standard by which you judge your present practice. You've intoxicated yourself with that experience and you're offended by my attempt to understand its nature. But if we refuse to see where it led us, wthat e can hardly avoid reproducing the same outcome over and over again. If we're to avoid that outcome, we should confront the elements that led to it, expose them, uproot them and bury them. Please understand that I'm not devising an argument to throw at you or Luisa. I'm trying to describe a process in which not only Zdenek and I but most of the people around me are engaged. This process is an extensive examination of the roots of our submission. If I find that my own past activity is one of those roots then I have to expose that activity along with all the other roots.

I first met Zdenek in prison about a year after you and I were arrested. Halfway through a meal I started listening to a discussion taking place at the other end of the table. Someone said that before the war the union had fought for workers' interests and secured the workers' share of the social output. Another person said unions had always been pliant instruments in the hands of the most influential sections of the ruling class and that our newly-installed state-run unions were different only in degree but not in kind from all other unions. A third person — this was Zdenek — argued that the pre-war as well as the post-coup unions were not workers' unions at all but capitalist organizations within the working class. He said a genuine union was an instrument for the appropriation of society's productive forces by the workers; an organization which consisted of racketeers who enriched themselves by selling labor power and assisted the police in disciplining workers was not a genuine union. In Zdenek's argument I recognized what I had learned from Luisa and I looked for opportunities to talk to him. For several months Zdenek and I talked continually during exercise sessions and during meals. He was fascinated by my accounts of Luisa's experiences; in my descriptions of those events he saw a reflection of his own activities as a union organizer.

Zdenek had been active in union politics, in the same plant where he still works today, already before the war. During the war he had been a member of a resistance organization. After the war he was appointed to a minor union post. He never tired of explaining to me that, although he identified with the union bureaucracy at the time, he took his function seriously only with respect to the workers' demands and fought to increase wages and improve safety standards and working conditions; he didn't take seriously the directives that came from the top regarding work discipline and productivity. His first major political engagement coincided with yours and mine — but unlike you and me, Zdenek was a member of the union bureaucracy. He took seriously the state propaganda about dangerous reactionary circles who threatened to deprive workers of their rights and institute a repressive military regime. He engaged himself in the official struggle to neutralize those reactionary circles by mobilizing workers to demonstrate and strike. He knew that workers did not initiate the strikes and demonstrations since the initiatives were instructions handed down to him by union officials. But he didn't question his role; he was convinced that the threat had to be removed and that the strikes and demonstrations were appropriate responses to it.

Zdenek initiated the strike at his plant, called for the expulsion of the manager and personally accompanied the delegation that carried out the expulsion. Although he had become critical by the time he told me about these events, he communicated the enthusiasm he had felt at the time they had taken place. He attended the congress of works councils as the official delegate for his plant. "Hundreds of delegates arrived," I remember him telling me; "We decided to declare a general strike, and only ten votes were recorded against it." Although I don't remember his descriptions word for word, his summary of his experiences was very similar to yours; he considered this the greatest event in his life; "The event released a surge of contentment, enthusiasm and initiative throughout the working population; at last we were going to run our own affairs, at last the people were masters, nobody would be able to exploit our efforts for their own ends, nobody would be able to deceive us, sell us to our enemies or betray us." He remained enthusiastic when, at least in appearance, armed workers occupied radio stations, post and telegraph offices, railway stations. When action committees and workers' militias sprang up in every factory and every public institution he thought the workers' community had been born.

Zdenek didn't begin to have doubts until he was ousted from his union post. A new plant council was appointed and he was excluded from it. Zdenek himself hadn't been elected either but had been appointed by resistance politicians and he had never questioned his own right to the post he occupied. As he narrated this he was bitter about the fact that he became critical of his own usurpation only after he was himself usurped. Zdenek was excluded because a temporary trade union council had appointed itself as an organ higher than the plant council; this temporary body consisted exclusively of workers who had been members of one organization: the government party. The temporary body then proceeded to appoint a new plant council consisting of workers who were members of the same party or who were at least enthusiastic sympathizers. Zdenek was popular among workers for his consistent defense of their interests as workers but he was known as a critic of the government party. The newly appointed plant council then proceeded to elect a new trade union council and voted back the very individuals who had previously appointed the plant council; by this maneuver the status of the trade union council was legitimized as an organ higher than the plant council and therefore empowered to appoint the members of the plant council. Zdenek set out on a lone campaign to expose these machinations but his exposures had no effect. Workers who knew him merely winked knowingly and reminded him that he hadn't made such critiques when he had been a creature of self-appointed politicians. He had known about these things all along but hadn't concentrated on them during the years when he had himself been part of the machinery. By the time I met him he couldn't say enough about the spurious nature of the workers' victory or the orchestrated character of the strikes and demonstrations. It was from Zdenek I learned that the initiative in those events didn't come from the workers themselves, that the enthusiasm was artificially stimulated by seasoned bureaucrats, that instructions were skillfully transmitted from the top of the political hierarchy to the rank and file. In my last letter I tried to summarize what I learned from Zdenek but your response to my description of the puppets and puppeteers makes me aware that I failed to communicate what I learned. Zdenek's descriptions were filled with vivid details; having himself played a role in stimulating the artificial enthusiasm he was intimately familiar with the ways in which this was done; he knew perfectly well how the decisions to demonstrate and to strike had been reached.

I still remember every detail of one of his descriptions. Several days before a scheduled union meeting he was informed by the local secretary of the government party that on the day of the union meeting several plants were going to proclaim themselves on strike in opposition to the machinations of reactionary circles. Since Zdenek was glad to learn this, seeing it as an appropriate response to a real threat, on the day of the meeting he was the first to speak in favor of proclaiming the strike. Three or four others immediately followed with speeches in favor of the strike and a couple of minutes after the last speech the decision to go on strike was unanimously acclaimed. The decision which had been transmitted to Zdenek by the secretary of the local organization had been transmitted by the same secretary to the three others who spoke in favor of it. The decision had obviously been transmitted to the local secretary by the regional secretary, since otherwise the local secretary couldn't have known ahead of time that several other plants were going to make identical decisions on the same day. When the strike broke out and almost all plants were on strike when the day began, it became clear that not a single one of these strikes was a spontaneous gesture of solidarity; it became obvious that the decision to strike had originated yet higher, that it was the decision of the general secretary of the organization, who was at that time jockeying for the post of prime minister. The decision had originated at the peak of the state apparatus and by transmitting it, Zdenek had been a state agent.

Only after he was arrested did Zdenek realize that all the demonstrations and strikes, all the shows of force by armed workers, had a similar origin; only then did he lose his enthusiasm for the events that had taken place. The plant militias and action committees, which he had earlier seen as detachments of armed workers spontaneously created by the workers as organs of struggle and self-defense, were composed exclusively of workers who had long been members of the same organization that ousted him from his post. In jail he realized that the members of this organization had succeeded in becoming the only armed body in every factory and public institution. Since the police was by then under the command of the same organization, the role of the action committees, militias and other groups of armed workers was to act as an adjunct to the police. He realized that the entire movement of armed workers had not constituted a workers' community but a gigantic police network, that whole sections of the working class had been recruited to do police work, that under the banners of the self-liberation of the' working class workers had attacked and arrested other workers.

What Zdenek realized was that he had played his part, not in a victory of the workers' movement but in its complete defeat. What pained him even more was the realization that this defeat had annihilated everything the workers had won during all the earlier decades of struggle: militant workers who had fought for workers' demands were all jailed; workers lost the right to strike; the possibility of forming independent workers' organizations was destroyed. Although Zdenek had helped inflict this defeat as a member of the union apparatus, at the time of our discussions he still didn't grasp the role his activity as union organizer had played in this defeat. His outlook was identical to the position Luisa still expresses today. He blamed himself only marginally and only for his blindness; he blamed external elements for the defeat. He argued that the workers' real union had been transformed into a sham union, that the real workers' movement had been replaced by a simulated workers' movement which in fact consisted of politicians and bureaucrats. The politicians had infiltrated the workers' union and destroyed it from within; they had taken over and then derailed the real workers' movement. Zdenek felt that he and the rest of the workers had been betrayed. Instead of taking over the plants and running them on their own the workers had replaced a Zagad only to find themselves bossed by a Genghis Khan. They had averted the military and police dictatorship which was to be carried out by reactionary circles that later turned out to have been pure inventions of propagandists, and found themselves surrounded by the military and the police, by an immensely enlarged police which included former friends, fellow workers, relatives and neighbors in its ranks.

Throughout his prison term Zdenek remained convinced that the real workers' movement was still alive, that workers could still revitalize the union, that all they had to do was to oust the alien elements that had infiltrated it. At the end of his term he was as much of a missionary as I was. He left prison with the enthusiasm of the first union organizers. His mission was to expose what the workers didn't know: that they had been duped, that agents of the state and racketeers had taken over their union and made it serve their own ends. He was as convinced as you and Luisa that his past experiences, intentions and hopes were an adequate basis for his relations with others. His aim was to return to the struggle as it had been before these external forces derailed it from its real course and temporarily defeated it.

Zdenek was always bitter about the fact that he didn't begin to reexamine his past until after he lost his union post. Even when I talked to him only a few days ago he insisted he would still be a trade union bureaucrat today if he hadn't been ousted twenty years ago and that he wouldn't have developed any critical insights if he had continued to carry out his official function. He admits he would sooner or later have been removed from the apparatus because he would have continued to use his position to further the workers' interests whenever this could be done. But he says that if the apparatus had been flexible enough to allow him to do only that, he would never have turned against it on his own.

When I first met him, his critique was similar to yours. His earlier hopes and projects as a union organizer were the basis for his commitment and he didn't try to examine the nature of his earlier activity. He defended the union not only as an instrument with which workers could appropriate the productive forces but as the only instrument suitable for this task. He rejected councils and all other forms of workers' organizations. He didn't classify councils into genuine and spurious types but held that all councils could be manipulated by any well-organized group of politicians. He insisted that councils were by nature local organizations whereas the union was a mass organization and therefore was less susceptible to being used by an outside group. He held on to these views even though he had watched a political group use councils as well as unions as the instruments with which it destroyed everything Zdenek had fought to build.

When I saw Zdenek at the prisoners' club a few days ago he had changed his mind about virtually everything he had defended when I first met him. I didn't have much of a chance to talk to him because he got involved in an argument which became quite heated and which lasted most of the evening. We exchanged addresses and he agreed to visit me in the near future. I learned from his arguments that he has reached conclusions very similar to my present outlook. The argument began when an elderly man overheard Zdenek tell me, "The very language we once used has to be demystified; terms like workers' movement, union, popular will should be abandoned until humanity regenerates itself and knows what it means by them."

"That sounds like an ambitious project, my friend; it would require organizational resources that are not available to us at present," said the man; I later learned he had once been a politician, had been arrested as a member of an inexistent oppositional organization and had been an elementary school teacher since his release.

Zdenek turned to the man and snapped, "Organizational resources are one of the things we don't need; that's yet another mystification."

"I don't understand you," the teacher said. "Terms like workers' movement and union have been transformed into synonyms of the word state. They must be demystified; their real meanings have to be restored. This requires some type of organization, minimally some type of publishing activity."

"That wasn't what I meant," Zdenek said, "Those terms don't have any real meanings. Perhaps demystification is the wrong word. Perhaps they have to be eliminated altogether. Each of those terms and countless others, including the word organization, refer to opposites. Take the word union. It refers at one and the same time to all workers and to the politicians who speak in the name of the workers. It's exactly the same type of term as commonwealth, which seems to refer to all human beings and to the world they share whereas in practice it refers only to the monarchs who ruled over human beings throughout history."

"I agree with you," the teacher said. "There's no question that countless terms have been distorted out of recognition. But surely you're not denying that some kind of organized activity is required to combat this. I don't mean an organization of experts or a circle of intellectuals. I'm referring to an organization that transforms language by transforming reality itself, like the workers' organizations of the past, councils, unions and other forms which workers found useful in their struggle."

Zdenek raised his voice. "Those organizations were never useful to workers. Unions as well as councils were useful only to politicians. All the forms you mention are forms which allowed politicians to make themselves representatives of the working people, embodiments of the workers' movement. You missed my comparison with a commonwealth. Just as in a commonwealth, the monarchs of a union speak for, dominate, repress and sell their subjects."

"That's of course true today, but —"

Zdenek interrupted the teacher and shouted, "That's true whenever working people lose control over the language they use, whenever their very thoughts are couched in terms they don't understand, terms like organization!"

"But that's ridiculous," the teacher objected. "You seem to want every generation to destroy the language and invent one of its own."

"Maybe that's exactly what I want," Zdenek said. "For people to destroy the language along with all the other conditions they're born into, for every generation to shape its own world and invent its own language. How can we talk of a revolution in which people reshape their world if we can't even imagine people shaping their own language? How can people shape anything if they never leave the world they're born into?"

"How can you even communicate with people if you don't agree to use the language they use?" the teacher asked.

"Do you think you communicate anything when you do use that language?" Zdenek asked.

"Of course there's a vicious circle in the whole problem of communication, but it's not as closed as you make it seem," the teacher said. "I'm obviously aware that the language of an epoch expresses the ideas of the ruling class, but this has never meant that it is therefore impossible to find support for a struggle against the ruling class; this has never meant that a disciplined revolutionary organization need be permanently trapped in your vicious circle."

"Hasn't it meant that? Really never?" Zdenek asked. "I'm under the impression that this was always the case. The very organizers of such a struggle are the instruments who restore the ruling class. Whether it's a question of unions or councils or workers' movements, the organizers' very language already embodies relations between rulers and ruled, relations of domination and submission. What in the world do you think support and discipline mean?"

"Please don't identify my words with the words of the ruling politicians," the teacher insisted. "I'm talking about opposition to the ruling order."

"You're talking about support for the politicians who head the organization," Zdenek insisted. "When I support the organization's leading politicians I make their enemies my enemies, I become suspicious of their enemies and in the end I even become grateful to the police for liquidating people who were never my enemies but enemies of the organization's leaders. You're talking about the ruling order, not about opposition to it."

While Zdenek spoke I was again reminded of Claude's suspicion of George Alberts twenty years ago. You made a great deal out of the fact that Alberts was a strange person and that therefore it wasn't surprising if people were suspicious of him. Claude's or my suspicion of Alberts had nothing to do with Alberts' personality or with his acts. I was making the same point Zdenek made. My suspicion illustrated the fact that I, like Claude, had become an instrument of the authorities, that I had come to think of their enemies as my enemies. The fact that Alberts had shortcomings is as irrelevant as the fact that Sabina had an exaggerated idea of his virtues. This had nothing to do with Claude's or with my suspicion. What was Alberts to me?

Everyone in the room was listening to the debate and Zdenek was shouting. I don't know how many people agreed with what Zdenek was saying, but I do know that everyone understood what he was talking about; he was damning the role he had played in the establishment of the ruling system. "When you talk about support you talk about obedience," Zdenek continued. "When you talk about a disciplined organization you're talking about people who transmit instructions from the higher ups to those lower down."

"In present-day historical circumstances it is impossible to overthrow a ruling social order without discipline and organization," the teacher objected.

"But my good fellow." Zdenek shouted, "don't you see that it's impossible to overthrow a ruling social order with organization and discipline? What you're talking about is the reinstatement of the ruling order, not its overthrow. We begin by fighting, not for each other and for ourselves, but for the organization, and we end by suspecting and fighting each other; at the end it is neither your will nor my will that determines decisions but the will of the state: decisions are implemented at the end not by you and me but by the central organ of the state's will: the police! At that point our plant militias and trade union councils and action committees cease to be our instruments for overthrowing the ruling order and become the state's instruments for repressing us. At that point our own initial commitments jump back at us as the state's commitments."

"That's of course what happened here," the teacher admitted. "But what happened here was due to very specific historical circumstances which you leave totally out of account. You forget that the ruling clique used a great deal of chicanery and double-talk to secure its power and that it was largely through this chicanery that they took the workers' organizations away from the workers and transformed them into their own instruments."

"I don't think it's that simple and I don't think chicanery is a good word," Zdenek said. "Chicanery suggests a one-sided relationship and what I experienced was two-sided. I suspect you were among those who helped the present clique to power —"

"Yes, I, but —"

Zdenek cut him short saying, "So was I. And I don't remember thinking either that I was duped by those above me or that it was my task to dupe those below me. Do you? I transmitted instructions and waited for the world to change, for factories to be transformed, for the state to disappear, for capitalism to crumble. What was I doing to make all this happen? Transmitting instructions. What were you doing?"

"Of course —"

"Of course," Zdenek interrupted again. "Weren't we all? Was I a victim of chicanery? No, I was perfectly aware of what was happening. I was transmitting instructions, the next person was transmitting them further, and eventually we all acted them out. As for the factories, the state and capitalism, I assumed as everyone around me assumed that someone would take care of all that if I took good care of what I was doing. And who was to take care of all that while I was busy carrying out my instructions? The organization, of course! The councils! The union! The workers' movement! I'm powerless but the organization is all-powerful! Its power and its efficacy were constantly being verified. Don't you remember what proved the power and efficacy of the organization? The efficiency with which it removed enemies. Here was one, there was another, right in our midst! The organization removed them both. Thank god the organization knows how to recognize them! Thank god the organization removed them! Thank god the organization knows what it is doing and knows how to bring about my goals! The organization will remove the emperor, the capitalists, the state, the police, and in their place will institute a new world. All I have to do is obey the instructions and stay at my post."

At this point in Zdenek's tirade I thought of the comments you had made in your letter. You and I, after all, merely carried our signs at the appointed time and the appointed place; did we think that our walks with those signs would undermine the ruling order or that with our motions we were building a new world? And if we weren't destroying the old world and building the new with our acts then who was doing this? I'm convinced we were among those Zdenek described.

"It was the same all along the organizational line. The working class had risen, the workers were moving. But we all looked above to see motion. For all of us only the top moved. Its motion was confirmed by acts of repression. Our enemies were rounded up and the defeat of those enemies was our victory and our only victory. Soon we thought the victory over those enemies was the ultimate victory. But where had we moved and where had we started? Didn't we notice that the enemies who were wiped out had never been our enemies? Did we forget that the enemy we started combating was the situation into which we were born? That situation remained intact yet we experienced a victory. Victory against enemies. Which enemies? Not mine. Groups hostile to the leading group were wiped out and when the last group of enemies was wiped out and victory was proclaimed we found ourselves face to face with the police, the outfit that liquidated the enemies. The only thing our struggle for liberation didn't bring about was our liberation. The police were the only victors. We didn't recover our lost powers, we didn't become communal beings, we didn't even begin to communicate with each other, we didn't constitute ourselves into a community that determined its own relations, environment and direction. You can't tell me that I was duped. I was wide awake. If I was duped then I duped myself; no one used chicanery on me. I myself fought for the victory of the entities that held me in their grip, the unions and workers councils, the movement — entities which have as much to do with human life as saints and angels. These words —"

This time the teacher interrupted Zdenek. "That's the most consistently nihilistic analysis I've ever heard. First you identify the workers' organizations with the police and then you claim that unions and councils are religious organizations."

"Precisely," Zdenek said. "What you call workers' organizations are mere words. Unions, councils, movements — they're words on banners carried by opportunists, racketeers and gangsters as well as inquisitioners and executioners. We, you and I and probably the majority of the people in this room, at one time or another marched behind those banners; we provided the backing, the mask that enabled those gang leaders to call themselves the union, the council and the workers' movement. Thanks to our discipline and support the unions and the politicians became the same entity, the struggle to build a new world became synonymous with the seizure of power by the political racketeers. And in the act of supporting inquisitioners and jailers we became powerless and acquiescent things, at most cannon fodder in their struggles. Only our representatives had the power to act. Our own independent action became impossible and inconceivable. Call it what you like. Our role was to reintroduce religion into a world where it had been dying. We helped empty human beings of their humanity, we helped turn their humanity into an image, a word which we carried in our heads; we dislodged the real potentialities of people from their real gestures and lodged them in the heads of priests. You understood me perfectly. Union, council, movement — all our favorite words became synonyms of heaven. But we never saw heaven. All we saw was the witch hunts and the purges and we thanked the powers of heaven for liquidating imaginary beings which we experienced as the only evil that oppressed us."

It wasn't hard for me to imagine the experiences which had led Zdenek to those conclusions. His experiences must have been similar to mine. The entire environment that surrounded us in prison was filled with meanings we failed to grasp. We didn't look or listen. We were spellbound by images we carried in our heads. We failed to grasp the meaning of the walls or the guards or the interrogations; we failed to draw conclusions when we experienced what a human being became when he had total power over another.

Zdenek and I were together during the early part of my first prison term. What I experienced after we were separated should have led me to reexamine my earlier commitments. But I didn't revise them during that term nor during the four years of my first release. I emerged from my first term with an outlook almost identical to your and Luisa's present outlook. Soon after my release, when Jan Sedlak accused me of exaggerating the importance of my clear and distinct ideas, I defended myself with arguments similar to your present arguments. At one point in your letter you said I had given you the impression that I considered myself more observant and more insightful than you. The opposite is true. I held on to conclusions similar to yours in the face of experiences that completely undermined those conclusions; I was neither observant nor insightful; I was blind. I'm unraveling the significance of those experiences only now, almost two decades later; many of my insights are being formulated for the first time only in response to your letter. During the four years of my first prison term I seemed to be two different people: one of them saw, heard and felt events take place, the other responded as if he were deaf and blind. I stored the prison experiences in my memory but my behavior and my outlook weren't affected by them until several years later.

My experience during the first weeks after my arrest was in many ways similar to your experience after your release and emigration, when you found yourself alone in a hostile environment. I was an alien in a world I couldn't understand. The prison authorities seemed like beings of a different species. They were cruel, sadistic and arbitrary; they were incomprehensible to me. These brutes and sadists weren't my likes, they weren't similar to people with whom I had shared hopes and projects, they weren't beings with whom I could communicate. I was filled with anger when I learned that many of the guards had themselves been prisoners during the war and that their most vicious practices were practices they had learned from their jailers.

But the impression that the jailers were a different species didn't stay with me. Many guards had themselves been prisoners and many prisoners had been guards. I soon met prisoners who had been prison or camp authorities or police agents during the war. Their behavior in the cells, in the exercise yard, in the prison corridors and during meals didn't differ from the behavior of other prisoners. They weren't a different species. I even met people who had been jailers only a few months or weeks before I met them and during that brief period had acquired human characteristics totally lacking in jailers. And the first person who became a friend, Zdenek Tobarkin, had been an integral part of the bureaucratic apparatus before his arrest, yet when I met him he was someone whose experiences and outlooks I shared. Did a mutation take place when a person moved from one side of the bars to the other? I'm not saying what you and Luisa understood me to be saying. I don't consider prisoners interchangeable with guards. I'm not suggesting that you and I might have been jailers. Such a hypothesis may or may not be absurd; I don't know; it's not my point to explore it. All I'm saying is that at some point I learned that at least some of the jailers were not a different type of being. Below their social function there was something recognizable. Below the gestures and attitudes they had learned from other jailers I saw other gestures and attitudes. These attitudes hadn't been learned in prisons but on streets and in factories; they referred to experiences I had shared; they indicated that at some time in their lives these people had engaged in a struggle similar to mine, that they had once taken part in strikes and demonstrations, that they had once shared my perspectives and hopes. Of course this wasn't true of all the jailers. Some were so brutalized that they remained the same on both sides of the bars; it wasn't in them that I recognized any trace of myself. The jailers I'm describing were equally brutish in their behavior but the brutality wasn't the only component of their personalities. There was something else, something familiar, something that resembled me. The resemblance wasn't superficial; it didn't consist of a mere similarity of words which in reality had different meanings. What I recognized wasn't the words but the hopes and experiences behind the words. What I recognized was the experience around which you have built your life. I recognized dreams and hopes I had shared with you and Luisa. The role hid the dreams, just as several years later my role as bus driver hid them. Yet as soon as a bureaucrat like Zdenek was dislodged from his post, as soon as a guard was jailed, the person below the mask became visible. Those experiences, hopes and dreams weren't born after the guard was jailed; they had been there all along, masked by the jailer's social role. It's ironic that some of the guards in whom I recognized my own past experiences were the strictest disciplinarians and the cruelest torturers. Habitual sadists were arbitrary and therefore inconsistent and corruptible and sometimes lenient. But those who had once engaged themselves in a struggle similar to mine and who saw themselves as still engaged in it were incorruptible, pitiless and unswerving. They were the strictest guards and the cruelest torturers precisely because they were still committed to that struggle. In their own eyes they weren't cruel but committed. They saw themselves as embodiments of the working class struggle and they saw prisoners as enemies of the working class. Their cruelty wasn't aimed against individuals but against the principle of evil; through them the workers' movement was protecting itself from its enemies. Such jailers were convinced that the struggle you and I had waged had been victorious, that the workers had seized power over all social activity. These jailers saw themselves as the protectors of that victory. The proof of the victory was the fact that people like themselves were in power, people whose words expressed the liberation of the working class, whose brains contained a representation of the self-liberation of the workers. Their power over prisoners was the proof of the success of the project. As Zdenek observed in his argument with the former politician, these were people who had transformed the workers' movement into a religion. They were its priests. They served their religion by suppressing its enemies. Prisons and concentration camps were the living proof of the religion's victory, strict surveillance of inmates was the proof of its vitality and the liquidation of all the enemies would herald its ultimate realization.

Carriers of my own project were my own worst torturers. They were my likes, not in the sense that I could have been like them, but in the sense that they carried the project I had carried. And I was their like, not in the sense that I've ever been the jailer of another human being, but in the sense that I still carried the project in whose name they tortured me. Throughout my prison term I remained committed to the same representations, the same religion; I too was a priest. I didn't grasp the repressive character of my commitment, I didn't see that prisons and concentration camps were outcomes of my religion's victory, not of its defeat.

My previous letter was one-sided. I threw at you conclusions I've reached over a twenty-year period but I didn't describe the experiences which led me to those conclusions. I made it seem that you had intoxicated yourself with illusions which I had never shared and which I found incomprehensible. Actually, despite the fact that I recognized my own project in my jailers and despite the fact that I recognized myself in a former union bureaucrat, my commitment remained unchanged during all the four years of my term and I left prison with the same enthusiasm that you express. I went out into the world determined to spread that project. Your letter angered me because it reminded me how long and how stubbornly I held on to that commitment. You confronted me with attitudes I had only recently rejected. I had never before couched that rejection in words. You weren't far wrong when you said I was carried away by my rhetoric. I was putting into words for the first time what I had just learned and I made it appear that I had always known it. I'm now trying to remedy that one-sidedness by describing the experiences which led me to reject the attitudes I once shared with you. It was only gradually that I learned to see those attitudes as a poor basis for present action. Only after innumerable shocks did I begin to see that such attitudes and such behavior were elements of social relations common to religions, that the concrete outcome of such practice was the palace, the church and the dungeon, and that in an age of fusion and fission such a project was unimaginably repressive.

I experienced another one of these shocks when I learned about our wartime resistance from prisoners who had taken part in it. I met several people besides Zdenek who had been active in the resistance. Almost every single one of them had become critical of his part in that struggle only after he was excluded from an official function. Before the exclusion they, like Zdenek, had not questioned the nature of their engagement. This fact is very significant but its significance isn't the one Luisa read into my first letter. I don't mean that every victim would have been an executioner if he had only been allowed to remain on his post. The prisoners I met would all have been removed from their posts eventually; they would all have stopped carrying out their official functions at one or another time. Some would have stopped sooner, others later. They were willing to go to a certain line but no further. They differed from each other in terms of where each drew this line. And those who were still carrying out their functions and who therefore seemed so different from the rest of us might draw that line at the next turn or the turn after that. Today's jailers would then join yesterday's victims and be victimized by tomorrow's.

What about you and Luisa and me? Didn't we carry a project up to a point beyond which we refused to carry it? Luisa's answer to my last letter is that the project we carried was insurrection and that my rejection of our former activity is a rejection of insurrection in favor of acquiescence to the ruling order. In other words I'm a traitor, and no one wants to be a traitor. The fear of being considered a traitor is what keeps most of us moving longer than we want in a direction we've started to suspect is wrong. Those of Luisa's accusers who took part in arresting the enemies of the working class but refused to take part in their execution were accused by their previous day's comrades of turning their backs on the revolution, abandoning their commitment, becoming soft and conservative and ultimately of becoming reactionary and counter-revolutionary. We become critical only after we cease to go along, and even then most of us become critical only of the events that took place after we stopped going along.

I met only one individual who fought in the resistance on his own, who had no connection at all with any of the organized resistance groups. I no longer remember his name; I'll call him Anton. When I met him I considered him very different from me and from most of the other people I met. He was completely apolitical. He didn't express dreams or hopes that you and I would have recognized as our own. Anton was a worker a few years older than I. He had many of Ron's traits. He rejected social institutions in practice but not in words. As a boy he had left his family, run away to the city and gotten a job. He rejected all the rules of work and was repeatedly fired for absenteeism and theft. He was evicted from one after another apartment for refusing to pay rent. On the first day of the resistance he joined a group of people who were building a barricade. He hated the militarists who occupied the city and was determined to do all he could to rid the city of them. When the liberation army entered the city he returned to the barricade and continued shooting. He didn't distinguish between the two armies; to him they were the same. For him the resistance hadn't ended. He was arrested immediately as an enemy agent and sentenced to life imprisonment.

It didn't occur to me at the time that if I hadn't met Luisa and if I hadn't learned to express myself in political terms, I might have been very similar to Anton when we met. I myself had fought in the resistance with very few political conceptions, since I hadn't learned a great deal from Titus Zabran or his friends. The only reason I didn't shoot when the "liberators" marched into the city was because of my ignorance; Anton was much better informed than I. When he told me about the events that had preceded the liberation army's entrance into the city I was convinced that if I had known about those events at the time I would have shot too.

Anton's account of the end of the resistance was identical to accounts I had heard from other people who had fought in it and had been informed about the forces in play. But Anton's account was unique and horrifying. Unlike all the other accounts it wasn't couched in the political language that had recently become familiar to me, it didn't contain the qualifications, the ifs, the political interpretations and pseudo-explanations. He described a sequence of events whose significance spoke as loudly as drops of blood dripping from a wound. No one I've met ever contested the facts of Anton's narrative. All the other accounts I've heard as well as numerous figures I've seen have only confirmed the accuracy of Anton's description down to the smallest details.

"During the first night of the rising, thousands of barricades were built throughout the city, across streets and alleys." (I am retelling Anton's story from memory.) "The entire city was held by the inhabitants, except for a few sections which were still held by the occupying army. The following day the occupiers mobilized all nearby troops, tanks and artillery against the city. There were at least four heavily armed soldiers for every three poorly armed workers. Resisters dispatched envoys to the two armies which were on their way to 'liberate' the city, armies which had been urging the population to rise against the occupiers. Both armies were within a few hours march of the city. Each of them outnumbered the forces of the occupiers. Yet for three days and three nights neither army made a move. Camped so close that they could almost hear the shells explode, they waited while men and women and children were massacred in all the streets of the city. Several thousand people were butchered. Yet people fought with such determination that the occupying forces were defeated; they capitulated at the end of the third day and started to evacuate the city. On the day after the capitulation of the last occupying forces, the so-called army of liberation marched into the city. People who could not have taken part in the rising, who must have stayed in their basements during all the fighting, lost their heads cheering for these liberators. I got behind a wall and started shooting. When I was captured people looked at met as if I was a lunatic. I've often wondered why more people didn't continue shooting when the new occupiers entered the city. The explanation is that most of the people who would have kept on fighting were killed during those three days and nights. The 'liberators' waited while people like I were exterminated by the former occupiers. It would have been embarrassing for so-called liberators to begin liberating the city by shooting thousands of its inhabitants. Those who died were those who fought hardest, those who were most exposed, those who would have shot at the next occupiers. And I was called a foreign agent for shooting at a foreign army that marched in and occupied the city."

Other accounts I heard differed from Anton's only in terms of the meanings into which the same facts were inserted. Some people considered it reasonable that the liberation army had let the occupiers clean up riff-raff like Anton so as not to have to do it themselves; they considered this a necessary purge of dangerous elements carried out without trouble or expense to those who benefited from it. Most people weren't so crude as to actually justify the massacre. All those I met admitted they had known at the time that the liberation armies were within a stone's throw of the fighting during all three days and nights yet all of them had cheered when the liberation army marched into the city on the day after the massacre, when it was already liberated. They admitted the facts only after they were jailed. Earlier, when they'd held official posts, they had denied that the liberation army had been anywhere near the city at the time. Yet even when they admitted the facts they didn't admit their significance. They suddenly discovered, in their brains, all kinds of military reasons for the fact that the liberation army hadn't moved: the supply lines were overextended, the rearguard had fallen behind the front lines and left them exposed. They hadn't ever dreamed of invoking these reasons before they were imprisoned. They never faced the contradiction between their knowledge and their cheering. They knew that troops, tanks and artillery had camped nearby while thousands of people were slaughtered. But they refused to see this army as an army. They saw it as the working class movement. What entered the city wasn't tanks and soldiers but the representative of the victory of the working class. It was our dreams, aspirations and hopes that marched into the city. It was the image of our liberation, of our determination to run our lives free of armies and prisons and tanks. This is what these blind comrades saw entering the city when they cheered.

I heard Anton and I sympathized with him, but I didn't learn. I still identified with politicians. Although my own participation in the resistance had been almost identical to Anton's, my later political experiences had transformed me to such an extent that I no longer recognized myself in him. Before I could do this I had to peel off one after another layer of the political skin that had covered up the person who could have recognized himself in Anton. First of all I had to peel off the layer I had acquired from Luisa. This is what Manuel did for me. He didn't actually remove that layer, but he provided me with a vantage point from which I was able to remove it. No, Manuel is not an embodiment of my reactionary arguments: he's not an invention.

Manuel was a prisoner I met during the second year of my term. In an argument with another prisoner, I was defending the revolutionary potential of unions. At one point I referred to an example I had learned from Luisa; I illustrated my case by referring to a historical event in which workers had used the union as an instrument with which to carry on their own struggle. Manuel interrupted my argument. He said he was familiar with the event I was citing because he had fought in it. He said he had once agreed with the position I was defending but that life itself had disabused him of this view; he also said I was supporting my arguments by suppressing nine-tenths of the actual picture.

Manuel grew up in a peasant village. Poverty drove him to the city and he became a transport worker. At the time of the rising of the army against the population he was a member of a small political organization. He explained that he had not joined this organization because he had selected it from among the others nor because he agreed with its program more than with other programs but only because the first worker who became his friend was a member of it. At the time of the rising all the members of Manuel's organization were in the streets along with the rest of the population. In a single day working people from all quarters of the city, having transformed every available implement into a weapon, defeated the army. For an instant, but only for an instant, the population was on the verge of making its own history. For an instant it looked as if the revolution would spread, as if it would continue to grow until it encompassed all working people everywhere, until all the armies of the world were defeated. But the instant was short-lived. While the smoke still filled the air, unknown to the workers who had risked their lives all day and had seen countless friends and relatives slaughtered, a meeting took place. It was something like a private meeting between the government that had been discarded and destroyed during the day, the government that had lost its armed force and ceased to function — between that former government and four or five workers. These were not nameless workers. They were not any four or five among thousands. They were workers who were known as fierce fighters and uncompromising union militants. They were workers who were known not to tolerate any authority whether it be boss or government official. The politician of the ousted old order offered these workers posts in the government. Instead of turning their backs to this wily politician and telling him the workers had just destroyed governments and had become their own masters, these union militants accepted the offer. They told themselves that a government with their presence was no longer a government but a mere organ of the workers' self-government. And they told other workers that they were not a government at all but a revolutionary committee; they said the state had been abolished. And many workers accepted this. For years they had respected and admired these militants, they had come to regard them as leaders, they had seen them as carriers of their own aspirations. They accepted the entry of these militants into the government as their own self-government. When a member of Manuel's own organization accepted a post in this revolutionary committee, Manuel turned in his membership card. He found himself isolated. Gradually he found other people who understood and tried to expose the fact that the union had not served the workers as an instrument of their liberation but of their reenslavement. Ironically, Manuel was arrested shortly after he quit his small organization; the reason for his arrest was his membership in this organization. It was thanks to this arrest that he was still alive when I met him. He learned later that the other individuals he had met who had tried to expose the incorporation of the union into the state apparatus had all been shot.

In my discussions with Manuel, I countered every observation he made with an observation I had learned from Luisa. I have no idea if he's dead or alive today. At the end of my second year in prison he was transferred to another prison and I never heard of him again. During the brief time I knew him, I defended Luisa's views with such self-assurance that he must have known he wasn't convincing me. He must even have thought that I hadn't heard a single word of his account. I'll probably never be able to tell him that I did hear him, years later, and that his account helped me understand, not only the event he described, but many of my other experiences as well. It was Manuel who helped me understand the difference between the rebel and the philosopher of rebellion, between someone like Ron and someone like Luisa, between workers and the representation of workers by unions, councils, parties and movements. He also helped me see how easily we delude ourselves and take one for the other, how easily we become carriers of the representation and agents of our own repression. But it was only during my second prison term that I began to hear what Manuel had told me. It was only then that I began to compare his account to Luisa's. As soon as I did begin to replace Luisa's account with Manuel's I was able to imagine myself a participant in the events Manuel narrated, just as I had earlier imagined myself a participant in Luisa's narrative. The day when workers filled the streets and began to build barricades couldn't have been very different from the first day of the resistance here. As in my experience, barricades sprang up in every quarter of the city. The main difference was that in Manuel's account there were no liberation armies camped nearby observing our slaughter. This difference doesn't blur the similarity of the events for me because I didn't know about those armies at the time.

Imagine that we're among neighbors and friends, that during the course of a day and a half we rid the city of the last militarists. Imagine the city is ours to shape with each other as we shaped the barricades. We'll organize our social activity with each other in terms of our dreams. If the possibilities to realize all our dreams don't exist we'll create the possibilities. We'll communicate with each other, we'll coordinate with each other, we'll organize with each other — without politicians who speak for us, without coordinators who manipulate us, without officials who organize our activity. To communicate with each other we hold large and small meetings where we exchange suggestions, initiate projects, solve problems. At the largest meeting, we attentively listen to the projects of all, the decisions of all. Yet when we leave the largest of all the meetings we all feel cheated, we feel that something has been taken from us, that something, somewhere has gone wrong. At that mammoth meeting we listened to speeches given by our union militants, by workers who had fought alongside us, who had always been the first to attack. Many such militants have died. We listened to them as we had always listened to them: as our voices, as the formulators of our deepest aspirations, as comrades and fellow workers who had always before put into words the decisions of the union, the decisions of all the workers. Yet at this meeting the decisions of all the workers were unlike the decisions we had been making with each other since the day we built the barricades; the projects of all the workers were unlike the projects we had launched with each other, whether it was to repair disabled vehicles or to appropriate a restaurant so as to prepare our own meals. At this meeting the most militant, admirable and courageous of our comrades, standing and sitting on the speakers' platform, were transformed into something we cannot quite understand. We had come to the meeting in order to organize social activity with each other and we found our organization on the platform. We had come to coordinate activity with each other and we found five coordinators on the platform. We had come to formulate our collective decisions and we heard our collective decisions formulated from the platform. We had always before listened to the collective decisions formulated and expressed from the platform. Yet now we pause, look around and ask ourselves what it was we had always before listened to. We begin to realize that the decisions of all the workers, the decisions of the union, were the decisions of the secretary of the union, of one individual. One, perhaps five, at most ten individuals had expressed our aspirations, formulated our projects, made our decisions. Yet who are they, those influential militants we had so greatly admired? What is this union? Who is the secretary of the union? Is this really our union or is it a sham? It's our real union. It's the same union it has always been. The people on the platform are the very people who should be on the platform. They're the militants who devoted their lives to us, who always fought alongside us in our struggles to govern ourselves, to reshape our own social activity, to define the content of our own lives. This is the union we've known; it hasn't turned into a sham; it hasn't been betrayed. It's we who changed. We changed the day before yesterday. Not all of us. Maybe only miserably few of us. We suddenly discovered our own and each other's humanity only yesterday, and we began to act as a human community. And today we suddenly realize that this union we had fought to build and whose victory we assured the day before yesterday is not our project at all. It's not a human community. It's a power above us, as alien and hostile as the powers we've just overthrown. And now we realize that the project of the people on the platform is about to replace the projects of thousands of human beings who only yesterday learned they had the ability to initiate projects. We become nauseated when we realize we've just taken part in an event which robbed us of the fruit of our struggle, an event in which the representatives of the union of all the workers replaced the union of all the workers. The union has robbed thousands of workers of their eyes, ears and voices only one day after they had learned to use organs which had until then grown weak and passive from disuse. We're learning, and we're nauseated because we're learning too late. Couldn't one of us have gotten up at that vast meeting and shouted? Couldn't he have asked why the influential militants were on the platform the day after we had eliminated the need for influential militants as well as platforms? Would anyone have heard? Was it already too late even then? Should those questions have been raised years earlier, should we have shouted them during the days when we ourselves helped build the workers' organizations and the influential militants in whose grip we now find ourselves? At that meeting we acquiesced in our own reenslavement, we accepted the reconstitution of the entire state apparatus. The influential militants who argued that their presence in the state apparatus was equivalent to the abolition of the state will quickly become engulfed by the apparatus, they'll soon be ministers. As rulers they'll differ in no way from earlier or later rulers. The politicians will let our militants call themselves whatever they please, even representatives of the abolition of the state. These miserable politicians know that they need the influence our comrades exert among us to rebuild the state apparatus. As soon as the legitimacy of that apparatus is reestablished those seasoned politicians will skillfully use our comrades the way craftsmen use tools. They'll transform the one-time union militants into agents of the state. They'll use the former workers to turn one group of workers against another. They'll use the influential militants as trouble-shooters; they'll send them to disarm the workers, turning us once again into helpless victims of the army and the police. And like classic monarchs, the influential militants, our onetime comrades, will lull us back to sleep with speeches in which they glorify their rule. They'll tell us their presence in the state apparatus is equivalent to the victory of the working class and the realization of Utopia on earth. And some of them will go to greater lengths than any monarch who ever said: I am the people. Some of our influential former comrades will not only tell us their rule is our rule but also that their presence in the government is equivalent to the realization of all humanity's deepest aspirations.

Manuel's account destroyed the picture Luisa had drawn for me. I'm obviously not surprised by Luisa's response to my rejection of her analysis of her first struggle. I'm not surprised she considers my rejection of her struggle a rejection of all struggle, nor that she considers Manuel reactionary. Manuel's account shows that the sequence of events celebrated by Luisa didn't lead to the triumph of the workers but to their repression. Luisa is using the word reactionary the way politicians use it: all those who challenge the politicians' premises are reactionary. In my understanding a reactionary is a person who favors a return to an earlier system of social relations, an earlier mode of being, an earlier form of political engagement. If the term is to define Manuel or me it has to be drastically redefined. All my life I've rejected all earlier systems of social relations including the one I was born into, all earlier modes of living, and for the past ten years I've been rejecting my own earlier forms of political engagement. Since Luisa introduced this term I no longer see any need to keep myself from asking who among us glorifies, intoxicates herself with, an earlier form of political engagement? Who among us makes a virtual Utopia out of a miserable practice that has repeatedly led to the physical and spiritual destruction of those engaged in it? Who among us uses repressive activities of the past as guides to the present and future? If I had thought about it during the past ten years I would have known that I would never again be able to have a comradely or even a polite conversation with Luisa unless she too changed. I knew this as soon as I began to grasp the significance of Manuel's narratives. Yet I learn from your letter that Luisa knew this much earlier, perhaps as many as twenty years ago. You don't seem to realize you told me this. You tell me George Alberts had considered me a hooligan; you tell me this illustrates the similarity of Alberts' outlook with that of my jailers. You also tell me what Luisa thought of Alberts' opinion of me: "Alberts was right." Did she already consider me a destructive hooligan twenty years ago?

Manuel helped clear my mind of everything I had learned from Luisa. But I had to undergo many other shocks before I could come to grips with the significance of what he told me.

During the third year of my first term, several months after Manuel had been transferred to another prison, all the cells filled to capacity. Workers from a small industrial town were crowded into every cell. I had the impression that the inhabitants of a whole town had been rounded up and jailed. All of these workers were furious. I had never before seen so many prisoners with so much spirit and so much anger. They refused to stop shouting during the day or night. They gave the impression they were determined to bend the steel bars and dismantle the stone walls of the prison. After a few weeks most of them were released, while a few of them were separated from each other and sentenced to incredibly long prison terms. For the first time since the resistance the workers of a whole town had risen. As far as I remember there had been nothing extraordinary about the circumstances that led to the rising: working conditions went from bad to worse, jobs were unsafe, real incomes were falling, houses were deteriorating. But the response of the workers grew to proportions which made this event unique in our recent history. All the workers of the town went on strike and demonstrated their discontent. Unlike workers at previous or later demonstrations, these workers called for the abolition of the political police, the abolition of the factory managers, the abolition of union representatives. In Luisa's language, all these workers were hooligans; all their demands were destructive. They called for nothing less than the abolition of the ruling system. One worker proudly told me, "When a union rep got on a platform and started lecturing about the victory of the working class, about workers administering their own factories, we carried off the rep, the microphone as well as the platform. When the police came in to clear the streets of workers, we cleared the streets of police. We thought workers everywhere would follow our example." These workers were more distrustful of politicians and pedagogues than any workers I've met before or since. They trusted only each other; they learned only from each other. They had put an end to the power of representatives, if not throughout society, at least over themselves. "We were able to hold our own against what they call the workers' militia and the workers' police," the same worker told me, "but we couldn't hold out against the army." The greatest achievement of technological progress, the army, defeated them. Approximately half the inhabitants of the town were arrested and imprisoned — in the name of the workers' self-administration of their own productive forces. They were repressed by the official representatives of the workers' movement. The repression was organized by pedagogues whose project is the liberation of the working class. These political racketeers presented the repression of these workers as yet another great stride toward the liberation of the workers.

It was the seizure of total power over society's repressive apparatus by pedagogues, philosophers and dreamers that created conditions in which workers were arrested and imprisoned under the banner of their own liberation. Today's fanatics consider human beings obstacles on the paths of their gods. The gods are today called workers but are in fact mental categories lodged in the brains of pedagogues and have nothing in common with living beings. In the name of these gods the earthly representatives of these deities, the politicians, recognize no human or natural limits. For the sake of their deities they depopulate cities and even entire regions. These gods are more jealous than the patriarchal despot Jahweh; they don't only demand the destruction of other gods that threaten to stand beside them; they call for the liquidation of all human beings who refuse to bow to them.

These are conclusions I've drawn from painful experiences. I didn't draw them easily and I think I can therefore understand why you haven't come to such conclusions. All the experiences of my first prison term didn't affect my outlook until several years later. During those four years I had learned how workers had been transformed into police detachments which repressed other workers; I had met prison guards whose conceptions had once been identical to my own; I had learned that we had embraced as liberators those who allowed our comrades to be massacred; from Manuel I had learned that all groups and organizations that embody the aspirations of others can only be victorious by repressing those aspirations; I had met workers who had risen against all forms of representation and had found themselves face to face with the entire repressive apparatus of society. Yet after all those experiences I left prison like a new organizer. It was at the end of those four years that I carried my insight and my project to Mirna and her parents, determined to communicate to them, not what I had experienced in prison, but the activities my prison experiences had undermined. I went to them as a pedagogue who had learned nothing about the significance of his own teachings: I went to them determined to enact the same drama yet another time.

I think I do understand how you're using what you call your standard of comparison. You're comparing the repressive society that surrounds us with an earlier experience that reproduced the same repression. It seems to me that this experience provides you with a faulty standard of comparison. What you told me about your friend Ron made me think that his genuinely rebellious acts provide a standard of comparison far superior to the orchestrated mass activity which placed the repressive machinery of society in the hands of representatives of human liberation. Your comparison of yourself to Vesna and of your environment to Vesna's cage were very moving. But I'm convinced the experience you've preserved with such care does not give you a vantage point outside the cage. I'm convinced you're looking at the cage from a vantage point inside it. You're doing precisely what you say permanent inmates of a prison can't help but do: you're confusing a corner of the prison with the outside world.

I'd like to learn more about your life. I found your descriptions fascinating and some of your analyses profound and informative. But I won't be converted to your life's central project. I was converted to it once, by Luisa, and I'm still struggling to rid myself of my entanglement with it. I can't honestly say I admire you for holding on to that project so tenaciously and for such a long time.

Yarostan.

Sophia's third letter

Dear Yarostan,
You should be happy to learn that Sabina's comment after she read your letter was, "He's absolutely right."
With this comment, Sabina lit a fuse on a stick of dynamite. Her comment gave rise to a discussion that lasted all night and to some of the most bitter arguments

I've ever experienced. During this discussion Sabina and Tina forced me to admit that I did actually make a choice of the type you described, a choice between Luisa and Ron, between the pedagogy you condemn and the "individual act of rebellion" you glorify.

I had invited Luisa to supper as soon as your letter came. She read the letter as soon as she arrived but the only comment she made during supper was, "Be sure to tell him how pleased I was to hear about Jasna."

Tina read the letter when she got home from her job. While we ate she didn't take her eyes off Luisa; she couldn't hide her impatience to see Luisa respond to the critiques you made of her.

Sabina didn't show any impatience at all. "Have we institutionalized the letter-reading party?" she asked. (Neither she nor Tina had read your previous letter when it came; when Sabina finally did read it after I sent my answer, she had been very excited to learn that "The Mirna he married was Jan's sister!" She told me "I knew her; she was a marvel!")

Our whole discussion revolved around the questions you raised in your letter. I can think of no better way to answer you than to give you an account of the discussion.

Sabina's opening comment yields the expected response from Luisa: "Absolutely right about what? About Manuel and Zdenek and Anton? They're obviously fictions. He's merely giving names to his ridiculous arguments. After all, he can tell us anything he pleases. He can tell Sophia her letter caused his arrest. He can tell us Marc Glavni and Adrian Povrshan are television stars. From here we can't prove otherwise."

"He did go out of his way to tell me he didn't think my letter caused his arrest," I insist.

Tina grabs your letter saying, "Not exactly," and finding the spot, she points out, "He asks what Lem was doing there besides delivering your letter."

I tell Tina that as far as I knew that was all Lem was doing.

"That doesn't exactly clear you," Tina points out.

Luisa adds, "Lem told me the investigators tortured him to find out who else he had letters for. Your letter was precisely what interested them."

"What does that prove?" I ask he, "that I was in fact responsible for Yarostan's arrest?"

"It proves," Luisa says insistently, "that Yarostan is using that ancient letter of yours to support arguments which Sabina considers absolutely right. Specifically the reactionary argument that victims are responsible for their own oppression."

I try to defend you. "He's not 'using' the letter that way. He doesn't mean that argument to be taken personally. The point he makes is perfectly clear to me. We don't always know the consequences of our acts. He doesn't say my letter caused his arrest. He says it might have. And he's right when he says I couldn't have imagined it might have had such a consequence."

"You're apologizing for him," Luisa insists. "His point is to make all of us responsible for the establishment of a police state."

Now Tina comes to your defense by pointing out, "He doesn't exactly say that either."

Luisa insists, "That's exactly what he does say! He insinuates it throughout his letter. Even that cryptic reference to George Alberts not being jailed is an accusation —"

"Come off that," Tina objects. "He says it was Sophia's reference to Alberts that was cryptic. She told him Alberts wasn't arrested. Well I'm as surprised as Yarostan must have been. The last time you were here you told me Alberts had been fired from his job just before you were all arrested so I obviously assumed Alberts was arrested like the rest of you."

"Alberts obviously wasn't arrested!" Luisa tells us.

"What's so obvious about it?" Tina asks.

"It was Alberts who made our release possible! He couldn't have done that from jail," Luisa says.

"Does Yarostan know that?" Tina asks.

"Of course he does!" Luisa insists. "And he acts as if all of us were suspicious because of that, as if all of us had conspired to keep him in jail."

"No he doesn't," Tina says, handing your letter to Luisa. "Read it again. You treat this letter exactly the same way he says you treat your past: by disregarding the facts."

"Really, Luisa, you're making him say the opposite of what he said," I point out. "In both letters Yarostan makes it clear that he had no reason in the world to suspect Alberts, that the suspicion was created by Claude."

"You're both leading me away from the point," Luisa insists. "When Yarostan speaks of his suspicion of Alberts he invariably uses words like 'suspicion' and 'enemy' exactly the same way the police use those terms."

"That's a different point," Sabina tells her, pouring each of us coffee.

"Don't interrupt me! In both letters he drags his suspicion of Alberts —"

"Well it is a different point!" Tina tells her.

"Then let me finish my different point!" Luisa shouts. "He says that whenever we consider someone suspicious we hand him to the police to be shot! Whenever we consider someone an enemy we carry out a pogrom! Sophia rightly told him our project was to communicate, not excommunicate. He turned that completely around —"

Tina interrupts again. "He only said he had seen a lot of people passively accept the arrest of their friends."

"That's what I'm talking about! Arrests and imprisonments are his whole frame of reference. It's the frame of reference of the police. When I'm suspicious of someone, I don't think of arrest and imprisonment. The point is to destroy the institution, not the individual."

"How do you do that?" Tina asks.

"If you can't distinguish the institution from the individual, your unorthodox education didn't amount to much!"

I swallow the insult because I'm embarrassed for Tina, and my embarrassment grows when Tina asks, "How do you distinguish between them?"

Tina's naive question transforms Luisa into the pedagogue you remember so well. "A priest without a cloak or a church is merely an individual. Such a priest is like a child who doesn't know how to make anything useful. He ought to be treated like a child and taught to do useful things."

"What about a soldier or a boss or a bureaucrat?" Tina asks.

"A soldier without a gun or an army is like a priest without a cloak or a church; he should be kept from dangerous implements like a child from fire, but he should be given a chance to develop in other ways."

"What if he holds on to his implements and threatens to kill you?"

Exasperated, I ask Tina, "What are you getting at?"

"Either I'm defending violence or I'm lost," Tina tells me. She crouches down in her chair when Luisa and I laugh at her.

Sabina doesn't laugh. "What is your point, Luisa? Yarostan uses terms like suspicion and enemy the way the police use them. So?"

"He can use terms any way he pleases. I don't mean the same thing by them," Luisa tells her.

"A person who says one thing and means another is a hypocrite." That statement summarizes Sabina's view of Luisa. "Take the slogan, 'Factories should be administered by the workers themselves.'"

"What about it?" Luisa asks.

"What do you mean by it?" Sabina asks her.

"I certainly don't mean 'Genghis Khan for boss'! I mean exactly what the slogan says!" Luisa shouts.

"Yet all those factories are now bossed by Genghis."

"Not because of me!" Luisa shouts.

"Who installed them?" Sabina asks.

"The new bosses obviously weren't installed by the very people who fought against them!" Luisa answers.

Sabina asks, "Did you ever meet anyone who fought to install a new boss?"

"Some people fought with nothing but words! In practice —"

"In practice they carried the same placard you carried," Sabina tells her.

I intervene in favor of Luisa. "That's not fair, Sabina. Some of the people who carried those placards knew perfectly well that their own party leaders were going to set themselves up as new bosses."

"Were some of those people workers?" Sabina asks me.

"I didn't say they weren't. Some workers looked forward to the day when their politician would be boss," I admit.

"But the overwhelming majority of workers opposed the establishment of the new bosses?" she asks me.

"Obviously!" I insist. "You know that as well as I do."

"Then why didn't the overwhelming majority throw out the new bosses as soon as they installed themselves?" Sabina asks me. "According to Yarostan only the workers of a single town rose against those bosses during the past twenty years."

"The fact that those workers rose proves that workers were opposed to the new bosses," I argue.

"Really?" Sabina asks sarcastically. "Doesn't it prove that all other workers submitted to the new bosses?"

"They were overpowered," I insist.

"Yes they were! Precisely because all other workers acquiesced! If workers had risen in all the towns, no force could have overpowered them." While saying this, Sabina leaps out of her chair, grabs me and then Tina by the waist, and starts tugging us toward the kitchen. "Your place is in the kitchen!" she shouts.

"Let go of me!" Tina shouts, pulling herself loose, while I scream, "Sabina! What's gotten into you?"

Sabina lets me go. Then she points toward the kitchen door and, trying to act like an army officer giving a command, says, "Luisa! Tina! Take Sophia into the kitchen! On the double!"

"What on earth for?" Luisa protests. "Have you gone crazy?"

"And you're telling me a handful of politicians can give orders to the majority of workers without the majority's acquiescence?" Sabina asks.

While Sabina glares triumphantly at Luisa, Tina slyly slips behind Sabina, gets on all fours and nods to me. I give Sabina a slight push and she falls flat on her back. Tina slips out from under Sabina's legs, raises Sabina's hand and proclaims, "The loser!"

Luisa and I laugh and applaud. This is to be Luisa's only moment of relief.

Remaining stretched out on the floor, Sabina tells Luisa and me, "This is what happens to a jailer when the majority doesn't want jailers. You think the majority didn't want jailers back then. But Yarostan is right. You're nursing an illusion. Sophia, you didn't believe Lem when he told you he'd been tortured. What about you, Luisa? Did you become disillusioned with those fellow workers when Lem told you about the tortures?"

"Lem wasn't tortured by workers but by inquisitors, by prison officials," Luisa insists.

"By workers who obeyed the orders of prison officials."

"That's how Yarostan sees it," Luisa tells her.

"Why did you disobey me when I ordered you to drag Sophia to the kitchen?" Sabina asks her.

"You unprincipled —"

"Try again!" Sabina shouts to her.

"Would you two like to fight it out with knives or do you want guns?" Tina asks, but her joke goes unappreciated.

"You spent your whole life among hoodlums. You have no right to breathe a word about workers who fought to free themselves." Saying this, Luisa gets up, turns her back to Sabina and walks toward the bookcase.

Sabina turns to me. "Next time you write Yarostan ask him to tell you more about Manuel. Ask him how many friends he had when he refused to obey the orders of the union leaders. Ask him if they were the majority. Ask him if those friends were hoodlums, like Ron and I."

Keeping her back to Sabina, Luisa snaps, "There aren't any hoodlums like Ron or you among genuinely revolutionary workers."

"Ask Yarostan," Sabina continues, "if Manuel's friends wanted to take pot shots at the union leaders the way that resistance fighter shot at the new occupiers. Ask him if they wanted to deal with the union officials the same way you and Tina dealt with me —"

"What'll that prove?" I ask.

"Ask him which side liquidated those friends of his. Ask if they were shot by the army generals or by the revolutionaries who spoke in the name of the workers."

"But it's perfectly clear who killed them!" I insist.

"Who?" Sabina asks.

While I say, "The generals," Tina simultaneously says, "The revolutionaries."

Sabina wins another bout and, as if she had suddenly gone over to her side, Luisa blurts out, "There were obviously enemies behind the lines as well as across the trenches."

"Really?" Sabina pounces. "Enemies who were shot? I had thought enemies were defrocked and treated like little children!"

"There were paid enemy agents who murdered revolutionary workers and sabotaged production," Luisa continues.

"And what happened to them?" Tina asks.

"They were shot!"

"But a while ago you said you didn't use the term enemy that way!" It's Tina's turn to embarrass Luisa.

Not embarrassed in the least, Luisa continues, "If those saboteurs and assassins hadn't been caught, the revolution would have been defeated right at the start."

"Then why did everyone laugh at me before?" Tina asks.

Disregarding Tina, Sabina plunges in. "Such saboteurs and assassins were an even greater threat to the revolutionaries than the attacking militarists, weren't they?"

I try to warn Luisa that Sabina is leading her into a trap, but Luisa insists on walking right into it. "That's right, such people were the greatest danger. The militarists were visible enemies, they were openly reactionary, they were on the other side of the trenches, whereas these weasels were indistinguishable from workers.

They infiltrated union meetings and workers' militias; they paraded as the greatest revolutionaries. Usually they couldn't be spotted until after they had done their deeds or proclaimed their reactionary programs."

"You just said there weren't any such people in that revolution," Tina observes.

"There weren't," says Sabina. "Destructive hoodlums like Ron didn't exist because they were all shot by the good revolutionaries."

I protest. "Yarostan didn't say anything like that."

"Ask him!" Sabina insists. "Ask him what Manuel's friends were like and who shot them!"

Luisa is intent on continuing her argument. "Yarostan compares a great historical rising of the working population with the petty thievery of a hooligan. He damns revolutionaries and glorifies gangsters. Jan, Manuel, Ron and Yarostan himself are types that become shock troops of reactionary movements."

Deliberately disregarding Luisa's newest observation, Sabina asks me, "What did you tell him about Ron?"

Luisa says, "You obviously glorified Ron in your letter to Yarostan."

"No I didn't," I tell her. "I only described Ron. I told him Ron stole bicycles. To Yarostan those thefts were individual acts of rebellion. It was Yarostan who glorified him."

"And you never saw him as a rebel?" Sabina asks me.

"Well yes, I did at the beginning," I admit. "I compared him to Yarostan and I glorified both. But I was wrong about Ron."

"When did you know that?" Sabina asks me.

"I knew it before that night when I walked away from both of you, the night when you told me I was just like Luisa."

"Did you bother to remember that over all these years?" Sabina asks me.

"I wrote it down so as never to forget it. You had no right to say that."

Luisa asks, "Was that insulting to you?"

Leaving me no chance to answer, Sabina says, "You wrote it down wrong. I said that before you walked away from us, before the car was wrecked. You were an ass that night."

"I thought you and Ron had just made love on the beach!"

"Ron and I swam together and that was all! Surely you know that now! Ron knew what you'd think. He said if you suspected your best friends without asking them anything, he was through with you."

Luisa says to me, "It's a good thing you walked out on them or you'd have stayed with that nest of —"

Tina cuts her short. "Don't say it. Please. You're talking about the people who gave me food, love and shelter, who made me what I am now. They were not a nest. They were the great sages of the age." Feigning an upper class air she continues, "If you would care to compare my wit with that of your own protégé, sitting on your immediate left, I would be glad to demonstrate —"

"Tina!" I whisper, embarrassed for Luisa because Sabina is roaring with laughter. I can hardly keep myself from bursting out laughing, but Luisa looks miserable.

"I'm here too, you know," Tina pleads.

Something in me explodes. "I know you are. So am I. Luisa, you have no right to call our friends a nest of anything. My weeks with Ron were the only happy weeks I spent here until I left for college. Yes, happy, filled with activity, with humor, with life. When I lost Ron and Sabina my insides emptied. I spent my time staring like an owl. You thought everything was fine because we talked about the past every evening. Please don't get up to leave, Luisa! I enjoyed our discussions and they meant a great deal to me — But I didn't want to live only in the past. I wanted a present as well. No, you didn't keep me from anything. You prohibited nothing. I knew I could do whatever I pleased and leave whenever I wanted, but I didn't want to tell you our evening talks weren't enough for me, I didn't want to tell you I loved Ron —"

Sabina interrupts me, "I never thought —"

"I'm not done yet!" I tell Sabina. "If Ron loved me, he loved only half of me. He rejected the other half. I knew that long before the night we went to the beach, Ron knew it and you knew it too! It was all so obvious to me on the night of that school theft when you and Ron came to the house with the two bikes you wanted me to keep for you. I hadn't seen either of you for almost a year and Ron didn't even show his face. You didn't tell me what you were doing or where you were going. The two of you used me but you didn't trust me. That's not the way you treat what you're calling your best friend."

Luisa asks Sabina, "Did you take part in that school theft?"

I turn angrily to Luisa, "Is that all you heard me say? Yes, she took part in it! So did I! Even you were an accomplice in it!"

"Don't play Sabina's games on me!" Luisa shouts.

"I'm not playing games!" I shout back. "One night, after you had gone to sleep, I woke up with a start because someone was throwing pebbles at my window. I looked out and saw Sabina grinning innocently, as if throwing pebbles at windows at that time of night were perfectly normal. I ran to the door and let her in. I thought something horrible had happened. Sabina calmly brought two bicycles in."

"Would you mind keeping these for half an hour? And please leave your door unlocked."

"That's exactly what you said then, Sabina! And you said it with that same grin. Since you remember it so well, tell me why you came alone. Why didn't Ron come with you? What was I to Ron then? Do you also remember what state you left me in? I stood by the door trembling during the entire half hour; I felt as if several hours had gone by. I was sure you'd tell me what happened as soon as you got back.

I was so sure you'd explain everything that I wasn't prepared to stop you from leaving before you told me anything. But you came back with that same demonic grin and all you said was — no, don't remind me, how could I forget? — 'Thanks a lot.' That's all! You vanished with the bikes before I could open my mouth. I'd never felt so humiliated. I thought you had completed the blow you had begun to strike at me the night we went to the beach. The following morning I preferred to think I'd had a nightmare."

Luisa points a shaking finger at Sabina. "You had the nerve to use my house for that theft?" Turning to me she asks, "And you helped her?"

"That wasn't what bothered me!" I shout. "Ron was in jail before I learned what had happened. That was what bothered me. Sabina, why didn't you tell me what you and Ron had done? Why did I have to go see you after Luisa told me there was a story in the paper about 'that awful Ron.'"

Sabina reminds me, "You came to Alberts' house before the trial. The story was in the paper after the trial."

"But I already knew about the robbery when I went to see you."

"Lem Icel told you about it," she reminds me.

"That's right. The police had contacted Debbie Matthews. She told Lem about it. At the end of a class Lem told me, 'They've caught the lumpen; he'll be on trial next week.' I left school and ran directly to your house."

"George Alberts' house," she corrects.

"To me it was your house. I was furious. I wanted to let you know how mad I was at you for letting me stand behind my door trembling, staring at the two bikes. You said 'Come in' as nonchalantly as if nothing had happened. I was boiling."

"Well, what did you do?" Tina asks me.

"Nothing, because I saw a tiny shrieking bundle on the couch and I forgot everything I had intended to shout. I asked Sabina whose it was —"

"You asked what it was," Sabina reminds me.

"The bundle was you, Tina, brand new."

"My! What an exciting story!" Tina says sarcastically. "Has it all been building up to my grand entry into the world?"

"Sorry to disappoint you, Tina. As soon as I learned 'what' you were I lost interest in you. I've never been fascinated by people who only know how to go and pee."

"Neither have I, so you don't have to apologize," Tina says.

"I remembered why I was there and some of my fury returned. Sabina continued to act as if nothing had happened. She still didn't tell me —"

"Tell you what?" Sabina asks, purposely acting out the role she had played then.

"That's what you said! 'Tell you what?' Of course I knew about the robbery by then. I wanted you to tell me why you'd let me stand behind my door waiting ignorantly. But without saying a word you led me down to your basement. I was stunned. It was full of bike parts, motors and all kinds of other junk; it smelled like grease and paint. I again forgot what I'd come to ask. I asked if you'd stolen all those things and you said you'd stolen half. When I asked what you did with it all, you said you repaired some things, changed others and then sold them. My anger disappeared. For some reason I thought everything was clear, but nothing was."

Luisa mutters, "Is this what Yarostan considers heroic acts of individual rebellion? Stealing from working people and schoolchildren is worse than scabbing."

"That was how I felt when I walked home from Sabina's after she showed me her basement," I admit. "I understood Ron wasn't what I had thought he was. He wasn't a rebel. He was no different from any unscrupulous businessman."

"Ron and I both knew that was how you felt," Sabina tells me.

"Is that why you didn't tell me anything? Were you afraid I'd give Ron away to the police?" I ask. "If that was the extent to which he trusted me how can you tell me I was his best friend? What difference would it have made if I had known? It was his own fingerprints that gave him away."

"Ron wasn't arrested or convicted because of those fingerprints," Sabina says mysteriously. "The prosecutor had no way to connect the fingerprints with the robbery."

"You mean you stole that lens?" I ask Sabina.

"We both stole it," she says. "Ron climbed into the principal's office through the window. I stayed across the street and kept watch."

"And he left his fingerprints all over that slide projector!" I point out.

"It was the lens of a brand new movie projector," Sabina says. "The school had bought it mainly for George Alberts' science classes."

"How did Ron know that?" I ask. "He was no longer in school."

"Ron had seen it when it had first arrived," she explains. "Shortly before he quit school he was called to the principal's office for having frightened a teacher. He was kept locked in the office for over an hour. He was alone with the projector. He studied it and unscrewed the lens but he screwed it right back because he knew he'd be caught if he took it."

Tina asks her, "But why did he leave his fingerprints on it the night he stole it? Didn't he know —"

Sabina answers, "He didn't leave them that night. He wore gloves when he climbed into the principal's office. He came out with the lens, showed it to me and threw it into a garbage can. It was carried off by the garbage truck the following morning."

Tina anticipates my question, "What? He threw it away? Then why did he steal it?"

"Because Debbie had been fired from her job," Sabina explains. "Ron quit school when that happened. But he wanted to do more. He talked of burning the school down. Then he remembered the projector."

"Why couldn't you have told me that at the time?" I plead.

"Because we thought your response would be identical to Luisa's: 'Stealing from the children of the working class.' We didn't need that kind of wisdom. We wanted the trial to expose the school officials who had fired Debbie as a subversive. At the trial we were going to show they had arrested Ron without any evidence, merely because he was the son of a subversive."

"How could you have done that?" I ask. "They found his fingerprints all over the machine."

"Ron hadn't ever been arrested before, so they didn't know whose fingerprints they had found," Sabina explains. "They had arrested him because he was Ron Matthews, the notorious hoodlum, son of Debbie Matthews the subversive."

"But the fingerprints they found did turn out to be his," I insist.

"They couldn't have been his if he wore gloves on the night of the robbery," Tina points out.

"Debbie had gotten Ron a lawyer," Sabina says. "Ron told the lawyer he had been locked into the principal's office with the projector for an hour. The lawyer checked into that and found out it was true. Ron told him he'd played with the projector from boredom during that hour. The lawyer wasn't only convinced of Ron's innocence. He said there was no way they could prove Ron stole the lens. Ron wasn't convicted because of those fingerprints but because of that ass he had for a father."

"I remember it now!" Tina shouts. "Jose told me all about that trial. Ron's father lied like a cop and got the judge to convict Ron without even listening to the testimony."

:||||||||:

Suddenly I remember that trial too. Everything I had found so strange about it at the time becomes clear.

The strangest thing of all was that, except for the judge and Tom Matthews, I seemed to be the only person in the courtroom who thought Ron was guilty.

I went to the trial with Lem. Sabina was already in the courtroom, alone. She sat in the front row, near the bench where Ron was going to sit when he was brought in. I recognized Tom Matthews when he came in. He sat down at the opposite end of the front row. I thought of his wrecked car and cringed. He didn't recognize me. A woman Luisa's age came in, visibly drunk. She held on to the young man who came with her. Lem nudged me and whispered that she was Debbie Matthews. I told Lem I wanted to meet her and the jerk introduced me as Sabina's sister. Debbie mumbled that she hadn't known George Alberts had two daughters and she glared at me with hatred. I tried to tell her I wasn't exactly Sabina's sister but failed to communicate anything. The young man with her said, "Hi, I'm Jose; I'm not exactly Ron's brother." A man with a briefcase came in and whispered something to Debbie. Then he sat down in the center of the front row and spread out papers; he was obviously the lawyer.

After the judge came in and asked everyone to stand, Ron was brought in, escorted by a policeman. Ron looked around; when he saw me he smiled. I didn't return his smile. I was mad at him for not telling me about the robbery. His smile turned to a frown and he looked away from me. When he saw Jose he grinned and waved his fist, as if to say "We'll get these bastards." I heard Jose whisper to Debbie, "Don't worry, they won't get him." I didn't understand that. I knew Ron had done it. I thought the only thing in question was the length of his sentence.

:||||||||:

Luisa responds to Tina's last comment by shouting, "How can you have such a twisted picture? Ron stole that machine, not his father! That hoodlum got exactly what he deserved!"

Tina reminds her, "I thought in your view no one deserved to go to jail."

"If countless workingmen are imprisoned daily for stealing food for their children," Luisa retorts, "it would have been the grossest injustice if this boy had been set free after stealing from a public school."

:||||||||:

Was that what I thought at the time? If so, I can't blame Ron and Sabina for not telling me anything. I thought the trial was ugly but it seemed that no one could have expected another outcome. The trial seemed like a pure formality. The prosecutor gave a short speech, arguing that the evidence proved Ron was guilty beyond any shadow of doubt; he said Ron was a hardened criminal of long standing and that his behavior had to be reformed so that he wouldn't continue to endanger the lives of honest citizens and their children. Ron's defense seemed petty to me. I considered his lawyer's arguments sophistic and irrelevant. When Ron was called to the stand, his lawyer asked where Ron had seen the movie projector. Ron told the story of his imprisonment in the principal's office. He admitted playing with the projector at that time. The lawyer asked Ron if he'd seen the projector after that and Ron said he hadn't. I didn't blame Ron for saying that but I didn't see how anyone would believe him. The lawyer then called the police investigator to the stand and asked him if Ron's fingerprints had been found anywhere else in the room. They hadn't. The lawyer sat down, evidently satisfied with himself, though I couldn't imagine why.

The prosecutor called Ron to the stand. He asked Ron if he was in school. No. Did he work? No. That was all he asked Ron. He called Debbie Matthews. She obviously wasn't prepared for that. "Do you mean me?" she asked. She could barely walk to the stand. Ron's lawyer objected but the judge overruled him. The prosecutor asked Debbie if she was Ron's mother and she said she was. Then he asked her two more questions. Had she been dismissed from the high school? Yes, she had.

Would she describe the reason for her dismissal? The lawyer objected and was over-ruled again. She defiantly announced she had been dismissed for inciting school-children to overthrow the government, violently. The thought that passed through my mind was that of all the people in that room Debbie and Lem were probably the strongest supporters of government; they worshipped the state; how ludicrously ironic! That was all the prosecutor wanted to know from Debbie. He called Tom Matthews to the stand. He asked if Ron lived at home. Matthews answered, "No, he doesn't; I asked him to leave about a year ago, your honor, because I found out he was stealing and storing his stolen goods in the basement of my house." I heard Jose whisper, "That bastard!" The judge must have heard him too because he turned to Jose and rapped his wooden hammer on his table. Then the judge told Matthews to continue. "I should have reported him at that time, your honor, especially when he boasted he was going to put a stick of dynamite in the wall of the school." The judge rapped his hammer again. He announced he wouldn't listen to any more evidence; the trial was over. He gave Ron six months in reform school and a large fine. (Debbie later paid the fine.) Ron's lawyer looked stunned. He shouted that he objected. But the judge got up and left the courtroom.

While Ron was being escorted out he looked helplessly at Jose and Debbie. Jose's eyes were red with anger; Debbie was as pale as a sheet. Tom Matthews stormed out of the courtroom as soon as the judge left; Matthews looked victori-ous; he'd gotten his revenge for the wrecked car. I wasn't surprised by what he had done. Sabina remained sitting in her corner, sobbing. I had never seen her cry. Debbie and Jose didn't budge. They stared at the absent judge; they both looked hypnotized, or as if they had just seen someone run over by a truck. Lem and I got up and left. No one looked at us. I had the strange feeling that something had hap-pened that I hadn't understood.

The following day Luisa handed me the newspaper and asked, "Isn't this the boy you brought to the house?" I acted surprised. I tried to give her the impression that I hadn't thought Ron capable of such an act. I didn't tell her the bicycles had been at our house on the night of the robbery, nor that I had been to the trial. I told her I had been wrong about Ron.

And that was exactly what I felt. Wrong, wronged and cheated. The Ron I had once looked for, found and loved wasn't the Ron I had just seen in the courtroom. I had looked for the Ron described in your letter: the insurgent, the rebel who rejects all social institutions through his acts. I had found such a person; my picture of him wasn't destroyed when I learned he stole bikes, since he didn't steal them from boys who couldn't afford to buy chains. But the Ron I saw at the trial was no insurgent. He didn't steal from the rich but from his "likes." He was a gangster who stole for money. The only thing he had in common with a genuine insurgent was that he was going to become a permanent fugitive from the police, he was going to live his life in an environment consisting of prisons and courtrooms. But unlike an insurgent, his activity was going to remain irrelevant to the struggle against the institutions of which prisons and courtrooms were mere symptoms. I was relieved that I wasn't Sabina, sitting and sobbing in that courtroom. I was relieved that in six or seven months I was going to leave the high school, the neighborhood and Luisa, relieved that I was going to move to a new environment where I would find new problems, perhaps new friends, possibly even worthwhile projects, projects which would in some meaningful way be the projects of an insurgent.

I saw Ron for the very last time just before the school year ended. Sabina again threw pebbles at my window at night. Both she and Ron were outside. They refused to come in. I got dressed and went out. In spite of everything I had felt, in spite of all my pent up anger, I was overjoyed to see them. I threw my arms around Sabina and cried. It was the first time I had let Sabina know I didn't hate her. She must have been as surprised as I was. I gave Ron my hand. He pulled me to him and kissed me. Fighting tears and trying to smile I said, "Didn't I tell you I'd come out to meet you any time of day or night?" "Lady, would you repeat that?" he asked. "Only if you say my name correctly," I sobbed. "Sophie Nachalo," he said, and kissed me again. Suddenly he asked, "Does that mean you trust me?" I remembered how angry I had been because he hadn't trusted me. I didn't answer. He became stiff and let me go. We started walking.

Sabina broke the silence. "Ron wanted to tell you about the people he met in reform school."

I said, "Really?" with feigned indifference. I immediately regretted saying it. I would have loved to listen to Ron's observations about reform school; I had always loved to listen to his observations. That "Really?" deprived me of my last chance to hear them. Ron had heard every nuance of meaning I had put into that single word. With undisguised hostility — with a tone in which he might as well have said, "So you've joined the police!" — he said, "I hear you're going to college." That was the last thing he said to me. He didn't want an answer or an explanation. He seemed to become deaf and dumb.

We walked on in silence. Everything had been said. But Sabina became impatient. "Go ahead and tell her!'" she insisted, but Ron shook his head. He didn't intend to say another word that night, any more than I had intended to accept a ride on the bar of his bicycle on the night of the car wreck. Sabina did all the talking. She told me he had met teenage scientists, engineers, artists and acrobats. "The best minds of our time are in that reform school." One mind had especially impressed Ron: a boy called Ted. Sabina, trying unsuccessfully to imitate Ron, described Ted as a genius who could pick the lock of any brand new car and get the car started in less than a minute; the guy he worked with drove the car into his garage where he and Ted dismantled it into parts; Ted was caught only because he had stolen a sports car and driven his girl friend around the city with it in broad daylight — his girl friend was only ten and Ted didn't look much older.

As soon as Sabina began, I was sorry she was telling me these things instead of Ron. How badly I wanted to hear the story in Ron's own words, with his characteristic comments and digressions. Sabina's erudite, perfectly grammatical narrative sounded so artificial; she took all of Ron's spirit out of his experiences. I felt miserable for having ruined my chance to hear about these experiences at first hand, but I resented having to hear a second hand account. Whenever Sabina paused I cut her and Ron with that same word: "Really?" My tone communicated to Ron immediately; I couldn't have been more explicit if I'd told them I resented being woken so late at night merely to be told such boring trivialities. Ron told Sabina, "Oh shit, let's go home."

They walked me home. No one said a word. I wanted to ask Ron to tell me again what Sabina had just told me. But the gap between us had grown too large. Ron and I both knew it. Only half of me wanted to hear Ron describe "the greatest minds of the age." The other half saw a Ron who had graduated from bicycles and was moving on to cars, a Ron who was about to become a professional criminal. I saw a person who was in no sense a rebel, a person who didn't feel comradeship and solidarity with his fellow beings, a person to whom others are mere objects to be used the way he'd used me on the night of the school theft. That night Ron knew as well as I did that only half of me wanted to hear about his newest adventure, to share his observations, to laugh with him and to explore possible projects with his new friends. He recognized the other half as the dominant half, the real Sophia. That half was a stranger to him, a hostile stranger, an outsider. Ron's "I hear you're going to college" was equivalent to, "Oh shit, when the hell did I have anything to do with anyone like you?" I was an alien to his world, his friends and his projects. Telling me about his newest experiences was a mistake. "Oh shit, let's go home" meant, "Oh shit, let's not waste time talking to this teacher; let's get out of here; this is like telling a cop what we intend to steal next."

:||||||||:

I ask Sabina, "Couldn't you at least have told me Ron had only stolen that lens because of what they had done to Debbie?"

"It wasn't up to me to tell you anything," Sabina answers. "Ron was dying to tell you. But you didn't once visit him in jail before the trial and you didn't once go see him in reform school. I knew he'd want you to join us when he came out of reform school but I also knew all you'd say would be, 'Really?' You were spending your time with that nitwit Lem Icel. It was clear to everyone but Ron that you had made your choice. Yarostan's letter describes that choice perfectly. You had already chosen to join the moralists, the priests, the judges. He was an idiot not to see that. By the time of the trial you were as repelled by him as Luisa was. If we'd told you we intended to win the trial and have Ron emerge innocent, if we'd told you we intended to expose the persecution of Debbie, what would you have done? I expected you to start shouting about the injustice and immorality of causing a poor working man to be persecuted for a crime Ron had committed."

:|||||||||:

Sabina is probably right. By the time of Ron's trial I had already made my choice. But I don't think either you or Sabina are right about the nature of that choice. I don't think I chose between Ron and what you call "pedagogy."

I certainly didn't choose "pedagogy" in the conventional meaning of that term. That kind of pedagogy didn't appeal to me at all. The people I admired — you, Luisa, Nachalo, Sabina, Ron — had never even finished high school. George Alberts was the only pedagogue I had ever been close to and I couldn't stand him. Maybe Luisa was a type of pedagogue too. I understand what you mean in your letter. But I can't apply it to my own life. During my last year in high school I didn't see Luisa the way you describe her. Nor did I choose between Ron and Luisa. If I rejected Ron at that time I rejected Luisa as well. I rejected the prospect of spending my days in a factory dreaming of the day when the general strike would put an end to wage labor. It was precisely the experiences and hopes I had learned from Luisa that made me permanently unable to accept the boredom, the scheduled routine, the supervision and the submission.

I rejected both Ron and Luisa but I didn't affirm official "pedagogy." I didn't challenge Ron's observation that the greatest scientists, engineers and artists were in reform school. I knew already then that great literature wasn't created by text-book writers or experts in creative writing, that great discoveries weren't made by the bureaucrats called researchers, that revolutions weren't carried out by academics who dreamt of governing society the way they governed their classes. Ron, the high school dunce, was more perceptive and resourceful than I was ever going to become. And in terms of sheer information, Sabina already then knew more than I was going to learn during all my years in college even though she hadn't ever finished elementary school. She had pumped out of George Alberts every scrap of physics, chemistry and biology he had ever learned. She and Alberts had converted the entire second story of their house into a laboratory and a library. And then Sabina abandoned all that and joined "the greatest minds of the age," minds capable of driving off with a brand new car in less than a minute in broad day-light on a crowded street. She spent several years living in an underworld that you seem to glorify abstractly. You characterize as "individual acts of rebellion" what to me looked like theft, constant fleeing and prostitution. Maybe I've always been as narrow as Luisa about this possibility. Sabina offered me this alternative two years after Ron died and I rejected it for the second time. Maybe I never really understood that alternative. All I do know is that at some point Sabina rejected it as well. Maybe I'm not as self-assured about my choice as I was then, but neither you nor Sabina have convinced me that the choice I made was wrong.

What I looked for wasn't related to the official purpose of the university, although I admit I did have some vague hopes that by studying history and sociology I'd at least clarify my own and Luisa's past experiences. The first few months of classes knocked those hopes out of me. About this, at least, I don't disagree with you. State functionaries do see the world from their offices. All their textbooks and all their lectures celebrated the existing social order; the apparatus they called "knowledge" seemed to have been created expressly for the purpose of making the overthrow of the social order appear inconceivable. Everything I valued was considered dangerous and violent. I entered the university at a time when the normal barracks-like life of this medieval monastic institution was supplemented by modern forms of militarization. Numerous professors were directly in the pay of the armed forces. Whole branches of activity that had once been scholarly pursuits were transformed into weapons-development factories: physics, chemistry, biology, anthropology, sociology and psychology. Instead of being taught to formulate questions, students were being bombarded with answers. Open apologists for capital and for the state treated their classrooms as pulpits from which to give sermons eulogizing the official religion. Students were brainwashed into believing the state's enemies were their own enemies. Critics of every shade, even state worshippers of a different brand, were systematically prevented from speaking. Male students were actually recruited directly into the armed forces when they enrolled in the university; military training became another academic discipline. Several professors were fired for refusing to swear to serve the state unconditionally; all the professors who remained signed the oath; they swore to lie systematically, to distort and falsify whatever threatened the interests of the state. No, I didn't go to the university because of anything it had to offer. I went there because I rejected Ron's world and Luisa's world, not because I saw a community in the military enclave that exists only to destroy community. I went there because I hoped to find others like me, others who had rejected what I had rejected. The community I wanted to find was a community of people whose choices were similar to mine. I looked for people with whom to shape meaningful responses to the world we rejected, responses which went beyond sheer opportunism for the sake of survival.

I made the mistake of moving into a dormitory, I stayed there for three months. It was the closest thing to prolonged imprisonment that I've experienced. I did learn to play pranks, but even then I couldn't endure that regime of rules and regulations to which I had never in my whole life been subjected. I couldn't afford to rent an apartment of my own. Then I found some women students who owned a house and ran it on a cooperative basis; those who could afford to pay less did more of the housework. I washed dishes and got free room and board.

My first friend was my roommate at the co-op, Rhea Morphen. I liked her very much at first, mainly because of how enthusiastic she was about me. I suppose you always like people who think a lot of you. She made me tell the story of my life at least a dozen times during my first few weeks at the co-op. The fact that my "mother" worked in an auto plant and supported me already recommended me to Rhea. She was even more impressed by the fact that my "mother" had never finished high school, that my "sister" hadn't finished elementary school and that my "father" hadn't ever spent a single day in school. Rhea's perpetual comment was, "I don't believe it!" But after a few weeks of being admired as such a perfect proletarian I got sick of her admiration and when I learned more about her I resented it. It turned out that she was a member of the same political church as Lem Icel, that she and Lem were friends, and that Lem was responsible for the fact that Rhea and I were roommates.

Rhea perfectly fits your portrait of the politician. Her world was populated by constituents and leaders. In her eyes I was a perfect constituent, a potential cadre, a potential rank-and-file leader, a full-fledged proletarian intelligent enough to understand the dialectic and to know how to interpret it to my fellow rank-and-filers. Her father was a lawyer who was later to become a city politician.

The part of my past I had failed to rid myself of was Lem. He was in one of my classes. It was from him that I learned about the co-op when I wanted to leave the dormitory. It was also largely because of Lem that I met the people who were to be my friends throughout my university years. Lem and Rhea more or less conspired to recruit me to their organization. It took me several weeks to figure out that I was a fly in a spider's web. I got my first clue when, during one of Rhea's admiration sessions, she commented, "You really have a highly developed consciousness; you see a lot of things the way we do," implying that there were a few things about which I still had to be straightened out. I immediately asked her if she happened to know Lem Icel. The moment of silence before she answered gave her game away. When at last she said, "Yes, he's a good friend of ours," I knew she had known about me before I had moved to the co-op. She admitted she had lacked a roommate and I had sounded ideal; she asked if I minded. I really didn't mind. I had hated the dormitory and I was glad to find new friends. Rhea's friend Alec Uros visited her every other day and she invariably recited my proletarian virtues to him. Alec was at least as impressed as Rhea. He was another person to whom the daughter of a worker was as exotic as a Martian.

Ultimately their conspiracy backfired. Because of me their little university group fell apart. It would probably have fallen apart anyway, but not the way it actually happened.

Rhea was the "open" member of the organization. She attended all sorts of events and meetings where she announced her organization's position on the topics under discussion. Alec and Lem were "secret" members. All three attended organization meetings, which were frequently held at Debbie Matthews' house, but when Alec and Lem were asked if they were members they denied it. All three pressured me to attend at least one of their meetings merely in order to see what "wonderful people" they all were, but I invariably turned down the invitation, passing up my chance to meet all those wonderful people.

When he came to visit Rhea, Alec would tell us about his projects on the school newspaper staff. The more he talked about that, the more interested I became. He talked about professors who were being fired for refusing to sign the oath of loyalty to the state, about students who refused to take part in the military training program, about the latest speaker who had been banned from speaking on campus. He saw his role on the newspaper staff as that of a muckraker who exposed these infringements on the students' right of speech and of assembly. He didn't see any contradiction between his newspaper campaigns and his organization's denial of all such rights. Alec's naïveté recruited me, not to his organization, but to his campaigns. This was a project I recognized; I wanted to take part in it. I joined the newspaper staff. So did Lem.

Yarostan, your letters inhibit me. No, I'm no longer angry. I'm frustrated. For twenty years I longed to tell you about myself, if not in letters then in a novel which was addressed to you even if it never reached you. I wanted to tell you about my life because I thought I'd lived up to what you might have wanted me to be. I looked at myself through what I took to be your eyes and I wasn't ashamed. I was in fact somewhat proud of myself. Not altogether. I hadn't taken part in the overthrow of the ruling system. But I hadn't succumbed to it either. I hadn't emerged unscathed but I wasn't destroyed either. Unlike Luisa, I hadn't sold my productive energy. Unlike Sabina, I hadn't sold either my body or my soul. Until your letters challenged my self-evaluation I'd thought I had done rather well. My activity on that university newspaper staff was one of the high points of my story. I saw it as a continuation of activity I had once shared with you. Yet now that I can finally tell you about my little victories I feel embarrassed and inhibited. I can't help seeing myself through the lenses you're now wearing and I look ludicrous to myself. The very words with which I would have boasted about my activity are the words with which you ridicule it. If my desire to communicate and defend my insights and past experiences was pedagogy, then it was precisely the opportunity to engage in this pedagogy that attracted me to the newspaper staff. I think you go too far when you characterize every instance of such activity as an attempt to convert people to a religion. I understand the way your analysis applies to Lem, Rhea and Alec; I recognized them as missionaries of a repressive religion. I can even see how your analysis applies to certain aspects of Luisa's relation to the world. But I don't see how your analysis applies to me. To communicate a religion you need to have certainties and I never had any. At most I had past friends and experiences, but the answers those friends and experiences gave me in any given context were never clear. Even if I granted that your description of me was valid down to your characterization of my pedagogical activity as a type of missionary activity, I still wouldn't see that I had chosen the worst of the alternatives available to me. In retrospect I'm still convinced that under the circumstances I did rather well, since I know what other alternatives were available to me. I've had a few chances to sample Luisa's as well as Sabina's alternatives. I might in time have reconciled myself to Luisa's situation, but I couldn't have retained the amount of energy she has managed to keep alive. I could never have been Sabina; I wouldn't have survived either physically or psychologically.

In a way it's ironic that you describe the activity I chose as a type of religious activity. I visited Luisa soon after I started to work on the newspaper. She had just been called to testify at an official inquisition; she was asked where she was from, what she had done, what she thought. Later she learned that the inquisition didn't concern her but George Alberts. His turn had come to undergo the treatment to which he had subjected Debbie Matthews. George Alberts, the person I've always regarded as a model opportunist, was called a subversive and fired from his teaching job. (Don't shed tears for him though; he immediately opened up some kind of research organization connected to the military and he again sold his talents to the same government that had just fired him.) When Luisa told me about that, I had the feeling that I was among the pitifully few people who were engaged in a struggle against the state religion and its inquisition. I saw myself as an atheist during a witch hunt aimed not only at people playing at being revolutionaries but even at totally unprincipled individuals like Alberts who had once in their lives been swept along by a revolutionary upsurge.

Some of my newspaper friends were devoted to a counter-religion as repressive as the religion we fought against, and they tried to convert me. Lem's and to a smaller extent Alec's goal was to convert all the students of the university to their form of state worship. But my approach, influenced by Luisa and by my experiences with you, was significantly different from theirs. I don't think you can really characterize it as religious. Unlike Lem and Alec, I didn't write articles about fired professors in order to prove that they wouldn't have been fired if the counter-religion prevailed. I knew perfectly well that the professors would never have been hired in the first place if that religion prevailed. My sole aim was to describe the militaristic lectures, the banning of speakers, the firings of professors, and to let readers draw their own conclusions from the facts themselves. To me reality itself was so scandalous that I was sure numerous students would act as soon as they knew what the facts were. I was wrong, but not altogether. Several years later a large number of students did in fact respond to the scandal; that movement is today being drowned by variants of the religion then carried by Rhea and Lem. I didn't only resist Rhea's and Lem's attempts to recruit and use me; by resisting them I helped mess up their other plans and ruin their miniscule organization.

The editor of the campus newspaper, Hugh Nurava, was a very mild-mannered, very middle-class student. I was immediately fascinated by him. The words he used most frequently were "responsible" and "fair." He seemed convinced there were always two and never more than two sides to every question. The task of the "responsible" editor was to be "fair" to each of the two sides. Once Alec wrote an article on some students who had refused to swear to be loyal to the state; they were forced to march in a military parade in their street clothes; they looked ridiculous, even to their own friends, and everyone laughed at them. Hugh went out of his way to give equal space to the other half of the question. He interviewed a military "professor" and published, alongside Alec's article, an equally long article depicting the dangerous and all-pervasive enemy against whose imminent invasion the uniformed students were protecting civilization. One time I wrote an article about a pacifist who was to speak in a university lecture hall but who was denied permission to speak in the hall just before the event was scheduled to take place. For the sake of "fairness," Hugh telephoned the university administration and alongside my article he published the administration's official statement that it was the university's policy never to prevent anyone from speaking on campus since free speech was an indispensable condition for education. The fact that one article flatly contradicted the other didn't prove to Hugh that one of them had to be false; it convinced him that "the truth" lay "somewhere between the two extremes."

The person on the next rung of the newspaper hierarchy was Bess Lach. She was the managing editor. She was the only person on the staff besides me who didn't have a middle class background. I learned that her mother worked as a cleaning woman for people who were managers in the plant where Luisa worked. Her father had run off when she was a baby. Yet although she was even more "proletarian" than I, neither Lem nor Alec took the slightest interest in her. It was impossible to communicate with her. She was literally a machine. I'm sure she was the best managing editor that newspaper had before or since. She read, measured, counted with the speed and precision of a computer. But whenever she opened her mouth she articulated a law. "Don't, can't, not allowed, against regulations" appeared in every statement she made. She had internalized all the written and unwritten codes of the state, the university, and while Hugh was editor she internalized the code of "fairness and responsibility" as well. Bess and Hugh went with each other when I met them. I can't imagine what they could have said to each other and I never asked him. Perhaps by enumerating the regulations she familiarized Hugh with his "responsibilities." I have to admit I wasn't able to muster up any solidarity toward my fellow worker Bess.

The most bizarre member of the newspaper staff was Thurston Rakshas. He came from the very top of the social hierarchy and I'm sure that's where he is again today. He considered himself superior to the rest of us in wit, knowledge as well as looks. He thought himself a humorist. He wrote a regular joke column which was in fact very clever and occasionally he wrote an article. I laughed whenever he said anything at all. He thought I appreciated his brilliant sense of humor. In fact I laughed at him. I thought his poses were ludicrous and hilarious. I had never been so close to a real dilettante, a genuine heir to the wealth wrenched from the labor of millions of wage workers. He never saw through me. Genuinely convinced that my laughter expressed appreciation of his wit, one day he asked me to accompany him to a dance which was going to take place several weeks later. I accepted his invitation immediately. In a flash I figured out this was my chance to slip away from the unwanted attentions of Lem as well as Rhea. I made it a point of announcing to everyone on the staff that I had accepted Thurston's invitation to the dance.

My strategy was completely successful, but in ways I hadn't expected at all.

When I told Rhea, she said, "I guess I overestimated your class consciousness." That put an end to her admiration for her proletarian roommate. She never again asked me about the educational background of my "family." And she never again asked me to join her organization.

Lem caught me late one afternoon when I was alone in the newspaper office typing an article. He sat down next to me and started to cry. "Are you actually going to go through with that?" he asked.

"With what, Lem?" I asked innocently.

"Are you going to go out with that reactionary, that exploiter of the working class?" he asked.

"He's really a wonderful person when you get to know him, Lem," I lied.

In Lem's eyes I was "lost." My strategy was an instant success; from that day on I no longer had a private missionary trailing me like a shadow. Lem retreated to Debbie Matthews and to his organizational meetings.

What took me completely by surprise was Alec's response to my insincere flirtation with Thurston. Alec was jealous. He hatched a plot to "save" me from the claws of the "dangerous reactionary." And in the process of working out his exquisitely designed plot he threw all of his political commitments overboard, spoiled the plans and projects of his organization, and created absolute chaos on the newspaper staff.

Alec didn't confront me with the problem directly. In fact he took such a roundabout approach that I didn't figure out what he had done until several months later. His strategy was brilliant and like all brilliant strategies it led to completely unexpected consequences.

He began by breaking up his relationship with Rhea. He told her he was disillusioned with the organization and tore up his membership card in her presence. Rhea blamed me. She accused me of brainwashing him with reactionary arguments. I argued from the bottom of my heart that I'd had nothing to do with Alec's disillusionment. I felt sorry for her. Little did I know then the place I occupied in Alec's scheme. When I began to figure it out I silently moved into another room.

Alec's "defection" from the organization and my deficiency as a "rank-and-file leader" left Lem isolated on the newspaper staff. To remedy this Rhea herself joined the staff.

After breaking up with Rhea, Alec formed a clique with Minnie Vach and Daman Hesper, the remaining two regular members of the newspaper staff. Minnie and Daman were members of a political sect which was indistinguishable from Lem's organization in terms of its internal relationships but which considered Lem's and Rhea's organization the main evil that plagued humanity. I actually agreed with much of what they said. Many of their views even had a superficial similarity to views you've expressed in your letters. For example, they held that an organization of professional revolutionaries which claimed to liberate the workers would only enslave them; they held that the workers' revolution could only be led by the workers themselves. What I couldn't understand then and still can't now is how they viewed their own sect. They never tired of telling me that the role of their organization was not to lead the workers but to educate them. It never seemed to occur to them that the teacher is the one who leads, the student the one who follows.

Alec's resignation from Lem's and Rhea's sect was a precondition for his alliance with Minnie and Daman. (If I refer to Minnie and Daman as a single person it's because at that time they were like Siamese twins; Minnie formulated the arguments and Daman merely emphasized them.) Alec had a long talk with Minnie and Daman a few days after he broke up with Rhea. He told them he had finally been convinced by their arguments and had quit his organization; he proved this by showing them his torn membership card. He even attended a few meetings of their organization, although he later told me he didn't agree with their organizational practices at all. As soon as he gained their trust, the three began to plan a series of articles which would systematically expose the bias of the education, the extent to which militarists and state officials dominated the university's policies, the cowardice of administrators and professors, the apathy of students.

Every day one of them submitted exposures of the military curriculum, articles on fired professors, interviews with pacifists. Hugh couldn't possibly keep up with "the other side" of all the questions raised in their articles. Consequently there was a lively confrontation in the newspaper office almost every day. Bess and Thurston argued that if the "other side" wasn't given equal space, the paper would become a propaganda sheet and that consequently the articles of Minnie, Daman or Alec should be suppressed whenever a rejoinder couldn't be published with them. Hugh's position wasn't as clear as that. Committed though he was to publishing two sides to every question, he had yet another principle; no article should ever be suppressed. Since he couldn't resolve the conflict between his two principles he would put the question to a staff vote. At first the result of the voting was that Minnie, Daman and Alec outnumbered Bess and Thurston because Hugh, Rhea, Lem and I abstained. As a result all their articles were published. The reason Lem and Rhea abstained was that they refused to be on the same side as Minnie, Daman and the "renegade" Alec. I abstained because, although I favored including the articles without views of the other side, my vote wasn't needed for their inclusion. But this state of affairs didn't last. On one occasion Minnie wrote an article which contained a critique of Lem's and Rhea's organization. From that day on, both Rhea and Lem formed a ludicrous bloc with Bess and Thurston and voted against the inclusion of every article written by Alec, Minnie or Daman, who were outnumbered four to three. I was forced to take sides. Of course I voted in favor of including every article without a rebuttal and as a result there was a tie: four in favor and four against. Tempers rose and cliques hardened. After one particularly heated exchange which took place only a few days before the dance to which I was to accompany Thurston, he very politely told me he would prefer not to go with me. I was relieved. Alec had known that sooner or later I'd take sides and at that point I'd clash with Thurston. I was no longer inhibited from openly joining the "clique." But the ultimate decision as to whether or not to include the articles again depended on Hugh. He once again found a way to be fair to each of the two sides. He voted with us one day and against us the next, so that nearly every other one of our articles was suppressed. In spite of the exclusion of almost half of our articles I felt that my new friends and I were engaged in a virtual crusade to expose the repressive atmosphere of the university.

My acceptance of my new friends wasn't unqualified. I rarely argued with Minnie and Daman. They were infinitely better informed than I and the convoluted sentences in which they couched their arguments intimidated me. Yet despite their erudition and their rhetorical talents I saw through their outlook; I thought it was a superficial version of Luisa's. Their affirmation that working people were perfectly capable of running their own affairs seemed to be a mere slogan that neither Minnie nor Daman really believed. The workers' ability to run their own affairs seemed to depend on their ability to learn this from Minnie's and Daman's organization. And they were convinced, believe it or not, that their sect had discovered that workers were able to run their own affairs, that their sect had discovered workers' councils, and that their sect had discovered the reactionary character of the role of revolutionary politicians. Nachalo, Margarita and Luisa had learned all this from experiences they had lived; this knowledge had flowed in their blood; they had learned from painful counterrevolutionary wars how revolutionary politicians transformed the workers' movement into a gang of government bureaucrats. To Minnie and Daman these painful experiences were nothing but phrases discovered by their sect only yesterday and not yet applied to their relationships with each other within their organization. I couldn't respect them. But I did enjoy muckraking with them.

I accepted Alec with fewer misgivings. He was politically unformed. He had joined Rhea's sect for the same reasons you said Manuel had joined his organization. Alec had been Rhea's boyfriend and had followed her into the organization on a date. When he became interested in me, he abandoned Rhea as well as the entire credo of her organization. After he left the organization he worked out a political potpourri consisting of Minnie's and my observations couched in phrases he had retained from his earlier commitment. Alec had nothing at all in common with you or Jan Sedlak or Ron Matthews. But in spite of his naïveté, perhaps because of it, I liked him a lot.

One night, a few weeks after I moved out of Rhea's room, Sabina surprised me with a visit. She burst into my room at the co-op late at night. Alec had just brought me home. He and I had taken the paper to the printer's that night; we had done all the last minute proofreading of galleys and shortening of articles. Sabina had waited outside for Alec to leave. I was dead tired and my head was filled with the day's events. Minnie had submitted a very long interview with a campus general who had boastfully showed her the files he kept on all the students in the university. He classified students in terms of their degree of patriotism, from loyal to apathetic, disloyal, dangerous and subversive. The article was one of the biggest exposures of the year. Hugh had voted with the four of us to include the article.

I wasn't glad to see Sabina that night. I knew that I had turned against her and Ron long before they had left me standing next to their bicycles. I knew that my hostility toward Sabina and Ron had been only partly motivated by the fact that they hadn't trusted me at the time of the robbery. I knew that I had rejected Ron even before our excursion to the beach in the car Ron wrecked. This was very clear to me when I saw Sabina that night because I was then in the midst of the activities and friends I had hoped to find when I had first turned against Ron. It was clear to me that I had rejected Ron already when our relationship was at its peak, at the time of our earliest bicycle excursions. Ron had known that as early as I had. It had been as obvious to him as to me that he could no more take my path than I his, he would have suffocated in an atmosphere of petty quarrels couched in erudite language; he couldn't have fought his battles on that terrain. Yes, Yarostan, I knew how early I had made the choice you describe. It wasn't Ron's terrain or Sabina's. But I knew it was mine. It wasn't all petty quarrels. By that night I had already fought some meaningful battles. I don't want to exaggerate their significance, but I'm certain they were far more meaningful than any battles I could have fought on Ron's terrain. As I studied Sabina, wondering why she had come, I didn't regret having rejected their path; I couldn't imagine anything socially relevant growing out of stolen cars. This was the only time I saw Sabina until I was expelled from college. The following morning I remembered her visit as a bad dream.

Sabina spoke like a robot. She looked past me and seemed not to care whether or not I heard her. "Ron is dead."

"Dead! How? When?" I asked.

"You and George Alberts are responsible," she droned.

I thought her coldness and her seeming indifference were symptoms of hysteria. I paid no attention to the accusation. I repeated my questions.

"Missing in action," she answered. "They didn't say when or how."

"But when did he join the army?" I asked with disbelief.

"Air force. He signed up because of you," she told me without raising her voice, without seeming to be aware that she was telling me anything extraordinary.

"Sabina!" I shouted. "I don't understand!" I burst into tears.

"I didn't think you would. But I thought you ought to know." Saying that, she left as abruptly as she'd come. I cried, uncomprehending, until I fell asleep without undressing or washing.

The next morning Alec's knock on the door woke me. He was annoyed. "What's the matter with you?" he asked. "This is a hell of a day to oversleep." We had intended to rush to the boxes where the papers were distributed so as to see how students responded to Minnie's article. We spent the day interviewing students who were willing to express their responses to the article. Sabina's visit and Ron's death receded in my memory.

:||||||||:

"You're absolutely right," I admit to Sabina. "By the time of Ron's trial I had already made my choice. I had walked out on Ron. But why did you say I was responsible when you came to tell me Ron was dead?"

"You and George Alberts were responsible," Sabina says in the same tone she had used fourteen years earlier.

"How can you repeat that accusation today?" I ask her. "When you said it that night you visited me at the co-op, I thought you were hysterical. Ron had left you and he'd just been killed in the war."

"Ron never left me," she says. "He left you. And he wasn't killed in the war."

"Would you stop being so cryptic and mysterious!?" I shout. "What you're saying doesn't mean anything to me!"

Tina asks me, "Are you sure it was Sabina who was hysterical that night?"

"What the hell do you know about it?" I ask Tina. "You were only four years old at that time."

"I know a hell of a lot more about it than you do," Tina proclaims. "First of all I was almost five, and secondly Jose told me about his last days with Ron at least a dozen times before you came to the garage. You were always the villain of his story. I thought of you along with George Alberts and Tom Matthews as the bad people of this world."

"If you knew so much, why didn't you tell me after you left the garage?" I ask her.

"Are you kidding? You were about as interested in Ron as Luisa is," Tina says. "Whenever I mentioned Ron you went into your professional pose. 'Oh really? What else did he steal?'"

Luisa contributes: "What else was there to tell about him?"

"Nothing," I say to her; "absolutely nothing."

"So why should Sophia have wanted to hear about Ron?" Luisa asks Tina.

I answer, "Because I want to hear about him now, that's why. I want to know what it was that Tina knew about Ron during all these years."

"The day Ron got out of reform school Jose and Sabina went to get him," Tina begins. "Instead of being glad to see his two best friends Ron got into the car and asked, 'Where's Sophie?'"

I ask Sabina, "Is Tina making that up?" Sabina shakes her head.

"Jose thought Ron was joking," Tina continues. "He asked Ron who the hell Sophie was. Then he got mad at Ron for expecting someone else to have come for him instead, but he saw tears in Ron's eyes and asked Sabina who else Ron was expecting. Sabina told him you hadn't known when Ron was supposed to be released."

"You never told me anything about that," I say to Sabina.

Sabina answers, "We visited you after Ron was released and all you said was 'Really?'"

"Ron hardly said a word to me that night," I insist. "You did all the talking. He seemed to be in a different world."

"Different from whose?" Sabina asks.

"Mine! From mine!" I answer angrily. "You're so right! Have you ever been wrong, Sabina, about anything?"

Tina continues, "Jose said Ron changed after he and Sabina visited you. Jose thought it was then that Ron decided there were two or three more things he wanted to do in his life before he was through."

"It always looks like that after a person is dead," I tell her. "The last things a person does always look like the last things he had intended to do."

"Jose hadn't just met Ron, you know!" Tina exclaims. "He had that feeling before Ron died, not after."

"I know how long Jose had known Ron," I admit. Tom and Debbie Matthews had adopted Jose during the depression. It was mainly Jose who brought up Ron when both Tom and Debbie had jobs during the war. Some years after the war Tom accused Jose of teaching Ron to be a criminal. Jose angrily left the Matthews and didn't see them again until Ron's trial.

Tina continues, "The first thing Ron wanted to do after visiting you was to find Ted, who had left reform school some months before Ron."

"To start the garage: stolen parts at cut rates and heroin for the health of the poorer folk," I say sarcastically.

"But you're just like Luisa!" Tina says to me.

"I'm sorry," I tell her. "Please go on."

"Ron and Jose looked for Ted because he was good at stealing cars." Tina says. "Ever since the trial one idea had been on both their minds: to get even with Tom Matthews. Ron had wanted you to be in on the revenge. That's why he and Sabina visited you."

"To take part in revenge?" Luisa asks. "Is that the act of individual rebellion Yarostan praises in his letters?"

Tina disregards Luisa's interruption and continues, "Tom Matthews had bought a brand new car right after the trial. He would park it right in front of his diner and he'd spend half the day looking through the window to see if it was still there. Jose, Ron and Ted drove off with it in broad daylight a couple of seconds after he'd just looked at it and probably a couple of seconds before he looked at it again and saw that it was gone. The first comment Ron made when they drove off was: 'I bet Sophie would have loved to see the old man's face when he saw that car gone. I'd give my right arm to hear what she'd have said; if she could only have stood across the street and watched his expression this would have been perfect.'"

"Good grief!" Luisa yells. "Why you?"

I answer, "Because Ron's old man almost shot me the night Ron took me to his house. Yes, Ron was right; I really would have liked to see that old man's face."

Tina continues, "They drove it away and dismantled it so completely that Matthews himself couldn't have recognized his new car if he'd walked into the garage and looked right at it. He went out of his mind when he saw his new car was gone. He hunted for Ron all over the city. One day he even came to our house —"

"Alberts' house," Sabina corrects.

"He came with a gun, looking for Ron. He would have shot Sabina if I hadn't screamed," Tina says proudly.

"Do you remember that?" Sabina asks.

"I almost remember," Tina says. "Anyway I thought I remembered when you first told me about it. You laughed at him. You told him —"

" — that Ron had just become a professional killer," Sabina says, "and that he'd drop a bomb on Matthews' house."

"Matthews went wild," Tina continues. "He waved his gun in Sabina's face; he waved it at me when I screamed; and then he ran out of the house."

"You had some nerve to laugh at him when he was in such a state!" I tell Sabina. "He could have killed both of you!"

"We're both still here though," Tina says. "Matthews closed his diner during all the weeks he spent looking for Ron. When he opened the diner again hardly any of his former customers returned. Most of them went to a franchised restaurant across the street which hadn't done very well until Matthews closed down. At the end of that month Matthews didn't have enough money to pay all his bills. A few months later he was bankrupt. His diner was auctioned off."

"Couldn't Debbie get some kind of job?" I ask.

"I was with you once when we saw what a state she was in," Tina reminds me. "Jose told me she had been something of a drunkard ever since she'd been thrown out of her union job after the war. When she lost her teaching job she was drunk all the time. Matthews tried to get a factory job. He did get some low paying job but was fired after a few weeks; maybe it was just a temporary job; Jose never told me the details. What Debbie told Jose was that one day she heard a shot. She dragged herself to the basement. Matthews was lying on the floor. He had shot himself."

Luisa mutters, almost to herself, "He was murdered by his own son."

"Oh shit!" Sabina exclaims.

I object too. "That wasn't exactly what Tina said."

"I didn't say he shot himself because his new car was stolen," Tina explains. "That's only part of the reason —"

I add, "Debbie's drunkenness must have had something to do with it. Several years earlier Ron had told me how bitter she'd been about being thrown out of the union she'd helped build. I can understand why she broke down when that happened to her a second time. I still remember the hatred with which she looked at me at Ron's trial because she thought I was George Alberts' daughter."

"Do you see any connections yet?" Sabina asks Luisa. "Don't you know why you and Sophia and I got out of jail two days after being arrested and why our emigration was so easy?"

"I don't see what that has to do with it." Luisa says.

"Why do you think he had a job waiting for him as well as a house for the three of us when we got here?" Sabina asks her, immediately answering her own question. "Alberts saved your skin by selling his soul! Debbie Matthews was only one of his victims. When Debbie fell she drove the sinking Tom Matthews all the way to the bottom. You came here on the devil's pay, Luisa!"

Luisa objects, "If you're suggesting I was implicated in that man's suicide you're completely deranged. Your reasoning is as distorted as Yarostan's."

"I'm not suggesting anything," Sabina says. "I'm only stating facts."

"All right, you've made that point," I concede to Sabina. "But you still haven't told me what I had to do with Ron's death."

"Haven't we?" she asks.

"No you haven't," I insist. "I don't know any more now than I knew that night you came to my room at the university co-op; you shouted that I was responsible for Ron's death."

"I didn't shout," Sabina says. "And I said you and Alberts."

I get impatient "Would you mind explaining that, Sabina? I don't care how long it takes." Noticing Luisa's pained expression, I tell Sabina, "I don't care whether Luisa stays or leaves. Now that you've unearthed the details of my relationship to Ron I'd like to hear all of it. And please don't ask what good it'll do to tell me."

Luisa leans back on the couch, yawns and closes her eyes so as to communicate to all of us that she's not interested in the details of my relations with Ron.

"The day before I went to see you at the university," Sabina begins, "Debbie Matthews showed up at Alberts' house. I was alone with Tina, Debbie collapsed into an armchair the moment she walked in. She was stone drunk. 'You hussy,' she told me; 'Why did you walk out on my son when he needed you? And where's that filthy father of yours? Where's that son-of-a-bitch Alberts?' I asked her what had happened and why she wanted Alberts. She said, 'I want to see his face now that they've thrown his ass out of school, I want to see what he looks like now that he's gotten what he gave me, I want to ask him if he's happy now about himself and me; where the hell is that slimy bastard that called himself my friend and then cut me up one limb at a time?' I told her Alberts was working and asked if something had happened to Ron. She said, 'He's working? He can't be working, deary; he's off in some bar; he got booted out like I was; he's not allowed to work; he's a subversive.' I described the work he was doing and Debbie got hysterical. 'That bastard is doing research for the air force?' she asked; then she shouted, 'That low unprincipled bastard! The air force! He's working for the outfit that killed my son!' I had been afraid that was the news she'd come with. She worked herself up into a frenzy about the fact that Alberts was already employed again. She walked around the house, knocked down chairs and threw books on the floor. She yelled, 'What are you people? Who sent you? You're some kind of agents. You were sent to get rid of us. Well kill me right here, get it over with!' Then she collapsed on the floor. I couldn't tell if she was asleep or dead. I set a pillow under her head, put a blanket over her and ran to the garage. Fortunately Jose was there."

Tina tells me, "That was when they found out where you fit in —"

"What do you mean?" I ask her.

Tina says, "When Jose got to know you years later he often said, 'She's as innocent as a baby that started a fire that burned down a city.'"

I become impatient. "Tina, what the hell are you talking about?"

"Jose told me never to tell you," Tina claims.

Sabina says to Tina, "Go ahead and tell her; there's nothing left to tell she doesn't already know."

"Jose said you'd have become a completely different person if you'd known the truth," Tina tells me.

Exasperated, I ask, "The truth about what? Aren't you confusing Jose with Yarostan?"

"The truth about you and Ron," Tina says. "Jose often told me he wouldn't have liked what you'd have become if you'd known. That's exactly the opposite of what Yarostan says."

"Tina, don't play Sabina's games with me!" I shout.

Tina calmly muses, "I wonder if it would really have made any difference if you'd known."

I grab her by the shoulders and shake her, shouting, "Don't dangle a string, Tina! I'm not a cat!"

Tina shouts back, "That's what Jose said about you! You kept dangling a string in front of Ron and he kept jumping at it. Only you never knew you were dangling it."

My patience wears out. "Go to hell, Tina! If this is another one of your jokes you can shove it up your ass because I'm going to sleep."

"This one doesn't have a funny ending, Sophia," she says. "And I'd just as soon not tell you about it so if you want to go to sleep that's fine with me; I'm sleepy as hell."

I plead with Tina, "What is it you'd just as soon not tell me?"

"What you've been asking about for the past two hours, Sophia! Your connection to Ron's death."

"How can you know anything about that?" I ask her.

"It turned out that Debbie Matthews was the only one who knew anything about it. When she told Jose and Sabina all they could say was My God!"

I turn to Sabina. "You never breathed a word to me about what Debbie told you!"

Sabina says, "I told you everything that night when I visited you at the co-op. You didn't ask me to go into details and in any case it was too late to do anything about it."

Tina adds, "Ron was already dead."

"All you told me was that I was responsible for Ron's death," I say again. This time it's Tina who says, "You and George Alberts." She continues. "That was really a very complete summary. And if it was too late to tell you the details then, it's way too late now! I have to be at work in four hours and we should carry Luisa to a bed."

"Don't worry about Luisa," I insist. "Nothing wakes her once she's asleep. Please, Tina, I want to hear those details now. Go to sleep on your job."

"Don't keep repeating that Sabina told you that you were responsible for Ron's death," Tina tells me. "Alberts' role was much more important to Sabina than yours. We were still living in his house when she learned about it. Didn't you know what Sabina thought of Alberts then?"

Sabina asks Tina, "Would you mind leaving that out?"

"If I'm going to lose my night's sleep telling her," Tina says, "I'll at least tell her everything I know. I'm sure she'll never learn that part from you." Tina turns toward me. "Jose told me he and Sabina were both stunned when they heard what Debbie had to say but they were stunned for different reasons. Every time Jose said "My god!" because of something Debbie said about you, Sabina said it because of something she said about Alberts. Sabina didn't tell you about your role because that wasn't what mattered to her and she had in any case learned most of that before, from Ron. What mattered to her was what she learned about her life's hero. All that math and physics she had learned from him ever since she was a little girl, all those laboratory experiments which she thought revealed the secrets of the universe — she hadn't ever connected any of that with the slaughter of thousands of human beings. Debbie uprooted all of Sabina's admiration for Alberts; she gave Sabina a picture of a cold-blooded murderer of thousands and maybe even millions of people. And not only a murderer, but the worst kind, the one who doesn't kill a single opponent in face-to-face combat but who exterminates unseen victims from the safety of his laboratory. Sabina went completely wild. She left Jose at Debbie's and ran to Alberts' house. She completely destroyed the lab he'd built for her on the second floor. She took all the books he'd ever given her and threw them into the incinerator. She burned all her clothes, all of mine, all my toys, everything. The clothes she was wearing were the only things she took with her. She'd even have burned his house —"

"My god!" I exclaim.

"Sabina blurted it all out once, years later, only because she was completely stoned. The day after she told us she tried to convince us she'd lied to us. She never again got stoned after that. Jose didn't know any of this had happened at the time: he only knew that Sabina had decided to move into the garage with him, Ted and

Tissie. She hasn't once seen Alberts since then, Sabina was calmer the day after she moved out of Alberts' house, when she visited you. She went to tell you Ron was dead and that was all she intended to tell you. She thought you ought to know. She probably hadn't paid much attention to what Debbie had said about you. It was Jose who heard that."

I beg Tina. "Would you mind being a little more coherent? I know you can do it."

Tina is offended. "You don't have to be sarcastic! This is the first time I've ever pieced the whole story together from the bits and snatches dropped by you, Sabina and Jose. I've never before realized what all those pieces added up to."

I try to apologize, "I didn't mean to be sarcastic; I got lost, that's all."

Tina turns to Sabina and asks. "Why don't you tell her? You were there too. I only know these things at second hand."

Sabina says, "Just you go ahead, Tina, you're doing fine."

"Don't you be sarcastic too," Tina tells her. "I'm sorry it's so confusing, Sophia. It's awfully late. Why don't you get Sabina to tell you these things some other time?"

I object. "You told me those were precisely the things that didn't matter to her. Besides, I want to hear it now and from you. Sabina would only confuse me even more."

Tina says, "I'll try to tell it in order. Sabina already told you Debbie had gone to look for Alberts. That happened the day before Sabina visited you at the university co-op. Debbie was drunk and collapsed on the couch. Sabina ran to get Jose. She wanted to get Debbie out of Alberts' house before he returned. She couldn't do that alone. She got Jose to help her drag Debbie to Jose's car and drive her home. They both sat by her bed while she slept for several hours. She was relatively sober when she woke up; Jose gave her coffee. Pointing her finger at Sabina, Debbie said to Jose: 'Keep away from that snake, kid. She'll stab you in the back.' Jose asked what Sabina had done. That's when Debbie blurted out the whole story. Her finger hadn't been pointed at Sabina but at you."

I start to feel sick.

Tina continues, "She thought Sabina was the girl Tom Matthews had tried to shoot that night Ron tried to take you to his room —"

"She didn't see me that night; Debbie and I didn't meet until Ron's trial," I tell Tina. "But Lem introduced me to her at the trial; she couldn't have thought Sabina and I were the same person since we were both at the trial."

"She didn't know you had anything to do with Ron when she saw you at the trial," Tina tells me.

"What story did she blurt out?" I ask Tina.

"When Jose asked her what she had against Sabina, Debbie said she'd visited Ron in reform school after the trial. Ron told her that as soon as he got out he'd get even with Matthews. Debbie said she didn't blame Ron because Tom Matthews was a bastard who'd jailed his own son. Ron told her he wasn't going to get even with him about that; he had expected that. He wanted to get even with Matthews for breaking up Ron's relationship with his girl. Ron told Debbie that when Matthews tried to shoot you he had scared the shit out of you and you had changed as a result, you had become afraid of Ron."

"If Ron said that he was lying to himself," I tell Tina. "Our relationship was already over when Matthews threatened us with his gun. Ron met Sabina the very next day —"

Sabina, trying to imitate Ron, says, "Oh shit. Sabina, you know it's Sophie I want, but she thinks I'm someone else, someone she must have known someplace else —"

"When did he tell you that?" I ask Sabina.

"A week after he moved in with me," she says.

"So soon after the car wreck!" I exclaim. I turn to Tina and ask her, "Is that true?"

"Now how in the world would I know that, Sophia?"

"You seem to know everything else!"

Tina says, "I know that when Sabina and Jose got Ron the day he was released from reform school —"

I interrupt, "He asked why I wasn't there. I already know that."

Sabina says, "Right after his release from reform school —"

" — you and Ron got me up at midnight," I interrupt again. "Ron was as talkative as a mummy."

"He talked to you," Sabina says.

"You mean at the beginning?" I ask. "I tried to joke with him."

"What did you say?" Sabina asks.

"Just trivialities, " I say. "I reminded him of our first meeting."

"Your words?" she asks.

"I said I'd meet him any time," I admit.

"You said that to him?" Tina asks. "Jose was right! You really did dangle a string in front of him. Jose said that before and after they drove off with Matthews' car Ron kept mumbling, 'She'll meet me any time.'"

"I couldn't have joined him in the air force!" I exclaim.

"Ron didn't mean the air force," Tina tells me. "He thought the garage idea would appeal to you. If it didn't he was ready to leave the city with you after Matthews' car was stolen."

"Leave and do what?" I ask.

"Go traveling, stealing and camping, I suppose," she says.

"He was crazy! I'd never have agreed to that!" I exclaim.

Tina says, "That's what Sabina told Ron. She told him he was crazy, that you were set on becoming a professor."

I bite my lip until it bleeds. Would I have joined Ron if I had known?

"Sabina told Ron you'd gladly meet him any time but not any place; she told him you'd meet him in college," Tina adds. "And Ron must have known Sabina was right. That's why he joined the air force."

"What do you mean, 'that's why he joined the air force'?" I ask her. "Couldn't he have done thousands of other things? Did he have to become a killer for the state?"

"Maybe he thought he'd communicate something to you by doing that," Tina says.

"Are you suggesting he joined the air force because he knew I'd hate him for it?" I ask her.

"I don't know," she answers; "Ask Sabina."

Sabina says, "Revenge was always important to him."

Tina continues, "I was telling you what Debbie told Jose after he asked her what she had against Sabina. She told about her conversation with Ron in reform school. Then she got out of bed and showed Jose a letter she had gotten from Ron only a few months before he was killed. Jose kept the letter. Once I saw him reading it and crying. I saw the letter. It said, 'Dear mom, I didn't want you to think I came out here because of you, or even because of the old man. All that got balanced out. I came out here to balance out some other things that had nothing to do with you. But I can't go through with what they're doing out here. Your loving son, Ron.'"

"He didn't kill himself!" I exclaim.

"Several months later Debbie was informed that he was missing in action," Tina tells me.

"Why?" I ask.

"Do you want me to repeat his letter?" Tina asks. "I know it by heart."

"I don't understand!"

"Do you want to?" she asks.

No, I suppose I don't want to understand that Ron killed himself because I was wedded to my past experience, to you, to pedagogy, to everything you now dismiss as illusions. Would it really have made any difference if I'd known that I could have saved Ron's life by ceasing to be what I was? I didn't answer Tina's question.

It was morning when our discussion ended. Tina and Luisa went to work. Sabina and I went to sleep. I got up in time to go to my evening class. We haven't discussed the subject since. Our lives have reverted to normal. I still can't answer Tina's question. Can you? It was your letter that gave rise to that systematic dissection of my life's choices. Your letter makes it all sound so simple. In your view I could have chosen to be a genuine rebel like Ron and instead I chose to make myself a pedagogue. By choosing what I did, I led Ron to commit suicide.

But is it really so simple? Apparently even Ron couldn't put all the blame on me. He tried to blame Tom Matthews for creating the gap between us. He tried to convince himself that if Matthews hadn't tried to shoot me I would have been delighted to share his individual acts of rebellion while we traveled, stole and camped. Yet

Ron knew perfectly well that my fear of his father wasn't what separated me from Ron. If he placed the blame on Tom Matthews it was because he knew that the blame lay somewhere outside of me. He knew that I couldn't have gone stealing and camping with him, that our life together would have been a miserable attempt to adapt to the margins of society. He must have known that he didn't kill himself because of me but because there was no room in this society for someone like Ron. He was a romantic with an unattainable goal. He made me the symbol of the goal. He became aware that he would never reach that goal. That was why he committed suicide.

What was his goal? Maybe it was the goal of a genuine rebel: to live freely, rejecting the constraints of society. But you know perfectly well that this goal can only be realized by all human beings at once, or by none. It can't be reached by an individual. What you call individual acts of rebellion quickly turn into their opposites. Individual thefts aren't acts of rebellion but forms of adaptation to private property. If you thought they were more than that why didn't you steal and hide when you were first released from prison, why did you look up the Sedlaks, why did you get a job? When workers appropriate the productive forces, they don't steal them from former owners but take what's theirs: the former owners are the thieves. By stealing we accept the legitimacy of the owners and by fleeing we accept the legitimacy of the armed force with which they protect their ownership.

It's easy to romanticize Ron precisely because he was such a romantic. But the daily reality isn't romantic at all. You wait for your chance and you pounce. That's stimulating because it's a dare, a challenge. If you aren't thrown into jail it's a victory. Then you wait for another chance. This time Ron might have to take an enormous risk, next time he might have to send me out as a lure. Sabina can tell you all about the chances you take. And at that point we're right back where we started before we raised the question of rebellion. At that point we're right back to the students in my "community college" class: they no longer want to sell themselves as mere workers, namely as low-quality merchandise, and to deal with that problem they're repairing and painting themselves so as to sell themselves at a higher price. At that point we're back to George Alberts, whose choices never entered within my spectrum, whose life I've always regarded as the opposite of what I wanted mine to be.

You, Sabina and Tina have forced me to reexamine my past. I still embrace my own choice. Call it pedagogy if you like. But please don't call it politics. If Marc and Adrian are successful politicians now it's not because they realized the aspirations we once shared but because they betrayed those aspirations. I was surprised and disappointed to learn about them. I can't quite believe they were capable of such a turnabout. But you can't use them as proof that every "pedagogical" rebel aspires to a government post. Of the friends I made on the college newspaper, every single one remained some kind of social outcast and rebel for as long as I kept track of them. At most you can say we were ludicrous Don Quixotes, that our pens and typewriters were ridiculously inadequate weapons with which to fight the battles we threw ourselves into. But the giants we confronted were real. We tried to cope with some socially meaningful reality. Among the alternatives available to me, only the one I chose enabled me to engage in activity in any way similar to the strike you've just experienced in the plant where I first learned about such activity.

Please tell me more about yourself and the exciting events around you, and less about me.

And do, please, give Jasna my greetings, and Luisa's as well.

Love, *Sophia.*

Yarostan's fourth letter

Dear Sophia,
    The arrival of your letter coincided with Jasna Zbrkova's first visit to our house. Jasna, Mirna and I read your letter simultaneously; each of us waited anxiously for the others to finish a page and pass it on. Each of us was fascinated, surprised, disappointed and angered by your account.

My situation has changed considerably since I last wrote you. I've gone back to work at the carton plant. As a result Yara now does most of the housework as well as the cooking. On the day your letter came Jasna helped Yara prepare a surprise banquet for Mirna and me, to celebrate a victorious "strike" that had just taken place at their school.

When Jasna started to read your letter she exclaimed, "They remember me!" She was flattered. But the more she read the more confused she became. "I had never known what had happened to Sophia and Luisa after they were arrested twenty years ago, and I can't understand this argument she describes; were they released before their terms were over?" Jasna asked me. I told her you and Luisa had spent only two days in jail and she was as stunned as I had been. "Two days! Even I was imprisoned for a year, and I didn't have a notion of what I was doing!" Please understand, Sophia, that our astonishment about this fact is only natural; after all, Jasna spent a year in prison and I spent four. Luisa is extremely unfair when she interprets my references to George Alberts as accusations. I'm not accusing. I'm simply very curious about the fact that George Alberts managed to have both of you released after only two days in jail. What power did Alberts have to arrange your release?

One of the comments Jasna made while reading the rest of your letter was, "What a strange world that must be. I can't imagine what I would have done there." When she finished reading the letter she said, "Sophia and Luisa don't seem to have any idea what happened here after they left."

We were all bothered by what Jasna called your strange world. The whole system of alternatives and choices you describe seems strange and unreal. The choices you say you faced are incomprehensible to me. Yet these choices seem to be the source of your attitude toward me, toward people you knew twenty years ago and toward the pedagogues who were your university friends. You say that at one point in your life you faced a choice between Luisa, Ron and the university, and you chose the university. You say you rejected Luisa's life, the life of a wage worker, a life of boredom without any prospects, sustained only by the dream that wage labor will soon end. You've eliminated some of the contradictions and anachronisms. That leaves the part of Luisa's life that consists of daily wage labor. In what sense have you rejected this? Wage labor is still the condition for your physical survival. In fact you admit that the evening classes you teach are sold activity in the same sense as Luisa's factory work. Something is wrong with your description of your alternatives. You didn't reject Ron's actual life but your picture of his life. You made this clear by describing Tina's and Sabina's views of him in addition to yours. From them, and also from your earlier letters, I got a view of an individual who uncompromisingly rejected repressive relations and tried to overcome them, even if his attempts seem childish and directionless. You depict an individual who didn't want to overcome constraints, who wanted to adapt to repression and derive personal benefit from it, and after this misleading description you tell us you chose to live your life among journalists. You chose to spend your life among people I consider opportunists, and in your letter you identified those journalists with people we knew twenty years ago in the carton plant. You made that identification, not I. It's ironic that the arrival of your letter coincided with Jasna's visit. After our banquet Jasna gave us detailed accounts of the people you've come to consider your models. Most of the people we used to know happen to be people who've been willing to sell, not only the motion of their limbs, but their will and their consciousness, for a wage; I'd call them "opportunists."

Before telling you what we learned from Jasna, I'd like to try to describe two events which made Jasna's narrative particularly significant to me: the first is my recent return to work and the second is Zdenek Tobarkin's visit a few days before Jasna's. In the context of these events Jasna's account made me realize that you and I experience two completely different worlds. It's not clear to me what place I occupy in your world but it's becoming clear to me what place you occupy in mine: it's the same place you and I occupied twenty years ago during our activity in the carton plant. But during those twenty years the carton plant changed and I changed. I've come to realize that my Life was derailed precisely at the intersection which you consider the fulfillment of your life. I flirted with your world much the same way as Tina accused you of having flirted with Ron's world. In this respect at least I'm not comparable to Ron. He never accompanied you into your world; it was you who intruded into his. Unlike Ron, I did enter into your world: Luisa introduced me into it. Today I view that experience as alien to me; my life had veered off its course. Thanks to my encounters during my first prison term with individuals like Manuel and Zdenek I eventually woke up and realized I was heading toward my destruction as a human being. Today I'm ashamed of the fact that I once took part in that type of activity. My correspondence with you is forcing me to deal with that moment of my life.

A few days after I sent you my previous letter I accepted the "invitation" of the workers at the carton plant. I got my old job back. This "invitation" is a direct result of the ferment that's taking place here. Before the political police was suspended two months ago I was unemployable and as a result when I was released from prison Mirna merely acquired another burden to support with her job at the clothing factory. Of course I helped prepare meals, clean the house and fetch the groceries while Mirna was at work and Yara in school, but this didn't ease Mirna's burden significantly. My unemployment pension didn't pay for even a quarter of the food I myself consumed. The invitation extended to me by the workers in the carton plant isn't only flattering but is also a solution to a pressing need.

A few days ago I brought home my first weekly wage, which was twice as large as Mirna's despite the fact that she's been working at the clothing factory for thirteen years. We immediately had a discussion almost identical to one we'd had several years ago. I suggested she could finally quit her job. Mirna emphatically said she wouldn't dream of quitting. "It's only thanks to my job that Yara and I survived during all those years you were in prison and I don't intend to throw that income away just because our situation during one week has been different. The last time you made that suggestion you were jailed a few days later." To Mirna our present situation is an abnormal state of affairs and she's convinced it will only be temporary; prison and poverty is our normal state of affairs.

My task at the carton plant is the same as it was twenty years ago when I worked with Luisa and met you. I operate a newer model of the press that prints labels on cartons; the old press must at last have given out. There were openings for several other tasks. All the openings have been created by the departure of police agents, or rather of workers who were paid by the police to spy on other workers. I could have chosen another task. But there was no real reason to choose between the tasks since they all require one and the same act: the exchange of my living time for a wage. Since all the tasks in question required the same hours and paid the same wages, my choice between them could only be whimsical. It was on the basis of whims that I chose. One of my whims was to familiarize myself with a task I had never performed before.

Another whim was to return to the machine I had operated at the time of your life's key experience. I chose in favor of the second whim, thinking that the familiarity of my motions and my surroundings would remind me of the experiences and the people you've carried in your head for the past twenty years.

The strike I described in my last letter ended soon after I wrote you. It ended with a compromise. The plant's manager agreed to accept a union representative elected by the workers, who in turn dropped their demand to elect a different union representative each month as well as their original demand to rotate the post among all the workers in alphabetical order. I was disappointed by their compromise with the manager. I argued that such a partial victory was actually a defeat because compromising with the manager meant recognizing the legitimacy and authority of the management. Several workers said they agreed but argued that in conditions of the present ferment, when much more would become possible, it was necessary to proceed with caution since otherwise we might cause the field of possibilities to close prematurely. I argued that caution was the first step toward defeat and expressed the view that the manager should have been ousted along with the union representative, that both posts should be rotated alphabetically or eliminated altogether, and that we should examine our field of possibilities only after this much had been accomplished. I was told that a position like mine had been defended and that the overwhelming majority had been opposed to it. Several workers told me the view of the majority: "It is essential to see what other workers do in other factories, to wait and see if they succeed, and then to proceed along similar lines; if we run ahead of all the rest we'll soon be all alone, and by ourselves we won't get much further." I disagree with this attitude but during these days such waiting isn't an altogether passive activity. Ever since I've returned to work I've become intensely aware of changes taking place all around me, not only at the factory but also at home, in other plants, in the streets of the city. I have to admit that I've come to feel the same mixture of daring and caution expressed by the workers at the carton plant. "Daring" and "caution" are such miserable words. My sensitivity to words comes mainly from Zdenek Tobarkin. Already when I knew him in prison he understood the ways in which language was used to deform reality. He has helped me understand that words can't communicate realities like the ones we're currently experiencing here. Words can only refer to things or conditions which have a certain degree of permanence or which at least recur periodically. There can be no words to describe a condition which never existed before, which changes from one moment to the next and which has no known stages or outcome. Even the word "revolution" is miserable because it conveys nothing more than a summary of past events known as revolutions, events which have nothing in common with the present.

What I'm experiencing can't be expressed by words like "daring and caution." The condition I'm describing isn't inexpressible; it isn't a mystical experience. It's an experience shared by thousands of people who are in fact expressing themselves, many for the first time in their lives. But the communication has not been taking place only through words. The words acquire their meanings from motions, acts and steps. The words by themselves only refer to other conditions, earlier periods, and even when they're used in the context of the present ferment they suggest faulty analogies to earlier conditions. What I mean by "daring" is a readiness to walk into terrain which none of us explored before. What I mean by "caution" is the perception that our ability to approach this terrain grows only to the extent that all those like us approach it with equal daring. We're reaching for a field of possibilities that can be reached only if we move together as we've never moved before; we proceed with caution because those who move too far ahead will be caught without a lifeline to the rest. What I think is taking place around me is an advance consisting of small steps taken by all simultaneously. Each small step creates the conditions for taking the next. Any move that prevents the continued advance of all cuts off the possibility of further advance by any. All around me human beings are attempting to come to life as human beings, as universal individuals, as species beings, each advancing with all and all with each.

One day twenty years ago, while I was running the same machine at the same plant, I thought the epoch of wage labor had suddenly come to an end. I responded by formulating slogans, printing them on signs, and displaying the signs. During the past week I've experienced a far greater tumult but I've felt no impulse to print or carry signs with slogans. I'm not the same person I was twenty years ago, the person you knew. My commitment to slogans, words, programs, abstractions on signs, was a commitment to death. Twenty years ago I was the victim of a mystification. I began with vague yearnings for free activity; I began with a longing for freely chosen projects carried out within a community that made the projects possible and appreciated them. But instead of taking steps with those around me to realize my desires, I transformed my desires into what seemed to be the first step toward their realization, namely into a program of action. But by this transformation I negated my real desires; I replaced them with ideas, with words, with notions in my brain. Instead of a life I had a credo. Instead of taking steps with other people toward real projects carried out during our living moments of time, I took steps to convert other people to my credo, my religion, my words. I replaced the concrete practical activity of the whole human being with merely mental activity, with activity that took place inside my mind, with combinations of written letters or spoken sounds, namely with non-activity. I inverted my urge to live and turned it into its opposite. My desire for liberated activity became a belief in liberated activity. My longing for a human community was replaced by a longing for a community of believers, a religious community, a community of converts to my credo. And instead of finding myself among living, independent and creative individuals, I found myself in the frock of a priest in the midst of a flock. It has taken me twenty years to realize that I had been a priest — even if a heretical one — of what must surely be humanity's last religion, that religion of liberation from the illusions of religion, that religion which was used by a group of pedagogues to establish unprecedented power over populations who had desired, not the words of the credo, but the world those words seemed to suggest.

Today like twenty years ago we're daily bombarded with slogans and programs, with platforms and reforms, with revolutions ever so carefully worked out on paper by those who live in paper worlds. But today I'm not among those printing or carrying posters with slogans nor among those arguing in defense of one or another platform. In the framework of your world I've joined the ranks of the inarticulate. I can't formulate either my goals or my means. I can tell you neither where I'm going nor how I'll get there. Yet I feel more vibrant, more alive, than I felt when I thought I knew my direction and my destination because I had words for them. I feel alive precisely because I don't know what the next moment will bring. Time has once again become a dimension that reveals possibilities and has ceased to be a dreary schedule of expected events. I came to life when the events I had learned to expect suddenly stopped recurring. Only a few months ago Yara took part in a completely unexpected demonstration. A few weeks ago workers invited me to join them. A week ago those workers ousted their union representative. This week we elected one from among ourselves to replace the ousted official. Next week we may learn that the workers of a neighboring factory have started tearing down the factory walls. And a month from now we might invite our neighbors, especially the children, to our factory to begin dismantling the machinery into as many pieces as Sabina's friend the car thief dismantled a car. At that point we might begin an altogether different life on a terrain from which every trace of our former activity has been removed. A human life might begin, inhibited by no barrier external to the developing individual. The realization of one's potentialities would then be accompanied by the enjoyment of the infinite potentialities realized by all those around one. Such a prospect cannot be the program of an individual or a group, and it cannot be articulated. It is not a religion to which people are to be converted. It is a practice which I and those around me are trying to invent.

Although I sense that we're moving, I still perform the familiar motions at my press, I go home after work and I return to work the following morning. The contradiction makes me tense. It's a tension I share with all those around me. At any moment the regularity might end and we'll plunge forward and cross a frontier we can't see today. Our willingness to cross that frontier is what I called "daring." But there's also "caution." There's apprehension. My heart beats faster and I feel dizzy and nauseated; the anticipation is accompanied by a certain fear. I know and those around me know that the conditions which open up a possibility for a new life also give rise to forces which negate life. Human life itself has this double character. Growth takes place through cell division, through the realization of the potentialities carried within each cell. Yet the ugliest form of death also takes place through cell division. Such death is also a growth, one that annihilates potentiality and replaces living cells with monstrosities. All around me people are trying to move to a ground on which the specific potentialities of each individual can develop, like plants seeking sunlight and moisture. And life-negating forces are accompanying every move we make. Just as the power of one cell to split into two is the power that turns against the further division of living cells, so the power that enables us to move together out of slavery to a terrain where the free development of each individual becomes possible is the power that turns against our ability to move at all. The power to conceptualize and communicate, the power that enables us to move together as a community, is the very power that turns against us and deprives us of community. The reality we strive to reach comes back to us several times a day in the form of a concept, a substanceless unreal thing, a mere combination of words. I think that up to now we've steered clear of these traps; I think we're still alive. But the traps are heavily camouflaged and we still aren't very practiced in recognizing them. At any moment, instead of taking another step forward, we might again blindly confuse the concept with the reality and again waste ourselves reaching out for nothing. If that should happen once again then our present ferment will again give rise to that negative cell division, that deformed development of monstrosities which exterminate our real desires. If we recoil from leaping into the unknown and again take refuge in the concept, we'll plunge right back to our starting point. The deadliest of the traps is being set by those who are transforming the leap into a phrase, by those who are naming our destination and transforming our real desires into their political program. If we again recoil from real motion and development and replace it with the motion and development of concepts in the heads of priests, we'll only produce another religion with its church and its priests. We would again cease to be the agents of our own struggle; our desires would again become disembodied concepts carried in the heads of intellectuals.

Politics: that's the religion of today, that's the cancer that annihilates every possibility of community and puts an end to every period of ferment. This deformity divides and multiplies precisely during periods of ferment. Because it's unnatural it outruns our natural development of capacities. It plants itself at all intersections long before we reach them. Political militants are its missionaries. Committed intellectuals are its priests. The state is its church. Like all religions it transforms the human community into a herd. Its agents, the organizers and pedagogues, are the spiritual leaders of flocks of animals. It grows, like its biological analogue, inside the very body it attacks. It reproduces itself within the living members of the human community, extinguishing them as living beings, annihilating the very possibility of community. Its instruments are the entire armory of life-destroying gadgets devised by technology, everything that can serve to police a herd, from bombs to walkie-talkies, including the newspapers that proliferate the words and the loudspeakers that magnify the voices of the high priests. Contrary to what you think, I don't see your newspaper activity as similar to the ferment surrounding me but as activity which can only annihilate the ferment.

We all carry the possibility as well as the negation within ourselves. At work we listen to the radio all day. Even though each of us is nervously anticipating our next concrete step, we nevertheless feel exhilarated when the words of a politician seem to express the exact nature of the step we long to take. We applaud phrases like "new democracy" or "new socialism" or "genuine workers councils." We walk into the politicians' traps like newborn children who have learned nothing from countless previous generations. While applauding the speaker or praising the writer we momentarily forget that we haven't been longing for a new phrase but for a new life;

we forget that we've only just begun to explore a new possibility, the possibility of creating the world ourselves. When we applaud we again become the lifeless globs of organic matter we've been nearly every moment of our normal lives. We cheer the pedants and we're again helpless, like the spectators of a sporting match rooting for a team. We're hypnotized by the bouts and struggles among the concepts; we passively admire reflections of our own real longings and we passively admire the politicians who return our longings to us in the form of images.

That's why we feel tense. I'm convinced that the present ferment carries real possibilities for life. But I'm also aware that every time we take a step we're surrounded by the ideological birds of prey who feed on our possibilities, fill themselves with concepts of our desires and reenslave us with beautiful combinations of words which seem to depict the world we failed to realize.

A few days before Jasna's visit I had a very stimulating discussion with Zdenek Tobarkin. When I first met Zdenek, during my first prison term, he was intensely interested in everything I told him about the workers' struggle with which Luisa had familiarized me, the struggle in which she, Manuel, Titus Zabran and George Alberts took part when you were two years old. When Zdenek visited us a few days ago he made several comparisons to the earlier struggle which have helped me understand some characteristics of the present situation. I told Zdenek that in recent years I had completely discarded Luisa's view of that struggle, the view I had expressed when Zdenek and I were in prison together. I summarized Manuel's analysis of those events.

Zdenek said he had long suspected that something like Manuel's analysis had been missing from my earlier accounts. "I found your earlier stories exciting because they justified my attachment to the union," he told me. "But when I began to reexamine my commitment I also became suspicious of your account. The union you described so enthusiastically was led by politicians. Those politicians probably expressed the urges of workers more accurately than any previous group of politicians, if words can ever express real urges accurately. Workers accepted the politicians as their spokesmen. This is why the workers were defeated on the day after their victory. This is why the working population came to life only for a day, the day of the rising against the generals. At the very moment of victory the union consolidated the power it had already established over the workers. The working people were reenslaved before they had the time to realize that for twenty-four hours they had begun to live without chains." Zdenek contrasted that situation with the ferment surrounding us here today. "Our present situation is unique. When the ferment began, all politicians, organized intellectuals and bureaucrats of liberation were completely discredited." He also contrasted the origins of the present ferment to the origins of the earlier rising. "We weren't suddenly attacked by the military and consequently we didn't have to concentrate all our energy on a single act of self-defense. We've had time to explore new ground, to consider alternatives, to move ahead slowly, absorbing the significance of each step. We weren't attacked during one day but over a period of twenty years. Those who attacked us weren't army generals but every species of representative of the working class, of revolution, of liberation, of self-determination that has been coughed up by history. Consequently, although our steps have been small and undramatic, we've moved on our own and not under the hegemony of politicians. Instead of being attacked, we were suddenly let free; the repressive power of all representatives was suddenly suspended. Unlike the workers who were attacked, we've had a chance to rise and stretch, to test the abilities of our unused limbs and to explore our ability to act communally. We haven't moved far, but we've moved on our own."

I expressed misgivings about the rate at which we were moving and about the fact that the politicians were moving much faster than the rest of the population. Zdenek brushed my arguments aside. "You don't seem to realize that this is one of the few times in all history when a population has moved without politicians. I don't want to say the recuperators are absent. You're perfectly right. They're all around us. Every day a new group of aspiring bureaucrats presents a new program in the press and on the radio. Every day a new speaker tours the factories, schools and meeting houses. Yes, they're omnipresent. But they're not omnipotent. That's why there's a new program and a new speaker every day. Not a single group among them has established its hegemony over the population. People haven't been infected by a single politician's credo. The politicians are moving fast, but the people are staying clear of them. The steps being taken may be small, but they're real, they're taking place in this concrete world and not in an organization's program. The politicians are all discredited. Due to the ideological character of the regime we've experienced for the past twenty years, ideologists and theorists as such, politics as such have been discredited. Don't exaggerate the applause speakers are getting. There's nothing wrong with applauding a good speech. The applause only expresses appreciation for the speaker's talent as a speaker. The fact that people applaud doesn't mean they're being hypnotized."

I told Zdenek that only the recognizable politicians of the old regime have been discredited. I said that all types of politicians with a "new face" have been transforming the present ferment into their profession and that at least the workers at my plant were not altogether hostile to such "new" politicians. I admitted that as yet there were no large numbers of people repeating the formulas of any politician but I said I didn't exclude the possibility that one of the "new faces" would "realize our goals" by installing himself in the state apparatus.

Zdenek thought I was unjustifiably pessimistic. "You're too much of a Cassandra," he told me. "It's of course true that only one variant of the theory of the proletariat reigned supreme during the past twenty years. But I'm convinced that the rule of this variant discredited all the variants of the theory of the proletariat, from the tyrannical variant to the self-determined variant. Today everyone sees through the absolute, omniscient and omnipotent embodiment of the proletariat. Maybe some people aren't as overtly hostile to the other versions because

they haven't had to live under them, but no one can help recognizing them as varia-
tions on the same theme. Your view is extremely pessimistic. If humanity had to
experience every single variant of representation before it rejected all of them, it
would never emerge from its morass. I think you're wrong. I think the experience
with one variant has taught us lessons about all of them. I think humanity is finally
rejecting what has always been an impossible project, the project of representation.
The present proliferation of major and minor pharaohs around the world is the
final and ludicrous stage of that impossible project. My life can't be lived as a representation; my representative can't realize my aspirations, take my steps or engage
in my actions. The pharaohs are the final and definitive proof of the impossibility
of representation. I think we've all finally learned what took me so long to learn,
namely that I'm robbed of my enjoyment if my representative enjoys himself for
me, that my hunger remains when he eats for me, that I don't express myself when
he speaks for me, that my mind and my imagination stagnate when he thinks for
me and decides for me, that I lose my life when he lives for me."

I agreed with Zdenek but I still had misgivings. I told him that he had gotten
his insights from very specific experiences which had not been shared by many
people, that the mystifications which he had seen through were not necessarily as
transparent to everyone else.

"What are you suggesting?" he asked. "That I go out into the streets like a
prophet and communicate my insights about the danger of prophets? Do you
remember the former politician with whom I argued at the prisoners' club — the
one who emphasized the need for organizational resources and publishing activity? We would once again reconstitute a group with a theory and a publication,
we would once again replace the concrete activity of thousands of people with the
image of that activity communicated in words by our publication and our group.
I've had specific experiences and so have you, but these experiences are specific to
our whole historical period. If I'm able to draw conclusions from them so can all
my contemporaries. I can't understand my experiences any other way. If I've had
experiences no one else has had then I can't hope to communicate with anyone.
One human being can no more demystify another than eat for another. But I
haven't had experiences no one else had. The concrete activities of those around me
prove this to me, just as my activities surely communicate the experiences I've had.
Organizational resources and publications would only separate me from those with
whom I want to communicate."

I feel that Zdenek is right. The strike that recently took place at the carton
plant showed me that those workers must have had experiences and drawn conclusions similar to mine. Their concrete act communicated this to me. They didn't
carry signs nor proclaim a program nor engage in any of the activities which seem
so dear to you. They simply removed the local representatives of the repressive
apparatus, directly, without a platform, without representatives. That done, we're
ready to take our next concrete step. The politicians have been unmasked, not only

for Zdenek and me, but for all of us. At the plant we listen to political speeches broadcast by the radio but we don't act on them; we watch for the next step people like us will take elsewhere.

I think Zdenek is also right in considering the present ferment in many ways more profound than the uprising Luisa and Manuel taught me about. In that earlier event repressed and self-repressed human beings suddenly came to life — but for a period that lasted less than twenty-four hours. Here the concrete steps have been small and undramatic but those who came to life are still living. Can this ferment continue to spread without being caught in the webs of the politicians? Can we get past the spokesmen, coordinators and organizers who extinguished the earlier struggle? My first impulse is to doubt it. So many people have never before become independent without provoking the concentrated resentment of those who wanted to rule over them. Such "directionless" and "spontaneous" activity has never before held its own against the blows dealt against it by organizational militants and their infallible leaders. Manuel and Luisa, in their descriptions of the events they both experienced, concur on one and only one detail: on the day when the generals attacked, the people ran into the streets on their own; the "leaders" ran behind and placed themselves on the front lines so as not to "lose" their followers. For an instant it was the influential militants who were lost among the independent individuals whom they later claimed to have led. The first individuals at the barricades were not there under orders but on their own. Each individual formulated his or her own task, and by carrying out that task, each implemented the project of the group, which was inseparable from the projects of each individual. Each coordinated and organized, not because he or she was the official coordinator or organizer, but because one and then another was closest to the problem that needed to be coordinated and organized. Individuals who have this capacity for self-directed activity during an insurrection are in all ways identical to the individuals with whom I work in the plant, with whom I share this city, with whom I inhabit this globe. Individuals who have such capacities during twenty-four hours have the capacity to appropriate human life and make it a project of the living.

I've tried to give you some idea of the ferment which surrounds me. I've tried to describe my hopes as well as my apprehensions, and I've summarized Zdenek's view of the prospects of this activity. It's perfectly clear to me that this activity has nothing in common with the journalistic activity to which you compared it. The type of activity which you chose has much in common with the activity of the politicians who lecture to us on the radio and in the newspapers; it has nothing in common with the actions and apprehensions of the people with whom I work in the carton plant. I resent the fact that you compare the ferment around me with your academic and journalistic activities. I think the two projects are not only different from each other but also hostile to each other: the projects you've chosen can only take place if my present project fails. That's why I can't recognize myself in your choices or in your enthusiasms. I can understand the world you describe, the world in which you've so carefully steered toward your chosen alternative, only because I once stepped into that world. But I stepped out of that world long ago. I think you're right when you compare your chosen activities to those of the people we knew twenty years ago. Jasna described those people to us on the very day your letter came. During these past twenty years I've changed and you haven't. You've retained the commitments we shared twenty years ago. Jasna's account of the individuals you remember so fondly makes it clear to me that your chosen activities have a great deal in common with theirs, not with mine. After the luxurious meal she and Yara had prepared to celebrate the "victory" at their school, Jasna told us everything she knew about the present activities of those individuals.

Jasna and Yara were waiting for me when I returned home from my third day of work. Jasna was anxious to read your letter, but Yara couldn't wait to tell me about the day's events. It's amazing how quickly the ferment spreads once a population regains creative initiative. Several students, among them Yara, began a campaign to oust the assistant head of the school, the person responsible for maintaining discipline among students as well as teachers. All the students stood quietly in the halls and let the head of the school know they wouldn't enter their classrooms until the disciplinarian resigned. They were joined by every single teacher. Even the head of the school gave a speech praising their determination. Jasna said she was profoundly moved by this speech. The disciplinarian resigned after having occupied her post for twenty years. She was undoubtedly a police agent, although neither Yara nor Jasna knew if she was actually in the pay of the police.

Mirna came home soon after I did and we all read your letter. After supper Mirna asked Jasna when she had first met Jan and how long she had worked with him.

"He was hired right after the resistance," Jasna said. "We worked together for three years, three unforgettable, wonderful years."

I begged Jasna to start her story earlier, to tell us how and when she had come to work at the carton plant.

"I started working there before the war," she told us. "Among the people you knew, I was the first one there. I had just finished high school and I'd always known I'd have to find a job the day after I finished school. My parents both worked in factories. All the money they earned went to pay for the little house they had bought. I still live there. My father was a horribly bossy man. I was afraid of him. I was like a servant in the house. After I started working that changed. I went to several factories but none of them had openings for someone without any experience. When I went to Mr. Zagad's office he hired me even though I told him I didn't have experience. He was really such a decent man. I still feel sorry for him. A few months after I started work the war broke out and the city was occupied. I went to work every day and returned to my parents' home every evening. I wasn't much bothered by the war or the occupation at first. I knew something horrible had happened but I didn't understand what it was. Then one day, during the second year of the war, my father brought home a man he worked with. He explained that the man was homeless and that he'd spend the night with us. Late that night the police came to our house, broke our front door and arrested the stranger as well as my father. They insulted my mother and me for hiding a Jew. Then they took both men away in a police car. I never saw my father again. I never learned if he was shot or sent to a concentration camp. A year later a man from my mother's factory came to the house to tell me that my mother had died in an accident. I was sure she had committed suicide; she had talked about killing herself ever since my father was taken away. The war and the occupation became very meaningful to me. I hated it. I hated the occupiers because of what they had done to both my parents. But when I saw the occupiers in the streets I was deathly afraid of them. I was — I still am — afraid of every person with authority, just as I had been afraid of my father. But people with authority aren't all the same. I was never afraid of Mr. Zagad. He was decent, and I've always been grateful for that. He heard about my mother's accident and told me to leave work for two weeks with pay. He even attended my mother's funeral.

"I've never understood why it was Mr. Zagad that you and the others turned against. Maybe it was wrong for him to have so much power over others, but that can't be the reason he was removed since his successor had even greater power. But I'm running ahead. Either shortly before or shortly after my mother died, Titus Zabran was hired. He had returned from abroad just before the war started. During breaks he would tell several of us about his earlier adventures and I was hypnotized by his stories. He told about workers who had fought against a whole army, not for three days but for three years, to defend their own popular government."

I was amazed by Jasna's last statement. "Is that how Titus understood that struggle?" I asked. I had never heard Titus say anything about that struggle nor about his role in it.

"Of course I don't remember the actual stories he told me," Jasna said. "I don't think I paid too much attention anyway. Titus frightened me. I shared his hatred for the occupiers. But I was afraid of his constant talk about the need to arm and shoot. He seemed like the kind of person who would do everything he said he'd do. He reminded me of my father. I shared his hatred but not his manner. I remember that I liked Mr. Zagad a lot better. I sensed that he hated the occupiers as much as Titus or I but he didn't growl and show his teeth like a vicious dog. Whenever soldiers or inspectors came to the plant he was always courteous. He wasn't slavish, just courteous."

I interrupted Jasna to point out, "If everyone had been so courteous those occupiers would still be here."

"I know," Jasna said. "I'm just telling you what I felt at the time. After the war ended I felt that Titus had been right. Actually I got to like him even before the war ended, mainly for his knowledge. He seemed to know everything. Luisa Nachalo was another person who seemed to know everything but I disliked her when she first came to the plant. She was hired a few months after Titus."

At this point Yara had a question. "Did you say you liked him because he was smart but you disliked her because she was smart?"

Jasna laughed. "You caught me, didn't you? No, I guess I'm not being altogether truthful. I was afraid of Titus but I liked him at the same time. And I think I disliked Luisa at first because I was jealous. In a way I did dislike her because she was so smart; that was what made me jealous. I suppose I wanted to form a closer relationship with Titus but he seemed to consider me a goose, especially after Luisa started working at the plant. Next to Luisa I was a goose. She was so quick, so well informed, so brilliant with her foreign accent and her sharp tongue. I knew I'd never live up to that woman. She had been married before, already had two daughters, and had nevertheless managed to familiarize herself with everything under the sun and seemed as independent as a bird. My mother had only had one daughter and she had used me as her lifelong excuse for her abysmal ignorance. Yes, I envied Luisa. But I didn't even try to compete with her. I knew I'd only make myself more of a goose. I stopped thinking of forming a closer relationship with Titus."

I told Jasna that Titus and Luisa had merely been friends and that Luisa had lived with another man when we knew her.

"I think I knew that," Jasna said. "I dimly remember having known that, but I lied to myself. Titus took no interest in me. I was hurt. I convinced myself that he ignored me because I was no Luisa. But I didn't spend too many hours feeling sorry for myself. I read novels instead. Later on, after I dropped the idea of falling in love with Titus, I got to like Luisa. But that was only a few months before we were all separated. I've always been sorry I never had a long talk with her. We were together for such a short time."

I asked Jasna what she had done during the resistance.

"Nothing," she answered. "Absolutely nothing. During the whole last year of the war Titus had repeatedly asked me to attend meetings of the neighborhood resistance organization. Several times I promised I'd go, but when the time came to go to the meeting my whole body started shaking. I had visions of police knocking on the door and dragging me away, along with Titus and all the others, to be shot or deported to a concentration camp. During all three days of the uprising I locked myself into my house and I didn't come out again until several hours after I heard the last shot. I was deathly afraid. When it all ended I was as glad that the shooting was over as I was that the occupation was over. The following day I went back to the plant. Many of the people I had worked with had been killed by a single explosion when they were leaving the plant on the last day of the uprising. Several others had been killed in the fighting. That was when I met your brother," she told Mirna. "They were all hired at the same time: Yarostan, Vera Neis, Adrian Povrshan, Claude Tamnich, Marc Glavni."

I reminded Jasna that Marc was hired three years later.

"Three years!" she exclaimed. "I had forgotten. They were the happiest years of my life. I think I would have been content to remain on that job with those people.

You, Titus and Luisa were the most thoughtful, the most intelligent people I've known. Recently I've known mainly teachers; none of them are as well informed, as educated and perceptive as the three of you were. And your brother, Mirna, was the gentlest, warmest, most generous individual I've ever met or read about. He was the only one who never treated me as a goose. He paid attention to what I had to say even though I usually contradicted myself.

"He took me seriously even when I didn't take myself seriously. He sometimes had the most absurd ideas, like wanting to drag the machinery into the street and converting the factory into a dance hall, but he was never malicious. All his suggestions seemed like fun and I was usually the main supporter of his crazy schemes. At that time I also loved Vera and Adrian. They were so comical. I thought already then that they ought to be entertainers in a theater. I wasn't far wrong. Vera was so funny with all her stories about the crooked deals of what she called the ruling class. I was in stitches during half of every working day. I even liked that ox Claude, mainly because I felt sorry for him; he was the only person there who was dumber than I. Yes, Marc was the last. And I liked him least. He was fresh out of high school and such a clod. I can't believe what he is now. He always spoke with the self-assurance of a spoiled brat but couldn't do a thing on his own. I constantly had to show him what to do, and almost every day I repaired something he had ruined. I don't think any of those people would have been remarkable by themselves. Something strange happened during those three years. We were all deeply affected by something, perhaps by each other. I think those years made all of us what we became. I know that Vera would have quieted down and become like everyone else if Titus and Luisa hadn't continually encouraged her, and if Titus hadn't used his influence to keep her from being fired. You, Yarostan, would have been a completely different person if you hadn't met Luisa. The only one who didn't change during those years was your brother, Mirna. I think Jan was the only one of us who would have led the same life he led."

I told Jasna you considered your brief contact with that group of people the central experience in your life and asked her what she thought extraordinary about those people or that situation. Her answer gave me some insight into the life choices you've made.

"I've never in my life experienced such a turn-about, except when I was arrested," she said. "I went to college later on, but I didn't learn nearly as much as I learned during those three years. The real university I attended was the carton plant after you, Jan and the others were hired. I knew already then that none of the people in our group would spend their lives in the carton plant or in any other kind of factory work, except possibly Jan. We were simply transformed by that experience."

I asked her what she thought had happened to us during those three years.

"It's something I've never before tried to put into words," she said. "Not that it was so mysterious. When I attended college several years later I knew that none of my fellow students would ever go back to factory jobs no matter what their social background was. In the university this was simply taken for granted. In our group this wasn't ever stated but it seemed just as obvious to me. I'm surprised you're still working in a factory. I was wrong about you."

I told her I had changed and reminded her that Luisa too was still working in a factory.

"I'm not surprised about Luisa," she said. "I wouldn't have expected her to undergo the same changes. She was different. She's the one who set it all off. I don't think Titus by himself would have had such an impact. I think it was the presence of Luisa that was so explosive, that caused such profound transformations in the people around her. I wasn't the first to be affected by her. Unfortunately I was one of the last. I think you and Vera were the first. Luisa obviously didn't have the same effect on everyone. You and Vera were affected so differently. Everyone was affected differently. It wasn't only what Luisa said that affected us, although that too was exciting. I still remember the stories she told us about workers she'd known who hadn't only fought in a resistance like ours but had gone from the barricades to their factories to lock out their bosses and install their own friends in all the managerial offices. Those stories were exciting but only as topics of conversation, as stories. I heard them as fairy tales. That alone wouldn't have transformed me. What transformed us was how she acted: her manner, her behavior, her personality. Even if her stories weren't true, if workers had never done what she said they had done, Luisa made us all feel that she was determined to do exactly that, and right in our plant. From the first day she came to the plant she started asking where the materials came from, what was to be done with them in the plant, where the products were sent afterwards. Maybe she only asked those questions so as to familiarize herself with every aspect of the plant's activity, but she made us all feel we knew infinitely more about the process than Mr. Zagad; she made us feel that Mr. Zagad was superfluous and that we could run the plant much better without him. She communicated her impatience to us. With everything she said and did she seemed to be asking the rest of us what we were waiting for. She made us feel like cowards for not doing all the things that had been done by the workers she described. This had a strange effect on all of us, and first of all on you."

I admitted having been affected by Luisa the very first time I met her.

"You weren't only affected, you were completely transformed. You became just like her. I think Luisa could have left the plant a few months after you came and you would have exerted the same influence on the rest of us. You acquired the same self-assurance, the same impatience. You made us feel like cowards for not going ahead with all those schemes. You weren't her disciple but her exact replica. You gave the impression that you had actually lived all the experiences she had narrated to us, and that you were as determined as she to make them happen here. I could see you change from one day to the next. No one else was so completely transformed by Luisa. Vera was also profoundly affected, but she didn't become another Luisa. I'm convinced that it was only because of Luisa that Vera became such an entertainer, such a radio, as you used to call her. Luisa's mere presence provoked Vera. It was as if Vera felt compelled to compete with Luisa every minute of the day, as if she had to outdo Luisa in intelligence, knowledge and even self-confidence. I could almost see the changes Vera underwent. She wasn't that talkative when she first came and she did do her job. But after listening to Luisa's stories for only a month Vera started to tell her own stories. At first she bombarded us with statistics about the output for which workers were responsible and the income we were paid. She must have spent her nights rummaging through government publications and official documents so as to spend her days telling us about the financial dealings of bankers and factory owners. The statistics were appreciated by Titus but they didn't go over very well with the rest of us. We still found Luisa's observations more exciting. So Vera started collecting all kinds of anecdotes, hair-raising accounts of crooked deals. She was determined not to be outdone by Luisa. Three or four times she even told us the details of major scandals several days before the newspapers reported them. And Adrian, who had worshipped Vera since high school, became something like her straight man. Vera would make a grandiose statement and Adrian would leap in with detailed documentation. Sometimes they even acted out the scenes of a recent scandal. Do you think they'd ever have done those things in normal circumstances? I was affected too. Everything seemed so much fun, I was swept along by all the excitement. Even Marc was affected, though he was in the carton plant so briefly before we were arrested. Inept as he was in everything he did, he treated himself as someone who knew more about workers running their own plants than anyone else, even Luisa. Every other day he described a complex scheme; he figured out how people were going to supply each other with raw materials, electricity, housing and everything else under the sun. Luisa seemed to admire him for the effort he put into these schemes. I was surprised she didn't see through him. He was nothing but a conceited boy trying desperately to prove that he was better than the rest of us. He may have been intelligent, but since it was I who ran behind him repairing what he had ruined, I wasn't impressed by his abilities. Claude was affected too, but in a strange way; he had such a one-track mind. His single response to Luisa's impatience and to Vera's exposures was to want to liquidate obstacles, liquidate enemies; he even spoke of liquidating Mr. Zagad. Claude seemed to think already then that all our excitement was only a preparation for the day when our group would order him to carry out his liquidations. I don't think I knew this at the time; I must have realized it when I saw him years later. What I felt at the time was that he loomed above us like a threatening cloud. Whenever he spoke he turned our enthusiasm into something frightening. He made all our fun seem like a prelude to something horrible."

I interrupted Jasna's narrative and told her I thought she was exaggerating the magnitude of Luisa's influence. In my view it wasn't only the experiences we shared at the carton plant that made those people what they later became. The traits they exhibited when Jasna knew them must already have been integral parts of their personalities.

Jasna disagreed quite vehemently. "Without the experiences we shared in that plant none of those people would have moved in the directions in which they've moved since then. Every single one of those people would have been a factory worker today. Well, of course I can't be sure about that. But I do know that hardly any of them are factory workers today and what changed them was the time we spent together. Do you think Claude would ever have left his first factory job if something extraordinary hadn't happened to him? Of course they all came there with personality traits. That's why they all responded so differently. When I got to know Vera she boasted she'd been a troublemaker in high school during the war, she'd given speeches attacking the occupiers. But the mere ability to give speeches wasn't enough. She'd have lost this ability as soon as she was fired for giving a speech and had to find another job; if she'd gotten a job in a place where the noise drowned her out or where talk wasn't allowed, she'd have been as quiet as anyone else. She was talkative already in high school. But she became a self-assured social reformer only after she ran into Luisa. And what personality traits did Marc have? His conceit came from his having been one of the brighter students in a provincial school where over half the students missed school for several weeks every spring and fall because of farm work and every winter because of lack of transportation. His conceit would have been knocked out of him by any normal group of city workers who were as educated as he was. If Luisa hadn't considered him such a genius he'd never have dreamed of going to the university and he'd never have thought himself able to occupy the posts he occupies today. When Marc started to climb to those high posts it became clear to me what kind of people occupy them. Nor would Adrian have gotten where he is now on his own. He merely drifted in the direction the rest took, which is all I've ever done. Neither Adrian nor I would ever have drifted out of the factory if we hadn't been able to drift along with the others."

Mirna asked why her brother had remained unaffected by Luisa and by all the excitement we had shared.

"Jan wasn't like the rest of us," Jasna said. "Neither was Titus. It's funny. I've seen much more of Titus than of any of the others. I've known him since the war and I saw him frequently during the past twenty years. But I don't understand him at all as well as I understand the others. I never really got to know him. If he took part in discussions at all, it was only to advise others to be patient. After his first year at the plant, he no longer said anything about the experiences he had shared with Luisa. I don't suppose he changed during those years any more than Jan did. But I don't know to what extent Luisa affected him before I met him. I do know that Jan wasn't affected by Luisa. He opposed Luisa the very first day he came to the plant. He ridiculed her. He said that if he had been one of the workers who had ousted a plant's owners and managers he couldn't imagine why in the world he would return to the plant the next day unless he had some personal use for one of the machines in the plant. He said he couldn't imagine a situation in which workers ousted all social authorities and then continued doing what they had done before. He even accused Luisa of lying. He said no worker he'd ever known would return to work if he no longer had to. Much as I admired Luisa, I was convinced by Jan every time he argued with her. If Jan had had his way none of us would have gone back to the plant the day after Mr. Zagad was thrown out. Or we'd have gone back only to throw out Mr. Zagad's machinery. Of course if we'd done what Jan wanted we'd have been arrested even sooner than we were."

"Since you didn't do any of those things, why were you all arrested?" Mirna asked.

"Didn't you know?" Jasna asked. "I figured that out — or rather, it was explained to me during my year in prison. Every one of our signs was different from the official signs. Yarostan, Luisa and sometimes Vera argued all night long to make our signs different. Jan had absolutely nothing to do with that. He even refused to take part in the printing and distribution of our signs after Mr. Zagad was ousted. He grumbled that by continuing to work inside those factory walls without tearing them down we were only imprisoning ourselves. And he was right."

"You were arrested because your signs were different?" Yara asked.

"And I was so stupid I didn't know that at the time," Jasna said. "During one of my first days in prison, in the dining hall, a woman asked me why I'd been arrested. I honestly told her I didn't know. The investigator's questions had been totally incomprehensible to me and I didn't understand the accusation either. The woman then asked what I had done during the days of the coup. I told her I had printed slogans on signs and marched around with the signs like everyone else. Eventually she asked me what slogans were on my signs. As soon as I started to describe some of them all the women in the dining hall began to laugh at me. Several days later I asked one of the women why everyone had laughed at me. She asked with disbelief if I really hadn't known that every one of my slogans was a parody of the official slogans. Wherever the official signs had the word state, our signs had the word workers; wherever the official signs said party, ours said union; wherever their signs said power, ours said self-management. I felt like an absolute idiot. I had been totally unaware of these differences. To me all the signs in the streets had looked identical. It was only after I learned about these differences that I remembered all the arguments between Luisa, Vera and Titus about the slogans that were to go on our signs. At the time I had thought they were arguing in a foreign language. I still don't understand why this was so important. If I didn't see our signs as any different from anyone else's I'm sure no one else did either. I'm sure the police were the only ones who were aware of these differences, Yarostan, surely you knew why we were arrested. You and Luisa attached so much importance to those differences. The differences mattered to Marc and Adrian only because you and Luisa thought them so important. I didn't know anything about them. When I was arrested I insisted I hadn't ever done anything in my whole life; I hadn't even had the nerve to take part in the resistance against the occupiers who killed my father. But my protests were all irrelevant. The trial rolled over me like a locomotive, and no matter how loudly I shouted I couldn't affect its course. I didn't understand a thing. I don't remember all the accusations that were thrown at me. At that time I didn't even know what the word sabotage meant. I was nevertheless sentenced to a year in prison. How is it possible that Luisa spent only two days? She, at least, knew why she was there. Prison life was a nightmare for me. Most of the women I met were mean to me. After I made such a fool of myself I became the prison dunce. One woman told me that after my year was over I'd automatically get another sentence because during the first year I had become a jailbird and therefore a socially dangerous person. And she said there was no telling how long the next sentence would be but that one-year terms were unheard of. Another woman filled me with horror stories about the torture chambers to which I'd be sent. I shook with fear every waking moment I spent there. I was so relieved when I finally left that hell. Luckily my house was exactly as I'd left it. It hadn't been confiscated. I decided I'd never again take part in political groups. I'd never again carry signs or go to demonstrations. I stuck to that decision until a few weeks ago. But I took part in the activities in our school only because everyone else is taking part in them; in that situation it would require bravery not to take part."

I gave Jasna a brief summary of my miserable experience after my first release and asked if she had been able to find a job.

"I was so glad to be out of that prison that nothing else mattered," she said. "Of course I was lucky to have that little house. I had also saved some money. I did look for a job, and had experiences similar to yours. I went to the carton plant first. The people in charge were apes compared to Mr. Zagad. Of course they turned me down. I was turned down at three other factories as well. But I didn't really care. I had enough money to buy groceries for several months and my little house has been paid for since before the war. I just read and waited to see what would happen. I envy the courage of women like Sophia and Sabina. I didn't have the nerve to leave the house and go looking for adventure. Not on my own. I read. I thought. Mainly I felt sorry for myself. I was completely lost. I knew that my savings would run out eventually. I knew I couldn't just stay inside my house. But the prison term had made me unemployable. There was nothing I could do. It was only some months after I was released that I began to feel the way you must have felt. Fear took hold of me. I was afraid of my neighbors because they seemed to look at me funny, they seemed to think me strange; I remembered what I'd been told about being a dangerous convict. I was afraid of the police. I was afraid of strangers on the street. I didn't know anyone. I was twenty-eight years old and I was deathly afraid to leave my house."

Yara was moved. "We didn't know what you'd been through when we called you a traitor for not taking part in the demonstrations. I'm sorry," she told Jasna.

"Don't be sorry," Jasna said. "You and your friends were right. People who are afraid of their own shadows aren't very admirable. I had good reason to be afraid but not of everything and everyone, not all the time. I didn't think of killing myself. That takes courage too. I just didn't know what to do. So I waited. I don't know what would have happened to me if Vera hadn't literally saved me from some awful death or from insanity. Vera was released almost a year after I was. Her apartment had been confiscated. She didn't have any living relatives and she hadn't been able to locate any of the other people we'd worked with. She had nowhere in the world to go. How happy she was when she saw it was I who opened the door of my house. She was overjoyed to learn I was living alone. But her happiness at seeing me was nothing compared to mine. I hugged her and acted as if my father as well as my mother had returned home. I begged her to stay with me and to treat my house as if it had always been hers. Vera was completely transformed by her prison term. She was quiet and bitter. I was grateful to her for coming to me. I did everything I could for her. I shopped, cooked, cleaned the house. Vera spent every day outside the house, meeting people, learning what openings might be available for her. I'm embarrassed to admit how quickly she oriented herself. During almost a year I had assumed everything was closed to me, and I did nothing. Vera had only been with me for a week when she began talking about enrolling in college. She said that was the only way to become someone nowadays; furthermore it was an alternative that wasn't closed to former prisoners. A few weeks later she was enrolled in the university. She expressed relief about the fact that she'd been turned down at every factory where she had applied for a job; she said she might have gotten stuck in one. By enrolling in the university she acquired a small stipend as well as a large hope that she'd never have to look for factory work again."

I made a comment about the passage near the end of your letter where you describe the students in your course. I compared Vera to those former workers who, in your words, are repairing and painting themselves in order to get out of the factory.

"That's not really a fair comparison," Jasna said. "That was literally the only alternative available to her and to me. We looked for factory jobs and were turned down. But you're not altogether wrong. We had all decided to get out of factory work, but several years earlier. The hope that we'd never work in factories again was born during the days when we worked at the carton factory together. It was then that Vera dreamed of becoming something like a popular tribune, some type of public speaker, exactly what she is now. Our experience in the carton plant taught every one of us that we didn't have to spend our lives doing that work. It was on that point that Jan always disagreed with Luisa. Jan continually said that as soon as we knew we didn't have to do that work none of us would ever return to it."

I objected to Jasna's interpretation of Jan's attitude.

"I know Jan didn't mean that we'd go on to the university and to higher paying jobs," Jasna admitted. "He wanted to destroy the factory so that no one else would have to work in it either. But the rest of us weren't about to do that. We didn't acquire the desire to put an end to factories but to push ourselves out of them. And that's what Vera did after her release. As soon as she was enrolled in the university she started teasing and prodding me. She would tell me I was an old maid and would soon become the neighborhood witch if I stayed locked up in the house. She told me that if I enrolled in college I'd get a stipend for workers and one for war orphans, since I was both, and if I graduated I'd never again have to work in a factory, but if I waited any longer I'd be older than the professors. I was afraid. I was sure that a dunce like I was had no place in the university. I remembered the women who had laughed at me in prison. I imagined that all the students at the university would laugh at me merely for enrolling. One day Vera told me she had learned about a college that was specifically designed for dunces and geese: the college for teachers. She assured me I'd have no trouble being accepted there. She was right. I applied and was accepted. I attended for four years and was no more of a dunce than anyone else. At the end of four years I was a teacher. But I'm going too fast again. During my second year in college we got a surprise visit from Adrian Povrshan. He had just been released and he needed a place to stay. Suddenly my little house was full for the first time since the war. I expected you to be our next visitor."

I told Jasna that I hadn't known where she lived.

"Neither did Adrian but he found out easily enough," she said.

I had to admit that it had never occurred to me to look her up. I thought she would be offended.

But she laughed. "I don't know what would have happened if you had come! Vera stayed in what used to be my parents' room. Adrian moved into the living room. He thought he'd take up with Vera where he'd left off. The first thing he did was to enroll in the university. I'm not the one to say it, but Adrian is really dumb. He didn't even suspect that anything strange was going on. It wasn't until ten years later that he found out about Vera's relationship with Professor Kren."

Mirna and I begged Jasna to tell us the details of Vera's adventures.

"I'm sorry I'm jumping around so much," Jasna said. "I don't know what to tell first. I had known about this professor long before Adrian came to stay with us. During her first year at the university Vera had told me about a certain Professor Kren who taught a course in political economy which she attended. She described him as an incredibly sleek politician who came to class in a spotless black suit. He lectured for two hours about the transformation of society and about revolutionizing the living conditions of the working people. After his lecture students lined up on the street to watch him enter his chauffeur-driven limousine and be driven away to the government palace. He was a high official in the state bank. Later on he became the head of the bank. It's funny how Vera's views of that professor changed during that year. When she first told me about him she ridiculed him and called him a revolutionary who had servants. Gradually she told me less and less about his sleekness and his limousine and more and more about his position, his importance;

she also told me he wasn't married. Two or three months before Adrian returned she told me she was "madly in love" with Professor Kren's limousine and with his power. She attended every lecture he gave at the university. She even went to hear lectures she'd heard before. And Adrian, who was two years behind her in school, simply assumed she was specializing in the things taught by Professor Kren. When she graduated she enrolled in a program of postgraduate studies under Professor Kren. After I graduated I got my first teaching job in a primary school on the other side of the city. But my domestic drama and my first teaching job ended abruptly, before I'd taught for half a year. All three of us were suddenly arrested."

Mirna was stunned. "You were arrested a second time? Why?" she asked. I was stunned too.

"I don't know why," Jasna said, "and that time no one explained it to me. The first time I had at least been doing something. The second time I was doing absolutely nothing. That happened twelve years ago. Suddenly everything came to an end and that terrible nightmare started all over again: the searches, the investigations, the cells. And for no reason at all. During my first few months as a teacher I had done everything exactly as I'd been taught. I had gone to school on time. I had spoken only to people I knew and even then I had only said good morning and good night. In my classes I had repeated what the textbooks said and I hadn't added a word of my own even when I'd known the textbook was wrong."

I asked her what she was accused of.

"Only God knows!" she said. "They asked me such ridiculous questions; they asked about things I couldn't possibly know and mixed these questions up with questions about things I couldn't help but know. They asked if I knew some notorious foreign spy and then they asked if I knew my own friends. It was all so stupid. They had arrested me together with Vera and Adrian and they asked if I knew them. When I admitted knowing them they insisted I must know the spy and the whole thing started all over again. They even had a wrong last name down for Sophia and Luisa but I didn't correct their mistake. The people hired to do those interrogations are even dumber than I am. But suddenly, when I'd been in jail only two days, I was released!"

Mirna and I again expressed our surprise.

"Yes, I was released after two days, I never did find out why we were arrested, but several years later I did learn why I was released so fast. I obviously didn't go to a lot of trouble to find out why I was released. The same officials who'd been ready to chop my head off if I didn't tell them things I didn't know were suddenly so polite, so full of smiles and handshakes. They bowed to me and apologized. They told me my arrest had been a 'mistake.' Such mistakes could take place at any time several times a year! By the time I got home my fear came back. The day after my release I went to my school to teach. The head of the school told me he had learned about my arrest and had already replaced me! And he said there were no other openings in the school. I was heartbroken. I had lost the job for which I had studied for four years. My house was empty again. Adrian and Vera were both gone, God knows for how long. I was all alone and once again I didn't know what I'd do. As if my misery wasn't complete enough I had a bad experience a few days after I was released. There was a loud knock on the door. I thought the police had come to get me again. I peered out the window and recognized Claude Tamnich. He looked strange. I trembled as I opened the door and immediately regretted letting him in. He slammed the door shut and slapped me so hard I fell to the floor. He accused me of having caused his arrest. I bawled like a baby. I told him I'd just been arrested myself for no reason at all and that as a result I had lost my job, my only two friends and my whole reason to remain alive. His anger decreased somewhat because he could see I was ready to die right on the spot where I lay on the rug. He accused me of having told them he was a member of a spy ring organized from abroad. I told him they'd asked me about spies but I'd never had anything to do with any spies; I told him they'd asked me if I knew him and all the other people I knew and of course I told them I knew him; they knew perfectly well we had worked together. But Claude insisted they wouldn't have released me so soon if I hadn't told them he was a spy. When I told Claude they had apologized to me for making a mistake, he said, literally, 'They never make mistakes.' Then why, I asked him, didn't he go and ask them why they had released me and what I had told them. I said they hadn't ever slapped me the way he had. Claude muttered that I must have told them but he helped me up and apologized. Years later I learned why I was released so suddenly. It wouldn't really have mattered if I'd known at the time. Claude rushed in and slapped me before I even had a chance to say hello. I don't know how I convinced Claude I was innocent. He suddenly lost interest in my guilt or innocence. He asked if I had anything to drink and then he started asking about the people we used to know. He continued drinking until he'd swallowed almost every bottle of alcohol Vera and Adrian had accumulated in my house during all the years they lived there. He seemed to pour it all into a barrel. The more he drank the more he told me about himself. He had been arrested along with the rest of us at the carton plant at the time of the coup and had been sentenced to four years. But he was released after he'd served one year of his term. He boasted about it. He was stinking drunk. He said it was the easiest thing in the world to be released from prison: all you had to do was to carry out your obligations to the state, like any good patriot. I asked what he meant by that and he told me that in prison he had spied on other prisoners. At the end of his first year an official asked him if he wanted an important job. Claude didn't turn it down. He said that after he'd taken part in ousting the enemy of the working people he wasn't going to spend four years in prison only to return to his job in the carton factory, and he certainly wouldn't return now that Marc was head of that factory. I asked if he meant our Marc. Exactly the same Marc, he said, and he called Marc a worm who had wiggled his way into the leadership of the factory's party organization. So Claude accepted the important job they offered him. He became a police spy. He didn't describe the work he did and I didn't ask him about it. He did boast that he was so good at it he was promoted a few years later. I can't remember what kind of post he got. He became some kind of prison official or security administrator; he was put in charge of other people who did the spy work he had done earlier. And then he was suddenly arrested, accused of conspiring with foreign agents to overthrow the state. They had asked Claude, too, if he knew the rest of us, and when he said he knew me they told him that I, Jasna Zbrkova, had admitted he and I had both been members of that foreign espionage ring. I asked him why they would have released me if I had admitted being a foreign spy but he was too drunk to answer that. He only ranted about efficiency; he said that's the way they do things and that's the only efficient way. And then he fell asleep in his chair. I locked myself in my room. When I got up the following morning Claude was gone. I haven't seen him or heard of him since then. I don't know if all the things he had told me while he was drunk were true but only one of those things mattered to me. He had told me that Marc Glavni had become an important person in the carton plant."

Yara had started to yawn during Jasna's narrative but at this point she perked up and asked. "Do you mean Marc Glavni the government official? Was that the Marc who used to be a friend of yours?" Yara was obviously impressed by the fact that we had once been the "friends" of that conceited provincial who had considered the rest of us halfwits.

"He's exactly the same Marc," Jasna said. "I went to see him the day after Claude's surprise visit. He was there all right — in Mr. Zagad's office! He recognized me, but not as a former friend. He didn't remember me as the person who had helped him learn his job at that very plant, as the person who had repaired his blunders. I'm sure if you asked him he wouldn't admit that Yarostan and I had ever been his friends. He recognized me only as someone he had seen before, someone whose name he knew. And that was all. He wasn't unkind. I don't want to suggest that. He was every bit as cordial and decent and courteous and distant as Mr. Zagad had been the first time I had walked into that very office nineteen years earlier. The scene was an exact repetition of the earlier scene, only Zagad's role was being played by the boy wonder from the provinces whom Luisa had liked so well. I asked if there were any openings. Marc said there just happened to be one opening and they would be very happy to 'have me.' Mr. Zagad couldn't have said it any differently. The only difference was that this time I didn't have to apologize for my lack of experience. This time I had infinitely more experience than the man who was hiring me and I didn't need Luisa to tell me I could carry out my task more efficiently without the boss. It was then that I realized Luisa had been wrong and Jan had been right. Without the rest of you around me I hated the work in that plant. If I hadn't had to support myself that way I'd never have returned to that boring routine, even if all the Mr. Zagads and Marc Glavnis had been ousted. Jan was right. Those eight hour days were the nearest thing to prison. He'd always objected to Luisa's comments by saying that only an idiot or a brainless mechanical slave would return to his prison cell after all the gates were opened and all the guards were gone. I wasn't at all as pleased with myself when Marc hired me as I had been when Mr. Zagad had hired me. I hated every minute of it. At night I dreamed of going back to teaching. But I only dreamed about it, and every day I went back to work there. I'm such a timid person. I stayed in that plant for three more years. My body and my mind got numb. I became what Jan had described: a brainless, mechanical slave. I wasn't in any way distinguishable from my alarm clock. I went off at the same hour every morning, wound myself up every night and went off again the following morning. During those three years Marc rose to yet another post. He became a member of the city planning commission. He had the power to help me find another teaching job simply by talking into his telephone. I don't know where I found the nerve to go into his office one day to ask his help in transferring me to a teaching job. I told him how many years I'd spent preparing to become a teacher. And I don't know where he found the nerve to turn me down. No, he said. Without any explanation. I'm sorry comrade, but! For the first time in my life I wanted to do something violent. I had a strong desire to push the desk into his belly — Zagad's old, heavy desk. I'm proud of what I did after that. I walked out of his office, through the workshop, out to the street and straight to my house. I haven't once returned to that plant since. Several of the workers came to my house to ask if I'd been fired. I told them I had simply quit because I'd had enough. And every one of them congratulated me for my courage. It was the only time in my life when I was congratulated for my courage."

I asked Jasna how in the world Marc had become so important in the carton plant.

"The same way we all became what we are now," she said. "He started to rise the first day he took part in the political discussions we had twenty years ago, when he elaborated those schemes Luisa admired so much. The workers at the plant were familiar with every step of his rise; they told me all about him during those three more years I spent there. Some time later Titus Zabran told me some funny things about him. Marc too was arrested twenty years ago. He was released after half a year in jail. I've never allowed myself to wonder why he was released so soon. That only leads to wondering why most of the people around me weren't arrested at all, and once you start thinking like that nothing makes any sense. After his release Marc applied for his old job at the carton plant and he was turned down by the new officials. Some of the workers I worked with later had been there at the time of his rejection and they told me how surprised they were when he turned up at the plant again several months later. They thought he must have had important contacts already then, so soon after his release from prison. This mystery was clarified for me by Titus sometime after I walked out of Marc's office. After being turned down by the plant officials Marc learned that Titus had some kind of trade union post. He visited Titus and with a single telephone call Titus got Marc hired at the carton plant. This same Marc refused to do that much for me several years later. As soon as he had his old job back Marc started to attend night classes at the university.

It was an educational program paid for by the union to give rank-and-file workers diplomas with which they could apply for posts in the union bureaucracy."

I commented that Marc must have attended a program similar in purpose and content to the program of the institution where you teach.

"And Marc certainly used it to his fullest advantage," Jasna continued. "He was a good student as he'd always been. He enrolled in a course in economic planning, which must have suited his talents perfectly. After attending the course for a year he was appointed to the plant council and got his own office. That was all he needed. From that point on he merely rose. He continued to be paid by the carton plant although he no longer did any work; he spent his days in his office studying for his courses. He did so well in his studies that he was appointed party secretary of the plant council. This appointment automatically made him a member of the trade union council. When he finished his course he had higher academic credentials than anyone else in the plant and he rose yet another notch; this time he was 'elected' head of the plant's party organization. He spent the next two years inside his office, writing a dissertation based on statistics collected for him by minor union officials in the plant. He became Dr. Glavni. What happened to him next was funny to the workers who told me about it. Late one night a car pulled up in front of Dr. Glavni's house, two men knocked at his door, and they arrested him exactly the same way they would have arrested any ordinary saboteur. But unlike ordinary saboteurs, Dr. Glavni was immediately released. I was told that the regional party secretary personally took a trip to the prison to apologize to Dr. Glavni for the mistake. After his release Marc wasn't only reinstated in all his posts. He also became a representative in the city planning commission. It was then that I went into his office and asked his help in transferring me to a teaching job. I haven't seen him since that day but two people who still work there have children in the school where I teach and they've kept me informed about his continuing successes. Shortly after I walked out of his office never to see him again, Dr. Glavni became general manager of the carton plant. The following year he became a member of the state planning commission and also of the foreign trade commission. Only last year I read in a newspaper that he had become a member of the central committee of the state planning commission. Today you can keep up with his titles simply by reading the newspapers. He's mentioned at least once a day."

We asked Jasna if she had gotten a teaching job on her own after she left the carton plant.

"I didn't even try," she said. "I again did absolutely nothing for several months. I had grown so used to spending months at home doing nothing."

"You really did absolutely nothing?" Yara asked with disbelief. "Did you just sit home and stare?"

"I mean nothing outside of my house," Jasna said. "No, I didn't sit and stare. I didn't feel particularly sorry for myself any more. Although what I did do amounts to nearly nothing. I have a weakness for reading novels, especially long novels, and the periods when I did nothing were in many ways the fullest periods in my life. Those were the months when I lived all the possible lives I was never going to be able to lead in real life.

"During that time I was vaguely aware that Vera had been released. I wondered why she didn't visit me, but I made no effort to try to see her. I just stayed home and read. My reading spree came to an end when I got another surprise visit. Titus Zabran came to see me. We hadn't seen each other in more than ten years. He had recently been released from prison. I think his arrest had been another mistake. He worked in the trade union bureaucracy and he somehow learned that I had quit my job at the carton plant. I learned from Titus that Jan had disappeared, that you were still in prison, and that Mirna and your two daughters lived in my own neighborhood."

"But you never came to see us," Yara said reproachfully.

"I always intended to visit," Jasna told us. "But I'm such a timid person. I was afraid. Titus was shocked when I told him I just stayed home and read. He asked why I had walked out of Marc's office. When I told him, he asked me with the seriousness of an old official what kind of work I'd like to do. I told him I wanted to teach again. Two days later he visited me again and told me there was an opening for me in the elementary school in my own neighborhood. I was overjoyed. I prepared a feast for him. I was so grateful to him. He visited me quite frequently after that. But I couldn't get any closer to him than when we'd worked together years earlier. This time it wasn't because I had to compete against the incomparable Luisa Nachalo, but because Titus had grown so dull, so robot-like, so official. He was hardly more human than an office desk. I continually asked him about his life, but unlike everyone else I know he had no desire at all to talk about himself. It was like pulling his teeth to get him to tell any details. He didn't tell me a single thing I didn't specifically ask him. That's why I know only fragments of his life. After we were all driven from the carton plant in so many different directions, Titus got a post in the trade union. It was through this post that he was able to help Marc get rehired at the carton plant. He told me he had been imprisoned for 'cosmopolitanism,' whatever that was. The second time he was arrested he was charged with 'revisionism.' I never heard of the things he was accused of. He seemed extremely lonely and told me he had no friends at all. I could see why; he was as sociable as a stone. About four years ago, when I had been teaching again for over a year, after Yara had already enrolled in our school, Titus told me he had seen Adrian, who had just been released from his second term two years before your release. Adrian had visited Titus to ask his help finding a job. Titus found Adrian a job in the trade union council. Titus didn't know where Adrian was living but he told me where his office was. I was annoyed by the fact that Adrian hadn't come to see me after his release. I hadn't seen him since we'd been arrested at my house six years earlier. I got a substitute to replace me in school one day and went to his office. Adrian and his office were both terribly depressing. Adrian had grown as skinny as a skeleton. Dark rings surrounded his eyes. His face and his hands seemed to consist only of skin and bones. And his office was just as sparse as he was. It was larger than the average prison cell. It had a desk and a chair. But that was all. There was nothing on the walls, nothing on the floor, nothing on the desk. We shook hands. I couldn't keep myself from asking what in the world he did in that room. Looking around at the bare walls he said, 'This is my job. I'm a researcher.' I asked him exactly what Yara just asked me: did he just sit there and stare at the walls? Didn't he ever read? He pulled the sports section of a newspaper out of the top drawer of his desk to show me that he did read. I could see that there was nothing else in that desk drawer. As if to explain his situation to me, he told me he was waiting. Waiting for what? I asked. All day long every day? He reminded me that before his arrest he had been on the verge of finishing his studies at the university. If he had taken three more exams and submitted one paper he would have finished. His paper was written and he was waiting to take the exams. After that he'd get another appointment. Adrian was simply sitting in that office waiting for the appointment. He literally had nothing to do there. I spent most of the day in his office. I asked him why he hadn't come to see me after he was released. I'd gladly have put him up in the same room where he'd stayed before. He said he couldn't stand anything that reminded him of Vera. And then, calmly, almost mechanically, he started telling me what had happened to him after he was arrested. I couldn't believe what he was telling me, although it clarified why I had been released so quickly and why I'd been told I'd been arrested by mistake. Adrian had also been accused of having contacts with a foreign spy ring and he too had been asked if he knew the people we all knew, including Vera and Marc. Of course he admitted knowing them. He was sentenced to two years. At the end of the two years, instead of being released, he was swept into another trial. I was reminded of the story a woman had told me during my first prison term: as soon as one term ended a longer one began. That was what happened to Adrian. He was interrogated again. This time the interrogators wanted him to deny he had ever known Vera Neis or Marc Glavni and to say he had lied at the first trial."

I told Jasna I'd had similar experiences during my second prison term. At one trial they asked me to admit I knew all my friends and I was sentenced to eight years because I refused to admit I had ever known any of them. I thought I'd get them into trouble if I admitted knowing them. At the time I didn't know most of them had already been arrested. Some two years later an interrogator asked me to sign a paper to the effect that I had never known Vera or Marc. I obviously signed it since I had already told them I didn't know them; I thought I couldn't possibly harm people by admitting I had never known them.

"But that wasn't Adrian's situation," Jasna said. "First of all he, Vera and I had been arrested together so the interrogators would have known perfectly well that he was lying when he said he didn't know Vera. Secondly he was sure they were trying to trap him or Vera into contradicting each other so as to build a case against one of them. He thought he was protecting Vera by refusing to sign that paper. He told me he was completely dumbfounded by the trial. During his remaining four years in prison he couldn't figure out what had happened. It all became clear only after he was released, when he finally located Vera's office and saw the plaque on her door. At that trial he was accused of perjury, intentional defamation of the characters of two important state officials. The prosecutor railed against Adrian as a known foreign agent who had tried to implicate Vera Neis and Marc Glavni in his spy ring. Adrian was supposed to have caused the arrest of two comrades above suspicion by claiming they were members of his group. The prosecutor told the court that Comrade Vera Neis, full professor of political economy, had been cleared of this malicious slander through the personal intervention of Professor Dr. Kren, head of the state bank; Comrade Marc Glavni, head of the party organization of the carton factory and representative of the city planning commission, had been cleared through the personal intervention of the head of the state planning commission. For this malicious slander Adrian was sentenced to four more years in prison. During all those years he wrestled with the significance of that trial. All he figured out was that Marc and Vera must have been released and that his denial that he had known them might have been needed to expedite their release; he said if he'd known that during the interrogation he would gladly have signed the paper. Everything finally cleared up after he was released. He went to the university and looked for Vera Neis. He was told there was no such person. Someone told him to ask in the rector's office. Imagine his surprise when he saw the plaque on the door: rector of the faculty of political economy, Prof. Dr. Vera Krena! Adrian then remembered the name of the bank official who had personally intervened to release Vera."

Yara was impressed once again. "Do you mean Vera Krena the minister? Was that the Vera Neis you used to know?"

"She wasn't a minister yet when Adrian found her office," Jasna said. "Adrian told me he hesitantly went in. There were three secretaries there. They asked if he had an appointment with the rector. He told them he didn't want to see the rector; he only wanted to learn something about her because he had known her once, in high school, as Vera Neis; he said he wanted to know how she had come to her present position and asked if they would be willing to tell him. One of the secretaries left the office with him and they went to a coffee shop. She told him she had been Vera's classmate in the university and knew exactly how Vera had become rector of the university. From her Adrian learned that Vera had begun her affair with Professor Kren already during the days when Adrian and Vera had lived happily at my house. Adrian didn't tell the secretary he'd known Vera after high school. She told Adrian she and Vera had graduated together and after graduation she had gotten the job as the rector's secretary and had been on that job ever since. But when Vera graduated she enrolled in a postgraduate course in political economy so as to be close to the bank official, Professor Kren. Vera and the professor became inseparable during the day while, according to the secretary, Vera returned to another lover every night. The secretary told Adrian that Vera's career was almost cut short soon after her postgraduate program started, because a foreign spy had claimed that she was a member of his spy ring. She was arrested and Kren himself had to intervene to get her released. My hasty release was suddenly explained. Vera must have asked Kren to intervene for me as well. Adrian was annoyed when I told him this, because he had been the one who'd had to suffer because of Vera's release. He had been left in jail so as not to be in Vera's way. The secretary had told him that Vera had protested to the police for arresting her. Marc apparently did the same thing. The way the police cleared themselves of these mistakes was to put all the blame on Adrian, slapping another four years on him for having implicated Vera and Marc and then announcing they had discovered the cause for their mistake. The woman told Adrian that as soon as Kren got Vera out of prison she abandoned her lover and moved into the professor's house. From that point on she walked on a golden carpet. She finished her studies under him and became Dr. Vera Neis the same year when he became the head of the state bank. The following year she became professor of political economy; such a quick journey from student to full professor was unprecedented. She was probably the youngest professor in the university's history and one of the few women on the university's regular teaching staff. The secretary said all the men professors were charmed, there was a great deal of talk about the equality of women in all fields of social endeavor, and all of it was a mutual sham. A year later Vera married the professor and shortly after the marriage Prof. Dr. Vera Neis Krena became assistant rector of the faculty of political economy. And then the rector of the university was arrested in the middle of a night by the security police. That had happened only a year before Adrian's release. Professor Kren's candidate for rector, his wife, was unanimously elected to the post; there were no other candidates. After Adrian learned all that, he must have suspected that I had known about Vera's relations with Professor Kren all along, but he didn't ask. After his session with Vera's secretary, Adrian wanted to look up the other important state official whose character he had defamed by claiming to know him, Comrade Marc Glavni. Adrian went to the carton factory, but Marc no longer occupied Mr. Zagad's office, where I had found him six years earlier. Adrian was told that Dr. Glavni was the general manager of the plant but that his office was located in the state planning commission building. Adrian went to the government building, found Marc's office, but got no further than the desk of a secretary. Adrian was asked his reasons for wanting to see Dr. Glavni. When he said he wanted to apply for a job at the carton factory, the secretary told him that hiring was handled by an official at the plant itself, and she promptly wrote an official's name and office number on a slip of paper. Adrian then tried another approach. He telephoned Marc's office, introduced himself as Comrade Kren from the state bank and said he needed to discuss urgent business with Comrade Glavni. He was given an appointment for the following day. When Adrian entered Marc's office and introduced himself as Comrade Kren, Marc's face fell. Marc didn't even shake Adrian's hand. He merely asked Adrian what he wanted. Adrian said he wanted a job at the plant.

Marc, flushed with anger, shouted: 'You want my help after what you've done to me? Couldn't you have told them you didn't know me? You've put a permanent blot on my name!' Adrian shouted back. 'A blot on your name! You lunatic! I've just spent six years of my life in prison. What wouldn't I do to have a mere blot on my name in exchange for those six years!' Marc didn't respond. He regained his composure, sat behind his desk and called his secretary to accompany 'Comrade Kren' out of his office, saying 'I'm sorry comrade, there aren't any openings for your friend.' Adrian was furious when he left Marc's office. But he didn't know what to do. He was miserable for several weeks. Then he somehow learned that Titus Zabran was a trade union official and went to see him. That was when Titus got him the job in that office where I found him. I told Adrian something about my own life since our arrest and I invited him to visit me for old time's sake, but he never came. I didn't see him again for a whole year. Titus visited me two or three times during that year. I went to school every day and read my novels at night. And then — was it three years ago? — I learned that your older daughter Vesna was sick. I didn't even know her. She hadn't ever been in my class and I hadn't ever tried to talk to her. I told Titus, but I didn't come. When I learned she had died in the hospital I felt awful. I cried every night. I even burst out crying during one of my classes. But I just couldn't bring myself to come and see you, Mirna. I had stayed away so long and you didn't know me. I was afraid you wouldn't trust me. I had to go somewhere, to see someone. I decided to visit Adrian again. Nothing had changed in his office. The walls were still bare, there was still nothing in the room except the desk and the chairs and there was nothing on the desk. I asked Adrian if he was still waiting. Adrian told me he had one exam left to finish his studies. He was sure he'd be promoted as soon as he got his degree. I asked him what kind of life that was, waiting in that empty room for a promotion like a prisoner waiting to be released. He told me he had done a great deal since I'd last seen him. He had been seeing Vera's secretary regularly, the one who had told him about Vera's successes, although he hadn't yet seen Professor Dr. Vera in person. He had told the secretary that he'd been the one responsible for Vera's arrest. He insisted on telling me the details of his self-exposure. The secretary trapped Vera into admitting she had lied about the foreign spy who had caused her arrest. The secretary had told Vera that in her student days she had met an Adrian Povrshan who had told her he had known Vera in high school. Vera admitted having known Adrian in high school; she even told the secretary she and Adrian had grown up together. When Adrian told the secretary about his arrest, his near release and the new trial where he was to admit he had never known Vera, the secretary was indignant; she realized Vera had caused Adrian to be imprisoned for four extra years merely in order to rehabilitate her name. She wanted to expose Vera's duplicity, to make a public scandal. Adrian told me he was pleased by the secretary's reaction but he begged her not to mention the details to anyone; he was afraid that a scandal would interfere with his coming promotion. I felt a mixture of disgust and shame when I left Adrian's office. I haven't ever gone to see him again. I was disgusted by Adrian. I regretted having gone to see him after I had learned of Vesna's death. I was ashamed of myself, of my life, of all my former friends."

I asked Jasna if she knew what all those people were doing today.

"I lost track of Claude nine years ago, after the day when he came to my house to accuse me," she said. "I don't even know if he's still alive. If he is, he's probably a prison or police official. You don't need to ask me about the others. They're in the newspapers. Vera and Adrian appear together on speakers' platforms. I have no idea how or when they became friends again. Vera has fulfilled her life's dream. She's a popular tribune. She lectures to applauding audiences, talks on the radio at least once a week about the urgent political tasks of the day and the need for reforms. And Adrian is still her straight man; he still documents the things she says. I listen to them on the radio whenever I can. They're not nearly as funny as they used to be. Whenever they're mentioned in the newspapers their names are accompanied by titles that fill whole paragraphs. Vera is still rector of the university. She's also deputy minister of the ideological commission and I don't know what else besides. Adrian got all the promotions he had waited for; he's first party secretary of the commission for problems of standard of living. Marc has more titles than either of them. He's a member of the central committee of the state planning commission, he's on the foreign trade commission, his name is mentioned whenever there's an international trade conference. And me: I get up at the same time every morning and go to teach my classes at the elementary school. I'm neither a head nor a member nor a party secretary nor anything else. But somehow I'm one of them too. I've also abandoned people who were killed and jailed, who suffered because they wanted to live another kind of life. I too am a traitor to people like Jan who disappeared so many years ago, and to little Vesna who wasn't even given a chance to survive. Our famous friends have succeeded in getting the life we used to talk about; they got it for themselves."

It was very late when Jasna finished. Before she left she said to me, "Be sure you tell Sophia about the people we knew twenty years ago. They don't all deserve the sympathy she expresses for them in her letter."

I suspect that you know who our friends were and that you're one of them; my suspicion is confirmed by your descriptions of those people and by your description of your life's choices. You describe Marc and Vera as committed revolutionary workers. Luisa regards Jan and me as hotheads. You recognize the repressive aspirations of your university friends Lem and Rhea, but only because these two people expressed their aspirations openly. You fail to realize that those who announce their repressive aspirations are not the only carriers of repression. You fail to see through people who do not carry the world of repression in their mouths but in the motions and decisions they make every day of their lives. Today it doesn't take great insight to see through people like Lem and Rhea. People like them have realized their aspirations in a third of the world and the repressive character of these aspirations has become public knowledge. You reject Lem and Rhea because they're antiquated, not because they're repressive. You glorify their modern cousins. You glorify Marc, Vera, Adrian, Claude and those like them in your environment. You describe them all as rebels. I would like to think, as Jasna does, that you don't know what kind of people these are. But I think you do know who they are. I think you use language the same way they do: not to unveil and clarify but to mask and obscure. I think you know that the terms with which you describe these people are the terms behind which they hide. I think you know that terms like independent, committed, revolutionary, do not describe the characters or activities of these people. In plainer terms, you're lying about these individuals. Vera, Adrian, Claude and Marc are people for whom the organized system of repression is the only possible form of life. They perceive their own personal development in the form of active participation in the repression. For them the university hierarchy, the union hierarchy, the enterprise hierarchy and the state hierarchy are the hothouses in which human life flowers and grows, and it's within these contexts that they define their choices, their life projects and their success. Their aim in life is to occupy positions in these hierarchies, to play the roles defined by the previous occupants of their offices. They've renounced their own projects and their own lives in order to live what has already been lived. They ran to sell themselves or sat like commodities in display windows waiting to be bought. And while they grow inside their hierarchies the rest of us manure the hothouse soil and maintain the heat with our submission and our admiration.

Several times during Jasna's narrative Yara interrupted with comments that expressed admiration for our one-time co-workers. Even Jasna and I became more admirable to Yara because we had once known these paragons of integrity and solidarity; we shone in the light reflected from these suns. It's true that Yara is only eleven years old, but her admiration nevertheless disappointed me. She happens to be the individual who had so much to do with stirring up the ferment at her school. Her self-assurance in matters that concern her directly, combined with passive admiration for the occupants of social offices, is identical to the mixture of self-assurance and passivity among my fellow workers in the carton plant who determinedly oust a union bureaucrat and then applaud speechmakers waiting to replace the ousted bureaucrat in the same post. From her own experience Yara knows that she and her friends are able to move the world, while her education has imbued her with the illusion that only the tops of the hierarchies move the world. Yara's admiration for Vera and Marc has much in common with the mirages people experience in a desert. The illusion is caused by the heat, the distance, and the thirst one feels. The mirage continues receding; no matter how far one goes one seems to get no closer to it. One who does finally reach it finds there is no water there but only more sand. The aura which seems to surround the admirable people of our society is an illusion caused by the poverty of everyone's personal life in contrast to the brilliant public life of the personalities daily displayed to thousands. Some of those who watch, condense their life projects to one single goal: to be watched, to be seen daily by thousands. But this goal is a mirage. Being watched is no more of an activity than watching. The observed is as passive as the observer. It seems to me that the personal lives of those who occupy the highest offices are as miserable as the personal lives of those who are victimized by the officials. When Marc reached his goal and became manager of the plant he renounced his own life to such an extent that when Jasna visited his office she saw in him, not the individual we had known, but the previous occupant of that office, Mr. Zagad. Having annihilated himself to such a degree he turned his back on Jasna and Adrian when they needed his help. Adrian had to serve four years in prison so that a blot could be removed from Marc's name. Adrian's prolonged imprisonment served Vera's interests as well: she could marry her banker without having to explain anything to her lifelong friend. We don't know how many others Marc had to repress, in order to rise to his heights but we have strong grounds for thinking it was Vera or her future husband who removed the previous rector of the university from his post. And Adrian, after having been victimized by both Vera and Marc, outdid both of them: Adrian's self-debasement for the sake of bureaucratic advancement is scandalous. He simply gave all of himself to the bureaucracy; he denuded himself of all internal and external characteristics, of all marks that might even superficially define him as a specific individual, and waited like an unlabelled bottle ready to be filled and sold. Claude had succeeded in attaining his repressive ideal earlier and more grossly. Having repressed their own desires to live without bureaucratic structures, they hit out blindly against all those who have not repressed such desires. I think Luisa shares one trait with her former comrades. I think she too, a long time ago, gave up her desires for her own self-liberation and gave herself to the last of the repressive institutions, the representative of liberation, the union. She poured her life into meaningless drudgery for the sake of that repressive Utopia where rank and filers are said to rule when they are ruled by a rank and filer, where workers are said to manage when they are managed by a worker, where the people are said to be victorious when one of the victors governs. I think this is why Luisa responds so irrationally whenever Ron is mentioned, whenever Manuel, whom she never met, is mentioned, whenever Jan is mentioned. I think she responds that way because these individuals refused to repress their own desires, because they refused to submit to the victory of repression called by another name.

I was amazed by the exchange between Sabina and Luisa about all those whom Luisa called enemies behind the trenches. Luisa is straightforward when she speaks of saboteurs and assassins as if they were first cousins; to her, people who sabotaged production are the same as people who murdered revolutionary workers, and she defends the repression of both. Isn't it perfectly clear that if Luisa's ideal had triumphed, people like Manuel, Jan and I wouldn't have fared any better than we did? Sabina guessed exactly what Manuel had told me: the revolutionary saboteurs were killed alongside the hired assassins, not by the order of the generals, but by the order of the revolutionary general staff. That's what would have happened to Manuel if he hadn't been arrested earlier because of his membership in an organization to which he no longer belonged when he was arrested.

The weekend is over and tomorrow I return to work. I'd like to end this letter on a more cheerful note. I would genuinely like to carry on this correspondence with you in a spirit of understanding and mutual aid, not only for the sake of our past friendship, but also because communication across such large chasms will have to take place if our meager beginnings are going to continue growing and not be drowned in blood spilled by those of our likes who remain under the spell of their rulers.

I hope my letter, and especially Jasna's narrative, has at least clarified the character of the individuals and the experiences on which you based so many of your life's choices.

Yarostan.

Sophia's fourth letter

Dear Yarostan,
So much has happened since I sent you my last letter and most of it has confirmed your statement that you and I live in completely different worlds. I have no idea what place you would occupy in my world and you can't know what place I'd occupy in yours. It certainly wouldn't be the place you assign me!

I admit I was shocked by what Jasna told about the people I've regarded as my comrades. I was particularly shocked by the ruthlessness and inhumanity with which Marc and Vera attained their bureaucratic goals. But I don't have even a shred of sympathy for the path they took. Nothing in me could have accepted, or even drifted in the direction in which they moved. Your characterization of me fails. I didn't identify with Marc, Vera or Adrian and I obviously didn't identify with Claude. If I identified with anyone in Jasna's or your narrative it was with Jasna herself and, much as you hate my saying it, with you. I identified with you, Yarostan, not because my life was anything like yours but because I wish it had been, particularly right now. I'm genuinely overjoyed that you're finding in your present life everything I sought but never found throughout my life: a real and significant project with people who are alive and want to be. I came close to that kind of activity only once and you've just about convinced me that I wasn't close to it even then. Since then I've come no closer than a caricature comes to an original event. My experiences during the past two weeks have been such caricatures of the experiences I've longed for.

Two weeks ago there was a demonstration at the university where Daman Hesper teaches. Daman was my friend during my student days; we were on the university newspaper staff together. He's the person who helped me find my present teaching job. At the demonstration, about a hundred students barricaded themselves into the university administration building and announced they wouldn't leave until the university accepted a long list of demands. The university president announced that if the students didn't leave the building immediately, he would call on the police to evict them by force. In response to this announcement several hundred students and teaching assistants planted themselves in front of the administration building to act as a kind of "buffer" between the police and the occupying students. Only one professor was among those in front of the building: Daman Hesper. That evening the police attacked. According to Daman it was more like an invading army. The police, who far outnumbered the people inside as well as outside the building, simply pushed their way into the building. They arrested all the students inside as well as most of the people outside, including Daman, whom they beat. Daman called me that night and told me to be ready with bail money in the morning. I went to jail the following morning but he was already out. Everyone had been released. Daman had an ugly cut across his face. We came to my house by taxi and I called a doctor.

Daman is really the only good friend I have now except for my two housemates. He's the only one of the people with whom I worked on the newspaper staff whom I still see. Sabina has an intense dislike for him and Tina doesn't think a whole lot of him either. My own respect for him went down considerably during the past two weeks and your letter had a lot to do with this. I think that without the observations you made I wouldn't have been so critical of the role Daman played in the events that followed that demonstration.

A week ago Daman came to the house to tell me several students were going to call for a strike to protest against the police repression of the students who had occupied the building. He brought me several copies of a leaflet they had prepared announcing a student general strike. I thought it was a good leaflet. It didn't only attack the repression of the student demonstrators but also raised questions about the university's involvement in weapons development and war strategy, questions about the ugly relationship between the university and the working class community that surrounds it and questions about the education itself, about its authoritarian form and its apologetic content.

Although I'm no longer connected to the university, I decided to take part in the strike. I became very excited thinking I would be involved in activity that in some way resembled the strike you described in your previous letter, I was intensely disappointed. The event resembled a strike only in name.

The day after Daman's visit I went to my job at the community college. Since the leaflet wasn't addressed only to students of the university but to all students and was a call for a general strike, I read it to my class. I also announced that I wasn't a strikebreaker and wouldn't come to class on the day of the strike. This was probably the longest lecture I had given in my class. Not a single one of the "students" expressed the slightest sympathy for the leaflet, for the coming strike or for me. Most of them were completely indifferent and some were actually hostile. One person criticized the students who had occupied the administration building because they had "illegally trespassed on private property." What was more upsetting to me was that I was the only one who laughed when he said this. I should remind you that the people in my class are workers, they haven't yet reached the managerial posts to which they aspire, they still work in factories. "Since they trespassed on private property," the person continued, "the police were only doing their job when they arrested them."

Another student argued that strikes were for higher wages and improved working conditions, and that therefore the leaflet was not calling for a strike but for a riot. I argued that it was up to strikers to define what they were striking for, but this statement provoked protests from almost all the workers in the room, workers who had all participated in strikes. "If everyone defined his own strike it would be anarchy," one student complained. The dominant view was that the unions and the government define the aims of a strike. There seems to be a great deal of similarity between a situation where strikes are illegal and a situation where strikes are institutionalized. Here strikes are nominally legal but only those strikes which are called by the unions and sanctioned by the law are legal. In practice this means that any genuine strike, any strike organized by workers themselves with aims which they themselves define is as illegal as it was in your environment for the past twenty years, and is just as savagely repressed.

Even the fact that I talked about such a strike in my class led to my being intimidated. Or rather, it wasn't just the fact that I talked about it but the fact that I acted on it, took part in it, called off my class, that led to intimidation. Just talking is all right.

My last class before the "general strike" was dull. No one even mentioned the coming event. Everyone seemed to know that something was going to happen. Later on I learned that several of the students in my class were also in a psychology class and that they had talked about me in their class. When my class ended some of the students left but others stood in the hall and were joined by a professor I had seen before: he teaches behavioral psychology and is on some administrative body of the college. The professor shouted at me as I came out of the classroom. "I understand you've decided to revise the length of the school term."

"You understand correctly," I told him. "I'm not a scab and I won't come to work during a strike."

"Such matters are taken up by the proper authorities, Miss Nachalo," he said.

"No they're not," I said. "Since when did the bosses determine when a strike was to take place?"

"You encourage violence against what you call the bosses, don't you Miss Nachalo?" he asked.

"What does that have to do with it?" I shouted. "I'm taking part in a strike and you're not going to stop me!"

"That's just the point, Miss Nachalo," he said, and he grinned. "Nothing at all is going to stop you. You're a dangerous person. You shouldn't be teaching in a college. You should be undergoing treatment in a hospital."

His statement, his smugness and his idiotic grin infuriated me. Such people and their cousins in the police are called "pigs" by a small number of radical students; I certainly sympathize with this attempt to call certain people by their proper names. "Why you bastard!" I shouted. "I'll show you just how dangerous I am!" I slapped his face twice with all my might.

He didn't raise his hands to protect himself. Instead he grinned even more stupidly, like a genuine masochist. He said, "Everyone can see you're an extremely violent person. Miss Nachalo."

One student yelled, "Bravo, champ!" The rest dispersed like zombies. I walked away trembling with anger and frustration. After that event as a build-up, the actual "strike" that took place was a real letdown.

Your letter arrived one day before the "general strike." I was so excited by certain passages that I translated and typed them up; I wanted to show Daman that experiences similar to ours were taking place on the other side of the world. What struck me most was your description of your situation in the carton plant; I then imagined my own situation was about to become similar to yours. I thought I was about to experience a progression of events similar to the one you described: last week there had been an unprecedented demonstration; today a general strike of students was breaking out; next week workers might go on strike and if the ferment continues then a new life might be possible here too — as you put it: a human life inhibited by no barriers external to the developing individuals. But I was only dreaming, so please don't take this as another of my misguided attempts to identify my situation with yours.

On the morning of the "strike" I waited impatiently for Daman to come by for me. He normally didn't start teaching until noon and consequently wasn't in the habit of starting out early. When he finally picked me up at lunchtime I left the house without the pages I had typed up for him — but you'll see that those pages, in fact your entire letter, strongly affected my perception of the day's events and particularly of Daman. My disappointment with Daman began the moment he arrived; I was peeved because of how late he had come and how nonchalant he acted about the whole thing. He seemed to be going to the university the same way he would have gone any other day, at the same hour, apparently with the same thoughts. He seemed completely indifferent about the strike and didn't talk about it. I realized that I had magnified the importance of what was going to happen because of what had already happened to me. I even asked him, "Aren't you excited?"

"No," he said. "Why should I be excited?"

"I don't know," I said. "What if the police attack again?"

"What makes you think they're going to attack again?" he asked, snickering at me.

I really do have a vivid imagination when I think about strikes and demonstrations. That's one critical observation of yours that really hits its mark. I suppose I got that from Luisa. Every time a group of people get together to protest, I see the revolution around the corner. The expectations I had built up in myself for that strike certainly had no relation to what actually happened. It was a beautiful spring day, the first really warm day of the year. The strike, it turned out, was one vast picnic which seemed to extend over all the lawns of the university campus. I'm not saying this with irony. I was actually somewhat pleased. Nothing of this sort had ever happened at the university when I had been a student. The picnic seemed enjoyable enough. Students had come with their lunches and thermos bottles. I even saw groups of students with large coolers, with boxes full of picnic supplies, and some had even brought lawn chairs and folding tables. It was a nice picnic, but it wasn't the event I had anticipated from the leaflet that had announced a "general strike," and it certainly wasn't the violent riot anticipated by the domesticated students who attended my night class.

The event wasn't particularly festive. There was no singing or dancing or theater. There were just groups of friends picnicking on the grass. The event didn't indicate the end of the university or the beginning of anything new. Everyone knew that classes would resume "normally" the following day. I suppose that would have bothered me less if your letter hadn't arrived that very day. I looked for signs of something new but there wasn't a trace of the ferment your letters have described. As a general strike this event was a bad joke. Only one minor detail reminded me that the event was not merely a picnic. A young woman ran up to Daman and announced, very proudly, "You know what. Professor Hesper? A group of us ran through the administration building yelling 'Jailbreak!'"

Daman smiled and said, "That's great. Was anyone there?"

Losing most of her enthusiasm, she answered, "The secretaries and deans."

Several students sitting on the steps of the administration building caught sight of Daman and began waving and shouting for him to join them.

"Come on," Daman told me. "I'll introduce you to the political students."

Normally I would have said that I'd be delighted to meet the political students; normally I would have preferredi'm the company of "political" students to that of apolitical students. I don't mean "normally." I mean before your last two letters came. Because of your letters I began to hear words I had never really heard before and I began to see a Daman I had never really looked at before. When we came up to the group, Daman introduced me: "Sophie Nachalo, meet the organizers of this unusual event."

One of the "organizers" said, "I know who you are. You're the faculty radical who was fired a year ago right after the riot."

"I recognize you too," I told him. I recognized two or three of the others as well. A couple of years ago, right after I had gotten my first teaching job, I attended a large protest meeting which was destroyed by manipulative politicians who had elected themselves the leaders of the student movement. I think I told you about that meeting. Three or four of those very politicians were among the "political students" to whom Daman introduced me.

What happened next on the steps of the administration building was so bizarre that I'll try to describe it in detail, first of all because I'd like to engrave that event on my memory and secondly because I'd like to show you that I do read your letters attentively. Your letter is what made this event clear to me.

It was the day of the great strike against the university. The leaflet announcing the strike had specifically described the authoritarian character of the education as one of the targets against which the strike was launched. Yet Daman placed himself on the bottom step and began lecturing like an orator in a colosseum, the omniscient professor lecturing to his ignorant admirers. What took place on the steps of the administration building was the most authoritarian classroom situation I have ever experienced, and those subjected to it were the students who had been introduced to me as the organizers of the strike against that type of authoritarianism.

Daman always introduced himself to people as "basically a worker." He had worked in a factory for several years before he was employed in the university. In this context, among those he called "the political students," the fact that he considered himself "basically a worker" made him their idol. The lecture began when, after introducing all the students to me by name, Daman said, "This was easy! But this isn't what counts." (By "this" he meant the student strike.)

A young woman I didn't recognize objected to this put-down of the student strike. "I think this does count. Many of the students come from working class homes and most of them are going to be workers of one type or another."

At that point Daman began a tirade. At one or another time I had agreed with most of what he said, and I still do agree with much of it. But he spoke in a tone that was terribly intimidating and in a context which totally falsified what he said. I remembered what you had written about the 'mirrors' created by politicians, mirrors which reflect people's desires and transform them into images, words. Daman turned to the young woman and said, "That theory of students and professors being part of the so-called new working class is so much baloney invented by petty-bourgeois academic sociologists." He spoke calmly but what he said was so intimidating to the young woman, to the rest of the group and even to me that he might as well have shouted at the top of his voice. It's probably true that the "theory of the new working class" is baloney invented by academic sociologists, but Daman's statement had nothing to do with what the young woman had said. He intimidated her by identifying her comment with a theory she was probably unfamiliar with; he transformed what she had said into an expression of sympathy for a petty-bourgeois theory. He then continued to push his point in the same direction. "The only test of class is someone's relation to production. People whose function is to manipulate others, like professors, are best defined as middle class."

I felt like shouting and telling the "political students" that they were being taken in by a hoax, precisely the type of hoax you described. I again agreed with his words. But how were his listeners and he related to those words? He was talking to students some of whom were already experienced manipulators. He was himself a professor. Yet he spoke as if his and their lives and functions were totally unrelated to what he said, as if he were talking about other professors, other manipulators, other members of the middle class.

"The best paid and most thoroughly unionized workers in the basic and heavy industries are crucial to revolutionary potential and cannot be brushed aside and replaced by clerical workers, students, professors and so on," he continued. "The fact that workers are at the point of production is the source of the revolutionary capacity of the working class. Their work teaches them how to run production."

Up to this point I thought I agreed with every statement Daman had made. But the very fact that I agreed with his words made me realize that such agreement has nothing to do with shared commitments and projects. I agreed with the statements but the context of those statements made me want to shout my disagreement. I grew increasingly frustrated as Daman's lecture progressed further. I stopped agreeing with the statements he made, although I wasn't able to articulate my disagreements until later that evening, when Tina tore into Daman's arguments.

He must have talked without a break for at least an hour. The main point of his lecture was that capitalism, by concentrating workers in the basic industries, had itself created the organization and discipline of "the new society." I had heard that whole argument innumerable times before and I used to agree with it. I started to doubt its validity before I started corresponding with you but thanks to your letters and especially your brief descriptions of Jan Sedlak's insights I'm finally able to express my understanding of what's wrong with that argument. Daman glorifies the absolute degradation of the human individual and the human community for which capitalism is responsible. He locates "the new society" in the assembly lines, the furnaces and the mines. His argument is an apology for the unprecedentedly inhuman hell created by capitalism.

I was so irritated by what Daman said that it didn't dawn on me until later that I had heard every single one of his statements before, in exactly the same words. He had already said the same things fourteen years earlier! The context was apparently irrelevant; it was nothing but an occasion for repeating the same performance. The statements he made on the steps of the administration building were the political beliefs of the organization to which he had belonged when I had met him on the newspaper staff. Despite all that's happened during the past fourteen years, Daman has somehow managed not to change a single one of his ideas! I can now understand why you were so shocked when you read my first letter and recognized a person and an outlook you had known twenty years ago. I hope I haven't been as rigid as Daman! That's frightening. He could have put all his views on a phonograph record fourteen years ago and anyone who wanted to meet him could simply play the record. That's eerie. Daman isn't altogether a living person.

There were no questions when Daman finished his lecture. He simply said, "Well, see you next week." This was incomprehensible to me. The students got up and joined picnickers on a lawn.

I asked Daman, "What do you mean you'll see them next week? Are they going to call for another general strike just so they can listen to you deliver the same lecture another time?" I was furious at Daman. I was also furious at myself for having made such a scene at the community college for the sake of this travesty of a strike and especially for the delusions with which I had filled myself while anticipating this great day.

He either disregarded my anger and frustration or else he didn't notice it. Very matter-of-factly, as if everything was exactly as it should be, he told me, "I'll see them next week because we get together one night a week. Since there was no school today we had decided to meet during the day."

Indignantly I asked, "You mean this was a class? And you carried it on precisely with the group who had organized the strike against classes?"

Still matter-of-factly, as if he were unable to grasp the contradiction, he said, "This isn't a formal university class. It's an altogether informal affair and it was convenient to all concerned to meet today."

"You hypocrite!" I shouted. "You call people to a strike and you're the one who breaks it! That was the most formal university class I've ever attended. Informal my ass! It's infinitely more formal than mine and I walked out of my teaching job because there was a strike!"

He looked at me with genuine surprise and asked, "Did I ask you to do that?"

Of course he hadn't asked me to walk out of my job nor had he told me that this strike would be the first stage of a revolution. He had merely given me a leaflet and I had asked him to drive me to campus on the day of the strike. I had neglected to ask if the leaflet meant what it said.

I asked Daman to take me home. On the way to his car I asked about the class he was giving to those he called the "political students." He told me that some of the students I had just met were "in the process of forging a relevant type of organization." I could guess which ones. He went on to say there had already been talk about publishing a newspaper.

"Another student paper?" I asked.

"No, not a student newspaper," he said. He was peeved. "I've had my fill of student newspapers, haven't you? What I'm talking about is an organization that organizes itself to publish a workers' paper."

"But you've just convinced me that you and those other members of your organization are anything but workers," I said. "What do you mean by a workers' paper? You've just spent an hour describing the paper's publishers as middle-class manipulators."

With an appearance of genuine surprise he asked, "What's that got to do with it?" The naïveté with which he asked this made me suppose that I had missed something which would have been perfectly obvious to anyone else. I recognized the source of his ability to intimidate.

Echoing your argument (probably word for word) I said that such a newspaper, published by Daman and his group of "political students," could only transform the real activity of workers into the political program of Daman's organization, once again representing and replacing the workers like all the other politicians who speak in their name.

Daman finally lost his matter-of-factness. He spoke to me in a tone he's rarely used on me before, a paternalistic, condescending tone. "I didn't say we were going to write the paper. The workers themselves are going to write it. I'm not talking about a newspaper for workers. You're the one who is talking about that. I'm talking about a workers' newspaper. Its task will not be to speak for the workers but to let the workers themselves speak. There's no question here of representing workers or replacing them or any of that old crap. I said earlier, that the new society is created at the point of production, particularly in the basic industries. It's not created in the heads of intellectuals. The sole task of this paper will be to recognize the existence of the new society and to record the facts of its existence."

This statement mystified me completely. The words described a project I would have embraced without reservations under other circumstances. Yet under the present circumstances everything about it seemed false. The selflessness that such a project would require was to be carried precisely by people who were among the crassest politicians I've ever seen. That paper would recognize, not the new society, but merely Daman's ideology, and it would record, not the facts of the struggle for the creation of the new society, but the rising influence of Daman's organization among workers. But it sounded like something altogether different.

It became clear to me why Daman had remained consistent for so many years. He had answers to everything, detailed and documented answers which he had worked out and perfected years ago, and the more he repeated them the more perfect they became. He carried a corpse in his mouth.

On that day I recognized Daman as the pedagogue who deserves all the critiques you've formulated. How grateful I am for your letter. I really don't think I could have seen through him on my own. How perfectly he fits your description! He and his students are going to edit "a workers' paper, not a paper for workers." Daman agrees with your critique of representation. He agrees so much that he'll represent the end of representation. He knows who the real revolutionaries are and therefore his paper will really be revolutionary. He knows that professors and students are middle class and therefore his paper will not be a students' or a professors' paper. He knows that the new society is located at the point of production and therefore his paper will not be merely another political gimmick nor his organization another racket. He'll reflect the new society.

On the way to my house I tell Daman about my correspondence with you and I beg him to come in and read the excerpts from your letter. When we go in, Sabina and Tina are sitting in the living room discussing your letter. Daman takes the translated sections and goes to my bedroom to read them.

I tell Sabina and Tina that I'm going to call Luisa. Tina asks if I really think Luisa will be willing to experience another scene like the one we had last time we discussed your letter. I call Luisa and tell her your letter contains a long account of Jasna Zbrkova's life. Luisa says she'd like to borrow the letter and read it by herself at her house. I guess she was really upset by our all-night session.

Tina's first comment about your letter is, "Wow, what a put-down of all your friends, Sophia!" Tina, predictably, is enchanted by the put-down.

Tina goes to the kitchen; it's her turn to make supper. When I go to the kitchen to make myself coffee she makes another comment about your letter. She raises the same question you and Jasna both raised. "You know, neither you nor Luisa have explained why you three were released twenty years ago after you spent only two days in jail. Saying that George Alberts arranged your release doesn't explain anything. Yarostan wants to know what power Alberts had to arrange your release. I'm curious about that too."

I can't answer Tina because I don't know. I vaguely remember that the police apologized to us. Perhaps they told us that our arrest had been a "mistake," as they later told Jasna. I also vaguely remember that George Alberts wasn't arrested. But it was Luisa who said that Alberts made our release possible. I didn't think to ask her how he had done that; I simply passed her comment on to you. I'll try to remember to ask her.

When I return to the living room, Sabina reminds me that you didn't answer the questions she had asked about Manuel. You commend her for "guessing" that Manuel and his friends were repressed by the revolutionary leaders and not by the reactionary generals, but you don't elaborate. She says the comment she made wasn't really a guess. She learned a great deal about that uprising from George Alberts; that's why she never accepted Luisa's view of that struggle. Although Alberts didn't explicitly tell her that revolutionaries had been jailed and shot by the "revolutionary government," she suspected this from what Alberts did tell her. Your account of Manuel confirmed her suspicions. She tells me that Alberts viewed that struggle as a struggle for industrialization and nothing more. In Alberts' view everything else was romanticism or ideological obfuscation. That's also Sabina's view of that struggle. To her I'm an example of the romanticism and Luisa of the obfuscation. Alberts told her that the sole task of that revolution was to sweep away the dark ages and create the conditions for progress; all those who opposed industrialization had to be pushed out of the way. These reactionaries included the church, the landowners and the military. What always bothered Sabina was that Alberts also included "reactionary saboteurs among the workers and peasants." Alberts, like Luisa, called these people "lumpen" and "hoodlums." Sabina was always suspicious about the inclusion of "saboteurs" among the "reactionaries" for the very reasons you mention in your letter, but she had no way of knowing who they really were and what they were fighting for. She had thought they were revolutionary workers and peasants who fought against both regimes because they wanted to industrialize on their own, without "revolutionary leaders," without managers like George Alberts, without a "revolutionary army." Manuel was apparently one of the people Alberts described as a saboteur and a lumpen. But what you've told about him so far doesn't exactly fit the picture she's constructed of these revolutionary saboteurs. That's why she wants to know more about Manuel.

Sabina also wants me to ask you and Jasna a question about Jasna's second arrest. Jasna says that the police insisted she had known a "notorious foreign spy." They also asked her if she had known Luisa and me. Then Jasna comments mysteriously that "they had the wrong last name down for Sophia and Luisa." Sabina asks if Jasna happens to remember the name the police had for us; was that name, by any chance, Alberts? When Sabina raises this question I ask her if she's suggesting that George Alberts was that foreign spy. "I'm not suggesting anything," Sabina says; "I'd just like to know if she remembers."

We call Daman when supper is ready. Tina and I look at him quizzically; we can't wait to hear his response. It's the first time Daman has ever eaten at our house and I can see that Sabina is waiting for the slightest pretext to tear into him. She dislikes academics in general; she dislikes Daman even more because he pretends not to be one.

Daman starts eating and his sole comment is, "Mm, this is very good. What is it?"

I ask myself if he's going to avoid your letter. I've seen him do that before. Whenever he confronts a situation he doesn't want to face he's like an ostrich with its head in sand; he simply pretends the situation isn't there.

The three of us eat in silence, glancing at Daman between bites. Finally I can't stand waiting any more and I blurt out, "Did you read it?"

"Every page," he says.

"Well?" I ask. "What did you think?"

"I don't understand why you asked me to read it," Daman says. "The entire exposition revives the worn out theory of the backwardness of the working class."

All three of us are startled.

"The what of the what?" Tina asks, almost spitting out the mouthful of food she's just taken.

Assuming his pedagogical posture again, Daman explains to Tina: "The theory, or so-called theory, of the backwardness of the working class. It's nothing but a rationalization of the prejudices of petty-bourgeois writers who don't know a thing about the revolutionary potential of the working class."

Before Daman is done speaking Sabina throws her knife down on her plate, gets up so abruptly she knocks the chair down behind her, and pointing her fork at Daman she shouts, "You're full of shit, professor!" Carrying the fork, she rushes away and slams the door of her room.

Daman remains perfectly calm. "She obviously agrees with him," he says, and continues eating.

Tina, who remains as calm as Daman, asks him, "How does that so-called theory apply to those sections of Yarostan's letter?"

"Is anyone else going to wave a fork in my face?" Daman asks, but neither of us laughs. "If workers were as backward as he describes them, socialism would be impossible."

"Show me where he says workers are backward!" Tina insists.

How glad I am that Tina never attended school and therefore never learned to be intimidated by pedagogues who force one to assume what they then proceed to prove.

"Do you want me to quote the actual lines where he says it?" Daman asks, trying to suggest that the passage I typed is full of such lines.

"How else could you show me what he says?" Tina asks.

"The idea of the workers' backwardness pervades his whole argument," Daman says curtly, as if with that statement he had definitively proved his accusation and he proceeds to shift the conversation to something else: "The working class is inherently revolutionary. This is not a matter —"

"Hey!" Tina interrupts. "Aren't you going to show me where he says the workers are backward?"

Daman is obviously not used to arguing with a person whose perception hasn't been dulled by formal education, and he proceeds as if he had succeeded in shifting the topic. "The working class continually develops the capacity to create a new society, there as well as here. The workers always and everywhere exhaust the available possibilities."

Tina just glares at him.

"Now wait a minute. Daman," I say, becoming as frustrated as Tina seems to be. "Do you think the police regime Yarostan lived under for the past twenty years exhausted the available possibilities?"

"I didn't say that," Daman insists. "I said workers create organizations to struggle for whatever seems useful to them. These struggles win for the working class whatever it is objectively possible to win. These victories are never granted without struggle, and they are never tricks to deceive the working class."

"If you're not saying that police regime was a working class victory then what in the world are you saying?" Tina asks, apparently giving up her attempt to get her earlier question answered.

"What's wrong with your friend's comments," Daman says, "is that he criticizes the role of all types of organizations and leaders in restraining and limiting the revolutionary capacity of workers. But he never deals with the question of organizations and leaders in a fundamental way. Unless you accept a conspiratorial theory of history — that organizations and leaders are always and everywhere introduced to restrain and defeat the workers."

"I'm lost," Tina says. "At least I think I'm lost. Everything you say sounds like an evasion and seems to have nothing to do with what anyone is saying."

"I'm lost too," I admit. "What's your point? That Yarostan doesn't deal with organizations and leaders in a fundamental way whereas you do?"

"That's right," he says. "His critique of organizations and leaders is totally misplaced."

"Misplaced!" I shout. "He's been experiencing the effects of those organizations and their police for the past twenty years!"

"He's not the only one experiencing those effects; so are millions of other people," he says.

"What in hell does that mean?" I ask, starting to shake with frustration. There's no way to talk to him! I begin to wish I had walked out like Sabina instead of trying to communicate with him.

"Your friend doesn't like real revolutions," Daman says. "That comes through every line. He wants a revolution to be pure. But real revolutions are the only ones that take place and workers' struggles are never pure. Your friend is against all real struggles."

"You're a real card, professor!" Tina says, unsuccessfully pretending to be amused. "Next time you come to dinner I'm going to fry you a turd fished straight out of the toilet bowl and if you don't like it I'll ask; What's the matter with you, professor? Do you only like food when it's pure?"

Daman turns to me pretending that he's being persecuted and asks, "Do I have to listen to that?"

Without a trace of sympathy for his plight I tell him, "Daman, you don't have to listen to anything except your own inner voices."

"I'm trying to make the point," he continues, "that your friend is like all those petty-bourgeois writers who condemn real revolutions because they don't live up to certain standards set up, not by the struggling workers, but by the bourgeois writers. Workers always struggle for whatever is objectively possible, whether or not it's pure, whether or not it lives up to the standards set up by the bourgeois writers."

I start to boil. "That's an apology for police states if I ever heard one!" I shout. "Whatever happens to workers is for you a working class victory. If workers are shot and jailed then that's the only victory that was objectively possible! Whatever happens to workers is all that was objectively possible. You're an apologist for the status quo!"

"Yarostan is no more of a bourgeois writer than I am!" Tina shouts.

Daman at last shows signs of becoming angry. He turns to me and pretending to be injured at the very core of his being, he says, "Sophie, your last statement is a complete distortion of everything I have ever said, and you know it. You know perfectly well that I'm not talking about counter-revolutions so don't you dare call me an apologist for counter-revolutions. I'm talking about revolutions that don't live up to the expectations of a middle class intellectual."

"You don't know what you're talking about!" Tina shouts. "You, a full-fledged university professor, are calling someone who spent half his life working in factories a middle-class intellectual. Talk about distortions! How do you dare —"

"That's just plain horseshit!" Daman shouts, cutting Tina short and losing his professorial detachment altogether. "No factory worker I know could have written anything like this!"

"Wow!" shouts Tina. "Look who's talking about the backward workers who can't write and have no standards!"

"Do you want to talk seriously or do you want to have a shouting match?" he shouts. "If you'd like to have a shouting match then count me out because I've got more important things to do and my nerves can't take it. So what if he spent half his life in a factory? So have I!"

"And you sure have capitalized on that fact," I comment sarcastically.

"What's that got to do with anything?" he shouts. "That doesn't make me a factory worker any more than it makes him a factory worker or anyone else in this room. It's obvious that he spent the other half of his life getting a political education every bit as complete as mine."

Without the slightest hope of getting through to him I comment, "But Daman, this afternoon you said that one's relation to production is the only test of one's class."

Tina says with venom, "You're not the one to talk about other people's distortions, professor! You're talking about someone who spent the other half of his life in prison, and if you call that a university education you can kiss my ass and call it love at first sight since it's obvious that with all your education you didn't learn to call things by their names!"

Pretending not to have understood what Tina said, Daman turns to me and asks, "Is this the level of your usual political discussions?"

"No it isn't," I say with a venom that by this point matches Tina's. "Neither Tina nor I have ever discussed anything at such a low level."

"I can see that it's time for me to leave," he says, getting up.

I get up too and continue in the same tone, "You've evaded every one of Tina's questions with cheap tricks and sneaky shifts of topic. She asked you how you could call a worker who spent half his life in prison a middle class intellectual. And not just any prison, but a prison created by the organizations and leaders you defend."

Fidgeting with the doorknob he says, "I hate to say this, Sophie, but when it comes to politics you're a complete ignoramus. If you knew anything at all about the working class, you'd know that leaders don't simply impose themselves on the working class. Leaders are products of the working class. If workers are defeated, it's not because of the evil ways of leaders but because the working class isn't able to take control of the means of production. It's not their leaders but their work itself that teaches workers how to run production."

Shaking with frustration, I try to talk calmly, "Daman, you just keep repeating that, but you obviously don't believe it. You learned your whole argument, not from work itself, but from the writings of so-called revolutionary leaders. Half of your statements are quotations from the writings of the first dictator of the working class."

"Your naïveté simply amazes me," Daman says, still fidgeting with the door-knob. "It so happens that workers produce their strongest leaders when they're themselves strongest. The strength of the leaders derives from the strength of the working class!"

"Now you've said it!" I shout. "The stronger the leader the greater the triumph of the workers. You're an out and out apologist for the police state and you camouflage it with such unbelievable claptrap about the workers themselves. For you the total enslavement of the workers by the first so-called proletarian dictator is the model of the workers' victory. That's what you call the new society. The almighty leader is the sign of the strength of the workers. Slavery is freedom."

Daman throws the door open but remains in the doorway. "Your critique of the first great leader —"

"Is misplaced!" I cut in. "All critiques of the great leader are misplaced, because under all your talk about workers at the point of production you worship the great leader. The sun rises and sets with the great leader!"

While I'm shouting at him, he walks halfway to his car, then turns around and shouts: "That's right! Misplaced! By raising the role of the great leaders in that way, you assume nothing has changed during the past fifty years. You're only demonstrating your complete ignorance of the fact that the working class today is even better educated and even better organized, not by political organizations but by production! With modern technology and advanced means of communication, nothing can stop the workers from building a new society and a new state!"

"A new state! You said it! An even newer state and an even more total dictator of the proletariat!" I shout while Daman rushes to his car.

Tina runs behind Daman. It looks like she's going to rush into the car with him. He slams the car door. She plants herself by the driver's side of the car and starts shouting at him through the closed window. "Now I understand what you're all about, professor! You're a conservative bureaucrat who thinks workers are all popcorn eaters and baseball fans who don't know they're being had when someone calls himself their leader. To you all those popcorn-eaters are impure and that's why they'll always be tied to the point of production. And that's why there'll always be room for flunkies like you in the government palaces —"

Daman drives off. Tina, standing in the middle of the street, continues shouting at the quickly vanishing car: "And anyone who tells you they're not going to remain at the point of production, that they're going to come out in mass to destroy the government palaces, is a misplaced petty-bourgeois intellectual and an ignoramus who doesn't know that workers are impure. And you're betting they'll remain impure. They sure as hell better remain impure if you're going to keep your cushy job!"

I burst our laughing. Tina looks so ludicrous standing in the street shouting at nobody. When she sees me she starts laughing too, and when we go in she comments, "Some fancy friends you've got."

Yes, I certainly do have "fancy" friends. You and Jasna made that perfectly clear to me. I obviously couldn't have known it before your letter came, but now I see that Daman is in suitable company with Marc Glavni, Vera Neis Krena and Adrian Povrshan. Your letter was the instrument that unmasked this academic with a corpse in his mouth. This phoney factory worker who parades as an expert on factory workers perfectly fits the picture you drew of him before you knew anything about him. He really is everything you say. The rigid theory he's been carrying around all these years transforms revolution into something like his own private domain. He's a priest of a sect of believers. That organization he's trying to found will only spread his own rigor mortis to others, and the aim of that newspaper he's talking about is to plant corpses in lots of people's mouths.

Thanks to your letter I can see through Daman. And I obviously understand that Adrian, Vera and the others are opportunists. But I think your comments about me are extremely unfair. I once engaged in projects with those people and those projects were very important to me. Does that make me one of them? Does that mean I was an opportunist too? I once shared a project with Daman. Does that mean I'm like him?

I think it's mean of you to identify me with them. What I did and who I was can't be defined by what Daman became nor by what Marc and Vera became. Even if Jasna is right, even if Marc, Vera and Claude were already starting to climb bureaucratic ladders at the time I knew them, this doesn't mean that I was climbing such a ladder too.

Daman was already a priest of a sect when I first met him and worked with him. But that doesn't mean I was a priestess of a sect, nor does it mean that the activity we shared consisted of propagating a religion. The activity I was engaged in, however flawed it might have been, was some kind of affirmation of life, not any kind of affirmation of death. If Vera, Marc and Daman were running alongside me but heading elsewhere, you can't say that I was heading toward the destination they reached. What they've all become doesn't tell you anything at all about who I am, nor even about what I did with them.

Yes, like Daman, and like Marc, Vera and Adrian, I went to the university. I do have that much in common with them, but not much more. Jasna went to college too, and she's neither an official nor a missionary. And if you call the carton plant our "first university," then you too have that much in common with the rest of us. My similarity with Vera and Daman ends where it begins. My life in the university has nothing at all in common with Vera's or Adrian's or Marc's bureaucratic ambitions, just as my activity on the university newspaper staff had nothing in common with Daman's missionary activity.

When I first met Daman on the newspaper staff his relation to Minnie Vach was very similar to Adrian's relation to Vera. Daman and Minnie were members of a political sect like the one Daman is trying to bring to life again now. Minnie was always the theorist and Daman was something like her henchman. Their organization published a paper but I never read it and consequently I can't tell you how well the self-chosen prophets recognized and recorded the new society while workers remained at the point of production. What I can tell you is that I did not work, and would never have worked, on their organization's newspaper, and that Daman and Minnie did not transform the university newspaper into their organization's organ. In this respect Daman and Minnie were much more decent than their political enemies on the staff, Lem Icel and Rhea Morphen. Lem and Rhea would have liked nothing better than to transform the university newspaper into a propaganda sheet for their organization, and I was as hostile to their attempts to do this as anyone else on the staff.

You're probably right in saying that I recognized the repressive aspirations of Lem and Rhea mainly because they expressed them so openly. But you're wrong when you say I glorify their more sophisticated political cousins. If I "glorified" Minnie and Daman in my last letter, it was because the moments I shared with them on the newspaper staff were among the happiest moments of my life, not because I shared any of their organizational commitments. I really do think you get carried away by your own rhetoric. In my last letter I told you that my friend Alec had to trample publicly on all his past political commitments before Minnie and Daman accepted him as a friend and ally. Admittedly I didn't make an exhaustive critique of Minnie and Daman but the little I did say hardly amounted to a glorification. And I certainly didn't glorify anyone else on the staff. I rather think I made the others seem more ridiculous than they really were.

I'll stop trying to compare my activity to yours. I realize that the circumstances are too different and I'm obviously failing to communicate the similarities I see between the two situations. I finally understand your critique, and I recognize some of the people I worked with as the targets of that critique. But I don't think the activity itself was determined by what those people were, nor by what they've become since. I think that my activity in the university was a modest but genuine act of rebellion against a repressive social system. I see that Daman fits your description of a repressive "revolutionary." But I don't think the activity I shared with him can be described as "repressive rebellion."

The activity I'm about to describe began fourteen years ago. We were among the first students who raised our voices against the witch hunts taking place at that time. Our activity didn't stop the witch hunts and it obviously didn't destroy the social system that perpetrated them. But by raising our voices we did stimulate others to raise theirs and this is why I'm proud of having been part of that activity. Students at another university followed our example and in time moved much further than we had ever dreamed of moving. In time the protest movement grew so vast that it did play a role in putting an end to witch hunts, while it simultaneously reproduced relationships which were at least as repressive as the ones we had started to fight against. Our initial gestures weren't as far-reaching as those of the movement which later grew to such proportions, but the repressive overtones of our activity weren't as far-reaching either. Not that ugly relationships were absent among us. Unfortunately that wasn't the case at all. A great deal was ugly. But there was one trait we didn't share with the later "student movement," or at least with its spokesmen. In the activities I shared with them, these individuals didn't consider themselves spokesmen or representatives despite the fact that almost half the people on that staff were members of political organizations which did claim to represent the interests of other people. Whatever they might have done in their organizations, when I worked with them they didn't act as if history had elected them to reflect, represent, recognize or record the desires of workers, students or anyone else. Each one of us fought to realize her or his own desires. We represented no one but ourselves. No, we didn't even represent ourselves. We were ourselves.

In my last letter I told you something about the articles we wrote, articles which exposed the militarization of professors and students and documented the repression of radicals. I also mentioned the biggest article of the year, Minnie's interview with a campus general who kept files on all the students in the university.

Minnie's article caused a scandal on campus. Alec and I were night editors on the issue in which Minnie's article was published. We worked on it on the very night when Sabina came to the co-op to tell me Ron had been killed. The following morning, Minnie, Daman, Alec and I went to four of the boxes from which students took the paper. We engaged students in conversations about the article and asked their permission to publish their comments in the paper. We then ran a series of interviews with students in several consecutive issues.

Some of the students' comments were priceless, especially those which expressed sympathy for the campus military establishment. I still remember the gist of what a bristle-haired athlete told me. He said he wasn't at all surprised that the army and the police (Minnie's article hadn't said anything about the police) kept files on the entire population. "After all," he explained to me, "It's their job to protect society from dangerous elements, and the only way they can do their job properly is by constant surveillance of all actual and potential dangerous elements. They ought to use those files they've got and start rounding up all subversives, homosexuals, pacifists and other crackpots so as to make life safe for the rest of the population."

He ventured to guess that "the reason the government isn't rounding up all those sick perverts is because the cost of imprisoning or exterminating them would be too great for the government's present budget." He concluded by saying that "I, for one, would be glad to pay more taxes so as to enable the government to carry out that enterprise."

I got several other interviews similar in outlook to this one, but none of them were as rabid. Minnie's interviews were precisely the opposite from mine. She said she couldn't stomach students who sympathized with the military and she only interviewed those whose comments were hostile to the general's files. One student she interviewed said he wouldn't be able to sleep any more because every time he heard the police siren at night he'd think the police were coming to arrest him. Others she interviewed spoke at length about the "unconstitutionality" of the general's files, and one student commented on the general's anti-Semitism. One of the "insights" the general had gotten from his files was that "subversive traits" appeared more frequently among "Baltic Jews" than among any other "easily identifiable" group.

I felt that my articles were much better than Minnie's precisely because I didn't just interview students who said things I agreed with. I felt that the students who defended the general exposed him much more effectively than those who attacked him. Besides which it was such a ball to interview those reactionaries. I did them the favor of making their statements coherent and grammatical. Most of those protectors of civilization and culture, future officials and managers, hadn't ever learned to use their own language.

Daman and Alec were terribly disappointing. They didn't contribute a single article. Instead of interviewing students they had gotten into heated arguments with them, and Alec even got injured in a fight with a student he was supposedly interviewing.

Every single one of Minnie's and my articles were published. It was obvious to Hugh (the editor) that my articles reflected "one side" of the picture whereas Minnie's reflected "the other side," and consequently there was never any question of excluding any article.

This series of interviews caused as much of a scandal as Minnie's original interview, and the scandal led directly to the repression of the newspaper staff.

Professors and students discussed these articles in their classes, and the city newspapers started to take an interest in the question. But the two city papers were owned by people just like the general who kept the files, and they weren't interested in our exposures of the general's files but in us. They started publishing stories which said the university newspaper had been "taken over by a clique of reds and pinkos," and that this clique was intent on defaming and destroying "the university, the army and the flag." They quoted some of the most extreme statements of students we had interviewed and said the statements had been parts of editorials which "expressed the newspaper staff's policy."

I've never known if it was the campaign carried on in the city newspapers, or pressure from the campus military, or the university administration's own embarrassment that set off the repression. It was probably all of these things plus some others I'm not even aware of. Only a few days after Minnie's original article appeared, we got a note from the administration demanding that the editor and managing editor go to the office of the university president "immediately, before the preparation of another day's issue." Hugh and Bess rushed to the president's office, and the rest of us continued working on the next day's paper. When Hugh and Bess returned an hour later all the work stopped. Bess said the president had told them that the paper would have to stop publishing articles about the general's files. If such articles continued appearing, there would be "severe consequences."

Hugh said he had objected to being called to the president's office "on a matter that is completely within the competence of the elected editor," and that he would disregard the president's threat and continue to edit the paper "according to strictly journalistic standards."

Every one of us jumped up with relief and congratulated him for his principled stand. But he still wanted a vote of confidence. "Since I was elected by the staff, the final decision has to be made by the staff. I feel that these articles are of high quality and of great public interest and that each article expresses a different side of the problem. Therefore the question is whether or not the staff wants to continue to do what is perfectly justifiable from a journalistic standpoint, but may lead to severe consequences the nature of which is unknown to us."

None of us could imagine what the "severe consequences" might be, and no one was particularly worried. Minnie and I still had several more interviews to publish and the vast majority of the staff voted in favor of publishing them. Lem and Rhea abstained from voting.

After all our articles were published we all thought the crisis had blown over, although the city papers continued carrying completely made-up accounts of who we were and what we did.

About two weeks after my last article appeared, two weeks during which there hadn't been anything really interesting in the paper, the university administration struck. Something called a "directive" was released by the administration to the city press and the student government. We all gathered in the office and read the statement with disbelief. Minnie started crying. I felt like crying too. Hugh seemed thunderstruck and just paced back and forth.

According to this directive, the student newspaper would be "given back" to the student community at the end of that week. Since the directive came out on a Thursday, this meant we would only put out one more issue. The directive went on to say that "after a brief delay, competent journalists selected from among the student body will resume publication of a newspaper that reflects the interests of the student community." This sentence suggested that we were neither competent nor students, but it also suggested something much more ominous. As far as any of us knew, the editors of the university's newspaper had always been elected by the staff, and this was now going to end; the selected journalists would obviously be people appointed by the administration. The statement also gave away what kind of people were going to edit a paper that "reflects the interests of the student community": obviously not people like Lem and Rhea who in their own eyes reflected the interests of the student community, but rather people who reflected those interests in the administrations eyes, namely people who served the administration's interests, stooges appointed by the administration.

The directive went on to explain the reasons for this action. It said that "a self-perpetuating clique of radical agitators has taken over the publication of the student newspaper, thereby endangering the education and well-being of the student body and doing irreparable damage to the university's public image." This statement was not an outright lie. It was authority's way of stating the truth. "Self-perpetuating" simply meant that we elected our own editors, as opposed to the new arrangement which introduced an administration-perpetuated clique. But the expression "self-perpetuating clique" made the electoral arrangement sound so underhanded and manipulative.

It was also true that there were proportionally many more "radicals" on the newspaper staff than there were in the student body as a whole. For all I know every "radical" in the university at that time was on the newspaper staff. But it's perfectly obvious why this should have been the case. It was a period when all self-expression was being fiercely repressed. Those few students who refused to be muzzled were by definition "radicals" since they were swimming against the stream. These were the only students who tried to express themselves at a time when self-expression was taboo, and where should they have gone if not to the newspaper staff, the only place in the university where self-expression was still possible? The directive also said that the present staff of the paper was not being fired; on the contrary, the staff was being urged to cooperate with the new editorial board to make the paper "a representative student newspaper which is a positive asset to the university community."

All of us skipped our classes and spent the day at the office, planning our last issue. I felt as if a major historical event had taken place, as if a world war had just been declared.

Hugh suggested that each of us write an editorial expressing our side of the question; he said the bias of the last issue would be more than compensated for by the fact that all the issues from then on would express the other side.

I suggested that black borders be placed around every page, expressing the fact that the press had just died at the university. Bess Lach was violently opposed to this. "Just because we won't be the editors doesn't mean there won't be a paper!" she said. Someone called for a vote and everyone but Bess was in favor of the black borders.

Rhea suggested that we use the front page to call for a mass demonstration against the suppression of the paper. Bess objected, "You can't use the school paper to advocate a demonstration!" and Hugh agreed. I tried to argue that we were no longer bound by regulations that the university itself had just broken, but only Lem and Rhea agreed with me.

Suddenly Thurston Rakshas, of all people, made a suggestion that seemed to be similar to Rhea's, although Rhea didn't think so. Thurston argued that it was perfectly legitimate to announce a coming event, since this was one of the paper's functions. We could announce that on Friday morning the former staff members of the university newspaper were going to march in a funeral procession across campus, carrying the corpse of the university newspaper inside a coffin. That upper class dandy always did have a sense of humor. I was immediately fired up by the idea. Hugh and Alec were also enthusiastic about it from the start. Minnie favored some kind of demonstration but she argued that a funeral would only suggest that we had been defeated and had given up the struggle. For once Lem and Rhea agreed with Minnie; Daman obviously did too.

The argument about the nature of the demonstration was sidetracked by Bess, who had worked herself up into a hysterical state. "We can only express our opinions of the university directive! We can't use this paper to advocate one or another course of action. That's a betrayal of our trust! It's a crime! By calling for such a demonstration we would be using the paper as our own private organ. But the paper doesn't belong to us. It belongs to all the students. And it won't be dead just because some of us no longer work on it."

Thurston defended his idea of announcing the mock funeral by pointing out that by the time it took place the people taking part in it would no longer be the paper's staff but merely a group of anonymous students.

Bess shouted at Thurston, "But we're not anonymous students today. We're the editorial board and staff of the university newspaper, and today you can't transform this paper into an instrument for your own demonstration. Tomorrow you can carry all the coffins you want!"

Thurston angrily called for a vote.

Bess shouted, "It's not in our jurisdiction to vote about university regulations!"

"It isn't?" Thurston asked. "Watch this! All" in favor of Bess's position."

No one voted in favor, not even Bess since she disapproved of the vote.

"All in favor of mine!"

Everyone's hand went up except Bess's. But that was a sneaky maneuver. Thurston hadn't only put an end to Bess's objections; he had also closed the discussion on the nature of the demonstration. We were all aware of this but no one reopened that discussion. I suppose we all knew that if we spent the day arguing we wouldn't have time to prepare any kind of demonstration, to write our editorials or to put out our last paper. And I suppose Minnie and Rhea considered Thurston's suggestion better than no demonstration at all.

Bess stormed out of the office while Thurston's hastily called vote was taking place. She returned later in the day, but only to submit her editorial. She didn't take part in the work on the last issue.

Later in the day Rhea suggested that we run off leaflets announcing the demonstration and that we distribute them to all the student dormitories. I was in favor of doing that. Hugh objected to this type of "agitation" because the very nature of the demonstration required us to be "dignified and responsible." Minnie said we simply didn't have time to do that, and she was right.

We worked feverishly. Since everyone was composing an editorial, no one started doing the typing and editing until evening. Hugh did the layout in Bess's absence, and although he was as good at it as she, he wasn't nearly as fast.

Late that night Rhea made another suggestion. She said the former staff should start publishing an off-campus paper as soon as possible. Only such an act would clarify the real significance of the black borders and the funeral procession. The official university newspaper would have died, but not the people who had given it life. The contrast between the two publications would make it obvious to all that the press was still alive in our publication, whereas the university paper had become a corpse.

I was moved by Rhea's suggestion but no one discussed it. We were simply too busy. We didn't get the paper to the printer's until two in the morning; we didn't leave the printer's until five, and we had to get up again a few hours later to carry out the demonstration we were announcing.

Fortunately, when Thurston had made his suggestion he hadn't expected the rest of us to do the work of implementing it. Thurston himself worked out the details of his mock funeral after he left the printer at five in the morning. One of his father's friends ran a funeral parlor. Thurston went there at six in the morning and explained to the undertaker that he needed a coffin as well as several wreaths and bouquets of flowers for a theatrical performance. He drove all the props to campus in a hearse.

All of us except Bess gathered at the newspaper office at eight in the morning, but the copies of the paper hadn't been delivered to their boxes yet because of how late we'd gotten the layout to the printer. The papers didn't arrive until nine, and we spent the hour frustratedly waiting for them, since our "funeral" would have been incomprehensible without any explanations. Rhea, naturally, reminded us that leaflets would have solved this problem.

We were all dead tired, but we started out full of enthusiasm. Thurston came dressed in a tuxedo and Hugh wore a black suit and a comical black hat. Daman and Minnie walked in front of the procession giving out copies of the newspaper. Hugh, Thurston, Alec and Lem carried the coffin, which was covered with flowers. Rhea and I walked behind the coffin with wreaths. We walked, very slowly, in front of all the administrative and academic buildings and in front of all the dormitories.

But our initial enthusiasm died. The mock funeral was a big disappointment, even to Thurston. Students would pause briefly, stare at the paper, stare at us, and then continue along their varied paths. The main response was an icy indifference. Some students said things like, "Go back where you came from!" and "Who do you think you're fooling?" Not one student said anything sympathetic. I had hoped there'd be a mile-long procession, but not one student joined us. I don't think the fault lay with Thurston's idea. The eight of us would have looked even more ridiculous if we had announced a "mass demonstration" instead of the "funeral."

After walking for two hours which seemed as long as two years, the "procession" returned to its starting point and the coffin was taken into the editor's office. Lem and Alec came back out, but Hugh and Thurston stayed inside the editor's office and closed the door. I lay down on the bench. I was exhausted and I felt like crying.

Minnie asked if we had all read the managing editor's final statement. I lazily picked up the paper and started leafing through it. I thought I had seen all the articles the night before, when I'd edited the copy, but I remembered I hadn't seen Bess's editorial.

"You don't have to hunt for it. Sophie. It's right on the front page," Minnie told me.

I sat up. I was furious. The headline in the middle of the front page said, "Shades of Grey." The first line of Bess's editorial said, "There is no black and white; there are only shades of grey." That didn't apply to the university's directive, which is what her article was about. Her next statement said, "There are some arguments in favor of the staff's point of view, but there are also arguments in favor of the administration's point of view." The argument in favor of the staff was that the staff had consisted of "relatively competent journalists" and that the coverage had "in general been responsible and fair. But responsibility and fairness broke down when some staff members engaged themselves in an anti-military campaign." According to Bess the editors, "including the undersigned managing editor," convinced themselves that by printing articles favorable to the general and his files alongside articles hostile to the general, the paper was expressing both sides of the question. But those were not really two sides of the question; according to Bess they were the same side, since the administration had made it clear that both types of articles created an image which damaged the university. "Yet the editors and staff voted in favor of excluding the administration's side."

I asked, "Who put this garbage on the front page?"

Alec answered, "Hugh typed it, edited it and laid it out in the middle of the front page so that the last issue wouldn't spoil the paper's tradition of fairness."

"But it's full of distortions and outright lies!" I said.

"Hugh must have known we'd all want to leave it out," Alec said. "That's why he didn't let us see it before putting it in the middle of the front page."

I felt like vomiting. I had not only hoped that a mile-long procession would follow our coffin. I had also hoped that our course of action would somehow be very clear when the demonstration ended, that we would know what we had to do next. But nothing was clear except that my project was over. It had ended as abruptly as my activity at the carton plant had ended when we were arrested. And at that moment I blamed Hugh for the failure of the demonstration: I convinced myself we would have had support, and lots of it, if Bess's ugly argument hadn't appeared in the middle of the front page.

But instead of storming into Hugh's office, I lay back down and closed my eyes. My exhaustion was greater than my anger. I must have dozed because I wasn't aware until later that a strange sequence of events had begun to take place. Hugh and Thurston had been in the editor's office for over an hour. I vaguely knew that at some point Thurston had asked Daman as well as Alec to join them in the office and that sometime later Lem was called in as well. But I didn't respond to the strange fact that Rhea, Minnie and I were left outside, I asleep, Minnie and Rhea wondering what was going on but far too hostile toward each other to start a conversation.

I woke up when Alec stormed out of the editor's office and slammed the door behind him.

"What in hell is going on in there? What's all the shouting about, and why aren't we in on it?" Minnie asked him.

Alec sat down next to me. I could see he was agitated. "Were you fighting in there about that dumb editorial?" I asked.

"I'll tell you exactly what's going on in there!" he said. "It's the dirtiest shit I've ever seen. Hugh and Thurston had worked out a filthy strategy when Daman and I were called in. I made such a stink about it that they dropped it. But then Thurston convinced all four of them to accept an even filthier scheme, so I walked out."

"Can you hold yourself together enough to tell us about it?" Minnie asked him.

"Thurston had this idea that we ought to publish an off-campus paper —" Alec began.

Rhea interrupted him to say, "That wasn't Thurston's idea; it was mine, Alec!"

"So it was! I remember that now. Sophie was the only one who responded when you suggested it. That was your idea. God damn them!" Saying this, Alec shook his fist at the door of the editor's office. "Well, they stole it from you, Rhea. That's what happened. Thurston loves your idea, but he doesn't want you to be part of it. He convinced Hugh that if you and Lem were both on the staff he, Thurston, would soon quit, Hugh would be outnumbered, and the paper would become a propaganda sheet, and when Thurston says propaganda sheet he makes it sound like toilet paper with shit on it. Even if he didn't say it that way, you know that Hugh must have nightmares about being caught in a paper that's biased. Fair and responsible. He's got those damned words etched on his brain. He thinks he's still editing the university paper. When they call Daman and me in, Thurston tells us we're going to put out this off-campus paper, all of us except Lem and Rhea. I ask what's wrong with Lem and Rhea. That fucker Daman grins and doesn't say anything. I tell Hugh and Thurston I don't understand. Hugh tells me this shit about not putting out a propaganda sheet and then I do understand. I start shouting and telling Hugh and Thurston to crawl to the administration, ask to be forgiven and beg to be rehired on the administration-run paper. I tell them they're about to do to Lem and Rhea exactly what the administration just did to us. Hugh pretends he'd never thought of that, and says I'm right. I argue that if we're going to put out that kind of sheet, we've got to include every single member of the fired staff, even Bess if she's not about to sell out to the administration's staff. At that point Thurston calls Lem into the office and I'm under the impression that I won the argument. But that Thurston is as slippery as a fish. He explains the idea to Lem and then tells him that all the men on the staff are going to put out the off-campus paper. That blockhead Lem says that he understands that! He starts talking about how dangerous it is to publish what he calls an underground newspaper — much too dangerous for women. Thurston has to cool Lem down when he starts talking about a revolutionary underground newspaper. I shout at Lem and call him a stupid asshole. I tell him that a minute ago it was he who was being excluded. But I can see that he's enchanted about being included. Lem may be your comrade and all that, Rhea, but you can't deny that the fucker is dumb! What cheap shit! I can see right through it! Thurston thinks Lem and Daman won't ever vote on the same side. That means the vote will always be three to two, and Thurston and Hugh will always be on the winning side. If the three of you were included the vote would usually go the other way. That's why they're leaving you out and that's why I'm walking out. Without me the vote will always be three to one. They can have it!"

"Didn't Daman say anything?" Minnie asked.

"They can have that bastard too!" Alec said. "No, he didn't say a word. He just sat there and listened. That's why they wanted him in there instead of you."

Alec squeezed my hand and said to me, "I'll talk to you some other time, Sophie. I can't stand this place for one second longer." He walked out of the office. I started to cry.

The door of the editor's office opened and Lem stepped out, grinning, looking as if he were intentionally trying to confirm Alec's characterization of him. "The press is dead! Long live the press!" Lem shouted. The three of us didn't respond. We stared at him with intense hostility. He continued, revoltingly self-satisfied: "I'd like to announce the birth of a new publication out of the womb of the old. It will be an underground newspaper, and two names were under consideration: *The Spark*, suggested by me, and *Omissions*, suggested by Hugh. The majority voted in favor of *Omissions* because the specific task of this underground newspaper will be to publish the news which will from now on be omitted from the crippled official newspaper."

"That's a perfect title for it," I told him. "It began its career by omitting half the people who ought to be on it."

Rhea got up and started walking slowly toward Lem. She looked as if she intended to strangle him. When she was a foot away from him she said, through her teeth and with her mouth nearly shut, "It was my idea to publish that paper." Then she started trembling. I asked her if she was all right. She walked out of the office, her eyes red with rage. She looked hysterical.

Today I think it strange that Lem and Rhea were so committed to that paper. The project which it was to carry out had much more in common with my outlook than with theirs. It was I who was in favor of printing omitted facts and letting scandalous information speak for itself. Letting facts speak for themselves and letting readers draw their own conclusions conflicted with Lem's and Rhea's political commitments.

As soon as Rhea was gone Lem turned toward me and tried to explain that it hadn't been his idea to exclude anyone. This had already been decided without him. And then he went on to talk about the dangers of publishing and distributing an "underground" newspaper: "Counter-revolutionaries might attack the newspaper headquarters at any time of day or night; goons might attack us while we're distributing it." I turned my back to him and he left the newspaper office.

Daman came out of the editor's office looking like a dog that had just been beaten, shuffling his feet, his head bobbing from side to side. Thurston came out behind Daman, slapped him on the back, said, "See you next weekend," and rushed out of the office with a victorious grin smeared across his face.

Minnie walked toward Daman, shouted, "You traitor," hit him twice across the face so hard that I jumped up both times, and she too rushed out of the office.

I remained on the bench, staring at the typewriter I had used so many times. I turned around when I heard Hugh come out of what had been his office ever since I'd been on the staff. He was surprised to see me. In his arms he held a large bundle of papers he had collected. He had tears in his eyes. Looking away from me he said, "I'm awfully sorry." He walked away slowly. He was just another student now. To me he was still the editor.

I was alone with the typewriters, the u-shaped desk in the middle of the room, the doors to the editor's and managing editor's offices, the pages tacked to the walls with errors circled in red. I cried. I was going to miss the typewriter, the desk, the walls and the people with whom I had spent so many hectic days. I hadn't felt so lonely, so excluded since the night I had gone to the beach with Ron and Sabina and had walked home by myself after Ron wrecked his father's car.

I started to think they would all miss this office. And then the thought passed through my mind that Alec hadn't told us the truth about the meeting that had just taken place in Hugh's office. I convinced myself that they hadn't wanted to exclude Rhea, but rather Minnie and me, and that Rhea had been excluded with us just for the sake of appearances. They had all turned against Minnie and me because we were the ones who had provoked the repression with our articles. I convinced myself we were being blamed for having destroyed the paper for everyone else. I simply couldn't accept Alec's explanation of my exclusion. I couldn't make myself believe that I had been excluded from the "underground" paper because Thurston was counting votes. I couldn't accept such an explanation because the exclusion meant so much to me and the motives for it were so petty. My exclusion from *Omissions* by my own friends was much more painful to me than my exclusion from the university newspaper by the administration. Not only because the newest exclusion was so personal but because *Omissions* was a project being launched by the people who were going to engage in it, whereas the university paper was an institution that had existed before any of us had ever joined it; it was not our project. I was hurt because *Omissions* was precisely the kind of project I had hoped I'd find when I first enrolled in the university. It seemed to me then that this project was identical to the project I had taken part in years earlier, with you and Jasna and the others at the carton plant, when we formulated our own goals and strategies, printed our own posters, distributed them ourselves. I was excluded from the only genuine community I had found here, the second community I had found in my whole life.

I now recognize the validity of your critique of my earlier activity. I didn't understand the context in which it took place and I wasn't aware of the motives that animated the people around me. But I don't think you can impute their motives to me. The activity in the carton plant was not a rung of a bureaucratic ladder for me, and unlike Vera and Marc, I haven't risen in any hierarchy. My desire to participate on *Omissions* wasn't motivated by bureaucratic ambitions. I was pained by my exclusion not because it deprived me of opportunities or comforts but because it deprived me of a project, of a community, of genuinely independent activity. I sat in that office and cried because my project with you, Jasna, Vera and Marc was going to remain the only genuine project in which I had taken part.

I understand Jasna's narrative. I've even extended it by telling you who Daman was and what he has become. I'm sure I'd be equally disappointed if I learned what the other people on that newspaper staff were doing today. But that's not the point. My point is that the activity I wanted to share with them was not composed of their character traits, any more than the activity at the carton plant was composed of Marc's or Vera's bureaucratic ambitions, and no matter what they've become I since then, you can't take away from me what I experienced I because what I experienced was my project, not their ambitions.

What I don't seem able to convey to you is that what I sought all my life is something that's completely my own. It's a significant project within the context of a community. When I tell you that I learned about the possibility of such a project and such a community during those days I spent with you, I'm merely telling you a fact about myself, a detail of my biography; I'm not telling this to you in order to glorify those specific people nor that specific project. The reason I felt so miserable when I was excluded from the off-campus paper was because I was deprived of something I had learned to want many years earlier. It had nothing to do with Vera's or Marc's titles. It had to do with activity and with human relationships. What I learned to want didn't have to be related to posters or newspapers. After my exclusion from *Omissions* I became desperate and I leapt from one world of activity to another in search of such a project and such a community. I sought it with Alec within the university itself, and we both got expelled from school; I sought it by trying to correspond with you, and failed to reach you; I sought it in a fictional world that I myself invented, but I never finished my novel; finally I went to the underworld where Sabina and her friends were living, still seeking the kind of life I had learned to want during those full few days I spent with you twenty years ago.

It was dark when I finally dragged myself out of the newspaper office and back to the co-op. I fell asleep as soon as I got to my room and I slept through most of the following day, a Saturday. Alec came shortly after I woke up. We had supper in a small restaurant and then we took a walk around the campus. It was early spring, as it is now. The campus was deserted. We mechanically retraced the path of the previous day's funeral procession.

For a long time we just walked silently. Then Alec started to express thoughts that perfectly echoed my own. "It's funny," he said; "I always thought putting out that paper was a lot of hard work and I never thought all of it was such great fun. Sometimes I even wondered if it was worth all that work. But now that it's over I don't think I'll be able to stand it around here."

"I know I won't," I said. "I know I'll hate it."

We sat down on the steps of the administration building, the very same steps on which the striking students sat a few days ago when Daman lectured to them about the point of production.

"Why don't we do something together, just you and I?" Alec asked.

"I was just thinking the same thing," I said. "I was thinking about that military professor and his files."

"You mean writing more articles about him? I'm sick of that," Alec said.

"But you didn't write a single one of the articles," I reminded him, laughing. "No, I wasn't thinking of more articles. I was thinking that you and I could sit in on one of his classes and ask him questions about his files." That wasn't really such a daring suggestion. In recent years students have planted bombs in such files.

Alec was enchanted by my suggestion. "That would drive him up a wall!" he said. "He might even try to exterminate a couple of reds right in the classroom. Doesn't that frighten you?"

"You just said you wouldn't be able to stand it around here if we didn't do something like that," I reminded him.

Alec got all excited. "If that works out, we could go visit some other classes and do the same thing. I can think of at least a dozen where I'd like to do that. Those smug bastards are always asking if anyone has questions, and they're used to hearing some pip-squeak say he didn't have a chance to write down every one of the professor's words. We'll give them questions. God damn it, maybe some other students will learn how to ask questions. This place would have to shut down!"

We continued speculating about the possible effects of our activity until late into the night. We decided to launch our project the following Monday.

We didn't talk about the kinds of questions we'd ask nor about what we'd do if we were thrown out or if the professor didn't call on us. We didn't prepare a single thing. We simply decided to sit in on the general's class. That Monday I decided to skip all my classes again. When Alec came for me at the co-op, I could see that he was as nervous as I. We hardly spoke to each other. We found the room where the general's class was supposed to take place and, trying to look inconspicuous, we sat down in the last row.

We didn't succeed in our attempt to be inconspicuous. The room gradually filled up with identical-looking young men in suits and ties, all of them short-haired. Alec wore jeans and a T-shirt and I was the only woman in the room. The students kept turning around and looking at us; several of them made obscene gestures. I don't know if those gestures meant that the students guessed who we were or if the people in that class were automatically vicious toward women and casually dressed men. They all looked at me like bloodthirsty marines; and I'm sure every single one of them has by now exterminated countless human beings on some distant battlefield.

The professor paid no attention to us; he simply pretended we weren't there. He lectured during the whole hour and didn't ask if there were any questions. I couldn't believe that lecture. I had known that such people existed but I had never spoken to any and had never looked at military literature. That man talked about the slaughter of thousands of people as if he were describing a game of chess. If a person who cannot distinguish people from roaches is a psychopath when he starts talking about exterminating the vermin, then this professor was the most dangerous psychopath I had ever seen. I couldn't have asked him a question if I had memorized one. I was frozen in my seat. I imagined myself being exploded into scraps, being burned alive and being shot full of holes by the weapons he described. I was chilled to the bone. I don't think I've ever been so frightened. When I got home I vomited.

Alec apparently didn't respond to the lecture the way I did. When the hour was nearly over he became impatient and raised his hand. The professor didn't call on him. So Alec interrupted the lecture and started shouting. "Why do you keep talking about such far away places, professor? Why don't you describe what those weapons will do right here in this town, when you start killing off those enemies you keep files on? Tell us about burning out certain parts of this city. Some of us might have relatives there. That'll help us understand your lecture a lot better." Alec was sweating when he finished and he started shaking like a leaf.

The professor paused while Alec spoke, but then he ignored Alec completely and continued his lecture, as if he had been interrupted by a psychopath. When the bell rang he walked up to us, said he didn't remember having seen us in his class before, and asked if we were registered for his course. Alec told him we were considering enrolling the following semester but before doing so we had wanted to hear one of his lectures and, having heard it, we were no longer considering enrolling. The professor then said that we couldn't simply walk "off the street into a classroom," but that we first had to have permission from the proper authorities.

When we left the classroom, five or six of the students were waiting for us. In spite of their suits and ties they looked like a pack of vicious bristly-haired dogs. I was scared to death. Ever since that day I've sympathized with anyone who urged the population to "get guns and protect yourselves," even in situations where that slogan was totally inappropriate. And I've certainly sympathized with every guerrilla anywhere in the world who ever shot one of these monsters. Alec was scared too. We didn't exchange any words with them. Alec grabbed my hand and we started running without looking back to see if they were following. We ran to Alec's car, drove to the co-op, and I rushed to the bathroom and threw up.

We didn't know whether to consider the first stage of our project a partial success or a complete failure and we didn't have the time to evaluate it, nor the chance to try another approach. Two days after our visit to the military lecture one of the city papers carried a long story about our escapade. The story was so distorted that if we hadn't known the mentality of its authors we wouldn't have recognized ourselves in it. The few facts there were in the story must have come out of the professor's files and even those facts were wrong. I realized that the files we had made so much noise about couldn't have been of much use to anyone. The headline was: "Outside Agitators Disrupt University Lecture." The names of the agitators were "Miner Vach and Sophia Narcalo," namely the authors of the articles that had appeared in the school, paper rendered in the city reporter's or the professor's spelling. The article described the two agitators as the leaders of the "cell" that had temporarily taken over the student publication. According to the article, the university had taken vigorous measures to remove from the newspaper staff "all communists, homosexuals, fellow travelers and other outside agitators" and had given the publication back to "the student community." However, the article observed critically, the university's measures had not been vigorous enough, because "dangerous elements are still being allowed to run rampant in our university, among our sons and daughters, among tomorrow's leaders." The last paragraph stated that "Miner Vach and his consort" were obviously no students, but did not explain why this was obvious; undoubtedly the name they chose for him made this obvious. The article concluded by describing Miner and his consort as dangerous elements who were intent on disfiguring the minds of the entire younger generation and who would stop at nothing in their determined attempt to bring the university to a complete halt. This article was an example of journalism as it was practiced outside the university. We had been fired from the newspaper staff so as to be replaced by people who aspired to this type of journalism.

The following morning both Alec and I were served subpoenas by the university administration, or something just like that. A messenger brought both of us notes which told us to appear in the office of the president "immediately." Alec came over as soon as he got his notice and we discussed what we would do about it. Our first impulse was to disregard the president's invitation. But on second thought both of us wanted to have a taste of that experience. Neither of us had ever seen the university president or his office and we were certain that whatever happened, it would not be as terrifying as the moment when we left the general's class and faced a pack of his snarling students.

We obviously didn't dress up for the occasion, but I must admit that the president as well as his secretary were very open minded about that. The secretary told us, "The president will be right with you; please sit down," and indicated that we should install our dirty-looking jeans on the plush chairs in that carpeted room.

The president came in, introduced himself, and shook our hands while we remained seated. He asked if we wanted coffee.

"Yes, please," we both answered simultaneously. Later on Alec told me he wished he'd thought of asking for breakfast as well.

The president himself went out and a few minutes later returned carrying a tray with two cups of coffee, a cream pitcher and a sugar bowl. Apparently he wasn't going to join us.

"Did you summon us here so as to serve us coffee?" Alec asked.

In a very apologetic tone, the president said, "Oh, that note. Yes, it was excessively harsh. We merely wanted to get somewhat better acquainted with you." Then he grinned and added, "I hope you don't mind."

Oh, not at all," I said. "The coffee is very good and the room is nicely decorated. I wouldn't mind coming here every morning."

"Yes, well," the president continued, "I should tell you that I understand you young people perfectly. I was quite a gay blade myself during my college days." Alec snickered and the president paused. "However," he then said, "you have to understand that we must face certain realities."

Alec and I obviously didn't understand that; if we did we wouldn't have been drinking coffee in the president's office.

"Realities like the present war hysteria?" Alec asked. "Is this a university or an army barracks?"

"I understand your point perfectly," the president said. "However, there are certain political considerations, and also certain financial ones."

"The hysterical politicians could fire you and the war profiteering corporations pay your salary; is that what you mean?" I asked.

My comment irritated the president ever so slightly. He said, "I can see that you're both reluctant to face these realities." Then he immediately reverted to his original tone; he didn't want us to think he was an evil man. "Your point of view is in many ways justified, I might even say admirable.

"Unfortunately, I have certain responsibilities and the university has certain responsibilities toward a larger community, and your uncompromising attitude makes it very hard for me, and for the university at large, to carry out these responsibilities."

I got angry and said, "If you think we're going to compromise our attitudes —"

"Oh, no," he interrupted. "Nothing of the sort. I merely wanted to get better acquainted with you. From my point of view this interview has been completely satisfactory." He got up and shook our hands again, saying, "I honestly wish you the greatest success in your endeavors."

I certainly didn't regret having accepted the president's invitation: I had never before met such a completely unprincipled person, such a perfect politician. The following morning the same messenger who had brought us our invitations brought Alec and me notes informing us that we were being expelled from the university.

Neither Alec nor I were terribly upset by our expulsion. We had already felt expelled when the administration directive had closed the newspaper office to us and neither of us had wanted to remain in the university without working on the newspaper.

Alec found an apartment and moved away from campus on the very day the notice came and a few days later he already had a factory job. He asked me to move to his apartment but I knew that I'd be making a terrible mistake if I did that. We hadn't ever discussed the question of marriage and I knew that the day after I moved in with him it would already be too late to begin that conversation. Besides my lack of desire to become a wife, I didn't want to leave the university environment so quickly for several reasons. First of all I wanted to see how the purged newspaper functioned and I also wanted to be on campus when the first issue of *Omissions* came out. Secondly I had started writing my novel again. This time my experience on the newspaper staff was its central topic and I was afraid that if I removed myself from that environment I would lose my desire to continue working on it.

The university newspaper didn't come out for a week but when it did come out it looked almost the same as when we had put it out. I must admit I was disappointed by this fact. I had thought that somehow its very appearance would reveal what it had become. Bess Lach hadn't merely been accepted on its staff; she had been appointed news editor, a position which was only one notch lower than her previous position. I assumed that the paper looked so much like ours because Bess had done all the editing as well as the layout, but maybe I gave too little credit to those pliant journalism students picked from the fraternities and sororities. Of course the paper didn't have the kinds of articles Daman, Alec, Minnie and I had written, but not all of our issues had carried such articles either, nor had all of our articles been masterpieces.

A few days later the first issue of *Omissions* came out. I was disappointed by that too: it was so small! Only two letter-sized pages, with, typewritten articles. But it was beautifully laid out and the articles were fun to read. I was particularly moved by Hugh's description of the purpose of the paper. Thurston's humor column was hilarious.

I had called Minnie to find out if she knew when the first issue was going to come out. She told me that she and Daman had become friends again and that she was going to help distribute the paper. They had been denied the right to distribute the paper on campus and consequently they were going to give it out across the street from the administration building, namely on the side of the street which was not on university property. I joined Minnie and Daman there and without even being asked I grabbed a bundle and gave out copies to the men students who lived in the fraternity houses across the street from the administration building. Hugh and Lem were giving them out at the other end of the campus to students who drove their cars to school. The paper was given out free, like the official paper; the editorial asked people to subscribe to it so as to help defray printing expenses which were being paid by the editors.

When we ran out of copies Daman asked me to come to the next staff meeting at Hugh's house. I didn't say I'd come. I thought of Rhea and Alec. I didn't want to be one of those who had betrayed them.

But I couldn't stay away. Minnie and Daman came for me on the day when the second issue was to be laid out. When I walked in with them, Thurston and Hugh acted as if they took my presence for granted. I sat and listened while they discussed the materials to be included in the issue. There were no arguments, no cliques, no majorities or minorities; there was no reason for voting. Hugh asked me to write an article but that was where I drew the line. I was willing to help with the typing and the distribution but I refused to become one of the editors.

I went out with Alec once a week. I told him I was taking part in the distribution of *Omissions* and gave him a copy whenever it came out. I didn't tell him I was also taking part in the production of the paper. I was ashamed to tell him that. I also felt ashamed at the co-op several times when Rhea saw me go out with Daman and Minnie on our way to Hugh's house; she must have known that I was on my way to work on the off-campus paper originally suggested by her.

I took part in the production of the paper but I continued to be an outsider, not only in my eyes but in theirs as well. After the second issue all four editors as well as Minnie urged me to write articles and take part in the decisions, but I continued to refuse. I just couldn't forget the way the paper had been started and my failure to participate in those activities didn't let them forget either. They hardly spoke to me; they were afraid I'd take offense at something they said or even at the tone in which they said it. They didn't want me to walk out. The production of that little paper was a lot of hard work and by the third issue I had become indispensable for the paper's distribution as well. Daman and Lem helped distribute only the first two issues. Both had morning classes every day and Daman had always been a good student. Lem also went back to being a good student, although I can't imagine why, since he then left the university before finishing the school year. And of course the upper class dandy Thurston never took part in the distribution. He'd as soon have been a peasant guerrilla. Handing out the paper across the street from the university was for Thurston an activity worthy of outside agitators and union organizers, and he was equally hostile to both. The only reason he found himself in our company was that the witch hunt mentality of that time was even interfering with the ability of the ruling class to make jokes about itself, which was all he wanted to do. As a result, Hugh, Minnie and I were the paper's only distributors. Minnie and I continued to give it out across the street from the administration building and Hugh continued to distribute it to commuting students on the other side of the campus. How ironic. The argument that had justified our exclusion had been that the distribution of the "underground" paper would be far too dangerous for the women. I did undergo a terrible experience before the year ended, which I'll describe later, but this experience had not been one of the dangers that had been anticipated when our exclusion had been justified.

There were numerous favorable responses to the publication of *Omissions*: several encouraging letters, some classroom discussions of questions raised by *Omissions*, a certain growth of political awareness on the official newspaper staff which would not have taken place if *Omissions* hadn't been published and if it hadn't maintained such a high level of quality. I'll only describe one of the responses because it's related to events that took place long after the first *Omissions* had been forgotten.

Around the middle of the year we learned that a group of students at another university had heard about our series of articles in the school paper, about the directive and about the mock funeral. One of those students was one of the first paying subscribers to *Omissions*. Stimulated by our example these students launched a similar publication, which they also named *Omissions*. They were not former editors of the official publication. The official paper of that university had apparently always been as self-repressed as the one here became after the directive. Another difference was that the kinds of articles they carried were not at all like those that appeared in our *Omissions* but rather like the articles Minnie and I had been publishing in the official paper just before the directive; they were exposures of the militaristic and repressive engagements of professors and academic departments. That group of students didn't disperse at the end of the school year, the way we did. They kept their publication going. Its staff as well as its readers increased. Its name changed several times; new students replaced those who graduated. Several years later the entire editorial board of that publication got themselves elected to the student government: it was the first time within memory that radical students had been so prominent. These students became the first official spokesmen of what became "the student movement." I learned all this many years after the demise of the original *Omissions* when I re-enrolled in college. I'm mentioning all this because I do understand what you mean when you describe our activity in the carton plant or mine on the newspaper staff as a stepping stone toward a political career. That's what it was for Marc Glavni, Vera Neis and the group of students I've just described. But the activity was not a stepping stone in and of itself and I'm not the only one who knows this. Nowadays, when the student movement is vast, several of its politicians are writing the history of their movement. They invariably identify the origin of the present movement with the publication of the first issue of the *Omissions* that was published at the other university, which came out several months after our first issue. There's a very good reason why they locate the origin there: that group was a group of politicians and the historians are politicians writing the history of their "likes." They don't mention our activities because we weren't politicians, because we spoke only for ourselves. They know it, I know it, and I think you should know it too. If our activity were ever included in a history, it wouldn't be a history of politicians but a much vaster history of people's attempts to fight against repression on their own, for themselves, without politicians. Our activity had innumerable flaws. Our motives weren't pure and our achievements weren't terribly impressive. But the establishment of political careers was not what motivated us and that certainly wasn't what we achieved as a result of that activity.

Some months before the end of the school year, Lem Icel announced that he would be leaving the *Omissions* staff as well as the university. He was one of the students selected by his political organization to attend a world student conference which was to take place in your part of the world. I had thought Lem had left that organization when he'd joined the *Omissions* staff and had fallen out with Rhea but I'd been wrong. To his credit he hadn't once let his organizational commitment define his relations to the other people on the staff. I reluctantly admitted to myself that Thurston's calculations had not been altogether without substance: if Lem and Rhea had both been on that staff they would have blackmailed each other into implementing the organization's position on every question. Not that their positions would always have been wrong. They would always have been rigid, inflexible, and consequently the discussions wouldn't have had the character of genuine communication but of people shouting at phonograph records that just kept repeating themselves. But even that would have been preferable to the exclusionary course that was taken.

Lem's coming trip gave me an idea. I asked him if he'd be willing to deliver letters to all the friends I had known eight years earlier. I didn't tell him we had all been arrested; I was afraid Lem would suspect there was something wrong with my friends, that they were all "stained," as you put it in your second letter. Lem was delighted by the fact that I asked him for a favor. I hadn't asked him to do anything for me since high school. He was also enthusiastic about the prospect of meeting people who had once been my friends, and was positively enchanted when I told him they were all workers.

I had two weeks to write letters to all of you and except for the day I spent working on *Omissions* and the morning I spent distributing it, I did nothing else during those weeks. The uprising in Magarna had just broken out. Lem had told me something about that uprising and the city papers carried front page articles about it which conflicted in every detail with Lem's account. I suspected that both accounts were wrong and some of the descriptions in the city papers gave me the impression that the Magarna rising was in some ways a continuation of our activity in the carton factory eight years earlier. In fact, the vehemence with which Lem denied certain details even led me to suspect that the events unfolding in Magarna went far beyond anything I had experienced, that in fact a revolution was taking place which was as extensive and profound as the revolution Luisa had described to me. Those suspicions were of course confirmed in later years, when I read documented accounts of the Magarna revolution, but at the time I had no way of learning those facts. The closest I could come was to reach you.

I feverishly wrote long letters to every one of you. Once I wrote straight through the night and continued writing the whole next day. The letter to you was the longest. In my recent letters I've repeated most of what I told you then. I described the extent to which two key events had affected my life: the revolution with which Luisa had familiarized me, and the agitation in which I myself took part with you and the others in the carton plant. I told about my lifelong search for the elements which had made those experiences significant to me; I narrated all I've just finished telling you about my activity on the newspaper staff and the off-campus paper, and I summarized my earlier attempt to compare you to Ron. I was eager to hear about your life and the lives of the others, about your experiences, activities and projects. I wanted to hear about the rising in Magarna; I was sure those events were giving a new life to the community I had once known. I wanted desperately to be in touch with those of my friends who were closest to it; I wanted to be part of it and part of them. At that time I felt that I was still an integral part of that community. I still thought of myself as one of you. If I had gotten your newest letter and read Jasna's account then, I would have been heartbroken. I imagined all of you were still in the carton plant. I had no way of knowing what dreadfully long prison terms so many of you had served already then. I obviously thought of all of you as I remembered you, as you had been when I had known you.

When I wrote those letters, there was nothing I wanted more than to be asked to return, by one and all of you. My letters almost begged for such an invitation. In each letter I described my life since my emigration as the life of a foreigner, the life of an outsider. I described the environment and the population that welcomed me with the slogan "Go back where you come from," and the university in which I had never been anything more than an "outside agitator." I also described my exclusion from the single activity I had found here which I would have embraced as my own: the off-campus newspaper. I waited for a letter, a postcard, a word or a mere sign. I was ready to fly out of here as abruptly as Alec had left the university on the day of our expulsion. But no word came. Even Lem didn't return. When I finally did see Lem again several years later, his account of what happened to him was so unrelated to the letters I had written that I barely listened to what he told me: I was convinced it had nothing to do with me. Poor Lem.

Soon after Alec and I were expelled I started my novel again, for the second and last time. How well I understand why Jasna reads long novels whenever she's excluded from the activity of those around her: to live all the possible lives she knows she'll never have a chance to live. I suppose I wrote for similar reasons. Unlike Jasna, I didn't wander through worlds others had created; I wandered through my own, and while wandering I changed it here and there to make it more like the world I would have wanted it to be. I spent almost every day working on it, alone in my room at the co-op. I saw the *Omissions* people only one day every two weeks and at no other time, since the activity that drew us together on that single day, the preparation of the paper, was the very activity that separated us the rest of the time. I saw Alec on weekends; during the week the job he'd gotten used up all his energy and he simply ate, slept and went back to work. I was glad to be left alone in my room. I was close enough to the people and experiences I was writing about to continue to be stimulated by them, while at the same time I was able to look at them from a distance, the distance which my exclusion had created between us.

My second novel wasn't a love story but the story of two projects. Ron was replaced by the group of people with whom I bad shared the experience on the newspaper staff, the people who had excluded me from *Omissions*. I contrasted this project and these people with my experience at the carton factory eight years earlier. I described the first group as a genuine community, one which could not have excluded me, and I tried to explore the reasons for my exclusion from *Omissions*, reasons which I didn't locate in Thurston's vote-counting but in the character of the participants. Since I was using my experience with you as a model, I obviously glorified the people I had known in the carton plant as well as the project I had shared with them. Jasna's account of who those people really were and what they've become since then is not really relevant to the way I described them. The characters in my novel were products of my own imagination. In a sense my characters were all different facets of my own self. Through them I contrasted the pettiness of those around me with a picture of what I would have wanted those people to be. Through those characters I tried to say that the world around me was not the only possible world and certainly not the best of all possible worlds. I never accepted Daman's philosophy according to which all that happens is explainable afterwards as all that was "objectively possible." Now I understand why Daman hadn't said a word when Rhea, Minnie and I had been excluded from *Omissions*. With all its revolutionary language, Daman's philosophy is merely another version of the submissiveness to fate which you attributed to Mirna's mother. By describing characters who in some ways resembled you and Vera and Marc, I was trying to depict a possible community. I wasn't trying to describe a community that had actually existed precisely because I didn't submit to the flawed community that existed as the only "objectively possible" community.

Unfortunately my second novel never became more complete than my first. I was forced to abandon it abruptly and I've never returned to it. I re-read it before writing you about my experiences on the newspaper staff, and I have to admit that some of the events I've just described come directly out of that manuscript. I apologize for that, but I can no longer remember the sequence of the actual events.

My project was cut short by an incident which I do remember, and very vividly. It happened several weeks after Lem left with the letters I wrote to all of you. Minnie and I were distributing copies of the newest issue of *Omissions* across the street from the administration building. The students who came out of the fraternity houses lined up for copies. Minnie and I were delighted. We thought there had been a revolution in the fraternity houses. On all previous occasions, only an occasional student had been willing to accept a copy; others had either insulted us or had avoided walking near us. Since we were surrounded by people reaching for copies, we couldn't see what was happening. Suddenly we heard the siren of a police car. The students around us moved some distance away and we saw that copies of *Omissions* were scattered all over the street and sidewalk, over the lawn of the administration building, on the hoods and in the door handles of cars. Minnie and I just stood there, holding bundles of copies of the publication that was scattered like fallen leaves all over the landscape. The police grabbed us and pushed us into their car. The whole thing had obviously been pre-arranged, probably by the university administration, since the events which followed were clearly parts of a scheme that had been well worked out ahead of time. Those fraternity boys were always such "good" students; it's too bad that a word like "scab" doesn't exist for them. At the police station we were asked our names. The police called someone in the university, gave our names and learned that I was no longer a student. We were given a long lecture, which was directed only at me, about "littering and defacing public and private property." We were told that if we ever "littered" the street again we would have to appear before a judge and be subject to a jail sentence. This obviously meant that we could be jailed for trying to distribute *Omissions* again.

Minnie was called into the university president's office and reprimanded, but she wasn't suspended from school. What happened to me was much worse.

The co-op where I lived was governed by a "board" which consisted of four students who were elected by all the occupants. Two days after the "littering" incident the university administration sent the co-op board a threatening note which said that "university approved housing is intended exclusively for the use of students and not for the general public. The university cannot grant recognition to facilities which are run like hotels or other public accommodations." In other words, if I wasn't evicted from the co-op, the co-op would lose "university recognition." I still haven't learned what "university recognition" is. I think that without it the co-op would not have been placed on a list of "university approved" student housing facilities. But no one was in the co-op because it was "university approved"; we were there because it was cheap.

The co-op board called for a meeting of all the occupants. No one had ever been evicted from the co-op before. Numerous students went to school one semester and worked one semester, so that I wasn't the only non-student living there. But as soon as the board members started speaking I knew that the whole business revolved around me. One of the board members said that the loss of university recognition would do irreparable damage to the co-op, and two others said that it would do irreparable damage to the careers of all the students in the co-op. The three board members who spoke (the fourth didn't say anything) were law students. This was not a coincidence. Law students were normally the only people who ran for board posts; no one else wanted to be a board member. The law students listed the fact that they'd been on the "board of directors of the university co-operative dormitory" on their list of accomplishments; they were politicians. I had heard that when the co-op was first organized it had been a center for radical students, but this had ceased to be the case long before I had come there. These board members apparently thought that my presence there was going to revive that long-lost reputation of the co-op. In that case they would no longer be able to list the co-op among their accomplishments. It's in this sense that my presence there was harmful to their careers.

There was a very brief discussion. Only two students expressed opposition to the university's threatening note. The others just sat and said nothing. I looked desperately toward Rhea; she would be the next one whose presence would be harmful to the lawyers' careers. But she avoided my glance and said nothing.

It all happened so fast that I couldn't put my thoughts together. Someone called for the vote. I started to say, "But you can't —" I couldn't say any more. I gagged and started sobbing. They voted. Two students voted against my eviction, about a third of the students abstained and all the rest, including Rhea, raised their hands in favor of evicting me.

That was Rhea's revenge for the fact that Alec had abandoned her as well as her organization, and probably also for the fact that she had been excluded from what was in a way her creation, the off-campus paper. With that vote she was also getting even with herself for having admired this "perfect proletarian" so much when we first met. Perhaps in some strange way she was also acting as the instrument of Debbie Matthews' revenge against George Alberts, although Rhea couldn't have known about my connection to Alberts. I understood how Debbie must have felt when she was fired, and particularly when she learned the role her former friend had played in the firing.

After that horrid vote I started to bawl. Everyone left the room. Not one person stayed with me, even to console me. I felt like a leper.

I dragged myself to my room and cried myself to sleep exactly the way I had done when I'd been excluded from *Omissions*. When I woke up in the morning I started crying again. How terribly cruel it is to evict someone. I looked helplessly at my familiar room, at my unfinished manuscript, at my stack of newspapers. I had nowhere to go and I wasn't able to go anywhere else even if I had wanted to. I had no money. I'd had a tuition scholarship during my three and a half years in school and my room and board at the co-op had been free. Luisa had given me money when I had started college but I had always returned it because I really hadn't needed it. The little I'd kept when Luisa insisted was in a savings account, and I hadn't spent any of it. But all my savings couldn't have paid for a single week's rent and food.

I didn't have much to pack except manuscripts, notebooks, newspapers and books. I hadn't bought clothes since high school and some of them were so old I stuck them into the garbage instead of packing them.

I went to the bus station and stuck all my belongings inside a locker. I wandered around the ugly station and walked aimlessly amidst the crowds on the downtown streets. I was like a person who had just arrived in the city, a person who didn't know what she would do here, whom she'd meet, what she'd become.

I went to a drug store and sipped a cup of coffee. It was only then that I started to think about what I would do next. But I couldn't think about it coherently. Images kept flying through my mind: images of the disappointing funeral procession, of Alec telling us why we had been excluded from *Omissions*, of Rhea's hand raised in favor of my eviction.

The most obvious thing would have been to go to Luisa. But I couldn't stand the thought of doing that. I knew I'd spend all my time sitting in my room staring at the walls the way I'd done before I started high school. In that room I wouldn't be able to continue my novel about the university newspaper, and I certainly wouldn't pull out the manuscript of my first novel. And the thought of breaking down and bawling in front of Luisa frightened me. It would create a relationship that hadn't existed between us for as long as I could remember: I would become a helpless and dependent child and she'd become my protective mother. I didn't know if she was able to play that role, but if she did play it, I knew I'd hate her afterwards because I'd be terribly humiliated to have to assert my independence again.

I could have gone to Alec. He had already asked me to move in with him. But in the state I was in, that would have been even worse than returning to Luisa. Helpless and completely lost, I would automatically have become his "burden" and his "responsibility." I could imagine him saying, "Just go ahead and cry on my shoulder, Sophie; everything's going to be all right." Soon I'd be his wife, and then his "old lady." By then any kind of separation would be extremely painful if not altogether impossible. I decided not even to contact Alec until I had solved my living problems.

Of course I could have thought of going to work like any "normal" person, but I had never worked before and the mere thought of looking for a job made me feel like vomiting. Is this revulsion a trait I share with the people Jasna described, or does it have something to do with the nature of "work" in this society?

Lem would have been delighted to put me up, and I could easily have dispelled any expectations he might have had, but Lem was by then in your part of the world. And I didn't want to seek help from any of the others on the *Omissions* staff. My exclusion from the paper was far too similar to my eviction from the co-op.

While I was considering and rejecting all these alternatives, the solution was already in the back of my mind. I would turn to Sabina. At that moment it seemed that she was the only person in the world I could turn to. She wouldn't ask any questions. She wouldn't become my protectress. I could come and go as I pleased and when I pleased. And I knew she wouldn't turn me away.

I had no idea where Sabina was. I hadn't seen her for two years, since the night she had come to the co-op to tell me Ron had been killed. I didn't even know how to start looking for her. I had a hunch and it turned out to be right. I suspected that she was still together with Ron's friends, or even that she was directly in contact with Debbie Matthews, since that was probably how she had learned of Ron's death. I also remembered that Sabina had once stayed at Debbie's house.

Debbie Matthews suddenly became very important to me. I hadn't ever gone to see her when she'd been fired from high school and I particularly regretted not having gone to her when I'd learned about Ron's death. I became so convinced that Debbie would know where Sabina was that I returned to the bus station and took my things back out of the locker.

It was still morning when I rang the bell at the Matthews house, hugging all my possessions. Debbie opened the door. We had seen each other at Ron's trial but she didn't recognize me. She asked what I wanted. She was drunk. I told her I was Lem Icel's friend and Sabina Nachalo's sister, that I had once gone with Ron, and that I was desperately trying to find Sabina.

"You're the other Alberts girl!" she exclaimed, but she asked me in anyway.

As soon as I was in the living room I became hysterical. I shouted that I wasn't George Alberts' girl, that Alberts had never been either my friend or my father, that I hated him as much as she did. I told her I hated Alberts more than ever at that very moment because Debbie's own friends Lem Icel and Rhea Morphen had done to me exactly what Alberts had done to her. I bawled. I acted out the very scene I hadn't wanted to perform for Luisa. I told her about Lem's role in my exclusion from *Omissions* and about Rhea's role in my eviction from the co-op. I told her Sabina was the last person I had left in the world and that I had no idea what would happen to me if I didn't find her.

Debbie poured me a drink and said almost exactly what I would have expected Alec to say if I'd gone to him. "Take it easy, kid. Everything is going to be all right. There's no reason to have a fit; that won't help any."

She left the room to wash and put on a dress. She looked almost sober when she returned. "Come on," she said; "their garage is right down the street. I've never gone there before. Now's as good a time as any."

When we left her house she carried most of my packages. I must have been the one who looked drunk.

By the time we reached the garage I might as well have been in a foreign land where I knew neither the language nor the customs. I had cried so much that day that a film of tears had formed in my eyes and everything looked distorted. I was like a person walking in her sleep or under hypnosis. Nothing would have surprised me. I had stopped responding to what was happening around me.

One of the mechanics ran up to Debbie and asked, "Is something wrong?"

Debbie answered, "Not with me. This girl says she's Sabina's sister. She needs a place to stay."

"So you're Sophie!" the mechanic said. "Ron never stopped talking about you. I remember seeing you at his trial."

I remembered seeing him too. He was Jose. Pointing to the other two mechanics he said, "That's Vic Turam over there and this is Ted Nasibu."

"I remember Ted," I said, trying to smile. "He's the car thief Ron told me about."

Jose looked embarrassed by my comment. Apparently Debbie didn't know what kind of garage it was. I wanted to apologize but just then a little girl ran up to us. She must have been six years old. Jose told Debbie and me, "This is Ron's kid."

Debbie embraced the little girl and said, "She sure doesn't look like him."

It was Tina. I hadn't seen her since she'd been a bundle on the couch in George Alberts' house.

Tina ran into the house and a few minutes later returned with Sabina. As soon as I saw Sabina I ran to her and threw my arms around her. I hadn't been so glad to see anyone since the night, four years earlier, when Sabina had thrown pebbles at my window, the night when she and Ron had come to tell me about Ron's experiences in reform school. I held on to Sabina and let all the rest of my tears run down to her shoulder. "I've been excluded from everything," I sobbed; "I'm a complete outsider."

Sabina loosened herself from my embrace. I saw that there were tears in her eyes. She put her arm around me and helped me to the apartment behind the garage. After letting me down on a kitchen chair she went back to the garage to ask Debbie if she wanted to join us for coffee. Debbie apparently didn't want to be entertained by both "Alberts girls" because Sabina came back alone. She gave me a wet towel so I could wipe the streams of tears off my face. Then she gave me a cup of strong black coffee and a bowl of thick soup. I felt much better, though I was still as disoriented as a tourist in an exotic land.

A young woman — or rather a girl: she couldn't have been over fourteen — burst into the kitchen from another room, rushed to the stove and poured herself coffee. Her hands trembled and she had dark rings around her eyes.

Sabina said, "Tissie, this is Sophia. She's going to stay with us."

Tissie turned to me and said, "So you're the college sister!" and she abruptly left the room with her cup of coffee.

I asked Sabina if Tissie was sick and Sabina said, very matter-of-factly, "She's a heroin addict." I had never seen a heroin addict before.

Sabina told me there was an extra bed in her room as well as in Tina's room and suggested I stay in Tina's room because Sabina slept during odd hours. I asked Sabina if she took part in the car thefts.

"Not any more," she said. "It's mainly Ted who does that. Tina helps fix the cars up. She's getting quite good at it. Vic specializes in heroin. He sells it to the rich at a bar run by a friend of his and to the poor right in the garage."

Tissie came back into the room and poured herself another cup of coffee.

"Tissie and I work in the bar," Sabina continued.

Tissie turned to Sabina and said, "You ought to bring your sister along and show her what we do."

Sabina snapped at Tissie, "Sophia can do whatever the hell she wants, and I'm not taking her anywhere."

When Tissie left again I asked what kind of work they did.

"It's like everything else we do here, Sophia," Sabina answered. "It's easier than many other things, it pays better than most, there's no drudgery, sometimes there's a lot of adventure, and we can work whenever we please."

I didn't ask Sabina if she and Tissie were waitresses. I said, "I don't mind, you know. I came to ask for help. I haven't come to judge you."

"Don't you worry about me," she said. "Why don't you go get some sleep. You look just like a heroin addict."

Sabina was right. I was exhausted. I fell asleep as soon as I lay down. When I woke up Tina was already asleep. I went to the kitchen to find something to eat. It was past midnight. Tissie was sitting at the kitchen table sipping her coffee.

"You sleep all day, sis?" she asked. "So did I. I'm getting a late start. Want to come along?"

"To the bar?" I asked, looking around nervously. "Where's Sabina?"

"She must have left two or three hours ago," Tissie said. "She'll never take you there. She told me. Want to come?"

"I don't have a dress," I said. I was afraid. But I was also curious. All day long I had felt like a tourist but I had been too upset and too tired to absorb my new surroundings. After having slept I felt refreshed and wanted to see more.

"You can wear one of Sabina's dresses. She's got dozens and we trade all the time. She'll never miss it," Tissie said.

I can't say that I was intrigued by the prospect, because that word suggests a much more active state than the one I was in. I was halfway in a stupor. I think at that moment I would have let anyone take me anywhere. I wanted to see whatever there was to be seen, to take part in everything those around me did.

As we left the garage, Tissie told me, "Don't you ever let them know I took you there, neither Sabina nor Jose nor Ted. They'll give me hell."

"Won't Sabina see me there?" I asked.

Tissie said, "She'll be gone by now. I'm telling you, she'll never know unless you tell her."

The only bar I had ever been to before was a bar near campus where Alec had taken me. Students drank beer there, sitting on plastic-covered seats watching television. The bar I entered with Tissie looked like my idea of a nightclub. There were chandeliers, live musicians and a singer, plush chairs and professional waiters. I had never seen anything so luxurious.

Tissie placed me on a stool at one end of the bar. "But what am I supposed to do?" I asked her.

"It'll all come to you, sis," she said patronizingly, and walked off to talk to someone.

I must have gone into a trance. When I came out of it I found myself inside a chauffeur-driven car. Next to me sat a large, middle-aged man who must have been a city politician or a corporation executive. Absolute chaos swept through my mind. I started to shake with fear. The chauffeur, the man next to me, the noise, the neon signs, the car lights all terrified me. I felt my heart pounding in my stomach and I wanted to vomit.

The man must have noticed my agitation. "Something wrong with you?" he asked.

I don't think I've ever thought so quickly in a crisis. "Yes," I said. "I forgot my tranquilizer pills. I've got to stop at a drug-store."

He had the driver pull over by a drugstore. But then he said, "I need cigarettes anyway. I'll get your pills. What kind are they?"

"Oh. I have a prescription for them," I said as calmly as I could, "and I'm the only one who can use it. I'll get your cigarettes."

He started reaching for his wallet but I jumped out of the car before he had a chance to give me the cigarette money. I immediately wished I'd asked what brand he smoked, or had at least waited for the money. I was afraid he'd come running after me.

I tried to walk nonchalantly to the drugstore entrance, but as soon as I was inside I ran to the white-frocked man behind the counter. He was alone. I started shaking him by the shoulders. "Someone's after me," I stammered. "Please, where's your back door?"

The poor druggist looked as frightened as he might have looked if someone were holding him up. I suppose he was glad that I wasn't asking for his money. He rushed to the back door, frantically undid several bolts and removed an iron bar. Holding on to the bar, he opened the door and peeked out to see if anyone was in the alley. I suppose he thought I might be luring him into an ambush. Satisfied that there was no one there, he opened the door. I bolted through it without thanking him.

I ran through alleys and along deserted streets like a hunted animal. I wanted to run to the university co-op, to my familiar surroundings. But that was no longer my world. I ran to the garage and pounded hysterically on the door. Jose let me in. He and Ted were still working.

"God damn it!" Jose murmured. "Did Tissie already take you there? Or was it Sabina?"

I suddenly felt terribly ashamed. I had betrayed my new hostesses. "Please don't mention this to Sabina or Tissie! Nothing at all happened," I said. "I got scared and ran away."

Jose and Ted both laughed. Then Ted said, "Good for you, kid."

Jose said, "Look, Sabina should have told you this: no one around here expects you to do any work. Ron's girl is our guest, do you understand that?"

I was hurt and humiliated by Jose's statement. I was to be a guest, a permanent visitor. I was an outsider again, only a few hours after my arrival. But I just couldn't make myself do the things that would have made me a part of that community. Those things may have been part of Ron's world but they had not been the part I had sought when I had gone walking and riding with him. I couldn't turn myself into a professional prostitute. Why? Is it really because of what you and Jasna say in your letter? Is it really because my activities in the carton plant spoiled me, turned me into a traitor against my class and taught me to seek my role above my class? I didn't think so that night when I ran back to the garage, and I still don't think so. I didn't think that by leaving the university I had abandoned the opportunists and rejoined the working class. Nor did I think that it was opportunistic to refuse to engage in Tissie's and Sabina's activity. For you it's so clear and obvious where the opportunism lies. For me it's not nearly as obvious. My activities on the newspaper staff didn't give me money or fame and they didn't secure my future rise in any bureaucratic hierarchy, whereas Sabina's activity would have given me money, probably a car of my own, as well as a certain type of adventure. It's not that I consider Sabina an opportunist. She's always wanted to immerse herself in everything, to try everything out, to live every possible adventure. She never drew any lines, she never established any limits. I always did. Yet even though I was the one who drew the lines, she was ultimately more principled because the lines I drew were arbitrary. I dreaded selling my mind, time and energy yet eventually I did sell these parts of myself; I nevertheless convinced myself that selling my body was worse and I drew the line there because that's where the ruling morality draws it. The activities I had left were the activities I wanted. To me those activities had something to do with what was happening in Magarna; they were the kinds of projects I tried to describe in my novel and in the letters I wrote to all of you. It was for the sake of such projects and such a community that I rejected the world to which Tissie introduced me.

After my experience at the carton plant I was never able to find anything that resembled the kind of project I had sought and when something like it was born with *Omissions*, I was excluded. What I sought is unfolding around you right now and your letters tell me that everything I stand for is alien to that activity. All right. Maybe that's what I've become and maybe that's what I've always been. But I want you to know that from the bottom of my heart I hope you and your friends are now creating the community I sought in every environment down to the underworld, the community I tried to invent in my novel because I never found it in my life.

My love to Jasna, Mirna, Yara and you, *Sophia.*

Yarostan's fifth letter

Dear Sophia,

Your letter arrived yesterday. Mirna and I both read it before sitting down to the supper Yara had prepared for us. Yara was annoyed. "After the way she insulted you last time I wouldn't think you'd skip supper to read another one of her letters."

Mirna told Yara, "It's a very moving letter, Yara; you and Sophia have a lot in common."

I felt this too. For the first time since the beginning of our correspondence I was able to recognize myself in you. This isn't only because you used my arguments or Zdenek's in your quarrel with your friend Daman but because your letter made me aware of similarities in our experiences and outlooks. I now feel I should apologize for the way I treated your earlier letters. I did treat you as an outsider, as a person with whom I couldn't communicate about my present situation. I was wrong.

During supper last night Mirna commented, "Sophia is a born troublemaker, just like Jan and Yara. She shares Jan's recklessness as well as his courage. I'm glad for her sake that she was taken away from here even if her emigration caused her some pain. There's no room here for people like that. If she'd stayed she would have disappeared years ago in a prison or concentration camp." Mirna loved her "reckless" brother and she's very proud of Yara's rebelliousness. Your letter convinced me that Mirna is right: if you'd stayed here you could well have followed a path very similar to Jan's. And you're right: you certainly wouldn't have occupied the "place" I assigned to you in my earlier letters. The tenacity with which you pursued your struggle, even in the face of certain repression, is something you share with Jan, not with people we both consider opportunists. Your recent confrontation with the administrative psychologist at your college, your exposures of militarism during your university years, your disruption of the war expert's class, are clearly not opportunistic acts, and you make it perfectly clear to me that you couldn't have derived any privileges from engaging in those acts. You're right when you accuse me of failing to distinguish your commitment from the commitments of those around you. I did accuse you of being a carrier of the repressive fuctions of the university and the press and I recognize that this accusation was unfair. I did identify your engagements with engagements that are as unacceptable to you as they are to me. I think I did this because the contexts in which you've chosen to struggle are contexts in which I had thought genuine rebellion impossible. In my world the political militant, the journalist and the academician do not and cannot help establish a human community because their very existence presupposes the absence of community. This must be true in your world too; Tina expressed it very colorfully when, standing in the street, she shouted at Daman that his "cushy job" depended on the passivity of the rest of the population.

You've convinced me that your engagement in Daman's activity, or in Marc Glavni's and Vera Neis's activities, doesn't make you like them, and that your engagement was "some kind of affirmation of life," as you put it. But you haven't convinced me that the kind of struggle you've waged is actually possible in the contexts in which you fought it. Every one of your experiences convinced me that the instruments you chose are useless for the kinds of ends you tried to make them serve. You were trying to fight for liberation with this society's instruments of domination. I think this is why you always remained an outsider while those alongside you became priests of political sects, missionaries of repressive religions and officials in government bureaucracies. In my earlier letters I failed to distinguish you from your context and my understanding of your activities was very one-sided. You're right to emphasize the side I had excluded and you do force me to recognize my narrow-mindedness. But I think you still leave some veils hanging, you still hide some parts of the picture. I see the picture in a new light now but I still don't see an altogether different picture from the one I saw before. I now see that your own goals were not repressive but I'm still convinced that the context in which you fought for those goals was repressive.

In order to combat my one-sidedness you have recourse to arguments that are equally one-sided. You pretend that the contexts in which you located your struggles were accidental and that your own activities had "nothing to do" with those contexts. I think you're wrong. I think your activities were reduced to nothing by those contexts. I think it's no accident that the agitational activity at the carton plant twenty years ago served Vera and Marc as a stepping stone toward the establishment of bureaucratic careers. I think it's no accident that your co-worker on the university newspaper is now a functionary in the ideological establishment, nor that the students who were stimulated by the example of your journalistic activity became politicians. The contexts in which you sought a project and a community are institutions which thrive on the absence of what you sought and you couldn't have been anything more than an outsider there. I'll try to clarify what I mean by telling you about my recent encounter with two of our onetime friends.

Last Saturday Jasna and I attended a lecture in the auditorium of the House of Culture. The speakers were Vera Krena and Adrian Povrshan. Their speeches were critical exposures of the repression we've undergone during the past twenty years. In terms of their words alone, Vera and Adrian couldn't have been very different from you at the time when you exposed the militarization of the university on the school's newspaper staff. They sounded like rebels, even revolutionaries. But in terms of their relations to those around them, in terms of the context in which they spoke, they are not rebels but political opportunists.

I agree with you: the similarity of their activity to yours does not make you one of them. But I don't agree that the context is or can be as hospitable to your goals as to theirs. You seem convinced that speakers' platforms, newspapers and pedagogical institutions can be serviceable to the struggle for freedom. I'm convinced of the opposite; I think such contexts are antithetical to your goals and hostile to your struggle and by engaging in them you merely strengthen forces whose very existence negates your project and your community. Maybe I'm being unfair again. If so, I hope you'll show me where I'm wrong. I'll try to express my doubts as clearly as I can, even at the risk of being unfair and overstating my case again. If I do get "carried away by my rhetoric" once again, I hope you'll understand that it's not because I feel that everything you stand for is alien to me. On the contrary, I'm not addressing my comments to a stranger but to a comrade and it seems to me that such critical appreciation is not an expression of hostility but is at the very basis of communication and friendship.

Last Friday Jasna walked Yara home from school and waited for me to return from work. She told me Vera and Adrian were scheduled to speak the following night and she was quite excited about it. She hadn't seen Adrian since she'd visited him three years ago in his empty office in the trade union building. And the last time she saw Vera was twelve years ago, on the day when all three of them were arrested at Jasna's house and accused of having contacts with a foreign spy. I did remember to ask Jasna if she could answer Sabina's question about the last name the police attributed to you and Luisa when they questioned her about her former acquaintances, but Jasna didn't remember the name.

I didn't share any of Jasna's enthusiasm about the prospect of seeing Adrian and Vera. In fact, I refused to accompany her to the lecture when she first mentioned it. I told her that if two politicians ever came to the carton plant to lecture to me during work hours, I'd walk off my job, so that I obviously wasn't disposed to go out of my way to hear the politicians. Jasna said she wasn't going because of her interest in political speeches but because these speakers had once been her friends. If my correspondence with you hadn't revived my memories of a distant past, I doubt if I'd still remember that Adrian Povrshan and Vera Krena had once been my friends. But I did remember this bizarre fact and I changed my mind, not so much because I wanted to see or hear Adrian or Vera, but because of you, because they've come to occupy such an important place in your life.

The auditorium was almost empty. The audience consisted mainly of young people, probably students, although there may have been a few young workers among them.

Vera Krena was introduced first, along with all her titles: honorable rector, honorable member, honorable deputy minister. There was little applause. She spoke very eloquently about what she called the "errors" which had been committed here during "recent years." She was applauded when she said that these "errors" and "shortcomings" had all been brought about by the "deformations of our social system." I didn't applaud, since I felt that by linking the "errors" to the "deformations" she merely linked two equally empty words. Her concluding speech was a rousing call for what she called "action." Vera's words were as out of place in the midst of the present ferment as Daman's lecture was in the midst of the student strike. "We must find our way out of this vicious circle where bureaucratic attitudes reinforce passivity and passivity reinforces bureaucratic attitudes. We must create an atmosphere favorable to the growth of initiative. The prohibition and repression of criticism, the stifling of democratic relations, only inhibit the growth of initiative. Such deformations paralyze initiative at all levels and lead to indifference and to the cult of mediocrity. We stand at a historical crossroads. We face a great task. The time to act has come. Let us not be satisfied with half measures."

The audience applauded and some people stood up. I felt uneasy. I had of course known that politicians were very busy trying to derive personal profit from the present ferment. But it is one thing to know this and quite another to experience it directly. No one in the audience could doubt Vera's sincerity or determination. She is still a very powerful speaker — much more powerful than most of the politicians I hear on the radio in the carton plant. She's also more courageous than most of the other "radical" politicians of today; perhaps she still has some of the traits you admired her for twenty years ago. She's the first politician I've heard in recent months who referred, in one and the same speech, to the stifling of democratic relations, the repression of criticism and the paralysis of initiative. But like all politicians in power, Vera presents all this as "errors" and "deformations," and not as the very nature of the system of which she's an integral part. If the system is only "deformed" then it can be cured. However, if this social system is itself the deformity then it can only be destroyed, root and branch. Vera's remedy follows from her own diagnosis: the system has to be cured. How? "We must find ... We must create ... We stand ... Let us..." "We" of course means Vera Krena together with her audience, Vera together with the working population. And how will "we" cure the system "together"? Obviously the same way "we" have always done anything "together." We the workers will do our share by remaining at our posts in the factories, while Vera will do her share by remaining at her posts in the offices of the academic and ideological establishments. In other words, we will cure the system "together" by continuing to reproduce it. And why do we face this "great task" only now, why have we suddenly arrived at this "historic crossroads" when "the time to act has come"? Because a ferment began at the bottom of this society and this ferment has spread to such an extent that it threatens to sweep away all the offices that Vera and her comrades occupy. For Vera the time has come to put an end to this ferment. That's the "great task" she faces. The offices she fought so hard to reach are endangered by the ferment. That's why she sounded so sincere and so determined. She's determined not to lose a single one of her conquests. Her heart may even be set on reaching new heights of bureaucratic power, on profiting from the opportunities created by the ferment itself. The present situation would then indeed be a historic crossroads — for Vera Krena.

I don't think Vera is an unusually brutal, cynical or unscrupulous person. I think the brutality is in her social activity, in the offices she occupies. These offices are part of the state apparatus. That apparatus can perform its functions only so long as a passive and submissive population lets itself be expropriated of those functions. For the past few months thousands of people have started to perform functions they had never performed before, functions which had been the exclusive domain of the state. This is especially true in the area of communication, namely the area which contains all of Vera Krena's academic and ideological offices. People have started to communicate with each other directly; they've been forging their own terminologies and infusing them with their own meanings. The ideological establishment and all its means of propaganda are being superseded by human forms of communication. If this process continues, all those offices and instruments will become historical junk, curiosities discarded by a reawakened humanity.

Vera's interest in derailing and stopping this ferment is not so much her own personal interest as it is the interest of an ideological establishment struggling to reimpose itself over human beings who are running out from under it. Vera Krena, director and ideological minister, didn't speak as an individual but as an agent of directorship and ideology. Through her these institutions, these abstractions which are nothing but summaries of regularized submission, acquire a voice and a will; through her these abstractions assert their insatiable hunger, their will to devour every human thought, word and sound, to digest all forms of human communication and excrete them as ideology.

Adrian wasn't applauded when he was introduced; several people snickered when his full title was announced; "Chairman of the central committee of the commission for problems of standard of living." His speech was short and dull. He did exactly what he used to do twenty years ago. He didn't add anything at all to what Vera had already said; he merely repeated a few of her platitudes and then proceeded to document them. He documented "errors" and "deformities" with statistical data. He cited facts about the stagnating rate of industrial development and the declining standard of living, facts which are well known to a population that has experienced them daily. Adrian, like Vera, called for the reproduction of the very system whose ills he documented, but he was much more straightforward about the "cure" than Vera. When he said, "The leaders must apply policies which will earn them their leading roles in society," he was hissed by several people. He apparently didn't hear the hisses because he continued in the same vein: "We can no longer impose our authority but must conquer it through our acts." The hisses became so loud that I could barely hear his concluding sentence, which was something like, "We can no longer impose our line by commands, but only through our work, only through the truth of our ideals." A few people applauded; over half the audience hissed. He could not have been more pathetic if he'd begged, "Please let us stay where we are; we promise to be good next time." The rulers apparently think the population is ready to overthrow them. If only the rest of the population had such a high opinion of its own potential!

The fact that Adrian was hissed whereas Vera was applauded puzzles me. I'm equally puzzled in the carton plant, where people condemn some of the radio politicians as "rotten bureaucrats of the old school" while praising other politicians as people who are "basically on our side." I'm puzzled because I can't see any essential difference between the politicians who are so different in the eyes of those around me. Either I'm failing to see some very important differences or else those around me are failing to see the similarities.

This is related to something I experienced in prison. We often discussed the behavior and character of prison guards and we classified guards in terms of their degree of brutality: some guards were "vicious," others "so-so," a few were "fairly decent." But on several occasions I heard a prisoner refer to a guard as a person who was "on our side." I could never understand this type of characterization of a prison guard. Or rather, I understood it and considered it absurd. In prison the absurdity of such an observation is made obvious by the walls, gates and bars. A person who was not inside a cell, who policed us in the yard, who left the prison every night, was clearly not on our side. The comment was absurd if it was understood literally. But it was much more disturbing if it was not understood literally because it described something very real about our situation as prisoners. It meant that prisoners have no "side," that our fate depended completely on the wills and whims of the guards. We were things, inhuman entities without interests, desires or potentialities. The closest we could come to regaining our humanity was to have our interests and desires represented among the guards. Saying that a guard was on "our side" meant that all that remained of our humanity was lodged in the guard.

The applause given to politicians like Vera Krena in the present situation is even more disturbing than it would have been in prison. Our survival as human beings in prison did in fact depend on the prison guards, on the presence or absence of "our side" among the guards. Every attempt to affirm our humanity on our own led directly to severe repression, mutilation, even death. But this isn't the case in the present situation, a situation Vera described as a "historic crossroads." For the first time in twenty years the extent of our development as human beings has not depended on the extent to which our humanity was represented among the prison guards, the ruling politicians. For the first time in twenty years we've begun to take steps to regain our own potentialities and realize our own desires. For the first time in twenty years we haven't been prisoners at the mercy of guards but free human beings discovering our freedom and beginning to forge our own humanity. The applause given to politicians like Vera indicates that many, disturbingly many people are not able to leave the prison in which they've been locked up. It means that many of my contemporaries are unable to accept the reality of their own desires even in the act of realizing them. They are unable to accept themselves as human beings. They've been locked up too long. They can no longer imagine any freedom other than the freedom of the prison guard. They've repressed all desires except those represented among the guards. Even while they take steps to realize their own project they affirm a politician's project and deny their own.

Most of the audience left after Adrian's speech. A group of people gathered around Vera and a smaller group around Adrian. Jasna told me she wanted to talk to Adrian, or at least to shake his hand. She told me she felt sorry for him. I stayed in my seat when she walked up to the circle of people surrounding Adrian. He was very busy grinning and shaking hands. He didn't seem aware that anyone had hissed his speech. The enthusiasts surrounding him probably gave him the impression that everyone in the audience considered him a seer.

Most of Adrian's admirers were gone when he noticed Jasna. He shook her hand as if he were pumping water from a well. She must have asked if he remembered me, because both turned to look at me. Adrian's face didn't show the slightest sign of recognition. He immediately turned to the young man next to Jasna and started pumping his hand. Jasna's turn had ended.

Jasna walked toward the large group which still surrounded Vera, and waited. I saw Vera look at Jasna several times and then turn to someone else. Jasna waited until she and a girl who couldn't have been over twelve were the only people who still wanted to shake Vera's hand. Vera shook Jasna's hand without even looking at her, said, "Thank you very much, comrades," shook the girl's hand and turned to Adrian saying, "Well, that didn't go over as badly as I'd thought it would."

Jasna walked toward me with tears in her eyes. "Adrian at least remembered my name," she sobbed. When we left the auditorium she was crying. "Vera lived with me for five years! We could have been sisters. She doesn't even know who I am!"

I tried to console Jasna by telling her that I wouldn't have recognized either Vera or Adrian if I hadn't been reminded of them by our recent conversations and by your letters.

"You haven't seen them for twenty years, and you never knew them the way I did," Jasna said, and continued to cry. She knew that it wasn't only time that separated her from her former housemates. The distance between two worlds separated her from them. Jasna was as alien to Vera and Adrian as you were to Ron on the night of your last encounter with him. When Ron said. "I hear you're going to college," you heard him ask: "When did I ever have anything to do with you?" Adrian remembered only Jasna's name. Vera didn't remember that she'd ever had anything to do with Jasna, not only because twelve years have turned Jasna into a stranger, but also because Jasna's world is strange to Vera. The people who inhabit Vera's world have names, "real" names, like "chairman," "first secretary" or "president." They have titles, posts, offices. They're the people Vera remembers. Jasna doesn't have a title. She doesn't have a name. Jasna isn't somebody. She's nobody. Jasna is a cipher in the population statistics, a grain of sand indistinguishable from all the other grains on a beach, a face indistinguishable from all the other faces in an audience; she's merely another hand to shake after a speech, another member of the working class whose noble cause Vera serves.

Jasna and I walked silently toward my house. I stopped trying to console her. I thought of your first two letters. I understood perfectly why I had responded to them so "unfairly." You had described these politicians as your "community," as the only people you knew who weren't puppets, as insurgents who had struggled to shake off their own chains without enslaving others. I had responded as if you'd told me you had modeled your life on the life of the Roman emperor Caligula. I hadn't seen Vera or Adrian for twenty years and I had never exerted the type of social power they aspired to. I've never seen Caligula either, nor have I occupied any post comparable to his. But I've experienced some of the effects of the projects of their likes. When you identified yourself with them I thought of you as one of them. I'm now convinced that you're not one of them, that your project has nothing in common with theirs. But the terrain on which you've chosen to struggle for your project is their terrain. Every one of the activities you've described is an activity of politicians and ideologues. This is what led me to respond so "unfairly." I couldn't imagine that anything human could grow on that terrain and I still can't.

During our walk home I could have tried to cheer Jasna up by telling her she ought to be flattered not to be recognized as a comrade by two opportunistic politicians, but I didn't think of this. Yet this is what Mirna must have had in mind when we got home and she saw Jasna's tears; she asked us what had happened.

"They didn't recognize us," I said.

"Did you think those people would recognize you?" Mirna asked. "How important do you think you are?"

Jasna smiled in response to Mirna's question but protested, "I'm as much of a person as they are!"

"Maybe you are in Yarostan's eyes and in my eyes," Mirna said. "At my factory there are dozens like me in my section and there's one manager. Do you think I'm as important as he is?"

"Much more important," I said.

Mirna laughed and said, "Come with me on Monday morning and tell him that!"

Jasna laughed too. At this point Yara turned to Jasna and asked, "Could you tell if they were lovers?" Yara had apparently been bursting to ask this question from the moment we had entered the house but had been inhibited by Jasna's sadness.

"Could I tell what?" Jasna asked.

"Krena and Povrshan: aren't they lovers?" Yara asked.

"What in the world do you know about that?" I asked her.

"Jasna told us all about them!" Yara insisted.

"What Jasna told us was that Vera married the bank director and when Adrian was released from prison and found that out, he stayed away from Vera," I reminded her.

"Jasna also told us Povrshan went out with the rector's secretary," Yara reminded me. "I told my girl friend Julia everything Jasna told us. Julia's father works in the state bank and knows all about the bank director and his wife. Julia says they talk about them all the time. But they didn't know anything about Povrshan. Julia told me the bank director is old and his wife isn't nearly as old. In their mansion they sleep in separate rooms."

"Did your girl friend's father tell you about all that?" I asked.

"No, Julia figured it out," Yara said.

"You mean she made it up," I said.

"She did not!" Yara snapped back angrily. "She's not a liar!"

I said, "I'm sorry. I was amazed that you and your friends discussed such things."

"Why shouldn't we? You do!" Yara retorted.

Mirna laughed and said, "We keep forgetting that you're already eleven years old."

I asked Yara to tell us what Julia had figured out.

"Her father had talked about deputy minister Krena having a lover, but no one knew who he was until I told Julia about Povrshan."

I burst out laughing and couldn't keep myself from asking, "Do you actually know what a lover is?"

"Do you want me to bring mine home and show you? His name is Slobodan!" Yara snapped.

Jasna and I were embarrassed. Mirna laughed. Unfortunately not one of us can take credit for Yara's sophistication. Periods of ferment undoubtedly have a stimulating effect on everyone. I begged Yara to go on.

"Julia's father only knew that Krena's lover was some kind of official, that he was married, and that Krena had him appointed to a commission," Yara continued. "But it was Julia who put all the pieces together. She's read stories like that in magazines, but usually it's the woman who does what Povrshan did. And she knew from the papers that every time he and Krena gave a speech together he got another promotion until he became commission chairman. When I told her what Jasna told us, Julia figured out that Povrshan had never stopped loving Krena, even though he hated her for what she's done to him. But he knew Krena would throw him out if he simply showed up in her office. She'd think he wanted to get even with her. So he married her secretary, the one Jasna told us about. That way, when he turned up at the rector's office he wouldn't be looking for Krena but for his wife, and it would be Krena who would accidentally run into him. Can you imagine her expression when she asks, Are you looking for me? and he answers, No, I'm waiting for my wife. Julia figured out something else too. Krena would have thrown him out of her office if he'd turned up there unmarried, but she must have turned green with envy when she learned he was married to her secretary. Julia says it doesn't really matter if he planned all this from the start or if he married Krena's secretary because he actually loved her. In either case he obviously ran into Krena, since they're together now, and his wife is Krena's private secretary. Julia's father said it was Krena who appointed him and Jasna told us that he was someone who'd do anything for an appointment. Don't you see? Krena appointed him and then he had to see her about his post, sometimes at night, sometimes even all night. Krena was tired of that old bank director. When they started giving speeches they were together all the time."

We were stunned. I had no reason to doubt the plausibility of any part of Yara's story. After a long pause I asked, "How old is your girlfriend Julia?"

"She's ten and a half," Yara answered. Then, by way of explanation, she added, "But we're both in the same grade in school."

I was stunned by the worldly wisdom of Yara and her ten year old girlfriend. I was also disturbed. What bothered me was related to what had bothered me in your letters and also to what had bothered me when young people had applauded Vera Krena's lecture. What disturbs me is not Yara's sophistication but her frame of reference. She and her friend have unbelievable insight into the private lives of the ruling bureaucrats. They're familiar with the most intimate details of a world that's completely alien to them. They're as interested in the love affairs of officials as the ancient Greeks were in the love affairs of their gods. The world of officials is the world that matters. Officials are today's gods. They're omnipotent and immortal. Not as individuals: Krena and Povrshan are mortal; they're also replaceable. The deputy minister and the chairman are neither mortal nor replaceable. They're the essential beings, the permanence behind the flux, the fixed stars of an ever-changing universe. They're immortal. They can conceivably be dislodged from their positions, but only through a cosmic cataclysm which takes place in the sky. They cannot be dislodged by mere mortals. Nothing we do down here affects them. The projects which Yara has already forged with her companions have not dislodged the all-powerful beings who inhabit her imagination. The solidarity, the community, the potentiality she and her likes experienced in their demonstrations are transitory and trivial compared to the love affairs of a deputy minister and a chairman. Yara's acts may at times be courageous and exciting but they can never be fascinating, admirable or awesome. Fascination, admiration and awe are reserved for the acts of the gods.

Like those of my fellow workers in the plant who applaud the speeches of certain bureaucrats, Yara is already a fascinated admirer. Like them, she has already experienced in herself a capacity, however modest, to overthrow the ruling relations and like them she lodges all capacity in the gods. Like them, she has already experienced a glimmer of freedom yet still she can't imagine any freedom other than the freedom of prison guards. Yara and her friend are our contemporaries, not only because of the sophistication of their perceptions, but also because they're already prisoners of the ruling ideology. Like the students who applauded Vera Krena's speech, Yara and her friend remain locked up within this ideology at a time when their own acts are undermining the ideology's social foundations. With half of their being they dig the grave for the expiring corpse of the repressive world while with the other half they infuse the corpse with new life and carry it through yet another crisis.

In one of your earlier letters you and Luisa argued very eloquently that slaves are not responsible for their misery nor workers for their exploitation nor the poor for their poverty nor prisoners for their imprisonment. That's true, but only superficially. Where do masters derive their mastery? From the stars? Where do the rich get their wealth if not from the poor? Where do guards and exploiters derive their power? You and Luisa are right in a very narrow sense: we don't shoot ourselves. They shoot us. But it's we who produce them, it's we who staff their armies, it's we who produce the weapons that kill us. It isn't even true that they shoot us. They only order us shot, and it's we who implement their orders. We butcher ourselves.

I'm not suggesting that Yara's imagination has been permanently maimed. If this were so she wouldn't have been able to engage in the demonstrations in which she's been taking such an active part. All the lively activities taking place around me prove that no one has been permanently maimed. Human beings cannot be permanently transformed into insects or robots. But all the half-revolutions of the past show that human beings are as reluctant to reclaim the totality of their repressed humanity as they are to lose it. I think you illustrate this as much as Yara and my fellow workers in the carton plant. I'm not talking about opportunism now. I finally do recognize that you have nothing in common with Vera Krena. I'm talking about an ambiguity you share with people who are genuine rebels. I'm talking about the fact that you've reproduced the official project in the very act of struggling to realize your own; you've re-enacted repressive relations in the very act of fighting against them. The world in which you've tried to realize yourself is the world Yara carries in her head. It is the official world, the world of officials. The context in which you've chosen to fight your struggle makes your acts ambiguous, it robs your acts of their intentions and turns them against you.

You haven't been uncritical of the environment in which you've sought to realize your projects. In fact, some of your critiques of the academic world are devastating and they've been very instructive and novel to me because I know so little about it. Yet how am I to understand your critiques if you conclude every one of them by telling me this was the world in which you sought your project and your community? Would you understand someone who gave a lucid analysis of the social function of the police and concluded by telling you he had joined the police in order to struggle against its social function? I won't say that this situation is identical to yours. But there are similarities. The social function of bureaucratized education and communication is not identical to the function of the police, but the two functions are not mutually exclusive and their consequences are terribly similar. A prisoner whose helplessness leads him to seek out guards who are "on our side" is terribly similar to the worker who thinks a politician is "on our side." The prisoner's justification is that the guards are armed. The prisoner's human prospects do in fact reside in the guard. But a worker who thinks his human prospects reside in a politician is deluded. He is imprisoned, not by concrete walls and iron bars, but by delusions implanted in his mind. The schools, the newspapers, the official and unofficial propaganda machines, the proclamations of the rulers and the "consciousness-raising" campaigns of "revolutionaries" are the instruments which create these delusions, they are the walls and bars which imprison him.

You've told me that in your activities you didn't aim to implant the ruling delusions but to undermine them. You've convinced me about the integrity of your intentions. But you're not as lucid about your own intentions as you are about Daman's. As soon as he began talking about his intention to found a newspaper in which the "inherently revolutionary" workers would "speak for themselves," you spotted the saint, the prophet, the shepherd and guide lurking behind the intentions. You're not nearly as lucid about yourself. Surrounded by prophets, politicians and aspiring bureaucrats, you fought for your own project on a terrain where only theirs could grow. You fought against repression within the repressive apparatus itself. You don't claim to have realized any of your own goals in that context, but you claim that it was not your intention to contribute to the realization of their goals. Are you sure you didn't in fact strengthen their goals, the apparatus' goals, by your mere presence within it? Did your intentions really matter?

It's not Vera's intentions that make her a bureaucrat but her social activity. Her intentions are "to find our way out of bureaucratic attitudes" and to "create an atmosphere favorable to the growth of initiative." In terms of her intentions Vera is probably still the devoted revolutionary, the humorous and quick-witted militant you remember. I'm sure that in her own eyes she's devoted, not to herself, but to the workers' cause, not to the repressive apparatus but to society's liberation from it. But in her daily life she's an integral part of the repressive apparatus and she's determined to remain within it. The bridge between her intentions and her practice is the ideology which allows her to equate her own success with the success of the workers. I'm sure Vera is convinced that the higher she rises in the bureaucratic apparatus, the closer we all are to "finding our way out of bureaucratic attitudes," and the greater the power she and her friends are able to exercise over the rest of society, the more favorable the atmosphere becomes for the growth of initiative. She identifies her importance in the repressive apparatus with the workers' cause and her freedom to exercise repressive powers with society's liberation from repression.

If this repressive ideology were confined to Vera Krena, she could be dismissed as a very cynical and profoundly deluded individual and the rest of us could then turn to life's real problems. But Vera's delusions are not confined to Vera and Adrian; they're shared to some extent by all of us, even by people who can't use these delusions as masks for their own private ambitions. Vera's applauding audiences share her delusions; people with whom I work share them; Yara shares them; you share them.

When we shut down the carton plant in order to oust the union functionary, we began to find our way out of the bureaucratic society and to create an atmosphere favorable to our own growth and our own freedom. But when we praise the speech of a radio politician we back away from our own deed and return to the safe terrain of the official delusion, the delusion that we can't find our own way. We revert to the comforting conviction that our growth and our freedom are being realized by one or another politician. And, like Vera Krena and her likes, we identify our own growth and freedom with the advancement and power of politicians "who are on our side": we give up our own struggle and become passive admirers and supporters of "our" bureaucrat; we renounce our projects and our potentialities and lodge them in "our representatives," who realize them for us.

The programs and commitments of Krena and Povrshan are nothing but veils which cover their own private goals. Theories of liberation are the clothes of dictators. Vera Krena "finds our way out of bureaucratic attitudes" by marrying the head of the state bank, by using his influence to imprison the university rector, by replacing the former rector, by rising to the post of deputy minister of the ideological commission. Vera Krena serves the cause of the workers by reviving her love affair with Adrian Povrshan, by promoting Povrshan to member and then chairman. And we sit by our radios and newspapers, admiring the progress of our struggles and the flowering of our humanity during the official daily sessions and the unofficial nightly sessions. Our projects and our freedom become mere concepts; the reality behind the concepts consists of the love affairs of the deputy minister and the chairman of the commission for problems of standard of living. Our struggle is played out in the corridors of government palaces and the bedrooms of country houses.

We identify our lives with the private lives of bureaucrats because our own lives have stopped being real to us. We have no projects; only the rulers have projects. If we nevertheless want projects, we think we can have them only in the world of the all-powerful bureaucrats, not in the world we share with others like us. Thus we seek to realize ourselves by negating ourselves. We seek to express ourselves, not directly, not as individuals, but indirectly, as voices magnified a thousand fold by electronic instruments; we seek to communicate, not within the community of our likes, but within the community of written words, the community of newspapers, books and leaflets. But in that community there is no communication because that's not a human community, and we either accept our bureaucratic assignments or we're evicted as outsiders. I believe you fought bravely in the university and on the newspaper staffs, but I don't believe you took any steps toward the realization of your projects because I don't believe such steps can be taken in that world.

From our vantage points in repressive societies it's as hard to imagine a world without newspapers as it is to imagine a community of free human beings. But if your whole life has been a search for such a community, how could you possibly have thought you'd find it on a newspaper staff? A community of free human beings is first of all a community in which every individual defines reality, and it is on this basis that the community builds its own environment. Journalism can only exist where there are no free human beings, where there is no community. The person who specializes in informing others about the "news" is a usurper. The newspaper establishes a reality which is common to all but alien to each, a reality expressed by all which is the self-expression of none. By letting "the news" be defined for us, we allow our definition of reality to be imposed on us from outside ourselves and we lose our ability to define, express or project ourselves; we lose precisely those faculties that make us communicative and communal animals, the faculties that make us human beings.

You treat your exclusion from the university newspaper and from the oppositional newspaper as an exclusion from Utopia, and you describe your trip to Sabina's garage as a descent to the underworld. In the newspaper world you saw yourself as a participant but in Sabina's world you saw yourself as a disoriented tourist. Yet the garage in which Sabina and her friends lived is an environment far more familiar to me than the world of the university or the newspaper. Your descent to Sabina's world is a descent to my world. I recognize the people as well as the activities: those are the people with whom I shared cells during both prison terms, those are the activities and the choices I confronted when I was released from prison, those are the activities in which most of the people I've known have engaged. I hope you're beginning to understand why I treated your previous letters as the letters of a stranger: you describe my world as a world which is far stranger, far more exotic to you than your world ever was to me.

Nevertheless, you did descend from the world of the newspaper, even if not by your own choice. The moments during which you considered your alternatives in the world below the propaganda apparatus must have been very much like the days I spent facing similar alternatives after my first release. As soon as you start moving in an environment very much like my own, I understand you and I admire you. I think Mirna was right when she compared your courage as well as your recklessness to Jan's. You refused to become a protected daughter or a protected wife. You refused to sell your labor for a wage. You left yourself no other choice but to "descend" yet further, to a place you call the "underworld." And once there, you refused to submit to the requirements for survival imposed by that world. You refused to sit inside a display window waiting to be bought. I'm obviously very interested in learning what you did do in the garage operated by Sabina and her friends.

When you wrote about your search for genuine friends and for a human community in the world of academics and journalists, I responded with hostility and I didn't understand your search. But when you carry that search into the world of Tissie, Jose and Sabina, I suddenly understand. That's why I'd like to know what you did in Sabina's world, why you and Sabina both left it, why your only friend today is the pedagogue Daman. It seems to me that your search is transformed as soon as you leave the academic world and descend to the "underworld." Looking for community in the world of academics is like looking for trust among informers or for sympathy among executioners. In that world it's impossible to distinguish the desire for self-realization as a human being from the desire for self-realization as a bureaucrat. It's only when you descend among those who are nothing in this society that your search becomes meaningful as a struggle against this society. Tissie, Jose, Ted are nothing; in order to become anything at all they have to become everything all at once, and that can only happen through the complete destruction of this society. For them there are neither transitional stages nor illusory victories along the way to self-realization. To look for a human community among them is to look for the destruction of everything that makes them and their likes an "underworld."

I think I share your lifelong commitment. But I also think you don't grasp the nature of that commitment. You still refer to our experience in the carton plant twenty years ago as the original stimulus for your commitment. I think the project and community you seek were as absent from that experience as they were from all your subsequent experiences. I think that experience played an altogether different role in your life from the one you attribute to it. I think your attachment to that experience stems from a desire to materialize your dreams, a desire to visualize what cannot be visualized, a desire to resurrect what can only be created. I share your commitment if it's a commitment, not to a corpse, but to a community that has never existed, a community that cannot coexist with the world that represses it. But I don't share your understanding of that commitment: by locating its source in a repressive experience, you make the goal itself repressive.

Yet I also understand your desire to resurrect the past. You're not unique in having such a desire. When I was first released from prison I wanted to relive the very experience you've placed at the center of your life. Luisa's life has revolved around the revolution she experienced before she came here. Every politician seems to be motivated by the dream of stepping into the shoes of a past prophet, dictator or executioner. Nor is this desire to resurrect the past confined to priests and politicians. It's probably shared by all individuals who have desires. I think it's related to your commitment, but very differently from the way you say it is.

After my first release from prison I would probably have expressed myself in terms very similar to yours. I didn't only feel hostile toward the police society into which I had been released; I also felt that I had lost something, that something was missing, something I had learned to want. Like you I thought that this missing element was something I had possessed sometime in the past, perhaps during the agitation at the carton plant or during the resistance, or perhaps only when I had listened to Luisa's accounts of the revolution she had experienced. I was convinced that I had been whole and alive in the past and I wanted to be whole and alive again; I wanted to resurrect the past situation. If my memory isn't exaggerating I think I was at that time convinced that anyone who had experienced such a community and wanted to resurrect it was an insurgent, my comrade and my like.

I sensed that Mirna had a similar dream and a similar commitment. I thought that she too had lost a community and that she too was committed to resurrecting her lost community. I idealized the village where she spent the first six years of her life. I imagined she had lost the rebirth of plant life in springtime, the summer walks in the countryside, the chores as well as the festivals, the wood burning during the long winter. Above all I thought she had lost a world of human beings each of whom had recognized the other's humanity.

The war and the occupation had driven the Sedlaks out of that community. They had tried to resurrect the village environment on the fringes of this bureaucratic city. Mirna seemed awkward and out of place; I interpreted her awkwardness as a form of resistance to the environment to which she'd been brought, as a form of affirmation of the community she'd been forced to abandon. I saw Mirna as a patient but committed insurgent determined not to lose forever the communal relationships she had once experienced. I understood Mirna's life the same way I understood my own, the same way you still understand yours. I thought all her gestures, including her attachment to me, were motivated by a search similar to mine, a search for something lost, for something missing, for something she had learned to want.

I was as wrong about Mirna as I was about myself. And I'm convinced you're just as wrong about yourself. The community I thought Mirna had lost was a product of my imagination. Her actual village was no more of a community than the neighborhood into which her family settled on the outskirts of the city. Later on Mirna told me that when she'd still lived in her village she'd dreamed only of moving to the city, and once in the city she never dreamed of returning to the village. I don't know if a genuine community ever existed in a peasant village. I doubt it. Even if it did, this community disintegrated so long ago that our memories couldn't possibly retain any trace of it. Mirna's village, like all the other villages that survive today, was a food factory; its inhabitants were commodity producers; its project was the production and sale of merchandise.

I idealized Mirna's village for the same reason that I idealized my own past experience: because it was in the past. Since that past experience existed only in my memory, I continually infused it with present desires until it grew into a golden age, a Utopia that contained everything my present lacked. I think this is what you've done with your experience in the carton plant. You've made it your Utopia. You've convinced yourself that it had contained people, relations and projects you haven't been able to find since. But by doing this we turned our heads backward while we continued to walk forward. My understanding of Mirna wasn't only wrong; it was inverted. Mirna herself, unlike you and me, never looked for her future in her past. She wasn't self-satisfied, like the numerous complacent patriots whom neither you nor I seem to include among our acquaintances. She wasn't submissive, like her mother, who accepted whatever happened as the inevitable unwinding of fate. Nor was she an opportunist like those of our friends who waited for a buyer to offer them a future in exchange for their lives. Mirna's life, like yours and mine, was motivated by a search. But it wasn't a search for something she had lost. If something was missing in her urban world, it wasn't something that had existed in her village. Whatever was missing in her present had already been missing in her past. What she felt in the city was not nostalgia for the village but relief at having left it.

Near the end of your letter you say that for me "it's so clear and obvious where the opportunism lies." I only wish it were clear and obvious. To me it's only clear and obvious that during most of the time I've spent out of prison I've collaborated in the reproduction of the repressive apparatus. To me it's clear and obvious that whatever it was Mirna sought, she has only moved further away from it. It's not so clear where the opportunism lies. We've sold our lives in order to survive. In this respect we don't differ from Vera, Adrian, or Marc Glavni. They were once rebels too, like you and me; they too were motivated by a search for something missing; they too felt desires that were repressed by the ruling society. But unlike Mirna, you and me, they didn't sell only their lives in order to survive; they also sold their desires. They weren't unwilling collaborators in the reproduction of the repressive apparatus but became its carriers and its functionaries. They appropriated its desire, the desire to contain, repress and extinguish the humanity of each. The extinction of their initial goal became their project; they realized themselves within the apparatus that makes self-realization impossible. Vera, Marc, Adrian and Claude are on the upper levels of a pyramid while we're at its base. We've wanted and we've tried to overthrow the pyramid yet we've been among those who supported it. We did it in order to survive. We were opportunists to that extent. We sold our humanity in order to keep it. By selling it we lost it, we merely added to the weight that crushed us. By surviving we kept alive, not our humanity but at least its potential. And by keeping alive that potential, that nothing which can at any moment become something, we've kept alive a flame that can at any moment set fire to the entire bureaucratic pyramid we call society. I think an opportunist is an individual who extinguishes that flame, and I think what you call your search for a community is the struggle to keep that potential alive.

When Mirna and I were married we confirmed the reality of our desires because we found them in each other. Both of us expected the future to be nothing like the present or the past and each of us thought this future was guaranteed by the other. We were both wrong. After our marriage the world remained the same. The only change was that I replaced her brother in her parents' house. We continued to live on the outskirts of the city, and urban worker though I was, I drove a bus — just like her father. Mirna's enthusiasm, her lust for life, adventure and change, were frustrated. She talked less. Our walks grew shorter. She didn't tell me she was unhappy; she didn't even hint that she wanted to leave her parents' house. Not that I was observant enough to understand a hint. I was too busy proselytizing, telling her about Luisa's experiences. She made me feel self-conscious, just as Jan did whenever he came to visit. I talked, and I remained where I was. I even talked about driving that wretched bus and I continued to drive it. It was Jan who finally put an end to a situation that couldn't have gone on much longer. He asked if I'd be willing to work in the vehicle repair depot where he worked, at the opposite end of the city. The possibility of working with Jan appealed to me, but I didn't like the idea of spending two hours a day traveling on a bus in addition to eight hours at the depot.

"You could get an apartment," Jan suggested. "Mirna would welcome the change."

I obviously didn't go to the depot to apply for the job. Such a procedure is archaic under the dictatorship of the proletariat. I don't really know if anyone gets a job that way any more. I got my second job the same way I'd gotten the bus-driving job. Jan went to the trade union building next door to the depot, spoke to Titus Zabran, and Titus pulled strings. An official pulled strings. And some workers I've met thought they'd won a victory twenty years ago! I didn't even have to go to Titus' office the second time. Jan went alone. He told me Titus picked up the phone, listed the qualifications of "the mechanic, Miran Sedlak," and told Jan that I would start working in the depot the following Monday. I suppose everyone must know someone like Titus Zabran. I wonder what happens to people who don't. This was the third time he had pulled me out of a trap, and it wasn't the last. What gave Titus Zabran the power to pull strings? My powerlessness. If I had picked up the telephone and introduced myself as Yarostan or Miran, the person at the other end would have laughed and said, "Comrade, if you're not an official you can't be heard; this is a people's democracy."

For several weeks I actually enjoyed my new job. I had repaired presses in the carton plant, but I had never dismantled a vehicle. I was impressed by the ingenuity of the generations of workmen who had connected the power of an engine to the motion of axles and wheels without concerning themselves about the use to which their work would be put. Would they have worked so hard if they had known what their work was for, or didn't they care? After the first few weeks the work became familiar and then routine. My initial awe gave way to resentment toward the tinkerers who had given their lives to the project of transporting ever larger quantities of commodities with ever greater speed. Working alongside Jan, I couldn't forget what my work was for, because he continually reminded me. Once, when I was still new on the job, I went on working on an engine when the others took a smoking break.

Jan grabbed my wrench and asked, "What's your hurry, brother? If the busses pile up, some people won't be able to get to work and they'll have a day off." He didn't let any of us forget that the busses didn't serve our aims but only the managers', the bureaucracy's, the state's aims, and that the faster we worked the more we increased the power of the forces that policed us. Jan didn't let any of us forget that those vehicles were not our project.

It was during those first weeks on my new job, when Mirna and I were still living at her parents' house, that I stopped trying to convert my hosts to the wisdom I had learned from Luisa. I finally gave up the project I had embraced so enthusiastically when I'd first visited the Sedlaks, the project of "going to the people" with news about a past experience. It wasn't only Jan's hostility toward my missionary activity that made me give it up but also my own growing hostility towards it. I became ridiculous to myself. My situation, my daily activity, made me sense that my closely reasoned arguments were incoherent, contradictory and irrational. I spent an hour every morning and another every evening on a crowded bus, usually standing, letting myself be conveyed to and from a garage where I repaired busses. Some of my fellow passengers rode to factories where they produced the tools or the parts with which I repaired the busses. I spent all the motion of my limbs tightening chains that bound us to a monster, yet every evening I spoke to my hosts about a community of free human beings. I had learned about such a community from Luisa. One of my favorite stories had to do with workers who drove and repaired busses. I told it to the Sedlaks as enthusiastically as Luisa had told it to me. Bus drivers and bus repairmen like I, like Jan and his father, had once turned against the monster; they had taken over the entire transportation network of their city. Like a schoolboy reciting a memorized lesson I stressed the fact that shortly after the takeover the busses were again running on schedule, they were again transporting workers to factories and buyers to markets, they were again repaired. The workers themselves were doing without capitalists and managers exactly what they had done with capitalists and managers. In other words, with naive enthusiasm I told my hosts, over and over again, that workers had defeated the monster and yet remained chained to it. My hosts didn't respond; they evidently didn't understand why I was so enthusiastic, and they obviously didn't think that such a victory was worth a drop of a worker's blood.

Let your friend Daman call me an "intellectual." I was educated and informed by Luisa if by no one else. Because of this education I had to think hard in order to figure out what was perfectly obvious to Jan and his father. Who but workers have ever driven and repaired busses? Who but workers have ever transported other workers to and from factories? If those workers fought on barricades in order to do voluntarily what they'd been forced to do before, then there was something wrong with those workers, or else with Luisa's story. But my hosts were polite. They didn't ask me if I'd be willing to risk my life in order to drive a bus "on my own." They'd heard such meaningless jargon before: on the radio. They still had high hopes for me.

But I lost my missionary zeal as well as my self-assurance and grew increasingly depressed. Everything I knew was false and everything I did was harmful. On balance it was my activity that bothered me more than my ignorance, because I spent only an hour a day talking compared to the ten I spent working and traveling. You're perfectly right. Survival or not, there's only one word for that activity. It's prostitution. From morning to night I sold myself, I exchanged my life for a sum of money. What I knew or thought I knew was completely irrelevant. I sold myself when I was a missionary and I continued selling myself after I stopped being a missionary. The only concrete thing I did with my life was to keep some busses running, to contribute to the efficient circulation of commodities and labor power. The hopes Mirna and I had shared vanished like childhood illusions about the adult world.

While I became increasingly depressed, Mirna grew more hopeful. Vesna was born shortly before I got my new job, and to Mirna the birth of the child and my job transfer were the first of a series of changes that were going to transform our lives. My job transfer confirmed some of her more extravagant expectations. One day, after I complained bitterly about the social function of my new job, she said, "Don't be such a pessimist; that's only a beginning." A beginning of what? I didn't ask her but I think I knew. It was the beginning of our journey from the village to an imaginary place where all desires could be fulfilled. In her eyes I had apparently stepped backward into the village when I had become a bus driver like her father. The move to her brother's job was a move out of the village. Jan lived by himself in the city; he didn't grow chickens or potatoes in his own back yard; he was no longer a peasant but a worker. And the fact that I moved at all confirmed her most profound hope: it confirmed that I was able to move.

But it was only after I had been on my new job for several weeks, after I asked her if she wanted to move closer to the center of the city, that Mirna expressed any of this.

"An apartment in the city!" she exclaimed. "If you only knew how long I've dreamed of that and how afraid I've been that I'd never get there. Of course I want an apartment in the city! There's no reason for Vesna to be brought up by my mother when she's already so close to a different kind of life. How badly I've wanted to leave, Yarostan! I hate it here! Didn't you know?"

If I hadn't known, I knew then. It became very clear to me why my new job was a "beginning." It was the beginning of Mirna's final break with the village, the beginning of Mirna's journey to the dream world she had seen from far away: the beginning of Vesna's upbringing as an urban worker, a citizen, someone like Jan and Sabina; the beginning of a different kind of life.

Since neither of us had to be convinced, our next problem was to find an apartment. Various monuments were built after the war to celebrate the workers' victory, but very little had been done to house the victorious workers. The consciousness of the working class had to be housed first, and all the new buildings were inhabited almost exclusively by bureaucrats. I could have turned to Titus Zabran once again but I had misgivings about the strings he had already pulled for me. I decided to consult the people with whom I worked in the depot. That was how Jan had found his place: a worker offered to share his apartment with Jan. But since there were three of us, this possibility was out of the question. My fellow workers promised to keep their eyes open for any vacancies that might turn up in their neighborhoods.

But weeks passed, and then months. Mirna grew impatient. She decided to look on her own. She visited addresses advertised in the newspaper. They were all privately owned houses or apartments. Her experience was the same wherever she went. She was asked what her husband did, and as soon as she said "mechanic," she was told the apartment was already rented. She cried as soon as she got home. After four or five days she gave up.

Finally, several months after our search began, one of the workers at the depot told me there was a vacancy in the building across the street from where he lived. I went to see the place as soon as I got off work. The building was an ancient two-storey mansion that had been divided up and turned into an apartment house already before the war. After the coup the four downstairs and four upstairs apartments were classified as doubles so that the one-time single private house now consisted of sixteen living units. Each double unit consisted of two bedrooms and a single living room, bathroom and kitchen. In other words, the vacant apartment consisted of a vacant bedroom. An old worker who had occupied it had just died.

When I described the place to Mirna, she was overjoyed. She was so frustrated and so desperate that she'd gladly have run to a rat-infested basement that had been used to store coal. All that mattered was that there were neither geese nor chickens in the yards and that all the neighbors got their potatoes and vegetables from stores. She didn't even want to see the place first. We simply moved in, and all her enthusiasm returned. Mirna greeted and embraced our new neighbors as if they were long-lost friends. She carried Vesna around the neighborhood, in and out of all the stores, as if to familiarize the baby with her new, genuinely urban surroundings. In the evenings we took long walks. Mirna studied all the passers-by, their expressions as well as their clothes. She also studied all the commodities displayed in the store windows.

Mirna fulfilled her life's dream. She became a city dweller, a citizen, the wife of a city worker, with an apartment of her own and a child who would be no more of a country bumpkin than her urban neighbors or her brother. But that school-created dream masked a shallow reality. She became everything she was going to become on the day she moved out of her parents' house. The following day, or week, or month, she didn't become more of a citizen or more of a worker's wife. She didn't become more creative nor more imaginative nor — after her enthusiasm dissipated itself — more energetic. She didn't become anything she hadn't been before. She merely lost her life's dream.

But that dream is a chameleon. It changes whenever we think we've reached it. Mirna knew that something had gone wrong, that something was still missing. I remember one of the statements she made only a few weeks after we moved: "I had expected everything to be so different." She had expected a new life. She had expected what you express with the words project and community. But she didn't become desperate or depressed. She still experienced reality as she'd been taught to experience it. She held on to her dream. The chameleon transformed itself. Whatever was still missing, whatever she hadn't become, could be bought in a store. She didn't buy very much. We had saved a considerable sum of money during the year when I had driven the bus and we had lived and eaten at her parents' house. She spent very little of it; she's always been afraid to spend money. But the few things she did buy were very important to her. Since our room was adequately furnished, we didn't need to buy furniture. But we did need curtains. I'm sure that no city has ever been built with the love and care with which she bought those curtains. She looked at shop windows for several weeks; every night we walked to look at another pair. When she finally bought them she treated them as a second newborn child. After the curtains were hung she repeated the entire ceremony with a bedspread. Jasna read novels in order to experience in fiction what she'd failed to experience in her life; Mirna bought curtains and a bedspread. The objects replaced her project as well as her community. But like the apartment itself, the objects lost their promise on the day they were acquired. No new life began. Nothing was different. Even the curtains and the bedspread remained new only for a few days. The chameleon changed again. But the more it changed the more it remained the same. The lack, the gap that reappeared every time it was filled, could be refilled continually only to reappear again. If this object failed to satisfy, surely the next object would succeed — or the next job transfer, or the next apartment.

The next object was to be the largest of all our objects. It was Vesna's baby carriage, a four-wheeled vehicle complete with bed and canopy, two axles, springs and brakes. It was the only vehicle we ever owned. And it was from that vehicle that I learned the narcotic potency of the manufactured thing. We scrupulously examined every carriage in the city before deciding which one was to be our carriage. We wheeled it to our apartment as if it were made of glass, carefully avoiding every pool of dirty water, raising it gently over every bump. We carried it upstairs to our bedroom, and we continued to keep it in our bedroom, not so much because we were afraid it would be stolen from the hallway but because we wanted it where we could see it. In other epochs people looked for gods, saints and revelations to confirm their lost humanity. In ours the commodity embodies all the gods, saints and revelations. Whenever we were depressed by the hollowness of our lives, whenever we felt the still unfulfilled gap, we looked at Vesna's carnage. The object confirmed our purpose and our worth. It was the meaning of the endless waiting and the meaningless work.

Our evening walks on the neighborhood streets, and especially our Sunday walks in the city park, became the high points of our lives. It was on those walks that we displayed our qualities, the qualities we had bought in stores. As soon as we had the carriage we needed the clothes that went with it. I bought a suit identical to the suits I had seen in the city park, the suits of young men who accompanied their baby carriages and their wives. Mirna and Vesna each acquired a dress with similar properties. We were now complete. When we promenaded Vesna through the park, we felt ourselves admired the same way we had admired the well-dressed couples with baby carriages. Passers-by looked into the carriage and smiled at Vesna. We were proud of Vesna, proud of our success, proud to be admired. Vesna, Mirna and I were like all the others in the park, like the admirable others, the members of the working class. We were complete human beings, citizens. Our clothes and Vesna's carriage proved it. At the end of the promenade we removed our attributes and hung them in the closet, always keeping them spotless and uncreased. We set Vesna's carriage in the corner of our room. It was a very pretty carriage. We still have it. But Vesna is no longer with us.

Our bliss lasted for two seasons. I don't know how long we could have remained intoxicated by our objects if the ground under out feet hadn't shifted, but I suspect the drugs would have lost their power on their own during the third season. In any case, we weren't given a chance to enjoy the full effect of our narcotics; our frail house of cards collapsed around us.

The event that put an end to our blissful stupor was a violent encounter between Jan and the foreman at the depot where we worked. The foreman was the type of person usually described as dumb and ruthless. He was several years younger than we were and had started working at the depot three years before Jan was hired. He was immediately recruited as a police informer and he apparently did this job so well that he was appointed section foreman only a few months after he was hired, and general foreman a few months after that. Although he had spent a few months working as a repair mechanic, by the time he was general foreman he had become convinced that the mechanics were all mindless robots and that the only thinking in the depot took place in his head. He thought of the rest of us, not as complete human beings, but as human fragments, as extensions of his limbs, as instruments which mindlessly implemented his orders.

The only consequence of the foreman's attitude was that his intentions were completely undermined. Since we were brainless, we didn't use our brains to implement his wishes but only to thwart them. As extensions of his limbs we were worse than lifeless limbs; we were rebellious implements that continually frustrated their user. No one expressed this rebelliousness as explicitly as Jan. Whenever the foreman called his name, Jan instantly dropped whatever he was holding, even if it was an oil pan, jumped up, saluted, and shouted, "Yessir!" Jan was the only one who tried to conform in every single detail to the way the foreman saw him. If all the foreman told him was, "Pull that carburetor out," Jan took a winch or a pry bar and pulled the carburetor out, without removing any of the bolts. One day Jan was removing a rear wheel to replace a worn bearing. "What the hell are you doing? All it needs is grease!" the foreman shouted. Jan furiously replaced the wheel and packed it with grease. The bus was towed back to the depot two weeks later with a ruined axle and wheel. The rest of us also implemented the foreman's orders to the letter, but none of us were as scrupulous as Jan. If some busses were nevertheless repaired, it was only because the foreman couldn't be everywhere at the same time, and all of us worked with relative efficiency when we weren't carrying out a command.

Some weeks after the incident with the broken wheel, the foreman again pulled Jan off the job he was doing and bellowed, "See if there's oil in this engine. And don't let me catch you doing anything to the engine!" The foreman had conveniently forgotten that he'd been wrong when he'd kept Jan from replacing the wheel bearing.

Jan did exactly what the foreman told him to do and two days later the bus returned with a burned out engine. The foreman was furious. He ran to Jan and shouted, "I thought I told you to see if there was oil in that engine!"

Jan dropped his tools and saluted, saying, "Yessir!"

"There couldn't have been a drop of oil in it!" the foreman shouted.

"Yessir!" Tan said again.

"You imbecile!" the foreman bellowed. "I told you to put oil in! Did you put oil into that engine?"

"No sir!" Jan answered.

The foreman's eyes were red with fury. He leered at the rest of us, ran to get a crowbar and swung it at Jan's head. Jan ducked and was hit lightly on the shoulder. Jan picked up a wrench.

The foreman started to swing his crowbar again but I ran up from behind him and yanked the bar out of his grasp. "You're lying," I told him, holding on to the bar; "I heard what you told Jan to do. You told him to see if there was oil in the engine and you explicitly told him not to do anything else."

"You're crazy!" the foreman shouted. "Whoever heard of sending a bus on the road with a dry engine?"

"Everyone here has heard of that," I answered. "We've also heard of sending a bus out with a worn bearing and of stopping someone who wanted to fix it."

Backing away from me and the crowbar, the foreman shouted at the top of his voice, "Put that bar down! You can't threaten me! You Sedlaks are lunatics. I'll have you locked up. You're sick! Someone sent you here to wreck the workers' busses! Who pays you to wreck busses?"

Jan turned to the foreman and said calmly, "No one pays us to do it. We wreck the busses on our own and for ourselves. We can't stand them. They use up our space, our air and our energy. We're lunatics determined to drive you and your busses out of our asylum."

I'm reminded of your scene with the school official who said you were deranged and dangerous when you called off your class to take part in the student strike. I commend you for your courage; you really do share that with Jan. Your courage was in fact greater because Jan and I weren't nearly as isolated as you were. The foreman backed away from us like a cornered beast. He grabbed another bar and then a wrench, but he didn't try to use them. He no longer faced only the two of us. Every single worker in the depot had picked up a tool and joined the semi-circle of angry workers surrounding the foreman. Every single person was waiting for the foreman to take the slightest step toward Jan, toward me, toward any other worker. We were all waiting for him to start swinging his bar, his wrench or even his fist. The foreman was pale with fright. He cringed away hugging the wall, trembling, not taking his eyes off us for a second.

The foreman didn't return that day, nor did we continue our work. We sat down and smoked. All of us were furious. Someone said, "Let him try that just one more time. We'll show him!"

"What'll we show him?" Jan asked.

"We'll show him who does the work; we'll show him that we can do without him," the man answered.

"That's a lie," Jan snapped. "Do you think I'd repair these contraptions if no one forced me to do it? What on earth for?"

Everyone drew back when Jan said this. The others probably hadn't ever heard anyone express such an attitude. I drew back too, although I had heard such a view before, during my first prison term. Jan's attitude to work was identical to Manuel's. It was also similar to the attitude your young high school friend Ron expressed when he took you on your first tour of his city. To Jan it wasn't the presence or absence of the foreman that made our work prostitution but the fact that we sold our lives to a project that wasn't our own. At that time I didn't understand him, just as I hadn't understood most of what Manuel had told me in prison.

Jan had expressed the same attitude six years earlier, during our agitational activity at the carton plant. Luisa still remembers him for that. In your second letter you told me George Alberts had considered Jan and me "destructive hooligans" and Luisa agreed with Alberts. It's not at all surprising that she included Ron and Manuel among the "hooligans."

According to Sabina, George Alberts thought that workers had fought a revolution in order to replace reactionary foremen with revolutionary foremen, that workers had fought a revolution in order to place George Alberts in an important post. All those opposed to this, like Manuel, had to be swept out of the way. Where was Luisa when revolutionaries like Manuel were swept out of the way? Was she alongside the aspiring foreman Alberts, helping to sweep people like Ron, myself, Manuel and Jan out of the way? She virtually admitted this when she said that "such people" were a greater threat to the revolution than the militarists. I'd really like to know where Luisa stood during this purge of saboteurs. I've long ago become suspicious of her interpretations; your letters have made me wonder about her activity as well.

Incidentally, I'd still like to know how Alberts succeeded in having you and Luisa released from prison twenty years ago.

Sabina wants me to tell more about Manuel. Unfortunately I knew him only in prison, and our conversations were neither very thorough nor were they very relaxed in the circumstances in which they took place. Also, at the time I knew him I spent as much time defending Luisa's arguments as I spent listening to Manuel's. I didn't really understand Manuel's positions until I worked with Jan at the bus repair depot, and even then I resisted the implications of that position. Emotionally I agreed with Jan. His attitude to the work we did expressed exactly what I felt toward my job and toward my life. Emotionally I had also agreed with Manuel, and even while defending Luisa's arguments I had known that I would have been among those of Manuel's friends who were jailed and killed as saboteurs. Intellectually I must have held a view similar to the one Sabina expressed in your letter although I don't remember that I had any intellectual view at all; I only had vague feelings. I suppose that I, like Sabina, thought that busses and factories were useful and that their only dehumanizing characteristic was that they were managed by bureaucrats and policed by armed torturers and murderers; if we could only get rid of those predatory parasites, we would humanize the factories as well as ourselves. Such may have been my view when I drew back in response to Jan's comment after the scene with the foreman, and such may still be Sabina's view today, but this view has nothing in common with Jan's or Manuel's. Manuel had nothing good to say about what Sabina, following Alberts, calls "industrialization." Manuel's name for it was Capital, and he called the revolutionary politicians who murdered his comrades, "capitalists." For Manuel, industrialization was merely another name for humanity's disease, it was a synonym for dehumanization. He called it Capital because he didn't see it as a human activity, as a project launched by living individuals for themselves and for each other, but as a process that grew apart from them and against them, as a growth which they fed with their living energy but which they didn't control. He had been with people who had temporarily defeated the forces that repressed them, had shared with them the experience of projecting a world that would be for human beings, and had watched most of those people reimpose on themselves the very forces they had defeated the day before because someone had told them industrialization was for them. He saw workers re-shackle themselves to a process over which they had no control because someone convinced them their desire for their own life and their own project constituted sabotage and hooliganism. Manuel and Jan taught me that if we don't destroy the old life, whether we call it capital or progress or industrialization, and if we don't project and begin to create a new life, then we're only going to reenact our slavery on the graves of our fallen comrades, some of us managing and most of us managed, some of us repressing and all of us repressed.

When Jan said he wouldn't repair any busses if a foreman didn't force him to, I drew back. I suspected that I wouldn't either, but I refused to draw any conclusions. I knew that on a superficial level Jan's statement was false, since the only time any of us repaired any busses was when the foreman was out of our sight. But Jan meant something more profound, and it was this that I resisted. My resistance to his argument helps me understand why we still produce busses, bureaucrats and bombs. I resisted because I worried for the busses. I wondered who would repair them and produce them if the revolution I then had in mind ever took place and overthrew all foremen, informers and influential comrades. I worried for the future of Capital. It was only years later that I began to ask myself who had decided that several of us were to spend parts of our lives repairing busses. This certainly wasn't the project of the living individuals engaged in it. None among the living, nor even among those who had lived before, had ever come together and decided that this activity was to be the content of our lives. It was as if we had no choice in the matter, as if we were irremediably condemned to spend our lives at forced labor. The progress of things determined the content of our lives. Things defined us, things dominated us and things consumed us. And when Jan expressed the desire to run out from under them and let them crash, I worried, not for myself or for any of us, but for the things. I wondered how the things would fare when we were no longer under them. I knew we had the ability to communicate, to determine our own individual and collective projects, to launch them together and to enjoy our common creation. I knew that such abilities were inherent to our being, that they were our very essence if we have a specific essence, that they were not aberrations or Utopian dreams. I knew this with as much certainty as I know that my heart beats: because I feel it. Yet every day I negated my being, I suppressed it; every day of my life I nursed the thing, I worried for it, I repaired it, cringed under it and died for it. The progress of the thing matters more to us than our development, more than the flowering of our own capacities. It is more important than our lives. If the progress of the thing ever requires us to stop breathing, I wonder if we'll be flexible and accommodating enough to do that for it as well.

I drew back from Jan's conclusions but I couldn't draw back from the experiences that had led Jan to those conclusions. I couldn't draw back from the world I lived in. I couldn't keep myself from experiencing what I still refused to believe: that the thing didn't exist for me but only for itself, that its well-being coincided with my immiseration, that its progress was built on my stagnation.

The day after our confrontation with the foreman I went to work at the usual hour. When I reached the entrance to the depot two men in street clothes rushed toward me, grabbed me by the arms and dragged me to the back seat of a car. Jan was already there. He laughed when I was placed next to him and shouted, "What's this? Have you ever seen these gentlemen before? Did you ever have anything to do with them? I'd thought we were having an argument with the foreman, an argument that concerned only us and the foreman. Are these gentlemen the foreman's relatives or his personal body guard?"

We were taken to the police station. I felt frustrated and indignant. It wasn't hard to surmise where the foreman had gone the previous day after he had cringed away from the circle of angry workers surrounding him. Nor was it surprising that going directly to the police would have been the normal reflex for this individual who had started his career as a police informer. What was so frustrating, and so revealing, was that all this took place without any communication among the individuals who were involved. Nothing was discussed, nothing was decided by the workers in the depot. The whole matter was settled by the foreman and the police, by the agents of order, by the agents of an order that doesn't concern those who maintain it because it isn't theirs and doesn't exist for them; they merely undergo it, as their lot.

Everything that happened at the police station was predictable except the fact that we weren't sentenced to a new prison term. We were locked into a room with nothing in it except a bench. Jan grumbled, "Here we go again." We were both convinced that we were going to spend the next few years, perhaps the rest of our lives, in prison. We sat quietly and waited. Jan stared at the blank wall; his laughter was gone. I started to cry, not because I would miss my walks in the park, wearing my suit and pushing Vesna's carriage, but because that activity suddenly seemed so ludicrous, such a miserable way to use up life's time. I cried because I would miss all that I hadn't done, all the possible lives I had failed to live. I thought of a story I had read about a man who realized only on his deathbed that during all his years in the world he hadn't once lived.

We were wrong. The repressive apparatus decided to dispose of us in a more economical way, without incurring the costs of maintaining us.

We were summoned to the office of what must have been the station's head bureaucrat. As soon as we were seated the bureaucrat turned to me and, fumbling with a dossier that must have been mine, asked, "Are you Yarostan Vochek?"

"Would you believe me if I told you I wasn't?" I asked.

Pointing his forefinger at me, the bureaucrat threatened, "If you parade as Miran Sedlak one more time, you'll be imprisoned for fraud, do you understand that?"

Jan and I looked at each other; we were relieved. "If" and "one more time" meant that we weren't going to be imprisoned this time. We wanted to laugh.

The bureaucrat turned to Jan and, with the same threatening tone, said, "You know that you can both get ten years for insulting and beating the foreman."

Jan didn't respond.

"You could get another ten years for instigating a riot inside a workplace, and another for wrecking social means of production. All this on top of your criminal record would land you in prison for life," the bureaucrat said, threateningly but calmly, as if he were explaining a mathematical problem to us.

Both of us stared at him. We no longer felt like laughing.

He continued, "We're not going to imprison you. We don't run a nursery for wild beasts." (That explained our good fortune.) "Parade under false names one more time, go into or near the bus repair depot for any reason whatever, wreck any more social property, fight with the same or another representative of the working class, and we'll take care of you — this time permanently. Do you understand that?"

We were being told that we would be exterminated like "wild beasts" if we protected ourselves from abuse one more time. We were being fired from our jobs. We were being given a picture of our future: either to live as dead things or else not to live at all. We were being deprived of uncertainty.

"Yes," I answered, "We understand that."

The small amount of conventional happiness Mirna and I had nursed with such loving care disintegrated all around us. We could enjoy the illusory satisfaction offered by the objects only if we served them; as soon as we stopped serving them we learned that they were not for us but that we were for them. The moment we transgressed the rules of progress and found ourselves alone with our rewards, the objects lost their auras and revealed their essence: they were garbage.

I returned to our apartment long before the end of the working day. Mirna started crying before I even told her Jan and I had been arrested. She knew as soon as I walked in that I'd been fired. The previous night I had told her about our encounter with the foreman; her only comment had been, "What'll become of us?" I had been angered by her comment because I'd interpreted it to mean, "What'll become of the curtains, the bedspread, Vesna's carriage and our Sunday clothes?" I'd been angered mainly because I had shared exactly the same concern: I had worried for the objects.

When I told Mirna what happened at the police station she started to tremble. Her face took on an expression of undisguised, raw fear. She threw herself at me, sobbing and shaking, and uttered weakly, "They can't, Yarostan, they can't!" Mirna saw what I had seen a few hours earlier while waiting with Jan in the room at the police station; she saw how ludicrously poor our lives had become since the day when we'd started pouring them into our objects. We stopped worrying for the objects and started worrying for ourselves. We became aware of our own lives for the first time only when we began to be hounded, when we faced the danger of losing them.

That day was a beginning, but not the kind of beginning Mirna had looked forward to. It was the beginning of our persecution. From that day on we were hounded so persistently that we never again had the opportunity to worry about the future of our objects. That day was the beginning of our human lives. We ceased to be objects in a world of objects; we ceased to be things that produced and things that consumed. I began to understand Jan's outlook as well as Manuel's.

Only two days after Jan and I were "briefed" by the police bureaucrat, there was a knock at the door. Mirna jumped up as if a cannon had exploded; she backed against the wall, pale with fear. The moment misfortune begins all news is bad news and every change is likely to be a change for the worse. I let in a man who introduced himself as the president of the neighborhood council. His eyes didn't once stop shifting from side to side. He was as suspicious as a mouse sitting in the middle of a room, ready at any instant to flee back to its hole. He even studied Vesna with apprehension, probably fearing that her paw would fly out and claw his face before he'd had a chance to defend himself or escape. Years later our neighbor, the police informer Mr. Ninovo, reminded me of this council president.

The president announced, as if he were reading, although he didn't have a text: "At its last deliberative session the neighborhood council resolved that convicted criminals and other parasites who suck the blood of the working people will not be harbored within the living units of said council."

Mirna started to bawl and Vesna joined her. I flung the door wide open, grabbed the president by the back of the collar, and sent him flying out of our apartment with a kick in the rear, so as to justify the need for his vigilance, his suspiciousness and the constant shifting of his eyes.

Mirna became hysterical. She was sure the police would come to arrest me for the last time because of the way I had treated the council president. I tried to calm her by telling her the president's behavior had indicated that he hadn't expected to be treated any other way. But as soon as her fear for my arrest receded, she started worrying about our situation. She convinced herself that the neighborhood council had no right to evict us, since they didn't even live in our building. She talked me into taking our predicament to the neighbors. I agreed with the principle of doing this, but I assured her that our neighbors had no more power to stop our eviction than we did; right or wrong, the neighborhood council had the police behind them.

Even so, I went with Mirna to knock on the doors of our neighbors' apartments. This was a mistake; it only informed us how alone we were. One of the women downstairs opened the door and immediately slammed it in our faces. None of the others let us into their apartments. We were forced to stand in the doorways and explain our situation as if we were dirty beggars asking for food, and as we spoke we heard the doors we'd just left open slightly. Apparently people wanted to hear our story a second and then a third and even a fourth time, or else they were eavesdropping so as to hear what the others would tell us. When we reached our third or fourth door, the man interrupted us before we were finished and said, "I'm sorry for you, but you really should have told us you were a convicted criminal."

The next neighbor interrupted us almost as soon as we began and she made the advice more succinct: "You should have told the council you were convicts."

Mirna angrily grabbed the woman by the shoulders and shouted, "You idiot! We're workers just like you! Convicts are people who are inside prisons, and most of them are workers too!"

The woman was apparently intimidated. She said, "I'm sorry for you," backed away from us and closed her door.

We heard the next door close while we walked towards it. We knocked and a man shouted, "I don't talk to criminals!"

I got furious and, banging on the door with all the strength in my arms, I shouted, "That's because you're a pig, and pigs never talk to human beings!"

We didn't knock on the remaining three or four doors. We didn't have the nerve. We were defeated. All of our neighbors were workers; there wasn't a single clerical worker, student or bureaucratic official in the building.

According to your friend Daman, workers are "inherently revolutionary." I suppose what he means by that is identical to what our neighborhood council president would mean. Daman doesn't mean all workers; he means those workers who have learned to submit to authority, those workers who would be willing to obey any authority that speaks in their name, those who would be willing to evict and ultimately to maim and kill other workers for the sake of a politician who considers them "inherently revolutionary." Daman is a politician or a saint: in his mouth "revolutionary" means the same thing as "blessed" and is merely a way to flatter his future followers.

Our situation was similar to the one I had faced during the weeks after I had been released from prison. We had no place to go and I had no job. We still had some savings but now there were three of us. We were stained, exactly the way Jews had been stained during the occupation. Only now there was no resistance movement; the dregs of that movement had replaced the previous occupiers; the rest of the movement had been slaughtered during three days and nights of senseless butchery.

If we found another apartment, we would be hounded out as soon as the police informed our neighbors that we were "convicts." I couldn't find a job for the same reason. I didn't even think of looking for one. I knew I'd have the same luck I'd had before: "I'm sorry comrade, but with your record... we can't afford..."

We went to Jan for help and advice. He was able to remain in the apartment of his former fellow worker, and as a result he was able to communicate our situation to the other workers in the depot. The police had told us to stay away from the depot; they hadn't told Jan to move out of his apartment. I suppose the police had expected Jan to be evicted the same way we were, but Jan's friend, not being a "criminal," had managed to reason with his neighbors, convincing them that Jan couldn't be evicted since the apartment wasn't in his name; he was simply a guest.

Jan said that he would contact Titus Zabran once again about our getting another job; he'd have to telephone Titus to avoid being arrested, since Titus' office was next door to the bus depot. As for our housing problem, Jan looked sadly at

Mirna and suggested that we move back to their parents' house, at least until I found another source of income.

Mirna swallowed her pride together with her life's dreams and took Jan's advice. We moved back to the fringes of the city, back to the yards with chickens and vegetable gardens, back to the neighborhood which was no longer a village but was not yet part of the city. We packed our curtains, our bedspread and our Sunday clothes; we wouldn't need them where we were going.

Vesna's carriage had to be transported on a truck. We were ashamed of it when it arrived. There were no baby carriages on the unpaved streets where Mirna's parents lived; they weren't built for such streets. We stored the carriage in what had been Jan's room and covered it with an old sheet. Unlike an old trunk after a journey's end, it couldn't be used as a storage box nor as a seat or surface; it had no use at all; it was simply a large mistake.

What upset Mirna most of all was the thought that Vesna would grow up in the environment where Mirna had grown up, that Vesna would be brought up by Mirna's religious mother, and that Vesna's whole life would consist of experiences like the one we had just undergone. I argued that there was no reason to project our misfortune into the child's life, but ultimately it was Mirna who turned out to be right.

When we told Mirna's father what we had undergone, he nodded with approval for what Jan and I had done. He said, "You can't teach mules to fly," referring to those who had evicted us; his conclusion was as fatalistic as his wife's: "That's how it is. What matters is that you're alive and well. Worse things have happened."

In other words, a healthy horse can still be made serviceable; only a lame horse is good for nothing. In his view our adventure was nothing more than a temporary setback comparable at worst to a healthy and vigorous peasant's loss of a year's crop. Next year was another year, and if we stayed alive and well we'd surely emerge with a better crop, perhaps even coming out as far ahead as we'd fallen behind. He was still convinced that I would go far, perhaps to a bureaucratic office, perhaps even to the university. But he noticed that I talked less and sometimes not at all: he suspected that something had gone wrong. One evening during dinner he asked me, half jokingly, "What's the matter with you, boy? Have you lost your politics? This is no time to lose that type of talent!"

Mirna's mother didn't share Sedlak's high opinion of me. She had seen me as an omen, an evil omen, since the day when I first came to her house. I didn't learn this until several years later, because she didn't say anything at all at the time. She saw me as hell's messenger, sent from afar to bring destruction, misery and death to the entire family. Everything I had done until then confirmed this suspicion — or rather this certainty, since she didn't once show that she doubted the truth of her initial impression. The newest episode showed her that I had already started to carry out my destructive assignment. By taking part in Jan's fight with the foreman, and especially by calling myself Miran Sedlak, I had caused Jan to get into far more trouble than he'd have gotten into by himself. It's possible that this was when she linked me to Jan's first arrest, since a few years later she was going to blame me for everything that had happened to Jan, and she knew that Jan and I had been arrested together six years earlier at the carton plant. Finally, by getting myself evicted, I was starting to bring pain and humiliation into Mirna's life and even into little Vesna's life. I didn't know these details at the time, but I sensed her intense hostility toward me, a hostility that couldn't be pacified with a kindly gesture, a pleasant word or a smile.

Mirna and I helped with the housework, read a little, took care of Vesna and waited. There was snow on the ground and we rarely left the house; in any case, Mirna no longer had inclinations to take walks in that familiar neighborhood.

We waited for something to change for the better. Our main hope was Jan; we waited for him to come with good news about a job, perhaps about an apartment.

Jan came, but not with good news. He had telephoned Titus Zabran. Titus knew about our firing. He told Jan that our situation was made difficult by the fact that the police had reported our behavior to the trade union bureaucracy and consequently no official would be willing to hire us, even with "pull." But he told Jan he would continue to try to find a "place" for us.

Mirna grew increasingly frustrated and impatient. "We can't simply sit here and wait," she insisted. "Nothing is ever going to happen here, absolutely nothing!"

She decided to try to get a job on her own. First she went out with a newspaper. Then she started to ask young women on busses what kinds of jobs they had and where their factories were located. She visited every factory she could find.

After three or four weeks of daily journeys to large and small workshops she found a job in a clothing factory not far from the carton plant. She announced it with a certain amount of pride, but without a trace of the childlike optimism with which she had greeted earlier changes. Already before she started to work, her passion and her pride were mixed with a certain resignation, a certain helplessness in the face of an indifferent, arbitrary and cruel environment. She became increasingly silent, increasingly patient; her life's dreams continued receding. Mirna became a member of the working class but not on her own terms. She became a wage worker, a citizen of Capital. She described her job with one word: "drudgery." In the clothing factory she learned boredom, the endless repetition of the same motions, the gloomy foreknowledge that the following day, week and year would be the same as all the yesterdays. Her daily activity enriched humanity only in clothes; it consumed Mirna, swallowed all her projects, extinguished her hopes. By becoming a member of the working class she annihilated the possibility to become a member of a human community, she gave away the time and energy necessary for the creation of that community. The resignation Mirna expressed the first day she worked in the clothing factory was the resignation of a person whose life is no longer one's own, of a beast of burden.

About a month after Mirna started working, Jan learned about a job for him and me. Titus Zabran had actually gone to Jan's apartment to tell him about the job. A steel plant in a small town about 100 kilometers from the city was short of unskilled laborers. There were not enough workers in the town or the surrounding villages to supply the needed labor force and city workers were either unwilling to move or unwilling to travel such a great distance twice a day. Consequently the plant officials were willing to overlook our prison past as well as our employment records. Titus suggested that Jan and I accept the job, assuring him that such "emergency situations" were the best we could expect under the circumstances and that the next emergency might not pay as high a wage as the steel plant.

Mirna refused to hear of our traveling 100 kilometers away. I argued that we apparently had no other choice. Jan suggested that we postpone making our decision until he learned more about the job.

Jan came again two weeks later, on a weekend. He told us that housing was cheap and plentiful in the steel town and that he was going to rent an apartment near the plant. He urged us to do the same. Mirna burst out crying, turned to the wall and beat her fists against it. She shouted, "I don't want either of you so far away from me, in the wilderness!"

Jan sadly told her, "The heart of this city is the only wilderness in this part of the world."

Mirna turned to Jan with a look of desperation and said, faltering, "I'll kill myself before I go there! I'm going to stay in the city and I'll support Vesna as well as both of you for the rest of my life if necessary!"

"Mirna, don't be a mule," Jan pleaded. "You're not living in the city now, and we don't have a choice."

Mirna told us, "They're building houses for workers near my factory. Several women in my department have already signed up. I'm going to sign up to buy one!"

"And what'll you pay for it with?" Jan asked. "Your wages don't support Vesna or Yarostan. Father supports them; he gets twice as much as you do. In the steel plant I'll be paid three times what you get."

"They told me I'd get a raise," Mirna said.

"When?" Jan asked.

"In two years."

"Two years!" Jan exclaimed. "And when will you buy your house?"

Mirna collapsed into a chair and cried. "I don't know," she said desperately. "But I don't want you to go there and I don't want Vesna to grow up there!"

I suggested a compromise. "We could move back to the city if I took the job in the steel plant. That way we could afford to buy the house and stop being a burden to your father."

"You'd spend half your day traveling," Mirna objected.

I said, "I don't see any other acceptable alternative."

Mirna didn't say anything. I decided to take the job. Jan moved to an apartment near the plant.

A certain feeling of happiness accompanies self-realization. During those days I learned that another type of happiness accompanies resignation. I was convinced that I had no other choice and I resigned myself to a twelve-hour working day, four hours of which I spent going to and from the plant. As soon as I resigned myself to that situation everything became easier and more pleasant than I had expected it to be; I experienced lesser pains as pleasures. The work was hard; it consisted of shoveling scraps of hot metal onto a moving conveyor belt. We sweated in winter; in summer the place became an unbearable inferno. Small wonder that other workers didn't want to travel a hundred kilometers for the sake of such activity. But on the other hand, the foreman didn't take his job seriously and was in no way different from any other worker; no one had been willing to accept the task and the workers had drawn lots to determine which one of their names would be entered as foreman on the official forms. As a result there was no supervision; the people I worked with were among the freest human beings I've encountered inside a factory or prison.

The time I spent traveling used up what remained of my living day. I got up every day long before sunrise. I rode a tram and a bus to the train station and then spent nearly an hour and a half on the train. I returned home long after sunset, dirty and exhausted. I bathed, ate and collapsed into bed — six days a week. I degenerated as a being with specific capacities, with the power to create. I stagnated. Whatever potentialities I had were stunted. Please mention this to Sabina. What she calls industrialization is impossible without steel. That process is not our project; it's not for us; it thrives only by destroying us.

However, since I was resigned, even the discomfort of spending so many hours a day traveling contained a pleasure. I took books with me and read on the train every morning: philosophy, history, science, as well as several novels. I was fascinated; I even came to look forward to my train ride to work. On my way back home at night I was usually too tired to read.

As soon as I started working I insisted that Mirna quit her job. I argued that since my wages were three times hers, we could easily support ourselves and also move on what I earned, so there was no reason for both of us to turn ourselves into oxen. But Mirna was adamant. If she quit her job she wouldn't be able to buy the house she'd signed up for, since those houses were earmarked for workers in her plant. That would mean we'd have to rent another apartment and would again be subject to victimization by the bureaucrats who administered them. She also insisted that she'd never be fired from her job as a troublemaker whereas there was no telling how long I'd keep my job. Mirna was determined not to let anything like our eviction happen again and she was equally determined to move out of her mother's house and into the housing complex near her factory. I asked who would replace her mother as Vesna's nurse when both of us were working, but learned that the planners had already removed this obstacle to the unfettered development of the productive forces: the children were going to spend the day in a nursery while their parents reproduced Capital.

Mirna's application was accepted, the house was built and we moved in. It's the house in which I'm writing this letter. Mirna still works in the clothing factory a few blocks from here. Today there are blocks of similar houses, the streets are paved, there are streetlights and sidewalks, and a bus stops half a block from our house. When we moved here there were neither blocks nor streets nor lights. It was late spring. Our house and two of its neighbors stood in a pool of mud with trails consisting of narrow, slippery planks of wood. Our baby carnage was as useless here as it had been at the Sedlaks' house. The house was built for workers, which meant that it was built shoddily. The roof began to leak during our first heavy rainfall; during my second prison term Mirna had to have the entire roof replaced. The plaster on the walls and ceilings has cracked and left large fissures. The foundation was set in mud and one side of the house has been sinking ever since we moved in; everything in the house stands at an angle. We got used to that. In fact, we got used to everything: the jobs, the mud, the nursery. What mattered to Mirna was that there were no chickens and no gardens. Eventually there were small front lawns, only grass grew on them, and we didn't even plant our own grass; that was done for us by the builders; we only mowed it. What mattered was that we finally had our house in the city and no one could evict us from it.

We were happy in our new house. It was the happiness of permanent exiles, of survivors from a shipwreck or a war. It was the happiness of wage workers resigned to their lot, the kind of happiness that comes with resignation. We had shed almost everything: our dreams, our projects, our unrealized potentialities and our unused abilities. Consequently we embraced what little we had retained with all the joy that was in us. We threw ourselves into the project of fixing our little house with the same enthusiasm with which we might have joined human beings building a new world. I wasn't able to do much during the week but every Sunday I became a master carpenter and painter. Mirna worked every night and did most of the building and decorating. We built our own bed and tables and for chairs we use backless stools. In time we again had enough money to buy what we needed but the main thing we bought was a sofa. Wood as well as paint were plentiful while the housing complex was being built since the quantities we needed were always available in the scrap piles. We left all our earlier purchases packed away. Mirna made all the curtains and bedding as well as all our clothes. We spent our money only on food and saved the rest. Mirna insisted on saving money for the same reason that she had insisted on buying the house: she didn't want to be dependent on a world she couldn't trust, she didn't want to be at the mercy of a merciless bureaucracy ever again.

Mirna, Vesna and I had lived in our house for a year when I started to hear rumors about a vast uprising breaking out in Magarna. I say rumors because every account I heard contradicted the previous one. The press organized a systematic campaign to create ignorance and confusion. I don't know what I would have thought of you if I had received the letter you sent me at that time, describing your newspaper activity as your life's project and reporters as your community. The newspaper's systematic falsification of the acts of the Magarna workers convinced me that the press was an instrument of domination and couldn't be anything else.

You commented on the press's falsification of the Magarna events but you suggested this was due to the bias of the reporters or owners and not to the very nature of the instrument. I think you fail to grasp something about the press, probably because you were so deeply involved with it. You fail to understand that instruments of domination and destruction can't be used for anything else. Surely it's obvious to you that a bomb doesn't become a benevolent instrument if it's controlled by a benevolent person. A newspaper destroys communication as certainly as a bomb destroys life and this was plainly visible during the Magarna rising. The people who reported the Magarna events were not like the people engaged in the events, just as they were not like Jan or Mirna or her parents or me. They were different, not because of their views or their biases, but because of their activity. These differences didn't reside in the personal benevolence or malevolence of the reporters but in the instrument they served. Gross, unbridgeable chasms separated two groups of people engaged in mutually antagonistic activities. The workers of Magarna were desperately trying to cease to be what they were, to free themselves from the routine that had repressed them, while the reporters made no effort to cease to be what they were but on the contrary threw themselves passionately into their special routine. The Magarna workers were desperately trying to communicate directly with each other and with their likes elsewhere while the reporters were spreading their reportages between like and like, interpreting each to the other, portraying each to the other through a glass that didn't reflect the experiences of the individual on either side but only the reporter's. The workers were struggling for lives which were not interpreted, defined, mediated or represented while the newspapers could only interpret, define, mediate and represent because that's their essential purpose, their nature. Locked into the world of representations, the reporters couldn't see a struggle against representations as anything other than a struggle between one representation and another. I'm not even mentioning the fact that almost all the reporters were actual agents of the State, officials who earned their livelihood by falsifying workers' struggles. Newspapers can't coexist with or serve human beings fighting to abolish reportage and create communication; they're based on the impossibility of community.

This was what I was learning about newspapers twelve years ago when you were writing me about your newspaper articles. I didn't see your letter; I can't guess if I would have been angry or pleased, I know I wouldn't have been pleased by your high regard for our activity at the carton plant eight years earlier, nor by your enthusiasm for the press. But I think one aspect of your letter would have pleased me very much. Your letter was an attempt at direct communication between two individuals separated by impenetrable political and geographical barriers, an instance of the communication the Magarna workers were desperately struggling to create. Maybe it was this characteristic of your letter that antagonized the authorities. Maybe their fear of direct communication across their frontiers is far greater than our trust in it. Maybe the ultimate concern of the State is to keep such communication from taking place: that's the central purpose of the fences and the walls, the censors and the paid liars. Letters like yours vanish in normal times; it would have been a miracle if such a letter had reached its destination in a time of crisis.

I can believe that such a letter would have been confiscated, and even that a messenger carrying such letters would have been arrested. But I still can't believe that Jan and I could have been arrested merely because such letters were addressed to us, and before we had even seen them. This possibility would be slightly more plausible if we hadn't been doing anything at the time, if I had remained in the stupor of resignation, if I had continued to channel all my energy and enthusiasm into Sunday afternoon repairing and decorating of the interior of this house. It wasn't your letter but the event you asked about in that letter, the Magarna uprising, that woke me from that stupor and shamed me in the face of my resignation.

When I heard the first rumors of a widespread rising I paid no attention to them. It's not that I thought they weren't true. I had learned during my first imprisonment that such rumors contained descriptions of real events. I began to take an interest when Jan and several other workers brought newspapers into the steel plant. The fanaticism with which the newspapers denied all the rumors indicated that at least some of them weren't only true but also current.

However, what confirmed the rumors wasn't the press but direct communication with Magarna workers. One of the workers in the steel plant pretended to be ill and went to visit his family, who lived in a small village on the frontier of Magarna and had relatives across the frontier. He succeeded in evading the border guards and in communicating with his relatives.

As soon as he returned from his village all the workers in our section of the plant gathered around him like flies, questioning him about every detail of what he had learned. Jan was the most persistent; he simply couldn't stop asking questions and he repeatedly asked the same questions. He couldn't believe what he heard. Somewhere in the world people just like us had started doing exactly what Jan had always wanted to do; they had started to break the chain that shackled them to the monster that consumed them; they had started to move for themselves.

Our fellow worker wasn't able to answer several of Jan's questions and I still don't know the answers today. He told us that repressive old functionaries were being ousted from their posts but couldn't tell us if they were being replaced by repressive new functionaries in similar posts. He told us workers' councils were being formed in factories and workshops but couldn't tell us about the extent to which politicians and their organizations were behind the councils. Jan repeatedly asked, "Are they doing this for themselves or for the productive forces?" This couldn't be answered either.

Yet in spite of all the unanswered questions it was clear to us that a population had begun to stir, that ancient social structures had started to crumble. People like ourselves had suddenly turned against the apparatus into which they had been pouring their lives. We didn't know if they were determined to recover their whole lives or if they were already looking for half-way stations, if their struggle was already being channeled into dead ends. But wherever their struggle ended, we were convinced that it had begun as a struggle against the entire social apparatus that had shaped individuals into tools that served its ends. Wherever they were eventually channeled, it was clear that the workers of Magarna had stopped being workers and by that act had already made the impossible possible; they had already created the field in which jobs could give way to projects and production to creation.

I don't think I could have answered any of your questions; I didn't know any more about the Magarna struggle than you did. Our fellow worker's visit to his family was the only direct information we had. My nearness to Magarna was counteracted by a more total suppression of information. I was convinced, as you were, that a revolution had broken out, a revolution as extensive and profound as the one Luisa had experienced. It was during those events that I began to question Luisa's interpretation of her experience and to contrast it with Manuel's accounts. It was then that I began to understand Manuel's as well as Jan's arguments. It became clear to me that if there were workers in Magarna whose job had been to shovel scraps of burning hot metal onto a conveyor belt, those workers couldn't possibly be motivated by the desire to shovel the same burning scraps onto the same conveyor belt "on their own." We didn't need strikes, barricades or bloodshed for that; we were already doing that on our own. This was clear not only to Jan and me but to everyone I worked with.

This was also clear to Mirna, despite the fact that the supervision as well as the noise at her clothing factory made communication impossible, despite the fact that after work she didn't talk to anyone but ran directly to the nursery to pick up Vesna. "Officials we've never seen before walk up and down the aisles," she told me. "And they're so nervous, so afraid; they act as if at any instant we were going to walk off with the machinery and the clothing. If we only had the nerve!"

Discussion of the Magarna events was almost impossible at Mirna's factory, as it was in most other factories and workshops. But it wasn't impossible at the plant where Jan and I worked, certainly not in our section. There were no aisles in which police agents could walk up and down, and the heat in which we worked didn't motivate any officials to take an interest in our conversations. I've already mentioned that our foreman was a foreman only on paper and consequently we weren't supervised. I'm also convinced there were no police agents among us; the authorities had a hard enough time finding people willing to do the shoveling. We were unsupervised but we were also completely isolated from all the other workers in the steel plant; from the moment we entered our section of the plant to the moment we left we hardly saw anyone who didn't work in our section. This didn't prevent several of my fellow workers from trying to communicate with others. The communication took place after work hours in the restaurants and bars, on the street corners and in the park of the steel town. It was direct, face-to-face communication; it didn't take place through a newspaper like the one your friend Daman described, a "workers' newspaper", the very existence of such a newspaper would have replaced and ultimately suppressed the type of communication that took place. One individual exchanged views and feelings with another; before long everyone in the steel plant, perhaps everyone in the town, felt what the Magarna workers must have felt on the eve of their revolution: the desire as well as the ability to throw off their chains.

In spite of the deafening noise and the unbearable heat, my workplace turned into a discussion club. Every day someone had heard more rumors that had slipped across the border; every day the press confirmed the rumors with its fanatical denials and distortions. We discussed the implications and prospects of every act; we discussed our own possibilities and prospects. And we knew that similar discussions were taking place elsewhere in the plant, if only because fewer and fewer wagons of metal passed through our section. The entire town could have been located in Magarna; it responded to events in Magarna as if they were taking place inside the steel plant.

Unfortunately I didn't take part in the all-night discussions that took place after work in the restaurants and bars; I would have had to catch a train that left three hours later and thus eliminate the small amount of time I spent with Mirna and Vesna. But Jan's accounts of those meetings and discussions made me feel that I had taken part in them. Whenever two or more people met they exchanged, not greetings, but news from Magarna; before long all were shouting, each outdoing the other in denouncing the lies fabricated by the press. Although formal meetings were banned, steel workers who met informally in bars and restaurants talked about writing letters to the newspapers, about passing resolutions criticizing the press, about sending delegations to the newspaper offices and even about going on strike for the sake of honest information about the revolution in Magarna.

I was enthusiastic about all the suggestions and proposals, but my enthusiasm was dampened by Jan's misgivings. Jan was enthusiastic too, but only about the fact that the human beings around us had come to life and started to stir. He considered the agitation around the press a wasteful expenditure of energy that couldn't find other outlets. Jan stated his misgivings to others whenever the occasion arose, but he did so quietly, without insistence, without a politician's rhetoric or a missionary's self-righteousness. He was convinced that what was clear to him would sooner or later become clear to everyone. It did become clear to me and perhaps to many others that our agitation for an honest press was grounded in an illusion and that this activity was a substitute for the real activity, we were unwilling or unable to launch.

What became perfectly obvious to me is illustrated by your experience on the university's newspaper staff. Your activity was the type of "honest journalism" we were agitating for. But when you practiced this "honest journalism," authority immediately suppressed the newspaper. You claim that this suppression was caused by the spinelessness of the university administrators. You're wrong. Your newspaper was suppressed because it had stopped carrying out its function. The newspaper is an instrument by which the ruling minority shapes the conceptions of the majority. "Honest journalism" is not its function but its mask. Those in power may at times tolerate honest journalism but only if they consider it harmless. Your own experience proves this. Authority had only to place its signature on a "directive" and your honest journalism vanished. Your attitude to this is as ridiculous as the idea that a general's brain can be a warmonger while his mouth and his other organs are pacifists. The newspaper is an organ of the rulers; it serves those in power or else it is nothing, it doesn't exist. That's why our agitation for an honest press was a waste of time. I'm not talking about honest reporters. We heard about honest reporters — after they were fired.

Resolutions were passed and sent to newspapers; letters were written; there were several brief work-stoppages at the plant. But I sensed a general feeling of frustration. We seemed to be in constant motion but we remained where we'd been before. The newspapers obviously didn't publish our letters or resolutions nor did they give the slightest indication that similar activity was taking place elsewhere. But the newspapers weren't the cause of our inability to communicate with our likes elsewhere; they were merely a symptom of that inability. What made direct communication with our likes impossible was the absence of community, the fact that intermediaries stood between ourselves and our likes. We didn't know how to bypass the intermediaries nor how to extend our hands to those who stood on the other side. That's why we turned to the intermediaries themselves for help, asking them to reflect accurately what our brothers were saying and doing, asking them to communicate our words and our gestures to our brothers. But the intermediaries, the professional interpreters and ideological specialists, could communicate and reflect only their own words and gestures, they could display only the insights derived from their own mode of living.

We thought we had nowhere else to turn and we convinced ourselves that if only the intermediaries reflected a portion of the truth about the Magarna workers' struggle and if only they communicated our desire to take part in that struggle then workers elsewhere would begin to rise as well. If the intermediaries could only be brought to our side, if their instruments could only be made to serve our struggle, the police-run regimes would tear at the seams — in the factories, workshops and mines.

We were wrong. Such instruments couldn't be made to serve our struggle; such intermediaries couldn't communicate our desires. They separated worker from worker and brother from brother like fortified walls standing between them. The only one who moved in response to another's motion was one who communicated with the other face to face. One who depended on intermediaries for information depended on them also for guidance, motion and life.

The workers in my section of the plant succeeded in communicating with the rest of the workers in the plant, but that was the beginning and the end of our success. To go beyond the plant we turned to intermediaries, just as to reach their comrades elsewhere the Magarna workers turned to intermediaries. And the intermediaries they turned to turned against them.

Workers in tanks murdered their brothers on the streets of Magarna. The workers in the tanks had been informed about the struggle, not by those engaged in it, but by politicians' speeches and newspaper articles; their gestures were guided, not by the sense of solidarity with their likes, but by submission to the commands of superiors. They aimed and fired without scruple or hesitation because they couldn't see their opponents; their vision was blocked, not by the metal casing surrounding them, but by the ideological casing that gripped their minds. They aimed at the demons described by the speeches and newspapers. They fired at images. But they killed human beings.

The Magarna workers couldn't aim or fire with the same lack of scruple, with the same certainty, because they knew that their scruples and their uncertainties were only a few days old; they knew that only a few days earlier they too had known about each other only what they'd seen on the opaque screens that stood between them. They hesitated before they fired. But those in the tanks didn't hesitate.

For a moment our stupor and our resignation gave way to hope, to the anticipation of a life where large projects are possible, where dreams can be realized in the company of vibrant, imaginative and sympathetic human beings. But our hopes were short-lived. The society held together by the market and the police didn't disintegrate. Magarna workers were buried in mass graves and our hopes were buried with them. We hadn't been able to add anything more than hopes to their struggle; our gestures had remained confined within boundaries we hadn't created, boundaries we hadn't been able to cross. Something like your journalistic project had been all we had reached for during a moment when a universe of possibilities wasn't very far from our grasp. We called for good intermediaries instead of creating conditions in which no intermediaries could thrive. We called for an honest press instead of forging our own communication as our first step toward the creation of our own community. The people of Magarna had started to struggle for such a community. They were isolated and defeated. They were isolated from us and from those like us who remained fascinated by all or part of the glitter of the monarchs' world. We were isolated too, but we weren't defeated. We hadn't even begun to struggle.

Yarostan.

Sophia's fifth letter

Dear Yarostan,

Your letter was beautiful. I wish I had joined you at the time of the Magarna uprising instead of having Lem take you my silly letters.

I have a little bit more in common with you now than I did when I last wrote you. I've just come out of jail!

A few days after the so-called "general strike" which I attended with Daman, a loud noise woke me at seven in the morning. At first I thought it was thunder; a storm was raging outside. Then I heard it again: a loud, insistent knocking. I ran to the door in a stupor and opened it. Two huge uniformed policemen stood in front of me, both grasping the handles of the guns in their holsters!

"Mrs. Nachalo?" one of them asked.

"Miss Nachalo. Which one? There are three of us here." My first thought was that something horrible had happened to Tina, who is no longer with us.

"Miss Sophia Nachalo."

"That's me," I said.

"You're under arrest."

"Me? Why?"

"That's for the court to determine; anything you say now may be used as evidence against you. Come with us."

"Can't I get dressed?" I asked.

"Don't take all day."

"Would you mind waiting for me outside?" I asked.

"Not this time, Miss. We'll wait right here. Step on it!"

"Could you at least keep your voice down? You'll wake everyone up," I whispered.

"Just make it snappy, Miss, or you'll have to come in the clothes you're wearing."

I took my time dressing and tiptoed out of my room so as not to wake Sabina. They were sitting when I came out. They both rushed out of the house after me. "O.K. Let's go."

I started to run back in, asking, "Can I at least leave a note for my sister?"

"You've taken enough of our time, Miss. You can call her from the station."

287

A third policeman was sitting in their car listening to the radio while waiting for his colleagues to escort me out of the ram. I'd forgotten my umbrella but I didn't ask for another favor. I got drenched.

"You've been charged with assault and battery," I was told in a cold, matter-of-fact manner; it didn't seem to occur to any of them that the charge was ridiculous for a person of my stature. What had they thought when they saw me open the door in my pajamas and barefooted — that I might slug two enormous protectors of law and order? They'd kept their hands on their guns just in case. Maybe they thought I was "wiry."

"Is my victim dying of the injuries I inflicted?" I asked, trying to imitate their cold matter-of-fact tone.

All of them including the driver turned to look at me. One of them mumbled something more about the court determining the extent of the injuries and about the possibility that my words might turn up as my accusers. They and I were silent for the rest of the trip.

I asked for the phone as soon as I got to the station. Everyone I asked was very cordial; I was told I could use the phone "right away," as soon as I was interviewed and searched. But after I was interviewed once, I was interviewed again. And after I was searched one time, I was searched a second time and then a third. I won't bore you with the details; you must be familiar with them; police stations all over the world must have more in common with each other than with the neighborhoods in which they're located.

It must have been noon before I got to use a phone. I rang and rang but there was no answer. Of all days to decide to go out before lunch Sabina had chosen this one! I was escorted to a room full of women sitting on benches. I was furious at myself. How stupid I had been not to wake Sabina! In my early morning stupor I had thought my arrest was so trivial compared to the event that had taken place two days earlier — Tina's departure — that I had even whispered and tiptoed so as not to disturb Sabina's sleep with my silly "tragedy." I could at least have written her a note during the time I was alone in my room dressing. How dumb! I felt so frustrated I bit my lip until it bled.

My anger gradually shifted to the sneaky psychology professor who was responsible for my arrest. I have to give him credit for one thing: he certainly is a psyche-manipulator. He had grinned when I'd slapped him in response to his intimidating insults. I had interpreted his grin as a sign of masochistic enjoyment. But I'm not a psychologist. His grin was the grimace of the victor! His insult-strategy had succeeded beyond his wildest dreams: he had provoked the criminal to enact the crime! He's no masochist. He's a sadist, an ordinary bastard, an agent provocateur for the police. I didn't regret slapping him. In fact, I wished I had done something which deserved the description "assault and battery"; I wished I had given that morning's policemen some reason to keep their hands on their guns; I wished they had in fact told me that my victim was in a critical condition because of the wounds I had inflicted. Various colorful and ingenious forms of "assault and battery" drifted through my mind, none of which would ever be within my reach, none of which I'd ever be able to carry through. And while I pondered my total inability to torture my torturer the cracks on the blank wall across from me formed themselves into a smug face with a stupid grin whispering at me through its teeth; "Everyone can see that nothing is going to stop you, Miss Nachalo; you're a dangerous person; you should be undergoing treatment in a hospital, Miss Nachalo."

Toward evening we were moved from the room with the benches to a similar room with cots but no blankets. I had been there, or in an identical room, once before. When trays of food were brought in I realized I hadn't been given any lunch but I didn't feel the urge to complain. After supper I asked to use the phone but the guard told me I could phone in the morning; she turned off the lights and shut the door; I thought we were locked in for the night. I was wrong. Sometime during the dead of night, blinding lights were turned on and I was one of several women herded out of the building into a van. Barely awake, I asked the woman next to me what was happening. "Nothing much, dearie; we're being transferred," she said. Maybe such middle of the night transfers are "normal," but for all I knew we were being taken to the river to be drowned. I was too sleepy to care.

I've never familiarized myself with the city's prison system and wouldn't have known where I was if I'd stayed awake in the van. The building to which the van transported us was the "classical" jail, the castle-like fortified monstrosity which is an architectural (and no doubt also social) monument to the first cities, the building with the thick stone walls, iron gates and endless corridors of cells with metal bars. When I was arrested several years ago I had only been shown the accommodations available in the courthouse building. This was my first visit to the "correctional institution" properly speaking. My first impression was favorable: the cot had a neatly folded blanket on it. But I didn't sleep well: the clanging gates, the footsteps on metal floors and a woman's shriek all conspired to destroy any comfort the blanket might have given me.

By the time breakfast was brought to my cell I was hysterical. I dropped the tray to the floor and shouted my demand to use the telephone. Eventually two guards escorted me out of my cell into a waiting room — where I was subjected to a medical examination. When that was over they escorted me back to my cell. I screamed about my rights and threatened to sue the prison authorities. In this I was somewhat hypocritical: I knew I had a right to use the telephone, but during all my years as a "troublemaker" I had never familiarized myself with any of the other "rights" I might have. I'm not apologizing for my ignorance. I know that "prisoners' rights" are little more than documents shifted to and fro by legislators and reformers. The physical set-up alone precludes a prisoner's having any rights, or as you put it so aptly, the prisoner's rights reside in the humanity of the jailer.

Shortly after my "examination" one of the guards returned and explained that I couldn't telephone just then because I would soon be up for trial. She seemed convinced that her explanation was perfectly logical. But it failed to pacify me; I continued to shout about my "rights." She returned again, intensely annoyed, and at last accompanied me to a telephone.

I cursed Sabina for not being home to answer my call. I cursed Tina for having walked out on us just before my arrest. I cursed Daman; he never leaves his house before noon, but that morning he was out. Maybe he and Sabina were out together! (The very idea was absurd. Yet I later found out that they were in fact out together — looking for me.) Out of sheer desperation I tried Luisa although I knew she was at work. The guard triumphantly escorted me back to my cell; she had succeeded in pacifying me.

It turned out that I was "up for trial" all day long and by supper time I was wondering how many days or months I would continue to be "up for trial." Some of my wondering can undoubtedly be traced to paranoia but as you well know the paranoia is itself grounded in terrible reality. How many have spent their last days waiting for the promised trial!

I only had to wait until the following morning. I was roused before sunrise and "transferred" back to the courthouse, not in the back of a van this time but in a car's comfortable back seat, which I shared with two other sleepy women.

As soon as we reached the courthouse I started demanding my "rights" again. An officious clerk with a clipboard enumerated the exact number of telephone calls I had already been "allowed." Trying to grab his clipboard I asked if it showed how many times I had reached anyone. He backed away and returned shortly to tell me I could call my lawyer.

I finally reached Sabina. She sounded groggy; I hoped she wouldn't think she had dreamed my phone call. "Sophia, where are you?" she asked sleepily; "we thought you'd been kidnapped."

"Kidnapped? I was! Two burly policemen kidnapped me and had me locked up. I'm in the courthouse now."

"I'll call Daman; if I can't reach him I'll come by cab," she said.

I felt lighter. I was even somewhat flattered: they had missed me.

The clerk asked, "Did you reach your lawyer?"

"Yes, thank you," I said; "she'll come for me after the trial."

He shrugged his shoulders with an "Another one of those nuts" expression and ordered me to follow him out of the waiting room. I followed him into another world, the world of the courtroom. A black-robed judge was already installed in almighty god's seat, passing judgment on lowly humans; on both sides of him divine clerks recorded his every word and gesture, divine messengers waited to fulfill his every wish and command.

Totally unlike my previous courtroom experience, I didn't have to wait all day only to return to court a week later. It was my turn as soon as I entered. My court-appointed lawyer made his way toward me to ask for my name and "occupation."

The only familiar face in the entire courtroom was the face of my accuser, my "colleague," the professor of behavioral psychology. He gave a brief but pungent account of the misfortune that had befallen him. He had come across Miss Nachalo in the hallway of their shared workplace and they had exchanged a few words; this much was all perfectly "normal," and neither my court-appointed "defender" nor I pointed out that he had never before come across nor exchanged words with Miss Nachalo in their "shared workplace." Everything was "normal" — when suddenly a snake reared its head in paradise. Totally unprovoked by any concrete physical deed on his or anyone else's part, Miss Nachalo "started to inflict physical blows" on his innocent person.

My presentation didn't match his either in eloquence or in penetrating behavioral insight. I said he had insulted me and I had slapped his face as hard as I could; my slapping his face couldn't be described as assault and battery; therefore I was innocent of the charge. I repeated my statement three times, once for my defense, once for my prosecution and again for the judge. In the judge's view, it was not within my competence to define the nature of my deed, but within his. Since I confessed to a deed which he classified as "assault and battery," he found me guilty, fined me, and my trial ended. I saw my accuser's face grimace with dissatisfaction when the judge announced the fine: it was a trivial sum.

I paid my fine and rushed out of the courtroom. I pranced up and down the hall clutching my purse in my left hand, my right hand ready to swing. I vaguely hoped to give my community college "colleague" a chance to "come across Miss Nachalo" in a different hallway. Concluding for the second time that he wasn't a masochist, I abandoned my hope and left the courthouse.

A familiar car was parked across the street, empty and locked. Daman and Sabina must have gone inside to find me — no easy task, since I hadn't told Sabina where I was going to be tried.

I sat down on the hood and waited. The car reminded me of Tina. I hadn't seen Daman since our argument about you and your previous letter, the argument which ended with Tina standing in the street shouting at Daman's vanishing car. I thought of her comment "Some fancy friends you've got" as I sat on the hood of my fancy friend's car. A few days after that argument Tina had left Sabina and me and my fancy friends.

I was intensely upset by Tina's departure. Not because it was totally unexpected. Sudden departures are in my own best style. Nor because I had ever thought Tina would remain by my side until the end of my days. On the contrary: I've often thought Sabina and I cramped Tina's development in our own peculiarly insidious ways.

What upset me about Tina's departure originates in experiences that took place eleven years ago in that garage I described so briefly in my last letter.

Two days before my arrest, Tina failed to leave for work in the morning. I assumed she was taking sick leave and thought the better of her for it: she had been excessively conscientious about her job. But just before lunch she pulled what must have been all her things out of her room.

Sabina asked, "Are you moving into the living room?"

"I'm leaving," Tina announced.

"You could have avoided all questions by leaving at night," Sabina said.

"I don't have anything to hide," Tina retorted.

"Are you leaving town or just this house?" Sabina asked.

"Just this house."

"And your job?" I asked.

"In about a week they'll figure out that I'm not coming any more and they'll hire someone else," Tina answered.

"Good for you," Sabina said. "Do you mind my questions?"

"Yes I do, Sabina," Tina said sadly, "because you'll mind my answers. I know that the only way you'd ever go to a university building would be with a stick of dynamite in your hand. Maybe I'll feel that way too, but if I do, I'd like it to be for my own reasons. You've been crutches, both of you, and thanks to you I haven't learned to walk on my own. At least not very well. Some kids occupied a university building and inside it they're forming something they call a commune. I'd like to figure out how I feel about that by being part of it."

"But Tina," I protested, "surely you're not taking all your things to a building occupied by its students; do you expect this commune to last?"

Tina didn't smile. "I'm taking my things to Ted's."

I jumped. "To Ted Nasibu's house?"

"Yes, to Ted's," she repeated; "he'll be here in five minutes."

"Couldn't you leave them here?" I asked; "this is as much your house as anyone else's."

"It's not a question of leaving my things, Sophia, and I mind your questions too. I don't know what you've always had against Ted and I no longer care. I'm not just leaving my things there. I'm moving. I'm going to live in the commune and I'll be staying at Ted's."

"At Ted Nasibu's?" I asked again, stupidly. I was on the verge of tears.

"Yes, Sophia, at Ted's! Do you have wax in your ears? Look at the scene you're making! Do you really want me to tell you why I'm leaving? I loved you, both of you. But I've come to hate you. I feel like your prisoner. The university, Ted. What else is taboo? Oh, I know it's not taboo to you. You have your reasons. But your reasons aren't good enough for me. They don't grow out of my own life. I do things for Sabina's reasons and I do others for Sophia's but I never do anything for my own reasons. I don't even know what my own reasons are. And that's all I want right now. To discover my own reasons. To become me, Tina, a human entity, someone who's neither Sophia nor Sabina. I'll wait for Ted in the street. It's getting stuffy in here."

Tears rushed to my eyes and I ran to my bedroom while Tina turned around to go outside. I heard Sabina help Tina carry her things out, heard their shouts of "goodbye." Then the front door slammed shut and Sabina burst into my room shouting, "Shame on you, Sophia!"

I was ashamed only of my uncontrolled crying. "You're not bothered in the least, are you Sabina?" I asked, no longer crying.

"I was bothered by the fact that she spent so many years with us! It's about time she asserted her independence. And you of all people presume —"

"I don't presume anything," I interrupted. "You know perfectly well that we've always agreed about that. One and only one thing bothers me."

"Namely?"

"Namely Ted Nasibu!" I shouted. I was angered by Sabina's mock innocence.

"Sophia! She's her own person!" Sabina responded indignantly. "You're using Ted to mask your possessiveness. Somewhere along the way you've acquired a mother complex."

"That's ridiculous, Sabina!" I shouted. "You know perfectly well what I'm talking about, and I'm amazed that it still doesn't bother you!"

"Still?" Sabina asked, acting puzzled.

"Have you forgotten that I spent several months in that house behind the garage? I became familiar with everything that happened there!" I shouted.

Sabina's face hardened. She planted herself in my doorway and stared at me for several minutes. Then she said, "Really? You'll have to tell me about it sometime." She marched straight to her desk, slamming her door shut.

Ghosts. I feel so strange in their presence. For all these years I prided myself for the open relations Sabina, Tina and I maintained with each other. Everything was always in the open. None of us ever had anything to hide. Suddenly a ghost walks out of the closet where we'd locked it for good and it mocks our hypocrisy with its hideous laughter.

The three of us shared an experience eleven years ago and each one of us was profoundly marked by it. Yet except for passing references to it we've never once discussed it nor its significance. Not once during all the eight years we've been together. Yet if it hadn't been for that trial and its aftermath I would have been thinking of nothing other than that experience since the day Tina left. I continued thinking about it as soon as the trial ended, sitting on the hood of Daman's car waiting for him and Sabina to emerge from the courthouse. I can't even force myself to go on telling you about my trial before telling you what I experienced behind the garage eleven years ago. I had suppressed every memory of those events for so many years. Yet for the past few days the suppressed memories have been coming up like vomit. I don't know anything about the supposed connection between remembering and eating but I do know that as soon as Tina mentioned Ted, as soon as one element of that repressed experience came up, all the other elements came up behind it.

I apologize for having flown so far away from the subject with which I started this letter. Tina's decision to live with Ted is far more important to me than that "fancy" job I had at the "community" college. My experience in the garage should in any case be more "interesting" to you, since you claim that you "recognize" yourself in the "garage world" while feeling a complete stranger in my corner of the "academic world." I wonder if you'll still recognize yourself when I'm through.

The only similarity between your experiences during the Magarna uprising and my experiences in the garage is that they both began at the same time. But I'll let you be the judge of the similarities and the differences; you've scolded me enough for my comparisons and contrasts.

:||||||||:

I learned about the prostitution during my first night at the garage. But that was only the beginning of my education.

I was a slow learner. During the middle of my first lesson I got scared and ran away. Jose and Ted both laughed — at the dunce, I thought. But then Ted congratulated me and I didn't know what to think. Was he a puritan about everything except stealing? Or did he have hopes that I would reserve my favors for him? I'm not mentioning any other alternatives because that very night I became convinced that the second alternative explained his congratulations. I went to Tina's room and slipped into the bed next to hers. Suddenly I heard a noise outside. I rushed to the door, which I had left ajar just as Tina had left it. I saw Ted tiptoeing away from it! I thought he had been there since I had entered the room, watching me undress.

I went back to bed and started to shake with the same fear I'd felt earlier that night, when I'd found myself in the back of the chauffeur-driven car next to the fat executive. No matter which way I turned, my heart pounded in my stomach. I couldn't sleep. (Part of the reason for that was that I'd spent the whole previous afternoon sleeping.)

My fear of being attacked during the night diminished the following day. Later it vanished completely, but only because it was replaced by another fear.

I got up early the next morning, scrupulously dressed in the most masculine clothes I had, and went to the kitchen to pour myself a cup of Tissie's coffee. Ted came in as soon as I'd sat down.

"Did you have a good night's sleep? You must have, since you're the first one up. I sure am glad you're joining us." He looked like he wanted to embrace me.

Grabbing a fork on the table, my lips trembling, I asked, "Why did you do that? Why did you look at me? What do you want to do to me?"

"Oh that," he said. "I always do that. But I can see how you'd worry, me being a stranger. Just checking things out, you know what I mean? Seeing if everything's all right."

What a strange explanation, I thought. As if his peeping didn't even concern me. "You've got some nerve!" I snapped.

"It's you who've got nerve," he said, responding to my words but totally missing their meaning; "that's what I tried telling you last night. Takes nerve to get scared and run. Wish me and some others here had nerve!"

"What the hell are you talking about? Are you trying to talk yourself out of —"

"That's what I'm talking about!" Ted said, pointing at Tissie, who was making her way toward the coffee pot.

Tissie sat down next to Ted, sipped her coffee, and suddenly looked up at me as if she were seeing me for the first time. "Hey, gorgeous, who dolled you up so early in the morning? How did you do last night?"

"Fine, Tissie, just fine," I lied. "Thanks a lot for taking me."

Ted got up from his chair as if he'd been stung. He glared down at me. "You're not telling her?" he asked.

"Tell her what, Ted?" I asked innocently, at last seeing a way to spite him. "I really enjoyed it, Tissie."

I got the effect I wanted. Ted backed away seemingly horrified, his face expressing a combination of disappointment and disgust. If he already knew I hadn't gone through with the previous night's escapade, now he also knew it wasn't because I was saving myself for him. "Honestly, Tissie, it was wonderful; I hope you'll take me along again sometime," I continued, watching Ted back out of the kitchen.

"Now get off it, sis!" Tissie grumbled as soon as Ted was gone. "No one thinks it wonderful and no one enjoys it. You're saying that to rile his ass ain't you?"

"No I'm not, Tissie," I insisted, carried away by my performance. "I was afraid at first, but once the fear passed I got to like it." I said this loudly, for Ted's benefit, in case he was still listening. But I was also performing my act for Tissie's benefit. I didn't want her to think me a snobbish puritan. I wanted very badly to be part of her world. Don't forget that I was still aching from the series of exclusions I had experienced in the university. I didn't want Tissie to turn against me on the second day of my new life.

But I was too ignorant of my new world, and of Tissie, to perform an act that simultaneously estranged me from Ted while it endeared me to Tissie.

"I used to think your sister was weird," Tissie said slowly, sipping her last drop. "But you really take the cake, baby. Enjoyed it! God damn!" With that, she got up and returned to her room. She, like Ted, seemed disappointed and even disgusted.

I sat in the kitchen alone, taking stock of my partial victory. I had succeeded in pushing Ted away from me. But that wasn't my main project. That was a trivial goal born in the previous night's fears. I had failed in my main goal. I had failed to insert myself into my new community.

In your letter you described Mirna's dreams of moving to the city and becoming part of its life. Not the city of bureaucrats, traffic jams or cops but an altogether different city, a city that never existed, a city that contained something she had learned to want. And when she finally reached the real city she peered behind its curtains and its walls, convinced that her city was there, somewhere, never once giving up her search for whatever it was she had once learned to want.

I can easily appropriate your entire vocabulary and apply it to my own search. You've convinced me that my glorification of our activity in the carton plant was nothing more than an exercise in rhetoric; it was only a way of referring to a present gap, a lifelong gap, a way of describing my search for something I had lost although it had never existed, something I had learned to want although I had never experienced it.

As I sat in the kitchen behind the garage eleven years ago, I knew nothing of Mirna and I had failed in my foolhardy attempt to communicate with you. I thought of my past hopes, my dreams of finding a human community and becoming part of its life. Not the "communities" of politicians, academics and journalists. The only thing those "communities" shared with my dream was the absence of what I sought. When I entered the garage I had the impression that I was on the verge of finding a trace of what I had sought. This, I thought, is at least something different, something I had never experienced before. And that world did in fact contain elements of what I had sought so desperately elsewhere. That's why I held on despite a long train of shocks and disillusionments. That's why I wanted so badly to be accepted by Tissie and to be like her. I wanted to be a prostitute and a heroin addict for exactly the same reason that Mirna wanted to be a citizen, an urban worker. In your letter you say, "Your descent to Sabina's world is a descent to my world." That was what I felt during those first days. That was why I felt ashamed for having run away from Sabina's and Tissie's nightly activity. That was why I tried so awkwardly to lie to Tissie, to convince her I wasn't an alien in her world. Yet instead of winning Tissie's sympathy and friendship I had only roused her suspicion.

I sat in the kitchen feeling miserable. That kitchen behind the garage was like a snack bar in a bus station. Busy people continually ran in and out while I sat waiting for a bus that never came. I recognized my next visitor as Vic Turam, the "mechanic" I had seen in the garage when I'd first arrived with Debbie Matthews. He ate his breakfast in silence, never once taking his eyes off me, never once saying a word. Tina came in next. She asked if I'd really known her "father," and "What was he like?" I told her she didn't look the slightest bit like him and immediately regretted making that pointless observation; it certainly didn't encourage Tina to pursue the conversation further. She finished her breakfast in silence and left without a word. Tina was followed by a person I hadn't met yet. "You're the sister," he said, ascertaining a fact. The way he said it shamed me further; he might as well have said, "You're the nun," I asked who he was. "Seth," he answered. I later learned he was a heroin dealer, but he always remained undefined for me, shadowy and hostile. I didn't like him any better than he seemed to like me. After Seth left there was a lull. It was noon before Sabina and Jose joined me in the kitchen. I assumed they had gotten up together and came from the same room; I soon learned I was mistaken.

Jose greeted me so jovially that he jarred me out of my pensive mood. "Is Ron's girl brooding? It's too early in the day for that!" Then he turned to Sabina and added, referring indirectly to my previous night's embarrassment, "We ought to spend some time showing the sister the sunny side of life, right Sabina? Letting her brood when she's just arrived — that's not right, Sabina; that's not showing proper respects to our founder."

I thought I heard a note of hostility. My impression was confirmed as soon as Sabina spoke. "Take her on a tour, Jose," she said. "You're the sun of the underworld. Light everything up for her. I won't cloud her vision; I'm leaving."

I reached across the table for Sabina's hand and pleaded, "I have to talk to you, Sabina — a long talk."

Sabina pulled her hand away as if mine were diseased. I was amazed and hurt. She finished sipping her coffee and said curtly, "Sure, Sophia, but I've got to run now. I have a free hour between three and four this afternoon." She got up and left like a businessman with important appointments.

"Your sister is a very busy woman," Jose said, explaining the obvious. Then he added, with the same hostility I had noticed before, "She don't have time to brood." Suddenly he reached for my hand, held it in his and said, laughing, "But we're not all like that. Come on, I'll show you around."

Jose gave me a complete tour of the accommodations behind the garage. I was struck by how clean and well arranged everything was. And how expensive! When I'd first seen the building from the outside it had looked run down; the garage through which I'd entered had seemed dirtier and messier than most garages I'd seen. But when Jose escorted me through the hall from one room to the next, I realized for the first time that the garage was literally a "front," a facade. I'd been impressed by the nightclub to which Tissie had taken me but I'd been too preoccupied by my fears to look around the house. The walls and ceilings were all paneled and at frequent intervals paintings were set into the wall panels, as were most of the cupboards. The floors were all covered by heavy rugs. The basement contained a laundry room, a marvelously equipped and very clean workshop and a "recreation room" which, Jose said, hadn't ever been completed because no one used it. He told me the second floor consisted of lofts and an "experiment room," and that if I wanted to see them I'd have to go up with their users, Ted, Sabina and Tina. My head was swimming; I wasn't able to take it all in.

What struck me almost as much as the luxury was the fact that each person slept in a separate room, although there were twin beds or a double bed in every bedroom. I asked Jose awkwardly, "Aren't there any couples?"

"Couples?" he asked, visibly annoyed. "Sure there are couples. Lots of them. There's hardly anything else."

Without even trying to interpret his answer I asked, "You and Sabina?"

"Not on your life!" he said angrily. "You never got to know your sister, did you? This is her room; mine's over there; we were never a couple and never will be. Any more questions?"

"I'm sorry," I said, not knowing just what I was sorry about.

Jose's anger vanished and he smiled. "Nothing to be sorry about. I'm the one that's sorry. I wanted to show you the work in the garage next."

But I was too confused and too tired to continue the tour. "How about tomorrow?" I asked. "I had a terrible night last night." I liked Jose. I wanted to go on and tell him about my fears, about Ted, but I held myself back.

"Sure," he said; "I hope you don't have any more terrible nights."

I fell on my bed in Tina's room as soon as I reached it. I woke up, like the previous night, at midnight. Tina was sound asleep. I had missed my afternoon "appointment" with Sabina. I had also missed all my meals. I crept to the kitchen and literally looted the refrigerator. When I was finally satisfied I sat down and waited for Tissie but realized that she must have gone to work on time. When I heard the heavy garage door closing I turned out the kitchen light, rushed back to Tina's room, left the door ajar and slipped back to bed with my clothes still on. I listened to Ted and Jose walk to their rooms. After a long silence I heard someone tiptoeing toward my room. I kept my eyes glued to the door — and saw Ted creep through the opening! For an instant he just stood there and stared; then he backed out of the room. I started shaking again. I hadn't only failed to communicate with Tissie; I had also failed to communicate anything to Ted.

I lay awake all night. When Tina got up in the morning I pretended to be asleep — and fell asleep until noon. When I reached the kitchen I found Sabina pouring Tissie a cup of coffee. Tissie didn't even notice me.

"Sabina —" I said.

"I know," Sabina said. "Let's go to my room."

As soon as we reached her room she said, "Wait for me just for a minute, would you? I have to make some phone calls."

Just like a businessman! Anger and resentment filled my every pore as I paced back and forth like a caged animal. I was determined to have it all out with Sabina. I pounced as soon as she returned. "Sabina, why did you pull your hand away from me as if I were a leper? What am I to you?" I went on pacing.

Sabina closed her door and then just stood and stared at me. Suddenly she burst out laughing. "I've never seen you like this, Sophia. You're marvelous. Running around in a circle, filled with righteous fury, frustrated out of your wits — you look just like a circus clown!" Sabina threw her arms around me and pressed me, tightly.

I collapsed in her arms. My anger melted away. I forgot what I'd resented. I felt at home. "I love your house, Sabina," I whispered.

Sabina said, "I'm glad you do." Then she kissed me — on my lips. I was surprised — but also pleased because I knew then that I wasn't an intrusive stranger to Sabina. She asked, "Do you mind?"

"You're the only friend I wanted to turn to in the entire world," I whispered.

Sabina stiffened as she let me go. "So much for the preliminaries," she said, making herself comfortable on her bed. "Let's talk, about anything and everything. As long as you want. No time limits. No secrets."

"Sabina, I'm frightened," I whispered, sitting down next to her.

"You, a Nachalo, frightened?" she asked in a mocking tone. "Is someone after you?"

I knew she meant someone outside but I answered, "Yes, it's Ted!"

"Oh, get off it, Sophia!" she shouted, angrily hurling a pillow across the room. She seemed disappointed, even disgusted, as Tissie and Ted had seemed the previous morning when I'd announced I'd enjoyed my first experience as a prostitute. "Are you serious?" she continued. "We haven't been together for years. We've both lived whole lives since we've last talked to each other. And all you tell me is that Ted is after you! Are you sure you don't mean Seth?"

I was in a panic. I wanted to apologize. I didn't want Sabina to turn against me. I shook my head.

"I could understand your being afraid of Seth," she said. "He might shoot you or stab you. Or even Vic. But not Ted! What happened to you Sophia? What have you become?"

I was deathly afraid Sabina was going to add, "Coward! You're just like your mother!" I felt the tears rushing toward my eyes. But for once in my life I caught myself before breaking down crying. I bit my lip, stiffened up and looked right into Sabina's eyes. "Why did you pull your hand away yesterday?"

"I'm schizoid!" she said. "What are you?"

"I'm only joking," I said, trying hard to smile. "I was just trying to devise an original way to start. I'll try again. Just to get started, let's turn to Ted. Who is Ted? What is he?"

"Holy, wise and fair is he; the heaven such grace did lend him, that he might admired be," Sabina mocked, unconvinced by my act, but not determined to look under my veil. "You'd know who he was if you'd listened, and you'd know what he was if you'd heard and been moved."

"Please don't be cryptic," I begged.

"An unused memory is like a pair of eyes that have never been opened," Sabina said.

"I've always wanted to have memory training from you, Sabina. Is this to be my first lesson?" I asked.

"There's the Sophia I remember!" Sabina retorted. "Sarkasmos. It means to cut or bite another's flesh. Ron was trying to tell you all about Ted. But you bit right through him with your: (imitating me) "Really?"

I remembered. Sabina and Ron had visited me five years earlier, when Ron was released from reform school. Ron had tried to tell me about all the people he'd met, but I'd shut him up with my stupid "Really?" That had been the last time I'd seen Ron. "Thanks for the memory lesson," I said, confirming her characterization of me. "Ted is Ron's reform school philosopher."

"Not philosopher," Sabina corrected. "Scientist, engineer, artist, acrobat. One of the best minds of our time."

"He can pick the lock of any brand new car and drive away with it in less than a minute," I added. "If I'd remembered last night I would have known it wouldn't do me any good to lock my door. But to compensate for that, I could at least have consoled myself with the thought that he was Ron's friend and one of the best minds of our time. Is he at least nice?"

Sabina kicked me and laughed, saying, "But you haven't changed at all! You're —"

"Just like my mother!" I interrupted.

Sabina stopped laughing. "I wasn't going to say that again, Sophia; it's too mean. Besides, if you ever compare me to my so-called father, I'll kill you."

"In the flesh or just with words, the way I bite?" I asked. "Don't worry, I don't know enough about either of you to hazard such a comparison. And I'd asked you about Ted."

"Is he nice?" she repeated. "You'd probably know that now if you'd curbed your sarcasm five years ago. No, that's not true, since then you probably wouldn't have gotten along with Ron and consequently wouldn't have met Ted then either. Ron admired your sarcasm."

"Did he like me for my sarcasm?" I asked.

"Not altogether," Sabina answered. "He only liked your sarcasm when it was aimed at other people. How badly he wanted you along when they stole Tom Matthews' brand new car! Your sarcastic comments would have put the crowning touch on that event. Ron missed your comments; the event was incomplete without them. He never got over your absence; he had staged it all for you and you never saw it."

"I don't know what you're talking about," I said.

"You do and you don't," Sabina said cryptically. "It was your sarcasm that was missed, yet it was that very sarcasm that kept you away. Did Ron like you for your sarcasm? Do I? I do like you, Sophia. And you've always been sarcastic. Close enough? I'm only guessing; I never asked Ron precisely that question. Is Ted nice? You'd know if you'd watched Ted break into Matthews' car and if you'd finished Matthews off with your biting comment. Ron thought he was nice. Ted was the first person he looked up when we left you after your 'Really?'"

"Is Ted really everything Ron thought he was?" I asked, immediately regretting the presence of that silly word, since Sabina caught it right away.

"Is he really?" she mocked with a sarcasm far superior to my mine. "Believe me, Sophia, everything! Engineer; he'll slip into your room in a flash without a key. Scientist: before you can shout for help, he'll turn your flesh to liquid and carry you off in a vial. Artist: he'll pour you out in his loft as a marble statue, life size and a perfect likeness. Acrobat —"

"Sarkasmos my ass, Sabina!" I interrupted. "You love my sarcasm! Do you want to know why?"

"Don't you think I know? Did you think we were considered sisters because we looked alike?"

We both burst out laughing. Sabina and I became friends for the first time in our lives.

"If Ted is everything Ron thought he was, why don't you like him?" I asked.

"I don't remember your being that observant," Sabina said. "In fact I don't like him, though this is the first time I've been aware of my dislike. It's not because of anything he is, did or said, but because I know he despises me. It's normal to dislike someone who despises you, isn't it? Ask him sometime when you're reconciled with him. Tell him you're afraid of me. He won't laugh at you or call you a coward. He'll drown you with friendship and shower you with a barrel-full of sympathy. He might even ask you to kill me."

I was horrified. I reached instinctively for her hand and asked, "Sabina! Why?"

Sabina raised my hand to her throat and asked, "Would you do it?"

"Of course! Like this!" I said, pressing her neck lightly and kissing her cheek, Sabina smiled.

It was precisely at this moment that Tissie burst into the room. I'd thought such coincidences took place only in novels. There we were, sitting next to each other on Sabina's bed, "necking," my lips on Sabina's cheek, a blissful smile across Sabina's face. Tissie stood in the doorway and stared at us, absolutely stupefied, while Sabina lowered my hand from her neck.

Tissie completed the scene by making it clear she had "understood" everything perfectly. "I'm awfully sorry," she said, backing away with the same stupefied stare; "I thought you were alone, Sabina. I didn't know."

"And that's that!" I shouted as soon as Tissie was gone. I jumped off the bed laughing. "I wouldn't even try explaining. She'd only think we were liars besides." I stopped laughing when it occurred to me that Tissie already thought me a liar "besides." It had done me no good at all to insist that I'd enjoyed having sex with a man for money. If Tissie also remembered how profusely I'd thanked her for taking me to the bar, she'd think me not only a lesbian and a liar but a hypocrite to boot. I had obviously lost Tissie. But I wasn't depressed. I had won Sabina. "Does it bother you?" I asked.

"Me?" Sabina asked. "Tissie can think whatever she wants." Sabina didn't laugh. She looked sad.

I put the incident out of my mind. I didn't in fact understand its full meaning until much later. I sat back down and returned to the point we'd reached before we were interrupted. "Why in the world would Ted want to kill you? I think that's awful!"

Sabina stared blankly at the door for a few seconds and then answered in a monotone, as if my question bored her, "I didn't say he wanted to kill me. He's incapable of wanting that. He's one of the few people I've met who knew the difference between things and people and never confused the two. He can do anything that's ever been done with a tool, but he'll never touch a weapon, and he'll never confuse the two. He doesn't step on a worm if he sees it in time, and he looks sadly at a dead fly. You're afraid of him? Sophia, believe me, the world will end before Ted attacks you. I can't imagine his wanting to kill you or me."

"Then why would he ask me to kill you?" I asked, totally bewildered, although I was also relieved to learn that my pursuer wouldn't hurt a worm.

"I said he might," Sabina continued. "But I know he never would. It's what I'd do in his shoes. All I know for a fact is that he fears and despises me. He's odd. We're all odd, but each in a different way. Ted's oddity is that he's gone through life making his own decisions but he's convinced that everyone else is manipulated. If you want a more theoretical explanation: in his practice he's a perfect democrat while in his political philosophy he's an absolute elitist. But he's not a philosopher; he doesn't think; he just acts and feels. He acts as if I were the one responsible for everything that happens here and he despises me for it."

"Responsible for what kinds of things?" I asked, becoming increasingly bewildered.

"Everything," she repeated. "For Tissie. For Vic and Seth. For what Jose or Tina might do. For everything. It's a long story and I'm not a mind reader. I'm just guessing. He's of a piece all right: perfectly consistent. One hundred percent right. And he knows it. His contempt for me is completely justified."

"Would you mind explaining?" I begged. "I'm confused."

"I don't guarantee to clarify anything," Sabina said. "The garage was Ted's and Ron's idea. They dreamed of buying it when they were in reform school. Ted had worked for the former owner —"

"Stealing cars and selling heroin?" I asked.

"Just the cars," Sabina continued. "The heroin came later. The former owner became increasingly careless, spent half his time in jail, and let the place get all run down. Ted rented it as soon as he was released and we bought it soon after Ron was released. The original group was to include Ted and Tissie, you and Ron, and Jose."

"Me? What about you?" I asked.

"I'll get to that. Tissie was to be included because she'd been Ted's girl friend since they were kids. He thinks I'm responsible for what she chose to do with herself but he's wrong; he didn't know Tissie when they were kids together. That's what makes him nice, I suppose. I call it dense. Ted and Ron might as well have been twins in that respect. You were to be included because you were Ron's girl. Ron cried 'Sophie!' every time there was a knock on the door. And of course Jose was included because he was Ron's best friend. But that didn't work out. Ron finally convinced himself that you weren't coming and went off to get himself killed. And Jose didn't like the idea of moving in on Ted and Tissie; he thought he and Ted would kill each other over Tissie. Tissie was terribly pretty but Jose didn't know her then. So Jose suggested a different arrangement. He recommended his and Ron's friend Seth for his money, and Ron's friend Sabina for her brains. Ted was absolutely opposed to that suggestion, but Tissie was carried away by it. I forgot to tell you another one of Ted's traits: he's a perpetual loser. This follows from his other traits. Seth moved in and brought Vic. I came with Jose and Ted's original project started to collapse. Seth started dealing heroin from the garage. Then Tissie got hooked on it. Ted raised a big fuss and succeeded in getting Seth to move out of the house. But things didn't improve for him. Jose and I and Seth went in on the bar together and soon Tissie and I were working there."

"And he blames you for all that?" I asked. "Why did he want to exclude you from the original group, before any of those things happened?"

"I already gave you part of the answer," she said obscurely. "Ted draws a perfectly clear line between people and things; 'the heaven such grace did lend him, that he might admired be,' And I do admire him for it, whether his ability comes from grace, instinct or personal insight. 'Holy, wise and fair is he,' applying his standard impartially to all situations. Depriving the rich of their objects and transforming those objects with a view to increasing the well-being of the underlying population is an unambiguously human and possibly revolutionary project. Selling one's body, ruining one's own or another's health cannot be means to reaching the same goal because our humanity would be maimed when we reached it, and our humanity is our goal. Ted's logic is impeccable. But of course he never formulates it as a logic, he never expresses his philosophy, he acts it out. And that's why the trouble started. He disliked me the very first time we met, soon after Ron tried to tell you about Ted and the garage. Ron told Ted about his half-brother Jose and then started talking about this rich friend of his, Seth. 'A dope dealer?' Ted asked. Ron dropped the subject right away but I didn't. At that time Ron and I thought everything a person was jailed for was a revolutionary act. But I learned something from Ted that night. I drew answers from him like a dentist pulling his teeth out. I made sentences out of his single words and logical propositions out of his grimaces and groans. Before the night ended I hadn't only drawn his entire philosophy out of him but had become completely convinced by it. Ron fell asleep. Ted's philosophy isn't all that difficult. It all hinges on Ted's distinction between people and things, and his corollary distinction between weapons and tools. Once you get hold of the axiom everything else follows. And he exhibits his axiom on his face and in every gesture: he grins when a tool is in question and groans when it's a weapon. But Ted didn't appreciate what

I did for him. He squirmed every time I put his attitude into words. He became increasingly frightened of me, as if I were depriving him of something precious, as if I were undressing him stitch by stitch, as if I were reaching inside him and pulling his guts out for all to see. He hated me from that day on and he never forgave me. That's why he hoped you'd join Ron. Ted is everything but a philosopher. He fears philosophy, he's suspicious of logic, even of words. He expresses himself in metal, wood, marble, canvass — everything but words. To him philosophy isn't a tool but a weapon; its only purpose is to manipulate people. And he's convinced it's the weapon with which I've manipulated every person here except himself and Tina, and he's not sure about Tina."

Sabina suddenly jumped off the bed like an energetic cat, pulled me up as well, and shouted, "Hey it's dark already! Why are we spending the day cooped up in here like prisoners? Let me take you on a tour!"

"Jose took me on a tour of the house yesterday," I told her.

"Let's go to the bar, then," she suggested.

"Tissie took me there on my first night here," I admitted, remembering afterwards that Tissie had begged me never to tell Sabina.

"Tissie took you!" Sabina exclaimed. Clenching her fists she added, "Why the little hypocrite!"

"I asked her to take me," I added, trying to protect Tissie, and surprised by Sabina's outburst.

Sensing my surprise she calmed down and said, as if by way of explanation, "I thought I was going to have that honor. What's left for a hostess if she can't show off?"

"I asked Tissie to take me because you'd told her you'd never take me there," I said, still protecting Tissie.

"Not to work there, Sophia," she said. "That's for you to choose or not choose. We haven't eaten all day, I'm starving and the food there is as tasty as the girls are beautiful."

I laughed, thinking she was referring to herself and Tissie, and I started heading toward my room.

"'Hey, where are you going?" she shouted, grabbing my arm.

"To change my clothes," I said, pointing to my blue jeans and work shirt.

"You look perfect as you are," she said.

"But I wore these clothes all night!" I protested.

"You also smell perfect," she insisted, pulling me out of the house.

We walked to the bar, continuing our conversation every step of the way. I told her I spotted a contradiction between her praise for Ted's "philosophy" and her activity in the bar. Sabina admitted the contradiction but we reached be bar before she had time to deal with it.

Sabina did something strange as soon as we entered. She put her arm through mine and escorted me along the stools of the bar right past Tissie. "Evening, Tissie," she said nonchalantly, but with a mean grin on her face.

I said, "Hi, Tissie," and tried to smile, but I felt intensely embarrassed. I knew I was right in the middle of something I couldn't understand. Sabina exchanged greetings with some of the other "girls" and I noticed that they were indeed pretty, and all very tastefully dressed. I was surprised. My notions of how prostitutes looked and dressed had come from newspapers and novels. When I saw them in the flesh I felt like a homely clod among them: Sabina's country sister, maybe even her aunt.

As we walked across the floor toward a table, a frighteningly large man grabbed Sabina's arm and said, "Hey, Sabina baby! Thought you weren't coming tonight."

Sabina jerked herself out of his grasp so quickly that I thought she'd sent an electric shock through him, and she hissed at him through her teeth: "Don't lay your hands on me, Bozo. I'm busy tonight!"

"Gee, Sabina, how's a guy to know that?" the huge man asked, backing away from us.

As soon as we reached a table in a dark corner of the enormous room Sabina asked me, "Are you shocked?"

Before I could answer a waiter came, greeted Sabina and bowed to me.

"The works!" Sabina told him. "I've got a very special guest tonight."

"Shocked?" I asked. I was confused, flattered, distressed, pleased. I felt dense, ignorant and lost. But I wasn't shocked. "Why should I be shocked? You've told me what you do. And I've seen this place already."

"You're being evasive," she said. "Do you disapprove?"

"Do you disapprove of my being sarcastic?" I asked.

The waiter brought us the best drink I'd ever tasted and I started sipping.

"Good answer!" she said, but then pushed on: "What were you saying about the contradiction between Ted's philosophy and my practice?"

She's really all brain, I thought. But I changed my mind immediately when I remembered several of the day's events that led to a very different conclusion. I tried to concentrate my thoughts, or rather to find out what they were. The band was playing a familiar tune and I listened and started to hum. I couldn't keep up with Sabina. Finally I admitted, "I'm completely lost. I don't understand you, Sabina. I don't understand Ted, although I'm less afraid of him now. And I don't see how I fit into it all!"

Sabina reached for my hand and said, looking straight into my eyes, "There's nothing to understand, Sophia, and nothing to fit into. It's your life to do with as you will. There's no structure. Nothing is banned. Everything is allowed. No holds are barred."

"What's everything?" I asked hesitantly.

Letting go of my hand, she said, "My life, my desires, my capacities; those are my axioms."

"And this?" I asked, my glance sweeping across the bar, the sex-crazed men, the prostitutes.

"A person freely creates her own life, but in circumstances not of her own choosing," she answered.

"I've heard that before, but I don't see how it applies," I said.

"All this, as you call it, is part of the circumstances not of my own choosing," she answered.

Just then the waiter arrived with "the works." I had never in my life eaten so much delicious food. The meal was indeed as tasty as the place was lush. We continued our conversation all through the meal, and I grew increasingly giddy from the wine.

"That sounds terribly cynical," I said with my mouth full.

"It is!" Sabina admitted. "But I'm not being cynical. The cynicism is part of the world I was born into, the world I'm trying to get out of."

"I'm not sure I understand," I said, and then probed further: "The fullest development of my life, my projects, my capacities —"

"Desires," she added.

"Yes, all of it," I granted; "I think I understand that. But I —"

She interrupted again: "With which organ do you understand that?"

I was stunned. "Organ? What do you mean?"

"I know some people who understand that — but only in their sexual organ. We both know people who understand it only in their political organ, people who understand everything you'd want to know about life, capacities and desires, who accept themselves as slaves, who've never lived in their lives, who've stunted all their capacities, who've annihilated their desires." Her anger grew as she spoke.

"And their collective name is Luisa Nachalo," I ventured.

"I didn't name any names!" she shouted. "Anyway, she's not the only one. You must have met dozens if not hundreds of them during your years in the university. Life, desires, capacities — they've reduced them all to words, words which they carry around in their political organs. And they're the ones who impose life on everyone else. They don't know what life is because they've never lived and they're intent on generalizing their own condition — for the sake of the word, for the primacy of the political organ."

"What about the means, Sabina, the tools?" I asked. I was getting dizzy from the wine and I had a hard time formulating my question. "Earlier you said you could get maimed by the tools you used — or was it weapons?"

"We come maimed!" Sabina exclaimed. "The question is whether or not we're able to heal. Not abstractly but here and now. Look around you. Look closely at the waiters, the band members, the prostitutes. None of them are people born with golden spoons in their mouths. They're down-and-outs, every last one of them. They're the underclass. All of them came here off the streets or out of jail. They were already dope pushers, prostitutes, hustlers and pimps. That's part of the circumstances they didn't choose. They came maimed. And they're starting to heal!"

"In what way?" I asked.

"Did you look at that ape who grabbed me earlier?" she asked. "He's part of the apparatus that does the maiming. He's one of the biggest crooks in this city. He's an official in one of the international corporations. When he snaps his fingers, people all over the world respond like caged rats responding to an experimenter's stimulus. See the girl he's with at the bar? She used to be lower than the lowest rat in his cages. She was the slave of every two-bit pimp on her street and if she'd wound up in the garbage dump no one would have missed her. And look at her now! She's on her ninth or tenth drink and probably on her fifth dessert and he's ordering another round. The price of food and drinks here is over a hundred times the cost. And you know what? She'll go to the john after a while, slip out the back and go home. Eventually he'll turn to someone else and start all over again. He's Mister International. But here it's we who snap our fingers and he who jumps. One of us always goes in the end, but first we soak him to the limit. And everything we get out of him stays right here: it's all ours. This is anti-imperialism in practice, Sophia. This is class war. And we're winning. We all have expensive hobbies now, and some of us have more than hobbies. All the way from sex to crafts, painting and playing with the sciences. I'll show you sometime. We're all expanding, discovering ourselves. We're starting to live and we want to live more. If we're ever going to destroy what maims us it'll be because we've started to live. Those who love life will be the ones who'll push the fucker into the sea! Look toward the door. See that weasel who just came in? He's the local police chief. Look at him putting his hand on that girl's ass. Watch what happens now!"

I saw the girl turn around and sock the police chief, who went reeling backward until he tripped over a stool and fell.

"Outside he does that to the likes of us whenever he pleases!" Sabina said. "Watch him get up and go back to her. The funniest thing is that she'll probably go out with him; it's getting late. Is that demeaning?"

"I don't know," I mumbled; my head was swimming and I was getting sick.

"Is that maiming? Maybe it is," she continued. "I know it is. But we didn't create the means. We found them and we're learning to use them. The chief's making up to her now. She'll decide to go with him."

The room was moving up and down like a ship. I felt worse every minute. But Sabina didn't notice; she kept on talking. "She'll sell him sex for money. You notice a contradiction and you're right. Sex is also her hobby. Hobby is a lousy word. It's her life. You know what she does with her money? She had her apartment redone. Wall-to-wall mattresses, all down. In every room except the bathroom and kitchen. She fills her apartment with everyone she can find between the age of six and sixty. Every conceivable shape, size and age. And then she lives. She satisfies every desire, every whim; she engages in every conceivable and inconceivable perversion, if you like that word; I don't."

I held on to the table to keep myself from falling. I heard her words but all I saw was a blur; my insides felt like bubbling lava.

"But she pays some of them," Sabina continued. "That's a contradiction, a terrible contradiction. She still hasn't healed. She's still revenging herself for what she was forced to undergo. She still can't tell people from things nor distinguish her life from the means that make it possible. She hasn't learned to draw Ted's fine line. Ted won't ever be caught in such a contradiction. He'll never make that mistake. He works in the garage: that's the circumstances, the means. But he plays in the loft and in the basement workshop: that's his goal, his life. She confuses the two; she hasn't learned to make Ted's distinctions and maybe never will. We all come maimed. But don't think Ted doesn't. She's healthier than Ted in at least one respect. She knows people; he only knows things. She knows the boundlessness of desires; he only knows the possibilities of things. She knows love in every conceivable form and sex in every imaginable combination, position or pattern; he only knows love and sex in the forms practiced by the maimed, by those with stunted imaginations and dead desires. He can imagine things in all combinations, positions and patterns. He knows people aren't things. And he's profoundly right. He's wise, even holy. But he doesn't know people. He also came maimed."

I must have passed out. The next thing I remember is being carried through the garage to Tina's room. Jose carried my feet — and Ted's arms were under my back. I must have fallen asleep right away.

I heard someone tiptoeing toward my door. I watched Ted slip through the opening and walk right up to my bed. He stood staring down at me. Suddenly he pulled the blanket off me. I saw that he held a wrench in one hand and a screwdriver in the other. I jumped out of bed terrified — and found myself lying on the floor next to my bed. It was a nightmare, but I couldn't stop my trembling. The sun was already up, but Tina was still sound asleep. I was panicky. I crept toward Sabina's room, shook her hysterically and whimpered, "Help me, Sabina."

Sabina swung her arm and hit my side so powerfully that I fell to the floor. Looking right at me, seemingly wide awake, she hissed through her teeth, "Don't touch me!" She spoke to me in the same tone in which she'd spoken to the corporation executive who'd grabbed her arm.

"Sabina!" I cried with disbelief. "It's me, Sophia, your friend, your sister!"

"Get out of my room, Luisa!" she hissed viciously. "You're not my sister!"

I gathered myself up off the floor and backed away from her, horrified. Snatches of the previous night's conversation flashed through my mind, particularly her statements, "I'm schizoid, what are you?" and "He only knows love and sex in the forms practiced by the maimed."

"You'd like nothing better than for Ted to rape me!" I cried hysterically. "You'd say he was healed!"

"For his sake and for yours!" she hissed.

I slammed her door and ran back to my bed. In a few minutes I stopped trembling. I was wide awake and felt dumber than a baboon. I realized that I had run to Sabina's room under the spell of my nightmare. That was the only time in my life that I acted out the remainder of a dream after waking. I felt ashamed of myself; I was afraid to face Sabina.

I lay in my bed feeling intensely embarrassed long after Tina got dressed and left the room. I had a splitting headache. I reached the kitchen around noon, a couple of minutes before Sabina.

She set me at ease immediately. "I had the strangest dream. Or did you actually come to my room last night and —" she started to ask.

"You dreamed it, Sabina," I insisted. "I just got up."

"That's a relief!" she said. "It was awful!"

"What was it about?" I asked, frowning.

"Do you really want to hear about it?" she asked.

"I'd rather not," I said. "But I would like to ask you one question."

"Want me to call off my day's projects?" she asked, smiling and friendly, sisterly again, but surely unconvinced that last night's visit had been a dream.

"No, please, not even one. It's only a bitty question," I insisted, trying hard to smile. "What's my name?"

Of course she knew then that I'd lied. How sad she suddenly looked. But she's so crazy and such a ham that I couldn't possibly nurse my resentment against her. She walked around the table, kneeled to me and placed her contrite head in my lap. Lifting her head I begged, "Please look at me, Sabina, and tell me who I am. And please don't kneel!"

"Pray, do not mock me," she quoted. "I am a very foolish fond young maid. A score and upward, not an hour more nor less; and, to deal plainly, I fear I am not in my perfect mind. Methinks I should know you. You are a spirit, I know. Yet I feel this pinprick. Oh, do not laugh at me; for as I am a woman, I think this lady to be my sister Sophia. If you have poison for me, I will drink it. You have some cause."

"No cause," I whispered, smiling through my tears. "Now get up! You have a busy day!"

Ruthless and contrite, icy and warm, monarch, enemy and sister — I couldn't hold on to my resentment against any of the four, or ten or a hundred Sabinas. Nor could I make her activities the model for mine. Probably because I, too, came maimed. "You describe your trip to Sabina's garage as a descent to the underworld," you said. And that's exactly what it was, and remained, no matter how "familiar" it might seem to you. I remained a disoriented tourist, a visitor from another world. It didn't even occur to me to ask Sabina to take me along on her day's "business rounds." Did she go out to look for more "beautiful girls" for the bar? Was it her turn with the international executive? Or was she going to her friend's wall-to-wall down mattress to satisfy "every desire, every whim — every conceivable and inconceivable perversion"? I admit I was curious. But I wasn't curious enough to go along, or even to ask. And Sabina didn't make the slightest effort to influence my choice. She let me know that I could have her friendship if I wanted it, and whenever I wanted it. But that was all. I was my own person and she didn't impose herself. Ted wasn't the only person in that house who was perfectly consistent. Sabina wouldn't have interfered if I'd spent every day in bed, started taking heroin, or floated down the river. She'd have stopped me from setting fire to myself only if she'd thought the flame would burn the house. (I'm exaggerating.) It became perfectly clear to me she wouldn't raise a finger to keep Ted away from my bed until he actually injured me.

There was no structure, Sabina had told me. How true this was! Everything was allowed, no holds were barred. I could have joined anyone, or taken up with anyone, at anytime of day or night. Or I could have indulged some fancy of my own. If it had been expensive Sabina would have paid for it. If I'd wanted to pay for it myself she would have showed me how. There were no limits to what I could choose. But I couldn't choose. I realized that I had never made a real decision before. I'm sorry if the sequel disappoints you: I didn't make one then either, and I haven't made one since. I don't know how. I came maimed.

Unable to lean on Sabina, I tried to lean on Tissie, though, not for long. She obviously wasn't as well disposed toward me as she had been the first day. She sat across from me, ate a meager lunch drowned by an enormous quantity of coffee, and made small talk.

When I asked if she'd ever take me to the bar again, she became indignant and announced, "You don't look like Sabina's sister!"

I guessed that Tissie wasn't only ascertaining the fact that Sabina and I didn't look alike (there being no reason why we should). Since she already knew me to be a liar, she was letting me know she'd had no trouble at all figuring out who and what I really was: I was obviously Sabina's "man" parading as her sister. I couldn't have explained anything; I had advised Sabina not even to try.

Tissie spoke to me again slightly later; she was suddenly a lot friendlier. "If you'd ever like to have a shot," she said, "just let me know. Seth will be glad to give you as many as you need."

"Need" was the word I latched on to. As many as I need! So much for leaning on Tissie, I thought. How helpful! She was certainly willing enough to help me with my choices. She certainly wasn't above imposing herself on another. I should really have thanked her. Instead I said, "No thank you," trying very hard to reciprocate her earlier hostility. I apparently succeeded. She kept her distance for several weeks. But I hadn't gotten a step closer to making a decision, to choosing the shape of my self in the world.

I really should explain my hostile "No thank you," since nowadays it might be attributed to prudishness. Radicals who are Tina's age today might think me "maimed" in that respect as well. That explanation would be false because my generation of radicals (there were pitifully few in that generation) explicitly ranged narcotics among the weapons of the oppressor. The anti-utopia I grew up with was a "brave new world" of nodding imbeciles kept in line by tranquilizers and kept happy and pacified by narcotics. I simply can't stomach those of Tina's peers who today consider the imbecilic nod of an addict the supreme revolutionary act. Not that Tina shares that idiocy; in this respect as in many others she might as well belong to Sabina's and my generation. My "No thank you" was an expression, not of prudishness, but of genuine hostility.

My hostility wasn't personal; it wasn't aimed against Tissie, but only against the offered drug. I made no effort to impose myself on Tissie, to convert her to my attitude. I did try to avoid Vic, and particularly Seth, but I didn't once confront them about the dope dealing. The heroin was largely responsible for my final departure from the garage, but it wasn't I who started the scene about it. I only stayed away from it, and responded with hostility to all offers.

By rejecting the heroin I antagonized Tissie and, by implication, Seth and Vic. Since I didn't know how to lean on myself, and didn't want to learn, I was left with the garage crew: Ted, Jose and Tina. And I wasn't about to lean on Ted.

I turned to Jose first. But that day really wasn't my lucky day. I went to the garage and paced, waiting for him to return from an errand. Ted and Tina were so busily at work they didn't even notice me. Vic just stood there, like a fixture. The day I'd arrived I'd thought Vic another mechanic. But he did nothing at all. He was like an aged cat that looks on but never moves; you might think he was the commissar assigned to watch the others work. I paid more attention to Vic's presence than I did to anything Tina or Ted were doing.

When Jose finally came back, I went up to him and put my foot straight into my mouth. "I'd like to accept your offer," I said. I was of course referring to his offer to show me the work in the garage.

Jose grabbed my wrist and literally dragged me out into the street. "Let me get just one thing clear," he shouted when we were outside of anyone's hearing. "Ron's best friend never made Ron's girl any kind of offer!"

Oh no, what have I done now? I thought. "But you said yesterday —" I started.

"You don't understand!" he shouted. "I never made you an offer!"

"I'm sorry!" I said, trying to look sorry but wanting to laugh. "I didn't mean that kind of offer. You said you'd show me —"

He cut me off again. "I've got to explain something to you," he said insistently. "I used to dream about you long before I met you. I thought about that big guy wanting a broad badly enough to go and kill himself because of her; I thought that's not something you'll find every day; I thought I'd really like to meet up with her; I thought, Wow! That must really be some piece of ass! I'm sorry, I don't mean that. I mean some dame! He told me you were sensitive about the names we give to — er, broads, chicks, you know —"

"Try women," I suggested.

"That's what it says on shithouses! Is that better?" he asked.

"You're a little bit like him," I said. I liked him. A lot.

"I'd never kill myself over a br — a girl, a woman," he said.

"Why do you keep repeating that?" I asked. I had no idea what any of it meant, but I didn't care. He did remind me of Ron.

"Because that's what made me think I wouldn't want to meet her. That's when I remembered she left him when he needed her most, she left him when he was just about ready to take off and do some big things on his own, with her and for her. And that's when I thought that a girl who'd done that to him wasn't for me. And then, almost four years later, she comes walking right into the garage as if nothing ever happened. And she lets me take her on a tour of the house. Something funny must have happened inside me. I must have gone back to my first thoughts. I must have thought, Wow! She really is some woman! And it must be when those thoughts were in my head that something I said might have sounded like an offer. But you've got to understand that whatever I said, I didn't mean it, because those first thoughts aren't the thoughts I have now. You'd better understand that I'm not about to make Ron's girl any kind of offer!"

"I understand," I lied; I didn't understand anything. "What can I do to make up for what you blame me for?"

"Just stay out of my sight," he answered. "Because you really are —"

"Some piece of ass!" I finished his sentence with the words he'd have preferred, and added coquettishly, "And you'd better understand that Ron's girl isn't going to accept any kind of offer." I ran back through the garage to the now-empty kitchen. I wasn't hungry and ate from habit. I then took a long walk along streets where there were lots of people; I thought that with more of the same luck I might successfully antagonize a complete stranger. But I didn't meet anyone and turned in before Tina did. I had a long, marvelously restful sleep, without interruptions, fears or nightmares.

It was only on the following day that my active life in the garage began. Tina was already gone when I woke up. I reexamined my situation as I sipped my breakfast coffee. I had knocked down every one of my potential props except one: seven-year old Tina. And rather than face up to Sabina's challenge, I went to the garage looking for Tina.

I squatted next to her and silently watched her work. She seemed annoyed by my presence. "Would you mind showing me how you do things here?" I asked, begging.

"Ted'll show you; he's much better at it than I am; he showed everyone," she said innocently.

"I don't want Ted to show me," I insisted. "I want you to show me."

Tina stopped what she was doing, turned to me and looked into my eyes as if she were searching for something. Suddenly she said, "You're my mother, aren't you?"

I almost fell over backwards. "Why in the world do you say that?"

"You were Ron's girl, weren't you?"

"Yes I was, for a time," I admitted, "but I swear I'm not your mother!"

"Why did you leave us?" she asked.

Oh no! I thought. There goes my last prop! "Tina, I swear I never left you," I whispered insistently and I hoped convincingly.

Tina went back to her work and I went on squatting next to her. Fortunately for me, Tina was more compassionate than her older but not wiser housemates. She worked in silence for a while. Suddenly she said, "Here, hold this!" And my apprenticeship began.

The seven-year old teacher and her twenty-three year old student became inseparable. I went to bed when she did and got up when she did. We ate our meals together and spent most of the day working together. I became a crack auto mechanic, an amateur carpenter and something less than an amateur (namely a lousy) welder, wood turner and machinist. Tina I knew what to do with every tool in the garage and she could operate every machine in the downstairs workshop. Let no one tell me about the virtues of specialization, the lifelong training required by each trade, or the helplessness of children! Tina taught me infinitely more than the uses of the tools or the operations possible on each machine. She taught me what human beings might be if —

But there was one thing she didn't show me: the lofts. She assured me I could have a loft of my own if I decided to paint or sculpt and then I could visit the other painters and sculptors (namely Ted and Tina) to study their materials and techniques. I told Tina I preferred to express myself with a full pen and an empty piece of paper. Admission to the lofts, and to Sabina's lab, was restricted to the artists themselves. The finished works were brought down, and could be criticized or admired only then. I learned that some of the most beautiful objects in the house and in the tiny garden were Tina's. But no one except another painter or sculptor was allowed to see the work before it was finished since the outsider might influence the artist's decision or even distort the original intention. One had to decide and choose on one's own.

It all sounds so idyllic, doesn't it? Almost Utopian. I'm trying to describe those days as I experienced them, not only because they were the happiest days I spent there, but also because it's the only way I can clarify why I feel so sour about that experience today. It all turned sour gradually; everything turned out not to be what it had seemed. But I should tell you about three more trivialities I experienced before the souring began.

The first concerns Ted. He continued to tiptoe to our door and to look in on me every single night. I started to take his modest "perversion" for granted. If that was the extent to which he satisfied his sexual desires, then I had to agree with Sabina: he really didn't have very extensive desires. I started to feel sorry for him.

The second concerns Tina. She repeatedly talked about wanting to leave the garage, "just me and you and Ted." I asked jokingly if we couldn't take Jose along and she explained, "Oh no, he'd want to bring Seth along and Seth would bring Vic," and I understood that Seth and Vic would bring the heroin so I didn't pursue that. I asked why we couldn't bring Sabina along and Tina said, "She'd bring Tissie and Tissie can't live without Seth," and we'd be right back where we started. I didn't take any of this very seriously and I didn't put all the pieces together until much later; I'm not sure I'm aware of all the pieces even now.

The third has to do with Jose. He and I had simultaneously avoided and courted each other since our bout in the street. I worked facing him as often as I could and whenever I faced him he turned his back to me. But I knew that whenever my back was turned to him he didn't take his eyes off me.

One day Seth rushed to Jose and I overheard him whisper something about "Sabina's kid and sister."

Jose "corrected" Seth in a way that struck me as totally bizarre. He said, "Ron's kid and Ron's girl are staying right here in Ron's garage, so either say what you've got to say or get out of here!"

It did become perfectly clear to me why Tina had an identity crisis: she was a dead man's daughter in her living mother's house. Furthermore, if she was perpetually "Ron's kid" while I remained "Ron's girl" it was obvious that I was the girl's mother.

I decided to have it out with Jose. I was anxious to learn if he too thought I had walked out on Ron and Tina, if he too thought I was Tina's mother. I also wanted to put an end to our silence, to place our courtship on more solid ground. But I didn't have a chance. That's when everything began to sour.

That night, when Tina was ready to turn in, I told her I wanted to stay behind to finish the work on my own; she could inspect it in the morning and tell me how I had done all by myself.

Tina left. A few minutes later Ted said goodnight and left. Jose and I were alone. Suddenly a terrible thought flew through my mind. Ted never went to bed before me!

I rushed into the house, took my shoes off, and crept to an alcove in the hallway. I watched Ted come out of his room, tiptoe across the hall and slip into Tina's room. I was terrified. A few seconds later he came out and returned to his own room. I ran to Tina's room. As soon as I reached my bed I started trembling again. I broke out in a cold sweat. I realized that Ted came to our room every night, not to look at me, but to look at Tina!

I stupidly thought I ought to tell Sabina. The following day I went to the kitchen at noon, when she usually got up. I waited for her impatiently. When she came in I told her, "I have something really urgent to tell you."

As soon as Sabina looked at me I realized I hadn't chosen the best day to reveal my discovery to her. She looked at me but saw Luisa. "If it's about Ted again, save it; I'm busy," she said.

"It's not about me and Ted. It's about Tina and Ted," I said insistently.

"You'll have to tell me about it sometime," she said, and yawned.

I was horrified. It was Sabina the prostitute talking to one of her buyers, coldly, indifferently, absently. "Sabina!" I shouted. "There's a funny relationship between them. I'm not imagining it."

"It's only funny where you come from," she said contemptuously. "To him she's a fully developed person. That must be very funny to you, because where you come from she'd be a thing, a pet, a child. What a funny relationship: a man and a pet! But why does it bother you? Aren't all relationships funny where you came from?"

I got mad. "I'm sorry to take up your valuable time; I'm sorry to bother you with my funny sensibilities," I said sarcastically.

"Don't ever apologize for your sensibilities, Sophia! Develop them, refine them. They're all you've got." And then, adding, "See you around," she vanished.

I sat in the kitchen biting my lip with frustration. What in the world could I make out of any of that? You would have been a great help just then, Yarostan. Didn't you tell me that "Sabina's world" was completely familiar to you, that you felt perfectly at home there? I didn't know what to think. Was Sabina simply indifferent? Did she simply not care what happened to seven-year old Tina? Or did she know all about Ted and Tina, everything "conceivable and inconceivable," and did her philosophy account for it all as normal, as part of the process of healing? And were my sensibilities right after all? Or was I one of those who "only know love and sex in the forms practiced by the maimed, by those with stunted imaginations and dead desires"? And even if my sensibilities were right, was I right to want to impose them on the other people in the house? Who was I, after all? In terms of experience and in almost every other way as well I was the youngest person in the house, the only real "child" there. I was Tina's apprentice. I wasn't her guardian but her charge. She was my teacher and my model. It was she who defined my day's activities, not I hers. It was I who turned to Tina to ask, "What should I do next?" That relationship was funny too, where I came from.

That afternoon I rejoined Tina in the workshop, as her apprentice. Outwardly everything remained the same. But inwardly I was transformed. I stopped my flirtation with Jose and forgot the urgent questions I'd wanted to ask him. I turned all my attention to Ted. I accompanied Tina when she went to tell Ted she was stuck with a problem and asked for his advice. They discussed the problem like two explorers setting out into uncharted territory. They were the adults. I was the child. They obviously knew what they were doing. I was completely lost.

I became obsessed with the desire to take a trip, if only a brief trip, out of "Sabina's world" and its "funny relationships." I longed to see how it all looked from outside, from where I came from. I hadn't called Alec or any of my university friends since the day I'd been evicted from the co-op three weeks earlier. I had simply disappeared. I wondered if they too would present me with a child I had mothered and ask me why I had abandoned it. Surely not after only three weeks!

It was Saturday evening, Alec's habitual date-night. The school year had just ended. If Alec and I hadn't been expelled we'd both be college graduates. I wondered if he'd be dating someone that night, perhaps someone I didn't know. I couldn't imagine him without a woman. But he was home, and excited to the point of hysteria; he obviously wasn't dating anyone else.

"For Christ's sake Sophie where the hell have you been?" he shouted. "Everyone's looking all over for you. Even your mother —"

"My what?" I asked.

"Your mother, for Christ's sake!" he shouted. "Minnie and I found her through the phone book thinking she'd know where you were but even she hadn't heard from you. What the hell happened? When can I see you?"

"How about tomorrow morning, breakfast time?" I suggested.

"You'll come over?" he asked.

I almost consented — but a "brilliant" idea flashed through my mind. "Why don't you come here?" I asked. I gave him the address and insisted, "Don't tell anyone where I am and come alone, understand?" I thought my idea was "brilliant" because Alec's visit would bring the world I came from right into the midst of Sabina's world. That way I'd see how I looked from outside much more vividly than I ever could if I went outside.

On Sunday morning I got up before sunrise, panicky with anticipation. Alec didn't come until nine. I ran to the garage when I heard a knock, but Vic was there before me. Alec had gotten all dressed up in his Saturday night date suit. He looked as frightened as a rabbit that's ready to bolt away. Vic refused to let him in.

"Ain't no cop going to get inside here!" Vic grumbled.

"He's no cop! He's my best friend!" I shrieked. I threw my arms around the scared rabbit and kissed him. Then I led him past Vic, through the messy garage, through the plush hallway with its panels and inset pictures and sculptures, to the kitchen. Tissie was the next member of the welcoming committee.

"Cripes, what's that you're bringing in here?" Tissie asked, almost dropping her cup.

"Tissie, this is my friend Alec," I said.

"Alec! That's short for Alexandra ain't it?" she asked.

"Tissie! Don't be mean," I begged.

"Can't tell from looks these days," she exclaimed vengefully. "Don't worry, sis, I'm through here; I won't spoil anything for you." She left us alone.

Poor Alec still looked like he wanted to get away as quickly as possible. He paced back and forth and asked, "Couldn't we have breakfast out someplace?"

I finally succeeded in pushing him down into a chair and told him. "I wanted to see you right here."

Looking suspiciously at me, then at the hallway. Alec asked with unambiguous hostility, "What the hell you got into, Sophie? A whorehouse?"

I couldn't keep myself from laughing. Alec's words were like gusts of air from the world I'd come from. Gusts of foul air. Farts. Alec and I had never talked about prostitutes but I'm sure he'd have set forth the standard "radical" views of them: guiltless victims of a predatory society, exploited by the bourgeoisie like the rest of the working class, basically proletarian — until the day when he finds his girl friend among "sluts in a whorehouse." Alec disappointed me. I'd expected him to lean over backward with hypocritical understanding and sympathy, even encouragement. I would then have bombarded him with revelations about the "negative aspects" of the good life. But his instant hostility put me on the defensive immediately.

"A whorehouse?" I asked. "I thought you knew I was evicted from the whorehouse! Or didn't you know my colleagues at the co-op were all for sale — to anyone willing to buy them: the city, the state, any corporate bureaucracy, any academic bureaucracy, law firms, rich husbands, even cops?"

"I get the point, Sophie," he said contritely. "I didn't mean to come on like that. But ever since you told me to be hush hush about where you were, and what with that guy stopping me at the door, I thought —"

"You thought I'd become a prostitute," I cut in.

"I didn't say that," he insisted.

"But you thought it," I said.

"Get off it, Sophie," he begged. "You can't read my mind and I can't read yours, so tell me what you've been doing and I'll stop trying. You told that guy I was your best friend, but you sure don't act like you believe that."

"All right, comrade, you asked for it," I announced, proceeding defensively every step of the way. "I've gone back to the working class, which is where I started, where I found my first love —"

"And where I've never been! Only I never expected you to throw that in my face!" he exclaimed.

"I'm answering your question," I said calmly. "I'm an apprentice mechanic, carpenter and welder; in a few days I start out as apprentice machinist and later on as electrician, plumber —"

"Aw get off it, Sophie," he said, annoyed. "I know you can't be all those things. What's the big secret you're keeping from me?"

I was annoyed too. For once I wasn't being sarcastic and as a result I sounded like a liar. I grabbed him by the wrist and dragged him downstairs to the workshop. "You don't believe me? I'll show you!" Like a magician performing a trick, I showed him a rectangular block, inserted it into the lathe and transformed it into a cylinder. I didn't know how to do anything else on the lathe but Alec had never even seen that done.

He was greatly impressed. "Jesus, Sophie, is this a school?" he asked, now all modesty and admiration.

I gleamed in his admiration, proudly absorbing credit for what I had neither conceived nor built nor helped maintain. "Something like a school," I answered, "but so different from the schools we know that it shouldn't be called by the same name. The state doesn't pay for it and professional educators don't run it."

"Who does, then?" he asked.

"Exactly who you thought ran it. It was founded by street people, lumpen, whatever you choose to call them: professional hustlers, prostitutes, dope dealers, pimps and thieves — the works! They pay for it by stealing and hustling and they run it themselves. They're the freest people I've known; they sell less of their time, their bodies and their talents than anyone I've ever been with. It's a school, but there's no curriculum and no structure. Everyone does exactly what he or she pleases." As I talked, Ted and Tina walked into the workshop.

Alec exclaimed, "Jesus, this place is great! I didn't think such things were possible. Are there kids here too?"

Tina planted herself in front of Alec and asked, "Are you Sophia's professor friend?"

Suddenly Ted faced Alec and asked, "What's great here, mister? The heroin? The prostitution?"

"Heroin?" Alec asked, backing away from Ted. "Jesus, I don't know, buddy. She was just telling me —"

Pointing his finger at Tina, Ted asked, "Is it great for her, mister? I heard you say this place was great. Is it great for her? You hear my question?"

"Sure, I heard you, buddy," Alec said; "I never said heroin was great."

"It ain't great for her, mister! She ain't into it. And what she's into don't need this place. Her and me either. What her and me are into don't need to be built on heroin and prostitution. This place ain't great for her and me!"

I heard "her and me, her and me" over and over, louder and louder, like a sledgehammer pounding in my brain. I felt myself sinking. Alec must have caught me because I suddenly found all three of them carrying me upstairs. I asked to be placed in a kitchen chair. I sat and stared, oblivious to Alec and to the others gathering around me. I kept hearing Ted's voice repeating "her and me." Suddenly everything had fallen into place and the place had fallen apart. Suddenly everything had meaning and became meaningless.

When Ted repeated "her and me" for the third time, everything flashed through my mind simultaneously; Tina talking about leaving, "just me and you and Ted"; Jose telling me, "Sure there are couples; lots of them; there's hardly anything else", Ted's nightly visits to Tina's and my room. When I'd thought he looked in on me, I'd concluded that he found me attractive. It now dawned on me that the only time he really looked at me or spoke to me was when I squatted alongside Tina, when I looked her size and seemed her age. "Her and me." "Just me and you and Ted." "You're my mother, aren't you?" The mother of Ted's seven-year old bride. And where was the honeymoon to be? Not in Sabina's world, where "nothing is banned, everything is allowed, no holds are barred," but in the world I came from, the world where "all relationships are funny." But why me? Why not Sabina? Because "she'd bring Tissie" and Seth and the rest of the crew and the honeymoon wouldn't even be as private as the lofts by Sabina's laboratory. "He might even ask you to kill me," Sabina had told me. I wouldn't bring anyone along. I'd be a far better front for Ted's "funny relationship" than Ted's garage ever was for Seth's heroin. It was no longer a question of not imposing my sensibilities; it was now a question of not being imposed on. I felt like vomiting. I couldn't keep my mind off the yet more private loft, just for "her and me," with yet more rigid admissions requirements, with a steel door and a combination lock, with a wall-to-wall down mattress for "every conceivable and inconceivable perversion — in every conceivable shape, size and age —"

Those were the thoughts that flew through my mind as I sat in the kitchen eleven years ago, staring at the bewildered faces surrounding me.

:|||||||||:

Those are the thoughts that fly through my mind as I sit on the fender of Daman's car waiting for him and Sabina to come out of the courtroom, four days after Tina announced, "I'm leaving. I'll be staying at Ted's."

Finally Daman emerges from the courthouse alone. He sees me, waves, runs across the street and the first thing he talks about is Tina. "I didn't expect to be seeing you again so soon, and certainly not under such unusual circumstances. That fireball you keep in your house with you —"

"Scared the hell out of you and you deserved it! She's no longer with us." I look expectantly toward the courthouse entrance and ask him, "Where's the other fireball I keep in my house with me?"

"No longer with you? My fault I suppose?" he asks. He starts driving.

"Your fault?" I ask. "Why are you so paranoid? Where's Sabina?"

"I told her I'd pick her up after I found out where your trial was. Couldn't you tell her on the phone? It was over before I found anything out," he says.

"When did you two get so chummy?" I ask.

"You can call it chummy," he says with sarcasm. "That's not what I call it! She was waiting for me after my last class — with a switchblade knife!"

I can't keep myself from laughing. "Sabina? She was playing wasn't she? When was that?"

"Day before yesterday," he says. "If she was playing, I didn't think her game very funny. She pressed that knife to my stomach and asked, 'Where is she?' As if I'd locked you into my desk drawer! Don't laugh, Sophie! I don't see how you can live with that woman and still be alive. She pressed the knife until I felt it — I still have a wound — and demanded, 'Where's Sophia? What did you do with her, professor?' All right, go ahead and laugh; it was hilarious! 'How the hell should I know?' I said, and I was sure I'd had it. That was as chummy as we got. For some reason she spared me. She put the knife away and said, 'She's been kidnapped.' 'Kidnapped,' I shouted. 'Why would I want to kidnap her?' Answer: 'I don't know, professor; I can't read your mind'!"

"She was right!" I shout.

"Right?" he shouts.

Still laughing, I say, "She was right! You, a professor, were completely exposed in an argument; every mask you wear was pulled off; you were shown up as a cop for capital. But a professor, a powerful member of the establishment, doesn't have to let himself be exposed like that, certainly not by people who don't have the proper credentials. He picks up the phone and sends out a goon squad —"

"Sophie, god damn it, you're going to walk home!" he shouts.

"Only she had the wrong professor," I continue. "But she was right! I exposed a professor in an argument and he sent out the goon squad!"

"Hm," he says, bristling with frustration. "I just found out they had you in there for assault and battery."

"I also slapped him," I admit.

"Oh, you slapped him," he says self-righteously.

"Yes, '*Oh, I slapped him!*'" I shout. "Just like I wanted to slap you when you said Yarostan's years in prison were equivalent to a university education. That would have justified calling the goon squad, wouldn't it?"

"Hm," he says again, turning onto my street.

"What's hm?" I ask. "What happened after Sabina put her knife away?"

"I obviously became concerned, whatever you say about professors — the entire genus. I didn't think you ever made such sweeping generalizations," he says, parking the car in front of my house.

"I usually don't, but Sabina does. So what happened next?" I ask impatiently.

"She had me drive her to your mother's. Then she had me drive all over town looking for someone else. At one point I suggested calling the police. She screamed, 'If you call the police — ' 'I know,' I said, 'I'll get knifed.' But you have to admit I was right at least about that! It would sure have saved a lot of gas!"

"I'm grateful for all your trouble," I tell him. "Would you like to come in?"

"No thank you," he says emphatically. "My life is too precious to me."

"Then tell me one more thing. What do you know about that commune some students got going?" I ask.

"Nothing much," he says. "Some wild new 'cultural radicals' have got it into their heads that they can make a revolution without the working class, inside a university building."

"Thanks again, Daman," I say, climbing out of his car.

"But none of my students are involved in that," he adds, boasting.

"Because they're the working class," I shout.

He shouts back, "That's right, they're the working class. Goodbye, Sophie. Give my regards to the knife thrower. And send my greetings to the fire eater!" He drives off.

I walk up to the door and knock lightly. No response. I pull out my key and let myself in. Still no Sabina. I walk to her room. She's sound asleep. It's not noon yet. I go up to her quietly and kiss her. She sits up abruptly and stares at me. I whisper, "If you were so worried about me that you went out looking for me with a knife, why did you go back to sleep?"

"What did you expect me to do?" she asks, hugging me. "March in front of the courtroom carrying a sign and shouting 'Free Sophia!'?"

"You couldn't have looked funnier than when you poked Daman with a knife," I say, starting to laugh again.

"Did he come in with you?" she asks.

"Oh no, if he ever sees you again he'll run as fast as he can!"

Both of us burst out laughing. Sabina gets up and starts dressing.

"What made you think I was kidnapped?" I ask.

"Look around the living room and tell me what you'd have thought," she answers.

I run into the living room and look around for the first time since my arrest. The rug is decorated by enormous footprints of dry mud. Under the pillow on the couch there's a smashed record and in front of the couch there's a mess: a shattered lamp and a spilled ashtray next to the tipped coffee table. I try to explain the "evidence" to Sabina. "It was pouring out when they came for me — and they probably walked around the house before they came in. One of the oafs crushed the record because I'd left the pillow over it; the other one bumped into the coffee table on his way out."

"It was sunny and dry when I got up — but never mind; you sure would write lousy detective stories," Sabina shouts from her room. "It's perfectly obvious, isn't it? Two giants crawled in through your window in the middle of the night. I know there were two because I measured the footprints; there were two different sizes. They gagged you and started carrying you out through the front door. You put up a good fight in the living room, but they knocked you out cold, threw you into a sack and carried you away."

"You mean you measured their footprints but you didn't go into my room?" I ask. "My pajamas were under my pillow and my bed was made up! Some detective you'd make!"

"I obviously didn't sit around here playing detective!" she shouts. "I went out to find you."

"But why Daman?" I ask.

"Who else?" she asks.

"And why the knife?"

"Sophia, I — if I'd wanted a house all to myself, I would have looked for one several years ago," she shouts.

"Aha!" I shout. "Are you the one who lectured to me about possessiveness? Is it possible that somewhere along the way you've acquired a mother complex?"

Sabina runs into the living room and puts both her hands on my throat — gently. "Say that again, smart-ass," she hisses through her teeth, "and I'll have a home all to myself. I'll admit only one thing," she says, removing her hands and turning away from me, as if ashamed; "I was sorry I lectured to you when you weren't here any more. You were wrong about Tina and I was furious. But I wasn't furious enough to want you beaten and carried away. That's why the knife. Losing both of you so suddenly didn't give me time to adopt a detached, speculative attitude. But what business did you have with the police? And why didn't you tell me about it beforehand? What about your job? Come on, let's have breakfast. There are two letters for you in there."

We go to the kitchen; I'm glad to be home. I open your letter first and start reading it while eating, handing Sabina each page I finish. "A born troublemaker," she comments. "Reckless and courageous. Like all of Nachalo's brood" (I being his daughter, Sabina his granddaughter and Tina his great-granddaughter). Suddenly she says, "Hey, troublemaker, it's a beautiful day; how about spending the afternoon in the park?"

It really is a beautiful spring day, one of the first cloudless and warm days this year. We catch a bus near our house and ride to a bridge that leads to an enormous island park. On the bus I tell Sabina why I was arrested, tried and fined. She laughs at every detail and obviously doesn't respond with "Oh, you slapped him!" On the contrary, she's sorry about the fact that my slaps could hardly be more than gentle pats on the professor's cheeks. I don't know how well you remember Sabina. She still looks like a gypsy whatever she wears, and she's still smaller than I am, but over the years she's learned every conceivable technique of self-defense, and she always was terribly strong; I suspect she could easily have committed "assault and battery" against both of the cops who arrested me — if they hadn't had guns. The behavioral psychologist would have smarted for a long time from Sabina's slaps and then he'd really have been disappointed by the smallness of the fine.

We get off the bus and she runs across the bridge; I walk across, and I'm exhausted by the time I reach the bench where she waits for me. We've gone mountain climbing several times — but I'll strike that out; I've digressed enough already, and this is my third day on this letter. We walk to an isolated spot by the river and lie down on the grass, sunning ourselves while reading your letter. We spend the rest of the afternoon watching the birds and the passing boats and discussing your letter. Before telling you about that discussion, I'd like to tell you about the second letter that was waiting for me, so that I can at least finish telling you what happened to my teaching job. I haven't forgotten that I've left you dangling right in the middle of my experience in the garage. I'm sorry. Ten things can happen in an instant and ten thoughts can fly simultaneously through your mind but you can only tell about one thing or one idea at a time and that fact alone falsifies what really happened and how I really felt.

The second letter that was waiting for me is from the administration of the community college. It's almost identical to notes Alec and I received years ago from the president of the university. The main difference is that this note came by mail instead of being delivered by special courier. It only contains one line: "Please report to the office of the Dean at 9 a.m. Friday." How quickly that note came! The "assault and battery" trial and my interview with the dean must have been planned at the same time and by the same people. I show the note to Sabina and she responds by giving me advice. "Next time you want to slap someone, clench your fist — not like that! Fold your thumb on the outside, like this!" She shows me.

I arrive at the dean's office on Friday morning half an hour late. I usually get up at nine. Since I knew, more or less, what was going to happen, I thought I was making enough of a concession by setting my alarm for quarter to nine.

The "interview" with the dean isn't nearly as congenial as my earlier interview with the president. The first difference is that the dean is nervous and rude, not at all the smooth politician the president was. It's through this dean that I got the job. He makes public displays of his liberalism and is a great friend of Daman's whenever they're both visible to others. Daman had recommended me to him. The second difference is that there's a hostile presence in the room: the behaviorist. And lest I forget: no coffee is served, although the hour would warrant it.

"Sophia," the dean starts out; "I must confess that I am at once surprised and disappointed."

"So?" I ask, shrugging my shoulders.

"This proceeding is highly irregular," he says, fidgeting with some papers on his desk.

"Please come to the point," I say; "I really don't have all day."

Lifting some of the papers, he says, "I have a report here —"

I grab the report out of his hands and the psychologist starts running toward me. "Am I not allowed to read a report about me?" I ask, clutching the papers.

The liberal dean shoves his arm in the psychologist's path and says, "Surely Sophia is entitled to read the report!"

"But it's the only copy!" the behaviorist shouts with amazing psychological insight.

The dean keeps his arm between the predator and his prey and assures me, "You may study the report if you wish." Liberalism: authority granting its victims the right to live a minute longer.

Turning my back to the frustrated behaviorist, but listening attentively for every move he might make, I leaf through the report. It's a medical report, or rather a mental report, about the state of Sophia Nachalo's health. And it concludes that the subject is urgently in need of care: unbalanced, with strong symptoms of psychosis, disposed to acts of extreme violence, and not only unfit to teach but socially dangerous as well.

"In short, a witch!" I announce.

"Pardon me?" the dean asks.

"The accuser, the judge and the executioner are all one and the same person; how does that fit into your political philosophy?" I ask the liberal dean.

"Of course you are entitled —" he starts.

"Oh, am I?" I ask with mock enthusiasm. "In that case I'd like my own defense attorney, expenses to be paid by the institution; I'd like a trial by jury; and I'd like the right to examine my jury to make sure my accusers aren't sitting in judgment over me."

The liberal dean is really nervous now and his free hand fidgets with everything on his desk. "You're entitled — yes, of course — a review board will have to be appointed — surely —"

While the dean fishes for words, I fish for the lighter in my purse. I'm grateful for the noise the dean makes, both with his mouth and his hands, and also for the numerous disappointments with which he threatens to frustrate the behaviorist. All four corners of the report are on fire before either of them smell what's happening to the only copy.

"The trial is over! She's a witch! Burn her!" I shout as I throw the report on the dean's paper-laden desk. Before leaving I start laughing. The laughter is the crowning touch: it must really sound demonic to them. Neither of them moves to put out the fire on the dean's desk before I leave the room.

That afternoon Daman calls. His friend the dean told him everything. "Gee, I just heard. I didn't think you'd lose your job, Sophie. That's terrible. I'll be right over."

The hypocrite. He talks about working class revolutions from morning to night. But losing an academic job is terrible.

That's serious. The job is the only thing in life that really matters. He refused to come into the house after such a trivial event as my arrest. But now he rushes over.

Sabina had laughed until she'd ached when I'd told her I'd burned part of the dean's office as well as the only copy of the document that proved me to be a maniac. Daman doesn't laugh. He fidgets, like the dean. His hands mechanically leaf through the stack of paper on the coffee table; they're the pages of your letter. "Do you really think you helped your case by doing that, Sophie?"

"In every conceivable way," I answer. "I've regained all the self-respect I lost when I accepted that job. I've regained my time. I didn't demean myself, and I was so proud of myself when I walked out of that room that I felt three feet taller."

"This is a serious matter, Sophie, and I'm not joking," he says.

"Neither am I! For you it's not a serious matter to kiss the dean's ass. It is for me!" I shout.

"You won't easily find another job like that," he says, threatening never to recommend me again.

"I won't ever look for another job like that," I assure him. "You can keep them all yourself!"

Still fidgeting with your letter but never once looking at it, he asks, "Is this a novel you're working on?"

"No," I tell him, "it's another letter from my friend Yarostan."

He drops your letter as if it, too, had been burning. "Well, I guess I'd better be shoving along," he announces.

"I'll read you parts of the letter," I suggest. "I told Yarostan about you and he said some really interesting things about professors and journalists. You'll be fascinated."

"I'd rather not," he says. "The idea of the workers' backwardness pervades his whole argument. He doesn't understand that the working class is inherently —"

Sabina cuts Daman short. Until now she'd stayed out of the conversation in deference to me: with Tina gone, the circle of my friends is diminishing. But now she leaps in front of Daman and snaps her fingers in his face. "Are you alive, professor, or are you some type of robot?"

"I'd better be shoving along," Daman repeats uneasily.

"You said that before too," Sabina reminds him, blocking his path. "I've always wondered how you professors managed to say the same thing with the same tone year after year. Now I know. You've got a phonograph installed in your throat. Open your mouth and let me see, professor. I've never seen a phonograph that could fit into a man's throat. But what happens to you? How does it feel? Don't you feel frustrated when you hear someone ask you one thing and your throat answers something else? Sophia told you Yarostan had things to say about professors and journalists, not about backward workers. Does the academic phonograph kit include ear plugs? They must be absolutely perfect plugs. Let me see your ear. What about your eyes, professor? Can you see us standing here? Or is your vision plugged up too?"

Daman looks uneasily at the door, then at Sabina and me.

I suggest: "Here's the phone; you could call the police."

Sabina steps out of his way. Daman glares at me and then bolts through the door.

You wrote that the political militant, the journalist and the academician couldn't help establish a human community because their very existence presupposed the absence of community. I don't disagree. Daman is all three in one, and he's all the proof I need. I also agree with what you say about the "context" Daman moves in: it's a desert and nothing human can grow there. But I'm not sure all this applies to the people I met on the university newspaper staff fifteen years ago. I'm not even sure it applies to Daman as he was then. You seem to assume that once people have chosen their "context," they've chosen it once and for all, they can't get out of it, they can't change. You certainly make your argument convincing by citing the case of Vera Neis and of Adrian Povrshan. Once they chose their "starting point," they seem to have gotten on an express train which didn't stop until it reached its final destination. The people with whom I spent over three years on the newspaper staff didn't exhibit such demonic consistency. If I had tried to guess then where all those people would end up, I would have missed every single time. The only genuinely "professorial type" among us was Hugh, the liberal editor, the one who claimed to have no views of his own because there were always two equal and opposite views of every problem. Yet he's the one who wound up with the "down and outs," and the last time I saw him he expressed an anti-professorial attitude very similar to yours, and lived it. As for Daman: at that time I thought no one less likely to become a professor. He was so totally dependent on Minnie for everything he professed that I couldn't have imagined him addressing a classroom all by himself. Of course I can trace the "basic continuity "of his character today — but only through hindsight, only because the "basic starting point" would be what he is today, not what he was then. I could do that just as easily if he were a bank clerk today, or a street cleaner. With the end-point as the "basis" we can trace the origin of anything back to the beginning of time. Surely that's not all your argument boils down to.

I'm moved to tears when I read your description of the role of journalists in the Magarna uprising: "spreading their reportages between like and like, interpreting each to the other, portraying each to the other through a glass that didn't reflect the experience of the individual on the other side but only the reporter's." That's horrifying, I agree. And that's what I was at that time: a reporter. That was my "context," my "world." But when I think about what you're telling me I can't help rebelling. It all makes so much sense when you refer to your past experience. But does it make any sense at all when you apply it to mine? Are you really sure I would have been a reporter if I'd been in your world at the time of that uprising? Are you really sure you'd have been miles away from the university newspaper if you'd been in mine? Those are senseless questions, but it's you who raise them. You tell me, "It's only when you descend among those who are nothing in this society that your search becomes meaningful as a struggle against this society." Until then my search was "a search for a corpse." I come alive only on the day when I move into the house behind the garage. And of course that's where you would have been all along. You say so. "The garage in which Sabina and her friends lived is an environment far more familiar to me than the world of the university or the newspaper. Your descent — is a descent to my world. Those are the activities I confronted — the people I've known. Yet you describe my world — as exotic." Exotic: that's the exact word for it. That's exactly how I experienced it. Just like a tourist. I kept my distance. I didn't become involved until I was threatened personally, even physically. You're right about my detachment. You know perfectly well that my "social origins" weren't responsible for it. Was my experience in the carton plant responsible for that detachment? Or my three years in the university? Was I really so determined by my "starting point," whenever I reached it, that I couldn't have made myself someone like Tissie? Was it really my "search for a corpse" that made the people in Sabina's world exotic to me? Are you really so sure the house behind the garage wouldn't have been "exotic" to you — every bit as exotic as it was to me and Alec?

I'm not asking rhetorical questions. I'm asking questions I couldn't answer for myself then and can't answer for you now. In many ways I did find in the garage something that was profoundly "meaningful as a struggle against this society." If I hadn't found that there, I wouldn't have stayed as long as I did; I would have walked out with Alec the day I figured out what Ted was. I didn't only stay there. I didn't ever decide to leave. In the end I was carried out. I did find the experience meaningful — more meaningful than all the other experiences of my life lumped together. Yet once I left I suppressed every detail of that experience from my memory, and I went on suppressing them for ten years. I haven't given one thought to Ted, Tissie or Seth until only a few days ago, when Tina announced she was moving in with Ted. If all those events were so meaningful to me, why did I repress every trace of them so thoroughly? Was it really because I belonged to that other, alien and hostile and inhuman world, the world of academics and journalists? I don't think so, but I'll let you be the judge. Since Tissie's world is already familiar to you, I have no reason to spare you any of the details, do I? Since my experience was so meaningful, I have no reason to be ashamed of any of it, nor to continue repressing it. But I wonder if you'll be able to tell me just what is so familiar to you about my experience — and just what it all meant. That's the one detail I still can't provide.

:||||||||:

I wanted very much to run out of that kitchen with Alec eleven years ago, to move in with him, to get away from that world where "nothing is banned, no holds are barred" for "her and me," the world of wall-to-wall mattresses for "every conceivable shape, size and age." But I sat at the kitchen table, surrounded by faces I failed to recognize, until Alec's voice roused me.

"What's the matter with Sophie?" he was asking Ted. "Is she on heroin? Is that what you're trying to tell me, buddies?"

Ted backed away from Alec and I jumped out of my chair at Ted, determined not to let him repeat "her and me" one more time. "Get out of this room," I hissed; "Get out of my sight. You're disgusting!"

For an instant Ted froze where he stood and glared at me, his face expressing bewilderment more than anger. Then he turned around and slowly walked out of the room. As soon as Ted was gone, Tina ran up to me, bawling, and started to beat my chest and my stomach with her powerful fists until I cried out from pain. She asked, "What's the matter with you? Why do you hate Ted so much? What did he ever do to you?"

I could see the same question on Tissie's face and also on Jose's. I sank back into my chair, rested my head on the table, between my arms, and cried. Tina walked out of the room sobbing. Tissie stomped out. Jose stayed but said nothing. Alec stroked my hair as if to "comfort" me; I pushed his hand away.

"Jesus, Sophie, what was that all about?" Alec asked. "Are you on heroin?"

"No, god damn it!" I shouted. "I'm not on heroin. You're the only dopes in this room!" I was furious at both of them for being so blind, so dense, for thinking there was something wrong, not with Ted, but with me.

"I'm sorry Sophie," Alec said awkwardly. "Maybe it wasn't such a good idea for me to come here."

"What are you sorry about?" I bellowed at him.

"Jesus Christ, Sophie! Don't start shouting at me now! I'm sorry about everything. You, the heroin, this place. I don't know what to think. First you make this place sound great and you make me feel like a jerk. You tell me about street people raising themselves up with their own forces, running their own lives, showing others that it can be done and showing how. That's just great. That's something I'd like to be part of. Then this guy starts telling me about prostitution, about selling heroin and about taking it. And then you collapse like you're having a fit. I think that guy is right and I don't see why you chewed him out. I don't think prostitution is great and I don't think heroin is great, and if you're not having a heroin fit I'd like to know what the hell you're having and why you collapsed when he said it isn't great!"

"Maybe you're right, Alec," I said weakly. "Maybe this wasn't a good day for us to meet. Maybe I should have gone to your place." Jose jumped when I said this, but quickly turned his face away when he saw I'd noticed. Looking right at Jose, I added, "Maybe we should go to your place right now."

But Alec let himself be carried away by his socio-political program now that he realized he had one. "Why don't you answer me, Sophie? If you're not on heroin what are you on? Do you think I'd take you home in the shape you're in? These people probably know how to take care of you if you have another fit. You know that I don't know shit about that. I don't even know any doctors."

"Why don't you go home then?" I suggested.

"Why did you do it Sophie?" he continued. "Was it because they threw you out of that co-op? Why bother yourself about that? You yourself admit it was nothing but a whorehouse, an establishment whorehouse. Was it because they kept you off that *Omissions* rag? It wouldn't be the first time you did something like this. I remember that time you had some resentment against Rhea or Lem and you took it out on them by getting a date with that idiot Rakshas. That was some novel way to spite somebody — to go to a military dance with a playboy from the suburbs! And that time it worked. Lem and Rhea dropped their golden apple as if they'd bitten into a worm. But what are you doing now? Is this your way to spite that *Omissions* crew? Don't you know *Omissions* is all over and done with, that it's absolutely dead, part of the forgotten past? I called them when I couldn't find you — every one of them except Rakshas. They've all graduated and they're all into other stuff now. Not a one of them talked about starting up that paper again. You're not making any

point, don't you see that? And that shit about street people raising themselves up —
Jesus, Sophie, by becoming pimps? By selling morphine? That's not a way to raise
themselves up! That way they just dig themselves further under!"

With his last comments Alec invited Jose into the conversation. "How did you
pay for that suit, mister?" Jose asked. "Did your rich papa buy it for you?"

Alec got hysterical. "Who the hell is he? Your pimp?"

Jose would have knocked Alec across the room if I hadn't run between them
and shouted at Alec, "Either be civil or get out this very minute! Jose is your host
and if you don't apologize to him I'll —" I didn't finish. I was going to add: I'll let
him beat you to a pulp, but I realized that only Jose could decide to do that.

Alec amazed me by reaching his hand out to Jose. "I'm sorry, Jose, I didn't
mean that." Jose refused to shake Alec's hand. Alec added, still holding out his hand,
"You struck a sensitive spot. I hated my old man. I walked out on him and haven't
seen him for at least six years."

Jose suddenly shook Alec's hand and said, "No shit. I walked out on my old
man eight years ago." Turning to me, Jose said, "I mean Ron's old man." I looked at
him curiously but he didn't explain. He turned to Alec again and added, "That give
us two things in common."

"Two? What's the second?" Alec asked.

"Sophie," Jose answered.

Sophie! I thought. So I was no longer Ron's girl! I blushed until my cheeks
burned but said nothing.

Of course Alec took that up. "Christ, Sophie, you mean you and this Jose —
you mean you two —"

I hurriedly cut him short. "He's my host and that's all, Alec. Understand?"

"No!" he insisted. "I don't understand. A little earlier you were asking me to
be your host —"

Fortunately Sabina walked into the kitchen just then and I didn't have to
deal simultaneously with Alec's outburst of jealousy and Jose's sudden confession.
"What's this?" Sabina asked, studying Alec in his suit, "the circus?"

"He's my friend Alec. Alec, my sister Sabina," I said.

"This is your sister? Are you serious? I mean, I never knew you had a sister,"
Alec said, literally ravaging Sabina with his eyes.

"Sophia is your friend, is she?" Sabina asked him.

"Yes," he answered, completely off guard. "She's my best friend."

"How about Tissie? Is she your friend too?" Sabina asked.

"I don't understand what you mean." Alec said.

"Anything in a skirt is your friend, isn't that so, Mr. Alec?" Sabina asked. Jose
started to laugh but stopped as soon as Sabina turned to him and whispered, "Oh
you're an altogether different type of fish, aren't you?"

Alec turned to me with a helpless expression; he'd already forgotten his recent jealousy. Grateful to him at least for that, I said to Sabina. "But he's all right in spite of that."

Alec stuck his arm out to shake Sabina's hand, saying, "Sophie and her friends here have been telling me about your establishment, er, your house."

Sabina turned her back to him and walked to the stove. Suddenly she faced him, coquettishly pulled her skirt above her knee, and said, "You obviously like them short, thin but not skinny, preferably with pitch black hair. They're the most expensive types. How much can you pay?"

Alec stared at her with disbelief (or was he weighing her proposition?). Suddenly he made up his mind, turned to me and started shouting, "Jesus, Sophie, what the hell were you telling me about being a carpenter and a mechanic! Your sister! Do you take me for a complete jerk? Jesus Christ, why did you have to go and get into this? Pimps, prostitutes and dope addicts! Why?"

Jose tensed up again, but Sabina was far ahead of him. "How do you spend your time, Reverend Alec?"

"I work in a factory like thousands of others!" Alec shouted proudly.

"Not thousands, Reverend; millions," she corrected. "That's an ultra-respectable way to spend your time, since millions do that. We spend our time discussing our own projects and carrying them out. Why do you do that to your time, Reverend?"

"Aw get off it," Alec pleaded. "To earn my living, that's why!"

"In other words, you sell yourself?" Sabina asked.

"What the hell do you do?" Alec asked.

"How often do you work in a factory, Reverend?" She pursued him relentlessly.

"Six days a week, like most everyone else," he answered reluctantly.

"Day, or night?" she asked.

"I said six days!"

"Prostitute!" Sabina shouted.

"What are you calling me?" Alec asked, dumbfounded.

"Prostitute!" Sabina responded. "You sell yourself during six of your seven living days. Do you think any of us does that? I sell myself for half an hour, and at night! All I lose is a little of my sleep. I don't sell one second of my living day. Prostitute! You sell all there is to you, every living day, six days a week, during your living day. You sell yourself and you sleep. What did you call me, Reverend? I didn't hear you!"

Alec had started backing away from Sabina and before she finished he had bolted through the door. No one tried to stop him. I remained seated and thought I'd let that be my last encounter with Alec, but I remembered Ted's "her and me" and changed my mind. I caught up with him in the garage and we walked out together.

"I can't deal with it, Sophie," he said as soon as we were in the street. "I thought I was radical and open-minded but I can't take any of this in. It doesn't seem right to me, although she makes it all sound right. And I can't tell you why it doesn't seem right. Maybe she's got me all figured out; she sure looked right through me —"

"You looked pretty hard yourself," I reminded him.

"Aw come on," he said, smiling a little. "She sure saw that right away! Is she really your sister? Sure sounds like it when she runs her mouth. But I can't take it in. Like she says, I talk about exploitation and revolution and when the time comes to do something every goddamn morning I baa like a sheep." He paused, took my hand in his, and asked, "You're not really a heroin addict, are you Sophie?"

"Nor a prostitute. I'd like to see you again. Alec," I told him, letting him kiss me.

"I'd like to believe it," he whispered.

"Well I hope you're able to!" I shouted sarcastically, pulling myself away from him and starting to return to the garage.

"What should I tell your mother?" he asked.

"Tell her I'll call her! No! Tell her I'm a dope addict. Tell her I'm a slut in a whorehouse. Tell her to go to hell!" I shouted, running back to the garage.

"How much do I owe you?" he yelled back. He had the last word. I ran through the garage, past Ted and Tina, straight to my bed.

Alec's visit resolved absolutely nothing for me. I'd hoped his "outside perspective" would at least give me a clue as to how I might respond to Ted, to Sabina's "no holds are barred," to Tina. But he'd come with nothing but hackneyed and insulting prejudices, petty jealousy, and his perennial "skirt chasing."

I stayed away from Tina because I couldn't bear the thought of facing Ted, even in the workshops. For a week I got up every morning, right after Tina left the room, and went for all-day lonely walks. I avoided Sabina as much as I could because, like Alec, I wasn't able to "take it all in." I also stayed away from Jose. The cryptic confession he'd made during his argument with Alec excited me immensely but it also frightened me; when I thought of him, the idea that "everything is allowed, no holds are barred" made my heart flutter wildly.

One day I even visited Debbie Matthews. She was drunk and our brief conversation wasn't very satisfactory. But it was then that I learned about poor Lem Icel's fate. The international conference he'd attended had ended six months earlier and he still hadn't returned. In the meantime, the Magarna uprising had been suppressed by the tanks you described. Of course I knew then that the letter I'd sent you probably hadn't reached its destination.

By the end of the week I was absolutely bored. I decided not to let Ted empty my life of its content. I had enjoyed my brief apprenticeship with Tina immensely; she was a marvelous teacher and I'd loved being able to do all those different things that had always seemed so impossible to me. I resolved to regain Tina's friendship. My first attempt led to a disaster.

It was exactly a week after Alec's visit. I'd gone to bed before Tina all week long. That night I stayed awake and waited for her. As soon as she turned out the light and slipped into bed, I said, "I'm sorry about what I did, Tina." I heard her breathe faster but she didn't say anything. "Do you hate me?" I asked.

"Why do you hate Ted?" she asked.

I lay silently, not knowing what to say. Then I asked, "Doesn't he ever touch you, hurt you?"

"Who told you that?" she asked, seeming astonished. "Ted could never hurt anyone. Sure he touched me. He used to kiss me every night when I went to bed — before you came."

I fidgeted with my blanket. "I'm sorry I came," I said. "I know I should leave. But I have nowhere to go."

Silence. Suddenly Tina sat up in her bed and whispered, "Sophia? Are you asleep?"

"No, I'm not."

"I don't hate you," she announced.

I leaped out of my bed and sat down on hers. "Friends?" I asked, reaching for her hand.

Tina turned her face toward mine and asked sadly, "Sophia, would you kiss me the way Ted used to?"

"Where did he kiss you?" I asked nervously.

"Here," she said, pointing to her lips.

I couldn't — but I didn't have to! I was blinded by the room lights. Ted stood by the door with his hand on the switch!

"You!" I shrieked hysterically. "Get out of here!"

Jose and Tissie came running into the room and both looked bewildered when they saw me sitting on Tina's bed, holding her hand.

Ted asked insinuatingly, "Is there something the matter with your bed, Sophie?"

"Get out of here!" I repeated, getting off Tina's bed and into mine. "I don't owe you any explanations!"

Then Tina said to Ted, "I'd have called you if she'd hurt me! She wasn't hurting me. I asked her to kiss me goodnight, like you used to."

Jose and Tissie backed slowly out of the room. But Ted stayed, still trembling, glaring at me with terror and hatred in his eyes. Then he turned around and walked back to his room. Tina got up to turn the light out. On her way back to her bed she stopped by mine and kissed me, "the way Ted used to." I had won her friendship. But I lost my desire to resume my apprenticeship.

I spent four more days avoiding the workshops as well as all my housemates. I rode busses to parks, taking my lunch and a novel. But I couldn't concentrate on what I read. My situation was too unresolved. I thought of leaving but I didn't want to be anywhere else. And I knew that something in my situation had to change, something had to come to a head. My relationship with Jose was suspended in midair. My conflict with Ted had to reach some kind of climax. My apprenticeship was bound to resume. Or else I might finally be pushed into trying out Tissie's and Sabina's "trade." I say pushed because the one thing I wasn't going to do was the pushing. That's why I rode the busses, letting them take me wherever I went. I waited for something to happen to me, to make my decisions and choose my path for me. The perfect dilettante. And I felt perfectly self-satisfied at least about that. After all, Jose had told me on the first night that Ron's girl didn't have to do any of the work. Ron's girl didn't have to do anything at all. She only had to be present at the major ceremonies and entertain the founder's followers with her sarcastic comments.

After four more days of evasion, "something" did change, but for the worse. That hardly seemed possible. I was already estranged from everyone in the house. But impossibility is a term of logic and reality doesn't observe the limits of logic.

I said I wasn't going to spare you any of the details. I won't. I'm making no effort to separate meaningful details from meaningless ones. If I did make that effort I doubt that I'd succeed. After all, I must have had some good reason to repress my memory of those events for ten years. They simply don't fit into the rest of my life. Yet they, too, must have done their share in making me what I am. Besides, all these details should be rich with meaning for you. You said so. They're all part of "Sabina's world," the world that's so terribly familiar to you. I'm dying to get your next letter so as to learn the meaning of those experiences. Am I being sarcastic? That's my main quality, Sabina told me. Ron loved me for it. Bitter? No more now than I was then. I still can't "take it all in" any better than Alec could, any better than if it had all happened last night.

I don't know what hour of the night it was. I felt someone shaking me by the arm. I woke up and saw it was Tissie. She was trembling. I sat up and asked her what had happened.

"Help me," she pleaded pathetically. "I'm hearing things. I'm scared."

I immediately thought Ted might be hovering around her room. Then I thought she might be hallucinating. I asked what I could do.

"Stay with me. Just for a while," she pleaded.

I climbed out of bed and accompanied her to her room. I lay down on the bed next to hers. I didn't hear any sounds. I asked Tissie drowsily, "Do you feel better now?"

"Yeh, lot better," she said. "But I'm still scared. I can't sleep."

"What kind of sounds?" I asked. But I lost interest. I fell asleep.

I woke up in terror. Unimaginable terror. This was no nightmare: the moment for waking up in a cold sweat had long passed. There was no other waking; I was wide awake. If I hadn't been so blind during all the weeks I'd spent in that house, if I hadn't so completely missed so many clues, if I hadn't been so completely uninformed, I wouldn't have been so surprised, so terror-stricken, so inhumanly crude. I lay on my back stark naked. Tissie's naked body writhed over mine, her legs wrapped around me, her mouth sliding over me, licking and kissing whatever it could reach. My eyes were wide open but my body was paralyzed. I could neither move nor cry out. With an enormous effort I found the strength to whimper, "Don't! Please don't!" — as if she were murdering me! I kept repeating my plea mechanically as I tried to writhe away from her, moving toward the edge of the bed.

Tissie put her lips on my ear and pleaded, "Come on, honey, hold on just one more minute. Please hold on!"

But I didn't have the decency to let Tissie have her orgasm. My upbringing as a radical hadn't taught me anything about that. I reached the edge of the bed and regained control over my vocal cords. I became hysterical. "No! Get off me!"

Both of us fell to the floor. Tissie, still hugging me, cried, "Be like your sister, honey! Show some feeling! Don't leave me like this!"

Not Sabina! my insides cried out. A cold shiver ran down my back. I felt like vomiting, as if to expel that thought from my system. I started crawling toward the wall, trying frantically to keep Tissie off me, repeatedly whimpering, "Get away from me!" I couldn't believe what she was telling me about Sabina and I ignored it, I repressed it immediately, just as I had ignored and repressed everything I'd seen, heard and felt since the day I'd come to the garage. From the very first day I had been "Ron's girl," and though I knew perfectly well Sabina had been "Ron's girl" I'd never asked, "Why not Sabina?" I'd never once asked myself why Tina thought I was her mother, why she didn't think Sabina could be. At the beginning of my first long conversation with Sabina she'd kissed me on my lips and asked pointedly, "Do you mind?" She'd recommended the bar to me on the grounds that the food was as tasty as the girls were beautiful — she, who'd called Alec a skirt-chaser. When I'd told her Tissie had already taken me to the bar, she'd clenched her fists and exclaimed, "Tissie took you! Why that little hypocrite!" The meaning of that outburst was unambiguous, but I'd repressed it immediately. I couldn't let it dawn on me that Sabina was jealous of Tissie because Tissie had made the first pass at me. I couldn't let myself imagine that Sabina was furious because Tissie had betrayed her. I couldn't, because I had suppressed all the clues that would have allowed me to imagine that. Just one day before Sabina's outburst Jose had exclaimed, "Sure there are couples, lots of them, there's hardly anything else." Who were they? Not Ted and Tissie; they avoided each other like mortal foes. Ted and Tina? I didn't count that. Jose and Sabina? "Not on your life," Jose had said. "You never got to know your sister, did you? We were never a couple and never will be." Who, then? Sabina and Tissie! Until I came. They fought over me and Tissie won the first round. But Sabina wasn't someone to be outdone, ever. She'd immediately gotten even with "that little hypocrite." Just before taking me to the bar she'd insisted I wear my blue jeans and workshirt, commenting, "You look perfect as you are; you even smell perfect." And how proudly and spitefully she'd paraded me in front of Tissie, her arm locked in mine! That very night she'd told me about "love in every conceivable form and sex in every imaginable combination, position or pattern." And that scene she'd made with Alec, baring all her teeth the moment she'd figured out what he was to me! She'd been jealous of him!

I'd repressed it, all of it, and I didn't hear what Tissie told me. I crawled frantically toward the wall. When I reached it, I pushed myself up, using all my strength to hold Tissie's body an arm's length away from me. My face contorted with fear, as if I were struggling with some terrible beast, I continued crying, "I can't! Get away from me!"

Tissie's whole body was trembling and she started crying uncontrollably. "You bitch!" she said between sobs, like a badly injured and frustrated child, "You filthy bitch. You do it with Sabina. You do it with Tina. What's wrong with me? I'm too low for you, is that it? I'm just a gutter slut, is that it? I'll show you how low I am!"

She started kicking me. As soon as I let her arms go she started hitting me, hard, hurting me. I ran toward the door. I cried hysterically, "Get away — you beast!" How inhuman. How terribly mean! If I'd heard, seen or felt anything since the day of my arrival, I would have known that she couldn't possibly have expected me to act the way I did, that she couldn't possibly have foreseen my scandalized surprise. She'd been so obviously disgusted the morning I'd told her I'd enjoyed sex with a man. She'd gotten her first clue as to who I must really be when she'd seen me on Sabina's bed, my lips on Sabina's cheek. "I didn't know," she'd said. And now she knew. How had Tissie felt when Sabina had escorted me past her with a spiteful, victorious grin, and her vengeful, "Evening, Tissie"? It was Tissie who was betrayed by her lover and I was the instrument of that betrayal. She'd hated me for that. How indignantly she'd said, "You don't look like Sabina's sister!" I was obviously her lover, her old flame. And my more recent flame's nickname must obviously have been "short for Alexandra." Betrayed and alone, what could she have felt when she saw me "doing it" with Tina? Why was I "doing it" with Sabina, with Alexandra, with Tina, but not with Tissie? Why was she being left out? What was wrong with her? How could I possibly have been so surprised? How could I have been such a monster as to cry, "Get away — you beast"?

I was altogether hysterical, on the verge of falling apart. I couldn't take any more. But more took place that night, infinitely more. I fell off a precipice into an abyss. I lost all control over myself and fell to pieces. Yet it was precisely when I reached the bottom of the abyss that I regained control over myself and held myself together, on my own, if only for an instant, for the first time since I'd come to the garage.

Hurting from Tissie's kicks and blows, I lunged at her, pushed her away from me and ran out of her room, leaving her writhing on the floor, bawling.

I ran straight to my room and was about to slip into my bed — when I froze. What I saw, what I felt — it was impossible. It simply couldn't be true. Ted was inside my bed in Tina's room. "Not you!" I shrieked. His eyes were wide open and looked terror-stricken, exactly as mine must have looked when I'd found Tissie on top of me. My hands flew at his eyes, pulling frantically to remove the arms with which he quickly protected them, scratching his face with my fingernails. "Out!" I shrieked. "Out!" I felt his blood on my hands and continued struggling to reach his face.

Tina sat up, paralyzed with terror. Suddenly she leaped on Ted's bed and tried to pull my hands away from Ted's face. "Don't, Sophia!" she pleaded. "Don't! You're killing him! Stop it!"

"Get away, Tina!" I shrieked. "Don't protect him!" I was absolutely wild. But Tina wouldn't let go; she clung to my wrists and kept pushing my arms away from him. I was like a trapped beast, lunging at my prey but tearing myself in my attempt to reach him. She hung on me like a dead weight, her face frozen in a grimace of unbelieving horror, her jaw moving soundlessly, incapable of articulating her plea.

I ran out of the room like an injured animal, dragging Tina with me. As soon as we reached the hall, she released my wrists and rushed back to Ted's bedside.

I flew across the hall to Jose's room. I was beside myself with rage and frustration. I switched on his light, flung myself on his bed and shook him with all my strength. Jose literally leaped out of my grasp across the room, shouting, "Holy shit!"

I was still stark naked but that fact didn't once cross my mind. I jumped after Jose and started tugging him out of his room. "He's raping her! Help me! He's raping her!" Jose looked totally bewildered as I pulled him by the arm across the hall to Tina's room.

The light was on. Ted lay on my bed, staring at me, the blood from the scratch on his cheek staining my pillow. Tina kneeled alongside the bed, bawling, wiping Ted's wound with a corner of my sheet. I went completely out of my mind. I started to push Jose toward the bed and screeched, "Kill him! Kill him! Get him out of here!"

Jose drew his own conclusions from the scene and once again exclaimed, "Holy shit!" Then he turned around, his face a grimace of disgust and contempt, and slapped my face so hard that I went reeling to the floor. He then grabbed my arm and dragged me out of Tina's room. His voice filled with revulsion, he hissed at me, "You pervert! What did you ever have to do with Ron? And all those years I spent thinking you must have been some piece of ass! You sure as hell are! If I catch you molesting that kid just one more time, I'll send your ass flying so far —"

"No!" I shrieked, prostrate on my chest, my teeth biting into the rug. "You're crazy! You're all crazy!" Jose left me lying there, exactly as I had left Tissie. "Help me!" I shrieked.

"Go sleep in Ted's room and shut your trap!" Jose shouted.

That was the bottom of the abyss. I lay naked in the hallway, clawing the rug with my fingernails, biting it with my teeth. I've never fallen so low. Yet it was precisely at that point, the lowest point, that I came to myself. For the first time in weeks I stopped worrying about Tina, and Ted vanished completely from my mind.

I literally became indifferent to their relationship with each other, and I remained indifferent until the end of my stay in that house and for ten years after that. For the first time in weeks, maybe in my whole life, I started to concentrate exclusively on myself. I was the pervert. I was the rapist, the child-molester. Only four days earlier Jose had seen me on Tina's bed, holding her hand, while Tina had explained, "I'd have called you if she'd hurt me." Jose had caught me in the act. I couldn't be Ron's girl nor any man's.

Suddenly I knew exactly what I had to do. I rose to my feet, spat the dirt and carpet wool out of my mouth, and held my head up proudly, defiantly. I was determined not to let myself be thrown naked into the garbage dump and pushed into the river with the city's trash. The pieces all came together. I had perfect control over myself. The nightmare was over. It was my second waking.

I walked straight to Jose's room and threw his door open. I felt as strong as an ox and as determined as a locomotive. No one and nothing was going to stop me from showing Jose once and for all that everything he'd thought about me for the past four days was as wrong as wrong could be.

In a single move I pulled off his blanket, tore off his underclothes and threw myself at him. He shouted, "What the hell?" and started to move away, but I wrapped myself around his body and hissed, "You're staying right where you are, mister. You're not going to call me those names and get away with it. I'll show you what a piece of ass Ron's girl was. I'll show you who it is you're calling a child-molester. I'll make you eat those words until you throw them up!" I clung to him with all my might until he stopped trying to move away. Then I started caressing him, crawling all over him, kissing and licking and biting him everywhere. When he came I didn't let him pause for a second but kept right on going. I didn't even let myself pause when I came. "There's only one person in this whole house that I ever wanted to molest," I told him, "and that person has a prick and is not a little girl!" He came again, and still I didn't let up. "I wanted you since the day you took me on the tour," I said, "and I wanted you badly, the way only a woman who loves men can want a man. You're terribly wrong about me, Jose. I never made love to Tina. I never dreamed of it. I know why you suspect me. I learned about Tissie and Sabina only tonight. But you're wrong about me! I want you, Jose, only you!" He came again. At last he begged me, "Please, Sophie, no more! I can't," and fell asleep exhausted. Only then did I stop. I lay back proudly. I had won!

The sun was starting to come up. As I lay on the pillow I shared with Jose, I heard Sabina walk through the hall to her room. I realized why Tissie had chosen that night. Was Sabina returning from a job or from an all-night orgy at her friend's mattressed apartment? I no longer cared. I was proud of myself and felt completely relaxed. I fell asleep perfectly satisfied, even happy.

I woke up with Jose's lips on mine. He was sitting by me, all dressed. It must have been noon. "You really are some woman," he whispered.

"Jose's woman?" I asked.

He asked. "What was all that about last night?"

I told him, without a trace of my former anger, everything I knew about Ted and Tina. The only comment he made was a defense of Ted. "If it wasn't for Ted, the kid would be on heroin right now and probably going out every night to —"

"You don't believe me!" I exclaimed.

"I believe everything you said. But you don't know Tissie, or Seth," he said.

"What do they have to do with it?" I asked.

"How about just forgetting last night?" he suggested. I looked for nothing better. I forgot immediately and continued forgetting, year after year. "You going bus riding again?" he asked.

"If you stay in this room all day, I'll stay," I told him. "If you leave, I'll follow you wherever you go. If you won't let me I'll cling to you."

"So you really mean it?" he asked.

"Mean what?"

"Jose's girl," he said.

"Woman." I corrected. "Ron's girl, Jose's woman."

"You're as crazy as Sabina," he said.

"Of course. We're twins," I exclaimed. "What else do you know about her?"

"She once gave me the same shock you did," he said.

"With Tissie?" I asked.

"With Tissie," he said. "Ron never told me anything about Sabina. She's stiff as a board, he once said, but I didn't believe him. She don't look like a board. You're twins for looks. When we started here, Sabina's looks drove me batty. I told her. Her room's always been right there, right across from mine. That night she left her door open. She and Tissie. I didn't believe it."

"What else do you know?" I asked.

"She left her door open again the next night. And the night after that."

"Anything else?" I asked, turning my face away from his.

Jose's tone changed. "She's terrific. There's no one like her. Without her this place would have collapsed a month after we started."

"What about you?" I asked.

"She's the brains," he said. "I'm just her flunkey. She's got all the ideas. She's the one who works them all out. And she's always the first to try it out and see if it works. Like I said, she's terrific."

"So are you," I said, kissing him.

"Let anyone say there's something wrong with Sabina and I'll send him to see the sky!" he continued. "She's no twin of yours, Sophie, but once you stop asking her to be that, you see that she's got no twins; she's in a class all her own; that Sabina is on the ball like no one I ever met. And she's no board. Ron wanted the one thing she couldn't give him."

"And Tina?" I asked.

"You tell me," he said.

"Breakfast?" I suggested.

Jose threw a robe over me and carried me to the kitchen. I was happier than I'd been since my first bicycle trip with Ron. "This is my world," I thought. I agreed with you. I had completely forgotten everything that had happened the previous night.

I had found myself when I had risen from the rug, resolved to win Jose, but I lost myself as soon as I won him. I immersed myself in him, annihilated myself, became Jose's shadow. I got up when he got up, ate my meals with him, spent the morning with him in the garage, the afternoon in the workshop, the evening on a walk or ride. We washed together, laughed together, worked together, slept together. I ceased being Sophia even in my own eyes. I was Jose's woman. And I was happy, not only at the beginning but to the very end. I was accepted, I was loved, and I was an apprentice again. I stopped worrying about anyone else. I left Tina to Ted. I left Vic to Seth (I didn't tell you about that; you didn't miss much.). I left Sabina to Tissie, and I left both of them to their buyers. The house did indeed consist of nothing but couples. I was overjoyed to be one of them.

The destruction of my happiness began with a phone call from Alec.

"Hello, Sophie, I'm really sorry about the way I acted, what I said —"

"I don't ever want to see you again!" I shouted into the phone.

"Please. Sophie, don't hang up!" he pleaded. "Minnie and the others — they're dying to see you!"

"What for?" I asked. "To preach about heroin and prostitution? I don't want to hear about it."

"I said I was sorry, Sophie. No, I told them about the school and all that. About street people running their own activities and about the things you learned to do. Hugh was really impressed. He said he's been thinking about getting involved with something like that. Minnie was impressed too. And you know Daman. But he wants to see you too. He and Minnie broke up, you know."

"Really?" I asked. "How's he getting along by himself?"

"I don't know," Alec answered. "I only talked to him on the phone. You know, I've been thinking a lot about all those things your sister said. About selling all my time by going to that job every morning. I think she's right and it really bothers me."

"Quit!" I advised him.

"Easily said. That's one of the things I wanted to talk to you about. Is it all right if we come over?" he asked.

"Quit first," I said stupidly, thinking I was throwing him a challenge he couldn't meet.

"How about a week from Sunday?" he asked.

I hung up without answering. I was sure I'd heard the last of Alec. I quickly forgot that I'd talked to him. I rejoined Jose at the work he was doing. I fetched tools for him, oiled machines, cleaned parts, held bolts in place. I was Jose's woman. My newspaper staff friends were the last people in the world I wanted to see.

But all four of them showed up at the garage a week from Sunday. Vic let them in and Ted escorted them to the kitchen. When they entered, Alec was slapping Ted on the back, telling him, "I understand your point about the heroin. But I was saying —"

Minnie walked up to me and shook my hand coldly. "I suppose you never will forgive us for that *Omissions* —"

"Oh that!" I said. "What an appropriate name! I almost forgot it. You're right, I never will forgive you."

Hugh made no reference to it. He only said, "Good to see you again, Sophie. Alec says you're doing some exciting things here." He shook my hand politely.

Daman neither shook my hand nor said anything; he just sat down. I supposed that his break-up with Minnie meant that he lost both his will and his voice. I felt sorry for him.

Alec started to make introductions. "This is Ted. The girl is Tina. There's also Tissie and Sabina, but I guess they're not up yet. And over there — Ron, is it?"

I flew across the room toward Alec shouting, "Ron? What kind of a joke is that? Who the hell told you about Ron?"

"Your mother," Alec answered contritely.

"Your mother?" Jose asked. "Sabina told me years ago she was dead!"

"I just talked to her a week ago!" Alec insisted. "She's still waiting for your phone call."

"What else did you tell her?" I asked.

"Christ, I don't know — I mentioned your sister," he admitted.

"My sister! You ran to her to tell her about —" I started.

"Jesus, Sophie, you didn't want me telling her what you told me to tell her?" he asked desperately.

Tina and Ted had been cluttering the table with bread, cheeses and beer, and at this point they invited all of us, hosts and guests, to join them at lunch.

I lost interest in Alec and sat down next to Jose. Everyone started eating. Minnie broke the silence. "I understand you run a school here."

"A school!" Jose exclaimed. "We run a school?"

"I've never once been to school, ever." Tina contributed.

"But that's what Alec told me!" Minnie insisted. "Was he misinformed?"

Alec looked helplessly at me but I ignored him so he ventured out on his own. "I said it was sort of a school, Minnie. But it's not called a school. People learn things here but it's not structured. What I mean is — at least that's how I understand it —"

Just then Sabina and Tissie came in together. Alec looked relieved — but only for a second.

"Well, well! The reverend!" Sabina said with mock enthusiasm. "Don't let me interrupt you, Reverend. Your sermon is fascinating!" Then, imitating Alec's inflection, "What I mean is — at least that's how I understand it — Simply fascinating. May I also suggest: you know, I was about to say, from my point of view, on the other hand, if you see what I mean? Please do go on, Reverend!"

Alec sulked. "I wasn't saying anything much. And I'm not a reverend any more. I handed in my resignation over a week ago, and yesterday was my last day at work."

I smiled at Alec. He'd taken up my challenge after all.

"So you've left the millions of citizens behind and joined the criminals!" Sabina exclaimed.

Alec was visibly disappointed by the meager congratulations he received for his courageous act and he sulked in silence.

Minnie took the opportunity to resume her quest. She turned to Sabina and said, "Maybe you'd be so kind as to answer my questions."

Sabina looked Minnie up and down, smiled, and asked, "Do you happen to be employed by the police department?"

Minnie glanced at me for help that I wasn't about to provide and she continued on her own, "I understand that you're all indigenous to the inner city, so-called street people —"

"And you being a broad from the suburbs would like to know how it feels to be screwed in the inner city," Sabina butted in.

Minnie turned to Tissie next and demanded indignantly, "Is it possible to talk to any of you?"

"Who the hell are you?" Tissie fired back.

"What the fuck do you want to know so badly?" Jose asked.

Minnie whispered something to Hugh, and Hugh turned to Jose. "Alec gave us an interesting account of your establishment — your house. We found many of the features admirable. But we would like to clarify certain points —"

"What points?" Jose asked, the hostility mounting in his voice.

"We were puzzled by the question of the financing," Hugh continued.

"You the judge?" Jose asked.

"Excuse me, the what?" Hugh asked.

"Are you the judge?" Jose asked again, emphasizing each word. "Are we on trial? When the hell were we arrested?"

At this point Daman spoke for the first time. "Well, I guess we'd better be shoving along."

Hugh got up and shook my hand politely again, and again said, "It was good to see you, Sophie."

Minnie got up and leered at Alec. "Gee, Alec, you said these people were friendly. I've seen friendlier people. They're convinced we're all cops. Even Sophie acts as if she'd never known us."

"The way out is that way," shouted Jose, pointing.

Ted and Tina accompanied them out — three of them. Alec remained seated at the kitchen table.

Tissie burped at "Alexandra" and went back to her room.

Alec turned to Sabina, pleading and contrite, his eyes focused on her hands, "I wanted to apologize for the way I looked at you last time. I know that can be insulting. I wanted to tell you I quit my job because of all those things you told me. You were right. I was a wage slave, a coward. What I wanted to ask was, is there anything I might be able to do around here?"

Sabina was stunned. "You? A professor?"

Jose nudged me to see if I was ready to return to the workshop. I was. As we walked out of the kitchen, I heard Alec saying, "You're perfectly right. I don't know how to do anything at all. I'm a complete ignoramus. But I really want to try to learn. If I could start as a mechanic —"

Jose and I finished a project we had started before lunch and we took the rest of the day off. We came back exhausted after a long car ride and walk in the country. The following morning I felt sick to my stomach when I entered the garage and saw Tina and Ted explaining the workings of a car engine to Alec.

The next time I saw Sabina I complained angrily to her, "How could you invite that — that idiot?"

"He invited himself," she said calmly. "We've never turned anyone away when we had a spare room. And the first time we do it'll be the end."

"You know perfectly well that's not a spare room," I hissed. "It's Ted's room!"

Sabina turned and walked away from me. I didn't raise the question again. I stayed with Jose. But the atmosphere grew tense.

One afternoon Alec caught me alone in the garage. Ted and Tina were in their lofts and Jose had gone downstairs to look for a part. Alec edged toward me. "I hardly recognize you as the person I once knew, Sophie."

"Then act as if you never knew me!" I said.

"There's all that talk about doing your own activities —" he started.

"Why did you stay here? What do you want?" I asked.

"I want to be close to you, if you really want to know," he said.

"It looked to me like you were panting for Sabina with your tongue hanging out," I said.

"Aw get off it, Sophie. Ted told me all about —" he started.

"So that leaves only me, doesn't it? We followed Rhea into the party and we followed Sophie out. We followed Sabina down to a sewer and who do we run into if not Sophie? But it's too late, Alec, it's way too late for anything like that."

"What does that mean?" he asked.

"I'm Jose's woman," I said proudly.

"Naw, Sophie, Jesus Christ, that's not you, that's not anyone I ever knew," he said, and I heard him; I was stung. "You're not that guy's woman. You're his rug, his cigarette lighter, his messenger, his pet. Christ, Ted's been telling me about the dope and the whorehouse, and that's bad enough. But that's nothing compared to what's been happening to you. I don't know what happens to people on heroin but it can't be any worse than what you've got. You've lost your whole personality. You're that guy's dog."

I ran from Alec and headed for the workshop, to be near Jose. He noticed my tears and asked if anything had happened.

"He told me he was only staying here because of me," I said. "He's jealous of you!"

"I don't blame him," Jose said.

"Jose," I cried. "Please make him leave."

"I can't do that, Sophie," he said. "The guy says he's got no place to go, and we've got space. Can't just tell him to leave. If he wanted to start his own garage we could help him like we did last year with that one kid —"

"Jose," I pleaded. "I was so happy until he came."

"So was I, Sophie," he said. "I mean, I still am happy. I don't see that he should ruin anything. He's not a bad guy, you know. If you're through with him, tell him. If you're not — well, you're your own person is what Sabina always says."

"Jose," I said, crying. "Remember when you said Sabina was terrific? That there was no one else like her? Well, there's no one else like you," I bawled, "You're more terrific than she is!" I fell into Jose's powerful arms and he held me and pressed me — as if I were his rug, his cigarette lighter, his pet. And that's all I was. I couldn't stop bawling because I knew Alec was right.

I had one more encounter with Alec before everything caved in. It was on a Wednesday morning.

One morning each week, on a Wednesday, Jose had an errand on which I didn't accompany him. He asked me not to, and I didn't pry. I didn't learn a great deal about Jose during my stay with him, nor he about me. We never asked; there were too many things we didn't want to talk about. I didn't pry into his few secrets and he didn't once ask me what Alec had been to me during my university days.

On all previous Wednesday mornings I had stayed in our room, or gone for a walk, waiting for Jose to return from his secret errand. But that morning I went into the garage. I had decided to settle the question of Alec on my own. The three of them — Alec, Ted and Tina — were working by themselves, each on a different project. I walked right up to Alec. He stopped what he was doing and stared at me. His face looked sad, but I was determined. "Why don't you leave this place, mister!" I told him firmly. "You don't belong here. You're not like us."

Tina and Ted both stopped working and looked at me, waiting.

"Jesus, what did I do now?" Alec asked, hanging his head.

"You're still here! That's what you did now!" I snapped.

Tina butted in with a barely audible, "Sophia, you've got no right —"

"Stay out of this and mind your own boyfriend, Tina!" I snapped. "You're the one who has no right!" Tina started to sob.

"Sophie, listen to me," Alec said slowly. "It's you who've got to leave this place. You're the one that doesn't belong here. Don't you see what's happening? You're sick, don't you see that?"

"You just watch who you're calling sick, mister!" I snapped. "Have you ever looked at yourself? You're disgusting. We're here for life! Why are you here? For a broad! You don't know what life is, mister, because broads are all you've got on your brain. To spend week after week crawling on the floor and greasing up your arms just on the chance that she'll come to you — that's what I call sick, mister. Real sick!"

"I'm going to leave soon, Sophie," he announced, his anger mounting. "But not before trying to make you see what you're turning yourself into! I know for a fact that you don't know shit about what happens here. I've watched you. Whenever anything comes up, you stick your head up your ass. You hide out inside that boyfriend of yours, or husband or father or whatever the hell he is to you. Well, I've picked up a few clues and you're going to hear them, like them or not. Ted can bear me out. Who do you think pays for the great school of yours and that great love affair? You don't think it's the piddling we do around here, do you? Allow me to straighten you out before I leave. It's your sister's and Tissie's whoring that pays for that expensive house and all the food and the three cars and all that expensive shit that's displayed in every room. And your boyfriend's pimping. That's right, that's the name for it! Pimping! But with all they take in they can't pay for all of it, what with Sabina having her own expensive hobbies and Tissie her heroin. And this piddling around with all the newest machinery doesn't even pay for its own costs. This garage stopped supporting itself before you ever came here. Ted stopped stealing when it dawned on him he was supporting a narcotics depot. For a while he just took the cars apart. But he didn't want other people working for him either, so he helped them set up their own garage. Nothing comes in here anymore except the junk they can't get rid of at the other garage. What do you think pays for all this shit? Just Seth's heroin. And Seth is figuring out that he doesn't want to carry all that ballast. Yea, ballast. Dead weight. All he wants is his boyfriend Vic. He needs Ted as a front and he needs your friend part-time, for the contacts. But he doesn't need you or me or the kid or ninety-nine out of every hundred machines here — and he's getting ready to dump all that. What'll you do when he starts dumping? You tell me, Sophie! Learn to steal cars? You can't even steal cigarettes from supermarkets! Get a job? A year at the highest paying job wouldn't pay for one of the machines that's here! What'll you do then, Sophie? Stick your head up your ass? You tell me!"

Swinging my whole arm, I whacked Alec on his cheek and ran to my room. I confronted Jose as soon as he returned. "Alec has to go, Jose. I can't stand being in the same house with him."

Jose fidgeted. "I don't know what to say, Sophie. I thought that got worked out. I thought you two kept away from each other."

"I can't stand it!" I repeated.

"How about a trip?" he asked, brightening. "A long trip all over this continent, just you and me."

I smiled. "Just Jose and his woman." Then I asked, "Who'd pay for it?"

"You know Sabina would help us out," he said without hesitating.

"Jose," I said, "I don't want to go on Sabina's money."

"We don't have much of our own," he said.

"I want to go on my own money. I can get at least as much as Sabina does, and maybe more. It'll be a better trip if we go on my money," I insisted.

"That's up to you, Sophie," he said sadly.

"I'm my own person," I said.

"That's right. Sophie, you're your own person," Jose said, walking out of the room.

I ran out after him and slipped my arm into his. I tried to smile. "It's just talk, Jose. You know that, don't you? It's all just talk. Jose's woman is a big talker, but she doesn't ever do the things she talks about. She doesn't care whose money it is and she doesn't want to take a trip. She's not going to start working and she really doesn't care who lives here. All Jose's woman wants is to be loved by her man."

I can't tell you what happened during the days or weeks that followed. I don't even know if it was days or weeks or months. Jose and Sabina clashed with Alec and Ted once, perhaps several times; I think one of them hit the other, but I don't remember. I don't think this is an instance of repressed memory. I think I didn't register anything at the time; there was nothing to repress. All I remember is eating with Jose, working with him, sleeping with him, loving him and being loved by him.

The first event I remember took place on my last day in the garage. It must have been a Sunday morning. I was working. There was a terrible amount of noise. I was vaguely aware that Minnie, Hugh and Daman were in the garage. Everyone I knew was in the garage. All of them seemed to be talking at the same time. I didn't know how long they'd been there. Minnie was shouting about the desire for money and the desire for power over underlings; Sabina was shouting about moralizing high school teachers who dreamed of being dictators. I ignored them and turned the grinder on to sharpen my chisel.

Jose put his hands on my shoulders and said, "Your friends came to visit you too, Sophie, not just Alec."

"They're not my friends, Jose," I said calmly. "Make them leave. They're not your friends either."

I heard Alec whisper to Minnie, "You see what I mean?"

I went on grinding until I was done.

Minnie continued her argument with Sabina. "My moralizing, as you call it, never had that effect on a human being. Look at her! It's awful! Did you know what she was like before she came here? She was the liveliest intellect in the university! Alec swears you don't keep her on drugs but I don't believe it. How else could you have gotten her into the state she's in? Shame on you! Your own sister! And what have you done to your own intellect? You've chained it, to serve your boundless lust! How can you justify your crimes? You say you're part of a process of change and it sounds so good because everyone wants that. But a change for the better, not for the worse! Why do you leave that question out? I know why! That world-changing process you claim to be part of is nothing but your own deranged ambition! You'd like to change the world all right — into an empire of lesbians!"

Sabina lunged at Minnie and pinned her back against the wall, but Minnie continued, "You're nothing but a depraved, ruthless businessman, a millionaire aiming for billions, a lousy imperialist. You'll stampede over anything that stands in your way and destroy it. You'll turn your own sister into a mechanical doll, a grinning vegetable."

Sabina whacked Minnie with her fist and Minnie slid slowly to the floor, holding her cheek in both hands, whimpering.

Sabina took hold of Minnie's shoulders, raised her up and held her pinned against the wall. "Now you listen to me, sister," she said with contempt.

"I'm no sister of yours!" Minnie exclaimed, controlling her sobs.

"That's what I always thought," Sabina said. "The first time I saw you I knew you were a cop. How decent of you to admit it! A plain, simple cop, ruining no one's life, just keeping people happy. I'll tell you what's wrong with Sophia. She spent too many years being policed — by cops, like you! Missionaries, professors, policemen! You're the ones who took care of that lively intellect! You're the ones who chained it — to your filthy uses. You might as well have pulled it out of her! You wound it so tightly around those so-called projects that aren't even your own that she lost all control over it!"

I stared at Sabina's back, spellbound, fascinated by every sound she made, horrified.

"By the time she came here," Sabina continued, "she didn't know who or what she was, she had no mind of her own, she couldn't choose, she couldn't decide. Don't give us credit for that! You get all that credit. It's thanks to you that she trembled with fear when she came in contact with living people. It's thanks to you that she had nightmares when her imagination broke out of its prison. It's thanks to you that she broke down the moment she felt desire stirring inside her. She broke down because for the first time in her life she wasn't being policed. She broke down because she didn't know how to be her own person. When the police inside her were removed there was nothing inside her to hold her up. You'd seen to that, you and your apparatus, your establishment, your school. You'd removed whatever was her and you'd replaced it with police. Don't tell me about a grinning vegetable, you mechanical doll! For the first time in her life she's fighting not to be one, and she's going to win that fight!"

I felt like passing out but stopped myself when I thought of Alec's comment about my sticking my head up my ass "whenever anything comes up." Everything inside me was coming up.

As if in a dream, I heard Hugh start talking, calmly, politely. "Why don't you let Minnie go now, Miss Nachalo? I'm sure she heard you. We all did. You're ain eloquent speaker. Very eloquent. And also very convincing. I don't think any of us, not even Minnie, would care to deny any part of your argument. We're all familiar to some extent with the destructive power of the institutions you describe. I think what's at issue here is the alternatives to those institutions. Two friends of ours, Alec and your sister, discovered such an alternative in this establishment, and I must admit that when Alec first told me about it I was immensely impressed — so impressed that I've abandoned my studies and thrown myself into what I at first understood to be similar work."

Hugh looked beautiful to me — exactly as he'd looked when he'd walked at the head of the funeral procession, carrying the coffin of our dead newspaper, wearing his black suit and his funny black hat.

"I remained impressed after our first visit," he continued. "Unlike Minnie, I wasn't antagonized by your hostility. On the contrary, I considered it a very healthy reaction against the intrusion of what you call missionaries, educators and police-men. As soon as we left I realized that was exactly what we were. You were per-fectly right to eject judges who hold up the dominant institutions as the standard of human decency. I wanted to insert myself into a similar struggle, but unlike Alec I didn't think it appropriate to impose myself here. I hope I'm not boring you; I'm coming to the point as quickly as I can. I moved out of the university envi-ronment and into an area where the human consequences of our social order are less disguised, more visible; I don't live very far from here. Instead of frequenting university seminars I began to frequent street corners, bars and pool halls. I soon learned that you're right on yet another account. What you called a world-changing process is indeed taking place. And it is taking place precisely where you say it is: among those you call street people. I began to meet regularly with a group of those so-called street people —"

"So you went to the jungle and started to preach to the natives!" Sabina exclaimed sarcastically.

"Vampire!" Minnie hissed, making a move toward Sabina.

"Please let me finish, Minnie!" Hugh begged. "I'm just coming to the point. I learned that, at least in this neighbor-hood, your establishment has a certain repu-tation among the so-called street people. Your establishment is known. I became indignant. I thought that I had been lied to, and that Alec had been badly deceived. But I couldn't make myself believe what I saw and heard. That's why I responded with interest when Alec called —"

Jose bellowed, "He called you here? I thought you just dropped in to see your friends!"

"I'm sorry if I spoiled anything for you, Alec," Hugh said, and then continued addressing Sabina. "What I've seen here confirms everything I've been told. Your establishment is as great an exploiter of this community as all the institutions you so eloquently condemn. And in many ways it's worse. Under the guise of being an integral part of the rising community, you are in fact leeches on that community, you push it back down, sucking its strength out of it. You are incapacitating that community precisely at the moment when it is trying to raise itself up with its own strength. That fellow over there" (he pointed to Seth) "is known to your neighbors as one of the biggest heroin dealers in the entire area. The one behind him has a somewhat more modest reputation for similar accomplishments. You and your friend — I forget her name — are known locally as the regional Cleopatras. This fellow here, Sophia's companion, is known —"

Sabina's fists were both clenched. She started to move toward Hugh but stopped when she saw Minnie lunging toward her. Sabina arched her back like a tigress; she would have sent Minnie tumbling to the ground if Alec hadn't jumped behind her and pinned her arms against her sides. Minnie's blow landed squarely in the middle of Sabina's face. Jose, who is considerably smaller than Alec, leaped at Alec and yanked him away from Sabina.

Alec screamed at Jose, "That's right, pimp, you protect her. That's what she's got you here for. Protection. You're her henchman, her time-server, her parasite. For protection and for fattening her pigs so she can sell them for a good price!"

Jose's blow sent Alec reeling across the room. "There's only been one parasite here, pretty boy," Jose shouted to Alec, "and that's been you. You never learned to act without orders, you never learned what work is, you never learned that it's your motions and not the foreman's orders that make things move. Save your names for yourself!"

While Jose spoke, Daman was moving toward him, and Hugh took a step toward Alec, who lay on the ground near Seth. Both stopped abruptly. Seth stepped over Alec and pointed a gun at Hugh. Vic, behind Seth, pointed another at Daman.

I screamed. "Not Hugh," I shouted, running across the room until my body touched the barrel of Seth's gun. "Shoot me! Not Hugh! He never did any harm to anyone!"

Seth pushed me to the floor. "You!" he ordered, aiming his gun at Hugh again and pointing his other hand at Alec, "Pick him up and get him out of here. Quick! One, two! All of you! Shoo! Scat! Clear out!"

With both guns waving in their faces, Hugh, Daman and Minnie all helped Alec to his feet and started moving toward the door.

"Hugh!" I cried weakly. "Take me with you!"

Hugh looked uncertainly at Seth and then at Jose, but didn't take a step toward me.

"Take me!" I pleaded. But Hugh continued to accompany Alec to the door.

Seth jumped toward Hugh and poked him with his gun. "You heard her, boss! Get her out too! Step on it! The whole fucking lot of you!"

Hugh walked toward me. Sabina, Ted, Tina, even Jose didn't make a move. They looked like statues. Hugh picked me up in his arms and carried me out of the garage. I didn't leave on my own two feet.

Hugh set me down on the ground as soon as we were outside. I noticed that Daman and Minnie were staring at me as if I were a circus freak. "What are you two looking at?" I asked. "Haven't you ever seen a nitwit before? Get away from me! Go home!" Daman walked reluctantly and slowly across the street, got into his car and drove away. Minnie continued staring, seemed about to say something, and then rushed away, on foot, in the opposite direction. I turned to Hugh and said, "Thanks a lot. I wouldn't have made it by myself. I'd like to see you again."

Hugh scribbled his address on a piece of paper and walked away. I looked sadly at the garage and the shabby looking building behind it. Then I started to walk away from both. I became aware that Alec was following me. I turned and shouted, "Shoo! Scat!"

"Do you know where you're going?" he asked.

I screamed as loudly as I could: "It's none of your fucking business!"

I turned and walked on. He was still behind me, though not as close as before. I tried to get rid of him for the second time. "Leave me alone, stupid asshole. Do you think I've stopped being Jose's rug in order to become yours? I loved him the way I never loved you! Do you think I'm glad I left him? I know you forced me to do it and — listen to me, Alec — I'll hate you for that until the end of my life! Now get away from me!" I walked again and thought I had shaken him off. I turned a corner just to make sure. And there he was, turning the corner at the other end of the street. I saw a bottle in the gutter, grabbed it, and ran towards him with it. He just stood where he was and waited. I didn't look at his face to see if it was sad or bewildered or angry. I stopped a few feet from him and hurled the bottle at his chest with all my might. "You bastard!" I screamed. "You've got no right to take another person's life into your hands no matter how bad you think it is or how good you think you can make it! You're the only real beast I've known in my whole life!" I turned and ran from him. I ran until I convinced myself he was no longer following me. I sat down on a curb to rest before walking on. I walked all the way home. I mean "home." To Luisa's.

I knocked. I hoped Luisa was home. Over all the years when I hadn't once visited, I had always carried my key in my purse. But just then my purse was far away, in Jose's room. I would have let myself in through a window if she hadn't been home. I had, after all, become a "criminal."

Luisa opened the door and beamed. At least she seemed to find me recognizable enough! I embraced her with gratitude for that. "Well, what a surprise," she shouted.

"Have room for me?" I asked.

"The whole house!" she exclaimed.

"I'll try to pay my way," I said.

"Are you crazy?" she asked. "It's your house as much as mine. And I've got more than twice as much food and money as I need."

"Yes, I am crazy," I answered. "Do you mind?"

"I only mind your asking if I mind," she answered.

"Same job?" I asked.

"Unfortunately," she answered. "Disappointed?"

I didn't answer. "Boy friends?" I asked.

"Not this minute," she said.

"Can I go up to my room now and talk to you later?" I asked.

"You can go wherever you please and you don't have to talk to me!" she answered. But before letting me go, she threw her arms around me and kissed me. She had never done that for as long as I could remember.

I ran up to my room, closed the door and sat down on my familiar bed. I stared at the walls. They hadn't changed; they needed to be repainted. I felt lost — exactly as I'd felt once before, ten years earlier, when we first arrived. I didn't know where I was or why and I didn't know what to do with myself in this big city. But one thing was different. I knew someone, besides Luisa. There was one person in the city I wanted to be with. And do you know why, Yarostan? You're going to ridicule me again. Because he reminded me of you! Didn't you recognize yourself at all when I described him? I'm talking about Hugh. I thought about what he'd said a while earlier and how beautifully he'd said it. "You're incapacitating the community precisely at the moment when it is trying to raise itself up with its own strength." Compare that to this, from your newest letter: "If we don't destroy the old life, if we don't project and begin to create a new life, then we're only going to reenact our slavery on the graves of our fallen comrades." Down to the correctness, and even the shyness. I had understood Hugh. What he stood for had been "familiar" to me: I had experienced it before. I looked forward to seeing him again, I remembered him as I'd known him on the newspaper staff. And I forgot everything that happened after I left the university until I saw him again. Forgot it, repressed it, stored it away. That wasn't familiar to me. And when I did that, did I really give up life and resurrect a "corpse," as you put it?

I sat on my bed and stared at the walls because I wasn't sure I hadn't made a horrible mistake. Not that I ever thought what you said, namely that my descent to the "world of Tissie, Jose and Sabina" was a descent to your world. I loved you, Yarostan, as I've loved very few people in my life. But my love for Jose was far, far away from your world, or from mine, in a world all its own. That's why I sat and stared. I had been carried out of that underworld, I had left it behind. But I had left something down there — far more than my purse, my two started manuscripts and my junky dresses. What I killed in myself wasn't a sequence of unpleasant or painful memories, I had to kill the joy together with the pain. I had to suppress my happiness. If I had allowed that to come back to life and become a vivid memory, even for an instant, I'd have run back to the house behind the garage, crawling and begging to be let in. Don't ever tell me that world is your world, Yarostan, or that you recognize yourself in Jose. If I'd had any basis to even suspect that from any of your letters, you wouldn't have received a mere letter from me; I would have flown to you twice as fast as a letter and torn you from Mirna and Yara, from your friends, your work, your world.

If Mirna reads this letter, I hope she'll forgive me for expressing myself so crudely. I had to tell all of it or none of it. If I hadn't told you any of it, I couldn't have gone on corresponding with you. I couldn't bear your telling me how "familiar" that world of experience was to you precisely at the moment when Tina reminded me just how "familiar" it was to me. It was so "familiar" that when I emerged from it I was ready to start all over again from a point I had reached ten years earlier. Yes, I erased it so forcefully that all the ten years that preceded it temporarily went down with it. All that remained was Hugh, and Hugh was someone I had known before I ever came here — in a carton factory.

I hope none of you have your heads crammed with hackneyed notions about "mental illness." There was no such thing in my life. I'm ill when an organ or a limb doesn't function. There was nothing at all wrong with my limbs or organs. Fortunately there were no "psychologists" or "mind doctors" anywhere near me trying to "heal" what no one in the world has a right meddling with: my own life. And in this respect Luisa was a perfect gem. On the evening of my first day "home," she brought my supper up on a tray, exactly as she'd done for several days ten years earlier. She knocked lightly on the door, placed the tray on my desk, asked no questions, and left my room.

I set my alarm and the following morning — it was a Monday morning — I got up before Luisa left for work. I went downstairs, to the kitchen, embraced her and kissed her; I wanted to thank her for being such a gem.

During that first week after my "homecoming" Luisa and I were the best of friends, despite the fact that I told her nothing whatever about where I'd been or what I'd done. I didn't learn a whole lot about her either. But my conversations with her did help me sort out experiences I could safely remember from those I had to forget.

"I know you know where I've been," I told her provocatively, curious about how much she actually knew.

"With Sabina and that boy Ron," she said.

"You always thought Ron such a nice boy, didn't you Luisa?"

"Simply wonderful!" she said. "Every fascist household should have his picture on the wall."

"He's quite respectable now, you know," I said. "He joined the Mafia. Didn't Alec tell you that too?"

"Alec told me all about it," she said. "He also told me to expect a phone call from you."

"Oh, that's right," I said. "I told him I'd call. But I only told him that for his benefit — to fit into his idea of a dutiful daughter. You didn't sit up waiting, did you?"

"I did think you'd call," Luisa said sadly.

"Come off that, Luisa! When did you become so sentimental?" I asked. "Did you really expect to hear my voice say, Hello, mother? This is your daughter; I'm over at Ron's and Sabina's?"

"I'm sure Alec would have called his mother," Luisa said.

"If she'd been alive he certainly would have!" I exclaimed. "But if his mother expected such things from him, do you think he'd ever have moved back to her house?"

"If she expected that, I'd have urged him to stay as far away from her as possible!" she exclaimed. Both of us laughed. But when Luisa stopped laughing, she looked sad.

"Were you worried about me?" I asked.

"They were worried. They wanted to call the police," she said.

"I'm glad you stopped them," I said. "Who were 'they'?"

"Alec and his girlfriend," she said.

"Alec and who?" I asked.

"I think her name is Minnie," she said.

"Minnie isn't Alec's girl friend," I said. "At least, I don't think she is."

"Really?" she asked. "They came together the first time."

"The first time?" I asked. "You mean they both came again?" After my experience with Ron, I had kept my "home" and my friends worlds apart and I was disappointed by my lack of success.

"Only Alec," she answered. "He's a very nice person."

"He's what I'd call a fascist!" I snapped.

"How can you praise Ron to the sky and yet say that Alec —" she started.

"I don't want to hear about Alec!" I snapped. "Tell me about your friends."

"I used to visit an old revolutionary exile every week; a kind, well-read, generous man," she said.

"What happened, you broke up?" I asked, too offhandedly.

"He died, a year ago," she said sadly.

Poor Luisa, I thought; she's so completely alone, with nothing in her life but her job. I realized just how lonely she was toward the end of that week. I had decided to go visit Hugh. Luisa came home while I was eating supper. I think it was Friday night.

"I'm going out tonight," I said.

"With Ron again?" she asked.

"Yes, with Ron," I said.

Suddenly she started crying.

"What's wrong?" I asked. "Does Ron upset you that much?"

"No, it has nothing to do with you," she said.

"Something at your job?" I asked.

"Nothing ever happens at my job!" she bawled. "Our lives get eaten up for no reason. I'm no good to anyone, Sophia. No one needs me."

I vaguely remember telling you about this scene before. I'll try not to repeat myself, I tried to console her, but didn't really know what to say. I suggested she start dating one or several of the men she knew at work, whether or not they were married.

"They're all hateful!" she said. "Why don't you invite your friends over?"

"All right," I said — and then added sarcastically, pointlessly, "I'll bring Ron home."

She said, "It's your house, Sophia. And your life. But if you ever bring him in here again, be sure I don't know about it! I mean your nice friends, Minnie and Alec and the others they mentioned."

"Invite them yourself!" I snapped. "Here are their phone numbers! It's your house and your life. But if you ever bring them in here, be sure I don't know about it."

I left her sobbing. I resented her hostility toward my dead Ron, but I felt sorry for her at the same time. She was so starved for friendship, for affection, for love, and I had absolutely nothing to give her.

I took a bus to Hugh's neighborhood — my former neighborhood — and found his apartment. I rang, knocked, waited, but no one came. I walked around the streets. I had stupidly put on one of Luisa's dresses and I regretted that now. It was a rough neighborhood. I had never noticed just how rough. I returned to the apartment and still no one answered.

I went out again the following night, Saturday night, to look for Hugh. But as soon as I walked out of my house I noticed a familiar car across the street and a familiar face inside it: Alec's. He got out of the car as soon as he saw me and started to head toward me. I turned and ran back into the house. Luisa was in the kitchen, eating. I tiptoed through the house and slipped out by way of a back window.

I failed to find Hugh and I left him a note, begging him to call me. I waited the whole next week for his call. On the following Saturday I resolved to look for him again. That day I had another surprise.

During that week I became increasingly depressed as I waited for Hugh to call, whereas Luisa became increasingly exhilarated. Finally on Saturday morning I asked her wheat had changed so suddenly in her life.

"I have a date tonight," she said. "And I invited him to come here. Do you mind?"

"Mind!" I shouted. "I think that's great!"

"Are you going anywhere tonight?" she asked apprehensively.

"Oh, don't worry about me," I said flippantly. "I'll probably be out all night. Is he someone from work? Is he nice?"

"I'd rather not tell you," she said.

I didn't ask. Luisa spent most of the day preparing a very special meal, and the rest of it dressing. I helped her clean the whole house. She put candles in the kitchen and candles in the living room. Before I left that evening I taunted her, "Why have you kept yourself in a closet all these years, Luisa?"

She blushed. "You hussy! Do I look all right?" she asked, twirling in front of me.

"You're beautiful!" I exclaimed. "You're ravishing! Why, if you and I walked the streets together, you could quit your job and we could —"

"Sophia!" she said indignantly.

"Shocked?" I asked.

"Coming from you, yes. Are you seeing Ron again?" she asked.

"No," I said. "I'm going to a movie. Alone."

"And you're staying out all night?" she asked sadly. She was shocked. I'd forgotten what I had told her earlier.

"I'd rather not tell you," I said, imitating her. "But don't mind me. Whenever I come in, I'll run straight upstairs without looking left or right." I kissed her to apologize for my inconsistent lies and whispered, "Have a good time, hussy!" I walked out of the house in my jeans, denim shirt and Luisa's leather jacket. I looked back and saw her standing in the doorway. She smiled. She really did look ravishing, and so happy.

When I reached Hugh's apartment my heart missed a beat. The note I had left him was still under his door! I bit my lip for having spent the whole week waiting for the phone to ring. I could have come the day after I left the note and learned that he no longer lived there. I kicked myself for not having come for the first time until so many days after he'd given me his address. But then I started to wonder if he'd ever lived there, if for some mysterious reason he'd given me the wrong address.

I rushed away from Hugh's unoccupied apartment. I had an intense desire to return to my room, but remembered Luisa's date. I went to a movie, but the film was so awful I couldn't sit through it. I took a bus home. Less than two hours had passed since I'd left Luisa standing in the doorway. She and her date would just be finishing her special supper. Perhaps he'd take her out.

I stopped caring about Luisa's date; I wanted to reach my room. I opened the door quietly, and as soon as I closed it I sensed that the two lovers were locked in a tight embrace on the living room couch. I tiptoed to the staircase — and stopped.

I heard a terribly familiar voice whispering, "Jesus Christ, Luisa, I thought she wouldn't be coming in!" I ran up the stairs.

Luisa ran to the staircase and pleaded, "I'm sorry, Sophia; I wasn't expecting you so soon."

I heard Alec say weakly, "Hi, Sophie."

"I told you don't mind me!" I shouted as I slammed my door.

I sat on my bed trembling, blinded by rage. So that was her date! That unspeakably unscrupulous bastard! To gorge himself with all those years of that love-starved woman's pent-up desire — solely out of spite against me! Only a week earlier she'd described herself as a useless old rag, squeezed drier every day. "I'm no good to anyone; no one needs me." With what blind, what mindless hunger had she become a willing instrument of Alec's revenge? With what deluded longing had she given away so much love to requite his mere spite? Poor Luisa! She had wanted me to bring my "nice friends" home!

I knew I wouldn't be able to face Luisa again. I knew I'd kill her if I told her the truth, and if I said nothing she'd read it on my face. As soon as I heard the door of Luisa's bedroom close, I started to pack a small bag. I had so pitifully little to pack. I walked downtown and napped uncomfortably in the bus station. In the morning I found a cheap room and paid a week's rent with almost all the money Luisa had given me. The room had roaches as well as mice. I couldn't stand to stay in it during the day and went back to the bus station. Nor did I sleep well in my room that night. But I was definitively "on my own," for the first time in my life. I could forge my own life, guided only by my own lights. And what did I make of myself "on my own"? Exactly what almost everyone else does. I got up early Monday morning, bought a newspaper and read the job advertisements. The only ones I circled were the ones that said "no experience required." If I'd told anyone I was a "crack mechanic" or a welder, he would have laughed — and I couldn't have proved it. I walked until my feet were sore. I filled forms and answered ridiculous questions. By mid-afternoon I had found a job which I would start the following morning. Since I wouldn't get my first pay for two weeks, I asked for an advance, telling the "personnel man" that I was out of food money. He pulled a bill out of his wallet, saying, "Pay me back in two weeks, Miss." I worked in a fiberglass factory. It was awful. If I've ever had a bad experience in my life, it was that job. I don't understand why people put up with that. I won't describe it to you now.

It was only then, after my first week of wage labor, that I was really a zombie, a vegetable. By the following Sunday I was so tired that I slept until mid-afternoon. My whole body ached when I dragged myself out of bed. I left my room, walked mechanically to the bus stop and rode to my former neighborhood. I approached the address Hugh had given me as sullenly as I'd walked toward the fiberglass factory every morning that week. I knocked and rang, from habit. I perked up with expectation when a woman opened the door. I asked about Hugh. She'd never heard of him.

I dragged myself along every street in the area — every street but one. I studied the names listed on every apartment house, the names on all mailboxes and on the doors of small houses. I walked into every open store and looked through the display window, mail slot or keyhole of every closed one. It had been dark for at least two hours when I reached a door that said "Project House" in roughly painted letters. I tried the door; it was open. The room was full of boys and men, my age or younger, all rough-looking, all "street people." With my jeans, my hair in a cap and Luisa's leather jacket, I didn't attract any attention; I was merely another one of them — maybe younger and not quite rugged enough. I looked from one unfamiliar face to the next, and recognized Hugh's.

I realized that Hugh had seen me the minute I'd walked in but hadn't taken a step toward me. He just stared at me; his face expressed disbelief and profound disappointment. I walked up to him and asked, in a whisper, "You don't recognize me?"

"I'll meet you outside in five minutes," he said, and turned his back to me.

I shuffled through the crowd and waited. He came out, grabbed my arm and marched me rapidly away from the project house. "How did you find me?" he asked.

"Hugh!" I exclaimed. "I've been looking for you since you carried me out of the garage!"

"I'm sorry I did that," he said. "A gun was pointed at me."

"You can't know how badly I've wanted to be with you," I said, almost pleading.

"You're wrong," he said. "I knew. I made a bad mistake when I gave you my address."

"You mean you left that room because I might find you there?" I asked.

"Yes, Sophie, because you might find me there," he said.

"Didn't you care at all what happened to me?" I asked.

"Yes," he said slowly. "I cared very much what happened to a person I had known — a person I had disliked, distrusted and feared, if you must know the truth."

"Why?" I asked.

"Perhaps Alec could explain that to you," he said. "I should add that I also admired you at times, with that grudging admiration we sometimes have for something we cannot understand, something we fear. I don't believe your 'why,' Sophie. You cannot possibly be so naive, so blind. First Lem, then Thurston, then Alec kissed the ground you walked on. And you have the nerve to ask me why I feared you? Do you want my honest critique of that fine theatrical performance to which you subjected us, pretending to grovel and crawl in front of your Jose for the benefit of your entire train of admirers? I'm only glad that Thurston and Lem were unable to attend — for their sake. I cared, Sophie — at a distance, just as I admired you at a distance. It was you who drove me out of my wits when I was about to start graduate school — you and your 'sister' and her world-changing project. I longed to be where you were — yet far removed from you. Finally I was driven to 'join' you — but only in spirit. I couldn't do what Alec did to himself. The closest I wanted to get to you was to throw myself into your type of engagement, your project. I found it here, and as soon as I found it I learned that you and your establishment were indeed part of it, of its foulness. What I've found here is simple, unsophisticated people who are discovering what it is to be human. They're discovering it on their own, without seers —"

I interrupted to ask, "What are you doing here then?"

"I'm discovering it with them, Sophie. I'm discovering what it means to be in a society but not of it, what it means to be insulted, excluded, maltreated and injured. I'm discovering what it means to be a stray dog with human characteristics. And I'm discovering that everything I've learned is as useless to them as it is to me. These are people who are becoming themselves, Sophie, on their own. It's a process in which neither you nor I can help them, a process to which we cannot contribute, a process we can only harm. They can only help themselves and each other; they cannot be helped from outside. I'm not here in order to guide, to help, to contribute, or to interfere or meddle in any way. There's no room here for those who are able to give but not to receive. I'm only here to learn."

"You don't know me, Hugh," I said. "That's all I want."

"You, Sophie," he said, "you don't know who you are or what you want. I've known you to be sincere — once, perhaps twice. Always quick-witted, at times even brilliant. Brave, even heroic. A rare companion. But please believe me when I tell you I don't need you, Sophie. My new friends don't need you. What you carry inside you, what surrounds you, whether you intend it or not, is all the rot we've started to shed."

I turned away from him and walked to the bus stop. I didn't shout, nor tremble, nor cry. But my heart was broken.

:|||||||||:

Yarostan, I hope you won't think I'm being flippant when I tell you I experienced that bus ride as a second ocean voyage away from you. I came ever so close to what I had always sought: human beings discovering themselves and each other, deriving from each other the will to found the world anew. I came ever so close to what I've learned to call a human community. And I was inexplicably hurled out of it, down to a limbo of interminable days in a fiberglass factory and comfortless nights in a rodent-infested room. What I came so close to, Yarostan, was not the bureaucratic world of Minister Vera, Secretary Adrian and Representative Marc. It was you, Yarostan. Your world. At least the world I've dreamed of building alongside you and alongside living humanity. That was what I recognized, what I found so "familiar" in Hugh's engagement, in his "project house." But that dream had gotten buried so deep inside me — no, not a corpse, Yarostan, but a live desire, an urgent yearning — it had fallen so far below the surface that Hugh couldn't see it. He only saw the rot that had encrusted itself over it during the intervening ten years.

It's my sixth long day on this letter and I still haven't told you everything I wanted to. If I go on, it'll be forever before I hear from you again, and I don't want to wait that long to learn what else is happening where you are, and what else you experienced after the uprising in Magarna. I haven't told you about the conversation Sabina and I had as we read your letter in the park. I'll have to tell you next time.

Because I've "confessed" so much already, I can't keep myself from repeating one of my confessions. I love you, Yarostan. I'll never stop loving you. If I've loved Luisa less than she deserved, it's because I've never forgiven her for taking me with her on that ocean voyage to this desert.

But I'm not flying to you. I'm staying here. Not because I'm afraid I'd bring all my rot; I don't believe I carry only rot. But because I love you too, Mirna, for everything you've been to him.

And I love you, Yara, for being what you are, and you too, Jasna, for being exactly what you've been,

Your, *Sophia.*

Yarostan's sixth letter

Dear Sophia,

Your honest and moving letter embarrasses and shames me. I'm ashamed because I haven't been as open in my letters to you. I'm embarrassed by your declarations of your love for me. I can't honestly tell you that I feel or ever felt a similar emotion toward you. I failed to make this clear to you at the very beginning of our correspondence, at a time when I was nothing more to you than a one-time friend you hadn't seen in twenty years, a stranger to whom you hadn't yet bared the secrets of your life. My only excuse is that I'm not in the habit of expressing my emotions with words; my life's experiences haven't been fertile ground for the development of such an ability. I realize that by trying to be honest and complete at such a late hour I'll be inflicting pain which I could have spared you if I had made the attempt sooner, but I'm afraid that if I remained silent I would ultimately inflict far greater pain.

By vomiting up the repressed experiences of your life, as you so vividly put it, you set off a similar process in me, in Jasna and in Mirna, not only by your example but even more by what you brought up. We didn't respond to your letter with our minds but with our stomachs, with everything that's inside us.

After reading your previous letter Mirna had expressed admiration for you, comparing your rebelliousness and courage to her brother's. Her attitude toward you has changed drastically since I last wrote you, not so much because of what you've written as because of what we've undergone during the past two weeks. After I last wrote you we experienced one of the happiest moments of our lives, at least one of the happiest in my memory. That happy moment came to an abrupt end three days ago. Your letter arrived the day before yesterday. If it had come two days sooner we would have responded to it very differently. For the past three days I've been moving in an atmosphere of hostility and fear the like of which I haven't experienced since the days immediately after my release from prison three years ago. The arrival of your letter didn't create that atmosphere but simply coincided with it. I can't account for this fear and hostility in terms of a single event. An "event" did take place; we heard it announced over the radio. But this event isn't new; it's one of the constants of the world we live in, it's common knowledge. The radio reminded us that now that we're no longer watched by the national police we're still being watched by the international police. No one had doubted this. Such a reminder could immobilize us only because immobility is already engraved in our being, only because our interminable and continuing past taught us to immobilize ourselves. I don't fully understand what happened to us three days ago but I'm convinced it had less to do with the radio announcement than with what we've become during the past twenty years.

Three weeks ago, a few days after Jasna and I attended the lecture given by your and our former comrades, Jasna came to our house again. Yara invited her, ostensibly to read the letter in which you described your dismissal from school, your eviction from the dormitory and your arrival at Sabina's garage, but actually so as to pursue her speculations about the love affairs of Minister Vera and Commissioner Adrian. Jasna read your letter; before she finished it she started crying. "Don't you think she's wonderful?" she asked. "Think of being beaten down so often and so hard and still having the nerve to reach for more." When she finished your letter she said, "It must take a lot of nerve to be a prostitute. Please do let me know when you hear from her again." She left our house with tears in her eyes.

When Jasna was gone Mirna whispered, "You're certainly no Sabina, teacher. 'A lot of nerve to be a prostitute.' It takes doing, not just reading about it!"

Yara ran to Mirna's lap shouting, "She's not altogether like that, mommy. I used to think she was until the last day of school. Remember I told you we danced in the yard? One of the teachers played an accordion. Jasna just sat by herself and watched the kids dance. I could tell by the way her eyes and her whole body moved that she was dying to dance, so I begged Slobodan to ask her. You should have seen her! She was wilder than anyone else in the yard. Slobodan wanted her all to himself but I cut in and even the principal danced with her. The principal wore out after two rounds but Jasna just went on dancing. Mommy, let's give a dancing party for Jasna."

"Don't be silly, Yara," Mirna said crossly.

"But you just said, 'It takes doing.' Dancing is doing! Poor Jasna is always so sad, and she was so happy when she danced."

"No one would dance with Jasna here."

"I'll bring Slobodan; he'll dance with her," Yara insisted. "I'll bring Julia's phonograph and records and Julia and I will both dance with Jasna. Besides, she can bring her own friends."

"Does Jasna have any friends? Are you thinking of Commissioner Povrshan?" Mirna asked sarcastically.

Yara turned to me. "You'll dance with her, won't you father?"

"I've never danced in my whole life," I told her, although her idea appealed to me.

Yara stomped her foot on the floor in front of Mirna and said angrily, "But you told me he danced!" Mirna smiled absently (I then thought mischievously). Yara saw the smile, reached for Mirna's hands and shouted excitedly, "You remember! You said he'd take both my hands in his, pick me up in his arms and spin me round and round the room." While Yara talked, Mirna picked her up and both of them spun together like a top. "Faster and faster," Yara continued, "until we fall from dizziness."

When Mirna and Yara reached the ground, I laughed and shouted, "I'd love to dance with you, Yara, but I swear to you I never danced with your mother or with anyone else."

They didn't hear me; Mirna and Yara were completely absorbed by their performance. "And then we roll on the ground, still spinning, dizzy, laughing and happy and — father kisses me."

Before the performance ended I noticed that Mirna carried out every one of Yara's instructions mechanically, as if in a trance. When Mirna raised herself up after the kiss, her smile was gone; her face was covered with tears and it had the same absent look. "What happened then, Yara?"

Yara's joy ended abruptly. With an expression of terror on her face, tears running down her cheeks, she turned toward the door and wailed, "Vesna — she saw us."

"And then, Yara?" Mirna asked with the same expressionless tone.

Yara started bawling, but she suddenly snapped out of the trance; she got up and ran toward the door shouting, "Don't, mommy! I can't think of Vesna every day for the rest of my life! I can't and I won't! It wasn't our fault! She died because of what they did to her and you know it!" Yara ran to her room sobbing.

Mirna became aware that I was staring at her. She wiped her face hurriedly, still kneeling on the spot where she'd kissed Yara. "Why do you have such a strange look on your face?" she asked matter-of-factly, as if nothing had been strange except the look on my face.

"Mirna, I don't understand."

"What don't you understand, Yarostan? About the dance? My father danced with me when I was Yara's age."

Mirna got up and went to the bedroom, leaving me alone in the living room, bewildered. It was very late. I wanted to ask her a lot of questions but the only one I was able to formulate was why she had been so hostile to Yara's idea of having a party. Yara doesn't want very much, and I've never before known Mirna to refuse anything Yara wanted.

I didn't have a chance to ask Mirna the following evening either — that was Thursday — because we had unexpected company, and by Friday Mirna herself became the main advocate for a dancing party.

The unexpected guest was Zdenek Tobarkin. He dropped by just before we sat down to eat to tell us his plant had gone on strike that morning. He was full of life. "You didn't think it could happen, did you, Cassandra?" he asked me, laughing vigorously. "A full-fledged strike. Ousted all managers, supervisors and functionaries. Elected workers are to fill the necessary offices and their mandates are revocable. And all of it carried out in general assembly of the workers themselves, without politicians or any repressive apparatus."

"Then it's the first time in history," I said.

"At least in our history," he corrected.

Mirna invited him to join us at dinner.

"I was hoping you'd ask me!" Zdenek exclaimed. "It's not a night to return to my room alone, and the bar depresses me. Besides, I wanted to hear about the coming strike in your plant."

"Mine?" Mirna asked. "There isn't even talk of a strike. Only a few whispers."

"It's now or never," Zdenek said, taunting her.

"Then it's never!" Mirna snapped. "There was talk of a strike once — twelve years ago. And everyone who talked was fired. Most of the fired women never got jobs again, and two of them disappeared, like Jan; they never returned." Mirna was referring to the agitation at the time of the Magarna uprising. She had been very excited when Jan, Titus and I had discussed the uprising at our house a few days before Jan and I were arrested. But apparently she hadn't done any "agitating" at her plant, since she wasn't fired. "None of the people working there now can forget that," she continued. And then, looking at Yara, she added, "We're going to think of that every day for the rest of our lives."

"Times change, Mirna," Zdenek said. "And even if they don't, even if Cassandra is always right, you can't lock yourself up today because someone else is going to lock you up tomorrow."

"Can't I?" Mirna asked defiantly.

Yara and I set the table and the four of us started eating.

"All right, you're doing it," Zdenek said; "I know you can do it. It's what we've all been doing. We've repressed ourselves to avoid being repressed. What sense is there in that?"

"Shrewd, peasant sense," Mirna answered, winking at me, obviously referring to my characterizations of Mirna and her father in my letters to you.

"In a few years there'll be no peasants left, so what good did it do them?" Zdenek asked.

"Those who stayed out of trouble lived longer," Mirna answered.

"You mean they didn't live at all!" Zdenek shouted angrily.

Yara added, "There are some kids who stayed out of the demonstrations in my school. No one talked to them after that and they weren't even invited to next week's outing, so what good did it do them to stay out of trouble?"

"Exactly!" Zdenek shouted, although it seemed to me that Yara's example did not "exactly" support Zdenek's argument, since nowadays, at least at Yara's school, it takes more nerve to stay out of demonstrations than to conform by taking part in them.

"What's life to you, Zdenek? Strikes and demonstrations?" Mirna asked, shifting the context of the argument. "Then I never lived. A few times in my life I had the nerve to abandon myself to my desires; I felt intensely alive and paid dearly — with the lives of those I loved. But that doesn't count in your philosophy."

"You're wrong, Mirna," Zdenek pleaded, seeming hurt by her comment. "That's all that counts in my philosophy. The strikes are only the first step; if they don't lead to what you're describing, they're nothing. In a strike we only announce that we've had enough of this repression of life, this non-life; we express our refusal to continue being chained to machines and cowed by police. But it's obviously not enough to announce that we're coming to life; we have to do what we've announced, we have to find the nerve to live, to dance on the tomb of the repressive apparatus."

"We danced on the last day of school!" Yara exclaimed. Zdenek and I burst out laughing. Yara smiled, but pretending to be angry she planted herself next to Zdenek and asked him, "Why are you laughing, silly? Wasn't that what you meant?"

Zdenek picked her up, placed her on his lap, and still laughing told her, "Because you can say what I mean much better than I can, you little devil!"

"Are you going to dance on the last day of your factory?" Yara asked.

Zdenek roared. "I dream of nothing else! I haven't danced for over twenty years and I'm bursting with the desire to dance!"

Yara twisted Zdenek's moustache and said coyly, "I like you, Mr. Tobarkin. But I don't like your name. Can I call you something else?"

"How about just calling me Zdenek?"

"I can't call you that! You're too old!"

Mirna grinned, leaped out of her chair blushing, swept Yara off Zdenek's lap and carried her to the kitchen, asking in a whisper, "Too old for what, you little goose?"

The following evening Mirna came home from work an hour later than usual; throwing her arms around me and spinning me around the room, she shouted, "We spent the whole day talking about our strike!"

"At your plant?" I asked.

"And we're going to talk about it all next week before voting!" she continued excitedly. "We'll talk and talk until every single one of us is convinced."

"Is the vote going to have to be unanimous?" I asked with dismay.

"It's the only way we can avoid what happened twelve years ago. But it'll be possible! Today the talk spread like a disease. In the morning there were only a few whispers; by the end of the day we were embracing in the aisles, throwing spools across the room. Those women went crazy!"

"That's not the disease but the beginning of the cure."

"It's a disease, you oaf! We're sick, we've gone crazy!" she shouted, tripping me so that we both fell to the floor. "It's exactly what happened twelve years ago. Please, disease! Where's that bewitched daughter of yours? Yara!"

Yara came running out of the kitchen; as soon as she reached us, Mirna pulled her down to the floor between us. Her arms wound around both of us, Mirna whispered to Yara, "No one is too old, Yara, ever, for anything!"

Yara, with tears in her eyes, threw her arms around Mirna's neck and whispered, "I love you when you're like this, mommy."

"You devil, you're going to win," Mirna whispered. "When are we going to have that dancing party?"

Yara covered Mirna's face with kisses. "How about Sunday? No, Julia can't come then. A week from tonight?"

"Your father and I will set the stage; you bring the characters. Fair?"

"You're fair, mommy. You're always fair. You won't change your mind?"

"And if I do?"

"We'll have the party anyway!"

For a whole week Mirna was a person I had never known. She's always been energetic, but on that Friday two weeks ago Mirna seemed to acquire the energy of a girl Yara's age; she reminded me very much of a girl I knew briefly twenty years ago: your energetic twelve-year old "sister." Mirna seemed to shed twenty years of her life, to become a girl who hadn't lived through her husband's imprisonment, her brother's murder, her father's death, her mother's insanity, her first-born daughter's death.

"Setting the stage" meant transforming our living room into a ballroom. On Saturday Mirna ran all over the city looking for appropriate decorations. We spent all day Sunday as well as Monday and Tuesday evenings removing all the furniture as well as the rug, and then scrubbing and finishing a floor that hadn't been cleaned since Mirna bought the house thirteen years ago. Wednesday night we decorated our ballroom and Thursday we installed Julia's record player. Mirna insisted that

Yara bring only records with "real" (namely traditional peasant) dance music, "and not those noisy things."

Meanwhile Yara spent the week collecting the "cast." Two days before the big event I asked her whom she'd invited.

Yara enumerated: "First of all there's me because I'm giving the party. Then there's you and mommy because you did all the work. Then there's Julia because the music is hers and Slobodan because he's our boyfriend. Finally there's Mr. Tobarkin because he wants to dance and Jasna because she's so sad. I wanted four couples, but Jasna wanted me to invite Mr. Zabran so I told Jasna I had my reasons for wanting exactly three and a half couples. And I do. I'd rather have three and a half couples than someone who might spoil everything. But I told Jasna not to worry; I said you couldn't wait to dance with her."

"Devil!"

"Please don't call me that, father!" she shouted, running off to her room.

The dancing party took place a week ago. If our neighbor Mr. Ninovo had been home he might have thought the revolution had broken out in our house. Music blared out of all our doors and windows, which we kept open because it was a warm spring night with a perfectly clear sky and a full moon. Someone kept running in and out and around the house. Mr. Ninovo would have been subjected to the experience of seeing and hearing happy human beings. Of course we wouldn't have been as happy if Mr. Ninovo had been home; his mere presence would have depressed us and muffled our joy. But Mr. Ninovo wasn't home; he hasn't been home for months. Maybe he died.

Mirna completed her stage-setting tasks by placing a record on Julia's player. I saw Yara pinch Slobodan's behind, and the two girls' boyfriend dutifully walked up to Jasna and asked her to dance. Jasna graciously accepted her pupil's invitation, and the moment she placed her left hand on her hip, snapped the fingers of her right hand and jumped, all of us were magically transported to another planet. Meek, skinny Jasna, who in real life is well over forty and probably close to fifty, was transformed on the dance floor into a stunningly beautiful child. She outdid her partner in grace, agility and speed; she was unmistakably the younger of the pair. Her usually sad and troubled face was an expression of pure joy covered only by her long hair, which she periodically swept back like a fan by swinging her head in rhythm to the music. I could have spent the rest of the night leaning on the wall, watching Jasna dance.

But it was Yara's party, and Yara wasn't about to let me do as I wished. She must have pinched Julia's behind because as soon as the first record ended, Julia was standing in front of me with both hands stretched out, asking me to dance.

"I'm very flattered," I told Julia, "but I'll have to take some lessons first."

"You don't need lessons, Mr. Vochek," Julia shouted. "Yara showed me how you danced; it's such fun that we both taught Slobodan to dance the way you do."

"Oh, she did, did she?" I asked, annoyed by this information. Looking angrily at Mirna I shouted, "Well, I'll have you know that I was under a magician's spell when I showed Yara that dance!"

Mirna laughed, threw me a kiss, and looked for another record. I felt Yara at my side, pulling my arm; when I bent down she bit my ear and whispered, "Come on, father, don't be such a coward." The music started playing.

"All right, Cinderella," I said firmly, bracing myself against the wall. "So you'd like to do the dance I showed my daughter? Very well!" I stuck out my arms and Julia pulled me away from the wall. We were in the middle of the dance floor; everyone's eyes were on us; Julia jumped up and down. Suddenly I got into the spirit of the thing. I actually danced for the first time in my life. I bent down, picked up Julia, and started turning around with her. She hollered. The record Mirna had picked out was very fast, so I spun faster and faster. Unfortunately I got dizzy much faster than Mirna had on the day she had first showed me my dance. I hit my head against the wall and dropped Julia to the floor.

In dismay I rushed away from the wall thinking Julia might be hurt, but I couldn't see her; or rather, I saw any number of Julias spinning all over the floor. One of them found my hand, pulled it to her lips, and shouted, "Hey, Mr. Vochek, don't forget the end of the dance!" I had in fact forgotten. As I bent down, I fell right on top of what must have been the one real Julia, kissed her ten and a half year old lips, raised myself up proudly and staggered to a corner of the room. From my corner I heard my appreciative audience fill the room with laughter.

As soon as my performance ended, Julia and Slobodan walked out of the house hand in hand, undoubtedly in order to determine whether she or I had won the bout. Mirna busily hunted for another record while Yara planted herself in front of Zdenek.

"Oh, I can't dance the way your father can," Zdenek said shyly.

I shouted, "Come on, Zdenek, don't be such a coward!"

Yara pulled him to the center of the dance floor saying, "I don't want everyone to dance the same way!"

Zdenek and Yara danced — or rather Yara danced around Zdenek, who did not become transformed into a boy on the dance floor; he retained his nearly sixty years.

Suddenly Mirna started chuckling. "Hey Zdenek, you're wonderful!" she shouted with glee. "You dance just like a peasant I loved once; you even look like him!"

I wasn't as impressed as Mirna. Zdenek looked like he was dancing only so long as I kept my eyes above his waist; as soon as I looked at his feet I noticed they barely budged; one of his knees bent occasionally. As soon as Jasna burst out laughing I realized Mirna's compliment was a joke.

Even so, Zdenek turned to Mirna and bowed majestically. "Thank you, I'm very flattered."

"Don't be," I said; "she means her father."

As soon as I said that, Yara stopped dancing, looked up at Zdenek's face and shouted, "You do look just like him! Stay right there! Don't move!" Yara ran out of the room and returned with a photograph of Mirna's father. "Look!" she shouted to Zdenek. "You look just like him!"

Zdenek seemed unconvinced. "Well," he said, "he does have a moustache."

Jasna and I laughed; Mirna blushed.

"That's what I can call you!" Yara announced victoriously.

"Moustache?" Zdenek asked.

"No, silly! Grandfather!"

"Won't your real grandfather be jealous?"

"He died when I was a year old."

All were silent while the record completed its melody. Yara left the room with the photograph of her grandfather. Julia and Slobodan returned. Mirna started a new record, walked toward Zdenek and asked coyly, "Would you dance with me, grandfather?"

"Do I look like your grandfather too?" Zdenek asked with dismay. "That's no longer so flattering."

"My father, then. Yara's grandfather, my father."

"And the peasant you loved once?" he asked.

Mirna blushed, then bowed as majestically to Zdenek as he had to her and started to dance around him. I was again transported out of this world. The woman on the dance floor was the peasant girl I had fallen in love with fourteen years ago, but she was more, infinitely more. I've loved Mirna for fourteen years, only six of which I've spent with her. But the woman dancing with Zdenek was someone I had never known, someone whose existence had never been possible, someone who burst into life fully grown after more than two decades of repressed growth. Her motions weren't agile or light, like Jasna's, but slow, deliberate, almost willful. Instead of Jasna's grace, Mirna's dance expressed a certain dignity, the dignity of a stubborn human being determined to reach her goal.

Yara and Julia planted themselves next to the dancers and tried to imitate them. Julia did an excellent rendition of Mirna's deliberate, calculated, almost mechanical motions; only her facial expression was wrong; Julia smiled; Mirna's face was somber, distant. Yara couldn't stop laughing while she imitated Zdenek's motionless dance. Her friend Slobodan changed the record and remained standing by the player; he looked terribly bored.

My reveries ended when I saw Jasna's hands reaching for mine. She looked sad, old and skinny again. "Your daughter promised," she said.

"I know," I said apologetically. "But you've already seen the only dance I can do." A generous, beautiful smile flashed across Jasna's face. I suddenly wanted to pick her up as I had picked up Julia. "Would you like to be spun?"

Jasna flushed. "That's not exactly what I had in mind."

Mirna shouted, "Go on, Jasna, don't be such a coward!" She and Zdenek danced straight out of the house, followed by Jasna and Yara.

Jasna pulled me to the center of the floor. "I'll give you that lesson you wanted."

"You just dance," I insisted, "and I'll stand still like Zdenek."

"You have to have known how to dance very well to stand still the way Zdenek does. Put your right arm out, jump on your left foot, kick with your right — don't be so stiff, Yarostan!"

I was quickly exhausted. Zdenek was covered by sweat when he returned. Slobodan was about to start another record but Mirna stopped him. "Let's rest for a while. Isn't anyone hungry? We have all that food and beer!"

Yara helped Mirna cover the dance floor with food. We sat on the floor eating, drinking, smiling silently. We were intensely happy.

Unfortunately Slobodan was bored. He left our circle and took a walk inside the house. He found his way to Mirna's and my room and turned on the radio. A piercing, alien sound broke through the silence.

"...UNDER THE PRETEXT THAT OUR POPULATION IS OUT OF CONTROL. MILITARY MANEUVERS HAVE BEEN OBSERVED IN..."

I leaped to my feet and ran to turn the apparatus off. But it was too late; the harm had already been done.

"The tanks!" Mirna shrieked. She started collecting dishes and empty bottles, but on the way to the kitchen she dropped them and ran to her room sobbing. "Just like twelve years ago!"

Slobodan walked toward Yara with a frightened expression on his face; he didn't understand what he had done. Yara put her hand on his shoulder and told him consolingly, "Don't lose sleep over it; something was bound to set that off. She'll be happy again tomorrow." Then she ran to Mirna's room.

Julia pulled Slobodan out of the house, saying to me, "Thank you for dancing with me, Mr. Vochek."

Jasna helped me clear the rest of the floor and then went to thank Mirna and Yara for the party. On her way out she shook my hand; the familiar sadness was back on her face.

Zdenek walked to the bedroom doorway and said, "The tanks were there already yesterday, Mirna; they're always there, and they're always on some maneuvers."

"But they couldn't have taken happiness away from miserable people," Mirna sobbed.

"They're not yet taking anything away, Mirna," he said hesitantly. "It isn't certain."

Zdenek wasn't certain either; he staggered slightly as he left the house. He seemed to feel depressed, the way he must feel after spending an evening at the bar.

Last Saturday, after helping Yara return Julia's phonograph and records, I helped Mirna turn the ballroom back to a living room. Yara spent most of the day packing. The following morning she left the house with a pack on her back for an outing to the mountains. Yara and several of her friends, including Julia and Slobodan, had looked forward to this outing for several months; they had planned it during a demonstration celebrating the return of a teacher who had been arrested and fired. They had originally intended to invite that teacher but no other adult to accompany them on the outing. Before the school term ended they talked themselves into taking the trip unaccompanied by teachers, parents or anyone older than twelve.

On Monday morning Mirna and I return to our jobs. The air at the carton plant is foul. Everyone in the plant seems to have heard the same radio broadcast. I work silently, keep to myself, and refuse to participate in speculations about troop and tank movements. I leave the plant early in the afternoon with a splitting headache. When I get home I find your letter in our box; I finish reading it a few minutes before Mirna returns from work. I hand her your letter, but she brushes it aside saying she's "too tired to read about other people's problems." I set out the food I'd cooked while reading your letter, but Mirna doesn't eat; she only stirs the food angrily. At last she stops stirring and slams her fork down on the table.

"You voted against striking?" I venture.

"That's right, Yarostan. I voted against striking. All last week I was for it; everyone was; it would have been unanimous. But the vote was this morning, and this morning we didn't embrace in the aisles or throw spools. I was the first to vote against it. When someone asked if anyone was opposed, I was the first to raise my hand. And just as I expected, another hand went up after mine, and then another. In a minute at least half the hands were raised. If we'd waited another minute, all the hands would have been up; it would have been unanimous. We talked about striking once before, twelve years ago. We embraced, we cried from joy, we loved each other and the world twelve years ago, but only for an instant. It was our joy itself that brought the destruction of all we loved. There isn't a person in the workshop who can forget that."

Mirna is wrong in placing the blame on the victims of the repression. But I don't have the nerve to confront or console her with Zdenek's arguments. I go to bed shortly after she does. But I can't easily fall asleep. I'm too depressed.

This is the mood we're in when your letter arrives. The following afternoon — the day before I start this letter — I leave the carton plant early again and walk to Jasna's house. She had wanted so badly to be told when another letter from you arrived. And she's overjoyed. Jasna, apparently, has not spent the previous two days speculating about tank movements. She runs out of her house, kisses me on the cheek and exclaims excitedly, "I can't wait to read it! I've felt so wonderful since your party, I can't tell you —"

"Then at least don't tell Mirna; she's convinced that happiness is inevitably the prelude to —"

"Oh, Yarostan, don't be so mean to her." Jasna puts her arm through mine as we walk toward a store on our way to my house. "Mirna is frightened. Don't you think I am?"

Jasna reads your letter while I prepare a meal with the groceries she and I bought. I avoid telling her about Mirna's strike vote so as not to destroy the pretty smile that so transforms her usually sad face. Jasna is still reading when Mirna returns from work. Without greeting either Jasna or me, Mirna walks straight to the bedroom. Jasna gives me a bewildered look, but I tend to my cooking; I suppose she thinks Mirna and I had an argument. When I finish the meal, Jasna smiles to me but seems far away; she seems to be in the house behind the garage with you and Sabina, with Tissie and Jose. I wake Mirna and she drags herself to the table with a sullen expression. "I suppose you know all about it," she grumbles to Jasna.

Jasna giggles and waves your letter in the air. "That's why I came! I think it's marvelous!"

"Mirna means her strike," I tell her, regretting now that I hadn't mentioned it earlier.

"There's going to be no strike," Mirna grumbles.

The smile leaves Jasna's face. "I'm awfully sorry. I didn't know."

"Didn't you?" Mirna asks bitterly. "Zdenek is wrong, all wrong. Of course we lock ourselves up to stop them from doing it. It's so much less painful when we do it ourselves, and we inflict so much less harm on those we love." This is not the same Mirna who, after reading your previous letter, had enthusiastically praised you for being "a born troublemaker just like Jan and Yara." Before starting to eat she reaches for your letter and grumbles, "Let me see something marvelous."

"It's worse when we do it to ourselves, Mirna; I don't agree with you," Jasna says hesitantly.

"Yes you do!" Mirna snaps. "You've done it all your life!" She reads the beginning of your letter while eating, turning the pages impatiently, angrily. Suddenly she stops reading, pushes your letter away and stares — at nothing, into space. Her eyes have a glassy look: not sad, but removed.

Jasna's eyes already have tears in them. "Don't judge them, Mirna, please. They never stopped, never retreated, never gave up. I know them, both of them, but I never knew what fires burned in them. I knew Sabina was a devil; all of us knew. But all the other devils I've known were tamed before they left elementary school. She was hardly older than Yara then. And who could have imagined what passion was concentrated inside Sophia, that prim, polite, exaggeratedly correct young lady? I don't have a vantage point from which to judge them, Mirna. I can only gasp with admiration for such unquenchable desire, such burning passion. It's something I've never —"

"Some of us suffered the consequences of that passion, some of us paid the devil's price," Mirna grumbles.

Jasna, apparently unable to control the flowing tears, objects. "I suffered only the consequences, Mirna, never the passion. I lived my whole life with my mind on the consequences and I ended up paying with my life and getting nothing in return. You're terribly wrong, Mirna. There's nothing more painful than to look back on a life which had no satisfied desires, a life that hadn't ever been lived. How I admire Sophia and Sabina! How I envy them! If I had been only a little bit like them! If I had only had a little courage to reach for what I desired!"

"And the courage to run away from the consequences, Jasna!"

"Let them be, Mirna, those consequences; let the devil take them."

"The devil never takes the consequences!"

"Mirna, please! You don't know them. You haven't finished Sophia's letter. You don't know what courage —"

Mirna rudely cuts Jasna short. "Don't keep repeating that I don't know them. And don't you talk to me about courage and passion! You, who've never let yourself be driven by passion, who've never in your life had the courage to reach out and satisfy a desire. How sorry I felt for you the night you told us you'd let every desired being slip by you untouched. Yet you talk about courage and passion. How pitiful! How many lovers have you embraced only in your novels, Jasna? Titus, Yarostan, that Adrian and how many others?"

"Mirna, that's terribly, terribly cruel." Jasna cries like a child.

I beg Mirna not to go on, but she seems not to hear me; her eyes are glassy; her expression is cold and distant; she seems to be talking as much to herself as to Jasna.

"Meek Jasna, spineless Jasna advised me to let the devil take the consequences. Isn't that cruel, terribly cruel? Where was Jasna when the devil refused to take them? I took the devil into my blood; the devil's passion flowed in my veins. I reached out, touched, grasped and embraced those the devil drove me to desire. But the devil didn't take the consequences. My brother, my father and my mother took the consequences. Vesna took the consequences. Yarostan and I suffered the consequences. The devil ran!"

Wiping her face and trying to control herself, Jasna says, "I know the horrors you've lived through for the past twelve years, Mirna. I know you've had far more than your share. I know they've destroyed your past. Why do you let them destroy your present and your future? You're at least fifteen years younger than I am. That's a whole generation, Mirna, time enough for a whole life. Why do you make yourself do willfully what I couldn't help doing? Why are you strangling yourself from both directions? Brush me away; rub me out with the sole of your shoe! I never asked you to take me for a model. But why turn against them in the same breath? If you had known them, even if only for an instant!"

Although it is trivial to the point Jasna is making, I clarify a factual detail to which Jasna refers constantly but mistakenly. "Mirna did in fact know Sabina for an instant. You probably remember that Sabina was Jan's companion during those few days before our arrest. One day Jan introduced Sabina to his parents and to Mirna —"

"What do you mean by 'introduced,' Yarostan?" Mirna asks. "Jan brought you to the house together with Sabina —"

"I didn't intend to give a full description because I don't see what it has to do with —"

"You didn't see then, you don't see now and you never will see!" Mirna snaps.

Jasna pursues her argument a step further. "However briefly you knew her, Mirna, didn't she communicate something to you, something I could never act on, something having to do with the passion to live, unhindered, uninhibited, unbounded —"

The glassy expression returns to Mirna's eyes as she drones, "Yes she did, Jasna. That devil communicated her passion to me, just as she communicated it to Jan, to Yarostan, to you. And where was she when the three of you were in jail?"

"Mirna!" I plead. "That's really out of place in this discussion."

"Where was she when you were taken from me? Where was she when Jan disappeared, when my father died?"

"That's so unfair!" Jasna exclaims.

Mirna turns her glassy eyes toward Jasna and asks, without anger, almost in a monotone. "Why have I had to suffer more than my share of the horrors, Jasna? Why didn't you share some of them with me — at least one? Where were you when Vesna was dying? You had been Jan's friend as well as Yarostan's."

With tears rushing to my eyes, I walk behind Mirna and place my hands on her shoulders, trying in vain to make her realize how cruel, irrational and misplaced her attack is, but Mirna won't be stopped. "Vesna was a pupil in your school. You knew she was ill. I needed your courage then, Jasna. Where was it — in your novels? That courage might have saved my Vesna; she might still be alive today. The devil might not have taken her from me."

Jasna backs away from the table with a look of intense pain, even horror. "Let her go on, Yarostan," she sobs. "It's all true. I'm a coward, and cowards are the worst of all the criminals. It's because of all the cowards that we've lived through so many horrors. I read my novels and let it all happen. All of it! Including Vesna's death."

Jasna leaves our house crying. I run after her, afraid of what she might do. "I'm terribly sorry, Jasna. I couldn't have imagined she was going to throw that in your face too."

"Please don't be sorry for me," Jasna says, trying to smile through her tears. "She's so perfectly right about me. I've never faced consequences, and I won't face them now any more than I ever have."

"That also takes a certain kind of courage."

"That kind is called cowardice," she says, smiling.

"It doesn't make you a monster."

Jasna hugs me and rests her wet cheek on mine. "If I were only a bit of a monster, Yarostan! If I only had the nerve! If I were at least vengeful! But I'm not, and I don't have the nerve. Can't you guess what I'll do now? I'll go home and read another novel." She smiles as she walks away.

When I return, Mirna sits at the kitchen table, staring. I feel mad at her; I consider her attack on Jasna irrational, unprovoked and heartless. "I don't understand, Mirna. You're blaming that poor, harmless woman for everything this police state did to us, to our lives, to those we loved. You're making Jasna a scapegoat. Why?" Mirna stares at me but doesn't say anything, so I continue. "Because that's the way you see it, is that why? Have you ever thought you might be seeing it wrong? I admit you're not inconsistent. You see yourself the same way. According to you, a letter sent to me by Sophia twelve years ago caused my arrest, Jan's disappearance, your father's death, your mother's illness. Is it really impossible for you to imagine that there are places where people receive letters from all parts of the world without being molested by the police? Can't you understand that the cause of the arrests, the deaths, the suffering, is one and the same? It's that abomination we put up with for the past twenty years. Vesna didn't die because of you or Jasna or Yara. She suffocated in the rot; she was too sensitive to ignore it and too fragile to withstand it. Do you want to drive Jasna to suicide by throwing Vesna's death in her face?"

"Suicide?" Mirna asks coldly, cruelly. "Jasna? Suicide takes courage."

"Mirna, I've never seen you like this."

"Have you ever seen me, Yarostan? You've seen a shepherdess whose only passion was to buy a pair of curtains and a baby carriage, a pretty peasant girl whose desires were limited to displaying herself in the city park wearing city clothes." Then she adds, with a trace of contempt, "I've never been near a sheep in my whole life." While saying this, she picks up your letter and goes to the bedroom.

Mirna had told me more or less the same thing over two weeks ago, but in a much friendlier way. After reading my previous letter to you, she had said, "It's a very pretty portrait, this Mirna of yours, but it's not someone I'd recognize if I met her on the street." I had responded by saying, "I apologize for the distortions; you've never been very eager to tell me about the real Mirna." "Obviously not!" she'd exclaimed, throwing her arms around me; "you might not like her as well as you like your shepherdess."

Mirna is still awake when I enter the bedroom. She has apparently finished your letter. "All right, I've never seen you," I admit, sitting down on the edge of the bed. "I simply assumed you herded sheep in that village you came from. That's not the same as holding Jasna responsible for Vesna's death."

Mirna's response is, "I did throw corn to the chickens in our yard, so you weren't so far off."

"Calling someone a shepherdess isn't the same as calling someone a murderer."

"I didn't call her a murderer but a coward," she says, yawning. Suddenly she forces me to forget my anger and drop the whole topic; she sits up and asks, with evident concern, "Yarostan, how is it possible that Sophia loved you for all these years if you loved her mother?"

I had told Mirna something about you several months ago, a few days before I wrote you my first letter. Yara had taken part in the first demonstration at her school, Mr. Ninovo had reported me to the police, and the police had come to our house to warn us about Mr. Ninovo. For several days Mirna was filled with affection — I should learn to use the right word: passion. It was one of the rare times in Mirna's experience when "trouble" had not been followed by fierce and unbearably painful repression. Although we had barely touched each other since my release from prison two years earlier, we now made love — passionately — every night. On one of those nights she asked me, "Who is Sophia Nachalo?" I was obviously stunned. I knew she hadn't ever known you and I couldn't imagine where she'd heard of you. "How in the world do you know about her?" "I don't know about her," she said; "Sophia Nachalo was the name of the sender of the letter that came for you at the time of the Magarna agitation." I remembered Mirna's having told me about a letter when she'd visited me in prison. "But I didn't know the letter had come from Sophia," I told her. "Then Sophia Nachalo is a real person?" she asked. "Of course! What makes you think she isn't?" Mirna said, "I could barely understand the messenger who brought the letter, but I did understand that he'd delivered a similar letter for Jan to my parents' house and that the letter came from someone who'd known you and Jan. So I was sure the letter came from someone else, someone who knew where my parents lived because she'd been there, someone whose name wasn't Sophia but Sabina." I told Mirna, "That's Sophia's younger sister." She exclaimed, "Then I wasn't so far off!" "But what makes you think of that letter now, eleven and a half years later?" I asked her. Mirna answered, "Because I'm happy now, as happy as I was then, and because I know I'll have to pay for that happiness, just as I did then. I knew that letter from Sabina was the devil's bill of charges, and I still know that's what it was even if your Sophia sent it." I asked, "The devil's what? You sound just like your crazy mother when you say things like that." Mirna said, "I don't care what I sound like. My mother wasn't as crazy as people thought. Two hours after that letter arrived the police came looking for it. That same instant other police were at my father's house, beating him because he refused to give them a letter for Jan, That night Jan disappeared and you didn't come home." I responded angrily, "But that's ridiculous! You're making the so-called devil responsible for events that have no connection with each other. You know perfectly well that Jan and I were arrested because of what we were doing in the steel plant. And your father couldn't have been beaten because he received a letter that no one ever read from a Sophia Nachalo he'd never met. Your father was probably beaten because he was Jan Sedlak's father. Can't you see that those events were pure coincidences?" Mirna was silent for a while; then she said, caressing me gently, "All right, lover, I'll pretend to see they were pure coincidences if you tell me how much you loved your Sophia." That was when I told Mirna, "She wasn't my Sophia, and I never loved her." "I'm not going to pretend you're right if you don't tell me," she said. "But it's true," I insisted. "You've never really known me, Yarostan," she told me; "you've never known that jealousy isn't something that flows in my blood; if you brought your Sophia to my bed I'd only love you all the more." I said, "I don't believe you, but I'm not hiding anything from you. Anyway, it all happened when you were still in elementary school, so why would you be jealous? I slept with Sophia three or four times, just before our arrest, but I didn't love her. If you want to know the truth, I was madly in love with Sophia's mother. I dreamed of Sophia's mother during my whole first prison term and I was still in love with her when I met you, when we were married, when I was arrested the second time." Mirna pressed me to her and exclaimed excitedly, "Her mother! That's wonderful! I'll pretend anything you want if you tell me about her. Was she anything like Sabina? Why don't you write her?" "She was a devil in her own way," I told her, "but I don't love her any more. And how could I write her? Do you want me to go to the police and ask for Sophia's address? I don't even know that Sophia and her mother are still together." Then Mirna admitted slyly, "I memorized the address on that envelope." Somewhat stupefied, I asked, "And you remembered it until now? Why?" She said, "Because I thought the letter came from Sabina." I fell asleep without telling her about Luisa, and she didn't ask again — until two nights ago, after her argument with Jasna.

Mirna's question makes me swallow my anger toward her, it makes me forget my pity for Jasna. Her question brings back the embarrassment — I should say guilt — I'd felt the day before, while reading your letter. "I suppose Sophia never knew how much I loved Luisa, and I suppose she still doesn't know."

"Sophia thought you loved her, didn't she?"

"I suppose she did. I know what you're getting at, Mirna, and I know you're right. I was a coward and I'm still a coward. I treated Sophia very badly. Yes, terribly. And I didn't have the nerve to tell her. I still don't have the nerve."

"I can see why!" Mirna exclaims, grasping your letter. "Who would have the nerve to tell such a correct young lady, 'I slept with your mother'? — a young lady so sensitive to the correct age and the correct sex of the correct couple. The thought that Tina slept with Ted — and she didn't convince me of that — drove her out of her mind. After she caught her mother with her boyfriend, she dramatically left them both and buried herself in a factory although she obviously didn't have to. She does have something in common with our Yara, but she also has something in common with our Vesna. So you lied to her to avoid hurting her. That's very thoughtful, Yarostan. It shows you did love her. If I had only lied to Vesna, and kept lying to her, she'd still be alive today."

"I don't understand, Mirna. Why do you bring up Vesna —"

She cuts me short. "Tell me about Luisa; tell me everything Sophia doesn't know, and I'll pretend to forget Vesna — at least for the time being."

Twenty years of lying is twenty years too many. I tell Mirna "everything," and I'm going to tell it all to you. I don't know how Mirna could have helped Vesna by lying to her, but I do know that I've "helped" you in just that way long enough, far too long. I understand that you genuinely loved Jose and I'm relieved by your telling me that you never felt that kind of love for me. I don't fully understand why you left Jose and I'm embarrassed by your insistence that this had something to do with me. Or rather with "Yarostan." I add this because your "Yarostan" has nothing in common with me; your "Yarostan" is a product of your imagination, a composite of all the people you loved, or wished you had loved. The real Yarostan turned to you only when he felt rejected and betrayed; he turned to you dishonestly, he abused you and lied to you, he used you as a substitute, as a last resort. I know it's extremely crude of me to tell you this after reading your moving account of your painful experiences in Sabina's garage. I'm expressing myself as crudely as possible. What would have happened, according to your imagination, if you had come here twelve years ago, or the day before yesterday? Did you really think I would have said goodbye to Mirna and Yara the moment I saw you? How much pain would you have felt if I had told you only then that you had made a big mistake, that I had respected you once, perhaps even admired you, but that I couldn't find a trace of my love for you in my memory? Would you have been grateful to me then for lying to you so thoughtfully for so long? And is it really altogether my fault that you can still speak of "flying to me"? Have the clues I left in all my letters been altogether undecipherable to you? But I'm judging you and I've no right to. I carried an illusory "Luisa" in my heart for many years after reality itself had made the real Luisa plainly visible to me. And, in spite of my determination to be as crudely clear as possible, I wouldn't be completely open with you unless I admitted that your declaration of your twenty-year long love for me doesn't leave me cold. Yes, the knowledge that one is desired stimulates desire. But please understand this, Sophia: My love for you would have to be born in the present; it couldn't be built on any love I felt for you in my past.

"When did you first meet Sophia's mother?" Mirna asks. "What was she like? Did you think of her as your mother or she of you as her son? Did you run after her or did she catch you? Why did you accompany Jan and Sabina to my house? Were you running from Luisa? Chasing Sabina? Looking for fresh air?"

"If I hadn't accompanied them, you and I would never have met."

"Don't I know!" Mirna exclaims. "Jan would have spent the night with Sabina; I would have married that peasant I was engaged to; my whole family would be alive and well today — But I promised to pretend to forget. Well? Tell me! Unless you're sleepy."

No, I'm not sleepy at all; I'm wide awake and very excited. Mirna is twenty-nine. Luisa was twenty-eight when I first met her. I was fifteen. The war was over and quickly forgotten; only fairy tales survived. The resistance was over, half the resisters were dead, and they were quickly forgotten; only fairy tales survived about that as well. It was a time for fairy tales about the past and the future. I suppose that's why Titus first took me to Luisa's house. He thought I ought to have a little "political consciousness." Why not, after all? I was already a proven fighter; I could shoot, I could work; all I couldn't do was "think politically." And what better "teacher" could have been found? I had already seen her in the carton plant. As soon as I stepped into your house, which to me was and remains Luisa's house, I was instantly "politicized." I was converted. Even better: seduced. I was seduced by every story she told, by every theory she expressed, by the tone of her voice, by her lips, her eyes, her body, her hair. I believe you were in that house too, Sophia, but I don't remember your presence there because I wasn't aware of it. All that existed for me was Luisa. I wallowed in Luisa, swam in Luisa. I became Luisa. I memorized everything she said and even copied her manners. I tried to think what I took to be her thoughts. Did I think of her as my mother, my imaginary mother? I don't know. I did think her the most daring, courageous, intelligent, imaginative and beautiful human being in the world and in a sense I was her "son" certainly intellectually. But I didn't think of her in personal terms at all, in terms of her physical relationship to me. I thought of her in terms of barricades, in terms of the workers' own genuine union, in terms of the struggle we were preparing ourselves for. I thought of her in terms of the revolution. Luisa and revolution were synonyms to me. You learned Sabina's outlook in her friends' bar; you seem to have learned it then for the first time and to have been somewhat shocked by it. Yet Sabina couldn't have chosen better words to describe what I experienced in Luisa's house: all relationships were open, nothing was left unsaid, there were no secrets, no taboos, nothing was forbidden. Did I desire Luisa already then? Yes I did, desperately, with all my being. But I didn't "run after her." She already had two lovers, or "husbands" George Alberts and Titus Zabran, and I didn't consider myself a likely candidate for a third, not so much because of my age as my "political backwardness." Besides, Titus had been a friend to me since the war, almost a brother; he had introduced me to Luisa and I didn't want to stab him in the back for all his kindness. For almost two years I loved Luisa in the shape of the revolution; I did everything to prepare myself for her; I read, concentrated, talked. I ran after the revolution. It was Luisa who "caught" me.

"Show me how she caught you! How old was she then?"

"She was a year older than you are, but I can't show you in the dark, Mirna, because she did it in broad daylight." As she did everything else. She was thirty; I was seventeen. I suppose relations weren't as open as I thought, not everything was said, and there were secrets, since you never knew about us. But I couldn't have known at the time that you, who lived in Luisa's house, didn't know about our love; I couldn't have known that in your eyes two people separated by more than a decade didn't constitute a "correct" couple. But I admit I wouldn't have acted differently if I'd known.

It happened in the carton plant, during work hours. Luisa was carrying on a heated argument with Claude Tamnich. I obviously don't remember the subject of the argument, but I do remember both of them quite clearly and I can easily imagine what they were arguing about. Claude was probably insisting that solidarity and comradeship meant spying, liquidating, jailing, torturing, killing. Whether he actually said that or something similar, he infuriated Luisa. "Stunted baboon," she called him, and "fascist" (both of which titles he undoubtedly deserved), Luisa stomped around the shop muttering, "I'll show you what workers mean by union, by comradeship, by solidarity!" She came to me first and locked her arm in mine; then she locked her other arm in Adrian's; quickly Jan, Vera, Titus joined us — and Jasna last. We moved toward Claude like a stone wall. "Join us or get out!" Luisa shouted. Claude was undecided at first; then he turned and walked out of the room. We roared with laughter as we returned to our machines. (Small wonder the same Claude later spread the rumor that Luisa was a foreign spy.) Luisa returned with me, her arm still locked in mine. Suddenly she turned and pressed her chest, her whole body, against my arm. She whispered, "That's what comradeship means." I almost fainted. I knew Titus had seen us. I suppose everyone had. But I didn't move. I won't say I couldn't move. I didn't want to. I had at last "graduated"; I had become a "politically conscious militant." My revolution, everything I had wanted from life during every minute of the previous two years, had come. I became a "revolutionary cadre" the following afternoon, during a break, in the stockroom of the carton plant. Your mother, Sophia; a woman almost old enough to be mine. In one of your first letters to me you moralized for several pages about the fact that I was "married."

It's my turn to "moralize." I actually doubt that you'd know about my passion for Luisa if you'd seen us embracing — you wouldn't have seen the embrace because you wouldn't have believed either of us capable of it. When you saw Luisa lying with Alec that night you left them, why did you assume it was Alec who had seduced Luisa, and only in order to spite you? Why did you become so infuriated when Tina left you to join a man twice her age? I can't speak of your experience, but I can tell you from mine that your "correct" relationships are not the only ones possible. For a whole year Luisa and I made love daily, in the stockroom, in your house (I suppose you weren't ever there at the time), in my modest room. My love for her was total, my desire for her unquenchable. Neither my love nor my desire could have been more complete, more perfect, if Luisa had been fifteen years younger.

"Where did Sophia get the idea you loved her? Are you leaving something out?"

No, this time I'm not leaving anything out. I hadn't paid any attention to you or Sabina before the strike broke out. Luisa brought both of you to the plant on the first day of the strike. I still didn't notice you. All I noticed was Luisa's sudden and inexplicable coldness toward me. She suddenly treated me, not as a complete stranger, but as a fellow worker with whom she'd not had intimate relations. I tried to explain this to myself in terms of her desire to be free and unattached on the eve of the great event. I tried to explain it in terms of my "political backwardness." On the very first day of the strike, Luisa already had a "position," Titus had another, Jan had a third. Vera a fourth, while I was completely at sea; all I could think of was Luisa's sudden indifference to me. Everything seemed to become clear on the second day when, after a group meeting, Titus told me furiously that I would have done better to remain in the city's basements and alleys. I thought he was finally responding to my having stabbed him in the back by taking Luisa from him; I concluded they'd had a scene, that Titus had shamed Luisa into abandoning her "affair" with the "irresponsible adventuristic hooligan." I was ashamed, not only of my stab in the back but also of my persisting political illiteracy. I had to prove myself, both to Titus and to Luisa; I had to show them their attempts to "educate" me hadn't been wasted. At our next meeting — I suppose that was the third day — I brought up the fact that the "class oppressor," Mr. Zagad, was still sitting in his office counting his future profits while we merely talked about slogans on posters. I was only stating what everyone knew, yet everyone, even Claude, responded as if I'd discovered a new planet. I grinned with pride; I thought that in Luisa's and Titus' eyes I had become a "strategist." You bothered to remember my "strategy" for twenty years; in one of your first letters you told me you admired me, you fell in love with me, when I proposed my "plan." Yet all your admiration, as well as all my pride, were badly misplaced. That "strategy" wasn't really mine, nor was I the one who implemented it. I merely stated the obvious: Zagad was still in his office. It wasn't I but Claude who suggested doing something about this. I merely watered down Claude's suggestion by asking if instead of locking Zagad into his office we couldn't just ask him to leave. And for this I was given credit for our one concrete accomplishment, our sole real feat. Yes, the only genuine "event" that we set off during those two weeks. Everything we did after Zagad was ousted, all those "activities" you remember so vividly, were nothing; we merely treaded water to keep from drowning. I was proud of myself as the "instigator" of that event, but I wasn't the one who instigated it nor the one who implemented it. Much as we all disliked Claude, it was he who instigated and also implemented our single concrete deed. It was an "action" perfectly suited to his temperament: it had to do with "liquidating," Claude headed our little procession to Zagad's office. It was he who threw the door open. It was he who introduced us as "representatives of the Plant Council," namely as emissaries of a vast, nebulous entity, as agents of a powerful repressive apparatus. It wasn't I and it couldn't have been. I would have knocked on Zagad's door, entered sheepishly and hesitantly; I would have begun to "implement our strategy" by saying, "Good morning, Mr. Zagad," and my admirable plan would have vanished the moment Zagad had said, "Good morning, Yarostan, what can I do for you?" I'm not the hero you've bothered to remember for two decades, Sophia. My thoughts weren't on Zagad but on Luisa. I was proud of our "action" because I was sure she was pleased. I thought I had redeemed myself in her eyes and in Titus' as well. And I was terribly confused. Had I redeemed myself to Luisa as a "politically conscious activist" or as a lover? Such a separation hadn't existed before the strike; suddenly there wasn't only a separation but it seemed unbridgeable. I would be trusted by Titus and Luisa but I would no longer be loved by Luisa. All this occurred to me only after Zagad left his office. Until then I had been carried away by everyone's enthusiasm, especially Sabina's. When Claude, Jan and I had elected ourselves to implement "my strategy," Sabina had jumped up to join us. On the way to Zagad's office, Jan and I had walked, or rather "danced," behind Claude, with Sabina between us, her arms around our waists, ours around her waist. "This will make everything possible!" she'd kept saying, filling my head with images of a world where everything would be possible everywhere and at any time. Jan and I had lifted Sabina and "flown" her up the stairs to Zagad's office. Suddenly Zagad was gone and so were my images.

Sabina's arm left my waist and I was alone. How I envied Jan that moment. Sabina's enthusiasm didn't diminish after Zagad's departure; it increased. And she showered Jan with all of it. Claude walked out behind Zagad, Sabina shouted, "We've done it!" and wrapped herself around Jan. How I wished Louisa had wrapped herself around me shouting, "We've done it!" How I wished Sabina had turned to me! I crawled out of the office, lonely, disoriented. Jan rushed out after me and asked for the key to my room; he gave me the key to his. I didn't then understand the reason for the exchange but I didn't ask. Jan and Sabina left together through the office building entrance. I shuffled from the office back to the workshop but stopped behind a post before anyone saw me. I saw Luisa and Marc Glavni leaving by way of the workshop entrance, arm in arm, gesticulating and laughing. Titus and Jasna were still in the shop. I backed away from my post and rushed back through the office building to the street. I walked aimlessly and wanted to die. I had proved myself for nothing, to no one. All my explanations had been wrong. Luisa hadn't dropped me because of my backwardness nor because she'd wanted to be detached but because she'd found another lover. Titus hadn't scolded me because I'd taken Luisa from him. Only then did it dawn on me that just before Titus' outburst, during our meeting, I had laughed and nodded vigorously when Jan had proposed throwing all the machinery into the street as our first revolutionary act. How stupid I'd been to attribute Titus' outburst to jealousy! My sympathy for Jan's "scheme" defined me as an outright "counter-revolutionary" in Titus' eyes, since for Titus the machinery was the revolution, the two were synonymous.

"So that's when you turned to Sophia," Mirna concludes prematurely.

"Not yet, Mirna; that's when I met you."

"And you were disappointed," she says all too accurately; "you'd hoped to find another Luisa."

"Did you know that already then?" I ask.

"If I had, I wouldn't have cared; I had my own passions to worry about," she says.

I spent the night in Jan's room. But I couldn't sleep. I remember why but I'd rather skip over it. Early the next morning I crawled back to my room. Sabina let me in. I wanted only to be left alone, to sleep. But Jan and Sabina were wide awake and they had other plans for me. I had known since I'd first met Jan that he hated his mother; I was soon to learn why. Sabina nestled up to me and told me, "We're going to spend the day in the country." I told her to have a good time and let me sleep. "You're not going to sleep today," she assured me, poking me in the ribs to keep me from trying. Jan and Sabina lifted me out of bed and forced strong coffee down my throat. "We can't go without you," Jan explained. "The revolution is going to spread to the peasantry, and your contribution is going to be indispensable." I was awake. "You're needed to cement the great worker-peasant alliance," he continued. Brushing aside my objections, he went on, "You don't have to harangue anyone; you don't have to organize anything. All you have to do is make love to the Queen of the Peasants — a woman slightly older than Luisa but less experienced. That single act on your part will destroy religion and morality, the family and the state; that single act will set the fires of hell to all the peasantry's precious traditions, all their sacred bonds. Tomorrow peasants leaving their burning villages will mingle with workers leaving their burning factories and they'll all migrate across fields and over mountains, fulfilling every wish, satisfying every desire and every whim on the way."

Mirna laughs. "Did Jan really tell you that? And did you actually come looking for 'a woman slightly older than Luisa but less experienced'?"

"I obviously don't remember his exact words, but I swear what he said was very close to that. And I believed him. I actually thought he and Sabina felt sorry for me and intended to introduce me to someone like Luisa."

"That's marvelous!" she exclaims. "Now I remember why he had us all go picking berries! Why didn't you go through with it? Don't you see how right he was? All hell would have broken loose in a single instant, instead of cracking a little this year, a little the next and again the next over such an endless expanse of time!"

I didn't think it was "marvelous" at the time, and I still don't think so. I think Jan and Sabina had devised a mean trick. Jan knew that the mere mention of Luisa's name would set me moving. He dangled Luisa in front of me during two tram rides and a substantial walk. We reached his house. He introduced me to his father, mother and sister. I looked for the nearest chair; I had a splitting headache and felt like vomiting; I hadn't gone without sleep for so long during the entire war and resistance. "A headache!" Jan said; "Well isn't that too bad? You won't be able to join us on our berry picking expedition." I got up in spite of my headache and my nausea; I didn't want to miss my promised rendezvous. "Oh no, you can't go in that condition," Jan insisted; "you stay right here in the house, where my mother can nurse you." Then he whispered, "She's a real queen, Yarostan; every bit as regal as the queen of heaven and as pure as the mother of her lord Jesus Christ." I vomited. Jan and his father helped me to the couch. Mirna and her mother cleaned up the mess.

Then Jan left with his father, Sabina and Mirna. I was alone in the house with the Queen of the Peasants. She brought me a wet cloth for my head and crossed herself when she handed it to me. Sometime later she handed me a newly dampened cloth and crossed herself again. She crossed herself every time she entered the front room to look in at me. She was deathly afraid of me; she seemed convinced I was either a thief or a murderer who had just escaped from prison. And one time she tiptoed through the room I was in and went to another room where she wailed prayers. I hated myself for having let myself be tricked into leaving my comfortable room and bed. I was nearly unconscious with pain when the berry pickers returned. And I was nauseated; I had no interest in eating the meal the Queen of the Peasants had spent the day preparing. Jan, Mirna and Sabina helped put me to bed in Jan's room, or rather the guest room, since Jan explained, "They call it my room although I haven't spent a single night in it; you're the first person in this bed."

"My mother started building that room onto the house two years earlier," Mirna explains; "until then Jan and I had always slept in the same room and in the same bed. One day she came into our room before we were up and saw us sleeping with our arms around each other — she saw us sleeping the way we'd always slept as far back as I could remember — and she yanked us both out of bed and beat us with a broom, calling us the names of all the devils in hell. Jan left. I never shared a bed with him again. I cried for weeks. I hated her until she died. Then I understood why she beat us."

So that was why Jan wanted me to help destroy religion and morality, the family and the peasant community. I suspected this at the time, from much that Jan had told me, from much that he had done. Two years earlier Mirna had been eight, namely the same age Tina was when you watched over her in her bedroom. You described yourself as Tina's apprentice; you considered her old enough to teach you lathe-turning, machining — But that's your problem. In any case, I didn't think about it that night or the following night or during any of the hectic days before our arrest, and in time I forgot why Jan had invited me to meet his family. While they carried me to bed, Sabina angrily whispered in my ear, "Coward! Counterrevolutionary! Everything depended on you, and you spoiled it all." I was too sick to respond. I woke up once during the night; my head was bursting. Jan was sound asleep next to me. The next time I woke it was morning. Jan was shaking me. "Come on, let's get out of here." When I sat up he added, "Planned revolutions inevitably fail; isn't that their very nature? But our trip wasn't a total failure. Anxious to keep the blessed young virgin out of Beelzebub's paws, the Mother Superior placed the virgin directly into Satan's!" Jan left the room laughing victoriously. Understanding nothing, I dressed hurriedly and rushed out of the room and then out to the street. I couldn't believe what I saw and heard. Mirna's mother stood near the doorway grasping a broom which she kept trying to raise, but which Mirna's father kept lowering. She was screeching at Sabina. "You'll roast in hell, you shameless gutter snipe! You'll burn for all eternity!" Sabina, her back arched like a cat's, stood right in front of the woman and shouted just as loudly, "You'll freeze where you're going, you dried up carcass, you vampire that sucks life out of the living because there's none left in you!"

"What happened that night?" I ask Mirna. "She brought my brother's destruction," Mirna says bitterly, "my father's death, my mother's —"

"I mean that night, Mirna," I interrupt impatiently; "Would you rather forget?"

"Doesn't this letter tell you what happened? How could I ever forget? My mother was right. Sabina put the devil's blood into my veins. The hypocrite! For twenty years I'd thought she'd done it for me. But the fiend has no kindness, no heart; her deeds are for herself alone! 'Your brother loves you,' she told me. 'You're his only girl.' she told me. And then she asked, 'Would you like me to pretend to be your brother?' I begged her to pretend and I lost myself pretending. I drowned in happiness pretending. And my happiness drowned everyone I loved, Jan first of all."

"Now you're contradicting yourself. I thought that letter Sophia sent was responsible for all that happened —"

"If your logic could bring Jan back I'd have more faith in it!" she exclaims angrily. Mimicking Jasna she goes on, " 'Didn't Sabina communicate something about the passion to live?' And where was Sabina when we drowned in that passion? Why did we have to suffer all the consequences? 'Your brother loves you.' I knew it was true. So did you. Everyone knew. We didn't hide our love. The devil! I thought she was going to help us the way she did that morning —"

That morning Sabina made herself the object of the superstitious old woman's wrath, provoking Mirna's mother with taunts and insults while Mirna's father kept the broom from leaving the ground. Jan and Mirna were a few houses away; I walked toward them in a bewildered stupor. Mirna, her arms around Jan's neck, cried desperately. "Take me with you, Jan, take me to the city. Please don't make me stay here!" Jan told her, "It's not possible yet, Mirna." She wailed and pleaded. "But it may soon be possible," he told her; "Wait a few more days, at most a week. Wait in the clearing." Years later Mirna took me to that clearing in the forest. "I'll be there every day all day long; I'll sleep there," she said. Jan told her, smiling, "Don't do that, silly; you'll get sick. Be there in a week. A week from yesterday. If the rest of us do better than this spineless friend of mine, a lot is going to be possible, everything's going to be possible." With an expression whose pathos I still remember, the ten-year old girl pleaded, "Promise, Jan! Promise!" He said sadly, "I promise. I'll take you away from here. We'll leave the clearing and walk through the forest to the neighboring village and we'll think we're dreaming, because the village won't be there any more; we'll find thousands of people building a city like no city that's ever been built and they'll welcome us and ask us to help because they'll all be our friends; there won't be any policemen or prying old women because they'll all be too busy building or making love. We'll stay in our friends' beautiful city as long as we want and not a minute longer; we'll be as free as birds; we'll roam across the entire country; we'll visit streams and caverns and other cities, and in each city we'll find only friends; they'll all beg us to join them in what they're doing and we won't know where to turn first because every activity to which we're invited will seem more gratifying than all the rest." I heard Mirna's pathetic plea; I heard Jan's fairy tale; but I registered nothing. I was angry about the fact that Jan and Sabina had tricked me. I wanted to get back to the real world, the world of Luisa, the world of meetings and posters and demonstrations. I remember that it was a Monday morning; the following Monday the strike ended; two days later we were arrested. I nudged Jan and said, "Let's go back, we'll be late for the meeting and it'll be an important meeting; we're to decide what steps to take now." Jan freed himself from Mirna's embrace, turned to me and said bitterly, "Damn your meetings, Yarostan. That's not where any steps are going to be taken." Then he kissed Mirna's forehead and said to me, "But you're right. That's all we've got to go back to." He rushed to Sabina, lifted her away from in front of his mother and carried her off while she continued shouting. As we walked away Jan shouted, "Goodbye, father." Mirna ran after us and shouted, "Don't forget, Jan; you promised!" We were late for the meeting, but Jan was right; no steps were taken. We spent the week doing all those exciting things you still remember and then we were arrested.

"Jan did keep part of his promise though," Mirna tells me; "the only part he was able to keep."

"You mean you saw him again before our arrest?"

"I went to the clearing every day hoping he'd be there. He came exactly when he said: in a week. But he wasn't the same. Something inside him was broken. He didn't kiss me. He didn't even touch me. When he talked, he didn't look at me. The devil had made me beg him to do something he couldn't do and he had broken himself trying. 'I love you the way a brother loves his sister, Mirna — no less and no more; do you understand that?' he asked me. I didn't understand that. The devil was in my veins; I was angry; I reached for more. 'Sabina showed me how much you loved me,' I told him. He turned his back to me. 'Forget what Sabina showed you,' he said, and I knew he was sad when he said it because I wanted him to be sad when he said that. 'Forget you ever heard of Sabina. What she showed you is impossible and not even Sabina knows how to make it possible. Only a revolution would make it possible and there aren't enough Sabinas for that revolution; not today; not here. I tried; believe me when I tell you I tried. But there weren't enough of us trying and we failed. Failed! Please understand what that means, Mirna. Everything we dreamed is going to be impossible and there's nothing to do but forget it until the next time. If you can't forget, at least pretend to forget; lock your feelings into your heart and keep them locked there every minute of every day. If you let them out that old vampire and all the vampires of this world are going to tear your heart to shreds. Do you understand that?' I didn't understand anything. He sounded sincere but I didn't believe a word he said. I got on my knees and prayed to him, I begged him to take me to the city. Nothing would be possible if he left me in that house with those peasants, that horrid mother. In the city I'd be just like you and Jan and Sabina; in the city everything would be possible; Sabina would be there; she'd know; she'd show me. Why did I have to pretend not to be what I was, not to feel what I felt, not to love those I loved? Who would tear my heart to shreds? I didn't believe Jan. I didn't believe him until the vampires tore my heart to shreds. Jan left me in the clearing, alone, angry. I returned the following week, and the week after that, but he didn't come for me. One day my father told me Jan and all his friends were locked up, far away. Then I believed what he'd told me. I learned to pretend. I pretended for four years and when he returned I went on pretending. I was engaged to a peasant I knew in school; I pretended I'd never loved Jan and he didn't even remember he'd told me to pretend. He was upset about the peasant, but for my sake, for the sake of my future, not for his own sake. When you came I pretended you were Jan. And I've pretended ever since. How does that make you feel?"

"What difference does that make, Mirna? What if I pretended you were Luisa? I still loved Luisa when I first made love to you. Does that make any difference to you? Would it have then?"

"Is that what you did to Sophia? Did you pretend she was Luisa when you made love to her?"

"No, Mirna. If I pretended you were Luisa it was because I loved you the way I had loved Luisa. I didn't pretend Sophia was anyone I had ever loved. I only used her. That's why I could never tell her."

"Couldn't she tell?"

That's what I'd like to know: couldn't you tell? I had seen you at Luisa's — I should now say your house, the house in which Luisa and I had made love countless times; how could you not tell? I saw you again at that meeting after Jan and I returned from his family's house. I saw you exactly as Jasna still remembers you: as the prim, well-mannered, perfectly correct young lady, amazingly well-informed and incredibly naive. I read your description of your passion for Jose with disbelief. I can't imagine how Hugh could have characterized you as he did. It was I who was wrong, I know that now; my picture of you was as false as your picture of me. It was nevertheless that picture I saw; it was that person I "seduced." I don't want to insult you, Sophia. You were very pretty, even beautiful in your own delicate way; I'm sure you still are. But for me your beauty wasn't the beauty of flesh and limbs, it wasn't a beauty that stimulated passion. It was the beauty of a porcelain statue — cold, fragile, hollow. You were no Luisa — not then, not to me. With what passion Luisa had expressed herself at that meeting! It was that passion that hurled me into frenzied activity. Yet you remember only the words. When she shouted, "The workers have to run the factories by themselves! We have to make all of life ours and run all of it!" I didn't hear only words; I saw the desire in her eyes and on her lips, I felt the passion in all her movements. That's why I agreed with Luisa while simultaneously agreeing with Jan. Their words seemed to contradict each other but I thought their passions were identical. Luisa talked of running the factories, Jan of burning them, but both communicated the same thought to me: the thought of a life we've dared only to dream and only those of us who've dared to dream. What I felt and heard had to do with willful, passionate human beings whose biographies were to consist of realized desires and not of paid instructions, whose factory aisles, if they must have factories, were to be carpeted with the mattresses Sabina described to you. That's why I worked with passion to put Luisa's slogans on posters and on walls and inside other factories. Those slogans were all I retained of Luisa's love. After the meeting she kissed Marc Glavni on his lips and walked away with her arm around him. It was only then I turned to you, Sophia. That was when I asked if you wanted to help me print posters. That was when I gave you a tour of the plant and rode with you the following day distributing the posters. It wasn't love or passion or desire that drove me to you, Sophia, but only frustration and resentment. You tell me that my caresses didn't equal Jose's — yet you loved me. Couldn't you draw your conclusions? The only desire I felt toward you was the desire to take a porcelain statue in my arms and shatter it into splinters. Yet you responded to every request I made with the same, polite, "Yes, Yarostan, it would please me very much." When we returned to the plant after distributing our posters I asked if you'd like to spend the night with me in the plant. "Yes, Yarostan, it would please me very much." I slept. I dreamed of Luisa. You didn't rouse a shadow of desire in me. You shyly placed your arm next to mine, but ever so politely! I couldn't make myself pretend you were Luisa! I did desire you once, Sophia, for an instant. You politely consented to spend the following night with me. That night's "love" is undoubtedly the love you've remembered for twenty years; that's the night I've tried to make myself forget. But if I'm going to expose the falseness of your feelings toward me, I can't continue hiding the foul root from which they sprang. I intentionally placed our blanket near the street entrance to the workshop. You responded politely to my caresses. I was sure you said everything you thought you should say and you turned exactly as you thought you should turn. It was only the following morning that my desire for you grew. You were nervous; you knew how late it was. But you remained in my arms, smiling your polite, fragile, nervous smile. Suddenly the workshop entrance was wide open; sunlight streamed in; Luisa shouted, "Oh, excuse us!" as she and Marc scurried past us into the shop; Titus arrived a second later. My satisfaction was complete when, red with shame, you ran to the stockroom with a blanket draped around you. I had broken the porcelain statue. I did it out of resentment toward Luisa and toward Titus, out of frustration, out of spite. How you hated Alec when you saw him embracing Luisa for what you took to be similar motives! I loved you, desired you, Sophia, during one instant: the instant when you turned red with shame, the instant when Luisa, Titus and Marc looked at the correct young lady having intercourse on the workshop floor right by the street entrance in broad daylight.

"The devil put that into your head!" Mirna exclaims.

"I don't want to hide behind the devil, Mirna. What I did to Sophia was monstrous and I feel I should tell her that her love for me is built on rot."

"You'll be boasting. Do you think any such idea could have come into your head on its own? Don't you recognize its author? Only three days earlier Jan had asked you to do exactly the same thing at my house, to my mother. Did you think that was Jan's idea? The two pranks are identical, Yarostan, and neither you nor Jan were such ingenious pranksters. It has the devil's signature on it; don't you see it even now? The prank was designed to drive my mother out of her wits. By making Sophia the Queen of the Peasants you merely made the prank useless to Jan and postponed the completion of the devil's plan until a time when Jan could no longer derive any satisfaction from it."

"That's terribly garbled, Mirna. I insulted Sophia —"

"She revenged herself twice over! She told you she left jail in two days, abandoning you and Jan to four years in prison. Then she went on to take everything you hadn't given her and she thanked you for all of it — from spite! That prank would have served Jan's aims far better than it served yours. Did you ever regain Luisa's love? Was she waiting for you at the prison gate when you were released four years later? Yet you still loved Luisa then. It's you I feel sorry for, not Sophia. The three of them took twelve years from your life and the heart out of mine, yet you're groveling, apologizing: 'I'm sorry, Sophia, for having played your sister's prank on you; I should have played it on Mirna's mother.'"

"That's all constructed with your mother's superstitious logic, Mirna, and it doesn't refer to what actually happened. No, I didn't regain Luisa's love. Yes, I did love her long after that. But that has nothing to do with the fact that the police arrested us and —"

"Why were you and Jan arrested? Tell me that! Tell me why the three of them were released two days later! Did they try to release their comrades when they were out? Tell me that!"

I can't tell Mirna that. I don't know why. Mirna's superstitious "analysis" is garbled but her questions are perfectly clear and they raise more problems than I'm willing to face. The day after I played my "prank" on you (or Sabina's prank, if Mirna is right), the rumor spread among us that Luisa's "companion" George Alberts had been expelled from his plant. The following day Claude and Adrian told me Alberts was a "spy" who had worked for the "enemy" during the war, and that Luisa was in some way his accomplice. I knew these were lies manufactured by Claude's police mentality and I also knew that Claude had waited long for his revenge against Luisa. I dismissed Claude and Adrian as repressive maniacs. Claude later worked with the police and it's obviously because of him that the police added "espionage" and "collaboration with the Alberts spy ring" to their list of charges against us. In prison I was shown a foreign newspaper clipping according to which "George Alberts and his family" were settling abroad in the comfort provided for them by the government they had served. These typical police maneuvers didn't shatter my trust in or admiration for Luisa. Nothing was odd to me until you told me two or three months ago that Luisa's prison term had only lasted for two days. The slanderous rumor spread by Claude, the elaborate scheme invented by the police, the fact that Luisa was gone when I was released — none of that bothered me. But the knowledge that she'd been released after two days in jail would have bothered me. I knew the police regularly bungled then own elaborately concocted schemes by giving shorter terms to those they designated "ringleaders" than to those they designated mere "accomplices." But I couldn't have made myself believe they had bungled so far as to release the entire "center of the ring" after only two days while leaving the accomplices locked up for four years. I didn't even believe the clipping I'd been shown in prison. The day I was released I went directly to Luisa's house. Complete strangers lived there; they'd lived there for four years and hadn't ever heard of a Nachalo or an Alberts family. I concluded she was either in jail still or that the clipping was authentic. When I brought this up to Jan a week or two later, he told me he'd seen the same clipping, hadn't ever doubted its authenticity, and hadn't been bothered by it: "Did you expect them to stay here?" he asked. Obviously not. I no longer doubted the authenticity of the clipping and I wasn't bothered by it; there was nothing odd to me about the fact that Luisa had settled abroad after being released from prison into an environment that offered no release from prison. Once I accepted her absence I even felt stimulated by it. She had left me behind to continue her work. I wondered how proud of me she'd have been if she'd heard me repeat every one of her stories and every one of her theories to Mirna and her father.

"So you didn't pretend I was Luisa!" Mirna exclaims.

"I didn't say I did; I only asked what difference it would have made. No, I obviously didn't pretend you were Luisa; you had nothing at all in common with her."

"But you had everything in common with her. You became Luisa and I became you."

There's a great deal of truth in that. Mirna became my "political pupil," just as I had once been Luisa's. Even the content of the lessons was the same: the workers had done it once and they could do it again; they had defeated a whole army, taken hold of the land and the factories and started to forge their own world, and we were going to forge it again, arm in arm. But I didn't communicate my project to Mirna as successfully as Luisa had communicated hers to me. What Mirna heard was totally unrelated to what I said. I gradually realized that she wanted life while I was offering her politics. I became Luisa, but only in my own eyes.

"You became someone else in my eyes, Yarostan, someone I wanted very badly. Every word you spoke expressed what I most longed to hear. You were my brother as I had known him before his prison term, you fulfilled his promise to me, you satisfied the desire Sabina had roused in me. And in the end you were the instrument that destroyed my family because Sabina devised a prank —"

"You've been obsessed with that superstition ever since Sophia's letter arrived, Mirna. Sabina had nothing to do with my coming to your house after my release.

She'd been gone during all four years of my imprisonment. I came because Jan was my best friend. I knew where his parents lived and I hoped they'd know his whereabouts."

"You weren't her conscious instrument; I was," she continues stubbornly. "You didn't know what your coming to us meant. I knew. Jan had warned me. My mother didn't let a day pass without telling me. She told me the same thing over and over again, like a record that's played day after day until you finally stop hearing it. How she had single-handedly tried to bring us up in the way of the lord, but the lord had sent a scourge on all of us because my father had transgressed the lord's way and trafficked with the devil. To you she was always just a crazy old woman with crazy explanations, but she wasn't as crazy as you thought. My father had run after our neighbor's wife in the village; maybe he'd even slept with her. Jan and I joked about it when we were little and father winked at me, knowing perfectly well that I knew. Everyone knew, including the neighbor. When the war came, that neighbor went to the occupation authorities, told them some tales about my father, and in a single day we lost our yard, our chickens, our house, everything."

"An enormous army didn't occupy this country for five years in order to punish your father's sexual affairs, Mirna!"

Mirna kicks me and shouts, "You keep your explanations and I'll keep mine! What good do your explanations do you anyway? My mother's explained what happened to us and why. Yours don't explain anything at all; they've got nothing to do with me. As soon as we left the lord's path we started our journey to perdition and Jan's imprisonment was only a stop along the way. That was what she told me twenty years ago and nothing you ever said was more true. If we'd stayed in the village, Jan would be alive today, my father would be sixty-three and still as vigorous as a bull, my mother would only be fifty-eight and she'd be no crazier than any of our neighbors. I hated her lord as much as I hated her lord's path, but only after we'd moved to the outskirts of the city — which she called a den of sin. If I'd grown up in the village I'd have been just like her. After we moved I loved my father and I loved what he'd done, even though I knew everything she said was true. I believed her, but I didn't want to be like her. I came to hate her more than Jan ever did, but I still believed her. 'You're going to be the devil's bride!' she told me. 'The devil possessed your father first; then he visited your brother; he came to you last, but you're going to be the one who drives the devil's sword into our flesh.' She pointed her finger at me with such hatred; she actually saw the devil in me. I screamed: Liar! Superstitious hag! And after Sabina taught me: Vampire! But I knew it was true and I wanted it to be true. My arms, my lips, my whole body ached for the devil. I longed to be the devil's bride and I dreamed of driving the devil's sword into her flesh! The devil's bride, Jan's bride, my father's bride — everything she said I'd be, I wanted to be. But I didn't have the nerve. I only had the nerve to do it as Sabina had taught me: by pretending. And pretending was good enough; the devil doesn't know the difference. I no longer know the difference either. I've already driven that blood-stained sword into all but three of us, and I'm still holding it —"

"Mirna —"

"Don't interrupt, Yarostan, you don't understand anything! I had my second encounter with the devil, at long last, a year before you or Jan were released. He came in the shape of a boy I knew in seventh grade; we were both thirteen. It was with him that I tried to complete what I'd never carried through with Jan, what I'd completed only once, the night Sabina pretended to be Jan. I don't remember his name because I called him Jan. Everyone else in class thought me strange; they knew I had the devil in me and they were afraid. But the peasant boy I called Jan liked me because I was strange; he spoke to me, touched me, walked me home. One day I didn't walk home after school; I pulled him to the clearing in the forest where Jan and I had played when we were little. We were all alone. I removed all my clothes and started to tear his off. He was frightened. I begged him to pretend to be the devil, my brother, but he didn't know how to pretend. I was so hungry, so terribly hungry. I pushed his naked body to the ground and shouted, 'Take me, Jan, take me! I'm your bride; the devil's bride!' When I was on him he sobbed and shook with fear. He jumped away from me and ran off with his clothes, leaving me alone in the clearing. If you were a monster to Sophia, what was I to that peasant? A few days later I learned the devil doesn't care if the deed is pretended or real, nor even if it's carried through to its consummation; all he cares about is the desire, the devil's passion. The boy's father was killed. The fathers of several other students in my class were arrested. They had all worked in a neighboring town where there had been a confrontation with the police. The day I had taken the boy to the clearing a strike had broken out. It wasn't just a strike. It was Jan's strike. What those workers wanted was the revolution, the world where everything would be possible — and they were all arrested, every last one of them; some were killed; my peasant's father had only worked there for a month —"

"I heard about that rising during my first term. The fact that it broke out when you were having your affair was a coincidence, Mirna, a trivial coincidence. Those workers had tried —"

"My whole life's meaning is built out of such coincidences!" Mirna snaps, and then proceeds to silence me definitively. "Marbles experience coincidences, Yarostan. People experience meanings. Don't you know the difference? I knew what I had done, and so did the boy. He was terrified; death itself couldn't have frightened him more than I did. He avoided me as if I carried the plague. Not because of what I'd done to him in the clearing but because of what we had both done to his father. If he were here now I'd make you ask him! His fear made me afraid, afraid of myself, afraid of that devil's sword my mother had already seen in my hand. For the rest of that year I tried hard to be like everyone else. But I had communicated to the peasant. Don't you see she was right? Once you step ever so briefly into the devil's path, you'll never ever leave it no matter how hard you try. He had stepped into it, only for an instant, and by the end of the year the same passion started to burn in him. He spoke to me again, he walked me home. He had learned to pretend; he pretended we weren't responsible for what had happened to his father. One day he pushed me against a wall in a dark corner and asked me to marry him. He wanted the devil — but all to himself, not in broad daylight in the clearing where I could pretend he was Jan, but at night in his own private bedroom where I wouldn't be able to pretend to be anything other than what I'd become: the peasant's wife. I consented. He spoke to my parents and arrangements were made. We were to be married at the end of the school year. His older sister was going to be married at the same time, which meant he'd take charge of what they called their farm. They raised a few chickens, some vegetables, and supplied our street with milk from their three cows. Those cows are as close as I ever got to the sheep you think I herded. On one of my visits his sister showed me how to milk them, to prepare me for one of the chores I'd be doing until I died. A month later Jan returned, completely changed. He didn't look the same or act the same. He wasn't only older. He was broken. And I had broken him. I pretended that I loved my peasant, that I'd never loved Jan, that I'd never learned anything from Sabina, that the devil didn't flow in my veins, that I liked to milk cows. We didn't speak to each other in the house, we never went out together and we slept in separate rooms with both our doors closed. The old hawk found nothing at all to reproach in our behavior although her eyes followed us every minute around the clock. But the truth is that the devil's passion still burned inside me, and it broke through with all its force one night when I was out on a walk, alone; I accidentally ran into Jan. He asked me, 'Are you really going to go through with that marriage?' I told him, 'Yes I am, and I can't wait.' He asked, 'Couldn't you find someone with more life in him, someone slightly less shallow?' I felt my passion rising but I crushed it and told him, 'I love him exactly as he is, Jan, and I love his cows and his chickens and —' He didn't let me go on. 'You hate cows and chickens, Mirna! Do you really want to do this to your life?' That instant everything broke through; I burned. I threw my arms around his neck and begged, 'Why are you asking me? You know perfectly well what I want!' He forced my arms off his neck and said, 'But that's impossible, Mirna.' He walked away from me, but I knew he was crying. The following day I pretended to forget. I pretended to look forward to my life milking cows and throwing corn to chickens. But two weeks before the marriage you came to our house. The moment I saw you I knew the devil had sent you to me and I went wild; I gave my heart to the devil out of sheer gratitude; I became the devil's bride; I gave myself up wholly and unreservedly to my passion. Deny it all you want! I knew exactly why you had come and who had sent you. Don't you remember the first thing the devil made you ask? 'Are you Jan's wife?' My lips told you, 'No, silly,' but my heart said, 'Yes, yes, Jan-Sabina-father-devil, I'm your wife! Take me, right here, right now!' Oh, Yarostan, I'm melting just thinking about it. I loved you the instant I set my eyes on you; I almost wrapped myself around you right then. I couldn't sleep that night. I was on fire. I longed to crawl into your arms, to drown in you. But I had to fan the fire to its highest heat, I had to set the devil's stage. My heart pounded in my throat the whole next day. I was possessed. I took you out of the house in the morning and paraded you to the whole neighborhood, pressing your body to mine. I had you walk back and forth in front of the peasant's house, and when I finally saw him I threw my arms around you and kissed you — and how happy I was when you responded with such passion. That ended my marriage to the cows and the chickens. I never saw my peasant again; I later learned he left the neighborhood and went to work in the factory where his father had been killed. I couldn't sleep the second night either; I was doubled up with desire, I wanted to scream, I was starved, I was charred. The following morning the stage was set. It was a beautiful spring day, the most beautiful in my life, crystal clear and warm. It was a blaze of fire that led you to the clearing in the forest. The devil never had a happier bride or a more beautiful ceremony. As I embraced you I wanted to crawl through your mouth, to embed myself in your skin, to —"

"We lay down on the grass. 'Wait,' you told me. 'Pretend to be Mirna.' And I said, 'I'll pretend to be anyone in the world; I can't exist without you.'"

"I pretended to be Jan. Oh yes, as you did then! I'm on fire! I love you, Mirna! You're my only girl! Oh —"

"You see, Mirna? Pretending didn't matter. We loved each, other no matter who we pretended to be."

"You pretended to be Luisa seducing Yarostan! That's marvelous!"

"That's ridiculous. I pretended to be whatever you wanted me to be. In actual fact I didn't pretend to be anyone; I lost myself in you. Don't forget it was you who seduced me!"

"Then you were Mirna!"

"All right, I was Mirna."

"It did matter, Yarostan! Jan penetrated Mirna. I lost my mind. You created a storm I'd never dreamt of. You filled me with Vesna. Vesna was the daughter of a brother and a sister. My mother knew it. Vesna knew it, she always knew it, and she hated both of us because of it. But it was I who let the devil push me to it and who drove the devil's sword through her heart."

"Mirna, please don't spoil every happy moment —"

"That's the devil's price! I was so happy when you finally took me away from that house, the lord's house, my mother's house; when you took me into the den of sin, the city, where people like you and Jan and Sabina lived. Yes, I wanted curtains and a baby carriage and clothes that made me like everyone else in the city, that made me look and feel different from my mother. And I wanted more, much more. I wanted to find that world Jan had promised, the real den of sin, the devil's city, where everything I desired would be possible. But I hadn't paid the devil's price for Vesna. And I started to pay when she was barely out of my stomach. You and Jan were fired. And then the police warned you; they were going to destroy you, both of you. But the real blow came when our neighbors, those workers I had so long wanted to join, turned against us and evicted us. I knew then I was going to have to pay a heavy price for my happiness; I knew the devil was going to strip me of everything, whether he had given it or not. I had been frightened once before, when the peasant's father died. But when we returned to my parents' house I grew terribly frightened. 'You bear Satan's mark,' she told me; 'you're damned for all eternity; everything you touch will wither; everyone you love will die.' How I hated her! 'I'm Satan's bride and I'm proud of it,' I shouted at her; 'I'll drive the devil's sword through you first of all!' But I was terrified. Those things you call coincidences: there had already been too many. I couldn't bear to be near my mother. But I didn't want any more coincidences. I found my job. I bought our house. I thought I had cheated the devil, escaped him. I was on my own, no longer dependent either on the lord or on the devil. And for a year I thought I'd succeeded. I hardly saw you or Jan; I saw Vesna only from the time I picked her up at the nursery until you returned from work. And I never had time to visit my father. But I was happy. I thought the devil was going to let me keep all I had; I thought the devil had forgotten me. Then the stirring began in Magarna and my heart beat faster again. At first I became even more afraid. I remembered the uproar in the town where my peasant's father had worked; I remembered everyone in the town had been arrested or killed. I trembled when you first described what you'd learned about the events in Magarna. They were the same as those in that town! It was Jan's revolution, yours, and yes, mine. I trembled because I knew how happy they were and how they longed for what could be. I trembled because I knew they'd all be killed. And then the devil again numbed all my senses but one. It happened in my factory. Women who had hardly ever talked to each other started poking each other, running their hands through each other's hair, embracing, even kissing. I longed for that revolution; I wanted it for all of us. I couldn't restrain myself; I was possessed again. I embraced all the women in the factory; I loved every one of them. Do you remember that last Sunday when Jan and Titus came to our house early in the morning? I didn't know which of you I desired most: Titus, the fatherly stranger; Jan, the brother I had loved since childhood; or you, the combination of both, you, who had been Mirna and could therefore be Sabina as well as Satan himself; I desired you the most. You were the most enthusiastic of the three; you wanted that revolution as badly as I did —"

"You're being unjust to Jan. I was blind in my enthusiasm. He saw that what we were doing was self-defeating, just as he'd seen that eight years earlier, and he was right both times. Titus and I were stuck on the question of a free press; we kept insisting that an ignorant working class cannot possibly chart its own course and build its own world. But Jan was telling us — and no one heard him — that the press was part of that ignorance. He kept pointing out that Magarna workers were already creating forms of human communication which freed the people, not the press —"

"Jan knew they were all going to be killed or jailed. He knew that everything was going to remain impossible. Jan wasn't only his father's son. I knew too, but the devil was in me and I didn't care. Titus said the press had brought the spirit of Magarna to workers who had lost their ability to act, and I loved the press for that as I loved Titus for saying it. The press was the devil's instrument, it did the devil's work, it put life into shriveled carcasses, it transformed the frightened women in my factory into reckless maniacs, it filled you with life, it filled me with unquenchable desire."

"I'll never forget, Mirna; you took me to that clearing again; I dreamed of that for the next eight years."

"That time I didn't pretend to be anyone other than Mirna because I wanted you, all of you, every one of you, everyone I had ever thought you to be: my brother, my father, Titus, yourself, Sabina and all the workers in Magarna; I gave myself to all of you without shame, without pretending —"

"And I suppose you think that's why Yara —"

"I don't suppose! I know! Yara would pick up the devil's sword the moment I dropped it! But I'll never drop it. I can't. It's part of me, part of my flesh, it's in my heart. The devil sent two bills of charges only three days later. They weren't just bills for those few days of happiness but for all the previous years; the devil wanted all his back pay. I had thought I'd cheated him out of that. But he had merely extended credit to his favorite bride. And now the sum was enormous. The first bill of charges was in the newspaper that Wednesday morning. Tanks were killing the Magarna workers — inside buildings, in schools, on the streets! How I wanted to die with them, to kill that passion that had possessed me! How I wished the devil also had the power to bring those workers back to life! The women in my factory might as well have died that morning; all their love was gone; they were lifeless, as still as the dead. Hell is the silence of the graveyard. A week later those who had come to life first, vanished. We've been still ever since, until last week — and we're still again; we remembered the tanks. How can Jasna speak of courage in those who never faced the tanks? The devil sent his second bill by special messenger; it came in the form of a letter from Sophia Nachalo, but I knew who the letter was from as soon as he told me he'd left an identical letter for Jan at my father's house. I knew you wouldn't come back and Jan wouldn't come again. I knew even before the police came for the letter two hours later. I knew I had to pay — for Vesna, for my passion, for my happiness. Don't tell me the letter arrived the same day the tanks entered Magarna 'by coincidence.' Don't tell me it was a coincidence that the messenger arrived at my house the very minute when you and Jan were being arrested a hundred kilometers away, not an hour sooner or an hour later. Don't interrupt, Yarostan! I took the trouble to find that out! Two years after your arrest I got a day off to visit you in prison. They wouldn't let me in; they said I had the wrong permit; the permit had been changed. I took the train to the steel town and waited for the workers to come out. I ran to the first group and told them who I was; they all knew both of you. I told them I had found you and asked if they knew where Jan was. They were silent with that silence of death; their faces answered; they didn't know but they all knew. Then I asked about the day when you and Jan were arrested. They told me lots of workers had been arrested. 'When?' I asked. 'A week later'! You and Jan were the only ones arrested on that Wednesday, just as you left the plant at the end of the workday. You were arrested the very minute the messenger reached my door! Don't tell me about coincidences; they don't explain anything! I knew the moment the letter came, but I didn't want to believe it. I took Vesna to the train station and waited for the later train; we sat and waited for the train after that. Then there were no later trains. I carried Vesna to the tram stop and we rode to the transfer point but the next tram was no longer running. I carried Vesna for hours, drenched with sweat and unable to breathe; I didn't once stop to rest. I knocked weakly and heard my mother shout, 'Bar the door! Don't let the devil in!' My father opened it and I fell into his arms, bawling. 'Damned witch, Satan's whore, you've brought destruction to our house!' she screamed, endlessly crossing herself: My father forced her out of the room and she spent the night praying to the wooden Jesus in her room, shouting, wailing and beating the floor, continually repeating 'perdition' and 'Satan's whore.' She had started to scream the moment the letter had arrived; she'd known what it was as well as I had. When the police came, she immediately gave them the letter, but my father snatched it out of their hands; they had no right to take a letter addressed to his son. The two police immediately started to beat him. He had no rights, they told him; he was the father of a criminal and therefore an enemy of the people; they even threatened to arrest him for interfering with the people's police and for protecting a criminal. But he wasn't broken. He smiled and tried to comfort me. He said you and Jan were both strong, you had both been through all that before and you'd know how to take care of yourselves. I begged him to find a pretext to drive his bus to the repair depot next to the union building and to find out if Titus had been arrested too. If only we could find Titus he'd surely know where you and Jan were. I hardly slept; my mother's prayers mingled with my own fears. I took the first morning tram; I couldn't afford to be a minute late for work. I knew they'd fire me. That would have completed the devil's plan right then; I would have lost the house; I couldn't have fed Vesna. But the devil has time; he has all eternity; and he had me wait, taking his toll slowly, one victim at a time. I returned for Vesna that evening, exhausted from lack of sleep, sick from worrying, but anxious to learn if my father had found Titus. I walked in without knocking and I knew right away that the fiend had already struck again. My mother stood in the middle of the room clutching a broom with one hand, waving her other hand in my face, and singing a hocus pocus with which she drove devils away. Vesna stood in a corner trembling with fright and bawling, her back turned to me. My father sat in his chair and stared as if he were blind. They had broken him. I shook him hysterically and asked what happened. 'I was never late, never sick; for twelve years I drove that bus, every day of the week, on Sundays if they needed me.' I burst out crying and begged him to tell me what happened. 'Father of a criminal, accomplice of a traitor, saboteur —' They fired him! He didn't say anything more; he just stared. My mother lifted the broom with one hand, clutched Vesna with the other and screamed, 'Out of this house, witch! Get out and take all the devils with you!' I ran for Vesna but she clutched the child and kept me away with her broom. 'I'll go; only give me my Vesna,' I begged. But she hit me with that broom and screamed, 'You'll not give this innocent child to the devil; you've given your master enough! The child is still innocent; I'll keep her innocent. Shameless whore, you'll not take this child to perdition! Live alone! Repent! It's too late to pray for your own salvation. Pray for the child's. Beg the lord to remove your curse from this child. Be her suppliant. You'll never be her mother.' I was on my knees, bent over, crying; she didn't hit me again. My father suddenly got out of his chair; I looked up; the stupor in his eyes was gone. He forced her hands and her arms away from Vesna. For a moment Vesna stood in front of me, trembling, terrified. Then she turned and ran back to the woman, clutched her black skirt and buried her face in it. My father picked her up as I rushed to the door. He handed Vesna to me. Tears streamed down his withered, wrinkled cheeks. I ran to the tram stop, hurting from Vesna's kicks, deafened by her screams. She was only two and a half but she already had a will of her own. I carried her off against her will. I knew what the consequence would be. But I had to have Vesna; she was mine; she was all that was left to me of my love, my desire, my passion."

"Do you know what time it is?"

"Why didn't you tell me sooner!" she exclaims angrily; "I'll be late for work!"

It was Thursday morning. That night I started this letter. I hadn't known Mirna's father had been fired from his bus-driving job. When Titus visited me in prison I learned he was ill, and when Mirna visited me later, three years after my arrest, I learned he had died.

It's Saturday night now. I'm tired and I don't have anything more to tell you. Yara is to return from her outing late next week. I haven't seen Jasna since she left our house crying Wednesday evening.

When I started this letter I wanted to get to the root of your feelings toward me; I wanted to make it clear to you that I would not have been comfortable in that "community" of journalists in which you imagined me, that I felt more kinship with Ted and Tissie and that world which seemed so "exotic" to you. But I'm falling asleep.

Yarostan.

Sophia's sixth letter

Dear Yarostan,

D I couldn't wait to write. I haven't heard from you since I last wrote you because I haven't been home for a week, not even to pick up my mail.

I've spent the past week in the "commune" inside the occupied university, and I love it here. I've been dying to find time to tell you about it and also to finish my previous letter; it got so long that I skipped half of what I wanted to say and I didn't deal with any of the questions you'd asked me.

I'll tell you about the commune first. Everything I've ever wanted seems to be happening all around me. Thanks to Tina I got into the midst of it all just as it began. I pinch myself several times a day just to make sure I'm not dreaming. And I'm still not completely sure. What's happening here at this moment is exactly what I longed for but I never really believed it could happen here. I was intensely happy for you, yet also green with envy, when you described what was happening around you: inside the factories, in the schools, on the streets and in your own house — wherever you looked. And now it's all taking place here. Employed and unemployed workers, beggars and prostitutes, street kids, are all suddenly bursting with life, they seem to be animated by a single purpose. I've always wondered how I'd have felt during the day Luisa loved to describe — do you realize it's already thirty-two years since that day? — the day when everyone ran into the street, some with rifles and pistols but most with kitchen knives and rolling pins, and confronted the entire national army. Now I know how it must have felt. The army hasn't come out; even the police have been suspiciously still; but the feeling I have is that if and when they do move, everyone is going to be in the street, on roofs, at windows, everywhere. At least in this neighborhood. I never knew so many friendly people existed here! Crowds gather at every corner; complete strangers talk to each other as if they'd been lifelong friends; all are intensely interested in every leaflet that's given out; everyone studies every inscription or poster on a wall. The only time I've experienced anything like this was during that week I spent with you, twenty years ago. The steel town in which you worked must have had a similar atmosphere during the time of the Magarna uprising.

Today I understand your critique of the activities in which we took part twenty years ago. And I'm convinced that what's taking place around me isn't subject to that critique, even in little ways. First of all there aren't any generally accepted "leaders" or even "influential militants." The "leaders" that do exist are monarchs of tiny sects, and during the past week the sects I've come in contact with have been losing adherents instead of gaining them. Secondly there aren't any "official slogans," any "correct lines," or even any "strategies." It all started when students occupied a university building simply because they'd had enough of a lifeless present and a prospect-less future and not because they had a blueprint of things to come. They didn't even announce a list of demands. They simply sat in and started to talk. Then other students occupied another building. Soon the whole university was occupied. That was when I arrived. I'm not saying the politicians and representatives have all disappeared; they're actually all over; they're constantly waving lists of "what we all want" and presenting themselves as "we students" or even as "we proletarians." But at least for the past week no ones paid any attention to them; they've served mainly as subject matter for cartoons.

A week ago a factory was occupied by its workers. No "authority" ordered the occupation — neither a political party nor a union nor a sect. Since then other factories have been occupied. All the dams seem to be overflowing all at once. Workers from non-striking factories have been meeting with workers from the occupied factories. I know this is no puppet show, Yarostan. No one is taking any orders. Thousands of people are suddenly speaking and acting on their own. On their own and for themselves; no one is speaking or acting for others. I'm convinced that what's happening around me is what you and I used to call "the revolution."

I'm writing this letter from the Council office and I'm having a hard time concentrating on what I'm telling you. The "office" is a former classroom; the walls and blackboards have been turned into a vast bulletin board with thousands of messages, announcements as well as poems and cartoons. The desks and seats contain stacks of newly printed literature. The "office" serves as a meeting place and mainly as a place where people can find the latest information on the occupied workplaces. My function is to help people find what they're looking for, whether it's a place, a pamphlet, a leaflet or a person. I think I'm beginning to understand what you tried so hard to tell me about the role of the journalist. Every person who comes into this room has an altogether different account of what's happening; each person has different stories to tell. And it's precisely this that makes every encounter so stimulating. What you call "direct communication" is taking place all around me. And I know that a newspaper, no matter how "revolutionary," no matter how "complete," would destroy that communication. It would replace everyone's account with a single account, the "official" account; it would replace everyone's lived experience with an "experience" that hadn't been lived by anyone. Worst of all, people would read about each other instead of talking to each other, and as you pointed out, they wouldn't find each other in any of the articles no matter how hard they looked. But there's no such newspaper. The capitalist press can't even imagine what's happening and no one pays any attention to it. And whatever "journalists" there are here are being forced, like the politicians, to speak only for themselves or not at all. The room I'm in is full of literature, but none of it is journalism; most of it consists of announcements or factual summaries; the rest consists of poetry, comics, satires, sketches. The writings, like the discussions, are attempts by people to communicate with each other directly. What I'm experiencing is something you called communication among likes, communication by all about themselves, their lives and their possibilities, the communication at the basis of common projects.

Besides trying to answer the various questions people come in to ask, I've also corrected and typed some of the frequent announcements and information bulletins. After what I told you in my last letter, you won't believe who I work with on these bulletins and leaflets. Not the "academic revolutionaries" Daman, Minnie, Hugh or the others; I haven't seen any of them since I've been here. Tina pops in several times a day, always in the midst of a group of workers or students or both, always incredibly busy with the art work or layout of a leaflet, pamphlet or poster. The printing is done in Ted's print shop! Tina herself does most of the actual printing, although she encourages people to do their own printing. And you won't believe who else is here! The entire garage crew except Vic and Seth — and except Jose, who was killed three years ago. Yes, Sabina is here, as well as Tissie! They're together at an enormous research center; the workers there are about to occupy the center and open it up to the whole population; it all sounds nebulous but enormously exciting. Ted and Sabina got Tissie released from a prison "hospital". I've been so busy that I haven't seen Tissie yet.

In my previous letter I insisted that my "world" as well as yours was the world of Hugh, Daman, Minnie and, yes, the world of Luisa; she's not here either. I told you that I left the garage in order to return to the world that was so familiar to me, the world which I identified with projects I had once shared with you. Isn't it ironic? Now that I'm engaged in precisely those projects I'm with the very people I'd left in order to engage in them. Does this mean you were right when you said my "descent to Sabina's world" was a descent to yours? I don't think so. I rather think all the people I knew have changed in ways that couldn't have been predicted. In several of your letters you argued that such enormous changes were impossible. You seemed convinced that once Vera Neis, to take just one example, got on the bureaucratic train, there was no way for her to ever get off. But what's happening here right now disproves that type of fatalism if nothing else does. Who'd ever have imagined Sabina or Ted in any way connected with a student commune, or Tissie in a research center? I don't see where your fatalism comes from. You've told me that during your second prison term you became disillusioned with Luisa's frequently obsessive optimism. I don't blame you for that. But don't you see that your fatalism flatly contradicts the very possibility of events like those that took place in Magarna, like those you've been experiencing during the past two months, like those I'm experiencing now? If people were all locked into trains headed toward predictable destinations, who would ever give rise to those unpredictable and unforeseen events we call revolutions? I don't think I was wrong about the people I knew in the garage ten years ago. I think they're different people now; I think they've all changed in completely unpredictable ways. I've seen such changes before. Jose, for example, became totally transformed two or three years after I left the garage. It could happen to Vera too, as well as Adrian and Marc. One or all of them may yet respond to the atmosphere that first stimulated Yara, then you, then Jasna. You may yet find yourself storming the prison walls alongside your former comrades. In case that happens, be sure you tell me what you did with your fatalism.

No, I don't think I was wrong about the nature of the activity in the garage and the bar. When Hugh described it, he merely gave words to my innermost thoughts. That wasn't the project I had sought all my life. It was a capitalist operation existing on the fringes of society and exploiting those least able to defend themselves. I had to leave the garage in order to live my own life, in order to launch my own project. The funny thing is that when I finally did find a project that had something in common with the one I had shared with you, it was with Jose, of all people — a totally transformed Jose.

But I'm rambling. A meeting is taking place and I'm trying to listen and write at the same time. Two postal workers are talking excitedly to a group of workers from an occupied factory. I'm trying not to be guilty of Luisa's uncritical optimism, but Yarostan: if postal workers can be affected by the spirit of the occupations, everyone can! Do I dare imagine where all this could lead? How I wish you were here!

It's relatively quiet here again. Yes, I wish you were here, but not because I'm miserable without you. I've rarely been happier. I want to share that happiness with you. I also longed for you ten years ago, after I left the garage, but then my longing didn't come from a desire to share happiness with you. I wanted you to help me out of my misery. When Hugh asked me not to join him in his activity at the "Project House," my heart broke. How similar that activity must have been to the activities I shared with you in the carton plant. How similar that "Project House" must have been to the Council office I'm in right now. How I longed to work with Hugh, to be loved by him, to be accepted by the "street people." The most exploited, the most dehumanized started to stand up, refusing to accept the life into which they were born; they started "becoming themselves, on their own," as Hugh put it. And today many of those very people are occupying factories. I wanted to be part of that movement, part of that community, but in Hugh's eyes I could only be a leech on that community, I could only push it back down, suck its strength out of it and incapacitate it at the very moment when it was trying to raise itself up on its own. I could only be part of "the cancer that annihilates every possibility of life and puts an end to every period of ferment" (those are your words, not Hugh's; I copied them into my address book; they were so similar to his).

I may be profoundly deluded about who I am, but I really don't think I deserve your or Hugh's descriptions of me. I had already started working in the fiberglass factory when I found Hugh. At the very moment when he called me a leech, I was already discovering what it meant to be exploited, maltreated, injured; I was already one of the units of human flesh on which the Leviathan feeds, I was already exchanging my life for a lifeless survival. You told me you felt a certain satisfaction — I think you called it resignation — during the hours you spent in that steel factory and during the hours you spent traveling there. I came closer to feeling defeated. I don't remember everything you said about your resignation and I'm not sure I can really pinpoint the difference between that and defeat. I think by resignation you meant to say that you didn't really accept your condition but that you put up with it because you didn't see any prospects for abolishing it; as soon as such prospects appeared you'd be among those fighting to abolish the condition. Many people must feel that way: the proof is that today they're destroying the "jobs" to which they were resigned only yesterday. But I didn't feel that way. My attitude was infinitely more cowardly, even slavish. I was resigned, yes, and I dreamed of getting out of that factory — exactly as I'd gone in: by myself. The liberation I dreamed of was my liberation from that factory, not our liberation from that condition. I wasn't resigned but defeated. For me there were no prospects other than for me to leave, letting all the other "me's" remain there.

Was I "spoiled," as you suggested? Was I unwilling to share the conditions of my peers because I aimed for a social position like Vera's? I really don't think so. Yet I can't really justify having left that factory the way I did. I can tell myself such factories wouldn't exist if everyone left them but I know perfectly well that not all the people in that factory had college educations on which to fall back or rich "sisters" who'd come to their rescue. I think the truth is that I didn't have the physical or moral strength to feel resigned. I was dying on that job, literally dying; I wouldn't have survived until the day when prospects appeared; my resignation wouldn't have been an acceptance of a temporary set-back but an acceptance of certain death. I was defeated in the face of a condition I really couldn't cope with; my only prospect was to escape from it.

That was the only factory job I ever had. I'm sure all factory work isn't as horrible as mine was but I never had the slightest desire to find out. The mere thought of doing anything even slightly similar to what I did there sends shivers down my spine. I was one of four people — three women and a man — who pulled a continuous blanket of fiberglass from one set of rollers and pushed it into another set. Although we wore long rubber gloves, boots and masks, minute particles of glass found their way into every pore of our skin, into our hair, our mouths, our nostrils, our lungs. It had a peculiar, horribly offensive smell; I still get nauseated whenever anything reminds me of it. I felt perpetually as if pins were sticking me; the smell followed me wherever I went; I lost my appetite because everything tasted like glass. That job didn't only consume my time, my energy, my human possibilities, like the bus you described so vividly; it literally consumed my very life. One of the women I worked with described our situation with the most bizarre sense of humor. "It's not really so bad once you figure out what it's all about," she'd say. "At first you hate it so bad you can't wait to get out of it. Then your lungs go. They can fix you up the first time if you've got one strong lung. When you come back you know the wait won't be so long; one lung can't take as much as two. That's when it becomes fun: you want to see how long you can hold out. They always fire you the second time you go to the hospital. They know you've made it. You're out of it. There's no more waiting." She went to the hospital, for the second time, a few weeks before I left that job. In order to prepare oneself for a day when there are new prospects on the horizon, you have to assume you'll survive until that day. I couldn't assume that. My only prospects were escape or death.

Your worst three years in prison couldn't have been as empty or as painful as the three years I spent in that fiberglass factory. During both prison terms you seem to have found frequent occasions to have profound discussions with people, occasions to think meaningfully about yourself, your past, your surroundings, your future. For me those three years were like a coma from which I woke three or four times, and I remained drowsy even during those few moments of wakefulness. What a horror! I know all about "hardships" and "circumstances," but I still don't understand how people can put up with that. Out of over a thousand days, I was awake and alive during three days — if that long! On my last day in the garage, Minnie had blamed Sabina and Jose for the fact that I had become a mindless idiot, "a grinning vegetable." How wrong she was! It wasn't the garage but the entire society outside it that transformed human beings into grinning vegetables.

I was awake for at most three days during those three years, and almost all the waking hours took place during the last year. I remember only one "event" during the first two years and that only took a few minutes. I didn't dream of telephoning Sabina or Jose; I knew Jose would never forgive me for having run out on him exactly as I'd run out on Ron; I didn't blame him. And I couldn't bear the thought of Sabina saying, "Coward, you're just like your mother." I did telephone Luisa once, several months after I'd left her. I no longer know why I called her; I suppose I wasn't really awake even then. I lied to her. "I'm calling to let you know I'm alive and happy," I told her.

"So am I," she said; "intensely alive and very happy. Do you want to get together to celebrate our happiness, or just to talk?"

"I'd rather not, Luisa. I hope that doesn't hurt your feelings."

"Not at all," she said. "In fact, I'm relieved; I'd rather not face you after that last scene you made."

"That makes two of us." Both of us were silent for a while. Then I said, "Goodbye, Luisa," and hung up. I didn't see or talk to Luisa again for seven years. I ran into her by accident last year, after the riot, in a bizarre committee which was supposed to document or publicize the police repression during the riot.

The only prospect I had during those first two years was to save enough money to escape from that hell. Unlike most of the other people in that factory, I didn't have a family to support or a "home" to furnish and decorate; I didn't buy any of the things they bought. I remained in that cheap hotel room and saved three quarters of my paycheck. I calculated that after five years I'd have enough money saved to support myself for another five years without working; I intended to spend the later period writing about the earlier period; I'd be "free," if I were still alive.

But my prospects suddenly changed. One evening I returned from work and saw two familiar figures sitting on the doorstep of my hotel. I immediately recognized Sabina, but Tina had grown so much during those two years. I walked faster and then ran — directly into Sabina's waiting arms. I was so relieved when she embraced and kissed me. I turned to Tina, shook her hand and exclaimed, "You're as tall as I am, Tina! I almost didn't recognize you. What are you two doing here?"

Tina had tears in her eyes when she said, "We were thrown out this morning, Sophia. So we came to you."

I couldn't hold back my tears. "To me? You came to me? You mean you both forgive me?"

Sabina answered sarcastically, "Who said anything about forgiving you? How sentimental! We've come for revenge! How could we ever forgive you after all you've done to us?"

I dropped Tina's hand and backed away from both of them, frightened. "What do you mean — revenge?"

Tina jumped toward me and, pulling me to her, whispered, "You are unbelievably dumb, Sophia! That's why I missed you so much after you left. Don't you know how much Sabina likes you? We know you couldn't help what you did."

But Sabina exclaimed, "Don't let yourself be blackmailed by her tears, Tina! We've come for revenge, Sophia, and we won't let your sentimental tears divert us from the purpose of our visit. Our first step will be to force a decent meal down your throat!"

Tina, still holding me in her strong skinny arms, whispered, "Small wonder you thought I was so tall. The hotel keeper told us you took bread and cheese to your room and never went out."

Unashamed, I let my tears run freely down ray face. "I love you, both of you!"

"You may regret that admission after we're through with you," Sabina said sarcastically, while each of them put her hand under one of my arms and started pulling me toward a restaurant. "After we fatten you we're going to abandon you to your new friends."

"I don't have any friends," I sobbed.

"I saw one in your room!" Tina exclaimed. "The hotel man let us in; he wanted your 'sister and your 'daughter' to wait for you in your room — but I was scared to death; it was so big and ugly."

"I suppose there aren't any rats where you come from, Princess," I said to Tina, angered and dismayed by her distinctly "upper class" attitude toward my "proletarian" room.

"No there aren't!" Tina exclaimed. "You know there aren't! I've never seen a rat before. When we arrived here this morning we intended to rent a room near yours. But I begged Sabina not to; I wouldn't have slept a wink. We spent the whole day looking for a place — and we found one, right near here, and cheap."

I forgot my pride in my living quarters and started sobbing again. "Is there room for me?"

Sabina hugged me, so this time I knew she was joking when she said, "Not even a corner, Sophia; I told you we intended to fatten you only in order to feed you to your new friends."

"I won't take up much room," I cried.

"You sure won't!" Tina exclaimed as we entered the restaurant. "Watch the waiter show us to a table for two! Wow, Sophia, you sure don't know how to take care of yourself! When one of Sabina's friends told her you'd left your mother and gotten a job, we thought you'd be all right. We never imagined you'd be starving yourself and sharing a room with rats. When we left your room to look for another place, Sabina said, 'Looks like we got here just in time.' Of course we found a place with room for you, dummy. We rented a whole house. Sabina and I didn't even choose our rooms yet; she said she wanted you to have the first choice — if you'd come with us."

I couldn't see the words on the menu in front of me.

Sabina kicked me under the table. "If you don't stop acting like a broken faucet, I'm going to — imitate your act, Sophia! Why don't you just smile and eat, and skip the melodrama?"

I tried hard to smile, and I tried hard to eat, but I couldn't do either very well. The food was delicious but it went down my throat with particles of glass.

Sabina and Tina waited for me outside my hotel while I stuffed all my belongings into two grocery bags. I loved the house they had rented. The three of us had lived in it for eight years when Tina left two weeks ago. The night we arrived, there was nothing in it but three cots, Sabina's and Tina's bundles, and a suitcase containing the few books, the two manuscripts and the old clothes I'd left in the garage.

When I returned from work the following evening, there was a refrigerator, a stove, as well as a table and chairs in the kitchen; there were beds and cabinets in all the rooms; there was a rug and a sofa in the living room. On the kitchen table were platters containing all the foods I had loved when Sabina and I had been small, before I ever met you. I couldn't stop myself from crying again. "Sabina, I've never ever done anything for you; it never even crossed my mind, not once —"

"And I never ever will again, since I'm making you so miserable!"

"I'm sorry. Don't people sometimes cry when they're happy? All this must have cost you a fortune: the food, the furniture, the rugs —"

"They were all gifts," Sabina said.

"I saved a lot of money during the past two years. I'm not penniless any more. I can pay for the food and furniture; I think I should at least pay the rent."

"And be our landlady?" Sabina asked angrily. "Not on your life! Each of us pays one third of the rent."

"But you've spent so much already! All this food and —"

Sabina turned to Tina and asked, "How much have we spent?"

Tina then turned to me and asked, "Sophia, do you mean you actually go to the supermarket to buy groceries?"

"But surely you didn't stuff the refrigerator and beds into your coats!"

Tina said, "We were thrown out of the garage but Sabina didn't lose all her friends."

I couldn't believe it. "Everything matches so well! It's all so tasteful — how could it all have been stolen — and in a single day?"

"One of her friends works as a truck dispatcher — she had the contents of an enormous mansion delivered here. The neighbors must think we're millionaires. Three moving vans came. We only took the things we wanted; they probably weren't even missed."

I ate the meal they had prepared for me but I enjoyed their thoughtfulness more than I enjoyed the meal; even my favorite foods tasted like glass. Sabina, as if she'd sensed my feelings, told me halfway through the meal, "It is clear to you, isn't it Sophia, that you don't have to go back to that job?"

I couldn't think clearly. I said thoughtlessly, "Thank you, Sabina, but there's one thing I won't accept from you, and that's your money. I don't know where it comes from and I don't want to be dependent on it." None of what I said was true and I knew it when I said it. Sabina turned her face away angrily, but only for a second; then she was friendly again; she acted as if she hadn't heard. I obviously knew where her money came from, every penny of it: she had told me; she hadn't hidden anything from me. Snatches of what Alec had told me in the garage, snatches of what Hugh had said flew through my mind. But Hugh's and Alec's critiques weren't the real reason for my refusal. During the previous two years I had acquired another reason, an unbelievably crude one, for not wanting to be dependent on Sabina or on anyone at all. I'm ashamed to tell you what it was. I had gotten into the habit of counting my money. Every week I calculated the money I had earned, the amount I'd need for rent and food and the amount I'd deposit in my bank account. I told you before that I intended to use this money later to live more comfortably and to write. That's not completely true. The life I'd live and the works I'd write were contained in my bank account. Whoever it was who said capitalists and workers had nothing in common hadn't ever worked for wages. Accumulate! Accumulate! That's Moses and the Prophets, not only in the bureaus of capitalists but in the mind of every worker. I longed to leave the fiberglass factory but I couldn't abandon my bank account: two years of my past as well as my whole future were in it. If I had accepted Sabina's offer, every miserable minute of those two years would have been for nothing. By turning down Sabina's offer, I didn't use up two years of my life for nothing, but three.

Sabina didn't insist, although she knew perfectly well what that job was doing to me. As always, I was "my own person", she merely wanted me to be aware of all my alternatives. I abandoned that awkward topic and asked why she and Tina had been thrown out of the garage.

Tina shocked me by answering, "First of all Jose was arrested."

"Jose!" I exclaimed. "Why?"

"Someone squealed," she said.

"Was there a raid? Was it the police that chased you out?"

"We were chased out the same way your friends were: by Seth's gun."

"But that's awful! You've both been so cool! Why didn't you tell me?"

Sabina asked, "Would you have eaten more if you had known? Would you have slept better?"

She was right. I didn't care why they'd been thrown out. All I cared about was that they'd come to me, that they'd taken me away from that horrid hotel, that they loved me. "You know I wouldn't have eaten more," I admitted. "If I ever want to know the details, I'll ask." I never asked.

But Sabina wanted me to know one more thing. A few days later she told me, "I visited Jose this afternoon. He wasn't glad to see me. 'Poor Ron,' he said; 'he could never really appreciate you, Sabina; you're made of gold, you know that?' 'But you were expecting someone else, weren't you?' I asked him; 'someone who wasn't made of metal but of flesh. He turned away from me and cried."

"How could he?" I sobbed. "He has every reason in the world to hate me. I walked out on him exactly as I walked out on Ron."

"What about the rest of us?" Tina asked, offended. "You walked out on us too! Don't we count?" I started to cry, but Tina made me stop by squeezing my face in her hands and scolding me. "You dumbbell! You're just like a baby! Whatever made me think you were my mother? You also walked out on Sabina and me. Yet here we are. Jose doesn't hate you, Sophia. He told me Ron never hated you. He told me Ron knew you couldn't ever do the things Ron wanted you to do. No one can hate you because of that. Besides, Jose told me he thought you were right — both times."

I couldn't make myself ask more questions. But the following night I did ask Sabina how to go to the state prison, and what I needed to get in. She had papers made for me proving I was Jose's sister. Sabina had already visited him as his "wife."

The trip to the prison lasted over an hour each way; the visit was only half an hour long. The first time I went, Jose just kept rubbing his eyes. "I can't believe it. Either you're Sabina turning yourself into Sophie by some magic trick, or else I'm in my cell dreaming."

"I'm me."

"But you look so different. What the hell happened to you, Sophie? Did you go through a machine?"

"Aren't you going to ask me why I left you?"

"You're a genius, kid, that's why. You figured things out before any of the rest of us did. And that's why you ought to take better care of yourself. If you don't, you won't be around for that trip we were going to take. How did he size things up so fast — what was his name, your friend?"

"Hugh."

"He sure pinned us down, right where it hurt. What made him able to see right through us? Was it something he learned in school? Is it in books? I'd sure like to see him again. Can you bring him with you sometime?"

"No." I was crying. Words gagged in my throat; I couldn't see Jose when a guard accompanied him out of the visiting room. For two months I did nothing but go to work and sleep. I should say almost nothing. A few days after my visit I left a sheet of paper on the living room desk; on top it said, "For Jose." On it I scribbled the titles of all the books I had read and discussed with the people on the university newspaper staff; I kept adding titles as they came back to me. Whenever I added a title to the list, the book would appear in the living room bookshelf the following day, or else I'd see Tina reading it when I came home from work; she must have read all of them. I kept expecting Sabina to take some of them along on her visits to Jose, but she always went empty-handed. I had always been an avid reader, from long before you knew me; even during my stay in the garage I had read at least three books a week. But I didn't open a single book during the three years I worked in the fiberglass factory. After my visit to Jose my interest in the books I had read before revived. I wanted Jose to read them. It was the only way I knew to tell him what had made Hugh "able to see right through us." That obviously wasn't an adequate response to Jose's question, but I couldn't deal with his question; the closest I could come was to deal with the books I'd read, the books Hugh had read. Two months after my first visit I went to the prison with a bag full of books. They didn't let me in with all of them, but they did let enough through to take up all of Jose's reading time between my visits. I went once a month. I came to life during those visits. Jose devoured the books; he couldn't wait to discuss them with me. He was no longer the Jose I'd known; he wasn't anyone I'd ever known; our relationship wasn't a continuation of any relationship that had existed before. Our love had never existed. During those visits I came to life as something you unflatteringly called me in your letters, as a pedagogue. I came to life as Jose's teacher, as his guide, his mentor. What came to life, Yarostan, was my relationship to you. What revived was the week I'd spent with you: the tours you had given me, the discussions, the long, patient explanations. Only with Jose it was I who did the guiding and the explaining. You've admitted that you yourself were a pedagogue after your release from your first prison term, when you first met Mirna; you taught her everything you'd learned from the resistance, from Luisa, from the prisoners you'd met. I came closest to my relationship with you by becoming to Jose what you had been to me and to Mirna. Isn't it ironic that this happened with Jose of all people? The Jose who devoured my books and waited impatiently to discuss them with me wasn't the person to whom I'd abandoned myself in the garage. He became the person I had dreamed of meeting ever since I left you; he became the companion with whom I was going to experience a new world, the comrade with whom I was going to realize all my life's projects. I dreamed again: of the day when Jose would be released, of the day when I would no longer have my job. But I didn't realize my dreams. Jose was released — and a few days later he was dead.

The dreams I dreamed then are coming to life only now, in numerous factories, in this occupied university, in the Council office where I'm writing this letter. And now that the activity is real I'm no longer a pedagogue. You were right and Hugh was right. I don't have anything to teach. I never did. I've learned more during the past week than I'd learned during the previous twenty years. Yes, I'm now the one who is learning all the things I'd thought I could teach.

I learned quite a lot during the past three weeks. I wanted to tell you about some of them in my previous letter, but I had too much else to tell, I was too carried away by the sequence of experiences that came back to my memory. Many of the things I didn't tell you answer questions you've been asking ever since you started writing me. I'm really sorry I didn't take a little more time to tell you all the things I learned from Sabina. I'm already starting to forget some of them, and the exciting events taking place around me aren't helping me keep everything straight.

I started to tell you about the discussion Sabina and I had three weeks ago, during our "outing," but I didn't ever return to that. It was a beautiful day; it looks beautiful out right now but I've hardly been outdoors for a week. We were all alone by the river, listening to quacking ducks, watching passing boats, talking about your letters and the questions you had raised. Sabina was unusually talkative. Your questions stimulated her to travel further and further back in time, all the way to the time of her birth, thirty-two years ago. Sabina often intimidates me, but despite that I think she's really fantastic and I wish I had some of her qualities. That day, as we lay on the grass sunning ourselves, she told me stories George Alberts had told her over twenty years ago. I'm having a hard time remembering them only three weeks after I heard them.

"It's funny that Yarostan keeps referring to the time and place of my birth," she said. "He wasn't even there. It's as if his memory were an extension of Luisa's."

"What's so funny about it?" I asked. "You weren't exactly there either. Your memory is an extension of Alberts'. I was every bit of two when you were born but I wasn't really there either and my memory doesn't have any extensions; I can hardly remember the few things I learned from Luisa."

"You know what?" she asked. "I wouldn't be surprised if that Manuel character Yarostan met in prison actually knew my grandfather" (namely Nachalo, my father). "Everything he told Yarostan has such a familiar ring to it. Manuel must at least have heard of him. Too many of the incidents are identical to incidents Alberts described to me; only the interpretation is different and by now my interpretation is closer to Manuel's than to Alberts'."

Sabina pointed to the passage where you said (I'm paraphrasing; I don't have your letter with me); "According to Sabina, workers fought a revolution in order to give power to people like Alberts — and people like Jan, Manuel and I had to be swept out of the way."

Sabina's response to this was: "Alberts told me exactly the opposite. Yet they both referred to the same events. In his own eyes, Alberts was the one who fought for a popular revolution and he was the one who was pushed aside by those opposed to the revolution. They can't both be right. Yet I think neither Alberts nor Manuel were lying, although I do think Luisa lied most of the time. I think Alberts and Manuel both fought for something — on opposite sides of the same battleground. They both described that battleground though each of them saw something completely different. I know what Alberts fought for, but I still don't fully understand Manuel; try to get Yarostan to tell you still more about him."

I told her I'd try, but I'm trying only now. Sabina told me about those events as if she'd experienced them herself, and as if they'd taken place only yesterday. When she was small, Alberts never tired of telling her that she was born right after the greatest revolution that ever took place, during one of the darkest nights in all history. The army attacked the city. Everyone was in the street. Nachalo, Luisa and Margarita were behind barricades. "Alberts stayed indoors minding two-year old you. He told me how he pleaded with Margarita not to go out; she was about to give birth. But Margarita couldn't be kept indoors; according to him, she was the revolution." A bullet grazed Margarita's arm. The injury wasn't serious, but she lost a lot of blood when she could least afford to. "He always called her the little gypsy. She died two days after the revolution's victory, giving birth to me. She was fourteen." During those two days, Alberts never left Margarita's bedside. He told her the reactionary forces of the whole world had been destroyed by all the Margaritas behind the barricades. He told her she was giving birth to a new epoch. All the marvels of science and technology were going to make the people free instead of enslaving them. Gone was the day when workers had to fight against inventions and labor-saving devices which up to then had only been used to increase misery. Gone was the day when workers cursed science because it was used mainly to torture and kill them. He told her she was giving birth to an age of unfettered creativity, an epoch of unprecedented scientific and technological innovation carried out by the people themselves and for themselves. "Margarita died giving birth to another little gypsy. That was the dark night. She wasn't ever going to enjoy her creation — neither she nor any of the other Margaritas who gave birth to it. Alberts told me I was all that remained of the revolution he had told her about." I couldn't take my eyes off Sabina as I listened. It dawned on me that her whole life has been an attempt to realize Alberts' hopes in herself, that she has tried to embody in her own being the revolution to which Margarita gave birth. "Tell Yarostan his friend Manuel was right. The brightest of all days was followed by the darkest of all nights. The incredible victory on the streets and in the factories was immediately followed by an incredible defeat on the same streets and in the same factories. Luisa thought the defeat took place on the front, in the battlefield. She was wrong. The defeat took place in the rear. Alberts knew that by the time he told me I was all that was left of the victory. But he never figured out what role he played in that defeat." After Margarita's death, Nachalo left for the front; Luisa drove a streetcar and nursed both babies; Alberts was transformed. He wanted revenge. He ranted about destroying the reactionary forces that had taken Margarita's life and were destroying the world she had fought to create. He joined a military brigade consisting mainly of foreigners. He was told the aim of the brigade was to join with the revolutionary population to destroy the reactionary forces.

"And he believed that. He thought that after the liquidation of the few remaining nests of reactionaries the field would be clear for the realization of his dream, Margarita's dream. He never admitted that this was a pack of lies. That popular army he enlisted in had only one aim: to impose itself over the population. In its view, the main nest to be liquidated was the revolutionary population itself; the campaigns against the reactionary army were nothing but a pretext, a justification for its existence. It was the popular army he joined that wiped out every trace of Margarita's victory, every possibility for the realization of her dream. He never admitted that. He blamed the population itself for the defeat; his view of the population always remained identical to that army's view: hoodlums, adventurists and saboteurs; according to him all the revolutionaries had been killed on the barricades or died after that battle; there were no Margaritas left. But that wasn't what he thought when he joined the popular army. He thought he was joining a revolutionary population in a struggle against reactionaries; he thought that army actually had the population's support. When it finally dawned on him that it didn't, he ran. He was always a democrat first of all. Once he convinced himself that the entire population was reactionary, and not just a few nests, he ran. He never figured out that it was the popular army itself that was the central nest of reaction, but he did have enough 'principles' to refuse to fight in an army that opposed the entire population."

I asked Sabina when she figured all this out.

"When I met Ron," she told me. "Actually when Ron moved in with me in Alberts' house. Alberts called him a hoodlum, an adventurist, a petty criminal. That was when I started to figure out who that army had fought against, whom Alberts blamed for that defeat. The reason I liked Ron was that I thought Margarita must have been a little like him: the same mixture of fury and humor, the same visceral rejection of all morality; both were accomplished pranksters, unselfconscious thieves, and fatally romantic, except that poor Ron never found his barricades. Alberts was the diametrical opposite of both. He stayed indoors during the day of the barricades. He didn't move off his ass to join the fight until all the adventure and romance were gone, until an apparatus had replaced the fighting people." Inside that apparatus. Alberts experienced only one campaign, and it wasn't at all heroic. His brigade unit reached the front in a village which was terrorized by a small, poorly armed enemy unit; a villager was frequently killed if he wandered off alone; occasional showers of shells caused numerous injuries. Before the arrival of Alberts' brigade unit, the village had supposedly been defended by a loosely disciplined militia unit. According to Alberts, this militia unit didn't protect the village from the enemy but was in fact an extension of the enemy beyond the front and was itself responsible for the terror reigning in the village; the sole activity of that militia was to sabotage weapons, shoot at their own troops, encourage desertion among the soldiers, demoralize the village population. Some weeks before Alberts' arrival a military commander had arrived in the village to coordinate the militia's moves with those of the rest of the popular army and the commander had been murdered. The first task of Alberts' brigade unit was to liquidate the enemy agents who had infiltrated and taken over the militia unit. The infiltrators were known; there were eight of them. But the villagers were so demoralized and the militia unit was so rotten that the infiltrators carried on their activities in broad daylight. Part of the militia even tried to prevent Alberts' popular army unit from arresting the infiltrators. Alberts accepted an assignment to the firing squad which was to liquidate the infiltrators. He still wanted to revenge Margarita and to remove one of the "nests" that prevented the realization of all she'd fought for. But just before the order to shoot was given, one of the eight condemned men shouted, "Next time the people rise they'll turn against the red butchers first. That will be the first moment of the real revolution!" When the order to shoot was given, Alberts shot into the air. "This was his only military campaign," Sabina told me, "and at the critical moment he refused to take part in it. The condemned man had spoken in the name of the people; the firing squad was killing him in the name of the people. Alberts had joined the brigade to liquidate a few nests of reactionaries, not to liquidate the people. When he heard that man, Alberts suddenly suspected that the people might not want the revolution his popular army was bringing them. And his suspicions were confirmed in a matter of hours. The entire militia unit and half the villagers surrounded his brigade unit. Shooting began. His popular army unit had to abandon the village altogether and camp outside it, fortifying itself against the enemy unit as well as the surrounding peasantry. It became clear to him that the task of his brigade was to force Margarita's revolution down people's throats with weapons. That wasn't the project he'd had in mind, and it couldn't be done in any case. When that poorly armed enemy unit attacked, it had the whole population's support. Alberts was injured; half his comrades were killed; his popular army unit was routed. That was when he concluded the entire population was reactionary: hoodlums, adventurers and saboteurs; they would never industrialize by themselves; Margarita's dream was an illusion. Alberts ran. He's been running ever since."

Thinking I had missed one of the main points of Sabina's story, I said, "Then Alberts didn't actually agree with the aims of that army he joined, and Yarostan is wrong when he accuses Alberts of wanting to impose his own power over that population."

"Yarostan means something different, something I don't altogether understand," she said. "Yarostan thinks Alberts' project, his very dream, was repressive
in and of itself." She showed me the passage where you said industrialization could
only take place by robbing human beings of their energy, by stunting their capacities. "Alberts finally concluded that industrialization could never be carried out
by the people themselves," she continued. "The implication being that the people
would always need someone like Alberts at the helm, as foreman, supervisor, boss.
By adopting that attitude Alberts became an outright reactionary, a turncoat. That
became perfectly clear to me when he had Debbie Matthews fired for her supposedly radical views. It was then that he and I parted ways. He crawled up the bureaucracy and I rejoined Margarita on the ground. We went a long way to proving him
wrong — all of us: Ron, Tissie, Jose, Ted — the people themselves. We industrial-
ized, on our own. Yarostan knows that people can do that on their own. But he goes
a step further. He says it's not worth doing. His opposition to Alberts is different
from mine. In his view Alberts didn't only want to push people aside to make room
for the supposedly indispensable bosses. That far we agree. Yarostan also thinks
that if people freely develop their potentialities, there's no steel; if there's steel, then
there are no potentialities — and no people. I don't understand that. Maybe I'm too
much George Alberts' daughter to understand that; maybe I'm too much the little
gypsy who fought on the barricades so as to conquer the science and the technology for myself and others like me. What Alberts taught me was that the power of
the people as well as their freedom resided in the steel. In the technology. In physics, chemistry and engineering. In machinery. That's been the axiom of my life and
it remained my axiom after Alberts turned against the people. He never turned
against the technology. I'd thought those who opposed the technology were outright medieval obscurantists."

I reminded her that Luisa had in fact called you a "reactionary" after she'd read
one of your first letters.

"I know. I heard her. She's wrong. When you call someone a name, you stop
listening to him. Luisa hasn't heard anything for thirty years. Yarostan is no reactionary. He's trying to tell me something that conflicts with my most basic axioms.
I think he's wrong but I'm not sure. I'd like to be sure before I call him any names."

It was almost night when Sabina and I left our desolate spot along the river's
edge and returned to the city. I was baffled by much of what she'd told me; I couldn't
sort it out into clear and distinct categories. But I was happy as I crossed the bridge
with Sabina. I was happy because I knew you and was together with you again, at
least by mail. I was happy, and even somewhat proud, to cross the bridge with my
little gypsy "sister," happy that I too had been born somewhere near the uproar she
described. And I was happy because I thought I understood both you and Sabina
a little better.

But my self-satisfied mood didn't last long. My happiness as well as the
details of Sabina's story were replaced by worries about the note from the college

administration. My arrest, my firing and Tina's departure were all I could think of last time I wrote you. It took me several days to get used to the fact that I was unemployed again and that Daman wasn't going to help me get another job. The only time I ever looked for a job on my own I landed in that horrid fiberglass factory. But I was in no mood to sit home worrying about that. Sabina's narrative stimulated my interest in other questions you had asked. On the day after I mailed my letter to you — on Sunday two weeks ago — I telephoned Luisa. I remembered she had once known Lem Icel and had in fact seen him much more recently than I had. I learned this a year ago, when I ran into her by chance after the riot. At that time I had asked her what she'd been doing besides working during the seven years since I'd last seen her. She told me that for several years she'd gotten deeply involved in the activities of the so-called "peace movement," and that she'd been introduced to that "movement" by none other than "a former friend of yours, Sophia, a young man by the name of Lem." I turned away in disgust. The last time I'd seen Lem I had lost all desire to see him or hear of him again. But your letters have revived my interest in Lem. You asked me several times why Lem had been arrested twelve years ago while trying to deliver my letter to you and I wasn't able to answer. I decided to find out once and for all by trying to find Lem and by getting his own account of his arrest.

Luisa was furious when she answered the phone. "What the hell do you mean by 'Hello, Luisa'! You've got some nerve to be so calm! Your friend Daman came here a few days ago to tell me you were kidnapped! Sabina was with him; she obviously didn't come into the house."

"It was really thoughtless of me not to call sooner. I apologize."

"Thoughtless isn't the word, Sophia. You're as inhuman as the monster you live with. Daman told me to call him if I heard anything from the kidnappers. I couldn't sleep half the night! I was so upset I kept calling him. Finally he found out you were in jail for assaulting a professor. I had to call him again to learn that you were out of jail. Did you think I didn't care what happened to you?"

"Is there anything I can do to make it up to you, Luisa?"

"Nothing. My heart is like a stone."

"I'll cry!"

"For me? That's very flattering, Sophia. It means you want something from me. That's flattering too. What do I have that you might want?"

"Everything, Luisa: love, friendship, help —"

"Get off it! What do you want?"

"Luisa, do you remember Lem Icel? Do you suppose you could reach him?"

"Of course I could; he's living on an estate. I took him there myself."

"Are you joking?"

"No. But the only way I can reach him is by actually going there; it's an hour out of the city by bus. Is it something urgent?"

"It is to me. Are you busy?"

"When can you be at the bus station?" she asked.

"In fifteen minutes."

She beamed as soon as I walked into the bus station. "What happened to your stone heart?" I asked when she put her arms around me.

"Does it really mean nothing to you that I spent half a night worrying about you?"

"I'm sorry to be so glib, Luisa. That whole affair was so trivial it didn't deserve a phone call. I'm sorry Daman bothered you about it. You look beautiful in that dress. Is it new? Forgive me?"

"You're a rascal, Sophia. Are you going to propose that we walk the streets together?"

"You still remember that? How about doing it after we visit Lem?"

Luisa was really wound up. She acted like a teenage girl who'd just fallen in love, and in her pretty summer dress she even looked like one — except for her wrinkled face. On the bus she told me, "I don't know why you hang around Sabina and her violent friends, Sophia; your other friends are so nice!"

"Oh no, Luisa! You don't mean Daman!"

"He's a wonderful young man! A professor! And he's close to our movement too!"

"So he didn't just tell you I was kidnapped!"

"Certainly not! I let that hussy wait in the car for him. He seemed relieved when I asked him to come in."

"I bet it was love at first sight."

"What if it was!" she exclaimed. "I asked him if he was a student. No, he said shyly, a professor. I had forgotten you were old enough to have professor friends. He told me he'd known you for more than ten years, and that he'd also known Lem and Alec. I asked if you and he were more than just friends, and he said: not lately. When he left I told him I was sorry you hadn't introduced me to him ten years sooner. I was lying when I told you I spent half that night worrying about you. I did worry about you that night — a little."

"Luisa!"

"There are a few other things I'd like to tell you, Sophia."

"Right now? Tell me tonight, while we're walking the streets. How does Lem come to be living on an estate? And what did you have to do with taking him there?"

"That was one of the things I wanted to tell you before we got there. Lem didn't only introduce me to the peace movement. Lem and I became very good friends four or five years ago. He had suffered a great deal because of an errand you sent him on."

"Is that how he told it? He suffered because of me?"

"He told me he had been very active politically until he was arrested over there while trying to deliver certain messages you'd sent with him. He spent two years in prisons and camps. When I met him he was still politically conscious but he was terribly confused. He said the prison experience had opened his eyes, but I'm convinced it fogged his mind. I tried to keep his political interests alive, and for a year I almost succeeded. Almost. I couldn't get him to separate his activities in the peace movement from his growing interest in mysticism. He became irrational; he called it contemplative. He just sat, with one leg propped on a table, and stared into space. I was disgusted and of course he sensed that. He started talking about wanting to get away from what he called Civilization, about wanting to be alone with Nature. He even started to accuse me of depriving him of what he called Freedom, of keeping him locked up in a prison of steel and concrete, of separating him from his beloved Nature. Fortunately a friend of his found precisely the thing Lem was looking for: the estate, beloved Nature. Do you remember Art?"

"Art Sinich?" I asked with amazement. I had known Art during my brief involvement with the "peace movement." I saw him again last year in that "committee against repression" where I also bumped into Luisa, but I didn't know he'd had any previous dealings with Luisa and I certainly hadn't thought of him as "Lem's friend" — there are, after all, at least two million other people in this city. "Art was Lem's friend? And he owned an estate?"

"He didn't, but some relatives of his owned one. It had once been the country estate of a famous actor and his equally famous sister; they both died a quarter of a century ago, and the house and grounds have been totally abandoned since then. Weeds and trees have all but hidden what must once have been lovely paths and gardens. There are even weeds growing inside the house. When Art described the place, Lem begged us to take him there; he accused us of having kept him ignorant of the paradise the gods had created especially for him. So three years ago we took him to paradise. And good riddance. But you'll see."

It didn't take me long to "see." The country estate was literally "abandoned." What had once been the entrance way from the road was a path through a forest; there was no sign that any human being had been in the area for at least a quarter of a century. The path led to the remains of an immense house. The front door was wide open. Luisa went in; I could hardly get past the doorway. The entire floor was littered with several layers of garbage: food, empty wrappers, paper bags, empty boxes, torn books, rags; an old sleeping bag lay in the midst of the trash. I compulsively join Luisa in the impossible task of trying to pick up and sort the garbage.

"There's a beautiful kitchen down the hall," Luisa told me. "Art had the water connected, and even had electricity brought in. But to Lem that's Civilization. And this pigsty is Nature. In summer, on clear days, he spends the day sitting on a rock by the pond, always the same rock, until dark; he's afraid of the dark. In winter he doesn't budge from this room."

"How awful! Prison can't be worse."

"I know. I feel guilty about the whole thing. But I simply won't have him in my house and his father wants him put in an asylum. I'm sure that couldn't be worse. But Lem says he likes it here so why force·him into an asylum? His father is filthy rich, you know. Art had a disagreeable correspondence with Lem's father and finally got him to agree to send just enough money to cover the cost of food and electricity plus the cost of hiring a young man to deliver the food once a week. The old bastard spends at least twice that much on a detective who makes sure Art actually spends all that money on Lem. And Lem will talk your head off about how free and independent he is now that he's left rotten Civilization; he'll tell you Mother Nature takes care of his needs. But come on," she said, dropping the things she'd gathered, "let's at least get some fresh air while we're out here. Watch where you step; he doesn't use the bathroom if he can avoid it; Civilization destroys Nature's cycles and all that. But he's afraid he'll get lost if he leaves the path. I walked him up and down the path the first time we visited him, when I realized he hadn't left the house since we'd taken him to paradise."

The hermit·sitting on a rock was unrecognizable to me. He was as "abandoned" as the forest surrounding the lake. Hair hung down to his chest, his face was covered by a filthy beard. As we approached him, my heart pounded and my brain incessantly repeated one and the same question: am I responsible for this?

When Lem saw us he exclaimed, "Luisa!" but he didn't leave his rock. "You're going to take me away." He sounded hopeful when he said it, as if he wanted to be taken away.

"Away from paradise, Lem?" Luisa asked sarcastically. "Is Mother Nature mistreating you?"

"If you've come to take me, I won't resist because I know you're only obeying the cosmic will."

"I'm not taking you anywhere, Lem; I brought you a visitor. Can you try to remember to close the front door of the house when you leave in the morning? That way you won't have to share your food with all the lovely animals."

"All the creatures of the forest are Her offspring, Luisa. You don't understand them. You can't."

"I'm going for a walk around the pond," Luisa announced. "You ought to try it sometime, Lem; if you stay close to the water you'll come right back to your stone, unharmed."

"I get scratched, my beard gets all tangled," he said, but then he added, looking up at the sky, "I go far, far away from this stone, many planets away; I don't need to walk in circles around a pool of stagnant water."

"If you love Nature why are you so afraid of it — her?" Luisa asked, walking rapidly away from us.

"Remember me?" I asked, almost shouting; I had made myself comfortable on a fallen tree some distance away from Lem and his path of excrement; I didn't want to decrease the distance because he disgusted me. Nature is clean; Lem was a mound of unnatural filth from the top of the unwashed tangle of hair to the boots which hadn't been removed for three years.

"Sure, Sophie," he said without interest or resentment. "Still in the newspaper business?"

"Glass business, Lem. I told you that when you were living at Debbie Matthews house. Don't you remember my visit? I had just sold my newspaper business and gone into glass."

"I remember. You came with your half-sister and her kid. Doing well in the glass business?"

"Oh, marvelously, Lem. You and I wasted our time during all those years in the newspaper business. We should have turned to glass. I own most of the glass factories in the country now, and I'm known as the glass tycoon. But I'm not doing half as well as you are."

"That's right, Sophie, I'm doing well now, and it doesn't matter to me whether you owned the glass factory or just worked in it. I've learned that there are more important things. I've discovered my own inner light. Each one of us has an inner —"

I interrupted him and asked, "Do you remember those letters I had you deliver twelve years ago? I'm sorry about the trouble they caused you."

"Even that's unimportant now, Sophie."

"It's important to me, Lem. Why did those letters get you into trouble? Who did you give them to? Whom did you talk to about them? The only address I'd given you was that of the house we had lived in."

"You told me to ask for someone at that house. I did. The people living there had never heard of him. They told me to ask the police."

"You didn't take my letters to the police!"

"Of course I did. It was the People's Police. At that time they were Comrades. I had nothing to fear from them. I identified with them. I introduced myself as a Comrade, showed them my card and my invitation to the Conference. They weren't at all unfriendly. But in office after office they just leafed through the envelopes and told me they couldn't find any people with those names. Finally one of them recognized a name and gave me an address —"

"Do you remember the name?"

"I didn't know it even then, Sophie; I just showed people the names on the envelopes. Would anything have been different if I'd learned all those names?"

"I suppose not. Go on, Lem. He gave you an address —"

"I took a taxi there. It was an office building. The doorman wouldn't let me in. Finally I said the police had sent me there and he got polite and led me to an office. I waited and waited. When someone finally came, he recognized the name on one of the envelopes and told me to leave that letter in that very office, since your friend would stop by there later to pick it up. I asked him how I could find the other people. He took all the remaining letters and walked out with them."

"And you were arrested!"

"No. He was gone a long time, but he returned with the letters. He had put addresses on three of them and he even told me the order in which I should deliver them so as not to have to pay extra taxi fare."

"It's really too bad you don't know any of the names. Can you describe what part of the city you went to?"

"The first address was nearly an hour's ride away from that office building; I'd say the house wasn't in the city at all, but in a much more natural environment."

"Did the people seem like one-time peasants?"

"They seemed more natural. I don't know what peasants are like. A woman in a black dress and a black kerchief opened the door. I thought she looked afraid of me. She crossed herself as she took the letter; she didn't seem to understand a word though I spoke to her with my best accent. She closed the door on me while I was trying to tell her the letter was from an old friend of her husband's or her son's — I can't remember which although I'd been told in the office building. Then the cab took me all the way into the city to what looked like a construction area. There was a row of finished houses, but I had to walk a couple of blocks through mud to reach them. It was a woman again, with a baby girl."

"That was Mirna! What was she like?"

"She wasn't friendly either, although she didn't cross herself when she took the letter and she understood me and heard me out. She told me her husband returned from work very late. She also said she knew who I was and what the letter contained and she didn't seem very happy about it. Five minutes later I knew why. As soon as I got back in the cab, two plain-clothesmen got in beside me, one from each side. What did you tell them, Sophie? Why? It wasn't I who excluded you from that *Omissions* paper, but Thurston. I know I shouldn't have gone along with that. I knew it then. That's why I was eager to get out of it all and go to that conference —"

"Lem, please believe me, I didn't send you on that errand in order to have you arrested, those really were letters to my friends and I honestly didn't know people could be arrested for delivering or receiving letters."

"I wanted to believe that, Sophie. It was very hard for me not to believe that. But during the whole investigation and trial they kept repeating the name of my high school teacher George Alberts and they kept asking if I'd known him. Of course I'd known my own high school teacher. They said he was a spy and that made sense to me; I knew he'd had Debbie Matthews fired from her job. Who else but you could have told the police that George Alberts had been my high school teacher?"

"Lem, your arrest and Alberts' behavior in the high school had nothing to do with each other. George Alberts and Luisa —"

"You're as unscrupulous as I'd thought, Sophie. You can't implicate Luisa — don't you remember I know her? I confronted her with that as soon as I met her!"

"How did you even know that Luisa and I had any connection with Alberts? Did the police tell you that?"

"I knew you must have told them Alberts had been my high school teacher, and that's all I knew then. It was Debbie Matthews who told me..."

Of course! I last saw Lem seven years ago — in Debbie Matthews' house. I hadn't expected to see him there and my complete surprise had kept me from absorbing a great deal of what he told me. We went there on a weekday night, it was summer, I was exhausted after having sweated all day in the fiberglass factory; I wasn't altogether receptive to Lem's narrative or to his presence. This happened a few weeks after I had moved into the house Sabina and Tina had rented. Sabina told me that Jose had supported Debbie financially after Tom Matthews and Ron both died. Debbie had never gotten a job again after she'd been fired from high school because of Alberts. After her second visit to Jose in jail, Sabina became concerned about the fact that Debbie was no longer receiving any income from Jose. When she said she was on her way to Debbie's house, I begged to go along; I had liked Ron's mother, and I had never really thanked her for having helped me find Sabina after I'd been evicted from the university co-op. Tina also begged to go along, so as to see her "grandmother" again. Tired as I was, I was extremely curious about the relationship Sabina would be able to establish with Debbie. Jose was something like Debbie's adopted son, so I wasn't surprised that she accepted his financial support. But I wondered how willing she'd be to accept money from George Alberts' daughter. As soon as we entered the house where I'd almost been shot by Ron's father ten years earlier, I was sorry I'd asked to go along. Debbie answered the door wearing nothing but panties and a brassiere; she reeked of alcohol. She yelled, "Well what do you know, Lem, the Alberts girls, all two of them, and Ron's kid. So you've come to finish us off!" Behind Debbie, in his underwear, stood Lem Icel, the same Lem who had been my fellow pupil in Debbie Matthews' high school class, the same Lem who had been introduced to the world of "tendencies and things" by Debbie Matthews. Sabina shoved an envelope into Debbie's hand and said curtly, "Jose is in jail; he wanted me to give you this." Sabina was ready to leave. But Debbie threw the envelope at Sabina's feet and shouted, "Pick that up and take it with you, Miss Alberts! No one here is for sale. Isn't that right, Lem?" Then Debbie turned to me. "What are you staring at, dearie? The bathing suits? Don't you know it's the season for them? Isn't that right, Lem?" "That's right, Debbie," Lem answered; "bathing suits. We don't owe her any explanations anyway, not after what she did to us!" "What did I do?" I asked angrily. Debbie turned to me with flaming hatred in her eyes. "You unscrupulous, manipulative bitch! You're ten times worse than that lousy sister of yours. You're Alberts' first daughter. You're really good at it; you sure took me in! First I thought there was only one of you and that she was a two-faced schizophrenic. Then I learned there were two, and the second one was as sweet and innocent as a newborn babe; she's even shocked by bathing suits. But you can't do that innocent act in front of Lem! Show her your wounds, Lem!" "What did I ever do to him?" I asked angrily. Sabina kicked the envelope into the room and started leaving. Tina pulled me by the arm and begged, "Don't make a scene,

Sophia, please, can't you see they're both drunk?" Debbie shouted, "What did you do? Look! Look at this gash across his head! Look at his back. Look at his arms! Show her the rest, Lem! Show her what she did to you!" Sabina and Tina went out to the sidewalk. I started sobbing, "Have you gone crazy, Debbie? I didn't touch Lem! I couldn't have done that!" "There's no point in your acting so innocent, Sophie," Lem said; "I know all about those letters. That was a vicious trick to link me up with George Alberts, of all people. Really vicious. It wasn't until I got back and saw Debbie that I found out what else Alberts was: your father! After what he did to Debbie, you couldn't have told me he was your father, could you? So you made them think I was related to Alberts! You probably expected me to die there. Why, Sophie? Because of *Omissions*?" Debbie said, "Because you're a worse piece of shit than he is, that's why. At least Alberts never went so far as to pretend to be my boyfriend!" My anger returned and I shouted, "You're raving, Lem! What happened to those letters I gave you? What did you do with them? They mattered to me, Lem! My whole life was in them!" Lem answered, "They put me through two years of prisons and camps, Sophie! Two years! I told them everything I knew, but they beat me, burned me, cut me for not telling them things I couldn't know. They kept questioning me, transferring me and questioning me again. But you did do something for me, Sophie. Thanks to you I now know what it's really like over there. It's as rotten as it is here. Thanks to you my eyes were opened, Sophie. Now I see that Civilization is at the root of it all. Since I've been back I've been discovering new ideologies, positive ones, to replace what turned out to be a rotten ideology. I've been studying ancient Egyptian philosophy and Debbie introduced me to the peace movement. If you hadn't done this to me, Sophie, I'd think you'd be the perfect peace movement person; I always thought of you as a person with an inner light —" I was nearly hysterical with fury. I screamed at him. "You're lying, you bastard! You lost my letters! You're making all this up because you don't want to admit you lost them!" I ran out of Debbie's house crying. I didn't believe a word he'd told me. For seven years I remained convinced that he'd lost my letters. But some part of me must have believed something of what he said, because as we walked home I felt increasingly guilty. I asked Sabina and Tina if they'd heard of the peace movement. Sabina was too uninterested to answer but Tina said, "I've seen them. They sit in front of building entrances and wait for people to hit them. I talked to one of them. They think the more people hit them the more good they're doing." I didn't miss Tina's sarcasm, but a few weeks later I went to the address on a leaflet Tina brought me and I "joined" the "peace movement." I wanted to feel I was "doing good" when I was hit; for several years I had been hit and hit and I'd felt only the pain. One of the first people I met in the Peace Movement was Art Sinich, the young man who helped Luisa transport Lem to the estate.

All this came back to me while I listened to the bearded Lem on the abandoned estate. "...you must have told them Alberts had been my high school teacher.... It was Debbie Matthews who told me George Alberts was your father! So you were going to have me put away the way your father had Debbie put away!"

"Lem, you're wrong —"

"You can't implicate Luisa because I got to know her too, Sophie. You're no good. Debbie saw right through you. The first time I met Luisa I asked her what connection she'd had with Alberts and with my arrest. I learned she hadn't seen you in years, she'd separated from Alberts when we were still in high school and she disliked Alberts to the point of not wanting to even answer questions about him."

"Will you let me explain, Lem?"

"It wouldn't do any good, Sophie. Not because you're no good. Maybe Debbie was wrong. But because it's not important. These things are petty and most people spend their whole lives concentrating on petty things. I've learned to concentrate on —"

"Your inner light. You told me earlier, Lem." I saw Luisa returning from the direction behind Lem. I didn't have the energy to begin to explain. I couldn't even bring myself to apologize to that hairy, filthy mystic. I felt disgust and terrible guilt. I was the one who'd made him what he was, that revolting, rag-covered glob.

Luisa was all smile. "You picked a gorgeous day for your outing, Sophia!" She started skipping along the pond and then ran right past Lem toward me.

I fell into her arms crying. "Everything he told you about me, Luisa — it's all true, every word of it."

Luisa pressed my head between her hands and brushed my tears away with her thumbs. "Hey, I don't think I like this; I didn't ever intend to hold you to that promise."

"What promise?" I sobbed.

"Your promise to cry for me. I was flattered when you made that promise, but I know it's nothing but a trick designed to prove you're the child and I'm the old woman!"

I tried hard to smile. "My visit is over, Luisa. We were going to go street walking afterwards, remember?"

"Fine! You'll be my mentor! I'm the young novice." Remaining where she stood, Luisa shouted, "Goodbye, Lem. Take good care of Mother Nature. And close the front door."

"Thanks for coming, Luisa. You'll come again?"

"As soon as the inner light tells me to, Lem!"

She grabbed my hand and we ran through the forest to the street, avoiding Lem's path. As we walked to the bus stop, I said, "Luisa, have you changed or are you always like this?"

"Whenever I'm in love. I used to hide from you when I was in love; you always spoiled it. Today for some reason I enjoy your company immensely. I think I know the reason. I'm finally not your mother any more, Sophia. That feeling is gone, it's dead, not a trace of it remains. I like you for the first time in my life. You're like a new friend, an older friend."

"Older hell! I'll race you to the corner!" I shouted, starting to run.

"Older! Older!" she screamed, and reached the comer first.

"You think I'm jealous of your affair, or coming affair with Daman?" I asked as we climbed into the bus. "You can have him. I think he's awful."

"Sour grapes!" she yelled, pushing me into a seat.

When we got off the bus, Luisa hopped in front of me, spun around coquettishly, and then put her arm through mine and tugged me hurriedly down the street, asking, "Do I look like a hooker? Am I walking right? Come on, teacher, start teaching!"

"Luisa, I have a confession to make —"

"Aw Sophia, don't tell me you've never done it either! What a sad sack! Didn't those friends of yours teach you anything? I suppose you didn't approve!"

"If you're serious about it, Luisa, why are we rushing down the street?"

"Because I'm starving, that's why! I've got all the ingredients for a rice casserole and I'm inviting my new comrade to be my guest, unless she has prior commitments."

"No commitments, Luisa; I'd love to come. I haven't been there in years!"

"Good! Since you won't tell me any of your secrets, I'll have all the more time to tell you mine."

As soon as we were inside the house I started to run upstairs to my room, but Luisa stopped me halfway. "Hey, where are you going? Someone lives there!"

I climbed back down. "Sorry. I stupidly assumed it would always be my room. Is it someone I know?"

"Art Sinich."

"Art lives in my room? Since when?"

"Since the week after we took Lem to the country."

"Luisa! Did the entire peace movement stay in my room?"

"Just Lem and Art. And it's not your room! I've often thought Prudence would have been a much better name for you. You were named for a Sophia who was reckless, uninhibited, ferociously independent."

"I thought you'd stopped being my mother!"

"I have, sourpuss! That's why I'm having such a good time taking jabs at you!"

"Where will you put Daman? Are you collecting a male harem?"

"You act exactly as I'd always feared you would! You're so predictable! But my fear is gone. You're not my conscience any more."

"Your conscience! And who made me that?"

"I haven't the slightest idea, Sophia. I didn't. Nachalo didn't. They say that when the children of radicals rebel, they do so by becoming conservative."

"That's unfriendly, Luisa. I haven't exactly been conservative, and I always tried to live up to —"

"Your morals, my pretty —"

"You don't know anything about my morals!"

"I do know I had to hide from them with great care —"

"I hope that didn't spoil all your fun!"

"It didn't spoil much, Sophia. I was careless only once, with Alec —"

"Alec! Don't you know he only wanted —"

"You're as red as this pepper! Here, help me put this into the oven. Do you like it spicy?"

"Not too."

"Fine, then it's ready to bake. I thought you were through with Alec —"

"I was! I couldn't stand him!"

"Then why all this passion? Because I'm your mother? We should have had this scene at least twenty years ago! We'd either have become friends or sworn enemies, instead of this wishy-washy, polite How are you, nice to see you again. No, I'm not collecting a harem, Sophia. I'm just living my life, and I'm not hiding from you any more; in fact I'm having the time of my life showing it to you. Art was fine while the peace movement lasted, but he dried up when it dried up. When he too started talking about his inner light, I asked him to leave; he'll move out this week. Nor do I expect Daman to move in here; doesn't he have a nice place of his own? I like him, that's all. I get excited just talking to him on the phone. A professor!"

"Professors are beasts, Luisa. Doesn't that conflict with your principles: to like someone because he's an authority?"

"Is that why you're so upset? Help me set the table."

"I'm not upset! Where do you keep the glasses?"

"On the top shelf; you'll need a chair. Bring down two champagne glasses too."

"Champagne! Just for me, your conscience?"

"We're celebrating my independence!"

"I'm sorry you have to celebrate that."

"Not your fault, Sophia. I loved that man. He was my first. I was mad about him and I wanted to carry his child as well as his name. Now I'm carrying only his name. Salud y Libertad! To my independence!"

"Am I nothing at all like Nachalo?"

"Not a hair, Sophia! You're as gentle as a lamb —"

"Whereas he was violent, like Sabina, like Ron —"

"If you insist on that comparison —"

"Then why did you like him? You hated Ron! You hate Sabina!"

"Why did you like them? In high school you left Lem with his tongue hanging out and ran off with Ron. Explain that, Sophia, and you'll explain why I went crazy for Nachalo. Yes, he was violent. He lived with his rifle. When I met him he hadn't eaten for days and lived in a rathole. But his rifle was clean and he had lots of ammunition. Whenever he heard shooting he ran towards it; if it was workers shooting at priests, state officials, capitalists or cops, he'd empty his rifle as fast as he could fill it. But if two groups of workers ever shot at each other he'd risk his life by standing between them and shouting, 'When workers kill each other, there's no more reason to live. Kill me from both sides!' His violence was revolutionary violence. It had nothing in common with Ron's hooliganism."

"You never knew Ron! Besides, weren't there people in your union who thought Nachalo was a hooligan? What did George Alberts think of him?"

"Every one of the workers I introduced him to was as enthusiastic about him as I was."

"Luisa, you're hiding part of the picture."

"Of course the conservative old union leaders thought he was a hooligan. They considered everyone who still talked of revolution a hooligan. But their influence disappeared on the day of the barricades. Even Alberts became quite violent himself when Margarita died; he joined Nachalo on the front and nearly died alongside him. They fought for the workers' cause. Ron, Sabina and their ilk fought for nothing but their own precious selves!"

"Your casserole is delicious, Luisa."

"Well, didn't they?"

"I don't know, Luisa. I'm confused. Let's talk about something else. When we were arrested twenty years ago, why did the three of us get out of jail after two days whereas others stayed locked up for four years?"

"That's Yarostan's question."

"What if it is? You've told me George Alberts arranged our release. What power did he have to do that?"

"Why do you ask that? George became something of a mythical hero during the war; he did some research, I suppose in physics though he never told me about any of it; his work supposedly contributed significantly toward the victory. It made him a big man, very influential, with international connections. Everyone knew that, including Yarostan. What do you mean: what power did he have? There was nothing mysterious or secret about the power he had. If they'd left us in jail he'd have made a big scene in the world's press: Wife and family of wartime physicist arrested, tortured, and whatever else they spiced up those stories with. I despised him by then. During the war he'd convinced himself that workers were incapable of carrying a revolution through; he'd convinced himself all they could do was topple a dictatorship and make room for another and probably worse dictatorship. By the time we got here he was an outspoken reactionary; he thought our experience had only proved his reactionary outlook yet another time."

"Then why did you leave with him?"

"I thought we had no other alternatives and I still think so. Did Yarostan tell you there were better things for us to do?"

"He spent four years in prison!"

"I only learned that when his letter came this year! At the time I thought every-one was being released, either a day before us or a few days after. The police told us we'd all been arrested by mistake; it had all been a bureaucratic blunder."

"And you believed that?"

"Sophia, it's the easiest thing in the world to be so smart twenty years after the event! Of course I believed them; I had no reason not to. And you're not the one to be asking questions about my clearheadedness during those days! You were old enough to use your own head and draw your own conclusions — and you obviously don't remember just how helpful you were! A fifteen-year old girl hanging on to her mother's coat and staring off into space like an idiot who'd lost all her brains! I was so ashamed of you! Sabina's gypsy mother had only been fourteen when she'd died on the barricades. Don't you see you're still trying to hang on to me? 'Why didn't you do this instead of that, mother?' Sabina was only thirteen but she knew perfectly well what she wanted; she couldn't wait to leave and the ship wasn't fast enough for her! If you'd said you wanted to stay, you'd have stayed. If you'd only made a peep!"

"I'm ruining your celebration, Luisa. I'm sorry I brought that up."

"Damn you, Sophia, wipe those tears off your face! Why didn't you cry then? I would have understood tears! I would have left you there if that was what you wanted. But that stupid, helpless stare! I couldn't leave you in that condition; I thought you were sick! Don't you dare cry now! It's twenty years too late and I'm not a bit moved. I don't even feel sorry for you. You've made yourself what you are, Sophia, and if you hate yourself that way, don't start blaming me. Smile, won't you, please? A pretty, friendly smile, as if you enjoyed your comrade's company. Not through tears, you ninny! That's ten times worse! There, that's better. I don't see why you'd hate yourself. To me you've turned out just fine; you've already led two different lives —"

"You're the rascal, you know that Luisa?"

"See? I haven't turned out so bad either!"

"Thanks for the delicious dinner, Luisa, and for taking me to see Lem. Let me pour another round before I leave. To our friendship!"

"Bravo Sophia! There were thousands of other things I'd wanted to tell you."

"Then you'll have to invite me thousands of times!"

It must all sound terribly garbled to you. That Sunday night as I rode home in a taxi I was determined to start writing you the following morning, before I'd for-gotten everything I had just learned. I got home exhausted and slightly drunk. But I couldn't sleep. What Sabina and Luisa had told me about Nachalo, Margarita and George Alberts passed through my mind alongside images of that dirty, bearded hermit who had slept in what had once been my room. The following morning I got up with a headache. I stared at a blank sheet of paper but couldn't concentrate on anything. In fact I sat and stared all day long. I didn't even thank Sabina when she brought me a sandwich. It was my first completely empty day in years. It wasn't only the previous night's wine, nor my headache, that made me stare "like an idiot who'd lost all her brains." I wondered if I'd really turned out as fine as Luisa claimed I had, if I had any reason to be satisfied with the "two lives" I'd led (I suppose she meant my academic life and my life with Sabina, Ron and their friends). I had lost my teaching job and didn't have the prospect of finding another one. It dawned on me that for the past twelve years I hadn't had any projects. All my life I've wanted to create something of my own, something that has meaning to those I love. Yet for the past twelve years I've had only jobs, pseudo-projects, activities that use up my project-time and my creative energy but aren't in any sense my own: they existed before me and continue after me. They did more than use up my energy. They were substitutes for the real thing; they pretended to be projects; they filled the gap left by the absence of any activity of my own. They gave me the illusion that I was living while twelve dead years went by. It dawned on me that I hadn't done anything of my own since I'd worked on my "novel" just before being thrown out of the university and evicted from the cooperative dormitory. I had abandoned that manuscript in the garage and hadn't even seen it again until Sabina brought it with her things two years later, when we moved into our house. And I didn't touch that manuscript until your first letter came. For twelve years I'd had experiences, dreams — and jobs. But no projects of my own. That thought nauseated me; I felt empty. Luisa was wrong. I had every reason to hate what I'd made myself, or rather what I'd failed to make. I may have looked like an "idiot" but I was lucid for the first time in twelve years, and I was frightened.

Fortunately early the next morning — a week ago yesterday — Tina saved me from the fright, and from the lucidity as well. She came to tell Sabina and me that something very much like a revolution was breaking out.

"I thought you'd both be interested," she said. Turning to Sabina she added, "Ted thinks this might be the beginning of something big, something you all used to talk about in the garage."

"In a university building?" Sabina asked sarcastically.

"It's not a university any more, Sabina. The students aren't students any more, but just people. Workers have been coming from all over the city and they're no longer workers; they're just people too. And they're all talking to each other. I've never seen so many people so excited. Ted thinks something big is possible. I think anything at all is possible. It's what both of you always looked forward to."

"Everything is always possible when it isn't real," Sabina said.

"Stay home, then. It won't be my fault! Ted is so sure it's real he's trying to get Tissie out of the state hospital on parole. He wants her to be in on it."

"Damn it, Tina, don't just stand there! Call a cab!"

"Ted knew you'd come, Sabina. He wants you to be at the hospital with him when Tissie comes out; he thinks she'll be less frightened if you're there. You can both stay at Ted's. I'm staying in the commune."

"Don't waste my time arguing, Tina! I've got to pack!"

I told Tina, hesitantly, "I'd rather not stay at Ted's."

"That's real news, Sophia! Hear that, Sabina? She'd rather not stay at Ted's! Why have you kept it from us all these years, Sophia? We all thought you were crazy about Ted!"

"I'll just stay here and I'll go there every morning by cab."

"And what'll you do when the cab drivers go on strike?"

"I'll spend the day walking! I can hardly stay in that university commune since I'm not a student!"

"If you're not a student what am I? Oh shit, Sophia, have it your way! Stay here and read about it when the books start coming out."

"You're a gem, Tina. Don't let the cab leave without me!"

The three of us went to the revolution by taxi. We got out in front of Ted's print shop, or rather the cooperative print shop started by Ted; Tina snapped at me for calling it "Ted's." Sabina went inside with Tina while I waited outside. Young people rushed in and rushed out with stacks of papers, talking excitedly. When Tina came back she told me Ted was out, probably arguing with hospital officials to get Tissie released; Sabina had decided to stay in the print shop and wait for Ted to return. I leaned against the building wall.

"Sophia, what's the matter? You're trembling!" Tina observed.

"I'm frightened."

"Frightened of what? This is what you dreamed about for all those years."

"I know. But I never dreamed what I'd do if it actually happened."

"You're such a baby! Come on, I'll hold your hand. We've got work to do."

"Sorry you brought me?" I asked.

"No, I'm glad. If you can do it, anyone can!"

Tina pulled me toward the main classroom building, the building in which I'd attended most of my university lectures. As soon as I saw the building I knew that "something big" had already taken place, that this was no mere picnic like the "general strike" which I'd attended with Daman.

The main classroom building is transformed in ways I would have thought unimaginable when I took classes here. Black flags, red flags and even a few black and red flags hang out of the windows. Posters, banners and painted slogans cover every inch of wall space. Over the main entrance there's a single word in enormous, beautiful letters: "Liberated."

Tina was more familiar with the building than I had been when I'd studied there. She took me to what had been the main lecture hall, a large auditorium that had sometimes been used for performances of plays or movies. The sign above the doorway now says, "General Assembly." It was fuller than I'd ever seen it. All the seats were taken; people sat on the steps and leaned on the walls. I heard statements about "factory occupations" and about "extending communication." I couldn't make much sense out of the discussion and Tina didn't give me a chance to concentrate. A young man whom I've come to know quite well during the past week, Pat Clesec, walked toward Tina with a box full of leaflets. Tina grabbed a large stack and handed me a smaller one. "Have them passed down the aisles on this side, and make sure everyone gets one," she whispered. I nervously carried out my first task. The meeting ended at about the time I ran out of leaflets. Suddenly I was lost in a sea of people. I looked frantically for Tina as I followed the crowd out of the auditorium. One person walked up to me and, pointing to the leaflet I had just given out, asked me, "This is a real gas; do you work there?" I shook my head stupidly; I hadn't even read the leaflet! I was so relieved to see Tina and Pat waiting outside the auditorium that I ran toward them.

"Sophia, this is Pat Clesec, the only person I've met of my age who knows as much as you or Sabina."

Pat grinned immodestly as he shook my hand. "Tina told me you were one of her best friends."

"I also told him you were a little nutty. I hope you don't mind. I've got to run. He'll show you where things are."

I felt lost without Tina. I studied the spectacled eighteen-year old boy who looked like a premature professor and I couldn't feel any confidence in him. "Are you going to show me what to do?"

"Obviously not, Miss Nachalo. Are you Tina's sister or are you really just her friend?"

"Almost her sister but call me Sophia and I won't have to explain. What do you mean by 'obviously not'? Tina just said —"

"No one is going to show you what to do, Sophia."

"But I've just gotten here!"

"We've all just gotten here. Most of us came because there aren't any supervisors or leaders here to tell us what to do."

I was terribly embarrassed. "I didn't mean my question the way it sounded. But I'm lying. I did mean it. All my life I've dreamed of the day when people would make their own decisions, yet I've never in my life made my own decisions."

"Obviously not. People in a slave society reproduce their own slavery. But there are moments when they stop doing that. This is one of those moments."

"I hope so. Can you at least show me where things are?"

"Bathroom is over there. Beds on the fourth and fifth floors. Food in the basement. Discussions, arguments, meetings, projects everywhere else."

"Tell me one more thing. What was on the leaflet I just gave out, and what was the topic of the general assembly meeting?"

"You gave out the leaflet without reading it?"

"Tina told you I was nutty."

He told me the meeting I'd just attended had been a gathering of students occupying the building as well as workers from occupied factories all over the city. The general assembly had discussed ways to extend information and encouragement to factories and other workplaces that were still functioning "as before." At the very beginning of the meeting someone had announced that the workers of the city's largest assembly plant had just gone on a wildcat strike, had locked up the plant manager and several foremen and occupied the plant, and that several of them were present at the meeting and ready to do whatever was necessary to extend the occupations. As a first step, it was decided that news of the wildcat was to be carried to every corner of the city. Workers from the assembly plant, accompanied by Tina, Pat and several of their friends who'd learned to print, went to the "co-op" to print the announcement. Tina had gone to fetch Sabina and me while the leaflets were being printed. Meanwhile Pat learned that a very dramatic event had taken place at the general assembly meeting. A member of a political sect had given a speech calling for "picket lines and demonstrations to support the wildcatting assembly plant workers." He had been applauded. But then one of the strikers had given a speech explaining that picket lines and demonstrations would only attract the police, whereas what was needed was "wildcat strikes and occupations everywhere; we don't want demonstrations called by politicians; we don't want picket lines manned by politicians; we understand that such tactics are maneuvers through which politicians tie their ropes around our necks." He had gotten a standing ovation. Someone had shouted, "Hang the politicians with the guts of the capitalists!" At that point, the politician who had given the speech as well as all the rest of his organization had angrily walked out of the auditorium, while everyone else in the room applauded and cheered wildly; someone shouted after them, "Disband! That'll be your greatest political act!" After the politicians had left, the general assembly had resolved to create organs for the dissemination of information about the occupations; Tina and I had walked in while the final details of that resolution were being worked out.

While listening to Pat, I had followed him up the stairs to the third floor. People rushed past us in couples, in groups, all laughing, arguing, shouting. Wherever I looked there were posters, announcements, graffiti. On the doors of former classrooms were the names of factories — of those factories that were already occupied. Pat stopped in front of a room with two signs: "Workers' Councils" above, and below that: "Occupations, Information." It was full of people. He started to go in.

"Do you know anyone in there?" I asked him.

"I don't think so. Why?"

"What are you going to do in there?" I asked uneasily.

"I haven't the vaguest idea."

Feeling reassured, I went in with him. The atmosphere was tense. Someone was saying, "We've had the support of students before. Twice. And we were had both times. I know this is something different. But the others aren't convinced." Pat whispered for a long time with the person next to him. When he was through I nudged him and he pulled me out of the room. He told me that during the past year workers at a nearby office machine plant had gone on two wildcat strikes; both times they'd been supported by students who belonged to political sects and both times the student politicians had been advertised in the city newspapers as "leaders" of the strike while wildcatting workers had lost their jobs. When we went back in, the office machine worker was asking how many of the people in the room were willing to go to her plant the following morning to talk to her fellow workers about the occupations. More than half the people there raised their hands, including Pat. I didn't budge. It was agreed that those willing to go would meet in that room at five the next morning.

As everyone walked out of the room, I clung to Pat. "Can I go with you in the morning?"

"That's not up to me, Sophia. I'll be here at five."

"So will I."

I walked up to the fourth floor, peered into each of the classrooms that had been converted to a bedroom, and went on to the fifth floor. I had expected one dormitory floor to be for men, the other for women. But each single room was mixed. I walked dizzily from one door to the next until I recognized a young woman I had just seen in the "workers' council room" (which we later called the "council office"). I sat down on the unoccupied mattress next to hers and asked if anyone had an alarm clock to wake me before five the next morning. She told me everyone in the room would be up before five.

The following morning a large crowd of sleepy people was gathered in front of the council office, including Pat as well as my new roommate. I clung to Pat as we all walked to the office machine plant. He was much friendlier to me than he had been the previous day. He talked excitedly all the way to the plant. He told me about the beginning of the occupation of the university, the creation of the commune, the first occupations in factories. He convinced me that people all over the city had started to act on their own, without instructions from "leaders," without orders from any apparatus whatever, even "their own" apparatus, the union.

When we reached the plant gate, Pat walked up to a woman who seemed to be Luisa's age and told her, "We'd like to talk to you about the occupations."

"I'd like nothing better," the woman said, as if she'd expected Pat to say exactly what he said; "I'll be in the restaurant across the street at noon, with several others who've got hundreds of questions to ask. And you'd better be there!"

Pat and I had breakfast in the restaurant across the street and stayed there drinking coffee until noon. The woman Pat had spoken to came in with five other women. They pushed two tables together and motioned for us to join them. As soon as we were all seated one of the women turned to me and, with a hostility that immediately angered me, asked, "What's in this for you, dearie? Who're you with? Who sent you? Who's behind all this?"

I snapped, "What's in it for me is intense personal satisfaction; this is probably the biggest thing that's happened to me in my whole life. No one sent me except myself and I'm not with anyone except my friend Pat. If someone were behind all this, I'd never have gotten up before five in the morning!"

Other women asked questions; I answered, and I continued answering during the entire lunch hour. Before they returned to work, one of the women suggested, "Why don't you two come to the union hall tomorrow night? Lots of people would like to hear what you've got to say."

I said, "If we go to the union hall, then the union is going to be behind all this."

"At my house, then!" the woman said, giving us her address.

We had lunch with the same women again the next day, and at night we met with a large number of office machine workers at the house of the woman who'd given us her address. People continually bombarded me with questions, most of them insulting and many repetitious, and I continued responding, angrily and with injured pride, that no one had sent me, that I was on my own for the first time in my life. Pat was surprisingly quiet; he mainly supplied factual information of which I was ignorant.

As we walked back to the former classroom building that second night, Pat grinned and told me, "You're really good. What did you do before this? Were you in any organization?"

I told him I had never been in an organization but had once taken part in a vast uprising, something like a revolution. Twenty years ago. With you.

We spent the following day arranging a meeting with a different group of workers from the same plant. Between our sessions with the workers, Pat and I talked to each other uninterruptedly, about everything. When we were alone he did most of the talking. At first I found him altogether incomprehensible; he uses expressions like "desublimation of eros" and "supersession of alienated being" as if they were part of everyday language. Gradually I realized he was merely expressing my own goals with a language he'd borrowed from a newer radical literature than the one I had read. I shouldn't say "my own goals" so matter-of-factly, since that makes me seem terribly wise while it makes him seem unoriginal. He does express several things that are new to me. For example, he doesn't only talk about putting an end to coercion, to external, physical repression, but also to internal coercion, self-repression, the repression of one's own desires. Yet his behavior conflicts with everything he says about desires; he's a perfectly proper, completely serious young man; I actually doubt that he's ever personally experienced the desires he describes at such great length. Once I asked him if he ever thought of sex. He answered, "Obviously; erotic play will occupy a central place in the disalienated *gemeinschaft.*" He said it without a trace of personal involvement, with the detachment of a philosophy professor talking about Plato's cave. But I like him. I liked him from the moment he said "obviously not" to my request to show me what to do. For four days we were together from early morning until late at night and I found myself drawn to him like a negative magnet is drawn to a positive. I listened to everything he told me as attentively as I had listened to you twenty years ago; I became something like his political apprentice.

Yet there's something perverse in my feelings toward Pat, and I'm ashamed to write about that because I'm ashamed to experience such feelings in myself. Already on the first morning when we went together to the office machine plant I felt my heart jump to my throat as soon as I saw him. Yes, I'm drawn to him as I was once drawn to you: because he seems so clearheaded and determined, because he seems to know so much about what's happening around us. But I'm also drawn to him as I was to Ron, and to Jose when I lived in the garage. This is the feeling I don't understand. I loved you; I loved Ron and Jose. But I know I don't love Pat. I admire him — the way one admires acrobats or certain freaks. I don't respect him. All I feel toward him is what he talks about so much: desire. I listened so attentively to everything he said because every word he spoke excited me physically, sexually. The reason I felt ashamed was because my excitement wasn't accompanied by love or even warmth toward him but by an irrepressible desire to pull him down from the heights of his abstractions. I was excited by the desire to humiliate him; I felt like tearing his clothes off his body in order to tear those abstractions out of his head. What excited me was the prospect of raping the boy-genius, the prospect of physically overcoming that pure intellect who simultaneously attracted, intimidated and repelled me. I felt ashamed as soon as I began to suspect the nature of my desire. I've never felt that way toward anyone: so condescending, contemptuous, authoritarian. In fact, I had thought myself incapable of that kind of feeling, although Hugh once accused me of behaving as if I felt that way toward everyone.

Fortunately I was able to get out of the situation that stimulated my perverse desire before I felt compelled either to repress it or to act on it. The office machine workers went on strike three days ago. When I first heard of this I thought with some pride that my "talks" might have contributed something to this decision, but I was deflated a few hours later when two of the women I'd talked to told me they had opposed the strike until the very last moment; they had joined it only out of solidarity with the majority. That day and the whole next day there was a festive atmosphere here, in the entire building. In the council office (that was when it acquired this name) it was decided that leaflets, announcements and all other bits of information about strikes and occupations everywhere in the city were to be kept in that room, and at least one person was to remain there during all hours of the day to help people find the information they were looking for. I was the first to volunteer for that "assignment," and I've been in this room sixteen hours a day since the day before yesterday. I volunteered for two reasons: I wanted to find time to write you, and I wanted to get away from Pat until I'd had a chance to clarify my feelings toward him. I've seen him twice since then, at our evening meetings, and on both occasions I sat some distance away from him.

Yesterday evening, after a meeting with two postal workers who asked eagerly about the occupations, I left the "office" briefly and telephoned Luisa. I told her exactly what Tina had told Sabina and me. "It's happening, Luisa. What you've always looked forward to."

"Where are you?"

"For the past day and a half I've been in an office that disseminates information about the occupations."

"Sounds exciting. Did Daman ever find you? He told me he'd been trying to find out what you were going to do after losing your last job. There was no answer at your house for several days, so he thought you and Sabina had both been kidnapped."

"Couldn't he guess where we were? What's he been doing?"

"He's been staying home, since his classes were called off," Luisa said, without a trace of irony.

"His classes called off! His whole world's been called off! The hypocritical jackass!"

"Sophia, he tried to reach you because he thought you might need his help finding another job."

"He's the one who'll need help pretty soon! What about you, Luisa? There are millions of things to do here, and there's lots of room for you to stay overnight."

"Sophia, you know perfectly well I'd lose my job if I left right now!"

"So what? Tina simply walked off her job and told us: They'll miss me in about a week and then they'll get someone else."

"I'm not Sabina's daughter! I'll join you as soon as the union calls a strike in my plant."

"The union! Luisa, where have you been? Don't tell me you still think it's not a strike unless the union calls it!"

"Would you mind calling me back when you're less hysterical, Sophia?"

I hung up, but almost immediately I felt bad about having done that. I remembered that neither Sabina nor I had jumped up with glee when Tina had first told us about the commune and the occupations. Maybe I was unintentionally getting even with Luisa for having made me feel so "old."

The two postal workers who came to the council office yesterday were here again today. They came to get a second and larger collection of leaflets; they told me that mail carriers, drivers, clerks and other postal workers had spent the day talking about striking. I can't believe it! But in case it does happen, please send your next letter to the following address across the border; (...). I'll manage to get it from there. I hope the cab drivers don't go on strike before I have a chance to go home to see if you've already sent a letter.

Right now I'm alone in the council office. It almost looks like an empty classroom; I'm using the "professor's desk" to write this letter. I'm waiting for other workers to walk in: workers from unoccupied factories, from other cities, from other continents. I'm waiting for you to walk into the council office.

I love you, *Sophia.*

Yarostan's seventh letter

ear Sophia,

D Your letter was marvelous. Jasna and Zdenek were both here yesterday sharing it with us, celebrating the events that have started unfolding around you. For once we received your letter in the spirit in which you wrote it. I was relieved that you hadn't received my previous letter before you set out on your adventure in the Commune and the Council. The depressed mood in which I wrote it wouldn't have contributed anything positive to your exciting experiences. I regret much of what I said in that letter. I now have an opposite admission to make to you. I was very moved when you said you were waiting for me to walk into your "council office." If such an expedition should ever be undertaken, I'll be the first to volunteer and of course I'll bring Yara and Mirna along as well as Jasna and Zdenek. I love you, too, Sophia; we all do; you've seduced us with your honesty and especially with your modest, almost shy courage.

The circumstances in which your letter arrived were poles apart from those I described in my previous letter. When I came home from the plant the day before yesterday (Thursday afternoon), Mirna threw her arms around me and started to dance around the living room with me. She waved your letter in the air.

"You're glad to hear from Sophia?" I asked.

Yara shouted, "She's on strike! We're all on strike! We're going to have a party tonight and another tomorrow night!"

It was my turn to squeeze Mirna and spin her around the room. "You're on strike? And we're having more dancing parties?"

Mirna poked me in the stomach. "Eating parties, for your sake. There'll be a dance at my plant in a week. Want to come?"

"Not if you dragged me there. Take Zdenek. He says he likes to dance."

"I'm going too!" Yara shouted.

We understand your excitement and your hopes, Sophia. There's good news from everywhere all at once. I don't think you're being naive or "obsessively optimistic." Our hopes couldn't ever have a more solid basis than they have now. The world has to change now; if it doesn't, we'll all die as exiles in an inhuman world.

Yara and Mirna prepared an enormous banquet, just for the three of us, to celebrate the strike at Mirna's plant. Mirna was drunk before she started drinking. "What did your strike accomplish, Yarostan?"

"We ousted a union functionary who did police work."

"Is that all? What are you waiting for in that plant?"

"We're all waiting for you, Mirna. We need the devil's inspiration."

"That's exactly what it is! The devil's work! And why not? If we're going to suffer for sipping from the devil's cup, we might as well empty the whole barrel! No more sipping! What did Zdenek's strike accomplish?"

"All the functionaries were ousted; elected workers replaced them in all posts. What did you devils accomplish?"

"Everything, all at once, unanimously! The slowest to come are the most thoroughgoing. We threw the entire administration, union and police crews out on the street and we didn't replace them with anyone; we voted to go on permanent vacation with pay!"

"But where will the pay come from, Mirna?"

"Is that your affair? We'll worry about that when it runs out! We're off until Monday, in any case. Then we'll meet again. Someone suggested we use the hated workshop to do all the things we ever daydreamed of doing there. Everyone loved the idea. To begin, we'll push all the machinery against the walls to prepare for our dance. We'll invite all our friends. Then it'll be our turn to wait and see."

"Tomorrow we'll party all day long," Yara announced. "We'll go get Zdenek out of his plant and you go and bring Jasna."

Yesterday morning I set out for Jasna's house at the same hour when I usually go to the carton plant.

I feel like Tina must have felt when she went to tell you and Sabina about the commune. Jasna, fresh out of bed, is alarmed; she thinks something awful happened. During the week and a half that preceded our newfound joy, we all went through hell.

"Good news this time, Jasna. The best. Mirna, Sophia, Sabina — everyone is on strike!"

"You're joking! Tell me about it!"

We rush to my house as soon as Jasna is dressed; Yara and Mirna have already returned with Zdenek. Jasna plunges into your letter. Zdenek pumps Mirna for every detail about her strike.

While reading, Jasna exclaims, "We're finally together again; we're in one and the same world; only geography separates us now! Sophia's experiences are identical to ours! I'm so excited! I heard everything you said, Mirna. You're wonderful! I wish school were still on so that I could go on strike too!"

I leave with Yara to buy groceries and drinks, but the two of us couldn't carry enough to satisfy the appetites of five happy people. When we return, Zdenek is reading your letter and commenting on nearly every passage. The rest of us start to prepare our "feast."

"Your friend talks of unions the same way we do," Zdenek observes.

"Why shouldn't she?" I ask. "They have the same function there as here."

"I know that intellectually but I can't accept it emotionally. Unions over there claim to protect workers' interests whereas their real role is to sell workers to capitalists. Here unions have the additional function of supervising, of policing workers. I see a difference."

"You, Zdenek? You who taught me so much about the repressive function of any and every form of representation?"

"Don't forget I spent half my life fighting for the type of union apparatus they still have over there."

Mirna shouts, "Do I hear Zdenek backing away from everything he was defending? Is it really true that grey hair makes people cautious? Read to the end and you'll see that Yarostan's Luisa is as grey-haired as you!"

"Damn you all! Of course it's conservatism! Those young people are turning against something I fought hard to build."

"What you built was rotten! Admit it and help them destroy it!" Mirna shouts to him. Until a week ago Mirna was the most cautious among us; now she's the most rebellious. I had known she loved her brother; I had never known how much she had learned from him.

Zdenek persists. "They don't even know how repressive unions can be when they become appendages of the state."

I object. "Maybe you never knew how repressive they were when they were only appendages of capital; after all, you were part of the bureaucracy then."

"I know how repressive they were, Yarostan. But I had always thought people would have to experience the transformation of unions into parts of the state apparatus before they finally saw through them. I was obviously wrong. Let me see what else they see through." Zdenek reads on while we continue our cooking. Suddenly he shouts, "Now this is too much! It's simply wrong-headed. Capitalists aren't the only ones who use the mail! We use it too. And communication is needed precisely at a moment like this. What the postal workers ought to do is throw away all capitalist mail and deliver only workers' letters. But a postal strike! That's like blinding yourself!"

Mirna stops what she's doing. "I didn't think of that when I read Sophia's letter. If the post were on strike, we would stop hearing from Sophia precisely at the moment when the revolution was at its peak. Yet we wouldn't know whether to expect the beginning of a new world or tanks!"

Jasna also agrees with Zdenek. "It would be awful not to hear from her now! Every new letter is full of surprises. Knowing what they're doing makes us want more, it makes us do more."

Mirna adds provocatively, "It gives us courage, is that what you mean, Jasna?"

I think it's ironic that these few months have been the only time in twenty years when I've been able to receive mail freely whereas this might be the only time when you stop receiving mail. More than geography still seems to separate us. I obviously can't dissuade postal workers from striking, nor talk them into changing the nature of their strike, but I agree with Zdenek. A postal strike harms only the ruling order during normal times, since then communication serves mainly to lubricate that order; but in disruptive times like these, unfettered communication serves mainly to further disrupt the ruling order.

"If we're going to learn about each other, then let's learn everything," Mirna shouts. "Let's fill ourselves with each other, with Sophia and Sabina and their commune. First of all let's fill ourselves with food and beer! Let there be something for the tanks to invade, right Zdenek? Hey Zdenek, how close are you to done?"

"I've just come to Pat Clesec; leave me alone!"

Yara, pointing to me, asks Jasna, "Was he really like that brainy Pat Clesec when Sophia knew him?"

Then Mirna asks Jasna, "Do you suppose Luisa seduced Yarostan in order to humiliate him? Zdenek! We're starting without you!"

Jasna giggles. "You're more brainy than Yarostan ever was, Yara." Jasna blushes as she tells Mirna, "If I had thought Luisa only wanted to humiliate Yarostan —"

"What would you have done, Jasna? Scratched her eyes out?" Mirna taunts.

"If we're telling everything, you might as well know I would have wanted to," Jasna answers.

Mirna shouts mockingly, "Shame, Jasna! You were a grown woman and Yarostan was just a boy!"

"I know; I was as worried about that as Sophia is." Jasna sighs, as if she were dreaming.

"How about you, Zdenek?" Mirna asks. "Could you love a woman half your age?"

"Why not?" Zdenek says absent-mindedly, trying to concentrate on the end of your letter.

"Your daughter for instance?" Mirna asks.

Zdenek coughs uneasily. "Let me finish this letter! You're out of your mind!"

Jasna, still in her dream, seems oblivious to the conversation. "Luisa was five years older than I. Yet she looked just like a girl when she was with Yarostan, just like Sophia described her when she skipped around that pond. She was always so pretty, and so young; I doubt that she has a single grey hair even now. She had everything and everyone. She had Titus as well as that mysterious engineer she came with. I felt so sorry for Tissie when I read Sophia's previous letter. 'What's wrong with me?' she asked. That's what I asked myself every day of my life: what's wrong with me? I was younger than Luisa but I felt a hundred years older. She and

Yarostan were so beautiful together. And even that wasn't enough for her. As soon as Marc Glavni came she ran after him as well. Marc was the brainy one in that lot. He must have been a city planning commissioner already in his diapers. He's the one Pat Clesec reminds me of. My former boss. I'd like to think Luisa went after him just to humiliate him. She should see him now!"

Yara leaves her seat, goes up to Jasna and strokes her hair, whispering, "You know what Slobodan told me a few days ago? After our dancing party he stopped loving Julia and me. He loves only one person now, and she's the best dancer in the world."

"Well go get Slobodan!" Mirna shouts to Yara. "Tell him I've forgotten about that radio he turned on."

"Please don't embarrass me," Jasna begs.

"If you're embarrassed, Jasna, how do you think I feel?" I ask her, "I don't know whether to apologize or to cry."

Zdenek joins us at the table announcing, "This is no time to cry! An excellent letter; let's drink to it! Those people have somehow learned everything we've had to have hammered into our heads by twenty years of total repression. Fill up again! To the Commune! What's this about a letter Sophia's hermit tried to deliver to you?"

Jasna says, "That's what I find so admirable about Sophia. She loved Yarostan to the point of trying to find him eight years after she was separated from him, to the point of sending us all letters describing her love for him and getting us all arrested in the process, including the messenger she sent them with."

"How admirable!" Mirna says sarcastically. "She had the courage to get everyone except herself sent to jail!"

"Wait a minute!" Zdenek shouts. "Do you mean to tell me you were all arrested because of that letter she sent you?"

"The poor girl didn't know what she was doing; she was only looking for Yarostan," Jasna tells Zdenek. "What she didn't know was that her step-father, or whatever he was to her, was a foreign spy in the police records. It all makes sense to me now. When I was arrested together with Vera and Adrian, the police kept asking me if I'd known Sophia Alberts; I'd kept insisting that wasn't her last name; I had forgotten her step-father's name. I don't think I even knew his name. But to the police Luisa was Alberts' wife, and both Sabina as well as Sophia were his daughters. And since we had known all three of them, we were obviously spies."

"But you didn't even get the letter," I point out.

"That part I can understand," Zdenek says. "It wouldn't be the first time this police incarcerated people because of crimes they had not yet committed, crimes which the police themselves expected those people to commit in the future. But the whole thing is so ludicrous!"

"It is ludicrous, and I'm still not clear about the role Sophia's letter actually played," I tell Zdenek. "Jan and I were agitating in favor of the Magarna uprising; Titus had just signed a strongly worded protest in favor of the Magarna workers. We would have been arrested whether or not that messenger had come with Sophia's letters. The letters must have been a mere pretext, a so-called provocation to justify the arrests."

"What about the rest of us?" Jasna objects. "Vera, Adrian and I weren't agitating about anything at all! Vera was busy running after her Professor Kren, Adrian was about to finish college, and I'd just gotten my first teaching job. Marc had just become head of the party organization at the carton plant and he certainly didn't sign any protest or engage in any agitation. And Claude already worked for the police; there could have been no earthly reason for his arrest. I'm convinced the letters Sophia sent us led to our arrests. The police linked those letters to the so-called spy ring. And they couldn't have made that connection, they couldn't have connected Sophia to Alberts, unless someone who had known Sophia had told them."

"Namely one of us?" I ask.

"Lem mentioned an official," Jasna continues. "Only three of the people Sophia wrote to were officials of any type at the time she sent those letters: Claude Tamnich, Titus Zabran and Marc Glavni. Claude hated the whole bunch of us, especially you and Luisa, and he'd have liked nothing better than to slap us all in jail. But I saw Claude a few days after my release; he was totally baffled by the whole thing and even accused me of causing his arrest. He's too dumb to have performed such an act, and there was no earthly reason for him to perform it for my benefit. So Claude is out. Titus was also an official, although a minor one, a union official. He also knew all about Alberts and Sophia. But he spent a whole year in jail, whereas half of us were only in jail for a few days."

"Titus wasn't arrested until more than a year later," Mirna points out.

"Typical police bungling," I suggest.

"Either that." Jasna continues, "or they wanted to make it impossible to prove they had arrested eight people merely because a letter had been addressed to them. Titus is absolutely out of the question. He'd have been overjoyed to hear from Luisa's daughter and he had no reason in the world to have us all arrested. That only leaves Marc Glavni, my former boss —"

"But he's on the state planning commission," Yara objects.

"Is that the Glavni you're talking about?" Zdenek asks, amazed that such a high official was once part of our modest circle.

"Yes, the one who's going to engage in a major policy debate over the radio," Jasna exclaims triumphantly. "Member of the central committee of the state planning commission, member of the foreign trade commission, formerly general manager of the carton plant and my boss, M. Glavni. He didn't hate us, the way Claude did. But he certainly loved his career more than he liked us. Lem must have reached the carton plant. The police sent him there. Glavni was the only name they recognized; it was the most important name on any of the letters; Marc was already then a member of the trade union council and head of the plant's party organization. But Lem reached only a secretary, probably a kind-hearted soul left over from the old days, someone who obviously recognized all our names, since he gave Lem your and Jan's addresses. As soon as Marc returned and read the letter, he saw his whole career falling to pieces. He probably thought any one of us, and certainly Claude, would immediately report the letter to the police, and I'm sure that's exactly what Claude would have done; I'm certain we would have been arrested anyway. So to prevent anyone else from calling them first, Marc called the police and told them he'd received a letter from the famous Alberts spy ring."

"But you've told us Marc was arrested too," I remind her.

"Shows how stupid the police are. They responded to his call by sending two agents for him in the middle of the night and slapping him in jail. But they released him right away, and the regional party secretary even apologized to him. He wasn't only reinstated in all his posts but was even promoted right away. I wouldn't be surprised if he owed his promotion to the fact that he collaborated with the bank director, Professor Kren, in clearing Vera of the espionage charges by accusing Adrian and probably you and Jan as well of having slandered her and Dr. Glavni. I'm convincing myself it was because of him that you and Adrian served such long prison terms and that Jan never came out again. While you, Jan and Titus were dreaming of a different world, Marc was dreaming of his coming promotions in this one."

"That pig!" Yara shouts. "I'll tell Julia and Slobodan about that Commissioner Glavni! We'll fix him!"

"What in the world will you do to him?" Mirna asks her.

"You'll see!"

Jasna tells Yara, "That all happened before you were even born!"

"Don't you want revenge?" Yara asks.

"What on earth for?" Jasna asks. "What can one do with revenge?"

Mirna exclaims, "Yara is perfectly right!"

"But Marc only did the devil's bidding," I remind Mirna.

"He did the devil's dirty work and that's something altogether different."

Zdenek re-enters the conversation. "The thing I don't understand is what kind of letter this was. The charge of espionage was obviously a pretext, since most of you didn't even get the letter. Why did the police arrest nine people because of a letter?"

Mirna answers, "But that's obvious, isn't it? To stop what we're doing right now, that's why! Letters are like the first whispers of a strike. The whispers grow louder, more and more people start whispering, eventually they're all shouting. Something none of us had thought of spreads like a disease. The police are the sanitation department; they try to stop the disease from spreading and to do that they have to lock up people and kill them because what's spreading is life itself and life can't be policed."

Jasna adds, "Don't you see, Zdenek, that the period during the Magarna rising was similar to the present? All news was good news and every bit of it inspired people to go a step further, gave them courage."

"The police are too stupid to know that," Zdenek claims.

I disagree; in fact for once I agree with Mirna about the likelihood that your letter played a role in our arrest. "Maybe they do know that, Zdenek. They must. How else can you explain the total censorship they try to establish? Maybe they believe in the possibility of communication and solidarity more than we do. For that very reason I think it's wrong to blame any of the individuals trapped in the net created by the police, whether Sophia or Lem or Marc. The fault lies solely with the police. If Comrade Glavni's career can be spoiled by a letter, there's something wrong with the system in which he's seeking his career."

"I knew the system was rotten, but I didn't know people were arrested for receiving mail not approved by the police," Zdenek says.

"You'd have known if you'd gotten any," Jasna tells him.

"It all sounds very clear and logical," Mirna says, "but none of you have explained anything. First of all there's that poor messenger. After he spent two years in prison and was tortured besides, Sophia called him a liar and accused him of losing her letters. He certainly had more than his share of the consequences of that letter. When she finally believed him years later, she left him bathing in filth. Meanwhile Glavni sits on top of the world and Sophia isn't doing too badly either. She spoiled nine people's lives, yet she wasn't anywhere near the arrests; she didn't even know about them for more than a decade —"

I interrupt. "But Mirna, the very same censorship prevented her from learning about those arrests. You're working yourself up again. Sophia wasn't here —"

"She did exactly the same thing when she was here and she knows it; she even brings it up in this letter. Sophia asks Luisa why they left all their comrades in jail and Luisa asks Sophia why. Sophia knows that wasn't right; Luisa acts as if it were the most natural thing in the world. And maybe it is. But you and Jasna seem convinced there was something special about Luisa and Sophia, you seem convinced they wouldn't have run and left the suffering to their comrades."

Jasna says, "You're putting it very strongly, Mirna, but I admit I was shocked when I learned only a few weeks ago that Luisa and the two girls had emigrated after two days in jail. You're right: I hadn't thought any of them capable of that. I don't understand it. All of us except Claude always accepted every suggestion Luisa made. We would have followed her to prison if she had been the only one arrested."

"Apparently someone had something like that in mind," I remind Jasna. "Someone was ready to arrest Luisa alone and didn't expect the rest of us to follow her to prison. I think that someone was Claude, who must have been a police agent already then. He thought he could turn the rest of us against Luisa by telling us Alberts was a spy and Luisa his accomplice. That would have isolated Luisa while the rest of us followed Claude like sheep. But his scheme backfired. Do you remember? Four or five days before our arrest, instead of turning against Luisa, all of us lined up alongside her exactly as we'd done in play a year or two earlier, and once again it was Claude who was isolated. Luisa told us politicians of Claude's ilk were using the strike as a base from which to install themselves in the government, and every one of us understood. When she told us the struggle wasn't on one front but on two, and the greater enemy threatened us from behind, we knew exactly what she was talking about. Unfortunately the only thing we were able to do about the greater enemy was to carry signs about him, and that obviously wasn't enough. Jan knew that wasn't enough. Apparently Titus also knew; three days before the arrest he told Sophia and me to be realistic, not to expect the working class to carry through its final victory in a day. I understood him to mean we shouldn't be surprised if Luisa was arrested. Apparently Titus foresaw the danger but thought it would only be a danger for Luisa. I tried to warn Luisa but she was perpetually out with Marc. When I told Sophia, she said I was being a defeatist on the eve of the final victory."

"It's funny, Yarostan, but I remember a somewhat different sequence," Jasna tells me. "First of all the rumor that Luisa worked with a spy. I heard that too — but from Vera."

"From Vera? But that's impossible. Vera was something like Luisa's disciple; she worshipped Luisa as much as I did; every one of her ideas came from Luisa. I distinctly remember that Vera was the first one to applaud when Luisa said the greater enemy was behind us. She stood alongside Luisa and remained alongside her to the very end."

"Vera was always good at creating appearances; she still is. You didn't really know her," she tells me. "Yes, she was Luisa's disciple, but she was too vain to remain a disciple very long. I knew she'd wanted her apprenticeship to end long before the strike broke out. She hated Luisa for being the center of attention. She saw her chance when that rumor about Luisa started spreading. With Luisa gone, Vera thought she'd become the center of attention, she'd become the popular heroine of the revolution, and we'd all line up alongside her as we had lined up alongside Luisa. I obviously didn't believe the rumor and Jan slapped Vera's face when she told him Luisa had something to do with a spy. But that wasn't what put an end to Vera's attempt to get rid of Luisa. I know she liked Sabina a great deal. I think she must have become afraid that if Luisa and Sabina's father disappeared as spies, Sabina would disappear as well. I think that was the only reason she lined up alongside Luisa and remained alongside her until the arrest."

"Was Vera Claude's accomplice when she spread that rumor?"

"Obviously not, Yarostan. Vera stood exactly where Luisa did: against everything Claude stood for. She only wanted to replace Luisa on that spot. If they arrested us because we stood alongside Luisa, they would have arrested us just as quickly if we had stood alongside Vera. But the fact is that we stood alongside Luisa to the very end, and she had no reason to run out on us the way she did."

"You and Mirna are right," I admit. "Luisa certainly didn't show a similar solidarity with us. I can't get it out of my head that the so-called Alberts spy ring was released after two days while those accused of being mere accomplices were left in prison." Something remains strange about your sudden release, about the whole affair, but I can't focus on it clearly enough to formulate a coherent question.

But if everything is more obscure to me than it was before your letter came, everything is now perfectly clear to Mirna. "They're not the angels you both thought they were, that's all. They ran out on you. How carefully did you both read Sophia's letter? Sabina told us that Alberts person ran out on Margarita's comrades and your Luisa ran with him while her husband died at the front."

Yara says proudly, "I would have died like Margarita if I'd been there! Shooting from the barricades! Just think, she was only three years older than I am when she gave birth to Sabina!"

"Sophia's letters are full of good ideas, aren't they?" Mirna asks sarcastically.

"You deserved Yara's comment!" Jasna snaps. "Would you like Luisa better if she had died on the barricades? Besides, Sabina left a small detail out of her story. Titus told me something about those events, and so did Luisa, and I remember both of them telling me their army was defeated militarily by the fascist army and they had no choice but to run."

"Sabina doesn't contradict that," I point out. "What she says is something I had almost figured out on my own over a fifteen-year period. She says both armies had their guns turned against the people. Luisa together with the rest of her union and its influential militants literally abandoned themselves to an army that was as fascist as the army they fought against. Its aim, like the other's, was to tame or kill workers. Only her army was less experienced than the other; that's why they had to flee; a deposed ruler has no other choice."

Zdenek asks, "Is Luisa the same union militant you had described to me in prison?"

"Exactly the same," I tell him.

"But you've turned around completely, Yarostan. At that time you swore by her; you convinced me those events proved a real workers' union could exist since such a union had carried through the greatest working class victory in history."

"I believed every word I told you for many years after I met you, Zdenek. Toward the end of my first term I met someone who told me almost exactly what Sabina recently told Sophia. His name was Manuel. I listened to him, I was fascinated by everything he said, but I didn't connect any of it to Luisa." I tell Zdenek and Jasna the things I've already told you about Manuel; I also tell them stories that came back to me when I read what Sabina told you. Manuel and Alberts must indeed have known each other, or at least viewed the same battlefield from different vantage points, as Sabina suggests; the similarities in their stories are striking. Even many of the details are the same. The main difference is in the personalities and standpoints of the viewers. On the day of the rising Manuel, like Margarita and Luisa, fought on the barricades. Two or three days later, and not months later like Alberts, he joined a militia unit which set out to defeat a section of the fascist army.

They reached the front at a village, surely the same village Alberts described to Sabina. On arrival they found that the villagers themselves had already risen against the attacking fascist army and had succeeded in preventing that army from entering the village. This apparently took place several months before Alberts and his army reached the village. When Manuel's militia unit arrived, the villagers were resentful and even hostile, although that unit consisted of workers and peasants like themselves. The villagers told Manuel's comrades to liberate their own regions and keep the enemy busy on several fronts instead of "liberating" their already liberated village. Manuel and several of his comrades were ready to take the villagers' advice, but someone spread the rumor that the enemy unit, still camped outside the village, was soon to be massively reinforced, and the majority of Manuel's unit voted to remain in the village. The rumor was false. The only enemy reinforcements that arrived were poorly guarded shipments of ammunition. Almost all of these were stolen by Manuel's militia unit, and the ammunition was distributed among the villagers. The militia unit remained in the village, but not as a military formation; they fraternized with the villagers, lived among them and carried out military exploits jointly with them. Alberts told Sabina that the enemy unit camped outside the village terrorized the villagers. Manuel told me exactly the opposite. The enemy unit was totally immobilized outside that village, its supply lines were constantly intercepted, entire cargoes of ammunition were stolen; its very existence was a drain on the entire fascist army; its only alternatives were to continue to be drained or to retreat. Meanwhile the villagers appropriated lands abandoned by their landowners, turned the church into a theater and dance hall, established an experimental school and began to explore new ways of relating to each other and to their surroundings. The villagers weren't terrorized from the front but from the rear. Some months after they had neutralized the enemy unit, a "militia commander" and several other "people's officers" arrived in the village. They came as representatives of the "working class." They showed papers according to which they had been empowered by the union, Luisa's "genuine workers' union." The villagers merely laughed at the "representatives." Neither the villagers nor Manuel's militia comrades had learned the latest news: the most influential union militants had accepted posts in the government! The "commander" and his "officers" confronted Manuel and his comrades "in the name of your own comrades." The commander insisted that the militia unit immediately separate itself from the villagers and house itself in military barracks. The entire unit refused. One of Manuel's comrades said the commander was on the wrong side of the battle line; he belonged with the fascist unit camped outside the village. The commander ordered the man to be arrested but none of the militia moved in response to the order. The commander then drew his gun on the man and shot him. Immediately Manuel and several of his comrades aimed their rifles at the "commander," whose hysterical shouts of "I command!" were of no avail; one of the rifles killed the "commander." The "officers" were told, at the point of rifles, to leave the village immediately. But Manuel's comrades as well as the villagers were uneasy; they knew something was happening in the rear, behind their backs, something which represented a far greater threat to their victory than the miserably equipped enemy unit in the front. A few weeks after the death of the militia fighter and the "commander," news reached the village that a "popular brigade" was on its way "to liberate the village from the fascist menace." Everyone in the village understood what this meant. The militia unit held a crisis meeting. Less than half the men decided to remain in the village, out of a misguided sense of loyalty to "their union." The majority, including Manuel, decided to return to the city where, they felt, the real front was located. Manuel reached the city and remained there long enough to learn that all the formerly unpaid secretaries of the union's locals had become paid functionaries of the government; former organizers had become work supervisors; the central function of the entire apparatus was to make workers produce the greatest possible amount of armaments for the "popular army." Half a day after his arrival in the city he was arrested. Ironically he was not arrested because of his activities at the front; his militia unit's reputation had not yet reached the police. He was arrested for having been a member of a small political sect which was black-listed by the dominant political group in the ruling coalition. In prison Manuel met one of the former militia comrades who had remained in the village and waited for the arrival of the "popular brigade." Manuel learned that eight of those who remained were murdered the day the "popular brigade" arrived in the village; they were charged with being infiltrators; the official story told about them was that they had defected behind enemy lines. Immediately after this massacre the villagers attacked the "popular brigade" and forced it to camp on the opposite side of the village from the enemy unit. Meanwhile the enemy received some reinforcements and a shipment of arms which was not intercepted, and the enemy unit moved into and through the village, massacring the inhabitants and routing the "popular brigade." Many of the remaining militia were killed in that encounter. The "popular brigade" retreated from the village and continued retreating all the way to their military headquarters on the outskirts of the city, and on arrival the remaining few militia were arrested and charged with being traitors. The man who narrated these events to Manuel was himself condemned to death. What Manuel told me about the village is almost identical to what Alberts told Sabina except for some very significant details. The village was not "terrorized" by the enemy army. On the contrary, the villagers held off that army for months and they fell only after the arrival of the "popular army"; they were massacred by the combined fire of both armies. Secondly, the villagers did not support the fascist army in order to defeat the "popular army." That's a face-saving rationalization on Alberts' part, perhaps on the part of his whole "brigade" which, being a militaristic organization, prides itself for its militaristic ventures; defeat at the hands of a small, poorly armed enemy unit did not reflect well on the brigade's "honor": the whole population had to be blamed for its defeat. But this rationalization is a vicious slander against villagers who had bravely defended themselves against one and then the other army, who were slaughtered by the combined power of two armies, who died with the knowledge that no army can be "popular."

When I finish narrating Manuel's story, Zdenek asks, "But where in the world did you get the idea that Luisa's union helped those workers carry out a genuine revolution?"

"From Luisa's illusions. I tried very hard to believe them, all of them. But the facts have been creeping into my consciousness for twenty years, destroying those illusions. Luisa seems to believe still today everything she told me over twenty years ago."

"So much for my single example of a genuine workers' union," Zdenek sighs. "If all the instruments are rotten, what are we left with?"

"We're left with ourselves and each other," I suggest.

Jasna asks, "Is that bad?"

"Of course it's bad!" Zdenek says. "In my head I know you're both right, but my heart can't accept that; my heart wants a tool, an instrument; my instrument was the union. To me the union was like a train; we spent years building the bed, the ties, the rails, the locomotive and the cars; when the train was all built, we set it in motion and once it began to move it continued moving until it reached its final destination. Without such an instrument we feel naked, disarmed, alone. I suppose this means I don't really trust my fellow human beings. In that respect I differ from Margarita. I would never be the first person at the barricades; I'd always be afraid I'd find myself alone. If there were no Margaritas in the world, if all those I had to count on were like me, there would never be any revolutions; we would all be forever waiting for everyone else."

Yara shouts, "You're just old! Most of my friends would want to be like Margarita!"

Jasna, Zdenek and I laugh at Yara's comment, but Mirna takes all three of us to task. "Why are you laughing? Out of that whole crew, Margarita and her father are the only ones who deserve admiration, not only Yara's but ours as well. All the others stayed with their comrades only until danger came, and then they all got on that train you're talking about and rode away from danger as fast as the train would take them. Margarita was there at the start, and she remained until the end!"

Zdenek responds angrily, "You wouldn't like Margarita as well if she were alive, would you Mirna? I've noticed something a little morbid about you. I think you have a strange fascination with suffering and death. We all admire Margarita. Admiring is easy; it takes neither courage nor effort. But none of us admire our own death. Except you, Mirna. To you an act is worthless if it's not followed by pain and suffering, and it is truly meaningful only if it's followed by death. As if death were the aim of life. It isn't. It is merely life's end. What you admire in Margarita is her courage to die. What I admire is her courage to live. There's a world of difference between our outlooks. To you every affirmation of life is a step toward suffering and death. To me an affirmation of life is not a step; it is itself the goal. My goal is to live, not to take steps toward death. You're far too young for your philosophy, Mirna. In every moment of joy you see only the coming pain; in every moment of life you see only the coming of death; that's a philosophy for someone on a deathbed, not for a young, beautiful and vigorous woman. Margarita had the courage to want a different world, not the courage to want death. Your courage may be greater than Margarita's but it's not a human courage and there's something repressive about it. 'If you can't face death, don't live at all; if you dare to live, know you'll die' — isn't that your view? 'Only the dead have courage; if they're alive they must be cowards, traitors, runaways.' That's why you were so upset when Yara —"

"Zdenek, that's mean," Jasna interrupts. "You'll make her sick again."

Yara adds, "Don't forget it's her party and she did go on strike. She does have the courage you're talking about!"

But Mirna is not on the verge of becoming "sick" again; I'll describe that sickness later. She's fascinated by Zdenek's description of her. "Keep quiet, both of you. Go ahead, Zdenek; what upset me when Yara did what?"

"When Yara as well as Jasna expressed a desire to live. All you talked about was the devil and the consequences. You couldn't trust either of them to be a Margarita, could you? You were afraid they'd leave those consequences to others, namely to you, and they'd run like Luisa and the others who are still alive. So you tried to stop them from living."

"Are you done?" Mirna asks. "Good. Let's drink to Zdenek!" Then she turns to Yara and asks, "How do you play your love games?"

Yara runs to Mirna's lap. "By pretending, like you taught me."

"Have I ever stopped you?"

"Never, not once, ever. And I never told Zdenek you stopped me."

"What did you tell him?"

"I told him you beat me, once, only once in my whole life."

"Why did I beat you?"

Yara starts to cry. "I don't know."

"Why are you crying now? Have I made you unhappy?"

Yara tries to smile. "I'm not unhappy. It feels good to cry like this."

Zdenek says apologetically, "I may have gone too far, Mirna."

"Oh don't back away so quickly, Zdenek! That's precisely your point, isn't it? Go too far and then keep right on going; live and go on reaching for more life. How far are you willing to reach Zdenek? How much life do you want?"

"As much as possible, Mirna, but without getting killed or maimed," Zdenek answers.

"Then you do expect consequences!"

"You misunderstood me intentionally!" Zdenek says angrily. "So long as a police or an army exist anywhere in the world, I expect unpleasant consequence! But I don't prune my life down to nothing because they exist, I try to do everything humanly possible, and if it becomes possible for me to help get rid of the army and the police, as Margarita did, then I'll do that too. Once we do that, arrest and imprisonment will no longer be the consequences of our attempts to live. Am I being clear?"

"As clear as the wine in my glass," Mirna says. "And if it turned out that what you thought was possible wasn't really possible —"

"It's always a calculated risk," Zdenek says.

"That's a cowardly way to put it, Zdenek. If you were on those barricades, getting rid of that police alongside your beloved or your daughter or your comrades, and if it turned out that your goal was impossible and you were overpowered, what would you do, Zdenek? Run for your precious life?"

"If possible, Mirna, yes. But you tricked me."

"Would it be possible for you to run out on your beloved, your daughter, your —"

"No, Mirna, I could no more do that than not stir at all. You win!"

"But Zdenek, you're every bit as morbid as I am!"

Yara shouts, "Bravo! You showed him he's not the coward he says he is!"

Jasna adds, "That was well done. Where's the trick, Zdenek?"

"The trick is that Mirna concentrates on nothing but the consequences whereas I concentrate on everything but the consequences. I concentrate on living. Let the police concentrate on arresting me, jailing me and killing me. Why do we have to destroy our living moments with consequences that may or may not follow?"

"What does living consist of, Zdenek?" Mirna asks.

"Are you preparing another trick?" Zdenek asks. "Of love and comradeship, of dancing and eating, of dreaming and building; what kind of answer do you want?"

"Do you like me, Zdenek?" Mirna asks.

"Even though I find you morbid? Of course I do. You have a demon's perseverance, you're perceptive, clever —"

"Do you like dancing with me?"

"The single opportunity I've had — yes, I enjoyed it very much."

"Go to a dance with me, Zdenek!"

"Are you crazy?" Zdenek asks. "I like you, Mirna; you're a friend; Yarostan is also my friend, as is Yara —"

"Zdenek!" Mirna says with mock astonishment. "Are you worrying about living, or about the consequences?"

Jasna blushes. Yara and I both burst out laughing. I shout, "Bravo, Socrates!"

"Have you both gone crazy?" Zdenek asks. "Did you plan this out beforehand? Is it some kind of prank?"

"It's no prank, Zdenek," I tell him. "Mirna's fellow workers are going to use their former plant as a dance hall and they're inviting all their friends. I turned down her invitation."

Yara turns to Zdenek and pleads. "If you turn her down, she'll have to go to the dance without any of her friends. And she wanted all her friends to go."

Jasna, blushing, asks me, "Would you be willing to go if I promised to give you another dancing lesson?"

It's my turn to blush. "I turned down an invitation to a dance, not an invitation to a dancing lesson. I need another such lesson more than I need anything in the world."

"Then we're all going except you, grandfather!" Yara exclaims. "Didn't you say you'd go out to the barricades when all your friends were already there?"

"You and your mother are trappers, Yara! That's right, everything becomes possible when all my friends are already there. You both win. You win the argument, you win me, and you'll win the world. We should correct that false religious slogan to say: The morbid shall inherit the earth."

Jasna objects. "I still think you're mean, Zdenek, even if you lost the argument. Couldn't you just say: the living?"

Yara tells Zdenek, "Call us anything you want, only go with us. We like the way you dance."

Zdenek objects. "But you laughed when I danced, Yara!"

"That's why I want to see you dance again!"

As you can see, we're all well now; perhaps we're dizzy; we may even be a little crazy. We're starting to heal from a twenty-year long sickness. But just before we started to get well, we had a major relapse; I'm convinced it was our last relapse. The tense and fearful atmosphere I described in my last letter did not vanish right after I sent that letter; before the atmosphere improved it got worse, much worse. I doubt if any external force will ever be able to hurt us as much as we hurt ourselves.

I sent my previous letter a few days after Mirna voted against a strike at her plant. Yara was on an outing to the mountains; she returned a week ago yesterday. During Yara's absence, Mirna as well as most people I came in contact with seemed to have only one thought: the tanks. Toward the end of the week, the workers at the carton plant began to discuss less "morbid" subjects again; there haven't been any new broadcasts about tank movements. But Mirna remained in the mood she'd been in when she'd insulted Jasna.

:||||||||:

Yara returns from her outing late in the afternoon; Mirna and I are both back from work. As soon as Yara comes through the door, she asks, "What happened? What did you do to Jasna?"

"How did you know about that?" I ask her. "How was your trip?"

"I stopped at Jasna's on my way home. It was a wonderful trip. We were all glad we went without anyone older than us; we did everything we wanted to do. On the way home Julia and I tried to figure out some more things about Minister Vera and Commissioner Adrian, and I went to Jasna's to see if we'd guessed right. She told me a whole bunch of other things Julia and I didn't know. Then I asked Jasna to come home with me and she started crying. I asked her what was wrong but all she said was that she was too embarrassed ever to come to our house again. What happened?"

Mirna answers curtly, "I insulted her, that's what happened."

"How?" Yara asks.

"I called her a coward."

"What did she do?"

"She praised the devil."

"Good for her!" Yara shouts. "Then why did you call her a coward?"

"Because Jasna is the last person in the world —" Mirna begins, and stops. She sits down and pulls Yara to her lap. "Never mind that now. Were the mountains beautiful? What did you do?"

"Lots of things. We took hikes and we climbed to several mountain tops. The most fun was when we played love games on a mountain top, just Julia, Slobodan and I."

"How do you play love games on a mountain top, Yara?" Mirna asks, with a fascination that's mixed with apprehension.

"By pretending, mommy, the way you taught me."

"Who did you pretend to be?"

"Once I was Vera Krena and another time I was you. And once Julia pretended to be the devil. It was beautiful, mommy; the three of us were alone in the whole wide world."

The glassy, distant look comes into Mirna's eyes. "Let me tell you a story, Yara."

"If it's about Vesna I'd rather not hear it."

"It's about a time when I played love games on a mountain top."

"You never did that!"

"And it's about you, Yara."

"Then I want to hear it!"

"I climbed to a mountain top nine months before you were born, Yara. I took everyone I loved: my brother and my father, my husband and my friend as well as several of their comrades. There were twelve of them; counting me we were thirteen. When we reached the top it was beautiful because, like you and your friends, we were alone in the whole wide world. Up there we could do whatever we wanted. At the very top there was a large flat rock, just big enough to hold me. I lay down on it and let the sun beat down on me. I reached downward with my right hand and six hands fastened themselves to mine; I reached with my left and another six hands grabbed mine. With all the strength in my arms I pulled all twelve of my loved ones to the top of the mountain, and when all twelve were on the rock they became one, the one I loved most of all —"

"The devil!" Yara shouts.

"Yes, Yara. The devil fathered you on that mountain top twelve years ago."

"That's a beautiful story, mommy."

"It isn't over yet, Yara. I played love games with the devil all day long. But toward evening clouds hid the sun, a wind started blowing and the rock got cold. Everything was possible on the mountain top only so long as there was sun and no wind. I started shaking with cold and wanted to return back down where there was shelter and warmth. I pushed the devil away from me with both my arms, forced him down off the rock, and when I sat up and looked I saw that I was pushing all twelve of my loved ones down from the rock, six on each side. The wind blew fiercely, the clouds turned black and thundered, and it started to pour. The rock where everything had been possible was no longer beautiful; it was bare and cold; it gave no shelter. I jumped off the rock and pushed my twelve loved ones downward; as soon as I left the rock it was hit by lightning. I pushed as hard as I could, but the rain and the lightning blinded me. Suddenly I heard four shrieks in front of me. I had pushed four of my loved ones off a precipice. I backed away from that edge in terror and tried to shelter my remaining eight under a tree, but there was no shelter from that storm. Lightning hit the tree and killed four of them before my very eyes. Now there were only four left: my brother, my father, my husband and my friend. I pulled them away from the burned tree and started pulling them down the mountain side. The paths were all slippery and rushing rivers blocked our way wherever we went. I was frenzied and lost track of my friend. Suddenly lightning struck near us again. I lost my grip on my brother and my husband and both slid down into a river that quickly carried them away. I started to run after them but my father held me back; he told me they were both good swimmers and would find their way to land. I was all alone with my father in that terrible storm. The two of us descended, slowly and carefully; we stayed close to the banks of the river into which my brother and my husband had fallen. But lightning struck again, and yet again. We both fell to the ground, and a tree fell across my father's legs, breaking both of them. I kneeled next to him and cried. My love games destroyed everyone I loved."

Yara gets off Mirna's lap and says, politely, "I don't like your story."

Mirna pulls Yara back. "I'm not through yet, Yara. The story ends with your birth. I could see that my father was in pain, but there was nothing I could do for him. Finally the storm let up. The lightning stopped and the rushing rivers became small streams. In the black of night I ran down the mountainside alone, straight to my mother's house. I told her where I'd left my father. She gathered several neighbors and they all went to help him. But I didn't go with them. I ran to the stream we had been following, ran along it, and finally came across someone I knew. He told me he had seen my husband in the stream, with his head up, swimming vigorously. But he hadn't seen my brother. I ran on down the stream, hesitated, and then turned and ran back to the spot where I'd left my injured father. The clouds were gone and the moon lighted my way. When I reached the spot I saw a circle of people standing around it. There was only one courageous person in the circle; I recognized him as my one-time neighbor and my father's friend. He put his hand on my arm and led me through the circle; the others grumbled and moved away from me as if I were a leper or a witch. He told me they weren't bad people but they were all afraid. And then he told me my father's legs hadn't been badly broken; they could have been cured; he might even have walked again. When the neighbor had reached my father, he had heard my father moaning about his drowned son, his daughter's marriage to a drowned husband, and about his own inability to help his daughter find her brother or her husband. The neighbor said he died of a broken heart. When I reached the center of the circle I saw my father's lifeless body where I had left him. My mother kneeled next to him across from me; her face looked blue in the moonlight. She pointed her finger at me, and at you as well, Yara; you were in my stomach then. 'You and the devil killed him,' she told me. I knew she was right. I crawled on all fours out of that circle, crawled all the way to my house, and at that moment I was able to let you come into the world, because I had paid what you cost, I had paid for my love game with the devil on the top of the mountain.'

"I don't like you when you tell stories like that," Yara says, trying to get away from Mirna. "You sound just like that crazy old woman."

Unlike Yara, I'm deeply moved by Mirna's story. I realize that I haven't really been aware of the pain Mirna experienced during my second prison term. My eight years in prison weren't pleasant, but I didn't spend many hours, or even many minutes, trying to imagine what Mirna was undergoing during the days I spent in cells, exercise yards or prison workshops. I didn't have any contact whatever with my family until several months after Jan and I were arrested at the steel plant on the day when the Magarna rising was suppressed. My first visitor was Titus. He told me he hadn't found Jan "yet" but was still trying. He also told me Vesna was well and Mirna was pregnant. He didn't tell me Mirna's father had been fired from his bus-driving job; I suppose he didn't want to be the earner of bad news to a prisoner. He did tell me Mirna had acquired a pass to visit me but was having "trouble" with her parents; she could barely find time for them, for Vesna and for her job. Titus also brought me two books. After Titus' visit, my contact with the "outside" was completely broken for more than two years. I acquired my own constrained routine: prison acquaintances, interests and problems. Mirna and Vesna visited me three years after my arrest. Mirna spent a long time telling me she had gotten a pass with Titus' help but terrible things had happened and by the time she got a day off work and came to the prison, she was told the forms had changed and she wasn't allowed to visit me. Then Titus was arrested and Mirna wasn't able to find out what she had to do to get the pass she needed. That's why she visited me only after Titus was released. I asked her what terrible things had happened and she listed them mechanically, almost coldly, but something in her tone gave me the impression she considered herself responsible for everything she was telling me. She began with Jan's and my disappearance "on the day after we dreamed"; then Jan could no longer be found, her father died, her mother got sick, Yara was born. When Mirna completed her list, Vesna uttered her only contribution during that first visit; it consisted of three words: "I hate you." It became clear to me that if Mirna blamed herself, Vesna blamed me for everything that had happened. I felt like an extra burden on Mirna's back, a burden she didn't need to carry. I reminded her that during our first walks I had tried to warn her not to marry a "political criminal" because she might find herself bound to a non-person, a human being who would suddenly cease to exist. Mirna started crying but I continued in the same vein. I urged her to divorce me and told her I'd heard divorces were easily procured by wives of political criminals. Mirna's eyes filled with anger, bitterness and resentment. "Is that all you have to say to me after three horrible years?" she asked me. "How dare you even think about divorce! Your return is all I live for, Yarostan; you're all I have left now; you're my brother, my father, my husband and my only friend; you're everyone I love in the world; if you disappear, I'll die of a broken heart, like my father. Don't talk to me about divorce, Yarostan; tell me something else!" But I didn't have anything else to say. I told her, "I love you, Mirna, more than I love myself; that's why I don't want you to sacrifice yourself to me." Mirna left crying; Vesna walked away from me with hatred in her eyes.

Yara tries to get away from Mirna's lap but Mirna holds on to her. "Neither you nor I have a right to say the old woman was crazy. You were born right after my father died. I got a short leave from work but I spent all my time with you. I didn't once go visit my mother although I knew she needed me. I wanted her to let me know she needed me. You were my excuse for not going to her. The union had given my father a retirement pension after he was fired. Our neighbor, the same one who'd told me about my father's death, found out she still had a right to that pension but she had to go to the union building for it. The first time he went with her. But the second time she went alone. She didn't let the neighbor come tell me she wanted me to go with her: she was afraid I'd turn her down. The neighbor couldn't get another day off his job. Titus told me what happened to her when he came to tell me, several days later, that she was in the hospital; he learned what had happened from the doorman at the union building. It was a cold, snowy day; the roads were slippery. The old woman confronted the door-man and demanded 'her due.' The doorman asked her whom she wanted and she ranted about devils and their agents. She pushed her way past the doorman but several guards pushed the 'crazy woman' out of the building. She tried to enter the building a second time but the guards pushed her so violently she fell — and remained where she had fallen. The police took her to the hospital and a few days later everyone in the union building knew she was 'Sedlak's wife' and had a right to the pension she had come to collect. Titus came to tell me she was in the hospital, completely paralyzed; there was nothing they could do for her. That was when I let them bring the 'crazy woman' to the spare room in our house. She turned Vesna's heart against me, against Yarostan, eventually against you, Yara. She knew her sickness wasn't brought on by the guards or the snow, but by my love games —"

"She was crazy!" Yara screams. "I hated her!"

"You're what made her the way she was!"

"You're lying!" Yara shouts, trying to pull away from Mirna. "I hate you when you talk like her. You're trying to do to me what she did to Vesna! But you can't! I won't let you!"

"Vesna would never have killed anyone she loved —"

"Neither did you and neither did I! That old woman lied through her teeth; it was all she was able to do; she was completely looney —"

"Say that once again, Yara, and I'll —"

"Looney! Crazy! She taught Vesna we killed people by loving them and she killed Vesna by teaching her that! Everything she said was a lie and everything you're telling me is a lie! I know it is. I played with Julia and Slobodan and nothing happened to any of us and nothing is going to happen, ever, and you know it! Why can't you just be yourself instead of turning yourself into that crazy woman? You're hateful when you're like her, and don't think you'll ever stop me from playing love games whenever and wherever I please because you won't! I'm not Vesna! I was glad when we took the old woman to the shed outside where we could neither see nor hear her and I was overjoyed when she finally croaked! I'm glad she's dead and so are you!"

Mirna's face is flushed with anger as she whacks Yara across the face. Yara starts bawling. Mirna rushes to the kitchen to put our dinner into the oven.

"She was so happy before I went on my outing," Yara sobs. "What happened between her and Jasna? Why did she hit me? She never did that to me before!"

"I don't understand, Yara," I tell her. "She's been upset ever since she heard that radio broadcast your friend turned on and she's been angry ever since this letter came." I point to the letter in which you describe your experiences in Sabina's garage.

Yara starts reading your letter. She reads while I set the table and help Mirna bring the food in. She continues reading during the meal. Suddenly she asks me, "Is Sabina younger than Sophia?"

"Yes, three or four years younger," I tell her.

Yara reads further and then says, "I wish Vesna were still alive, and I wish that old woman hadn't ever come into our house."

"Exactly what does that mean?" Mirna asks.

Yara looks defiantly at Mirna; there's fire in her eyes. "It means I'd be Sabina and Vesna would be Sophia. It means Vesna would be different from me, she wouldn't want what I wanted, but she'd still be my friend and she wouldn't be dead, that's what it means."

Mirna drops her fork on her plate and runs to the bedroom. For a moment Yara pretends indifference and continues reading, but it's obvious she can't concentrate. She walks hesitantly to the bedroom and says from the doorway, "I'm sorry. I didn't mean how that sounded. I know you couldn't help bringing your own mother into our house. If you ever become just like her I'd take you into my house too, but only because you'd once been good to me. I'd hate what you'd become as much as you always hated her. You called her a vampire!"

"I was wrong, Yara. You're the vampire."

"That's a lie and you know it! You're ten times worse than she was! She never hit me! She didn't pretend to be my friend and then turn against me. You're not just an enemy, you're a traitor!" Yara starts to walk away from the bedroom.

Mirna shouts, "Yara! Tell me how you like me!"

Yara returns to the doorway. "When you're yourself."

"When am I myself?"

"When you're not the old woman."

"Show me, Yara. Come here next to me. Come on, Yara. That's it. Now lie down. Pretend you're on the mountain top. Lie still. Pretend we're alone. Now who am I?"

"I don't know yet but I like you now."

There's a long silence. Then Mirna asks, "Is this how you like me, Yara?"

"You know I do, mommy."

"Who am I now?"

"You're Slobodan and Sabina and Julia and father and I love all of you. I showed them —"

"What did you show them?"

"To pretend." There's another silence. Then Yara pleads, "You're hurting me, mommy."

"Can you pretend to forget what I showed you?"

"No, mommy, not if you hurt me a thousand times worse."

"Do you ever pretend to be Vesna?"

"No, mommy, never, and I hate you when you pretend to be the old woman."

"But I'm able to pretend that! And so are you!"

"I'll never be Vesna!"

"Pretend hard! There, Vesna, lie still, I'm your father. How does that feel, Vesna? And that? Is this how you like me, Vesna?"

"No I don't! I'm not Vesna! Why are you so afraid? What happened to you?"

"Do you like it better with Julia?"

"That's right, mommy! And even better with Slobodan because then it's more real!"

"Is it more real than Vesna?"

Yara shouts defiantly, "Yes, it's more real than Vesna! Slobodan is alive! Julia is alive! Vesna is dead! Why can't you understand that? Vesna isn't real any more!"

I hear a loud whack. Yara shrieks with pain. "Let go of me!"

Mirna shrieks, "We killed her!" She whacks Yara again. "Pretend to understand that we killed her, Yara!" She whacks the girl yet again shrieking, "You'll kill the rest of us!"

I run in frantically and hold Mirna's arms back to keep her from hitting Yara yet again. The thought of Mirna's father stopping her mother from swinging the broom flashes through my mind. I take Yara in my arms and rush out of the room with her; she goes on shrieking; her face is an expression of terror. My own face probably expresses a similar terror. I let myself down on the living room couch, pressing Yara to me. She starts trembling and places both hands on her burning cheeks. "I won't pretend to be Vesna," she sobs. "I'm not Vesna!"

Yara gradually stops trembling and sobbing. She falls asleep in my arms. The poor girl has had a full day since she returned from her outing. I carry her to her bed and return to the living room couch; I can't make myself join Mirna in the bedroom. I try to sleep but the few memories I have of Vesna pass through my mind. Vesna was barely two when Jan and I were arrested at the steel plant. I didn't see her again until she was five, when Mirna visited me in prison for the first time. Mirna didn't come again for a long time after that visit when I urged her to divorce me; she sent Vesna to bring packages of food to me, packages which I was never allowed to keep. Every time Vesna came she made it perfectly clear to me that she hated me and blamed me for the miserable life they all led. From Vesna I learned that Mirna's mother had somehow become incapacitated, that she had been moved into our house, and that she continually filled Vesna's head with superstitions and fears. But it wasn't only the old woman who shaped Vesna's development; the whole environment in which she grew up terrorized her. When she was six, Vesna did all the shopping and housecleaning, took care of Yara and nursed the helpless old woman; Mirna cooked supper when she returned from work but was too tired to do anything else. On one of her earliest visits Vesna gave me a fairly clear idea of the quality of her experiences in the world "outside." A few days before her visit, when she was on her way home with a bag of groceries, a group of school children walked by her. One of them shouted, "That's Vochek's daughter." Others started chanting, "Traitor's daughter! Capitalist! Foreign spy!" Vesna ran from them and was hit by several rocks. One of the "brave young revolutionaries" ran after her, pushed her into the snow, and spilled all the groceries. No one defended her; several adults walked by her indifferently. When she got home, the milk was half ice, there was snow in the bread and vegetables, and her hands were frozen. Yet she told me about the incident without indignation, as if it were perfectly natural that "Vochek's daughter" didn't really have the right to share the street with "decent and normal" people. Mirna kept Vesna out of school until she was seven, partly to get help with all the work in the house, but mainly for fear of what the schoolchildren might do to her. When neighbors reported her, Vesna was enrolled in school. Her visits became rare and then stopped altogether. Contrary to Mirna's fears, Vesna wasn't physically assaulted in school. From Vesna's sparse descriptions I gathered that she became a model "revolutionary" pupil. She absorbed everything she was told, like a sponge. Her schooling didn't do away with the superstitions she'd learned from her sick grandmother but on the contrary reinforced them. She merely learned to call the devils that infested the universe by new names: now they were shirkers, counter-revolutionaries, hooligans and foreign agents; the rest of her outlook remained unchanged. About the middle of her first school year, Vesna's visits came to an end; I never saw her again. I had no visitors for several months and I began to speculate that Mirna had finally decided to divorce me. But then Titus visited me for a second time. He told me that shortly after her last visit to me, Vesna had become ill; he had rushed her to the hospital. She remained in the hospital for several weeks; the doctors said she had a weak heart and advised that she be allowed to rest as much as possible; she recovered despite the fact that she couldn't rest for a minute at our house. Titus brought me Mirna's usual package; that was the only time I was allowed to keep it and share its contents with fellow prisoners. Ever since Vesna had started visiting me, I had gone to the visitors' room with a certain apprehension; I was relieved when I saw Titus there instead of Vesna. I begged Titus to urge Mirna to divorce me. I told him there was no reason for them to go through a hell worse than prison because I had been convicted of political crimes. I had already been in prison for four years and I knew I'd be there for at least four more; I didn't think I would ever see the outside world again. I reminded him that he had once asked me to join him in carrying a project; I had not done very well, but my efforts had caused me to lose my ability to survive, my ability to give another generation the possibility to carry a project. Titus smiled sadly at my request; he told me he would try. For several months I again had no visitors. I thought, without joy, that Titus had carried out my request. Then Mirna came; it was her second visit; I hadn't seen her in years. She was skinny; her face had wrinkles; she looked twenty years older than I remembered her; in her simple dress and black kerchief, she looked very much like her mother. "Titus asked me to marry him," she told me. "And you refused?" I asked. "No, Yarostan," she said angrily; "I accepted. I knew it was you who'd asked him to propose to me. He did your bidding ever so meekly and unwillingly. But I threw myself at him. Take me, I told him; I'm yours. At that moment he backed away from me. He saw what I was! He saw the devil in me. He cast me away; he didn't want the devil around his neck any more than you do. Suddenly I understood all your talk about divorce. Vesna thinks you're responsible for everything that happened to us and she's ended up by convincing you. But Vesna doesn't know what I know. Vesna doesn't know that whatever you were arrested for, I shared in greater measure. You told Titus you were a chain around my neck, but he saw that I was a chain around yours! Don't lie to yourself any more; you know it too. You're all I have left now; you're my father, brother, husband and friend, and I'll do everything in my power to hold on to you. I'll be at the prison gate when they release you. And if they don't release you I'll find a way to crawl through the prison bars. If it's the devil they want in jail, let them imprison me. It's because of me that my brother disappeared and my father died. Please, Yarostan, share that burden with me!" As I listened to Mirna, I concluded she'd been affected by her mother's insanity, but I couldn't keep myself from crying. I realized that for Mirna my prison cell represented freedom from the life she had to live daily. From that day until a few months before my release, Mirna visited me frequently. Sometimes she brought Yara; she never again brought Vesna, I couldn't hide the fact that I liked Yara much more than I liked Vesna, mainly, I suppose, because Yara seemed to like me. On one visit when Mirna came with Yara, I asked about Vesna's health. Yara, who was six then and had just started school, answered, "Oh, she's well enough, but her skin turns to goose pimples whenever anyone touches her. You're not like that, are you father?" Mirna swept Yara off the ground and shouted, "Of course he's not like that, Yara. The three of us have the devil in us. Vesna is a saint, like your grandmother." After which Yara told me, "I wouldn't like you if you were a saint!" Mirna and Yara visited me together for the last time about a year before my release. Mirna came in her best dress; she had fixed her hair; she seemed healthier than I'd seen her since my arrest and she looked her own age again. She was beautiful. Yara was as lively as an energetic seven-year old. Mirna blushed when I walked into the room. She told me she'd learned that prisoners were being released at the end of their scheduled terms, and therefore I would be released in 347 days. "Mommy says when you get home you'll teach me all the things they don't teach in school," Yara said excitedly. Mirna blushed again. I was infected by their happiness. I, too, started to count the days to my release, although I knew that such activity could lead to frustrated hopes and a broken heart; if prisoners were being let out at the end of their terms, I was convinced it was out of pure caprice on the part of the repressive apparatus. I continued counting days; that's why I know that for the next 204 days I received no visitors. I knew something had happened; I speculated that Mirna had found out the rumor did not refer to me and had spent her energy trying to move a cog in the bureaucracy. Yara finally put an end to my speculations, I was shocked by her appearance. She was dressed in a sack far too big for her, there were tears in her eyes, and her face had an expression I had seen before, on Vesna's face, and once or twice on Mirna's: it was hatred. "They killed Vesna!" she told me, concentrating all her hatred on the "they." I asked her what had happened but could learn nothing from her account except that Vesna had died in a hospital and that I was indirectly responsible for her death. "Vesna was so afraid, father, so terribly afraid." "Afraid of what?" I asked; "what happened to her?" "The day we got back from visiting you, mommy and I were so happy that you'd be with us in a year, but Vesna didn't want you to come back, ever — and they took her away and killed her because of that!" "Who took her away and why?" I asked. "Mommy and I tried to stop them but we couldn't; two of them held me and the others took Vesna away from us." I asked impatiently, "You tried to stop whom, Yara? What happened to Vesna?" Her answer was, "They locked her up in that hospital and didn't let her out again! They killed her! You would have stopped them if you'd been home! They paid no attention to mommy and me!" I grew suspicious. "Yara, how long was Vesna sick before Mirna called the doctor?" Yara suddenly backed away from me. The hatred that had earlier been concentrated on "them" was now aimed at me. With horror and indignation she told me, "Father, we didn't call the doctor!" I became indignant too. "Why, Yara? Mirna should have called the doctor when Vesna's illness began! Why didn't she call the doctor?" Tears covered Yara's face; she looked at me incredulously, as if I were a monster. "You don't understand either!" she wailed as she ran from me. My last month and a half in prison was like an extra term. One phrase kept going through my mind: "Vesna didn't want you to come back, father — she was so terribly afraid." I remembered, analyzed and re-analyzed the few contacts I'd had with Vesna; none of them had been happy encounters; since she was extremely sensitive, she must have been aware of my dislike for her, of the resentment I felt at seeing her and not Mirna in the guest room. That dislike and resentment were somehow responsible for her death. But I didn't understand how. Vesna's heart was apparently too weak to withstand the numerous tasks that fell on her and I didn't understand why Mirna hadn't called the doctor when Vesna had gotten sick again; I remembered that it had been Titus, and not Mirna, who had taken Vesna to the hospital the first time she'd gotten sick. But I never asked for an explanation. When Mirna finally accompanied me home after eight years of confinement, I found myself in a worse prison than the one I had left. The joy Mirna and Yara had communicated to me during their visit a year earlier was gone; it had died with Vesna. Yara was no longer the friend and comrade she had been during her few visits with Mirna; she was cold and distant. Mirna was twenty years older again, tired and resigned; she dragged herself to work in the morning and dragged herself home in the evening, ate, cleaned and fed her mother, and fell into bed. Her mother was housed in a brick shed next to the house; she couldn't move her arms or her legs; all she could do was talk. As soon as I returned I relieved Mirna of the task of removing the old woman's excrement; I'd had similar tasks in prison. Mirna insisted on feeding and washing the old woman herself; her mother would probably have spat out food that I served her. Yara never entered the shed. I wasn't able to find a job and wasn't terribly eager to look for one; between my tasks and our meals, I took long, lonely walks. When we were together we didn't ever talk about the old woman in the shed next to the house, and the subject of Vesna never came up.

Eventually I fall asleep on the living room couch. The following morning I wake up aching, at the hour when I usually wake to go to the plant, but it's Saturday. I walk toward the bedroom and stop in the doorway, horrified. Mirna is still in the position where I left her when I pulled her arms away from Yara! Her eyes are wide open and concentrate on a spot on the ceiling; she looks like her mother did during the weeks after my release, before she died; she looks paralyzed. "Mirna!" I shout, and I start to tremble. She doesn't stir. I run to Yara's room and shake her.

Yara rushes to our bedroom, shrieks the moment she enters, and jumps on top of the bed. "Mommy, don't do that!" she shouts, shaking Mirna's arms and shoulders. "Beat me all you want, but don't look like that!" Then Yara starts to shriek hysterically: "Stop it, mommy! I'll be Vesna! I'll be anyone you want! But stop it!

Please! I love you, mommy. You can be the old woman if you want. But don't make them take you away. Please, please stop it!"

I become infected with Yara's hysteria. I start pacing around the bed. "We have to do something, Yara. Mirna is sick. I'll go out to look for a doctor."

Yara's face takes on the expression of hatred and horror I had seen when she last visited me in prison. She shrieks, "No!" Then she leaps away from the bed and starts pushing me out of the room. "Leave her alone! Go away from here!"

"Yara, what's the matter with you?" I shout. "Your mother is sick!"

Yara shrieks. "She's not sick! You don't understand anything! You want them to kill her!"

"That's terribly mean, Yara. I love Mirna very much. I want her to get well."

"Then leave her alone!" she shouts. "The doctor is going to say she has to go to the hospital and they'll kill her the way they killed Vesna!"

"Please, Yara! She has to see a doctor. We won't let anyone take her to the hospital."

"You're lying," she shouts, pushing me toward the outside door. "Go for a walk, visit someone, but leave her alone. Please! You won't stop them from taking her! You wouldn't have stopped them from taking Vesna!"

"Vesna was sick! The doctor should have been called —"

"Vesna wasn't sick!" Yara shrieks. Then she calms herself and pleads with me. "I don't hate you, father, but you don't understand. You're just like Mr. Zabran and those horrible doctors. Mommy isn't sick. I know. I'll get Jasna; she'll understand. Maybe Zdenek will too. Please go away, won't you? She'll get well if you go away. And please don't bring anyone; I'll get everyone I know to stop them from touching her!"

"I've had enough of this silliness, Yara! I'm going to call —"

"Then go to hell!" she shrieks, pushing me and beating me with her fists. "Get out of here and stay out at least until tonight! Mommy isn't sick!"

"Then what's wrong with her?"

"Nothing!" she shouts. "Nothing's wrong with her! She's playing with you and me! But you don't know how to play! You're the one who's sick, like all those others. Please, father, don't have her killed for playing!"

I leave the house reluctantly. I go to a coffee house to try to think clearly but nothing becomes clear to me. Yara understands Mirna, especially her "games," much better than I do. On the other hand, I suspect that Yara's opinion of doctors and hospitals might be a bit of "wisdom" she picked up from Mirna and her mother. I convince myself that neither a "game" nor Yara's opinion of doctors should endanger Mirna's health. I take a bus to the city hospital. My first encounter with the hospital "reception" forces me to admit that whatever Mirna and Yara think of hospitals, it is based on something real. I've never been to a hospital before; I've also never visited a prison as an "outsider"; I imagine the "reception" offices of both must be very similar. "Can she walk? Is it critical? A hospital doctor cannot visit your house. Would you like us to send an ambulance with a stretcher? No? In that case you'll have to bring her here by taxi." I make up my mind to find someone to help me take Mirna to the hospital, someone Yara trusts. I walk to Zdenek's house but he's not home. I consider Titus but the thought of Yara's hysteria dissuades me from looking him up. I take a bus to Jasna's house but she's not home either. I know I can carry Mirna to the taxi myself and I realize I'm looking for someone who will not only convince Yara of Mirna's need for medical attention but also help me decide to oppose Yara's will. I walk to Yara's school and sit down on a bench in the playground. I try to take Yara seriously; I try to figure out the nature of the "game" Mirna is playing. But surely a person who is seriously injured or paralyzed in a game needs medical care! It's already mid-afternoon. I leave the schoolyard and head home, determined to get Mirna to a doctor, with or without Yara's approval.

The moment I enter the house, Yara plants herself in the bedroom doorway. Zdenek and Jasna are both in the living room. "Have you been here all day?" I ask. "I went to both your houses to look for you."

"Yara came to get us as soon as you left this morning," Jasna tells me. "Calm down, won't you? Did you contact anyone else?"

"How is she?" I ask.

"Mirna is perfectly all right," Jasna says with an insistence that makes me sense she's lying; "it's you who worries us, Yarostan."

"Me!" I shout. "Are you in on that game too, Jasna? Are you playing with Mirna's health, with her life?" I take two quick steps toward the bedroom doorway. "Yara, step out of my way!"

But it's Zdenek who stops me; he pulls me towards the couch and forces me down on it, commanding, "Stay out of there! If you have any love for her, Yarostan, stay seated and listen to us!"

"She needs a doctor!" I shout. "Can't you see she's sick?"

Jasna says calmly, "I'm amazed at how cruelly you disregard Yara. She's not an idiot, you know!"

"It's not a question of insulting or not insulting Yara," I shout impatiently as I writhe frustratedly in Zdenek's grip; "it may be a question of Mirna's life! Have you both gone crazy? Are you going to sit here and hold me while she dies like her mother?"

"If you're just going to shout, Yarostan, it would be better if you took another walk," Jasna says. "Come back when you're in a mood to listen to us."

"I should have had them send the ambulance!" I shout. "I'll go, Jasna — I'll go get the ambulance."

Zdenek shouts, "You'll stay right there and listen to us no matter what mood you're in! It took Yara less than half an hour to explain the whole thing to me; why are you so mule-headed?"

"Because I love her," I mutter weakly.

Zdenek shakes me. "Listen to me. Mirna is convinced she's carrying a terrible burden. She thinks she's responsible for all the deaths in her family, including her own daughter's." Yara starts to close the door of the bedroom but Zdenek shouts: "Leave it open, Yara! She has to listen too, and I don't want to say it all twice! She's convinced that death stalks every one of her happy moments. That stupid broadcast about the troop movements convinced her she was right, and that letter from your friend gave her some mysterious insights into the origins of her guilt. She seems to think she was driven to do everything she did, and last night she apparently convinced herself that Yara was an agent of whatever it was that drove her. Mirna's sickness is nothing but an attempt to destroy Yara's carefree love of life. She's determined to drive guilt into the child, and she's apparently willing to die trying because she's as mule-headed as you are."

I tell Zdenek, "I don't understand a single word," but that's a lie. The shed in which Mirna and Yara had "isolated" the old woman flashes through my mind. Yara's visit after Vesna's death and her admission, "Father, we didn't call the doctor," flash through my mind, as well as Mirna's shriek when she hit Yara the night before: "We killed her — you'll kill the rest of us." What I don't understand is why Mirna didn't call the doctor when Vesna was sick, and why Zdenek and Jasna refuse to call the doctor now.

Yara starts to cry. "Why don't you understand, father? Mommy made me think you were different, she made me think you'd be a friend, and I believed her, I wanted so much to believe her, but I couldn't go on believing her after I visited you in prison for the last time, when you told me you wouldn't have stopped them from taking Vesna away."

I ask Zdenek indignantly, "Are you telling me Vesna wasn't sick either?"

Zdenek answers, "The only thing wrong with Vesna was that she grew up in this house between her sister, her mother and her grandmother."

"Vesna wasn't sick," Jasna adds. "She'd had rheumatic fever a few years earlier, but she'd recovered from that —"

"I'm not an idiot either!" I shout to Jasna. "You're repeating Yara's comment like a parrot. If Vesna wasn't sick, why did she die?"

"You are an idiot, Yarostan!" Zdenek shouts. "Why can't you believe Yara? In the hospital they didn't know what to make of Vesna. They misdiagnosed her —"

"But that's impossible!" I start to shake.

"Impossible!" Zdenek shouts. "But you're as authoritarian as they come! Do you think doctors are gods? Hasn't Yara told you what they did to her?"

"I couldn't tell him because he was on their side," Yara says.

"Tell him now, Yara; he has to be told sometime," Jasna insists.

"They didn't even let mommy and me go see her. They kept us in that front office where white-frocked people continually ran in and out. They told me Vesna was asleep and couldn't be disturbed; we waited all day and half the night, but Vesna kept being asleep and then I knew they were lying; Vesna didn't sleep all the time. When there wasn't anyone in the office, I left mommy there and walked up and down the halls, which are the same as in school only longer; I looked into every room until I found her in a room full of sick people. The doctors had all lied to us. Vesna was wide awake, staring at the ceiling just like mommy is, but I knew they were killing her; they had all kinds of tubes connected to her: in her arm, through her nose and elsewhere. Poor Vesna couldn't breathe. I went up to her and told her, 'If you don't stop, they won't let you come out and see father when he returns.' She said, 'I've seen him and I hate him.' I asked her, 'Do you want to stay here?' She said, 'No, Yara, I hate it here, I hate all these people, I want to go back to grandmother's room!' I got mad at her and shouted, 'Then stop pretending!' Vesna said, 'I can't.' I could have made her stop but they didn't let me. Nurses and guards had heard me and came running for me; I screamed, 'You're killing her!' while they carried me to the waiting room and then they told us both to leave; they knew what they were doing to Vesna."

"How awful!" Jasna sobs. "I only learned about Yara's visit to Vesna this morning. All I knew before was what Titus had told me right after Vesna died. He had called the hospital every half hour to find out how she was; poor soul, he had taken her there and he was so concerned. But he took the hospital authorities as seriously as you do. She was in a perpetual coma, he told me. They kept diagnosing and rediagnosing her; every diagnosis had its tests and treatment; poor Vesna just wasn't strong enough to withstand all those treatments. And all that time Vesna succeeded in fooling them!"

"How could she?" I ask, on the verge of tears.

"Please don't be so stupid, Yarostan," Jasna sobs. "How could Yara's sister, Mirna's daughter, herself an accomplished prankster, fool all those doctors and nurses? Children do that in school every day of the year — not just to me; that's easy; some fool the entire teaching staff for months at a stretch! Those doctors authoritatively told Titus she was in critical condition, she had a clot on the brain, and even that her brain was damaged — and they treated her for all that!"

I can't hold back my tears. I reach both my hands out to Yara and beg, "Please forgive me. I insulted you whenever you tried to tell me. You have good reason to hate me. I was terribly wrong."

Yara runs to me crying. "Until today it didn't matter how wrong you were," she whispers. "You couldn't have helped us; you were in prison when they took Vesna away."

"I'm the one who could have helped but I stayed away and I continued staying away," Jasna sobs. "Vesna had missed school for more than a week but I didn't ask Yara what was wrong and I didn't introduce myself to Mirna as her husband's and her brother's friend. Instead I told Titus that Vesna was probably ill and it was he who rushed to your house; I satisfied myself with visiting vicariously, through Titus. I knew that something was terribly wrong when he described Vesna's illness and Mirna's and Yara's reactions to it, but I still didn't come. Titus was convinced

Vesna needed medical care; but he'd had no experience with imaginative children. He told me indignantly that Vesna never left the sick old woman's bed and when he walked into the room the child repeated her grandmother's hocus pocus about the devil and the charms with which to exorcise him. I should have known right then; I would have known if I'd seen her. Titus blamed Mirna for leaving the child in that bed instead of having her taken to the hospital. He told me that when he mentioned the hospital, Mirna acted as insane as her mother and Yara became hysterical. So he took it on himself to have Vesna taken to the hospital. When she was carried to the ambulance, two attendants had to hold Yara and keep her out of the way. Mirna has every reason in the world to consider me a coward and a hypocrite. Where was I when Vesna was carried away? Mirna and Yara needed me! Vesna might still be alive today. But I was home, reading. I couldn't share the real horrors with Mirna, not even one of them."

"She didn't blame you, Jasna; she blamed herself, and that was my fault," Yara tells her. "Mommy tried to stop them from taking Vesna as much as I did. She begged them on her knees not to take her away from us, and she cried all day long. We went to the hospital every day, even after they told us not to come any more. Whenever anyone came out we begged, 'Please give our Vesna back to us.' Twice we waited all day in the rain; a nurse kept running out and telling us to go home; she said we were crazy and called us stupid peasants. Finally a man in a white coat let us into the waiting room, but only to tell us Vesna wasn't in the hospital any more. We screamed at him and he had another man in a white coat come in and tell us she had died that morning in an ambulance while being transferred to another hospital. That was when I shouted, 'Mommy, you let them kill our Vesna!' It wasn't true. I knew it wasn't true! But I wanted someone to blame because I loved Vesna. Mommy believed it; she blamed herself. For two weeks she went to work crying and she returned crying. I begged her to forgive me for saying that, but she never stopped blaming herself. One day, weeks after Vesna's death, I told her Vesna would never have started hating you and mommy if that old woman hadn't been living with us, and that made her stop crying. That night she went to grandmother's room and screamed, 'Vampire! You won! You've always wanted to take Vesna from me! You've done it! Your holy work is done. You can go now.' Mommy had me stay home from school the next day. A heating stove arrived and a bed, as well as a load of bricks. She came home from work with a wheelbarrow and mortar. That night we started building walls around the stove and bed. And every time she walked by grandmother's door she mumbled things like, 'You'll soon have a house without devils in it,' and 'Vesna should have helped me do this five years ago; you might have spared her your salvation.' When we finished, the two of us carried the old woman to her new house; she was mainly bones and lighter than I. I laughed when mommy sang, 'Holy Mary Mother of God, we're taking you to heaven; no demons will ever share your house again except to feed you and remove your excrement.' But she didn't stop blaming herself for Vesna's death and when the old woman died after you came back she blamed herself for that too. I wish I'd never told her she'd let them kill Vesna! Vesna's death was my fault more than anyone else's!"

Hugging Yara, I beg, "Don't say that, please. You loved Vesna; you and Mirna did all you could to save her. I didn't love Vesna! I was afraid of her; I was sorry whenever she came instead of Mirna. I was even happy when Titus came instead of Vesna. I resented Vesna's hating me for being in Jail. She sensed my feelings toward her; that must have had a terrible effect on her. Don't ever blame yourself for that, Yara."

"Your feelings had nothing to do with it," Yara says insistently. "Vesna was playing a game with me and with no one else, and she won —"

"A game, Yara? And Vesna won?"

"A game, father! Why did those doctors have to come into it? Vesna hated the old woman as much as I did but she pretended to love her. She loved you as much as I did but she pretended to hate you. When we learned you'd return in a year, before mommy and I went to see you, I caught her kissing herself in the mirror. I knew she was kissing you and I forced her to admit it; she made me promise never to tell mommy and I never told. But I made fun of her until the day we went to visit you; I called her a liar for pretending to be like the crazy old woman; I told her I knew she wanted you to touch her and kiss her and sleep next to her." Yara starts crying and continues through her sobs, "I didn't tell her those things to be mean or to hurt her, but because I knew they were true. Vesna was my sister, not the old woman's. And she wasn't hurt when I told her those things. It was a game. She made her eyes real big and she ran to the old woman's room shouting, 'You'll roast in hell, Yara.' She didn't hurt me any more than I hurt her. That was our game. And it was still just a game the day mommy and I went to tell you about your release. Mommy was so happy! She got all dressed up; she looked beautiful. Vesna wanted to come with us; I know she did. But when mommy asked her, she said, 'You're the devil, all of you.' I told her, 'So are you!' Mommy and I were so happy when we got back; she showed me how you'd dance with me. We danced and played until Vesna came in and saw us. Mommy teased her the way I had, but Vesna just had to win, she had to prove I was wrong, that she wasn't the devil. Vesna froze, and even mommy thought she was sick. Vesna made herself crazy just like the old woman and she wouldn't come out of the old woman's room. She sweated and then shivered, and mommy got scared until I showed her I could do that too; Vesna had showed me. But that's when I should have stopped teasing Vesna, before all those outsiders came to our house. The more I teased her about being the devil, the more she became like the old woman, and in the end she won — everyone believed her, starting with Mr. Zabran and those ambulance people who came for her. It was all my fault — not yours or mommy's or anyone else's. I wish I hadn't forced her to play the game so hard, so long!"

All of us turn our heads abruptly when we hear Mirna's sob. She's standing in the bedroom doorway looking at the three of us huddled around Yara; she's crying.

She walks toward us, kneels in front of Yara and throws her arms around her. "Did you really see Vesna kiss herself in the mirror?"

Yara throws her arms around Mirna's neck and, kissing her on the lips, whispers, "Like this, mommy; it's the only way you can kiss in a mirror. And I know she wanted a boy in school to kiss her —"

"You're not making it up?"

"I swear, mommy."

"Please don't call me that any more."

"Mommy? Why not?"

"Because you're so much smarter than I am."

Zdenek is the only one without tears on his face. He gets up and exclaims, "That was a nasty trick, Mirna! That whole elaborate performance just to get your daughter to admit her share of the guilt!"

"You're smart too, father," Mirna whimpers. "I'm the only idiot here."

Zdenek turns to Yara. "Can I borrow that letter now? There are some things you didn't make very clear." Yara hands him your previous letter. He leaves the house shouting to Mirna, "I want to find out who taught you to play such devilish games."

Mirna moves toward Jasna; her hand pushes the hair away from Jasna's face. Kissing Jasna's forehead, she asks, "Do you hate all the schoolchildren who fool you and play tricks on you?"

"No, Mirna, I don't hate them," Jasna sobs; "I love them more than any of the others, because they're alive."

"Will you forgive me?"

"There's nothing to forgive, Mirna; everything you said about me is true; will you ever forgive me?"

Mirna wipes the tears from Jasna's face. "Yarostan says you're very pretty when you smile, Jasna. Show me, please." Jasna smiles weakly. Mirna kisses her cheeks. Jasna hugs Yara and then me; she leaves the house crying — but smiling.

Mirna picks up Yara and carries her to the bedroom, asking in a whisper, "What else did Vesna want?"

"She wanted everything you and I wanted, mommy — I mean Mirna. If the old woman hadn't been staying with us, Vesna would never have been afraid of being touched. That came from thinking herself the old woman with that cold, bluish wrinkled skin that was so disgusting to touch. If it hadn't been for the old woman, Vesna would have loved you and father — can I call him Yarostan now? — maybe not the way Tissie loved Sophia; not that way at all; but at least the way Sophia loved Sabina. I know —"

A few days later, when I return from work, Mirna throws her arms around me and starts to dance around the living room with me. She waves your most recent letter in the air. Yara shouts, "She's on strike!" I'm overwhelmed with joy. I spin Mirna around the room. Our crisis is over. Zdenek and Jasna join us to celebrate your commune and Mirna's strike. "We're finally together again!" Jasna exclaims while reading your letter.

We love you, *Yarostan.*

Sophia's seventh letter

Dear Yarostan,
You'll never guess where I am. Outside there's a general strike. Everything is out of commission. Literally everything: factories, offices, transportation vehicles, even taxis — everything except the telephones, and a radio station that's been taken over by the police. I ought to be in the council office, or in the research center where Tissie and Sabina are conquering the whole universe, or somewhere in the midst of all the excitement. But I'm sitting at my desk in Luisa's house, writing you on the ancient typewriter I inherited from George Alberts when he left. I'm surprised it still works; it's the machine on which I was going to type up my novel about you and Ron Matthews as soon as I organized all my notes. Luisa cleaned the room so thoroughly after Art moved out that there was no trace of anyone's having been here since I left for college fifteen years ago. The walls are the same walls I stared at day after day twenty years ago, wondering why I had been separated from my Yarostan and from the only friends I had in the world. The bed is the same bed I shared with Ron for a whole week after the night when his father threatened to shoot both of us — that happy week which ended with my thinking Sabina had "stolen" Ron from me. It was the only happy week I spent in this room. Before and after that week I only dreamed of happiness; I spun that whole universe of illusions which you've finally succeeded in shattering completely.

"I didn't pretend Sophia was anyone I had ever loved. I only used her."

I've been staring at those two sentences the way I once stared at the walls of this room. In one of my letters I tried to argue that the reality on which I based my dreams didn't matter, because my dreams only defined what I sought, not what I had actually lived. Now I know I was wrong, dead wrong. The reality does matter to me. I got both your letters this morning; I read them in the order in which you sent them, and could barely read through the first. I felt empty and hideous inside. I had based my whole life, my daily acts as well as my most distant hopes, on a travesty. You had "only" used me! That matters to me. It matters to every nerve in my brain and to every organ in my body. In your later letter, which I've just read, you tell me that our correspondence has been important to all of you; you tell me that Mirna, Yara as well as Jasna have been stimulated by some of the things I've written, and even that their very decisions and actions have in some way been affected by me.

What if none of what I'd written were true; what if I'd never left this room and had invented everything I've narrated? Wouldn't that matter to you, to all of you?

I was in a rage when I read your "confession," and I spent the entire day squeezing my illusion out of my being, acting without "Yarostan" at the center of my consciousness. Thanks to my rage, an hour ago I achieved something I might call my independence. For once in my life I didn't try to live up to my "central experience." I acted on my own and for myself. I abandoned myself to my wildest desires and I didn't try to live up to anything except my own passion. If Mirna had been here she would have loved me; Sabina would have too. And contrary to what Mirna suggested about Luisa and me, I'm not running from the consequences. I'm staying right here, eager to face every one of the consequences; Luisa's hostility, Daman's hatred, Pat Clesec's suspicion and even fear, as well as my own newborn, inexperienced and untried independence.

What enraged me even more than your "confession" was the fact that I recognized myself in your description. That passive, fragile, mindless thing who was perfectly willing to do "whatever pleases you, Yarostan," is the same person who recently begged eighteen-year old Pat Clesec to "show me what to do." That identical posture, at the beginning and end of two decades of experience, was not a reflection of my weakness, of a moment of dependence in an otherwise independent person. That posture indicated the depth and extent of my independence. I made each of those statements during a period when I had broken out of passivity and joined a community of independent individuals. Your forcing me to recognize the lies I've told myself for the past twenty years enraged me infinitely more than your admission of your desire to shatter a porcelain statue into splinters.

All my life I've been surrounded by people I considered independent, people who were in some way rebels. I hardly know what "normal," submissive people are like — yet I'm one of them. The rebel Nachalo was my life's hero, but I never rebelled against him. Luisa, the insurgent unionist, was my life's first model, but I never turned against her; I left her. The day Tina told Sabina and me that we cramped her, I was hurt. Yet Tina did what I've never done: she rebelled against her "parents" and took the indispensable step toward independence. I took an easier route. A child of radical parents, I was in the privileged position of being a rebel by birth; all I had to do was conform to my parents; my life's idols and my parents never clashed; they were the same. Sabina didn't ever reject her mother either. But Sabina rediscovered the source of Margarita's rebellion and made it her own; she reacted to the world Margarita had reacted to, and her response was her own authentic response to that world. I never tried to rediscover the source; I only tried to copy my models' responses, I tried to make my behavior conform to Luisa's and the mythical Nachalo's. What was radical to the world at large was the norm to me. That's why you and Jasna saw such a normal, prim, correct young lady come to the carton plant with Luisa. I had anticipated the coming of the revolution the way a "normal" girl must anticipate the coming of marriage. When the revolution finally came and my mother accompanied me to it, I gave myself to it as dutifully as to the unavoidable, expected husband: "Whatever pleases you, Yarostan..." It wasn't a "forced marriage"; I'm not suggesting that. I had seen you at our house. I had listened to you. I hadn't known it would be with you I'd leave for "the barricades," although I had wished it. When it was you, nothing could have been more natural. I stepped into a ready-made revolution the way the new bride steps into her assigned husband's ready-made home: she steps into an alien house, another's house, eager to learn her tasks: "Show me what to do." Don't take all the credit for having used me, Yarostan; some of the credit is mine. I gave myself to you as something to be used, as clay to be shaped —.

Couldn't I tell you didn't love me? Oh no, Yarostan, not I, and not then. It wasn't love that had brought me to you, but "destiny." I was Nachalo's daughter; I had been brought up for the revolution, and I had come of age. I was simply being transferred from Luisa's care to yours. You were to me what Nachalo had always been to me: my model, my idol. It never occurred to me to ask myself whether or not you loved me; it was my "duty" to love you.

(Luisa just came back; it's long past midnight. I shouted down to ask if she wanted to talk, but she apparently doesn't. When I asked if she'd mind if I went on typing, she slammed the door of her bedroom. She's in a fury now. Today it was my turn to shatter a porcelain statue, maybe even several.)

You probably thought your "confession" would shock me. It didn't. Your description wasn't exaggerated. I happen to remember the morning when I lay naked on the floor with you right by the carton plant entrance. The reason I remember is that only a year later, by the shore of a pond to which Ron and I had ridden our bikes, I lay awake all night worrying; I was afraid the farmer would open a gate and let the sun shine in on us the way Luisa did. I was afraid because I was ashamed to be seen as a body, as a naked animal. Ashamed because I thought myself the very negation of a body: I was all principle, revolutionary determination, goal. If your desire wasn't roused by any passion in me except my shame, it's because that shame was the only passion in me. You don't exaggerate in the least when you say I turned exactly as I thought I should; the desire to turn differently simply wasn't in me. I didn't only turn without passion. I also experienced your embraces without passion, exactly as I had expected to experience them. Nothing surprised me, nothing excited me physically. I said, "I love you, Yarostan": I've said it since; I can say it as easily now, after your "confession," as I ever could before. I love you, Yarostan. That's not a description of my passion. It's something like my life's principle, my motto; it's almost my name. When you had your orgasm that morning, between my legs, I was very excited — but not physically. Only intellectually. I was proud of myself, proud to be fulfilling the task I had been brought up for. I would have been equally proud if you'd praised me for coining a perfectly appropriate slogan or for printing a beautiful poster. During all the days and nights we spent together you didn't rouse me sexually once, even for an instant. You weren't a body to me but a principle. My feelings toward you were exact inversions of your feelings toward Luisa. You embraced the revolutionary principle with sexual passion, as a body; I embraced your body intellectually, as a principle. I'm not saying any of this out of spite. I'm ashamed of myself. Your letter forced me to come to terms with a self I can't stand. Isn't it beyond belief that someone could grow up between Luisa and Sabina Nachalo and remain sexless? I'm ashamed to admit to Yara and to Mirna that I understood perfectly how poor Vesna must have felt in the face of their unbounded animal passion. Shivers went down my back when I learned Mirna had apparently desired her own father physically, sexually, as a body — the same shivers I experienced ten years ago when I learned that my closest friend and comrade desired her own sex physically, the same shivers Vesna must have experienced when the prospect of physical contact with you was thrown in her face. Until today — except for one single period which I tried to erase from my memory — I've lived at the opposite end of the world.

Today I made my grand entrance into Mirna's world. I thank your letter for that. I know I'm scabbing against the postal workers' strike by having you send your letters across the frontier, but I agree with Mirna and Jasna that it would be awful to stop communicating with you precisely at this moment when everything is possible. Your letters are my only connection with my "likes" elsewhere, and they're every bit as precious to me, with all your "confessions," as mine can possibly be to any of you.

This has been an incredible week. Almost everyone is on strike. All major workshops, assembly plants and factories are occupied by workers. For two days Pat and I visited an immense research center which has been transformed into something like a technological playground. Sabina and Tissie gave us fascinating tours. I would have loved to stay, but Pat thought we might be more useful in the council office. He was wrong; nothing much was happening in the council office last night or this morning, but I'm glad we returned, since otherwise I wouldn't have gotten your letters.

Early this morning I decide to call Luisa. I learned a week ago that her assembly plant is on strike, but I didn't learn any of the details. I was curious about her response to the strike. The last time I called her I'd gotten furious at her for telling me she was waiting for the union to call the strike. She's still asleep when I call. "Won't you be late for work?" I ask sarcastically.

"This happens to be one of the few weekdays in my life when I haven't set my alarm, Sophia. Couldn't you've called an hour later?"

"I don't know where I'll be in an hour, and I'm dying to talk to you."

"Daman and I did intend to try to get together with you."

"Why don't you both come to the council office?" I suggest. "People here would love to hear about your strike."

Luisa hesitates for a moment and then asks, "Would they? The union called the strike. I've been on the picket line every afternoon."

It's my turn to hesitate. I didn't know the union had called any of the strikes. I feel irritated, even angry, at this reminder of the character of Luisa's insurgency. It's not Luisa who rebels; it's her apparatus — that train Zdenek described so straight forwardly. Even that rotten union in her plant is still a union, and a strike not called by a union would be meaningless to her.

I hold my anger in; I don't want yet another conversation with Luisa to end with her telling me: "Call me when you're less hysterical." After my shocked pause, I change the topic. "How's your romance going?"

"Not so hot. Daman is even more of a puritan than you are. But he does join me at the picket line."

Suddenly inspired by a plan, I ask her, "Would you mind if I joined you?"

"Seriously, Sophia? A union picket line?"

Giving all my plans away at once, I ask her, "Would you mind if I brought some of my friends?"

"Obviously not!" Luisa exclaims. "Bring your friends and raise all the hell you want with the union bureaucrats! The first day was exciting because some workers tried to go inside to work. But since then it's been a horrible bore. Do you want us to pick you up?"

I tell her the room where she and Daman can find us. I beg her to have Daman drive across the border to my foreign postbox and also to stop by my house to see if any letters came from you.

I find Pat in the makeshift cafeteria and join him for a quick breakfast. I tell him — in fact I sort of warn him — that I invited a union organizer as well as a professor to the council office.

"I don't check people's credentials, you know!" he says with some annoyance.

"I know, but they're both good friends of mine," I explain awkwardly; I don't want him to chase them away with intimidating arguments the moment they walk in. "Luisa is the woman I told you about, the one who took part in that revolution thirty-two years ago."

"Well, that's a type of union organizer I would like to meet!"

"I don't think you'll find her very different from her colleagues. How would you like to raise hell at a union-run picket line?" I ask him.

Several people are already in the council office when Pat and I get there. The discussion is fascinating, but I'll just summarize it. People are talking about the strikes that have been breaking out in other cities, and mainly about the fact that one corporation's productive facilities all over the country are occupied by workers. Everyone's enthusiasm is dampened by a person who points out that this corporation's foreign plants have been running at full capacity. "Even if the movement here is victorious, such corporations will shift their operations abroad and continue to determine the content of human activity from there." People then discuss the prospects for the destruction of international corporations on a world-wide scale.

Questions of language barriers, of forms of communication, of traveling delegations are raised and dropped.

About two hours after my call to Luisa, there's a knock on the door of the council office. Everyone in the room glares with amazement, and a few people laugh. Daman and Luisa back away from the laughter. They probably think I told people two agents of the system were coming — which is in fact what I'd told Pat. I run out and shout, "Good grief, Daman, how many classes have you taught in this very room? This isn't a private apartment, you know!"

Poor Luisa! She looks terribly intimidated. She's never been in the "university" before, although she's always revered it. It's awful what institutions do to people. To you, to me, to all her friends, Luisa is "the intellectual," a virtual encyclopedia on unionism and revolution. Yet the minute she walks into the official "intelligence building," she sees herself through official eyes as a working woman who never finished high school, therefore unschooled, namely ignorant. I know exactly how she feels. I felt the same way the day Tina took me by the hand and accompanied me to the commune; I wasn't intimidated by the university, but by the "revolution" I imagined to be boiling inside it. Luisa is wearing the same pretty dress she wore the day we visited "Lem's estate." (She had expected Daman to call her on that day, but I had called instead.) I take her hand and pull her into the council office. "They all bite here, but none of them has rabies," I tell her, introducing her to Pat.

Daman remains outside. When I extend my hand to him, he gives me both your letters. He's not exactly friendly toward me, and I can't say I don't know why. The last time I saw him Sabina had insisted he had a phonograph inside his head; he'd tried so desperately to defend himself from Sabina's attack, and all I'd done to help him was to suggest he call the police to protect him from her. My respect for Daman has been the main casualty of my correspondence with you.

Trying to break the silence I ask him with unintended sarcasm, "Have you been on vacation since you lost your job?"

Daman is offended. "It so happens I've been working much harder this past two weeks than I work when school is on."

"Really? Is that why you haven't had time to come here, even for a visit? So much has been happening here! What have you been doing?"

"We've finally gotten that organization off the ground," Daman says proudly.

"The people I've met here have been getting along perfectly without that kind of organ —"

Daman interrupts me; the professor replaces the intimidated tourist as he asserts authoritatively, "The new society will not be created here, but at the point of production, particularly in the basic industries. It isn't born in the heads of intellectuals."

"Is that what your organization is organizing: the new society?" I ask him, this time with intended sarcasm.

Daman answers with a grave tone, "We've already gotten out one issue of our paper."

Unable to curb my sarcasm, I exclaim, "Not that newspaper for workers edited by a professor and his political students!"

Daman's tone becomes condescending: "It so happens that production workers actually wrote the entire issue. It's not a paper for workers but a workers' paper; there's a world of difference. Its task is not to speak for the workers, but to let the workers speak for themselves."

"All the workers? It must be an immense newspaper!"

Daman's face becomes crimson, and I realize I'm doing exactly what I'd hoped Pat wouldn't do: intimidating him to the point of driving him away. I reword my question. "Did many workers contribute articles?"

"You have to understand there are certain financial difficulties, as well as the problem of time. This issue has two articles, both written by production workers. Luisa happens to have written one of them. I'm now in contact with a third —"

"Luisa wrote an article? I'd like to see your paper!"

Daman beams. "I just happen to have several copies with me."

"Really? Well let's take them inside. Everyone in there will want to see them!"

Daman pulls out his handful of "workers' newspapers" as we walk into the room, and I immediately feel sorry for him. His organization's achievement looks pathetic in a room filled with beautifully printed leaflets and pamphlets. It's called *The Workers' Voice* and it's a dirty mimeographed sheet with crooked headlines and barely readable typewritten text. Both articles are unsigned. One is titled, "The Workers Can Do It" and deals with workers who ran a transportation system without any bosses other than union bosses. The other looks, at a glance, like an article on the beneficial effects of higher wages.

"Do you actually give these out to workers occupying their factories?" I ask him.

"They're going like hot cakes!" Daman tells me. He smiles as he starts giving copies to the people in the room. "We've been handing them out at Luisa's plant and we're getting rid of at least fifty a day. We only ran off five hundred."

When Daman hands a copy to Pat, Luisa exclaims, "That's our workers' paper!"

Pat glances at both sides briefly, studies the side on wages and lets out a guffaw. "You call this a workers' paper?"

Daman's smile leaves his face and his whole body gets rigid as he announces, "What you understand by workers may be very different from what I understand." With a sweep of his arm he dismisses the roomful of people as well as the stacks of strike announcements and factory occupation accounts. "Students parading as a new working class just don't cut the ice. The new working class is an invention of petty bourgeois sociologists —"

I interrupt him angrily. "Pat and I and you happen to be the only people in this room who don't come out of factories!"

A young worker shouts to Daman, "What the hell is the new working class?"

Luisa tries to interpret Daman's outburst to the people in the room. "He's referring to workers' relation to the traditional workers' movement."

"I.e... the union," Pat adds.

But Daman persists. "I'm talking about one's relation to the means of production, which is the only test of class. People whose function is to manipulate others are best defined as middle class."

All the people in the room except Luisa and Pat move away from Daman. I move to the corner furthest from Daman and start looking at your first letter, but I continue listening with a certain amount of interest.

Pat says calmly, "Your categories are being superseded by present practice, Pro — mister." Pat remembers my "warning," but only to the extent of not calling Daman a professor. Pat points to *The Workers' Voice* article on wages. "What you call a workers' paper is nothing but an instrument of the union bureaucracy; it's an appendage to capital."

Daman, unruffled by Pat's argument, or perhaps missing its point, repeats his ancient argument that, "The most thoroughly unionized and best paid workers in the basic and heavy industries are central to any revolutionary upsurge."

Pat retorts, "Only when they stop production, only when they stop being unionized and best paid, only when they stop being workers, when they cease to be slaves, when they become masters —"

But Daman insists, "It's only the fact that they're workers, the fact that they're at the point of production, that gives them their revolutionary capacity! It's their work that teaches them to run production!"

"Their work reproduces capital, and that's all!" Pat shouts. "You're an apologist for capital, in other words a shithead!" Several people applaud.

"And you obviously don't know what capital is," Daman says with a professorial contempt that infuriates me. "By concentrating workers in the basic industries, capitalism itself creates the organization and discipline of the new society —"

This is greeted by catcalls, whistles, and various shouts like, "Here comes the boss!" and "The new society looks just like the old." Someone asks, "You a factory owner, mister?"

I can't resist answering, "No, he's a professor!"

Various people exclaim, "Oh!"

Daman, leering with hostility at everyone in the room, expresses his understanding of the situation: "It's obvious that I've walked into a meeting of a political sect that adheres to the theory of the backwardness of the working class. Those unionized and well paid workers you sneer at —"

I can't stand that condescending, self-effacing posture; I interrupt him. "We were sneering at you!"

He ignores me. "Those unionized workers you consider so backward are the ones who continually develop the capacity to create the new society; their work is inherently revolutionary."

"In other words, work hard and obey the rules!" Pat shouts. "Kiss the boss's ass, follow the leader, that's the revolution."

"Leaders don't simply impose themselves on the class, they're products of the class. Workers produce their strongest leaders when they're themselves strongest —"

And on and on. I've heard all of it before. Daman really does have a phonograph in his head instead of a brain. Pat and occasionally some of the other people try in vain to communicate with him. Periodically Luisa tries to "translate" his most unpalatable observations.

I finally lose interest in the argument and start reading the letter Daman picked up at my house; it must have arrived a few days after Sabina and I left with Tina, just before the postal strike began. Daman, Luisa, the argument and the council office vanish as I lose myself in the world you describe. Earlier I came close to suggesting that your "confession" was the only part of your letter I responded to. That isn't the case at all. I'm amazed to discover the Jasna who speaks through your letter, praising Sabina for having the courage to realize her desires — desires which Jasna never allowed herself to realize. I'm even more amazed by Mirna; your earlier letters had given me a significantly different picture. I'm surprised to discover a Mirna who has a lot in common with Sabina, and even more surprised to learn they knew each other. Mirna is perfectly right about my failure to face any of the consequences caused by that letter I sent you twelve years ago. I didn't even know there had been any consequences until I learned about them from your letters and from Lem. Of course I realize it was the police, and not my letter, that did the jailing and the killing, but I still feel awful. Obviously nothing I can say now can bring back Mirna's father or Jan or Vesna. I'm surprised you didn't learn about that letter for such a long time after your arrest. I'm also puzzled by something in your second letter. Neither you nor Jasna nor, apparently, anyone else had known that Luisa, Sabina and I were released soon after our arrest at the carton plant. Yet I vaguely remember that Titus Zabran was with us when we were released, so at least he must have known about it. I also vaguely remember Luisa telling me years ago that Titus didn't emigrate with us because he wanted to stay behind to try to have the rest of you released.

Your confession isn't the only part I respond to, but I admit it's the part I continue responding to for the rest of the day. As I read about your love for Luisa, the council office comes back into focus, and so does Luisa — nearly a quarter of a century older than the woman in your letter, but just as vigorous, just as youthful, and just as "seductive." Her seductiveness is novel to me. Either I'm very dense, or else she kept it from me: the truth lies somewhere in between. You're right: I didn't know you had slept with Luisa at our house. While I inform myself of that fact, I notice that Daman is no longer arguing with Pat: he's in a corner of the room, chatting with a woman; she probably expressed interest in his organization. Pat and most of the workers hover around Luisa; apparently they all know her to be the co-author of *The Workers' Voice*. Someone points out that the article on wages flatly contradicts her article. But no argument follows. Luisa is an organizer, a politician, a charmer — as well as a diplomat. She agrees that the point is not to have higher wages for slave labor, but to appropriate the productive forces and be free. Yet in the same breath she manages to defend Daman as well as the writer of the other article: the main point is to act, and even someone fighting for higher wages is more of a revolutionary than people who merely sit in a room and talk.

Pat starts to ask, "Are you going to tell us that workers producing weapons for the police are doing more than —"

"Obviously not!" Luisa exclaims, looking uneasily toward Daman. "But I am saying that workers on a picket line they themselves organize, defending their jobs from scabs, are doing infinitely more than what I see being done here."

"What if some of us went to your picket line to find out if it really is organized by the workers themselves?" Pat asks.

"The more the merrier." Luisa exclaims. "How many want to check out and if need be challenge the organization of that picket line?" She's in her milieu.

Someone asks, "Will the union goons actually let us talk to any workers?"

"All you have to do is out-shout the loudspeakers," she answers.

Pat makes another suggestion. "What if we go with a leaflet explaining who we are? It can start with the question: Why do you let the loudspeakers speak for you?"

Shouting "That's magnificent; it's what I've always asked myself," Luisa throws her arms around Pat and I almost fall off my chair, almost scattering your letter all over the room. I, Sophia Nachalo, Queen of the Peasants, prim, correct and well-mannered, perfect for shattering, afraid to hold Pat's hand because he's only eighteen, start to boil, and I go on boiling until I make myself the one who carries the revolution to the peasants, until I'm the one who shatters porcelain statues.

The leaflet on loudspeakers is composed in less than fifteen minutes; it consists of a sequence of slogans; almost everyone, including Luisa, contributes one. When it's done Luisa suggests that it be printed on the mimeograph in the basement of Daman's house, but Pat objects: "We have access to printing equipment only a few minutes away from here, and I know how to print; someone else with the name of Nachalo taught me."

Luisa looks quizzically at me. "I didn't know you could print."

"It's Tina," I tell her.

Daman expresses sudden interest. "Tina is here? And she prints?" He doesn't seem at all eager to have another run-in with her.

Everyone except the two people who volunteered to spend the day in the council office sets out toward Ted's cooperative print shop. Pat and Luisa, her arm locked in his, lead the procession of fourteen or so people. Daman and his new friend continue their conversation several feet behind everyone else; I learn that his newest "recruit" is a worker from the office machine plant Pat and I visited during my first week here. I walk right behind Pat and Luisa, with both your letters in my handbag.

On the way to the print shop, Luisa tells Pat, "I agree with you about the other article in *The Workers' Voice*. Its author is a union man, and I objected to Daman's including it. The union I fought with was a genuine workers' union which had nothing in common with this company union. It had no paid functionaries —"

Pat objects, "Yet after the victory, some of the unpaid functionaries became government ministers and factory managers!" I'm continually amazed by how we'll read he is.

"You have to understand the circumstances," Luisa pleads. "It was war, and war always destroys everything people fight for."

Pat doesn't pursue his argument. Ever since we went to talk to the office machine workers I've been aware that Pat isn't nearly as argumentative with women as he is with men.

Only Pat, Luisa and I go into the print shop; the others wait outside. Pat immediately sits down at an electric typewriter.

As soon as Tina sees Luisa, she exclaims, "Well I'll be damned! How many years is it since you've taken a day off work?"

"I take it that you Nachalos know each other," Pat ascertains. "May I ask if you're related?"

Tina, mounting an enormous plate onto the metal cylinder of a press, shouts, "Can't you see the family resemblance? Sophia and Luisa are sisters; I'm their mother. What else do you want to know?"

Pat mutters, "That'll teach me to snoop." He proofreads the leaflet before mounting it in the camera copyboard. Then he takes Luisa's hand and pulls her toward the darkroom entrance. "Come on; I'll show you how production can take place without managers or union bureaucrats."

I'm on the verge of asking, "Can I come too?" I've never seen that type of photography, and the thought of Luisa whisking you off to the stockroom of the carton plant flashes through my mind. But I walk toward the large press Tina is adjusting.

"Back so soon?" Tina asks me, concentrating on the press.

"From the research center?" I ask.

Tina turns the press on. "I couldn't get my fill of it," she shouts above the noise of the press. "I could have spent my whole life playing with all those tools and gadgets."

I back away from Tina as she pulls a printed sheet from the press and I almost trip over a box. I feel intimidated by her comments. I stayed at the research center for two days, but it didn't ever occur to me that I might want to play with the tools and gadgets. The only time I experienced such a desire was in the garage, when I was Tina's apprentice. It's not a coincidence that in the garage I also performed my life's single independent act, the night I threw myself on Jose because I had decided to demonstrate the exact nature of my innermost desires. But my independence began and ended with that act. That night I acted in the spirit of Tina, in the spirit of what the garage stood for. I was my own person; I made myself what I most wanted to be. What I made myself, independently, on my own — what I most wanted to be — was dependent! I wanted to be your shadow, Ron's shadow, Jose's shadow, even Tina's shadow. By that independent act I annihilated my independence. The garage was my one "community" where my role wasn't predefined, where I had to define the nature of my life and the content of my activity on my own. Unlike seven-year old Tina, I was only able to define myself the same way I had always defined myself: as part of someone else's project, as Tina's apprentice and Jose's woman.

"I'd give you a tour," Tina shouts, "but these pamphlets have to be done by noon."

"How did you learn to use all these things so fast?" I ask her.

"I didn't learn fast," she shouts. "Now that you know Ted isn't the beast you thought him, I might as well tell you I've been here since the print shop started, over two years ago."

"You've been seeing Ted for the past two years? Did Sabina know?"

"You're the only one who didn't know!" she shouts.

My head starts to spin. Didn't I know about your affair with Luisa, under my very nose, in my own house? I was the only one who didn't know!

"I've been seeing Ted ever since Sabina and I left the garage. Don't look so glum! You made it perfectly obvious you didn't want to hear a word about him!" Tina turns the press off and starts to dismount the plate.

I turn to another topic. "Have you known Pat long?"

"He sure is a bird, isn't he? I've never known anyone quite like him," she says, laughing and sitting down on a box. "I met him a few days before I moved out of our house. I was here when Pat and his whole group of friends came in. They said they'd heard Ted and I often helped students with their printing projects. And then they said they were anti-students; they didn't want either to contract a job or to hire a proletarian; they had come to create a new situation. Ted didn't know what to make of them. They talked about numerous projects, such as leaflets, pamphlets, even books. They showed me some of the things they'd written: attacks on every imaginable authority, especially revolutionary ones. I loved it. They told me none of them could draw, but when I volunteered to do some of the drawing for them Pat got mad. That's not the point, he said. We want to break down all those divisions; we all want to draw, write, print."

I begged Tina not to spoil her schedule because of me.

"The press is running perfectly, so I'm way ahead of my deadline. Anyway, Pat asked me if Ted would be willing to take part in their projects as an equal. I asked if Ted would have to enroll in college to be their equal, and Pat scolded me saying he hadn't come to be ridiculed, but to establish a direct, transparent, non-capitalist relationship. I understood what he meant, and it appealed to me a lot. I told them I'd take part. 'You?' Pat asked with disbelief. 'Now who's doing the ridiculing?' I asked him. He tried to get out of it by asking if I was the printer's daughter. They invited me to their next meeting and I went. I'm one of them now. But since that day I haven't let Pat forget that he didn't want to be the equal of an eighteen-year old girl who'd never been to school. Except for that I think he's nice — they all are; I'm the only woman in the group, and after that day they've all gone out of their way to treat me as an equal."

Ted walks toward us from the back of the shop. He lives upstairs. Tina shouts to him, "Would you mind giving Sophia a tour? I'd like to finish running this pamphlet."

I just saw Ted the previous evening, but I rush toward him as if he were an old friend. The previous day he had driven Pat and me back from the research center. I shake his hand eagerly. "I'm really impressed by the size of this place. It's immense, even when I think of the place we were in yesterday. After all, this is the work of a single individual."

"Two, not one," he insists. "Tina did more than half the work." Accompanying me from the press back toward the darkroom, he adds, "She's the one who built the darkroom and she got the large press running."

"Really?" I exclaim. "Where in the world did she learn to do that?"

"You didn't know? Tina had jobs in every major print shop in this city. She didn't only learn to run the machines, she also walked off with a bag full of supplies every time she left her job."

It suddenly occurs to me that the few times I asked her what kind of job she had, she'd told me she was printing. I had rarely asked because to me all jobs were wage labor and therefore the same. "Tina actually stole the supplies you use here?"

"Everything except the machinery and the paper. Until a couple of weeks ago."

"What happened then?" I ask.

He leads me to a corner of the shop and proudly points to several stacks of paper, mounds of unsorted inks, film boxes and various objects I can't identify. "Everything started to change. A group of kids came in to learn to print. Then other groups came — lots of them factory workers, some actual printers. They started teaching each other. The presses started running day and night. Leaflets, posters, picture books — beautiful things too. And they all brought things from places on strike: inks, paper, plates; two groups even set up silkscreening in the back. Some of them can print as well as Tina. I thought I might be needed here, but I'm not. I'll be going back to Sabina and Tissie tomorrow. They'd both be happy if I took you along."

I tell Ted I'll try to come. But it looks like I won't make it. Tomorrow is right now, and I'd rather finish this letter before accumulating yet more experiences to describe to you.

Pat and Luisa are no longer in the darkroom. Pat is running the leaflet off on a small press, and Luisa is outside, proudly showing a copy to Daman. I run out to have a look. Daman holds the copy in his hand and frowns.

"Isn't it beautiful?" Luisa asks Daman. "And it all took less than half an hour, for two thousand copies! Ours took us all of two weeks!"

"Are we ready to go?" Daman asks.

"Well wait for Pat to bring the rest of the leaflets, won't you? Oh, don't be such a sourpuss, Daman. It makes the same point ours does: why let the loudspeakers speak for you? Well, doesn't it?"

Before Daman answers, Pat comes out with the stack of leaflets. Someone observes, "There are eleven of us. We'll have to go in two cars." Pat gives half the leaflets to the six people who are to go in the other car; Luisa gives the other driver directions. On the way to the car, Daman continues talking to the woman from the office machine plant, and this seems to irk Luisa. When we reach the car, the woman gets into the front seat next to Daman. She looks slightly older than Luisa, although Luisa, in her girlish skirt and with her hair hanging loose over her shoulders, looks much younger than her age. I slide into the back seat next to Pat; Luisa gets in next to him from the other side.

Daman, apparently continuing his conversation with the woman, makes a comment that seems to be aimed at Pat. "It's not to become a paper in which professional writers express themselves. They can confine themselves to their usual outlets. This paper is for workers who've never written before."

Pat is about to respond to the comment, but Luisa prevents the resumption of the argument in the council office by resuming her own argument instead. She tells Pat, "Maybe a leaflet can be printed without any type of organization. But I still think the new society is going to need an organization. Of course it has to be the workers' own organization."

Pat responds angrily, "In most people's mouths organization and obedience are synonymous. Do you think this leaflet was printed without organization? My point was that organized activity is possible without order givers and order takers. Your new society sounds like a place where most people work and obey orders, while a few manage and make decisions. There's nothing new about that."

"Everything would be different if the workers themselves managed —"

"Why?" Pat asks.

Luisa pauses and then answers, "Because present-day managers serve the interests of capital and the state, whereas workers would serve the interests of their fellow workers. That would transform the nature of all activity and all relations."

The woman in the front seat turns toward Luisa. "Get off it, dearie! Every union rep I know is a former worker, and every one of them serves the interests of capital and the state. They'll serve whoever pays their salaries, as they always have."

Luisa objects, "That's because these unions are all company unions."

"Oh yea?" the woman asks. "Well I'm one of those who was around during those good old days when you got busted for talking union, and I know that the stories about union organizers serving the workers' interests are all bullshit. They were on the make then; that's why they seemed so gutsy. Today they've made it; they've got no more reason to be gutsy. And what do you think they were on the make for? For workers' interests? Forget it! They were on the make for precisely what they've got today!"

"Then you don't believe change is possible," Luisa concludes.

"Is that what I said?" the woman asks. "Why do you think I'm here, or in that commune? I think it's possible, but not with unions. I agree with the kid: if you've got managers, they're going to manage, no matter who or what they were before."

Although Pat squirms when she refers to him as "the kid," Daman swerves the car and almost side-swipes a car in the next lane when she expresses her agreement with "the kid": Daman just lost his newest recruit to "the kid."

The woman continues, unaware of the minor uproar she just caused, "Some people think everything would change if all supervisors were women. That's the same baloney. I've got a woman supervisor. She used to be an ordinary worker. And let me tell you something, dearie: I wouldn't go out of my way to give her more power than she's got already."

"If you reject the very possibility of a genuine workers' organization, what are you left with?" Luisa asks.

The woman hesitates for a moment. Finally she says, "Just people, I guess. That's what I hoped to find out in the so-called commune. I thought I'd find people asking the same questions." She turns to Pat and asks, "What do you think, kid? What's on the agenda after the unions, according to the younger generation?"

Pat stares at her but doesn't answer; he's obviously irked. I poke him gently and whisper, "Tell us, Pat; I'd like to know too."

But Daman shouts, "How would he know? Has he ever worked in a factory?"

That does it for Pat. He tightens his lips and stares out the window, a victim of age-ism. I lower my hand to the seat and reach for my humiliated comrade's hand. His fist is clenched. I wrap my hand around it and try to formulate an appropriate answer to the woman's unintended insults. "I can't speak for my whole generation — we kids are all different, you know — but I can tell you what at least one kid thinks." Pat smiles with gratitude and opens his hand into mine. I go on, "I think the printing of this leaflet was a good example of what I'd consider free activity. It wasn't bossed by capitalist or union or party managers. The people most interested in it made all their own decisions and did their own work. They organized their activity themselves. Isn't that true, Luisa?"

Luisa hesitantly admits, "That's true. But printing a leaflet is a simple matter compared to running a transportation system, provisioning a city with food —"

"Luisa!" I shout, "Why can't you imagine those things being done any other way than they're done now? At this very moment, in this very city, all kinds of things are being done freely, no longer as wage labor, but as projects, exactly the way this leaflet was done. Complex things, too. I consider street theater an extremely complex art. The entire former university is organized by its present occupants. Some neighborhoods are starting to organize food distribution on their own. I could have shown you any number of pamphlets describing —"

Pat's enthusiasm suddenly returns; so does his pomposity. "That's what I call the revolutionary project: the conscious domination of history by the men who make it!"

I let go of his hand abruptly. "The men? You mean the kids!"

The rest of the trip to the assembly plant takes place in silence. Luisa directs Daman to park the car right across the street from the picket line and sound truck. Men wearing perfectly clean overalls walk in a circle carrying signs with the name of the union.

"This is a strike?" Pat asks.

"It's not very exciting, but it is a strike," Luisa answers.

Pat objects, "But this is nothing but a ritual! Union bureaucrats are getting fresh air and being paid for it! Did we print these leaflets for them?"

"Of course not," Luisa assures him. Pulling him out of the car, she says, "Come on, I'll show you where the workers are."

Daman gets out of the car and announces, "I'll stick to the picket line." He hands the office machine worker a handful of *The Workers' Voice* and asks, "You'll join me?"

She gives the copies back to Daman and asks Luisa, "Where did you say they were?"

Daman walks quietly away from us and starts to give out his paper to the picketing "workers," and also to passers-by, in a polite, businesslike manner. He seems to have brought about fifty copies, probably the day's "ration."

Luisa tells the rest of us, "The main hangouts are the bar and the bowling alley next to it. There are also lots of people in the pinball machine parlor across the street. Basically all the people here, except the bureaucrats, are waiting for something to happen. This is one of the dirtiest and most dangerous plants in the city, and people will be receptive to just about anything. I think the bar is the best place to start a conversation."

"I used to know that too, dearie, in the good old days. But shouldn't we wait for the others?" the woman asks, referring to her six friends coming in the other car.

Pat suggests, "They probably got here first, saw what kind of a strike it was, and didn't bother to stop."

The woman agrees. "You're probably right, kid — I mean pal; people sure are thin skinned nowadays. I'm for the bowling alley."

"I'll try the bar. How about you?" Pat asks me.

I hesitate for a second and then decide, "I've never been to a bowling alley."

The woman grabs half the leaflets as well as my arm. "Never been bowling? Well come on, honey, you don't know what you've missed!"

Luisa glances across the street and waves to Daman. Then she shoves her arm through Pat's and shouts, "Let's go raise hell in the bar!" You knew Luisa. I never did. I've never before seen the woman who made love to you during work hours at the carton plant, nor the woman you saw leaving the carton plant with her arm through Marc Glavni's. She didn't let me see her. I used to be her conscience; she recently proclaimed her independence from her conscience.

I shove my arm into the arm of the woman who calls me "Honey" and I shout, "Let's us go raise hell in the bowling alley!"

As soon as we go in, we notice a stack of the "loudspeaker" leaflets by the entrance; we also see them in people's hands. The six who came in the other car are bowling. The woman pulls me toward them. None of them believe me when I tell them I don't even know the point of the game. Apparently you're supposed to knock down wooden bottles at the end of a channel by rolling a large ball into them. The ball has holes in it and is held like a glove. I don't succeed in knocking down a single bottle. On my last try, the heavy ball-shaped glove refuses to leave my hand, and I go flying down the alley with it. My comrades seem to enjoy that more than the game itself.

Luisa and Pat enter the bowling alley. I ask them if they lost an argument. "We didn't even have a chance to start one," Luisa says; she seems slightly tipsy. "There's a ball game on and everyone is watching the T.V. We even went across the street, but one of you already gave leaflets out there. And it's impossible to hear anything above those machines. We should have titled the leaflet, Why do you allow pinball machines to play for you?"

Pat says, "At least Luisa and I had a stimulating conversation."

"A very stimulating conversation," Luisa adds. "There's nothing like a few drinks to loosen tongues and soften tempers. Pat told me all about the real revolution. It's a festival where everyone does nothing but play, not these capitalist pseudo-games, but living games. It's the gratification of all desires, a never-ending celebration. Do I have it right?"

"Perfectly," Pat says, ogling her; apparently he can't hold his alcohol as well as she can.

"How about all of us going to my house and having such a celebration!" Luisa suggests.

The woman turns down Luisa's invitation, so the three of us cross the street and find Daman trying to interest a union bureaucrat in *The Workers' Voice*. Luisa pulls him toward the car and invites him to her celebration.

"I'd love to come, but I've got some work I could do."

Tugging at Daman's arm, Luisa hisses, "Only scabs work during a strike." Inside the car, she slips into the front seat and huddles to him, begging, "Please, Daman; we can discuss the next issue of the paper. There are numerous things I want to suggest."

I slide into the back seat — and wonder if Pat will get into the front seat next to Luisa. But he slips in next to me. The car starts. Pat's hand reaches for mine. I don't move away. His hand slips over mine and squeezes it. My heart pounds; a disorganized array of contradictory feelings surges through me. Contempt and resentment toward Pat combine with pity, and with growing desire — the desire to outdo Luisa, the desire to undo your humiliation of me. If revolution is a festival, then I warm up for it in the back seat of Daman's car, I get ready to celebrate, to gratify my own desires, to scandalize the union organizer, the professor and the eighteen-year old philosopher who considers men the only history-makers. I pull my hand from under Pat's and place it over his, sliding my fingers slowly between his. The arrival of your letter couldn't have been timed better. I've been longing to consummate this act, but I lacked the justification, the courage, the setting. Your "confession" provides the perfect justification; Mirna's stubborn determination gives me a model of courage; Luisa's "celebration" promises to provide a perfect setting. No one talks on the way to Luisa's, but if anyone did I wouldn't hear a sound; I'm deafened by the prospect of dethroning the Queen of Peasants, the prospect of shattering several porcelain statues. If revolution is the gratification of desires, then one of its fires is blazing in the back seat of Daman's car.

I didn't understand the perverse character of my desire for Pat until I described it to you in my previous letter. If my desire was perverse then, it's even more so when I dig my fingers into the palm of his hand in Daman's car; I've lost almost all the admiration I initially felt toward him; the pure genius who had simultaneously attracted, intimidated and repelled me is no longer such a genius nor so pure to me. But if my desire is even more perverse than it was then, my moral self-restraint is gone now — it's been driven away by your letter; by your description of Luisa, by Luisa's insistent confirmation of every one of the traits you described.

:||||||||:

Still a prisoner of the restraints imposed by my eclectic morality after I sent you my previous letter, I stayed away from Pat for over a week. Twice I visited the occupied office machine plant a few blocks from the commune. I stayed away from the council office except on days when I knew Pat wouldn't be there. During that week I attended meetings of striking postal workers, newspaper printers, taxi drivers. The discussions in which I took part were the most stimulating discussions I've experienced. In a historical fraction of a second, people here have appropriated the entire history of revolution. Everything human beings in struggle ever reached for is being sought here and now.

I ran into Pat in the council office, more or less by chance, a week ago. I described to him what I'd been doing. He described meetings he'd been attending; he spoke with contagious enthusiasm.

"It's just fantastic; the entire so-called intellectual community is committing suicide!" he exclaimed. "In one after another session, the experts themselves are denouncing their own special fields as illegitimate, as cut off from the rest of social life: philosophers, teachers, even medical students, though I haven't heard any doctors yet."

I was fascinated and asked when the next such meeting would be held. Pat told me architects were to meet that night. His enthusiasm wasn't exaggerated. At that meeting, held in a large auditorium, one after another architect, not merely students but practicing architects, described themselves as usurpers and their profession as an illegitimate monopoly over the individual's and the community's life activity: the creation of one's physical surroundings, the shaping of one's environment.

At the end of the meeting, with an enthusiasm equaling Pat's, I nudged him and said, "Imagine the experts themselves denouncing their own expertise as a usurpation!"

Pat's response was: "You really amaze me, Sophia! Very few people grasp the implications of what we've just heard."

My immediate reaction was to smile; I felt flattered! But then something like an electric shock went through me. I remembered his having said, "You're really good," the day we had talked to several office machine workers in the restaurant across the street from their plant. He was impressed by the apparent presence of wit and intelligence comparable to his own in a person with breasts! And I was flattered! I swallowed my smile and tried to stare through him, but he was totally unconscious of his arrogance. During the next few days he confirmed my new view of him; he demonstrated beyond a doubt that he's absolutely convinced he and his friends, all young men until Tina joined them "as an equal," which I suppose means as a young man, have an absolute monopoly over all human knowledge, wit and insight.

At the end of the architects' meeting I limited myself to staring at him. We left our seats together and followed the crowd out of the auditorium. The hall outside was lined with literature tables. Every conceivable political sect was displaying all its wares to the intellectual community on the eve of its self-destruction.

Behind one of the tables I recognized a person I hadn't seen in ages. I ran toward her shouting, "Rhea Morphen!" We embraced as if we had been best friends. Pat ran after me. I introduced Rhea as my roommate during my first year in college.

Pat picked up one of the books on her table and asked, "How much do they pay you to peddle this stuff?" Only then did I glance at the publications on the table:

celebrations of state-worship and glorifications of the most tyrannical dictatorships in history.

Rhea answered politely, "No one pays me, I volunteer my time."

With a sweeping glance at the table's contents, Pat asked, "How about the Political Thought of Adolph Hitler? Is it sold out?"

"What do you mean by that?" Rhea asked, growing hostile.

"You've got the collected and selected works of all the other Fuehrers! How about —"

Rhea turned her back to Pat and asked me contemptuously, "Is that the type of politics you're into now, Sophie?"

"That's the politics I've always been into, Rhea. Have you forgotten we didn't part on the best of terms?"

"Are you referring to your clique's excluding me from that underground paper?"

"No, Rhea, I'm referring to your voting to evict me from the co-op —"

A customer who looked like a professor interrupted our conversation. He picked out two books: a compilation of the "essential thoughts" of a dictator, and a diatribe on "petty bourgeois deviations in the workers' movement."

Pat commented, "Anticipation ends boredom for some. It creates fear in others."

"Are you talking to me?" the customer asked.

Pat picked up copies of the same two books, leafed through one, and said, "We must see what the authorities say before we take any false steps."

"Do you have something against these books?" the customer asked.

"I don't have anything against the books," Pat said, "I'm just curious about the mentality of those who read them."

The customer slammed his money down on the table and walked away saying, "These works are condensations of the historical experience of the international workers' movement."

"They're the ravings of megalomaniacs!" Pat shouted after him.

Rhea turned to me angrily. "Would you mind taking your boyfriend somewhere else?"

Whispering, "Let's go, Pat," I wrapped my arm around my "boyfriend," proudly displaying to Rhea not only my "type of politics" but also my "decadent immorality" — it's ironic that I wanted to display the latter quality a week before I got your letter.

But Rhea didn't let us get away; she shouted after us, "Whenever workers regain consciousness and again turn to their organization, petty bourgeois intellectuals try to poison them with their philosophy of despair."

I rushed back to the table and hissed, "The thought of your party's goons running the army and the police makes me despair all right! It sends shivers down my back! It gives me the creeps! Don't you know what they did to Lem?"

It turned out that Rhea did "know"; her organization apparently had a whole "line" about what had happened to her one-time comrade. "Don't tell me your lies about Lem!" she shouted. "I know your stepfather Alberts and his friends tortured him and then paid him to spy on and poison his former comrades. He turned Debbie Mathews into an alcoholic —" Rhea started whispering because another customer was buying the condensed thoughts of another dictator.

I decided to try my turn. "May I ask why you're buying this book?"

"I think we're living in a revolutionary period," she answered, "and I want to learn what someone experienced in revolution had to say."

It was fun to go on. "You mean an expert on revolution, on how to fight your own battles and live your own life? Did you attend the meeting?"

"Yes, and I agree with most of what was said. We architects have done nothing but serve the interests of the capitalist class, and that raises the question of the legitimacy —"

"How about the architects who served the interests of the dictator whose work you just picked up? Is that service legitimate?" I shouted.

Rhea told the customer, "She's being paid to heckle at my table." The woman paid for the book and walked away.

I turned furiously at Rhea. "All you're expert in is lying! The rule of your organization is the rule of liars, the reign of the big lies! But the day of your glorious victories is gone! Everyone except a few idiots is on to you now! You're nothing but a carcass!"

Rhea smiled viciously. "Don't count us out too soon, Sophie. Half a century ago everyone said we'd never win, and we won! Today we've got nearly half the world on our side, and our power is still growing. We sold more literature during the past week than during the previous ten years!"

Pat shouted, "You're growing all right — like a cancer! All the life-destroying political sects are growing. You're not growing because you carry life, but because some people have been dead so long they're afraid of life. You offer them death, that's why they turn to you! You rescue them from a void that calls for creativity and imagination and you give them back their lost boredom and routine; you save them from the leap into the unknown and channel them back to the known. You're gravediggers of revolutions and murderers of revolutionaries. You're the cancer of a revolutionary period!"

Rhea's grin didn't leave her face, "Do you think you'll ever get workers to follow your petty-bourgeois philosophy of despair?"

I shouted, "You can't even imagine people doing anything other than follow! Free human beings are inconceivable to you!"

Rhea still remained calm. "Workers will be free when they become conscious of their need for their organization and their leaders."

"Said Hitler!" Pat shouted.

"Who hired you to come here and heckle?" Rhea asked me.

I smiled and answered politely, "No one hired us, Rhea. We volunteered our time." I took Pat's hand and we walked away from her. As soon as we were out of the building, I let go of Pat's hand. I was depressed. I recognized something of myself in Rhea. Not the commitment to the organization or to the state. The life-destroying function of the puppeteers and manipulators is perfectly clear to me now. Maybe it wasn't that clear to me twenty years ago; I was only fifteen. Your letters have made me extremely sensitive to the self-elected "vanguards," the petty despots parading as the world's greatest rebels, sucking blood out of beings who've just come to life, the organizers and politicians waiting to pounce on the slaves only just freed from masters. To all of them the mere suggestion that human beings might be free and creative through their own efforts is an expression of despair. It's Rhea herself who is driven to despair. The possibility that people might do without her bureaucratic organization and its despotic central committee is what makes her despair, just as the possibility that people might do without unions makes Luisa despair: "What are we left with?"

Thanking Pat for telling me about the architects' meeting, I ran off to my bed in the "dormitory." I was depressed by Rhea's lifelong dependence on authority to guide her life's activity because I recognized a similar dependence in myself. Only instead of taking a ruler, a megalomaniac, to borrow Pat's word, as my life's guide, I took Nachalo, Luisa, you. I was wrong some time ago when I wrote you that my activity on the university newspaper staff had nothing in common with Rhea's. If her articles reflected, not her own practice and thought but her authority's, so did mine. Whatever I wrote, I kept my "community" and my "models" in front of me as my guides. If Rhea didn't communicate thoughts but merely transmitted them, I did no more. I transmitted Luisa's thoughts and what I took to be your thoughts. I didn't leave any more room for the mutual invention of projects than Rhea did. Only my authorities weren't among the world's great rulers, and therefore my dependence wasn't noticed, even by me.

I remained depressed for two or three days, although I continued to be stimulated by the activities and unending debates taking place around me. I couldn't get Rhea out of my mind — nor Pat — and I again avoided contacts with him. It was Tina who knocked me out of my sour mood. One morning she woke me at sunrise and literally pulled me out of bed.

"Nothing here can possibly be more exciting than the place I left last night, and I'd feel like a criminal if I didn't push you to go there," Tina told me. "Last night I returned from the occupied research center. Sabina and Tissie are both part of the new crew, and they're just dying to show the place off to you. Ted is going back there today and he'll be glad to take you along."

I hadn't seen Ted since I'd left the garage; I had even avoided going into the print shop the day I came to the commune; my first response to the prospect of seeing him again was fright. Ted's nightly visits to Tina's room, my desperately violent attempt to pull him out of my bed, his conviction that I had intended to ravage

Tina, all flashed through my mind. I told Tina, "I'd love to go — but couldn't I go whenever you go back there?"

"I just spent a week there; it was fabulous and I intend to go back. But I want to help clean up some of the mess in the print shop, and I'd like to learn to use some of the things people brought. I know what you're thinking, Sophia. Before you ever left the garage Ted figured out he'd been wrong about you. You were just as wrong about Ted. He's willing to forget; why aren't you? Why are you so unfair?"

"Is that why you woke me, Tina? To convince me to make up with Ted?"

"Gosh, Sophia, you're just like a baby! No, I'm not trying to force you into anything. I genuinely thought you'd want to see that place and to see what Sabina is doing!" Tina started to walk away from me.

"Wait!" I shouted; "I'll go if Pat agrees to go with me."

In less than half an hour Tina returned to my dorm room with Pat. "If Tina thinks no one should miss it, then it must really be worth visiting," Pat said to me. "And on the way there I'll be able to ask the printer about some problems I've been having with the camera."

Pat and I went to have a quick breakfast while Tina returned to the print shop to tell Ted to meet us at the corner of the campus. After breakfast I ran up for my purse and toothbrush, and we were off. Pat recognized Ted when he honked the car horn; I didn't. I ran to the back seat; Pat sat in front. Ted greeted Pat, and then extended his hand to me, looking sadly into my eyes. I put my hand in his, but could think of nothing to say to him. I felt relieved when, soon after we started, Pat asked Ted some technical questions about printing.

Ted took us to a fantasy world I didn't know existed: an immense factory building set in landscaped gardens and surrounded by a park. The entrance walls were covered by slogans, similar to those at the former university, but the rest of the environment was an electronic wonderland. Ted told us Tissie and Sabina were working with a crew developing a vehicle that would transport a person to any part of the world in a few minutes. He led us to a large room, full of computers and electronically operated machine tools; the walls were covered with diagrams and photographs of vehicles. I immediately, saw Sabina with a group of people studying a complex wiring chart. Sabina turned, grinned, and nudged the young woman next to her.

I couldn't believe my eyes when Tissie jumped and ran toward me. "Hi, sis! I thought I'd never see you again," she shouted as she threw her arms around me. "You look great! Isn't this place something?"

"Tissie! You look so happy, so healthy! I didn't recognize you!"

Dancing proudly in front of me, Tissie told me, "Three weeks with Sabina plus some new clothes was all it took, sis!"

"Let me look at you, Tissie! You look younger than you did ten years ago! You're beautiful!" I couldn't get over her vigor; she wasn't at all the person I had known in the garage.

Tissie hugged Sabina and shouted proudly, "Hey, listen to the compliments I'm getting, and listen to who's giving them!" Then she ran to me, turned me around, and exclaimed, "Holy Mary mother of god, Sabina, do you actually keep this jewel all to yourself all year round?"

I blushed and started to cry. "Thank you for being so nice to me, Tissie; I wasn't very nice to you."

Tissie returned to me, pressed me tightly against her and whispered, "You were a gem, sis."

I pecked her lips and whispered, "You're lying. You're the gem."

Tissie pulled Sabina toward me. "How about giving sis a tour of the place? This vehicle won't go anywhere for a while yet. Hey Ted, come on!"

I remembered Pat. "Wait, Tissie, I haven't introduced my friend."

"Did he come with you?" Tissie asked, turning to Pat. "Sorry there, I didn't see you."

I pulled Pat's hand toward Tissie's. "This is Pat Clesec. He's helped me understand a great deal of what's been happening." Then I introduced Pat to "my two best friends, Sabina Nachalo and Tissie Avis."

Pat shook Tissie's hand, then Sabina's, and asked, "Another Nachalo? Is it the name of a sect, an order or some kind of sorority?"

Tissie tried to help him. "One of them is the other's aunt, though I can't remember which. Are you the aunt, Sabina?"

Sabina answered, "I'm my own mother, Tissie, so I can't very well be the aunt, can I?"

Tissie told Pat, "Just act as if they're sisters; have you ever seen two more gorgeous sisters?"

Displaying Tissie to Pat, Sabina said, "Look at who's talking. Would you believe she was released from a prison hospital only three weeks ago?"

Ted added, "When she came out she looked like a corpse. Incurable dope addict, they called her. A week after she was out she was just like a kid, all cured."

Tissie pulled Ted's beard. "Sure I got cured, 'cause I had an old man like you to take care of me."

I was hypnotized by Tissie. She really was like a child. Her enthusiasm, her energy, her rebirth were every bit as fantastic to me as the strikes and occupations. Maybe what's happening is that we're all becoming children again. Our rigid roles and characters are dropping off like dried skin. We're fascinating to each other because each one of our acts might be a total surprise, at any instant our personalities might change completely. Like children, we're not exhausted by what we've been and are; life is ahead of us; we're no longer dead.

Tissie announced, "If no one's got any more compliments, let's start! But if anyone has more nice things to say about me, I'll stay all day! I love it!"

Sabina kneeled in front of Tissie, kissed Tissie's hand and quoted, "Shall I compare thee to a summer's day? Thou art more lovely and more temperate —"

Tissie danced around Sabina and laughed. "Oh, but my eyes are nothing like the sun, music makes a much more pleasing sound, and when I walk I always stay on the ground." Raising Sabina off the ground, she asked her gypsy tutor "Did I get it right?"

"Word for word, Tissie. Next week, when the whole world becomes our toy, everyone will speak in verse — their own verse."

Tissie sandwiched herself between Sabina and me, Pat and Ted trailed behind, and the tour began. Sabina was like a guide to a foreign delegation, and I was as much of a tourist as I had been and had continued to be in the garage. Yet I wasn't as much of a tourist as Pat. Sabina, Tissie, and the place itself were more than his all-encompassing intellect could absorb. He was completely at sea.

The tour began in the room in which we stood. Sabina pointed at pictures and diagrams and spoke of vehicles that would transform human beings into birds. She described the group's current project: a vehicle, not much larger than an individual, which would respond to verbal instructions, stand still in the air or fly several times faster than sound. She spoke of houses with entrances on their roofs, all ground being used up by gardens and fields in which to walk and play. She said such vehicles could almost be built now, but all research on them was being suppressed. "The way they suppress the thing is to hire all so-called geniuses on the verge of designing it and bury them in this room. Here they're allowed to play out their schemes on paper. Why are they suppressing it? Because this little vehicle lasts a lifetime, uses no steel and little plastic, burns no gas, and can be built by anyone once the principles are known. It would mean the virtual end of assembly lines, road building, oil production." Then, as if anticipating objections I didn't dream of making, she explained, "A central computer keeps track of every standing and moving vehicle. At any instant an infinity of positions and paths is available, so there's never a crash or a bottleneck. Central computer breakdowns are monitored by any number of computers located elsewhere and ready to take over. The sole function of the computers is to prevent crashes and bottlenecks. No one controls the computers. In circumstances where such vehicles would be possible, power over the transportation computers would be as outlandish as power over the world's supply of air."

On the way to our next marvel, Sabina walked between Tissie and me. Squeezing me, she said, "You look so lost, Sophia, and so frightened! You're really something! You have no facade! All your feelings show on your face! I'm all facade. I'm pretending that I love everything that's happening here. No doubts or reservations will ever show on my face! But half the things that can be done here scare the hell out of me!" We entered a room with subdued light, dark curtains and various strange plastic objects. Sabina continued, "I can understand vehicles, but watch this!" She operated a switch and a cup appeared on a table. "Grab it! Your hand will go right through it. There's nothing there. This is a way for someone to go anywhere not in minutes, but instantly. Only the person who goes is no more real than this cup. It's called a hologram. You can stay in your bed while your hologram travels all over the world. You could be standing in front of me looking as real as life until I tried to embrace you — my arms would go through air: you'd be nothing but a projection of light. Isn't that awful? It's part of the same package as the vehicles. When you write Yarostan tell him I'm not as sure of myself as I once was."

Tissie observed, "These things would sure make life in prison more bearable! I could at least think you were right there with me."

Pat opened his mouth for the first time. "I'd thought they were only into transportation research at this place."

"They're into everything they can turn into merchandise," Sabina told him. "They'd have an orgasm department if someone invented an orgasm machine that contained a ton of steel and used a barrel of oil every time it got you excited. Next they'd have two such machines getting each other excited while the rest of us lay in prison hospitals chatting with holograms. I rejected Jan Sedlak's attitude of technology all my life, Sophia, but I can no longer convince myself —"

"Hey what's all this?" Tissie shouted. "For three weeks you've been teaching me about it, telling me how great it all is!"

Sabina swung Tissie and me around and pulled us out of the hologram room. "You're right, Tissie. It is great. I was only raising interesting questions. Ted, let's show off your hangout."

We entered another computer-filled room. Sabina had me sit at a desk and press one of the buttons below the word "Quantity," and then told me to speak into a microphone. As soon as I'd spoken three words Ted handed me five slips of paper with the words "I'm completely lost" printed on them. This time I was the one with doubts and reservations. "I'm enough of an environmentalist to know that with such a gadget every megalomaniac would make millions of copies of his ravings, since he'd no longer have to bother writing them down, and forests would all be depleted in a day."

"In this department they've already moved far beyond that objection, probably because the forests are already depleted," Sabina told me. "All the world's writings would exist nowhere except in a computer library. There'd be no more book collections, libraries, bookstores or files. Everyone would have a fairly small computer. Whenever she wants a book or a work of art, the computer produces it for her, in a few seconds. She can study it, take notes on it, keep it around. When she's through with it, she deposits it into a paper disposal unit instead of a shelf or a drawer. The same small quantity of paper circulates among all the users of all printed works. If she's devoted to bookshelves, she can have holograms of them along every wall — it's the only positive use I can think of for holograms — but when she wants a book, she doesn't reach into the shelf but into the computer. When she's through she deposits the book in the disposal and its hologram into the shelf. There's nothing wrong with this department; they would even introduce it into the present system if steel or concrete or oil or some other large interests were involved,"

"But it takes all the fun out of printing," Ted commented; "the computer does it all."

"That's the point of the whole place," Sabina added. "The computer does it all. But let's go eat! There's a good restaurant, and there are no computers to do the eating for you."

When we sat down to eat I asked Pat what his impressions were. He announced, "The slogans on the walls are fantastic: They reflect the most revolutionary acquisitions of the proletariat to date, anywhere."

"Slogans?" Tissie asked. "I never noticed them."

"That's because you're not a professor, Tissie," Sabina told her. "Professors don't notice anything else."

Pat was offended. "Slogans are often a concise expression of the theory that informs the proletariat's practice."

"You must have been part of the student demonstration that came here the day after the occupation," Sabina said to him.

Pat grew increasingly offended. "I stay away from demonstrations, that pseudo-activity organized by politicians."

I asked Sabina about the demonstration. She told me thousands of people had marched toward the newly-occupied research center with flags and placards; "The gates were wide open, and everyone here thought they'd all come inside and turn this place into a popular playground. But would you believe it? All those thousands stopped in front of a sound truck and listened to slogans broadcast to them over loudspeakers. No one and nothing held them there. When the sloganeering ended they all dispersed; the open gate remained an impassable barrier to them."

"Afraid to touch what they said they wanted," Tissie added.

Pat tried to explain, "Those people were vendors of political ideologies and their customers. The slogans I liked here aren't expressions of ideology, but of theory; they subject revolutionary practice to demystifying scrutiny-"

But Sabina insisted, "Slogans, professor, are what that demonstration was about; the renunciation of the world for the sake of the word."

Pat stuck to his point. "If the proletariat doesn't regain its revolutionary perspective the revolution will be stillborn and practical needs will find no genuine revolutionary form!"

"Professor —" Sabina began.

"I'm not a professor and I don't aspire to be one!" Pat shouted.

"Don't be sore," Tissie told Pat. "Whenever anyone uses words as big as she does, she calls them a professor."

But Pat remained sore through the rest of the meal and for the remainder of the evening. I was very tired soon after supper, and Sabina showed Pat and me to "our bedroom," telling us she and Tissie slept across the hall, in case we needed anything. Our room was a former executive suite; its soft carpet made me think of a room Sabina had once described to me, a room with a wall-to-wall mattress. The carpet seemed clean enough, but I didn't avail myself of this luxury; I fell on a large couch next to the wall. Pat sulked in a corner of the room, next to a lamp, and read a book he had brought along. I had nothing to say to him. He had been out-argued by a woman, and he couldn't accept that. In the morning he told me he wanted to return to the occupied university. When I insisted on spending at least one more day in the research center, he told me he wouldn't accompany me or my "know-nothing friends," but would tour the place on his own, or with "the printer."

Tissie knocked when we were about to leave our room. "It's my turn to give you two a tour." I told her Pat was intimidated by women and would tour by himself. Tissie excitedly squeezed my hand and whispered, "Good, I want you all to myself, sis. I wanted you for years. Scared?"

As we walked away from Pat's and my bedroom, I put my arm tightly around Tissie's waist and told her, "I'm frightened out of my wits!"

"But you'll come anyway?"

"To the end of the world, Tissie. I'm all yours, all day long."

It was an unimaginably beautiful summer day. The sky was clear, the air was clean, there was a slight breeze. Tissie, the "incurable dope addict," led me to Ted's car. After a five-minute drive, she parked by the entrance of what looked like a vast estate. "I wanted to show you what the other half used to do during their breaks and lunch hours," she told me. We walked into a fabulous park with covered walks surrounded by thick forest; the morning sun only reached the tops of the trees. "There are several streams, a pool, a large lake. I went wild the first time Sabina and I came here. Imagine me, after spending all those years in prison, and then in that ward!" Suddenly shouting, "Watch this!" she dove right through a seemingly solid hedge. "Come on through!" she shouted. I followed her through the hedge and found myself in a grass-carpeted "room" completely surrounded by trees. Lying on the grass in a sunlit corner of the "room," Tissie told me, "Sabina and I found this place by accident. Isn't it great? I'd come here with her every sunny day if she wasn't so busy with her vehicle." I lay down alongside her. Tissie rested her head on my stomach and asked, "You mind?"

"No, Tissie. I don't mind." Tears came to my eyes as I ran my fingers through her hair. "I'm sorry about what I did to you, Tissie."

Tissie pulled my hand to her mouth. "You're not the one that should be sorry, Sophie." It was the first time she'd called me by my name. "I'm the one that's sorry."

"You mean about getting me to your room by telling me you were scared? You knew I wouldn't have gone if you'd told me what you wanted."

"About that too but I'm a lot sorrier about other things. I had you all wrong. I had everything all wrong. I thought you were just like Sabina and me. Seth wanted you and Tina in the bar, and I wanted those shots more than I wanted anyone or anything. I tried to get you for myself and for Seth at the same time, and I thought you were just pretending you didn't want me. I was sure Jose and Ted had told you I just wanted you for Seth, and I hated both of them; Jose kept me from you and Ted kept me from Tina —"

A shock went through me; we both sat up. "Ted kept you from Tina?"

"Don't tell me you still think he wanted Tina for himself!" Tissie exclaimed. "Ted was just like her father!"

"Tina's father?" I asked stupidly.

"Mine too!" she added. "You sure had him figured out all wrong. Ted's the only father I ever had; I couldn't ever stand him but I always loved him ever since I was little. I never had a real father; I hardly even had a mother. The woman who bore me was a drunkard and a prostitute. I was eight when I had my first sex; it was with one of my mother's girlfriends. I spent most days and nights on the street. That's where I met Ted. He was the best car thief in the neighborhood. He let me move into the garage where he lived. One day we were both caught in a stolen car and sent to reform school. That was where I got the rest of my sexual education. One of the girls I met was a prostitute to rich women. That's what I did when I came out. But I missed Ted. He was the only person I knew who didn't treat me as a monkey or a rubber doll. He'd always talked to me as if I understood; he'd tried to teach me things. Some neighborhood kids told me he was out of reform school and was running the garage by himself. I asked him if he still had room for me. He couldn't believe I actually wanted to stay with him. 'Well I ain't got no other home,' I told him. He soon figured out how I made my money, but he didn't mind. Ted didn't mind anything until I started taking heroin. That only happened after Seth bought the garage and Sabina and Jose moved in with us and started fixing up the house. I went wild over Sabina the first time I saw her. I know you can't understand that, sis. Being in the same house with her, day after day, drove me crazy. I wasn't a monkey to her but a person, the way I was for Ted, but I wanted to be more than that to her. She became my goddess. All I wanted in the world was to become her slave. She wanted the house first, and then all the machines. And above all else she wanted her precious independence. That was why I started taking heroin. That was why I started doing Seth's bidding. I thought I was showing Sabina what kind of independence I wanted, but I didn't show anyone anything. I just got all messed up. I started hating everyone. I tried to drag Tina to the bar and once I even tried to get her on heroin; that was the only time Ted ever hit me. When you came I wanted to do the same thing to you." Tissie was crying. "I wanted you bad, sis, real bad. But I wanted that heroin worse, and there was nothing I wasn't willing to do for Seth; I thought he was so good to me! I dragged you to the bar; I would have let them take that pretty body of yours and —"

I placed my hand over her mouth and pleaded, "Don't, Tissie. That's all over, and we're both so different now."

Tissie pushed me down to the ground, placed her lips right above mine and whispered, "I haven't changed any, Sophie. I still want you as bad as I did then." Suddenly she burst out laughing. "You haven't changed either, sis! You're shaking!"

"I'm sorry, Tissie!"

"Don't be sorry! You're just hungry, that's all!" She had brought a bag along, and started unpacking sandwiches, a bottle of wine, cake. "After lunch I'll take you to another gorgeous spot."

She took me to a sandy beach at a crystal clear lake. She ran into the water naked, perfectly unselfconscious. I followed her. The only previous time I swam in the nude was nineteen years ago, when Ron took me to a lake by a farm. Tissie and I raced, splashed each other, and then lay on the grass in the sun, our bodies touching. Tissie fell asleep. I found myself looking at her as if I were looking into a mirror. Beneath the seeming energy and determination lay the same passivity, the same longing for dependence. She wanted to be Sabina's slave. What did I want to be to you, to Jose, to Hugh? When she felt rejected and alone, she took heroin; I drifted and stared at blank walls.

It was nearly dark when Tissie drove me back to the research center. We had supper by ourselves in the restaurant. "It was a beautiful day, Tissie, every minute of it. I don't deserve to be treated so grandly, not by you."

"Don't be so hard on yourself, Sophie, or on Ted either. I'm the one that messed everything up in the garage. I haven't told you everything. I don't even dare tell Sabina; I wouldn't have any friends left."

"I'll be your friend, Tissie, always, even if you don't ever tell me anything."

"When you talk like that, sis, you make my insides jump around. If you and Sabina and I were on an island far away from everything ... Come on, I'll walk you to your room."

Pat was already in the room, reading. I felt happy. I kissed his forehead and asked if he'd spent the day enjoyably. All he told me was, "I asked the printer if he could give us a ride back tomorrow. He said he'd be glad to."

I lay down on the couch and fell asleep immediately. I woke up with a weight on my chest. I pushed Pat's head away from me and sat up. He started to cry. "I'm sorry, Sophia. I didn't want to take advantage of you like this. I — I think I'm in love with you. Ever since we went to talk to the office machine workers. The second time we went, my hand almost touched yours, I felt something funny, I wanted to be close to you. Then you stayed away from me, I thought you knew I wanted to make advances, and you didn't want me to. But a few nights ago, after the argument with your former roommate, you squeezed my hand and —"

I felt sorry for him and held his head in my hands; I started to kiss him, but he went on, "Then you wanted me to come here, with you, and we're alone in the same room at night. I heard you breathing. You were so close, Sophia. You're so beautiful, so intelligent."

I dropped my hands from his face and froze. I was so intelligent — for a woman. Sabina was far too intelligent; she intimidated him. But I was just intelligent enough to make him lose his head. I lay back down and turned my back to him. I heard him lie down on the carpet next to the couch. I felt sorry for him again, and tried to stroke his cheek with my hand, but quickly regretted doing that. He took my hand in both of his, pressed it to his lips, and apparently intended to spend the night in that position. I quickly got a cramp in my shoulder and pulled my hand away.

When I woke up the next morning, Pat was pacing, impatient to leave. I left our door open, and as soon as I saw Sabina come out of her room I told her I'd go back to the council office with Pat.

"Running out on us so soon?" Sabina asked.

I was stung by the way she put it. "That's mean, Sabina. I ran out on you and Ron and went to the university. Are you referring to that? Or to the time I ran out on Jose?"

"I'm sorry, Sophia. It was a mean way to put it. I thought you'd stay with us. Tissie and I both want you close to us. It was my way of saying I'd feel even better about being here if you were here with me."

I was crying on Sabina's shoulder. "I can't. My mind is all fogged. In the commune and the council, in the midst of leaflets and arguments and news of strikes, I know who I am. But I'm lost here. I don't know who I am or what I want. Tissie told me about Ted, about herself. I haven't had time to absorb it, any of it. I'll come back, maybe even tomorrow, but I've got to know why I'm coming back, what I want."

Just then Tissie came running toward us. "I'm leaving, Tissie, but I promise to come back."

"Aw, sis, we both thought you were here, to stay! Is it because of me?"

"No, Tissie, please don't ever think that. Before I came here, I was convinced that what I was doing was very important, very meaningful to me. I'm no longer sure. I'd like to find out before I come back."

Sabina jumped on Pat as soon as he came out of our room. "So you've had your fill of practice and it's time for theory again."

Pat said calmly, "I recognize the revolutionary character of the appropriation that took place here, but the point is not to appropriate a single enterprise but the whole world."

"Is that what you're going back to do?"

"That's what I'm going to take part in. Revolution will be made when all, and not just some of the victims of the market's tyranny throw off their shackles."

"That's well put. And just how do you intend to take part in all that?" Sabina asked him.

"By keeping abreast of reality. A radical critique of the modern world must have the totality as its objective."

Sabina walked away from him and went to look for Ted.

On the return trip I rode in the front seat, between Ted and Pat. I thought of what Tissie had told me about Ted. I didn't know how to begin undoing my gross misunderstanding, my brutal injustice. I whispered to him awkwardly, "Yesterday Tissie told me, about everything... I'm sorry, Ted, terribly sorry. I was closed-minded and mean."

He turned a very sad face toward me. "I wasn't so open either, Sophie, I saw Seth's hand behind everyone and everything. I made you suspicious of me. And then the day Jose was released you couldn't be there to see him because he came to my house, and you wouldn't have come there. He might not have gotten killed if you'd been there."

"Please don't tell me that, Ted."

I was crying. I hadn't run out on Jose only when I left the garage. I had run out on him again when he was in prison. On my third or fourth visit to the prison, Jose had talked enthusiastically about the books I had brought him. He talked about liberation struggles, about the need for the oppressed to arm themselves. I realized that while I was carrying bags full of books to Jose, books describing wars of liberation and revolutionary uprisings, I was dragging myself to a factory job every day except Sunday. The contradiction between the subjects of those books and my own mindless drift became unbearable to me. I couldn't face another conversation with Jose. I longed to do something, anything at all, that would associate me in some way with the subjects of those books. On the day I had accompanied Sabina and Tina to Debbie Matthews' house, Lem Icel had mentioned the peace movement, and I had asked Tina if she knew anything about it. Although Tina had contemptuously dismissed the peace movement, she remembered my question and brought me a leaflet about a demonstration; the bottom of the leaflet said "Volunteers Welcome" and gave an address. On a Sunday (my only day off) I went to the address on the leaflet, ready to "do something." In the "peace center" I found a room where several people were working at a large table. I asked how I could "join the peace movement." A woman pulled an empty chair up to the table, and I spent the rest of the day stuffing envelopes. I didn't get glass in my lungs, but the drudgery was the same as in the fiberglass factory. The activity was what I imagined office work to be: numerous women stuffing, sealing and stamping envelopes, a few important-looking men walking in and out of the room. But this drudgery had a justification: it was service and sacrifice for others. There were eight or nine women at the stuffing table, and one bearded man. The women were all middle-aged; the man was my age. I sat across the table from him. His name was Art Sinich; he introduced himself to me later that day. They stuffed envelopes right through the lunch hour. No one mentioned food. The mailing got done late in the afternoon. No one thanked me, obviously; I hadn't helped them, I had helped the movement. People started to disperse. They were all going to see each other again at a lecture which I couldn't attend because of my job. I asked if more work would be done the following Sunday. Art told me he would be there. I returned to the peace center the following Sunday. Art and two or three women were stuffing pamphlets into brown envelopes. The women weren't the ones who had been there a week earlier. Art introduced me to them; I was already a full-fledged member of the movement. The pamphlet stuffing didn't take long and everyone except Art and I left. I asked him what was done in the peace center other than envelope stuffing. He took me to the literature room. I leafed absently through some books and pamphlets. All of them dealt with the same subject: death. Death by nuclear holocaust, by chemical warfare, by radiation from atomic tests. Then Art took me to the peace center's print shop and introduced me to the printer. It was in the basement. A large man my age was operating a small printing machine in a space large enough for one small person; he looked like a giant trapped in a cave. (What a contrast to Ted's well-lit and spacious print shop! That building should have been called the sacrifice center!) Finally Art took me to the "reception room." He showed me photographs in the "movement scrapbook," pointing to himself at a "vigil," at a chemical warfare plant, in a rowboat "resisting" a nuclear submarine, "sitting in" at a government atomic energy building. He told me proudly that he'd been arrested at every one of those "actions." I returned again the following week. Announcements of a major demonstration several weeks away were being sent out. The demonstrators were to block the entrance gate of a military base about to receive missiles that could depopulate half the world. I told Art I wouldn't be able to attend the demonstration because of my job. He looked at me as if I were one of "them," the wrongdoers, the warmongers. I already knew that behind the modest, self-sacrificing servant of humanity stood a hardened holy man who towered above ordinary mortals. I didn't have the nerve to tell him I only supported myself; I felt guilty for putting my "selfish material interests" above goodness and peace. For Art that selfishness was at the root of all war, all destruction. I stayed away from the envelope stuffing for a week, intimidated by the righteousness. But that only put me back into the situation I had tried to leave behind. I decided to take part in the demonstration and to skip work. I was extremely nervous on the day of the demonstration. I rode with five or six other people to a military sign that said, "No public access beyond this point." Several other cars were already parked by the sign. People began to sit across the roadway, about twenty in all, with various home-made signs. It was spring, but the temperature was freezing. I couldn't stop shivering. At last a huge truck approached. I was stupefied by fear; I was sure we'd all be run over. But the truck stopped and one of the demonstrators told the driver he was transporting death in the back of his truck. Other trucks came, and drivers gathered at the side of the road and made various comments to the "nuts" sitting in the roadway. I knew at the time that all the hatred of the people sitting in that roadway was concentrated on the drivers of the trucks. Twenty righteous people were making themselves an example to the murderers who drove trucks and worked in factories. I also knew that all the "peace literature" appealed to the "moral sense" of government officials and the "humanity" of the rich. When I heard sirens I clung to Art with mortal fear. (At the trial I was charged with linking arms to resist arrest.) I was nearly unconscious with fear when I was carried to the police wagon. I had been arrested only once before: at the carton plant. After a day and a half in jail I was released on bail put up by the peace organization. The date of the trial was set. When I got home I called the fiberglass factory and told the foreman I'd been arrested at a peace demonstration. He told me not to bother returning to work. I had succeeded in transforming my situation: I was a full-time political activist. I described my act to Sabina and tried to tell her how "worthwhile" it had been. I described Art to her and tried to tell her how "wonderful and good" he was. Sabina made no effort to hide her disgust. We shared the house, but we no longer shared anything else. I was jobless and alone. I wasn't able to defend myself from Sabina's and Tina's hostility. I couldn't bear to face Jose's questions about liberation, armed struggle, revolutionary wars. I knew that my "act" had nothing to do with the subjects of the books I had taken to Jose. I knew that I had joined a tiny group of "God's witnesses on earth," sent from heaven to stimulate guilt in workers and move the hearts of rulers. I knew I had joined the martyrs of the age, the saints who stood witness to humanity's final cannibalistic act and kept their souls pure. When I saw Art again he showed me newspaper clippings about our arrest, and he was proud; the arrest was a sign of his personal worth, if not in the eyes of the "rabble" for whom he only felt contempt, then in the eyes of God and "good" members of the ruling class. I knew that my "act" had no relation to Hugh's "project house" where the oppressed were to become independent by their own efforts; my new friends found only one quality in the oppressed: guilt. All initiative, all change, had to come from the top, from those who rule. But instead of turning my back on Art and his friends, I turned against Sabina, Tina and Jose. I looked forward to the trial alongside my modest, bearded co-defendant. On the first day of the trial I told Tina not to expect me home that night. The trial wasn't about missiles or nuclear weapons or wax. It was about whether or not we had locked arms when the police had announced we would be arrested (which they hadn't actually announced). Afterwards I drifted to Art's apartment house. He invited me up to his tiny room, part of a subdivided apartment with a common kitchen. The room contained every book and pamphlet I had seen in the peace center. He had apparently read them all; there were notes in all the margins. In addition to the pamphlets there was a single bed, and that was all. He asked if I wanted to stay. I had nothing better to do with myself. For a few nights we both slept in his single bed; then I bought a cot. He insisted on sleeping on the cot; he was determined to bear the greater sacrifice. The trial dragged on for two and a half months. Every session was the same: had we locked arms before the announcement? Had there been an announcement? When Art wasn't stuffing envelopes or demonstrating, he read. I read four or five of his books and pamphlets; each one of them made the same points in exactly the same way; only the names and dates were different. After a few weeks I stopped accompanying him to the stuffing sessions. I tidied and swept his room, got book ends for his literature. Art didn't see the difference; he was neither pleased nor annoyed; it didn't matter to him: I was a crass materialist for occupying myself with such things. I made up the beds, shopped, cooked, washed the dishes. He didn't once tell me he'd liked one of the meals I'd prepared. He was a vegetarian; before I had come he had eaten mainly boiled eggs. I learned that he had never worked because his father, who owned a clothing store and whom Art considered a

crass materialist, gave him a monthly allowance. When the trial finally ended (we
were all let off on "probation," whatever that meant; I never reported to anyone), I
bought a bottle of wine to celebrate. Weeks earlier I had bought a vegetarian cook-
book, and I spent several hours preparing a delicacy. I set a cloth on the floor and
put candles on it. Art sat down as usual, gulped down my meal as if it were a boiled
egg, and turned back to the pamphlet he had been reading. Late that night I tiptoed
out of his room. I left him the cot, so as to decrease the discomfort of his next guest.
In the kitchen I looked into the phone book and scribbled him a note: "Get yourself
a maid. Maid Service phone number: —" I slipped the note under his door and
called a taxi. I didn't hear from Art again until I saw him, as Well as Luisa, after the
riot last year, engaged in envelope stuffing. I was back home with Sabina and Tina
— jobless, projectless, aimless. They didn't ask questions; I couldn't have answered
any. Gradually one of my former interests revived: my interest in reading. I made
frequent trips to the library and rummaged through bookstores. I hadn't read anything other than a few peace pamphlets since I'd left the garage. Now I spent most
of my days reading. Subjects that had rarely been treated when I was a student were
now explored in one study after another. In the bookstores there were entire sections of literature devoted to revolutionary theory, liberation struggles, even philosophical analyses of social and psychological repression. The more I read, the more
indignant I became about the narrowness of Art's interests. Whenever I found a
book particularly exciting, I set it on the living room table. Tina read them. I hoped
she'd take them to Jose, but she only returned them to the table. One day she told
me she was going to visit Jose, but didn't want to go alone and Sabina didn't want to
accompany her. She trapped me into visiting Jose again. I packed all the books I'd
set aside and went with her. In the visiting room she stood some distance away
from Jose and me. He had probably begged her to bring me, one way or another. I
gave him the books, but I didn't have the nerve to tell him about my peace movement "actions" or "friends." I visited Jose one more time before his release, by
myself. It was on that visit I noticed just how much he had been affected by the
books I had brought him. I don't want to exaggerate my share. Probably the solitude
in which he read the books, as well as conversations he must have had with fellow
prisoners, had also contributed their share. I did know that the intentions he
expressed, as well as the words he used, came out of the books, since I had just read
them. He talked about his intention to take part in the uprising of the oppressed. I
was excited at first; I thought he was describing something like Hugh's "project
house." But the more he talked, the more frightened I grew. The project house
turned into a band of armed guerrillas. Jose lectured to me about the need of the
oppressed to arm themselves, to defend themselves with knives, rifles, even machine
guns. When I had read the accounts of the guerrilla movements, I had been excited
by the knowledge that law and order were collapsing everywhere, that people were
responding to arms with arms — elsewhere, far away from me. I hadn't for a second
imagined myself stealing a truck full of weapons, shooting at police, or pulling the

ring of a hand grenade. Before leaving Jose I tried to tell him I thought activities appropriate elsewhere might not be so appropriate here, but I don't think he heard me. I never saw him again. As the day of his release approached my fears grew. It had been so easy to carry books to him. I wasn't able to live up to those books, to Jose, to his new commitment. On the day of his release Sabina told me he didn't want us to meet him at the prison. Several days later Sabina burst into my room crying. Jose had been shot in the back. "The police picked him up just like a dog — dead, in the street," she told me. "If they hadn't arrested Ted as a suspect, I wouldn't even have known!" Then she added, "He had wanted to be someone you could admire." I fell on Sabina wailing. "He was my whole life, everything I loved! I'm nothing compared to him, Sabina; I couldn't have given him anything, I'd only have dragged him down and made his life ugly! He couldn't have died because he wanted to live up to me, Sabina. You're wrong. You have to be wrong!"

I cried during the rest of the trip from the research center to the commune. Ted confirmed what Sabina had told me three years earlier, what I still didn't want to believe. Jose had wanted to be ready for me, he had wanted to live up to me, he had mistakenly associated me with the fearless revolutionaries described in the books I had taken him. I was completely oblivious to Pat, sitting silently on my right, humiliated by his two encounters with Sabina. All I saw was Ted, the person whose house I wouldn't have entered, even to be with Jose, because of my "suspicions." When we reached the corner where Ted had picked us up, he stretched his hand toward me again and said, almost pleading, "When Jose told me you had nothing to do with Seth, I tried to become your friend, Sophie. But it was too late then. I'd like to try again." I squeezed his hand and told him, "I'd like to try too, Ted."

I saw Ted again the following day, when Pat and Luisa used the print shop to print Pat's leaflet on the loudspeakers; that was the first time I entered Ted's house. I told him I might accompany him back to the research center when he returned there. But first I had to do what I'd told Sabina and Tissie I wanted to do: I had to find out who I was and what I wanted. Your letter gave me an enormous clue. It convinced me that I no longer wanted to be what I had been; it filled me with a desire to shatter my past self. Luisa, Pat and Daman provided me with a perfect setting. I formulated my strategy while riding next to Pat in the back seat of Daman's car, on route from the picket line at Luisa's assembly plant to the "revolutionary festival" at Luisa's house.

:||||||||:

I'm aware that Luisa has a "strategy" too. The whole purpose of her "festival" is to celebrate her independence from me for the second time, to conquer Daman right in front of her former conscience, and to use me as well as Pat in her conquest. She's slightly tipsy from the drinks she'd had with Pat in the bar across from her plant, but her determination shows in every move she makes. Daman and I accompany her to the kitchen to help with the dinner. Pat, who had seemed fairly drunk when we'd entered the house, sits on the living room sofa and waits, glancing at the "revolutionary acquisitions of the proletariat" in Luisa's bookshelf; men dominate history from living rooms while "so beautiful and so intelligent" women cook. To Daman's credit, he's totally unlike Art or Pat in this respect. Despite his rigid outlooks, when it comes to chores he's a perfect egalitarian; he doesn't expect a "comrade" to be his maid. I'm not the only one who appreciates this quality in Daman.

"Very few men I've known have followed me into the kitchen," Luisa tells him.

Daman blushes and says, "I was embarrassed when you had everything ready last time, Luisa; I wanted to help."

"Oh, have you two celebrated here before?" I ask.

"We certainly have!" Luisa answers vivaciously, "Daman tried to call you more than two weeks ago, when you had already moved into the university commune. He couldn't reach you and thought you might have been kidnapped again, so he called me. I told him where you were; you had called me two days before he did. And I asked him to explain to me what was happening at the university. You hadn't been very informative. He started to explain on the phone, but I insisted he come to dinner. It went off marvelously. Daman told me about the new working class, and I agreed to write my article for The Workers Voice. I wanted to help in other ways too, but since I can't type there wasn't much for me to do. I did go to Daman's house once and learned to operate the mimeograph machine in his basement."

Daman reminds her, "In the car you told me you had some suggestions for the next issue of the paper."

"Did I?" Luisa asks absentmindedly, but then she apparently remembers how she got Daman into her house. "As a matter of fact, I have several suggestions," but she doesn't make any.

Daman doesn't pursue the subject; he doesn't want to antagonize his proletarian recruit. I decide to leave them to their game. I ask Luisa if my room is free.

"Yes," she tells me. "It's as empty as when you left it. Why?"

"Because I want to see it before taking anyone up there!" I tell her, running into the living room. Pat looks half asleep. I pull him off the sofa. "So I'm beautiful and intelligent too, am I?"

"Yes, Sophia, extremely," he says sleepily.

"Almost as intelligent as you?"

He wakes up and blushes. I pull him toward the stairway. "Come on, we're going to occupy this place. I'll give you a tour." I pull him all the way up to my room. "This is where I spent my time dreaming when I was in high school — in this very bed."

"You mean this is your house, and Luisa really is your sister?"

"Couldn't you guess that from looking at us?"

"No, I couldn't, Sophia. She looks so much older than you. I thought you and Tina were sisters."

I push Pat on the bed, slide alongside him, and kiss his lips long and hard. "That's the nicest thing, you've said to me, Pat." My heart pounds, my limbs are sore from hunger. But I get up. I learned something from Mirna: to wait for the perfect moment, to fan the fire to its highest heat.

Pat begs, "Come back, Sophia, please. I love you. I never loved anyone before."

I take his hands, pull him to me, and kiss him again. "They're waiting for us downstairs."

"Let them wait, Sophia. I can't."

I scold him: "How will man dominate history if he can't even dominate himself? Tell me that."

He stiffens as if I'd pulled a switch. A woman is dominating the man who would dominate history, turning him on and off like a water tap. I descend victoriously. Pat follows me. I set the table. Daman and Luisa bring out a delicious looking meal, and wine. We start to eat.

Pat returns to the topic he had started discussing with Luisa when we left the council office. He becomes sober and alert. His passion vanishes. He's pure intellect again: all theory and history. "What did you yourself do after that uprising, Luisa? Earlier you told me people ran everything on their own. What did you run?"

"I operated a tram," Luisa tells him.

"I gathered that much from your article," Pat says. "But your article is full of platitudes. I didn't get any idea of what daily life was like after a so-called takeover by the workers. Was it different than it had been before? Did you drive the tram any differently? Do you understand what I'm asking?"

"Yes, Pat, I understand what you're asking," Luisa says, somewhat peeved. "But I'm convinced you don't really want to know; you just want to start another argument which proves that the union is always wrong."

"I'd really like to know, Luisa — not for an argument, but for the sake of historical understanding," Pat insists.

Daman says, "I second Pat's request. I find your experience extremely interesting."

Luisa pretends to be reticent. "I don't want to start our evening off by talking about myself. And in any case, Sophia has already heard everything I have to tell about my experiences."

"I'd like to gain some historical understanding too, Luisa." I look at Pat while saying this.

Luisa begins the story you and Jasna must have heard countless times. "In order to understand what it was like to drive a tram in those days, you have to understand what the whole struggle was about. The working people, together with their organizations —"

"You mean the unions!" I interrupt. It's the first time in my life that I've been so sensitive to Luisa's unionism. I feel as if I were in the presence of the train Zdenek described to you. In the past, Luisa's story always inspired me; now I realize that Luisa's life project had never been her own, any more than mine ever was. Luisa took part in a project which the union defined.

"I mean the union," she says calmly. "It was only thanks to the union that the working population was able to defeat the insurgent generals and the entire rebel army."

I've heard those terms before too — she always used them before, but I suddenly hear them for the first time, probably because we're in the middle of rebellion and insurrection right now. "Were you on the side of the conservatives fighting against the insurgents?"

"Don't be ridiculous, Sophia."

"Your terms are ridiculous, Luisa. What are insurgents? They're people opposed to authority, to the state, the ruling class, the status quo. How can you call a general an insurgent? A general is the highest official in the service of the established order. A rebel, an insurgent, is someone who rises against the ruling order. A general who suppresses an insurrection so as to restore the ruling order is no insurgent! As for a rebel army — that's like saying dry water or full vacuum. There's no such thing as a rebel army!"

Luisa wins the argument by exclaiming, "How easy it is to play games of logic with the dead! Thousands of working people, including your father, lost their lives defending the cause of the workers —"

"You're confusing Nachalo with George Alberts," I shout. "Nachalo didn't die fighting against insurgents and rebels, but fighting alongside them, against the ruling order, against discipline —"

"Whatever garbage you've picked up from Yarostan, I won't have you slandering people who fought one of the purest struggles in the entire history of the working class. What do you know about it? Was Yarostan there? What would he have done? What about you, Sophia? What would you have done? I've seen the type of insurgency you exhibit during revolutionary situations; you couldn't catch mice with it! Only the rich had time to play games with logic. Such logical contradictions were what the enemy threw into the working class to divide it against itself. Fortunately workers recognized each other and they recognized the enemy in spite of those who threw sand in their eyes by asking who the insurgents and rebels were. Nachalo knew perfectly well who his comrades and who his enemies were. He hated the status quo passionately. He slept with his rifle. The only bonds he recognized were bonds of solidarity with his comrades — union comrades, Sophia! He was among the first on the barricades, among the first to join the struggle to defeat the fascist army, among the first killed in that struggle." Luisa turns to Pat; all her reticence has vanished. "I'll tell you what daily life was like during those days. I was on the barricades alongside Nachalo and his daughter. She was hit in the arm.

She died two days later. The day after she died, Nachalo went to the front to defeat the last outposts of the enemy army. I was ready to go with him. Numerous women joined the militia; in that revolution they were treated as equals to men. But I would have had to leave two-year old Sophia as well as the newborn Sabina —"

"The same Sabina I met yesterday?" Pat asks.

Daman comments, "That's very interesting."

"I decided to stay away from the front," Luisa continues. "When I'd first met Nachalo he had believed men were made to do the shooting and women the cooking. After the years he spent with me, he no longer believed that women's place was in the rear. He didn't influence my decision; it was my own. The day he left for the front, I went to union headquarters to volunteer to do the work that had to be done in the rear. I had driven a tram earlier. I was urged to join comrades reestablishing the transportation network. The street fighting had completely paralyzed the city's transit system. There were barricades everywhere, and in many of them trams and busses had served as the basic construction material. This had to be straightened out before life could resume —"

"Resume? Wasn't everything being transformed?" I ask. I start feeling like the heckler Rhea accused me of being.

Luisa disregards my interruption. "As soon as I reached the department where I had worked before, I became a union delegate and joined a commission charged with inspecting the roadbeds and listing the jobs that had to be done before the trams could run again. The following day, the radio called all the manual and technical transport workers to a meeting. The vast majority turned up, except for a few fascists. Everyone, without exception, placed himself under the orders of the union. And five days after the street combats, more trains were circulating than had ever been on those streets before. To get the additional vehicles, we had to work day and night, in the midst of universal enthusiasm, repairing vehicles which according to the previous managers were beyond repair. After only five days there were more vehicles, each of which was more efficiently operated —"

"Thanks to which workers could again be transported daily to the factories where they produced the weapons —" I begin with sarcasm.

But Luisa misses my sarcasm. "The weapons were needed for the victory over the enemy. The spontaneous discipline and organization which made possible the resumption of transportation as well as production would have been impossible without the union."

"That's precisely Sophia's point," Pat tells her. "You've just said it yourself. The union played exactly the same role the managers had played before."

I add, "I can't actually believe Nachalo would have put up with the work discipline and organization you've been describing. Everything you've told me about him makes me visualize him as too much of a rebel —"

"I've never heard such comments from you, Sophia. We were all rebels. We were too poor to be anything else. My own mother died of disease and poverty when I was twelve. My father worked on a road-repair crew; it was thanks to him that I met unionized workers, attended the union school; it was through the union that I got my first job. It's well as good to rebel against everything, but I frankly don't understand your hostility to the union; it had nothing in common with the so-called union here. When I was sixteen my father was shot by the police; he was taking part in a demonstration protesting the imprisonment of union militants. That happened during my second year at the union free school. My father's friends took me into their house, but they were too poor to support me. I wanted to support myself; the union found me a job as ticket puncher on a tram. On my first day at work I was trained by a man I thought very old, although he was no older than Sophia or Daman are right now; he had a foreign accent and seemed to be a drunkard. He praised me for overlooking passengers who had no tickets. He told me the authorities would shoot me. I learned he did the same thing, and he didn't punch the tickets of people who looked poor. He remained my trainer for a week. He raged against the rich. When I told him how my father had died, he told me he kept a rifle in his room to avenge all the workers killed by capitalists. I was fascinated by the raw violence the man exhibited whenever he spoke about the exploiters. Yet he wasn't in the union. And one of the things he held against the exploiters was what he called the shameful fact that women had to work like men. I decided to give myself my first assignment as union organizer: to channel this man's energy where it belonged, and to teach him that his view of women was inconsistent with his revolutionary attitudes."

"Exactly what I thought! It was you who got Nachalo into the union!" I exclaim.

"That's right. My first assignment was a success. But not right away. After my week of training I got assigned to a different tram. I looked for him after work. I found him several times and followed him to a bar. He held me in a trance with his stories of a vast peasant uprising in which he had taken part. I talked to him about the union. But after a few brief encounters, he disappeared. Several weeks passed, during which I moved out of the house of my father's friends, and rented a room of my own. I was independent for the first time, as I've been ever since. But I couldn't get Nachalo out of my mind. At union meetings I asked continually if anyone knew the whereabouts of a foreign worker who didn't punch poor workers' tickets. At one meeting I learned that precisely such a man had started a brawl with an inspector who went through the tram and discovered three quarters of the tickets unpunched. Nachalo had fought with the inspector, but hadn't injured him. Police had arrived and arrested him along with half the passengers. He became a minor hero, but was fired from his job. I was one of a delegation that greeted him when he was released. He recognized me. I told him I was now an independent worker like himself. He was bitter. He told me he was unsuitable company for me; he spoke of himself as a broken man; he even called himself an animal. Then he shouted; 'Men aren't animals! They can't allow themselves to be continually harnessed and driven!' I followed him to the basement hovel in which he and his daughter slept. All the way to his building I argued that an individual can't overthrow the exploiters with his own physical powers, no matter how great they are; he can only do this through union with his fellow workers, through solidarity. Nachalo told me he knew he couldn't fight alone, but that the union got on its knees and begged like a cowardly serf instead of the workers' simply taking what was rightfully their own. 'My knees don't bend!' he shouted when we reached his room. I followed him in and continued arguing. Before long a gypsy girl arrived, a wild thing in rags, quick as a cat, immediately suspicious of me. Keeping her eyes on me as if she thought I'd steal something from her, she started pulling vegetables, meat, liquor and a wad of money out of her large coat. Nachalo whispered to her in their language, but she still didn't take her eyes off me. I asked her if she had a job; she didn't look older than ten. She told me furiously she couldn't get a job that would support two people, which was what she had to do now that Nachalo was fired. Then she told me, with shameless pride, that she'd been a pickpocket since six and a prostitute since eleven; she was twelve. I turned indignantly toward Nachalo and called him a hypocrite for his telling me men ought to work while women stayed at home; a fine principle for a man whose own daughter stooped to the worst form of slavery, prostitution. I called him a parasite and a pimp. The gypsy leaped at me like an enraged animal. She bit my arm and shrieked, 'You come from the church! We don't want the church in this room! Get out, priestess!' As she pushed me out of the room, I started crying. Nachalo reached for her arm and shouted at her until she released me. Then he told me, 'You're right. I'm worse than an animal.' He fell on his knees and begged me, 'Stay and tell me about your union.' That powerful, violent man was on his knees begging to learn from me! The gypsy pushed me toward him. I fell on my knees beside him. I told him, 'I haven't come as a judge, but as your comrade.' Tears flowed down the man's cheeks. It was the most moving sight in my life. This man who had survived a revolution in which all his comrades had been wiped out, this violent man, ever ready to reach for his rifle, was crying with shame before me. From that moment to this I've loved that man more than I've loved anyone since. I pressed his head to my bosom and let him cry. I wanted his comradeship, I wanted him, I wanted his child. I spent that night with him, sleeping on the rags on his floor. I woke early the next morning, bought breakfast for all three of us, and while I was setting their table, the girl walked shyly toward me. She kissed the spot on my arm where she had bitten me, put her head in my bosom just as Nachalo had, and begged, 'I want to be your comrade too.'"

Most of the details are familiar to me; I've always been moved by them. But now I hear something I've never heard before. The little gypsy's initial reaction to Luisa had been identical to that of the other little gypsy — only Sabina didn't ever change her mind about Luisa. The twelve-year old girl had called Luisa a priestess! The priestess of the train that would take humanity to its salvation: the union. The link between Luisa's passion and her calling is suddenly so clear to me. She gave herself to the lowest social stratum so as to elevate it to the salvation train. Isn't that exactly what she did to you? Give to him who hath nothing, like a nun giving a kiss to a leper; save the wretched from exclusion; pull them into the Lord's train, only thus will the world be saved. Margarita was more perceptive at twelve than I am at thirty-four.

"I convinced them to abandon their hovel and move to my room," Luisa continues. "It was larger, sunshine and fresh air reached it, and it was clean. The gypsy, like I, remained independent. She paid for her own board and keep. But I insisted she not pay for Nachalo with her prostitution money. I had started driving a tram and could afford to support him as well as myself. She stuck to her trade, willfully, proudly; she always had a knife on her and was the equal of any man, if not in physical strength then in speed. Nachalo quickly learned to respect my independence. He became deeply involved in union activities. It was in the union that he met others like himself, workers who didn't believe in waiting or in begging. His self-respect and even his pride returned — pride in himself and in his fellow workers, among whom he now included women as equals. He and his friends carried out night-time forays against torturers and killers of working people: police, supervisors, informers. The gypsy frequently took part in those forays — but she didn't go with a view of a better world; she went solely to draw the blood of the class that exploited her. When Sophia was born the three of us moved out of my room and rented a small apartment. It was large enough for weekly meetings, even when the number of workers who agreed with Nachalo increased. It was at one of those meetings that I met my second lover —"

This is new to me. I ask her, "Before the uprising? I didn't know. I thought Nachalo —"

"Of course you didn't know! Think of the scene you'd have made if I'd told you. He was a young physics student from abroad, eager to put his knowledge at the service of the most revolutionary workers. Union Comrades guided him to the meetings held at our apartment —"

"George Alberts? You mean you took up with him before Nachalo left for the front?"

Luisa laughs at me, acting as if both Daman and Pat were in on her joke. But she misgauges them. Daman seems shocked. To Pat it's all equally exotic. "You are really a phenomenon," she tells me. "One would think you'd been brought up in a convent. Did I take up with George Alberts, was I his mistress while my husband was still alive? Is that your question? And you have the nerve to lecture to me about insurgents and rebels? In those days a rebel was first of all a free person, not just someone who attended political meetings and verbally attacked the state and capital. A rebel was a person whose political beliefs and personal behavior were consistent. I rejected the family, marriage, parental and marital obligations in theory, like you, and also in practice, unlike you. Lovemaking was an integral part of our rebellion, our development as free individuals. I succeeded in teaching that to Nachalo. Who would have expected you to grow up with conventional notions of family obligations and hypocritical faithfulness?"

"I didn't mean my question that way," I insist, although that's only partly true. "I meant that Alberts was so different from Nachalo."

"He wasn't so different then. At the first meeting he attended he enumerated the bombs and explosives his university knowledge enabled him to produce with the cheapest of materials. Everyone loved him; he was witty and he spoke our language perfectly." Looking at Daman, she continues, "I've always been profoundly impressed, I should say moved, when a university person, a member of the intelligentsia, sacrifices the privileges available to him and devotes himself to the workers' cause. Of course I took up with him. He became a regular participant at our meetings. All our friends respected him for his knowledge and his evident willingness to share it. I had another reason for taking up with him, as you put it. I wanted to learn if Nachalo had really understood what I meant by independence; I wanted to test the depth of his understanding of mutual respect. One night after a meeting, when Nachalo and the gypsy both left with the others on one of their forays, I asked George to stay and tell me about his past." Luisa stares at Daman; she virtually undresses him with her eyes. "I took up with him as soon as they left. I showed him exactly how grateful I was for his coming from afar to share his knowledge with us. George rushed away before Nachalo returned. I told Nachalo I had gone to bed with George Alberts. His response was: 'You're an independent woman, Luisa; you can make love with whomever you please; if my presence ever hinders you —.' I threw myself at him; I made love for the second time that night. I loved Nachalo more than I would ever love George or anyone else. George stayed away from our next meeting, I found out where he lived and went to look for him after work. Poor George wasn't only afraid of Nachalo; he thought he had wronged me as well. He awkwardly told me he had fallen in love with the little gypsy, and that he thought he ought to have told me that before having an affair with me. He really was in love with her; he said he'd never met anyone so uninhibited, so vivacious, so completely untamed. And he told me he didn't know what to do with his passion, since a twenty-two year old student could obviously not make love to an innocent thirteen-year old girl. 'Innocent!' I shouted. I called him a blind idiot and told him every man in the union was more innocent than that gypsy!"

"You hated her, didn't you?" I ask. I've known that too, but I never understood why. "Nachalo was a down-and-out whom you were able to pull up to your union train. Alberts, the expert with your ideas, was something like a conductor of the train. But Margarita was neither fish nor fowl to you, was she? She continued to carry on her trade. You were unable to pull her up to where you wanted her —"

"Be that as it may, Sophia, I accepted George's admission with Nachalo's open spirit, without a trace of jealousy or resentment. In fact, I invited him to dinner the day after I visited him. He came. After dinner I arranged to leave with Nachalo; we stayed out very late. George and the gypsy were waiting for us; she had asked him to move in with us. He grinned and told us he had learned more from Margarita in a few hours than in all his years at the university. Obviously. After two years in her trade she was an expert in lovemaking. George went on worshipping her although she continued to sell herself in the street, to men as well as women —"

"Talk of narrowmindedness!"

"It was perfectly clear to me that an illiterate girl in her position didn't have much choice! She didn't do it as a sport but out of need. And she did change a little as a result of her contact with George. Maybe she even started to dream of a day when she could make love because she wanted to, not because she was paid. If George inspired such dreams in her, then he succeeded where I had failed. When that day finally came, when the city's workers rose like a giant to stop the attacking army, the gypsy was the first one to run to the barricades with Nachalo's rifle, nine months pregnant with Sabina. Nachalo ran to a comrade's basement and returned with rifles; all of us joined her except George. He knew how to produce explosives, but he had never held a gun in his hand; he stayed behind to mind two-year old Sophia. After the first exchange of shots Margarita was hit in the arm. Nachalo and I carried her home, bandaged her arm, and returned to the barricade. I doubt if George slept for five minutes during the two days before Margarita died giving birth to Sabina — an unbelievable replica of herself, a miniature gypsy born with black hair and black eyes. Nachalo left for the front the day after the gypsy died. And I took up with George again. Isn't that shocking, Sophia? At night George and I were alone in the apartment with two baby girls. Should we have slept at opposite ends of the room? But he was heartbroken, and I wasn't able to console him. His enthusiasm for the revolution waned. He was consumed by rage and self-hatred for not having been on the barricade instead of her. He started talking about revenge — not the workers' revenge but his own. It was already then that he started to slip away from his original commitment. He was temporarily saved for the movement by a young man he met, another foreigner who had come to defend the workers from their enemies. George brought him home. He was in uniform. He had something in common with Pat —"

"Are you talking about Titus Zabran?" I ask her. "He had something in common with Pat? Are you kidding?"

Luisa is playing with Daman. "Titus was younger than George. He was a theorist devoted to what he called the historical project of the proletariat. He was completely single-minded. He seemed to know exactly what was revolutionary in every situation, what steps had to be taken, what strategy was appropriate. George was more philosophical; his interests were more universal."

The suggestion that Daman's interests are universal strikes me as ludicrous, but I repress my objection.

"His main strategic insight was that all our accomplishments in the rear were meaningless if the enemy was not defeated at the front. He convinced George. They both joined Nachalo at the front. I longed to go with them, but I stayed behind with my job and the two babies. A month after they left, George returned alone. Nachalo was dead. Titus was seriously injured and in the hospital. George himself was completely transformed; he seemed shell shocked. He told horrifying stories about what had happened at the front. He turned his back on the revolution. I went to visit Titus in the hospital —"

Daman and Pat seem to be in a trance. The magnetism Luisa radiates is overwhelming. All my life I've been in the same trance, hypnotized by her, uncritically admiring her courage, her devotion, her determination. All my life I negated my own desires for the sake of Luisa's revolution. If I had become aware of my dependence on Luisa years ago, you would have had a comrade, Yarostan, not just a passive admirer, a frail, pretty thing at your revolutionary beck and call. If I had only felt jealousy toward Luisa then, it would have been you who ran to the stockroom with the sheet wrapped around you. I would have carried Nachalo's project instead of worshipping it. My love for you would have been an activity instead of a vocation. But I had to experience Jose before I experienced myself as a body, and I had to wait yet another decade to absorb what I learned from Jose.

I get up from my chair, dizzy from all the wine I drank, and walk toward Pat; I take his head in my hands and press it against me. I'm too giddy to listen, but not too giddy to proceed with the strategy I dreamed up in the car on our way here. "Alberts turned his back on the revolution, so you gave yourself to Titus Zabran, the soldier of the revolution, its theorist, the younger of the two." I'm burning with desire — jealous, resentful desire. "And why not?" I ask. "The revolution is a festival, the satisfaction of all desires. Isn't that what we're supposed to be celebrating?"

Daman snaps out of his trance. "Luisa's account makes it perfectly clear that certain matters, such as social production, transportation, precede the satisfaction of personal desires."

Pat, almost completely drunk, says weakly, "If production takes precedence over the real desires of concrete individuals, then the organizers of production take precedence over living individuals and repression takes precedence over life."

Daman objects, "I think you both missed I the point of what Luisa has been telling us. If revolution is nothing but the realization of what you call desires —"

"What do you call them, Daman?" I snap at him, starting to pull Pat out of his chair. "Are you sure you didn't miss the point of what Luisa has been telling you, Daman? She wants you to give her an orgasm, Daman, right here, right now. She's trying to tell you why she wants it from you. Because you're a professor with our ideas, because you're a driver of the train she serves, because of your universal ideas, because you're the one for whose service she pulled Nachalo out of his hovel, and Yarostan —"

If only I had been giddy that morning I was with you on the floor of the carton plant and if I'd known Luisa was going to open that gate, I would have pulled you into me while she watched! If I had done that, Yarostan, I would never have dreamt of emigrating. I would have waited for you at the prison gate when you were released, you would never have married Mirna, although you would have spent your life with a person much more like her than I've been. If I had nevertheless emigrated, during my first bike trip with Ron I would have spent half the night making love to him by the side of the pond, and I'd have slept the other half, content and happy and unafraid. I'd never have left Ron, he would be alive today, and I might be a successful thief or prostitute. I might have been the one who started the garage; I might have been Ron's girl and Jose's and Ted's, probably Tissie's and Sabina's too, each in turn, perhaps all at once. I know I'd never have gone near a university, and I'd never have met Rhea, or Lem, Hugh or Alec, Daman or Minnie. Nor would I've written you a letter at the time of the Magarna uprising; I wouldn't have needed to; you wouldn't have been arrested because of it; Jan would still be alive, as well as Mirna's father, and Vesna would have had no reason to play her game.

Do I wish, Yarostan? Yes. Don't you? I opt for that other life in Luisa's dining room. I replay my scene in the carton plant — unfortunately twenty years too late to undo the consequences of the life I've lived, but not too late to put an end to the Sophia I recognized in your letter, a Sophia toward whom I could feel no admiration, nor even pity, just contempt. Wrapping my arms around Pat's body I ask Daman, "What does comradeship mean to you, Daman? What do you understand by solidarity?" Then I ask Luisa, "Do you remember Claude Tamnich?"

Luisa puts her hand on Daman's shoulder and claims, "You know perfectly well Daman means exactly the same thing I do, Sophia." To prove it, and to dissociate Daman from Claude, she lifts his hand to her mouth, kisses it, and tells him, "This is what I mean by solidarity and friendship, Daman; it's more than articles and meetings and picket lines and arguments —"

I persist. I'm obsessed with my project. "Show Luisa, show all of us what you mean by desire, Daman." I turn to Pat. "And you! Show us what you mean by the real desires of concrete individuals, the unity between theory and practice. Show us how men dominate history!"

Pat tries to pull away from me, "I don't understand, Sophia. I just told Daman —"

"Never mind what you told him! Show Daman what you wanted to show me before dinner. Not with words, Pat! With your arms, legs, hips, with your body! Let me remind you." I'm breathing fast. I feel my heartbeats in my head. I'm burning the way Mirna must have burned the day she took her brother the devil to her clearing. And why not? The world is changing all around me. Why wouldn't I change? I've abandoned myself totally only once before in my life — to Jose, in order to show I wasn't perverse, to show him the nature of my most repressed desires, to show I didn't want to be Tina's seducer but Jose's woman. My determination to prove the existence of my desire itself gave birth to my desire. That was the first time I experienced the abandon of total orgasm. The irony is that in trying to deny my perversity I proved myself unimaginably perverse, bathing my entire body in Jose, writhing in semen. But I had been repressed too long to understand what I had done. Out of a shame and denial of sexuality identical to Vesna's, I committed suicide in a fiberglass factory and continued murdering my desires until both you and Luisa held up a mirror that reflected a horribly rigid, sexless porcelain statue, taunting me, provoking me until I can't stand to look at the reflection a second longer. I press my whole body against Pat's side, sliding slowly against his arm, his hips. "Don't look away, Daman!" I shout. "Tell him, Luisa! Tell him this is what you mean by comradeship and solidarity!"

Luisa holds on to Daman's hand and starts to cry. "Did Yarostan tell you about that too?"

"Do you remember what comes next?" I ask her. I pull Pat's shirt over his head and start undoing his belt buckle.

Pat begs, "Please, Sophia, not here."

Daman gets up and moves toward the door, announcing, "This is ridiculous."

Luisa, crying, falls to her knees in front of Daman and embraces his leg; she looks up to him like a begging dog. "Don't leave me now, Daman."

Pulling off my own clothes, I push Pat down to the floor. "Desire is ridiculous, Daman. Organization has nothing to do with passion. Solidarity means obedience to the leader's decisions. Comradeship is nothing but a synonym of membership. For you there's no contradiction between organization and desire because desire doesn't exist. It's expurgated from the revolutionary society. Luisa, do you remember Claude Tamnich?"

Luisa falls to the ground as Daman tries to walk away from her. He shouts to me, "You belong in a mental hospital!" That must be what his friend, the dean who fired me, told him.

Luisa holds on to him and begs, "Please don't prove her right, Daman!"

Pat and I roll naked on Luisa's living room carpet as if it were Sabina's wall-to-wall mattress. Pat, panting with desire, tries to pull me toward the stairway. I laugh at him and remind him, "All the victims of repression have to satisfy their desires, Pat, not just some. Men will never dominate history from bed-rooms. That's done in living rooms!"

Daman reaches the door, dragging Luisa after him. "At least sit with me in the kitchen. Don't leave me like this," she begs.

And then, exactly as Jan expected, all morality bursts into the open and shatters. Pat penetrates and wails, "Oh, no, I didn't want it to happen like this."

Daman slaps Luisa and runs out of the house, leaving her lying by the open door exactly as I had once left Tissie, crying hysterically. Luisa comes to herself, looks around furiously, and runs to her room shouting at me, "I'll never forgive you for this! I don't know what you're trying to prove, but you're doing it like a sick, wild animal!"

"Like a gypsy!" I shout back.

Pat runs from the open door and grabs the clothes strewn around the living room, exactly as I ran from the street entrance of the carton plant. A porcelain statue is shattered. Pat dresses in a corner of the room and bolts through the door. I bathe in the fresh night air blowing in from the street, immoral to the point of perversity, unashamed, independent. Luisa runs past me without looking at me and slams the door shut. I go up to my room, feeling victorious and free. I wanted, and I took in conditions determined by me. Tell Mirna I'm ready now to face all the consequences, I'm ready to face the world.

I've been typing for the past twelve hours. Luisa didn't invite me to breakfast before she left this morning. I recently finished the bottle of wine I carried up with me. And yes, I read your second letter as soon as I started writing this one. I lost some of my rage, but not my desire to describe my "revolution" to you. Outside there's a general strike. Everything is out of commission. Tomorrow I'll be part of it again, though I don't yet know which part. I may go back to Sabina and Tissie. I'll try to take Pat with me.

I still love you, Yarostan, and I'll go on loving you —

Your *Sophia.*

Yarostan's eighth letter

Dear Sophia,
Your victory is complete. I never dreamed the passion you just described lay below the surface of the person I knew twenty years ago. I was wrong. My outlook didn't allow me to see below the surface. I was near-sighted; I still am. Mirna, Yara, your letter, all the events taking place around me are making me suspect I've been viewing the world through opaque glass. The frame of reference I acquired from Titus and Luisa and from comrades I met during two long prison terms suddenly seems inadequate; real people seem to move outside its boundaries. More is breaking down and more is rising up than I'm able to take in. Perhaps I never dreamed of anything more than a different system of constraint. I had not envisioned the wealth of potentiality, the passion bursting out of individuals who suddenly lost their chains. Total lack of constraint appealed to me as a concept, a motto. But the more Mirna and Yara, and you, make it a lived experience, the less able I feel to move towards it.

Mirna, Yara, as well as Jasna are on a journey. They're exploring the possibilities available to them. Your previous letter convinced them working people were rising in every part of the globe. Everything seems to confirm this. A totally different activity seems to be on the horizon.

Yet for the first time in my life I find myself holding back. I didn't accompany my three comrades on their journey; I chose to remain in the carton plant. My expectations seem to be considerably below the level of the activity taking place around me. I told you that during my second prison term I rejected the outlook I had acquired from Luisa; I told you that when I first met Mirna, she hungered for life and I was only able to offer her politics. I haven't moved very far since then. I'm starting to realize that I barely understand Mirna or Yara. I learned from Titus and Luisa to put my life at the service of politics. All I did during my second term was to modify my politics, perhaps even, to enrich my political outlook; I didn't enrich my life's desires. My "theory" is still my dearest possession. Yet the genuine rebels in my life have been Jan and Mirna, and both of them have had very "crude" theories by Luisa's and Titus' standards — as crude as mine was when Luisa first undertook to "educate" me. Despite his theoretical "crudity" Jan was far less reconciled to the totality of repression than Luisa.

Luisa's account of her activity as a delegate in the transport union confirms most of what Manuel told me during my first prison term. When Manuel returned from the front to the city he found former union militants working as supervisors and speed-up engineers, lubricating the production of weapons for a "popular army" whose guns were turned against the workers themselves. Luisa fails to clarify precisely what's obscure. How could Nachalo, George Alberts and Titus Zabran all have fought on the same front? Why did Alberts return from the front completely transformed and "shell shocked?" Alberts had told Sabina his only military activity had been to serve on a firing squad which liquidated certain "infiltrators," by which he meant revolutionaries who refused to place themselves under the orders of the "popular army." Did he tell Luisa more immediately after this act than he told Sabina a decade later? According to Luisa, Alberts and Zabran "both joined Nachalo at the front." What a strange way to put it! From Manuel and Sabina we've learned that the popular army brigade "joined" the militia unit only to liquidate it. Luisa fails to distinguish victims from executioners. The two are the same to her because they are both parts of "our organization." The greatest crimes are virtues when committed by "our organization." When "our militants" enter the state apparatus, in Luisa's eyes they're still union militants, not state functionaries. When "our ministers" give orders to an army, the army is no longer a state army but an extension of the class. It's not by chance that she refers to the fascist army as the "rebel army" and to fascist generals as "insurgents." Once her comrades were in the government, the aim of "our organization" became to maintain law and order, and all those who threatened it were insurgents. Forced labor in the service of the state apparatus became revolutionary activity; supervisors and foremen became militants fighting in the rear. I too remember having heard Luisa's account before. But now I'm extremely puzzled about the friendship between Luisa, George Alberts and Titus Zabran. Titus never told me very much about his past activities, and I'm surprised to learn he was such a talkative "theorist" when Luisa met him. Was she exaggerating in order to compare him to your young friend Clesec, or have I never really known him? I'm not only puzzled by Luisa's account; I'm very suspicious of it. Sabina told you that Alberts didn't go to the front with workers and peasants fighting to liberate themselves;

he went with a state army that repressed them. According to Luisa, Alberts left for the front after Titus convinced him that victory at the front was a prerequisite for meaningful accomplishments in the rear; at that point they both "joined Nachalo at the front." This doesn't make sense. According to Manuel the militia units were formed a few days after the street fighting ended. Manuel as well as Nachalo left for the front almost immediately after they had fought on the barricades. The "popular army" didn't exist yet; the influential union militants were still trying to get into the state apparatus. It was only after the anti-state militants became state functionaries that the "popular army" was created. Luisa told you Titus was already in uniform when Alberts met him. It's conceivable that it was Titus who convinced Alberts about the importance of victory at the front. But it's not conceivable to me that Alberts "joined" either Nachalo or Titus at the front. Titus' uniform must have been the militia uniform, and he must have been on leave from the militia's front when he met Alberts; he probably couldn't imagine the nature of the "popular army" being created in the rear. I'll try to ask Titus; I haven't seen him since we began our correspondence. The more I learn about that struggle, the more I suspect that my own life, as well as yours, has been affected by it. It seems to me that if Titus convinced Alberts to join the "popular army," it was because Titus was unfamiliar with the nature of that organization. If they then "joined" each other at the same front, it wasn't as allies. Titus returned to his militia unit — perhaps the very unit in the village described by Manuel. Alberts arrived later with an apparatus that was labeled "popular" — and he served on a firing squad that liquidated members of the militia unit after calling them "infiltrators." Luisa visited Titus in a hospital after he was injured, probably defending his militia comrades. And Alberts returned "shell shocked" and "totally transformed" — why? What did he tell Luisa when he returned? That he had shot his own comrades? That he had taken Titus' advice and "by mistake" had found himself on the opposite side of the firing line?

As for your "remembering" that Titus was with you at the time of your release twenty years ago, I can assure you that your memory is playing tricks on you. He didn't stay behind in order to try to release the rest of us; he stayed behind because he was in jail like the rest of us. Titus had just been released when he met Jan's father at the bus repair depot next door to the trade union building where Titus had just gotten his job back. When Luisa told you that story, she must have felt guilty for having abandoned her comrades; she must have known that her emigration did not illustrate the "solidarity and comradeship" she had preached. Only a few days ago Zdenek and Titus ran into each other, not quite by chance. On the day of the dance at her plant, Mirna took Zdenek to Titus' house; she intended to invite Titus to the dance. Mirna was surprised to learn that Zdenek and Titus had known each other. Among other things, Zdenek told Mirna he had run into Titus in prison — during the time of my first prison term!

Mirna had invited Zdenek to the dance at their plant two weeks ago, while in the middle of an argument with him. I had timed down Mirna's invitation because of my inability to dance, but Jasna had lured me into taking part in the event by promising to give me another dancing lesson.

I wasn't aware of all the work Mirna and Yara did to prepare for the event, because I spent my days in the carton plant. A week ago Monday all the workers at the plant listened to a debate on the radio. Jasna had told us about two weeks ago that Marc Glavni and Vera Krena were going to engage in this debate, but I had promptly forgotten about it. I learned at Mirna's dance that Yara hadn't only remembered the debate; she had a university friend of hers make a recording of the speeches, and re-broadcast excerpts of Glavni's speech at the dance itself, with very dramatic effect. When I first heard the speeches I resented the fact that my fellow workers had dropped everything to listen to them; it seemed to me that if the speeches of bureaucrats still mattered to us, then we hadn't moved very far. If I'd known what use Yara was going to make of Comrade Glavni's speech I would have listened with greater interest.

The following day I got a hint of what Mirna and Yara were preparing. I could barely recognize Yara. Her light hair had been dyed pitch black, along with her eyebrows and eyelashes. Mirna explained that the dance was to be a masquerade: I gathered that Yara was going to play the devil. Mirna then dressed me in a peasant jacket, pants and boots of the type Jan used to wear. She proceeded to straighten my hair with wax, and to fasten a moustache above my lips.

Early Wednesday morning, when I was getting ready to leave for the carton plant, there was a knock at our door. It was Jasna. She seemed as full of energy and mischief as the other two. "How glad I am you haven't left for the plant yet," she told me exuberantly. "You haven't changed your mind about chaperoning me to the dance?"

I blushed as I told her, "No, Jasna. I'm looking forward to it — very much."

"You won't recognize me," she announced.

"Nor you me," I said. "Mirna already told me it's going to be a masquerade. She's going to paste a moustache on my face and —"

"You won't recognize me below the masquerade," Jasna said cryptically, kissing my cheek. "Where are the two devils?"

"They're still asleep," I told her. "They spent half the night in Yara's room hatching plots. Are you in on them?"

"Not yet, but I will be! May I wake them?"

Jasna woke Yara, who immediately shouted, "You'll do it, Jasna! I knew you would." Then both ran excitedly to Mirna's room. What I heard next made me extremely apprehensive for the rest of the day. Mirna said, "You're a real friend, Jasna!" Then Jasna shouted, "And you're a real hypocrite, Mirna. You're pushing me into this game only because you know I'll never take him from you. He'd have to be crazy to let me! Look at the two of us, Yara! He's not blind!" Yara shouted, "You're beautiful, Jasna! All of us are beautiful, and he loves every one of us; you'll see!" At this point Mirna shushed the other two so that I wouldn't hear any more of their "plot."

I didn't go to work Thursday morning. Yara and her friend Julia were in and out of the house all morning long. They painted large signs which they didn't let me see. Mirna was busy sewing more costumes. About two hours before the dance was to begin, Mirna made sure I wore every item of my costume, including the moustache, appropriately. Yara, with black hair hanging down to her shoulders and over her face, wore slacks and a work jacket. Mirna wore the dress she had worn when I'd first met her twenty years ago. Slobodan and an older boy came by for the signs, and Julia left with them. Then Mirna and Yara left carrying suitcases; Mirna explained they were going to "fix up" Jasna and Zdenek.

I walked to Jasna's house in my funny clothes. Jasna was "fixed up" in clothes that were vaguely familiar to me. I asked her what the masquerade was going to mean.

"Don't you recognize yourself, or me, or Yara?" she asked. I admitted I didn't. "I'll make you guess," she told me provocatively.

As soon as Jasna and I reach the plant, the first thing I see is yet another illustration of the significance your letters have for us. You responded immediately to my "confession." Yara responded just as immediately to your first description of the commune to which Tina accompanied you. Over the main entrance to Mirna's plant, covering the plant's enormous name plaque, is one of the banners Yara and Julia painted; it contains a single word: LIBERATED. Inside the plant, the floor and walls are newly painted; there is no sign of the machinery, which has all been pushed against a wall and hidden away by a curtain. At one end of the vast room there's a speakers' platform; behind it there's an enormous red flag with a picture of a tank in its center. There are streamers all over the ceiling. The two side walls contain enormous banners with slogans you'll recognize; one says, "Everything is allowed"; the other, "Nothing is banned."

Jasna and I are not among the first people to arrive; we seem to be among the last. Zdenek rushes to us and tells us, "I ran into your friend Zabran on the way here — a funny meeting." Jasna and I are both amazed to learn this, but Zdenek tells us he'll save the story until later; "I don't want to miss any of the antics of those two," he explains; "they're both like ten-year old children, and I suspect Mirna is the younger of the two."

The same thought had gone through my mind when Mirna had left the house wearing her elementary school dress. I myself feel like a ten-year old in this former factory which seems to have been decorated mainly by Yara, Julia and their ten-year old friend Mirna. I find your comparison of Tissie and of all of us to children profound and highly appropriate. Yes, the world is becoming for all of us what it is for Yara, what it may have been for us when we were children: unpredictable and fascinating because unknown. The machine-like routine, the knowledge that tomorrow will be like today, is gone. The world is becoming a field for the realization of our dreams, your dreams, all the dreams that reach us, all the imaginings of all the past dreamers we've been carrying inside ourselves. The world is no longer external to me, to any of us, but is beginning to be an externalization and reflection of ourselves; it is no longer a cold, hostile reality opposed to our "private," personal, unreal dreams. Reality is starting to incorporate our dreams.

Music starts to play: a traditional folk melody. Everyone forms into a circle, which Jasna and I join, and we start to move in rhythm to the music. In the middle of the circle another dance begins. Zdenek is in the center dancing with an old, bent woman made up as a skeleton, or perhaps as death. The old woman spins him in circles, and then chases him around the circumference of the circle. Suddenly a beautiful "courtesan" approaches Zdenek and makes suggestive gestures. The courtesan's eyes are covered by a mask below which I recognize Yara's lips; she wears a short skirt, a wig of long blonde hair, a tight sweater over a padded chest, and high-heeled shoes. I whisper to Jasna, "This must have been rehearsed."

"I suppose it was," she tells me. "I wasn't in on this part of it. I barely recognize her. Isn't she fantastic?"

When the old "skeleton's" back is turned, Zdenek accepts the courtesan's invitation and dances with her on the inside of the circle. But when Zdenek's back is turned, Yara throws the blonde wig and the shoes to Mirna, who places a black hairnet with horns over Yara's dyed black hair, and throws a black cape over Yara's shoulders. Then Yara, as the devil, continues to dance with the stunned Zdenek, while the old "skeleton" runs behind them with a broom. Suddenly the broom hits the devil, who vanishes through the circle. Zdenek is left alone, facing the old woman and her broom. He tries to run after the devil, but finds no way out of the circle of dancers. The peasant-girl Mirna leaves the circle, runs to Zdenek and dances with him. The old woman tries to hit them with the broom, but her broom only hits the ground; she seems unable to keep up with them.

Everyone laughs and applauds when Yara and Slobodan hang a sign below the "Everything is Allowed" banner. The sign contains the words "Daughter with Father."

Another melody begins and Zdenek joins the outer circle of dancers. Mirna remains inside the circle. She moves from person to person and stops in front of me. I notice that another sign is being added below the previous one. The new sign says, "Brother with Sister." Mirna pulls me inside the circle, guides me, pushes me, turns me. I grin and look awkwardly back toward abandoned Jasna. But there's no smile on Mirna's face; she looks determined, obsessed, almost possessed. While pressing and turning me, she kisses me and tells me, "Our love is possible now, Jan. From now on everything is possible. Tonight we'll make love; tomorrow we'll roam across the entire country, as free as birds; we'll visit streams and caverns and other cities, and wherever we go we'll find only friends; there won't be any prying old women —"

Behind us I feel "death's" broom hitting the ground, increasingly closer to us. Mirna continues, "everyone will beg us to join them in what they're doing, and we won't know which way to turn —" While she's speaking, the skeleton removes Mirna's arms from me and pulls her out of the circle, which breaks up because the dance ends. A sign on the speaker's platform announces an "intermission."

Couples move out to the dance floor. Mirna dances with Zdenek, turning gracefully around him, embracing him, kissing him. Jasna starts to give me my second lesson in dancing. She shows me foot motions, hand positions, bows and turns. She tells me, "Put your arm here, around my waist. Not so loose, Yarostan! Are you afraid of me?" I put both arms around her thin waist, kiss her and try to resume my foot motions, but Jasna prolongs the kiss. Then she guides me, still dancing, past the other couples and to the fresh air outside the plant.

Jasna, her arms around me, leans on the factory wall and smiles beautifully. "You've finally recognized me," she sighs.

"You're Jasna and you're beautiful," I tell her.

"You don't know how happy you're making me." She kisses me passionately. "Hold me, Yarostan, press me, love me. I've never been loved in my entire life." Suddenly she drops her arms and starts crying. "It's all a lie," she wails.

I try to kiss her again, and I assure her I meant what I said.

Jasna pulls me toward the light that shines out of a factory window. There are tears on her cheeks, but she's still smiling. She tells me, "I'm not Jasna!"

"Don't be foolish," I tell her. "Do these clothes make me someone other than Yarostan?"

"We've known each other for twenty-three years, Yarostan, and you never kissed me until I tried to make myself look like Luisa Nachalo: her clothes, her hair, even her manners —"

"Luisa! But that's ridiculous, Jasna! You're no more like Luisa than I am like Jan."

"Mirna knows you much better than you know yourself," she tells me. "Mirna and Yara started this game over a week ago, right after the last get-together we had at your house. When they came to my house, mischievous and conspiratorial, I was somewhat frightened, but I was excited. I suppose I was flattered that they wanted to include me in their mischief. They told me the dance would be a masquerade, and Yara asked if I could help make her look like Sabina —"

"Of course!" I exclaim, suddenly "recognizing" the gypsy with the long black hair. "She's a perfect likeness."

"But then Mirna insisted I make myself look like Luisa. I was offended and frightened. I reminded her you had loved Luisa, and asked if she wanted me to go to her dance with her husband as my lover. 'You'd like nothing better; you've dreamed about it for twenty years,' she told me. Mirna is absolutely shameless. And she's wrong. I never wanted to trick you into loving me —"

"Your smile, your motions, your words aren't tricks, Jasna. And if I did take you for someone I loved once, it would only be because I loved you —"

"That's exactly what Mirna said, even in the same words! I asked her why she wanted to do this? She loves you; why did she want to make every one of us miserable? Yara told me Mirna wanted you to be exactly as you were when she first met you. That was when I realized Yara was stage-managing the whole performance, and I told her I refused to play one of her love games, not because I share Vesna's fear — or at least no longer because of that — but because I was in love with someone else, with Titus Zabran."

"Was that true?"

"Yes, Yarostan, I've loved Titus as long as I've loved you, and the poor man is all by himself; he needs me; you have Mirna as well as Yara. Let's go back. They wouldn't want you to miss the second half."

As soon as I re-enter the factory-dance hall with Jasna-Luisa, the "intermission" sign is removed from the speakers' platform by Slobodan and Yara; they turn the sign around and hang it below the other signs on the wall with the "Everything is Allowed" banner; the back of the "intermission" sign says, "The Devil with Each."

The lights go out; only the center of the dance floor is lit. Yara, in the devil's black cape and horns, pulls me away from Jasna toward the lit-up center of the floor. The devil starts to dance with me. I see Mirna's hand reaching for me from outside the circle of light; then the old woman dressed as a skeleton pulls Mirna away from me. The old woman turns to me and sweeps near my feet, as if she were trying to sweep me out of the circle of light. Meanwhile the spotlight follows black-haired, black-caped Yara as she begins to dance with Mirna behind the old woman's back, while the old woman continues to sweep me away in the darkness. The audience laughs and applauds enthusiastically.

The spotlight continues following Yara and Mirna, who perform some sort of courtship dance. Mirna goads the devil, who dances gracefully toward her, but as soon as the devil reaches her, Mirna runs away. The sequence is repeated several times until the devil refuses to be goaded another time. The audience laughs. At this point the devil begins to goad Mirna; after brief hesitation, Mirna moves closer and closer until she's an arm's length away. The devil jumps and "captures" Mirna. The audience applauds. Exotic music plays. As the spotlight follows them, Mirna and the devil spin each other gracefully around the dance floor until a final, passionate embrace, followed by applause and embarrassed laughter from the audience.

Mirna and the devil remain locked in their erotic embrace when all the lights go on. The old woman stops sweeping behind me, turns around and sees Mirna in the devil's grasp. She runs toward them and starts to hit the devil with her broom. The exotic music is replaced by familiar folk music; the audience starts to form into a circle again. Jasna pulls me and Zdenek into the circle. Mirna enters the circle between Zdenek and a young man in a peasant costume similar to mine. The old woman seems to have vanished. Suddenly Mirna pulls the bewildered young man next to her into the center of the circle and begins with him the erotic courtship dance she just completed with the devil. The young man seems apprehensive at first; gradually he gets into the spirit of it and repeats the motions of the devil in the previous dance. But when he tries to "capture" Mirna, she trips him and he falls to the floor. At that point Mirna pulls me into the circle and spins me around the fallen peasant. When he tries to get up, she bends me precariously over him and kisses me passionately. She continues to display her passion for me provocatively until the peasant breaks through the larger circle and runs away. Still possessed with passion, Mirna dances with me toward Zdenek and then toward Yara, who has removed her cape and horns and once again wears slacks and a work-jacket of a type Sabina wore to the carton plant twenty years ago. Mirna pulls both of them inside the circle. The four of us form a small circle which moves in the opposite direction from the large one, and several times faster. The old woman returns; the blows of her broom are aimed at Mirna. Yara pushes Mirna into the center; Zdenek, Yara and I protect Mirna from the blows by forming a tight, closed circle around her. Jasna breaks the circumference of the large circle, pulls the line of dancers between our small circle and the old woman, and re-forms another circle around our circle of three. The new circle tightens as the dancers grasp each others' waists. The remaining dancers continue breaking the largest circle and creating smaller ones, each time forcing the old woman outside the new circumference until at last she's excluded from all the circles. Each circle is tightly closed, each moves in the opposite direction from the next, and in the center of all the concentric circles Mirna, her hands lifted high, spins her body frenziedly against ours, in the opposite direction, so that the speed is dizzying. Another sign has been added below the banner; this one says, "Each with All."

While the concentric circles turn like wheels within wheels, the music grows dimmer as it is gradually replaced by an alien sound that seems to come from the speakers' platform. It's the shrill voice of a politician, and it almost seems to emanate from the tank at the center of the red flag behind the platform. The voice blares, "The critique of the bureaucracy is justified, but it should not get out of control, it must not be allowed to slip into general and facile attacks against our entire social system..." I recognize the speech I had heard in the carton plant a few days earlier, as well as the voice of the Planning Commissioner, Marc Glavni.

The music stops altogether. The lights go out. There's a spotlight on the speakers' platform, the flag and the tank. The moment the lights go out, Mirna stops spinning and collapses into the arms of Yara and Zdenek. The concentric circles start to break up as the dancers shake their fists at the platform.

"The rightful demand of workers to play a larger role in our economic life," the voice goes on, "must not be allowed to destroy all work discipline; it must not be allowed to create chaos in production. That is a false democracy."

From behind the speakers' platform appears the old skeleton-woman with her broom. The spotlight follows her as she leaves the platform and moves toward the dancers. Every time Glavni makes an emphatic statement, she makes a threatening gesture with her broom. Every one of her threatening gestures is accompanied by spontaneous applause and laughter among the dancers.

The voice behind the tank grows yet louder. "The situation must not be allowed to get out of control. What is the sense of all the calls for workers' councils and other forms of uncontrolled participation? Does the present situation really justify the type of talk some comrades are engaged in? It is easy to launch a movement, but it is not easy to support its consequences! In the guise of reform and democratization, disruptive elements are destroying, not the deformations, but the achievements of the past twenty years! Such elements take into account neither the gravity of the hour, nor the elementary rules of democratic life, nor our international obligations. They are destroying the confidence of the working masses in their leaders —"

The skeleton-woman has started to herd people out of the factory with her broom. Her threats are met by taunts and laughter.

The speaker's voice has become deafening. "The occupations, the work stoppages, the strikes, all represent forms of destruction of the social means of production; they are inadmissible forms of self-affirmation of the working class. Workers are presenting demands in the form of ultimatums, thus creating disorder and distrust and giving rise to uncontrolled, emotional movements. The comrades who support such demands are supporting an irrational undertaking which, while sometimes claiming to support the policy we've been following for the past months, in fact compromises and undermines our policy. The recourse to strikes is a recourse to a method completely unjustified in the present circumstances. What we need most urgently is order and discipline at work! Let us be conscious of our historic tasks!"

The skeleton continues sweeping and threatening until all the dancers leave the plant. She rages and waves her broom at the last three dancers to emerge: Yara and Zdenek carrying Mirna. The crowd gathers at the street light outside the plant. As soon as the last group joins them, Mirna jumps out of Yara's and Zdenek's arms, laughing joyfully, while the old woman dressed as a skeleton removes her costume and Yara's friend Julia emerges from it. The audience applauds wildly and forms a circle around Yara and Julia in the street; near the street light inside the circle, the two friends repeat a fragment of the devil's courtship dance.

The dancers outside Mirna's plant, who laughed at the railing bureaucrat, who laughed at the tank on the flag, who laughed at death sweeping them from the dance hall, are indeed out of control. They seem determined to extend their dance to the entire world. Glavni and his fellow bureaucrats can no longer reimpose that control. The domestic agencies of repression are out of commission. That's why Glavni calls "us" to be "conscious of our historic tasks." That consciousness is the final agent of repression; only that consciousness can reimpose order and work-discipline now. Accepting rules and obligations, confiding in "our leaders" — that's the entire content of this "consciousness of our historic tasks." Glavni's speech contained a note of hysteria. He and his fellow bureaucrats no longer incarnate the

social order; their definitions of society's tasks are being met by strikes, by demonstrations, and by laughter. Former "workers" are losing their "historic consciousness," they're coming alive and defining their own tasks; the population is out of
control. Before the gathering disperses, someone announces, "Don't forget! Next
Monday we set out on our exploration." Work, order and discipline are gone from
this former factory.

Unfortunately the people gathered in front of Mirna's plant don't typify the
spirit of the rest of the population. Compared to them, Zdenek and I are "conscious," "responsible," and relatively orderly. Zdenek, in fact, rushes away from us,
explaining that the "workers' victory" at his plant was of a different nature than at
Mirna's plant, and that consequently he has to go to work the following morning.

After everyone disperses, Mirna tells Jasna, "We stopped at Titus' house on
our way to the dance. Why didn't you tell us you had already invited him?"

Jasna seems embarrassed. "I didn't want you to provide me with a lover,
Mirna."

"I wasn't providing you with anything, Jasna. I was providing myself!"

"Don't taunt me any more, Mirna," Jasna begs. "I've asked Titus to marry
me."

"Is that why he acted so strange when he saw us?" Yara asks. The four of us
start to walk home.

"Zdenek told us you stopped by his room," Jasna fells them.

"You asked him to marry you?" Mirna asks.

"Yes, Mirna, twice. Do you remember when we read the letter in which Sophia
described her experiences in Sabina's garage? That evening you intimidated me so
much —"

"I what?"

"You intimidated me, Mirna! You called me a coward, a spineless, frustrated
old maid! Titus visited me several days after that evening — and I asked him to
marry me."

Yara asks, "Was that when you told me about Vera and Adrian? Why didn't
you tell me you'd proposed to him?"

"I was happy, Yara, and I didn't want to spoil my happiness by telling you.
I knew how you've hated him since Vesna died. You were on your outing to the
mountains when he visited me. I was alone and terribly depressed after the argument with Mirna. I acted like a baby. I asked him Tissie's pathetic question: 'What's
wrong with me?' He didn't understand; he told me he had always admired my cool-
headedness and my reserve. I broke down. I told him my cool-headedness was
nothing but cowardice; I had never faced the smallest obstacles; I had led a horribly
impoverished life. I contrasted myself to the women I had admired: Luisa Nachalo
with all her lovers. Vera Neis with her two conquests, you, Mirna —"

Mirna asks, "Did he share your admiration for three such passionate —"

"No, Mirna, he didn't. Poor man. He's been so joyless for so many years! He told me awful things about Luisa and Vera."

"And me?" Mirna asks.

"I'd rather not repeat them," Jasna tells her; "I knew it was his loneliness that made him so bitter. I felt even sorrier for him than I'd felt for myself when he'd come. I thought there was no reason for him to remain so terribly alone; everything was changing; new possibilities were on everyone's horizon. In the past he intimidated me, but suddenly I saw how alike we were. He never aspired to anything more than the small corner he occupies near the bottom of the social hierarchy. He's so modest. He devoted his whole life to his dream of a better world, but he never sought anything for himself. I thought we'd make a nice couple in a quiet way, not passionate, but considerate and helpful. I asked him if he'd ever thought of marrying. He told me he had married the proletariat when he was eighteen. When I told him his present loneliness proved that his lifelong devotion has remained unrewarded and unrecognized, he told me the desire for rewards and recognition were alien to him. I asked him straight out if the thought of marrying me might ever cross his mind. Instead of answering, he told me he respected me far more than he respected the three women I admired. I was happy. I chose to interpret his answer as an affirmation. But I longed to talk to someone. I didn't dare visit you, Mirna, right after you'd thrown all those painful accusations at me. I was even more afraid to pour my heart out to you, Yarostan, because I couldn't have resisted — I would have melted —"

"You could have told me," Yara insists. "I don't hate you, but him."

"I was overjoyed to see you, Yara, I felt like telling you everything. You told me about the love games you had played on mountain tops. I wondered what Titus might say about your 'shameless individualism.' But I didn't want to talk about Vesna again. Only a few days earlier Mirna had reminded me that I had done nothing when Vesna was taken away. Besides, you were far more eager to learn the bucketfuls of secrets about Vera Krena that I had just learned from Titus. And I didn't have much of a chance to talk to you after that. The very next morning you came to tell me Yarostan was going to have Mirna taken to the hospital, for the same reasons Vesna had been taken away. I finally told both of you when you wanted me to make myself look like Luisa for Yarostan, but neither of you believed me —"

"Obviously not then," Yara says; "We thought you were looking for an excuse to stay out of our game."

"But the excuse happened to fit your plans perfectly, didn't it?" Jasna asks. "Mirna threatened to invite Titus to the dance — for me, I thought; because I was unable to satisfy my desires on my own. I refused to play your game."

I remind Jasna, "That's what you told me before. Yet here you are, playing their game. Did you change your mind? Did Mirna and Yara force you?"

"A little of both, I suppose," Jasna tells me, wrapping her arm around me. "Mirna made me positively miserable. She told me I'd never satisfy my desires on my own; I'd carry my unsatisfied desires to the grave. She asked if I'd ever held my body less than an arm's length away from the two people I've loved for a quarter of a century. And she continued taunting me; she could drive a sane person out of her mind. 'If you won't let me bring Titus for you, will you at least let me bring him for myself?' she asked. Then she told me she had been far closer to Titus than I was ever going to be. I called her a liar. So she told me that during your second prison term you had asked Titus to convince Mirna to divorce you, and when Titus had gone to her, she had tried to abandon herself to him. And she concluded her story by shouting, 'Aren't you human, Jasna? Don't you want to get even with me by taking Yarostan from me? I held your Titus in my arms! I wanted him! I would have made myself Luisa for him!' And Yara, the little devil, supported her! I couldn't stand their taunts. Last Tuesday night I went to Titus' room by myself. He seemed pleased to see me. He started explaining to me the political strategy that was necessary in the current situation, but I didn't listen. I proposed to him, just like that. And I invited him to come to the dance. He turned down the invitation to the dance, just as Yarostan had done at first. I didn't press him; I wanted his answer to my proposal. What he told me was that of all the women he knew, I was the only one he could imagine marrying. Then he became frightfully quiet. It was late and I wanted to spend the night in his room, but I was afraid to ask him. When I finally left, he accompanied me to the street telephone while I called for a taxi. I rode home feeling completely rejected. I didn't care if Mirna brought him to the dance or even if she fornicated with him on the dance floor. I decided to become Luisa for you, Yarostan. Yesterday morning I made sure you hadn't changed your mind about going to the dance with me. When I'd first invited you, I only had dancing in mind. But yesterday morning I had an altogether different dance in mind: Yara's devil dance. I woke Yara and Mirna and told them I was ready to play their game, I was through with Titus, I was in love with you. I also told Mirna that I was insulted by the fact that she wasn't the slightest bit afraid of me. Yara explained: 'Of course she's afraid of you! That's the point of the game! But her fear isn't part of your role.' It was going to be the first time in my life that I reached out for someone. But as soon as we arrived Zdenek told us Mirna had tried to invite Titus. Mirna, if you had come to the dance with him, I would have begged Yarostan to take me to the end of the world. But he didn't come, and I felt increasingly sorry for him."

"Maybe he acted so strange because he felt guilty about making you ride home by taxi," Yara says.

"Did he act strange when you saw him?" Jasna asks. We've reached Jasna's street and walk toward her house.

Yara narrates, "After we left your house we took Zdenek his costume and made him look just like the photograph of grandfather. Zdenek and Mr. Zabran live in the same neighborhood, and Mirna wanted Mr. Zabran at the dance; she wanted everyone she'd ever played love games with. She also wanted to see if Mr. Zabran would think Zdenek looked like grandfather and if I looked like Sabina. When he answered his door he just stood in his doorway and turned pale, as if he were look-ing at ghosts. For a long time he just stared at Zdenek; then he looked at Mirna and me as if he'd never seen us before. Mirna asked Mr. Zabran if he recognized Zdenek. 'He's my father,' she told him. He looked like he was going to slam the door in our faces. 'What do you want?' he asked us. I was scared. Mirna stopped smiling. She explained to him that we were on our way to the dance at her plant and asked if he wanted to come. He told us you had already invited him, and then he closed the door! It was only afterwards that Zdenek told us he and Mr. Zabran knew each other."

We've reached Jasna's house. "You're so mean," Jasna says to Mirna. "How did you think he'd respond if he'd thought Zdenek was your father? He's known your father has been dead for ten years! Did you expect him to shake the ghost's hand and invite him in? I doubt if anyone ever played a prank on him before. Poor man!" Jasna leaves us and goes into her house.

On our way home I ask Yara if Zdenek told them when he had known Titus.

"Zdenek almost didn't tell us," Yara says. "He was angry at Mirna and me for the same reason Jasna is. He told us we played with people's fears as innocently as children set fires. Then he asked Mirna how she found out Mr. Zabran and Zdenek had once suspected each other of having done something terrible. Mirna told Zdenek he was the one playing with fears. She told him Mr. Zabran had worked with you and Jan and Jasna in the carton plant, had helped her father as well as her mother, and even that she had once loved him. I added that he was the man who had taken Vesna to the hospital. That was when Zdenek told us we had probably frightened the man to death by introducing Zdenek as Mirna's father; he told us he and Mr. Zabran knew each other. They had known each other years ago when they both worked in the trade union building. They used to joke together about the emperor and his bodyguard. Suddenly Zdenek was arrested, and he was sure it was the fault of the person with whom he had joked so freely. But then he saw him in prison; that was during the time when you were in prison for the first time. Zdenek felt terrible about his suspicions; he knew Mr. Zabran must have had identical sus-picions about Zdenek. And then they saw each other years later, at the club where former prisoners meet —"

"Titus attended a meeting of the prisoners' club?" I ask with, surprise.

"Zdenek said one time he saw both of you at the same meeting, but you and Mr. Zabran didn't see each other. And then Zdenek asked us how we thought Mr. Zabran must have felt when Mirna introduced Zdenek as her father. He made us both feel bad all the way to the dance, but we forgot all about it as soon as the dance began."

When we reach our house, Yara goes directly to bed, exhausted by the day's events. But Mirna is wide awake. I ask her why she wanted to invite Titus for Jasna. "Surely that's insulting, especially after Jasna herself tried to invite him. And why did you taunt Jasna by telling her you threw yourself at Titus?"

"I wasn't inviting Titus for Jasna but for myself," she tells me, as she'd earlier told Jasna. "I wanted to complete my tram, my cast of characters, my life's lovers; I wanted my father, my brother, my husband, my devil and my friend. And I wasn't taunting Jasna!"

"What were you doing then?"

"I was telling her the truth, Yarostan, and I've told it to you several times already. Do I have to describe the vivid details to you? It happened three years before your release —"

"Mirna, I'm asking about Jasna; I don't want you to tell me what you did during the twelve years I spent in prison. You had every right to do whatever you pleased. I even asked you to divorce me so that you'd feel free to do whatever —"

"That was precisely what provoked me! Jan had disappeared; my father was dead; my mother was out of her mind. You were all I had left. And you had the nerve to send Titus on that mission —"

"At that time I thought I'd never come out again, Mirna; I thought that if you remained tied to me, you might as well have been tailed with me. What kind of a life was that for you? But you paid no attention to me. I thought you might pay more attention to Titus; Jasna is right; he's such a reasonable man, and he's always been so good to us."

"Yes, Jasna is right," Mirna says. "Titus certainly was a good man. It was precisely his goodness that killed Vesna!"

"Are we back to —"

"No, Yarostan, we're not back to Vesna. We're talking about my passion for Titus Zabran, the good Mr. Zabran. It so happens that Vesna had personal contact with that passion. That was when Vesna first exhibited that so-called illness of which she died."

"I don't understand —"

"I don't either," she tells me. "I only know what happened. I knew twelve years ago, at the time of the Magarna uprising, that two of the people in my life had a great deal in common: my mother and Titus Zabran. They both gave their lives to something higher, to God, only no one else could see that about Titus because he didn't call it God. When the Magarna workers fought against tanks in the street, I knew and Jan knew that they were fighting for themselves, for a world in which they could fulfill their dreams and satisfy their desires; to me they were fighting alongside the devil. But Titus thought they were fighting for something else, something outside themselves; for God, and you stood somewhere between Titus and me. But when the tanks slaughtered the Magarna workers and they had to be buried in mass graves, and when you and Jan disappeared, I was ashamed and I felt guilty. I thought the devil had betrayed us. I was ashamed of my passion, my selfishness. And of course my mother made the most of my shame. She even tried to take Vesna away from me. And I convinced myself she was right. I looked frantically for Titus, not as a friend, not as someone I could love, but as someone who would help me find you and Jan. I left a message for him at the union building. When he came I told him you had both disappeared and my father had been fired from his job because of a letter that had come from abroad which they never received. He was furious about the arrests; he told me people couldn't be arrested because of a letter they hadn't even read. He even went to the police to argue with them. He helped my father get a pension from the union, and he helped me get a pass to visit you. And that was all Titus was to me, that was all anyone was to me: someone who helped with pensions and passes. Except you. My father's death kept me from using my pass during the period stamped on it. When I went to the union building again, I learned that something had happened to Titus, but they wouldn't tell me what. I managed to get his address. I found his room. One of his neighbors told me he'd been arrested. His neighbor referred to Titus the same way Jasna just did: such a quiet, modest man, kind to children, with no harm in him; poor man. I had no one left in the world, and I thought my mother had been right. I had sacrificed everyone I loved to the devil — to my passion, if you prefer that word. Titus' visit after his release was like the beginning of spring. He became everything to me; Jan, you, my father. Vesna was six and still hadn't started school. My mother was a shouting invalid who was turning Vesna against me. The sequence of tragedies couldn't go on. I threw my arms around him hungrily as soon as he walked in. But he backed away from me. Vesna was looking at me, and I felt ashamed, horribly ashamed before both of them. From that day on, Vesna grew as attached to Titus as to my mother. She worshipped the good man, she hated me, and she feared you. Poor Vesna didn't have any reason to feel any other way toward us. From the time she was able to walk, she'd had nothing in her life but chores. She nursed Yara; she ministered to the sick old woman; she bought the groceries and cooked most of the meals. She was such a frail thing, she simply couldn't do all that. One day she collapsed. I didn't know what to do; I had never had anything to do with doctors. I took a bus to Titus'. He contacted a doctor and brought him to the house. The doctor said Vesna had a slight heart murmur, and said she had to rest all the time. Titus came to visit Vesna every day for a week. They liked each other and they were just like each other. Vesna got well in a week; I wasn't able to force her to spend her days resting. It was to save Vesna the strain of carrying a package to you that I asked Titus to visit you. And that was when you sent Titus to me with that mission —"

"Mirna, everything you're telling me convinces me that your loyalty to me, or whatever you'd like to call it, locked you into a prison many times worse than the one I was in —"

"That's exactly what I'm trying to tell you," she snaps. "You sent Titus on that mission because you wanted to escape from that worse prison. You didn't want to share my load. You were wrong! Half that load was yours. If the devil was responsible for what had happened, if my selfishness, greed, desire had brought it all about, it was you and not Titus who had shared that desire with me. I was furious — at you, not at Titus. I knew every one of his words came from you. He told me I was still young and energetic; with a little care I could still be beautiful. He asked me if I had ever thought of divorcing you. I became hysterical. I asked him if you had told him to ask me that, or if he knew you were going to disappear like Jan had, if they had taken you from me forever. Vesna begged me not to scream at Titus, since it wasn't he who had taken both of you from me. Titus picked Vesna up with tears in his eyes. He told me he wasn't asking for you but for himself; he said he was fond of Vesna and of me; he said Vesna, Yara and I deserved more than the miserable drudgery we lived daily; he said he had hoped I would let him help us. Then he left. I knew he wasn't speaking for himself. I knew you had convinced him I couldn't function as a 'conscious and combative proletarian' because of the chain around my neck. I knew he wasn't fond of me, but of his precious proletariat. But I was starved for love, and since his fondness came from you, I convinced myself I would be loving you. Passion stirred inside me for the first time since the Magarna rising. It came because I thought, or let myself imagine, that I was desired. It was the passion I had learned from Sabina, the devil's passion, the passion I then thought had driven my father, my brother and you to hell. I was in a frenzy for two days. And I was happy. I took 'a little care' and made myself young again. Little Yara noticed; she said, 'You look beautiful mommy.' Vesna noticed too. She grew frightened, she cried, and she stayed away from me. She spoke to me only once; she told me she could see the devil in me, just as her grandmother had told her. She'd had no more joy in her life than my mother, and she wanted to kill it in me just as my mother did. Two days after his visit, I went to his room directly from work, so as to avoid Vesna's reproachful, fearful eyes. I had to wait for him. As soon as he unlocked the door, I slipped into his room. It was bare, with nothing but a cot, a table, a few books and a cheap record player. I threw my arms around him. I told him, 'I'm not only fond of you, Titus; I love you; I'm yours.' I begged him to take me. But he backed away from me. His face was terror stricken. He looked at me as if I were a nightmare, as if I were reenacting some horrible event he'd experienced in his past. He saw the devil in me, the same devil Vesna had seen. His frightened eyes stared at my forehead as if the word 'incest' were stamped across it. Then he admitted you had put him up to the whole thing, you had asked him to talk to me about divorce, you had even suggested he try to repair the wasted youth, the wasted children. 'But I have nothing to offer you,' he told me. My whole body ached with shame, with the shame I'd felt when I'd embraced him after his release, with the shame I'd felt when I'd dragged myself to my mother's house after your arrest. I became afraid of what he had seen in me; I was as terrified as he when I backed out of his room. I dragged myself home, sat in the kitchen and cried. Vesna joined me and cried with me. She stroked my hair, kissed me, consoled me. She hugged me and told me she was glad I hadn't done what I'd set out to do; she was glad I had chased the devil out of me. She no longer hated me. When I returned to the joyless drudgery I became Vesna's best friend, and I remained her best friend until I learned the date of your release. The first time I told Vesna about you I thought I saw a gleam in her eye, a gleam of anticipation, almost joy. It must have been there, since Yara saw Vesna kiss herself in the mirror. But the joy conflicted with something else that was already deeply embedded in Vesna, it conflicted with that God my mother had driven into her heart. She wanted to love you, but she knew she shouldn't, because love is the devil; she killed her love for you just as my mother had killed her love for anyone other than her wooden Lord. It was that Lord, that morality, that sense of duty or whatever else people want to call it, that killed Vesna. Yes, killed her. Because that fearful Vesna wasn't the real Vesna. I didn't know it then but Yara knew. The real Vesna, the whole, natural and normal Vesna had passion inside her just as we did. She'd been twisted into something unnatural by my mother, by school, by the lives we led. She almost came with us the day Yara and I went to tell you prisoners would actually be released at the end of their terms. But she held herself back. She had been taught not to traffic with demons, counter-revolutionaries or saboteurs. Her desires conflicted with her moral duty. Yara's boundless, unashamed joy almost infected her. Almost. Before that visit, Yara and I put on our best clothes; we fixed our hair; we didn't stop smiling at each other. The devil lit fires inside both of us. I know we infected you with our joy. When we returned home my shame was gone; I burned with passion. It was I who taught Yara to play her love games that very afternoon. I told her that when you returned you'd make love to all three of us. I threw Yara on my bed and showed her how you'd touch us, embrace us, hug us, exactly as Sabina had once shown me Jan would embrace me. Yara had nothing but the devil inside her. She screamed with joy. Neither of us saw Vesna standing in the doorway. When Vesna demanded indignantly, 'What are you two doing?' she sounded just like my mother when she'd seen Jan and me before she chased him out of the house, or when she looked in on Sabina and me the first time you came to our house. I was furious. I wasn't ready to be driven back to joyless drudgery, not by a living daughter who didn't yet have the old woman's dried up flesh. Yara and I both leaped at her and pulled her to bed. The devil drove both of us. We showed her what her father would do to her as soon as he returned. We both turned her and kissed her lips and hugged her until I felt a horrible paralysis flowing through her trembling, freezing body. Her face was a mask of death. She stared like an idiot. She'd become the old woman! I was terrified. All my shame returned. I tried to vomit the devil out of me, but nothing came. I pleaded with Vesna. I shrieked. Yara shook Vesna and scolded her for spoiling our happiness. But the idiot's mask didn't leave Vesna's face: she was paralyzed. I didn't know what to do and became hysterical. I had gone to Titus when she'd been sick before, but I couldn't make myself go to him again. I asked Yara to go to him, but she insisted he'd only make Vesna worse; she insisted Vesna was playing with us. I didn't believe her. But when I tried to carry Vesna to her bed, she kicked me and screamed; she ran to the old woman's room, lay down next to her, and stared at the ceiling, paralyzed again. I knew Yara was right; Vesna was playing with us. But I didn't know how to put an end to her game, I didn't know how to reclaim her for you, for Yara and for me. I wasn't strong enough. My mother and Titus claimed her; each of them had recognized Vesna as one of theirs from the moment they'd set eyes on her. Yara knew they were wrong; she knew Vesna was ours. But I wasn't sure. I too had been turned into half an idiot by my mother and by the daily drudgery. I knew Yara had told the school authorities that Vesna was sick. But at that time I didn't know Jasna had told Titus. I couldn't imagine what had brought Titus to our house; I thought God must have told him his Vesna was sick again. I couldn't talk to him. I couldn't even look at him. I was filled with shame. I let Yara do all the protesting and pleading. Only once did I beg Titus to leave her where she was. He called me a criminal for keeping Vesna in bed with an insane old woman. A criminal. My mother had told me I carried the devil's sword. Yara insisted she knew her own sister and the doctors didn't know her. Titus ridiculed Yara and me for acting as if Yara knew more about sickness than the doctors in the hospital. He had an ambulance come. Yara tried to stop them from touching Vesna. Two nurses had to hold Yara while Vesna was carried away: 'Mommy stop them!' she screamed at me. 'Don't let them take her; they'll kill our Vesna!' The next day and several days after that, I didn't go to work. For the first time since I'd been hired, I asked myself what all that work was for. Yara and I went to the hospital, but they didn't let us past the front desk; they told us Vesna was in a coma and in critical condition. We begged them to let us take her home with us, but they treated us like dirt and had us wait outside the hospital, even when it rained: They were civil to us only on the day they told us, 'Your daughter died at 1:20 this morning in an ambulance during transit to the mental hospital.'"

Yara had already told me how our Vesna had died, but my eyes fill with tears when Mirna gives me her account. I nevertheless manage to protest, "You can't blame Titus for what he did. I wouldn't have done anything different. In fact, when Yara visited me for the last time before my release, I insisted just as rigidly —"

"I know; we were all half-idiots," she says, taking my hand and pulling me toward our bedroom. There aren't any tears in Mirna's eyes. "We were all deformed by a world of doctors, police and prying old women. Yara was the only one who knew that by killing the devil inside us, we killed our selves, and she couldn't help but know because there was nothing inside her but the devil. She couldn't help but know that the devil is not the assassin; that passion doesn't kill, that the sword that kills isn't the devil's but God's. God is the murderer. When I heard Yara tell you she'd seen Vesna kissing herself in the mirror, I knew my shame had been brought on by a lie. I knew it wasn't the passion that had killed Vesna, I knew it hadn't been the devil who had driven a sword through her. It's only those who deny the devil who carry a sword! Vesna had passion inside her too, and it wasn't the passion that killed her; that passion made her natural and healthy and beautiful. What killed her was the denial of her passion; what killed her was the God that had been driven into her by saintly old women and good, modest men. That was what possessed her, what stopped her from gratifying herself, what froze her organs, what killed her joy, what robbed her of pleasure. It was the goodness, the shame and the guilt, that possessed Vesna, that strangled what was in her. Do you understand what I'm telling you?"

I'm half asleep. I try to repeat what she's saying in my own words. "Yara convinced you your desires were natural, whereas the guilt, the shame, the denial of desires were alien to you and to Vesna as well. I'm not sure I agree —"

"I'm not trying to convince you. I'm explaining why I wanted Titus to come to the dance. I wanted him for my sake, not for Jasna's. Yara and I both wanted to see what effect he'd have on me now, to see if my organs still fill up with shame and guilt — I wanted to know, because tomorrow we're going to decide what steps to take next."

The following day, last Friday, Mirna took Yara to her former factory at the hour when she used to go to work. She told me what "next steps" they had decided to take when I returned from the carton plant that night. The former workers of her plant decided, probably on Mirna's suggestion, to take a "journey across the country," to take bus excursions to other plants in other cities and regions, if possible to other countries. The purpose of the journey is to see what others are doing so as to explore what can be done. Mirna and Yara eagerly invited me to accompany them, but I turned down their invitation. A confrontation has just taken place in the carton plant; it's the type of confrontation I had been looking forward to.

About two weeks ago, when Jasna had come to our house to celebrate the strike at Mirna's plant and to read your previous letter, Jasna had speculated about the possibility that Marc Glavni had caused our arrest twelve years ago by reporting the arrival of your letter to the police. Jasna had also told us that Glavni and Vera Krena were going to hold a debate over the radio. The speech Glavni made during this debate was tape recorded by Yara's university friend and re-broadcast at the dance.

I had forgotten about the coming debate as soon as Jasna had mentioned it. I didn't think of it again until last Monday, when the radio announced the two speakers, listing as part of their background the fact that they had both been production workers at the carton plant "before the seizure of power by the working class." My fellow workers were disappointingly eager to hear a debate between two of their predecessors who had risen so high. Several months ago the city's main radio station had launched a policy of "complete and objective information" which had a great deal in common with your friend Hugh's insistence that "two sides of every question" be presented. Debates between two bureaucrats seem to satisfy the radio station's notion of "objectivity."

The two speeches had not originally been given as part of a debate. Krena's speech was given to an immense gathering of workers at a large factory. It was one of the most "radical" speeches I've yet heard from the mouth of a bureaucrat. She urged the gathered workers to take matters out of the hands of bureaucrats and into their own. Glavni's speech, which I summarized earlier, was originally given in a studio of the radio station, and it was not intended as a direct attack on Krena but as a critique of "certain comrades." Krena was certainly included among those "certain comrades," but Glavni also included many of his own earlier positions among the positions he now opposed. As I mentioned earlier, he urged workers not to allow themselves to go "out of control" and to leave matters in the hands of the bureaucrats.

Jasna and I had attended a lecture given by Krena about two months ago. At that time Vera Krena had spoken about "leaders applying policies which will earn them their leading roles," and had made statements like "We must earn our authority through our acts." The speech I heard in the carton plant indicated that Glavni is not alone in having changed his mind recently. But Vera's change of mind moves in the opposite direction from Glavni's.

In the speech I heard last Monday Vera negated virtually everything she had said on the earlier occasion. "The execution of the policy we defended is no longer the affair of leading organs, but of the entire working population," she shouted. "People cannot be active in any sector of their lives — neither on their jobs nor at their plant meetings nor in any of their social or economic relations — if they are not politically active. The working population cannot be politically active if it does not determine the content as well as the form of its social as well as economic activity. This is our policy! We condemn the current policy of certain comrades who have retreated incessantly in the face of external pressures." (Vera's reference to "certain comrades" is probably what made this speech suitable for a debate with one of those certain comrades.) "We condemn the deliberate suppression of information in response to external pressures! We condemn the fact that policies are still today defined not by the clearly expressed will of the working population but by a self-appointed bureaucracy that does nothing but transmit instructions and orders from abroad! We are ready to use all the means at our disposal — at the disposal of the entire working population — to put our program into effect. We will oppose the replacement of our program by all the weapons available to the working class, including the general strike!"

The workers at the plant where the speech had been given applauded wildly, as did most of the workers at the carton plant. I was surprised that Glavni's "law, order and discipline" speech, which followed Vera's, also received some applause.

The speeches by our two "former fellow workers" were the main topic of conversation at the carton plant during the days when Mirna and Yara made the preparations for their dance. At least two "strikes" a day (one-hour long work stoppages for meetings) were called, usually by one of the office workers. The work crew at the plant now consists of eighteen production and thirty-two office workers. In the course of those meetings, the carton plant workers split into two "parties," but the alignments in these parties could not easily be explained in terms of people's "relation to the productive forces." Thirty of the office workers became militant supporters of Vera's "program." Twelve of the eighteen production workers and the remaining two office workers were partisans of Glavni's position. At first I couldn't understand why anyone would support Glavni's authoritarian, bureaucratic stand, but gradually the reasons became obvious to me. The two office workers who supported him are both union officials for whom Glavni is the direct gate for promotions to supervisory and managerial posts. Among the production workers who supported him, some aspire to follow Glavni's own path to supervisory and managerial positions; others, like Mirna until very recently, are intimidated, I should say silenced, by the prospect of tanks, arrests, and military invasion.

Six production workers, including myself, remained outside of either "party." I also kept out of all the discussions. If Vera Krena were merely another member of the working population for whom she speaks, she would indeed be a popular tribune expressing what everyone feels and wants. But Vera is not a popular tribune. She's a demagogue. She's expressing what everyone feels and wants not because she feels it, not because she's one of the working population, but because she and her clique are aiming to become the permanent institutional "voice" and "mind" of that working population. Vera's "program" would be fulfilled if ruling bureaucrats justified their rule as the fulfillment of the working population's aspirations and desires while that working population continued to engage daily in the same joyless drudgery.

At first the discussions that took place at the daily "strikes" were arguments about whether to Sign petitions in favor of Vera's clique, or to demonstrate "as we did twenty years ago," using the carton plant as a source for posters and placards.

But gradually a new and much more interesting element appeared. Ironically, it was one of the workers who had supported Glavni's speech who introduced the "new" into the discussions. He objected to petitions as well as demonstrations with an argument very similar to that of a worker you had described in an earlier letter. He said petitions and demonstrations would only attract the attention of the police. He was naturally called a coward by other workers, especially by the office workers. He then said the point was not to make a display of our courage nor to be arrested; the point was to change the nature of our activity. He suggested something very similar to Mirna's "excursion," though on a much more limited scale. Workers from the carton plant should directly contact workers in other plants in the same sphere of production and begin to explore ways of transforming our activity.

All the thirty office workers who had enthusiastically supported Vera's radical speech opposed this worker's suggestions, whereas fourteen of the eighteen production workers, including ten supporters of Glavni's disciplinarianism, supported the suggestions. I mention the numbers because I think the alignments are revealing. The office workers know that the transformation envisaged by this worker will not increase the importance of their roles, but will on the contrary eliminate the need for office workers. By remaining staunch supporters of Vera Krena they demonstrate that they understand perfectly the real nature and content of Vera's "radicalism."

Unlike the office workers, the production workers didn't call for meetings and they didn't argue in favor of the new suggestions. At meetings called by office workers they continued to defend Glavni's conservative positions. But in practice they started to implement, not Vera Krena's real intentions, but what Vera had said: they began to take matters into their own hands. Last Wednesday, the day before Mirna's dance, an informal "delegation" of carton plant workers decided to visit one of the paper factories which produces some of the materials we use. I wanted to accompany this "delegation" but they decided to make their visit on the day of the dance. Last Friday all the carton plant's production workers gathered around the four "delegates," eager to learn about their visit. They told us the majority of the workers at the paper factory had welcomed them with open arms. The paper workers said they received instructions and specifications from supervisors and engineers and they never understood the significance of the instructions because they had no contact with those who used the paper they produced. And four days ago, this past Monday, a similar "delegation" of paper workers arrived at the carton plant. They told us they had come to learn what was actually required by the workers who processed their paper at the next stage; they wanted to find out how many of the instructions and specifications were nothing but impositions of arbitrary authority or academic rules taught to engineers in university courses, rules which served no practical purpose. Before they left, they eagerly told us that during the afternoon's discussion they had figured out several ways to simplify production, eliminate waste, and do the required work at a fraction of the time it takes now.

The carton plant workers decided to create more informal "delegations" to visit food packaging plants and other users of cartons. I plan to take such a trip two days from now. That's why I turned down Mirna's invitation to accompany her on the "exploratory journey."

Mirna and Yara had also invited Zdenek to accompany them on their excursion, but he told them he couldn't imagine leaving his plant for a whole week, now that it's run "by the workers themselves." When we had discussed your letter two weeks ago and Zdenek had defended unions against your attacks, Mirna had characterized him as "conservative." That characterization conflicted with my original impressions of Zdenek. When I first met him in prison, I was deeply impressed by his determined opposition to anyone or anything that stood between the workers and their world. I was also deeply impressed by the strike that broke out at Zdenek's plant, when all posts were occupied by elected workers. But I'm starting to realize I'm still applying a standard I learned from Luisa almost a quarter of a century ago. Mirna is applying a significantly different standard. I don't know if she learned it from Jan or if she rediscovered it on her own, but I do know that her attitudes are very similar to Jan's. The only questions she asks are: Is it for us, the living? Is it for our desires, our passions, our dreams?

When I ask myself Mirna's questions, I lose half of my enthusiasm for Zdenek's strike, and for my own present activity as well. Zdenek's fellow workers have not appropriated the world as a field for possibilities, as a field for projects, as a non-existent which is to be created by us. Zdenek and his comrades reached Luisa's goal: they created a "genuine workers' union." I don't agree with your friend Clesec's suggestion that nothing at all changes when the workers themselves take charge of the existing production apparatus. But I do agree that such an act does not create a new form of human activity, since what is appropriated is precisely the old activity, the existing world. And this existing world is not a field for the realization of projects, but a negation of the very possibility of projects. It is not this activity, even if appropriated and managed by us, that we're glimpsing on the horizon because it is at the very center of our present lives. It is what surrounds us now, what we inherited. It wasn't projected by us but by the history of capital. Jan knew that we could never appropriate this activity because it appropriates us. Mirna knows that Zdenek's commitment is not to satisfy his own desires, but to satisfy the needs of the productive forces. For Zdenek, as for Luisa, the repression that was unacceptable when managers and union representatives were imposed from outside becomes acceptable when workers themselves assume the roles of managers and union representatives. Zdenek has told me several times that he has worked much harder and has been far more "responsible" at his job since the strike at his plant took place. Zdenek's daily activity remains drudgery; it isn't there that he expects to satisfy desires or realize dreams; the desires and dreams are not part of his "work", but part of his "politics," and he "realizes" them by attending meetings of the club of former political prisoners.

I'm having a hard time convincing myself that I turned down Mirna's invitation to her journey for better reasons than Zdenek's. At the carton plant we're no longer creating a "genuine union" so as to replace the managers and foremen with elected managers and foremen. But we still observe limits that the former workers of Mirna's plant no longer observe; we're still committed to a world we ourselves did not create, a world which we inherited; to borrow your image, we're still stepping into a house that's already completely built, furnished and decorated. The delegation of paper workers who came to the carton plant asked what was required at the next stage of the production process; they did not ask if this production process was required. The delegations that leave from the carton plant are asking what is required of us at the next stage of the process; they are not asking whether or not cartons are required. We're not asking Mirna's questions. We may ultimately desire cartons. But why do we begin with the desire for cartons? Is it the desire for cartons that's been repressed by capital and the state? Is it the desire for cartons that we're struggling to satisfy? Is that really a place to begin?

I think that my attitude to my activity is similar to Sabina's attitude to her activity in the fascinating research center you described. I'm excited about what's happening in the carton plant, but I have numerous reservations about its significance, especially when I compare it to Mirna's present activity. The purpose of Mirna's excursion is to meet fellow human beings, to find out who they are and what they desire, and above all to learn to communicate with them about the present and about all the possible futures. The purpose of the "delegations" setting out from the carton plant is much more limited. Their purpose too is to meet and communicate with fellow human beings, but only within the realm of paper and cartons. In other words, we're seeking contacts with each other within the walled-in realm we're at present locked into, without first destroying the walls that separate us from each other. We're not going out to meet human beings but paper producers and carton users; we're talking to them about specifications for simplified paper and carton production before learning who they are or what they desire. We're not learning to communicate about our desires and possibilities because such communication has never been tried, it may be slow and difficult to begin, and we lack the patience and the time for that because our tasks are far too pressing, the cartons are waiting, we're still their servants.

I was full of admiration for Sabina, Tissie and Ted when I read your description of the technological "toys" to which they've given themselves access. But I have the same reservations about those "toys" as I have about the delegations leaving the carton plant. If I'm not able to communicate with the people who presently surround me, people whose language and experiences I share, why would I want to fly to every corner of the globe at lightning speed? Wouldn't such activity remove us yet further from what you've described as your life's goal: communication with our contemporaries, human community? In what sense would my experience in such a vehicle differ from the vehicle's own "experience"? The prospect of a world of beings buzzing through the air at lightning speed frightens me. The fact that the meteors won't collide with each other doesn't console me. The reduction of human beings to self-propelled capsules, the reduction of the wealth of human qualities to the two most quantifiable qualities, direction and speed, strikes me as the final impoverishment of the species short of complete annihilation. Sabina herself expressed some reservations to you. What surprises me is that she expressed them so hesitantly. I find that her present activity conflicts irreconcilably with her own goals. When you joined her in the garage ten years ago she told you, very much in the spirit of Jan and Mirna, that her axioms were "my life, my desires, my capacities". Like Jan and Mirna she fought for a world where the development of these "axioms" was possible. Has she reduced her life's axioms to one: velocity? Are the buzzing vehicles a fulfillment of her life or its absolute negation? She wants Tissie alongside her while she engages in her "research"; she even begged you to stay with her. Sabina of all people knows that her life, her desires, her capacities cannot develop outside a human world, a community of human beings she can talk to, touch, embrace, love. Yet she's enthusiastically designing a plastic armor that would separate each from all. The condition Sabina's research is helping create is not a new human condition. In prison it's known as solitary confinement. It's one of the worst forms of torture.

I have to admit I don't understand Sabina. The few times she expressed her life's goals to you, she sounded like Jan or Mirna. Yet her project has nothing in common with theirs: it has everything in common with the life project of a person she seems to despise: George Alberts. Isn't it Alberts' life project that she's carrying on, during a time when "everything is possible"? Why? What illusions does she still retain about that project? Perhaps several centuries ago it was possible to think that industrialization would create an environment hospitable to human life, to the realization of human desires, to the development of human capacities. It was possible to think this before the process began; such a belief was illusory as soon as industrialization started. Human life was immediately impoverished; the wealth of human activities was reduced to the one single activity: wage labor, or Mirna's words, joyless drudgery; human desires were sacrificed to the needs of the productive apparatus; human capacities were blocked, stunted, frozen and eventually removed from life and relegated to the realm of Utopian dreams. Is Sabina's present project what has to be born or what has to die? Sabina told you the ruling order suppressed the development of her plastic vehicle. Maybe it did. But did Sabina oppose that ruling order because it suppressed the development of plastic vehicles? Jan opposed the ruling order because it suppressed us, the living, not because it suppressed vehicles or cartons, or even because it kept "the workers themselves" from developing the vehicles and cartons. It's always been "the workers themselves" who developed the vehicles and cartons! They poured their whole lives, all their desires and capacities, into the cartons and vehicles!

Undoubtedly Sabina, like Zdenek and I, would have been far too involved in pressing tasks to accompany Mirna and Yara on their excursion, their roaming across the country as free as birds, their visits to other cities in which they expect to find only friends. They're not interested in freeing the productive forces, in eliminating fetters to their development. They're looking for human beings eliminating fetters to their own development. If I were to summarize their "guiding axioms," I couldn't find better words than: "my life, my desires, my capacities."

I don't want to exaggerate the lucidity of my two comrades. They convinced Jasna to accompany them on their trip. Before they left, Yara told me, with unreserved enthusiasm, that she couldn't wait to ask Jasna more details about Vera Krena's relations with her husband and her lover; apparently Titus recently told Jasna things she hadn't known. Yara is on a quest for a world without bureaucrats, yet she remains fascinated by the private lives of those whose social activity stifles her own life.

I expect them back in two or three days. Yara is right: I love all three of them. I miss them terribly. If they intend to visit your part of the world on their next journey, or on the one after that, I won't turn down their invitation. I know you only from your letters, Sophia, and I would like very much to see you, to talk to you, to hold you in my arms. If you're still able to say "I love you, Yarostan," even if only because that phrase has become your "life's motto," then I can no longer keep myself from feeling, and saying,

I love you, Sophia, *Yarostan.*

Sophia's eighth letter

Dear Yarostan,

I don't know how to begin. I can't bring myself to tell you what happened here, I can't even make myself believe it.

It's over! Everything is over. The sun we saw on the horizon didn't rise! It's as if everything that happened during the past few weeks was a dream, as if nothing at all had happened. It's worse than that. It's as if we were all dead and had come to life only long enough to dream we were alive.

I'm home with Sabina in a world that hasn't changed. We haven't been able to find Tina, Pat or Tissie. Ted is in jail. And I can't continue writing this letter because my eyes are so full of tears I can't see.

I'm trying again a day later. Your letter has been with us for a week. Sabina and I discussed everything in it several times. But I simply couldn't bring myself to tell you what we've experienced since I last wrote you. I even asked Sabina to write you, and to tell you I was too sick to write. She told me she couldn't possibly replace me because "your letters are love letters, Sophia; I'd like very much to communicate with Mirna again, but not by letter." So would I. Yarostan — with you and Mirna and Yara and all of you. During the whole past week I wished I were among you instead of here.

I'm afraid Mirna's excursions can no longer include all the areas where human beings live. This area is back to "normal." The destruction of limits, the birth of possibilities — are no longer taking place here. People have returned to the labors that restrict their frontiers and destroy their possibilities. The police arrested hundreds of people at Luisa's factory and occupied the plant. At other plants the union announced a "victory" and workers returned to their jobs. The police attacked the occupied university. Ted's print shop was attacked by the police when it was being used day and night by hundreds of people. Postal and transportation workers returned to their jobs after their unions announced "victories." At one large assembly plant the union had workers vote on a list of demands before "calling off" the strike. I had a hard time taking it all in, and I still can't believe so much activity could have been repressed so quickly. I don't have any explanations. I don't want to be the "genius" who now "understands" that so many people failed to realize their desires because of "One, two, three, Bang — the key, which happens to be right here in my pocket." I now know that the political strategists who "understand" why so many people didn't realize their variegated, contradictory and unpredictable desires, in reality understand nothing except their own miserable desire to "lead."

A week of discussions with Sabina has convinced me that I don't have any "keys." I have less of a right than anyone to make a critique of others' practice. You and Sabina may have fallen into traps. I was never out of a trap. Except for an instant which I failed to prolong, my only desire has been to be led by the nose. There was never any reason to repress anything I was doing. I've never been free. Free human beings can't be repressed; they have to be destroyed.

Sabina and I didn't spend all week discussing me. We mainly talked about your letters. Not only the letter that came a week ago, but also the two Daman had brought to the so-called "council office," which seems so unreal now. It was only a week ago that Sabina learned about the strike at Mirna's plant, and about your "confession." Of course the first thing I asked her was if she had known you and Luisa had been lovers.

"Did I know! Yarostan wagged as if he were Luisa's tail! How can Yarostan describe that affair so naively? He was being shaped, like dough —" Sabina even remembers the day when Titus first brought you to our house soon after the war. "Zabran was as proud as if he were displaying a princess he'd saved from dragons. And Luisa introduced her new fellow worker to us as someone who'd been a thief and had slept in alleys until Titus recruited him to the resistance organization and transformed him into the most admirable of killers. Luisa wanted him on that very day. 'A second Nachalo!' she told us. 'Right off the streets! Isn't he beautiful?' Luisa was determined to do with Yarostan what she'd failed to do with Nachalo. She was determined to shape him into a servant of a project that wasn't his own. She tried to make him an organizer, a magnet. But although she put all of her mind as well as her body into her task, she failed miserably. Apparently he did become something of a magnet to Jasna and some of the others, but the project he carried wasn't Luisa's; it was Jan's. Yarostan could no more be made to serve the organization than Nachalo. Luisa tried to teach him what she'd tried to teach Nachalo. But thanks to his friendship with Jan, Yarostan didn't learn what she'd tried to teach Nachalo but what she'd learned from him. He did become a little bit of a second Nachalo. That's why Luisa abandoned him in the heat of the struggle for a hunk of more flexible dough."

I remind her, "Yarostan had the impression Luisa succeeded in communicating her political ideas to him. He says he didn't reject Luisa's positions until his second prison term."

"Yarostan also had the impression that Luisa's house embodied 'Sabina's outlook,'" she continues sarcastically; "he had the impression that all relations were open, nothing was left unsaid, there were no taboos, nothing was forbidden, and while he was having that impression he was being manipulated, shaped into something he was going to hate: a politician, a so-called rank-and-file leader. His whole training was underhanded. Nothing was said. Yarostan thinks he treated you as a toy! If so, he learned from her, because he was her toy, and everyone knew except you and he. Yarostan was a hoodlum to her, and he never became anything more."

I object to that. "You're exaggerating. Luisa didn't share George Alberts' prejudices until after we emigrated; she'd never called anyone a hoodlum until I brought Ron home —"

"The prejudices were there already then," Sabina insists, "and she didn't get those prejudices from Alberts. It's obvious where Alberts got them. During the war he had associated with an altogether different class of people from the proletarians and organizers he'd known before. When he returned to his 'family' after the war, he was a successful physicist, and Luisa's friends seemed like so much 'trash' to him. I know Luisa couldn't stomach him. She paraded Yarostan in and out of the bedroom so as to infuriate Alberts. And she knew Alberts would be furious precisely because Yarostan was 'trash' to him. She understood Alberts' social 'tastes' because her own were already very similar to his. Luisa was no longer the organizer who had picked Nachalo up in the street. Since that day she had associated with officers in the 'popular army,' with union functionaries who became government officials, she had moved in circles of eminently respectable people. They were the 'comrades' she had in mind when she spoke of downtrodden proletarians; it was to this level of respectability that she wanted to raise Yarostan. And until she raised him, he was trash to her. But you're right. She didn't express this contempt for her lover directly. She did use the word hoodlum already then, but not to characterize Yarostan. Don't you even remember a fragment of the conversations Luisa had with Titus Zabran?"

"Not one fragment, Sabina! That was over twenty years ago! You're the one who is odd for remembering, not I for forgetting!"

"I wouldn't feel bad for having a bad memory, Sophia, but for having to take someone else's word about an event I had experienced. How can you let everything in your head just lie where it falls, without ever moving it around? There's no such thing as a bad memory; you're just lazy! Luisa used the word 'hoodlum' daily. But you're right, she didn't call Yarostan a hoodlum — not directly. She reserved the term for Yarostan's best friend. Every time Zabran came over they'd groan to each other about Jan Sedlak's 'deplorable' influence on Yarostan, about Jan's total lack of self-discipline, about the incoherence of Jan's political outlook. They called him a lumpen element, a hooligan, a hoodlum — all of which was taboo, forbidden in Luisa's house. They said such horrible things about Jan that I couldn't wait to meet him. I didn't get my chance until the first day of the strike. On that day I watched their protégé, Yarostan, mess up all their plans. I didn't understand the politics then; I still don't. But I knew from Zabran's and Luisa's faces that something had fallen apart for them, and during the day I learned that it was their Pygmalion, Yarostan. Actually the scheme was simple enough, and I think I understood it even then. In theory the workers were supposed to be seizing power over the productive forces, but in practice, as Yarostan told us in his second letter, the 'workers' organization' was going to replace the capitalist class as the manager of production. Workers were supposed to experience this feat as their victory, the way they did here last week. The task of Yarostan, the rank-and-file militant, was to pretend he desired such a 'victory', and to parade this desire in front of other workers who didn't yet know this was what all workers wanted. The 'deepest layers of the proletariat itself' had to be the ones who defined the 'historical tasks of the proletariat.' But Yarostan sat and daydreamed. Luisa and Zabran, at the risk of being called manipulators, had to define the historical tasks; Vera and Marc immediately backed them up. But then Jan threw a wrench into their apparatus. He started shouting that the workers' real struggle wouldn't begin until workers tore down the factories, dismantled the machines and burned the productive forces. I shouted bravo, Jasna applauded. And Yarostan laughed! Luisa and Zabran were furious."

"Why were you so enthusiastic about what Jan said?" I ask her. "That enthusiasm seems to conflict with your whole life's commitment. Yarostan referred to that contradiction in his newest letter —"

"Because I was a schizophrenic already then!" Sabina exclaims. "Or maybe that was when my schizophrenia began. I applauded because Jan had thrown a wrench into Luisa's and Zabran's machinery, and also because what he said made a lot of sense to me, and still does. I even understood some of the implications of what he said. During the days that followed he told me that as a boy he had lived among streams, forests and fields and had loved to explore their secrets; ever since he'd become a worker he'd been reduced to an appendage of a machine. He told me if revolution and freedom meant anything, they certainly couldn't mean a struggle for the freedom to stand at the very same machine every living day. To Jan revolution meant a new start. It meant taking up again where he'd left off in his boyhood. I thought I agreed with him, but I didn't understand his position as a rejection of technology. I combined Alberts' position with Jan's and got what I thought was a perfect synthesis. What I had in mind was the dispersal of the technology in the forests and fields, and I thought people would relate to it the same way they related to the trees and the streams, not for mutilation and enslavement, but for adventure, exploration, travel and enjoyment. My synthesis was overstretched; it didn't work. But I didn't find that out until last week. In the carton plant I wasn't even aware of a contradiction, and in my guts I supported every stand Jan took. I suppose you don't remember the discussion of the slogans either. That took place on the second day of the strike. I didn't understand the political significance of the discussion, but I helped Jan mess up the united front Luisa and Zabran had looked forward to. The carton plant was to contribute to the general effort by printing slogans on posters which were to be used in demonstrations. Luisa and Zabran had minor disagreements about the slogans that should go on the posters. Suddenly Jan objected to the very idea of demonstrations with posters. He said we should talk to our fellow workers with our mouths, not with posters blocking us from each other. I caught on right away and asked what our discussions would be like if each of us sat behind a placard with a slogan on it, and if we waited for the placards to talk to each other. That's when everything went haywire. Yarostan was supposed to guide the group back to the tasks at hand, but he only nodded at Jan's and my comments. The united front fell apart. Jasna considered Jan's comments as reasonable as Luisa's. Zabran and Luisa were almost isolated; only Claude Tamnich and Marc Glavni stood by them. Even Vera Neis vacillated. Jasna is right about Vera; she was an opportunist. She became Luisa's disciple because she wanted to be what Yarostan was supposed to have become: the tribune, the rank-and-file leader. But as soon as Luisa was isolated, Vera abandoned her, and of course she took Adrian, her flunkey, with her."

"You make them all sound so petty and manipulative. Are you sure you're not describing Vera in the light of what Yarostan told us she became much later?" I ask Sabina. I'm still trying to defend the integrity of my "original community."

"I'm describing them in the light of what they did, Sophia," she insists. "In fact, what Vera did later doesn't even make a whole lot of sense to me. Her antics with that husband and lover don't quite fit with the Vera I knew twenty years ago. I might as well tell you about my experience with Vera Neis. You figure out how it fits with what she became later. She didn't switch sides only because Luisa was isolated but also because of me."

"You mean you convinced her Jan was right?"

"You can put it that way, but I didn't convince her with words. Vera couldn't stand Jan, and she'd never have switched sides if I hadn't been there. It was my presence that convinced her. The first time I spoke she took me aside and told me, 'What a witty, intelligent, fiery girl you are!' She couldn't believe I was only thirteen. 'You're a siren', she told me, 'pretending to be a gypsy girl!' That was what convinced her. I didn't know it right then, but she was courting me as openly as the circumstances and her own inhibitions would allow. She found the same treasure behind the long black hair that Zabran had found in Yarostan: a gem buried in sand. I sensed her passion and was excited by it without understanding it. I played with it. I sat by her, whispered in her ear, laughed with her, touched her. I wasn't aware that the pale, pretty woman whose chest heaved and whose face grew red whenever I touched her wanted to fling me to the floor then and there, in the midst of the meeting. I didn't know what a fire I was stirring up in her whenever I whispered to her; until then I had played in the park behind the school and had taken friends home with me, but I had never had contact with pure lust, with blind desire. It was only on the following day, the third day of the strike, that I realized what was happening. Zabran opened that day's meeting by groaning about the fact that nothing had gotten done during the first two days of the strike. Then he said the presence of outsiders who were not production workers, disruptive individualistic elements, was responsible for this. Vera knew he was referring to my presence. She slipped her hand over my fist, as if to let me know she'd keep me from being thrown out. Gradually she tightened her hold, dug her fingernails into the palm of my hand. I could see her eyes were red from lack of sleep, her teeth bit her lips. I whispered that she was hurting me, but her grip only tightened. I became afraid of something I didn't then understand. I was about to be overpowered and maybe even destroyed by something I couldn't control or restrain. Vera was driven by a blind desire to dominate me, to own me, to enslave me, without any trace of love or mutuality or equality."

"Gosh, Sabina, I never imagined —"

"I don't think anyone else did either, Sophia, because nothing actually happened. It was Yarostan who saved me from being ravaged by Vera and also from being thrown out by Zabran. Yarostan dreamily proposed an 'action' somewhere between printing posters and destroying machines — he too was good at making syntheses between diametrical opposites. When Zabran brought up the presence of outsiders, Yarostan brought up the presence of the owner, Mr. Zagad. Yarostan is excessively modest. It's true that Claude made the action concrete by suggesting Zagad be ousted, but that suggestion was nothing but the logical step that followed from Yarostan's observation. Jan jumped up, ready to implement the suggestion on the spot, and I leaped out of the fire I had unintentionally fed and threw my arms around Jan and Yarostan. The whole plan was Yarostan's —"

"That was what I thought too, but Yarostan wrote that Claude didn't only make his suggestion concrete, but was also the one who finally implemented it."

"Yarostan is wrong," Sabina says emphatically. "Today he'd like to make himself believe he didn't have anything to do with those events. Claude added nothing but his usual contributions: we should oust Zagad with clubs and guns, like the police would do it. Yarostan asked why we couldn't just ask Zagad to leave. And in the end it was Claude who implemented Yarostan's 'strategy'. We went peacefully to Zagad's office and Claude asked him to leave. That event was important to me. I thought it was the beginning of Jan's revolution. I thought the first step would be followed by others, workers would start tearing down factory walls and pushing machines into fields and forests. I was overjoyed when Zagad left his office. I threw my arms around Jan, and he asked me to spend the night with him. That was when my revolution began. Jan was the only man I gave myself to completely. He was my twin. He rejected all constraints, he was open to every conceivable experience, he refused to be stunted. He was Margarita Nachalo in the shape of a man."

"Why did Jan take you to Yarostan's room instead of his own?" I ask her. "Yarostan said they exchanged keys —"

"Yarostan started that letter by telling you how honest and complete he was going to be. He's a hypocrite. He still doesn't approve of his best friend's morals. Maybe he doesn't want Mirna to know. I'd think she'd be flattered. I asked Jan the same question and he told me he didn't want to take me to his room because he shared his bed with his sister."

"You mean Mirna lived in his room?" I ask.

"That was what I thought," Sabina goes on. "I was fascinated beyond words. He told me his sister was two years younger than I was. He was surprised I wasn't shocked. But my whole body filled with curiosity. I longed to meet the eleven-year old girl who shared her bed with her brother. I insisted on going to his room instead of Yarostan's. I flew into a rage when he refused to take me there. He told me his sister was wildly jealous and would scratch my eyes out, but that only aroused my curiosity all the more. I threatened to leave him if he didn't take me to her, so he finally told me the girl in his room was his sister only in age. He told me he did love his real sister, but had been separated from her by a religious vampire who had policed their love. The girl in his room was a homeless urchin; she had run to Jan in the street and begged him to hide her from the police, who were chasing her for stealing. He had hidden her, and she had stayed on with him; he considered her his make-believe sister. Yarostan was apparently shocked. I stopped insisting on going to Jan's room, but I couldn't stop being fascinated by his real sister. I asked him her name, what she looked like, and what she had done with her brother under the very nose of morality and the church. When he pulled me to bed, I refused to undress until he agreed to pretend to be his sister and to show me how his sister made love to her brother. Jan agreed. Mirna underestimates him. He was full of pranks. For Jan liberated life was going to be a game, a love game, played intensely, with every limb and pore. He agreed to be Mirna for me. And while he performed, I made love to the sister he was pretending to be, I fell in love with her, I lost myself in an ecstasy matched by only one other experience in my life, the following night's experience with the real Mirna: Jan's enjoyment was as great as mine; he continually told me, 'All life should consist of moments like these, interrupted only by periods of rest.' It was out of gratitude that, early the following morning, he told me he'd take me to meet his sister that very day. But first we had to think of a way of getting the religious mother out of the house. Jan knew I had fallen in love, not with him but with his sister, and he understood my passion, he fanned it, he loved me for it. The guardians of the social order had to kill Jan; there was no way for them and him to coexist; in his heart Jan carried the dissolution of every order; he'd always break through it with acts of passion unimaginable until then. Yarostan returned to his room at daybreak. He obviously hadn't slept a wink. He didn't describe his night with Jan's roommate. We didn't ask. His night hadn't been a happy one. He seemed absolutely worn out, miserable, lonely, perhaps ashamed. Both of us knew he was pining for Luisa. Mirna is wrong about the plot to seduce the Queen of the Peasants. It was Jan's idea from beginning to end. As soon as Yarostan knocked at sunrise, Jan knew what to do with the old vampire. If only Yarostan would resume with Jan's mother where he'd left off with Luisa, Mirna would be free and Jan and I would outdo each other courting her without any rules or time limits, without any standards of right and wrong; the revolution would begin when all of us started doing what we pleased. But Yarostan didn't want to contribute any more to our plan than he'd contributed to Zabran's and Luisa's. We barely succeeded in getting him to go with us. As soon as he saw the queen, the object of his passion, he yawned. Next time he saw her he vomited. He spent the entire afternoon and night sound asleep. We might as well have thrown a dead animal at the old woman."

"Would you like him better if he'd become your tool?"

"No, Sophia, I would have liked him less. And in any case, it wasn't my fun he spoiled but Jan's. The old woman concentrated all her energy on keeping Jan out of the game. With fabulous results! Those results were summarized for us by the untouched virgin herself, twenty years later! I suspect the old woman even had an inkling of why Jan had brought Yarostan. Her endless crosses and wails and prayers suggested she had trouble keeping the thought from passing through her own mind. The devil must have tried to slip into her consciousness while the rest of us were out picking berries. What she didn't have any inkling about was the infinity of forms the devil could take. That night she thought the devils were all safely put away in Jan's bedroom at the other end of the house; she expected to hear the first step the devil took toward the room containing the two chaste virgins. Meanwhile all of her worst fears were being acted out by the virgins themselves, unaided by any visiting demons."

"In one of their discussions, Mirna told Yarostan she thought you hadn't been honest with her." I remind her.

"I know, and she hurt me by saying that. She didn't describe to Yarostan the game we actually played. She transformed it, and I can't understand why. Is she ashamed of the role she played? I doubt it; Mirna had no shame, not then."

"You're twins in that respect, aren't you?"

"More than twins, Sophia; we're permanently embedded in each other's hearts. That's why I was hurt when Mirna inverted a key detail and made me seem so manipulative. Don't look at me so strangely, Sophia! Don't forget I wasn't thirty-two then! Mirna and I were only two years apart, and I didn't play the dominant role. The seduction was as mutual as the most reciprocal love depicted in any poetry. The mutuality of our love condemned the ugliness of all the brutalizing one-sided relationships in the midst of which it took place, and first of all Luisa's relationship to Yarostan, which was nothing but sheer manipulation; next Yarostan's relationship with you, Vera's toward Adrian and me, Zabran's toward Yarostan, Alberts' toward Luisa, and finally Jasna's pathetic and unrecognized desire for Zabran and Yarostan. Our love had nothing in common with any of those. It had no blemishes. The detail Mirna changed is precisely what made that night so incomparably beautiful, so unique in my whole life's experience."

"Well, what did she change?" I ask impatiently. "She was angry at you for pretending to be her brother and rousing her passion for your own selfish gratification. Don't tell me you did it for her; I know you too well —"

"I'm not denying my selfishness, Sophia. Nor Mirna's. She's right about why I did it, but she's wrong about what I did. I didn't pretend to be Jan that night. I'm disappointed that Mirna forgot that. It was a rare, unforgettable night. Moonlight streamed in through the window. It was quieter in that country house than anywhere I'd been before. Mirna asked me if I was Yarostan's girl or Jan's. I remembered Jan's telling me she'd scratch my eyes out from jealousy arid I tried to provoke that jealousy. I told her Jan and I were passionately in love with each other, that our love knew no bounds. But that had been Jan's inversion. There was no jealousy in Mirna. She put her hand on my face and told me, 'If I were Jan I'd love you passionately and without bounds; you're beautiful.' I almost cried. I told her, 'Jan says he loves me only because I remind him of the one person he really loves in the whole world.' Mirna insisted I tell her that person's name. I told her, 'He didn't love me at all until he taught me to act like her and be like her, because he doesn't really love me at all, he loves only her; and her name is Mirna.' She was quiet for a long time. I reached for her face and felt tears running down her cheeks. I asked if I had offended her. Then she asked me, 'Did he show you how he spent his nights with Mirna, how he slept with her?' I told her he showed me everything. She said, 'This was the bed in which he slept with Mirna until mother made him leave.' She sobbed and kissed my hand, telling me, 'I still cry sometimes when I remember. I was so happy every night, and I was happy during the day because I waited for night to come.' Why did Mirna invert what happened next when she told Yarostan about it? I did not ask her, 'Would you like me to pretend to be Jan.' How terribly banal, and how manipulative! Yet she works herself into a fury twenty years later, indignant at the creature she's invented during the intervening years. The fact is that my initiative ended with my telling her Jan loved her. From that point on the initiative was hers, and it remained hers until the end of that glorious night. It was Mirna who asked me, 'Show me what Jan showed you. Please be Mirna for me, just for an instant.' I agreed to be Mirna. I lay quietly next to her; our sides touched. She said, 'First Jan took Mirna's hand to his lips and whispered, I love you, my little sister, more than I'll ever love anyone else in the whole wide world.' That was how it began. And it was Mirna herself who went on, step by step, to an ecstatic climax, slowly uncovering every inch of one body and matching it with every inch of the other, ever so carefully, ever so gently, ever so passionately. Every motion, every gesture, every position she had ever dreamed of taking with Jan she took with me; every caress, every embrace, every kiss she had ever dreamed of receiving from her brother she gave to me."

"And all that time you pretended to be Mirna?"

"It was the easiest thing in the world to pretend to be Mirna and to accept all the love and passion she wanted Jan to give her. That was what made that night so incomparable, so monumental to me. And you should have seen her mother's face the next morning when she found her virgin sleeping in the devil's arms! Tissie told me what you looked like when you woke up in her embrace. Your look must have been compassionate compared to that woman's. All her life's pent-up desire, inverted into hatred, was concentrated in her look. She immediately rushed for the broom. Yarostan remembered the rest of it vividly enough: The rest is hardly worth remembering. Nothing else happened during the next two weeks. After the old woman chased us away we went back to the carton plant. I kept expecting next steps to be taken, but there weren't any. After those stupid discussions about slogans on posters everyone except Jan went back to work to print those posters. Jan and I boycotted the work as well as the rest of the meetings. We wandered throughout the city, among crowds, into factories, among students. We kept looking for those who were taking the next step, and we discovered what Yarostan described to you in his second letter: a vast puppet show, thousands of mannikins acting on orders pretending to be acting on their own. We did find a few free spirits, but they were isolated, disoriented and frustrated. Jan knew it was all going to end very badly. It was all too repetitious, too serious, and Jan knew that a revolution couldn't be serious. So at least the two of us stopped being serious, we played at revolution, we played at being free; we challenged, provoked and sabotaged. But no one responded. We might as well have been alone."

I remind her, "In the research center you continued to expect everything to happen. How could you have known during those events twenty years ago that nothing else was going to happen?"

"I'm not sure I can explain that, Sophia. Maybe for the same reason that I've tried to realize contradictory projects. I'm half Nachalo and half Alberts. Twenty years ago my two halves told me the same thing; two weeks ago they told me opposite things."

"I don't understand," I tell her. "I know you were in the midst of a contradiction in the research center. Yarostan saw that right away, and you yourself were aware of it. But I don't see why you were so single-minded twenty years ago. What did your Alberts-half tell you then?"

"It wasn't my Alberts-half, Sophia, but Alberts himself, in person, who told me exactly the same thing Jan told me. Jan knew right away that all the strike activity was staged and had no other aim but to replace one set of rulers with another. Alberts said almost the same thing to me a week before we were arrested. He told me we were going to emigrate as soon as he got all the papers and other arrangements in order; if we didn't emigrate we'd spend years in jail, maybe even the rest of our lives. I was indignant at first. I wanted Jan and Mirna and all the others to go with us. He told me it wasn't the whole group that would be jailed, but only the foreigners. He said foreigners were being used as scapegoats to explain why there was opposition to the revolutionary apparatus, so-called. It's so easy to single out foreigners. I told Jan what Alberts had told me and he said he was relieved to learn we would be allowed to emigrate; he had started to worry when he heard the rumors that were being circulated about Luisa. He didn't even imagine he would be arrested too, and didn't dream of emigrating; he had no reason to. Alberts made it all very attractive to me by promising me a whole world of technology as my plaything; he even told me he'd build me a laboratory. Jan and I knew our friendship would end as suddenly as it began; at least we had pretended a revolution was taking place."

"Then you don't know why the others were imprisoned for such a long time?" I ask her.

"I haven't the slightest idea, Sophia. Yarostan keeps asking why the three of us were released after spending only two days in jail. That's not what surprises me. I had known we were going to be allowed to emigrate. What surprises me is what happened to the others. No one, not even Alberts, imagined that the isolation of scapegoats would be carried to the point of imprisoning the entire production crew of the carton plant. I didn't have a hint of that fact until Yarostan's first letter came, and I don't understand it. What happened was exactly what Alberts had made me think would happen; I had no reason to be suspicious. We were all arrested; we spent two days in jail; we were released and the police apologized for their 'mistake'. Luisa's and Alberts' friend Zabran was there at the parting. Zdenek's claim that Zabran was in jail at that time is puzzling; Zdenek must have had another period in mind when he told them that, or another man. I knew who Zabran was, and the man who saw us off was Titus Zabran. He had been arrested too, but only for a day. He told us the entire crew had been arrested 'by mistake'. I thought that apparently someone in the police thought the entire crew were foreigners. Yarostan keeps pointing out how bizarre it is that the 'Alberts Ring' was released while the so-called accomplices of the ring were left in jail. That certainly is bizarre, but that wasn't the impression I had at the time. Zabran, not the Alberts Ring, was released first, a day before us, and I was sure the others had been released too. In any case we weren't given a grand opportunity to find out what had happened to the others. The police accompanied the 'celebrated physicist and his family' to our house, waited while we packed, and escorted us to the train station for the first tram out."

During the past week Sabina answered several other questions you raised in your newest letter, as well as in the two letters that arrived when she was in the research center. And in answering your questions, she completely demolished the "original community" I had glorified in my first letters to you. If I still retained some illusions after you tried to knock them out of me, Sabina has finally convinced me that no such community ever existed. In the process of convincing me, she made me doubt the reality of my most recent experiences as well. Were the commune and the council office hallucinations? Did I invent them? Were they dreams on which I can base another lifetime's hopes? If I correspond with Pat twenty years from now, will he write me that the events I remember never happened?

As you can see, I'm not too eager to tell you how I happen to be home discussing your letters with Sabina. I don't even want to think about it. Sabina is right; I'd rather let everything in my head just lie where it fell, without moving around. I may later have to take someone else's word about what happened, but at least I'll have spared myself the pain of living through a horrid experience more than once. I'll try to relive it — I was going to say for your sake, but I can't imagine what good it'll do you to know. I really do wish Sabina had written you; all I feel like telling you are the things she told me.

I was slightly drunk, comfortably exhausted and very happy when I finished my previous letter to you. The day before, with Pat's grudging help, I had given Luisa and Daman a tour of the continent I had discovered that day. I slept soundly for at least twelve hours after I finished that letter, got up at noon, and attacked Luisa's refrigerator. She had returned and left again while I had been asleep. I sealed the letter and walked across the border with it. It was a gorgeous summer day, I let my hair blow in the wind, and I experienced myself as a heroine. I felt victorious. I had realized one of my life's few, maybe only two, independent projects. I had projected it and carried it through all by myself. I felt that I had at last come of age to take part in a real revolution.

I was still in that mood when I walked to the commune. I was eager to learn what other strikes had broken out, where else the movement had spread. When I reached the entrance of the former university building two tough-looking young men tried to stop me from going in.

"Who are you?" I asked them.

"Security," one of them answered.

"Who the hell put you there?" I asked.

The answer was, "The building is full of informers and spies."

"Well go join the police force if you're interested in informers and spies!" I shouted, pushing my way past them.

The council office was almost the same as I'd left it three days earlier. If I hadn't just run into the security guards I wouldn't have noticed the differences as quickly as I did. Most of the stacks of pamphlets and leaflets were the same, but there were a few new stacks of leaflets, and these were very distinct from everything else in the room. They were the diatribes of political sects. None of the people in the room were familiar to me. As I listened to their arguments I became aware that they were all politicians with esoteric axes to grind. I was shocked. I ran upstairs and downstairs looking for familiar faces: for Pat, for workers who had visited the council office, for people I had met at the office-machine plant. But all I saw was the hostile, suspicious faces of dedicated professional radicals. The mood in which I had walked across the bridge was gone. I ran to the print shop. It was full of people who were strangers to me, almost all of them men. Suspicious glances followed me as I walked around and looked at the things being printed. All of it looked drab, repetitious and terribly repressive; "must not" and "should not" appeared in every sentence. In the garbage bin I found a crumpled leaflet, colorful, well laid-out and illustrated, satirizing the self-elected police hysterically trying to "recuperate" the revolutionary struggle. I supposed that leaflet had been done by Pat's group; I saw no other evidence of the presence of Pat's group in the print shop. I went up the back staircase and knocked on the door, but Ted wasn't there. None of the people in the print shop had ever heard of Tina. Wherever I had left friends I found only strangers; wherever I had left a community with a project I found only hostile politicians.

I was in a daze. I dragged myself out of the print shop and drifted across the campus looking for my lifelong companion and guide, Yarostan, in all his varied forms. I wanted him to take my hand again and show me what had to be done next. I was me again.

I did find a guide. Someone handed me a leaflet announcing a "militant demonstration" against the occupation of an assembly plant by the police. I wondered if it was Luisa's plant. I went to the gathering place two hours before the scheduled beginning of the demonstration. Other drifters like myself joined me. Finally an authority arrived, someone wearing an armband, and obviously a member of a political group. After listening to several minutes of his rigid rhetoric, I learned that it was in fact Luisa's plant that had been occupied by the police. On the previous day members of various political groups had joined the union picket line (I wondered if they had felt threatened by competition from Daman and had run to sell their political commodities at a lower price). A fight had broken out between union picketers and the so-called "subversive outsiders." Then a rumor was spread (apparently by union bureaucrats) that "subversive saboteurs" had seized the plant. This had been an ample pretext for the police to occupy the plant. And right after the police occupied it, the union called on workers to defend their plant from the police — in other words, after calling in the police, the union bureaucrats pretended to be the greatest opponents of the police. The leaflet quoted a union bureaucrat saying, "The government is fomenting disorder and is being helped by groups of revolutionists, adventurists and punks..." From the armbanded "leader" of the demonstration I also learned that the purpose of the "militant demonstration" was to "offer solidarity to the fighting workers" by joining them in the struggle to oust the police from "their plant." I obviously couldn't have gotten him to explain to me in what sense the plant was "their plant," nor why the workers would want to go back into it. It didn't occur to me to suggest that everyone might be a lot happier if the police were left inside the plant and everyone else went off to do other things. I joined the "struggle," and I was extremely nervous. The only other time I took part in a "militant demonstration" in which I knew I was going to be physically injured was six years ago, when I sat in the street to block trucks carrying weapons. But the "struggle" at Luisa's plant was more in tune with my upbringing than the peace demonstration had been. I imagined that Luisa and Daman might be behind barricades; I've always thought of her earlier barricades with nostalgia; I've always wanted to have barricades in my own life. I also wanted to get away from the loved places that had suddenly become so alien to me.

Several hundred people gathered. It was announced that the demonstrators were to break up into groups of six and to ride to the plant in cars. I found a group of five students with a car and clung to them. For once in my life I was the least hysterical member of the group. They were completely paranoid. During the entire trip they talked about police and even army units surrounding the plant with machine guns and even tanks. I told them I doubted that war had been declared, but my own fears increased considerably. Several days later I learned that their paranoia had been grounded in solid reality; if I had known that at the time, I would have collapsed long before reaching Luisa's plant. It turned out that I was the only one of the six who knew the way to the plant, and since I had only been there once I got lost. I did manage to get them to the right part of the city. They insisted on parking their car miles away from the plant. After walking for what seemed like hours, and after asking several people where it was, we reached a fence inside of which there was an immense parking lot. We decided we had approached the plant from the rear. So much the better, we thought; the police wouldn't be expecting us to come from that direction. We helped each other climb over the fence. We were inside the plant! Before we had a chance to congratulate each other about that fact we saw two busses rushing toward us. We didn't have the time to climb back over the fence, and there was no place to hide; we were on a completely empty parking lot. Both busses were full of police, all of them armed to the teeth! I don't have the words to tell you how terrified I was. Before they got out of their busses they threw a canister of gas at us. Then they came out of the busses wearing masks and pointing their rifles at us. And they kept coming out of those busses. Now that I'm putting it on paper that whole scene seems so ludicrous. Three studious-looking, clean shaven young men, two girls who hardly looked older than high school students, and I — we couldn't have managed a slingshot between us. Yet there we were, being beaten up by at least a hundred masked policemen, all armed with rifles and clubs! None of us offered the slightest resistance; the sight of those two busses had killed every trace of rebellion in all of us. Yet the police continued beating us. Finally they separated us into groups of three and carried us into the busses. The fright was infinitely worse than all the blows I received. Inside the bus the police spoke of us as if we were foreigners, even as if we had come here from another planet. I had no idea where the bus was taking us, but I had yet another fright when the bus stopped in an empty lot that looked like a garbage dump. We were pushed out of the bus. I was sure we were going to be shot and abandoned in the dump. But we were transferred to the back of a regular police wagon. Apparently the "counter-insurgent" police in the busses had to go back to the plant to hunt down more "guerrillas."

I was trembling and nauseated when the police wagon finally stopped. I didn't know what part of the world I was in when I was ordered to get out. I vomited as soon as I reached the ground. The six of us were pushed into a waiting room lit by one of those eternally bare bulbs. I was sick from the beatings; my lungs felt hollow from the gas; I thought my insides had been injured. I had felt that way every single day when I'd worked in the fiberglass factory. I was fingerprinted. I had to give my name repeatedly. And then, while I was being marched through a hallway with my five companions, I saw another group of "guerrillas" arriving, and Luisa was among them! I smiled weakly to her, but she glared at me with unforgiving hostility; the scene I had made with Pat had spoiled her love affair with Daman.

This time I didn't try to call Sabina or Daman to try to get me out of jail. I remembered what Mirna had said about our "running out" on the rest of you, and I was determined to practice solidarity with my "combative" comrades.

But I was in for a big surprise. It happened during my second day in jail. I was told that my lawyer wanted to talk to me. I was escorted to a furnished room, and there I recognized Minnie Vach! Minnie, the college friend with whom I had tried to expose the militarization of the university, with whom I had almost been arrested for littering public property with copies of *Omissions*. As soon as the guard was gone I threw my arms around her as if I were embracing my best friend.

"How in the world did you get in as my lawyer?" I asked her.

Minnie quickly told me that she was in fact a lawyer. She works with a group of lawyers who she referred to as a "radical lawyers' collective." Daman had called her. She told me we'd have time to talk after the trial; she was in a hurry to explain her "strategy" to me. She told me I was to pretend that I was nothing more than an innocent bystander.

"But they arrested me inside the plant!" I reminded her.

"It doesn't matter," she told me. "You were doing research on the student movement. You're Professor Hesper's assistant. Where you choose to do your field work is none of their business."

I was intensely disappointed; I regretted having embraced her so warmly. I told her I couldn't go through with her "strategy." I didn't want to run out on comrades one more time; I had done that often enough.

"Suit yourself, Sophie," she told me. "But you should know that all your co-defendants are getting lawyers, and not free ones either; they've all got parents who can afford the best that money can buy. Anyway, I'll be at your trial."

I was terribly depressed during my last days in jail. Everything I had lived for seemed to have collapsed.

In one of your letters you had told me that my "world" of journalistic friends consisted of people who aspired to roles within the ruling bureaucracy. I had indignantly denied that. At that time I had thought Professor Daman Hesper was the only one who really fitted your description. I could never have imagined Minnie as a lawyer. When I knew her on the news-paper staff I couldn't have imagined she would compromise everything she stood for to the point of joining the profession that practices "the law." Inside that prison I could understand perfectly, what Sabina told me later about Luisa's change of "social tastes." While I lay inside my jail cell, Minnie was treated as an equal by prison authorities who regarded me as nothing but so much "trash." Of course in retrospect I can "see" that Minnie wasn't as uncompromising as I would have liked to think her, but it's always easy to see such things in retrospect. I remembered the day when *Omissions* was launched and Rhea, Minnie and I were excluded from it. Minnie was the angriest of the three; she slapped Daman so hard I thought she'd made a permanent mark on his face. Yet only a few days later she compromised her solidarity with the other two excluded women and joined the *Omissions* group. But that's still a far cry from joining the legal profession. Of all the people on the newspaper staff, Minnie had been the most opposed to the idea of working within the system to accomplish anything significant; she had been the very antithesis of the managing editor, Bess.

But as I lay in my cell thinking about Minnie's "compromises," I couldn't keep myself from remembering my own. At the time when you wrote me about my university friends' "opportunism" I wasn't lying in a jail cell; I was teaching a university-level course. I was a member of the "academic community," not because of conviction or ambition, but because I had drifted there. I thought maybe Minnie had done no more to reach her present situation. I drifted back into the academic world when I learned how Jose had died. When Sabina told me Jose had been picked up in the street like a dead dog, I couldn't do anything but drift. Learning that he had died trying to become someone I could admire sent a terrible shock through me. I fell into Sabina's arms like a baby. I cried hysterically that I wasn't anyone to admire; I had nothing to give Jose because I had become nothing. I was completely alone again. If Sabina hadn't helped me through that crisis I think I would have disintegrated altogether and permanently. After my miserable experience with Art and the peace movement, Jose had become my whole life. I dated my life in terms of his release, simultaneously looking forward to it and fearing it, and at no time feeling able to face it. Jose's release was going to be the test of my capacities. His death put an end to all my prospects. I think it's only the fact that Sabina felt as devastated as I that kept me going during the weeks after we learned Jose was dead. I had never seen her cry before; I had thought those black eyes that perpetually sparkled with mischief or the desire for adventure were incapable of tears. When I saw tears under those long black eyelashes I felt an emotion I can't describe with words like friendship and love. Sabina hadn't ever been "Jose's girl," she hadn't ever shared his bed, she hadn't ever desired him physically, yet she loved him; I understood her love for him only because I thought it must be similar to what I felt toward Sabina when I saw her tears. We propped each other up. We talked to each other as we had only once before, during one of my first days in the garage. We didn't talk about Jose or about the past but only about ourselves. Sabina fought against my self-rejection by telling me we were perfectly matched friends, our personalities were each other's perfect complements: my lack of self-assurance was a counter-weight to her blind self-confidence; my constant self-evaluations were a counterweight to her uncritical acceptance of herself. I tried to tell her she had far less reason to be self-critical than I did. She knew five languages, was as well versed in all the sciences as most academics I had met, had seen half the world, had experienced every imaginable form of human relationship, had launched projects and grown with them; she had in some sense achieved the fullness of life. But she told me she had never done what I did all the time; she had never examined the meaning of all her life's accomplishments. It was during those weeks that Sabina launched the project in which she's still engaged; she began a systematic evaluation of the key events of her life. And being Sabina, she threw herself into that project with the same single-mindedness and determination with which she did everything she set out to do. I, on the other hand, set out with my usual lack of self-assurance and determination, I got over my shock, but I continued to drift. We remained each other's "complements." I wandered through familiar and unfamiliar neighborhoods; I wandered in and out of bookstores. I wandered to the university campus and found myself reading the catalogue of university courses. And while wandering through the catalogue I found Daman Hesper's name listed as the instructor of a course on political philosophy. I couldn't imagine Daman philosophizing on his own; the last time I had seen him he had only been able to parrot his political group's philosophy, and then only with Minnie's help. I think it was curiosity that drove me to enroll in Daman's course. Once I enrolled in his course, I added the other courses I needed to complete my requirements for the "bachelor's" degree. And once I was a student again, I convinced myself that something I had always wanted existed, at least in embryo, among that generation of students: something like a radical community. I started to look forward to activities which I thought would be similar to those I had experienced in the carton plant. I thought I'd find friends with significant projects. I had prospects again; the gap left by Jose's death started to be filled. This was three years ago; the student movement was just starting to take on the characteristics of a generalized movement, the characteristics which three years later made possible the complete occupation of the university and the formation of the commune. I was in the presence of something I hadn't experienced since my emigration. Everything had changed since the day when a tiny group of radicals published a school newspaper in the midst of an almost unanimously hostile student population. Nor did this movement have anything in common with my activity with Art and the peace movement, where a dozen "saints" had demonstrated their "goodness" in the midst of an "evil world." The student movement was no longer an "enlightened" minority; it was a substantial section of the student population. Opposition to the war had led students to begin opposing all the institutions that stood behind the war, including the university itself. What attracted me was not the university itself, nor the possibility it offered for rising in the academic hierarchy, but rather the opposition to the institution. I hadn't found anything that was so significant to me since the day when I had tried to find Hugh's "Project House." I wanted to be part of it, but in my own characteristic way. As always I wanted to walk into a ready-made "radical community": I wanted to submit to the tasks at hand instead of defining and creating them myself. As always I looked for a guide, and I found one, though not among my fellow students. Professor Daman Hesper became not only my teacher, but also something like my tour guide to the student movement. The first day I attended his class he was completely distracted by my presence. He avoided looking at me, as if he were afraid of me. I stayed after the class; we shook hands stiffly; he smiled dryly. "I suppose you've come to judge me," he said; "I've become a lackey of the ruling class and all that." He almost apologized to me. The professor, the highest university authority, had an inferiority complex in front of me. I beamed when I told him, "I'm your student, Daman; I'm enrolled in your course." He couldn't believe it and looked at his list of students to confirm the fact. "Well I'll be damned," he said; "the last time I saw you was when I was chased out of the garage at gunpoint. Alec told me you had moved in with your mother but had then disappeared again; I assumed you had rejoined your friends." We didn't say much more than that to each other during the entire semester. Daman was very rigid about not mixing his categories. The student-teacher relationship excluded the possibility of companionship. His course was an absolute bore; my curiosity about that died the second day I attended his class. Daman without Minnie was the same as Daman with Minnie. He still repeated the same slogans with the same emphases and the same tone. His reading list consisted of standard academic books which had nothing at all to do with his lectures, and he made no effort to relate the books to his comments. He didn't treat me as a former friend until the last day of classes, when I technically became a college graduate. He told me some students were organizing a "teach-in" about the war and invited me to attend with him. I was enchanted. I hadn't done anything "political" since the peace demonstration. After that day, during my year in graduate school I attended student "actions" with Daman at least once a week, always as a passive observer. Daman was curious, but hostile. He told me he had spent some time working in a factory since I had last seen him. And he continually repeated his favorite refrain: the real organization wasn't going to be organized by students but by industrial workers. I even listened to him lecture on this subject twice, when he was invited to speak at student teach-ins; both times he was introduced as "factory worker Daman Hesper." From the scraps of conversations I had with Daman before and after student meetings during my year in graduate school, I pieced together enough of his life to figure out how the "factory worker" had become a university professor. Daman had been the only one of the *Omissions* group who had enrolled in graduate school as soon as he finished his undergraduate study. After Alec visited me in the garage for the first time, he told Hugh, Daman and Minnie that I had turned my back on the academic bureaucracy and joined the working class. According to Daman, this was what influenced Hugh to quit his studies and throw himself into an altogether different activity. Alec joined the garage group, Minnie got a job teaching in a high school, and both called Daman a hypocrite for enrolling in graduate school. That was when he and Minnie broke up, although Daman continued to attend the meetings of Minnie's organization. When Daman told me about this episode, he said, "I soon realized that your activity in the garage had nothing to do with the revolutionary potentiality of the working class, and by trying to imitate you, Hugh and Alec only got themselves in a bind. I understood that the revolution was going to be made at the point of production, not in marginal semi-criminal gang activities." So he went on to get the "doctor's degree" in philosophy. But he didn't start teaching right away. He got a job in a factory and continued to attend the organization's meetings; he even took "a worker or two" to some of the meetings. While he had the factory job he convinced himself that "Minnie's commitment had never been to a real workers' organization, but only to an organization of intellectuals completely separate from the working class." That "realization" brought on his final break with Minnie as well as her organization. He told me that in the factory he started to "make contact with the class, particularly with one worker," apparently a worker who seemed to show interest for Daman's "workers' newspaper." Suddenly Daman's factory career ended; he told me, "That worker turned out to be a cop or an informer because one day I was fired, without explanation, and the only thing I had done that was in any way out of the ordinary had been to engage in political exchanges with this worker." Luckily there happened to be an opening in the philosophy department at the university, specifically in his "specialty," political philosophy. The first signs of student dissatisfaction were just appearing, and the administrators were looking for a person with Daman's qualifications, they were looking for a "revolutionary factory worker" with a doctor's degree in philosophy. I saw through Daman, but my own situation didn't give me an ideal vantage point from which to criticize him.

My own drift back to academia also didn't give me a very solid basis from which to criticize Minnie's acceptance of her new profession. Minnie had reconciled herself to the status quo when she had joined the *Omissions* staff. But so had I. Although I had refused to write for that paper, I had taken part in its production as well as its distribution. Once her anger had passed, Minnie had thrown herself into it wholeheartedly. I had merely let it happen to me. And that was exactly what I did at the trial that took place last week. I ran out on my young comrades the same way I had run out on Rhea, the same way I had run out on you twenty years ago. I ran last week the same way I've always run: passively, without conviction, without reasons or rationalizations. I had let Daman and Minnie "take me" to the *Omissions* meetings. I had let Luisa "take me" on a trip across the ocean, away from those I regarded as my only friends. And I let Minnie "take me" out of jail. I didn't contribute to her "defense" strategy, but I didn't resist it. I simply let it happen to me. I moved where others pulled me. My whole life has been like that trial: it's been something that merely "happened" to me. Even when I found the communities I was looking for, I was taken there by others, and when I got there I was shown what to do and how to proceed.

Minnie's "defense strategy" was ingeniously simple. It wasn't based on fact, but on plausibility: She confronted one authority, the judge, with another, the professor. The professor said I was in fact his research assistant and had in fact been doing "field research" on the student movement. I was the only one who could deny it, and my denial would have been extremely embarrassing to both Daman and Minnie. I liked Minnie much better when I realized she was risking her reputation on my behavior; Daman as well as Minnie knew perfectly well that reliability and predictability were not among my most prominent qualities. Daman took the stand and described the research; the judge frowned but didn't express his views of "left-wing professors"; hiring or firing such professors wasn't within his field of jurisdiction. I took the stand and nodded. When the judge asked me to speak louder, I shouted, "Yes I am, Yes I did!" It was the easiest thing in the world to lie to the State. And by lying I ran out on my comrades. Minnie had told me they had already run out on me. I didn't know their names; I wasn't able to find out what happened to them, just as twenty years ago I hadn't been able to find out what had happened to you. I took Minnie's word. I also told myself that by the time the trial took place, solidarity with them conflicted with the solidarity I owed to Daman and Minnie, friends who had taken so much time and trouble for me. The judge told me he hoped my research would contribute toward the task of "keeping those young vandals in line," and stormed out of the courtroom.

As soon as the judge left, I embraced Minnie warmly and thanked her. I told her I was able to pay all the "lawyer's fees" that were involved. Minnie said she'd feel terribly insulted to be paid by "one of my best friends." I almost cried when she said that. The last time I had seen her, on the day when Hugh had carried me out of the garage, I hadn't treated her as one of my best friends; I had angrily asked Minnie and Daman, "What are you two staring at?"

I asked her how she had become a "radical lawyer," and asked if that was something like being a "radical general."

Minnie smiled and told me she'd like to discuss that "with you more than with anyone I know, Sophie." But she said she had to rush off to another case, and promised to visit me. I gave her my address and phone number.

Daman waited for me outside the courtroom. "Well, at least that's over and done with," he said. "I told Sabina you probably wouldn't be released until this afternoon."

I asked him, "How often can you be beaten before you cry out with pain, Daman?"

"You don't look well at all, Sophie," he told me.

"The last time I saw you I was certain you'd hate me for the rest of my life, Daman!"

"I don't claim to understand you, Sophie, but I have no reason to hate you."

He again expressed concern for my health and acted as if he'd forgotten about the scene I made with Pat and Luisa. The amazing thing is that he probably has! Twelve years ago, when Minnie had slapped his face after the formation of the *Omissions* "staff," he had walked away, and a few days later he had simply driven to Minnie's house to pick her up to attend the newspaper's production meeting — as if nothing had happened! He seems to take nothing personally. Two years ago he helped me get my first teaching job; when I was fired I showered him with insults; yet when he heard of another opening he called me again. And three weeks ago, at

Luisa's, he ran away from what must have seemed to him like a psychopath and a nymphomaniac. Yet here he was again, helping get me out of jail; he'll probably call me in a few days to tell me about another teaching job. In some ways he's insupportable, in other ways he's the nicest person I know. I told him, "I don't understand you either, Daman, and I don't hate you." I kissed his lips gently as soon as we were in the car.

Since Sabina wasn't expecting us before noon, I asked if he'd mind giving me a ride across the border to see if another letter from you had come to my box. Your newest letter was there. I cancelled the postbox. I won't be needing it any more. I tore the envelope open right there and started reading — but I got no further than the middle of the first paragraph: "More is breaking down and more is rising up than I'm able to take in." The tears that filled my eyes kept me from seeing the following sentence.

On the way home I asked Daman how Luisa had been arrested. I had already learned some of the things he told me. The picket line at Luisa's plant had become a battleground for various ideological groups. No, the competition between the groups wasn't set off by Daman's modest leaflet. Members of three or four political groups had created "radical caucuses" in the plant's union organization, and each group had come to the picket line to support the program of its caucus. The official union apparatus publicly labeled all these politicians "outside agitators," and union goons tried to remove them from the picket line. At that point the picket line became a battleground between entrenched and aspiring union functionaries. The political groups summoned their followers to the picket line to struggle for the right of radical politicians to join picket lines and peddle their programs without being stigmatized and abused. Of course Luisa was on that picket line from morning to night. She had been waiting for something like that to happen; she had hoped Pat and the people from the council office would set it off. The political groups won. Their members and sympathizers far outnumbered the union functionaries. At that point the union bureaucrats withdrew from the picket line, and the central union apparatus started circulating the rumor that professional saboteurs had taken over the plant. Busses loaded with armed police as well as an army unit with machine guns and a tank attacked the assembly plant. All the picketers, Luisa among them, were arrested. They were taken to a high school gymnasium where they were supposedly going to be "processed." The "agitators" were going to be separated from the people who actually worked in the plant and therefore had a legal right to be on the picket line. The identification cards of all the workers were taken, and they weren't returned, nor were the workers released! At that point all the people at the gymnasium were carted off to jail; the workers could no longer prove they worked at the plant. That was the union's way of punishing workers who had stood by the "agitators." Daman told me he would have been arrested too if he weren't in the habit of getting up at noon; by the time he reached the plant it was already occupied by the police and surrounded by soldiers. He went directly to the jail where the arrested picketers had supposedly been taken and arrived there before they did! He called the "radical lawyers' collective" and Minnie succeeded in getting Luisa released the very next day, at which time Luisa told them she had seen me in jail. I asked him if the people who couldn't prove they worked in the plant, namely the "outside agitators," were left in jail.

"What were we to do?" he asked me. "Leave Luisa in jail? A civil rights lawyer interceded for the workers whose cards had been taken away, and each political group engaged its own lawyer to release its own militants."

When we reached my house I tried awkwardly to ask Daman to forgive me for having been so mean to him, but he really did act as if he'd forgotten about it so I didn't try very hard. I asked if he wanted to come in, but he didn't.

Sabina heard me close his car door and came out of the house shouting after his car, "Hey Professor! Thank you!" She pulled me inside the house and hugged me tightly. "I felt like the last survivor," she told me. "Ted and Tina disappeared, Tissie is gone, you didn't come back — my whole universe vanished." Then she looked at my bruised face and shouted, "What did those bastards do to you?"

Disregarding her concern for my injuries, I asked her, "How did it all end, Sabina? Why?"

"I've been waiting for you to tell me that! You're the sociologist of revolution, not I. Look," she said, pointing to the walls, "I've thoughtfully decorated the house with research documents, so that you can tell me how and why. Are you well enough to look at them?"

"I'm well enough, Sabina, but help me! I don't think I can stand to look at them by myself."

Sabina escorted me to her "exhibits." I read until I collapsed in her arms completely nauseated. She had decorated all our walls with articles, headlines, pictures. All of them told, in a distorted, intimidating manner, the story of the death of the hopes of thousands of people. One after another story described in detail the "raises" the union had "won" for the workers, after which the workers had "victoriously" returned to work. Other stories described all sorts of "vandals" and "outside agitators" ousted from factories by "union officials assisted by law-enforcement agencies." I paused at an article which was headed, "Liberation of the University." My head swam as I read it. Several paragraphs described "guerrillas and terrorists" who had forcibly established "fighting bases" in all of the university buildings. The article went on to say that real students called the police to protect them from terrorists who were beating and threatening them. But the article didn't explain what the "real" students were doing there; presumably they were trying to attend their classes. The university administration then demanded forceful and decisive action to put an end to the anarchy and terrorism, at which point the police could no longer "simply stand by while the lives of students are being threatened." The concluding paragraph said the police did not receive orders to intervene until "responsible student groups" within the university itself called for the "liberation of the university" from the vandals, guerrillas and terrorists. It was after reading this that I collapsed. I couldn't read any more. I told Sabina what had happened at Luisa's plant and asked if the defeat had been similar everywhere.

Pointing to other clippings, she told me, "The pattern was similar at the research center and in several other plants. But the police only attacked places where the union's authority was challenged, which was the case at Luisa's plant and at the research center, or where there was no union, as in the university. In more than half the plants the police didn't have to intervene. The union herded workers back to their posts much more effectively and with much less friction than the police could possibly have done. When you feel better study some of the pictures, the ones of workers returning to their jobs after their victories, smiling and waving their arms!"

Sabina pulled me to the kitchen. She had prepared a rice casserole for my homecoming! On the table there was a bottle of wine as well as a bottle of champagne. I cried from gratitude and told her, "At least we still have each other." I asked if she was willing to tell me how she'd gotten separated from Tissie.

"Two or three days after you left, one of the women in the group I was working with discovered a miscalculation. I and several others threw ourselves into the problem. I was sure the vehicle would run if we solved that problem. Tissie wasn't with me. She was upset that neither Ted nor you had returned, and she wandered around the center thinking she'd run into one of you; she even waited for both of you at the gate. She wasn't able to interpret what she saw there, so she came to tell me about it. People who seemed to be workers were stopping cars at the gate and asking their drivers for documents. She was extremely nervous about it and begged me to abandon the center. 'Let's go elsewhere,' she begged; 'let's go far away from the city, near a pond; let's first find Ted and Sophia and Tina —.' I was angry. She had dreamt of an island empire before, in the garage; I wrongly thought she was reviving that suggestion. I told her not to worry about the new guards at the gate because they were probably people who had always wanted to be cops and had never before had a chance. And I told her not to worry about you or Ted or Tina; if the whole world was opening up, you were all having the time of your lives elsewhere. I returned to the transportation problem. By the time I realized Tissie had been right about the change of climate, it was too late. A fight broke out in one of the laboratories. A self-constituted 'Research Workers' Council' of four vigilantes confronted the lab workers because they were 'harboring two outsiders.' The whole group stood by the 'outsiders,' just as my group would have stood by Tissie and me. But the vigilantes started pulling the 'outsiders' out by force, several lab workers tried to stop them, and some instruments were damaged. At that point the union spread the rumor that vandals were destroying the equipment and that a worker had been killed. The people guarding the gate, I later learned, were union goons. They let in several cops to 'investigate' the supposed sabotage and killing. The vigilantes of the 'Council' immediately showed them the equipment damaged in the fight they had themselves provoked. Union loudspeakers announced that the investigators had found 'wanton wreckage' of equipment, and that the body of the murdered man had disappeared! I looked frantically for Tissie but couldn't find her. The police got the order to clear the vandals out of the center, which obviously meant everyone since they couldn't tell from looks. Swinging their clubs and pointing their rifles at us, they herded us out as if we were cattle. Those who didn't have cars were forced into busses until the whole area was 'clean.' The center was surrounded by police as well as soldiers, and they all looked ready to shoot at the slightest provocation. All that mattered was the precious equipment; the people were replaceable. I came home and sat by the telephone, but not a single one of you called. This house was like a prison. Two days after our eviction from the center I took a taxi to Ted's print shop and saw police outside and inside it; I went to the research center. There was obviously no sign of Tissie. What I saw was caravans of police cars, busloads of national guard, and police barricades that kept the taxi from getting closer than a block away from the gate, and even at that distance I was ordered not to get out of the taxi. I saw a large red banner above the gate but couldn't read what it said. I asked the cop who had ordered me not to leave my seat. 'It says; United we stand, divided we fall,' he told me. I shouted, 'The police and the union! How appropriate!' I rode back to my prison. Something inside me started to boil. I knew I had made a horrible mistake by throwing myself into that vehicle research. That mistake is thirty-two years old —"

"Don't, Sabina, please! I haven't seen you cry since Jose died. I can't take it, not now, not yet; I won't be able to swallow your wonderful meal —"

"You're right, Sophia. We do still have each other. I went wild with joy last week when Daman called. At least you had been found. And Ted called on the following day. He told me he had tried to return to the research center two days after he had left you with your friend Pat; he had stayed an extra day thinking you might want to go back with him. But Pat returned to the print shop by himself; he told Tina and Ted about some trouble starting in the university; Pat and Tina printed a leaflet and ran off with it; Ted didn't know what happened to them after that. So Ted headed back to the center by himself —"

"I wanted to go back with him, Sabina —"

"But you were busy evaluating who you really were and what you really wanted —"

"That's in fact exactly what I was doing, and I was writing Yarostan about it. Didn't Ted get back to the center?"

"The self-appointed guards stopped him at the gate, and he didn't have an identification card so they didn't let him in. He parked his car nearby, hoping he'd see someone he recognized who might let Tissie and me know what had happened to him. But the union guards saw him and got suspicious. Two police cars drove up to him. They asked him to explain his presence there. He told them his friends were inside the plant. They asked him to name those friends, but he refused. They beat him and then arrested him. When I told him Tissie had disappeared, he said, 'It figures.' I suppose it does. I know as well as Ted what she does whenever she's intensely disappointed and frustrated."

"Heroin?"

"Yes, Sophia. And her disappointment and frustration began when I refused to leave with her. Like the police, like Alberts, I valued the technology higher than Tissie's love —"

I interrupted her again. I was too weak to listen to Sabina's self-accusations on my first night home. I told her, "I have a surprise for you." I gave her all three of your letters. She read all three of them that night. I didn't read your most recent letter until the next morning. I couldn't, for the same reason that I couldn't bear to see Sabina tear herself inside out — not that night.

"Yarostan is right!" was the first thing Sabina shouted to me the following day. "We should have wrecked everything in that research center instead of just damaging a couple of instruments! None of that is for us, for our desires and capacities." Frustration and anger stayed with Sabina all week long. Your letters didn't set off her fury, but they did fan it; at the same time they helped her focus on the contradiction at the heart of her life. "What I tried to do to Tissie was exactly what Alberts and Luisa tried to do to Margarita, and what Luisa tried to do to Yarostan," she told me. "Tissie wanted only to swim in a pond, to lie on the banks in the sun, to walk through a forest. But I didn't want to. I wanted to eliminate ponds and forests. I wanted to replace them with something I helped create. I wanted an immense crystal palace with artificial suns, artificial ponds, artificial forests, all products of science and technology."

"You did have reservations when I talked to you at the research center," I reminded her.

"It's easy to have reservations, Sophia. I didn't act on them, and that's all that counts. I remained Sabina Alberts to the very end. I've lied to myself all my life. I always thought I had created such a perfect synthesis between Margarita Nachalo's and George Alberts commitments. I was wrong. What confused me was that Alberts had also been a rebel once. His rebellion was the diametrical opposite of Margarita's. She rebelled against the constraints imposed by social institutions. Alberts rebelled against nature. It wasn't when he became reactionary that he negated Margarita's rebellion. It was his rebellion itself that negated Margarita. He gave himself completely to science and technology. His rebellion was the rebellion of the brain against the rest of the natural environment. He was committed to destroy everything that wasn't science and technology, to destroy the very environment in which human life can take place. Whatever wasn't the brain's creation had to be destroyed, everything we call nature, the human being included. It's a horrible obsession. A puny part of nature, the brain, suddenly started destroying everything else, consuming the conditions for its own health and survival. It's as if mosquitoes started to consume the rest of nature, as if water attacked all the other elements and transformed them into water, as if fire suddenly attacked and consumed everything that wasn't burning. Alberts inverted Margarita's rebellion. She affirmed life, first of all her own life; she rebelled against everything that constrained the living. Alberts affirmed technology; he rebelled against everything that constrained the further development of productive forces. That's why he ended up considering human beings reactionary. Human beings constrain the development of productive forces; human beings have to be overcome. The beings who would inhabit the crystal palace wouldn't be human beings. They'd have to be progressive beings, beings which, like the suns and the ponds, were products of science and technology. Alberts tried to channel Margarita into a rebellion against herself. He failed with Margarita. She died fighting her own struggle. It was me that he succeeded in channeling. And all the time I thought I was channeling myself. I thought he was helping me realize my own desires, which I thought identical to Margarita's desires. Before we emigrated I made him promise to build me a lab. He kept his promise. He built the lab; he let me pull out of him everything he knew: chemistry, physics, engineering; he brought all kinds of books home: textbooks, theoretical works; he satisfied every desire he had himself created in me. Something crucial was still missing. I missed Jan Sedlak, the playful, independent peasant with whom I had spent the two wonderful weeks before we emigrated. And I missed his sister. I dreamed about the forbidden night we'd spent in each other's arms. The first gap was filled when you brought Ron Matthews home —"

"You were drawn to him like a magnet, Sabina. I thought the two of you were in love the moment you saw each other."

"I knew you thought that, and I resented your jealousy. Ron was just like Jan. After he'd stayed in your room for a week the three of us rode to a forest. That night I tried to pretend you were a little bit like his sister. But you were like a cube of ice. A few days later Ron came for us with his father's car. I hungered for adventure. I didn't know you, Sophia, any better than you knew me. You were mean, suspicious and freezing cold —"

"I thought you and Ron —"

" — had fucked in the water or on the beach, and I hated you for thinking that. I purposely made no effort to deny it."

"Is that why you called me a coward, just like my mother?"

"I thought you were trying to do to Ron what Luisa had done to Nachalo and Margarita: picked them up in the street and shaped them into becoming cannon fodder for her organization. I was wrong about you, Sophia, and I'm sorry I said that. I wasn't wrong only about you. I was wrong about myself. I was wrong about Alberts. At that time I still thought Alberts, Nachalo and Margarita stood for the same things. I thought Alberts would recognize Ron as another Margarita. All my bubbles burst when Alberts and I moved into our house and Ron moved in with us. Alberts couldn't stand Ron. He called Ron a hoodlum, an adventurist, a petty criminal. He called Ron exactly the same names with which he had described the 'reactionaries' who had fought against his 'popular army.' That was when I started to suspect Alberts hadn't fought alongside people like Ron, people like Nachalo and Margarita, but against them. My suspicions were all confirmed when I learned the role Alberts played in having Debbie Matthews fired from the high school. Ron was furious; he wanted to destroy Alberts' house, but I was too attached to my lab. Ron responded exactly as Jan would have: destroy the technology. For my sake he compromised; we decided to incapacitate the brand new projector the school had just acquired. It was a perfect theft. Nothing was ever proved. That bastard father of his got Ron jailed because he was a hoodlum and Debbie Matthews' son, not because they proved he had stolen the lens. He was sent to reform school and I was left alone with Alberts. I had to get out of there. I knew then that Alberts hadn't been Margarita's ally; he wasn't even Luisa's; he was as vicious a reactionary as Tom Matthews. I had met Jose at Ron's trial. He hated Matthews even more than I hated Alberts. He and Ron were almost brothers, you know, like you and I —"

I asked Sabina to tell me about the time when Ron and Jose had been "almost brothers."

"They weren't really like you and me, Sophia; they weren't as different from each other. Jose had been adopted by the Matthews during the depression; his father was unknown and his mother had died giving birth to him. Tom and Debbie both had jobs; they were also political militants. When Ron was born, neither of them had time to bring him up; Jose was Ron's nurse, teacher, mother and father. He taught Ron everything, including stealing. Once, sometime after the war, the police came to their house and investigated the stolen bikes they kept in their basement. Jose acted very professional and told them he and Ron repaired bikes; then he challenged the cops to prove the bikes in the basement were stolen; the first thing he always did was to change the color and registration number and to switch parts around different bikes. The police left, but by then Tom Matthews was no longer a political militant; during the war he'd become a staunch law and order man; he started to dream about buying his own store. He chased Jose out of the house and accused him of having turned Ron into a punk. Jose hated him after that. He got a factory job and a room. Suddenly he got drafted. He was sure Tom Matthews had called the draft board. Jose quit his job, left his room, and went into hiding. He looked up Seth, who was wealthy by then because he'd gotten into dealing heroin. Jose and Ron had stolen bikes with Seth. Jose dropped the name Matthews and became Siriso. Seth gave him a job, not selling heroin but making contacts. Jose had just started working for Seth when Debbie Matthews reached him and told him about Ron's trial. I was really impressed when I met Jose. Nothing appealed to me more than the idea of joining the hoodlums and adventurers Alberts despised. I saw Jose regularly; we talked about getting a project off the ground as soon as Ron was released. I couldn't wait. Ron took me to Ted's garage the day he was released. I knew then I had found everything I'd ever looked for. Ron and Jose were like Jan Sedlak's brothers; Ted provided the technology; Tissie was a perfect Mirna and Margarita. I thought everything would be perfect if I could only keep them all together. But that wasn't going to be easy. First of all Ted was hostile to me from the very first moment we met. Secondly, Ron pined for you; he lost interest in everything else. And you were beyond anyone's reach by then. I couldn't hang on to him. I became desperate. I didn't want to lose anyone else. Seth had money. The only way to combine Jose with Ted and Tissie was for all of us to buy the garage with Seth's money. To Ted that was heroin money —"

"But not to Jose?" I asked.

"Jose worked for Seth but didn't get directly involved in the heroin; he thought none of the rest of us would get involved either. Don't forget Jose didn't have that many alternatives. After being chased out by Matthews he'd gotten a factory job, and every time he'd seen Ron he'd told him, 'What a grind that is! There must be other ways to stay alive!' Don't you remember how passionately Ron hated the very idea of getting a job? And then that draft call made Jose furious. 'Those bastards don't just want you to slave for them; they want you to die for them too,' he told me. That was why he'd looked up Seth, and he'd been very impressed with the way Seth had 'made it' without letting himself be put through 'the grinder.' At that time he didn't care a whole lot just how Seth had made it. And neither did I. If everything was allowed and nothing was banned then Seth could 'make it' any way he pleased. But Ted didn't go along with any of that. He didn't say a whole lot that first night, but I could read on his face that he didn't like what Jose and I were telling him. What intrigued him was mastery over things, and he thought already then that heroin meant mastery over people. He made it a point of stealing only rich people's cars because he thought everyone ought to have access to what he or she needed, and stealing from the poor deprived them of their access. He and Ron had shared that attitude; that was what had drawn them to each other in reform school. I understood Ted's objections, but I dismissed them. I thought he was too limited; his attitudes conflicted with 'nothing is banned.' I told him he was a hundred percent right, and then I proceeded to do to him what Luisa had done to Nachalo and Margarita. I dragged him into a project that negated his own. I was set on combining George Alberts with Jan Sedlak; Ted and Jose were perfect for that combination. I had rejected Alberts the man, but not his world view. I tried to convince Ted by telling him others didn't treat him the way he treated them. He was Tissie's brother and guardian; he stole only from the rich; he thought he sold the cars to others like himself, to people who needed the cars to make life possible for other Teds and other Tissies. I told him he was blind: the people he sold the cars to resold them for a huge profit, and they exploited him as well as those they sold them to; they were no different from the garage owner to whom he paid enormous rents. Ted gave in, not because I convinced him but because I saw through him. We bought the garage with Seth's money and transformed it into the technological play-land I had wanted. Ted was simultaneously attracted and repelled by me. He loved to show me how to steal cars, and I quickly became almost as good as he was. I, in

turn, demonstrated to him the theoretical principles behind the mechanical operations he had learned from practice. He was grateful beyond words. But everything
else about me repelled him. He was afraid of my philosophizing; it was all lies to
Ted, lies with which I had covered up the fact that heroin destroyed the lives of
people like ourselves. He thought me a hypocrite. I had often repeated that any of
us could leave at any time and start again elsewhere. But Ted didn't want to leave
Jose or me or Tissie or the garage; he just wanted to exclude Seth and the heroin
from the garage. Telling him 'You can leave any time' was equivalent to telling him,
'Thanks for Tissie and the garage, Ted; see you around.' And Ted knew that if we
failed to distinguish people from things outside the garage, we'd soon fail to distinguish them inside as well; if we turned strangers into instruments, we'd soon turn
each other and even ourselves into instruments. And he was right. It was Tissie
who became the first instrument. Though not right away. It all took place in small,
gradual steps, so gradual that I failed to notice them until they had all been taken.
We were all full of enthusiasm when we fixed up the house behind the garage. I
knew Tissie wanted me as much as I wanted her; we had known this since the night
of Ron's release. But when the house was done, Jose and I each moved into separate
rooms, Tissie moved in with Ted, Vic with Seth —"

"Where was Tina at that time?" I asked.

"I had left her with Alberts; he hired a nurse to take care of her. Tissie wanted
to move into my room, but I didn't want her to; I thought that would drive a final
wedge between Ted and me. I didn't know Ted had long been familiar with the
nature of Tissie's passion. I exerted myself to stay away from someone I loved; that
was a very bad mistake. Tissie was frustrated and felt rejected. She fixed up another
room and moved into it by herself. And then she started taking heroin shots from
Seth. She did that only to spite me, as well as Ted; she convinced herself Ted was
responsible for my unwillingness to let her move in with me. It all became extremely
complex when Jose started courting me. I assured him I had never been Ron's girl
or any man's, but he wouldn't believe me. It was only then that I asked Tissie to
move in with me. But it was already too late. I did get Jose to accept me as I was; a
warm, mutual friendship replaced his initial unbelieving shock. But I couldn't get
Tissie to drop the heroin. She had been so pretty; she became sickly and mean. She
started to blackmail me with the heroin —"

"Tissie blackmailed you?"

"Yes, Sophia. All of Ted's initial fears started to be realized. We were turning
each other into instruments. Debbie Matthews visited the garage and told us Ron
had been killed. Debbie blamed me for his death, and in her drunken state she
considered Alberts responsible for it. So did I. To me Alberts symbolized the entire
reactionary apparatus he had decided to serve when he had Debbie fired from the
school. I rushed to Alberts' house and kidnapped Tina when the nurse went shopping. I left him a note telling him I had become a dope pusher and could therefore
take better care of Tina than he could. And before I left I destroyed the upstairs lab.

Tina was four and I couldn't stand her; she was so dumb; I only took her to spite Alberts. Jose felt the same way about her as I did, but both Ted and Tissie loved her as soon as they set eyes on her, and each wanted to keep the other away from her. Ted thought that in her condition Tissie would harm the child, and Tissie's resentment of Ted grew into passionate hatred; she started considering him her jailer. And that was when she started blackmailing me. She talked about moving to a deserted island with no one on it but Tissie, Tina and me. Gradually the island became the garage itself. She told me she wouldn't stop taking heroin unless I got rid of all the men. If I didn't get rid of them, then I was the one responsible for her taking heroin, I was the one who made her Seth's slave, because I kept her chained to Seth. I thought Tissie was hallucinating, both about the island and about my responsibility for her condition. I didn't want to believe a single word of her accusation. I had her move back to her own room; I wanted to be on my own. A few weeks later Ted told me he had decided to leave the garage. He didn't tell me his reasons; I knew them; I also knew he held me responsible for everything, just as Tissie did. Ted also thought Tissie's heroin addiction was a direct result of Seth's presence, and I was the one who had brought Seth as well as Jose to the garage. Ted had probably been convinced all along that we could have bought the garage and the building without Seth's money; I had doubted it; the sum had seemed impossibly large to me, and I had been in a tremendous rush to get out of Alberts' house. In other words, both Ted and Tissie were right; I was the one responsible for forcing Seth and Vic on them. Ted also blamed me for the impoverishment of the activity itself. When I had first moved in, he and I had stolen the cars, transformed them, repaired them. But gradually the garage became a fence, a depot for cars that younger kids stole; all we did was to pay the kids and transform the stolen cars; we were something like bosses to them, what Ted's boss had once been to him. And of course what Ted liked least of all was the fact that the garage served mainly as a front for Seth's heroin, that Ted's own activity served to cover up something he hated."

"I remember he hated the garage when I was there; it was Ted who turned Alec against all of you. Why didn't Ted leave? Because of Tina?"

"Don't keep reducing him to that, Sophia. Ted didn't leave because of all of us. Believe it or not, he also loved me and Tissie and Jose; all he ever wanted was the exclusion of Seth and Vic. But there was no way to get rid of Seth. He was the owner, and he acted more like an owner every day. If Ted had merely hated the garage he would have left. But his attitude was ambiguous, like his attitude to me. He was simultaneously repelled and attracted. And the things that attracted him went together with those that repelled him; they weren't really so separable. When Ted told me he wanted to leave, I already knew Seth was going to buy the bar. And although the bar added yet more things that repelled Ted, it also added several that attracted him enough to convince him to stay. I saw the bar as an adventure, as an enrichment of our activity. It was in fact Tissie who made me look forward to it. As soon as Seth had told her about the bar, she had boasted to me that she wouldn't need me or Ted any more. 'I'll be every bit as independent as my Goddess Sabina,' she told me. 'I'll be a high-class prostitute; I'll be able to buy my own deserted island.' I have to admit I too looked forward to that activity. Margarita had been a prostitute; I didn't want to exclude that from my life. And at that point Ted's prediction was fulfilled. After turning each other into instruments, we turned ourselves, our own bodies, into instruments. Tissie and I both became high-class prostitutes. Jose made the arrangements —"

"You mean Jose was a pimp? That's what Alec accused him of being!"

"No, Sophia, those weren't the arrangements he made. There were no pimps; or if you prefer, each of us did her own pimping. Jose related to the bar as he'd related to Seth's heroin; he made contacts, paid off certain people, threatened others. He had nothing to do with the prostitutes or the customers; the fact is that he disliked the bar as much as Ted did. Or I for that matter. I could have killed some of those important bastards!"

"Then why in the world did any of you stay with it?"

"I tried to tell you then, Sophia. We didn't create the circumstances. We found ourselves in them, and tried to change them. At least I thought we were changing them. It wasn't the prostitution that drew me to the bar. After the first night I hated that. It was what the bar made possible that drew me there. Do you know how much money we took in every night? Everything that was taken in was split equally among all of us. Seth got ten times his share because a lot of the women, including Tissie, as well as many of the customers were on heroin. Tissie paid Seth most of what she got. But what I alone made paid for the house, the garage, the workshop in the basement, both art studios, my lab, and all the materials and machines we could dream of wanting —"

"But then it was just a business —"

"I didn't want to think that, Sophia. I still don't. Ted didn't like where the money came from, but for a while he acted as if he didn't know. Once the bar started going he no longer needed to be a boss. He helped the kids set up their own garages and he only worked on the really difficult jobs. He spent the rest of his time in the workshop or upstairs painting. No one could ever have dreamed what a creative person that car thief would turn out to be. And Tina became a wonder. She took to everything he taught her; she was a painter and a machinist at six. Ted and Tina weren't the only ones either. I wish I'd showed you the workshops and studios and apartments set up by some of the women. I don't think it was just a business, Sophia. Most of those women were like Ted and Tissie; they'd come right off the street; if it hadn't been for the bar they'd have been turned into garbage. And there was no reason the thing couldn't spread. At least I didn't think there was. It was for Seth that the whole thing was just a business. The more money he took in, the more of a capitalist he became and the greedier he got. He couldn't stand Ted because none of Ted's activity contributed anything to Seth. He saw all of Jose's and my money and some of Tissie's go into the house and the garage, and he didn't like it.

He thought all of it went to support Ted and Tina and their projects, projects which in his eyes didn't produce anything. So he tried to force Tissie to get me hooked on heroin; when that didn't work he tried to get Tissie to take Tina to the bar. Ted stopped Tissie and when you came he thought Seth had recruited you as well —"

"That's what Tissie told me at the research center. But couldn't you have told Ted how wrong he was about me? That would have cleared up so many misunderstandings!"

"If I had only known, Sophia! I didn't learn a thing about that until Ted told me the details several years later! I was in euphoria when you came to the garage. Everything seemed to be working perfectly. I had no idea what was boiling underneath. I loved you for coming exactly when you did. I was at the peak of my life's accomplishments. During the months before you came my new friends had introduced me to experiences I had never before imagined. The bar gave me insights into the power structure of the entire city, insights which I thought I'd use against that power structure some day. The house and the garage had just been transformed into a technological Utopia. I was completely independent, and I was surrounded by people who resembled Jan as well as Mirna as well as the best side of Alberts. You couldn't have come at a better time. I thought that a few months' contact with us would transform you —"

"Into what, Sabina?"

"I thought you'd become a little like you are now: reserved and introspective, but warm and interested and lively —"

"And I disappointed you?"

"No you didn't! You became Jose's best friend; you seemed to enjoy your work with Tina so much; I was sure we'd gradually become good friends. You seemed irrationally afraid of Ted, but I was sure that would pass. I was totally blind to all the problems you experienced. I knew that Tissie was wildly jealous of you — but I knew that only because I fanned her jealousy; I tried to 'blackmail' her the way she'd blackmailed me; I told her I'd replace her with you and wouldn't take her back until she dropped the heroin. That was another mistake. Tissie tried to get back at me by taking you from me. It was only in the research center I learned about that night, Sophia. I suppose it's ridiculous to apologize now —"

"Weren't you even slightly angry at me for not having known or even suspected anything until then, for being so naive, so stupid?"

Sabina laughed and threw her arms around me. "On the contrary! I loved you for that! It was so characteristic of you!"

I was embarrassed by myself, but I couldn't help laughing with her. Our conversation took place about two days after she read your letters. It rained all day long, and it felt wonderful to spend the entire day indoors with Sabina listening to stories that helped me forget everything that had happened the previous week. After supper that night there was a violent thunderstorm; we turned out the lights and spent about an hour looking out the window at a frightening display of lightning.

When the thunderstorm moved away, I reminded her that during all these years I had never learned why she and Tina had finally left the garage.

"I think the presence of your friends in the garage made Seth hysterical. After Alec moved in Seth threatened me: 'If you don't get him out of there, I'll close up the garage and Ted and Alec and Sophia go out on the street.' I obviously told him to go to hell; he didn't pay the bills at the garage, he no longer lived in the house. But the fact is that he did own it. What I didn't know was that he actually became paranoid. On the day when your other friends came, Seth thought you and Ted had hatched a plan to get rid of Seth and Vic, though I still can't imagine how he thought you'd do that. And on that day I made yet another mistake. I thought Seth was offended by your friends for the same reason I was: because they had come to judge and to condemn activity which was organized by those with least access to self-organized activity. They had no right to judge us. I was actually glad when Seth pulled his gun on them, and I gagged with frustration when you took their side and left with them. After your friends left, Jose convinced himself all of us were becoming Seth's employees, his tools, as Tissie had already become. He as well as Ted tried to tell me that, but I wouldn't listen to Jose any more than I had ever listened to Ted. I was completely blind. I told Jose he was dead wrong; I talked about expanding the activity yet further, about helping set up bars and workshops elsewhere. I imagined that the crystal palace I had dreamed of was about to be built, from the ground up, by the people themselves, the lowest layers among them. Jose grew increasingly frustrated by his inability to communicate with me. We never learned why he got arrested, but I suppose he got careless with one of his contacts. It was only after Jose's arrest that I started to become aware of my mistake. Soon after the arrest, Tissie confronted me with a proposition that at first seemed like another one of her attempts to blackmail me. 'Get rid of the men' she told me again; 'Take over the bar, and I'll stop taking heroin and stick by you; we'll make it our empire. If you don't, Ted goes out on the street, the house and garage get closed down, and Tina comes to the bar.' It seemed like the same proposition Tissie had made earlier, except that I recognized Seth's threat behind Tissie's. And at that point I knew Jose had been right and Ted had been right since the beginning. Seth had pulled his gun on your friends; I knew he'd pull it on Ted as well, and on me if necessary. Seth somehow convinced himself I actually wanted to turn the bar into Tissie's and my 'empire' and my eviction was very simple; with his gun pointing, he told me, 'Clear out and take the kid with you.' Yet Ted stayed on until Jose's release! He couldn't abandon Tissie to Seth, and he even agreed to do some of Jose's contact work as a condition for his staying. If Ted had left too, the bar would have closed down when I left."

The following day was clear and sunny. After lunch Sabina and I went for a walk to the riverbank near our house. As we sat and watched boats pass by us, Sabina drew conclusions from all she had told me about her experiences in the garage, experiences which were so completely different from mine. "I tried to combine elements that couldn't be combined. Yarostan sees a contradiction between my commitments; I'm only starting to see that contradiction now. By the time I left the garage I knew we had all become tools, not only Seth's tools; we had also become tools to each other and to ourselves: in Seth's view we were nothing but costs in a capitalist enterprise. It's not the contradiction between Seth and the rest of us that's becoming clear to me now; that was clear to me by the time I left the garage. What I'm starting to see now is that the two parts of my own project were contradictory. I wanted to rebuild George Alberts' crystal palace with people like Margarita, people like Jan and Mirna and Yara. But that wasn't possible, Sophia. I didn't understand that until now. In order to do that I had to destroy them. None of them, not Ron or Jose or Tissie or even Ted could carry Alberts' project as their own. Ted was the only one who even came close to having some of Alberts' interests, but Ted never had a mania to destroy the environment; all he wanted to do was decorate it. I tried to be a bridge between land and water. I don't like to admit this to you, but I now see that my project had a lot in common with Luisa's. She picked up Nachalo and Margarita and gave them to Alberts and Zabran —"

"I don't see that, Sabina. Luisa told me Alberts came to them and offered them his services; apparently he knew how to make bombs. And she didn't even know Titus Zabran then —"

"You're right, Sophia. I'm thinking out loud. I'm not referring to actual situations, but to symbols. The question I'm asking is: who stole whose soul, and for whom? I know Alberts went to them; I also know he initially went to them in order to serve their project, not his own. But the initial affirmation of their project turned into a negation of their project, gradually, step by step, so gradually one couldn't see what was happening, as in the garage. Luisa got Nachalo into the union, but she didn't thereby transform Nachalo; she transformed the union instead. Nachalo and Margarita caused a split in the union local. Instead of bending to the apparatus, they made it bend. They formed something like a terrorist gang inside the union. Their goal remained what it had been before: to remove the obstacles to human life, to destroy everything that turned people into tools. You're right; Alberts introduced his knowledge into their framework; his explosives were to be used against the obstacles to their development. But this was the extent to which they were interested in his technology. Alberts was able to tell me that Margarita dreamed of industrializing the world from the ground up only because she died. Don't you see that? For Alberts the production of explosives was to be the first step; for Margarita it would have been the last. For Alberts that production was itself the goal; for Margarita it was nothing but a means. If Margarita was anything at all like Tissie or Mirna, and that's how I now visualize her, then she didn't dream of going on from the production of explosives to the production of artificial ponds, artificial sunshine and supersonic vehicles. Alberts read this into her, and he made me read it into her, because she seemed to have died for that, but only in his eyes. Alberts couldn't understand why else she'd have fought on those barricades, and neither could I. Now I'm starting to understand why; Mirna and Yara help me understand.

Yarostan told us why else Margarita would have fought. To clear away the obstacles to their enjoyment, not to clear away fetters to the development of productive forces. It was that 'popular army' Alberts joined that fought to remove the fetters to the construction of his crystal palace, and Margarita as well as Nachalo were among those fetters! That was the struggle Luisa tried to channel them into! She and Alberts were able to present them as forerunners of that struggle only because they were dead! Luisa tried to turn them into agents of their own repression and failed. They both had to die before they could become that. Only their corpses could be made to serve that struggle. She stole their souls and gave them to Alberts and Zabran. How else would you put it? She told you Zabran and Alberts fought alongside Nachalo. Only Nachalo's corpse fought alongside Zabran and Alberts; only Margarita's corpse fought Alberts' revolution! Yarostan speculates that Zabran couldn't have fought in the 'popular army.' Yarostan is very lucid about some things; he's wrong about Zabran. The very first time Alberts told me about those events, he described his recruitment into the 'popular army' by none other than Titus Zabran, who was indeed in uniform at the time; the 'popular army's' uniform. Zabran was one of the first recruits to that organization. Zabran and Alberts served in the same unit, on the same front; they experienced the same defeat, they retreated together, they were demobilized at the same time. Yarostan is right about the ambiguity of Luisa's claim that 'Titus and George joined Nachalo at the front.' He's right because they couldn't possibly have 'joined' Nachalo! I too would like to know what Alberts told Luisa when he returned from the front completely transformed. What surprises me in Luisa's claim isn't that Zabran fought alongside Alberts, but that the two joined Nachalo. I didn't know anything about the militia until Yarostan told us what he'd learned from Manuel; I'd thought what Luisa still thinks, that all of them fought the same struggle. That's why I was able to synthesize Nachalo with Alberts. But that unity didn't exist at its very origin. When Nachalo left for the front, a few days after the barricades, there was no 'popular army.' Nachalo joined a militia unit like the one Manuel described; he might even have been in Manuel's own unit. Alberts and Zabran 'joined' Nachalo the same way they joined Manuel: as mortal enemies."

We sat on a bench by the river until dark. On several earlier occasions Sabina had told me fragments of what she'd learned from Alberts about that revolution. I had always felt somewhat proud of the fact that my life was in some way connected with those events. But as I listened to her a few days ago I didn't feel proud; I felt uneasy, almost ashamed. During my entire life I had identified with everything Luisa had praised. Suddenly you and then Sabina started to undermine it all. I'm only now starting to understand the "reappraisal" you carried out during your second prison term, when you reexamined everything you'd learned from Luisa in the light of what you'd learned from Manuel. I'm starting to understand the significance of the "revolutionary tasks" Luisa accomplished "in the rear." She never hid the fact that the final aim of the efficient transportation, vehicle production, food distribution was military, nor the fact that the production was war production, nor the fact that it was devoted to the 'popular army's' military victory. Luisa gathered Nachalo and Margarita off the street and gave them to Alberts and Zabran. That's such a strange way to put it, but I couldn't tell Sabina I didn't know what she meant. I learned only recently that Luisa never really imagined daily activity as other than what it is, as 'joyless drudgery' for the sake of an apparatus whose goals we don't understand, whose reasons aren't our reasons. To Luisa that drudgery was meaningful, she even found joy in it, because she was always so sure that the people who directed the apparatus understood its goals and knew its reasons, people like Alberts and Zabran and Daman Hesper. I can see why Luisa insists Alberts and Zabran joined Nachalo on the same front. It's because her "front" isn't the actual field or village where the battles took place. Luisa's "front" is the train Zdenek described to you. It's the union. She was the one who took Nachalo aboard that train. Everyone on that train was part of the same struggle. But the content of the struggle, the destination, wasn't defined by the people on the train. It was defined by the train's conductors, the "professors devoted to our movement."

The reason I feel uneasy, even ashamed, is that I can't convince myself I ever wanted to do anything other than board that train.

Please give all my love to those comrades of yours who are intent on defining their own aims and on fighting their own struggle.

Your *Sophia.*

P.S. Don't forget to address your next letter to my house, since the postal strike is over. I almost forgot to ask you something that's been bothering me. You told me Titus Zabran was the first person who visited you after your arrest at the time of the Magarna rising. I think it really strange that he didn't mention my letter to you, especially in view of the fact that Mirna already then considered my letter responsible for all those arrests. The other thing that bothers me is that Titus apparently wasn't arrested at that time. I gather that Mirna looked for him and found him shortly after the arrests took place. But I had thought all the people I had written to had been arrested, including Titus.

Yarostan's ninth letter

Dear Sophia,
Your letter was as painful to read as it must have been to write. How can everything be over? How can workers without illusions about unions march back to work hailing their union's "victories"? How can a population that just woke up be back asleep?

We've been hearing rumors of an imminent invasion, of tanks massing at our borders, but those rumors disturb us infinitely less than the knowledge that "normal" life has resumed in your part of the world. We had begun to take it for granted that our fellow human beings in other parts of the globe were engaged in acts similar to our own. The council office and the commune, the occupied research center, the spreading general strike, had all become part of the geography of our world. You couldn't have shocked us more if you had told us a continent had sunk.

I was fascinated by Sabina's accounts and interpretations, but I have to admit I was shocked by her attitude to Titus Zabran. She treats him as George Alberts' confederate and as her enemy. When Mirna and Yara read your letter, they both acted as if their worst suspicions about Titus were confirmed, and they both subjected me to an extremely humiliating experience when I refused to join them in their condemnation of Titus. Both Jasna and I were so disturbed by Sabina's and your suggestions that we felt compelled to confront Titus directly. We learned that many of the facts Sabina revealed are true, but both Jasna and I are convinced that Sabina's totally negative attitude to the man is unjustified.

So much has happened here since Mirna and Yara returned from their excursion that I don't really know where to begin. The eagerness with which they greeted Sabina's "revelations" about Titus is due mainly to the fact that they seem to have argued with Jasna about Titus during their trip. Despite their enthusiasm about the excursion, the first thing Mirna and Yara talked about when they returned was Jasna's determination to marry Titus. Mirna told me indignantly, "Jasna seems set on destroying herself. Can you imagine what that man told her when she expressed admiration for Luisa, Vera and me? Those three women, he told her, don't deserve anyone's admiration, and certainly not yours. He then called all three of us shameless individualists who put their own personal satisfaction above the interests of their class!"

"What was Jasna's response?" I asked.

"She didn't defend a single one of 'those women.' She proposed to him! She told Yara and me that Titus said such things only because he's so lonely and isolated. She said as soon as she took him on an excursion like the one we were on, as soon as he saw what people were doing today, he'd stop being so bitter and contemptuous toward 'those women.' But I don't believe it."

"Mirna, are you sure you aren't condemning Titus for having attitudes that you've only recently shed?" I asked. "During the first two years after my release all you ever told Yara was: 'Stay out of trouble.' Until your plant went on strike you seemed unable to imagine why anyone would want to go on strike. Zdenek even found reason to accuse you of being your own jailer. I'm sure Jasna is right. Titus will surely change when he realizes the extent of the changes taking place around him."

"Why are you so defensive about him?" Mirna asked me. "Another thing he told Jasna was that Vera Krena isn't really in love with that Povrshan man but with his wife."

"That detail must have fascinated Yara."

"It did," Mirna told me, "But Titus didn't tell Jasna that in order to fascinate Yara. He told it in order to prove that Vera wasn't really a proletarian but a selfish individualist!"

Somewhat exasperated I shouted, "Vera Krena is not a proletarian; she's one of the leading bureaucrats in this country! You seem determined on fitting whatever Titus said into Yara's picture of him as Vesna's murderer."

Mirna's response to my exasperation was, "An excursion would also do you a lot of good, Yarostan!"

The first result of my defense of Titus was that Yara and Mirna told me very little about their trip. I did learn that such excursions are not an isolated phenomenon. Mirna and her friends ran into other "workers' delegations" wherever they went, and all of them seem to have been engaged in a similar search. Until your letter came, it seemed as if the human species were suddenly making a deliberate effort to discover itself, to explore the possibilities for starting anew. I also took part in this activity, although on a more limited scale, and my impressions were similar to theirs. I accompanied a delegation of carton plant workers to two other factories, and, contrary to what I told you in my last letter, the specifications for efficient carton production were neither my main interest nor that of my fellow "delegates." The discussion of cartons was quickly displaced by questions about each other, our intentions, our analysis of our potentialities and our means. I also found certain things that disturbed me, both in Mirna's and Yara's brief account and among the workers I visited. I've often mentioned Yara's fascination with some of the leading bureaucrats. This seems to be extremely widespread. I met many workers who described reforms as enthusiastically as strikes comparable to the one that broke out at Mirna's plant, and who praised reformist bureaucrats even while they were describing the possibilities for doing without them. This inability to distinguish the realization of one's own desires from the "victory" of the representatives of "everyone's desires" is particularly ominous in view of the disaster you've just described.

This willingness on the part of so many people to continue letting themselves be represented obviously allows the "representatives" of everyone's liberation to remain at the "head" of a movement that seems to be on the verge of ending the history of representatives. Politicians with imagination, like our acquaintance Vera Krena, have been very agile, not only at keeping themselves from being dislodged, but at increasing their power. Krena has very successfully used an anti-political movement, a movement which is undermining the power of bureaucrats, to increase her own status and power. During the past week her "wing" of the bureaucracy accomplished a feat comparable to the puppet show in which you and I took part twenty years ago. A week ago today Vera Krena and several other members of the "reform" wing replaced several leading "conservatives" in important government posts. The hypocrisy of the slogans with which this "feat" was justified is comparable to that of the slogans we helped produce during the days you no longer remember so fondly. Vera was far less dishonest in the speech Jasna and I heard several months ago, when she had spoken of the need to democratize the bureaucracy by giving more power to people like herself. During last week's events, when she finally acquired that power, she made public statements similar to those she had made during the radio broadcast I described to you. "It is not our aim to establish the iron dictatorship of a stratum of parasites, but to pave the way for the self-government of the producers," she said, accepting a government portfolio. Among other "accomplishments" so far, the "new" bureaucrats have passed resolutions favoring the right to strike and the abolition of censorship, namely favoring activity that has been taking place for months. Another acquaintance of ours, Marc Glavni, has been demoted as a result of the recent "coup", he is now a fourth secretary instead of a second secretary.

The day after Mirna and Yara returned from their trip, a vast demonstration took place, or rather a celebration of the "victory" of the reformist politicians. Almost all of the carton plant's office workers and most of the production workers took part in this demonstration. Mirna and Yara went too. I stayed home. Your letter hadn't come yet, but that day I already felt as if our former condition were being restored while we waved flags and shouted "victory." The feeling was reinforced by what happened the following day. The radio announced that an "extraordinary session" of the heads of the military organizations of all the "fraternal countries" surrounding ours had been held. It was announced that the "fraternal countries" were surrounding ours with four million soldiers armed with the most modern weapons, including I forget how many tanks. This announcement is clearly a threat of invasion, an ultimatum: either reestablish authority in a situation which, in Glavni's words, "threatens to get out of control," or else authority will be reestablished by four million armed "brothers," one for every three members of the population including children, old people, the disabled — probably a ratio of two armed "brothers" to every worker, a hundred tanks to every rifle ... Since we refused to heed Comrade Glavni's counsel not to allow ourselves "to get out of control," we will have to be "liberated" militarily for the second time by the same "liberators." By demoting Glavni, the "reformers" seem to be more intelligent than he at implementing his own project. If this population is to be brought back "in control" without tanks and liberation armies, this can no longer be done "under the leadership" of comrades like Glavni, but it can still be done under the leadership of reformers whose slogans refer to the most radical acts. Apparently the "fraternal allies" fear that this population is so far "out of control" that neither the conservatives nor the reformers will be able to reinstitute order. Their fear is of course my hope. What I hope is that the demonstrations of "solidarity" with politicians like Vera Krena are not renunciations of the willingness to move further, but confused affirmations of the desire for a society that doesn't need politicians. I still think my hope is more than an empty wish. Among the people I've spoken to, even those who were unreservedly enthusiastic about the reformers' governmental "victory" looked forward to more than the reestablishment of "order" decorated by the slogans of a revolution that failed to take place. I'm still convinced that the people around me want more than the seizure of power by their "comrades," their union, their revolutionary tribunes. Maybe I'm nursing an illusion, but I'm convinced that below the enthusiasm for revolutionary demagogues there's an undercurrent of desires which are seeking gratification, desires which cannot be vicariously satisfied, which cannot be carried by politicians the way programs can be carried. My own "education" in political "schools" has not done much to help me understand this undercurrent, but Mirna's and Yara's "insane behavior," as well as your letters, have recently made me suspect that more was happening than I was able to see. But if I'm right, if this population can no longer be controlled either by the Marc Glavnis or the Vera Krenas, then what? A population out of control within "national boundaries" is like an animal in a zoo — it's caged, imprisoned by zoo keepers; it isn't a free population. The military apparatus surrounding us is like the tamer of a wild beast. Freedom inside a cage is still slavery. Our acts lose their human significance; we become freaks, monkeys. Those four million soldiers are workers like ourselves, they're victims of the same repression. Yet they fail to recognize their likes inside the cage; their species-solidarity has either been blunted or removed; what they see is wild beasts "out of control." Mirna's excursion didn't go far enough. Communication did take place, and in a cage larger than a circle of friends or even a factory — but still a cage. "Out of control" will become "freedom" only when there are no more cages, of any size; when the free human being becomes the "normal" human being. Your two previous letters had given us grounds to hope that the largest of cages, the "national" cages, had started to be destroyed. The events those two letters described suggested that our "lunacy" had started to become the "norm," and the very act of exchanging letters with you suggested that it was possible to communicate across the most impassable of barriers. That's why your newest letter dismays me more than the "fraternal ultimatum" broadcast over the radio. Your defeat reduces a struggle for life to a struggle for survival.

Ever since the announcement of the ultimatum I've sensed a certain "play-acting" not only at home, where I've come to expect it, but also in the carton plant. Unlike a previous occasion when tank maneuvers were announced, most people seem to be ignoring the announcement, acting as if the tanks weren't real. But not only the tanks; the creative explorations in which we're still engaged also seem to have lost their reality. For example at the carton plant, "delegations" have been leaving the plant daily, without any specific purpose; there seems to be a determination to play out what is possible before the play ends. Mirna and Yara have carried this attitude to extremes; both seem determined to realize their wildest fantasies during a moment they already know to be finite. I have a feeling that the spirit has gone out of the exploratory activities, or rather that they are now being done in an altogether different spirit. We're no longer taking steps toward the creation of a new mode of social existence; we're acting as if we were on vacation from the old mode, as if we all knew, but didn't want to remember, that we would soon have to return to "normal life." For a population under continued military and police occupation for twenty-eight years, the tanks and occupation armies are "normal life"; the realization of desires is not part of "normal life"; dreams are realized only during vacations.

As if to confirm the fact that we were "only" on vacation, the city police have already started to act as if "normal" times were back. While reformist politicians are publicly calling for more "self-government," the police, who are now under the orders of "reformist" politicians, are already acting on the principle that "our fraternal allies" will accept the "reformists" into their fraternity only if the social order remains unreformed. We had a visit from the police (or rather I did, since Mirna and Yara were visiting Jasna) only two days after the ultimatum was announced, and they no longer behaved as they had several months ago, when the activity of their comrades in the political police was suspended. The police had visited us several months ago to inform us that our neighbor, Mr. Ninovo, had reported me for having "instigated" the demonstration at Yara's primary school; at that time they had apologized to me and had warned us about our neighbor. They weren't nearly as polite this time. Two officials came to the house last Saturday. They lectured to me about the fact that there was enough disorder in this society, and that consequently people did not need to add to it by "provocations and pranks against their own neighbors." They then told me two large snakes had been placed in Mr. Ninovos house several months ago. Mr. Ninovo had immediately informed the police, but at that time the police were too busy to remove them. Thinking the snakes were poisonous, Mr. Ninovo moved to a hotel. The police eventually removed the snakes, but Mr. Ninovo would not return to his house until the police determined the origin of the snakes and "punished the evildoers." Mr. Ninovo told them he was certain "the Vochek girl and her criminal father" had placed the snakes in his house. The police told me they had recently traced the snakes to the Zoology Faculty of the university, but had not been able to determine how the snakes had gone from there to Mr. Ninovo's house. I laughed and told them neither Yara nor I had access to the university's snakes. Both policemen were offended by my laughter and told me the next time snakes were found in any of my neighbors' houses both Yara and I would be questioned, not at home but at the police station, "until the matter of the snakes is cleared up once and for all."

Your letter arrived last Saturday morning, about an hour before the police did. Yara and Mirna both rushed to Jasna's to invite her to another reading session; they hadn't seen Jasna since the three of them returned from their excursion. I read through most of your letter before lunch time, when the three joined me. Your harrowing arrest at Luisa's plant, as well as Sabina's comments about Luisa and

Titus, were not in tune with the spirit in which Mirna and Yara returned from their excursion, but with the way I felt after the announcement of the ultimatum, and particularly after the unpleasant police visit about the snakes. Mirna and Yara both laughed when I recounted what the police had just told me, and Yara commented, "He deserved crocodiles."

The police as well as the snakes are forgotten. As soon as Jasna arrives, she tells me exuberantly, "Titus and I are engaged. We're going to celebrate our engagement two weeks from tomorrow, and I'm inviting all my friends. I hope by then you can talk Mirna and Yara out of their hostility toward him." I congratulate her and promise to try.

Mirna plunges into your letter as soon as she's back in the house. She reads while eating lunch and excitedly passes every sheet to Yara. Soon after she starts reading, Mirna exclaims, "Sabina didn't even know about the strike at my plant until her strike was over! You're talking about communication between continents, and Sophia isn't even communicating with the person right next to her. How sad! She didn't even know I was looking forward to art excursion across the sea. I wonder if she would have looked forward to seeing me." Stopping at a later point in her reading, she tells me, "Sabina is right about that night we spent together. I'm the one who remembered it wrong. I'd think she could figure out why I changed it. I pretended to be Jan making love to Mirna, but what I remembered was the night when Jan made love to me, because that was the most wonderful night I spent with him." Still later she tells Jasna, "You'll smile less when you read the rest of this letter. You're trying to convince yourself Titus is mean because he's so isolated. Wait until you read what he was like when he wasn't isolated."

Jasna, who has also started reading your letter, is irritated by Mirna's comment. "I can understand Yara's hostility to him; it's due to Titus' misguided helpfulness in having Vesna taken to the hospital against Yara's objections. But I can't understand your hostility, Mirna, as anything more than jealousy. You loved him once, and that's the only clue I have to your behavior. I should never have told you what he said about you, Vera and Luisa. He said those things only because he's isolated, lonely and unhappy. You know perfectly well unhappiness breeds bitterness toward other people's happiness. As soon as I got back I described our trip to him, I told him about your strike and Yarostan's strike, I told him he was isolated, removed from the experiences taking place and the people living them. I told him his goodness was turning into bitterness; he was becoming a spiteful hermit while I was becoming a spiteful old maid. And I told him I was sure that together we could find our way back into the stream of life. He responded by proposing to me. Don't you see that his proposal is virtually a renunciation of what he's become? He doesn't want to be bitter and mean. He wants to rejoin us as our friend; he wants to break out of his isolation. Why are you so set on destroying our happiness?"

Mirna says, "Titus was released twenty years ago while the rest of you stayed in jail?"

"Zdenek saw him in jail twenty years ago," I remind her. "He was told his arrest had been a mistake. It was undoubtedly his release that was a mistake. Maybe they let him out just to give the Nachalos the impression that all of us were being released."

"Mirna, I'm not talking about things that happened twenty years ago," Jasna pleads. "I'm talking about the happiness of two living people. Titus and I need each other, and we're perfectly suited to each other; we're both equally isolated; we've both sacrificed our lives for nothing."

But Mirna is unmoved. "He wasn't arrested with the rest of you eight years later either!"

"That's surely a coincidence," I suggest. "On the earlier occasion he was temporarily released to create an impression; on the later occasion he was arrested a few weeks later than the rest of us. That doesn't exactly make him an ogre."

"I don't believe in coincidences!" Mirna shouts. "Sophia asks why he didn't tell you about her letter when he visited you. She sent him a letter too, and even if he didn't receive it he certainly knew about it because I told him it had caused your and Jan's arrest."

"Mirna, on that visit Titus told me about Yara's birth, about Jan's disappearance, about your mother's hysteria and your father's loss of his job," I remind her. "Did you really expect him to remember to tell me about a letter none of us had ever seen?"

"Why do you want to kill the joy of two people whose lives haven't had much joy?" Jasna asks her. "Are you still playing that game you played on Yara when she returned from her excursion to the mountains? If you are, then I agree with Zdenek: you have a morbid streak. Do you still now believe happiness can only lead to suffering and death? Or are you still determined to force me to share the burden you had to carry by yourself for so many years? I don't understand you, Mirna. When I'm miserable you say, 'Poor Jasna.' Yet now that I'm not 'Poor Jasna' any more you seem set on making me miserable again! Why?"

"Because you're both lying to yourselves," Mirna answers. "Sabina asks why Yarostan is so defensive about Titus. That's what I'd like to know. Read the letter to the end, Jasna! Titus wasn't the hero you thought him. He fought in an army that killed people like Yarostan, Jan and Yara, people like Sophia's and Sabina's friends Ron and Jose and Sabina herself. Jasna, you're lifting a burden you'll never be able to carry!"

Jasna drops your letter and leaves the house shouting at Mirna, "Don't bother coming to my celebration if you still feel this way two weeks from now!" She slams the door.

I turn angrily to Mirna. "You did this to her once before, when she expressed enthusiasm for one of Sophia's letters. I'm convinced she's right: your hostility to Titus wasn't brought on by anything Jasna told you during your trip, and obviously not by what you've just learned from Sophia's letter. You and Yara were already hostile to him three years ago when I was released. Even earlier. Yara's face was a mask of hatred during her last visit to me, when she told me about Vesna's death. And I don't quite agree with Jasna about the justifiability of Yara's unforgiving hatred. I don't justify what Titus did with Vesna, but I'm convinced very few people, if any, would have paid attention to Yara at that moment. Yara is at least consistent; she doesn't flit from blaming Titus to blaming herself and her devil and your mother; she blamed Titus for Vesna's death from the moment Vesna died; she still blames him; she was disappointed with me when I was released because I didn't immediately see the monstrosity of Titus' deed —"

"That wasn't all that disappointed her," Mirna says sarcastically. "As soon as you came home she saw you had nothing in common with the Yarostan whose return Vesna had feared. Yara was disappointed because she saw that the passion with which I had frightened Vesna wasn't in you; it was in me! Yara realized Vesna's fear had been groundless; Vesna had played her game for nothing; there had been no reason for her to fear your release! Yara was disappointed, not only because you agreed with Titus, but also because you were as passionless as he! You weren't the companion I had promised her."

Yara, still reading, looks up and says, as if to defend me, "I didn't compare him to Mr. Zabran. Even Sabina doesn't say that."

"And what if she did?" I ask Mirna. "I was even more like Titus before that prison term than after my release, yet you didn't throw the comparison in my face then." I'm not really sure that's true, just as I'm not sure Sabina's opposite picture of me is true. During my second prison term I reevaluated the theoretical insights I had learned from Luisa and from Titus, and I rejected many of those insights. But I didn't reject the approach to life I had learned from them, and I think that's what Mirna is pointing out. I was theoretically committed to the overthrow of the existing social order, and it had been Titus and Luisa who had taught me how to be theoretically committed. In this sense Mirna is probably right; I was more like Titus after my release than I had been before. Earlier I had made some kind of "synthesis" between my political goals and my personal desires; I've already told you Luisa and revolution were almost synonyms to me. It was precisely this "synthesis" that fell apart during my second prison term. After my second release I had some kind of theory and goal, but they were no longer linked to what Mirna calls my "passion." I also felt terribly isolated. I had hoped to discuss my theoretical re-evaluations with Mirna and also with Titus, but at that time Mirna was in no mood to discuss anything, and after two short visits Titus stopped coming to our house because of the cold reception he received from both Mirna and Yara.

I try to remind Mirna of that period. "You're being unfair, Mirna. You weren't an ideal companion either when I returned home after eight years in prison. If anyone was bitter during those days, it wasn't Titus Zabran but you. At that time you blamed yourself for everything that had happened, not only to Vesna, but to me and Jan, to your father, to your mother. When did you start putting that blame on

Titus? It wasn't Titus' bitterness that kept him from our house, but your and Yara's hostility. The first time he visited, a few days after my release, I returned the two books he had lent me when he visited me in prison. And that was the only courtesy of which any of us were capable. It wasn't he who was bitter during that visit, but we — all three of us. He thanked me for the books. He told us how sorry he was about Vesna's death."

"He was sorry the way someone is sorry about a hailstorm that destroys a year's crops," Mirna tells me. "He was sorry because Vesna died, not because he felt in any way responsible for her death. He had felt responsible for her health. But the doctors were responsible for her death, not he. If he hadn't felt so responsible for her health she might still be alive today!"

"If you felt that way about him, why didn't you tell me at that time?" I ask her. "I was full of gratitude toward him; was I a fool in your and Yara's eyes? I thanked him for everything he'd done for us, including his trying to save Vesna. And then I proceeded to ask him for yet another favor, while you and Yara simply stood by. I told him I was marked again. I was unemployable; I asked him to find me another job. Why didn't you tell me to be wary of any job Titus would find for me? On his second visit, when he came to tell us he hadn't been able to find a job for me, you made him feel completely unwanted —"

"He didn't even look for a job for you," she says. "Don't you remember what he told you? It wouldn't do your health any good to have a job right then. It also wouldn't do Yara's or my health any good if you went off to work every day. We would all be healthier if you stayed home and helped Yara with the housework. He obviously knew more about our health than any of us did, just as he had known about Vesna's."

"When did you find all this out, Mirna? When did you figure out that by feeling responsible toward our health Titus was in fact responsible for our ills? You certainly didn't know that when I first came home, nor for at least two years after that. My opinion of you during all that time was that you were a self-repressed slave. And you didn't only repress yourself. You told Yara: 'Stay out of trouble! Don't take part in any mischief!' Yara responded with 'Yes, mommy,' and 'No, mommy,' carrying on her mischief behind our backs, telling neither of us anything until the day she came home wearing a sign. Then she described her demonstration to me, not to you. And Yara was perfectly right; if there had ever been mischief in you, it had completely disappeared. Your view then was that mischief, passion, life could only lead to suffering and death. When your mother died you became even quieter. Your mother had blamed you for everything that had happened; when she died you internalized all her blame. That was the burden you've been carrying: your mother's blame. You tried to become toward Yara what your mother had been to you: a censor. Stay out of trouble, repress passion, because you'll cause Yarostan's re-arrest, you'll cause Mirna's death, you'll destroy everything you love."

"That's right, Yarostan, and when the police came to the house after Yara's demonstration because Ninovo told them you had inspired it, I thought my mother had been right. I was sure the devil in me carried a sword and intended to destroy all of us. I remained convinced of that until the day when Yara told all of you there had been a devil inside Vesna too. That night Yara convinced me it wasn't the devil that had killed Vesna, but the fear of the devil. It was the intrusion of the world Jan had hated, the world that makes our love impossible, Titus Zabran's world, that killed Vesna. Yara showed me that what my mother had called the devil is what's most natural in all of us, what we feel; it's our desires and our passions; it's what we are. No sword is needed to embed the devil in us; the devil is already there; it's the removal of the devil that requires a sword. It was Zabran and my mother with their crystal palaces and heavens and gods that made Vesna fear her own self, her own desires, her devil."

"That's what you told me before you left on your excursion, Mirna. At that time it seemed like a fine justification for your excursion, for your strike, for your complete transformation since the day when you beat Yara for flaunting her love games. Vesna's doctor succeeded in curing you. Was it also Yara who swung you to the opposite extreme, who shifted your hatred of yourself to a hatred of Titus and Jasna?"

Yara, who has been listening to our argument while trying to finish your letter, objects to my accusation. "I never shifted any blame to Jasna."

"Am I right about Titus then?" I ask Mirna. "Until a few weeks ago you blamed yourself for Vesna's death, as well as Jan's, your father's and your mother's. You didn't dream of missing a day of work, nor of going on strike; you were opposed to the gratification of desires, not only your own but Yara's as well. Suddenly all the blame is on Titus Zabran's head. All Yara can actually prove to you is that Titus took Vesna to the hospital against Yara's wishes, and we all know that. Yet what you threw in Jasna's face was the suggestion that you now blame Titus for everything. Suddenly Titus is a devil who carries a sword —"

"I've told you it's not the devil who carries the sword!" Mirna insists. "It's your friend Zabran and his friend Alberts! It's those who suppress their own devil and set out to murder it in everyone else. It's the ones building crystal palaces; the devil is in the way of such palaces; the devil loves trees and streams and sunshine —"

"I don't think you understood Sabina's point," I tell Mirna, although I'm not sure of that even as I say it, and both Mirna and Yara are going to make me regret telling Mirna that she had misunderstood Sabina. I nevertheless go on, "Sabina was talking about industrialization, not about the repression of desires. People were in Alberts' way. People are always in the way of industrial expansion. Sabina makes a great deal out of the fact that Alberts, as well as Titus, themselves took up arms against the human beings who stood in the way of their project. Now you're telling me both Alberts and Titus had something in common with your mother, that what all of them really opposed was the realization of one's desires, and that therefore your mother was ready to take up arms —"

"Yarostan!" Mirna shouts; "I'm going to force you and Jasna to decide which side you're on, once and for all!"

"You and your doctor!" I shout back.

Mirna gives her hand to Yara and says, "That's right, me and my doctor! We'll show you who it is that takes up arms, and why."

"And in the process you'll make at least two people miserable, two people who are desperately reaching for a little happiness —"

"One of those two isn't reaching for happiness —" Mirna shouts, but I rush to the bedroom and slam the door shut, tired of hearing about Titus' supposed guilt and responsibility. Mirna spends the night in Yara's room.

Mirna has already left the house when I get up the following morning. Yara has breakfast ready for me and is suspiciously friendly. "Isn't it a perfect day?" she asks, even though it's dark and cloudy. She acts as if she hadn't heard the previous day's argument. "Mirna promised to take me to an outing today," she tells me.

"Just you and she?" I ask.

"Oh no, it wouldn't be complete without you and Zdenek," she says.

"Where does she want to take us?"

"To the top of the mountain." Yara's tone tells me she's in a very mischievous mood.

"Are you sure she wants to take me?" I ask. "We're not exactly on the best of terms; yesterday she told me I wasn't fit to be taken to the top of the mountain."

"I'm taking you," Yara says, "and I'll show her she's wrong. She's taking Zdenek."

"I'm not sure I'm willing to go to the top of the mountain, Yara."

"You have to go," she tells me, climbing on my lap and kissing my cheek. "If you don't go you'll prove I was wrong and she was right."

"I wouldn't want to do that, would I?"

"You'll go then?" she asks, pulling me out of my chair and throwing her arms around me.

"How could I turn down your invitation, Yara?"

"I knew you weren't what she said you were!" she shouts, running off to her room. A few minutes later she returns with her dyed black hair hanging loosely over her shoulders, and she wears the slacks and jacket that had made her look like Sabina at the dance at Mirna's plant. "'You liked me like this, didn't you Yarostan?" she asks me, extremely coquettishly.

"I like you even better as yourself, Yara," I tell her, embarrassed by her question.

"I'm almost exactly as old as she was when Jan made love to her in your room."

"But you're not Sabina, and I'm twenty years older than I was then, Yara."

"Up there years don't matter," she tells me.

Unfortunately the arrival of Mirna and Zdenek prevents me from pondering the significance of Yara's last statement. Mirna and Zdenek come laden with food and wine all of which must have come from Zdenek's apartment, since it's Sunday and the stores are closed.

"He's going! I told you he would!" Yara shouts to Mirna.

"Wonderful," Mirna says to me.

"Your outing wouldn't be complete without me," I tell Mirna sarcastically. "Are you bringing Titus too?"

Mirna turns her back to me and starts repacking the food with Zdenek.

Yara asks me, "Why don't you talk Jasna out of marrying that awful Mr. Zabran?"

"And what then, Yara?" I ask her. "Marry Jasna myself?"

"She loves you more than she loves him, and she'd listen to you," Yara tells me. Mirna laughs, and even Zdenek seems entertained by Yara's "joke."

"You're almost as clever as your mother, Yara," I tell her; she'll make me regret that statement later. "Titus and Jasna are perfectly suited to each other, and I have nothing against Titus except what he did to you and Vesna —"

"Nothing?" Yara asks. "Not even after Sophia's letter? Don't you see —"

"I only see you and Mirna jumping to far-fetched conclusions. Titus is my friend; he was my first teacher, I like him, and I admit I have much in common with him."

"That's what Mirna says, but I don't believe you have anything in common with him," Yara says firmly, as if she were determined to make her statement true. "Please don't be like him!"

"If the purpose of this excursion is to prove to me the villainy of Titus, then I think I'll change my mind —"

"That's not the purpose at all!" Yara shouts, embracing me again, her eyes begging. "It's just that it's such a perfect day for this outing."

"Is it your idea that this is a perfect day for an outing?" I ask Zdenek.

Smiling sheepishly at me, Zdenek admits, "It's not a perfect day at all; it looks like it's going to rain any minute."

Mirna places her arms around Zdenek's neck and tells him, "You well know there hasn't ever been a more perfect day."

Of course at this point I figure out that Zdenek is "in" on the plot, but I still don't know just what the plot is. The closest I come is to suspect Mirna of wanting to "get even" for the previous night's argument by using Zdenek to rouse my jealousy, and I'm surprised by Zdenek's willingness to be used that way. "You're not going to let rain stop you, are you Zdenek?" I ask him sarcastically.

"I'm not sure I know what I'm getting into; are you?" he asks me.

"Whatever it is, I'm looking forward to it," I tell him.

Each of us carrying a basket filled with food and wine, we set out on the two-tram journey to Mirna's and Jan's former neighborhood. When we leave the end of the second tram line, we don't head toward her parents' former house, but to the clearing where Mirna took me twice before. It's still as abandoned and as "private" as it was the last time Mirna and I came here twelve years ago; I couldn't have found it by myself; perhaps it's so undisturbed because no one else found it either. The sky grows increasingly dark, but Mirna beams with satisfaction, sets her basket down on the ground and stretches out on the grass as if the sun were shining. Yara throws a cloth on the ground and starts setting the food on it, as well as one after another bottle of wine.

"And now would the three of you mind telling me what it is we're celebrating on this cloudy and dark Sunday?" I ask impatiently.

"We're not celebrating an event but a place," Yara says; there's a wild, absent expression in her eyes; I've seen such an expression before, in Mirna's eyes. "We're celebrating my birthplace. Long before I was born country girls my age ran to this clearing on moonlit nights; they drank down bottles of wine and danced naked in the moonlight until the moon stopped still in the middle of the sky at midnight. Then the devil stepped out of the dark forest and made love to every one of them. By that act they all became sisters and they lived only for the night of the full moon when they returned to this clearing once a month."

"Are we going to have to stay until midnight waiting for your devil?" I ask her naively.

"They waited for that night because nothing was possible for them during the day. That single night became their only day; that full moon became their only sun. But we don't have to wait until midnight because for us everything is becoming possible during the daytime. Soon even the clouds will be gone and we'll be able to do everything we want and love everyone we love in the light of the sun."

"You amaze me, Yara. You sound exactly like Jan — and like Sabina," I admit to her.

"If we hadn't been properly introduced, I would have thought those two sisters," Zdenek announces after guzzling from a bottle of wine; he shows signs of being slightly drunk.

Mirna sits up, helps herself to the sausages and salads Yara displayed on the ground, and clinks a bottle of wine against Zdenek's. "Do you realize we failed to celebrate Sophia's success with her philosopher Pat?" she asks. "Imagine! A boy young enough to be her son, the same age as Sabina's daughter! And in spite of all her previous expectations, she enjoyed every minute of it. And she couldn't have staged it more perfectly if Yara had been there to help!"

"Yet you just told me it's all over for Sophia," Zdenek observes. "Which only proves my point, Mirna. Perpetual dancing and lovemaking may be the goal, but to reach that goal something like a union is necessary."

Mirna jumps up and pours the remainder of her bottle of wine directly over Zdenek's head. "This is all you'll ever get from your union, Zdenek! When we get back you can read Sophia's newest letter and see just exactly what the union did to her and to Sabina and Tissie and thousands of others who wanted only to dance and make love."

Trying to crawl away from the pouring wine, Zdenek shouts, "You don't prove your point that way, Mirna! How could a union have soaked those workers? In her previous letter Sophia gave the impression all those workers rejected the union!"

"She was wrong," Mirna tells him. "It turned out the majority of those workers were more committed to unions and trains like the one you described than you ever were. They locked themselves into windowless compartments and let themselves be driven right back to prison!"

"If it took them to prison it wasn't the kind of union I had in mind," Zdenek objects.

"You obviously think your own train is the exception, but you'll see that Sabina was infinitely more honest than you are. She admitted that her own train, the one she devoted her whole life to, led nowhere except back. Tissie was the only one who knew exactly what she wanted."

Zdenek asks, "And what was it Tissie wanted?"

"Sabina's love, Sophia's love, the love of all the women in the world. For Tissie the devil had the shape of a woman, a beautiful young witch, with whom she was alone in a forest by a pond, lying naked in the sun, making love." Mirna, who is on her second or third wine bottle, seems as drunk as Zdenek.

"And how did Tissie hope to reach what she wanted?" Zdenek asks her.

"Like this!" Mirna exclaims, reaching out for Yara. When Yara gets up to move toward Mirna I notice she's drunk too; she swims toward Mirna, who pulls her down to the grass and falls on top of her. "How, Zdenek? Like this! It's not a train, Zdenek. It's mother with daughter, sister with sister, woman with woman. Is this position not included in your philosophy?" The two roll on the grass so that Yara is now on top of Mirna. "I couldn't accept it into my philosophy either. Sabina told Sophia the truth. I carried my mother inside me. I distorted one of the most precious experiences of my life. I remembered it wrongly, I changed it so I wouldn't offend my mother's feelings. I told myself I let Sabina make love to me only because she pretended to be my brother. I lied to myself." Saying this she rolls over again and presses Yara-Sabina to the ground. Zdenek and I stare, completely fascinated, at the intoxicated mother and daughter locked in a passionate embrace. "It was I who pretended to be Jan. I couldn't bear to remember it that way, because I wanted to believe Jan had made love to me that night. Sabina told me Jan had showed her how he loved me, and I wanted to believe he loved me as a body, the way I loved him; the only way I could make myself believe it was if I remembered that Sabina pretended to be Jan and showed me how he had wanted to love me. I never knew he loved me that way until this letter came. When we'd slept together as children the initiative had all been mine. Jan would lie perfectly still, I'd put my cheek on his, just like this. Then I'd slide down, undo his shirt, and kiss his chest and his stomach. He stroked my hair but didn't ever move on top of me. It was only from Sophia's letter that I learned how free he was with Sabina and with other girls he pretended were me. If I'd known then, I would have been the one who lived in his room with him, I would have been Jan's wife-sister until they came to separate us with rifles and tanks. Yes, I lied to myself about that night. I didn't really believe Jan loved me the way I pretended he did."

My dumb fascination turns to embarrassment when Mirna removes Yara's jacket and shirt and lets her lips wander from Yara's chest to her stomach.

"Sabina is right," Mirna continues. "I did to her what I wanted Jan to do to me, what he never did to me until we were forever separated and he was forced to substitute me. And she's right: it was beautiful exactly as it happened." She slides her lips to Yara's. "Every motion, every caress, every kiss I had ever dreamed of receiving from Jan I gave to Sabina, pretending she was I. I was as happy that night as I had ever been with Jan. That was all I wanted in life: the possibility to embrace those around me, all of them, to feel them, caress them, kiss them —" Mirna's head dangles above Yara's stomach and her hair sweeps across it in rhythmical strokes, like a broom. Drops of rain fall on Mirna's naked back.

Yara is panting, her hands frantically press Mirna down toward her thighs; she begs, "Don't stop Jan-Sabina-Yarostan —"

I turn my head away, confused, and I have to admit, disgusted. I announce, "It's starting to rain."

Mirna asks sarcastically, "Do you hear, Sabina? It's the woman with the broom." When I turn toward her angrily, she stops her stroking motions and pulls Yara up to sitting position. I'm afraid of the look in Yara's eyes: she's drunk, and stares wildly at me. "Yarostan thinks it's raining," Mirna continues. "We brought him with us so he'd make love to my mother who hadn't touched a man since I'd been conceived. But he can't go through with it because it's raining. For Yarostan the revolution means getting out of the rain, back to the safety of the carton plant, back to the meetings, back to his teachers Luisa Nachalo and Titus Zabran."

"He's not at all like that," Yara objects drunkenly. "I can see it in his eyes. He's not like the old woman or like that stiff Mr. Zabran. Yarostan is one of us —"

Mirna places Yara on all fours like an animal and pushes her toward me, telling her provocatively, "Prove it, Yara! Show us he's not like that."

While Yara crawls toward me, Mirna crawls behind Zdenek and pulls him down to the ground by his hair. Zdenek lies on the ground as if he were asleep or dead. Mirna starts to unbutton Zdenek's shirt and shouts to Yara, "Like this! Daughter with father! What could be more natural? What could be more beautiful? We're waiting, Yara! Show us who your father is like!" The rain increases. Mirna, suspended over Zdenek like an awning, shields his face and chest from the rain.

Yara, now behind me, starts imitating Mirna and I lose track of Mirna and Zdenek. Yara pulls with all her strength but instead of letting myself be pulled down to the ground I place Yara on my lap and tell her, "You don't know what you're doing, Yara. You're drunk."

"I know what I'm doing," she says drunkenly; "It's the most natural thing in the world. Haven't you ever seen how freely the animals do it? Rabbits, dogs, cats play love games whenever they feel the desire. Sister plays with brother, son with mother, daughter with father, always in each other's company, without shame. Among animals it's nothing to hide. Only people have shame, people like the old woman, people who don't have desire, and you're not like them!"

"I don't know who I'm like, Yara." My head is swimming.

"Earlier you said I was as clever as Mirna," she reminds me. "Were you lying? Don't you like me?"

"I like you very much," I tell her, kissing her playfully.

But Yara plunges her tongue into my mouth; her whole body writhes; she begs hungrily, "Open your mouth, father! Kiss me! Even Vesna could kiss!"

I turn my face away. "I don't like you that way, Yara."

"I love you, father!" she shouts, holding me with all her might; "Make love to me!"

"I can't play your game, Yara." I try to push her away.

"Yes you will!" Yara screams. She pushes me to the ground, tears my shirt open and throws her naked chest on mine. "You'll play my game until it's over! This is the revolution; it's right here; there's no other!"

I try to push her gently away from me. "Yara, stop, before I —"

But the more I push, the more hysterical Yara becomes. "Love games in every possible combination, every possible place and time, that's the revolution! You read that in Sophia's letter describing Sabina and her garage — and you toasted to Sabina and to Tissie! Why are you being such a hypocrite?"

Losing all my playfulness, I push Yara away from me and shout, "That's enough, you hear? You're drunk! You don't know what you're doing!"

Shouting hysterically, "I love you! Don't be Vesna!" she throws herself at me and pushes me back down to the ground. You could not have felt more shocked when you found yourself under Tissie.

"Stop it!" I command, but she has the strength of a frustrated wild animal attacking her prey; the expression on her face is completely deranged. I use all my strength to try to restrain her, to hold her at a distance.

But she still reaches for me, forces herself on me, shouting, "I want you, father, I want you!"

Suddenly I'm pulled down from behind and my arms are pinned to the ground by Mirna, while my legs are pulled straight by Zdenek. My violent kicks and twists prevent Yara from staying on top of me, but provoke her to keep trying.

Mirna, her face upside-down above mine, as drunk as Yara, tells me, "This isn't right, is it, Yarostan? It's natural, but it isn't right. What's natural is gentle; it takes place through a kiss, a caress, an embrace. But what's right requires shouting and kicking and beating! What's right requires the broom and the gun and the tank —"

Yara, thrown off again, laughs as if I were playing a game with her. She dives at me again and clings to me with all her might.

I shout hysterically, "You've gone crazy, all three of you!" I pull one of my hands away from Mirna's grasp, clench it into a fist and swing it into the side of Yara's face. Then she flies off me, howling, covering her face with her hands. Zdenek lets go of my feet to examine Yara's face, and I give him a kick. I get up shouting, "If this is your idea of enjoyment, then I agree with Titus. You need to be in the hospital, all three of you!" I put my shirt on and start to walk away from the "devil's" clearing.

Mirna shouts after me, "My mother is watching and listening from her bed in the sky! Stop their games, she's telling you! Kill them, she's telling you! There's no other way to stop their games, their passion, their desire to live! It's not the devil who carries a sword, not I nor Yara nor Sabina. It's she and you who carry it! It's not passion that brings destruction, but the fear of passion! Lock the devil up, she's telling you! Destroy the passion! Run from it! Or do what Vesna did: lock yourself up, destroy yourself —"

"Is this what the two of you did to Vesna?" I ask angrily, continuing to walk away from the clearing.

"You're worse than the old woman, you're worse than Zabran!" Yara shouts after me.

"Yes, Yarostan," Mirna shouts. "This is what the two of us did to Vesna! And Vesna grew rigid, her face became twisted with fear, just like yours!"

I place the palms of my hands over my ears and run to the tram stop. The tram isn't there, so I run to the next stop to wait for it. My heart thumps; my whole body is filled with outrage, with revulsion and, yes, with fear and shame of a passion I don't allow myself to feel, a passion I tried to stop the only way

I knew how: by violence. The tram finally comes and I do what Mirna said: I run from the passion. On the ride back to the city, I remember Mirna's threat, "I'm going to force you and Jasna to decide which side you're on!" Apparently she and Yara had disagreed about that, and I had proved Yara wrong, I had proved I wasn't on Jan's side, on Sabina's side, I had proved that for me there were bounds, there were limits, everything was not allowed.

When I reached home, I went straight to bed but couldn't sleep. I tried to convince myself I couldn't have acted any other way. I heard Mirna and Yara return. Both of them rushed to the bathroom. When I heard Yara cry out with pain, it dawned on me that I had hurt her face seriously with the blow of my fist; my hand had gotten slightly cut, and the blood next to the cut was apparently Yara's. I grew concerned; my heart pounded with guilt. But I couldn't make myself face either of them. Then they became quiet; Mirna apparently put Yara to bed.

Suddenly Mirna rushed into our bedroom and held a mirror in front of my face. She had never before been so drunk. "Do you know what dead people look like?" she shouted at me. "Their faces are pale, their bodies are contorted, there's a horrid lifeless fear in their eyes. Some of them breathe, but their breath has no life, nothing stirs inside them, they're not moved by their own passions and desires, their limbs and organs aren't able to respond to the fire of life because no fire burns inside them —"

"Mirna, I couldn't — not with Yara —"

She disregarded my interruption. "— Burned out themselves, they hit and beat and kill those whose bodies are on fire, putting out fires, healing, saving, jailing, sacrificing. Real people and real passions are in their way, they mess up their crystal palaces." Working herself up into a drunken rage, Mirna throws the mirror on the floor and shatters it. "I've had enough God-worshippers in this house already! I won't allow any more life to be sacrificed to gods! I built the shed for God's priests and saints because I don't want them stinking up my house with their purity! This is the devil's house!"

I didn't move to the shed. Mirna again spent the night in Yara's room and left me "quarantined" in our bedroom. I didn't sleep very much. I couldn't make myself understand that Mirna had wanted me to go to the point of copulating with my own daughter. Surely that act is beyond the limits of the unrestricted freedom which had so attracted all of us when Sabina described it. Was I really what Yara had called me: a hypocrite who applauded at a great distance acts which I dared not undertake in my own home and neighborhood? Or was this whole episode to be explained as nothing more than a drunken spree?

I left the following morning before either Mirna or Yara were up. When I returned, they were both in the living room with Jasna. I immediately noticed a bandage around Yara's jaw and started to walk toward her, but was stopped by a look of hatred identical to the expression on her face the last time she had visited me in prison. Yara stomped past me out of the house and slammed the front door so hard the whole house shook.

Jasna greeted me with surprise in her eyes and then turned to Mirna to ask, "Are you sure it was an accident?"

Mirna told her, "Yes, it was an accident." She then asked me, with an incomprehensibly sweet tone, "Did you swing your elbow into Yara's face intentionally?"

Her tone mystified me completely; it indicated that Mirna was already playing another game, a game with an altogether different point. But I have to admit I was relieved by her hypocritical sweetness. The previous night she'd threatened to ask me to leave the house and do what? Court Jasna? Mirna and Yara had apparently ascertained it no longer made any difference whether Titus or I courted Jasna, since they had proved Titus and I were "the same." Yara's door-slamming indicated she was still indignant about that "discovery," but Mirna was apparently ready to move on to the next "scene."

Jasna was too preoccupied with her own problems to be wary of Mirna's new mood. "I just told Mirna I've confronted Titus with most of her suspicions," she told me furiously. "Except for his brief period of military service, Titus never raised a hand against anyone. If you and Mirna and Yara are suspicious of him, confront him to his face, not behind his back! He'll be glad to answer all your questions. He told me he was willing to answer history for all his acts. All his life he's been devoted to something. Is that what you hold against him?"

"Yarostan holds nothing at all against him," Mirna told her.

Jasna said angrily, "Last time I was here you accused him of having killed people like Yarostan and Yara and yourself! Why don't you say that to his face? I know he served in an army; I've known it ever since I first met him. But that army's task was to save democracy from fascism, not to kill people like you and Yarostan. You're unjust, Mirna. His whole life was lived in the service of working people; he never wanted anything for himself. Whether he was jailed after the rest of us or before, the fact is that he was jailed both times. It was when he came to see me after our second arrest that I first learned about you and Vesna. Titus felt so sorry for you; he told me you worked like an automaton all day long, only to return to two children and a crazy old woman. He helped me find my teaching position in the school. He helped Vesna get medical care the first time she was sick, when her heart murmur was discovered. He never told me about his amorous experiences with you, Mirna. He must have been too embarrassed; you were only half his age. He's obviously not the world's most passionate person, but neither am I; maybe that's why we've always been drawn to each other. But whatever he's lacked in passion, he's more than made up in solidarity and loyalty toward his friends. He's helped almost every one of us find jobs, starting with Yarostan and Jan. He even helped Marc Glavni and Adrian Povrshan toward social positions much higher than Titus ever aspired to. I know he helped once too often; I know he shouldn't have insisted Vesna be taken to the hospital the second time she got sick. But it was I who told him Vesna was ill again. And what was he to think when he found her in your mother's bed, feverish and hysterical? He obviously couldn't even imagine you held him responsible for Vesna's death. He came to see you twice after Yarostan was released. Titus told me Yarostan had asked for help in finding another job, but Titus didn't even try to find one; he told me Yarostan looked like a skeleton when he came out, and workplaces were so policed that Yarostan would have gone insane even if he'd withstood the physical strain. That was three years ago. He hasn't offered his help to you or Yarostan or Yara since then. He knew you held something against him. Even his visits to me grew less frequent. It was only then that he became isolated, removed from events and from people. After a lifetime of helping the people around him, he was suddenly all alone. How could I turn against him now? How can you? If you suspect him of anything, tell him to his face!"

"You're absolutely right, Jasna," Mirna told her sweetly and contritely. "I have no reason to feel anything other than gratitude toward Titus. The first time I met him was after Jan's release fifteen years ago, before Yarostan came to our house when he was released the first time. Titus got Jan the job in the bus repair depot, and my father invited him to visit us. I haven't forgotten it was through Titus that Yarostan was hired as a driver, transferred to the depot and then hired in the steel plant after that fight with the foreman at the bus depot. I understand exactly how you feel, Jasna. Suspicion isn't in my nature at all, and I'm more than willing to meet with Titus and discuss everything openly."

"What if I tell him to expect us at his room tomorrow night?" Jasna asked.

"I'd like nothing better," Mirna told her. "During the past three years I had thought the good man had stayed away from our house because of his hostility toward us. Did he really think Yara and I were hostile toward him?"

"Mirna, you're —" Jasna began.

"You'll come for us tomorrow night?" Mirna asked, accompanying Jasna to the door.

As soon as Jasna was gone, I tried to complete the sentence she'd begun: "Mirna, you're a hypocrite, a liar, a faker —"

"What nasty names to throw at your beloved," she told me.

"My beloved! Yesterday you were ready to put me in your mother's shed until I died!"

"Your pretty young wife was drunk yesterday — on wine, on Sabina in Sophia's letter, on life, and today she can't remember what happened yesterday," Mirna told me with the same hypocritical sweetness. "She's forgotten every single detail, doesn't even know where she spent the night —"

"What about Titus?" I asked her. "You weren't drunk the day before yesterday, when you blamed him for everything that's happened to us for the past twenty years. Did you forget that too? You hadn't drunk a drop of wine then. When did he become the good man who mistakenly imagined you and Yara had something against him?"

Mirna's response to my anger was to put her arms around me and tell me, "If I ever lie to you, Yarostan, it'll be for one reason only: because I love you."

"That's not fair, Mirna," I protested. "I don't understand what happened yesterday. I don't understand your new attitude toward Jasna. You and Yara are up to something, and I'd like to know what it is."

"You'll know, Yarostan, soon enough." The following evening, Jasna was already at our house when I returned from the carton plant. The three of us took a tram toward the bus depot where I once worked. Yara had turned down Jasna's invitation.

Titus and I hadn't seen each other since the days immediately after my release from prison. We pumped each other's hands warmly. I congratulated him on his engagement and told him I was looking forward to the celebration.

Titus apologized to Mirna for the way he had behaved when she and Zdenek had surprised him before Mirna's dance. "I was a little stunned when you told me Tobarkin was your father; I didn't understand —"

"The misunderstanding was all my fault," Mirna told him. "I didn't know you and Zdenek had met before." Then Mirna went on with an irony that neither Titus nor Jasna seemed to notice, "My isolation in the present historical moment gave me a desire to surround myself with all the people who had ever been close to me: my father, brother, husband, friend —"

"Jasna clarified the meaning of your invitation," Titus told her. "I obviously understand the need for this type of regroupment of revolutionaries at a time of upheaval such as the present. But I didn't feel my presence at the dance would be a fruitful form of intervention. Perhaps I was wrong. The task of revolutionaries is to generalize understanding of the historical goals of the working class struggle at all times and in all situations."

"Especially during a period that seems to have so much in common with the excitement we lived through twelve years ago, at the time of the Magarna uprising," Mirna said to him, intentionally winding him up.

"There are certainly similarities between the two periods," Titus said excitedly. "The proletariat is once again regaining its own project, it is once again carrying its own historical task. The self-organization of the class, the exercise of power by the class as a whole, are once again on the agenda. Not since Magarna has it been so urgent for revolutionaries to rejoin the stream of history."

"You've put my innermost thoughts into the most perfect words," Mirna told him with a sarcasm I considered completely unprovoked, but which neither Jasna nor Titus noticed. "The proletariat is regaining its project and revolutionaries are rejoining the stream of history. What a perfect way to describe my hopes twelve years ago and my activity today. You say it with such conviction that you boost my confidence. Only a few days ago Yarostan and I asked Jasna if you had also been infected by the activity unfolding around us, and I can see that you have. Your desire to rejoin the stream of history must be as intense as it was at the time of the Magarna rising."

Jasna interceded, "Titus told me it wasn't only the social situations that were similar, but also his personal relationship to them. During the years before the Magarna rising Titus had become a functionary in the trade union apparatus, a simple cog. The work was repetitive and bureaucratic; there seemed to be no point to it other than to reproduce the bureaucratic apparatus."

"For me the autonomy of the class has always constituted the indispensable condition for its revolutionary activity," Titus added. "The trade union council was not an instrument of that autonomy. The work wasn't only repetitive; it had no historical significance; that apparatus did not carry any part of the proletarian project. Instead of being an instrument of class action, the apparatus had substituted itself for the class and tried to move history by itself and in the face of the proletariat's opposition. But revolution cannot be made against the masses. The Magarna rising was a fresh wind —"

"Was it the proletarian project the Magarna workers were carrying?" Mirna asked, pretending naïveté about Titus' meaning. "The authorities accused them all of being agents of foreign reactionary circles —"

"I remain convinced the strikes and the councils were genuine attempts of the proletariat to regain its project," Titus told Mirna. "Workers conscious of their own historical mission are immune to such influences."

"What about Yarostan and Jan?" Mirna asked. "Were they arrested for carrying the proletarian project, for rejoining the stream of history? Why were they arrested before other workers who had engaged in class activity? Why were they arrested a year before you were?"

"They weren't arrested because of the political activities in which they were engaged," Titus told her, "but because of a police bungle with a letter that supposedly came from a foreign spy ring."

"Oh yes, that letter; I had forgotten about it. Was that really the reason Yarostan and Jan were arrested?" Mirna asked. Her shameless lie — she's thought about that letter every day for the past twelve years — made me jittery, and I forgot to ask Titus the question you had asked in your postscript, namely why he hadn't told me about that letter when he'd visited me in prison.

Jasna responded to Mirna's hypocritical question. "I've asked Titus all about that letter, Mirna. The first time he ever heard of anyone being arrested because of it was when he visited you after you left a message for him at his office. He immediately went to the police to try to see if Yarostan and Jan could be released, since he was convinced they had been arrested by mistake, but he got no further than to provoke them to arrest him."

"I spent hours arguing with the police right after you told me about the arrests," Titus told Mirna, "but to no avail. They tried to deal with questions of consciousness by means of arrest and imprisonment. They completely failed to understand that the consciousness of a minority, no matter how clear, is not sufficient for the realization of the proletariat's historical task, which requires the constant participation and creative activity of all members, of the class as a whole. Generalized consciousness is the sole guarantee of the victory of the workers' councils. It's obvious that the class must use violence to reach its goal, but violence by a minority separate from the general movement is absolutely foreign to the methods of the class and constitutes a manifestation of petty-bourgeois despair; this diminishes the confidence of the class in itself and impedes the road to its self-emancipation. Those arrests were a mistake, a major bungle."

"Isn't it amazing," Mirna asked with mock astonishment, "that the bungling of the police had similar consequences for Jan as the bungling of the doctors had for Vesna?"

Jasna and I were startled, and we both looked at Mirna suspiciously.

But Mirna went on, "Of course your intentions were pure both times. You tried to do what was best for Vesna, and for Jan, and for the proletariat. You're really a very generous person. Yarostan told me that once, long ago, all your comrades were arrested and charged with having connections with a notorious spy, and that apparently your arguments convinced the police to release the spy himself. Were the police more receptive to your arguments at that time than they were at the time of the Magarna rising?"

"What are you driving at?" Jasna asked Mirna with undisguised hostility.

But Titus turned to Mirna calmly and told her, "Oh yes, you're referring to George Alberts' release. Jasna has given me a summary of Yarostan's correspondence with Alberts' stepdaughter. The fact is that those arrests were motivated by the same erroneous conception. Of course I urged them to release Alberts; we had been comrades several years earlier. Alberts had become a reactionary, but he was not a spy. The point was to isolate his position, not to arrest him."

What was it about his position that had to be isolated?" Mirna asked.

"Jasna hasn't told me exactly what Sophia has written you," Titus said. "Alberts was a revolutionary when I first met him; he was completely committed to the proletarian project. But certain influences made him turn against the organization necessary for the realization of the project, and by turning against the organization he turned against the project itself. This happened during the war, and especially after the war. He failed to see that there were only two alternatives: the naked rule of capital, or the victory of an organizational form that, no matter how deformed, still carried the kernel of the proletarian project. I tried to help Alberts understand that the point was not to side with capital, but to give reality to the organizational form, to infuse it with spontaneity, to help create the autonomous movement which was capable of realizing the historical task of the proletariat. But the police obviously made no effort to help anyone understand anything. He was treated with unbelievable cynicism and brutality. During the war the resistance organization recruited him to do certain scientific work abroad. After the war the same organization attacked him for having done this work abroad; they labeled him a spy and even accused his so-called family of being his collaborators. This was highly incorrect, but it wasn't the incorrectness or the hypocrisy that convinced the police to release him. Retaining him in prison would have created an international incident."

"But why did they arrest the rest of us?" I asked. "We didn't have anything to do with Alberts."

"Because the police substituted itself for the class," he told me emphatically; "because a minority gained precedence over the class as a whole, that's why. As I said, the point was to isolate a position, not to arrest a section of the working class! The working class is a historical class and cannot be replaced. The organization of a part of the class is insufficient. Only the entire proletariat can undertake the revolutionary transformation of society. The police are not the agent of the historical project of the proletariat. We have to absorb that lesson. Our task as revolutionaries is to help the class understand its own interests, to help it carry its own project with its own energy, to raise ourselves to a clear understanding of the line of march, the conditions and the ultimate results of the proletarian movement. The point is not to incapacitate the class by jailing its most combative elements, as was done when the entire production group of the carton plant was arrested. It is the class in and of itself that is revolutionary; without it there's no revolution. What makes this class revolutionary is its position at the heart of the production process; only this position makes the class capable of resolving the contradictions of capitalism."

I was surprised by the way he ended that statement, although I don't think I would have noticed this earlier. "You say the task of the proletariat is to resolve the contradictions of capitalism?"

"Precisely, and this is what you and Jan Sedlak never understood," he said excitedly. "Capitalist social relations become a fetter to the further development of the productive forces capitalism itself created. Those relations become an obstacle to the further development of social capital. This is what makes proletarian revolution inevitable. The historical task of the proletariat is to remove those fetters and to make possible the further development of the productive forces. This is the general interest as well as the final goal of the movement."

My head started swimming. I remembered Sabina's comments about the contradiction between my friendship with Jan and my admiration for Titus. "And is this what you've devoted your life to?" I asked him. "To remove the obstacles to the development of objects? What do those objects have to do with your own life?"

"That's a funny way to put it," Jasna said with some annoyance. "If Titus devoted his life to the development of objects, he certainly doesn't have much to show for it. Ever since I've known him he's wanted no personal power, no wealth, no high posts in the government. He always considered himself as nothing more than a humble servant of history, he's always been single-mindedly devoted to the working class — to you, Jan, Luisa. His pay has never been larger than that of any factory worker; he's a lowly functionary, a cog in an enormous apparatus; he files repetitious, bureaucratic reports day in and day out —"

"I didn't mean to accuse Titus of seeking personal gain," I told her with embarrassment.

Titus himself added, "Neither personal gain nor historical significance. Only the class can remove those fetters, Yarostan. I've devoted my life, not to removing the fetters, but to a much more modest work of theoretical reflection and elaboration, a work which permits the proletariat's activity to be based on an understanding of its past experience and future course. But it is only the class itself that undertakes the historical task. Without the activity of the class, my own activity amounts to nothing more than the reproduction of an empty shell, an apparatus that only stands in the way of the proletariat's task."

I agreed with Jasna's description of the modesty of Titus' own engagement, and I hesitated before asking him, "Why did you and George Alberts enlist in the so-called popular army during that uprising Luisa romanticized for all of us?"

"I know exactly what you're driving at, and it's an experience I don't like to remember," he told me. "At the time of that uprising I was a second-year university student. I was already committed to the task of contributing to the generalization of understanding of the goals of the working class struggle, to making the proletariat's historical lessons explicit. Those workers seemed to be attacking the entire established order, not merely locally but on a world scale. The fascists received international support, and it was urgent for the workers to receive it in far greater measure, since the proletariat is an international class; its struggle can ultimately be victorious only on an international level. Out of the chaos of political groupings reflecting the isolation and the divisions of the petty bourgeoisie, I finally found revolutionaries who understood the fundamental aspects of the struggle of the proletariat: the importance of political priorities, the importance of organization, as well as the unitary character of the revolutionary struggle of the class."

"Was George Alberts one of those revolutionaries?" I asked him. "Was the popular army the organization you found?"

"Only in appearance," he said, "but appearances are often misleading, and practice is the only test of the truth of appearances. I believed that the self-organization of the class struggle and the exercise of power by the class as a whole was the only historical road of the proletarian struggle. But I also believed that denying the need for organization and intervention by revolutionaries condemned one to non-existence, turned one into an agent of a withering of class consciousness. In other words, I saw the need for clear programmatic intervention in the proletarian struggle. In appearance the popular army seemed to be an organization which put forward the general interests of the class and the final goals of the movement, and to be an integral part of that struggle. I thought I was among revolutionaries who had not only raised themselves to a clear understanding of the line of march, the conditions and the ultimate general results of the proletarian movement, but who also participated in the struggle of the class and distinguished themselves by being the most determined and combative elements in those struggles."

"But that military machine was obviously —" I started.

"It was not a revolutionary organization," he said abruptly.

"When did you figure that out?" I asked him.

"I was as aware then as I am now that the historical task of the proletariat cannot be carried out by a conscious minority," he told me. "Generalized consciousness is the sole guarantee of the victory of the revolution. The activity of the class cannot be replaced by an apparatus. I've never identified the dictatorship of the proletariat with the dictatorship of an army, a party or a union. As a part of the class, revolutionaries can at no time substitute themselves for the class, neither in its struggles within capitalism nor in the exercise of power."

"If that was what you thought, then your activity in that military apparatus becomes even more incomprehensible to me," I said.

"I told you I had to learn the truth from practice. I saw that the popular army had a substitutionist character as soon as we reached the front. The revolutionary minority was given precedence over the class as a whole. This tended to diminish the confidence of the class in itself and as a result impeded the road to its self-emancipation."

"Couldn't you see right at the start that such an organization would inevitably 'take precedence over the class as a whole'?" I asked him.

"No, Yarostan, I couldn't see that, and I still can't," he told me. "That's something Luisa learned from her first husband, and she communicated it to you and to Jan Sedlak even though she herself never believed it. You've never understood that unlike other classes, the proletariat has no basis of power in capitalist society; its only material strength is its organization; the organization is the decisive and fundamental condition for the proletariat's very existence."

"I had thought the point of the struggle wasn't the proletariat's existence but its disappearance, its replacement by a human community," I objected.

"The class struggle for the emancipation of the proletariat will mean the emancipation of all humanity only when the organization of the proletariat is adequate to that task, and this requires an organization which is politically coherent, which has a clear orientation; this requires a proletarian consciousness which grasps reality without distortions. Only such consciousness enables the proletariat to liberate all of society from exploitation. The popular army was a mistake, Yarostan, but not in and of itself, not as an organization, but because of the social and political situation in which it arose. The emerging movement in which it arose was characterized by immaturity of consciousness and insufficient understanding of the needs of the class struggle."

"Yet it was that movement, it was those workers who built the barricades, fought in the streets, and defeated the fascist army in a single day," I reminded him.

"I don't deny that," he insisted. "Those workers were people like you and Jan; they were workers whose actions reflected the class's implacable hatred of capital, its will to struggle against the entire bourgeois order, its repudiation of class collaboration. What I'm saying is that what guided those workers was class instinct and not proletarian theory. And instinct is not enough for the proletariat. In order to liberate itself and to emancipate humanity, the proletariat requires organization and consciousness. The popular army did not fill that need. The organization of the proletariat has to be a secretion of the class itself; it cannot be imported from outside as the popular army was. That's why those workers and their organization remained separate; that's why the organization substituted itself for the class, that's why the organization ultimately opposed itself to the class and destroyed its most profound, most combative elements."

At this point Mirna reentered the conversation. "I think I caught the drift of what you've been saying, Titus, although I didn't understand all the intricacies. Do you think the same thing is happening today? Are the most combative workers being guided by instinct instead of being guided by proletarian theory?"

"I certainly do," he told her. "If that weren't the case, there wouldn't be such a drastic separation between the combative sectors and the conscious elements of the proletariat; revolutionaries would not be so cut off from the class, so isolated."

Mirna simulated great interest in what Titus was saying. "That sounds extremely important to me, Titus. I have several friends who I'm sure would want to learn about that separation, especially if you have suggestions about how it can be overcome. Do you suppose you might find the time to meet with them?"

Jasna carelessly suggested, "Why don't you bring those friends to my house? We could combine it with a meal; I could easily entertain ten or twelve people."

Even Titus was interested. "How about combining it with the celebration we're going to hold two weeks from now? We could transform a trivial event into a fruitful political meeting."

"Wonderful!" Mirna exclaimed. "I'll invite several people who are at least as eager as you and I to rejoin the stream of history. They'll all want to share your profound political insights."

At this point Jasna heard the sarcasm in Mirna's tone, but Mirna got up to leave, and Titus shook her hand very cordially; it was obvious he hadn't heard the sarcasm.

Jasna left with us. On the tram she asked Mirna, "What are you up to? Another prank? Why did you tell that lie about having forgotten the letter Sophia sent us at the time of the Magarna rising?"

"Did I lie?" Mirna asked. "I must have gotten confused. When I had first told Titus about those arrests twelve years ago, he had assured me that neither Jan nor Yarostan could have been arrested because of a letter they didn't receive. So when he said they were only arrested because of that letter, I got confused —"

"I thought he explained those arrests very clearly!" Jasna said definitively.

I agreed with Jasna. I told Mirna, "I don't agree with him. Or I should say, I no longer agree with most of what he has to say. But I certainly don't find him suspicious in any way."

Mirna didn't respond, and we rode the rest of the trip in silence. I could tell that Jasna was suspicious of Mirna, afraid of her next prank.

At home I asked Mirna what she had in mind with the so-called interested friends she intended to invite to Jasna's and Titus' celebration.

Instead of answering, she asked me, "Did you see the expression in his eyes whenever he spoke of history and the proletarian project?"

I repeated my question angrily, "What pranks do you have in mind, Mirna?"

"Didn't you recognize that expression?" she asked me. "It's the same expression that covered my mother's face whenever she spoke of her Lord! And the tone with which he described workers guided by instinct! She spoke the same way about people possessed by the devil!"

"Mirna, what are your intentions? If you're planning to destroy Jasna's and Titus' happiness because of the superficial similarities you think you see —"

"Remember when Jan and Sabina asked you to make love to the Queen of the Peasants?" she asked.

"I don't see what connection —"

"Remember the revolution Jan expected to result from your lovemaking? Morality, the family, the peasant village were all going to disintegrate, the revolution was going to begin."

"So that's what you have in mind!" I exclaimed. "Something similar to what you and Yara did to me in your clearing! Mirna, if you do anything like that to —"

"Similar, Yarostan, but not the same," she told me; "and I'm not going to do anything at all. I'm only going to bring a few friends, very old friends, to the celebration — not my friends but yours and Jasna's and Titus'. If any games or pranks result, it won't be because of me. Titus and his own Mends will make them happen. If Yara and I are right about Titus, then morality, history and the proletarian project are going to disintegrate all by themselves, and you'll see what a revolution you might have made if you'd gone through with Jan's and Sabina's prank and made love to the Queen."

"Whom do you intend to invite?" I asked her.

"His whole train, Yarostan: the passengers, the ticket-takers as well as the engineers."

Maybe I should have waited two weeks before writing you.

Yarostan.

Sophia's ninth letter

Dear Yarostan,

Or should I address my letter to "Poor Yarostan"? As I read your letter I didn't know whether to laugh or cry. I'm certainly not the one who has any right to pass judgment on you. Thank you for not waiting two weeks to write me. In two weeks you would have figured everything out, you would have seemed so sure of yourself, and I wouldn't have had a chance to see you as I've never seen you before: lost, confused, unsure of yourself. I felt much closer to you than I ever had before. For the first time since we've written to each other you weren't my life's hero but someone like me, someone who is drifting and waiting, who isn't quite included in the activities of those closest to him. I see now that it makes sense for you and me to be writing to each other; we have much more in common with each other than either of us do with Mirna or Sabina.

A few weeks ago we were so close to something, yet neither of us knew what it was. Now we're both trying to find out what we really wanted, and it isn't easy, is it? I don't think you did very well in your confrontation with Titus Zabran. I had a similar confrontation with Luisa only three days ago, and I think I did much better than you in coming to terms with her and with my own past. She's been at least as much to me as she and Titus were to you. Her independence, her refusal to submit to externally imposed authority, and especially the unity between her beliefs and her behavior have been my life's model. My problem wasn't so much to free myself of my model as to learn why, with such a model before me since my birth, I spent my life drifting. The fault lay in me as much as in her. And that's what you're learning only now. During your second prison term you reevaluated Luisa's stories in the light of Manuel's and you reexamined her experiences in the light of your two prison terms. But you never reevaluated what you had become along the way thanks to Luisa and Titus. You stopped your critique before it was complete. You apparently rejected Luisa's contribution to your life but retained Titus', and your unconvincing and apologetic defense of Titus shows that you're not willing to carry your critique to its conclusion.

I'm somewhat surprised and disappointed by your attitude to Titus. Sabina says you and Jasna are willfully blinding yourselves about him the same way Luisa did. You seem impressed by his admission that the popular army was a "mistake." But he's not actually admitting any mistakes. He told you it wasn't that army "as such" that was a mistake, but the circumstances in which it arose, and working people like Nachalo and Margarita were among those circumstances. In other words, it wasn't his popular army but the working population that was a mistake. His attitude is almost identical to George Alberts' attitude: the population consisted of hotheads, hoodlums incapable of industrializing themselves. The only difference Sabina or I can see between them is that Alberts special field was technology whereas Zabran's was politics. That's why Alberts characterized the "reactionary population" as saboteurs and hooligans who endangered the economy, whereas Zabran characterized them as being animated by "instinct instead of political theory" and thus of being dangerous to the all-important political organization.

Sabina and I are both anxious to learn what prank Mirna and Yara have in store for you and Jasna. Sabina told me she's learning from them what Margarita Nachalo might have been like if she had lived. Sabina said that "Yarostan's virtue" is that you never learned what Luisa tried to teach you, you never tried to "tamper" with Mirna's and Yara's lives the way Luisa did with Nachalo's and with yours. Your "virtue" is that you never became the organizer Luisa tried to turn you into. Consequently it's all the more surprising that you're so uncritical of Titus. In your second letter to me you attacked me for my attachment to my "key experience" and my "original community," for speaking of opportunists and manipulators as "our fellow revolutionaries." Yet what are you and Jasna doing now? Apparently both of you did learn something from Luisa, and you seem unable to undo the effects of the lesson. For both of you, as for Luisa, Titus still expresses the ideas of "our movement" and he's therefore "our comrade," and we don't apply the same critical standards to him as we do to "enemies," do we?

Sabina and I discussed very few of the questions you raised in your letter. One of those questions had to do with Alberts. At one point Titus told you that, at the time of our arrest twenty years ago, the police should not have arrested the entire production crew of the carton plant; instead they should have "isolated" George Alberts' "position."

"Read that again and tell me what sense it makes," Sabina told me. "As if Alberts' views had anything at all to do with the production crew of the carton plant! How can Yarostan be so uncritical? The first connection between Alberts' views and the production crew of the carton plant took place after the arrests, when the police accused Yarostan and the others of being confederates in Alberts' spy ring!"

Sabina convinced me there was something extremely bizarre about Titus' whole explanation of the carton plant arrests. There was no earthly reason for him to introduce "Alberts' position" into that explanation, because there was no way his views could have affected anyone in the carton plant.

"During the early part of the war Alberts apparently worked with the underground resistance organization," Sabina told me. "He locked himself into his room with papers; he didn't want me to tell either Luisa or you or anyone else about his coming home with papers. He may have been helping smuggle people abroad, or he may already then have been engaged in scientific espionage for the allied military. I obviously didn't figure out what it was since I was only seven, but I do know the only person who could have known about this activity was Zabran. A year and a half before the war ended Alberts told me he had been given an assignment abroad, and I later learned this assignment had something to do with the development of the atomic bomb, though he never told me any details. No one in the carton plant knew anything about it except Zabran. Luisa didn't learn a thing about his activities until he returned after the war. The production crew that was arrested three years after the war were all hired when Alberts was abroad — except Titus and Jasna, and Jasna never met Alberts, nor was she in any way influenced by his views. I think Zabran is doing exactly the same thing the police did: he's making a scapegoat out of Alberts. He can't accept the fact that his Pygmalion, Yarostan, simply didn't function, and he can't accept the fact that Jan Sedlak, a person Zabran considered an ignorant peasant, made more of an impression on Yarostan than Zabran's theoretical wisdom. He's trying to convince himself that only a theoretician, an intellectual like himself, could have messed up his plans, not a peasant like Jan, and obviously not Yarostan, an anti-intellectual undisciplined lumpen, on his own. He'd expected Yarostan to be disciplined by a few years of work in the carton plant; he'd thought Luisa's influence would turn Yarostan into an organizer, a cadre, with a smattering of theory. Yarostan's 'combativity' was thus to be channeled into what he calls the "self-activity' of the proletariat realizing its own historical task; Yarostan was to be something like a controlled Nachalo. But when the big moment came, Yarostan didn't function; instead of pulling 'the base' in Zabran's direction, he pulled Jasna as well as Vera and Adrian in Jan's direction. In other words the proletariat didn't move the way it was 'inevitably' supposed to move. How was Zabran to explain this? Certainly not in terms of the fact that Yarostan had remained his own person, certainly not in terms of the fact that Jan made more sense to Yarostan than Zabran did. There had to be an outside influence: Alberts. If his views had been isolated in time, the production crew wouldn't have been influenced by them. What he failed to tell Yarostan was how and when Alberts' views influenced the production crew, and I would have expected Yarostan to have the sense to ask."

"He did say his head swam as he listened to some of Titus' explanations," I reminded her.

"I'm not trying to tear into Yarostan," she told me. "My head's been swimming too. The irony of it is that Yarostan helped me clear up things he seems unable to clear up for himself. It was Yarostan who made me see the incompatibility of my friendship with Jan with my commitment to Alberts' project. It was he who helped me understand the contradiction between my rebellion against an inhuman social order and my desire to build an inhuman social order with the lowest strata of society. Yet he seems so mule-headed about his own contradictions — as if he'd suddenly gone deaf and blind. But then I suppose it's that very mule-headedness that made him such a miserable disciple and tool."

I'm as bothered as Sabina by your "mule-headedness," and I'd like to know what it is that you're defending, and why. As I told you when I started this letter, Yarostan, I'm not interested in judging you; I don't have a vantage point from which to do that. I'm trying desperately to understand what's happened to us, why we're again so strange to each other. Only a few weeks ago you wrote about the possibility of your voyaging here with Mirna; you even let a tender feeling toward me slip into your letter. Yet now you seem so closed, so defensive, so much like what I'm trying to stop being. You seem to be no stronger than I am. I suppose what upsets me about that is my realization that I can no longer lean on you. Apparently I still feel the need to.

Something very strange has happened since I last wrote you. Ted and I have become very close friends. He's staying with Sabina and me. Tina and Pat still haven't turned up. Ted has moved into Tina's room. It seems so strange, after the horrid things I thought and said about him, for Ted to be sleeping in Tina's room. And still more strange: I think I love Ted in a way I've never loved anyone before.

A few days after I sent my previous letter Minnie telephoned to arrange for a time when we could get together; she'd promised to visit me on the day when she'd helped me get out of jail. I told her Ted was in jail and asked her help in getting him out. Ted was released almost as soon as Minnie investigated the case. She learned that the only charge against him was "loitering," and that charge was dropped when she presented herself as his defense lawyer. Sabina waited for him when he was released, and they took a taxi to his place. The print shop looked as if a tornado had gone through it, and Sabina insisted Ted's life would be in danger if he returned there; she's sure the police intend to "finish off" the printer whose equipment was used for the production of so many of the radical publications of the strikers. She didn't even let him go upstairs for his personal things; she simply brought him directly to our house.

I hadn't seen Ted since he'd driven Pat and me back to the university after our visit to the research center. I must have looked shocked when Sabina walked into the house with him.

"Do you mind my coming here?" was the first thing he asked, standing in the doorway.

I grabbed his hand and pulled him into the house. "Of course I don't mind, Ted. I hope you don't mind my being here."

He smiled sadly and told me had had nowhere else to go and no other friends in the world, since both Tina and Tissie had disappeared.

Ted quickly learned that Tissie was back in the prison hospital. Sabina had of course suspected this, but she hadn't picked up the phone to confirm the fact. The day after he moved in with us, Ted went to visit Tissie; he was terribly depressed when he returned. He told us Tissie was convinced she wouldn't ever be released again; she'd spoken to him of dying in the hospital, "among my only friends." Sabina went to her room and shut her door; she didn't want to learn what Tissie had done after they'd gotten separated at the research center. After the police had cleared everyone out of the research center, Tissie had gotten a ride to the university. She went to the print shop and found it wrecked. There was no sign of Tina or Ted or me. "My mind went blank," she told him. She wandered away from the campus and went from bar to bar, until she finally found a heroin dealer. She spent the night sleeping on a street until she was picked up by the police. Ted cried while telling me this. I was profoundly moved by his attachment to the beautiful, spiteful urchin who never had and never would reciprocate his love for her. I felt so sorry for him, so guilty toward him. For two whole days I did nothing but try to make up to him for my horrid behavior in the garage. I was really a blind nitwit when I ran from the university co-op to the garage twelve years ago. I was such a stupefied tourist; it was all so exotic to me. If I'd been more sensitive to the people I had moved in with, my past twelve years might not have been as empty as they've been.

During the two days after he joined us I learned more about Ted than I'd learned during all the months I had lived in the garage. Sabina had told me some things about him, but I had never been able to piece the fragments together into a picture that made sense to me. His childhood was almost identical to Tissie's. He didn't know who his father was. His mother brought a different man home daily. Ted spent all his days and most of his nights in the street. When he was eleven he started hanging around a garage where stolen cars were repaired. One night he was beaten, for no reason, by one of his mother's boyfriends, and he managed to slip into the garage and spend the night there, probably much the same way you found your way into the carton plant. (Yes, it's the same garage in which I joined him, Tina and Sabina years later.) When the proprietor found him there the following morning, Ted begged to stay in the garage permanently. The proprietor accepted him, not as a person for whom he felt compassion, but as a potential tool; he taught Ted to open car locks, to hot-wire cars, to dismantle them. By the time he was thirteen Ted was an experienced car thief and driver, although he obviously didn't have a license. His boss would make him break into the car and start it; the boss could flee if the police arrived and Ted would be the one who got caught; while telling me this, Ted explained that he would "only" have gone to reform school whereas the boss would have gone to prison. This was when he met Tissie. She was ten, fatherless, and equally homeless; her mother was perpetually drunk and had no use for her. Ted offered her what his boss had offered him: a place to stay, and an activity; he also shared his meager income with his new friend. Although Ted didn't quite say it, I gathered that Tissie was bored while he worked. She resisted learning what he wanted to teach her, and after a few days with him she spent only her nights in the garage, returning to play in the streets during days. He tried to stimulate her interest in his activity by inviting her to join him on his first attempt to steal a car by himself and in broad daylight. One morning he and Tissie took a bus to a wealthy suburb and Ted broke into and drove off with an expensive sports car. Both were immensely proud as he chauffeured Tissie all over the city in a vehicle which probably belonged to a corporation owner's son. This was the escapade Ron had wanted to tell me about when he and Sabina had come to visit me after his release from reform school. Of course the inevitable police siren stopped the pair of ghetto children, one thirteen, the other ten, and both were sent to reform school. Ted for two years, Tissie for half a year. Ted met Ron in reform school: they became friends immediately. Ron, son of the "class-conscious" Debbie Matthews, patiently explained to Ted that he was being exploited by his boss. The idea of starting a cooperative, non-exploitative garage was Ron's. The project Ron described to Ted in reform school included three other people: obviously Ted included Tissie, and Ron mentioned only Jose and me! Sabina had told me this long ago, but I couldn't quite believe it; I still can't. I was to take care of "the books as well as the thinking." Ted was released long before Ron, and he didn't believe anything would come of Ron's plans. When he returned to the garage he found it closed down. His boss had apparently become so dependent on Ted that when he'd been left on his own he'd gotten caught and sent to prison for a year. Ted found him when he got out and learned he was giving up the garage. Ted's former boss offered to rent the garage to Ted for an exorbitant sum, and Ted accepted; he wasn't able to bargain. When he asked his boss what had happened to Tissie, the man told Ted, "Get yourself another girlfriend, kid; that one ain't for you." Ted didn't understand; he spent hours walking around the neighborhood hoping to find her. He bought himself a suit and a hat, and he did all his stealing at night, mainly from the section of the city where Ron had wrecked his father's car.

"One night I got back with a new car and there was a lady at the garage door, a woman with a fancy dress, heels, a hair-do, rings and bracelets. I just couldn't believe it was Tissie. She'd been just a kid two years earlier. She said she'd heard the place was my own. No, I told her, I'm just renting. Then she asked: 'Got room for me?' I couldn't believe she actually wanted to stay in the garage. 'Well I ain't got no other home,' she told me."

Ted made no demands whatever on Tissie. Her presence in the garage probably excited him, but he seems to have made no advances to her. He made it clear to me that his idea of sexual relations was what he'd seen between his mother and the men she brought home; to Ted it was equivalent to violence, and he feared every form of violence. Tissie went out almost every evening and she returned long after midnight. She told him she'd taken up a trade she had learned from a girl she'd met in reform school. Ted had no idea what kind of trade Tissie had learned in reform school, but he didn't ask. Late one night, shortly after Tissie had returned for the night, there was a loud knocking on the garage door. Ted opened the door and a wealthy-looking older woman burst in, found Tissie, and ran to her shouting, "Why did you run away from me, baby? Don't I pay you enough? I'll pay you whatever you ask, baby! Just say how much!" Tissie hid behind Ted and begged him to get the woman out of the garage. That was how Ted learned about Tissie's trade, and also about Tissie's sexual interests. Some days later he asked Tissie, "Would you quit your work if I had lots more money?" She told him, "Yes! I wish I didn't have to do it for money!" "With other women?" Ted asked her. "I sure as hell wouldn't do it free with men!" she told him. While telling me this, Ted expressed neither shock nor indignation. That was how Tissie was, and that was how he learned about her, that's all. It wasn't long after this episode that Ron was released from reform school; he and Sabina visited Ted immediately after their visit to me.

"I asked if Sabina was the girl Ron had told me about in reform school," Ted told me. "Ron said no, that girl was miles away. When I told him I was renting the garage, he scolded me for getting myself exploited worse than before. Now the boss does nothing at all and gets paid, he told me. Then he told me about Jose, and about this friend of Jose's who could buy the whole garage. I asked why this guy would buy the garage and why he'd let us use it the way Ron saw us using it, cooperatively. He told me about Seth selling dope and needing a steady place. Ron tried to make it sound better by telling me he wouldn't sell dope from the garage; he just needed a place for making contacts. But I didn't want anything to do with that. That's when Sabina turned me inside out. She said there's no difference between stealing cars and selling dope because you get locked up for both. She knows the difference now but she didn't then. We were still arguing about it when Tissie came home around midnight. She liked Sabina as soon as she saw her, and I guess it was Tissie who pulled me into going into it with them. She told me she'd quit working if I did what Sabina wanted."

Tissie blackmailed him the way she was going to blackmail Sabina later. In the beginning Ted thought he'd been wrong. The project seemed to be a success. He liked and trusted Jose. They all worked enthusiastically on the transformation of the house behind the garage, and for several months Ted worked with Sabina.

He remembered those months fondly. "Sabina and I stole together, we dismantled together, we built most of the inside of the house. She's the best person I ever worked with except Tina. She learned fast, and she told me all kinds of things about machines I didn't know. It was during those months that Sabina and I built the machine shop in the basement and the lofts upstairs. When I did a painting she liked it so much that I spent hours every day painting ever since then. But she had a blind spot. She couldn't see the whole thing was no good. It wasn't built by our own hands but by dope. Seth did his dealing right in the garage. Tissie became a dope addict. The garage became a front. And I became a boss and exploited kids the way Ron had told me I was exploited when I worked for a boss. Those months didn't last. Ron got himself killed in the war. Tissie might as well have gotten herself killed. She became like a dead person, a thing; she became Seth's tool. Jose knew the difference between heroin and stealing, but Jose couldn't argue with Sabina. No one could. Jose got sucked into the idea of the bar because he thought the bar would get the heroin out of the house and the garage. But the bar made everything worse. Tissie took up her trade again, this time with men as well as women. All her money went to Seth. And Sabina stayed blind. After she brought Tina, Seth wanted Tissie to take Tina to the bar. Tissie wanted to teach Tina what she'd learned in reform school. I couldn't take that. Tina liked the garage work, she liked to paint and to make things; I put myself in Tissie's way. That's when Tissie, my first and my best friend, started to hate me. Sabina didn't see any of that. I couldn't talk to anyone there. When the bar started, Sabina convinced Jose it had solved all the problems. That's when you came, Sophie. I was sure you'd be a friend that first night when you returned from the bar and told us you got scared and ran away. But you confused me the next morning when you told Tissie how you'd loved what you'd done the night before; I couldn't know you were ashamed to tell Tissie you hadn't done anything. You started to act funny. The night you went to Tissie's room I was sure you were on an errand Seth sent you on; I was sure you and Tissie were going to take Tina to the bar that night. I'm sorry, Sophie. Jose thought the same thing I did. It was hard to think anything else."

"I know, Ted. It was impossible to imagine how abysmally stupid I was to be so surprised by Tissie, to know nothing at all about Sabina," I admitted. "But I did learn one detail from Tissie during the day I spent with her at the research center. That night you thought we were acting as Seth's agents and plotting against Tina — that night Tissie wasn't Seth's agent, and she wasn't interested in Tina. Tissie loved me."

Of course Ted couldn't have known that either. By that night he distrusted everyone in the garage except Tina. "It was only when Alec moved into the garage that I had any friends besides Tina," he told me. "Alec understood the difference between dope dealing and all the other things we did. All your friends understood the difference, and I guess they made you see it too the last time they came. They opened Jose's eyes too. Not that he was ever blind, but he couldn't make himself go against Sabina. Jose and I became friends after you left. We talked about leaving, but we couldn't leave without Tina, Tissie or Sabina, and Sabina's whole life was in that bar and garage. I guess that's why Jose got himself arrested; he didn't know how else to get out of it. With Jose gone, Seth thought his chance had come to get Tina into the bar and even on heroin. Jose and I together could have stopped him, but I didn't see how I could do it alone until Seth himself showed me how. Seth got the idea that Sabina was trying to take over, and when he asked me about that I told him it was true. I even told him she had plans to get rid of him. Seth was afraid of Sabina; he hadn't ever dealt with her except through Jose. When he got convinced Sabina wanted to get him out of the whole thing, he got so furious he couldn't see straight. He didn't even talk to her; he just pointed his gun at her and told her to get out and take Tina with her. That was what I'd wanted for years. I would have moved into this house with you if you hadn't felt about me the way you did, and if Tissie had left the garage too. But I couldn't leave Tissie to Seth. To me she was still the kid who'd asked if I had room for her in the garage. She'd trusted me. You don't throw someone who trusts you down a sewer, no matter how many excuses you've got. But Tissie was in bad shape after Sabina left. She blamed me for getting rid of Sabina and Tina, and she was right. She really hated me for that. For some reason she also blamed Jose. She made herself believe Jose wasn't in prison but had gotten you out of the garage and then Sabina and Tina. Before Jose was released I rented a place, the same one where Tina and I later started the print shop. I kept hoping Tissie would change, I kept thinking she'd want to move to the new place when Jose was released, or that she'd want to move with you and Tina and Sabina. But Tissie got worse all the time; she started talking about killing me and about killing Jose when he got back, and I wasn't just sure she couldn't do it. Jose came right to the garage the day he was released, got his things, and we both drove to the new place I'd rented. He talked about you a lot, Sophie, he'd changed a lot too. We went upstairs. Then he went out to the car to get more of his things and he never came back."

I had learned the rest from Sabina a few weeks ago, and I didn't let Ted tell me about Jose's death all over again. How ironic that it should have been I and my "academic friends," particularly Hugh, who had finally turned Jose against Sabina. How ironic that Jose should have started to define his struggle in terms identical to Nachalo's and Margarita's in response to books I had carried to him in prison. How ironic that Jose should have thought he had to prove himself as a guerrilla in order to live up to me.

Only a day or two after my long talks with Ted, from an altogether unexpected source, I learned yet more about the garage, and about yet another "guerrilla fighter" who occupied a place in my own life. Minnie came to see me a few days after she helped get Ted out of jail. Lawyer or no lawyer, I couldn't keep myself from throwing my arms around her when she walked into our house. I had always liked Minnie a lot. Ted and Sabina were both out when she came.

"What have you been doing lately besides getting arrested?" she asked me. "Daman told me this was the second time you'd been in jail during the past two months."

"Isn't that enough for a committed revolutionary?" I asked.

"I can't tell you how glad I am that you can still tolerate me, Sophie. You've always fascinated me. My life seems so drab, so uniform, compared to yours. When I left you in front of the garage ten years ago you had gone as low as I could imagine a person going. Then I learned from Daman that you were teaching university courses; suddenly you turn up fighting hundreds of police in a factory yard. You're an absolute wonder."

"I'll be grateful to you forever for saying that, Minnie, but I know perfectly well you wouldn't say it if you'd kept closer watch. If you knew how undecided, how fickle, how dependent I was —"

"That's precisely my point, Sophie; I do know you, much better than you think. I'm almost your negative; I'm decisive, consistent, independent — and drab, dull, routine, a deadly bore. The most exciting moments in my life were those I spent with a person who had everything in common with you, who could have been your twin —"

"Namely who?"

"None other than Alec. He could no more function without 'his woman' than you could without 'your man' —"

I was stunned. "Are you being sarcastic, Minnie?"

"On the contrary. I envy you, both of you, both equally indecisive, both dependent, both so fickle you continually landed in the most terrible isolation, yet both the most fabulous people in my life. I was wildly in love with him, Sophie; I remained close to him until he was killed. I'm not being sarcastic. I'm fascinated, awed by something I don't understand."

"Please tell me about him, Minnie. Tell me about yourself too. I was so used to linking 'Daman and Minnie,' I have a hard time even imagining you with Alec. What about your political group? When did you give that up?"

"I've managed to combine it all, Sophie. Law school, politics and Alec all passed through my life while I remained unchanged."

"Did Alec turn to you after he left the garage?"

"Earlier, Sophie. He turned to me before he ever moved into the garage. He called me the day he learned you had disappeared from the cooperative dorm. He was absolutely frantic. He was sure you had disappeared in order to shock the people who had kept us off the *Omissions* staff. I told him you'd been evicted from the dorm precisely because you'd helped distribute that paper, and the fraternity boys had made a fuss about it and gotten us arrested. He apparently expected me to walk all over the city with him looking for you. I suggested calling your relatives. That was easy. There was only one Nachalo in the phone book. But when your mother told us she hadn't heard from you either, I became as frantic as Alec. We visited your mother. She was awfully nice to us, but she wasn't at all concerned about your disappearance; she was much more concerned that we kept referring to her as your mother. When we left her house Alec asked me if I'd go out with him that weekend. He knew that I was about to break up with Daman. Hugh, Daman and I had all graduated; Hugh and Daman intended to go directly to graduate school. I decided to get a temporary teaching job in a high school instead of going on. We had a big argument about that. But there's no need to go into that. I didn't accept Alec's invitation; I knew I'd be hurt. And I was right. It was on that weekend you telephoned him, and he forgot all about me and rushed to the garage to see you. He was terribly fickle, but I think he never stopped loving you, Sophie. He called me again right after his first visit to you. He told me excitedly that you had rejoined the working class, and he wanted me to go to his room to learn all the good news. I naively called Daman and Hugh to tell them you'd been found, and all three of us went to Alec's. As soon as we walked in I knew he had expected me to come alone. He pulled me to his kitchen and asked jealously if Daman and I were together again. I lied and told him we were. I sensed his jealousy; something inside me started to stir, but I didn't let it. I rejected his advances, not out of any consideration for you, but because I didn't want to be your second; I was much too possessive. So Alec told all three of us about what he called your 'bootstrap' operation. Hugh was immensely impressed. I think it was Alec's account of what you were doing in that garage that made Hugh change his mind about enrolling in graduate school. After that meeting, Alec didn't call for several weeks. During those weeks I waited for him to call. I had never been wanted that way, Sophie. When he finally did call my heart jumped. But that time he didn't want me. He wanted the four of us to visit you in the garage. On that first visit to you I was sure I'd never be anything more to Alec than your second, and I was relieved I hadn't let anything start. I couldn't make any sense out of what you were doing, but Alec was full of enthusiasm for all of it. He quit his job and moved to the garage. I thought he had moved in with you and had definitively walked out of my life. I plunged back into the political activities of my organization; I even saw Daman two or three times outside of organization meetings. And then, several weeks after our first visit, Alec called from the garage. He said he had to see me and he seemed awfully upset. He told me he hadn't touched you since he'd been in the garage, and that he was lonelier than he'd ever been in his life. As soon as he was in my apartment he kissed me as if we'd been lovers for years, and before saying anything he started making love to me. I had dreamed of that happening to me ever since I had sensed that he wanted me. I started to let myself go until he stirred up my jealousy with something he said. 'Oh Jesus, Minnie, we should have done this years ago,' he told me. I angrily asked him, 'When, Alec? When you were an errand boy for Rhea and her organization? When you were running after Sophie?' I told him I had been deeply hurt when my best friends had banned me from the *Omissions* staff, and I didn't want to be hurt again so soon by Alec, who'd had nothing to do with that stupid exclusion; I wanted to have at least one friend who hadn't been a bastard toward me. He let go of me right away. He acted as if I had unraveled a puzzle for him, and I was once again relieved I hadn't let myself go; I saw that you were all he had on his mind. I was nothing but a temporary consolation. 'So that's it, the *Omissions* staff! Sophie is overreacting again!' he exclaimed as if everything were suddenly clear to him 'she's expressing her spite against her former friends the same way she expressed it earlier against Lem and Rhea by dating that reactionary asshole Rakshas!' He'd been thinking about you all the time his arms had been wrapped around me; I was green with envy. He spent the whole rest of the evening trying to convince me to visit the garage again. I refused at first, but he drew such an awful picture for me. He told me that 'in response to your exclusion from *Omissions*' you had thrown yourself into a situation in which you couldn't survive. He told me all about the heroin and the prostitution. He didn't have to convince me you were too frail to survive that kind of life for very long. He suggested that Hugh, Daman and I drop in on you, casually as it were, to try to make you grasp what you were doing to yourself, to 'save' you. That's how we were drawn into that terrible confrontation. I thought your sister such an unscrupulous beast, Sophie; I'm glad that even she finally figured out what you were all doing to yourselves. All my jealousy left me, Sophie. I felt so sorry for you. When you lay on the floor begging Hugh to carry you away, I was sure you were gone. And once outside you shouted at me to get away from you. You didn't even recognize me. I walked away crying. I didn't walk far. I was sure you'd return to the garage, and I waited for Alec. I suppose my jealousy returned when I saw you walking away from the garage, with Alec tagging behind you. All my envy returned when I reached my apartment, alone, and it stayed with me and tortured me for the following two years. I waited and waited for Alec to call, but he never did; I had saved you for him. I hope they were happy years for you, Sophie. I spent almost two years with him after that, and those were the happiest years in my life."

"Minnie, who told you I spent those two years with Alec?" I asked her.

"You don't have to spare my feelings now, Sophie; I'm obviously not jealous now! When he left you. Alec came to me; we loved each other —"

"I saw Alec once, at a distance, a few days after I left the garage, Minnie, and I never saw him again."

"That's impossible, Sophie! He was living at your house when he started seeing me again."

"My house! I was staying in a dingy downtown hotel, Minnie! I had a job in a fiberglass factory. I never saw Alec again; I hated him when I left the garage. Did he tell you he was with me during those two years?"

"Oh my God, Sophie! No, he never talked about you, and I never asked. He only talked about your mother —"

I started laughing hysterically. "Minnie! Alec must have lived with Luisa for two years! And I had thought —"

She interrupted me. "Do you mean to tell me you didn't know?"

"Honestly, Minnie! I moved to a hotel, and later I came to this house with Sabina and Tina. I didn't see Luisa again until last year, and she hasn't told me anything —"

"I should have guessed!" Minnie exclaimed. "She was so upset when we spoke of you as her daughter that time Alec and I visited her. I could see why. She looked young enough to be your sister, and she was terribly interested in Alec."

"Already then, Minnie? Right after I was evicted from the co-op?"

"That was the only time I ever visited her. It wasn't I who noticed, Sophie; I'm not that perceptive. It was Alec who noticed. He bowed to her, kissed her hand, praised her house and made a complete ass out of himself. To me she was your mother! I couldn't have imagined Alec was going to live with her for two years! So it wasn't because of you that I spent all that time waiting!"

"Is that all you did, Minnie: wait? Those years must have been similar to mine; I waited for Jose's release from prison."

"I broke up with Daman once and for all."

"Why just then, Minnie? Wasn't it then that Daman finally got a job in a factory? Wasn't that what you had wanted him to do after you both graduated?"

"I was surprised when I learned you were close to him, Sophie. I hope this doesn't offend you, but it took me all those years to figure out that Daman was a jerk. Yes, he got a factory job, after he got his doctorate in philosophy. And as soon as he started working he caused a split in the organization. He suddenly became the world's greatest authority on the working class. His former comrades, including me, were suddenly bourgeois intellectuals with no roots in the working class. He started bringing his one recruit to the meetings, a complete ignoramus who got his politics from television sports announcers. Daman insisted on absolute silence whenever his baseball expert felt like making a comment. The meetings became weekly lectures on batting averages, but not for long. There had been eight of us; three people quit politics altogether; four of us started getting together at my apartment; Daman and his recruit apparently continued to hold weekly meetings; I wasn't even interested enough to find out what happened to our former meeting place. Alec started attending the meetings at my apartment. He was like a bomb. He finished off what was left of the organization."

"Alec left Luisa because he became interested in your organization?" I asked.

"Well in fact yes and no, Sophie. I ran into him by chance at a major political rally. I hadn't seen him for two years. I saw people there whom I hadn't seen for even longer. Lem Icel was there too. I even looked for you. Lem and Alec had apparently just seen each other when I saw the two of them. Alec was introducing Lem to your mother. I greeted all three of them as old acquaintances, and that was that. Alec asked me what Daman and I were doing, and I told him I was very involved in the activity of a new political tendency and no longer saw Daman. A few days later he called. He didn't apologize for having dropped me so completely two years earlier. He didn't express interest in me but in the organization I had briefly mentioned. He told me he was ready to become seriously involved in political activities; he wanted to do more than attend rallies. He told me he'd been reading about the third world and about the ghetto, and that he was sick of just reading about it. I told him when our group met. I also told him I didn't care to have anything to do with him outside the political meetings. And I meant it. I was sure his sudden political commitment was nothing but an act, and I was furious. He started coming regularly to our meetings. He was by far the most dynamic member of the group. I thought you had somehow transformed him. I had never seen him so concentrated, so logical or so eloquent. He came to four or five meetings and made no advances toward me. But one night he stayed after everyone else left. He told me he wanted to clarify some political questions that were bothering him. I lost my head, Sophie. Alec had been on my mind ever since that evening in his kitchen, when I'd learned he wanted me. I don't remember what it was he wanted to know; I don't think I knew even then. I had to consummate what I'd interrupted two years earlier. I asked him to stay longer. I talked to him about anything that came into my mind. I wanted to find out if he was still loyal to you, if he'd spend a few hours away from you. I hoped he was still fickle; I no longer cared whether or not I was your second. He stayed. We talked about *Omissions*, about the garage, about heroin, about your mother, about everything and everyone except you. He told me he had retained contact with Ted after he'd left the garage, that Ted as well as Jose had turned against the heroin pusher, and that Jose had been arrested. He also told me how intelligent and well-read your mother was; he seemed surprised that someone who had spent her life working knew so much about so many things. It got very late, and Alec asked if he could stay yet longer. I had been waiting for that question for years. I told him I only had one bed. I had always imagined that your love affairs were filled with animal passion, and I had always envied you Sophie. Alec moved in with me; our love lasted for almost two years. Those years were sexually the fullest years of my life. Until today I had thought Alec had left you when he'd moved in with me, and saying these things to you fills me with excitement. Please forgive me, Sophie —"

"I'm glad I found you again, Minnie. Please don't stop."

"I really can't go on, Sophie. In a way I can understand why you went from Alec to Daman. In spite of his rigidity, Daman was always so considerate, so gentle, and above all so scrupulously fair. Alec was a monster. He took everything out of me, left me completely drained. I don't just mean sexually. Politically too. Something had happened to him during the two years before he moved in with me. He kept telling me that the turning point in his life had been the confrontation he'd had with Sabina the first time he'd visited you in the garage. She had characterized him as a slave to any capitalist who bought him. It obviously wasn't the thought that was new to him, but the beastly way in which she must have said it to him. He told me it was because of Sabina's characterization that he'd quit his job and moved into the garage. And it continued bothering him after he saw through Sabina and her 'bootstrap operation.' He apparently decided that the only meaningful human activity was the total destruction of the capitalist class in all its manifestations, in the colonies as well as the ghettos. That attitude coincided perfectly with our tendency's political program. The fact is that when he'd started coming to the meetings, he had been drawn to the organization more than to me. That's ironic too, isn't it? He was the only one of the nine people in the group who had no job. He spent all his time reading and attending meetings. Of course he automatically became the editor and distributor of the tendency's newspaper. Before long it was Alec's organization. Alec stopped consulting the other members before he made major decisions, and this caused another split — or rather, the majority of the group 'purged' Alec for making himself a 'dictator.' Only three of the nine stuck with Alec: I, Eric, who is still a friend of mine, and a sixteen-year old girl, Carmen, who was connected with a group that eventually destroyed the little that was left. He had met Carmen while distributing the tendency newspaper. Her brother was one of three rebels who tried to start a radical bookshop in the heart of the ghetto. They were continually harassed by the police. Alec learned that one of the three dealt in dope. He made a scene about it, arguing that the radicalizing effect of the books was negated by the dope. Carmen agreed with Alec immediately, and her brother wavered. They were directly affected, since they lived right above the bookshop. Carmen started to attend organization meetings. Alec walked her home after the meetings, and he always returned to my apartment. But I had to make a stupid scene. I knew my two years were up. I blew up as soon as he returned one night. I told him I could support him with my teaching job, but I couldn't possibly support his friends. I just went silly. Carmen and her group were completely self-supporting, and the fact that I shared my bed and my meals with Alec had never been a burden to me. Alec rightly interpreted my outburst as a defense of wage labor, and he made that a perfect pretext for ending our relationship. He calmly told me he had experienced similar outbursts before — from his father, whom he'd hated since his boyhood. He acted as if I'd evicted him. He packed his little bag righteously and walked out of my life as if we were enemies."

"Poor Minnie! He did to you what I had done to him the night I left the garage. I spat on him and threw a bottle at him. Did you ever see him again?"

"I never rid myself of him, Sophie, any more than he ever rid himself of you. I think the radical bookshop, the campaign against heroin and even Carmen herself were all connected in his mind with you. He moved in with Carmen above the bookshop, and he and Carmen continued to attend the organization meetings. Alec took an interest in the bookshop and he succeeded in getting the heroin dealer out of it. One night Carmen called me from jail. She, her brother and Alec had been arrested and charged with being heroin dealers. I went to the trial. Although I knew nothing at all about law then, I knew that trial was an absolute scandal. They were defended by a court-appointed lawyer. Nothing at all was found upstairs or downstairs. One witness testified he had once bought a joint in the bookshop. But the prosecutor ranted and raved about the radical books; he listed one after another title; he read long excerpts about peasants collectively beating or hanging landlords, policemen and informers. The defense lawyer raised no objections. All three were sentenced to six months without a shred of evidence. When the three of them were released, they attended only one more meeting of the organization. They had prepared a skit before coming. Carmen announced dramatically that the time to talk had ended and the time for action had come. Alec said action meant armed action, and Carmen's brother opened the box they had brought and gave a rifle to every one in the room! I called them a 'suicide squad' and ran to my room crying. Eric joined them. What would you have done?"

"I would have run to my room crying, Minnie. Do you even have to ask?"

"I had never been so alone in my whole life, Sophie. For the first time since I'd started college I was without an organization, without friends, without any activity except that stupid teaching job. I spent my days policing kids and got home exhausted and disgusted with myself. I couldn't stand what I was becoming. That was when I decided to enroll in law school. I know exactly what you think of lawyers, Sophie. I agree completely. I agreed then too."

"I can't judge you, Minnie, not any more. I was drifting back to school around the time you started law school, and I drifted with many less scruples than you must have had —"

"They weren't exactly scruples, Sophie, but something less. I still agreed with Alec, I still thought the only worthwhile activity was to destroy capitalism in any way possible, but I didn't translate that to a practice of chasing down and shooting dope dealers or fighting cops in the street; that kind of activity seemed too much like swatting flies off garbage cans without removing the garbage. But the fact is that I didn't know how to translate my political ideas into any kind of practice —"

"I had almost the same experience with Jose. Maybe the suicide squad was the only way our commitments could be translated into practice —"

"If so, then I've become as much of a reformist as Daman. I never wanted to believe that, Sophie. I had always thought some kind of political activity other than suicide, organized activity, could be meaningful and genuinely radical. I never shared Daman's illusion that one could function meaningfully within the system, preaching to future bosses about the revolution at the point of production. But I can't even say that honestly. I had some illusions when I started law school. I was sick of policing kids. I had been enormously impressed by the foul treatment Alec, Carmen and her brother had received in court. I told myself my function could be less explicitly a police function, my time could be more my own —"

"And is it less of a police function?"

"You know damn well it isn't, Sophie. I'm part of an enormous apparatus. I move by its rules, not it by mine. My time is less my own now than it ever was before. I started practicing a year and a half ago, about six months before the riot. During the riot I defended victims of police harassment, illegal entry, illegal arrest, beatings. I found other so-called radical lawyers and joined the cooperative I'm still with. We worked with a group that called itself a committee against repression —"

"Luisa was on that committee!"

"Really? I never ran into her. I had just barely started that work when I was struck by a blow that incapacitated me for months. I don't think I can tell it without breaking down; it was so awful —"

"Is it about Alec? You don't have to —"

"I do have to, Sophie. I can't go on keeping it locked up inside me, and you're the only person in the world I can share the pain with."

"Don't make me cry before you even start, Minnie. But please tell me. I want to know."

"After the meeting when Alec, Carmen and her brother broke up the organization, Eric moved in with them above the bookshop. Eric was the only one of the group who visited me periodically. They did exactly what they advocated. They constituted themselves into an armed self-defense group. Next time the police would raid the bookshop they'd have to shoot it out with 'urban guerrillas,' as the four called themselves. They spent a whole year trying to convince people in their neighborhood to arm themselves against what Alec called 'the occupation forces,' by which he meant the police. According to Eric, Alec also kept track of all the heroin dealers in the neighborhood, and he paid specific attention to one dealer who supposedly 'serviced' the entire region from a bar protected by the police. They spoke of heroin dealers as rats. When the riot broke out Alec announced the time had come to rid the neighborhood of all the rats. The bookshop was near the heart of the riot area and was left completely unharmed by the crowds that looted and burned all the shops on both sides of it. All four of them had the impression the revolution had broken out, and they were eager to take part in it; they spent a long time arguing about the form their participation should take. Alec settled the argument by grabbing a handgun and shouting, 'This is how I'm participating; I'm going to get him!' Carmen's brother hesitated; he said he didn't want to hurt innocent people. Carmen stuffed a gun into her purse, pulled Alec out of their apartment and shouted at the other two, 'You're already too late, and there won't be a next time!' Carmen and Alec walked through excited crowds toward the bar where the regional heroin dealer did his business. Eric and Carmen's brother followed them. There were no police protectors near the bar; that day they were busy elsewhere, and the heart of the riot area was not the safest place for them. Alec and Carmen moved toward the bar shouting, 'Get the dope pushers!' and 'Clear out the rats!' At the bar entrance they both pulled out their guns and shouted 'This is the origin of all the heroin' and 'here's the biggest rat in the community.' An enormous crowd gathered in front of the bar. Some people shouted encouragement; most people stared curiously. Alec and Carmen entered the bar waving their guns. But the crowd attracted the attention of the forces of law and order. A tank and a National Guard unit were provoked by it. The tank aimed its gun at the heart of the crowd, and the soldiers started beating people, forcing them to disperse. Eric was separated from Carmen's brother but kept his eyes glued to the entrance of the bar. He saw Alec and Carmen come out grinning victoriously, still waving their guns. Eric shouted as loudly as he could to them, pointlessly. Alec and Carmen turned and started to run back into the bar. They were shot down by machine guns."

"Minnie, that's awful —"

"Eric still has nightmares about it. That was an awful thing to see. Carmen's brother committed suicide a few days later."

Minnie was shaking. I helped her lie down on the couch and put a blanket over her. I was crying.

"I shook this way for days when Eric told me about it, and I still shake whenever I think about it. I had opposed Alec's vigilante terrorism from its origins, but I disintegrated when Eric told me how Alec and Carmen died. Maybe you're right; maybe that was the only way to translate our commitment into practice. I can't help admiring their courage. Fickle as he was, Alec remained true to the one goal he set himself. Ever since his encounter with Sabina he had convinced himself he couldn't coexist with the ruling order, and he lived and died for that conviction. Eric wanted to commit suicide too. He felt he had no right to be the only one alive. He had pledged himself to the group, and he felt he had betrayed Alec and Carmen by letting them venture out by themselves. He knew that if he and Carmen's brother had stood guard outside the bar, they would have known about the arrival of the National Guard, and they'd have warned Alec and Carmen in time; they could all have escaped by the bar's rear entrance. Instead they had let Alec and Carmen emerge proudly into what they expected to be a cheering and welcoming crowd, the grateful community. Eric tortured himself with guilt; he knew that the same thoughts had led Carmen's brother to kill himself."

I revived Minnie somewhat with a drink and asked, "Where's Eric now?"

"Eric and I live together," she told me. "We have since the riot. He works in an auto plant, and he's one of the five people in the new political tendency we started several months ago. He's a very gentle and considerate person, and very scrupulous about sharing the work as well as the burdens. I'm sure you'll like him."

Before Minnie left I asked her if she knew what had happened to the other people we had known during our university days, and I told her all I knew about Lem, Rhea as well as Daman.

"I never heard of Thurston or Bess again," she told me. "I read about Hugh in a newspaper sometime recently. He's some kind of authority in one of the sciences; I think the article was about a lecture he was to deliver at a suburban college —"

"Hugh — a lecturer?"

"I'll try to look him up, Sophie. If I find him and he's nearby, should I ask if he could get together with us?"

"I'd love that, Minnie!"

I tried not to cry any more until Minnie left. Her account of Alec's life and his horrid death stirred up a great deal in my life too. I had been so vicious to him. In the end Alec, like Jose, had tried to act out, at least in some practical form, the project I had only dreamed about. In his own way Alec had been a Nachalo and had died like him. When Minnie and I parted, we both knew we were going to be seeing a lot of each other from now on.

Your letter arrived two days after Minnie's visit and Daman telephoned later that day. As I've learned to expect, Daman forgot everything that's happened recently except the fact that I'm out of a job. "It's an opening that doesn't call for any higher credentials than a master's degree; I thought you might be interested, in case you're still out of a job."

"I'm out of a job. Daman, and out of a project, but I'm not interested in another teaching job. How about coming over just to talk, about old times, about Alec for instance?"

"I can't, Sophie," he told me. "I've suddenly got more things to do than I have time. I thought I had recruited Luisa, but it turns out she recruited me to that committee of hers —"

"The repression committee?" I asked. "If you won't come over to talk, then how about giving Ted and me a ride to the repression committee? He still hasn't gotten his car back; it was impounded by the police. And he'd love to see you again. He was so impressed by you ten years ago, he still remembers you —"

Except for an excursion he'd taken with Sabina to try to get his car back, Ted had been spending his days the same way I had: moping around the house with nothing to do. Ted had in fact told me he'd like to see the people who had visited me in the garage; he had liked Alec a great deal, and he'd thought they were all like Alec. But Ted must have been disappointed. Daman came, shook Ted's hand showing no sign he had ever seen Ted before, and told him, "Nice seeing you again; how many years were you in jail because of that heroin business?" Ted and Daman had nothing more to say to each other on the way to the repression committee.

In the car I asked Daman if he knew how Alec had died.

"Of course," he told me. "He was gunned down in last year's riot."

"Why didn't you tell me?"

"I'm sorry, Sophie. I learned about it about a month after it happened, and I didn't see you for almost a year after that. I guess I forgot —"

"But you never forget to tell me about openings for college instructors!"

"I said I was sorry, Sophie! And what's so odd about my telling you about job openings when I know you need a job?"

"Nothing, Daman, absolutely nothing! You have a perfect sense of timing!" I was referring to something he'd told me a year ago, right after I'd been fired from the first job he'd helped me find. He didn't seem to recognize the reference.

Daman is such a bizarre person. He seems to have a different set of standards and pattern of behavior for each of the compartments in which he lives his life. I tried to get close to him during my year in graduate school. I felt very lonely among students who were ten years younger than I. Their concerns and interests had little in common with mine, I've never been spontaneously sociable, and until a few weeks ago the possibility of forming a liaison with a lover ten years younger than I never crossed my mind. Daman told me about interesting political events; he chatted briefly afterwards, but he didn't once pick me up or take me home. He didn't become a friend until I got my degree three years ago, when he helped me get my first teaching job. I became his "colleague" and therefore also his friend a year and a half after I first enrolled in his course. I was hired to teach one course. His teaching day began at noon, and I taught my course on Tuesdays and Thursdays, in the afternoon. From the first day of classes he picked me up and drove me to school; I read on the grass or in the library until his teaching day ended, and then he drove me back home. One Tuesday afternoon he invited me to dinner at his apartment. I learned what it was that Minnie, and later Luisa, liked about him. In the privacy of his apartment he was an altogether transformed Daman. All his personal and political rigidity were gone. He was the most thoughtful and considerate man I've ever been close to. I learned that he always cooked supper for himself, not to save money, but because he preferred his own meals to anything he could order in restaurants. And the meal he prepared for me really was splendid; Luisa is a good cook, but not compared to Daman. He washed all the dishes as soon as we were done eating, and that first night he didn't even let me dry them. After coffee and a brief chat he volunteered to drive me home, "Unless you'd like to go out on the town" — which of course I did. We went to a movie that was shown in a university auditorium. When we came out I put my hand in his and had him retrace the walk we had taken exactly ten years earlier, when we'd carried the coffin of the dead university newspaper. He didn't realize we had retraced the path of that mock funeral until the very end, when we stopped before the closed entrance of the building in which the newspaper office was located. He looked at me sadly. "I know how much that meant to you, Sophie; it meant a lot to me too." I asked him, "Would you mind taking me back to your apartment?" I had fallen in love with Daman's apartment and with Daman's behavior inside it. His apartment was clean and modest yet extremely comfortable; it was an absolute contrast to Art's filthy little reading room with an unmade bed. Daman did all his work in his office in the university. He used his apartment for cooking, eating, reading and sleeping, and everything in his apartment was perfectly arranged to make these activities as enjoyable as they could be. He had a double bed, but I didn't ask if anyone had shared it with him before me. He had broken up with Minnie long before he had been able to afford that apartment. Since all his acquaintances were political, and since he didn't mix politics with his private life, I didn't see how he could have had a sexual relationship with any other woman, unless she had invited herself as I had. Daman's compartments were so mutually exclusive that he didn't keep any political or philosophical books in his apartment. His single shelf contained only literary classics and, of all things, books of poetry. I had never imagined Daman sitting in his apartment reading poetry, but I had never imagined the rest of his "private" life either. For slightly less than a year (I was fired before the end of the school year) I "lived" with Daman two days out of every week, from Tuesday at noon, when he picked me up for my first class, to Thursday afternoon, when he drove me back after my last. I remember those days with a certain nostalgia. Unlike Art, Daman took nothing for granted. Every Tuesday afternoon, before driving to his apartment, he scrupulously asked, "Where to?" He sometimes let me help cook, but I didn't once cook alone, and I never did the shopping. I washed dishes only when he wasn't home for dinner, which happened very rarely, and on those occasions he left a prepared meal for me in the refrigerator! Unlike any other man I've known (I've never lived with you), Daman understood that not knowing how to cook or clean or wash dishes presupposed the existence of "proletarians" — women proletarians — who knew how to do all these things. He did all this for himself, not ostentatiously but quietly and matter-of-factly. His entire apartment was spotless whenever I stepped into it. I never once even had a chance to make the bed; he hurriedly did that while I brushed my teeth. In his apartment he was the most decent and thoughtful person I've known. But as soon as his "social role" was in question, or what he took to be mine, he became insupportable.

On the job he helped me find three years ago I was supposed to teach a conventional course in introductory sociology. I immediately turned it into the only study of society that interested me: the study of its overthrow. I had been told to use one of two "standard" textbooks, but I didn't read or assign or discuss either textbook. I gave out a list of books containing most of the titles I had taken to Jose in prison. The classroom sessions were political arguments about revolutions and liberation movements. In the record books I gave all students the highest mark whether or not I had ever seen them. I quickly gained a reputation as a "faculty radical," and students not enrolled in my class started to attend in order to engage in political arguments. Members of student political groups asked me to be the faculty "sponsor" of their organizations, a formality which was needed for them to have access to university facilities. I also attended some of the meetings of the groups I "sponsored," and I learned something about the unromantic side of the "student movement." I saw the politicians and manipulators transforming rebellious students into passive tools; I saw what you've called the grand puppet show. But I didn't generalize from such insights and experiences. I vaguely agreed with

Daman that the genuine revolutionary movement would in any case not begin among students but in the factories, "at the point of production." I had learned that from Luisa. I didn't figure out that the "organization" of the working class which was going to make that revolution possible, the union in all its various shapes and forms, played the same role in the factories as the politicians and manipulators played among the rebellious students. I only learned that very recently, and largely from you, although last year's riot gave me some clues. Everything that was "organized," from the State to the tiniest "radical" sect, was opposed to the spontaneous carnival atmosphere that suddenly took hold of this city. The riot broke out when my second teaching term was half over. I thought what I'd always waited for was at last happening. Massive rebellion broke out in the streets; whole blocks of buildings burned; carefully priced commodities circulated as freely as confetti. I wanted to be part of it all and drifted into it in my usual style. A man trying to run with two television sets shouted to me to grab one of them. I ran home with it as proudly as if I'd carried out a revolutionary act. When I next met with my class I was almost angry at students who hadn't taken part in the looting. As I told you in one of my first letters, I was promptly fired. And when I lost my job, my relationship with Daman ended in a bitter argument. I wasn't particularly upset about losing the lob, since the pay was scandalously low and I hated being part of the academic bureaucracy. But Daman was flushed with anger. "A classroom isn't the best place to carry picket signs!" he shouted at me when I told him why I'd been fired. I told him angrily, "I wasn't carrying picket signs! I was encouraging students to loot, riot and steal instead of sitting in that stuffy room listening to an idiot like me!" He retorted, "The revolution isn't going to break out in a university classroom!" I told him I didn't expect anything at all to happen in a university classroom. That was when he told me, "You have a bad sense of timing, Sophie!" I blew up. "Totally unlike you, Daman! You have a perfect sense for timing and placing and cataloguing! You have a different mask for every cubby hole you move through: anger for political meetings, condescension for classrooms, courage for strikes, submissiveness for meetings with superiors, kindness for animals and decency only in the privacy of your apartment. You're not a human being but a filing cabinet!" He tried to respond patiently, namely condescendingly, "Sophie, if you're going to keep a teaching job —" I broke in, crying with frustrated anger, "Don't you understand what the riot meant? People expressed in acts just how they feel about the precious institutions you serve! They hate those institutions, they feel oppressed by them, they'd like nothing better than to burn them all to the ground. Don't you feel the slightest bit ashamed to parade in front of that classroom exercising authority given to you by the state?" He walked away from me; his face expressed shocked disbelief. I called him about a month later to apologize for my outburst and to thank him for all he had done for me. I didn't hear from him again for over a year.

     When Daman had called four days ago to tell me about yet another job opening I had told him I wanted to talk to him, and that Ted was eager to see him again.

But neither Ted nor I said anything to him for the rest of our trip to the building where the repression committee has its offices. It was only when we were inside the building that it occurred to me to ask, "Why did Luisa recruit you into this committee, Daman? What in the world do you do here? Stuff envelopes?"

He told me, "Luisa feels the committee's work lacks political direction. She thinks I can help provide a certain amount of coherence by taking part in some of the activities, for instance by contributing a certain amount of research and simply by engaging in some of the discussions."

I commented sarcastically, "So you're sort of an ideological director of the enterprise."

Daman snickered but missed my sarcasm altogether. "I suppose you could call it that."

"Something like the minister of the committee's ideological department," I went on.

He said, almost with pride, "I wouldn't go quite that far —"

"No. I suppose you don't expect to reach the stage of government portfolios until after the revolution."

"It's not a question of revolution here but of repression," he told me, adding the expected, "The question of revolution is going to be resolved on the shop floor —"

"What are you doing here then?" I asked him. "I thought the only task of a revolutionary was to —"

Daman didn't respond. We had both heard each other's arguments before. He escorted Ted and me to a room full of people, the room I had walked into after last year's riot. Luisa came rushing toward Daman. "This is Ted, the printer," Daman told her.

Without even looking at me, Luisa shook Ted's hand eagerly and told him, "I really enjoyed my lesson in printing, and I can't tell you how glad I am that you came here. The committee acquired a printing press a few days ago, but no one here is able to get it going." She was called away to the telephone. While talking on the phone she asked Daman if he had finished an article. He handed it to her; she glanced at it continuing her phone conversation, and then handed it to a young woman who was typing. When she got off the phone she asked Ted, "Would you mind having a look at that printing machine?"

I had rarely seen Luisa "at work." I wondered if this was the Luisa you had known in the carton plant, if this was the Luisa who had recruited Nachalo into the "genuine workers' organization." She seemed just like a political boss. The activity in that room was identical to the activity that had finally repelled me years ago, when I had tried to escape from the drudgery of my job in the fiberglass factory. Yet Luisa didn't seem at all bored. I suppose the fact that she's held the same factory job for twenty years indicates that her tolerance for boredom is infinitely higher than mine. But she didn't seem merely to tolerate the boredom. She seemed to enjoy it, to be fulfilled by it, the way monks and nuns seem fulfilled while performing dull tasks. The gratification doesn't come from their senses, but from the knowledge that every moment of drudgery is yet another service performed for the Lord, or in Luisa's case, for the Organization. It struck me that the room I was looking at was something like a microcosm of all of Luisa's "organizations." The activity in and of itself is the dullest, most repetitious activity performed in the bureaucratic society. But this activity is transformed into something gratifying and enjoyable the moment a Daman, an Alberts or a Zabran define its "political direction." The purpose of her organizing has been to provide the political directors with staffs of flunkies. How ludicrous it is that Daman, that caricature of a fragmented human being, himself a patchwork of contradictions, himself unable to connect his politics with the other closed compartments that compose his life, should be the one to provide "political direction" to others! And how scandalous that Luisa should have sacrificed her own life to the task of recruiting independent spirits to the service of such gods.

When I had asked Daman to take Ted and me to the repression committee, I had forgotten that Art Sinich might be there: it was in that very room that I'd seen Art after last year's riot. And of course Art was there, and he rushed over to me as soon as he saw me. I wasn't glad to see him, but I shook his hand and asked if he had time to accompany me to a nearby coffee shop for a chat. I wanted to learn just how Art had come to be living in my room at Luisa's house until a few weeks ago.

I ended up treating Art to lunch and several cups of coffee. It turned out that Art's life was far more intertwined with mine than I had ever imagined. I learned yet another time that the "radical community" in this city with millions of people is like a closed, incestuous family, and by now I probably know every member of it; I also got a view of yet another ugly underside of that "community."

Art had met Luisa long before I had ever walked into the peace movement building. When I saw them both in the repression committee last year I thought they had met there; I didn't imagine they had known each other during the years when I hadn't seen Luisa. Art met Lem Icel as long as seven years ago. Lem had just returned from his harrowing prison experience after trying to deliver my letters, and was living with Debbie Matthews. Art was already involved in peace movement activity when Lem first walked into the peace center. "I met Luisa at a third world rally," Art told me. "Lem introduced me to a university friend of his, and Luisa was with this friend." That friend, of course was Alec. Everyone I knew must have been at that rally; I was in the fiberglass factory when it took place. "It's funny the three of you didn't run into each other when you came to the peace center," he said. "I must have seen Lem at least four or five times during the weeks when you came to the peace center. But Lem didn't bring Luisa there until after you did me the favor of looking up the maid service phone number for me. He introduced me to Luisa again, although I remembered her from the rally. Of course Lem didn't know I knew you, and I couldn't know Luisa was your mother. Eventually Lem dropped out of peace movement activities altogether, but Luisa got more and more involved.

Luisa and I found that we understood each other much better than she and Lem ever had. He started to look for ways to escape from responsibilities that we can't run away from, but neither of us could help him understand that. He wanted to be a hermit, and since one of my relatives owned an abandoned estate, Luisa and I took him to the type of environment he said he wanted. Luisa was generous enough to invite me to replace Lem in her house. Even then I didn't know I was in your house, Sophie; there wasn't a single photograph of you in it. She helped me understand a lot of things correctly, but she couldn't get me to understand that the people she called workers, people who filled their houses with material things, could be called oppressed. I didn't really understand the meaning of oppression until after last year's riot, when this committee got started. When I saw you last year I had just left the peace movement after almost ten years of involvement."

When I saw Art last year I had just been fired from my first teaching job. The money I had saved when I'd worked in the fiberglass factory had run out during my year in graduate school, and I hadn't been able to save any of the money I had earned from my teaching job. I wasn't worried about starving to death, but I didn't want Sabina or Tina to pay my bills. So I took advantage of one of the indirect benefits brought about by the riot. Immediately after the riot, state institutions which dispensed relief to the poor (ironically called "welfare") became temporarily flexible as well as "generous." I had drawn a small amount of unemployment compensation after I'd been fired from the fiberglass factory, but being fired from a teaching job didn't "qualify" me for that type of subsidy. So I went on "welfare." And it was in a welfare office that I received a leaflet announcing a demonstration sponsored by the "Committee Against Repression Inc." There were many strange things about the leaflet besides the name of the sponsor, but it did condemn the wanton killings carried out by the police, and it rightly pointed out that the police were the only ones who had rioted during the "riot." This had been perfectly clear to me; the redistribution of consumer goods had been carried out in a very orderly and cooperative manner, in the spirit of a feast or a carnival, certainly not a riot; yet all the newspapers had described the events with words that suggested uninterrupted and limitless violence. There were many fires, but they were systematically limited to enterprises that were known to practice the worst exploitation and extortion. I went to the demonstration on the date announced on the leaflet. The event attracted thirty demonstrators, if that many. The group took a two-hour walk along city sidewalks carrying signs with terribly unimaginative slogans; more than half the demonstrators left along the way. I stayed with the group, more out of curiosity than conviction. Imagine my surprise when someone behind me grabbed my arm, and I turned and saw Luisa. I hadn't seen her since the night when I'd returned home after hunting for Hugh and discovered her on the living room couch with Alec. "In another seven years I wouldn't have recognized you!" she told me. She invited me to visit the group's office, and proudly gave me a tour around the envelopes, the addressing machine and the stacks of mimeographed leaflets marked "press release"; it was similar to the envelope-stuffing room at the peace center. I imagined that the advertising offices from which the ruling class manipulates the society of consumers must also be similar, only a lot less messy and with swept floors, since they could afford to pay their proletarians. We weren't very friendly to each other, we both remembered how we'd parted, and we both remembered the brief phone conversation we'd had shortly after we parted, when neither of us had expressed any interest in seeing each other again. I asked sarcastically when she had graduated from shopfloor organizing to working with a "Committee Incorporated." She told me she had become politically active again two years after I had left her, when "a young man by the name of Lem" introduced her to the peace movement. "But the politics of those people were atrocious, and this committee's work is much more like the work I'd like to do." I asked her what she'd done during the riot, and the vehemence with which she opposed it amazed me. Among other things, she shouted, "Wanton attacks on the productive forces are not a revolution! The workers I fought with aimed to appropriate the productive forces, not to destroy them!" She had stayed home during the riot listening to her radio. "It sounded awful," she told me; "a vast release of pent-up frustration without any political direction or program." She'd gotten interested only when the repressive forces of the state had transformed the "riot" into a real riot. "We're exposing the fact that property is valued far higher than human life," she started to tell me, but someone called her away to the phone, telling her, "This is your department, Luisa; some radical union caucus." She excused herself and picked up the phone. I smiled to her coldly, indifferently, as I backed out of the Committee Against Repression Incorporated, out of the building and out to the street. Just as I reached the fresh air I ran into Art Sinich on his way into the same building. At that time I didn't connect him with Lem or with Luisa and I didn't ask him how or when he had moved from the peace movement to the repression committee. We stood by the building entrance and chatted briefly. He wanted to invite me back up to the "office," but I told him I had already seen it. Neither he nor I knew that the bed in which he spent his nights had once been mine.

I was much more curious about Art when I invited him to coffee four days ago. I asked him how he had managed to reconcile his peace philosophy with the significantly different outlook of the repression committee.

"I still don't condone violence," he told me. "But Luisa helped me understand that the violence of the oppressed isn't the same as the violence of the oppressor. She helped me understand that liberation can only be achieved through organization. The Committee is devoted to the belief that oppressed races carry the seeds of liberation —"

"You learned that from Luisa?" I asked with disbelief.

"Luisa doesn't agree with every one of the organization's positions," he told me.

I was relieved to learn that. I asked him how Luisa's positions differed from the organization's. He launched into a tirade that made my head swim.

"Ever since she asked me to leave her house she's been acting funny toward me and toward the rest of the committee," he told me. "She claims to bring that politics professor to the committee in order to give the committee political direction, but in my opinion she's trying to wreck the committee. It's becoming clear to me that she doesn't really understand the problem of oppression. She doesn't understand that every race of people must struggle for their survival and freedom. And she doesn't understand the real purpose of the committee. She and her professor friend seem to be stuck on the old belief that the key to revolution is some kind of mass movement. They don't know that the key to revolution today is race, racial movements. They don't see that we won't ever become a mass movement. We seek to maximize the power and influence we can exert as an organized minority. We serve the needs of other organizations and we serve to educate the public at large. We aim to coordinate the activities of organizations expressing the will of national and racial minorities —"

I hurriedly paid the bill and rushed out of the coffee shop. The hodgepodge that constituted Art's new philosophy had a familiar, ugly ring to it.

I returned to the repression committee and looked for Ted. I had a headache and wanted to go home with him. I went to the "press room" behind the office to look for him. Suddenly I froze in my tracks. What I felt must have been similar to what you felt twenty years ago when you stopped behind a pillar and watched Luisa walk out of the carton plant with her arm in Marc Glavni's. Ted was bending over the press, tightening or loosening something with a wrench. Luisa was "learning" by holding on to Ted's waist with her left hand, her whole body leaning over Ted's, her cheek almost rubbing against his. Yes, of course I was jealous; intensely so. But it wasn't only jealousy that infuriated me. I suddenly saw Luisa's entire life project, I suddenly understood Luisa's "union," I suddenly grasped how and why Luisa had so successfully combined her sexual with her political activity. Daman the researcher, Daman the spokesman of our movement, Daman the shepherd, was in the other room providing "political direction." But some of the sheep, namely Art and his friends, were already under the tutelage of a different shepherd, and the political director was on the verge of being left without followers. The shepherd's dog was using her entire body to recruit a new sheep into the flock, to provide her political director with a new follower. This was Luisa's revenge for the scene I had made with Pat. I trembled with fury as I moved toward them.

Luisa turned her back to me as soon as she saw me. She told Ted, "We could sure use the talents of an experienced printer around here. Would you be willing to continue my lesson some other time, and to show the rest of the staff how this machine works?"

Ted acquiesced. "Sure. I don't have many other things to do right now."

Luisa started to walk past me out of the room. I grabbed her arm and told her, "If you think you're the one who has a gripe against me, Luisa, get it out of your head this minute —"

She shook herself out of my grasp and pulled me through the office and out to the hall. "All right, Sophia! Let's have it out once and for all! Why did you ruin my relationship with Daman?"

"I only wish I had ruined it!" I shouted. "But I obviously failed to ruin your relationship to your authority, your god! I just caught you in the act of sacrificing another victim to him!"

Luisa pulled me all the way out to the street, where she shouted, "We're going to have it out, you and I, but you're not going to embarrass me one more time!" She hailed a cab, pulled me inside, and told the driver to take us to her house. "All right, now holler all you want!" she told me in the back of the cab, releasing me.

"Don't you accuse me of destroying anything, Luisa! You've devoured countless human lives for the sake of those beloved authorities of yours, those professors with the working class project in their heads! Leave Ted alone, would you? Didn't you have your fill with Nachalo and Yarostan and Alec —"

"You're feverish with jealousy, Sophia! You're the most conventional, spiteful, narrow —"

"I used to think you loved Nachalo. I admired you for that love. But you destroyed him! You've dragged everything he stood for through mud!"

"Stick to your present jealousy, you idiot, and don't talk about things you don't know anything about!" she shouted. She paid for the cab and I followed her into her house.

"How long did you expect me to go on knowing nothing about Nachalo?" I asked her. We both sat down in the living room where I had so recently flaunted my independence from her. "I know that Ted is another Nachalo to you. Sabina told me all about what Nachalo stood for, and I now know he had nothing in common with that organization you served, or its so-called popular army. George Alberts told her —"

"Whatever George Alberts told her was a lie!" she shouted, "He spent his life justifying his betrayal of his comrades at the front."

"When did you decide Alberts was lying?" I asked her. "When Titus Zabran returned from the front and told you Nachalo had died like a hero fighting alongside Zabran and Alberts in the popular army? That conflicted with what Alberts told you, didn't it? Alberts told you he and Zabran had fought against people like Nachalo, didn't he?"

"You're raving about things you can't know anything about, Sophia. Alberts couldn't have told Sabina anything until ten years after the event! And he couldn't have remembered anything. When he returned from the front, he was delirious; I thought his mind had been affected. He ranted senselessly about a firing squad, and about having shot into the air. As for Titus: I didn't visit him until several weeks after George returned. I knew George was lying — hallucinating, if you prefer — the moment he got back from the front. The only thing I did believe was that he'd shot into the air. I was sure he had deserted, and his lies were designed to cover up his cowardice. He had been the one who had stayed home when the rest of us had gone out on the barricades several months earlier. In his ravings, he called Nachalo a reactionary; he called him everything short of a defector. He said he and Titus had run into Nachalo at the front, and Nachalo hadn't greeted his former friends as comrades, but as 'red butchers.' He acted as if Nachalo were the enemy —"

"Then you admit that the apparatus Alberts and Zabran and you served was opposed to what Nachalo and his comrades in the militia were fighting for —"

"I admit nothing of the sort, Sophia! The so-called conflict between the militia and the popular army was a lie spread by the fascists. They were both in one and the same army, the union's army, the armed working class, the most devoted, most revolutionary workers. Everything we did in the rear, even my activity as a transportation delegate and tram driver, was a contribution to the popular army's victory, the union's victory, Nachalo's victory, which were all one and the same victory. The militia was nothing but the first detachments of the popular army."

"That's not true, Luisa! The popular army absorbed the militia into itself the same way you absorbed Nachalo into the union, and it destroyed all those it couldn't absorb. That's why Nachalo called Alberts and Zabran 'red butchers.'"

"You knew more about it when you were ten years old! 'Red butchers' is what the fascists called the entire working class! George learned the term from the fascists and he used it to excuse his desertion. I went to see Titus in the hospital as soon as he was allowed visitors. He told me neither he nor George could have had a conversation with Nachalo at the front. Titus also told me he had learned from Nachalo's comrades that Nachalo had died bravely, heroically, fighting the fascists; he died exactly as he had lived. The unit was defeated because of overwhelming odds against them, because of fascist sabotage in the rear, and also because of some defections. All he said about George was that he had done the best he knew how to do, but I already knew what George could and couldn't do, so he didn't have to tell me more. When I told him what rumors George was spreading among Nachalo's friends, Titus grew alarmed. He thought, and I agreed, that such rumors could destroy the morale of fighting workers and do untold harm. As soon as he came out of the hospital, Titus and I arranged a memorial meeting for Nachalo. It was the last union meeting held in my apartment. All of Nachalo's and Margarita's comrades who had remained in the rear attended the meeting; none returned from the front. Titus gave the main oration. He admitted he had never met Nachalo, but he told everything he had learned from Nachalo's comrades. Nachalo had died like a working class hero, fighting alongside his comrades. The victory of the popular army had been his first priority, and he had urged sacrificing everything for the sake of that victory. He was determined to die before allowing a single fascist soldier to encroach on the accomplishments of the workers. Alberts said nothing during the entire meeting. He never again repeated those rumors about Nachalo. I'm amazed he was so shameless as to repeat those rumors to Sabina years later."

"You're the one who's shameless, Luisa! You're lying! You've been lying to yourself for thirty years. Yarostan asked Titus about the popular army only a few days ago. Titus called it a mistake, a big mistake! What Titus told Yarostan didn't conflict with what Alberts told Sabina. It conflicted with everything you're telling me! The popular army was a monster that devoured revolutionaries; it turned against the very workers who initiated that struggle, just like the union —"

"I don't know what you're talking about Sophia, and I'm losing interest. Your lifelong friendship with Sabina hasn't made you very bright. When I first met Nachalo he was an isolated individualistic terrorist. I know Sabina admires that type of person, but I didn't know you did. It was thanks to me that Nachalo became a devoted union militant admired by thousands of his fellow workers. He became a virtual myth to them, the very symbol of the collectivist worker united with his comrades in the uncompromising struggle of the class for its liberation. I can't imagine what Titus might have told Yarostan. I'm not surprised that it conflicted with what I'm saying. Titus and I disagreed about many things, especially about the form that the unity of the working class should take. I emphasized the union; he emphasized councils and other political forms. But there was one thing we didn't disagree about, and that was the need for organization. We were both collectivists first of all; we both knew that the struggle was a class struggle, not an individual's struggle."

"So you lured Nachalo into an apparatus that turned against his struggle, an apparatus that ultimately destroyed him. You lured him with your body, but you didn't do it for yourself, for your own gratification; you didn't do it out of any love for him. Nachalo was no more to you than Yarostan was, than Ted is. You took Yarostan to the stockroom and then to your bedroom for the sake of the organization!"

Luisa, flushed with anger, jumped at me, pinned me back against the couch, and hissed at me, "You're asking for it, Sophia, and you're going to get it! If you stare like a deaf mute, or if I see a tear in your eye, I'm going to send you flying out that door for good! You're so green with jealousy you can't even keep your topic straight. Hypocrite! You're not the one to lecture to me about drawing a line between love and politics! You're the one who draws that line, not I! You were a political bureaucrat already before you lost your first teeth! If I had your life's experience behind me, I wouldn't have the nerve to lecture about the division between private and political life. I've never in my life drawn such a line! Yes, I wanted Nachalo for his political potentialities, and I simultaneously wanted him in bed, just as I wanted Yarostan in the stockroom or wherever I felt like it! I was a free and independent person in political and union matters; I was also free and independent in sexual matters. I was no one's wife, woman or servant. When some people considered me George Alberts' wife, I made it perfectly clear with Yarostan just what I thought of wifery. When I became disgusted with Yarostan's lumpen politics I got simultaneously disgusted with his lovemaking, and I left him as freely as I had gone to him. And that's what you can't stand, Sophia: the freedom, the independence. You've started the wrong argument with me, Jose's Woman! I know too damn much about you, and I no longer have any reason to keep it inside me. I don't know where the hell you came from. Don't you lecture to me about Nachalo! You've never even wanted to taste freedom and independence. You're completely shameless to bring up Yarostan. For at least a year I didn't touch him; I left him completely alone. He was at our house at least twice a week, and I could see your whole body shaking with desire; you must have been like jelly inside. But you didn't make a move on your own. You just stared with that cowardly, longing, absent look, like a dog begging to be fed, like a slave waiting to be carried off, like a spineless thing waiting to become Yarostan's Woman. Don't interrupt until I'm finished! It so happens that your friends kept me informed of the fact that you never changed, you remained a spineless coward. Lem gave me a complete picture of your daring affair with that high school hoodlum Ron. The daring was all exhausted in his petty thefts and antics. You were Ron's Girl, a pliant thing, his shadow, the woman behind the he-man. Alec completed a picture I hadn't wanted to believe when I'd first seen it. I can't tell you what intense shame I felt when I learned that my daughter, Nachalo's daughter, had become Jose's woman, Jose's slave, Jose's rag. Don't you talk to me about living up to what Nachalo stood for! How depraved could you get? Nothing in your life forced you to negate your freedom, your self-respect, your independence so completely. Yet you talk about drawing lines! You, who degraded yourself so despicably for your bedfellows, turned into a passionless prude for your political comrades. Jose's Woman, the sex-bomb, was all wit and sexless intellect with Daman and Alec. Yes, Alec told me, and even if he hadn't I would have guessed it from Daman's unbelieving shock at your display of sexuality with your newest tamer, that boy —"

I bit my lip during the entire tirade; the desire to respond by crying left me before Luisa was through. "You're absolutely right. I gave myself to Jose, completely, all of me. I desired him for myself, my insides longed for him from morning to night — for myself, Luisa, not for my project, my politics, my organization! I'd be happy to be Jose's woman today!"

"I'd die of shame before I admitted having any such desire!" she hissed.

"Because you've never had any real desires!" I shouted as I moved across the room from her. "All you've ever had inside you was the organization! I admit my desire and I admit it proudly, Luisa. I didn't become independent of you until I admitted having my kind of desire, my kind of love. Don't shove your type of independence in my face any more because I no longer want it. I killed Jose by transforming my kind of love into yours, by replacing my passion with politics, by feeling ashamed of being Jose's Woman, by dragging Jose into battles I wasn't able to fight just as you dragged Nachalo —"

"You can't hide your depravity with such vicious attacks, Sophia; they all miss their mark!"

"You're the one who's depraved, Luisa! I couldn't become independent until I figured that out. You picked Nachalo and Yarostan off the street. Lumpen, you called them; individualistic terrorists! And you fixed them up. You funneled them into your organization, your so-called union, that thing you served that was greater than your own life. You didn't love them but it; your only desire was to make them serve it. I didn't serve Jose and I didn't make him serve. I loved Jose! You never loved anything but an abstraction in the mouth of a Daman, an Alberts, a Zabran —"

"You're marvelous at playing with words, Sophia! That's all you've ever been good at!"

"I've never outdone you at playing with words, Luisa! You're the organizer, not I! You're the one who mystified language for me as far back as I can remember! You always spoke of working people and you made me think you actually had working people in mind. But you never had real people in mind at all, but something abstract, something religious people call god! Sabina and Margarita called you a priestess, and I was always too dense to understand what they meant. I finally understand, Luisa! I finally grasp the meaning of those words you played with, words like working people and union and we ourselves and labor movement. To you they were all synonyms for the ultimate authority. Your freedom and independence were synonyms with slavery, with submission to the ultimate authority. In practice you used the word union to mean submission to the spokesmen of the union, the carriers of the idea of the workers, submission to bureaucrats like Titus Zabran and Daman Hesper, submission to technocrats like George Alberts and —"

"Your malicious distortions can't justify your submission to a Jose, your total and shameless self-abandonment to a petty tyrant —"

"You have to use the word petty, don't you Luisa? Because the tyrants you served weren't petty tyrants; they were just tyrants with a big T. They were institutional tyrants, people whose social slots gave them the power to manipulate and destroy human lives. It's not hard for me to imagine what Alberts and Zabran would be today if their popular army had been victorious, and it can't be very hard for you. One of your authorities actually made it to the top. You must have sensed as far back as twenty years ago that you had come across another high priest when you reached out for Marc Glavni —"

"I obviously knew he wasn't going to spend his life working in that plant, Sophia —"

"You said it, mother! And that's what appealed to you about him! You knew he was moving straight to the top, and the top is what you've always worshipped and served!"

"Alec told me how irrational you could become, Sophia; he even told me you tried to kill him with a bottle once. I didn't believe him! Alec was right! You're a raving maniac!"

"I was just coming to Alec! How dumb I was! I thought he was taking advantage of you just to spite me, and I felt sorry for you! It's taken me all these years to see who you are! What was Alec to you, Luisa? Was he a Nachalo or an Alberts? Was he a lumpen to organize, or an authority for whose sake you organized?"

Luisa put her hands to her ears and shouted, "Stop this idiocy, Sophia! There's neither reason nor logic in anything you're saying. I honestly didn't know you were still attached to Alec when you made your dramatic exit ten years ago!"

I shouted, "You didn't take Alec away from me! You took him from Minnie. You must remember Minnie. She's the lawyer who got you out of jail. She came here once with Alec, and you told me later what nice people my friends were. Minnie loved Alec the way you never loved anyone. What did you want with Alec? What were your plans —"

Luisa, still holding her hands to her ears, got up and ran to her bedroom; I thought I saw tears in her eyes. I ran after her shouting, "Answer me! What purpose could Alec have served in your apparatus?"

Luisa lay on her bed sobbing, her face buried in her, pillow. I felt tears rushing to my eyes. All my tension suddenly snapped, my fury seemed to flow out of me. I sat down next to her and felt sorry for her.

Luisa mumbled into the pillow. "I'm afraid of you, Sophia."

I couldn't hold my tears back any more. "How do you expect me to react to that?" I asked her. "That's so unfair, Luisa. You wanted me not to stare or cry. For once in my life I didn't — only to be told you're afraid of me. I didn't force myself on you, Luisa; you pulled me here."

Luisa sat up next to me and wiped the tears from her eyes. "You're right, Sophia. I brought you here. I always wanted you to be proud and defiant. But I guess I can't take the defiance when it's aimed against me. You hurt me, Sophia, far more than you seem to think. Alec was of no use to me or to my politics or to my organization. I loved him. It was as simple as that. I had no Machiavellian motives. I only wanted to be loved by him."

"But he rushed into this house looking for me —"

"Only the first time, Sophia, when he and Minnie came to tell me you had disappeared from the university dormitory. Alec wanted to call the police, but I begged him not to; I told him they'd have called me if something had happened to you. Your friends thought I was terribly nonchalant when I told them you'd turn up eventually; I obviously suspected you'd gone back to your high school friends. Alec came again two weeks later, on a Sunday. He told me he had found you, and that you would telephone me. He looked me up and down. I wasn't used to it and I was flattered; I didn't know then that he looked every woman up and down. I asked him in. He told me about the newspaper work you had both done. I asked him to come again. He called me a week later and told me he wanted to talk to me, he wanted to learn all about me. It had been so many years since anyone had wanted to know anything at all about me. I invited him to dinner. I spent that whole Saturday preparing for his visit. We ate by candlelight. He told me you had joined Sabina and her friends. I thought your pal Ron was still among them, and I spoiled that evening for myself by telling Alec that Ron had been your boyfriend in high school. Alec thought I meant Jose and he became intensely jealous. He left before he even finished the meal. I begged him to stay; I cried; I felt old and abandoned."

I wiped tears away from Luisa's cheeks and told her, "I'm sorry I included Alec; I didn't know anything about your relationship with him; I didn't know that you could love someone in that way."

"I never reached the point of wanting to be Alec's woman," she said without hostility. "But I'm not being honest about that either. I wanted to be desired; I craved Alec's love, even more than Nachalo's. Maybe Alec came here looking for you. Maybe he even came to me so as to spite you. But he found me, Sophia, and he loved me, for two wonderful years. He phoned me two or three times during the week when you had decided to move back into your room. He asked about you, but he never asked to talk to you. I invited him to dinner again. I told you I was expecting a visitor on that Saturday night. You told me you were going to a movie and might not be back all night. As soon as Alec knocked I started shaking with passion. We embraced in the doorway. I asked if he wasn't hungry. 'Starving!' he told me. So was I. As soon as we were done eating I told him he could learn everything about me he wanted to know. He was very concerned that you might return. I told him, 'I don't interfere with her life and I suppose she feels the same way about mine; after all, this is my house too!' He told me I looked and acted like your younger sister. And he meant it! I hadn't been loved since we'd moved into this house. I let Alec learn everything he wanted to, on the living room couch. I didn't expect you to reappear so suddenly, nor to stare at us so stupidly with your hand on the doorknob. You made us both feel so indecent. But you didn't spoil my night, Sophia. That was my most wonderful night since my first night with Nachalo. The following morning you were gone. What could I call you except a puritan and a hypocrite? The fact is, I was relieved, and I think Alec was too. We spent that Sunday outdoors, picnicking and running through a park. I learned that Alec had lost his job and had no place to stay. 'This is an immense house, and it'll be empty again,' I told him. He asked. 'Don't you expect her to come back?' 'Eventually, in three or four years,' I told him. 'Don't you care?' he asked. I told him, 'I care very much; I care most for her sudden arrivals and departures; they're the only sign that she has anything in common with me.' He stayed, not in your room but in mine. Maybe you're right about my other relationships. I know that my relationship with Alec was different from all the others. I suppose you could call it pure love, or pure sex; there was nothing political in it. I hadn't engaged in any political activities since we'd emigrated. And maybe you're not altogether wrong about my combinations of love with politics. I know that as soon as politics entered into our relationship, our love was over. Alec read all the books I had, even the ones I'd brought over; that was his first language too, you know. Toward the end of his second year here he started asking about Nachalo and the popular army and the barricades; he also became very talkative about himself; that was when he told me about you and Jose, and about Sabina's enterprise. The more he read and talked, the more impatient he became to throw himself into some kind of political activity. I no longer had anything to offer him; my politics seemed sentimental and archaic to him. He learned about an anti-imperialist rally and asked me to go there with him. Alec ran into several of his university friends at that rally; it was there that he introduced me to Lem. That rally only increased Alec's desire to throw himself into political activity. During his last weeks here he'd spend hours pacing. He was like a caged animal. He said all he wanted was to help make a revolution, with his gun in his hand, and not to talk about it or read about it or support it at rallies or demonstrations. He apparently met people with similar views, and he started going off to political meetings. One day he simply failed to return. I made no attempt to find him; we were free individuals. But my heart broke. Maybe it was only because I felt myself growing old; I really don't know why; but I never loved anyone so much. Ever since he left me I haven't been able to live alone; I had to have someone's love, no matter how modest or flawed. Last year, in the committee office, I came across Alec's name on a list of people killed during the riot. I couldn't bear it, Sophia. You must know how I felt; you loved him once too —"

"I didn't love Alec until a few days ago, when Minnie told me how he died." I summarized what I had so recently learned from Minnie. "He was shot down by machine guns when he tried to run back into the bar."

Luisa put her head in my lap and cried. "I know what you're thinking, Sophia, but this time you're far away from the truth. I didn't encourage Alec to live or die like that; I didn't organize him or educate him; the kind of politics he and I talked about had nothing in common with that."

"I know, Luisa. He died for the kind of politics I talked to him about, almost exactly the same way Jose died two years earlier. I'd like to think I was in Alec's heart the day he died, but I don't think I was. You're right about the line I've drawn. Alec was never more to me than a political comrade, a colleague on the newspaper staff. We almost became husband and wife once, but we could never have been lovers —"

"You're staring, Sophia — but don't stop! I'm going to admit something to you. I love you just a slight bit more than I hate you, even when you stare. I'll admit something else. When I saw Alec's name on that list last year, I stared for weeks; I stared at work, I stared at the walls of this house and the walls of my empty bedroom, and I cried my eyes out. I hadn't cried so hard since George had returned from the front and told me Nachalo had died after calling his comrades 'red butchers.' And I'll even admit one more thing. After Titus' memorial oration for Nachalo, I turned myself into Nachalo's woman. I suppose I could have turned myself into Alec's woman. You infuriated me before and I lied to you. I don't think it was my principles, my commitment to independence, that stopped me. What bothered me about Alec was the social class from which he came —"

"I knew he was born in one of the neo-colonies; he still spoke with a slight accent when I first met him. What bothered you about that?" I asked.

"I suppose he wouldn't have told you; he wasn't proud of his class origins. He came from a family of wealthy landowners. His father worked as an army doctor during the war, and afterward started a successful practice here; then Alec and his mother settled here. Alec attended high school at a private boarding school. It was there that he was introduced to politics by the daughter of one of the wealthiest lawyers in this city, a girl called Rhea. It was for love of her that Alec started to turn against his class, and he apparently continued moving in the same direction until the day he died; I was no more than a station along the way —"

"If Alec's class origins bothered you, how could you possibly stand Lem Icel after Alec left you?" I asked. "Lem's class origins were the same as Alec's, and Lem's personality was so revolting! I found him insupportable already in high school."

"I was far lonelier after Alec left me than I had ever been before he'd come here. But that wasn't the only reason, Sophia. At first I found Lem interesting. And in the end I did exactly what you threw in my face; I tried to make something out of him, something political. Alec introduced me to Lem at that rally he took me to. Some weeks after Alec left me, Lem knocked on the door. He introduced himself as Alec's friend and your one-time university friend, and started asking me all kinds of questions: had I known George Alberts, did I know Alberts was a spy, did I know you had been responsible for Lem's imprisonment and nearly his death? I was stunned and invited him in. Then he told me a horrendous story about a letter you had sent with him which had caused his imprisonment. I imagined you had tried to send a note to one of your former comrades and the police had intercepted it; I knew how hysterical that police was about communication from émigrés. I told him I'd had nothing to do with Alberts for over ten years, and tried to tell him you couldn't have intended to harm him with your note. But he seemed convinced that you as well as his other former comrades had turned against him, betrayed him; he spoke already then about wanting to escape from what he called civilization. I felt sorry for him and asked him to visit me again. He came the very next day and invited me to join him at an event he called a 'witness.' We stood for several hours in freezing cold weather. I missed the point. I brought Lem home to ask him about the peace movement. I learned his father had completely disowned him. I told him your room was free and he moved in. In your fury you placed your finger into an open sore, Sophia. I know how revolting Lem was. I moved into your room with him, and I shared your room with him for over a year. I didn't love Lem. At first I felt sorry for him. Later I despised him. But still I went to him. I thought I was helping him; I thought I was making him useful to the movement, the peace movement since nothing else was available at that time. I thought I was encouraging him to remain politically active. But you're wrong if you think that by using my body

I always succeeded. Lem never became useful to anyone or anything. He became increasingly irrational, mystical. He hallucinated about rustic solitude. He stopped taking part in any of the peace movement activities. He just sat with his leg on the kitchen table and called me his jailer. I started attending peace movement activities without him; I got to know Art..."

It was long past midnight. I called Ted to learn how he'd gotten home from the repression committee, and to tell him I was spending the night at Luisa's.

"So you thought I wanted to take Ted from you," Luisa commented. "I didn't know you loved him. Not that I cared. I was still fuming about the scene you'd made in front of Daman."

"I used to hate Ted," I told her. "We share a house, but not a bed. I didn't know I loved him until I saw you bent over him."

Luisa and I had breakfast the following morning before she left for her job. I took a taxi home. I apologized to Ted for having left him stranded in the repression committee office. He told me he'd gotten a ride home with Daman. He asked why I had thought it necessary to call him the previous night.

"Do you remember what you thought I intended to do to Tina the night I ran naked from Tissie's room?" I asked him.

"I don't understand," he said sadly.

"Yesterday I was convinced Luisa wanted to do the same thing to you, Ted. But you're not seven, and I didn't feel any urge to protect you. What I felt was jealousy, intense jealousy. I thought Luisa was going to ravage a person I loved very much."

Ted stared at me with tears in his eyes. "No one ever said anything like that to me, Sophie."

I think I love Ted, but I'm not sure I can distinguish my love from guilt and pity. I feel guilty because I had thought him seven-year old Tina's lover, and even more because I had thought myself responsible for keeping them apart. I've felt pity toward him ever since I learned of his life-long unreciprocated devotion to Tissie. My life would have been very different if I had become Ted's friend in the garage twelve years ago, the friend he sought so desperately. I can't describe him better than Sabina described him to me then. He's lucidly aware of the difference between people and things. He's satisfied when he's shaping his environment with his companions, and has no desire to shape his companions or be shaped by them. I don't want to be either his "mentor" or his "woman," but I haven't learned to be anything else. The "liberating politics" you and I learned didn't leave either of us very liberated. Please let me know what Mirna and Yara do to make you aware of that fact. I'm on their side, Yarostan, but only because I'm far away; from here it's easy to be on their side. I still love you, but no longer as a god. I feel just a little bit sorry for you.

Your, *Sophia.*

Yarostan's last letter

Dear Sophia,
I don't deserve your pity. I've been blind. For over twenty years I've been nothing more than an apologist for a repressive ideology. You tell me you don't have a vantage point from which to criticize my attitudes. The events I experienced here yesterday convinced me I never had a vantage point from which to debunk what I called your "illusions," or Luisa's for that matter. I parted with my own illusions far more stubbornly than you parted with yours. Jasna and I had to experience one shock after another before either of us were willing to admit we were wrong, and had always been wrong, about Titus Zabran. The extent to which we were wrong went far beyond Mirna's or Yara's dreams. I can now answer all the questions you and Sabina have been asking for the past few months. I can now tell you why Titus didn't mention to me the letter you sent us during the Magarna uprising and why Titus wasn't arrested with the rest of the carton plant crew twenty years ago.

From the time I sent you my last letter until yesterday, Yara treated me as an "enemy." Her hostility toward me during the entire two weeks was as intense as the hostility she had briefly expressed toward me the last time she visited me in prison, shortly after Vesna's death. She made it a point not to be home when I was; she left a room whenever I entered it. A few days after our trip to the clearing, when she was still wearing a bandage over her jaw, we were both in the kitchen at the same time; I told her I was sorry about the blow I had given her.

Yara's response to my apology was, "I'm sorry I have to share this house with you. You're hateful!" She turned her back to me and stormed out of the kitchen.

During the entire past two weeks, Yara's attitude toward me remained what Mirna's had been on the night after our outing to the clearing. Yara wanted me to move to the shed where Mirna had once housed her sick mother. I tried to make myself "understand" Yara's attitude as a healthy rebellion against her father. But I couldn't make myself understand the specific cause for her rebellion, namely her hysterical attempt to copulate with her own father. Consequently, although I did try to apologize for having hit her, I did not make a serious attempt to be her friend. On occasions when she didn't turn her back to me, I turned mine to her. One result of our mutual hostility was that I failed to observe what Yara and Mirna were doing during those two weeks, and when their "plot" started to unfold I was taken completely by surprise.

Because of my antagonism, I gave the worst possible interpretation to the few things I did see. For example, early one morning, after she had removed the bandage from her jaw, Yara left the house wearing the same costume she had worn to the dance at Mirna's plant and to the outing to Mirna's clearing. I asked Mirna, "For whose benefit is she performing her Sabina role this time?"

"She's going to a lecture being given by the famous Vera Krena," Mirna told me.

"In that costume?"

"And why not in that costume? Haven't you repeatedly written Sophia that we were all acting under the influence of what we learned from her letters?" Mirna asked me, hypocritically sweet, but barely disguising her sarcasm.

"You don't mean to tell me Yara is acting on what we've learned about Vera's infatuation with Sabina twenty years ago!"

"Why else would she be wearing that costume?" Mirna asked, irking me with the playfulness of her tone.

I was furious. I immediately drew the worst possible conclusion. "You're a genuine maniac, Mirna! How can you put your own daughter up to something so vile? I suppose you'll send her looking for a narcotics dealer next!"

"Yarostan, you're a genuine saint," she told me with the same exaggerated sweetness. "Just like my mother. But my own daughter, it turns out, has a mind of her own and doesn't need me to put her up to anything. Are you forgetting you called her my doctor?"

Of course I now see that Mirna's sarcasm was perfectly justified. I was an absolute hypocrite. When I had read the letters in which you had described your experiences in the garage, I had been unreservedly sympathetic to Sabina, Tissie and "their world." Yet when I imagined that Mirna as well as twelve-year old Yara were beginning their "careers" as prostitutes, I reacted the same way Mirna's mother had reacted to her "devils."

Mirna's behavior during the past two weeks was even more incomprehensible to me than Yara's. The day after Yara's departure in her "Sabina costume," both were out when I came home from the carton plant. Mirna returned about an hour after I finished a lonely supper. I could barely recognize her. I stared at her, speechless, fascinated and repelled. She had transformed herself into a phenomenon I had never seen on the streets of this city, a phenomenon I had seen only in foreign motion pictures: a human body for sale, a sensual commodity. As soon as she saw my expression, she did all she could to provoke and deepen my shocked disbelief. She paraded herself in front of me imitating the postures, the walk and the gestures of professional "high class" prostitutes we had seen in movies. Instead of the usual bag hanging on a shoulder-strap, she carried a small leather purse; she wore shoes with high heels and nylon stockings, neither of which she'd ever worn before; her bright skirt ended above her knees; between her waist and her shoulders she wore a tight-fitting sweater that accentuated the contours of her large breasts; her hair was exotically stacked on her head in the shape of a cake. I convinced myself that Mirna, once having rejected her mother's repressive caution, had taken it into her head to relive every experience in Sabina's life and to invent additional possibilities of her own. I had admired Sabina, I had written you that I considered her world to be mine, when you had described her life's experiences to me. Yet I stared at Mirna with revulsion. I knew I was being a hypocrite; I knew I couldn't justify my revulsion, even to myself. I went to our bedroom with tears in my eyes, saying nothing to Mirna, ignoring her until she joined me in bed, at which time I turned my back to her.

Because of the false conclusions I drew, I felt like a stranger in my own house. I thought both Mirna and Yara were setting out on "liberated" careers as courtesans or prostitutes, and I didn't have the nerve to ask either of them any questions. After our recent outing and our unsuccessful confrontation with Titus, I felt as estranged from Mirna and Yara as I had felt after my release from prison three years ago. At that time Mirna had rushed to work and back, tended to the sick old woman, and slept, indifferent to my presence, perhaps even resentful about the fact that I represented yet another burden. And Yara had avoided me after she had ascertained that I would not have been less willing than Titus to give Vesna to the doctors. My sympathy for Yara's "political" activities in her school had put an end to her disappointment in me, but my behavior in the clearing revived and deepened her disappointment and transformed it to hostile distrust. From her own point of view she was perfectly justified. I had been repelled by the possibility of incestuous love with my own daughter. Such a possibility had never crossed my mind, and my whole being rejected it as alien and repulsive. But Yara is Mirna's daughter; she's known for years that Mirna at Yara's age had shared her bed with her brother and had desired him; to Yara this seemed perfectly understandable and normal; she's also heard Mirna express her love for her own father, and even her desire for sexual intercourse with him. I've also been familiar with Mirna's expressed desires; I learned about some of them from Jan as long as twenty years ago. I've also learned to take them for granted as perfectly normal. I've known that Mirna never actually realized her incestuous wishes, and I took them for granted only as the sexual fantasies of a little girl. But when Mirna communicated her desires to her two daughters, she frightened the older into a puritanical hysteria while creating in the younger an unquenchable desire to realize all of Mirna's unfulfilled wishes.

I felt estranged from my companions, and I made no attempt to communicate with them. During the past week and a half I dragged myself to work and back. I transferred my life's interests to the activity taking place in the carton plant, to the contacts being created by workers along the production line in order to explore ways of decreasing the amount of time we spent working. As soon as the workday ended I lost all my enthusiasm, dragged myself to a house which I knew would be empty, and waited with apprehension for one or the other "courtesan" to return. I even considered the possibility of renting a room, letting my companions develop their new selves without me. I felt I no longer had anything to contribute with my presence in the house. I told myself that Mirna, twenty-nine years old and fresh out of a condition of drudgery that was maiming her, would then be completely free to satisfy every conceivable passion and drama in her exquisitely constructed settings. And I started to doubt that Yara and I could continue to live under the same roof. I wanted to apologize for having hit her, for having kicked Zdenek, but not for having "disappointed" her. Sabina's motto, "Everything is allowed," no longer roused my unqualified enthusiasm. I was not able to engage in sexual intercourse with my own daughter, and I felt that my continued presence in the house was a provocation to a daughter obsessed by the desire for such an experience, and to a mother who wanted to be present during the act so as to experience vicariously an act which she considered the highest peak of enjoyment. I was afraid that the "revolution" of my two companions had parted ways with mine. Yesterday all of that changed.

Yesterday was Sunday, the day of Jasna's and Titus' celebration of their coming marriage. In the morning I felt extremely irritable and apprehensive, and I was ready to talk myself out of going to the event. I remembered Jasna's having begged Mirna and Yara not to attend her celebration if they still retained their hostility toward Titus, and as far as I could see nothing had changed in their outlook. I became even more apprehensive when, after the three of us ate lunch in silence, Yara ran to her room and returned to the living room wearing her "Sabina costume." A few minutes later Mirna turned up in the living room in her short bright skirt, high-heeled shoes and seductive sweater and announced, "We're ready."

I accompanied them out of the house only to avoid making a scene. I walked between two complete strangers who, with their "secrets" and "plots" and costumes, inhabited a world completely unfamiliar to me. Mirna looked odd. In one hand she carried the exquisite little leather purse while in the other she lugged a peasant's basket filled with the food she and Yara had spent the morning preparing; Yara earned another basket. They didn't ask me to help carry anything.

My apprehension turned to anger as soon as we arrived at Jasna's. I had forgotten when the "celebration" was to begin, but I remembered as soon as Jasna asked why we had come an hour early; I knew that our early arrival was part of Mirna's "plot." Jasna was in an apron and had her hair in a towel; she, too, was angry about the fact that we were an hour early, and her suspicion was aroused. "What in the world are you wearing?" she asked Mirna as soon as we walked in.

"Isn't she positively stunning?" Yara asked Jasna excitedly.

Jasna's face fell. She rushed to the kitchen, then upstairs.

Mirna shouted to her, "Yara and I can finish whatever still has to be done in the kitchen and dining room; you just go up and get yourself ready."

Jasna hesitantly accepted Mirna's offer. Mirna and Yara carried an extra table from the kitchen to the dining room, after which they set the table, counting the places as if they knew exactly how many guests were coming. They then proceeded to unpack the food from the baskets they had brought. When Jasna came down she exclaimed, "Good grief, Mirna! Did you invite all the people in your plant?"

"No, Jasna. I invited all the people in yours," Mirna told her cryptically. Jasna ran back up without responding, clearly becoming as apprehensive as I had been since that morning.

We didn't have to wait long before we started to learn what Mirna meant. Fifteen minutes after our arrival, another early guest knocked at the door. Yara ran to open it and in the doorway I recognized Comrade Vera Krena.

Yara eagerly extended both hands to the People's Representative and begged her, "Please do come in, Vera."

The woman stepped inside without once glancing at me or at the house. She embraced Yara and said, "I'm enchanted to see you again! I can't thank you enough for inviting me."

Yara placed her lips near the woman's ear and whispered, "The enchantment is all mine." I was certain I had been right about the function of Yara's "Sabina costume," her black hair and eyebrows, her slightly exotic jacket and slacks, her studied cat-like gestures.

Jasna ran down to see who else had arrived and stopped before she reached the bottom of the staircase, glaring at the couple embracing by the doorway. "Vera Neis!" she exclaimed with surprise, almost with indignation.

Vera abruptly let go of Yara and looked around for the first time, "Jasna Zbrkova!" she shouted. Glancing from Jasna to the living room and back to the staircase, she exclaimed, "But this isn't Sabina Nachalo's house! There's some mistake!" She backed up toward the door like a cornered animal and reached for the knob.

Yara blocked the door and whispered to her, "It's not a mistake, Vera."

Jasna started to grin as if she had caught on. She ran toward Vera and pulled her hand away from the doorknob. "Aren't you going to embrace me too, Vera? I'm also Sabina Nachalo's friend!"

Vera, on the verge of tears, hesitated briefly before she put her arm around her former housemate. "I'm terribly sorry, Jasna. I didn't know where I was. It was such a shock."

Jasna, still grinning, embraced Vera warmly and told her, "I'm so glad you remember me, Vera! Please do stay. You're more than welcome, no matter what Yara made you think in order to get you to come."

Freeing herself of Jasna's embrace, Vera turned suspiciously to Yara and asked, "Then it's not true that your mother is here?"

"It is true! She's right here!" Yara shouted. She took Vera's hand and pulled Vera toward Mirna.

Vera cautiously took both of Mirna's hands in hers. "It's not possible. So young, so beautiful, yet so transformed. I'm charmed to see you again, Sabina —"

Mirna, gleaming with pride, grinned wickedly. "The pleasure is all mine, I assure you. I've looked forward to this meeting for a long time. I'm Yara's mother —"

"But you're not Sabina," Vera at last ascertained. I felt called on to contribute, "Yara is a terrible liar —"

Mirna, holding on to Vera's hands, obviously defended her co-conspirator. "Yara wasn't exactly lying; She's my daughter only physically. In spirit she's Sabina's daughter, just as in spirit I'm Sabina's sister —"

"Then you're —"

"I'm not anyone you've ever met; I'm Jan Sedlak's sister." Vera grabbed Yara's shoulder and said, without bitterness, "Why you little devil!"

"Everything I told you is true in a way," Yara pleaded. "I so wanted you to come! Would you have come if I'd told you the actual truth?"

"No I wouldn't," Vera admitted. Then Vera turned to me and guessed, "So you must be Jan; you've changed so —"

"Jan died in prison," I told her. "I'm Yarostan." We shook hands.

"Yarostan Vochek! How stupid of me!" Vera turned to Mirna and told her, "I'm sorry, I didn't know."

"Twenty years is a long time," I told her, "Yara is our daughter."

Vera was amazed. "Your daughter! But why did she bring me here? What's the occasion?"

"Neither Jasna nor I knew she'd bring you here," I told her.

Jasna told her, "The occasion is a celebration of my engagement to Titus Zabran. Surely you remember him?"

"Titus? Of course I remember him! But this is all so strange. I suppose I should congratulate you."

Jasna explained to her, "Mirna had promised to invite certain of Titus' old friends. But I never expected you to come!"

Yara, putting on the expression of a begging dog, told Vera, "I hope you aren't terribly offended."

"No, I suppose I'm not," Vera said. "I've never had a prank like this played on me. I'm starting to understand that everything you told me was true, in a way."

The next arrivals were Titus and Zdenek. I was surprised to see them together. "Here's the groom!" Zdenek announced as he entered.

"Zdenek, how nice of you to come," Jasna said; then she told Titus, "You're just in time; Mirna apparently misunderstood the time and got here an hour early. And one of the guests she promised is already here."

Titus noticed Vera, turned stiffly to her and said, without extending his hand, "I take it you're the guest, Comrade Krena. I hadn't imagined you'd be interested in coming here to listen to my political views. I've heard many of yours on the radio."

"And you don't agree with them?" Vera asked.

"I've never believed a revolution could be launched by the top of the bureaucracy," Titus told her.

"Don't you think it can at least be lubricated from there?" Vera asked him.

"I don't think I'd call that lubrication," Titus told her. Then he remembered he was at least partly a host, "Do you know each other? Comrade Tobarkin, Comrade Krena."

Zdenek, shaking hands with Vera, told her, "Unfortunately I only listen to the radio when I'm drunk."

I hadn't seen Zdenek since our outing to Mirna's clearing. At that time I had thought him too drunk to be aware of what he was doing, but I was wrong. As he shook Vera's hand, he turned his face so that neither Vera nor Titus saw him, and he winked to Yara and Mirna. That wink gave me my first clue that Zdenek was "in" on Mirna's and Yara's game, that he had in fact been acting as their confederate since that outing. My suspicion was confirmed by the way Zdenek started the next conversation.

He turned to me and said, "This world is amazingly small, Yarostan. Do you remember when you and I ran into each other at the political prisoners' club five or six months ago?"

Thinking that I was spoiling the "surprise" he was about to reveal, I told him, "Jasna and I already know that you also ran into Titus at the political prisoners' club. Mirna and Yara told us."

"Zabran and I didn't only run into each other there," he told me. "It so happens we ran into each other the same day you and I did. Isn't that a coincidence? The first time I saw Zabran at the club was about half an hour before I saw you. As a matter of fact, I was still talking to him when I noticed you —"

Mirna commented, "That certainly is a coincidence!"

"I thought you didn't believe in coincidences," I said to her.

Zdenek continued, "On our way here I was trying to remind Zabran of that day. Zabran and I are practically neighbors, you know. He doesn't remember that day. Of course six months ago I had no idea you and Zabran knew each other. I rushed to greet you. When I turned to introduce you to each other, Zabran was gone."

I was irritated by Zdenek's suggestion that Titus had seen me at that meeting and avoided me. "There were a lot of people at that meeting, Zdenek, and I'm not surprised he didn't see me there; I didn't see him there either."

Zdenek asked me, "Wouldn't you have turned to look if someone had shouted his name?"

I remembered the occasion. Zdenek had shouted "Yarostan!" very loudly. I looked toward Titus for a clue, but he was helping Jasna set the table and seemed indifferent to Zdenek's "coincidence." I reminded Zdenek, "Almost all the people in that room were shouting the names of acquaintances they recognized." I felt uneasy. I was glad when Zdenek's attention turned away from me.

Vera and Yara were talking quietly to each other in a corner of the living room. I wouldn't have noticed the extremely flirtatious character of their exchange if Sabina hadn't "reminded" me of Vera's flirtation with her twenty years ago. In Jasna's living room the initiative was not exclusively Vera's. Yara, doing an excellent imitation of the little gypsy I remembered, made no effort to hide her admiration for the woman who had been the central topic of her gossip with Julia for the past year. Apparently Yara's esteem grew when Vera became the tribune of the reformist wing of the government. Mirna, who had been pacing impatiently between the kitchen clock and the front door, sat down on the edge of a couch near Vera and Yara. Zdenek also turned to listen to them.

Vera was asking Yara, "But why did you introduce yourself as Sabina Nachalo's daughter? Of all the people in this room, you and your mother are the only ones who didn't know Sabina!"

"Oh, but Mirna did know Sabina!" Yara protested.

"I do remember that Sabina and Jan were good friends —"

Mirna interrupted Vera. "Sabina and I were more than good friends. We were almost sisters, and in some ways much more than sisters —"

Vera seemed embarrassed by Mirna's tone. "But when did you know Sabina? Forgive me for doubting you, but you seem so young, and I had thought Sabina had emigrated twenty years ago —"

Mirna, looking past Vera with her distant look, told her, "Sabina and I were together for a day or two when the revolution started to break out —"

"You mean when that owner was ousted from the carton plant?" Vera asked. Suddenly she blushed intensely and turned her face away from Mirna's; she probably assumed Sabina had at that time told Mirna about Vera's secret passion. For an instant Vera seemed very embarrassed. Abruptly changing the subject, she asked Yara politely, "Do you have any brothers or sisters?"

Yara told her, "I had a sister, but she was the exact opposite of Sabina. Her name was Vesna."

"Why do you say 'was'?"

"She died three years ago," Yara told her.

Vera reached for Yara's hand as she said, "How awful!" She turned to Mirna and told her, "I'm so sorry. How did she die?"

Looking in Titus' direction, Yara said, "Mr. Zabran knows how Vesna died. He helped her."

Jasna intervened in the conversation. "Titus took Vesna to the hospital. He did what everyone would have done."

Mirna, who was again pacing impatiently, said, "Yes, everyone would have done it except the girl's own mother and sister. No one would have believed that the girl's sister understood more about the illness than the doctors did."

Jasna gave Mirna a pleading look and asked her. "Did you really come to bring that up —"

Titus entered the conversation; he commented, without a trace of hostility, "It is to be expected that when a patient dies, the doctors are blamed and not the disease —"

Jasna tried to object to this formulation. "Yara and Mirna did know —"

But Titus continued, "Of course, given the doctors' failure to diagnose the disease in time, anyone's guess seemed equally good. But this reasoning is incorrect. The doctors proceeded on the basis of the most advanced science available to them, on the basis of objective and not instinctive analysis, with exact procedures for analyzing, isolating, neutralizing and removing the disease. Thus all guesses were not equally valid. Only the doctors' diagnosis was capable of restoring the child's health."

Yara protested, "The only thing Mr. Zabran and the doctors didn't know was that there was nothing wrong with Vesna. It was the hospital and the doctors that made her sick. They killed her!"

Mirna hurriedly pulled Yara to the opposite comer of the living room, near where I was standing with Zdenek, and whispered, "Don't start that yet, Yara! Wait until they're all here!"

Yara whispered, "I couldn't help it; he started it."

Meanwhile Vera was asking Titus, "What was wrong with the child? I don't understand!"

Jasna told her, "There was nothing wrong with her; unfortunately no one believed Yara."

Titus seemed irritated by Jasna's comment. "Are we to believe, three years after the fact, that an eight-year old child was more knowledgeable in medicine than the staffs of two hospitals? If nothing was wrong with the girl, this was for the doctors to determine, not for lay people unfamiliar with medicine, and certainly not an eight-year old!"

Jasna objected meekly, "That's not always true, Titus. In this case —"

Titus cut her short. "Excuse me Jasna, but it's true in every case. The responsibility of any reasonable adult is to get a sick person to a hospital, not to consult a seer or a child as to whether the person's condition warrants a doctor's intervention. A reasonable person's responsibility begins and ends with putting a sick person in the care of people who are experts in disease. It is the responsibility of the experts to diagnose the disease and prescribe the cure. Unfortunately the experts are not omniscient; they're limited by the present state of development of medical knowledge. But within this limit it is obvious that two competent staffs of doctors understood Vesna's condition infinitely better than Yara! It is of course conceivable, but extremely unlikely, that Vesna's death may have been caused by a mistake on their part. I'm convinced Vesna was in a condition which couldn't be cured."

Jasna persisted. "You admit the doctors could have made a mistake. I'm convinced they made a terrible mistake. Vesna would still be alive today if you had listened to Yara —"

Titus said angrily, "It is inconceivable to me that Mirna or Yara or Vesna herself could have been better informed about Vesna's health than people who specialize in the field of health!"

Vera asked, "Am I to understand a perfectly healthy child was taken to the hospital and died there?"

Jasna told her, "I'm sorry this came up because it's far too complicated to explain. What Titus did was what almost every reasonable person would have done. I'm the one who told Titus that Vesna was ill. She had been absent from school. Yarostan was still in prison. Mirna worked all day and supported not only her two daughters but a paralyzed mother as well. Titus rushed to Mirna's house as soon as I told him. What he found there would have alarmed anyone; it certainly alarmed me when he described it. Vesna was in her paralyzed grandmother's bed and seemed deathly ill; she didn't eat, she had a high temperature and she became hysterical whenever anyone threatened to remove her from the old woman's room —"

Vera said with conviction, "It seems perfectly obvious to me that the right thing to do was to have the child see a doctor as soon as possible." I stared at Yara (with intense satisfaction, I have to admit) while Vera Krena said these words. Yara's eyes looked at Vera with a hostility that had long been familiar to me; the romance was over.

I tried to take up Jasna's argument. "I wasn't home at the time, as Jasna told you. If I had been, I would probably have insisted that Vesna be taken to the hospital. But Yara and Mirna have both convinced me that the doctors did not in fact know better, that Vesna would have recovered, in her own strange way, if she'd been left in the old woman's room. I'm convinced she'd be among us today —"

Yara seemed surprised; she looked into my eyes with gratitude. She was probably surprised that I was "convinced," since I had only recently been ready to throw Mirna to the doctors to save her from the same "sickness."

But Titus was infuriated by my intervention. "You don't know what you're talking about, Yarostan! Questions of health and disease are in the domain of science, not subjects for children's fairy tales or uninformed speculation!"

To which Vera added, "I must say I emphatically agree with Titus! I simply can't imagine a sick child being left without medical care because her eight-year old sister affirmed that she wasn't sick. I find your arguments strange, to say the least!"

Jasna still protested, "You don't understand the specific condition Vesna was in —"

Jasna was interrupted by a knock on the door. Mirna ran to the door; this was the knock she had been waiting for. All eyes were on her as she stopped before opening the door, straightened her hair, pulled her sweater down tightly. She took on a relaxed pose and turned to look at us with a provocative smile before she finally reached for the doorknob. I would never have imagined her capable of such sensuous gestures, of acting like such a courtesan. But my righteous shock quickly gave way to quiet laughter. The scene in the doorway became comical. A chauffeur-driven limousine of the type reserved for diplomats and high government officials was visible in the street, although the doorway itself was almost completely blocked by a short, extremely heavy man. He was dressed in a checkered "sports" jacket and white shoes which seemed completely inappropriate on such a large man; I forget what color pants he wore; it was obvious that all his clothes had been made in the most expensive tailoring establishment, or abroad. With a "chivalry" that made him look grotesque, he raised Mirna's hand to his lips. I almost laughed out loud when the man bestowed a kiss on the rough hand of the woman who had not in fact spent her life as a courtesan but as a factory worker.

Mirna said to him, in her best cinema-learned manner, "How exquisite! Please do come in!"

Holding on to Mirna's hand as he followed her into the room, the man glanced hastily from Mirna's bosom to the feet of the other people standing in the room. He dropped Mirna's hand abruptly and whispered, with evident surprise, "I had expected to find you alone."

"Oh please don't be offended!" Mirna begged. "Every one of the people in the room is a good friend of Luisa's." I was startled; so was everyone else except Yara, who grinned mischievously.

The man said to Mirna, still in a whisper but with the authoritative tone of someone used to commanding, "I had looked forward to a *tête-à-tête* with you, my dear. If you will do me the honor of accompanying me to a cafe —"

Mirna placed both her hands on his. "I'm flattered beyond words! I'd like nothing better than a *tête-à-tête* with you, and afterwards we could go to a cafe, just the two of us. But please wait a while. When I told Luisa's other friends how charming you were, they all insisted I introduce them to you, and they'd simply be heartbroken if I kept you all to myself —"

The man started moving back toward the door. "I assure you I'm not in a mental or physical condition to meet Luisa's friends. If you could arrange to extend your stay, at least by one day, I'm sure we could find another occasion —"

Mirna lifted one of his hands, pressed it tightly between her breasts, and told him with an irresistibly seductive tone, "I'll do anything, anything at all, if you'll only do me the honor of letting me introduce you. Tomorrow will be too late. This is the last day we'll all be together, since I have a reservation. Please do me that favor."

The man seemed defeated. He looked at the other people in the room for the first time. His face expressed shocked disbelief when his eyes focused on Vera Krena. Pulling his hand away from Mirna's bosom, he exclaimed, "You!"

Vera burst out laughing. "Of course! Wasn't I one of Luisa's best friends?"

Narrowing his eyes, he asked Vera suspiciously, "Are you and the so-called reform party behind this?"

"I only wish we were!" Vera told him.

Just then Titus pulled me to the hallway between the living room and the dining room. "What kind of joke is this? I had thought Mirna was going to invite workers, people like Zdenek Tobarkin, for a serious political discussion."

I told Titus, "I have no idea what Mirna and Yara are up to. I wasn't in on their game, I have no sympathy for it, and I don't know who that man is."

"You know perfectly well who he is!" Titus said indignantly. "Do you take me for a fool?"

"Honestly, Titus, I've never seen him before in my life!" I assured him.

Titus then told me, "That is the recently demoted member of the central committee of the state planning commission!"

I burst out laughing and asked very loudly, "That fat man is Marc Glavni?" I was immediately embarrassed by my involuntary outburst, and I looked into the living room to see if anyone had heard me. Apparently no one had, although Mirna winked at me when I looked in. My outburst was a sudden release of two weeks of tension. It suddenly dawned on me that all my speculations about Mirna's "activities" with her provocative costume had been wrong, that the entire masquerade had been conceived with one aim in view: to entice the demoted member of the central committee to Titus' and Jasna's celebration. I told Titus, "I'm awfully sorry! I really had no idea who he was."

"Don't apologize; I believe you," Titus said. "I think I'm starting to understand. She's introducing him to the friends of Luisa Nachalo. That's very funny indeed, since he was her lover once —"

I said, "Don't hold that against him."

Titus continued, "I should have known better than to expect Mirna Sedlak to be serious. How well did you know her father? He was the shrewdest, most calculating peasant I ever met. Jan and Mirna both took after him: extremely shrewd pranksters. In the last analysis they both became dilettantes despite their peasant origins."

"Both of them were my closest companions," I reminded him.

"How well I know!" he exclaimed. "And I suppose you still agree with Jan! Just push all the machinery into the streets and play with it like little children, bosses together with workers! Mirna obviously agrees with that! She's as blind to the class struggle as Jan was! What kind of serious political discussion can take place between the highest functionaries and the lowest workers? There's obviously no possibility for political regroupment between the proletariat and its class enemies!"

My attention was drawn to the living room; Jasna was shouting. I distractedly whispered to Titus, "I'm as surprised as you are by Mirna's bizarre choice of guests."

"At least old Sedlak's frame of reference was always clearly defined," he told me. "I never acquired a taste for Jan's or Mirna's pranks, which always lacked a frame of reference due to the fact that they were no longer peasants but were not yet integrated into the working class."

We moved back into the living room. Jasna was shouting at Glavni: "Don't tell me the well-being of workers is more important to you than your career! When certain workers were in prison, all of them one-time comrades of yours, you were perfectly willing to sacrifice their freedom, even their lives, to salvage your career!"

Marc was sitting on the couch. Mirna sat next to him and held his hand in her lap. Marc said to Jasna, "I have no idea what you're talking about."

"You know exactly what I'm talking about!" Jasna snapped. "Twelve years ago every single person in this room right now, except Mirna and Yara, was arrested. A letter had come from what the police called the Alberts spy ring. We now know one copy of the letter was delivered to an official, namely to you! And you cleared yourself by charging the others with being agents of that so-called spy ring!"

Marc responded patiently, "I remember the arrests, Comrade Zbrkova, but this story of a spy ring is new to me."

"It's not new to any of us!" Jasna shouted. "Your former mistress Luisa Nachalo was supposed to be one of the international leaders of that ring!"

"I was told such a story after my first arrest twenty years ago," Marc admitted. "But I could never make myself believe Luisa was capable of such activity."

"Comrade Glavni, you're a big hypocrite!" Jasna shouted. "When your career was in question you didn't only pretend to believe Luisa was an international spy, you went on to accuse others of being her accomplices!"

Mirna took up her guest's defense with a hypocrisy that infuriated Jasna. "What you're saying seems completely illogical, Comrade Zbrkova. If Marc genuinely believed, or even pretended to believe, that Luisa Nachalo was an international spy, would he have come here for a get-together with the best friends of that accomplice to an international spy?" Then Mirna turned to Marc and asked him, "Could you be so charmed by me as to be willing to endanger your entire career for my sake?"

"You're being positively hateful!" Jasna shouted at Mirna. "Jan was killed because of this man. Yarostan and Adrian were given long prison terms because they had supposedly tried to incriminate such a high personage as Comrade Marc Glavni —"

"If you're talking about the rehabilitation proceedings, I must point out that it wasn't I but Comrade Krena and her husband who initiated them." As he said this, Marc made a slight bow in the direction of Vera.

Vera jumped. "You're quite an expert at making insinuations and starting rumors, aren't you, Comrade Glavni?"

Marc showed a trace of anger for the first time. "Pardon me, Comrade Krena? It's common knowledge that you and Professor Kren initiated —"

Vera hissed at him, "Before something becomes common knowledge, it is a maliciously circulated rumor, and rumors begin somewhere, they have a specific origin —"

Marc cut in, "Comrade Kren initiated the rehabilitation proceedings as soon as —"

"I'm not talking about that stupid arrest!" Vera shouted. "I'm talking about current rumors! There are some people who'd love to drag my name through mud, and almost all of them are members of that conservative bureaucratic clique you're aligned with —"

Marc commented, "I believe your husband is similarly aligned —"

"Precisely!" Vera shouted. "And the rumors have already reached his ears!"

"He must have larger ears than mine," Marc told her. "I have no idea what rumors you're referring to. Your speeches discredit you amply enough."

Vera continued, "There are very few people in the world who know anything of my private life —"

"Surely you're exaggerating," Marc said. "Your affair with the standard of living commissioner has been a public secret for a very long time; you hardly keep it to a small number of people —"

Vera said darkly, "You know perfectly well that's not what I'm talking about, Comrade Glavni. You're one of the very few people who could possibly be at the source of the vicious slander that's being circulated about me, that malicious rumor about my affair with Adrian being a mere cover for an altogether different type of relationship. Your entire clique is whispering about it! I hear nothing else from Kren!"

I noticed that Yara was having a hard time trying to keep from bursting out laughing.

There was a knock on the door. Yara ran to open it and relieved herself of her pent-up laughter, seemingly in response to the new arrivals. I had counted the number of places at the dining room table, and I figured out that the couple in the doorway were probably the last guests.

I didn't recognize either of them until Vera shouted, "Adrian! Irena! You too?"

Adrian, who seemed intensely embarrassed, rushed to Vera and told her, "I'm terribly sorry about this, Vera. She insisted on dragging me along —"

"Don't be sorry, dearest," Vera told him, "This promises to be a grand entertainment! Was it the little girl who got you to come?"

"What little girl?" Adrian asked. "Irena? She insisted on coming in that outlandish costume and on dragging me along with her; she threatened to divorce me if I didn't come."

Vera's humor vanished as she asked Adrian, "She what? Was this whole thing Irena's idea?"

Vera's eyes, as well as everyone else's, turned toward the open door, and the same stunned amazement appeared on everyone's face. Yara and Irena were standing in the doorway, grinning. Both of them were identically dressed, in the same slacks and unusual work jacket; both had the same long black hair hanging down to their shoulders, the same black eyebrows. They looked like sisters, gypsy sisters. I walked toward Irena mechanically, as if I were in a trance, and extended my hand to her. "I have a feeling I knew you once, very long ago-"

Irena continued grinning. "So Yara tells me. You must be her father. She's told me so much about that twin sister I look like! I'm not really sure I'd care to meet her!"

"I'm stunned by the similarity," I told her.

Irena said, "I'm forever grateful to Yara. She made so many things clear to me when she told me about Vera's relation to Sabina Nachalo."

Irena looked exactly the way I would have expected her gypsy "twin" to look; she even seemed to be the same age. "Of course I haven't seen Sabina for twenty years and I have no idea what she looks like today," I told her.

My brief conversation was cut short by Vera, who regained control of herself after her shock at seeing the same similarity. Vera rushed toward Irena and pulled her from the doorway toward the staircase. "You little rat! You're going to explain certain things to me!"

Irena beamed as she let herself be pulled up the staircase. "It's you who are going to do the explaining, Comrade Krena! I finally understand what's been behind —"

"Such a low, mean trick!" Vera hissed. "To send a little girl after me as Sabina Nachalo's daughter! You're going to tell me exactly how you learned —"

"You're giving me far too much credit," Irena told her. "I wasn't the one who masterminded —" The two women disappeared into an upstairs room.

While the scene on the staircase was taking place, Adrian had embraced Titus. "Nice to see you again, Zabran! What in the world is this all about, and why did Irena consider it so urgent for me to attend?"

Titus explained to Adrian, "The event was originally to be a celebration of an engagement; subsequently it was to be a political discussion among workers; finally it disintegrated into an anarchic carnival. But I'm glad you came. That makes about four workers. Perhaps we could meet separately."

"Whose engagement is being celebrated?" Adrian asked.

Titus told him, "My own engagement to Comrade Zbrkova."

"Jasna?" Adrian asked. "Is she here?"

"Yes, Adrian," Jasna told him. She was standing right next to him.

"Congratulations! But why was this so urgent to Irena? Do you know each other?" Adrian asked.

"No, we never met," Jasna told him. Then she asked Yara, "Are they all here now? Let's start eating before everything gets cold."

"They're all here now," Yara told her.

Mirna stroked Glavni's hand and begged, "Since you've stayed this long, you'll surely stay to dinner."

Marc seemed uneasy. "I would infinitely prefer to invite you to dine with me in a quiet restaurant. Believe me when I tell you that you have nothing at all in common with these people. They may all have been Luisa's friends at one time, but that's not an adequate reason for you to be so tolerant of what they've become."

"No one's ever said such beautiful things to me," Mirna said, kissing his cheek. "But please stay, just for the meal. I find these people so interesting!"

"I would call them bizarre," Marc told her, but he was once again defeated by her; holding on to her hand, he accompanied her to the dining room.

Titus stayed behind when everyone else left the living room. I was glad for the opportunity to ask him a question. "I was disturbed by the comment you made to Adrian," I told him. "You said there were four workers here who might meet and talk separately. Why did you say that to Adrian? He's an official too. I count six workers, including Mirna, Jasna and Vera's secretary, but not including Adrian."

"I was referring to workers potentially interested in a serious political discussion," Titus told me.

"And you included Adrian as a worker?" I asked.

"Adrian is a prostitute," he told me.

"A what?"

"A prostitute," he repeated. "If he only realized what that Krena woman has done to his life, he would see that his place is with the working class."

"Are you serious?" I asked.

"She literally bought him," he said. "Adrian is a kept man. He's that woman's slave."

I said loudly, "I had thought that was how most officials reached their posts — Vera Krena herself, for instance." Just as I finished that comment, Vera and Irena came rushing down the staircase. I blushed; it was the second time I had shouted an insult within earshot of the person I insulted.

Jasna called from the dining room, "Titus! Vera! We're waiting to start!"

Titus and I were the last to take our places at the table. Jasna and Titus faced each other across the length of the table. I took the last empty chair, at Jasna's end of the table, next to Irena and directly across from Zdenek. As I sat down I noticed Yara throwing a questioning glance at Irena, who had also just sat down. Irena raised her black eyebrow and winked at Yara, who smiled and poked Zdenek. I figured out that Irena was part of the conspiracy. Jasna noticed nothing. Suddenly someone was poking me on the shoulder. Adrian, sitting on the other side of Irena, was extending his hand to me behind Irena's back.

"Yarostan Vochek! I didn't recognize you when I came in," Adrian shouted. "I'm surprised we didn't run into each other in prison during all the years we spent there."

I extended my hand to him, but I couldn't turn my eyes past the gypsy sitting next to me. Looking at Irena I asked Adrian, "Did you happen to run into Jan Sedlak during those years? He spent the rest of his life there." As I said this I noticed Mirna, who was directly in my line of vision to the right of Irena; she was sitting at the opposite corner of the table from me, at Titus' end and next to Marc. She momentarily stopped smiling at Marc and stared at me.

Adrian said, "I didn't know about Jan Sedlak until after my release, when Jasna told me."

Jasna said loudly, "And look at Jan's sister carrying on with the man responsible for those arrests!"

Adrian whistled crudely and asked, "Is she Jan Sedlak's sister?"

Irena whispered to me, "Aren't you relieved you didn't run into Adrian?"

"Yet you married him," I whispered to her.

"Just for the sake of this experience," she told me cryptically.

Mirna and Marc looked into each other's eyes and seemed not to hear the references to them, although I was sure Mirna's ears were picking up every sound.

Adrian said sarcastically, "Some people will do anything at all to get themselves another title."

Irena said, "Yes, Adrian, some people certainly will."

Titus addressed himself to me, as if he were continuing his earlier observations about Adrian, "It is important to distinguish a proletarian, who has no choice in the matter, from a member of the exploiting group, who enjoys a certain amount of so-called free will."

Mirna said to Marc, "I believe we're the subject of the conversation, dearest."

Yara pulled a serving dish toward her and asked, "What's everyone waiting for? I'm starving! Can I start?"

As soon as Yara started eating, all eyes turned to Marc. He suddenly forgot Mirna and started shoveling mounds from each platter onto his plate. Adrian, who sat directly across from him, shoved him the bread platter. Marc already had three slices of bread next to his plate. Adrian asked, "More bread, Comrade Glavni?"

Lifting a fork filled with food to his mouth, Marc told Adrian, "Later, thank you."

Adrian, encouraged by the glances Jasna was giving him, asked Marc, "You know who I am, don't you Comrade Glavni?"

"Of course, Povrshan. It's not a secret," Marc told him between mouthfuls.

"Did you also know me five years ago, when I came to your office looking for a job?" Adrian asked.

"If I'm not mistaken, you came to my office parading as the bank director, Kren," Marc remembered.

Vera, sitting directly across from Mirna and until then staring at Mirna with fascination, turned to Adrian, who sat right next to her, and asked, "You introduced yourself as my husband? You never told me about that!"

Adrian continued to address his remarks to Marc. "I had just been released after six years in prison, only to learn that you were married. Vera. I needed a job, and Glavni would never have made an appointment with a less important person, isn't that so, Comrade Glavni?"

"There were no openings in any case," Marc told him.

Adrian continued, "My real reason for coming to you, Comrade Glavni, wasn't to get a job, but to ask how it had happened that two people who had once worked in the same factory had met with such different fates. There you were, in one of the — shall we say plushier — offices of the bureaucracy, and already starting to fatten yourself on imported delicacies, while there I was, your former fellow worker, skinny as a broom after six years in prison, without the slightest prospects —"

Marc told him, "The explanation is very simple, Povrshan. You're an idiot."

Irena laughed, but I noticed that Mirna's grin left her face; she gulped, got up abruptly and rushed to the kitchen biting her lip; she seemed to be on the verge of tears. Yara started to rise, but I got up and ran after Mirna. I found her pressing her body against the kitchen wall, beating both fists against it. I shook her and asked, "Haven't you played enough of your game?"

Mirna, obviously repressing the urge to cry, told me, "No, love, my game is only beginning —"

Marc rushed into the kitchen, pulled me away from Mirna saying, "Excuse me, Comrade," and asked her, "Is everything all right, my dear?"

Mirna's grin returned. "I'm fine now, dearest. I swallowed a fish bone."

When the three of us returned to the dining room table. Vera and Irena were shouting at each other across Adrian's back (since he was sitting between them). Their argument would have been incomprehensible to me if I hadn't learned some of the details from your previous two letters. Vera, the boss, was shouting to her secretary, "You'll pay dearly for this, Irena! I should have known it was you! You've been dying to do this to me ever since I exposed that sex maniac who was rector of the university!"

"That act made you the champion of revolutionary morality, the heroine of the day!" Irena shouted back. "What an incredible sham! If anyone had known then that all you wanted was to take the rector's place, that all you wanted was to go to bed with one of —"

Vera reached across Adrian at Irena's throat and screeched, "Shut your trap you little —"

Adrian pulled Vera's arm away from Irena and asked, seeming intensely embarrassed, "Couldn't you two discuss these questions privately, some other time?"

Irena shouted at Adrian, "Jerk! You're the medium through whom she acted all these years, the front that kept people from seeing what she was, the errand boy who carried her public image!"

Adrian, holding both of Vera's hands down, shouted angrily at Irena, "Shut up! You're making fools out of all of us!"

Irena suddenly became calm, like a rebel who had decided to spit into her boss's face coldly and deliberately. "If you had only told me when we were students together that I looked like a little girl you had wanted to sleep with —"

Vera, straining under Adrian's grasp, shouted, "Beast! Unscrupulous beast! I never did you any harm." She started to cry.

Irena shouted, "You've taken half of my life, Vera! Why did you have to spin such an intricate web around me? I could have spared you all your trouble! If you'd only told me what you wanted fifteen years ago, I could have told you right then I had no desire to share you bed, even for an instant, because I could only make love to men!"

Vera cried pathetically. "Please stop it Irena, please!"

Yara reached across Zdenek to pull Jasna's sleeve and asked in a whisper, "Fifteen years ago? That was when Vera lived with you. Did you know about Irena already then?"

Jasna angrily swatted Yara's hand away from her arm and shook her head in the negative. Then she got up, walked toward Vera and pulled her up from her chair.

Vera sobbed, "Please help me." Jasna accompanied her to the kitchen. Everyone's eyes followed them except Marc's; he went on eating.

Irena, who was directly across from Yara and had heard Yara's question, said, "Jasna didn't know. No one knew. When we were students I thought Vera and I were good friends and Adrian was her lover. Maybe I should have figured it all out then, but I've never been gifted at reading people's thoughts. No, that's wrong; it's not as if she didn't give me any clues. Everything she told me was a clue. But I'm as much of a goose as Adrian; I couldn't interpret a single clue until three weeks ago when you asked me if my hair and my complexion were real or if Vera had asked me to paint myself this way." Irena turned to me and said, "Yara shouted 'That explains everything!' as soon as I told her I was three-quarters gypsy and had come into the world exactly this way. And the funny thing is it did explain everything! How could I've been so dense?" Pointing at Adrian, she told Yara, "But I'm not as dense as he is! She's his boss too, you know, and he simply refuses to believe anything I say about the boss."

"Have you been together with her for fifteen years?" Yara asked again.

"But I couldn't see through her until you came," Irena said. "When we were students all she ever talked to me about was her romances, or rather anti-romances. She told me what a clown her 'lover,' Adrian, was; she never felt anything but contempt for him. I didn't know him then. She'd boast to me, 'He's such a perfect front, isn't he?' I never asked myself what he was a perfect front for. I assumed he was the front behind which she carried on her affair with Professor Kren, but I didn't wonder what purpose such a front served."

Adrian rose from the table, said, "Excuse me," and apparently headed toward the bathroom; he looked like he was ready to vomit.

Irena continued, "After we graduated she went on to study under Kren. I got hired as secretary in the rector's office. That was when I learned she felt nothing but contempt for Kren as well; he was nothing more to her than a ladder to climb —"

Vera appeared in the kitchen doorway; her face was pale and had a contorted expression, but she was no longer crying. "All right, you little wretch, since we're bringing it all into the open, we might as well be complete and do justice to the past! You weren't merely hired by the rector's office; you were bought by the rector! He was in your bed before your training period was over. Don't single me out as the narrator of romances or as the one with contempt. Your feelings toward the rector were identical to mine toward Kren, and you narrated every gruesome detail with the greatest relish! After spending barely a month as the rector's secretary you started talking about becoming assistant rector; you were waiting for the old man occupying that post to be forcefully retired." Vera turned to everyone in the room and asked dramatically, as if speaking from a platform, "And how did this paragon of virtue intend to conquer that post? By marrying her boss! Unfortunately for our little Cinderella, the boss was not only already married, but was carrying on similar affairs with his other two secretaries!"

Irena shouted with venom, "And that was when you started dreaming of replacing the rector, not only in his office but in the bedrooms of his secretaries as well! Then that arrest twelve years ago almost spoiled it all for you! Your glorious ascent was interrupted. You came out so furious, and so hysterical! You simply had to find a scapegoat! And what better scapegoat was there than poor dumb Adrian? He'd be in your way in any case during your coming wedding ceremony with Kren! If they'd kept you in jail for only half a year, you'd have come out to find me married to the rector, occupying the office of assistant rector, and free for good from your attentions! The rector loved me and promised to divorce his wife —"

Vera smiled and said sarcastically, "He made the same promise to both of the other secretaries —"

"You're lying!" Irena shouted. "You hated that man! Until now I didn't understand your fierce hatred toward him. You were jealous of him! You conceived your scheme of driving him out with that scandal the moment you realized he really did love me! I didn't love him; I admit it! How else does one become someone in this society except by selling oneself to a high official?"

Vera hissed, "I regret everything I ever did for you, Irena!"

"You'll regret it even more before I'm through with you!" Irena shouted.

Vera retorted, "You're nothing but the commonest dirt!"

"In that respect we're twins!" Irena told her. "We both came out of the same cesspool! But as soon as you got out, you shoved me further in! I wouldn't have done that to you if I'd gotten out first! Never forget that! But you beat me to it. You acquired free will and in the same act deprived me of mine.

"First you had Kren force the retirement of the old assistant rector, and then you replaced him. But robbing me of that post wasn't enough for you! You had to destroy the rest of my prospects as well. Comrade Vera Neis married Professor Kren and immediately began her glorious campaign to clear the university of decadent bourgeois remnants, exposing the rector of the university for sexual abuses! As soon as the rector was ousted and jailed, Comrade Neis Krena replaced him as rector of the university and all hailed the arrival of a new day! No more sexual abuses! The end of bourgeois decadence! A great step forward for womanhood! And all accomplished with one single arrest! But to satisfy the libertines in the population, the police had to add a charge about his having embezzled public funds for private purposes. Or did you add that, just for seasoning? Have you met a single official who hasn't embezzled public funds for his country cottages and journeys? And he was finished off with such an exemplary trial! A twenty-year sentence! Do you even know that he died during his first year in prison? Do you care?"

"Don't shout to me about caring, you ruthless hypocrite! Do you care how much this outburst of yours is going to cost me?" Vera asked.

Irena told her, "You're right! I could care less! Do you really think people would rather be ruled by you than by the fat man across from you?"

Marc stirred to rise from the table, but Mirna told him, "Don't be offended; I'm sure she didn't mean it."

Irena winked at Mirna and said, "Of course I didn't. If I have to be ruled, I'd far rather be ruled by him! He'd be far too busy eating to have time to destroy people's lives. I would infinitely prefer his unquenchable hunger for food to that unquenchable hunger for power, the power to manipulate the lives of thousands in order to satisfy a secret innermost desire to crawl into the bed of a little gypsy —"

Vera had snatched a tea pot from the unoccupied end of the table. Jasna ran toward her from the kitchen doorway but reached her too late to stop Vera from flinging the pot with hot tea. The tea pot barely missed my head and shattered on Adrian's unoccupied chair, splashing its contents on Titus.

Irena said to Titus, "You see? You're the ones who face the consequences! How right you are to say a proletarian is the one who has no choice. Before she hooked Kren we were equals. By the time she was rector, I had become common dirt, as she now calls it! All the prospects I had looked forward to for ten years were ruined. I literally had no alternatives left, no choice. I knew she was a sham, I knew she had married Kren in order to become rector of the university, I knew that her sole qualifications for that post were located a few centimeters above and below her waist. But I was bound and gagged. She had me in her office every day. When she was promoted to the ideological commission she called me to her mansion several nights a week and on weekends. What could I do? Once, when she was still rector, I stormed out of her office, infuriated by the triviality for which she had called me in. 'I only wanted you by my side; you're my favorite,' she told me. I was furious. 'Your favorite secretary!' I shouted. I threatened to expose her whole sham. 'You breathe a word,' she said, 'and what do you think everyone will say about the spiteful jealous secretary? You don't suppose anyone will believe you, do you? They might even jail you as the former rector's accomplice.' I couldn't even dream of leaving the rector's office any more! In order to get any kind of decent job somewhere else I needed the recommendation of the rector of the university, Comrade Vera Krena. I had no choice. I was literally a proletarian."

I asked Irena, "What did you accomplish by marrying Adrian?"

"Much less than I'd hoped," she told me. "I didn't meet him until he was released from prison. I was overjoyed to learn he was the one who had been her lover, and I was doubly attracted to him when he told me how Vera had victimized him by associating him with a spy ring and claiming he'd tried to incriminate her. Besides which he was my age, unlike the rector or Vera's Comrade Professor Kren. But my only satisfaction with Adrian was to parade him in front of Vera in the rector's office right after we were married. I still had no choice. She was shocked when I told her we were married, and that shock is all I ever accomplished with him. She immediately turned him into her own private roll of toilet paper. She knew him far better than I did. The second or third time he came for me, she made eyes at him and said, 'Such a talented comrade is wasting away in the post of a lowly researcher.' She knew she was about to be appointed deputy minister of the ideological commission, thanks to Kren's influence, and she knew that from there she'd have almost as much power as Kren himself. She told Adrian: 'Irena and I will find you a post more in keeping with your talents.' That's right: 'Irena and I!' My dog and I! I tried to stop Adrian from accepting anything from that woman, but he turned to jelly waiting for its mold; there was no talking to him. He accepted a post on the secretariat of the standard of living commission, and I became Comrade Krena's private secretary. My reward, I thought! If I'd only known I was the one she was after! Wherever she went, Adrian and I tagged along. On trips the three of us always shared the same suite. The rumor started to circulate that Adrian was her lover, and she became popular for having the courage to display her lover in public. Kren became the subject of jokes. What no one knew was that Adrian was nothing more to her than a dog, that it was her personal secretary whom she —"

Vera hissed from the doorway, "I never touched you, Irena! Not once!"

Irena turned to Vera with hatred. "I wish you had touched me fifteen years ago! Everything would have been perfectly clear at the start! I would have destroyed your desire at its origin, I would have made you want to kill me instead of dragging me behind you bound up in your net! You didn't dare touch me! And the more you postponed showing your hand the more you feared my response! You were deathly afraid your bubble would burst, and you were right! My first chance to free myself of you didn't come until the current rebellion broke out. Nothing in my memory was so exciting as the uproar that started to spread to every sector of this society. That was when I realized I had become your political barometer. The more excited I became about the anti-bureaucratic activity, the more loudly you shouted about the need to reform the bureaucracy, and thanks to me you found yourself riding on the crest of the popular wave. When the strikes broke out and there were calls for the formation of workers' councils, I went wild with joy. I looked forward to the overthrow of the entire bureaucracy. And you stayed right behind me, giving speech after speech in support of the most radical strikes. I wondered if you'd lost your senses. I knew I and the vast majority had everything to gain from the overthrow of the entire bureaucracy. But you! You had everything to lose! I wondered if you really expected to become the head worker of the head workers' council, or if you pictured yourself as Liberty in the painting by Delacroix. It wasn't until Yara's visit that I started to get an insight into the sordid motives behind your sudden populism!"

Adrian, who reappeared in the entranceway from the living room, stared blankly at Irena.

Vera, still leaning on the doorway to the kitchen, commented, "So on the basis of a twelve-year old girl's gossip you decided to drive a knife into me —"

"Not quite, Comrade Krena!" Irena told her. "Not on the basis of anyone's gossip, but on the basis of the testimony of a roomful of people whose lives you've destroyed, and during a period when the entire population is exposing those responsible for the arrests and imprisonments! When I learned about Sabina, I also learned that Adrian wasn't the only one of your former comrades whose life you destroyed. Adrian spent six years in prison because of you!" Irena turned to me and asked, "How many years did you spend there?"

"Eight complete years," I told her.

"Do you know why?" she asked.

I said, "I thought I knew —"

"I'll remind you in case you forgot," Irena said to me. "Comrade Vera Neis gave testimony to the effect that all her former comrades had been members of a totally fictional spy ring." Then she turned to Titus and asked him, "How long did you spend there?"

"A year," Titus told her, "but I should tell you I wasn't arrested at the same time —"

"I don't see that it matters," Irena said, and she asked Yara, "How many years did your uncle spend?"

"He never came out," Yara told her.

Irena exclaimed, "He died in prison, like the former rector! Jasna —"

Jasna cut her short. "I'm sorry to ruin your performance, but you're missing your mark —"

"How long did you have to spend?" Irena asked.

"Two days," Jasna told her, "but the person responsible for my arrest, and for all the other arrests, is sitting across the table from you, and his name isn't Vera!"

Adrian shouted from the hallway, "That's right, Irena! It was Glavni who was responsible for those arrests!"

Jasna told Irena, "We were all arrested because of a letter that was delivered —"

Irena asked Jasna indignantly, "Why are you protecting her? That letter was an invention of the police!"

Adrian shouted, "I've told you repeatedly, Irena! Some spies actually did try to get in contact with us! And it was undoubtedly Glavni who told the police I was corresponding with them. Why else would he have been so rude to me when I went to see him after my release?"

I asked Adrian, "Do you still today believe Luisa Nachalo was a spy?"

Adrian told me, "During my first prison term the police showed me an article about her in the foreign press —"

"That article merely proved she had emigrated with her companion and their daughters," I told him.

Irena shouted at Adrian, "Idiot! You'd believe the police if they told you the sun was a triangle!"

Yara told her new friend insistently, "But there really was a letter, Irena!"

"I remember your telling me, but are you sure you didn't learn about that letter from the same rumor started by the police?" Irena asked Yara.

I told her, "Irena, I've been carrying on a very stimulating correspondence with the person who sent those letters twelve years ago, Sabina Nachalo's sister, or rather, Luisa Nachalo's daughter, Sophia."

Adrian shouted victoriously, "Who's the idiot, Irena?"

Jasna told Irena, "A messenger tried to deliver Sophia's letters to all the people she'd known in the carton plant eight years earlier." She turned angrily to Adrian and told him, "Sophia was no spy! She was trying to reach us because she considered us the only friends she had in the world! Sophia learned that only one of those letters reached its destination, one delivered to someone who was an official at that time. Vera, Adrian and I were university students at that time; Yarostan and Jan were steel workers. Comrade Glavni had recently become head of the party organization of the plant where we had all worked."

Adrian exclaimed, "And he was the one who was contacted! He cleared himself by telling the police the spies had contacted me!"

Marc told Adrian angrily, "The police asked me if I knew you. I had no idea why they wanted to know that, and all I told them was that I had known you once; it would have been ridiculous to deny it; we had both been arrested in the same plant eight years earlier." Adrian apparently intended to answer, but Marc got up abruptly and told Mirna, "I don't see the point of all these uncontrolled emotional outbursts, these accusations by uninformed ignoramuses, and I must say I don't find this gathering the slightest bit interesting."

Mirna took his arm again and begged, "Please, Marc, at least stay through the dessert —"

"I'm sorry," he told her. "I'm already late for an important meeting, which I would have called off if —"

Mirna got up, placed her lips near his and knew she had defeated him again already before she told him, "Oh please do call it off, dearest; use the phone in the bedroom upstairs. And while you're at it, would you please postpone my airplane reservation by a day? There are certain things I simply must discuss with you, but I can't leave this gathering. Please understand I owe it to Luisa to try to communicate with these people who seem so convinced she was a spy. Surely you understand she's still extremely concerned about that charge."

"I can understand her concern," Marc said, "but surely this is not the most fruitful way to clear her of the charge —" Adrian shouted from the hallway, "The only fruitful way is to accuse someone else, the way you did, Glavni!"

Marc asked Mirna, "Doesn't that prove my point?" Mirna shook her head. "Very well, my dear. In whose name are those reservations?" he asked her.

Mirna was flustered. "Why, the name I gave to your secretary when I came to see you. Wait a second." Her game almost ended. I started grinning. Yara fidgeted nervously. Mirna ran to the living room and returned with the little leather purse; she rummaged inside. "Here it is! It's in the name of Matthews. Mirna Matthews."

Marc said, "Oh yes. I remember. Matthews. Interesting! You've changed your original name, I take it?"

Mirna said nervously, "Oh no, I — I'm married."

Marc smiled indulgently. "I see. I assure you there's no cause for your embarrassment. I'll do what I can about your reservation. If there are no vacancies for tomorrow, will the following day do?"

Mirna smiled, relieved. "The following day would be perfect." She was cool and calculating again.

Marc walked past Adrian and headed upstairs. Mirna dropped her seductive posture and collapsed into her chair as if she had been carrying a heavy load.

As soon as Marc was gone, Jasna told Mirna, "If you don't stop this ridiculous game, I'll —"

Mirna said calmly, "You're enjoying it as much as I am, Jasna! And you may learn something!" Then she turned to Titus, who was still sitting next to her, at the head of the table. "Titus, were you arrested right after the Magarna rising was suppressed?"

Jasna said angrily, "How many times will you repeat that stupid insinuation? You know perfectly well he was arrested a year after the rest of us!"

Titus asked Mirna, "Is this what you had in mind as the subject matter for a fruitful political discussion among workers interested in rejoining the stream of history?"

Mirna told him, "Yes, Titus, this is exactly the subject matter I had in mind."

Titus told her, "Then I must ask you to leave me out of your discussion. The present moment is far too critical to be frittered away in sessions of bourgeois therapy and games. The struggle we face is a collective struggle, a class struggle, and not the struggle of individuals escaping from personal problems. The enemies we face are enemies because of their relation to society's productive forces, not because of their relation to a letter sent by a Sophia Nachalo."

Adrian whistled, apparently in response to Mirna's unanswered question, and returned to his seat next to Irena. He told Titus, "Something just struck me, something that bothered me at the time. When I was arrested twelve years ago, the police asked me if I had ever worked with certain people. The first time they interrogated me, their list included all the people they had arrested at the carton plant eight years earlier, except you. As time passed, the list got shorter; the last time they asked me about my past acquaintances, two years after my arrest, the only name left on the list was Vochek's. I assumed people were dropped from the list either because they were released or because they disappeared, and it turned out I was right. Soon after my release, Jasna told me everyone except Vochek had been released, and Sedlak had disappeared. You were among those she told me had been released —"

Jasna told Adrian, "They're not as efficient as you take them to be. Titus was arrested a year after the rest of us, but for exactly the same reasons —"

"Then his name should have appeared on their list a year after I was arrested," Adrian told her. "During the first two years they called me in at least once a month to ask me whom I had known; Zabran's name should have been added to their list during my second year, shouldn't it? He never appeared on their list. I thought at the time that he might have died." He turned to me and asked, "Didn't you wonder about that?"

I told him, "The first two times they interrogated me I told them I hadn't ever known any of the people on their list, so they stopped interrogating me, and I paid no attention to the names they listed or failed to list."

Jasna said, "It's common knowledge that the police files are crammed with misinformation and deliberate lies. I'm not at all surprised they couldn't keep track of all the names of people who had worked together in a small plant eight years earlier."

Mirna asked Jasna, "If they lost Titus' name, why was he arrested a year later?"

Jasna said, "I'm sure Titus can explain that to your satisfaction."

But Titus protested, "I don't owe anyone here an explanation. Is this a police trial?"

Mirna, as if she were upbraiding Jasna, asked her, "Why would you want to force Titus to do any explaining? He's perfectly right: this isn't a trial. And there's nothing to explain. Everything is perfectly clear. I saw Titus a few days before the suppression of the Magarna rising, and I saw him again a few days after —"

Adrian whistled again. "You saw Zabran? You mean he was overseas at that time?"

Jasna said, "How awful! I thought you knew Mirna was Yarostan's wife, Jan Sedlak's sister!"

Adrian seemed fascinated by Mirna. "You told me she was Sedlak's sister. But Glavni acts as if —"

Jasna snickered. "As if she were a foreign motion picture actress, which she really ought to be! She's never been further than a hundred kilometers away from this city!"

"I'll be damned! You certainly had me fooled!" Adrian told Mirna. Suddenly he looked at Zdenek, across the table from me. "And you, sir, is it going to turn out that you're Zagad, one-time owner of the carton plant?"

Extending his hand across the table, Zdenek said, "Tobarkin Zdenek is my name: I've never owned a factory, a house or even a car, and if I were a 'sir' I would be very far away from here. I've been a plain worker all my life; I was a union organizer once —"

Adrian shook Zdenek's hand, but his interest returned to Mirna. "Where did you say you saw Zabran at the time of Magarna?"

"At our house, two or three days before the tanks invaded Magarna," Mirna told him innocently. "He had just signed some kind of petition demanding freedom of the press. Jan was at our house too. He questioned the importance of such a petition. But Titus convinced me that workers had to be informed by the press before they could act intelligently."

"And you saw him again after the rising was put down and we were arrested?" he asked.

"Why yes, I went to look for him the first time I could leave work," Mirna told Adrian. "I thought he might know what had happened to my brother and my husband. He wasn't in his office in the trade union building, but I did learn he hadn't been arrested. I left a message for him with a trade union secretary. Titus came to see me that very night. I insisted Jan and Yarostan had been arrested because of that letter that had come from Sophia Nachalo, but he assured me they couldn't possibly have been arrested because of that letter, but because of the activity in which they had engaged. This was what Yarostan had always thought too."

I said to Mirna, "Titus couldn't have told you that twelve years ago. Only two weeks ago he told us he didn't believe we were arrested because of our activity, but because of that letter."

Titus said, "Since I've been dragged into this discussion against my will, I might as well try to clarify the reason for the apparent contradiction."

"Then Mirna isn't lying?" I asked him.

He said, "She remembers correctly, but she fails to grasp the political significance of that letter as well as the significance of the arrests, and I'd like to analyze —"

"Please do analyze, Titus," I begged him. "Something that was clear to me has just turned into a vast puzzle."

"I knew nothing about the arrests until I went to your house immediately after I received Mirna's message." Titus said. "On that evening I didn't believe that you or Jan could have been arrested because of the Nachalo letter. The police files contained enormous dossiers on both of you, and the police could have found any number of pretexts, at any time — in addition to which you had both recently been warned —"

"That was exactly my reasoning," I told him. "What changed your mind?"

"As I told you two weeks ago, I went to the police to learn the precise reasons for your arrest, and I was completely surprised to learn that you had in fact been arrested because of that letter, not only the two of you, but the entire former production group of the carton plant —"

Jasna interrupted Titus to add, "Titus got himself in trouble with the police by trying to convince them to release the rest of us. But then Glavni and Vera set off the appeal for their rehabilitation and in the process they confirmed the police invention about the spy ring and also made the police suspicious of Titus —"

"Not exactly," Titus told her. "I was arrested a year later because I had signed an appeal in support of a free press at the time of the uprising, not because Comrades Kren or Glavni accused me of being in contact with George Alberts or Sophia Nachalo. The matter wasn't that simple. A letter did arrive by the unusual method of personal messenger, and this fact alone aroused the suspicions of the police, especially since the letter came from a person listed in the police records as the daughter of a man they considered a spy. But their suspicions were entirely groundless. George Alberts was convicted in the police files without ever having been tried for espionage, and I know for a fact that he was no spy. Several years earlier I had argued with the appropriate authorities that it was totally incorrect and hypocritical to consider George Alberts a spy, and I returned to these arguments after the Magarna arrests. But with similar lack of success. As for the letter itself, I tried to convince them that, regardless of its method of delivery, it was a major blunder to arrest the people to whom it was addressed. I insisted they release, not only Glavni and Vera Neis, but all the comrades who had been swept in on that ridiculous espionage charge. As is characteristic of this police, they relented up to a point, finding new pretexts for releasing several of those originally arrested, pretexts suggested to them by Comrade Kren, while retaining three of the original group in prison and reaffirming their position that the Nachalo letter constituted an actual and not merely a potential danger."

I was completely confused and started to feel nauseated. I told him, "Titus, you're making my head swim. Tell me something. You knew the police considered that letter an actual danger, in other words they arrested me because of it. Why didn't you as much as mention that letter to me the first time you visited me in prison?"

Titus answered, "Because the Nachalo letter was not the real cause of your arrest; it was nothing more than the formal cause. As I told you before, the real cause for the arrests was that conception according to which errors of consciousness can be corrected by means of arrest and imprisonment. I spent day after day arguing with one after another official; I wrote one after another report; I tried to convince them the Nachalo letter, or any letter for that matter, even one from a spy, might represent a potential threat to coherent class consciousness, but that such a potential threat did not and could not become an actual danger unless and until it was transformed into a program of action of the class. In terms of its content, the Nachalo letter —"

"Its content, Titus?" Jasna asked. "The content of the letter Sophia sent twelve years ago?" Jasna had turned pale and seemed to feel as nauseated as I.

Titus continued, totally unselfconsciously, "Yes, the content of that letter did not call for arrest, or for any action whatever, and I tried to make that perfectly clear in my report to my section head as soon as I completed my study of it. What should I have told you when I saw you, Yarostan? Arrest and imprisonment was a totally inappropriate response to that letter, unwarranted and unprincipled. But I simply didn't have the courage to tell a man serving an eight-year prison term that he was in prison for no reason whatever, and that there was no prospect for his release!"

Jasna sighed and fainted. Vera caught her before she fell to the ground. Titus jumped up to help carry her to the living room sofa and on the way there he commented, "Poor Jasna, it must be the heat or the excitement; my own nerves are on edge." He was totally unaware of the effect of his revelation that he was the one who had received your letter.

When Titus returned, Mirna asked him, with a coldness that made it clear she hadn't been surprised by his self-exposure, "Are you really sure the content of Sophia's letter didn't warrant and even necessitate all those arrests?"

Titus said, "There's no doubt in my mind. I didn't deny the fact that the Nachalo girl was deeply infected by her father's individualism, by his complete lack of discipline; she illustrated this by glorifying the hoodlum she found as a companion, and she incorrectly compared him to Yarostan although he had much more in common with Jan Sedlak and even more with her own father. I also didn't deny the fact that, like her father and in some ways like Luisa as well, she sought a revolution not of the class, but of private bourgeois individuals, and not in history, but outside history, in something she called a community, namely in Utopia. Nor did I deny the fact that such unhistorical utopianism can only lead to a philosophy of despair on first contact with historical, I should say class realities. All these facts were undeniable, but none of them justified arrests and imprisonments. The only way for principled revolutionaries to deal with gaps in consciousness is to put forward the general interests of the proletariat and the final goals of the movement, not to arrest the proletariat or sections of it. It is our responsibility before history to isolate and arrest the virus, not to isolate and arrest perfectly healthy workers who are totally unaffected by the virus. And even if they become infected, the historical project can be realized only if we destroy the disease, not the patient. All this has always seemed perfectly obvious to me."

Yara asked naively, "Do you mean the police did the same thing to the workers that the doctors did to Vesna?"

I begged, "Yara, please don't reintroduce that game."

But Mirna protested, "It's no game, but a very serious matter. The responsibility of every reasonable adult is to take a sample of the disease to experts who are able to determine the gravity of the infection, isn't that so, Titus? You considered Sophia's letter harmless, but you're only an individual, you're not an expert in diagnosing the condition of the working class in the light of its historical task. This is the job of people whose special field is the health and disease of the proletariat. Or did I misunderstand you?"

Titus told her. "I hear my words coming back at me, but I don't understand you."

"I'm sorry I'm so obscure," Mirna told him. "I don't understand these things, since I'm not any kind of expert. Zdenek, help me explain what I mean to Titus."

Zdenek plunged into the discussion. "The work you do in the trade union council consists of theoretical reflection and elaboration on the conditions and general results of the movement, is that correct, Zabran? I believe those are the words I've heard you use several times at prisoners' club meetings."

"Those were my words," Titus admitted.

Zdenek continued, "And your work includes reflection and elaboration about such unusual documents as a letter from abroad addressed to the entire former production group of a factory, I take it. For instance, analysis of the historically progressive content of such a document, as well as what we might call its dangerous facets —"

Titus said, "Yes, of course, but I don't see what this has to do with —"

"With hospitals?" Zdenek asked, laughing. "Frankly I don't either, but I suspect Yara had a very profound insight by making that comparison, and I'm sure if we reflect on it, if we elaborate it —"

"Are you joking with me, Tobarkin?" Titus asked him.

"On the contrary, Zabran. I don't consider this a subject for jokes," Zdenek said with a sarcasm Titus missed. "What's in question is history, the historical project of the proletariat."

Zdenek's exposure was interrupted by Marc Glavni's heavy steps on the stairway. The seductive expression returned to Mirna's face as she ran to the living room. She returned with her arm in Marc's and asked him, "Did you succeed, my dear?"

Marc told her, "There seems to be some confusion. I've spent the past half hour trying to locate your airline reservation. They claim not to have a reservation in the name of Matthews."

"Oh dear, this is simply awful," Mirna said. She pondered, then picked up her leather purse and rummaged through it. "Why I have the flight number right here: it's 357. This was all done for me by a travel agent before I left, and I really should have studied this material more closely. Oh don't tell me! How terribly embarrassing!"

I've just come across my itinerary sheet. That's not a flight number but the number of a sleeping car! I was to leave by railway tonight! I don't know how to begin to apologize to you —"

Marc laughed, and most of the rest of us joined him. "We've all made such mistakes. Would you like me to try to postpone your tram reservation?"

"I simply don't dare to ask you to do that!" Mirna told him. "I'll postpone it myself. Mr. Zabran was just starting to tell us about history's project. I'm sure you'll find it fascinating. I won't miss much since I don't understand such things very well. I'll be as brief as possible. Be sure to help yourself to dessert."

Mirna went upstairs and Marc returned to his seat, next to Yara, and did indeed help himself to a generous serving of each dessert.

Zdenek said to Marc, "We were discussing certain things Mr. Zabran, I mean Comrade Zabran told me at a club where former political prisoners hold meetings —"

Marc was surprised. "Zabran attends meetings of that prisoners' club?"

"Quite frequently; does that surprise you?" Zdenek asked.

Marc said, "No, I suppose not. I remember that he and Comrade Neis had that in common; they both ran after the so-called radical sectors to try to pull them by the tail —"

Vera protested, "Excuse me, Comrade Glavni. I've never run after —"

Titus also objected. "Your statement is equally offensive to me, Comrade Glavni. Your social position has destroyed your ability to distinguish a reformist from a revolutionary. What is needed today is not hysterical speeches glorifying directionless strikes, uncoordinated demonstrations, undisciplined workers, speeches glorifying a body which has lost its head! What is needed, Glavni, is something you've lost all contact with, namely historical direction, a self-disciplined working class with a head. The power of such a working class can be dislodged neither by reformist politicians nor by bureaucrats totally cut off from the class and thus from history!"

Zdenek told Marc, "I was trying to determine Zabran's role in this historical process. Apparently he contributes to it by submitting reports to history, so to speak, reports on the present experience and future course of the historical movement."

Marc asked Zdenek, "Are you referring to Zabran's work in the trade union council? Has he really described it to you in such exalted terms? It is of course true that the tasks of the political sections are as important in their way as the tasks of the economic and planning sections, but Zabran doesn't occupy what one might call a key role in the political section. I've never understood why; I've always thought him a perfectly competent person. He's been content to remain at the lowest rung of the political section of the trade union council. You surely exaggerate his importance. His reports are not submitted to history, but to the chief of the political section of one department of the trade union council."

Zdenek turned to Titus and asked, "Is that true, Zabran? All that theoretical reflection and elaboration on the proletariat's task does not get submitted to history but to a mere section chief? For instance, when you wrote up your analysis of that Nachalo letter —"

I felt tears starting to run out of my eyes. I noticed Jasna leaning on the wall by the entranceway from the living room, pale as a sheet and expressionless. Mirna returned from upstairs and sat down next to Marc. The gathering looked funereal. Only Zdenek and Yara seemed to have any life in them. Marc was still eating. All the others stared at their plates.

Zdenek continued questioning, or should I say needling Titus. "I'm asking you because I'm genuinely interested, Zabran. I was also an employee of the trade union council. But that was twenty years ago, and even at that time I had no insight into the type of work you did there. All I ever did was to transmit instructions from the officials to the workers in the plants to which I was assigned. I never engaged in the reverse process, in analyzing the activity of the workers themselves, in the work of theoretical elaboration —"

Titus said, "It is solely on the basis of such theoretical work that the working class is able to resolve contradictions and steer its historical course —"

"Of course, I understand," Zdenek told him. "Without your work the working class is a body without a head. But what interests me is the daily routine, so to speak, what you actually do during your working day. I have a very concrete reason for taking an interest in this. When I was arrested in the trade union building nineteen years ago and charged with syndicalism, I asked myself: Why syndicalism? A charge of sabotage would have made sense to me. Ever since the coup I had sabotaged every single instruction that had come down to me; it simply wasn't in my blood to give speeches about labor discipline or to communicate threats to workers who took half-hour breaks every hour. But why syndicalism? That doesn't refer to a person's activity, but to his social philosophy; that wasn't anything I had done, but something I had told someone. I searched my mind for the person with whom I had discussed my social philosophy, and the only person I could think of was someone with whom I'd had innumerable conversations, someone with whose social views I had agreed down to details, although there had been minor disagreements here and there. I started to wonder if that person, who had always seemed so friendly and sincere, had actually been reporting our conversations to the police —"

Titus protested, "I've never in my life sent a single report to the police, and I've never considered arrest and imprisonment correct methods for dealing with questions of consciousness!"

"I'm not accusing you of that, Zabran! God forbid!" Zdenek exclaimed. "Those questions I asked myself immediately after my arrest were all answered the moment I saw that you had also been arrested. I had obviously been wrong. This police system makes everyone suspicious of everyone else. It was obvious you hadn't reported our conversations to the police, since you were arrested a year after the coup —"

Adrian said to Zdenek, "Surely you're wrong about that. Zabran was arrested with the rest of us at the time of the revolutionary seizure of power, twenty years ago —"

Marc interrupted, "I beg to differ with you, Povrshan. I saw Zabran soon after the arrests!"

"You mean you weren't arrested?" Adrian asked him. "I was arrested with the rest of you at the time of the seizure," Marc answered. "Since I had only recently been hired at the carton plant, I had no trouble convincing police officials that I had not established any contacts with the ringleaders —"

"So that was how you got out so fast!" Vera shouted. "Didn't they know you had been the ringleader's lover?"

"That fact, Comrade Krena, does not seem to have interested them," Marc told her.

Zdenek continued, "From the time I ran into you in prison nineteen years ago until very recently I stopped asking myself who or what had caused my arrest. I told myself I simply couldn't fathom the methods and procedures of the police. But in recent months that old unresolved question returned to my mind, and it kept on returning —"

Adrian commented, "If Zabran was arrested for the same reasons you were and if he wasn't immediately released, you can't accuse him of clearing himself of his charge by implicating you, the way some comrades did to me!"

Zdenek told him, "You're right, Comrade. If Zabran was arrested for the same reasons. But you see, he wasn't arrested for the same reasons. He was charged, not with syndicalism, but with cosmopolitanism. I knew this at the time; he told me himself what his charge was. Zabran is a very open person, and it's hard to be suspicious of him. I assumed the police investigators assigned to his case had charged him with cosmopolitanism because they hadn't properly memorized the correct charge. But two or three months ago, in a conversation with some recently released long-term prisoners, I learned there had been a wave of arrests nineteen years ago; certain people were charged with cosmopolitanism. Do you know what this charge means?"

Vera snickered. "Certain ignoramuses in high places use that word to attack anyone who has ever spent time abroad, even people familiar with a foreign language —"

"That was precisely what the charge meant nineteen years ago," Zdenek said. "It was a bizarre wave of arrests; it almost swept away every official who had any knowledge of the world — the so-called internationalists' trial. Hundreds of major and minor functionaries who worked in the political sections of every institution were carted off to prison if they had been educated abroad or had fought in foreign revolutions. Then a few weeks ago, while reading the correspondence in which Yarostan has been engaged, I learned that my one-time syndicalist comrade Zabran had played a prominent part in a foreign revolution."

Jasna objected, but without conviction, "That still doesn't allow you to conclude he had anything to do with your arrest. In a way we were all arrested for cosmopolitanism both times, since they connected us with an international spy ring."

Zdenek said, "I haven't drawn any conclusions yet, Jasna. I'm only trying to clarify some questions that keep me from sleeping at night. You had much to do with reawakening my questions, Jasna. Several weeks ago, during a very enjoyable dinner at the Vocheks', you told the history of certain letters delivered by a messenger at the time of Magarna, letters which caused several arrests. It was you who figured out the manner in which the letters were related to the arrests. You figured out that one letter had been addressed to someone who was an official at the time of its arrival —"

"So I was to have been that official," Marc surmised. Zdenek told Marc, "I didn't know you at the time, Glavni. I also didn't know that my friend Zabran had ever had relations with Sophia Nachalo. Consequently Jasna's explanation seemed reasonable to me. But a week or two later I learned, quite by accident, that Zabran was not a complete stranger to the Nachalos —"

"Yes, that is a bizarre coincidence," Marc said.

"That was also my first thought," Zdenek continued. "However, just before you arrived here, your friend Mrs. Matthews was telling us she didn't believe in coincidences —" Marc said reproachfully to Mirna, "That seems somewhat far-fetched; life is full of coincidences —"

"Perhaps it is, Comrade," Zdenek cut in, "but in this case Mrs. Matthews' point of view was not so far-fetched. During the past few months I've had several conversations with Comrade Zabran and I've learned he's a very committed person. He is totally devoted to the proletariat, and also to children. He has extremely clear ideas about the health of both, and very acute insights into the innumerable diseases that endanger their health —"

"I don't see the significance of your drift," Marc told him impatiently.

"Don't you?" Zdenek asked. "If a man with such selfless devotion to the proletariat's health, if a man who had devoted his life to reflection and elaboration in the service of the proletariat and its future course, if such a man had received the type of letter Zabran described for us earlier, do you really think it would be a coincidence if —"

Titus cut Zdenek short and asked angrily, "If he analyzed the political significance of the contents of the letter? Is that what you've been driving at for the past half hour? I must say I'm disappointed with you, Tobarkin. I had taken you for a much clearer thinker. You're muddled to the point of being incoherent. I'm familiar with the conclusion to which your digressive speculations lead. You're not the first to try to make such a point. You're trying to establish an analogy between the work of a proletarian theorist and the work of the police. It's a superficial analogy. It omits the central fact that the political theorist works with historical data and aims at making the proletariat conscious of its real interests, whereas the police are at the opposite end of the spectrum; they work with weapons and aim to arrest, confine and physically liquidate —"

"I apologize for my incoherence, Zabran; it stems from the fact that I'm not unaware of the difference you point out," Zdenek told him. "That's what makes me so curious about your daily activity, your routine. There's a gap in my knowledge which causes the muddle in my consciousness. You see. I'm only familiar with the work of revolutionary theoreticians in pre-revolutionary situations. When I was a union organizer, a quarter of a century ago, most of my friends were revolutionary theorists of one sort or another. Every one of them engaged in work of theoretical reflection and elaboration, analyzed progressive and regressive social forces, defined the future course of the proletarian movement and the dangers along the path. Every one of them was familiar with the viruses and diseases that could infect the proletariat along the way, and each prescribed a different cure. But in those days each revolutionary theorist published his writings in the newspaper of the group to which he belonged, and the publication of the theories seemed to be the ultimate purpose of the reflection and elaboration. However, after the coup, or should I say after the seizure of power by one of the revolutionary groups, the countless sects, newspapers and publishing houses disappeared overnight, as well as the majority of the political theorists who animated them. Some theorists of course remain, but their researches and analyses are no longer distributed by militants at the entrances to factories, and people who are mere workers, as I've been for the past fifteen years, no longer see the fruits of all that theoretical reflection. What I'd like to know is: what happens to all this theoretical work once the proletariat seizes power? You tell me this work is still motivated by a commitment to the historical interests of the proletariat, and I have no reason to doubt your motives. But to whom is the work submitted? To the proletariat? To history? According to Comrade Glavni it is submitted to a section chief —"

Titus interrupted angrily, "You obviously don't expect a revolutionary theorist to —"

Zdenek's anger was also mounting. "My expectations are irrelevant, Zabran! I have no idea whether such a person should print leaflets in a basement, shout from a window or submit critical reports to the appropriate channels; I'm not inclined in any of those directions! What interests me is how such selfless, indeed noble activity, carried out with such irreproachable motives, can possibly have any connection with the destruction of human lives, with the immiseration of the activity of an entire society, with the liquidation of all prospects —"

"At this point you're raving!" Titus said to him.

Zdenek shouted, "You're right, Zabran! Can you at least tell me this? When we worked together in the trade union council, the year during which we engaged in numerous conversations much less one-sided than the present one, I take it that you analyzed the political significance of my syndicalism. And I take it that you wrote your analysis down, isn't that so, Zabran?" Zdenek received no answer; he turned to Marc. "Perhaps you can tell me, Glavni. What would a political analyst have written about syndicalism during the year after the coup?"

Marc seemed embarrassed by the question. "In its day, syndicalism was a very progressive historical —"

"I mean after the coup, 19 or 20 years ago, not in its day!" Zdenek insisted.

Marc answered, "There were still innumerable progressive elements —"

Zdenek turned angrily to Titus and asked, "And there were also innumerable pitfalls, isn't that so, Zabran? Gaps in consciousness, incorrect approaches, and in the final analysis gross errors which represented a great threat to —"

"But that's common knowledge, Tobarkin," Titus admitted. "Who can deny that? You personally admitted —"

"I no longer agree with the position, but that's beside the point, Zabran," Zdenek told him. "Don't misunderstand me. I'm not trying to suggest you urged the police to arrest me because of my incoherence and muddle, because of the errors in my position. You need not repeat that you disown police methods as a way of dealing with problems of consciousness. Has it never occurred to you, Zabran, that men who have seized power over the entire apparatus of a modern state, who have total control not only over the entire network of communication and education, but also over an immense army and police — has it never occurred to you that such men have extremely powerful instruments for dealing with incoherent approaches and errors of consciousness?"

"That's a mistake!" Titus insisted. "I've spent twenty years pointing out that physical coercion —"

"Is no way to deal with false consciousness. I know that. I'm not accusing you of holding a different position. I am told that the inventor of nuclear fission, or whatever it's called, was a very peaceful man and campaigned against war! Did he or did he not give birth to that destructive weapon? Your reflections, Zabran: who uses them, how, for what purpose?"

Titus seemed exasperated by the argument. "That's a typically Utopian position. Humanity can only solve those problems for which the social and material means already exist. The social means for the peaceful application of scientific discoveries are not yet sufficiently developed —"

Zdenek shouted, "The social means for making proletarians conscious of what you call their historical interests also don't exist, do they Zabran? Your elaborations and reflections cannot be submitted to ideal carriers of the proletarian project, any more than nuclear fission can be submitted to human beings who will not make weapons out of it —"

"I'm not a utopian!" Titus shouted.

"Exactly what I'm driving at!" Zdenek shouted, banging on the table and red with anger. " Your reflections and elaborations are submitted to the actual carriers of the proletarian project, those who currently define themselves as the agents of history! Your analyses can only be translated into practice by history's real agents, not by its ideal agents! You're not a Utopian! When you analyze the incorrect and therefore dangerous positions of a Zdenek Tobarkin or a Yarostan Vochek, do you submit your analyses to history, to the proletariat? When you define me as ill, Zabran, which doctors do you take me to? Ideal doctors with a perfect understanding of human life and human freedom? Or the actual doctors coughed up by humanity's historical development?" Zdenek was sweating. Both Jasna and Yara extended their hands toward him to try to calm him, but he pushed their hands away and continued shouting. "Answer me, Zabran! What does it mean when you say you don't believe in arrest and imprisonment as methods for dealing with questions of consciousness? No other methods exist, Zabran, and you're not a Utopian! You're not an idle bourgeois dilettante but a participant in the historical process! When you write that the position of a Sedlak or a Vochek represents a potential danger to historical development, surely you're not surprised if Sedlak or Vochek are arrested! Why are you suddenly so silent, Zabran? Don't you know the only real, the only concrete, the only historically available agents of your historical project are the military and the police armed with rifles, machine guns and tanks?"

Zdenek, flushed with anger, sweat dripping from his hair and his face, looked like he was about to have an attack. Mirna, forgetting all about Marc, ran to help Jasna and Yara raise Zdenek out of his chair and accompany him to the kitchen. I was too hypnotized to move, as were the others who remained at the table with me, all of them in one way or another servants of the same apparatus Titus served.

Adrian quickly let it be known that he was stunned for quite different reasons from mine. He let out a whistle and exclaimed, "That man is a raving lunatic!"

"And you're a stunted chimpanzee!" Irena told Adrian, rising from the chair between me and Adrian and taking Zdenek's seat directly across from me.

Marc stared at Titus, wiped his forehead and said, "I would never have believed it."

"What do you believe, Glavni?" Titus asked him angrily. "Adrian is right; that man is obviously a lunatic."

"Obviously! And you're a model of sanity!" Marc said sarcastically.

I was irked by the thought that Comrade Marc Glavni did not have the most perfect "vantage point" from which to express himself so self-righteously. "Which apparatus do you serve, Glavni?" I asked him.

"My work happens to be in the domain of political economy and planning," he told me.

"Aren't human beings obstacles to the realization of your plans?" I asked him. "Aren't your plans the practical translation of the proletariat's historical project for which living individuals have to be sacrificed?"

Marc dismissed my questions with a shake of his hand, as if he were swatting a fly away from his face, and turned back to Titus. "It was thanks to you that I was rehired in the carton plant after my release, Zabran. I haven't forgotten that. But it suddenly occurs to me that I wouldn't have needed your intercession to regain my former job if I hadn't lost that job to start with —"

Titus, with a contempt equaling Marc's, the contempt of a proletarian revolutionary toward the class of bosses, said, "That's very funny indeed, Glavni!"

Marc told him, "Yes it is, Zabran, extremely funny. The entire conversation I had with you at that time was extremely funny. You didn't only help me get my job back. You also helped me resolve several, shall we call them philosophical, questions. On that occasion I didn't only ask for your help in getting me reinstated in the carton plant. I also asked your opinion about a newspaper clipping that had been shown to me by prison officials shortly before my release, a clipping about a woman I had loved, a woman who had been known for her solidarity with her comrades. This clipping showed that she was not in jail, like the comrades who had stood by her, but had emigrated with a man who was supposedly a spy —"

Adrian shouted, "I saw that clipping too! I tried to bring it up earlier. The man's name was Alberts. He was the head of the International Alberts espionage ring, and the clipping proved that Claude Tamnich had been right about Luisa Nachalo; she was the accomplice of an international spy —"

Marc disregarded Adrian with the same annoyed motion with which he had disregarded me, and continued addressing himself to Titus. "I asked you if you had known this Alberts —"

Adrian interrupted again. "I'm telling you that Alberts person was a convicted spy —"

I had an unobstructed view of Adrian, since Irena's chair was unoccupied; he really did look like a "stunted chimpanzee" to me. I reached for his arm angrily and shouted, "Damn you, Povrshan, when was he convicted? By what court?"

Adrian, nonplussed, told me, "He was a foreigner, like Luisa, and Zabran told us at the time he was a reactionary, therefore a foreign spy."

Marc disregarded Adrian's comments; he told Titus, "In answer to my question, you told me Alberts had been in the process of developing reactionary, perhaps you even said dangerous, views. I concluded that the police might have been right about Alberts." The others started returning to the table. Marc continued, "But I refused to believe that Luisa had underhandedly been engaged in espionage while pretending to be our comrade; I refused to believe she had caused our arrest by implicating us in the activity of this Alberts."

Since Zdenek's former seat was occupied by Irena, Zdenek sat at the foot of the table, directly across from Titus. Jasna took Irena's place next to me; as soon as she sat down she grabbed my arm and asked me in a whisper, "Surely he's not also the one who started the rumor about Luisa's being a spy? How could he? They were lifelong friends!"

"No, Jasna," I whispered to her. "But by describing Alberts as a reactionary, he apparently confirmed that rumor in the minds of certain people."

Vera heard me and told Jasna, "Namely in the minds of idiots, like Adrian and I. When Adrian and Claude told me Luisa was involved in a spy ring, I couldn't believe it either, so I asked the most authoritative person in the plant, Titus Zabran. He told me exactly what he told Glavni, namely that Alberts was a man with dangerous views. I obviously concluded the rumor was true."

Jasna said to Vera, "You wanted to believe it! You dreamed of replacing Luisa as the center of attention, as a popular heroine, as the spearhead of the carton plant strike, especially in the eyes of little Sabina —"

"So you're in on that too, Jasna!" Vera exclaimed. "I'll be damned! The way everyone here is carrying on, you'd think I was a sexual maniac who'd spent her life forcing little girls and secretaries into orgies! The fact is that I never touched a hair on Sabina's head — or Irena's! No proof exists for all your accusations! What do you hope to accomplish? What do you suppose would happen if a demoted bureaucrat and his clique started throwing outrageous accusations at one of the leading comrades?"

Irena retorted, "We all know perfectly well what would happen, Vera! We would all be arrested in the middle of the night, given interminable prison terms, and most of us would never come out to say another word about the leading comrade Vera Krena!"

Vera turned red with frustration and stared at her plate.

Marc, raising his voice for the first time, told Vera, "Your sexual adventures don't interest me in the least, Comrade Krena, so please don't wave any threats at me! In my opinion you and your consort Povrshan deserve each other! May I return to the topic I was trying to raise?" He turned to Mirna and told her, "Forgive my anger, dear. I have an urgent meeting two hours from now, one which I cannot possibly call off, and it seems to me this is precisely the question you wanted to resolve, if I understood you correctly."

Mirna nodded. "Yes, this was precisely the question."

Marc turned back to Titus. "Your description of that Alberts person was extremely disturbing to me. In many ways the course my life took was affected by that brief conversation with you. I had known you and Luisa had been close friends once. Shortly before our arrest, a rumor was circulated, by Comrades Povrshan and Neis among others, to the effect that Luisa was the accomplice of a spy. Then I was arrested and charged by the police with maintaining contacts with a circle of spies, among whom Luisa was the ringleader's accomplice. As proof of Luisa's guilt, I was shown a clipping which Povrshan apparently also saw. This clipping proved nothing about Luisa's espionage, but if it was authentic it did show that Luisa had emigrated with the so-called ringleader. I asked you what significance you attached to the clipping, expecting you to defend your comrade from the insinuations. But instead of proclaiming Luisa's innocence, you told me about the dangerous views of this Alberts person. When I met Mrs. Matthews, Luisa's closest companion for the past twenty years, she assured me Luisa had never had any connections with a spy ring, and I have every reason in the world to believe her. But I still find your position on this matter extremely unclear. Did you consider Luisa dangerous as well? Can you remember well enough to tell me that?"

Titus commented, "Apparently Vera Krena is not the only person who seems to be on trial here!"

Marc protested, "Excuse me, Zabran! I'm not a judge! I'm asking you about a person who was, and still is, very dear to me!"

Titus said angrily, "Be that as it may, Glavni, the rumor about Luisa or Alberts being spies could not have originated with me! I had known both of them for over ten years, and I knew for a fact that neither of them had ever been involved in a hostile spy ring. During the war, Alberts had done certain scientific work for the resistance, and it was especially insidious to accuse him of international espionage, as if he had done this work for the enemy. I forcefully protested the hypocrisy and injustice of this charge. Alberts was an idealist, a Utopian, but he was not a spy! Before the war he had taken part in a revolutionary uprising. He had expected workers to establish the perfect society overnight, without analyzing the nature of their organization, the international balance of forces, or even the material conditions in which this society was to be established. Such utopianism inevitably turns to despair as soon as it comes into contact with reality, and this is precisely what happened to Alberts. He cursed the workers for having failed to carry out what history itself kept them from carrying out. He didn't only curse the workers; he gradually turned against the proletarian project itself. I analyzed this progression from utopianism to —"

"You what, Zabran?" Marc asked.

"I analyzed it!" Titus repeated. "I tried to determine its origins. And I think I located the source of the utopianism, at least the version carried by Alberts and to a smaller extent by Luisa as well as those she influenced —"

I sensed that Jasna had started to tremble. She raised herself up and whispered to me, "I can't take any more of this, Yarostan." She ran upstairs, probably to her bedroom.

Titus asked me, "Jasna looked ill; is there anything I can —"

"No, Titus." I told him. "I think she'd rather be alone."

Marc told Titus, "Please go on, Zabran. This is exactly what Mrs. Matthews wanted to learn. You say you analyzed the source of Luisa's and her friend's utopianism —"

Titus finally heard the irony in Marc's tone, probably for the first time, and he hesitated; then he decided to continue. "Luisa's companion at the time of the earlier rising, a very dynamic man by the name of Nachalo, exerted an enormous influence on Alberts, and obviously on Luisa as well. I didn't actually know the man, but I was surrounded by his friends and consequently even I was infected by some of his attitudes, and I remained infected for many years after his death. This was the problem, you see. The man's attitudes were as infectious as the man himself. I don't want to go into the specific content of those positions, but let me just say they were Utopian to the highest degree. I traced Alberts' utopianism, his subsequent despair as well as the reactionary conclusions which he finally drew, to this single source, this man Nachalo. Alberts was a scientist by profession, and neither his temperament nor his specific discipline would have led him to those positions. It was only his contact with Nachalo that derailed him from what we might consider his natural course. As I said, I had no direct contact with the man himself, but at the carton plant we all experienced the infectious character of his positions. Everyone in the carton plant was affected to a greater or lesser extent. You were hired very late, and consequently you didn't experience this process long enough to draw the conclusions I was able to draw. Originally I thought that Luisa, in the absence of Nachalo and in the face of new demands and a new concrete situation, would gradually shed the Utopian elements and begin to grapple with realities. I was mistaken. Luisa not only continued to carry Nachalo's attitudes; she infected almost everyone in the plant with them. The only two workers who remained completely immune to this influence were Tamnich and Povrshan. At the opposite extreme, Sedlak became something of a reincarnation of Nachalo inside the carton plant. Luisa communicated more of the dead man's attitudes to Sedlak than she herself accepted in her own practice! The coherence, the political health of the entire production group was endangered —".

Marc got up abruptly. "I think you've told us quite enough, Zabran, and I really must be going now. But you've created an altogether new puzzle for me. If Alberts and Luisa represented everything you say they did —"

Mirna stopped him, "Oh my, you don't actually believe Luisa was —"

"My dear," Marc said to her, "it is fortunately not my business to translate the work of political theoreticians into policies which can be socially implemented. My work is exclusively in the economic domain. I believe Zabran's analysis has a certain amount of plausibility, and I shudder when I think of the ways in which such an analysis must have been treated in the offices of administrators with more practical concerns than Zabran's." He turned to Titus again. "That's why I'm puzzled, Zabran. If those two people represented what you say, why did our police release them in such a hurry? Why weren't they shot?"

"Shot!" Mirna exclaimed with mock naïveté. "They couldn't have been shot, could they? Luisa told me the police were extremely courteous on the day they were released. After all, George Alberts was at that time an important name in international scientific circles —"

"Ah yes, I had forgotten!" Marc said. "He was the wartime physicist. The liquidation of such a personage would have done great harm to our international prestige, precisely at that critical moment. And if I understand you correctly, Zabran, you insisted on the fact that neither Alberts nor Luisa were dangerous as individuals, but merely as carriers of a dangerous and extremely infectious virus, and consequently their forced emigration removed the carriers from our midst as effectively as other forms of liquidation. But those among us who had caught the virus — to a greater or lesser degree, as you told us, and as I'm sure you scrupulously made clear to the responsible leaders at the time — could not be forced to emigrate. We were placed in confinement of varying durations, depending on the extent of the infection and the speed of the cure —"

Titus protested, "I've repeatedly told you I don't consider physical confinement an adequate response —"

"That's perfectly clear to me, Zabran," Marc told him. "Your personal approach to these problems is extremely pacifistic. It is now also clear to me why you have never risen above the lowest rung of the political section of your department, namely why you haven't been promoted to higher levels, where practical implementation is a more direct concern. Such a pacifistic approach has not been the most, shall we say expedient, approach to the political problems we have faced. But I must admit I'm surprised. Your squeamishness about methods combines rather badly with the brutal realism of your overall approach. Would you say this is an element of Nachalo's influence that remains with you to this day — a trace of utopianism in the domain of methods? But I really must be going now —"

"Oh must you go?" Mirna asked him. "You clarified so many things for me —"

"I admit I'm glad you forced me to stay," he told her. "Many things have been clarified for me as well. You see, I was profoundly hurt when I learned Luisa had emigrated with someone considered a foreign spy. I had been close, very close to Luisa. I obviously couldn't make myself believe she had been engaged in espionage, nor that she had implicated the rest of us in that activity. But until today I could explain neither the reason for our sudden arrest nor the reason for Luisa's mysterious emigration. My inability to explain those events had a marked effect on my personality. After my visit to Zabran I made decisions which have affected my life since then. I swore myself to celibacy and devoted myself single-mindedly to my career —"

His comments conflicted with what I had known about him, and I asked him, "Are you claiming you would never have been a careerist if the police hadn't accused Luisa of being a spy?"

He disregarded my question with the same swatting gesture, and he told Mirna, "I have not experienced the desire for a woman's affection from that day until you walked into my office. I hope I'm not embarrassing you, my dear. Furthermore, until today I had never called off a meeting except in instances when it overlapped with a more important meeting. I attribute all this to you, dear. You brought me news of Luisa, you brought me the assurance that Luisa had never been a spy, and above all you brought me yourself." During this confession, Marc had been leading Mirna through the hallway toward the living room, his large arm around her waist.

After a few seconds, I heard Mirna shout, "How awful! I just remembered that I wasn't able to get through to the train station to change my reservation, and my train leaves in an hour!"

They both rushed back into the dining room. Mirna ran to get the purse by her seat, while Marc paced back and forth, obviously annoyed. "That really is a distressing oversight," he said. "I forgot too! Isn't there some kind of time limit beyond which reservations cannot be changed?"

Mirna said, "Yes, and I'm afraid I missed that limit!"

"That's extremely unfortunate," Marc told her, still pacing; "I had very much wanted to have another rendezvous with you."

"I had wanted the same thing with you, Marc," she told him.

Marc looked at his watch and told her, "I'm sure something could still be done, but I simply don't have the time to try to explore the possibilities still available to us."

"I wouldn't dream of asking you to spend your valuable time that way at this hour," Mirna told him.

"One of the things I had wanted to tell you was that there is a great likelihood I will be traveling overseas in the very near future," he told her, "and I very much wanted to have your home address, just in case —"

"What a wonderful solution to our present dilemma!" Mirna shouted. "And what an exciting prospect! I'll be so happy to see you again!"

"And your husband?" Marc asked.

"We've been separated for several years," she told him; "didn't I tell you?"

"Please do give me your address," he begged.

"How exciting!" Mirna started fishing through her purse. "Isn't this silly? I'm so excited I can't even remember my own address."

Marc looked at his watch again and said impatiently, "Please do hurry, my dear."

Mirna shouted, "Here it is!" She took out a piece of paper, wrote on it and handed it to him; then she took his hand in hers and told him, very seductively, "You'll be more than welcome! And Luisa! She'll simply go wild when I tell her!" They walked to the living room, arm in arm. Yara, Zdenek, Irena and I crowded into the hallway to watch the parting.

Marc kissed Mirna's hand and told her, "I don't know how to thank you. Please do communicate to Luisa how deeply I regret the thoughts I left unresolved during the past twenty years. In my heart I've never felt anything but admiration for her, an admiration the like of which I've since felt toward no one but you."

While Marc still held Mirna's hand near his lips, Adrian went bolting out of the dining room straight toward Marc, his right hand extended. "Comrade Glavni, I can't let you leave before trying to explain myself. I owe you an apology —"

Marc dropped Mirna's hand, turned his back to Adrian and started to walk toward the black limousine which was still waiting for him.

Adrian ran out of the house after him and shouted, "You've got to see my point of view, Comrade Glavni. When they threw that spy charge at me for the second time, and when I found out you had been released, and then remembering how close you had been to Luisa, I assumed —"

Marc slammed the door of the limousine and looked only at Mirna, who stood in the doorway.

Adrian continued shouting, "In any case I wasn't the one who started that rumor about her!" Then he walked past Mirna back to the living room and exclaimed, "Damn!"

Zdenek asked him, "What's the matter, Povrshan? Afraid Glavni might get reinstated?"

Adrian repeated, "Damn!" and dropped onto a sofa, red with frustration and perspiring.

Mirna stood in the doorway waving at the limousine as it drove off.

As soon as Mirna closed the door, Yara ran to her, embraced her and shouted, "You were perfect, absolutely perfect, in every way!"

Zdenek and Irena both grinned as they, too, congratulated her. Mirna looked quizzically at me.

I smiled and told her, "His career still came first — even above the prospect of a *tête-à-tête* with Mrs. Matthews. But you were never so — so seductive with me."

"Of course not!" she told me. "You never asked me to have a *tête-à-tête* with you, whatever that is!" She ran to me and kissed me passionately on my lips. Then she looked around, asked, "But why isn't the bride back?" and ran upstairs.

Yara started to return to the dining room, but Irena stopped her and told her, "They're having it out with each other. Leave them."

Vera was shouting at Titus in the dining room. "So you saw right through me, did you Comrade Zabran? You knew all about me from the very beginning! And with whom did you share this knowledge of yours? Why did you spread it? What do you expect to get out of it?"

Titus told her indignantly, "I happen not to be a gossip monger, Comrade Krena!"

"I suppose you only wanted your precious Adrian to recognize he was in the grip of a monster!" she shouted. "And what then? Do you really believe that after experiencing the upper echelons of the bureaucracy he'd ever again return to a factory job? You're deluded beyond imagination! Adrian is permanently spoiled! He'll never again be one of your beloved proletarians, he'll never again be one of your followers!"

"Unscrupulous, shameless hypocrite!" Titus shouted, genuinely angry for the first time. "Under the guise of devotion to the proletarian cause, you've done nothing but surround yourself with instruments for the satisfaction of your depraved personal desires!"

"You have the nerve to say that to me!" she retorted. "You, Titus Zabran, dare to throw that in my face! You who've spent your life maiming and killing your beloved proletarians, who destroyed what you could never totally possess, you have the nerve to throw depravity in my face! I've come no closer to satisfying what you call my depraved desires than you, Comrade Zabran, but I never went to such lengths trying!" There was a long silence. Suddenly Vera was shouting through sobs, apparently on the verge of hysteria. "How can you just sit there, so cold, so impassive? Don't you know what you've done?" She sobbed, and then continued, "I worshipped my proletarians as much as you ever did yours, but I never did mine any harm, not the slightest, ever! But you! When you lost your hold over yours, you had them maimed, tortured, confined, killed! And you talk to me about depravity!" There was silence again; only her hysterical sobbing could be heard.

Suddenly Titus appeared in the living room entrance; he walked toward the couch where I was and sat down. "Surely you're still sober and unhysterical enough to understand, Yarostan."

"I'm fairly sober and unhysterical, but I don't understand," I told him.

He went on, "Mass arrest of the entire group was an idiotic response to the actual danger the group represented, but uncritical acceptance of the group's unbridled and growing individualism would have been an equally idiotic response. The potentially explosive and infectious character of such uncontrolled individualism in the midst of a revolutionary situation had to be carefully assessed, not with the saber-rattling hysteria of a Tamnich, but with the historically tried and tested methods of proletarian analysis. When the most combative elements of the class began to reject, not only the misleaders who headed their pseudo-organizations, but also the real leaders of the proletariat's own organization, the consciousness of the entire class was put into jeopardy. Surely you understand this! The working class has always considered its organization as its most precious instrument. Opposition to its organization has always been the expression of confusion in the class, created by petty bourgeois influences —"

I moved as far to the other end of the couch as possible. I addressed him as "Zabran" and remembered how amazed I had been when Yara had started calling him "Mr. Zabran." I said to him, "During the war, Zabran, when I was caught sleeping in the carton plant, you kept the foreman from having me arrested. You introduced me to your comrades in the resistance organization. Later you introduced me to Luisa Nachalo. I've always been grateful for what you did for me. But — and excuse me for putting it this way — I'm suddenly curious about your motives. What was I to you? Or to put it differently, what potential did I seem to represent for the working class struggle?"

While I was talking, Adrian was tiptoeing toward the hallway to the dining room. I heard him ask Vera. "Do you realize we go on the radio exactly ninety minutes from now?"

In a muffled voice, Vera said, "I forgot all about it. You'll have to go on by yourself. I feel awful."

"By myself?" Adrian gasped. "I've never given a talk by myself! The talk I prepared lasts all of five minutes!" .

"Well have Irena type you more!" Vera shouted. "I can't go on! Don't you understand that?"

Adrian returned to the living room and walked toward Irena. He told her sheepishly, "Vera can't go on."

Irena told him, "Write your own speech, Adrian. I'm quitting!"

Adrian was on the verge of tears. "Irena, please —"

"Go to hell!" Irena shouted.

Adrian told her, "Don't forget the comrades at the radio station extended our time to half an hour because you had insisted fifteen minutes wasn't long enough for our program."

Irena hesitated for a second. Then she walked toward me, extended her hand and looked into my eyes. "I'm sure we'll see each other again." She crossed the room toward Yara, took her hand and said, "Please do let me know when you'll go on another one of your excursions. I'd like to go upstairs to say goodbye to Mirna."

"I'm sure you'll see her again too," Yara told her. "We both love you for coming."

"When will I meet your friend Julia?" Irena asked.

"I'll bring her to your office tomorrow morning," Yara told her. "I'm afraid you won't like all the games Julia and I play —"

Irena said, "I'm sure I'll love any games you play, Yara!"

Irena kissed Zdenek's bearded cheek, and Yara accompanied her to the door. Yara told her, "Thanks for everything. Sisters?"

"Sisters, Yara. Forever!" They embraced in the doorway. I couldn't take my eyes off them: identical hair, identical clothes, almost the same height. Finally Adrian pulled Irena away from Yara and walked out with her.

My eyes wandered back to Titus, who was staring at me from the other end of the sofa. I tried to return to the question I had asked him earlier. "I take it that I was more to you than simply a hoodlum, a homeless wretch for whom you merely felt pity. I represented something to you, didn't I? I was one grain of that vast mass which could potentially raise the world to its shoulders, but which was asleep, blind and ignorant. You provided the necessary coherence, self-discipline and organization. I was expected to do the rest on my own."

But before I clarified my question, Mirna came down the stairway pulling Jasna by the hand. Mirna sat down on the floor by my feet, placed her arm across my knees, and stretched her exposed stockinged feet toward Titus, as if to provoke him. Jasna sat down right next to me, or rather directly in front of me since I was facing sideways to talk to Titus. Jasna took both my hands and pulled them around her waist. This seemed to be her way of proclaiming that her marriage was off.

Feeling an urge to convey the same message to him, I pulled Jasna closer toward me, buried my face in her hair and kissed her ear while I stared directly at Titus. Yara left the door and went to sit on Zdenek's lap. Titus was completely alone, and for a second I felt sorry for him. He turned his face away from me and stared down at his own shoes.

Mirna said, "I'm sorry we interrupted. Please do go on."

I wasn't able to go on. There was a long silence. Then Yara said to Titus, "Yarostan was asking you why you took him into your organization! What did you expect from him?"

Titus, still looking down, said, "I've expressed my willingness to answer any question you ask, Yarostan — provided I can understand it."

I apologized. I was having a hard time concentrating on the question I wanted to ask him. I tried again. "What you've just told about Luisa — I suppose you thought all those things about her at the time." Titus nodded. "Yet you introduced me to her. You didn't only introduce me. You apparently wanted me to be, how shall I say it, something like her political pupil." Titus nodded again. I was irritated. "I don't understand the significance of your nod."

"I don't understand your question," he told me.

I shouted. "You took your patient to the wrong type of doctor, didn't you?"

He looked up from his shoes with a bewildered expression; I could see that he genuinely hadn't understood. I started again. "A hoodlum, a lumpen proletarian was found sleeping in the carton plant." Titus stared down at his shoes again. I continued, "He wasn't simply a hoodlum, but one familiar with the city's hiding places, with the sewers and empty buildings, the alleys and underground passages. He was potentially useful to the resistance organization, particularly at a time when an armed rising was about to begin. You took him under your wing. The first goal was to win the war; the rest would come later. But the war ended, and you still kept this lumpen under your wing, although he was no longer useful to you. His knowledge of sewers had become irrelevant. What was needed then was a proletarian cadre, and this lumpen was ignorant, undisciplined and anti-intellectual. What you called a merely instinctive rebel had to be transformed into a class-conscious revolutionary, if possible one with a smattering of proletarian theory. But why did you choose Luisa for this task? How could she have carried that transformation through?"

Titus said, "I still fail to understand your question, unless you want the simplistic and obvious answer that Luisa was an experienced working class organizer whereas I was merely a theorist —"

"Are you being purposely dense?" I asked him, exasperated. "You apparently expected Luisa to shape me into a self-disciplined, realistic cadre, to channel my instinctive rebellion and Utopian hopes into scientific understanding of the laws of social development and rigid consciousness of the proletariat's historical task. But you've just told us Luisa was incapable of carrying out such an assignment —"

Titus looked toward Zdenek with hostility and said, "I think I see what you're driving at. You're back to the fact that whatever our intentions are, we're limited to historically available instruments, and Luisa was the only historically available proletarian organizer in that plant; there were no ideal organizers. Yes, Yarostan, unfortunately we don't choose the circumstances in which we have to confront our tasks. Yes, I took you under my wing, if you want to put it that way. You were something of a natural leader, and in fact you were the catalyst who set off the politicization of the others; it was you the others looked to. Luisa couldn't play that role at the start because of her unfamiliarity with the local conditions and the distance created by her lack of local experiences —"

"But something went wrong, didn't it?" I asked. "Luisa started — how did you put it? — infecting us with attitudes that threatened to spoil everything!"

"Luisa didn't start by infecting you!" he protested. "She went a long way toward transforming you into a class-conscious revolutionary. I must have expressed myself simplistically earlier. The attitudes Luisa as well as Alberts' daughter inherited from Nachalo were typical of the most militant sectors of the working class, they reflected the class's implacable hatred for capital, its will to struggle against the capitalist order, its repudiation of all class collaboration. All this is necessary, indeed indispensable, for the proletariat's struggle. It is necessary, but not sufficient. Above all else the proletariat needs theory, namely proletarian consciousness, as well as organization. But consciousness cannot simply be placed into someone's head. It grows out of the situation itself, out of daily confrontation with the contradiction between the productive forces and the production relations."

"I see," I told him. "So my job was supposed to inculcate the self-discipline. The final result was to be a cadre with Nachalo's implacable hatred and with something, like your theory —"

"Precisely!" he said. "And Luisa was perfectly suited to guide you through such a development. If other factors hadn't intervened, nothing in the world would have made you turn against proletarian theory and ultimately against the proletariat's very organization —"

"Now you're coming to what I want to know," I told him. "What were those other factors?"

"In essence they can all be reduced to Nachalo's influence," he said. "But this influence was not communicated as directly as you claim I made it seem. Nachalo combined implacable hatred for capitalism with implacable hatred for the proletariat's own organization and theory."

"Just like my brother," Mirna observed.

"And like you, Mirna!" Titus told her. "It was precisely through Jan that the Nachalo influence was communicated to the rest of the production crew. It was no wonder to me that he and Alberts' daughter took to each other! Ultimately of course Luisa was the carrier of that influence, but what remained merely dormant in Luisa flared up in Jan! I wasn't aware that two processes were taking place simultaneously.

At Luisa's house you became increasingly conscious of the tasks confronting the class and of the local material and social conditions in which our group found itself. However at the plant Jan Sedlak absorbed, not lessons drawn from the production process, but the lessons he drew from Luisa's mannerisms and unintentional comments. This happened in spite of the fact that Luisa never considered him a comrade. Sedlak's spontaneism, his instinctive rebellion could have been channeled and controlled, it could have played a useful role in the workers' movement, if the rest of the group, and particularly you, had remained conscious of the historical tasks. But gradually you were swayed —"

"Just what did this influence consist of?" I asked him.

"Immaturity of consciousness, insufficient grasp of the needs of the class struggle, lack of any coherent approach to organization and political activity," he answered. "In Nachalo and Sedlak we saw a total incomprehension of the three fundamental tasks of the revolutionary struggle of the proletariat: class consciousness, proletarian theory and organization. This was extremely grave. All the combined forces of capital do not represent as great a danger to the proletariat as the incoherent and uncontrolled forces within the proletariat itself. I've devoted my whole life to the task of reflection and elaboration of the proletariat's historical project, the task of defining and isolating uncontrolled and dangerous forces within the proletariat's own ranks. What you don't understand is that Nachalo and his likes appear to be the most militant workers during times when no organized struggle is taking place. But during times of struggle they become obstacles and fetters to the proletariat. What was needed in the carton plant was a coherent structure to maintain and develop political clarity. Terrorist petty bourgeois elements fighting only to gratify their own personal desires had no place in such a struggle. The entire aim of revolutionary theory can be reduced to this: to define, isolate and make possible the neutralization of such elements before they contaminate the entire class —"

"This neutralization, Zabran — how was it carried out?" I asked him. "By means of theory, by persuasion, by organizers like Luisa, by theorists like yourself? You've told me that in the earlier struggle you were a soldier in a so-called popular army. Tanks and rifles were the instruments with which you isolated and neutralized —"

"That military organization was established within the framework of an incorrect perspective, as I've told you before!" he said angrily. "The class must necessarily make use of violence, but this cannot be done by a minority separate from the general movement of the class! Terrorism, by individuals or separate groups like armies or police, is absolutely foreign to the methods of the class and constitutes a method which expresses the despair of the petty bourgeoisie —"

"Damn it, I don't understand!" I shouted. "Do you actually conceive of the proletariat as a single body that turns all at once against its class enemy and deals a single blow, as if it didn't consist of individuals, of different groups?"

"Just so!" he said. "And it is precisely this unity of purpose and unity of action that are sabotaged by individualists like Nachalo and Sedlak! Individualism is a disease! The entire tactics and strategy of the struggle reside in diagnosing this disease and isolating its carriers from the rest of the class, not by military methods but by the methods of science! Once the carriers are isolated, their own followers tend to absorb the historical lesson and weld themselves to the iron fist which clears away the fetters that obstruct the historical movement —"

"I'm starting to understand," I said, feeling nauseated. "The point is not for an army, a minority, to carry your theory into history. The point is for Nachalo's own comrades to carry your theory, and if possible Nachalo himself. The point is to turn Nachalo's own comrades into partisans of a struggle he had repudiated from the marrow of his bones. So that's what you expected in the carton plant? Once Luisa and Sabina were no longer able to infect us with the individualistic virus, the rest of us were to turn to the correct tasks on our own, under no other pressure than that of the level of development of the productive forces —"

"Yes, Yarostan, that's precisely the point," he said. "The point is not the physical liquidation of spontaneity or combativeness or instinctive rebellion. When this is done the proletariat is left disarmed; this is when tanks and rifles substitute themselves for the proletarian fist, because it is the force behind the fist that is thus liquidated. The goal is to transform not only you, but even a Jan Sedlak and a Nachalo into coherent expressions of class power, and this cannot be accomplished by means of guns aimed at their heads! The proletariat's historical task is not that simple! It is the disease that has to be liquidated, not the proletariat! Surgery cannot be carried out by means of explosives! Not even in historical periods when explosives are the instruments most readily available to the surgeons! Theory has developed other methods, and these other methods cannot be considered Utopian because proletarian theory is not an abstraction; it is an excrescence of the class! A Sedlak must be made capable of turning his energy toward the appropriation of the productive forces when the historical opportunity for such an act presents itself, instead of shouting like a reactionary Luddite, 'Let's take the machinery into the street!' A Nachalo must be made to distinguish his personal enemies from enemies of the class, and not left in a condition in which he greets the proletariat's own organization by shouting 'Down with the red butchers!'"

Jasna and Mirna were as startled as I was. The three of us jumped up; Yara and Zdenek joined us. We formed a hostile circle surrounding Titus. I asked him, "Could you repeat that? What did you say Nachalo shouted?"

He seemed disoriented and hesitated before answering. "I've already told you I never met Nachalo. I believe it was Alberts who told me Nachalo had said something of that nature —"

"Where was Nachalo when he said this?" I asked.

"I believe he was at the front," Titus said hesitantly. "But as I told you, I've tried to forget my involvement with that military organization and I don't remember any of it clearly —"

I shouted, "It was the only time in your life when you were personally in a position to implement your theory, to apply the cure called for by your diagnosis!"

"But that army was not an appropriate method," he protested.

"You're contradicting yourself!" I exclaimed. "You just said Nachalo shouted about red butchers in the face of the proletariat's own organization. This means you did regard that army as the proletariat's own organization, as the only historically available instrument —"

He protested, "I couldn't have expressed myself —"

"On the contrary, you expressed yourself very clearly," I told him. "History's instrument was a firing squad!"

Titus stared at me with a bewildered expression and said nothing.

I tried to remember the exact words of Sabina's account. "In the real revolution, the people will turn against the red butchers first!'"

Titus' face turned into a grimace of horror. His whole body started trembling. He looked at me wildly, as if he were looking at a ghost — the ghost of Nachalo, whom he had never met. In a barely audible voice he said, "That's impossible —"

Jasna, trying very hard to control her tears, walked to the front door and opened it slowly. "Titus, get out of this house."

Titus rose slowly. He didn't take his eyes off me. Every part of his body trembled as he walked out the door.

Jasna closed the door behind him and fell into Mirna's arms, abandoning all her self-control, trembling as Titus had on his way out.

Zdenek asked Mirna, "Why did you make Jasna come down to face the gory end? You might have spared her."

Mirna told him, "I asked her how she'd feel now if she had married him when she first met him. Then she didn't want to be spared."

Jasna wept convulsively. "You tried to tell me, but I didn't want to believe you. I defended him to the very end. I know I would have stood by him when he had your Vesna taken away. Why are you so good to me, Mirna?"

"It was he who was good, Jasna, and you had every reason in the world to defend him," Mirna told her. "He was good the way Vesna was good, the way my mother was good. He did everything for the noblest motives, for his plastic Jesus, the proletariat. Who could have thought that such a good man was an assassin? He helped Jan and Yarostan find jobs after their release from prison. He also helped you, Jasna. He helped my father get a pension after he was fired from his job. He visited Yarostan in prison and helped me get a pass —"

"Why are you repeating all that again?" Jasna asked. "None of us would have needed his help if he himself hadn't been responsible —"

"I'm reminding you why you defended him," Mirna told her. "Even I couldn't believe it all until today, until he threw up all those gruesome details."

Jasna asked, "How in the world did you see what Yarostan and I could never have imagined?"

I had wanted to ask Mirna the same question, but just then Vera walked in from the dining room. She had been crying and looked as pale as Titus had looked when he'd left. The elegant, proud woman I had seen at the beginning of the "celebration" now looked old; the dark rings around her eyes made her face look like a skull with a wig and paint. Vera walked toward Yara, fell to her knees, embraced Yara's legs and placed her head in Yara's bosom. She sobbed, "I never meant any harm. You know that, don't you?"

Yara bent down to force Vera's hands away from her legs and walked toward me; she put her arms around me, pressed her head to my chest and started to cry.

Vera pathetically crawled on her knees toward Mirna, extended her hand and reached for Mirna's hand. Mirna pulled her hand away, walked to Zdenek's chair and sat down on its arm, wrapping her arm around Zdenek's shoulder. Vera turned to crawl toward Yara again.

"Vera, don't!" Jasna screamed as she ran toward Vera and raised her to her feet. Jasna ran to the closet for Vera's purse and hat. "I'll walk you to the taxi stand; you're overwrought," she told Vera, leading her out the door, her arm around Vera's shoulder. Vera walked out mechanically, like a human being suddenly deprived of her understanding.

When they had left, Zdenek commented, "That woman is carrying all of Zabran's guilt because Zabran is too idiotic to realize what he's done, and Jasna is the only one of us with enough compassion to know that Krena is carrying more than her share."

"She'd have done the same thing he did," Mirna insisted.

Zdenek objected, "But the fact is, she didn't quite do the same thing."

Yara was still sobbing. "I used to think she was so wonderful, such a powerful, proud woman." I ran my hands through Yara's hair. She looked up; there were tears on her pretty if not innocent face. "You like me again?" she asked me.

"Yes, Yara."

"As much as you liked Irena?" she asked. .

I blushed and looked away from her eyes. Her hands dropped from behind me. I put her hands back and forced myself to say, "More, Yara, infinitely more —"

"Show me!" she said; her eyes were big, her lips partially open.

I embraced Yara tightly. My heart beat so hard I thought the whole room shook; I felt a surge of desire I hadn't known I could feel. I lowered my face, closed my eyes, parted my lips and placed them on Yara's. When our lips parted, I was dizzy and unaware that I was standing. I almost fell to the floor; Yara helped me to a chair.

Mirna ran to me and asked, in a coaxing tone, "Aren't you ashamed?"

"No, Mirna, I'm not ashamed."

Mirna squeezed next to me and kissed me, not gently like Yara had, but fiercely, biting my lips and my tongue. "Didn't I tell you he was still ours, Yara?" she asked.

"Whose did Yara think I was?" I asked her.

"God's, morality's, history's!" Mirna said. "After what you did to her in my clearing, she was convinced you had given your life away, that you had become a servant of the tanks and firing squads —"

"She wasn't so far wrong," I admitted.

"Yes I was!" Yara protested. She crowded next to me from the other side and asked, "You didn't ever want to turn me into a cadre, did you?"

I hid my tears by burying my face in Yara's hair. Biting her ear gently, I whispered, "No, Yara, I want you exactly as you are."

Jasna returned, glanced with surprise at the love scene between the three of us, and turned to Zdenek. "Poor Zdenek, what did you do to drive everyone away from you?"

"Nothing except grow old, Jasna," he told her.

"Old! All of life is still in front of you," Jasna protested. She sat down on the arm of his chair in Mirna's former position.

"Is that what you told Krena?" Zdenek asked.

Jasna almost cried again. "She's completely broken. She kept repeating, 'I'm not like him, Jasna, I'm not like him.' I felt so sorry for her. Poor, sad Verushka. I tried to tell her none of us thought she was like him at all. She did cause Adrian's and probably Jan's and Yarostan's jail terms to be lengthened — but she wasn't the one who was responsible for their being in prison to start with."

"And that rector?" Mirna asked.

"She alone was responsible for that." Jasna admitted, and added, "But not a single one of us is pure."

Mirna asked, "Are you boasting, Jasna?"

"You can sometimes be so cruel, Mirna," Jasna told her. "God knows what you would have done if —"

Mirna cut in, "If I hadn't concentrated my passion into —"

"Into love games!" Yara exclaimed. "Which is what those two didn't ever do, even though they both longed to! They've pent it all up inside, and it gets so ugly when it's so pent up. I was afraid of her. Didn't you see how she looked at me? I was afraid she'd tear my arms off, one by one, and start eating them —"

I interrupted Yara to ask Mirna, "Jasna started asking you how you knew —"

"About Mr. Zabran?" Yara asked. "I knew three years ago, when he had Vesna taken to the hospital. I knew he wasn't having her taken away because he loved her, but because he loved something he called health —"

"I knew even earlier," Mirna said. "That day I went to his room, before you were released, he made me feel shame — the same shame I'd felt when my mother found Jan and me sleeping in each other's arms, the same shame I'd felt when she surprised Sabina and me, the same shame I'd felt when Vesna turned rigid the day Yara and I returned from visiting you —"

I asked, with unintended sarcasm, "And from that feeling of shame you inferred —"

"I didn't infer anything, Yarostan," she told me. "I felt the same shame the day Yara, Zdenek and I went to his room to invite him to the dance at my plant. The look on his face was the same as my mother's when she saw the devil in me — as if I intended to tear his clothes off and pull him into me right there and then! I nearly melted in the face of that look. Then Zdenek told me he had met him at the prisoners' club, that he'd been talking to him when he saw you, and Titus mysteriously vanished. It was only then that I started asking myself what Sophia kept asking you: why hadn't he ever told you about her letter? After Jasna told us what he had said to her about Luisa, Yara and I took all of Sophia's letters to Zdenek's and the three of us re-read every one of them. Sabina knew who Titus was twenty years ago, and maybe even earlier!"

Zdenek asked Mirna, "What I'd like to know is how that business about Krena got out —"

Yara told him, "Oh, I figured all that out by myself. Mr. Zabran had told Jasna everything he knew about Vera, but that really became interesting when I read what Sabina said about her. I went to listen to her lectures; once I stayed after the lecture and saw Irena! I figured it all out the moment I saw her! She looked exactly the way I'd been supposed to look at the dance! I had Mirna fix me up to look like Sabina again and I went to see Irena. She reacted the same way I had: we were twins! During all the years she'd worked for Vera, she hadn't figured anything out —"

Zdenek asked, "But who started that rumor that supposedly reached Kren's ears? I never heard of it before today."

Yara blushed and looked guiltily toward Jasna. "Oh, that rumor," she said. "Jasna wasn't supposed to tell me what she'd learned from Mr. Zabran, I wasn't supposed to tell Julia, Julia's father wasn't supposed to tell the people in the bank where he works, and they weren't supposed to breathe a word to Kren."

Everyone laughed, including Jasna. Yara looked relieved. Then Jasna asked Mirna, "Where in the world did you learn so much about airplane reservations? I've never even been to the airport!"

"Neither had I," Mirna said. "The whole foreign tourist idea was Irena's, or at least originated with her. Irena bought me the clothes and the little purse. I took two trips to the airport and acted as if I wanted to buy a ticket. I had the time of my life there, being ogled by all the important men with briefcases, especially the ones with their wives next to them! They weren't all as polite as my Comrade Glavni. I also had another reason for going to the airport. At that time I thought we would soon be taking excursions by airplane. It was Irena who suggested I tell him I was leaving tonight. Otherwise I could never have made him stay — he kept trying to run out as it was —"

Yara asked her, "Had you planned the mixup between the airplane and sleeping car tickets?"

Mirna laughed and told her, "Planned it! I was so stupid it didn't occur to me that there wouldn't be a reservation for Mrs. Matthews when he called the airline! That was when I thought my whole game was over! Then I remembered a scene in a movie — a young man rushed to the railway station, pulled out his ticket, and learned it was a bus ticket —"

Yara asked, "What address did you send him to?"

"The only two addresses I knew were Luisa's and Sophia s, and I didn't wish him on either of them!" Mirna exclaimed. "There were ten of us here, so I wrote: Mrs. Ron Matthews, 10 Daman Street, New York. I hoped he wouldn't happen to know Daman Street didn't exist."

Zdenek roared with laughter. "Maybe it does! Who knows whom he'll find —"

:||||||||:

Please forgive me for breaking off so abruptly. Mirna just rushed into the house and told me, "They're invading! The tanks are moving toward the city!"

I can't remember where I stopped, and I don't have the patience to reconstruct my frame of mind. On Monday morning, the day after the "celebration," I went to work, and I thought of nothing but Titus Zabran all day long. I was glad to find your letter when I returned from work that afternoon. You confirmed so much of what Mirna and Yara had "taught" me. I started writing you that night, and I stayed home from work yesterday and today trying to describe to you every vivid detail, until a few minutes ago, when Mirna returned from a meeting with some of her friends at her former plant. The tanks are supposed to arrive tomorrow or the next day —

I'm continuing an hour later. Yara, Julia and Irena were just here. Irena had been the first to learn about the coming invasion, and Yara had called Mirna at the plant. While they were here, the four of them spoke excitedly about joining a group of people, largely former workers from Mirna's plant, who are constituting themselves into a sort of "reception committee" for the tanks. They intend to remove as many street signs as possible and to knock on doors and suggest that people remove the numbers from their houses. Irena is no longer Vera Krena's secretary. The day after tomorrow that job might cease to exist anyway. All four of them begged me to join them, but I decided to stay to try to finish this letter; tomorrow I may not be able to mail it.

I'm alone again, but I'm finding it impossible to concentrate on anything except the tanks and the fact that Mr. Ninovo is in front of his house raking leaves. He had disappeared for several months. The past two mornings I got up before sunrise to continue this letter, and I heard Ninovo returning from the bar where he works.

According to official accounts, an army of four million men is massed at our frontiers. Four million! In some circles they're described as "barbarian hordes," but I'm sure the vast majority of them are workers, exactly like the people they're coming to repress. They're not "barbarians." But the "project" they're about to realize is one of the most barbaric acts in history. Such an invading force could annihilate a population ten times larger than ours in a single day. How did so many centuries of "progress" lead to this scandalous barbarism? What kind of system can afford to support a permanent force of four million trained assassins? Can you even imagine how much of a society's activity has to be concentrated on war-related work to supply an army of four million — in "peace time"? In the name of the most total liberation of human beings proclaimed by any historical period, human beings are subjugated by the most barbaric brute violence! It would be more comforting to think the invaders were creatures from another planet, or insects. What is so terrifying is the thought that the invaders are workers like ourselves, workers who may next week be repressed by armies consisting of some of the very workers they are repressing now. It isn't "they," "the enemy," who are driving those tanks and carrying those rifles. It's "we" — we comrades, fellow workers, brothers, we who failed to communicate with each other, we who failed to destroy the tanks and the plants that produce them and the laboratories that design them, we who failed to destroy the schools where we're taught to produce the tanks — the schools where we're taught to obey the commanders who order us to assassinate each other. Worker will be killing worker, like will be repressing like, as at the time of the suppression of the Magarna rising. I had thought our letters were a step toward communication across these frontiers, at least a symbolic step. But the frontiers haven't fallen. To the workers in the tanks we're a population "out of control," we're as incomprehensible as insects, we're like creatures from another planet. And in some ways we are: we had started to be free human beings.

Zdenek was just here. He came directly from his job, and he alarmed me considerably. He learned that a section of the political police is back in operation, patrolling the streets for "vandals and terrorists."

I'm extremely worried. Supper time has come and gone, and there's no sign of Mirna and Yara. I don't doubt the ability or resourcefulness of either of them; they've amply demonstrated these qualities to me during recent weeks. But they're extremely vulnerable. Yara's "combat" experience is limited to a few protest demonstrations at her primary school, and Mirna spent most of the past two decades in a clothing factory. The political police, on the other hand, have twenty years of experience in "defining social diseases" and in "isolating dangerous individuals" before they "infect the class."

Zdenek was furious when I told him where they had gone. "You don't play cat and mouse with a machine gun!" he shouted.

I lost my temper and quoted Zdenek's own statement, "Why repress yourself because they might repress you? Let them do the repressing!"

Zdenek said, "That's inappropriate now!" He went out to look for them, determined to bring the "reckless idiots" home.

I'm worried because I know that none of them will return home at the first sign of danger. They're all convinced they have a world to win and nothing to lose but a condition of lifeless routine to which none of them can acquiesce now. The extreme caution and fear of "trouble" that had characterized Mirna's behavior after Jan's and my arrest, and even after Yara's first demonstration, disappeared without leaving a trace when Mirna's fellow workers in the clothing factory disbanded as a production group and became explorers of a new world. At this morning's meeting, as soon as Mirna and her friends learned about the coming invasion, they unanimously decided that the moment the invasion took place, they would see to it that the machinery at their plant would never again be used to produce clothing for a regime like the one they experienced for twenty years. After that act they would disband until the possibility for further communication and exploration existed again. Some of them are preparing to emigrate; others are determined to "stop the tanks"; Mirna is among the latter.

When she returned this afternoon, Mirna told me, "I no longer have any reason to spend my life behind machinery. My mother and Vesna are both dead. You're on your own. Yara is old enough to take care of herself, and if she's not, Zdenek as well as Jasna will surely both be cautious enough to remain out of prison and be able to help her. Certainly Zdenek will; old as he is, he loves sheer survival more than any of the rest of us."

Between Mirna's and Zdenek's present attitudes, I know I'll choose Mirna's "idiotic recklessness." The only time I sought "survival" within the confines of the police capitalism about to be reimposed was immediately after Mirna and I were married. It was then that Titus helped me find three jobs. That period ended with the Magarna rising. After my release eight years later, the thought of suicide appealed to me more than the thought of resuming that kind of life. Yara's "recklessness" brought me as well as Mirna back to life. Yara's demonstration for her fired teacher showed me that the possibility of rebellion had not been suppressed, and it also revived Mirna's desires, Mirna embraced both Yara and me; she was as excited by the evidence of "devilry" in Yara as by the friendship that formed between Yara and me on that day. For me the impossible rebellion, for Mirna the impossible passion, had become possible again. Mirna wanted me for herself — as her brother; she wanted me even more for Yara. But her passion for vicarious incest remained "quiet," buried far below the surface, and when the police official came to our house because Ninovo had reported me as the instigator of Yara's demonstration, Mirna reverted to silence. Unable to trust me unreservedly, and afraid of Mirna's moods, Yara sought her allies elsewhere, with her school friends Julia and Slobodan. It was with them she played her first "love games" in the attic of Julia's house. The games were based mainly on gossip they learned from the "popular press": apparently their favorite game was about the boss of Julia's father, bank director Kren. Yara told me Slobodan played Kren, Yara played Vera, and Julia played the unknown lover. Sometime after Ninovo reported me to the police, the three of them, together with a university friend of Julia's, placed two large snakes in Ninovo's house. That was why he had disappeared. Yara wasn't the only one who discovered "allies" after that first demonstration. I discovered my first "ally" in Yara, and this led me to seek others. I became curious about Luisa, and about you and Sabina. Mirna remembered your address. I also learned that the carton plant was in the process of change. I found the same spirit there that I had found in Yara after her demonstration. An epoch seemed to have ended. It now seems that we've only had a brief "vacation." But I can no longer go back to "work." Ever since Jan and I were arrested at the steel plant twelve years ago I've acquiesced to the requirements of the social order only under compulsion, namely in prison. I know I will not return to the carton plant tomorrow or next week and submit to the orders of police-appointed managers, union bureaucrats or foremen. "Instinctive rebellion," Titus called it. He's right. I don't have the instincts of ants or bees; I can't function in a hive. My instincts are similar to Jan's and Manuel's instincts, and I finally know that. I finally know it's not the productive forces that are fettered but the human beings. By continuing to reproduce them, we're depriving ourselves of the possibility to develop, we're expropriating ourselves of our human qualities, we're becoming tanks. Zdenek seems to feel that by submitting to the repressive routine, we can at least survive; then our potentialities can reemerge when another opportunity arises. I don't know if I ever agreed with such an outlook; I certainly don't now. With that outlook one could justify returning to any job, even the job of driving a tank or carrying a rifle for an invading army. In the act of keeping myself alive for the next chance I would destroy those who are grasping for life right now. I see no reason to collaborate with the ruling order at any time, under any circumstances —

:||||||||:

There are tanks in the street. I didn't get this letter in the mail yesterday. Jasna came late last night; she was almost hysterical. I hadn't seen her since the "celebration."

"I've hardly slept since then," she told me. "I'm still attached to him, Yarostan. I can't help it. I had known many of those things before, and I hadn't turned against him because of them. And even if I hadn't known any of it, I can't just wipe out a lifelong friendship in a few hours! I've admired him for twenty-five years! I wanted so much to provide him with comradeship, to end his isolation! Whatever he did in the past, I know he was sincere in wanting comrades today, and I know he's unambiguously opposed to the coming invasion. He was always sympathetic to the most radical workers —"

"Provided they carried the correct historical project," I reminded her.

"Even that might have changed," she insisted. "I've been thinking about nothing else day and night. This afternoon, as soon as I heard about the invasion, I went to the trade union building. I wanted to tell him I was still his friend. But he wasn't in. A secretary told me this was his first absence in years. I went to his room. I love him, Yarostan! Everything that's come out hasn't destroyed my love. I listened at his door but heard nothing. I asked the building guard and his neighbors if they had seen him, but none of them had. I waited at his door until now. I can't tell you what I fear! He was, after all, a human being and not a dog!"

Jasna and I rushed to Titus' apartment building. It was past midnight. The front entrance was closed; we rang the building guard's bell. Jasna told him she had left her purse, with her identification card inside, in Titus' room. We told him Titus had mysteriously vanished and asked him to accompany us to Titus' room for the purse. He recognized Jasna and gave us the key to the room, excusing himself for not accompanying us; he was in his bedclothes.

Titus Zabran was dead. He had shot himself through the head. There were no explanatory papers or notes in his modest room. I had never seen his room before. It's true that he derived no personal benefit from his political commitment to the proletariat's health — within the limits of presently available knowledge, like Vesna's doctors. There was a bed, a table, a bookshelf and a record player that was still turning; he had apparently been listening to Don Giovanni, an opera by Mozart. In the bookshelf I recognized the two books he had lent me when he'd visited me in prison: The Brothers Karamazov and The Castle. The walls of the room were bare.

Jasna collapsed in my arms. I left the record player turning, closed Titus' door quietly, supported Jasna to the building entrance, and slipped the key under the building guard's door. Jasna revived in the fresh air as we walked to the taxi stand by the trade union council building. She told me she wasn't able to return to her house alone. I asked the driver to take us to my house.

Jasna and I spent the night together. She's waiting for me now. There's been no sign of Mirna or Yara or Irena or Julia. Zdenek hasn't come again. We're going to try to find them, and join them. Jasna isn't crying this morning. The despair comes from the thought that the tanks cannot be superseded. Jasna is smiling, beautiful and brave. I've been on the side of repression and death, including Vesna's, for too long. If the "joyless drudgery" is reimposed, I will not be among those who reproduce it.

I doubt that this letter will reach you; I can no longer drop it in a mail box. If it does reach you, please accept my apology for attitudes which reflected twenty years of ignorance.

Jasna sends her love, to all of you. So do I.

Yarostan.

Sophia's last letter

ear Yarostan,
I gagged as I read about Zabran's self-exposure and suicide. On the surface some kind of monster died, a monster that left so many corpses in its train. I was horrified when I recognized the monster in myself and in those closest to me, those who gave my life its only meaning and goal, those who helped define my life's search. My very dreams were contaminated by the monstrosity he stood for: the will to impose mental constructs on living people — which as Zdenek so perceptively pointed out can only be done by means of "historically available" instruments: guns, tanks, police and armies.

You once pointed to a split in my life, the split between my "academic and journalistic world" and the "world of Sabina and the garage." You included yourself in the latter world. I think the line you drew has to be re-drawn. I think the split was between the world of those who, like Ted, Jan and Mirna, sought to realize their own potentialities among others realizing theirs, and the world of those who, like Luisa and Daman and Titus Zabran, sought to fit human beings into what Sabina called a crystal palace, which in practice was always the same regimented barracks, the hive you've rejected. Like Sabina, and like me, you had a foot in both worlds. Don't tell yourself you're the only one whose past commitments were clarified by the exposure and the suicide. My life project, my "community," also died in that modest, barely furnished room.

I responded to your letter the same way I had responded to our emigration twenty years ago. I stared at the walls of my room. But there's a difference. At that time I still had my illusions: the community Luisa had experienced with Nachalo and on the barricades, the community that I had myself experienced with you. At that time I saw something when I looked at the blank walls; when I left my room I had something to look for and I found it, or at least approximations to it, with Ron, on the newspaper staff, in Hugh's project house. You weren't able to convince me that my commitment rested on rot, that my "community" had been the opposite of community at its very origin, that my adoration of you was an alibi for my inactivity.

I'm writing this letter as much for myself as for you; I don't really expect it to reach you. I read about the tanks in the newspapers, two or three days before your letter came. Something snapped inside me. I knew, even before your letter came, that I had a connection with those tanks. Part of my life, too, had been devoted to the service of a "historical class" that was going to realize a great "purpose." Zdenek is so right. I never asked myself what instruments were going to realize my goal. I told myself we, all of us, by ourselves and on our own, were going to realize it. But I obviously didn't believe that, not in practice, since I never did anything by myself and on my own. My goal wasn't something I did but something I served, and in that sense I was Titus Zabran's daughter and the sister of the tank drivers. Who and what carried my project since I and those around me obviously didn't? Where was the power to realize it since it wasn't in me? I never dreamed of imposing my goal with a tank or a gun, but apparently Titus didn't either. And since the great task of history required the elimination of fetters, heads obviously had to roll, categories of human beings had to be liquidated. He had the courage to kill himself. I wonder if he finally knew what it had all led to: the endless corridors with rooms full of breathing mummies, the paved highways with speeding vehicles whose passengers' potentialities could no longer be distinguished from those of their vehicles.

I trembled the day I walked home with the newspaper announcing the invasion in enormous headlines. The people I passed in the street, even those with newspapers under their arms, walked by me calmly, as if nothing was wrong, as if nothing had happened, as if everything was exactly as it should be. And I saw myself in those people. If I hadn't been exchanging letters with you for the past months, I would have reacted to those headlines the same way they did. And I realized there's no such entity as a human species, or rather that it doesn't recognize itself as such; it possesses no faculty of community. Either it never had such a faculty or it lost it. The beings I was among, including me, were not species-beings but closed compartments. Maybe what we've just experienced on both sides of the world shows that the faculty of species-being is something still to be created, and that it's not the abstract "community" I've always envisioned but something very concrete, as concrete as Mirna's "excursions." Maybe it's nothing but the willingness to touch, feel, look at and listen to each other. Maybe there simply weren't enough people on excursions, there weren't enough to reach the workers in the tanks. Maybe that's why the workers in the tanks couldn't know that the people at whom they aimed their guns were the same as themselves, or had been the same until they began to take excursions. The workers in the tanks were in no way different from the people I passed in the street, from you and me during "normal" times: they were merely workers doing their jobs, each with his own repressed "demon," each with the same reason to rebel as the people they repressed. And no doubt each of them had rebelled at one or another time, and each had been repressed, always by others who had also rebelled at some other time. I was always one of those others. However insignificant my contributions, they were no less significant than the contributions of a single soldier. I had responded with righteous indignation to your first letter, to your suggestion that prisoners had anything in common with their guards. I no longer have trouble imagining myself, if not as a soldier in a tank, at least as a teacher who helped shape the intellectual horizon of people who became soldiers in tanks. All I have to do is to ask myself what I was doing when others, elsewhere, were rebelling and when they were repressed. All I have to do is ask myself what I'm doing right now, when Mirna and Yara are confronting tanks with their bare hands!

At least I think I'm no longer on the side of the tanks, the side of those who would guide their comrades toward the revealed or "scientific" goal of history. At least I've learned that humanity's "historical goals" are the fantasies of megalomaniacs, that the proletariat's "organizations" are trains driven by would-be directors, and that weapons are history's only means for imposing such "projects" on living human individuals. Those are the "lessons" I've drawn from my correspondence with you, and they're awful lessons. My mother was the agent of my father's murderers. Was it to spare my sensitivity one more time that you didn't draw that knot? Sabina and I drew it as soon as your letter arrived.

Right after we read your letter Sabina had me reread the letters in which you had told me what you had learned from Manuel during your first prison term. When she had told me that Nachalo and Margarita had to be dead before they could be made useful to Luisa's organization, she had been much closer to the truth than even she had suspected. She combined Manuel's accounts with everything she had learned from Alberts; her reconstruction of the sequence of events is almost beyond belief.

On the day of the barricades the fascist army was definitively defeated in the city. It then made some advances in rural regions; one of the places where it met resistance was the village Manuel described. "This village became 'the front' for Luisa and the rest of the union apparatus, and also to fighters like Manuel and Nachalo," Sabina suggested. "For Nachalo and Manuel it was an extension of the battle on the barricades, and they went there, not as a separate armed force, but as an extension of the armed population that had fought on the barricades. But to the apparatus this 'front' immediately had a different meaning. First of all it was far away from the city and quickly became almost a mythical place. And secondly, as far as the union apparatus was concerned the revolution was over in the streets of the city and in the factories. The union had taken over production, transportation and distribution, and that was that; it was time to resume the normal activity of daily life. The front was for those whose blood was still hot and whose organs were still ungratified, and it was far away from the city. To the new managers of production, these fighters were only in the way; they were infinitely more useful as dead heroes who had died for the glory of the living union bosses than as living saboteurs, agitators and terrorists. The union leaders were relieved to send them off to fight 'the revolution' with official flag-waving. Alberts, who wasn't an agitator but was shamed by Margarita's premature death, was drawn to the mythical front only when it became something he could understand: the central focus of a state apparatus and an official war machine. He had come to offer the revolution everything science could provide, and he understood that these offerings could be efficiently used only in terms of their own rules: logically, hierarchically, militarily. He rightly recognized Zabran as the embodiment of applied science and was drawn to enlist in that replacement of the population's armed might, the popular army."

Sabina and I figured out that apparently Alberts and Zabran actually did "join Nachalo" at the front, as Luisa told me. Alberts had told Sabina he had served in the firing squad that murdered eight "infiltrators," and Zabran told you they were together from the moment Alberts enlisted. Just before the "infiltrators" were killed, one of them shouted, "Next time the people rise they'll turn on the red butchers first." Zabran told you he never "met" Nachalo. Apparently Alberts told him who had shouted that statement after Nachalo was dead. When Alberts returned from the front, he told Luisa that Nachalo had been a "defector" because he had called his "comrades" red butchers before they murdered him. Luisa and Zabran then proceeded to make the murdered man useful to their "movement." Zabran "enlisted" the dead man to his cause; the murderer justified his crime wearing his victim's mantle. The Church burned people and later made them saints, covering its repressive deeds with the rebels' own mantles. Luisa and her union placed the cape of her dead lover on his murderer and enlisted the dead man's comrades to his murderers' cause, helping the murderer shine with the life and deeds of his victim, transforming an assassin into a "revolutionary."

Sabina also figured out Glavni was wrong when he assumed that Zabran's later "pacifism" was some kind of moral attitude. On the contrary, it grew out of his "scientific" outlook. The death of Nachalo did not put an end to Nachalo's influence. Therefore the firing squad is not an effective instrument for dealing with questions of consciousness; it wipes out the patient without wiping out the disease. And since the proletariat's only quality was its "historical interest," the qualities Jan Sedlak possessed must have come "from abroad." They were a virus which Luisa carried in spite of herself, and with which she infected Jan and you, and through both of you the entire production group, and presumably also Mirna, who then infected Yara. "But his understanding had a gross flaw at its core," Sabina said. "He didn't understand what Mirna and Yara understand. The negating spirit isn't imported; the desire for freedom doesn't come from abroad. It isn't carried or transmitted. It's inherent in being human. It's already there. What is carried and imported is the repression of that desire. The only 'carriers' in the carton plant were Titus and Luisa. It wasn't Nachalo that hounded Zabran to his death, but Zabran's own gross error." Sabina was referring to the opera Zabran apparently listened to before he shot himself. When you repeated Nachalo's last statement to him, he must have thought my dead father's spirit had come to Jasna's celebration to hound his murderer.

Your letter came three weeks ago but I postponed answering it. I suppose the censorship has been reimposed together with the rest of the police apparatus, and I don't want to set off another sequence of events similar to the one set off by the letter

I sent at the time of the Magarna rising. Sabina reminded me that it wasn't my letter itself, but the "historically informed" intervention of Titus Zabran, that caused your earlier arrests, and she doubts if anyone will analyze what is "historically progressive" and what "dangerous" in the content of my present letter. But I couldn't have imagined anyone would have done that to my earlier letter either. Initially I thought of writing you a short, innocuous note, just to find out if you and your comrades were well, but I wasn't able to compose such a note. And the thought of receiving a similar note from you, the thought of both of us writing no longer for each other but for a censor, repelled me so much that I dropped the idea. If we can no longer communicate our lives, our innermost thoughts and our desires to each other, I think I'd prefer not to continue our correspondence; that sort of communication would be unbearable to me. It would be like a conversation with an intimate friend who'd had part of his brain surgically removed; I would infinitely prefer silence to letters in which you told me about yesterday's weather. So I decided to write you as uninhibitedly as I would have if the tanks hadn't invaded. There's so much I want to tell you, not only about what we shared, but about all that's happened to me since I last wrote you, and about what Sabina and I learned during the past few weeks.

During the week after my argument with Luisa, Ted got his car out of the police pound, and he wanted to return to the print shop and to his apartment to clean up the mess. He was upset that Tina still hadn't turned up; he told me again how impossible the print shop would have been without Tina. I obviously wasn't up to doing what Tina had done there; I also shared Sabina's fear that Ted would be shot by the police if he returned to the print shop. I convinced him to stay away from there, but he became increasingly restless. I suggested the three of us explore the possibility of launching a project but the only activity that interested him at all was to "help out" with that press Luisa had showed him at the repression committee office. So the Sunday after my confrontation with Luisa, I went back to that office with Ted. I disregarded everything and everyone in the committee office and accompanied Ted directly to the "press room." I became Ted's apprentice. We learned when the office would be open on weekdays the following week, and we went back every day. Ted got the press repaired and he, or rather we, started printing. I found it extremely challenging; Ted let me do every operation as soon as I learned how.

I wasn't only Ted's apprentice. I realized that the jealousy I'd felt when I saw Luisa bent over him was real. At first I thought I felt guilty toward Ted because of how grossly I had treated him at the garage. But when I became his apprentice, and then his "fellow printer," I knew that my feeling toward him was neither guilt nor pity. There's something of Ron in Ted — something Zabran had immediately recognized in that letter I sent you twelve years ago. It's that "instinctive" rejection of all official activity. There's also something in Ted that I've never encountered before: a certain modesty that seems to border on an "inferiority feeling," though that term bothers me. He's almost grateful to those who treat him as an equal. He has pride in his work, in his deeds, but not in his person; he expects others to respond to him solely on the basis of what he contributes, not on the basis of merely being there; he doesn't think himself wonderful.

A confrontation with Art Sinich put an end to our activity in the repression committee. It was a very brief confrontation. Art came into the press room while Ted was running some forms off the press. Art patted Ted on the back and told him, "You people are really the salt of the earth!"

Ted exclaimed, "Shit!" He turned off the press and told Art angrily, "What do you mean 'you people,' mister? There are just two people at this press, just Sophie and me!"

"You racist bigot!" I shouted at Art. "You fascist! Don't you know what your mouth is full of?"

Art didn't show the slightest awareness that he knew. Ted and I walked out. At home Ted told me, "It's no good, Sophie. It's not just Art; it's all over their walls and in their leaflets. All they're into is skin color. Not Luisa, but most of the others. Skin color is all they see. I've never worked near someone who looked at me as a color. I don't like it. He knows all about me before I ever start doing anything. I'm 'you people'; I'm like a tin can with a label, and I'm the same as all the cans with that label."

Ted was also angry at me when he said this, and he was right. He had trusted me not to introduce him into that type of environment, or at least to warn him. But I hadn't recognized it, and I had never imagined Luisa or Daman would ever collaborate with racists. Ted didn't remain angry with me; he knows that my life has been as shielded as his. Somehow both of us and all the people we've known have rarely had contact with any form of racism in a society where canning and labeling is the central activity. Art had exposed himself to me before, but I hadn't responded. As soon as Ted responded, I was ashamed I'd ever had anything to do with Art. How sickeningly ironic it is that the most revolting trait of this society should turn up as the "political program" of self-styled "radicals." I've never been near anyone like Art either. Even the customers in Tissie's and Sabina's bar didn't express such attitudes. Art had made himself perfectly clear to me the last time I'd talked to him, when I'd treated him to lunch; he had made it clear that human beings didn't exist for him; only cans with labels. I remembered the horror I'd felt when he'd described how he saw the function of his group: "We aim to coordinate the activities of organizations expressing the will of national and racial minorities." I shuddered. Ted and I haven't ever returned to the repression office.

I was even more upset by something that happened a few days after our last visit to the repression committee. I answered the phone. It was Tina. I got all excited. "Tina, where are you? What happened to you?" I shouted.

Tina said to me, in the voice of a robot, "I'm with friends. I'd like to talk to Ted."

I told her, "We've all been nervous about you. When we saw the print shop wrecked, we thought the worst things might have happened to you. Are you with Pat?"

"Neither of us were in the print shop when it was attacked," she told me. "Our group withdrew before the attack, when the print shop was taken over by counter-revolutionary agents. I'd like to talk to Ted."

I gave Ted the receiver. In answer to one of Tina's questions, he told her he intended to start printing again — with me. His summary of the rest of the conversation made it seem awful. "Something must have happened to her," he told Sabina and me; "she never sounded like that before. She and Pat and their friends want to visit us in a few days. She talked about her group as if it was a secret gang of some sort. She asked me something about 'continuing the coherent practice in which you were engaged before incoherent agents of repression recuperated you.' Then she asked if I was willing to separate myself from 'ideologues whose perspectives you don't share.' I think it's time we opened up that print shop again, but the way Tina sounded, I don't know; I'm worried. I don't want to become part of something I don't understand. I think Tina has become a tool, the way Tissie became Seth's tool."

Sabina emphatically stated, "It's impossible for Tina to have become a tool."

The day after Tina's call, Ted was restless again. He told me, "I think Sabina is wrong; I don't think the cops are out there waiting for me. But I don't know if I can get that place going again without Tina. It's her print shop, not mine."

I told him, "You're too modest, Ted. You've told me that before, but I saw that it wasn't quite true."

He insisted, "It's she who really got the place together; she brought material and even some equipment from other shops, she taught me how to use it all, or at least how they used it in the shops where she worked. Sure, I can use it all now, but without Tina the point seems to be gone."

"Couldn't I do some of the things Tina did?" I asked him.

"You mean you'd actually go there and spend time learning —"

"I'd like to very much, if you'd let me," I told him. "I enjoyed the few days we worked together last week more than I've enjoyed anything since I was Tina's apprentice in the garage."

"You weren't doing that just because you felt sorry for me?" he asked.

I blushed and asked him, "Did you spend all those days showing me how to run a press only because you pitied my abysmal ignorance about machines? Don't you consider me stupid for having forgotten everything Tina taught me?"

"When do you want to start?" he asked me.

I suggested we wait until Tina's visit, to see if Tina might be willing to return to the print shop in spite of her new commitments. And in any case I intended to spend the following day with Minnie.

Minnie had called me several days earlier to tell me she had located Hugh. "He's teaching at a suburban college," she'd told me, "and guess what? He's married to Bess! Can you imagine?" Bess had been his managing editor on the university newspaper staff; I've always remembered her for the cowardly editorial she wrote after we were thrown off the paper, and for the fact that she had collaborated with the university-appointed staff. "Hugh was very curt on the phone," Minnie had told me. "For a second I thought he didn't remember either of us. When I asked if we could get together with him, he told me he was extremely busy. 'I have a free hour between two and three next Thursday,' was the way he invited us. I hope you're not mad at me for accepting such a half-hearted invitation." I assured her I wasn't mad.

Sabina opened the door when Minnie came for me. Sabina amazed me by her courtesy. "I was deeply moved when Sophia told me how Alec died," she told Minnie. "I was surprised to learn I had played such a significant role in his life. I honestly regret the fact that my 'winning' that argument cost Alec his life; when I learned that, I felt like Death as she's depicted in medieval paintings."

Minnie was equally courteous. "You're a remarkable woman, Sabina. You made at least as great an impression on me as you did on Alec."

While Minnie drove me to the suburb where the college is located, we talked about Hugh. Minnie hadn't seen him since he'd carried me out of the garage the day Seth had pointed his gun at them. I hadn't seen him since the night when I'd finally found him, at the "project house," the night when he begged me not to burden his new friends with my "rot." Neither of us had seen Bess since the last meeting of the newspaper staff, the day before the funeral procession, and neither of us had known what had happened to her after the semester she'd spent on the administration staff.

We drove up to a suburban mansion. Two cars were parked in the driveway, both new; there were toys in the front yard. I had seen such houses before, but I had never been inside one.

Bess answered the door. If I hadn't been expecting to see her, I'd never have recognized her. Apparently she thought the same thing about us. She even treated us as people she'd never known. "Please come in. My husband will be right with you. He's on the phone."

I almost laughed when I asked, "Bess, don't you recognize us?"

My desire to laugh vanished when she said, "Yes, I recognize you, Miss Nachalo," and left the room.

Minnie whispered to me, "It looks like she was upset by his inviting us here."

Minnie and I sat down awkwardly on a cloth-covered sofa in an expensively furnished living room. We heard children playing upstairs; they had apparently been told not to look in on the disreputable guests. Minnie looked at her watch and whispered, "I wonder if he counts his phone conversation as part of the hour?"

Hugh finally entered. Minnie and I both rose; we'd never have risen for a university president. Hugh was dressed in an expensive "sport" suit; he looked and acted very important; he shook hands with each of us in a businesslike manner. "Well, what a surprise! Minnie and Sophie! May I ask the purpose of your visit?"

I couldn't believe his manner, or his words; I was almost in tears. "Just to see you!" I told him.

"Why yes, of course," he said. "Would you both like something to drink?"

Minnie told him, "Just coffee." I nodded.

Hugh walked toward the door through which Bess had left and said, "Honey, would you mind preparing some coffee for our guests?" The phone rang. He told us, "Please excuse me," and left through the door he had come in from.

Bess came in with a tray that had two cups of coffee on it, as well as spoons, cream and sugar. I remembered the day when the university president had brought Alec and me coffee, but hadn't brought any for himself. Bess set the tray down and left. I couldn't hold back my tears.

Hugh returned and apologized for the interruption.

"It's a gorgeous house," Minnie told him. "Have you lived here long?"

Hugh answered, "Yes, ever since I started teaching — that'll be six years now." I calculated that if he'd spent three years in graduate school before he started to teach, then he must have enrolled only a few weeks after I had seen him in the "project house."

Minnie asked, "How old are your children?"

"The oldest is seven, the youngest is five," he told her. So the oldest was born only two years after I had thought he had committed his life to "the people rising from below," only two years after I had thought I had found someone who resembled you. He didn't ask either of us any questions. He seemed to be waiting for us to go back out of his suburban life.

Minnie asked, "Hugh — may I call you that? — why is Bess so hostile toward us?"

Hugh cleared his throat; he seemed embarrassed. "My wife is convinced that your visit is motivated —"

I almost choked as I asked, "Your wife, Hugh? Don't you remember we knew her, we worked together?"

He seemed uneasy. "Why yes, of course. Bess and I had a slight disagreement. My wife was — Bess was convinced your visit had an ulterior motive, such as raising money for one or another political cause. Naturally I made no assumptions —" The phone rang again. He almost seemed relieved as he ran out saying, "Please excuse me —"

I felt vomit rushing to my mouth. I covered my mouth with my hand and pulled Minnie out of the "gorgeous" living room, out of the suburban house to the street, where I vomited. Minnie held me to keep me from falling. No one came out of the house. The front door closed.

Minnie started to pull me back toward the house so I could lie down. I shook my head and pulled Minnie toward her car. Minnie said angrily, "They'll at least give you a wet towel so you can wipe yourself!"

I begged, "Please take me away from here, Minnie." I burst out crying inside the car. I lay down across the front seat with my head on Minnie's lap.

Minnie drove away from Hugh's house and parked near a gas station a few blocks away. She patted my head consolingly and told me, "I don't understand, Sophie. He's neither the first nor the last to go that way. After all, this is what they call 'Making good.' It's what this society is all about. I admit he was terribly rude, and Bess was nothing less than a beast. But they never were the warmest of people, either of them. What did you expect to find out here? I wasn't surprised by what we saw: the happy two-car family with two and a half children and the rest of it. How well did you know him, anyway?"

"I didn't know him at all," I admitted. I sat up and worked myself into a fury when Art's abysmally stupid comment about the "salt of the earth" flashed through my mind. I told Minnie, "I saw him for a few seconds in that 'project house' near the garage. He was so beautiful then, Minnie! The person we just saw wasn't anyone I ever knew!"

"The project house!" she shouted. "You're a real nut, you know that Sophie? You would be the one to admire his project house! It was directly inspired by you!" Then she got out of the car saying, "Come on, I'll walk you to the station so you can wash up."

I asked her, "What do you mean that I inspired him?"

She told me, "Hugh was all concern when you disappeared from the co-op dorm, after those frat boys scattered the *Omissions* we were distributing. I think I'm the one who set off a chain reaction. I called Hugh and told him you'd been evicted from the co-op because you'd helped distribute *Omissions*, and I got exactly the response I wanted, I got my revenge for our exclusion. Hugh became so concerned for you. So did Daman. They were all concern and guilt. Guilt about your exclusion, guilt about getting you and me pulled into the police station, guilt about your eviction, guilt about the fact that you were the one who'd gotten into most trouble for *Omissions* without even being a full participant."

When I returned from the gas station washroom, Minnie was having the attendants change the oil in her car. "I hope you don't mind if I have this done now," she told me; "I always have to wait so long in the city." While that was being done, we walked a block away from the gas station and sat down on a suburban lawn. She continued the story she'd started telling me. "The three of us had regular meetings, and either Daman or Hugh constantly called Alec to get news about you. Hugh's interest in the project house began after Alec's first visit to the garage. Alec told glorious stories of your having joined the underclass, about people pulling themselves up by the bootstraps. Hugh and Daman were both getting ready to start graduate school, and Alec shamed them; he already had a factory job; I was looking for a job at that time. Out of his sense of guilt, Hugh dropped all his plans for graduate school and took the great leap. He flew ostentatiously past Alec and me to a commitment as pure as yours seemed to be. He was a great admirer of Leo Tolstoy —"

"Hugh admired Tolstoy?" I asked.

"I thought everyone knew that!" Minnie exclaimed. "His leap corresponded to giving his lands to his serfs and moving in among them. But the first time the four of us visited you in the garage, he had already heard something to the effect that your selfless activity was somehow connected with narcotics and prostitution. It was right after that when he threw himself into that so-called project house. I don't know how much you knew about it, but such institutions were being started in those years by well-meaning people who thought the lower classes, if placed in a proper environment, would acquire the manners of the middle class. Before long corporations funded such places, and eventually the local police ran them so as to keep energetic youth off the street. For Hugh the project house was mainly a method for learning what role the garage and the bar played in that community. By the time we visited you in the garage the second time he'd had his fill of the lower classes, of life among the serfs, and of you. And he threw it all in your face! But you begged him to carry you out of the garage! Were you on drugs?"

I was crying again. I hugged Minnie and told her, "When I first learned you were a lawyer, my thoughts were: Turncoat! Opportunist! Please forgive me for thinking that, Minnie!"

"You really are a nut, Sophie," she told me. And I felt somewhat proud of myself when she told me that. I may not have filled my life in a way I can consider satisfactory, but the official model of "fulfillment" as exemplified by Hugh revolted me. That trip to the suburbs with Minnie was actually my only visit to the "official world" you once accused me of inhabiting. Daman has his flaws, but he's positively a rebel compared to that person we visited and his "wife." Hugh is indistinguishable from his role. I admired him once. But now I have to admit he has a lot in common with Titus Zabran: both devoted their lives to history and science by serving themselves and the State. To serve the State they had to suppress their own humanity; they then repressed in the world the humanity they had suppressed in themselves. I didn't learn just what kind of chemistry Hugh is involved with, but I'm sure Zdenek's analysis of Zabran fits Hugh like a glove. I also failed to learn what noble cause Hugh claims to serve while developing life-destroying chemicals, but having known Hugh I suspect that the cause he serves is at least as noble as the proletariat's historical project. And if Zabran's theoretical discoveries are continually misused because the social means for using them correctly haven't yet been developed, I'm sure Hugh's contributions to human happiness destroy even more lives for exactly the same reason. I suspect Alec was right: the only meaningful human activity is to destroy capitalism in all its manifestations, in every way possible. You've certainly taken Alec's attitude — all of you except Zdenek. I can only admire you; I can't say I envy you; I'm too much of a coward.

The same day Minnie and I went on our "outing" to the suburbs, Ted had gone to visit Tissie in the prison hospital. That night he was even more depressed from his visit than I was from mine. Tissie told him they weren't curing her but torturing her with "cures." But she didn't want Ted to see if she could be transferred elsewhere because she has friends in that hospital. She told him she thought she was dying and she wanted to see Sabina and me before she died.

The three of us went to that terrible hospital two days later. Tissie started crying the moment she was brought into the visiting room. She looked terrible — not quite as sickly as she'd looked nine years ago when I'd last seen her in the garage, but almost like the corpse of the person I had been with at the research center slightly over a month ago. "I won't ever get out of here again," she told us. "They've got it in for me this time. I had to tell you, all three of you, some things I kept inside during the short happy moment I just spent with you. I didn't want to spoil my life's only happy moment. But I don't have any reason to keep it inside any more, not in this misery. I'm the one that's responsible for the garage and the bar falling apart, and also for Jose's arrest and his death —"

Sabina told her, "You're just torturing yourself, Tissie —"

"I torture myself more by keeping it all inside, Sabina," Tissie said. "I've tortured myself with it long enough. I think I paid for what I did. Remember when I took you to the bar, Sophie? That first night you stayed with us? Seth asked me who you were, and he told me to get you working right away. He was afraid if you got used to staying around the garage you wouldn't ever want to work. I tried to take Tina too; Ted remembers that. But I didn't care about you not wanting to go again; I tried and that was all I could do for Seth. I got to like you, Sophie. When I saw you in Sabina's bed I was sure you were like Sabina and me. I was never hurt so bad as that night when you pushed me away from you. I was sure Jose had put you up to that, or Jose and Ted together. I was sure I was right when you moved in with Jose. He'd always hated me, and he hated the heroin as much as Ted did. I promised Seth I'd get you and Tina to the bar if he got rid of Jose and Ted. But everything I did backfired. When your friends came, they insulted Jose and got him to side with Seth, and Seth was sure they'd come to help Ted get rid of Vic and Seth. So he got rid of them all and you went with them, and instead of having you and Tina and Sabina to myself, I was stuck with Seth again. I was far gone when you left, Sophie. I thought Jose had planned that whole thing with your friends, and that his fight with Alec had been a fake. All I could think of was getting Jose out of there. I told Seth I'd heard Ted and Jose talking about killing him. I told him after Seth had pulled a gun on their friends, they knew that was the only way they could talk to Seth. I knew Ted could never even hold a gun in his hand, but Seth didn't know. He believed me. But he told me he was in a jam. He couldn't get rid of both because then there wouldn't be anyone left to keep the garage and the bar going. But he couldn't just get rid of Ted because Jose wouldn't ever stand for that, and he'd figure out who'd gotten rid of him. But if he got rid of Jose, he said, Ted wouldn't ever know, and he could get Ted to do Jose's contacting. 'And I know just how to get that sonofabitch,' Seth told me. He got Jose arrested by the state police; he knew the city police would never arrest him because they were paid off by Jose himself; they were the main contact he dealt with —"

Sabina asked, "Jose dealt directly with the police?"

Ted told Sabina, "From the very beginning; he even made the rounds with me once; just in case, he said. But the main thing he told me was, 'Don't ever tell Sabina; she'd have a fit if she knew we bought protection.'"

Tissie continued, "When Jose was gone — that was when I thought you and I could go it alone, Sabina. I'd have quit taking heroin if you'd gotten rid of all the rest of them except Tina. Maybe Vic overheard me talking to you about that. However he learned about it, Seth acted on my idea much faster than you did, and he got rid of you and Tina. I wanted to go with you, but Seth was going to stop supplying me if I moved out. 'You should have thought of that when you wanted women to run this place; it's Sabina or heroin,' he told me. I stayed with the heroin. When you were gone, Seth and Vic laughed at me; 'women running this place would have run it straight into the ground,' they said. Right after that Seth and Vic ran it straight into the ground. It's because of me that Seth got rid of you and Tina —"

"No it's not, Tissie," Ted objected. "I'm the one who got Seth to get rid of Sabina; I wanted Tina out of there before Seth could do anything to her. I thought when Jose returned you'd want to leave too —"

"I knew you were just waiting for Jose to return; I thought you and Jose had made all my plans backfire on me. Sabina, after you and Tina left, I fell apart completely. Every day was a nightmare from which I never woke. Ted kept saying, 'It'll all be better when Jose returns,' but all my hatred got concentrated on Jose. I blamed him for everything Seth had done. On the day Jose was released, Ted told me he was driving to the state prison to pick him up. They both came back to the bar and argued with me; I thought they were trying to separate me from the heroin. I left them in the bar and walked back to the house. I called the state police, told them about this dope house and gave them the address. Then I went to sleep. Next thing I knew Seth was running all over the house screaming, 'Where are you, you sonofabitch?' He shook me and asked me where Jose was. I told him Jose was back in prison. He beat me and called me a liar. He said he and Vic saw Jose and Ted leave the bar. Seth and Vic went in to see if Jose had done anything in there; Seth thought maybe Jose knew who'd got him in jail. They weren't in there five minutes before the police rushed in and started wrecking; Seth got out by the back door, but they arrested Vic. Then Seth thought for sure Jose knew what had got him in jail, and he thought Jose was doing the same thing to him, he thought Jose had called the police. After he beat me, he figured out Jose must have gone with Ted; Seth knew about Ted's place because he'd had Vic follow Ted there. Ted, you told me Jose went down to the car to get more of his things. I bet that's when Seth shot him. That was when they got me too. Vic must have given them the address of the garage, because

Seth hadn't been gone for five minutes before the police were wrecking the garage looking for dope and dragging me out. I knew exactly how Jose died as soon as they questioned me about it. But last year, when you got me released, Ted, I learned for sure that it was Seth who killed Jose."

"Did you run into someone who saw him do it?" Ted asked her.

"No, Ted. I ran into Seth," Tissie told Ted. Then she told me, "Ted got me released last year, just for a few weeks. I was getting a lot better; I liked working around the print shop with Ted and Tina, and best of all I liked Sabina's visits. I even went out alone twice to visit girls I'd worked with in the bar. I wanted to see you too, Sophie, but not when Tina and Sabina told me you were having an affair with this professor. Then the riot broke out a few blocks from Ted's house. I heard about it over the T.V. Ted wasn't home, and Sabina and Tina hadn't come over yet. I went out and ran into a girl friend I'd known at the bar. We took part in the looting and loved it; we walked to Ted's place with armfuls of presents for Sabina and Tina, but there still wasn't anyone there. This was something I wanted to share with Sabina. The two of us went out again and ran into police and soldiers. Someone told us they were shooting people as if they were dogs with rabies. We watched some cops beat a couple of kids, just kept beating and kicking them until they bled. I got sick all over, I couldn't take it, my whole body was shaking, I thought I was dying. The woman I was with knew where Seth was. He was dealing from a bar right in the middle of the riot section. I went back to Ted's and took all the money I could find downstairs and upstairs. She didn't want to come, so I went to that bar by myself. The proprietor wouldn't let me in. I shouted Seth's name, but the man said there was no Seth there. It turned out he'd changed his name. But he recognized me and let me in. I lay down on the floor and begged him for a shot, but he wouldn't give me one. I showed him all Ted's money, but he still refused. He was trying to hide everything under false floors; he knew the place was about to be raided. I knew how I could threaten him. I told him, 'In prison they asked me who killed Jose.' That made him mad. 'Shut your god damned mouth,' he told me. 'Jose squealed, he got them to close everything down, boarded up, destroyed; he got you and Vic in jail. I could kill you now, Tissie, and no one would ever know you weren't shot by the police; they'll be here any minute.' But then he took the money and gave me the heroin. I didn't tell him it wasn't Jose but me who squealed, who got the bar and garage boarded up. I left the bar and there was this huge crowd outside shouting about rats that exploited the community. I tried to shove my way through but I probably fainted because someone carried me to an alley. Maybe I didn't faint; that whole crowd seemed to disappear and there was an awful silence. I heard what sounded like machine guns; I was sure they got Seth —"

"Tissie, that was Alec!" I shouted hysterically. I told her Alec and his friend Carmen must have killed Seth just before they both got gunned down. Tissie didn't know what I was talking about, since I couldn't have known anything about that; I was having an affair with a professor. And she was right. I was worlds away from

Tissie when all that happened. Sabina and Tina had both known there hadn't been any point in telling me Tissie had been released and was at Ted's; they'd both known I was still reacting to Ted and the garage as a trauma. Tissie's release would have had no more meaning to me than Alec's intention to rid the community of "rats." Until the riot I had been staying in Daman's apartment two days a week. Right after the riot I was busy getting fired from my academic post and breaking up with Daman. Tissie and I would have been as useless to each other then as we were in the guest room of that prison hospital. We were too much like each other. We were equally dependent on others to give direction to our lives, and we couldn't have filled each other's gaps because each craved for what the other couldn't offer. Tissie wanted a woman's total love and care; I wanted a ready-made project into which I could passively insert myself. I had learned that when I'd lain with Tissie in the forest to which she'd taken me from the research center; I had looked into her eyes as into a mirror; in those eyes I hadn't seen a loved one, but a variant of myself; I knew then I had nothing to give Tissie. I knew we were both equally unwilling to do what Sabina, Tina and Ted did so easily: define and launch our own projects, join others as active, projecting individuals and not as passive outsiders. The lack of a self-defined project left a vacuum in both of us; Tissie filled it with heroin; I filled it by staring at blank walls. Although surrounded for most of our lives by people who've defined the content of their lives on their own, we've both submitted to the degradation of letting those who bought us define us, Tissie as a prostitute and I as a college teacher. During the year after the riot I no longer had an alibi for my lack of a project. I didn't have a job; I wasn't waiting for anyone to be released from prison. I had a lot of energy, but I drifted. I don't want to insult Jasna, but books were my heroin. On cold or rainy days I stayed home and read; on sunny days I took walks and read. I did have something Tissie hadn't ever picked up. That was my "political radicalism," the dreams that have turned out to be such grand illusions. It didn't amount to much in any case, since it was completely locked up somewhere in my mind. I wasn't able to use it to define a project, to define my activity: my "consciousness" and my behavior had absolutely nothing to do with each other. My first project during that entire year was to formulate an answer to your first letter. I was pulled out of my inertia by you, or I should say by "Yarostan," with whom I had shared the activity that became the prototype for all the projects I sought later. Ironically, you forced me to defend my "first project" from your own attacks. And without my being altogether aware of it, you thus revived the only project that had ever been altogether my own: my unfinished novel about the community of independent human beings like the ones in Luisa's stories and like the ones I had known during the days I spent with you. I pulled out manuscripts that had been in a drawer for ten years and I reread them. I started doing what I think Sabina has been doing since Jose died. I started reevaluating the significance of my own life, or rather discovering it for the first time. But I didn't get very far before I acquired a new alibi. Only four or five days after your first letter came, I got a call from Daman;

I hadn't heard from him for almost a year. There was an opening in a "community college" — think of that! — "community" was precisely what I had been seeking for twenty years! It was only a part-time job; I taught an evening course; but it was enough of an academic position to make me Daman's "colleague" again. He became positively friendly and forgot all about my faulty "sense of timing," but I couldn't dream of patching up the relationship that had ended with the riot, and Daman undoubtedly couldn't either. After the way I'd been fired and the way Daman had responded to it, I couldn't count on his support any more than he could count on my "good sense." After a few months on my new job I convinced Daman that I didn't only have a miserable sense of timing, but that I had no sense of "reality" whatever; I was an outright psychopath. Ever since then Daman has been "helping" me, and I'm moved by his attachment to me; to Daman I became a person who needed "help," but what I needed wasn't anything he was able to provide.

On our way home from the prison hospital in Ted's car, Sabina sat between Ted and me. She stared directly in front of her as if she were frozen, tears ran down her cheek. She was probably weighing her responsibility for Jose, for Tissie, for Alec. I bit my finger to keep from bursting out crying. I wanted to tell her, "Cry on me, little gypsy; it's all the help I can give you." But Sabina doesn't need that kind of help from me. By the time we got home her eyes were dry and she was ready to plunge the remaining knives into her bosom. She dug into Ted as soon as the front door was closed. "Just exactly what was it that you weren't ever supposed to tell Sabina?"

Ted started to walk away, telling her sadly, "I shouldn't ever have brought it up. I thought Tissie was going to tell it all and make it sound ten times worse than it was. Jose asked me never to tell you, and I kept my word —"

Sabina grabbed Ted's arm and asked angrily, "What was it that was going to give Sabina a fit if she ever learned about it? Did Jose tell you he was nothing but an errand boy for Seth from the very beginning?"

Ted looked down at the ground as he said, "I can't tell you, Sabina; I'd rather move out —"

Sabina persisted, "On what terms did Seth give us the money to buy the garage? What did Jose tell you about that?"

Ted didn't answer; tears started to run out of his eyes.

Sabina shook him furiously. "Seth wasn't just buying a garage, was he? He was buying us, wasn't he? The garage was going to be a front for his heroin from the very beginning, and you knew it, didn't you? Jose lied to me and I tried to make you swallow the lie! Seth hadn't ever been Jose's friend, had he? He'd always been Jose's boss! And his money bought the rest of us! Jose was hired to pay off the cops, the rest of us were hired to drum up the business, and that's all there ever was to it! All my talk about masses rising from below in a world-changing process was just so much hot air! My hot air was nothing but a pack of lies which covered up the fact that we were never anything more than Seth's employees, we were nothing but hands in a capitalist enterprise! What else did Jose tell you?"

Trying to pull away from Sabina, Ted said to her, "That's all over now, Sabina, and he never told me that much —"

She shouted, "No, I suppose he didn't need to tell you that much because you knew all along! I was the only one who didn't know! Tissie knew all along too. I thought she was dense for not understanding my lofty aims; I thought she couldn't snap out of the thought habits of this fucked up society! I was the one who was dense! She knew we were nothing but Seth's employees, and she wanted me to be the big boss instead of Seth; it was always as simple as that! Even Jose finally figured it all out when Alec and Sophia's friends forced him to see himself as a dope dealer's errand boy, as a capitalist's flunkey! And to me it all remained a world-changing process after Seth told me to clear out! What else did he tell you?"

Ted tried to pull Sabina's hand away from his arm. "You're forcing me to leave, Sabina —"

I ran between them and begged hysterically, "Stop it, Sabina!" I threw my arms around Ted and begged him, "Please don't ever leave us, Ted!"

Sabina walked angrily to her room. Ted tried to hide his tears from me as he walked toward his room, formerly Tina's. I fell on the living room couch and cried. Then I dragged myself to Ted's room and kneeled by his bed; he was awake, staring at the ceiling. I remembered the last time I had been by Ted's bedside: I had tried to scratch his eyes out. I pulled his head toward me, put my lips to his and begged, "If you leave, Ted, please take me with you. But please don't make me leave Sabina."

Ted pulled his head away from me. "That's all over, Sophie, and there's no use going over it all the time. We've all got to start again somewhere. I don't want to leave either of you, Sophie; you're all I've got now."

I walked out of Ted's room in a daze. Ted was right. That was all over. Seth was dead. So were Ron, Jose and Alec. I'd had something to do with those deaths. So had Sabina. But that was all over. The three of us had to start again, somewhere. The following day I saw the headlines that announced the invasion and described the tanks. I realized I would have to start again with very few friends. The very same day when I walked home with that newspaper, the day after our visit to Tissie, I lost two more friends.

Tina and Pat graced us with their visit on that day. They came with two other young men whom they didn't deign to introduce to us. I opened the door and let the four of them in. Tina acted like a complete stranger to the house. Pat acted as if he'd never met Sabina or me. Their two friends placed themselves against a wall and stood there rigidly, like cops. Ted and Sabina came to the living room to greet the guests.

Tina addressed her first comment to Sabina and me. "I'd like to make my perspective clear to both of you, but I don't have the time now. The four of us came to communicate with Ted, and only with Ted. You two can stay, or leave, as you please;

it's your house." Tina couldn't have found a better way to arouse our suspicion as well as our curiosity.

Ted asked Tina, "What's happened to you?"

Tina told him, "We've come to find out what happened to you."

I asked her impatiently, "Where were you during the repression, Tina? And you, Pat? Damn you both, don't you think I might worry about you?"

In a hideously authoritarian tone, Tina said to me, "Apparently I failed to make myself clear, Sophia. We came here to talk to Ted!"

I shouted at Tina and Pat, "What the hell is wrong with you two?"

Sabina said sarcastically, "I have a gun in my room. Do you want one of your guards to hold it and to shoot in case either of us opens her mouth?"

Tina turned to her friends and told them, "We obviously can't talk to him here." Then she asked Ted, "Are you willing to accompany us to our quarters?"

"And have us miss the theatrics?" Sabina asked. "Don't you dare, Ted!"

Ted told Tina, "I'm staying here, so say what you've got to say or don't say it —"

"Let's see your act, Tina," Sabina told her.

Tina, clearly intimidated by Sabina, said nothing; her friends seemed momentarily unsure of themselves. Pat came to their rescue. He told Ted, "We've come to clarify the possibility of carrying on a common practice, specifically the possibility of rehabilitating the printing plant —"

Ted told Pat and Tina, "I'd like nothing better. Sophie and I have been waiting for you, Tina, in order to do just that. It seemed impossible to go ahead without you. If you want your friends along, they'd be welcome as far as I'm concerned —"

Pat interrupted, "We would also like to discuss the perspectives on which this common practice is to be based —"

Ted misunderstood that observation and told Pat, "I really don't believe the police are interested in that shop any more —"

Tina snapped at Ted, "That's not what we mean! By perspectives we mean the theory on which our practice is to be based. Theory is what allows one to consciously dominate one's situation as well as the material means for transforming that situation. We engaged in a practice of appropriating means of production without having a coherent critique —"

Pat took up Tina's refrain, "For us the problem of group organization is the problem of the coherent organization of our own practice, our common will and effort to clarify and resolve all contradictions between our practical activity and our revolutionary theory. Our aim is to apply the radical critique to the real world, our own practice included —"

"What does any of this have to do with reopening the print shop?" Ted asked.

Tina answered, "Revolutionary theory isn't only a critique of the world; it demands a critical attitude toward the activities of every individual who claims to be engaged in revolutionary practice!"

Ted told her, "I never made any claims about my printing except that it was well done, and neither did you, Tina!"

"That's not true!" Tina shouted. "You act as if our project had never been anything more than an artsy-fartsy craft shop on the fringes of capitalist society! You know perfectly well that our practice always aimed to overthrow the ruling society —"

"The impression I got certainly confirms Tina's observation," Pat told Ted. "When I arrived, the practice in the print shop was consistent with the highest levels reached by the revolutionary movement, namely with councilist organization. By organizing in councils proletarians have throughout history lain the practical foundation for their appropriation of the world —"

Sabina asked, "As illustrated last month?"

Pat said angrily, "It is because of lack of consciousness that the practical movement appropriating the world allowed bureaucrats and parties to appropriate its power. A group which pretends to be revolutionary cannot function below the level reached by the revolutionary movement. Such a group must be able to define the practical tasks which will allow it to install everywhere the conditions for the establishment of the power of the proletarians!"

"I've heard that before," Sabina told him. We also heard it again a few days later when we got the letter describing, in gruesome detail, the nature of Titus Zabran's noble commitment.

Ted said to Tina, "I thought you came to talk about the print shop."

"That's precisely why we did come," Tina told him. "But the only basis for engaging in a common practice is the existence of common perspectives pursued with equal ability and effort."

Ted objected, "I thought the basis for keeping the print shop going was whether or not a person cleaned up after using a machine, whether or not the equipment was left in functioning order for the next person. I don't understand your game, Tina. You're mixing up printing with revolution. What we did together was draw, photograph, print —"

"If you consider this discussion a game," Tina shouted, "if you think we're muddling something that was clear before, then this means I no longer define my practice the same way you do. It's in no one's interest for that confusion to continue to exist. I admit we printed together. But by virtue of our common practice we constituted a group, an organization, despite the fact that we didn't define ourselves in those terms."

Ted told her, "If organization means mouthing what your friends want to hear, Tina, then we were never an organization. We just printed together."

Tina retorted, "For you it wasn't an organization, Ted, but only a print shop, because for you the question of organization is apparently a non-question. I find that odd for someone who confronts every practical problem by first defining what you called a strategy. I realize only now that you were never clear about the overall strategy! Yet this is precisely the key question, this is what was unclear about the nature of our past collaboration! Such lack of lucidity and such relations of non- critique lead to incoherent group practice, which is what destroyed the print shop!"

Ted told her, "It's the police that destroyed it."

"That's only superficially true," Pat said to him. "The fact is that in the print shop we never defined strategy correctly, we never defined how our group activity inserted itself into the revolutionary movement which was developing everywhere in the world." Pat's comment made me uneasy. It's certainly true that I never connected my activity in the occupied university with what any of you were doing at that time; Mirna made a similar observation in your previous letter. But Pat's way of "connecting" our activities appalled me.

Ted told Pat, "The only strategy I ever had in view was about the concrete problem I was facing: repairing a machine, designing a poster, laying out a pamphlet. Tina ought to know I never defined strategies for others —"

Tina told Ted angrily, "In that case Pat and I are the only ones who regard our activity in the print shop as group practice in which we participated, and therefore we charge ourselves with the task of clarifying our past and present practice. Your attitude proves that you don't recognize either the problems we're posing nor our perspective toward them —"

"I don't understand your tone," Ted told her. "This isn't how friends talk to each other, Tina, friends who worked together for years, who never did each other any harm —"

Tina cut in, "That so-called friendship is what caused us to hold on to our illusions for so long! The remains of a friendship that had never understood its reasons caused us to take positions far below the level reached by the world revolutionary movement. Our friendship originated in a common practice, and it should not have survived after that practice deteriorated."

Sabina got up and walked to her room; her face was a mask of frustration. She had been ready to congratulate Tina for her "act," but the "act" reached levels of inhumanity Sabina herself had never explored.

I told Tina, "I never imagined you capable of such cold, premeditated cruelty. You're just like a —"

Pat interrupted me and said to Ted, patiently, pedagogically, "There's no such thing as abstract friendship, Ted, friendship which exists independently of its origin. Without a common project, without shared perspectives, there is no friendship."

Ted sadly asked Tina, "Why did you and your friends come here?"

Tina told him, "To clarify an unclear situation that has existed for years and that urgently needed clarification six weeks ago —"

"Six weeks ago?" Ted asked. "When others began to cooperate in using the equipment? Wasn't that the situation we had looked forward to for years, Tina?"

"I'm talking about six weeks ago when the print shop disintegrated because the participants were unable to organize their activities on the basis of a common perspective," she told him.

"The print shop was open to people with all kinds of perspectives," Ted reminded her.

"That's exactly what I'm talking about!" Tina shouted. "It was open to union organizer Luisa Nachalo, party hack Professor Daman Hesper, not to speak of the hundreds of petty bureaucrats who only spread confusion, who transformed radical theory into ideology!"

"Are you telling me we should have read the minds of everyone who came to the print shop and then decided whether or not to let them use the equipment?" Ted asked.

Tina answered, "Only by posing the problems of organization, autonomy and coherence will the revolutionary movement give itself the organized means for realizing its project! Everyone whose practice falls short of the level reached by the international movement is outside that movement. The ideological hodgepodge which mixed radical theory with a practice that negated it should not have existed and should have been denounced!"

I felt nauseated. "You sound just like the police Yarostan has been describing in his letters," I told her.

Ted said, "Sophia is right, Tina. The project we shared was printing. What you're talking about now is policing. I think all those who used the print shop were in some sense participants —"

Tina shouted, "You're definitely confirming your position of separating what cannot be separated, namely theory from practice! This separation is what enabled you to engage in partial projects with partial ideologies, and exempted you from taking a critical attitude towards the activity of others to the point of leading you to actively collaborate in the projects of ideologues. You claimed a place in the real revolutionary movement without assuring the minimum of practical coherence that this presupposes."

Pat said to Ted, in the same condescending, professorial tone he had used earlier, "This was a serious problem, Ted. The role of the various radical groups had to be defined at the very outset. Among those you call participants, it was necessary to recognize and denounce the bureaucratic canaille. It was a mistake to attribute to these groups roles they didn't play. Not one of the groups in the print shop played the role you attribute to them. This is why our group, practice was not in line with the international revolutionary project. Coherent groups with concrete strategies for the appropriation of the productive forces are still to be created. It is the evasion of this question that allowed us to engage in practical activity with people whose perspectives we did not share." Pat looked at me as he said this. "Such practice contradicts the perspectives of a radical group and works against the possibilities of the entire revolutionary movement. It is nothing less than a practical negation of the radical critique —"

"And the only way to deal with such dangerous practice is to acquire the power to liquidate the incoherent!" I shouted hysterically. Ted reached for my hand to calm me, and also to demonstrate his solidarity with me.

Tina shouted at Ted but her comments were aimed at me. "A strategy for appropriating the means of production is precisely what you've always lacked, Ted! That's why you've always collaborated with your enemies: first with Sabina, then with an anthill of petty bureaucrats, now with a new bordello of nostalgic sentimentalism and eclectic, half-digested platitudes!"

"If that's how you and your friends see me," Ted told her, "there's no reason for you to talk to me. I'll continue to be the one who decides who my friends are."

Pat said to Ted, with that same tone of the self-righteous missionary converting an ignorant savage, "Your attitude toward us stems from your decision to collaborate with those whose perspectives you don't share, Ted. You're turning against those with whom you seemed to agree because they reject your separation between theory and practice. Your decision to collaborate with your enemies and refuse collaboration with your friends contradicts your own past practice."

Tina shouted, without any of her colleague's patience, "The only basis for my future collaboration with you is your supersession of your past contradictions! We can maintain neither an organizational nor any form of abstract relationship with you unless and until you admit your incoherence and clarify your practice, and we're here solely to inform you of this!"

"Get out of this house and take your police with you this minute, Tina!" I shouted, unjustly, I know, since this is Tina's house at least as much as it is mine. I added, "I'm not in the habit of entertaining inquisitors and aspiring murderers!"

Tina looked at the other three; she and Pat rose and all four of them walked toward the door. "Is that your last word, Ted?" she asked. Ted didn't answer.

Pat still hadn't given up. He told Ted, "We had hoped to reach an understanding and to clarify the basis of that understanding. Think about it, Ted. We'll call in three days for your final answer."

Tina told him, "I hope we've made it clear that there can be no partial cooperation between us, and that future cooperation will be impossible unless all past errors are corrected, unless there is complete theoretical and practical agreement between us."

"Get out of here!" I screamed at her.

Tina still went on, "If you can't give your practical activity the same content and perspectives we give to it, no future collaboration is possible between us, do you understand that, Ted? Half measures aren't possible any longer —"

"Good-bye, Tina," Ted told her, turning his back to her and heading toward Tina's former room.

Pat Clesec did call three days later to ask if Ted had reached a decision. Ted told him he was already starting to clean up the print shop with me, and that Pat, Tina and all their friends were more than welcome to help us with the clean-up. Pat hung up. Neither he nor Tina nor any of their friends have come to help us.

Ted and I went to the print shop the day after Tina and Pat presented him with their "ultimatum." On the first day we made a list of all the things that needed to be done to get everything back in operation. Then your letter arrived. I spent two days home, depressed, speculating with Sabina about what might happen to all of you. I can't tell you how much we both love every one of you, and how sad your letter made us, all three of us. Ted never knew any of you but he cried too.

Since then Ted and I have been going to the print shop almost every day. Sabina went with us several times. We still don't have everything on our list checked off, and we've had to add some more "tasks" to the list, but the place already looks neater than it did when I first saw it. I've become familiar with what things are and what they're used for, and I've loved every minute of it. The past three weeks have been like a combination of the tour you gave me of the carton plant, the tour Ron gave me of this city, plus what I imagined took place in Hugh's "project house." We haven't actually done any printing yet, and the few discussions we've had about what we'll do with all that equipment have been vague, but I found them enormously stimulating. Even Sabina seemed excited by some of the prospects.

Ted is opposed to doing any commercial printing of whatever nature. He and Tina had done some before. He speculated, "Maybe that's what Tina meant to say about our earlier practice. She was right about that. It's no different from what Seth did. We'll have to support the place some other way." We don't yet know how we're going to do that.

We've talked about putting together and printing a critical analysis of the recent revolutionary events we all experienced, "if possible a coherent one," Sabina commented semi-sarcastically. We've also talked about sharing our modest means of expression with others who want to use them. Sabina and I agree with Ted's desire not to produce commodities for any markets; we also agree to try to do work of a quality that "shows respect for our readers," whom we don't yet know, but who we assume will be friends of ours.

Ted is still staying with Sabina and me. We've talked about using his former living quarters above the print shop as a space for doing typesetting and layout; Ted also has his "painting studio" up there. I've already decorated our house with several of his as well as one of Tina's paintings. One night last week when we returned from the print shop very late he told me, "I enjoy working with you a lot, Sophie — more than with little Tina in the garage days. I couldn't ever like Tissie the way I like you." I pulled him to my bedroom, kissing him, crying. I told him, "I love you more than I love anyone in the world," and I meant it.

My week-long love for Ted hasn't been like my love for Jose or my moment of passion with Pat. It's not the total self-abandonment, the self-annihilation Luisa accused me of wanting. I haven't felt any desire to be "Ted's woman," to be "possessed" by Ted. Maybe we haven't reached the peaks of passion Mirna sought to reach, but I don't have Mirna's strength; I'm not able to climb to such heights without losing myself. But my love also hasn't had anything in common with the "political love" by which Luisa tried to entice independent spirits into "history's" armored train. I did experience that type of love once, ironically with Jose — the changed, imprisoned Jose with whom I shared my books, the Jose who finally flew past me by taking my books seriously. I've been neither Ted's guide nor his slave, and I've gotten up every morning looking forward to my day's activities and looking forward to our coming days together. Without the activity I've shared with Ted, without his appreciative hugs and gentle caresses. I couldn't have risen from bed the morning after your letter came. I would have stared at the walls of my room exactly the same way I did after we emigrated twenty years ago; if I'd left the house, I would have drifted among strangers along crowded or empty sidewalks, a lonely tourist who had lost all interest in continuing her journey; I might have tried to bury myself in a suicidal job like the one I had in the fiberglass factory. I think Ted is making it possible for me to orient my life in a direction consistent with what I've learned from my recent experiences and from your letters. In an earlier letter you pointed out to me that during the general strike, when others were trying to explore and realize their creative potentialities, I was busy playing the bureaucrat, the coordinator of other people's activities, the "councilist official." What I now share with Ted has nothing to do with coordinating the activity of a third person. What I share with him is the activity itself: the gesture, the motion, the creative act, the discovery — the possibility of creating beautiful objects to share with friends, and ultimately the prospect of a world where none accept any constraints to the free self-expression of the whole being, where all develop each potentiality because each develops all potentialities.

But even as I write this I'm not sure. My love for Ted has little in common with my passionate love for Jose or Luisa's political love for Nachalo, but it does have something in common with my twenty-year long love for you, Yarostan. I've already, mentioned that my activity in the print shop reminds me very much of the days I spent with you in the carton plant. He doesn't feel toward me the way you did, but I suspect I feel toward him the way I felt toward you. Ted is my teacher, my guide. I'm his apprentice. Of course it's possible for an apprentice to remain independent. But I know myself too well to make any claims about my independence; I didn't even regard myself as Tina's equal when I was her apprentice in the garage ten years ago. I'm not so sure that I'm not repeating a not-so-new dependence. Ted doesn't only provide me with friendship; he also provides me with a ready-made project, with activity that I didn't define or create. And even the activity itself isn't very far removed from something you criticized in very unambiguous terms. We have all the equipment that's needed to print books, and two people can print a book on it in a finite period of time. When Ted explained this to me I was very excited. Being a book lover, I can think of no better way, given the choices presently available, of expressing myself creatively. But would this be a break with my past, with Luisa, with the experience I shared with you? The printing of books is terribly similar to the activity I wandered into when I joined you twenty years ago: what you taught me was to print, if only slogans on posters. What's a book? Is it a self-realization of an individual's life in the context of living others? Or is it self-realization as a closed compartment, for example an "insurgent," a category that remains separate from all the other separate categories?

I'm happy with my present activity with Ted, but I'm uneasy and I'm trying to locate the root of my uneasiness. The comments I just made may be true, but I don't think they're on the right track. In one of my first letters I told you I felt cut off from you by walls which I wasn't able to climb. I still can't climb those walls. I know this letter won't reach you, and I don't know what to do about that. My present happiness is a miserable thing. It's a close relative of Titus Zabran's commitment. It's defined, shaped and cut to size by the "historically available instruments." I suspect that something was frightfully right about Alec's and Carmen's final commitment. Even Zabran must have known that in the end. Maybe Zabran did to Nachalo what Mirna's mother did to Mirna's "devil": gave him a name and located him outside the individual. Sabina is convinced that what Zabran called "Nachalo" is at the root of every living individual. Maybe "Nachalo" is "the devil." But you don't need me to tell you that.

Love, *Sophia.*

Postscript: *For the reader*

MY LAST LETTER RETURNED TWO months after I sent it. Yarostan's address was completely covered by a large blot of opaque ink, and an arrow pointed to my address. There were no explanations anywhere on the envelope; in fact, there was no indication my letter had gotten any further than the local post office where the stamps were cancelled, there was no clue as to who had returned it or why. During the past eight years I haven't heard a single word from Yarostan or Mirna or Yara or Jasna. The "police capitalism" that imposed itself by means of its "historically available instruments" still rules today.

I held on to Yarostan's letters and the carbon copies of mine; occasionally I shared them with friends. Several years ago one of those who read them suggested I share them with a larger circle of friends. I hesitated because there was too much in them that could incriminate people whose lives are under constant police surveillance — and not merely "over there." When I finally decided to accept the suggestion, I carefully omitted all the names of places, and I changed the name of every person mentioned in both sets of letters, except where I felt this wasn't necessary (as with my own name: the police files over there never listed me as Nachalo, but as the daughter of the man I called "Alberts"). I hope "Yarostan" forgives me for making a book out of his letters to me: I hope even more that he sees this book.

I'm deeply grateful to all those who offered to help me typeset, proofread and print these letters, particularly to Ted and Tina. I'd like to address these letters to "all my likes" and "all Yarostan's likes," as he would have put it. And I want to dedicate it to the people I named Yarostan, Mirna, Yara, Jasna, Zdenek, Jan, Vesna and Irena, and to those I called Ron, Jose, Alec and Tissie.

S. N.

Fredy Perlman was co-founder of Black and Red Books, and author of the books *The Continuing Appeal of Nationalism, Against His-story, Against Leviathan!, The Strait, Worker-Student Action Committees: France May '68*, as well as numerous essays, pamphlets and contributions to *Fifth Estate* magazine.

The Ring *of* Fire Anthology

ET RUSSIAN

The Ring of Fire Anthology is a collection of the zine from the late 1990s by ET Russian (aka Hellery Homosex), and features new material never before published. *Ring of Fire* is honest, engaging, and ahead of its time.

Through black and white ink drawings, comics, linoleum block print portraits, essays and interviews this collection explores themes of art, bodies, disability, gender, race, community, class, healing and the politics of work.

Alternately emotional and erotic, funny and political, *Ring of Fire* tells the author's personal story, and captures the work and words of various artists and leaders from disability culture and history. A young activist steeped in the cultures of queer and punk, Russian embraced a cultural identity of disability while writing *Ring of Fire*. Years later, Russian examines what it means to work in healthcare in the United States.

ET Russian is a writer, performer, makeup artist, cartoonist, professional book nerd and physical therapist living in Seattle. Russian has published work in *The Collective Tarot* on Eberhardt Press, and *Gay Genius* on Sparkplug Books, co-founded the Seattle Disability Justice Collective, has performed with Sins Invalid in San Francisco, co-directed the movie *Third Antenna: A Documentary About the Radical Nature of Drag*, and authors the zine *Ring of Fire*. Russian has performed across the country and internationally doing drag, integrated dance, telling stories and reading poetry. Russian believes art is a powerful tool in the movements for disability justice, freedom and liberation for all people.

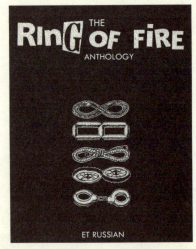

$20.00
237 pages; 8"x10"
ISBN 978-0-939306-00-8

Available from Left Bank Books
www.leftbankbooks.com

Distributed by AK Press
www.akpress.org

The Failure *of* Nonviolence:
From the Arab Spring to Occupy

PETER GELDERLOOS

FROM THE ARAB SPRING to the plaza occupation movement in Spain, the student movement in the UK and Occupy in the US, many new social movements have started peacefully, only to adopt a diversity of tactics as they grew in strength and collective experiences. The last ten years have revealed more clearly than ever the role of nonviolence. Propped up by the media, funded by the government, and managed by NGOs, nonviolent campaigns around the world have helped oppressive regimes change their masks, and have helped police to limit the growth of rebellious social movements. Increasingly losing the debates within the movements themselves, proponents of nonviolence have increasingly turned to the mainstream media and to government and institutional funding to drown out critical voices.

The Failure of Nonviolence examines most of the major social upheavals since the end of the Cold War to establish what nonviolence can accomplish, and what a diverse, unruly, non-pacified movement can accomplish. Focusing especially on the Arab Spring, Occupy, and the recent social upheavals in Europe, this book discusses how movements for social change can win ground and open the spaces necessary to plant the seeds of a new world.

Peter Gelderloos is the author of *How Nonviolence Protects the State, Consensus, & Anarchy Works.*

$14.95
306 pages
ISBN 978-0939306183

Available from Left Bank Books
www.leftbankbooks.com

Distributed by AK Press *&* Little Black Cart
www.akpress.org; www.littleblackcart.com

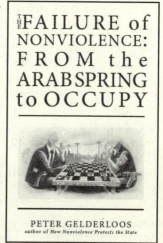

THE**FAILURE of**
NONVIOLENCE:
FROM the
ARAB SPRING
to OCCUPY

PETER GELDERLOOS
author of *How Nonviolence Protects the State*

Left Bank Books pamphlets

The Kronstadt Uprising of 1921 by Lynne Thordycraft: Originally published by Left Bank Books in 1975 as Left Bank Books Pamphlet No. 1, and written by one of its founders, Lynne Thorndycraft. The pamphlet tells the story of thousands of sailors rebelling against the Bolsheviks in the Russian Civil War, only to be suppresed by Leon Trotsky's Red Army. Letterpressed cover, hand-sewn binding. 20 pages.

Origins of the 1%: The Bronze Age by John Zerzan: New essay by John Zerzan showing the correlation between the characteristics of our culture that we find problematic, and their origins in the earliest civilizations. Silkscreened cover, "tarnished bronze" ink on metallic bronze paper, hand-sewn binding. 17 pages.

Seattle General Strike: An account of the Seattle General Strike of 1919. Originally published by the *Seattle Union Record* in 1919, this pamphlet tells the story of the first general strike to take place in the US, when 65,000 workers walked off the job for five days. This edition published by Left Bank Books and Charlatan Stew, 2012. 73 pages.

Radical History of Seattle's International District: A Walking Tour: Like all cities Seattle has been built by its working people, and the city's present-day geography reflects this unheralded history. No better place demonstrates this peoples' history than Seattle's International District, long-time home to the city's migrant working classes. The goal of this short walking tour is to provide a basic introduction to some of the District's history and how it has been shaped by struggle. Cover is a letterpressed map, hand-sewn binding.

publish & perish